"You get across and you're gonna find a place— another Alhambra. You got to go in that place. It's a scary place, a bad place. But you got to go in."

"Why do I have to go there, if it's so bad?"

"Because," Speedy said, "that's where the Talisman is."

"I don't know what you're talking about!"

"You will," Speedy said. He took Jack's hand. The two of them stood face-to-face, old black man and young white boy.

"The Talisman be given unto your hand, Travellin Jack. Not too big, not too small, she look just like a crystal ball, Travellin Jack, ole Travelin Jack. Here's your burden, here's your cross: Drop her Jack, and all be lost. . . ."

Speedy laughed and keyed the ignition. He backed up, turned around, and then the truck was rattling back toward Arcadia Funworld.

Jack stood by the curb, watching it go.

He had never felt so alone in his life. . . .

6w00 759063

W0006517

Also by Stephen King and Peter Straub
*Published by Ballantine Books:*

BLACK HOUSE

# THE TALISMAN

**Stephen King**
**Peter Straub**

BALLANTINE BOOKS • NEW YORK

This book contains an excerpt from the hardcover edition of *Black House* by Stephen King and Peter Straub. This excerpt has been set for this edition only and may not reflect the final content of the hardcover edition.

A Ballantine Book
Published by The Ballantine Publishing Group

Copyright © 1984 by Stephen King and Peter Straub
Excerpt from *Black House* by Stephen King and Peter Straub
© 2001 by Stephen King and Peter Straub

www.ballantinebooks.com

ISBN 0-345-44488-4

Manufactured in the United States of America

First Ballantine Books Edition: August 2001

OPM   14   13   12   11   10   9   8   7   6   5

This book is for

RUTH KING

ELVENA STRAUB

Well, when Tom and me got to the edge of the hilltop, we looked away down into the village and could see three or four lights twinkling, where there was sick folks, may be; and stars over us was sparkling ever so fine; and down by the village was the river, a whole mile broad, and awful still and grand.

—MARK TWAIN, *Huckleberry Finn*

My new clothes was all greased up and clayey, and I was dog-tired.

—MARK TWAIN, *Huckleberry Finn*

# CONTENTS

## PART III: A COLLISION OF WORLDS

## PART IV: THE TALISMAN

# ONE

# JACK LIGHTS OUT

# 1

# The Alhambra Inn and Gardens

## 1

On September 15th, 1981, a boy named Jack Sawyer stood where the water and land come together, hands in the pockets of his jeans, looking out at the steady Atlantic. He was twelve years old and tall for his age. The sea-breeze swept back his brown hair, probably too long, from a fine, clear brow. He stood there, filled with the confused and painful emotions he had lived with for the last three months—since the time when his mother had closed their house on Rodeo Drive in Los Angeles and, in a flurry of furniture, checks, and real-estate agents, rented an apartment on Central Park West. From that apartment they had fled to this quiet resort on New Hampshire's tiny seacoast. Order and regularity had disappeared from Jack's world. His life seemed as shifting, as uncontrolled, as the heaving water before him. His mother was moving him through the world, twitching him from place to place; but what moved his mother?

His mother was running, running.

Jack turned around, looking up the empty beach first to the left, then to the right. To the left was Arcadia Funworld, an amusement park that ran all racket and roar from Memorial Day to Labor Day. It stood empty and still now, a heart between beats. The roller coaster was a scaffold against that featureless, overcast sky, the uprights and angled supports like strokes done in charcoal. Down there was his new friend, Speedy Parker, but the boy could not think about Speedy Parker now. To the right was the Alhambra Inn and Gardens, and that was where the boy's thoughts relentlessly took him. On the day of their arrival Jack had momentarily thought he'd seen a rainbow over its dormered and gambreled roof. A sign of sorts, a promise of better things. But there had been no rainbow. A weathervane spun right-left, left-right, caught in a crosswind. He had got out of their rented car, ignoring his mother's unspoken desire for him to do something about the luggage, and looked up. Above the spinning brass cock of the weathervane hung only a blank sky.

"Open the trunk and get the bags, sonny boy," his mother had called to him. "This broken-down old actress wants to check in and hunt down a drink."

"An elementary martini," Jack had said.

" 'You're not so old,' you were supposed to say." She was pushing herself effortfully off the carseat.

"You're not so old."

She gleamed at him—a glimpse of the old, go-to-hell Lily Cavanaugh (Sawyer), queen of two decades' worth of B movies. She straightened her back. "It's going to be okay here, Jacky," she had said. "Everything's going to be okay here. This is a good place."

A seagull drifted over the roof of the hotel, and for a second Jack had the disquieting sensation that the weathervane had taken flight.

"We'll get away from the phone calls for a while, right?"

"Sure," Jack had said. She wanted to hide from Uncle Morgan, she wanted no more wrangles with her dead husband's business partner, she wanted to crawl into bed with an elementary martini and hoist the covers over her head. . . .

*Mom, what's wrong with you?*

There was too much death, the world was half-made of death. The gull cried out overhead.

"Andelay, kid, andelay," his mother had said. "Let's get into the Great Good Place."

Then, Jack had thought: *At least there's always Uncle Tommy to help out in case things get really hairy.*

But Uncle Tommy was already dead; it was just that the news was still on the other end of a lot of telephone wires.

## 2

The Alhambra hung out over the water, a great Victorian pile on gigantic granite blocks which seemed to merge almost seamlessly with the low headland—a jutting collarbone of granite here on the few scant miles of New Hampshire sea-

coast. The formal gardens on its landward side were barely
visible from Jack's beachfront angle—a dark green flip of
hedge, that was all. The brass cock stood against the sky,
quartering west by northwest. A plaque in the lobby announced that it was here, in 1838, that the Northern
Methodist Conference had held the first of the great New
England abolition rallies. Daniel Webster had spoken at fiery,
inspired length. According to the plaque, Webster had said:
"From this day forward, know that slavery as an American institution has begun to sicken and must soon die in all our
states and territorial lands."

## 3

So they had arrived, on that day last week which had ended
the turmoil of their months in New York. In Arcadia Beach
there were no lawyers employed by Morgan Sloat popping out
of cars and waving papers which had to be signed, *had* to be
filed, Mrs. Sawyer. In Arcadia Beach the telephones did not
ring out from noon until three in the morning (Uncle Morgan
appeared to forget that residents of Central Park West were
not on California time). In fact the telephones in Arcadia
Beach rang not at all.

On the way into the little resort town, his mother driving
with squinty-eyed concentration, Jack had seen only one person on the streets—a mad old man desultorily pushing an
empty shopping cart along a sidewalk. Above them was that
blank gray sky, an uncomfortable sky. In total contrast to New
York, here there was only the steady sound of the wind, hoot-
ing up deserted streets that looked much too wide with no
traffic to fill them. Here were empty shops with signs in the
windows saying OPEN WEEKENDS ONLY or, even worse, SEE YOU
IN JUNE! There were a hundred empty parking places on the
street before the Alhambra, empty tables in the Arcadia Tea
and Jam Shoppe next door.

And shabby-crazy old men pushed shopping carts along
deserted streets.

"I spent the happiest three weeks of my life in this funny
little place," Lily told him, driving past the old man (who
turned, Jack saw, to look after them with frightened
suspicion—he was mouthing something but Jack could not

tell what it was) and then swinging the car up the curved drive
through the front gardens of the hotel.

For that was why they had bundled everything they could
not live without into suitcases and satchels and plastic shopping bags, turned the key in the lock on the apartment door
(ignoring the shrill ringing of the telephone, which seemed to
penetrate that same keyhole and pursue them down the hall);
that was why they had filled the trunk and back seat of the
rented car with all their overflowing boxes and bags and spent
hours crawling north along the Henry Hudson Parkway, then
many more hours pounding up I-95—because Lily Cavanaugh Sawyer had once been happy here. In 1968, the year
before Jack's birth, Lily had been nominated for an Academy
Award for her role in a picture called *Blaze. Blaze* was a better movie than most of Lily's, and in it she had been able to
demonstrate a much richer talent than her usual bad-girl roles
had revealed. Nobody expected Lily to win, least of all Lily;
but for Lily the customary cliché about the real honor being
in the nomination was honest truth—she did feel honored,
deeply and genuinely, and to celebrate this one moment of
real professional recognition, Phil Sawyer had wisely taken
her for three weeks to the Alhambra Inn and Gardens, on the
other side of the continent, where they had watched the Os-
cars while drinking champagne in bed. (If Jack had been
older, and had he had an occasion to care, he might have done
the necessary subtraction and discovered that the Alhambra
had been the place of his essential beginning.)

When the Supporting Actress nominations were read, according to family legend, Lily had growled to Phil, "If I win
this thing and I'm not there, I'll do the Monkey on your chest
in my *stiletto heels.*"

But when Ruth Gordon had won, Lily had said, "Sure, she
deserves it, she's a great kid." And had immediately poked her
husband in the middle of the chest and said, "You'd better get
me another part like that, you big-shot agent you."

There had been no more parts like that. Lily's last role,
two years after Phil's death, had been that of a cynical ex-
prostitute in a film called *Motorcycle Maniacs.*

It was that period Lily was commemorating now, Jack knew
as he hauled the baggage out of the trunk and the back seat. A

D' Agostino bag had torn right down through the big D'AG,
and a jumble of rolled-up socks, loose photographs, chess-
men and the board, and comic books had dribbled over all
else in the trunk. Jack managed to get most of this stuff into
other bags. Lily was moving slowly up the hotel steps, pulling
herself along on the railing like an old lady. "I'll find the bell-
hop," she said without turning around.

Jack straightened up from the bulging bags and looked
again at the sky where he was sure he had seen a rainbow.
There was no rainbow, only that uncomfortable, shifting sky.

Then:

"Come to me," someone said behind him in a small and
perfectly audible voice.

"What?" he asked, turning around. The empty gardens and
drive stretched out before him.

"Yes?" his mother said. She looked crickle-backed, leaning
over the knob of the great wooden door.

"Mistake," he said. There had been no voice, no rainbow.
He forgot both and looked up at his mother, who was struggling with the vast door. "Hold on, I'll help," he called, and
trotted up the steps, awkwardly carrying a big suitcase and a
straining paper bag filled with sweaters.

## 4

Until he met Speedy Parker, Jack had moved through the days
at the hotel as unconscious of the passage of time as a sleeping dog. His entire life seemed almost dreamlike to him during these days, full of shadows and inexplicable transitions.
Even the terrible news about Uncle Tommy which had come
down the telephone wires the night before had not entirely
awakened him, as shocking as it had been. If Jack had been a
mystic, he might have thought that other forces had taken him
over and were manipulating his mother's life and his own.
Jack Sawyer at twelve was a being who required things to do,
and the noiseless passivity of these days, after the hubbub of
Manhattan, had confused and undone him in some basic way.

Jack had found himself standing on the beach with no recollection of having gone there, no idea of what he was doing
there at all. He supposed he was mourning Uncle Tommy, but
it was as though his mind had gone to sleep, leaving his body

to fend for itself. He could not concentrate long enough to grasp the plots of the sitcoms he and Lily watched at night, much less keep the nuances of fiction in his head.

"You're tired from all this moving around," his mother said, dragging deeply on a cigarette and squinting at him through the smoke. "All you have to do, Jack-O, is relax for a little while. This is a good place. Let's enjoy it as long as we can."

Bob Newhart, before them in a slightly too-reddish color on the set, bemusedly regarded a shoe he held in his right hand.

"That's what I'm doing, Jacky." She smiled at him. "Relaxing and enjoying it."

He peeked at his watch. Two hours had passed while they sat in front of the television, and he could not remember anything that had preceded this program.

Jack was getting up to go to bed when the phone rang. Good old Uncle Morgan Sloat had found them. Uncle Morgan's news was never very great, but this was apparently a blockbuster even by Uncle Morgan's standards. Jack stood in the middle of the room, watching as his mother's face grew paler, palest. Her hand crept to her throat, where new lines had appeared over the last few months, and pressed lightly. She said barely a word until the end, when she whispered, "Thank you, Morgan," and hung up. She had turned to Jack then, looking older and sicker than ever.

"Got to be tough now, Jacky, all right?"

He hadn't felt tough.

She took his hand then and told him.

"Uncle Tommy was killed in a hit-and-run accident this afternoon, Jack."

He gasped, feeling as if the wind had been torn out of him.

"He was crossing La Cienega Boulevard and a van hit him. There was a witness who said it was black, and that the words WILD CHILD were written on the side, but that was . . . was all."

Lily began to cry. A moment later, almost surprised, Jack began to cry as well. All of that had happened three days ago, and to Jack it seemed forever.

## 5

On September 15th, 1981, a boy named Jack Sawyer stood looking out at the steady water as he stood on an unmarked beach before a hotel that looked like a castle in a Sir Walter Scott novel. He wanted to cry but was unable to release his tears. He was surrounded by death, death made up half the world, there were no rainbows. The WILD CHILD van had subtracted Uncle Tommy from the world. Uncle Tommy, dead in L.A., too far from the east coast, where even a kid like Jack knew he really belonged. A man who felt he had to put on a tie before going out to get a roast beef sandwich at Arby's had no business on the west coast at all.

His father was dead, Uncle Tommy was dead, his mother might be dying. He felt death here, too, at Arcadia Beach, where it spoke through telephones in Uncle Morgan's voice. It was nothing as cheap or obvious as the melancholy feel of a resort in the off-season, where one kept stumbling over the Ghosts of Summers Past; it seemed to be in the texture of things, a smell on the ocean breeze. He was scared . . . and he had been scared for a long time. Being here, where it was so quiet, had only helped him to realize it—had helped him to realize that maybe Death had driven all the way up I-95 from New York, squinting out through cigarette smoke and asking him to find some bop on the car radio.

He could remember—vaguely—his father telling him that he was born with an old head, but his head didn't feel old now. Right now, his head felt very young. *Scared*, he thought. *I'm pretty damn scared. This is where the world ends, right?*

Seagulls coursed the gray air overhead. The silence was as gray as the air—as deadly as the growing circles under her eyes.

## 6

When he had wandered into Funworld and met Lester Speedy Parker after he did not quite know how many days of numbly drifting through time, that passive feeling of being *on hold* had somehow left him. Lester Parker was a black man with crinkly gray hair and heavy lines cutting through his cheeks. He was utterly unremarkable now despite whatever he had accomplished in his earlier life as a travelling blues musician. Nor had he said anything particularly remarkable. Yet as soon as Jack had walked aimlessly into Funworld's game arcade and met Speedy's pale eyes he felt all the fuzziness leave him.

He had become himself again. It was as if a magical current had passed directly from the old man into Jack. Speedy had smiled at him and said, "Well, it looks like I got me some company. Little travellin man just walked in."

It was true, he was not *on hold* anymore: just an instant before, he had seemed to be wrapped in wet wool and cotton candy, and now he was set free. A silvery nimbus seemed to play about the old man for an instant, a little aureole of light which disappeared as soon as Jack blinked. For the first time Jack saw that the man was holding the handle of a wide heavy push-broom.

"You okay, son?" The handyman put one hand in the small of his back, and stretched backward. "The world just get worse, or did she get better?"

"Uh, better," Jack said.

"Then you come to the right place, I'd say. What do they call you?"

*Little travellin man,* Speedy had said that first day, *ole Travellin Jack.* He had leaned his tall angular body against the Skee-Ball machine and wrapped his arms around the broomhandle as though it were a girl at a dance. *The man you see here is Lester Speedy Parker, formerly a travellin man hisself, son, hee hee—oh yeah, Speedy knew the road, he knew all the roads, way back in the old days. Had me a band, Travellin Jack, played the blues. Git-tar blues. Made me a few records, too, but I won't shame you by asking if you ever heard em.* Every syllable had its own rhythmic lilt, every phrase its rimshot and backbeat; Speedy Parker carried a broom instead of a guitar, but he was still a musician. Within the first five seconds of talking to Speedy, Jack had known that his jazz-loving father would have relished this man's company.

He had tagged along behind Speedy for the better part of three or four days, watching him work and helping out when he could. Speedy let him bang in nails, sand down a picket or two that needed paint; these simple tasks done under Speedy's instructions were the only schooling he was getting, but they made him feel better. Jack now saw his first days in Arcadia Beach as a period of unrelieved wretchedness from which his new friend had rescued him. For Speedy Parker was a friend, that was certain—so certain, in fact, that in it was a quantity of mystery. In the few days since Jack had shaken off his daze (or since Speedy had shaken it off for him by dispelling it with one glance of his light-colored eyes), Speedy Parker had become closer to him than any other friend, with the possible exception of Richard Sloat, whom Jack had known approximately since the cradle. And now, counteracting his terror at losing Uncle Tommy and his fear that his mother was actually dying, he felt the tug of Speedy's warm wise presence from just down the street.

Again, and uncomfortably, Jack had his old sense of *being directed*, of being manipulated: as if a long invisible wire had pulled himself and his mother up to this abandoned place by the sea.

They wanted him here, whoever *they* were.

Or was that just crazy? In his inner vision he saw a bent old man, clearly out of his mind, muttering to himself as he pushed an empty shopping cart down the sidewalk.

A gull screamed in the air, and Jack promised himself that he would *make* himself talk about some of his feelings with Speedy Parker. Even if Speedy thought he was nuts; even if he laughed at Jack. He would not laugh, Jack secretly knew. They were old friends because one of the things Jack understood about the old custodian was that he could say almost anything to him.

But he was not ready for all that yet. It was all too crazy, and he did not understand it yet himself. Almost reluctantly Jack turned his back on Funworld and trudged across the sand toward the hotel.

# 2

# The Funnel Opens

## 1

It was a day later, but Jack Sawyer was no wiser. He *had*, however, had one of the greatest nightmares of all time last night. In it, some terrible creature had been coming for his mother—a dwarfish monstrosity with misplaced eyes and rotting, cheesy skin. *"Your mother's almost dead, Jack, can you say hallelujah?"* this monstrosity had croaked, and Jack knew—the way you knew things in dreams—that it was radioactive, and that if it touched him, he would die, too. He had awakened with his body drenched in sweat, on the edge of a bitter scream. It took the steady pounding of the surf to reacquaint him with where he was, and it was hours before he could go back to sleep.

He had meant to tell his mother about the dream this morning, but Lily had been sour and uncommunicative, hiding in a cloud of cigarette smoke. It was only as he started out of the hotel coffee shop on some trumped-up errand that she smiled at him a little.

"Think about what you want to eat tonight."

"Yeah?"

"Yeah. Anything but fast food. I did not come all the way from L.A. to New Hampshire in order to poison myself with hotdogs."

"Let's try one of those seafood places in Hampton Beach," Jack said.

"Fine. Go on and play."

*Go on and play,* Jack thought with a bitterness utterly unlike him. *Oh yeah, Mom, way to go. Too cool. Go on and play. With who? Mom, why are you here? Why are* we *here? How sick are you? How come you won't talk to me about Uncle Tommy? What's Uncle Morgan up to? What—*

Questions, questions. And not one of them worth a darned thing, because there was no one to answer them.

*Unless Speedy*—

But that was ridiculous; how could one old black man he'd just met solve any of his problems?

Still, the thought of Speedy Parker danced at the edge of his mind as Jack ambled across the boardwalk and down to the depressingly empty beach.

2

*This is where the world ends, right?* Jack thought again.

Seagulls coursed the gray air overhead. The calendar said it was still summer, but summer ended here at Arcadia Beach on Labor Day. The silence was gray as the air.

He looked down at his sneakers and saw that there was some sort of tarry goo on them. *Beach crud,* he thought. *Some kind of pollution.* He had no idea where he had picked it up and he stepped back from the edge of the water, uneasy.

The gulls in the air, swooping and crying. One of them screamed overhead and he heard a flat cracking that was almost metallic. He turned in time to see it come in for a fluttering, awkward landing on a hump of rock. The gull turned its head in rapid, almost robotic movements, as if to verify it was alone, and then it hopped down to where the clam it had dropped lay on the smooth, hard-packed sand. The clam had cracked open like an egg and Jack saw raw meat inside, still twitching . . . or perhaps that was his imagination.

*Don't want to see this.*

But before he could turn away, the gull's yellow, hooked beak was pulling at the meat, stretching it like a rubber band, and he felt his stomach knot into a slick fist. In his mind he could hear that stretched tissue screaming—nothing coherent, only stupid flesh crying out in pain.

He tried to look away from the seagull again and he couldn't. The gull's beak opened, giving him a brief glimpse of dirty pink gullet. The clam snapped back into its cracked shell and for a moment the gull was looking at him, its eyes a deadly black, confirming every horrible truth: fathers die, mothers die, uncles die even if they went to Yale and look as

solid as bank walls in their three-piece Savile Row suits. Kids
die too, maybe . . . and at the end all there may be is the stupid, unthinking scream of living tissue.

"Hey," Jack said aloud, not aware he was doing anything
but thinking inside his own head. "Hey, give me a break."

The gull sat over its catch, regarding him with its beady
black eyes. Then it began to dig at the meat again. *Want some,
Jack? It's still twitching! By God, it's so fresh it hardly knows
it's dead!*

The strong yellow beak hooked into the meat again and
pulled. *Strettttchhhhhh—*

It snapped. The gull's head went up toward the gray September sky and its throat worked. And again it seemed to be
looking at him, the way the eyes in some pictures seemed always to look at you no matter where you went in the room.
And the eyes . . . he knew those eyes.

Suddenly he wanted his mother—her dark blue eyes.
He could not remember wanting her with such desperation
since he had been very, very small. *La-la,* he heard her sing
inside his head, and her voice was the wind's voice, here
for now, somewhere else all too soon. *La-la, sleep now, Jacky,
baby-bunting, daddy's gone a-hunting. And all that jazz.*
Memories of being rocked, his mother smoking one Herbert
Tareyton after another, maybe looking at a script—blue
pages, she called them, he remembered that: blue pages.
*La-la, Jacky, all is cool. I love you, Jacky. Shhh . . . sleep.
La-la.*

The gull was looking at him.

With sudden horror that engorged his throat like hot salt
water he saw *it really was looking at him.* Those black eyes
*(whose?)* were *seeing* him. And he knew that look.

A raw strand of flesh still dangled from the gull's beak. As
he looked, the gull sucked it in. Its beak opened in a weird but
unmistakable grin.

He turned then and ran, head down, eyes shut against the
hot salt tears, sneakers digging against the sand, and if there
was a way to go up, go up and up, up to some gull's-eye view,
one would have seen only him, only his tracks, in all that gray
day; Jack Sawyer, twelve and alone, running back toward the
inn, Speedy Parker forgotten, his voice nearly lost in tears and

wind, crying the negative over and over again: *no* and *no* and *no.*

### 3

He paused at the top of the beach, out of breath. A hot stitch ran up his left side from the middle of his ribs to the deepest part of his armpit. He sat down on one of the benches the town put out for old people and pushed his hair out of his eyes.

*Got to get control of yourself. If Sergeant Fury goes Section Eight, who's gonna lead the Howling Commandos?*

He smiled and actually did feel a little better. From up here, fifty feet from the water, things looked a little better. Maybe it was the change in barometric pressure, or something. What had happened to Uncle Tommy was horrible, but he supposed he would get over it, learn to accept. That was what his mother said, anyway. Uncle Morgan had been unusually pesty just lately, but then, Uncle Morgan had *always* been sort of a pest.

As for his mother . . . well, that was the big one, wasn't it?

Actually, he thought, sitting on the bench and digging at the verge of the sand beyond the boardwalk with one toe, actually his mother might still be all right. She *could* be all right; it was certainly *possible*. After all, no one had come right out and *said* it was the big C, had they? No. If she had cancer, she wouldn't have brought him here, would she? More likely they'd be in Switzerland, with his mother taking cold mineral baths and scoffing goat-glands, or something. And she would do it, too.

So maybe—

A low, dry whispering sound intruded on his consciousness. He looked down and his eyes widened. The sand had begun to move by the instep of his left sneaker. The fine white grains were sliding around in a small circle perhaps a finger's length in diameter. The sand in the middle of this circle suddenly collapsed, so that now there was a dimple in the sand. It was maybe two inches deep. The sides of this dimple were also in motion: around and around, moving in rapid counterclockwise circuits.

*Not real,* he told himself immediately, but his heart began to speed up again. His breathing also began to come faster. *Not real,* it's one of the Daydreams, that's all, or maybe it's a crab or something . . .

But it wasn't a crab and it wasn't one of the Daydreams— this was not the other place, the one he dreamed about when things were boring or maybe a little scary, and it sure as hell wasn't any crab.

The sand spun faster, the sound arid and dry, making him think of static electricity, of an experiment they had done in science last year with a Leyden jar. But more than either of these, the minute sound was like a long lunatic gasp, the final breath of a dying man.

More sand collapsed inward and began to spin. Now it was not a dimple; it was a funnel in the sand, a kind of reverse dust-devil. The bright yellow of a gum wrapper was revealed, cov-ered, revealed, covered, revealed again—each time it showed up again. Jack could read more of it as the funnel grew: JU, then JUI, then JUICY F. The funnel grew and the sand was jerked away from the gum wrapper again. It was as quick and rude as an unfriendly hand jerking down the covers on a made bed. JUICY FRUIT, he read, and then the wrapper flapped upward.

The sand turned faster and faster, in a hissing fury. *Hhhhh-haaaaahhhhhhhh* was the sound the sand made. Jack stared at it, fascinated at first, and then horrified. The sand was open-ing like a large dark eye: it was the eye of the gull that had dropped the clam on the rock and then pulled the living meat out of it like a rubber band.

*Hhhhhhaaaahhhhh,* the sand-spout mocked in its dead, dry voice. That was not a mind-voice. No matter how much Jack wished it were only in his head, that voice was real. *His false teeth flew, Jack, when the old WILD CHILD hit him, out they went, rattledy-bang! Yale or no Yale, when the old WILD CHILD van comes and knocks your false teeth out, Jacky, you got to go. And your mother—*

Then he was running again, blindly, not looking back, his hair blown off his forehead, his eyes wide and terrified.

4

Jack walked as quickly as he could through the dim lobby of the hotel. All the atmosphere of the place forbade running. it was as quiet as a library, and the gray light which fell through the tall mullioned windows softened and blurred the already faded carpets. Jack broke into a trot as he passed the desk, and the stooped ashen-skinned day-clerk chose that second to emerge through an arched wooden passage. The clerk said nothing, but his permanent scowl dragged the corners of his mouth another centimeter downward. It was like being caught running in church. Jack wiped his sleeve across his forehead, made himself walk the rest of the way to the elevators. He punched the button, feeling the desk clerk's frown burning between his shoulder blades. The only time this week that Jack had seen the desk clerk smile had been when the man had recognized his mother. The smile had met only the minimum standards for graciousness.

"I suppose that's how old you have to be to remember Lily Cavanaugh," she had said to Jack as soon as they were alone in their rooms. There had been a time, and not so long ago, when being identified, recognized from any one of the fifty movies she had made during the fifties and sixties ("Queen of the Bs," they called her; her own comment: "Darling of the Drive-ins")—whether by a cabdriver, waiter, or the lady selling blouses at the Wilshire Boulevard Saks—perked her mood for hours. Now even that simple pleasure had gone dry for her.

Jack jigged before the unmoving elevator doors, hearing an impossible and familiar voice lifting to him from a whirling funnel of sand. For a second he saw Thomas Woodbine, solid comfortable Uncle Tommy Woodbine, who was supposed to have been one of his guardians—a strong wall against trouble and confusion—crumpled and dead on La Cienega Boulevard, his teeth like popcorn twenty feet away in the gutter. He stabbed the button again.

Hurry *up!*

Then he saw something worse—his mother hauled into a waiting car by two impassive men. Suddenly Jack had to urinate. He flattened his palm against the button, and the bent gray man behind the desk uttered a phlegmy sound of disapproval. Jack pressed the edge of his other hand into that magic place just beneath his stomach which lessened the pressure on his bladder. Now he could hear the slow whir of the descending elevator. He closed his eyes, squeezed his legs together.

His mother looked uncertain, lost and confused, and the men forced her into the car as easily as they would a weary collie dog. But that was not really happening, he knew; it was a memory—part of it must have been one of the Daydreams— and it had happened not to his mother but to him.

As the mahogany doors of the elevator slid away to reveal a shadowy interior from which his own face met him in a foxed and peeling mirror, that scene from his seventh year wrapped around him once again, and he saw one man's eyes turn to yellow, felt the other's hand alter into something claw-like, hard and inhuman . . . he jumped into the elevator as if he had been jabbed with a fork.

Not possible: the Daydreams were not possible, he had *not* seen a man's eyes turning from blue to yellow, and his mother was fine and dandy, there was nothing to be scared of, nobody was dying, and danger was what a seagull meant to a clam. He closed his eyes and the elevator toiled upward.

That thing in the sand had laughed at him.

Jack squeezed through the opening as soon as the doors began to part. He trotted past the closed mouths of the other elevators, turned right into the panelled corridor and ran past the sconces and paintings toward their rooms. Here running seemed less a sacrilege. They had 407 and 408, consisting of two bedrooms, a small kitchen, and a living room with a view of the long smooth beach and the vastness of the ocean. His mother had appropriated flowers from somewhere, arranged them in vases, and set her little array of framed photographs beside them. Jack at five, Jack at eleven, Jack as an infant in the arms of his father. His father, Philip Sawyer, at the wheel of the old DeSoto he and Morgan Sloat had driven to California in the unimaginable days when they had been so poor they had often slept in the car.

When Jack threw open 408, the door to the living room, he called out, "Mom? Mom?"

The flowers met him, the photographs smiled; there was no answer. "Mom!" The door swung shut behind him. Jack felt his stomach go cold. He rushed through the living room to the large bedroom on the right. *"Mom!"* Another vase of tall bright flowers. The empty bed looked starched and ironed, so stiff a quarter would bounce off the quilt. On the bedside table stood an assortment of brown bottles containing vitamins and other pills. Jack backed out. His mother's window showed black waves rolling and rolling toward him.

Two men getting out of a nondescript car, themselves nondescript, reaching for her . . .

"Mom!" he shouted.

"I hear you, Jack," came his mother's voice through the bathroom door. "What on earth . . . ?"

"Oh," he said, and felt all his muscles relax. "Oh, sorry. I just didn't know where you were."

"Taking a bath," she said. "Getting ready for dinner. Is that still allowed?"

Jack realized that he no longer had to go to the bathroom. He dropped into one of the overstuffed chairs and closed his eyes in relief. She was still okay—

*Still okay for now,* a dark voice whispered, and in his mind he saw that sand funnel open again, whirling.

## 5

Seven or eight miles up the coast road, just outside Hampton Township, they found a restaurant called The Lobster Chateau. Jack had given a very sketchy account of his day— already he was backing away from the terror he had experienced on the beach, letting it diminish in his memory. A waiter in a red jacket printed with the yellow image of a lobster across the back showed them to a table beside a long streaky window.

"Would Madam care for a drink?" The waiter had a stony-cold off-season New England face, and looking at it, suspecting the resentment of his Ralph Lauren sport coat and his mother's carelessly worn Halston afternoon dress behind those watery blue eyes, Jack felt a more familiar terror needle him—simple homesickness. *Mom, if you're not really sick, what the hell are we doing here? The place is empty! It's creepy! Jesus!*

"Bring me an elementary martini," she said.

The waiter raised his eyebrows. "Madam?"

"Ice in a glass," she said. "Olive on ice. Tanqueray gin over olive. Then—are you getting this?"

*Mom, for God's sake, can't you see his eyes? You think you're being charming—he thinks you're making fun of him! Can't you see his eyes?*

No. She couldn't. And that failure of empathy, when she had always been so sharp about how other people were feeling, was another stone against his heart. She was withdrawing . . . in all ways.

"Yes, madam."

"Then," she said, "you take a bottle of vermouth—any brand—and hold it against the glass. Then you put the vermouth back on the shelf and bring the glass to me. 'Kay?"

"Yes, madam." Watery-cold New England eyes, staring at his mother with no love at all. *We're alone here,* Jack thought, really realizing it for the first time. *Jeez, are we.* "Young sir?"

"I'd like a Coke," Jack said miserably.

The waiter left. Lily rummaged in her purse, came up with a package of Herbert Tarrytoons (so she had called them since he had been a baby, as in "Bring me my Tarrytoons from over there on the shelf, Jacky," and so he still thought of them) and lit one. She coughed out smoke in three harsh bursts.

It was another stone against his heart. Two years ago, his mother had given up smoking entirely. Jack had waited for her to backslide with that queer fatalism which is the flip side of childish credulity and innocence. His mother had always smoked; she would soon smoke again. But she had not . . . not until three months ago, in New York. Carltons. Walking around the living room in the apartment on Central Park West, puffing like a choo-choo, or squatting in front of the record cabinet, pawing through her old rock records or her dead husband's old jazz records.

"You smoking again, Mom?" he'd asked her.

"Yeah, I'm smoking cabbage leaves," she'd said.

"I wish you wouldn't."

"Why don't you turn on the TV?" she'd responded with uncharacteristic sharpness, turning toward him, her lips pressed tightly together. "Maybe you can find Jimmy Swaggart or Reverend Ike. Get down there in the hallelujah corner with the amen sisters."

"Sorry," he'd muttered.

Well—it was only Carltons. Cabbage leaves. But here were the Herbert Tarrytoons—the blue-and-white old-fashioned pack, the mouthpieces that looked like filters but which weren't. He could remember, vaguely, his father telling somebody that he smoked Winstons and his wife smoked Black Lungers.

"See anything weird, Jack?" she asked him now, her overbright eyes fixed on him, the cigarette held in its old, slightly eccentric position between the second and third fingers of the right hand. Daring him to say something. Daring him to say, "Mom, I notice you're smoking Herbert Tarrytoons again—does this mean you figure you don't have anything left to lose?"

"No," he said. That miserable, bewildered homesickness swept him again, and he felt like weeping. "Except this place. *It's* a little weird."

She looked around and grinned. Two other waiters, one fat, one thin, both in red jackets with golden lobsters on the back, stood by the swing doors to the kitchen, talking quietly. A velvet rope hung across the entrance to a huge dining room beyond the alcove where Jack and his mother sat. Chairs were overturned in ziggurat shapes on the tables in this dark cave. At the far end, a huge window-wall looked out on a gothic shorescape that made Jack think of *Death's Darling*, a movie his mother had been in. She had played a young woman with a lot of money who married a dark and handsome stranger against her parents' wishes. The dark and handsome stranger took her to a big house by the ocean and tried to drive her crazy. *Death's Darling* had been more or less typical of Lily Cavanaugh's career—she had starred in a lot of black-and-white films in which handsome but forgettable actors drove around in Ford convertibles with their hats on.

The sign hanging from the velvet rope barring the entrance to this dark cavern was ludicrously understated: THIS SECTION CLOSED.

"It *is* a little grim, isn't it?" she said.

"It's like the Twilight Zone," he replied, and she barked her harsh, infectious, somehow lovely laugh.

"Yeah, Jacky, Jacky, Jacky," she said, and leaned over to ruffle his too-long hair, smiling.

He pushed her hand away, also smiling (but oh, her fingers felt like bones, didn't they? *She's almost dead, Jack . . .* ). "Don't touch-a da moichendise."

"Off my case."

"Pretty hip for an old bag."

"Oh boy, try to get movie money out of me this week."

"Yeah."

They smiled at each other, and Jack could not ever remember a need to cry so badly, or remember loving her so much. There was a kind of desperate toughness about her now . . . going back to the Black Lungers was part of that.

Their drinks came. She tipped her glass toward his. "Us."

"Okay."

They drank. The waiter came with menus.

"Did I pull his string a little hard before, Jacky?"

"Maybe a little," he said.

She thought about it, then shrugged it away. "What are you having?"

"Sole, I guess."

"Make it two."

So he ordered for both of them, feeling clumsy and embarrassed but knowing it was what she wanted—and he could see in her eyes when the waiter left that he hadn't done too bad a job. A lot of that was Uncle Tommy's doing. After a trip to Hardee's Uncle Tommy had said: "I think there's hope for you, Jack, if we can just cure this revolting obsession with processed yellow cheese."

The food came. He wolfed his sole, which was hot and lemony and good. Lily only toyed with hers, ate a few green beans, and then pushed things around on her plate.

"School started up here two weeks ago," Jack announced halfway through the meal. Seeing the big yellow buses with ARCADIA DISTRICT SCHOOLS written on the sides had made him feel guilty—under the circumstances he thought that was probably absurd, but there it was. He was playing hooky.

She looked at him, enquiring. She had ordered and finished a second drink; now the waiter brought a third.

Jack shrugged. "Just thought I'd mention it."

"Do you want to go?"

"Huh? No! Not here!"

"Good," she said. "Because I don't have your goddam vaccination papers. They won't let you in school without a pedigree, chum."

"Don't call me chum," Jack said, but Lily didn't crack a smile at the old joke.

*Boy, why ain't you in school?*

He blinked as if the voice had spoken aloud instead of only in his mind.

"Something?" she asked.

"No. Well . . . there's a guy at the amusement park. Funworld. Janitor, caretaker, something like that. An old black guy. He asked me why I wasn't in school."

She leaned forward, no humor in her now, almost frighteningly grim. "What did you tell him?"

Jack shrugged. "I said I was getting over mono. You remember that time Richard had it? The doctor told Uncle Morgan Richard had to stay out of school for six weeks, but he could walk around outside and everything." Jack smiled a little. "I thought he was lucky."

Lily relaxed a little. "I don't like you talking to strangers, Jack."

"Mom, he's just a—"

"I don't care *who* he is. I don't want you talking to strangers."

Jack thought of the black man, his hair gray steel wool, his dark face deeply lined, his odd, light-colored eyes. He had been pushing a broom in the big arcade on the pier—the arcade was the only part of Arcadia Funworld that stayed open the year around, but it had been deserted then except for Jack and the black man and two old men far in the back. The two were playing Skee-Ball in apathetic silence.

But now, sitting here in this slightly creepy restaurant with his mother, it wasn't the black man who asked the question; it was himself.

*Why aren't I in school?*

*It be just like she say, son. Got no vaccination, got no pedigree. You think she come down here with your birth certificate? That what you think? She on the run, son, and you on the run with her. You—*

"Have you heard from Richard?" she broke in, and when she said it, it came to him—no, that was too gentle. It crashed into him. His hands twitched and his glass fell off the table. It shattered on the floor.

*She's almost dead, Jack.*

The voice from the swirling sand-funnel. The one he had heard in his mind.

It had been Uncle Morgan's voice. Not maybe, not almost, not sorta like. It had been a *real* voice. The voice of Richard's father.

### 6

Going home in the car, she asked him, "What happened to you in there, Jack?"

"Nothing. My heart did this funny little Gene Krupa riff." He ran off a quick one on the dashboard to demonstrate. "Threw a PCV, just like on *General Hospital*."

"Don't wise off to me, Jacky." In the glow of the dashboard instruments she looked pale and haggard. A cigarette smouldered between the second and third fingers of her right hand. She was driving very slowly—never over forty—as she always drove when she'd had too much to drink. Her seat was pulled all the way forward, her skirt was hiked up so her knees floated, storklike, on either side of the steering column, and her chin seemed to hang over the wheel. For a moment she looked haglike, and Jack quickly looked away.

"I'm not," he mumbled.

"What?"

"I'm not wising off," he said. "It was like a twitch, that's all. I'm sorry."

"It's okay," she said. "I thought it was something about Richard Sloat."

"No." *His father talked to me out of a hole in the sand down on the beach, that's all. In my head he talked to me, like in a movie where you hear a voice-over. He told me you were almost dead.*

"Do you miss him, Jack?"

"Who, Richard?"

"No—Spiro Agnew. Of course Richard."

"Sometimes." Richard Sloat was now going to school in Illinois—one of those private schools where chapel was compulsory and no one had acne.

"You'll see him." She ruffled his hair.

"Mom, are you all right?" The words burst out of him. He could feel his fingers biting into his thighs.

"Yes," she said, lighting another cigarette (she slowed down to twenty to do it; an old pick-up swept by them, its horn blatting). "Never better."

"How much weight have you lost?"

"Jacky, you can never be too thin or too rich." She paused and then smiled at him. It was a tired, hurt smile that told him all the truth he needed to know.

"Mom—"

"No more," she said. "All's well. Take my word for it. See if you can find us some be-bop on the FM."

"But—"

"Find us some bop, Jacky, and shut up."

He found some jazz on a Boston station—an alto saxophone elucidating "All the Things You Are." But under it, a steady, senseless counterpoint, was the ocean. And later, he could see the great skeleton of the roller coaster against the sky. And the rambling wings of the Alhambra Inn. If this was home, they were home.

3

# Speedy Parker

1

The next day the sun was back—a hard bright sun that layered itself like paint over the flat beach and the slanting, red-tiled strip of roof Jack could see from his bedroom window. A long low wave far out in the water seemed to harden in the light and sent a spear of brightness straight toward his eyes. To Jack this sunlight felt different from the light in California. It seemed somehow thinner, colder, less nourishing. The wave out in the dark ocean melted away, then hoisted itself up again, and a hard dazzling streak of gold leaped across it. Jack turned away from his window. He had already showered and dressed, and his body's clock told him that it was time to start moving toward the schoolbus stop. Seven-fifteen. But of course he would not go to school today, nothing was normal anymore, and he and his mother would just drift like ghosts through another twelve hours of daytime. No schedule, no responsibilities, no homework . . . no order at all except for that given them by mealtimes.

Was today even a schoolday? Jack stopped short beside his bed, feeling a little flicker of panic that his world had become so formless . . . he didn't *think* this was a Saturday. Jack counted back to the first absolutely identifiable day his memory could find, which was the previous Sunday. Counting forward made it Thursday. On Thursdays he had computer class with Mr. Balgo and an early sports period. At least that was what he'd had when his life had been normal, a time that now seemed—though it had come to an end only months ago— irretrievably lost.

He wandered out of his bedroom into the living room. When he tugged at the drawstring for the curtains the hard bright light flooded into the room, bleaching the furniture. Then he punched the button on the television set and dropped himself onto the stiff couch. His mother would not be up for at least another fifteen minutes. Maybe longer, considering that she'd had three drinks with dinner the night before.

Jack glanced toward the door to his mother's room.

Twenty minutes later he rapped softly at her door. "Mom?" A thick mumble answered him. Jack pushed the door open a crack and looked in. She was lifting her head off the pillow and peering back through half-closed eyes.

"Jacky. Morning. What time?"

"Around eight."

"God. You starving?" She sat up and pressed the palms of her hands to her eyes.

"Kind of. I'm sort of sick of sitting in here. I just wondered if you were getting up soon."

"Not if I can help it. You mind? Go down to the dining room, get some breakfast. Mess around on the beach, okay? You'll have a much better mother today if you give her another hour in bed."

"Sure," he said. "Okay. See you later."

Her head had already dropped back down on the pillow.

Jack switched off the television and let himself out of the room after making sure his key was in the pocket of his jeans.

The elevator smelled of camphor and ammonia—a maid had tipped a bottle off a cart. The doors opened, and the gray desk clerk frowned at him and ostentatiously turned away. Being a movie star's brat doesn't make you anything special around here, sonny . . . and why aren't you in school? Jack turned into the panelled entrance to the dining room—The Saddle of Lamb—and saw rows of empty tables in a shadowy vastness. Perhaps six had been set up. A waitress in a white blouse and red ruffled skirt looked at him, then looked away. Two exhausted-looking old people sat across a table from each other at the other end of the room. There were no other breakfasters. As Jack looked on, the old man leaned over the table and unselfconsciously cut his wife's fried egg into four-inch square sections.

"Table for one?" The woman in charge of The Saddle of Lamb during the day had materialized beside him, and was already plucking a menu off a stack beside the reservation book.

"Changed my mind, sorry." Jack escaped.

The Alhambra's coffee shop, The Beachcomber Lounge, lay all the way across the lobby and down a long bleak corridor lined with empty display cases. His hunger died at the thought of sitting by himself at the counter and watching the bored cook slap down strips of bacon on the crusty grill. He would wait until his mother got up: or, better yet, he would go out and see if he could get a doughnut and a little carton of milk at one of the shops up the street on the way into town.

He pushed open the tall heavy front door of the hotel and went out into the sunlight. For a moment the sudden brightness stung his eyes—the world was a flat glaring dazzle. Jack squinted, wishing he had remembered to bring his sunglasses downstairs. He went across the apron of red brick and down the four curving steps to the main pathway through the gardens at the front of the hotel.

What happened if she died?

What happened to him—where would he go, who would take care of him, if the worst thing in the world actually took place and she died, for good and all *died,* up in that hotel room?

He shook his head, trying to send the terrible thought away before a lurking panic could rush up out of the Alhambra's

well-ordered gardens and blast him apart. He would not cry,
he would not let that happen to him—and he would not let
himself think about the Tarrytoons and the weight she had
lost, the feeling that he sometimes had that she was too helpless and without direction. He was walking very quickly now,
and he shoved his hands into his pockets as he jumped down
off the curving path through the gardens onto the hotel's
drive. *She on the run, son, and you on the run with her.* On the
run, but from whom? And to where? Here—just to here, this
deserted resort?

He reached the wide street that travelled up the shoreline
toward the town, and now all of the empty landscape before
him was a whirlpool that could suck him down into itself and
spit him out into a black place where peace and safety had
never existed. A gull sailed out over the empty road, wheeled
around in a wide curve, and dipped back toward the beach.
Jack watched it go, shrinking in the air to a smudge of white
above the erratic line of the roller-coaster track.

Lester Speedy Parker, a black man with crinkly gray hair
and heavy lines cutting down through his cheeks, was down
there somewhere inside Funworld and it was Speedy he had
to see. That was as clear to Jack as his sudden insight about
his friend Richard's father.

A gull screeched, a wave bounced hard gold light toward
him, and Jack saw Uncle Morgan and his new friend Speedy
as figures almost allegorically opposed, as if they were statues
of NIGHT and DAY, stuck up on plinths, MOON and SUN—the
dark and the light. What Jack had understood as soon as he
had known that his father would have liked Speedy Parker
was that the ex-bluesman had no harm in him. Uncle Morgan,
now . . . he was another kind of being altogether. Uncle Morgan lived for business, for deal-making and hustling; and he
was so ambitious that he challenged every even faintly dubious call in a tennis match, so ambitious in fact that he cheated
in the penny-ante card games his son had now and then
coaxed him into joining. At least, Jack *thought* that Uncle
Morgan had been cheating in a couple of their games . . . not
a man who thought that defeat demanded graciousness.

NIGHT and DAY, MOON and SUN; DARK and LIGHT, and the
black man was the light in these polarities. And when Jack's
mind had pushed him this far, all that panic he had fought off

in the hotel's tidy gardens swarmed toward him again. He
lifted his feet and ran.

### 2

When the boy saw Speedy kneeling down outside the gray
and peeling arcade building—wrapping electrician's tape
around a thick cord, his steel-wool head bent almost to the
pier and his skinny buttocks poking out the worn green seat
of his work-pants, the dusty soles of his boots toed down like
a pair of upended surfboards—he realized that he had no idea
of what he had been planning to say to the custodian, or even
if he intended to say anything at all. Speedy gave the roll of
black tape another twist around the cord, nodded, took a battered Palmer knife from the flap pocket of his workshirt and
sliced the tape off the roll with a flat surgical neatness. Jack
would have escaped from here, too, if he could—he was in-
truding on the man's work, and anyhow, it was crazy to think
that Speedy could really help him in any way. What kind of
help could he give, an old janitor in an empty amusement
park?

Then Speedy turned his head and registered the boy's presence with an expression of total and warming welcome—not
so much a smile as a deepening of all those heavy lines in his
face—and Jack knew that he was at least no intrusion.

"Travellin Jack," Speedy said. "I was beginnin to get afraid
you decided to stay away from me. Just when we got to be
friends, too. Good to see you again, son."

"Yeah," Jack said. "Good to see you, too."

Speedy popped the metal knife back into his shirt pocket
and lifted his long bony body upright so easily, so athletically,
that he seemed weightless. "This whole place comin down
around my ears," he said. "I just fix it a little bit at a time,
enough so everything works more or less the way it should."
He stopped in mid-sentence, having had a good look at Jack's
face. "Old world's not so fine right now, seems like. Travellin
Jack got buckled up to a load of worries. That the way it is?"

"Yeah, sort of," Jack began—he still had no idea of how to
begin expressing the things that troubled him. They could not
be put into ordinary sentences, for ordinary sentences made
everything seem rational. One . . . two . . . three: Jack's world

no longer marched in those straight lines. All he could not say weighed in his chest.

He looked miserably at the tall thin man before him. Speedy's hands were thrust deep into his pockets; his thick gray eyebrows pushed toward the deep vertical furrow between them. Speedy's eyes, so light they were almost no color at all, swung up from the blistered paint of the pier and met Jack's own—and suddenly Jack felt better again. He did not understand why, but Speedy seemed to be able to communicate emotion directly to him: as if they had not met just a week before, but years ago, and had shared far more than a few words in a deserted arcade.

"Well, that's enough work for now," Speedy said, glancing up in the direction of the Alhambra. "Do any more and I just spoil em. Don't suppose you ever saw my office, did you?"

Jack shook his head.

"Time for a little refreshment, boy. The *time* is *right*."

He set off down the pier in his long-legged gait, and Jack trotted after him. As they jumped down the steps of the pier and began going across the scrubby grass and packed brown earth toward the buildings on the far side of the park, Speedy astonished Jack by starting to sing.

> *Travellin Jack, ole Travellin Jack,*
> *Got a far long way to go,*
> *Longer way to come back.*

It was not exactly singing, Jack thought, but sort of halfway between singing and talking. If it were not for the words, he would have enjoyed listening to Speedy's rough, confident voice.

> *Long long way for that boy to go,*
> *Longer way to come back.*

Speedy cast an almost twinkling look at him over his shoulder.

"Why do you call me that?" Jack asked him. "Why am I Travelling Jack? Because I'm from California?"

They had reached the pale blue ticket booth at the entrance to the roller-coaster enclosure, and Speedy thrust his hands back in the pockets of his baggy green workpants, spun on his heel, and propped his shoulders on the little blue enclosure. The efficiency and quickness of his movements had a quality almost theatrical—as if, Jack thought, he had known the boy was going to ask that particular question at that precise moment.

> *He say he come from California,*
> *Don he know he gotta go right back . . .*

sang Speedy, his ponderous sculptured face filled with emotion that seemed almost reluctant to Jack.

> *Say he come all that way,*
> *Poor Travellin Jack gotta go right back . . .*

"What?" Jack said. "Go back? I think my mom even sold the house—or she rented it or something. I don't know what the hell you're trying to do, Speedy."

He was relieved when Speedy did not answer him in his chanting, rhythmic sing-song, but said in a normal voice: "Bet you don't remember meetin me before, Jack. You don't, do you?"

"Meeting you before? Where was this?"

"California—at least, I *think* we met back there. Not so's you'd remember, Travellin Jack. It was a pretty busy couple of minutes. Would have been in . . . let me see . . . would have been about four—five years ago. Nineteen seventy-six."

Jack looked up at him in pure befuddlement. Nineteen seventy-six? He would have been seven years old.

"Let's go find my little office," Speedy said, and pushed himself off the ticket booth with that same weightless grace.

Jack followed after him, winding through the tall supports of the roller coaster—black shadows like the grids of tic-tac-toe diagrams overlaid a dusty wasteland sprinkled with beercans and candy wrappers. The tracks of the roller coaster hung above them like an unfinished skyscraper. Speedy moved, Jack saw, with a basketball player's rangy ease, his head up and his arms dangling. The angle of his body, his posture in the crisscrossed gloom beneath the struts, seemed very young—Speedy could have been in his twenties.

Then the custodian stepped out again into the harsh sunlight, and fifty extra years grayed his hair and seamed the back of his neck. Jack paused as he reached the final row of uprights, sensing as if Speedy Parker's illusory juvenescence were the key to them that the Daydreams were somehow very near, hovering all about him.

Nineteen seventy-six? California? Jack trailed off after Speedy, who was going toward a tiny red-painted wooden shack back up against the smooth-wire fence on the far side of the amusement park. He was sure that he had never met Speedy in California . . . but the almost visible presence of his fantasies had brought back to him another specific memory of those days, the visions and sensations of a late afternoon of his sixth year, Jacky playing with a black toy taxi behind the couch in his father's office . . . and his father and Uncle Morgan unexpectedly, magically talking about the Daydreams. *They have magic like we have physics, right? An agrarian monarchy, using magic instead of science. But can you begin to understand how much fucking clout we'd swing if we gave them electricity? If we got modern weapons to the right guys over there? Do you have any idea?*

*Hold on there, Morgan, I have a lot of ideas that apparently have yet to occur to you. . . .*

Jack could almost hear his father's voice, and the peculiar and unsettling realm of the Daydreams seemed to stir in the shadowy wasteland beneath the roller coaster. He began again to trot after Speedy, who had opened the door of the little red shack and was leaning against it, smiling without smiling.

"You got something on your mind, Travellin Jack. Something that's buzzin in there like a bee. Get on inside the executive suite and tell me about it."

If the smile had been broader, more obvious, Jack might have turned and run: the spectre of mockery still hung humiliatingly near. But Speedy's whole being seemed to express a welcoming concern—the message of all those deepened lines in his face—and Jack went past him through the door.

Speedy's "office" was a small board rectangle—the same red as its exterior—without a desk or a telephone. Two upended orange crates leaned against one of the side walls, flanking an unplugged electrical heater that resembled the grille of a mid-fifties Pontiac. In the middle of the room a wooden round-back school chair kept company with an over-stuffed chair of faded gray material.

The arms of the overstuffed chair seemed to have been clawed open by several generations of cats: dingy wisps of stuffing lay across the arms like hair; on the back of the school chair was a complex graffito of scratched-in initials. Junkyard furniture. In one of the corners stood two neat foot-high piles of paperback books, in another the square fake-alligator cover of a cheap record player. Speedy nodded at the heater and said, "You come round here in January, February, boy, you see why I got that. Cold? Shoo." But Jack was now looking at the pictures taped to the wall over the heater and orange crates.

All but one of the pictures were nudes cut from men's magazines. Women with breasts as large as their heads lolled back against uncomfortable trees and splayed columnar, hard-worked legs. To Jack, their faces looked both fascinating and rapacious—as if these women would take bites out of his skin after they kissed him. Some of the women were no younger than his mother; others seemed only a few years older than himself. Jack's eyes grazed over this needful flesh—all of it, young and unyoung, pink or chocolate-brown or honey-yellow, seemed to press toward his touch, and he was too conscious of Speedy Parker standing beside him, watching. Then he saw the landscape in the midst of the nude photographs, and for a second he probably forgot to breathe.

It too was a photograph; and it too seemed to reach out for him, as if it were three-dimensional. A long grassy plain of a particular, aching green unfurled toward a low, ground-down range of mountains. Above the plain and the mountains ranged a deeply transparent sky. Jack could very nearly smell the freshness of this landscape. He knew that place. He had never been there, not really, but he knew it. That was one of the places of the Daydreams.

"Kind of catch the eye, don't it?" Speedy said, and Jack remembered where he was. A Eurasian woman with her back to the camera tilted a heart-shaped rear and smiled at him over her shoulder. Yes, Jack thought. "Real pretty place," Speedy said. "I put that one up myself. All these here girls met me when I moved in. Didn't have the heart to rip em off the wall. They sort of do remind me of way back when, times I was on the road."

Jack looked up at Speedy, startled, and the old man winked at him.

"Do you know that place, Speedy?" Jack asked. "I mean, do you know where it is?"

"Maybe so, maybe not. It might be Africa—someplace in Kenya. Or that might be just my memory. Sit down, Travellin Jack. Take the comf'able chair."

Jack twisted the chair so that he could still see the picture of the Daydream place. "That's *Africa?*"

"Might be somewhere a lot closer. Might be somewhere a fellow could get to—get to anytime he liked, that is, if he wanted to see it bad enough."

Jack suddenly realized that he was trembling, and had been for some time. He balled his hands into fists, and felt the trembling displace itself into his stomach.

He was not sure that he wanted ever to see the Daydream place, but he looked questioningly over at Speedy, who had perched himself on the school chair. "It isn't anyplace in Africa, is it?"

"Well, I don't know. Could be. I got my own name for it, son. I just call it the Territories."

Jack looked back up at the photograph—the long, dimpled plain, the low brown mountains. The Territories. That was right; that was its name.

*They have magic like we have physics, right? An agrarian monarchy ... modern weapons to the right guys over there ...* Uncle Morgan plotting. His father answering, putting on the brakes: *We have to be careful about the way we go in there, partner ... remember, we owe them, by which I mean we really owe them ...*

"The Territories," he said to Speedy, tasting the name in his mouth as much as asking a question.

"Air like the best wine in a rich man's cellar. Soft rain. That's the place, son."

"You've been there, Speedy?" Jack asked, fervently hoping for a straightforward answer.

But Speedy frustrated him, as Jack had almost known he

would. The custodian smiled at him, and this time it was a real smile, not just a subliminal flare of warmth.

After a moment Speedy said, "Hell, I never been outside these United States, Travellin Jack. Not even in the war. Never got any farther than Texas and Alabama."

"How do you know about the . . . the Territories?" The name was just beginning to fit his mouth.

"Man like me, he hear all kinds of stories. Stories about two-headed parrots, men that fly with their own wings, men who turn into wolves, stories about queens. Sick queens."

*. . . magic like we have physics, right?*

Angels and werewolves. "I've heard stories about were-wolves," Jack said. "They're even in cartoons. That doesn't mean anything, Speedy."

"Probably it don't. But I heard that if a man pulls a radish out of the ground, another man half a mile away will be able to smell that radish—the air so sweet and clear."

"But angels . . ."

"Men with wings."

"And sick queens," Jack said, meaning it as a joke—*man, this is some dumb place you make up, broom jockey*. But the instant he spoke the words, he felt sick himself. He had re-membered the black eye of a gull fixing him with his own mortality as it yanked a clam from its shell: and he could hear hustlin, bustlin Uncle Morgan asking if Jack could put Queen Lily on the line.

Queen of the Bs. Queen Lily Cavanaugh.

"Yeah," Speedy said softly. "Troubles everywhere, son. Sick Queen . . . maybe dyin. *Dyin*, son. And a world or two waitin out there, just waitin to see if anyone can save her."

Jack stared at him open-mouthed, feeling more or less as if the custodian had just kicked him in the stomach. Save her? Save his mother? The panic started to flood toward him once again—how could *he* save her? And did all this crazy talk mean that she really was dying, back there in that room?

"You got a job, Travellin Jack," Speedy told him. "A job that ain't gonna let you go, and that's the Lord's truth. I wish it was different."

"I don't know what you're talking about," Jack said. His breath seemed to be trapped in a hot little pocket situated at the base of his neck. He looked into another corner of the small red room and in the shadow saw a battered guitar propped against the wall. Beside it lay the neat tube of a thin rolled-up mattress. Speedy slept next to his guitar.

"I wonder," Speedy said. "There comes times, you know what I mean, you know more than you think you know. One hell of a lot more."

"But I don't—" Jack began, and then pulled himself up short. He had just remembered something. Now he was even more frightened—another chunk of the past had rushed out at him, demanding his attention. Instantly he was filmed with perspiration, and his skin felt very cold—as if he had been misted by a fine spray from a hose. This memory was what he had fought to repress yesterday morning, standing before the elevators, pretending that his bladder was not about to burst.

"Didn't I say it was time for a little refreshment?" Speedy asked, reaching down to push aside a loose floorboard.

Jack again saw two ordinary-looking men trying to push his mother into a car. Above them a huge tree dipped scalloped fronds over the automobile's roof.

Speedy gently extracted a pint bottle from the gap between the floorboards. The glass was dark green, and the fluid inside looked black. "This gonna help you, son. Just a little taste all you need—send you some new places, help you get started findin that job I told you bout."

"I can't stay, Speedy," Jack blurted out, now in a desperate hurry to get back to the Alhambra. The old man visibly checked the surprise in his face, then slid the bottle back under the loose floorboard. Jack was already on his feet. "I'm worried," he said.

"Bout your mom?"

Jack nodded, moving backward toward the open door.

"Then you better settle your mind and go see she's all right. You can come back here anytime, Travellin Jack."

"Okay," the boy said, and then hesitated before running outside. "I think . . . I think I remember when we met before."

"Nah, nah, my brains got twisted," Speedy said, shaking his head and waving his hands back and forth before him. "You had it right. We never met before last week. Get on back to your mom and set your mind at ease."

Jack sprinted out the door and ran through the dimensionless sunlight to the wide arch leading to the street. Above it he could see the letters DLROWNUF AIDACRA outlined against the sky: at night, colored bulbs would spell out the park's name in both directions. Dust puffed up beneath his Nikes. Jack pushed himself against his own muscles, making them move faster and harder, so that by the time he burst out through the arch, he felt almost as though he were flying.

Nineteen seventy-six. Jack had been puttering his way up Rodeo Drive on an afternoon in June? July? . . . some afternoon in the drought season, but before that time of the year when everybody started worrying about brushfires in the hills. Now he could not even remember where he had been going. A friend's house? It had not been an errand of any urgency. He had, Jack remembered, just reached the point where he no longer thought of his father in every unoccupied second—for many months after Philip Sawyer's death in a hunting accident, his shade, his loss had sped toward Jack at a bruising speed whenever the boy was least prepared to meet it. Jack was only seven, but he knew that part of his childhood had been stolen from him—his six-year-old self now seemed impossibly naive and thoughtless—but he had learned to trust his mother's strength. Formless and savage threats no longer seemed to conceal themselves in dark corners, closets with half-open doors, shadowy streets, empty rooms.

The events of that aimless summer afternoon in 1976 had murdered this temporary peace. After it, Jack slept with his light on for six months; nightmares roiled his sleep.

The car pulled across the street just a few houses up from the Sawyers' white three-story Colonial. It had been a green car, and that was all that Jack had known about it except that it was not a Mercedes—Mercedes was the only kind of automobile he knew by sight. The man at the wheel had rolled down his window and smiled at Jack. The boy's first thought had been that he knew this man—the man had known Phil Sawyer, and wanted just to say hello to his son. Somehow that was conveyed by the man's smile, which was easy and unforced and familiar. Another man leaned forward in the passenger seat and peered toward Jack through blind-man glasses—round and so dark they were nearly black. This second man was wearing a pure white suit. The driver let his smile speak for him a moment longer.

Then he said, "Sonny, do you know how we get to the Beverly Hills Hotel?" So he was a stranger after all. Jack experienced an odd little flicker of disappointment.

He pointed straight up the street. The hotel was right up there, close enough so that his father had been able to walk to breakfast meetings in the Loggia.

"Straight ahead?" the driver asked, still smiling.

Jack nodded.

"You're a pretty smart little fellow," the man told him, and the other man chuckled. "Any idea of how far up it is?" Jack shook his head. "Couple of blocks, maybe?"

"Yeah." He had begun to get uncomfortable. The driver was still smiling, but now the smile looked bright and hard and empty. And the passenger's chuckle had been wheezy and damp, as if he were sucking on something wet.

"Five, maybe? Six? What do you say?"

"About five or six, I guess," Jack said, stepping backward.

"Well, I sure do want to thank you, little fellow," the driver said. "You don't happen to like candy, do you?" He extended a closed fist through the window, turned it palm-up, and opened his fingers: a Tootsie Roll. "It's yours. Take it."

Jack tentatively stepped forward, hearing in his mind the words of a thousand warnings involving strange men and candy. But this man was still in his car; if he tried anything, Jack could be half a block away before the man got his door open. And to not take it somehow seemed a breach of civility. Jack took another step nearer. He looked at the man's eyes, which were blue and as bright and hard as his smile. Jack's instincts told him to lower his hand and walk away. He let his hand drift an inch or two nearer the Tootsie Roll. Then he made a little stabbing peck at it with his fingers.

The driver's hand clamped around Jack's, and the passenger in blind-man glasses laughed out loud. Astonished, Jack stared into the eyes of the man gripping his hand and saw them start to change—*thought* he saw them start to change—from blue to yellow.

But later they were yellow.

The man in the other seat pushed his door open and trotted around the back of the car. He was wearing a small gold cross in the lapel of his silk suit coat. Jack pulled frantically away, but the driver smiled brightly, emptily, and held him fast. "NO!" Jack yelled. "HELP!"

The man in dark glasses opened the rear door on Jack's side.

"HELP ME!" Jack screamed.

The man holding him began to squeeze him down into a shape that would fit into the open door. Jack bucked, still yelling, but the man effortlessly tightened his hold. Jack struck at his hands, then tried to push the hands off him. With horror, he realized that what he felt beneath his fingers was not skin. He twisted his head and saw that clamped to his side and protruding from the black sleeve was a hard, pinching thing like a claw or a jointed talon. Jack screamed again.

From up the street came a loud voice: "Hey, stop messin with that boy! You! Leave that boy alone!"

Jack gasped with relief, and twisted as hard as he could in the man's arms. Running toward them from the end of the block was a tall thin black man, still shouting. The man holding him dropped Jack to the sidewalk and took off around the back of the car. The front door of one of the houses behind Jack slammed open—another witness.

"Move, *move*," said the driver, already stepping on the accelerator. White Suit jumped back into the passenger seat, and the car spun its wheels and squealed diagonally across Rodeo Drive, barely missing a long white Clenet driven by a suntanned man in tennis whites. The Clenet's horn blared.

Jack picked himself up off the sidewalk. He felt dizzy. A bald man in a tan safari suit appeared beside him and said, "Who were they? Did you get their names?"

Jack shook his head.

"How do you feel? We ought to call the police."

"I want to sit down," Jack said, and the man backed away a step.

"You want me to call the police?" he asked, and Jack shook his head.

"I can't believe this," the man said. "Do you live around here? I've seen you before, haven't I?"

"I'm Jack Sawyer. My house is just down there."

"The white house," the man said, nodding. "You're Lily Cavanaugh's kid. I'll walk you home, if you like."

"Where's the other man?" Jack asked him. "The black man—the one who was shouting."

He took an uneasy step away from the man in the safari suit. Apart from the two of them, the street was empty.

Lester Speedy Parker had been the man running toward him. Speedy had saved his life back then, Jack realized, and ran all the harder toward the hotel.

### 3

"You get any breakfast?" his mother asked him, spilling a cloud of smoke out of her mouth. She wore a scarf over her hair like a turban, and with her hair hidden that way, her face looked bony and vulnerable to Jack. A half-inch of cigarette smouldered between her second and third fingers, and when she saw him glance at it, she snubbed it out in the ashtray on her dressing table.

"Ah, no, not really," he said, hovering in the door of her bedroom.

"Give me a clear yes or no," she said, turning back to the mirror. "The ambiguity is killing me." Her mirror-wrist and mirror-hand, applying the makeup to Lily's face, looked stick-thin.

"No," he said.

"Well, hang on for a second and when your mother has made herself beautiful she'll take you downstairs and buy you whatever your heart desires."

"Okay," he said. "It just seemed so depressing, being there all alone."

"I swear, what you have to be depressed about . . ." She leaned forward and inspected her face in the mirror. "I don't suppose you'd mind waiting in the living room, Jacky? I'd rather do this alone. Tribal secrets."

Jack wordlessly turned away and wandered back into the living room.

When the telephone rang, he jumped about a foot.

"Should I get that?" he called out.

"Thank you," her cool voice came back.

Jack picked up the receiver and said hello.

"Hey kid, I finally got you," said Uncle Morgan Sloat. "What in the *world* is going on in your momma's head? Jesus, we could have a real situation here if somebody doesn't start paying attention to details. Is she there? Tell her she has to talk to me—I don't care what she says, she has to talk to me. Trust me, kiddo."

Jack let the phone dangle in his hand. He wanted to hang up, to get in the car with his mother and drive to another hotel in another state. He did not hang up. He called out, "Mom, Uncle Morgan's on the phone. He says you have to talk to him."

She was silent for a moment, and he wished he could have seen her face. Finally she said, "I'll take it in here, Jacky."

Jack already knew what he was going to have to do. His mother gently shut her bedroom door; he heard her walking back to the dressing table. She picked up the telephone in her bedroom. "Okay, Jacky," she called through the door. "Okay," he called back. Then he put the telephone back to his ear and covered the mouthpiece with his hand so that no one would hear him breathing.

"Great stunt, Lily," Uncle Morgan said. "Terrific. If you were still in pictures, we could probably get a little mileage out of this. Kind of a 'Why Has This Actress Disappeared?' thing. But don't you think it's time you started acting like a rational person again?"

"How did you find me?" she asked.

"You think you're hard to find? Give me a break, Lily, I want you to get your ass back to New York. It's time you stopped running away."

"Is that what I'm doing, Morgan?"

"You don't exactly have all the time in the world, Lily, and I don't have enough time to waste to chase you all over New England. Hey, hold on. Your kid never hung up his phone."

"Of course he did."

Jack's heart had stopped some seconds earlier.

"Get off the line, kid," Morgan Sloat's voice said to him.

"Don't be ridiculous, Sloat," his mother said.

"I'll tell you what's ridiculous, lady. You holing up in some seedy resort when you ought to be in the hospital, *that's* ridiculous. Jesus, don't you know we have about a million business decisions to make? I care about your son's education, too, and it's a damn good thing I do. You seem to have given up on that."

"I don't want to talk to you anymore," Lily said.

"You don't want to, but you have to. I'll come up there and put you in a hospital by force if I have to. We gotta make *arrangements*, Lily. You own half of the company I'm trying to run—and Jack gets your half after you're gone. I want to make sure Jack's taken care of. And if you think that taking care of Jack is what you're doing up there in goddam New Hampshire, then you're a lot sicker than you know."

"What do you want, Sloat?" Lily asked in a tired voice.

"You know what I want—I want everybody taken care of. I want what's fair. I'll take care of Jack, Lily. I'll give him fifty thousand dollars a year—you think about that, Lily. I'll see he goes to a good college. You can't even keep him in school."

"Noble Sloat," his mother said.

"Do you think that's an answer? Lily, you need help and I'm the only one offering."

"What's your cut, Sloat?" his mother asked.

"You know damn well. I get what's fair. I get what's coming to me. Your interest in Sawyer and Sloat—I worked my ass off for that company, and it ought to be mine. We could get the paperwork done in a morning, Lily, and then concentrate on getting you taken care of."

"Like Tommy Woodbine was taken care of," she said. "Sometimes I think you and Phil were *too* successful, Morgan. Sawyer and Sloat was more manageable before you got into real-estate investments and production deals. Remember when you had only a couple of deadbeat comics and a halfdozen hopeful actors and screenwriters as clients? I liked life better before the megabucks."

"Manageable, who are you kidding?" Uncle Morgan yelled. "You can't even manage yourself!" Then he made an effort to calm himself. "And I'll forget you mentioned Tom Woodbine. That was beneath even you, Lily."

"I'm going to hang up now, Sloat. Stay away from here. And stay away from Jack."

"You are going into a hospital, Lily, and this running around is going to—"

His mother hung up in the middle of Uncle Morgan's sentence; Jack gently put down his own receiver. Then he took a couple of steps closer to the window, as if not to be seen anywhere near the living-room phone. Only silence came from the closed bedroom.

"Mom?" he said.

"Yes, Jacky?" He heard a slight wobble in her voice.

"You okay? Is everything all right?"

"Me? Sure." Her footsteps came softly to the door, which cracked open. Their eyes met, his blue to her blue. Lily swung the door all the way open. Again their eyes met, for a moment of uncomfortable intensity. "Of course everything's all right. Why wouldn't it be?" Their eyes disengaged. Knowledge of some kind had passed between them, but what? Jack wondered if she knew that he had listened to her conversation; then he thought that the knowledge they had just shared was—for the first time—the fact of her illness.

"Well," he said, embarrassed now. His mother's disease, that great unspeakable subject, grew obscenely large between them. "I don't know, exactly. Uncle Morgan seemed . . ." He shrugged.

Lily shivered, and Jack came to another great recognition. His mother was afraid—at least as afraid as he was.

She plugged a cigarette in her mouth and snapped open her lighter. Another stabbing look from her deep eyes. "Don't pay any attention to that pest, Jack. I'm just irritated because it really doesn't seem that I'll ever be able to get away from him. Your Uncle Morgan likes to bully me." She exhaled gray smoke. "I'm afraid that I don't have much appetite for breakfast anymore. Why don't you take yourself downstairs and have a real breakfast this time?"

"Come with me," he said.

"I'd like to be alone for a while, Jack. Try to understand that."

*Try to understand that.*

*Trust me.*

These things that grown-ups said, meaning something else entirely.

"I'll be more companionable when you come back," she said. "That's a promise."

And what she was really saying was *I want to scream, I can't take any more of this, get out, get out!*

"Should I bring you anything?"

She shook her head, smiling toughly at him, and he had to leave the room, though he no longer had any stomach for breakfast either. Jack wandered down the corridor to the elevators. Once again, there was only one place to go, but this time he knew it before he ever reached the gloomy lobby and the ashen, censorious desk clerk.

### 4

Speedy Parker was not in the small red-painted shack of an office; he was not out on the long pier, in the arcade where the two old boys were back playing Skee-Ball as if it were a war they both knew they would lose; he was not in the dusty vacancy beneath the roller coaster. Jack Sawyer turned aimlessly in the harsh sunlight, looking down the empty avenues and deserted public places of the park. Jack's fear tightened itself up a notch. Suppose something had happened to Speedy? It was impossible, but what if Uncle Morgan had found out about Speedy (found out what, though?) and had . . . Jack mentally saw the WILD CHILD van careening around a corner, grinding its gears and picking up speed.

He jerked himself into motion, hardly knowing which way he meant to go. In the bright panic of his mood, he saw Uncle Morgan running past a row of distorting mirrors, turned by them into a series of monstrous and deformed figures. Horns grew on his bald brow, a hump flowered between his fleshy shoulders, his wide fingers became shovels. Jack veered sharply off to the right, and found himself moving toward an oddly shaped, almost round building of white slatlike boards.

From within it he suddenly heard a rhythmic *tap tap tap*. The boy ran toward the sound—a wrench hitting a pipe, a hammer striking an anvil, a noise of work. In the midst of the slats he found a doorknob and pulled open a fragile slat-door.

Jack went forward into striped darkness, and the sound grew louder. The darkness changed form around him, altered its dimensions. He stretched out his hands and touched canvas. This slid aside; instantly, glowing yellow light fell about him. "Travellin Jack," said Speedy's voice.

Jack turned toward the voice and saw the custodian seated on the ground beside a partially dismantled merry-go-round.

He held a wrench in his hand, and before him a white horse with a foamy mane lay impaled by a long silver stake from pommel to belly. Speedy gently put the wrench on the ground. "Are you ready to talk now, son?" he asked.

4

# Jack Goes Over

### 1

"Yes, I'm ready now," Jack said in a perfectly calm voice, and then burst into tears.

"Say, Travellin Jack," Speedy said, dropping his wrench and coming to him. "Say, son, take her easy, take her easy now. . . ."

But Jack couldn't take her easy. Suddenly it was too much, all of it, too much, and it was cry or just sink under a great wave of blackness—a wave which no bright streak of gold could illuminate. The tears hurt, but he sensed the terror would kill him if he did not cry it out.

"You do your weepin, Travellin Jack," Speedy said, and put his arms around him. Jack put his hot, swollen face against Speedy's thin shirt, smelling the man's smell—something like Old Spice, something like cinnamon, something like books that no one has taken out of the library in a long time. Good smells, comforting smells. He groped his arms around Speedy; his palms felt the bones in Speedy's back, close to the surface, hardly covered by scant meat.

"You weep if it put you easy again," Speedy said, rocking him. "Sometimes it does. I know. Speedy knows how far you been, Travellin Jack, and how far you got to go, and how you tired. So you weep if it put you easy."

Jack barely understood the words—only the sounds of them, soothing and calming.

"My mother's really sick," he said at last against Speedy's

chest. "I think she came here to get away from my father's
old partner. Mr. Morgan Sloat." He sniffed mightily, let go
of Speedy, stepped back, and rubbed at his swollen eyes
with the heels of his hands. He was surprised at his lack of
embarrassment—always before, his tears had disgusted and
shamed him . . . it was almost like peeing your pants. Was
that because his mother had always been so tough? He supposed that was part of it, all right; Lily Cavanaugh had little
use for tears.

"But that ain't the only reason she come here, was it?"

"No," Jack said in a low voice. "I think . . . she came here
to die." His voice rose impossibly on the last word, making a
squeak like an unoiled hinge.

"Maybe," Speedy said, looking at Jack steadily. "And maybe
you here to save her. Her . . . and a woman just like her."

"Who?" Jack said through numb lips. He knew who. He
didn't know her name, but he knew who.

"The Queen," Speedy said. "Her name is Laura DeLoessian, and she is the Queen of the Territories."

## 2

"Help me," Speedy grunted. "Catch ole Silver Lady right under the tail. You be takin' liberties with the Lady, but I guess
she ain't gonna mind if you're helpin me get her back where
she belong."

"Is that what you call her? Silver Lady?"

"Yeah bob," Speedy said, grinning, showing perhaps a
dozen teeth, top and bottom. "All carousel horses is named,
don't you know that? Catch on. Travellin Jack!"

Jack reached under the white horse's wooden tail and
locked his fingers together. Grunting, Speedy wrapped his big
brown hands around the Lady's forelegs. Together they carried the wooden horse over to the canted dish of the carousel,
the pole pointing down, its far end sinister with layers of
Quaker State oil.

"Little to the left . . ." Speedy gasped. "Yeah . . . now peg
her, Travellin Jack! Peg her down good!"

They seated the pole and then stood back, Jack panting,
Speedy grinning and gasping wheezily. The black man armed
sweat from his brow and then turned his grin on Jack.

"My, ain't we cool?"

"If you say so," Jack answered, smiling.

"I say so! Oh yes!" Speedy reached into his back pocket and pulled out the dark green pint bottle. He unscrewed the cap, drank—and for a moment Jack felt a weird certainty: he could see through Speedy. Speedy had become transparent, as ghostly as one of the spirits on the *Topper* show, which they showed on one of the indy stations out in L.A. Speedy was disappearing. *Disappearing*, Jack thought, *or going someplace else?* But that was another nutty thought; it made no sense at all.

Then Speedy was as solid as ever. It had just been a trick his eyes had played, a momentary—

*No. No it wasn't. For just a second he almost wasn't here!*

—hallucination.

Speedy was looking shrewdly at him. He started to hold the bottle out to Jack, then shook his head a little. He re-capped it instead, and then slid it into his back pocket again. He turned to study the Silver Lady, back in her place on the carousel, now needing only to have her post bolted securely into place. He was smiling. "We just as cool as we can be, Travellin Jack."

"Speedy—"

"All of em is named," Speedy said, walking slowly around the canted dish of the carousel, his footfalls echoing in the high building. Overhead, in the shadowy crisscross of the beams, a few barnswallows cooed softly. Jack followed him. "Silver Lady . . . Midnight . . . this here roan is Scout . . . this mare's Ella Speed."

The black man threw back his head and sang, startling the barnswallows into flight:

" '*Ella Speed was havin her lovin fun . . . let me tell you what old Bill Martin done. . . .'* Hoo! Look at em fly!" He laughed . . . but when he turned to Jack, he was serious again. "You like to take a shot at savin your mother's life, Jack? Hers, and the life of that other woman I tole you about?"

"I . . ." . . . *don't know how*, he meant to say, but a voice inside—a voice which came from that same previously locked room from which the memory of the two men and the attempted kidnapping had come that morning—rose up powerfully: *You do know! You might need Speedy to get you started, but you do know, Jack. You do.*

He knew that voice so very well. It was his father's voice.

"I will if you tell me how," he said, his voice rising and falling unevenly.

Speedy crossed to the room's far wall—a great circular shape made of narrow slatted boards, painted with a primitive but wildly energetic mural of dashing horses. To Jack, the wall looked like the pull-down lid of his father's rolltop desk (and that desk had been in Morgan Sloat's office the last time Jack and his mother had been there, he suddenly remembered—the thought brought a thin, milky anger with it).

Speedy pulled out a gigantic ring of keys, picked thoughtfully through them, found the one he wanted, and turned it in a padlock. He pulled the lock out of the hasp, clicked it shut, and dropped it into one of his breast pockets. Then he shoved the entire wall back on its track. Gorgeously bright sunlight poured in, making Jack narrow his eyes. Water ripples danced benignly across the ceiling. They were looking at the magnificent sea-view the riders of the Arcadia Funworld Carousel got each time Silver Lady and Midnight and Scout carried them past the east side of the round carousel building. A light sea-breeze pushed Jack's hair back from his forehead.

"Best to have sunlight if we're gonna talk about this," Speedy said. "Come on over here, Travellin Jack, and I'll tell you what I can . . . which ain't all I know. God forbid you should ever have to get all of that."

## 3

Speedy talked in his soft voice—it was as mellow and soothing to Jack as leather that has been well broken in. Jack listened, sometimes frowning, sometimes gaping.

"You know those things you call the Daydreams?"

Jack nodded.

"Those things ain't dreams, Travellin Jack. Not daydreams, not nightdreams, either. That place is a real place. Real enough, anyway. It's a lot different from here, but it's real."

"Speedy, my mom says—"

"Never mind that right now. She don't know about the Territories . . . but, in a way, she *do* know about them. Because your daddy, *he* knew. And this other man—"

"Morgan Sloat?"

"Yeah, I reckon. He knows too." Then, cryptically, Speedy added, "I know who he is over there, too. Don't I! Whooo!"

"The picture in your office . . . not Africa?"

"Not Africa."

"Not a trick?"

"Not a trick."

"And my father went to this place?" he asked, but his heart already knew the answer—it was an answer that clarified too many things not to be true. But, true or not, Jack wasn't sure how much of it he wanted to *believe*. Magic lands? Sick queens? It made him uneasy. It made him uneasy about his mind. Hadn't his mother told him over and over again when he was small that he shouldn't confuse his Daydreaming with what was really real? She had been very stern about that, and she had frightened Jack a little. Perhaps, he thought now, she had been frightened herself. Could she have lived with Jack's father for so long and not known *something*? Jack didn't think so. *Maybe*, he thought, *she didn't know very much . . . just enough to scare her*.

*Going nuts*. That's what she was talking about. People who couldn't tell the difference between real things and make-believe were going nuts.

But his father had known a different truth, hadn't he? Yes. He and Morgan Sloat.

*They have magic like we have physics, right?*

"Your father went often, yes. And this other man, Groat—"

"Sloat."

"Yeah-bob! Him. He went, too. Only your dad, Jacky, he went to see and learn. The other fella, he just went to plunder him out a fortune."

"Did Morgan Sloat kill my Uncle Tommy?" Jack asked.

"Don't know nuthin bout that. You just listen to me, Travellin Jack. Because time is short. If you really think this fellow Sloat is gonna turn up here—"

"He sounded awful mad," Jack said. Just thinking about Uncle Morgan showing up in Arcadia Beach made him feel nervous.

"—then time is shorter than ever. Because maybe he wouldn't mind so bad if your mother died. And his Twinner is sure hopin that Queen Laura dies."

"Twinner?"

"There's people in this world have got Twinners in the Territories," Speedy said. "Not many, because there's a lot less people over there—maybe only one for every hundred thousand over here. But Twinners can go back and forth the easiest."

"This Queen . . . she's my mother's . . . her Twinner?"

"Yeah, seems like she is."

"But my mother never—?"

"No. She never has. No reason."

"My father had a . . . a Twinner?"

"Yes indeed he did. A fine man."

Jack wet his lips—what a crazy conversation this was! Twinners and Territories! "When my father died over here, did his Twinner die over there?"

"Yeah. Not zackly the same time, but almost."

"Speedy?"

"What?"

"Have I got a Twinner? In the Territories?"

And Speedy looked at him so seriously that Jack felt a deep chill go up his back. "Not you, son. There's only one of you. You special. And this fella Smoot—"

"Sloat," Jack said, smiling a little.

"—yeah, whatever, he knows it. That be one of the reasons he be coming up here soon. And one of the reasons you got to get movin."

*"Why?"* Jack burst out. "What good can I do if it's cancer? If it's cancer and she's here instead of in some clinic, it's because there's no *way*, if she's here, see, it means—" The tears threatened again and he swallowed them back frantically. "It means it must be all through her."

*All through her.* Yes. That was another truth his heart knew: the truth of her accelerating weight-loss, the truth of the brown shadows under her eyes. *All through her*, but please God, hey, God, please, man, she's my *mother*—

"I mean," he finished in a thick voice, "what good is that Daydream place going to do?"

"I think we had enough jaw-chin for now," Speedy said. "Just believe this here, Travellin Jack: I'd never tell you you ought to go if you couldn't do her some good."

"But—"

"Get quiet, Travellin Jack. Can't talk no more till I show you some of what I mean. Wouldn't do no good. Come on."

Speedy put an arm around Jack's shoulders and led him around the carousel dish. They went out the door together and walked down one of the amusement park's deserted byways. On their left was the Demon Dodgem Cars building, now boarded and shuttered. On their right was a series of booths: Pitch Til U Win, Famous Pier Pizza & Dough-Boys, the Rimfire Shooting Gallery, also boarded up (faded wild animals pranced across the boards—lions and tigers and bears, o my).

They reached the wide main street, which was called Boardwalk Avenue in vague imitation of Atlantic City— Arcadia Funworld had a pier, but no real boardwalk. The arcade building was now a hundred yards down to their left and the arch marking the entrance to Arcadia Funworld about two hundred yards down to their right. Jack could hear the steady, grinding thunder of the breaking waves, the lonely cries of the gulls.

He looked at Speedy, meaning to ask him what now, what next, could he mean any of it or was it a cruel joke . . . but he said none of those things. Speedy was holding out the green glass bottle.

"That—" Jack began.

"Takes you there," Speedy said. "Lot of people who visit over there don't need nothin like this, but you ain't been there in a while, have you, Jacky?"

"No." When had he last closed his eyes in this world and opened them in the magic world of the Daydreams, that world with its rich, vital smells and its deep, transparent sky? Last year? No. Further back than that . . . California . . . after his father had died. He would have been about . . .

Jack's eyes widened. Nine years old? That long? Three *years?*

It was frightening to think how quietly, how unobtrusively, those dreams, sometimes sweet, sometimes darkly unsettling, had slipped away—as if a large part of his imagination had died painlessly and unannounced.

He took the bottle from Speedy quickly, almost dropping it. He felt a little panicky. Some of the Daydreams had been disturbing, yes, and his mother's carefully worded admonitions not to mix up reality and make-believe *(in other words don't go crazy, Jacky, ole kid ole sock, okay?)* had been a little scary, yes, but he discovered now that he didn't want to lose that world after all.

He looked in Speedy's eyes and thought: *He knows it, too. Everything I just thought, he knows. Who are you, Speedy?*

"When you ain't been there for a while, you kinda forget how to get there on your own hook," Speedy said. He nodded at the bottle. "That's why I got me some magic juice. This stuff is *special*." Speedy spoke this last in tones that were almost reverential.

"Is it from there? The Territories?"

"Nope. They got *some* magic right here, Travellin Jack. Not much, but a little. This magic juice come from California."

Jack looked at him doubtfully.

"Go on. Have you a little sip and see if you don't go travellin." Speedy grinned. "Drink enough of that, you can go just about anyplace you want. You're lookin at one who knows."

"Jeez, Speedy, but—" He began to feel afraid. His mouth had gone dry, the sun seemed much too bright, and he could feel his pulsebeat speeding up in his temples. There was a coppery taste under his tongue and Jack thought: *That's how his "magic juice" will taste—horrible.*

"If you get scared and want to come back, have another sip," Speedy said.

"It'll come with me? The bottle? You promise?" The thought of getting stuck there, in that mystical other place, while his mother was sick and Sloat-beset back here, was awful.

"I promise."

"Okay." Jack brought the bottle to his lips . . . and then let it fall away a little. The smell was awful—sharp and rancid. "I don't want to, Speedy," he whispered.

Lester Parker looked at him, and his lips were smiling, but there was no smile in his eyes—they were stern. Uncompromising. Frightening. Jack thought of black eyes: eye of gull, eye of vortex. Terror swept through him.

He held the bottle out to Speedy. "Can't you take it back?" he asked, and his voice came out in a strengthless whisper. "Please?"

Speedy made no reply. He did not remind Jack that his mother was dying, or that Morgan Sloat was coming. He didn't call Jack a coward, although he had never in his life felt so much like a coward, not even the time he had backed away from the high board at Camp Accomac and some of the other kids had booed him. Speedy merely turned around and whistled at a cloud.

Now loneliness joined the terror, sweeping helplessly through him. Speedy had turned away from him; Speedy had shown him his back.

"Okay," Jack said suddenly. "Okay, if it's what you need me to do."

He raised the bottle again, and before he could have any second or third thoughts, he drank.

The taste was worse than anything he had anticipated. He had had wine before, had even developed some taste for it (he especially liked the dry white wines his mother served with sole or snapper or swordfish), and this was something like wine . . . but at the same time it was a dreadful mockery of all the wines he had drunk before. The taste was high and sweet and rotten, not the taste of lively grapes but of dead grapes that had not lived well.

As his mouth flooded with that horrible sweet-purple taste, he could actually *see* those grapes—dull, dusty, obese and nasty, crawling up a dirty stucco wall in a thick, syrupy sunlight that was silent except for the stupid buzz of many flies.

He swallowed and thin fire printed a snail-trail down his throat.

He closed his eyes, grimacing, his gorge threatening to rise. He did not vomit, although he believed that if he had eaten any breakfast he would have done.

"Speedy—"

He opened his eyes, and further words died in his throat. He forgot about the need to sick up that horrible parody of wine. He forgot about his mother, and Uncle Morgan, and his father, and almost everything else.

Speedy was gone. The graceful arcs of the roller coaster against the sky were gone. Boardwalk Avenue was gone.

He was someplace else now. He was—

"In the Territories," Jack whispered, his entire body crawl-

ing with a mad mixture of terror and exhilaration. He could
feel the hair stirring on the nape of his neck, could feel a
goofed-up grin pulling at the corners of his mouth. "Speedy,
I'm here, my God, I'm here in the Territories! I—"

But wonder overcame him. He clapped a hand over his
mouth and slowly turned in a complete circle, looking at this
place to which Speedy's "magic juice" had brought him.

### 4

The ocean was still there, but now it was a darker, richer
blue—the truest indigo Jack had ever seen. For a moment he
stood transfixed, the sea-breeze blowing in his hair, looking at
the horizon-line where that indigo ocean met a sky the color
of faded denim.

That horizon-line showed a faint but unmistakable curve.

He shook his head, frowning, and turned the other way.
Sea-grass, high and wild and tangled, ran down from the
headland where the round carousel building had been only a
minute ago. The arcade pier was also gone; where it had been,
a wild tumble of granite blocks ran down to the ocean. The
waves struck the lowest of these and ran into ancient cracks
and channels with great hollow boomings. Foam as thick as
whipped cream jumped into the clear air and was blown away
by the wind.

Abruptly Jack seized his left cheek with his left thumb and
forefinger. He pinched hard. His eyes watered, but nothing
changed.

"It's real," he whispered, and another wave boomed onto
the headland, raising white curds of foam.

Jack suddenly realized that Boardwalk Avenue *was* still
here . . . after a fashion. A rutted cart-track ran from the top
of the headland—where Boardwalk Avenue had ended at the
entrance to the arcade in what his mind persisted in thinking
of as "the real world"—down to where he was standing and
then on to the north, just as Boardwalk Avenue ran north, becoming Arcadia Avenue after it passed under the arch at the
border of Funworld. Sea-grass grew up along the center of
this track, but it had a bent and matted look that made Jack
think that the track was still used, at least once in a while.

He started north, still holding the green bottle in his right hand. It occurred to him that somewhere, in another world, Speedy was holding the cap that went on this bottle.

*Did I disappear right in front of him? I suppose I must have.* Jeez!

About forty paces along the track, he came upon a tangle of blackberry bushes. Clustered amid the thorns were the fattest, darkest, most lush-looking blackberries he had ever seen. Jack's stomach, apparently over the indignity of the "magic juice," made a loud *going*ing sound.

*Blackberries? In September?*

Never mind. After all that had happened today (and it was not yet ten o'clock), sticking at blackberries in September seemed a little bit like refusing to take an aspirin after one has swallowed a doorknob.

Jack reached in, picked a handful of berries, and tossed them into his mouth. They were amazingly sweet, amazingly good. Smiling (his lips had taken on a definite bluish cast), thinking it quite possible that he had lost his mind, he picked another handful of berries . . . and then a third. He had never tasted anything so fine—although, he thought later, it was not just the berries themselves; part of it was the incredible clarity of the air.

He got a couple of scratches while picking a fourth helping—it was as if the bushes were telling him to lay off, enough was enough, already. He sucked at the deepest of the scratches, on the fleshy pad below the thumb, and then headed north along the twin ruts again, moving slowly, trying to look everywhere at once.

He paused a little way from the blackberry tangles to look up at the sun, which seemed somehow smaller and yet more fiery. Did it have a faint orange cast, like in those old medieval pictures? Jack thought perhaps it did. And—

A cry, as rusty and unpleasant as an old nail being pulled slowly out of a board, suddenly arose on his right, scattering his thoughts. Jack turned toward it, his shoulders going up, his eyes widening.

It was a gull—and its size was mind-boggling, almost unbelievable (but there it was, as solid as stone, as real as houses). It was, in fact, the size of an eagle. Its smooth white bullet-head cocked to one side. Its fishhook of a beak opened and closed. It fluttered great wings, rippling the sea-grass around it.

And then, seemingly without fear, it began to hop toward Jack.

Faintly, Jack heard the clear, brazen note of many horns blown together in a simple flourish, and for no reason at all he thought of his mother.

He glanced to the north momentarily, in the direction he had been travelling, drawn by that sound—it filled him with a sense of unfocussed urgency. It was, he thought (when there was *time* to think), like being hungry for a specific *something* that you haven't had in a long time—ice cream, potato chips, maybe a taco. You don't know until you see it—and until you do, there is only a need without a name, making you restless, making you nervous.

He saw pennons and the peak of what might have been a great tent—a pavillion—against the sky.

*That's where the Alhambra is*, he thought, and then the gull shrieked at him. He turned toward it and was alarmed to see it was now less than six feet away. Its beak opened again, showing that dirty pink lining, making him think of yesterday, the gull that had dropped the clam on the rock and then fixed him with a horrid stare exactly like this one. The gull was grinning at him—he was sure of it. As it hopped closer, Jack could smell a low and noisome stink hanging about it—dead fish and rotted seaweed.

The gull hissed at him and flurried its wings again.

"Get out of here," Jack said loudly. His heart was pumping quick blood and his mouth had gone dry, but he did not want to be scared off by a seagull, even a big one. "Get out!"

The gull opened its beak again . . . and then, in a terrible, open-throated series of pulses, it spoke—or seemed to.

*"Other's iyyyin Ack . . . other's iyyyyyyyyyyin—"*

*Mother's dying, Jack. . . .*

The gull took another clumsy hop toward him, scaly feet clutching at the grassy tangles, beak opening and closing, black eyes fixed on Jack's. Hardly aware of what he was doing, Jack raised the green bottle and drank.

Again that horrible taste made him wince his eyes shut—and when he opened them he was looking stupidly at a yellow sign which showed the black silhouettes of two running kids, a little boy and a little girl. SLOW CHILDREN, this sign read. A seagull—this one of perfectly normal size—flew up from it with a squawk, no doubt startled by Jack's sudden appearance.

He looked around, and was walloped by disorientation. His stomach, full of blackberries and Speedy's pustulant "magic juice," rolled over, groaning. The muscles in his legs began to flutter unpleasantly, and all at once he sat down on the curb at the base of the sign with a bang that travelled up his spine and made his teeth click together.

He suddenly leaned over between his splayed knees and opened his mouth wide, sure he was just going to yark up the whole works. Instead he hiccuped twice, half-gagged, and then felt his stomach slowly relax.

*It was the berries*, he thought. *If it hadn't been for the berries, I would have puked for sure.*

He looked up and felt the unreality wash over him again. He had walked no more than sixty paces down the cart-track in the Territories world. He was sure of that. Say his stride was two feet—no, say two and a half feet, just to be on the safe side. That meant he had come a paltry hundred and fifty feet. But—

He looked behind him and saw the arch, with its big red letters: ARCADIA FUNWORLD. Although his vision was 20/20, the sign was now so far away he could barely read it. To his right was the rambling, many-winged Alhambra Inn, with the formal gardens before it and the ocean beyond it.

In the Territories world he had come a hundred and fifty feet.

Over here he had somehow come half a mile.

"Jesus Christ," Jack Sawyer whispered, and covered his eyes with his hands.

## 5

"Jack! Jack, boy! Travellin Jack!"

Speedy's voice rose over the washing-machine roar of an old flathead-six engine. Jack looked up—his head felt impossibly heavy, his limbs leaden with weariness—and saw a very old International Harvester truck rolling slowly toward him. Homemade stake sides had been added to the back of the truck, and they rocked back and forth like loose teeth as the truck moved up the street toward him. The body was painted a hideous turquoise. Speedy was behind the wheel.

He pulled up at the curb, gunned the engine (*Whup! Whup! Whup-whup-whup!*), and then killed it (*Hahhhhhhhhhh . . .*). He climbed down quickly.

"You all right, Jack?"

Jack held the bottle out for Speedy to take. "Your magic juice really sucks, Speedy," he said wanly.

Speedy looked hurt . . . then he smiled. "Whoever tole you medicine supposed to taste good, Travellin Jack?"

"Nobody, I guess," Jack said. He felt some of his strength coming back—slowly—as that thick feeling of disorientation ebbed.

"You believe now, Jack?"

Jack nodded.

"No," Speedy said. "That don't git it. Say it out loud."

"The Territories," Jack said. "They're there. Real. I saw a bird—" He stopped and shuddered.

"What kind of a bird?" Speedy asked sharply.

"Seagull. Biggest damn seagull—" Jack shook his head. "You wouldn't believe it." He thought and then said, "No, I guess *you* would. Nobody else, maybe, but *you* would."

"Did it talk? Lots of birds over there do. Talk foolishness, mostly. And there's some that talks a kind of sense . . . but it's a evil kind of sense, and mostly it's lies."

Jack was nodding. Just hearing Speedy talk of these things, as if it were utterly rational and utterly lucid to do so, made him feel better.

"I think it did talk. But it was like—" He thought hard. "There was a kid at the school Richard and I went to in L.A. Brandon Lewis. He had a speech impediment, and when he talked you could hardly understand him. The bird was like that. But I knew what it said. It said my mother was dying."

Speedy put an arm around Jack's shoulders and they sat quietly together on the curb for a time. The desk clerk from the Alhambra, looking pale and narrow and suspicious of every living thing in the universe, came out with a large stack of mail. Speedy and Jack watched him go down to the corner of Arcadia and Beach Drive and dump the inn's correspondence into the mailbox. He turned back, marked Jack and

Speedy with his thin gaze, and then turned up the Alhambra's main walk. The top of his head could barely be descried over the tops of the thick box hedges.

The sound of the big front door opening and closing was clearly audible, and Jack was struck by a terrible sense of this place's autumn desolation. Wide, deserted streets. The long beach with its empty dunes of sugar-sand. The empty amusement park, with the roller-coaster cars standing on a siding under canvas tarps and all the booths padlocked. It came to him that his mother had brought him to a place very like the end of the world.

Speedy had cocked his head back and sang in his true and mellow voice, *"Well I've laid around . . . and played around . . . this old town too long . . . summer's almost gone, yes, and winter's coming on . . . winter's coming on, and I feel like . . . I got to travel on—"*

He broke off and looked at Jack.

"You feel like you got to travel, ole Travellin Jack?"

Flagging terror stole through his bones.

"I guess so," he said. "If it will help. Help her. Can I help her, Speedy?"

"You can," Speedy said gravely.

"But—"

"Oh, there's a whole string of buts," Speedy said. "Whole *trainload* of buts, Travellin Jack. I don't promise you no cakewalk. I don't promise you success. Don't promise that you'll come back alive, or if you do, that you'll come back with your mind still bolted together.

"You gonna have to do a lot of your ramblin in the Territories, because the Territories is a whole lot smaller. You notice that?"

"Yes."

"Figured you would. Because you sure did get a whole mess down the road, didn't you?"

Now an earlier question recurred to Jack, and although it was off the subject, he had to know. "Did I disappear, Speedy? Did you see me disappear?"

"You went," Speedy said, and clapped his hands once, sharply, "just like *that*."

Jack felt a slow, unwilling grin stretch his mouth . . . and Speedy grinned back.

"I'd like to do it sometime in Mr. Balgo's computer class," Jack said, and Speedy cackled like a child. Jack joined him—and the laughter felt good, almost as good as those blackberries had tasted.

After a few moments Speedy sobered and said, "There's a reason you got to be in the Territories, Jack. There's somethin you got to git. It's a mighty powerful somethin."

"And it's over there?"

"Yeah-bob."

"It can help my mother?"

"Her . . . and the other."

"The Queen?"

Speedy nodded.

"What is it? Where is it? When do I—"

"Hold it! Stop!" Speedy held up a hand. His lips were smiling, but his eyes were grave, almost sorrowing. "One thing at a time. And, Jack, I can't tell you what I don't know . . . or what I'm not allowed to tell."

"Not allowed?" Jack asked, bewildered. "Who—"

"There you go again," Speedy said. "Now listen, Travellin Jack. You got to leave as soon as you can, before that man Bloat can show up an bottle you up—"

*"Sloat."*

"Yeah, him. You got to get out before he comes."

"But he'll bug my mother," Jack said, wondering why he was saying it—because it was true, or because it was an excuse to avoid the trip that Speedy was setting before him, like a meal that might be poisoned. "You don't know him! He—"

"I know him," Speedy said quietly. "I know him of old, Travellin Jack. And he knows me. He's got my marks on him. They're hidden—but they're on him. Your momma can take care of herself. At least, she's gonna have to, for a while. Because you got to go."

"Where?"

"West," Speedy said. "From this ocean to the other."

*"What?"* Jack cried, appalled by the thought of such distance. And then he thought of an ad he'd seen on TV not three nights ago—a man picking up goodies at a deli buffet some thirty-five thousand feet in the air, just as cool as a cucumber. Jack had flown from one coast to another with his mother a good two dozen times, and was always secretly delighted by

the fact that when you flew from New York to L.A. you could have sixteen hours of daylight. It was like cheating time. And it was easy.

"Can I fly?" he asked Speedy.

*"No!"* Speedy almost yelled, his eyes widening in consternation. He gripped Jack's shoulder with one strong hand. "Don't you let *nuthin* git you up in the sky! You dassn't! If you happened to flip over into the Territories while you was up there—"

He said no more; he didn't have to. Jack had a sudden, appalling picture of himself tumbling out of that clear, cloudless sky, a screaming boy-projectile in jeans with a red-and-white-striped rugby shirt, a sky-diver with no parachute.

"You *walk*," Speedy said. "And thumb what rides you think you can . . . but you got to be careful, because there's strangers out there. Some are just crazy people, sissies that would like to touch you or thugs that would like to mug you. But some are real Strangers, Travellin Jack. They people with a foot in each world—they look that way and this like a goddam Janus-head. I'm afraid they gonna know you comin before too long has passed. And they'll be on the watch."

"Are they"—he groped—"Twinners?"

"Some are. Some aren't. I can't say no more right now. But you get across if you can. Get across to the other ocean. You travel in the Territories when you can and you'll get across faster. You take the juice—"

"I hate it!"

"Never mind what you hate," Speedy said sternly. "You get across and you're gonna find a place—another Alhambra. You got to go in that place. It's a scary place, a bad place. But you got to go in."

"How will I find it?"

"It will call you. You'll hear it loud and clear, son."

"Why?" Jack asked. He wet his lips. "Why do I have to go there, if it's so bad?"

"Because," Speedy said, "that's where the Talisman is. Somewhere in that other Alhambra."

"I don't know what you're talking about!"

"You will," Speedy said. He stood up, then took Jack's hand. Jack rose. The two of them stood face-to-face, old black man and young white boy.

"Listen," Speedy said, and his voice took on a slow, chanting rhythm. "Talisman be given unto your hand, Travellin Jack. Not too big, not too small, she look just like a crystal ball. Travellin Jack, ole Travellin Jack, you be goin to California to bring her back. But here's your burden, here's your cross: drop her, Jack, and all be lost."

"I don't know what you're talking about," Jack repeated with a scared kind of stubbornness. "You have to—"

"No," Speedy said, not unkindly. "I got to finish with that carousel this morning, Jack, that's what I got to do. Got no time for any more jaw-chin. I got to get back and you got to get on. Can't tell you no more now. I guess I'll be seein you around. Here . . . or over there."

"But I don't know what to *do!*" Jack said as Speedy swung up into the cab of the old truck.

"You know enough to get movin," Speedy said. "You'll go to the Talisman, Jack. She'll draw you to her."

"I don't even know what a Talisman is!"

Speedy laughed and keyed the ignition. The truck started up with a big blue blast of exhaust. "Look it up in the dictionary!" he shouted, and threw the truck into reverse.

He backed up, turned around, and then the truck was rattling back toward Arcadia Funworld. Jack stood by the curb, watching it go. He had never felt so alone in his life.

5

# Jack and Lily

### 1

When Speedy's truck turned off the road and disappeared beneath the Funworld arch, Jack began to move toward the hotel. A Talisman. In another Alhambra. On the edge of another ocean. His heart seemed empty. Without Speedy beside him, the task was mountainous, so huge; vague, too—while Speedy had been talking, Jack had had the feeling of *almost*

understanding that macaroni of hints and threats and instructions. Now it was close to just being macaroni. The Territories
were real, though. He hugged that certainty as close as he
could, and it both warmed and chilled him. They were a real
place, and he was going there again. Even if he did not really
understand everything yet—even if he was an ignorant pil-
grim, he was going. Now all he had to do was to try to convince his mother. "Talisman," he said to himself, using the
word as the thing, and crossed empty Boardwalk Avenue and
jumped up the steps onto the path between the hedges. The
darkness of the Alhambra's interior, once the great door had
swung shut, startled him. The lobby was a long cave—you'd
need a fire just to separate the shadows. The pale clerk flickered behind the long desk, stabbing at Jack with his white
eyes. A message there: yes. Jack swallowed and turned away.
The message made him stronger, it increased him, though its
intention was only scornful.

He went toward the elevators with a straight back and an
unhurried step. *Hang around with blackies, huh? Let them put
their arms around you, huh?* The elevator whirred down like a
great heavy bird, the doors parted, and Jack stepped inside.
He turned to punch the button marked with a glowing 4. The
clerk was still posed spectrally behind the desk, sending out
his dumdum's message. *Niggerlover Niggerlover Niggerlover
(like it that way, hey brat? Hot and black, that's for you,
hey?).* The doors mercifully shut. Jack's stomach fell toward
his shoes, the elevator lurched upward.

The hatred stayed down there in the lobby: the very air in
the elevator felt better once it had risen above the first floor.
Now all Jack had to do was to tell his mother that he had to go
to California by himself.

*Just don't let Uncle Morgan sign any papers for you. . . .*

As Jack stepped out of the elevator, he wondered for the
first time in his life whether Richard Sloat understood what
his father was really like.

## 2

Down past the empty sconces and paintings of little boats riding foamy, corrugated seas, the door marked 408 slanted inward, revealing a foot of the suite's pale carpet. Sunlight from

the living-room windows made a long rectangle on the inner wall. "Hey Mom," Jack said, entering the suite. "You didn't close the door, what's the big—" He was alone in the room. "Idea?" he said to the furniture. "Mom?" Disorder seemed to ooze from the tidy room—an overflowing ashtray, a half-full tumbler of water left on the coffee table.

This time, Jack promised himself, he would not panic.

He turned in a slow circle. Her bedroom door was open, the room itself as dark as the lobby because Lily had never pulled open the curtains.

"Hey, I know you're here," he said, and then walked through her empty bedroom to knock at her bathroom door. No reply. Jack opened this door and saw a pink toothbrush beside the sink, a forlorn hairbrush on the dressing table. Bristles snarled with light hairs. *Laura DeLoessian*, announced a voice in Jack's mind, and he stepped backward out of the little bathroom—that name stung him.

"Oh, not again," he said to himself. "Where'd she *go*?"

Already he was seeing it.

He saw it as he went to his own bedroom, saw it as he opened his own door and surveyed his rumpled bed, his flattened knapsack and little stack of paperback books, his socks balled up on top of the dresser. He saw it when he looked into his own bathroom, where towels lay in oriental disarray over the floor, the sides of the tub, and the Formica counters.

*Morgan Sloat thrusting through the door, grabbing his mother's arms and hauling her downstairs . . .*

Jack hurried back into the living room and this time looked behind the couch.

*. . . yanking her out a side door and pushing her into a car, his eyes beginning to turn yellow. . . .*

He picked up the telephone and punched 0. "This is, ah, Jack Sawyer, and I'm in, ah, room four-oh-eight. Did my mother leave any message for me? She was supposed to be here and . . . and for some reason . . . ah . . ."

"I'll check," said the girl, and Jack clutched the phone for a burning moment before she returned. "No message for four-oh-eight, sorry."

"How about four-oh-seven?"

"That's the same slot," the girl told him.

"Ah, did she have any visitors in the last half hour or so? Anybody come this morning? To see her, I mean."

"That would be Reception," the girl said. "I wouldn't know. Do you want me to check for you?"

"Please," Jack said.

"Oh, I'm happy to have something to do in this morgue," she told him. "Stay on the line."

Another burning moment. When she came back to him, it was with "No visitors. Maybe she left a note somewhere in your rooms."

"Yes, I'll look," Jack said miserably and hung up. Would the clerk tell the truth? Or would Morgan Sloat have held out a hand with a twenty-dollar bill folded like a stamp into his meaty palm? That, too, Jack could see.

He dropped himself on the couch, stifling an irrational desire to look under the cushions. Of course Uncle Morgan could not have come to the rooms and abducted her—he was still in California. But he could have sent other people to do it for him. Those people Speedy had mentioned, the Strangers with a foot in each world.

Then Jack could stay in the room no longer. He bounced off the couch and went back into the corridor, closing the door after him. When he had gone a few paces down the hall, he twirled around in mid-step, went back, and opened the door with his own key. He pushed the door an inch in, and then trotted back toward the elevators. It was always possible that she had gone out without her key—to the shop in the lobby, to the newsstand for a magazine or a paper.

Sure. He had not seen her pick up a newspaper since the beginning of summer. All the news she cared about came over an internal radio.

Out for a walk, then.

Yeah, out exercising and breathing deeply. Or jogging, maybe: maybe Lily Cavanaugh had suddenly gone in for the hundred-yard dash. She'd set up hurdles down on the beach and was in training for the next Olympics. . . .

When the elevator deposited him in the lobby he glanced into the shop, where an elderly blond woman behind a counter peered at him over the tops of her glasses. Stuffed animals, a tiny pile of thin newspapers, a display rack of flavored Chap Stick. Leaning out of pockets in a wallstand were *People* and *Us* and *New Hampshire Magazine*.

"Sorry," Jack said, and turned away.

He found himself staring at the bronze plaque beside a huge, dispirited fern . . . *has begun to sicken and must soon die*.

The woman in the shop cleared her throat. Jack thought that he must have been staring at those words of Daniel Webster's for entire minutes. "Yes?" the woman said behind him.

"Sorry," Jack repeated, and pulled himself into the center of the lobby. The hateful clerk lifted an eyebrow, then turned sideways to stare at a deserted staircase. Jack made himself approach the man.

"Mister," he said when he stood before the desk. The clerk was pretending to try to remember the capital of North Carolina or the principal export of Peru. "Mister." The man scowled to himself: he was nearly there, he could not be disturbed.

All of this was an act, Jack knew, and he said, "I wonder if you can help me."

The man decided to look at him after all. "Depends on what the help is, sonny."

Jack consciously decided to ignore the hidden sneer. "Did you see my mother go out a little while ago?"

"What's a little while?" Now the sneer was almost visible.

"Did you see her go out? That's all I'm asking."

"Afraid she saw you and your sweetheart holding hands out there?"

"God, you're such a creep," Jack startled himself by saying. "No, I'm not afraid of that. I'm just wondering if she went out, and if you weren't such a creep, you'd tell me." His face had grown hot, and he realized that his hands were bunched into fists.

"Well okay, she went out," the clerk said, drifting away toward the bank of pigeonholes behind him. "But you'd better watch your tongue, boy. You better apologize to me, fancy little Master Sawyer. I got eyes, too. I know things."

"You run your mouth and I run my business," Jack said, dredging the phrase up from one of his father's old records—perhaps it did not quite fit the situation, but it felt right in his mouth, and the clerk blinked satisfactorily.

"Maybe she's in the gardens, I don't know," the man said gloomily, but Jack was already on his way toward the door.

The Darling of the Drive-ins and Queen of the Bs was nowhere in the wide gardens before the hotel, Jack saw immediately—and he had known that she would not be in the gardens, for he would have seen her on his way into the hotel. Besides, Lily Cavanaugh did not dawdle through gardens: that suited her as little as did setting up hurdles on the beach.

A few cars rolled down Boardwalk Avenue. A gull screeched far overhead, and Jack's heart tightened.

The boy pushed his fingers through his hair and looked up and down the bright street. Maybe she had been curious about Speedy—maybe she'd wanted to check out this unusual new pal of her son's and had wandered down to the amusement park. But Jack could not see her in Arcadia Funworld any more than he could see her lingering picturesquely in the gardens. He turned in the less familiar direction, toward the town line.

Separated from the Alhambra's grounds by a high thick hedge, the Arcadia Tea and Jam Shoppe stood first in a row of brightly colored shops. It and New England Drugs were the only shops in the terrace to remain open after Labor Day. Jack hesitated a moment on the cracked sidewalk. A tea shop, much less shoppe, was an unlikely situation for the Darling of the Drive-ins. But since it was the first place he might expect to find her, he moved across the sidewalk and peered in the window.

A woman with piled-up hair sat smoking before a cash register. A waitress in a pink rayon dress leaned against the far wall. Jack saw no customers. Then at one of the tables near the Alhambra end of the shop he saw an old woman lifting a cup. Apart from the help, she was alone. Jack watched the old woman delicately replace the cup in the saucer, then fish a cigarette from her bag, and realized with a sickening jolt that she was his mother. An instant later, the impression of age had disappeared.

But he could remember it—and it was as if he were seeing her through bifocals, seeing both Lily Cavanaugh Sawyer and that fragile old woman in the same body.

Jack gently opened the door, but still he set off the tinkle of the bell that he had *known* was above it. The blond woman at the register nodded, smiling. The waitress straightened up and smoothed the lap of her dress. His mother stared at him with what looked like genuine surprise, and then gave him an open smile.

"Well, Wandering Jack, you're so tall that you looked just like your father when you came through that door," she said. "Sometimes I forget you're only twelve."

### 3

"You called me 'Wandering Jack,'" he said, pulling a chair out and dropping himself into it.

Her face was very pale, and the smudges beneath her eyes looked almost like bruises.

"Didn't your father call you that? I just happened to think of it—you've been on the move all morning."

"He called me Wandering Jack?"

"Something like that . . . sure he did. When you were tiny. *Travelling* Jack," she said firmly. "That was it. He used to call you Travelling Jack—you know, when we'd see you tearing down the lawn. It was funny, I guess. I left the door open, by the way. Didn't know if you remembered to take your key with you."

"I saw," he said, still tingling with the new information she had so casually given him.

"Want any breakfast? I just couldn't take the thought of eating another meal in that hotel."

The waitress had appeared beside them. "Young man?" she asked, lifting her order pad.

"How did you know I'd find you here?"

"Where else is there to go?" his mother reasonably asked, and told the waitress, "Give him the three-star breakfast. He's growing about an inch a day."

Jack leaned against the back of his chair. How could he begin this?

His mother glanced at him curiously, and he began—he had to begin, now. "Mom, if I had to go away for a while, would you be all right?"

"What do you mean, all right? And what do you mean, go away for a while?"

"Would you be able—ah, would you have trouble from Uncle Morgan?"

"I can handle old Sloat," she said, smiling tautly. "I can handle him for a while, anyhow. What's this all about, Jacky? You're not going anywhere."

"I have to," he said. "Honest." Then he realized that he sounded like a child begging for a toy. Mercifully, the waitress arrived with toast in a rack and a stubby glass of tomato juice. He looked away for a moment, and when he looked back, his mother was spreading jam from one of the pots on the table over a triangular section of toast.

"I have to go," he said. His mother handed him the toast; her face moved with a thought, but she said nothing.

"You might not see me for a while, Mom," he said. "I'm going to try to help you. That's why I have to go."

"Help me?" she asked, and her cool incredulity, Jack reckoned, was about seventy-five percent genuine.

"I want to try to save your life," he said.

"Is that all?"

"I can do it."

"You can save my life. That's very entertaining, Jacky-boy; it ought to make prime time someday. Ever think about going into network programming?" She had put down the red-smeared knife and was widening her eyes in mockery: but beneath the deliberate incomprehension he saw two things. A flare-up of her terror; a faint, almost unrecognized hope that he might after all be able to do something.

"Even if you say I can't try, I'm going to do it anyhow. So you might as well give me your permission."

"Oh, that's a wonderful deal. Especially since I don't have any idea of what you're talking about."

"I think you do, though—I think you do have some idea, Mom. Because Dad would have known exactly what I'm talking about."

Her cheeks reddened; her mouth thinned into a line. "That's so unfair it's despicable, Jacky. You can't use what Philip might have known as a weapon against me."

"What he did know, not what he might have known."

"You're talking total horseshit, sonny boy."

The waitress, setting a plate of scrambled eggs, home fries, and sausages before Jack, audibly inhaled.

After the waitress had paraded off, his mother shrugged. "I don't seem able to find the right *tone* with the help around here. But horseshit is still horseshit is still horseshit, to quote Gertrude Stein."

"I'm going to save your life, Mom," he repeated. "And I have to go a long way away and bring something back to do it. And so that's what I'm going to do."

"I wish I knew what you were talking about."

Just an ordinary conversation, Jack told himself: as ordinary as asking permission to spend a couple of nights at a friend's house. He cut a sausage in half and popped one of the pieces in his mouth. She was watching him carefully. Sausage chewed and swallowed, Jack inserted a forkful of egg into his mouth. Speedy's bottle lumped like a rock against his backside.

"I also wish you'd act as though you could hear the little remarks I send your way, as obtuse as they may be."

Jack stolidly swallowed the eggs and inserted a salty wad of the crisp potatoes into his mouth.

Lily put her hands in her lap. The longer he said nothing, the more she would listen when he did talk. He pretended to concentrate on his breakfast, eggs sausage potatoes, sausage potatoes eggs, potatoes eggs sausage, until he sensed that she was near to shouting at him.

*My father called me Travelling Jack,* he thought to himself. *This is right; this is as right as I'll ever get.*

"*Jack*—"

"Mom," he said, "sometimes didn't Dad call you up from a long way away, and you knew he was supposed to be in town?"

She raised her eyebrows.

"And sometimes didn't you, ah, walk into a room because you thought he was there, maybe even *knew* he was there—but he wasn't?"

Let her chew on that.

"No," she said.

Both of them let the denial fade away.

"Almost never."

"Mom, it even happened to *me*," Jack said.

"There was always an explanation, you know there was."

"My father—this is what *you* know—was never too bad at explaining things. Especially the stuff that really couldn't be explained. He was very good at that. That's part of the reason he was such a good agent."

Now she was silent again.

"Well, I know where he went," Jack said. "I've been there already. I was there this morning. And if I go there again, I can try to save your life."

*"My life doesn't need you to save it, it doesn't need anyone to save it,"* his mother hissed. Jack looked down at his devastated plate and muttered something. "What was that?" she drilled at him.

"I think it does, I said." He met her eyes with his own.

"Suppose I ask how you propose to go about saving my life, as you put it."

"I can't answer. Because I don't really understand it yet. Mom, I'm not in school, anyhow . . . give me a chance. I might only be gone a week or so."

She raised her eyebrows.

"It could be longer," he admitted.

"I think you're nuts," she said. But he saw that part of her wanted to believe him, and her next words proved it. "If—*if*—I were mad enough to allow you to go off on this mysterious errand, I'd have to be sure that you wouldn't be in any danger."

"Dad always came back," Jack pointed out.

"I'd rather risk my life than yours," she said, and this truth, too, lay hugely between them for a long moment.

"I'll call when I can. But don't get too worried if a couple of weeks go by without my calling. I'll come back, too, just like Dad always did."

"This whole thing is nuts," she said. "Me included. How are you going to get to this place you have to go to? And where is it? Do you have enough money?"

"I have everything I need," he said, hoping that she would not press him on the first two questions. The silence stretched out and out, and finally he said, "I guess I'll mainly walk. I can't talk about it much, Mom."

"Travelling Jack," she said. "I can almost believe . . ."

"Yes," Jack said. "*Yes*." He was nodding. *And maybe*, he

thought, *you know some of what* she *knows, the real Queen, and that's why you are letting go this easily.* "That's right. I can believe, too. That's what makes it right."

"Well . . . since you say you'll go no matter what I say . . ."

"I will, too."

". . . then I guess it doesn't matter what I say." She looked at him bravely. "It does matter, though. I know. I want you to get back here as quick as you can, sonny boy. You're not going right away, are you?"

"I have to." He inhaled deeply. "Yes. I am going right away. As soon as I leave you."

"I could almost believe in this rigamarole. You're Phil Sawyer's son, all right. You haven't found a girl somewhere in this place, have you . . . ?" She looked at him very sharply. "No. No girl. Okay. Save my life. Off with you." She shook her head, and he thought he saw an extra brightness in her eyes. "If you're going to leave, get out of here, Jacky. Call me tomorrow."

"If I can." He stood up.

"If you can. Of course. Forgive me." She looked down at nothing, and he saw that her eyes were unfocused. Red dots burned in the middle of her cheeks.

Jack leaned over and kissed her, but she just waved him away. The waitress stared at the two of them as if they were performing a play. Despite what his mother had just said, Jack thought that he had brought the level of her disbelief down to something like fifty percent; which meant that she no longer knew *what* to believe.

She focused on him for a moment, and he saw that hectic brightness blazing in her eyes again. Anger; tears? "Take care," she said, and signalled the waitress.

"I love you," Jack said.

"Never get off on a line like that." Now she was almost smiling. "Get travelling, Jack. Get going before I realize how crazy this is."

"I'm gone," he said, and turned away and marched out of the restaurant. His head felt tight, as if the bones in his skull had just grown too large for their covering of flesh. The empty yellow sunlight attacked his eyes. Jack heard the door of the Arcadia Tea and Jam Shoppe banging shut an instant after the little bell had sounded. He blinked; ran across Boardwalk Avenue without looking for cars. When he reached the pavement on the other side, he realized that he would have to go back to their suite for some clothes. His mother had still not emerged from the tea shop by the time Jack was pulling open the hotel's great front door.

The desk clerk stepped backward and sullenly stared. Jack felt some sort of emotion steaming off the man, but for a second could not remember why the clerk should react so strongly to the sight of him. The conversation with his mother—actually much shorter than he had imagined it would be—seemed to have lasted for days. On the other side of the vast gulf of time he'd spent in the Tea and Jam Shoppe, he had called the clerk a creep. Should he apologize? He no longer actually remembered what had caused him to flare up at the clerk. . . .

His mother had agreed to his going—she had given him permission to take his journey, and as he walked through the crossfire of the deskman's glare he finally understood why. He had not mentioned the Talisman, not explicitly, but even if he had—if he had spoken of the most lunatic aspect of his mission—she would have accepted that too. And if he'd said that he was going to bring back a foot-long butterfly and roast it in the oven, she'd have agreed to eat roast butterfly. It would have been an ironic, but a real, agreement. In part this showed the depth of her fear, that she would grasp at such straws.

But she would grasp because at some level she knew that these were bricks, not straws. His mother had given him permission to go because somewhere inside her she, too, knew about the Territories.

Did she ever wake up in the night with that name, *Laura DeLoessian*, sounding in her mind?

Up in 407 and 408, he tossed clothes into his knapsack almost randomly: if his fingers found it in a drawer and it was not too large, in it went. Shirts, socks, a sweater, Jockey shorts. Jack tightly rolled up a pair of tan jeans and forced them in, too; then he realized that the pack had become uncomfortably heavy, and pulled out most of the shirts and socks. The sweater, too, came out. At the last minute he remembered his toothbrush. Then he slid the straps over his shoulders and felt the pull of the weight on his back—not too heavy. He could walk all day, carrying only these few pounds.

Jack simply stood quiet in the suite's living room a moment, feeling—unexpectedly powerfully—the absence of any person or thing to whom he could say goodbye. His mother would not return to the suite until she could be sure he was gone: if she saw him now, she'd order him to stay. He could not say goodbye to these three rooms as he could to a house he had loved: hotel rooms accepted departures emotionlessly. In the end he went to the telephone pad printed with a drawing of the hotel on eggshell-thin paper, and with the Alhambra's blunt narrow pencil wrote the three lines that were most of what he had to say:

> *Thanks*
> *I love you*
> *and will be back*

## 4

Jack moved down Boardwalk Avenue in the thin northern sun, wondering where he should . . . flip. That was the word for it. And should he see Speedy once more before he "flipped" into the Territories? He almost *had* to talk to Speedy once more, because he knew so little about where he was going, whom he might meet, what he was looking for. . . . *she look just like a crystal ball*. Was that all the instruction Speedy intended to give him about the Talisman? That, and the warning not to drop it? Jack felt almost sick with lack of preparation—as if he had to take a final exam in a course he'd never attended.

He also felt that he could flip right where he stood, he was that impatient to begin, to get started, to move. *He had to be in the Territories again*, he suddenly understood; in the welter of his emotions and longings, that thread brightly shone. He wanted to breathe that air; he hungered for it. The Territories, the long plains and ranges of low mountains, called him, the fields of tall grass and the streams that flashed through them. Jack's entire body yearned for that landscape. And he might have taken the bottle out of his pocket and forced a mouthful of the awful juice down his throat on the spot if he had not just then seen the bottle's former owner tucked up against a tree, butt on heels and hands laced across his knees. A brown grocery bag lay beside him, and atop the bag was an enormous sandwich of what looked like liver sausage and onion.

"You're movin now," Speedy said, smiling up at him. "You're on your way, I see. Say your goodbyes? Your momma know you won't be home for a while?"

Jack nodded, and Speedy held up the sandwich. "You hungry? This one, it's too much for me."

"I had something to eat," the boy said. "I'm glad I can say goodbye to you."

"Ole Jack on fire, he rarin to go," Speedy said, cocking his long head sideways. "Boy gonna move."

"Speedy?"

"But don't take off without a few little things I brought for you. I got em here in this bag, you wanna see?"

"Speedy?"

The man squinted up at Jack from the base of the tree.

"Did you know that my father used to call me Travelling Jack?"

"Oh, I probably heard that somewhere," Speedy said, grinning at him. "Come over here and see what I brought you. Plus, I have to tell you where to go first, don't I?"

Relieved, Jack walked across the sidewalk to Speedy's tree. The old man set his sandwich in his lap and fished the bag closer to him. "Merry Christmas," Speedy said, and brought forth a tall, battered old paperback book. It was, Jack saw, an old Rand McNally road atlas.

"Thanks," Jack said, taking the book from Speedy's outstretched hand.

"Ain't no maps over there, so you stick as much as you can to the roads in ole Rand McNally. That way you'll get where you're goin."

"Okay," Jack said, and slipped out of the knapsack so that he could slide the big book down inside it.

"The next thing don't have to go in that fancy rig you carryin on your back," Speedy said. He put the sandwich on the flat paper bag and stood up all in one long smooth motion. "No, you can carry this right in your pocket." He dipped his fingers into the left pocket of his workshirt. What emerged, clamped between his second and third fingers like one of

Lily's Tarrytoons, was a white triangular object it took the boy a moment to recognize as a guitar-pick. "You take this and keep it. You'll want to show it to a man. He'll help you."

Jack turned the pick over in his fingers. He had never seen one like it—of ivory, with scrimshaw filigrees and patterns winding around it in slanted lines like some kind of unearthly writing. Beautiful in the abstract, it was almost too heavy to be a useful fingerpick.

"Who's the man?" Jack asked. He slipped the pick into one of his pants pockets.

"Big scar on his face—you'll see him pretty soon after you land in the Territories. He's a guard. Fact is, he's a Captain of the Outer Guards, and he'll take you to a place where you can see a lady you has to see. Well, a lady you ought to see. So you know the other reason you're puttin your neck on the line. My friend over there, he'll understand what you're doin and he'll figure out a way to get you to the lady."

"This lady . . ." Jack began.

"Yep," Speedy said. "You got it."

"She's the Queen."

"You take a good look at her, Jack. You see what you see when you sees her. You see what she *is*, understand? Then you hit out for the west." Speedy stood examining him gravely, almost as if he were just now doubting that he'd ever see Jack Sawyer again, and then the lines in his face twitched and he said, "Steer clear of ole Bloat. Watch for his trail—his own and his Twinner's. Ole Bloat can find out where you went if you're not careful, and if he finds out he's gonna be after you like a fox after a goose." Speedy shoved his hands in his pockets and regarded Jack again, looking very much as though he wished he could think of more to say. "Get the Talisman, son," he concluded. "Get it and bring it back safe. It gonna be your burden but you got to be bigger than your burden."

Jack was concentrating so hard on what Speedy was telling him that he squinted into the man's seamed face. Scarred man, Captain of the Outer Guards. The Queen. Morgan Sloat, after him like a predator. In an evil place over on the other side of the country. A burden. "Okay," he said, wishing suddenly that he were back in the Tea and Jam Shoppe with his mother.

Speedy smiled jaggedly, warmly. "Yeah-bob. Ole Travellin Jack is okey-doke." The smile deepened. "Bout time for you to sip at that special juice, wouldn't you say?"

"I guess it is," Jack said. He tugged the dark bottle out of his hip pocket and unscrewed the cap. He looked back up at Speedy, whose pale eyes stabbed into his own.

"Speedy'll help you when he can."

Jack nodded, blinked, and raised the neck of the bottle to his mouth. The sweetly rotten odor which leaped out of the bottle nearly made his throat close itself in an involuntary spasm. He tipped the bottle up and the taste of the odor invaded his mouth. His stomach clenched. He swallowed, and rough, burning liquid spilled down his throat.

Long seconds before Jack opened his eyes, he knew from the richness and clarity of the smells about him that he had flipped into the Territories. Horses, grass, a dizzying scent of raw meat; dust; the clear air itself.

## Interlude

# Sloat in This World (I)

"I know I work too hard," Morgan Sloat told his son Richard that evening. They were speaking on the telephone, Richard standing at the communal telephone in the downstairs corridor of his dormitory, his father sitting at his desk on the top floor of one of Sawyer & Sloat's first and sweetest real-estate deals in Beverly Hills. "But I tell you kid, there are a lot of times when you have to do something yourself to get it done right. Especially when my late partner's family is involved. It's just a short trip, I hope. Probably I'll get everything nailed down out there in goddam New Hampshire in less than a week. I'll give you another call when it's all over. Maybe we'll go railroading in California, just like the old days. There'll be justice yet. Trust your old man."

The deal for the building had been particularly sweet because of Sloat's willingness to do things himself. After he and Sawyer had negotiated the purchase of a short-term lease, then (after a gunfire of lawsuits) a long-term lease, they had fixed their rental rates at so much per square foot, done the necessary alterations, and advertised for new tenants. The only holdover tenant was the Chinese restaurant on the ground floor, dribbling in rent at about a third of what the space was worth. Sloat had tried reasonable discussions with the Chinese, but when they saw that he was trying to talk them into paying more rent, they suddenly lost the ability to speak or understand English. Sloat's attempts at negotiation limped along for a few days, and then he happened to see one of the kitchen help carrying a bucket of grease out through the back door of the kitchen. Feeling better already, Sloat followed the man into a dark, narrow cul-de-sac and watched him tip the grease into a garbage can. He needed no more than that. A day later, a chain-link fence separated the cul-de-sac from the restaurant; yet another day later, a Health Department inspector served the Chinese with a complaint and a summons. Now the kitchen help had to take all their refuse, grease included, out through the dining area and down a chain-link dog run Sloat had constructed alongside the restaurant. Business fell off: the customers caught odd, unpleasant odors from the nearby garbage. The owners rediscovered the English language, and volunteered to double their monthly payment. Sloat responded with a grateful-sounding speech that said nothing. And that night, having primed himself with three large martinis, Sloat drove from his house to the restaurant and took a baseball bat from the trunk of his car and smashed in the long window which had once given a pleasant view of the street but now looked out at a corridor of fencing which ended in a huddle of metal bins.

He had done those things . . . but he hadn't exactly been Sloat when he did them.

The next morning the Chinese requested another meeting and this time offered to quadruple their payment. "Now you're talking like men," Sloat told the stony-faced Chinese. "And I'll tell you what! Just to prove we're all on the same team, we'll pay half the cost of replacing your window."

Within nine months of Sawyer & Sloat's taking possession

of the building, all the rents had increased significantly and the initial cost and profit projections had begun to look wildly pessimistic. By now this building was one of Sawyer & Sloat's more modest ventures, but Morgan Sloat was as proud of it as of the massive new structures they had put up downtown. Just walking past the place where he'd put up the fence as he came in to work in the morning reminded him—daily—of how much he had contributed to Sawyer & Sloat, how reasonable were his claims!

This sense of the justice of his ultimate desires kindled within him as he spoke to Richard—after all, it was for Richard that he wanted to take over Phil Sawyer's share of the company. Richard was, in a sense, his immortality. His son would be able to go to the best business schools and then pick up a law degree before he came into the company; and thus fully armed, Richard Sloat would carry all the complex and delicate machinery of Sawyer & Sloat into the next century. The boy's ridiculous ambition to become a chemist could not long survive his father's determination to murder it—Richard was smart enough to see that what his father did was a hell of a lot more interesting, not to mention vastly more remunerative, than working with a test tube over a Bunsen burner. That "research chemist" stuff would fade away pretty quickly, once the boy had a glimpse of the real world. And if Richard was concerned about being fair to Jack Sawyer, he could be made to understand that fifty thousand a year and a guaranteed college education was not only fair but magnanimous. Princely. Who could say that Jack wanted any part of the business, anyhow, or that he would possess any talent for it?

Besides, accidents happened. Who could even say that Jack Sawyer would live to see twenty?

"Well, it's really a matter of getting all the papers, all the ownership stuff, finally straight," Sloat told his son. "Lily's been hiding out from me for too long. Her brain is strictly cottage cheese by now, take my word for it. She probably has less than a year to live. So if I don't hump myself off to see her now that I have her pinned down, she could stall long enough to put everything into probate—or into a trust fund, and I don't think your friend's momma would let me administer it. Hey, I don't want to bore you with my troubles. I just wanted to tell you that I won't be home for a few days, in case you call. Send me a letter or something. And remember about the train, okay? We gotta do that again."

The boy promised to write, to work hard, to not worry about his father or Lily Cavanaugh or Jack.

And sometime when this obedient son was, say, in his senior year at Stanford or Yale, Sloat would introduce him to the Territories. Richard would be six or seven years younger than he had been himself when Phil Sawyer, cheerfully crack-brained on grass in their first little North Hollywood office, had first puzzled, then infuriated (because Sloat had been certain Phil was laughing at him), then intrigued his partner (for surely Phil was too stoned to have invented all this science-fiction crapola about another world). And when Richard saw the Territories, that would be it—if he had not already done it by himself, they'd change his mind for him. Even a small peek into the Territories shook your confidence in the omniscience of scientists.

Sloat ran the palm of his hand over the shiny top of his head, then luxuriantly fingered his moustache. The sound of his son's voice had obscurely, irrelevantly comforted him: as long as there was Richard politely coming along behind him, all was well and all was well and all manner of things was well. It was night already in Springfield, Illinois, and in Nelson House, Thayer School, Richard Sloat was padding down a green corridor back to his desk, perhaps thinking of the good times they'd had, and would have again, aboard Morgan's toy train line in coastal California. He'd be asleep by the time his father's jet punished the resistant air far above and some hundred miles farther north; but Morgan Sloat would push aside the panel over his first-class window and peer down, hoping for moonlight and a parting of the clouds.

He wanted to go home immediately—home was only thirty minutes away from the office—so that he could change clothes and get something to eat, maybe snort a little coke, before he had to get to the airport. But instead he had to pound out along the freeway to the Marina: an appointment with a client who had freaked out and was on the verge of being dumped from a picture, then a meeting with a crowd of spoilers who claimed that a Sawyer & Sloat project just up from Marina del Rey was polluting the beach—things that

could not be postponed. Though Sloat promised himself that
as soon as he had taken care of Lily Cavanaugh and her boy
he was going to begin dropping clients from his list—he had
much bigger fish to fry now. Now there were whole worlds to
broker, and his piece of the action would be no mere ten percent. Looking back on it, Sloat wasn't sure how he had toler-
ated Phil Sawyer for as long as he had. His partner had never
played to win, not seriously; he had been encumbered by sentimental notions of loyalty and honor, corrupted by the stuff
you told kids to get them halfway civilized before you finally
tore the blindfold off their eyes. Mundane as it might be in
light of the stakes he now played for, he could not forget that
the Sawyers owed him, all right—indigestion flowered in his
chest like a heart attack at the thought of how much, and before he reached his car in the still-sunny lot beside the building, he shoved his hand into his jacket pocket and fished out a
crumpled package of Di-Gel.

Phil Sawyer had underestimated him, and that still ran-
kled. Because Phil had thought of him as a sort of trained rattlesnake to be let out of his cage only under controlled
circumstances, so had others. The lot attendant, a hillbilly in a
broken cowboy hat, eyed him as he marched around his little
car, looking for dents and dings. The Di-Gel melted most of
the fiery ball in his chest. Sloat felt his collar growing
clammy with sweat. The attendant knew better than to try to
buddy up: Sloat had verbally peeled the man's hide weeks
ago, after discovering a tiny wrinkle in the BMW's door. In
the midst of his rant, he had seen violence begin to darken in
the hillbilly's green eyes, and a sudden upsurge of joy had
made him waddle in toward the man, still cutting off skin, almost hoping that the attendant would take a poke at him.
Abruptly, the hillbilly had lost his momentum; feebly, indeed
apologetically suggested that maybe that-there l'il *nuthin* of a
ding came from somewhere else? Parking service at a restaurant, maybe? The way those bozos treat cars, y'know, and the
light ain't so good that time a night, why . . .

"Shut your stinking mouth," Sloat had said. "That little
nothing, as you call it, is going to cost me about twice what
you make in a week. I should fire you right now, cowpoke,
and the only reason I'm not going to is that there's about a
two percent chance you might be right; when I came out of

Chasen's last night maybe I didn't look under the door handle, maybe I DID and maybe I DIDN'T, but if you ever talk to me again, if you ever say any more than 'Hello, Mr. Sloat' or 'Goodbye, Mr. Sloat,' I'll get you fired so fast you'll think you were beheaded." So the hillbilly watched him inspect his car, knowing that if Sloat found any imperfections in the car's finish he would bring down the axe, afraid even to come close enough to utter the ritual goodbye. Sometimes from the window that overlooked the parking lot Sloat had seen the attendant furiously wiping some flaw, bird dropping or splash of mud, off the BMW's hood. And that's management, buddy.

When he pulled out of the lot he checked the rear-view mirror and saw on the hillbilly's face an expression very like the last one Phil Sawyer had worn in the final seconds of his life, out in the middle of nowhere in Utah. He smiled all the way to the freeway on-ramp.

Philip Sawyer had underestimated Morgan Sloat from the time of their first meeting, when they were freshmen at Yale. It could have been, Sloat reflected, that he had been easy to underestimate—a pudgy eighteen-year-old from Akron, graceless, overweighted with anxieties and ambitions, out of Ohio for the first time in his life. Listening to his classmates talk easily about New York, about "21" and the Stork Club, about seeing Brubeck at Basin Street and Erroll Garner at the Vanguard, he'd sweated to hide his ignorance. "I really like the downtown part," he'd thrown in, as casually as he could. Palms wet, cramped by curled-in fingers. (Mornings, Sloat often found his palms tattooed with dented bruises left by his fingernails.) "What downtown part, Morgan?" Tom Woodbine had asked him. The others cackled. "You know, Broadway and the Village. Around there." More cackles, harsher. He had been unattractive and badly dressed; his wardrobe consisted of two suits, both charcoal-gray and both apparently made for a man with a scarecrow's shoulders. He had begun losing his hair in high school, and pink scalp showed through his short, flattened-down haircuts.

No, no beauty had Sloat been, and that had been part of it. The others made him feel like a clenched fist: those morning bruises were shadowy little photographs of his soul. The others, all interested in the theater like himself and Sawyer, possessed good profiles, flat stomachs, easy careless manners. Sprawled across the lounge chairs of their suite in Davenport while Sloat, in a haze of perspiration, stood that he might not wrinkle his suit pants and thereby get a few more days' wear out of them, they sometimes resembled a gathering of young gods—cashmere sweaters draped over their shoulders like the golden fleece. They were on their way to becoming actors, playwrights, songwriters. Sloat had seen himself as a director: entangling them all in a net of complications and designs which only he could unwind.

Sawyer and Tom Woodbine, both of whom seemed unimaginably rich to Sloat, were roommates. Woodbine had only a lukewarm interest in theater and hung around their undergraduate drama workshop because Phil did. Another gilded private-school boy, Thomas Woodbine differed from the others because of his absolute seriousness and straightforwardness. He intended to become a lawyer, and already seemed to have the probity and impartiality of a judge. (In fact, most of Woodbine's acquaintances imagined that he would wind up on the Supreme Court, much to the embarrassment of the boy himself.) Woodbine was without ambition in Sloat's terms, being interested far more in living rightly than in living well. Of course he had everything, and what he by some accident lacked other people were quick to give him: how could he, so spoiled by nature and friendships, be ambitious? Sloat almost unconsciously detested Woodbine, and could not bring himself to call him "Tommy."

Sloat directed two plays during his four years at Yale: *No Exit*, which the student paper called "a furious confusion," and *Volpone*. This was described as "churning, cynical, sinister, and almost unbelievably messy." Sloat was held responsible for most of these qualities. Perhaps he was not a director after all—his vision too intense and crowded. His ambitions did not lessen, they merely shifted. If he was not eventually to be behind the camera, he could be behind the people in front of it. Phil Sawyer had also begun to think this way—Phil had never been certain where his love of theater might take him, and thought he might have a talent for representing actors and writers. "Let's go to Los Angeles and start an agency," Phil said to him in their senior year. "It's nutty as hell and our parents will hate it, but maybe we'll make it work. So we starve for a couple of years."

Phil Sawyer, Sloat had learned since their freshman year, was not rich after all. He just *looked* rich.

"And when we can afford him, we'll get Tommy to be our lawyer. He'll be out of law school by then."

"Sure, okay," Sloat had said, thinking that he could stop that one when the time came. "What should we call ourselves?"

"Anything you like. Sloat and Sawyer? Or should we stick to the alphabet?"

"Sawyer and Sloat, sure, that's great, alphabetical order," Sloat said, seething because he imagined that his partner had euchred him into forever suggesting that he was somehow secondary to Sawyer.

Both sets of parents did hate the idea, as Phil had predicted, but the partners in the infant talent agency drove to Los Angeles in the old DeSoto (Morgan's, another demonstration of how much Sawyer owed him), set up an office in a North Hollywood building with a happy population of rats and fleas, and started hanging around the clubs, passing out their spandy-new business cards. Nothing—nearly four months of total failure. They had a comic who got too drunk to be funny, a writer who couldn't write, a stripper who insisted on being paid in cash so that she could stiff her agents. And then late one afternoon, high on marijuana and whiskey, Phil Sawyer had gigglingly told Sloat about the Territories.

*"You know what I can do, you ambitious so-and-so? Oh, can I travel, partner. All the way."*

Shortly after that, both of them travelling now, Phil Sawyer met a rising young actress at a studio party and within an hour had their first important client. And she had three friends similarly unhappy with their agents. And one of the friends had a boyfriend who had actually written a decent filmscript and needed an agent, and the boyfriend had a boyfriend . . . Before their third year was over, they had a new office, new apartments, a slice of the Hollywood pie. The Territories, in a fashion that Sloat accepted but never understood, had blessed them.

Sawyer dealt with the clients; Sloat with the money, the investments, the business side of the agency. Sawyer spent money—lunches, airplane tickets—Sloat saved it, which was all the justification he needed to skim a little of the cream off the top. And it was Sloat who kept pushing them into new areas, land development, real estate, production deals. By the time Tommy Woodbine arrived in Los Angeles, Sawyer & Sloat was a multimillion-dollar business.

Sloat discovered that he still detested his old classmate; Tommy Woodbine had put on thirty pounds, and looked and acted, in his blue three-piece suits, more than ever like a judge. His cheeks were always slightly flushed (alcoholic? Sloat wondered), his manner still kindly and ponderous. The world had left its marks on him—clever little wrinkles at the corners of his eyes, the eyes themselves infinitely more guarded than those of the gilded boy at Yale. Sloat understood almost at once, and knew that Phil Sawyer would never see it unless he were told, that Tommy Woodbine lived with an enormous secret: whatever the gilded boy might have been, Tommy was now a homosexual. Probably he'd call himself gay. And that made everything easier—in the end, it even made it easier to get rid of Tommy.

Because queers are always getting killed, aren't they? And did anybody really want a two-hundred-and-ten-pound pansy responsible for bringing up a teenage boy? You could say that Sloat was just saving Phil Sawyer from the posthumous consequences of a serious lapse of judgment. If Sawyer had made Sloat the executor of his estate and the guardian of his son, there would have been no problems. As it was, the murderers from the Territories—the same two who had bungled the abduction of the boy—had blasted through a stoplight and nearly been arrested before they could return home.

Things all would have been so much simpler, Sloat reflected for perhaps the thousandth time, if Phil Sawyer had never married. If no Lily, no Jack; if no Jack, no problems. Phil may never even have looked at the reports about Lily Cavanaugh's early life Sloat had compiled: they listed where and how often and with whom, and should have killed that romance as readily as the black van turned Tommy Woodbine into a lump on the road. If Sawyer read those meticulous reports, they left him amazingly unaffected. He wanted to marry Lily Cavanaugh, and he did. As his damned Twinner had married Queen Laura. More underestimation. And repaid in the same fashion, which seemed fitting.

Which meant, Sloat thought with some satisfaction, that after a few details were taken care of, everything would finally be settled. After so many years—when he came back from Arcadia Beach, he should have all of Sawyer & Sloat in his pocket. And in the Territories, all was placed just *so:* poised on the brink, ready to fall into Morgan's hands. As soon as the Queen died, her consort's former deputy would rule the country, introducing all the interesting little changes both he and Sloat desired. And then watch the money roll in. Sloat thought, turning off the freeway into Marina del Rey. Then watch *everything* roll in!

His client, Asher Dondorf, lived in the bottom half of a new condo in one of the Marina's narrow, alleylike streets just off the beach. Dondorf was an old character actor who had achieved a surprising level of prominence and visibility in the late seventies through a role on a television series; he'd played the landlord of the young couple—private detectives, and both cute as baby pandas—who were the series' stars. Dondorf got so much mail from his few appearances in the early episodes that the writers increased his part, making him an unofficial father to the young detectives, letting him solve a murder or two, putting him in danger, etc., etc. His salary doubled, tripled, quadrupled, and when the series was cancelled after six years, he went back into film work. Which was the problem. Dondorf thought he was a star, but the studios and producers still considered him a character actor—popular, but not a serious asset to any project. Dondorf wanted flowers in his dressing room, he wanted his own hairdresser and dialogue coach, he wanted more money, more respect, more love, more everything. Dondorf, in fact, was a putz.

When he pulled his car tight into the parking bay and eased himself out, being careful not to scratch the edge of his door on the brick, Sloat came to a realization: if he learned, or even suspected, sometime in the next few days, that Jack Sawyer had discovered the existence of the Territories, he would kill him. There was such a thing as an unacceptable risk.

Sloat smiled to himself, popping another Di-Gel into his

mouth, and rapped on the condo's door. He knew it already: Asher Dondorf was going to kill himself. He'd do it in the living room in order to create as much mess as possible. A temperamental jerk like his soon-to-be-ex-client would think a really sloppy suicide was revenge on the bank that held his mortgage. When a pale, trembling Dondorf opened the door, the warmth of Sloat's greeting was quite genuine.

# TWO

# THE ROAD OF TRIALS

# 6

# The Queen's Pavillion

## 1

The saw-toothed blades of grass directly before Jack's eyes
seemed as tall and stiff as sabres. They would cut the wind,
not bend to it. Jack groaned as he lifted his head. He did not
possess such dignity. His stomach still felt threateningly
liquid, his forehead and eyes burned. Jack pushed himself
up on his knees and then forced himself to stand. A long
horse-drawn cart rumbled toward him down the dusty track,
and its driver, a bearded red-faced man roughly the same
shape and size as the wooden barrels rattling behind him, was
staring at him. Jack nodded and tried to take in as much as
he could about the man while giving the appearance of a
loafing boy who had perhaps run off for an illicit snooze.
Upright, he no longer felt ill; he felt, in fact, better than at
any time since leaving Los Angeles, not merely healthy but
somehow harmonious, mysteriously in tune with his body.
The warm, drifting air of the Territories patted his face with
the gentlest, most fragrant of touches—its own delicate and
flowery scent quite distinct beneath the stronger odor of
raw meat it carried. Jack ran his hands over his face and
peeked at the driver of the cart, his first sample of Territories Man.

If the driver addressed him, how should he answer? Did
they even speak English here? His kind of English? For a moment Jack imagined himself trying to pass unnoticed in a
world where people said "Prithee" and "Dost thou go cross-
gartered, yonder varlet?" and decided that if that was how
things went, he'd pretend to be a mute.

The driver finally took his eyes off Jack and clucked something decidedly not 1980's American English to his horses.
But perhaps that was just the way you spoke to horses.

*Slusha, slusha!* Jack edged backward into the sea-grass, wish-ing that he had managed to get on his feet a couple of seconds earlier. The man glanced at him again, and surprised Jack by nodding—a gesture neither friendly nor unfriendly, merely a communication between equals. *I'll be glad when this day's work is done, brother.* Jack returned the nod, tried to put his hands in his pockets, and for a moment must have looked half-witted with astonishment. The driver laughed, not un-pleasantly.

Jack's clothes had changed—he wore coarse, voluminous woolen trousers instead of the corduroy jeans. Above the waist a close-fitting jacket of soft blue fabric covered him. In-stead of buttons, the jacket—a jerkin? he speculated—had a row of cloth hooks and eyes. Like the trousers, it was clearly hand-made. The Nikes, too, were gone, replaced by flat leather sandals. The knapsack had been transmogrified into a leather sack held by a thin strap over his shoulder. The cart-driver wore clothing almost exactly similar—his jerkin was of leather stained so deeply and continuously that it showed rings within rings, like an old tree's heart.

All rattle and dust, the cart pulled past Jack. The barrels radiated a yeasty musk of beer. Behind the barrels stood a triple pile of what Jack unthinkingly took to be truck tires. He smelled the "tires" and noticed that they were perfectly, flaw-lessly bald in the same moment—it was a creamy odor, full of secret depths and subtle pleasures, that instantly made him hungry. Cheese, but no cheese that he had ever tasted. Behind the wheels of cheese, near the back of the cart, an irregular mound of raw meat—long, peeled-looking sides of beef, big slablike steaks, a heap of ropy internal organs he could not identify—slithered beneath a glistening mat of flies. The powerful smell of the raw meat assailed Jack, killing the hunger evoked by the cheese. He moved into the middle of the track after the cart had passed him and watched it jounce toward the crest of a little rise. A second later he began to fol-low after, walking north.

He had gone only halfway up the rise when he once again saw the peak of the great tent, rigid in the midst of a rank of narrow fluttering flags. That, he assumed, was his destination. Another few steps past the blackberry bushes where he'd paused the last time (remembering how good they'd been, Jack popped two of the enormous berries in his mouth) and he could see the whole of the tent. It was actually a big rambling pavillion, long wings on each side, with gates and a courtyard. Like the Alhambra, this eccentric structure—a summer palace, Jack's instincts told him—stood just above the ocean. Little bands of people moved through and around the great pavillion, driven by forces as powerful and invisible as the effect on iron filings of a magnet. The little groups met, divided, poured on again.

Some of the men wore bright, rich-looking clothes, though many seemed to be dressed much as Jack was. A few women in long shining white gowns or robes marched through the courtyard, as purposeful as generals. Outside the gates stood a collection of smaller tents and impromptu-looking wooden huts; here, too, people moved, eating or buying or talking, though more easily and randomly. Somewhere down in that busy crowd he would have to find the man with a scar.

But first he looked behind him, down the length of the rutted track, to see what had happened to Funworld.

When he saw two small dark horses pulling plows, perhaps fifty yards off, he thought that the amusement park had become a farm, but then he noticed the crowd watching the plowing from the top of the field and understood that this was a contest. Next his eye was taken by the spectacle of a huge red-haired man, stripped to the waist, whirling about like a top. His outstretched hands held some long heavy object. The man abruptly stopped whirling and released the object, which flew a long way before it thudded and bounced on the grass and revealed itself to be a hammer. Funworld was a fair, not a farm—Jack now saw tables heaped with food, children on their fathers' shoulders.

In the midst of the fair, making sure that every strap and harness was sound, every oven stoked with wood, was there a Speedy Parker? Jack hoped so.

And was his mother still sitting by herself in the Tea and Jam Shoppe, wondering why she had let him go?

Jack turned back and watched the long cart rattle through the gates of the summer palace and swing off to the left, separating the people who moved there as a car making a turn off

Fifth Avenue separates pedestrians on a cross-town street. A
moment later he set off after it.

## 2

He had feared that all the people on the pavillion grounds
would turn toward him staring, instantly sensing his difference from them. Jack carefully kept his eyes lowered whenever he could and imitated a boy on a complicated errand—he
had been sent out to assemble a list of things; his face showed
how he was concentrating to remember them. *A shovel, two
picks, a ball of twine, a bottle of goose grease* . . . But gradually he became aware that none of the adults before the
summer palace paid him any attention at all. They rushed
or dawdled, inspected the merchandise—rugs, iron pots,
bracelets—displayed in the little tents, drank from wooden
mugs, plucked at another's sleeve to make a comment or start
a conversation, argued with the guards at the gate, each
wholly taken up by his own business. Jack's impersonation
was so unnecessary as to be ridiculous. He straightened up
and began to work his way, moving generally in an irregular
half-circle, toward the gate.

   He had seen almost immediately that he would not be
able just to stroll through it—the two guards on either side
stopped and questioned nearly everyone who tried to reach
the interior of the summer palace. Men had to show their papers, or display badges or seals which gave them access. Jack
had only Speedy Parker's fingerpick, and he didn't think that
would get him past the guards' inspection. One man just now
stepping up to the gate flashed a round silver badge and was
waved through; the man following him was stopped. He argued; then the tone of his manner changed, and Jack saw that
he was pleading. The guard shook his head and ordered the
man off.

   "*His* men don't have any trouble getting in," someone to
Jack's right said, instantly solving the problem of Territories
language, and Jack turned his head to see if the man had spoken to him.

   But the middle-aged man walking beside him was speaking to another man, also dressed in the plain, simple clothes
of most of the men and women outside the palace grounds.

"They'd better not," the second man answered. "He's on his way—supposed to be here today sometime, I guess."

Jack fell in behind these two and followed them toward the gate.

The guards stepped forward as the men neared, and as they both approached the same guard, the other gestured to the man nearest him. Jack hung back. He still had not seen anyone with a scar, nor had he seen any officers. The only soldiers in sight were the guards, both young and countrified—with their broad red faces above the elaborately pleated and ruffled uniforms, they looked like farmers in fancy dress. The two men Jack had been following must have passed the guards' tests, for after a few moments' conversation the uniformed men stepped back and admitted them. One of the guards looked sharply at Jack, and Jack turned his head and stepped back.

Unless he found the Captain with the scar, he would never get inside the palace grounds.

A group of men approached the guard who had stared at Jack, and immediately began to wrangle. They had an appointment, it was crucial they be let in, much money depended on it, regrettably they had no papers. The guard shook his head, scraping his chin across his uniform's white ruff. As Jack watched, still wondering how he could find the Captain, the leader of the little group waved his hands in the air, pounded his fist into a palm. He had become as red-faced as the guard. At length he began jabbing the guard with his forefinger. The guard's companion joined him—both guards looked bored and hostile.

A tall straight man in a uniform subtly different from the guards'—it might have been the way the uniform was worn, but it looked as though it might serve in battle as well as in an operetta—noiselessly materialized beside them. He did not wear a ruff, Jack noticed a second later, and his hat was peaked instead of three-cornered. He spoke to the guards, and then turned to the leader of the little group. There was no more shouting, no more finger-jabbing. The man spoke quietly. Jack saw the danger ebb out of the group. They shifted on their feet, their shoulders sank. They began to drift away. The officer watched them go, then turned back to the guards for a final word.

For the moment while the officer faced in Jack's direction, in effect shooing the group of men away with his presence, Jack saw a long pale lightning-bolt of a scar zigzagging from beneath his right eye to just above his jawline.

The officer nodded to the guards and stepped briskly away. Looking neither to the left nor to the right, he wove through the crowd, apparently headed for whatever lay to the side of the summer palace. Jack took off after him.

"Sir!" he yelled, but the officer marched on through the slow-moving crowd.

Jack ran around a group of men and women hauling a pig toward one of the little tents, shot through a gap between two other bands of people approaching the gate, and finally was close enough to the officer to reach out and touch his elbow. "Captain?"

The officer wheeled around, freezing Jack where he stood. Up close, the scar seemed thick and separate, a living creature riding on the man's face. Even unscarred, Jack thought, this man's face would express a forceful impatience. "What is it, boy?" the man asked.

"Captain, I'm supposed to talk to you—I have to see the Lady, but I don't think I can get into the palace. Oh, you're supposed to see this." He dug into the roomy pocket of the unfamiliar pants and closed his fingers around a triangular object.

When he displayed it on his palm, he felt shock boom through him—what he held in his hand was not a fingerpick but a long tooth, a shark's tooth perhaps, inlaid with a winding, intricate pattern of gold.

When Jack looked up at the Captain's face, half-expecting a blow, he saw his shock echoed there. The impatience which had seemed so characteristic had utterly vanished. Uncertainty and even fear momentarily distorted the man's strong features. The Captain lifted his hand to Jack's, and the boy thought he meant to take the ornate tooth: he would have given it to him, but the man simply folded the boy's fingers over the object on his palm. "Follow me," he said.

They went around to the side of the great pavillion, and the Captain led Jack behind the shelter of a great sail-shaped flap of stiff pale canvas. In the glowing darkness behind the flap, the soldier's face looked as though someone had drawn on it with thick pink crayon. "That sign," he said calmly enough. "Where did you get it?"

"From Speedy Parker. He said that I should find you and show it to you."

The man shook his head. "I don't know the name. I want you to give me the sign now. Now." He firmly grasped Jack's wrist. "Give it to me, and then tell me where you stole it."

"I'm telling the truth," Jack said. "I got it from Lester Speedy Parker. He works at Funworld. But it wasn't a tooth when he gave it to me. It was a guitar-pick."

"I don't think you understand what's going to happen to you, boy."

"You *know* him," Jack pleaded. "He described you—he told me you were a Captain of the Outer Guards. Speedy *told* me to find you."

The Captain shook his head and gripped Jack's wrist more firmly. "Describe this man. I'm going to find out if you're lying right now, boy, so I'd make this good if I were you."

"Speedy's old," Jack said. "He used to be a musician." He thought he saw recognition of some kind flash in the man's eyes. "He's black—a black man. With white hair. Deep lines in his face. And he's pretty thin, but he's a lot stronger than he looks."

"A black man. You mean, a *brown* man?"

"Well, black people aren't really black. Like white people aren't really white."

"A brown man named Parker." The Captain gently released Jack's wrist. "He is called Parkus here. So you are from . . ." He nodded toward some distant invisible point on the horizon.

"That's right," Jack said.

"And Parkus . . . Parker . . . sent you to see our Queen."

"He said he wanted me to see the Lady. And that you could take me to her."

"This will have to be fast," the Captain said. "I think I know how to do it, but we don't have any time to waste." He had shifted his mental direction with a military smoothness. "Now listen to me. We have a lot of bastards around here, so we're going to pretend that you are my son on t'other side of the sheets. You have disobeyed me in connection with some little job, and I am angry with you. I *think* no one will stop us if we make this performance convincing. At least I can get you inside—but it might be a little trickier once we are in. You think you can do it? Convince people that you're my son?"

"My mother's an actress," Jack said, and felt that old pride in her.

"Well, then, let's see what you've learned," the Captain said, and surprised Jack by winking at him. "I'll try not to cause you any pain." Then he startled Jack again, and clamped a very strong hand over the boy's upper arm. "Let's go," he said, and marched out of the shelter of the flap, half-dragging Jack behind him.

"When I tell you to wash the flagstones behind the kitchen, wash flagstones is what you'll do," the Captain said loudly, not looking at him. "Understand that? You will *do your job*. And if you do not do your job, you must be punished."

"But I washed some of the flagstones . . ." Jack wailed.

"I didn't tell you to wash *some* of the flagstones!" the Captain yelled, hauling Jack along behind him. The people around them parted to let the Captain through. Some of them grinned sympathetically at Jack.

"I was going to do it all, honest, I was going to go back in a minute . . ."

The soldier pulled him toward the gate without even glancing at the guards, and yanked him through. "No, Dad!" Jack squalled. "You're hurting me!"

"Not as much as I'm *going* to hurt you," the Captain said, and pulled him across the wide courtyard Jack had seen from the cart-track.

At the other end of the court the soldier pulled him up wooden steps and into the great palace itself. "Now your acting had better be good," the man whispered, and immediately set off down a long corridor, squeezing Jack's arm hard enough to leave bruises.

"I promise I'll be good!" Jack shouted.

The man hauled him into another, narrower corridor. The interior of the palace did not at all resemble the inside of a tent, Jack saw. It was a mazelike warren of passages and little rooms, and it smelled of smoke and grease.

"Promise!" the Captain bawled out.

"I promise! I do!"

Ahead of them as they emerged from yet another corridor, a group of elaborately clothed men either leaning against a wall or draped over couches turned their heads to look at this noisy duo. One of them, who had been amusing himself by giving orders to a pair of women carrying stacks of sheets folded flat across their arms, glanced suspiciously at Jack and the Captain.

"And I promise to beat the sin out of you," the Captain said loudly.

A couple of the men laughed. They wore soft wide-brimmed hats trimmed with fur and their boots were of velvet. They had greedy, thoughtless faces. The man talking to the maids, the one who seemed to be in charge, was skeletally tall and thin. His tense, ambitious face tracked the boy and the soldier as they hurried by.

"Please don't!" Jack wailed. "Please!"

"Each *please* is another strapping," the soldier growled, and the men laughed again. The thin one permitted himself to display a smile as cold as a knife-blade before he turned back to the maids.

The Captain yanked the boy into an empty room filled with dusty wooden furniture. Then at last he released Jack's aching arm. "Those were *his* men," he whispered. "What life will be like when—" He shook his head, and for a moment seemed to forget his haste. "It says in *The Book of Good Farming* that the meek shall inherit the earth, but those fellows don't have a teaspoonful of meekness among them. Taking's all they're good for. They want wealth, they want—" He glanced upward, unwilling or unable to say what else the men outside wanted. Then he looked back at the boy. "We'll have to be quick about this, but there are still a few secrets his men haven't learned about the palace." He nodded sideways, indicating a faded wooden wall.

Jack followed him, and understood when the Captain pushed two of the flat brown nailheads left exposed at the end of a dusty board. A panel in the faded wall swung inward, exposing a narrow black passageway no taller than an upended coffin. "You'll only get a glimpse of her, but I suppose that's all you need. It's all you can have, anyhow."

The boy followed the silent instruction to slip into the passageway. "Just go straight ahead until I tell you," the Captain whispered. When he closed the panel behind them, Jack began to move slowly forward through perfect blackness.

The passage wound this way and that, occasionally illuminated by faint light spilling in through a crack in a concealed door or through a window set above the boy's head. Jack soon lost all sense of direction, and blindly followed the whispered directions of his companion. At one point he caught the delicious odor of roasting meat, at another the unmistakable stink of sewage.

"Stop," the Captain finally said. "Now I'll have to lift you up. Raise your arms."

"Will I be able to see?"

"You'll know in a second," the Captain said, and put a hand just beneath each of Jack's armpits and lifted him cleanly off the floor. "There is a panel in front of you now," he whispered. "Slide it to the left."

Jack blindly reached out before him and touched smooth wood. It slid easily aside, and enough light fell into the passage for him to see a kitten-sized spider scrambling toward the ceiling. He was looking down into a room the size of a hotel lobby, filled with women in white and furniture so ornate that it brought back to the boy all the museums he and his parents had visited. In the center of the room a woman lay sleeping or unconscious on an immense bed, only her head and shoulders visible above the sheet.

And then Jack nearly shouted with shock and terror, because the woman on the bed was his mother. That was his mother, and she was dying.

"You saw her," the Captain whispered, and braced his arms more firmly.

Open-mouthed, Jack stared in at his mother. She was dying, he could not doubt that any longer: even her skin seemed bleached and unhealthy, and her hair, too, had lost several shades of color. The nurses around her bustled about, straightening the sheets or rearranging books on a table, but they assumed this busy and purposeful manner because they had no real idea of how to help their patient. The nurses knew that for such a patient there was no real help. If they could stave off death for another month, or even a week, they were at the fullest extent of their powers.

He looked back at the face turned upward like a waxen mask and finally saw that the woman on the bed was not his mother. Her chin was rounder, the shape of her nose slightly more classical. The dying woman was his mother's Twinner; it was Laura DeLoessian. If Speedy had wanted him to see more, he was not capable of it: that white moveless face told him nothing of the woman behind it.

"Okay," he whispered, pushing the panel back into place, and the Captain lowered him to the floor.

In the darkness he asked, "What's wrong with her?"

"Nobody can find that out," came from above him. "The Queen cannot see, she cannot speak, she cannot move. . . ." There was silence for a moment, and then the Captain touched his hand and said, "We must return."

They quietly emerged from blackness into the dusty empty room. The Captain brushed ropy cobwebs from the front of his uniform. His head cocked to one side, he considered Jack for a long moment, worry very plain upon his face. "Now you must answer a question of mine," he said.

"Yes."

"Were you sent here to save her? To save the Queen?"

Jack nodded. "I think so—I think that's part of it. Tell me just one thing." He hesitated. "Why don't those creeps out there just take over? She sure couldn't stop them."

The Captain smiled. There was no humor in that smile. "Me," he said. "My men. *We'd* stop them. I know not what they may have gotten up to in the Outposts, where order is thin—but here we hold to the Queen."

A muscle just below the eye on the unscarred cheekbone jumped like a fish. He was pressing his hands together, palm to palm. "And your directions, your orders, whatever, are to . . . ah, to *go* west, is that correct?"

Jack could practically feel the man vibrating, controlling his growing agitation only from a lifetime's habit of self-discipline. "That's right," he said. "I'm supposed to go west. Isn't that right? Shouldn't I go west? To the other Alhambra?"

"I can't say, I can't say," the Captain blurted, taking a step backward. "We have to get you out of here right now. I can't tell

you what to do." He could not even look at Jack now, the boy
saw. "But you can't stay here a minute longer—let's, ah, let's
see if we can get you out and away before Morgan gets here."

"Morgan?" Jack said, almost thinking that he had not
heard the name correctly. "Morgan Sloat? Is he coming
here?"

# 7

# Farren

## 1

The Captain appeared not to have heard Jack's question. He
was looking away into the corner of this empty unused room
as if there were something there to see. He was thinking long
and hard and fast; Jack recognized that. And Uncle Tommy
had taught him that interrupting an adult who was thinking
hard was just as impolite as interrupting an adult who was
speaking. But—

*Steer clear of ole Bloat. Watch for his trail—his own and
his Twinner's . . . he's gonna be after you like a fox after a
goose.*

Speedy had said that, and Jack had been concentrating so
hard on the Talisman that he had almost missed it. Now the
words came back and came home with a nasty double-thud
that was like being hit in the back of the neck.

"What does he look like?" he asked the Captain urgently.

"Morgan?" the Captain asked, as if startled out of some interior dream.

"Is he fat? Is he fat and sorta going bald? Does he go like
this when he's mad?" And employing the innate gift for mimicry he'd always had—a gift which had made his father roar
with laughter even when he was tired and feeling down—Jack
"did" Morgan Sloat. Age fell into his face as he laddered his
brow the way Uncle Morgan's brow laddered into lines when he
was pissed off about something. At the same time, Jack sucked

his cheeks in and pulled his head down to create a double chin. His lips flared out in a fishy pout and he began to waggle his eyebrows rapidly up and down. "Does he go like that?"

"No," the Captain said, but something flickered in his eyes, the way something had flickered there when Jack told him that Speedy Parker was old. "Morgan's tall. He wears his hair long"—the Captain held a hand by his right shoulder to show Jack how long—"and he has a limp. One foot's deformed. He wears a built-up boot, but—" He shrugged.

"You looked like you knew him when I did him! You—"

"Shhh! Not so God-pounding loud, boy!"

Jack lowered his voice. "I think I know the guy," he said— and for the first time he felt fear as an informed emotion . . . something he could grasp in a way he could not as yet grasp this world. *Uncle Morgan here? Jesus!*

"Morgan is just Morgan. No one to fool around with, boy. Come on, let's get out of here."

His hand closed around Jack's upper arm again. Jack winced but resisted.

*Parker becomes Parkus. And Morgan . . . it's just too big a coincidence.*

"Not yet," he said. Another question had occurred to him. "Did she have a son?"

"The Queen?"

"Yes."

"She had a son," the Captain replied reluctantly. "Yes. Boy, we can't stay here. We—"

"Tell me about him!"

"There is nothing to tell," the Captain answered. "The babe died an infant, not six weeks out of her womb. There was talk that one of Morgan's men—Osmond, perhaps—smothered the lad. But talk of that sort is always cheap. I have no love for Morgan of Orris but everyone knows that one child in every dozen dies a-crib. No one knows why; they die mysteriously, of no cause. There's a saying—*God pounds His nails.* Not even a royal child is excepted in the eyes of the Carpenter. He . . . Boy? are you all right?"

Jack felt the world go gray around him. He reeled, and when the Captain caught him, his hard hands felt as soft as feather pillows.

*He* had almost died as an infant.

His mother had told him the story—how she had found him still and apparently lifeless in his crib, his lips blue, his cheeks the color of funeral candles after they have been capped and thus put out. She had told him how she had run screaming into the living room with him in her arms. His father and Sloat were sitting on the floor, stoned on wine and grass, watching a wrestling match on TV. His father had snatched him from his mother's arms, pinching his nostrils savagely shut with his left hand (*You had bruises there for almost a month, Jacky,* his mother had told him with a jittery laugh) and then plunging his mouth over Jack's tiny mouth, while Morgan cried: *I don't think that's going to help him, Phil. I don't think that's going to help him!*

(*Uncle Morgan was funny, wasn't he, Mom?* Jack had said. *Yes, very funny, Jack-O,* his mother had replied, and she had smiled an oddly humorless smile, and lit another Herbert Tarrytoon from the butt of the one smouldering in the ashtray.)

"Boy!" the Captain whispered, and shook him so hard that Jack's lolling head snapped on his neck. "Boy! Dammit! If you faint on me . . ."

"I'm okay," Jack said—his voice seemed to come from far away; it sounded like the voice of the Dodgers announcer when you were cruising by Chavez Ravine at night with the top down, echoing and distant, the play-by-play of baseball in a sweet dream. "Okay, lay off me, what do you say? Give me a break."

The Captain stopped shaking him but looked at him warily.

"Okay," Jack said again, and abruptly he slapped his own cheek as hard as he could—*Ow!* But the world came swimming back into focus.

He had almost died in his crib. In that apartment they'd had back then, the one he barely remembered, the one his mother always called the Technicolor Dream Palace because of the spectacular view of the Hollywood Hills from the living room. He had almost died in his crib, and his father and Morgan Sloat had been drinking wine, and when you drank a lot of wine you had to pee a lot, and he remembered the Technicolor Dream Palace well enough to know that you got from the living room to the nearest bathroom by going through the room that had been his when he was a baby.

He saw it: Morgan Sloat getting up, grinning easily, saying something like *Just a sec while I make some room, Phil;* his father hardly looking around because Haystack Calhoun was getting ready to put the Spinner or the Sleeper on some hapless opponent; Morgan passing from the TV-brightness of the living room into the ashy dimness of the nursery, where little Jacky Sawyer lay sleeping in his Pooh pajamas with the feet, little Jacky Sawyer warm and secure in a dry diaper. He saw Uncle Morgan glancing furtively back at the bright square of the door to the living room, his balding brow turning to ladder-rungs, his lips pursing like the chilly mouth of a lake bass; he saw Uncle Morgan take a throw-pillow from a nearby chair, saw him put it gently and yet firmly over the sleeping baby's entire head, holding it there with one hand while he held the other hand flat on the baby's back. And when all movement had stopped, he saw Uncle Morgan put the pillow back on the chair where Lily sat to nurse, and go into the bathroom to urinate.

If his mother hadn't come in to check on him almost immediately . . .

Chilly sweat broke out all over his body.

Had it been that way? It could have been. His heart told him it *had* been. The coincidence was too utterly perfect, too seamlessly complete.

At the age of six weeks, the son of Laura DeLoessian, Queen of the Territories, had died in his crib.

At the age of six weeks, the son of Phil and Lily Sawyer had *almost* died in his crib . . . *and Morgan Sloat had been there*.

His mother always finished the story with a joke: how Phil Sawyer had almost racked up their Chrysler, roaring to the hospital after Jacky had already started breathing again.

Pretty funny, all right. Yeah.

## 2

"Now come *on*," the Captain said.

"All right," Jack said. He still felt weak, dazed. "All right, let's g—"

"*Shhhh!*" The Captain looked around sharply at the sound of approaching voices. The wall to their right was not wood but heavy canvas. It stopped four inches short of the floor, and Jack saw booted feet passing by in the gap. Five pair. Soldiers' boots.

One voice cut through the babble: ". . . didn't know he *had* a son."

"Well," a second answered, "bastards sire bastards—a fact you should well know, Simon."

There was a roar of brutal, empty laughter at this—the sort of laughter Jack heard from some of the bigger boys at school, the ones who busted joints behind the woodshop and called the younger boys mysterious but somehow terrifying names: *queerboy* and *humpa-jumpa* and *morphadite*. Each of these somehow slimy terms was followed by a coarse ribband of laughter exactly like this.

"Cork it! Cork it up!"—a third voice. "If *he* hears you, you'll be walking Outpost Line before thirty suns have set!"

Mutters.

A muffled burst of laughter.

Another jibe, this one unintelligible. More laughter as they passed on.

Jack looked at the Captain, who was staring at the short canvas wall with his lips drawn back from his teeth all the way to the gumlines. No question who they were talking about. And if they were talking, there might be someone listening . . . the wrong somebody. Somebody who might be wondering just who this suddenly revealed bastard might really be. Even a kid like him knew that.

"You heard enough?" the Captain said. "We've got to *move*." He looked as if he would like to shake Jack . . . but did not quite dare.

*Your directions, your orders, whatever, are to . . . ah, go west, is that correct?*

*He changed,* Jack thought. *He changed twice.*

Once when Jack showed him the shark's tooth that had been a filigreed guitar-pick in the world where delivery trucks instead of horse-drawn carts ran the roads. And he had changed again when Jack confirmed that he was going west. He had gone from threat to a willingness to help to . . . what?

*I can't say . . . I can't tell you what to do.*

To something like religious awe . . . or religious terror.

*He wants to get out of here because he's afraid we'll be*

*caught*, Jack thought. *But there's more, isn't there? He's afraid of me. Afraid of—*

"Come on," the Captain said. "Come *on*, for Jason's sake."

"*Whose* sake?" Jack asked stupidly, but the Captain was already propelling him out. He pulled Jack hard left and half-led, half-dragged him down a corridor that was wood on one side and stiff, mouldy-smelling canvas on the other.

"This isn't the way we came," Jack whispered.

"Don't want to go past those fellows we saw coming in," the Captain whispered back. "Morgan's men. Did you see the tall one? Almost skinny enough to look through?"

"Yes." Jack remembered the thin smile, and the eyes which did not smile. The others had looked soft. The thin man had looked hard. He had looked crazy. And one thing more: he had looked dimly familiar.

"Osmond," the Captain said, now pulling Jack to the right.

The smell of roasting meat had been growing gradually stronger, and now the air was redolent of it. Jack had never smelled meat he wanted so badly to taste in his whole life. He was scared, he was mentally and emotionally on the ropes, perhaps rocking on the edge of madness . . . but his mouth was watering crazily.

"Osmond is Morgan's right-hand man," the Captain grunted. "He sees too much, and I'd just as soon he didn't see *you* twice, boy."

"What do you mean?"

"*Hsssst!*" He clamped Jack's aching arm even tighter! They were approaching a wide cloth drape that hung in a doorway. To Jack it looked like a shower-curtain—except the cloth was burlap of a weave so coarse and wide that it was almost net-like, and the rings it hung from were bone rather than chrome. "Now *cry*," the Captain breathed warmly in Jack's ear.

He swept the curtain back and pulled Jack into a huge kitchen which fumed with rich aromas (the meat still predominating) and billows of steamy heat. Jack caught a confused glimpse of braziers, of a great stonework chimney, of women's faces under billowy white kerchiefs that reminded him of nuns' wimples. Some of them were lined up at a long iron trough which stood on trestles, their faces red and beaded with sweat as they washed pots and cooking utensils. Others stood at a counter which ran the width of the room, slicing and dicing and coring and paring. Another was carrying a wire rack filled with uncooked pies. They all stared at Jack and the Captain as they pushed through into the kitchen.

"Never again!" the Captain bellowed at Jack, shaking him as a terrier shakes a rat . . . and all the while he continued to move them both swiftly across the room, toward the double-hung doors at the far side. "Never again, do you hear me? The next time you shirk your duty, I'll split your skin down the back and peel you like a baked potato!"

And under his breath, the Captain hissed, "They'll all remember and they'll all talk, so *cry*, dammit!"

And now, as the Captain with the scarred face dragged him across the steaming kitchen by the scruff of his neck and one throbbing arm, Jack deliberately called up the dreadful image of his mother lying in a funeral parlor. He saw her in billowing folds of white organdy—she was lying in her coffin and wearing the wedding dress she had worn in *Drag Strip Rumble* (RKO, 1953). Her face came clearer and clearer in Jack's mind, a perfect wax effigy, and he saw she was wearing her tiny gold-cross earrings, the ones Jack had given her for Christmas two years ago. Then the face changed. The chin became rounder, the nose straighter and more patrician. The hair went a shade lighter and became somehow coarser. Now it was Laura DeLoessian he saw in that coffin—and the coffin itself was no longer a smoothly anonymous funeral parlor special, but something that looked as if it had been hacked with rude fury from an old log—a Viking's coffin, if there had ever been such a thing; it was easier to imagine this coffin being torched alight on a bier of oiled logs than it was to imagine it being lowered into the unprotesting earth. It was Laura DeLoessian, Queen of the Territories, but in this imagining which had become as clear as a vision, the Queen was wearing his mother's wedding dress from *Drag Strip Rumble* and the gold-cross earrings Uncle Tommy had helped him pick out in Sharp's of Beverly Hills. Suddenly his tears came in a hot and burning flood—not sham tears but real ones, not just for his mother but for both of these lost women, dying universes apart, bound by some unseen cord which might rot but would never break—at least, not until they were both dead.

Through the tears he saw a giant of a man in billowing whites rush across the room toward them. He wore a red bandanna instead of a puffy chef's hat on his head, but Jack thought its purpose was the same—to identify the wearer as the boss of the kitchen. He was also brandishing a wicked-looking three-tined wooden fork.

*"Ged-OUT!"* the chef screeched at them, and the voice emerging from that huge barrel chest was absurdly flutelike—it was the voice of a willowy gay giving a shoe-clerk a piece of his mind. But there was nothing absurd about the fork; it looked deadly.

The women scattered before his charge like birds. The bottom-most pie dropped out of the pie-woman's rack and she uttered a high, despairing cry as it broke apart on the boards. Strawberry juice splattered and ran, the red as fresh and bright as arterial blood.

*"GED-DOUT MY KIDCHEN, YOU SLUGS! DIS IS NO SHORDCUD! DIS IS NO RAZE-TRAG! DIS IS MY KID-CHEN AND IF YOU CAD'T REMEMBER DAT, I'LL BY GOD THE CARBENDER CARVE YOUR AZZES FOR YOU!"*

He jabbed the fork at them, simultaneously half-turning his head and squinching his eyes mostly shut, as if in spite of his tough talk the thought of hot flowing blood was just too *gauche* to be borne. The Captain removed the hand that had been on the scruff of Jack's neck and reached out—almost casually, it seemed to Jack. A moment later the chef was on the floor, all six and a half feet of him. The meat-fork was lying in a puddle of strawberry sauce and chunks of white unbaked pastry. The chef rolled back and forth, clutching his broken right wrist and screaming in that high, flutelike voice. The news he screamed out to the room in general was certainly woeful enough: he was dead, the Captain had surely murdered him (pronounced mur-dirt in the chef's odd, almost Teutonic accent); he was at the very least crippled, the cruel and heartless Captain of the Outer Guards having destroyed his good right hand and thus his livelihood, and so ensuring a miserable beggar's life for him in the years to come; the Captain had inflicted terrible pain on him, a pain beyond belief, such as was not to be borne—

*"Shut up!"* the Captain roared, and the chef did. Immediately. He lay on the floor like a great baby, his right hand curled on his chest, his red bandanna drunkenly askew so that one ear (a small black pearl was set in the center of the lobe)

showed, his fat cheeks quivering. The kitchen women gasped and twittered as the Captain bent over the dreaded chief ogre of the steaming cave where they spent their days and nights. Jack, still weeping, caught a glimpse of a black boy (*brown* boy, his mind amended) standing at one end of the largest brazier. The boy's mouth was open, his face as comically surprised as a face in a minstrel show, but he kept turning the crank in his hands, and the haunch suspended over the glowing coals kept revolving.

"Now listen and I'll give you some advice you won't find in *The Book of Good Farming*," the Captain said. He bent over the chef until their noses almost touched (his paralyzing grip on Jack's arm—which was now going mercifully numb—never loosened the smallest bit). "Don't you ever . . . don't you *ever* . . . come at a man with a knife . . . or a fork . . . or a spear . . . or with so much as a God-pounding *splinter* in your hand unless you intend to kill him with it. One expects temperament from chefs, but temperament does not extend to assaults upon the person of the Captain of the Outer Guards. Do you understand me?"

The chef moaned out a teary, defiant something-or-other. Jack couldn't make it all out—the man's accent seemed to be growing steadily thicker—but it had something to do with the Captain's mother and the dump-dogs beyond the pavillion.

"That may well be," the Captain said. "I never knew the lady. But it certainly doesn't answer my question." He prodded the chef with one dusty, scuffed boot. It was a gentle enough prod, but the chef screeched as if the Captain had drawn his foot back and kicked him as hard as he could. The women twittered again.

"Do we or do we not have an understanding on the subject of chefs and weapons and Captains? Because if we don't, a little more instruction might be in order."

"We do!" the chef gasped. "We do! We do! We—"

"Good. Because I've had to give far too much instruction already today." He shook Jack by the scruff of the neck. "Haven't I, boy?" He shook him again, and Jack uttered a wail that was completely unfeigned. "Well . . . I suppose that's all he can say. The boy's a simpleton. Like his mother."

The Captain threw his dark, gleaming glance around the kitchen.

"Good day, ladies. Queen's blessings upon you."

"And you, good sir," the eldest among them managed, and dropped an awkward, ungraceful curtsey. The others followed suit.

The Captain dragged Jack across the kitchen. Jack's hip bumped the edge of the washing trough with excruciating force and he cried out again. Hot water flew. Smoking droplets hit the boards and ran, hissing, between them. *Those women had their hands in that,* Jack thought. *How do they stand it?* Then the Captain, who was almost carrying him by now, shoved Jack through another burlap curtain and into the hallway beyond.

"Phew!" the Captain said in a low voice. "I don't like this, not any of it, it all smells bad."

Left, right, then right again. Jack began to sense that they were approaching the outer walls of the pavillion, and he had time to wonder how the place could seem so much bigger on the inside than it looked from the outside. Then the Captain was pushing him through a flap and they were in daylight again—mid-afternoon daylight so bright after the shifting dimness of the pavillion that Jack had to wince his eyes shut against a burst of pain.

The Captain never hesitated. Mud squelched and smooched underfoot. There was the smell of hay and horses and shit. Jack opened his eyes again and saw they were crossing what might have been a paddock or a corral or maybe just a barnyard. He saw an open canvas-sided hallway and heard chickens clucking somewhere beyond it. A scrawny man, naked except for a dirty kilt and thong sandals, was tossing hay into an open stall, using a pitchfork with wooden tines to do the job. Inside the stall, a horse not much bigger than a Shetland pony looked moodily out at them. They had already passed the stall when Jack's mind was finally able to accept what his eyes had seen: the horse had two heads.

"Hey!" he said. "Can I look back in that stall? That—"

"No time."

"But that horse had—"

"No time, I said." He raised his voice and shouted: "And if I ever catch you laying about again when there's work to be done, you'll get *twice* this!"

"You won't!" Jack screamed (in truth he felt as if this

scene were getting a bit old). "I swear you won't! I told you I'd be good!"

Just ahead of them, tall wooden gates loomed in a wall made of wooden posts with the bark still on them—it was like a stockade wall in an old Western (his mother had made a few of those, too). Heavy brackets were screwed into the gates, but the bar the brackets were meant to hold was not in place. It leaned against the woodpile to the left, thick as a railroad crosstie. The gates stood open almost six inches. Some muddled sense of direction in Jack's head suggested that they had worked their way completely around the pavillion to its far side.

"Thank God," the Captain said in a more normal voice. "Now—"

"Captain," a voice called from behind them. The voice was low but carrying, deceptively casual. The Captain stopped in his tracks. It had called just as Jack's scarred companion had been in the act of reaching for the left gate to push it open; it was as if the voice's owner had watched and waited for just that second.

"Perhaps you would be good enough to introduce me to your . . . ah . . . son."

The Captain turned, turning Jack with him. Standing, halfway across the paddock area, looking unsettling out of place there, was the skeletal courtier the Captain had been afraid of—Osmond. He looked at them from dark gray melancholy eyes. Jack saw something stirring in those eyes, something deep down. His fear was suddenly sharper, something with a point, jabbing into him. *He's crazy*—this was the intuition which leaped spontaneously into his mind. *Nuttier than a damned fruitcake.*

Osmond took two neat steps toward them. In his left hand he held the rawhide-wrapped haft of a bullwhip. The handle narrowed only slightly into a dark, limber tendon coiled thrice around his shoulder—the whip's central stalk was as thick as a timber rattlesnake. Near its tip, this central stalk gave birth to perhaps a dozen smaller offshoots, each of woven rawhide, each tipped with a crudely made but bright metal spur.

Osmond tugged the whip's handle and the coils slithered from his shoulder with a dry hiss. He wiggled the handle, and the metal-tipped strands of rawhide writhed slowly in the straw-littered mud.

"Your son?" Osmond repeated, and took another step toward them. And Jack suddenly understood why this man had looked familiar before. The day he had almost been kidnapped—hadn't this man been White Suit?

Jack thought that perhaps he had been.

## 3

The Captain made a fist, brought it to his forehead, and bent forward. After only a moment's hesitation, Jack did the same.

"My son, Lewis," the Captain said stiffly. He was still bent over, Jack saw, cutting his eyes to the left. So he remained bent over himself, his heart racing.

"Thank you, Captain. Thank you, Lewis. Queen's blessings upon you." When he touched him with the haft of the bullwhip, Jack almost cried out. He stood straight again, biting the cry in.

Osmond was only two paces away now, regarding Jack with that mad, melancholy gaze. He wore a leather jacket and what might have been diamond studs. His shirt was extravagantly ruffled. A bracelet of links clanked ostentatiously upon his right wrist (from the way he handled the bullwhip, Jack guessed that his left was his working hand). His hair was drawn back and tied with a wide ribbon that might have been white satin. There were two odors about him. The top was what his mother called "all those men's perfumes," meaning after-shave, cologne, whatever. The smell about Osmond was thick and powdery. It made Jack think of those old black-and-white British films where some poor guy was on trial in the Old Bailey. The judges and lawyers in those films always wore wigs, and Jack thought the boxes those wigs came out of would smell like Osmond—dry and crumbly-sweet, like the world's oldest powdered doughnut. Beneath it, however, was a more vital, even less pleasant smell: it seemed to pulse out at him. It was the smell of sweat in layers and dirt in layers, the smell of a man who bathed seldom, if ever.

Yes. This was one of the creatures that had tried to steal him that day.

His stomach knotted and roiled.

"I did not know you had a son, Captain Farren," Osmond said. Although he spoke to the Captain, his eyes remained on Jack. *Lewis*, he thought, *I'm Lewis, don't forget—*

"Would that I did not," the Captain replied, looking at Jack with anger and contempt. "I honor him by bringing him to the great pavillion and then he slinks away like a dog. I caught him playing at d—"

"Yes, yes," Osmond said, smiling remotely. *He doesn't believe a word*, Jack thought wildly, and felt his mind take another clumsy step toward panic. *Not a single word!* "Boys are bad. All boys are bad. It's axiomatic."

He tapped Jack lightly on the wrist with the haft of the bullwhip. Jack, his nerves screwed up to an unbearable pitch, screamed . . . and immediately flushed with hot shame.

Osmond giggled. "Bad, oh yes, it's axiomatic, all boys are bad. *I* was bad; and I'll wager *you* were bad, Captain Farren. Eh? Eh? Were you bad?"

"Yes, Osmond," the Captain said.

"Very bad?" Osmond asked. Incredibly, he had begun to prance in the mud. Yet there was nothing swishy about this: Osmond was willowy and almost delicate, but Jack got no feeling of true homosexuality from the man; if there was that innuendo in his words, then Jack sensed intuitively that it was hollow. No, what came through most clearly here was a sense of malignity . . . and madness. "*Very* bad? Most *awfully* bad?"

"Yes, Osmond," Captain Farren said woodenly. His scar glowed in the afternoon light, more red than pink now.

Osmond ceased his impromptu little dance as abruptly as he had begun it. He looked coldly at the Captain.

"*No one* knew you had a son, Captain."

"He's a bastard," the Captain said. "And simple. Lazy as well, it now turns out." He pivoted suddenly and struck Jack on the side of the face. There was not much force behind the blow, but Captain Farren's hand was as hard as a brick. Jack howled and fell into the mud, clutching his ear.

"*Very* bad, most *awfully* bad," Osmond said, but now his face was a dreadful blank, thin and secretive. "Get up, you bad boy. Bad boys who disobey their fathers must be punished. And bad boys must be questioned." He flicked the whip to one side. It made a dry pop. Jack's tottery mind made another strange connection—reaching, he supposed later, for home in every way it knew how. The sound of Osmond's whip was like the pop of the Daisy air rifle he'd had when he was eight. He and Richard Sloat had both had rifles like that.

Osmond reached out and grasped Jack's muddy arm with one white, spiderlike hand. He drew Jack toward him, into those smells—old sweet powder and old rancid filth. His weird gray eyes peered solemnly into Jack's blue ones. Jack felt his bladder grow heavy, and he struggled to keep from wetting his pants.

"Who are you?" Osmond asked.

### 4

The words hung in the air over the three of them.

Jack was aware of the Captain looking at him with a stern expression that could not quite hide his despair. He could hear hens clucking; a dog barking; somewhere the rumble of a large approaching cart.

*Tell me the truth; I will know a lie,* those eyes said. *You look like a certain bad boy I first met in California—are you that boy?*

And for a moment, everything trembled on his lips:

*Jack, I'm Jack Sawyer, yeah, I'm the kid from California, the Queen of this world was my mother, only I died, and I know your boss, I know Morgan—Uncle Morgan—and I'll tell you anything you want to know if only you'll stop looking at me with those freaked-out eyes of yours, sure, because I'm only a kid, and that's what kids do, they tell, they tell everything—*

Then he heard his mother's voice, tough, on the edge of a jeer:

*You gonna spill your guts to this guy, Jack-O? THIS guy? He smells like a distress sale at the men's cologne counter and he looks like a medieval version of Charles Manson . . . but you suit yourself. You can fool him if you want—no sweat—but you suit yourself.*

"Who are you?" Osmond asked again, drawing even closer, and on his face Jack now saw total confidence—he was used to getting the answers he wanted from people . . . and not just from twelve-year-old kids, either.

Jack took a deep, trembling breath (*When you want max volume—when you want to get it all the way up to the back row of the balcony—you gotta bring it from your diaphragm, Jacky. It just kind of gets passed through the old vox-box on the way up*) and screamed:

"*I WAS GOING TO GO RIGHT BACK! HONEST TO GOD!*"

Osmond, who had been leaning even farther forward in anticipation of a broken and strengthless whisper, recoiled as if Jack had suddenly reached out and slapped him. He stepped on the trailing rawhide tails of his whip with one booted foot and came close to tripping over them.

"You damned God-pounding little—"

"*I WAS GOING TO! PLEASE DON'T WHIP ME OSMOND I WAS GOING TO GO BACK! I NEVER WANTED TO COME HERE I NEVER I NEVER I NEVER—*"

Captain Farren lunged forward and struck him in the back. Jack sprawled full-length in the mud, still screaming.

"He's simple-minded, as I told you," he heard the Captain saying. "I apologize, Osmond. You can be sure he'll be beaten within an inch of his life. He—"

"*What's he doing here in the first place?*" Osmond shrieked. His voice was now as high and shrewish as any fishwife's. "What's your snot-nosed puling brat-bastard doing here at all? Don't offer to show me his pass! I know he has no pass! You sneaked him in to feed at the Queen's table . . . to steal the Queen's silver, for all I know . . . he's *bad* . . . one look's enough to tell anyone that he's very, intolerably, most indubitably *bad!*"

The whip came down again, not the mild cough of a Daisy air rifle this time but the loud clean report of a .22, and Jack had time to think *I know where that's going*, and then a large fiery hand clawed into his back. The pain seemed to sink into his flesh, not diminishing but actually intensifying. It was hot and maddening. He screamed and writhed in the mud.

"*Bad!* Most awfully *bad!* Indubitably *bad!*"

Each "bad" was punctuated by another crack of Osmond's whip, another fiery handprint, another scream from Jack. His back was burning. He had no idea how long it might have gone on—Osmond seemed to be working himself into a hotter frenzy with each blow—but then a new voice shouted: "Osmond! Osmond! There you are! Thank God!"

A commotion of running footsteps.

Osmond's voice, furious and slightly out of breath: "Well? Well? What is it?"

A hand grasped Jack's elbow and helped him to his feet. When he staggered, the arm attached to the hand slipped around his waist and supported him. It was difficult to believe that the Captain who had been so hard and sure during their bewildering tour of the pavillion could now be so gentle.

Jack staggered again. The world kept wanting to swim out of focus. Trickles of warm blood ran down his back. He looked at Osmond with swift-awakening hatred, and it was good to feel that hatred. It was a welcome antidote to the fear and the confusion.

*You did that—you hurt me, you cut me. And listen to me, Jiggs, if I get a chance to pay you back—*

"Are you all right?" the Captain whispered.

"Yes."

*"What?"* Osmond screamed at the two men who had interrupted Jack's whipping.

The first was one of the dandies Jack and the Captain had passed going to the secret room. The other looked a bit like the carter Jack had seen almost immediately upon his return to the Territories. This fellow looked badly frightened, and hurt as well—blood was welling from a gash on the left side of his head and had covered most of the left side of his face. His left arm was scraped and his jerkin was torn. *"What are you saying, you jackass?"*

"My wagon overturned coming around the bend on the far side of All-Hands' Village," the carter said. He spoke with the slow, dazed patience of one in deep shock. "My son's kilt, my Lord. Crushed to death under the barrels. He was just sixteen last May-Farm Day. His mother—"

*"What?"* Osmond screamed again. "Barrels? *Ale?* Not the Kingsland? *You don't mean to tell me you've overturned a full wagonload of Kingsland Ale, you stupid goat's penis? You don't mean to tell me that, do yoooooouuuuuuu?"*

Osmond's voice rose on the last word like the voice of a man making savage mockery of an operatic diva. It wavered and warbled. At the same time he began to dance again . . . but in rage this time. The combination was so weird that Jack had to raise both hands to stifle an involuntary giggle. The movement caused his shirt to scrape across his welted back, and that sobered him even before the Captain muttered a warning word.

Patiently, as if Osmond had missed the only important fact (and so it must have seemed to him), the carter began again: "He was just sixteen last May-Farm Day. His mother didn't want him to come with me. I can't think what—"

Osmond raised his whip and brought it whickering down with blinding and unexpected speed. At one moment the handle was grasped loosely in his left hand, the whip itself with its rawhide tails trailing in the mud; at the next there was a whipcrack not like the sound of a .22 but more like that of a toy rifle. The carter staggered back, shrieking, his hands clapped to his face. Fresh blood ran loosely through his dirty fingers. He fell over, screaming, *"My Lord! My Lord! My Lord!"* in a muffled, gargling voice.

Jack moaned: "Let's get out of here. Quick!"

"Wait," the Captain said. The grim set of his face seemed to have loosened the smallest bit. There might have been hope in his eyes.

Osmond whirled to the dandy, who took a step back, his thick red mouth working.

"Was it the Kingsland?" Osmond panted.

"Osmond, you shouldn't tax yourself so—"

Osmond flicked his left wrist upward; the whip's steel-tipped rawhide tails clattered against the dandy's boots. The dandy took another step backward.

"Don't tell me what I should or shouldn't do," he said. "Only answer my questions. I'm vexed, Stephen, I'm most intolerably, indubitably vexed. Was it the Kingsland?"

"Yes," Stephen said. "I regret to say it, but—"

"On the Outpost Road?"

"Osmond—"

*"On the Outpost Road, you dripping penis?"*

"Yes," Stephen gulped.

"Of course," Osmond said, and his thin face was split by a hideous white grin. "Where is All-Hands' Village, if not on the Outpost Road? Can a village fly? Huh? Can a village somehow fly from one road to another, Stephen? Can it? Can it?"

"No, Osmond, of course not."

"No. And so there are barrels all over the Outpost Road, is that correct? Is it correct for me to assume that there are barrels and an overturned ale-wagon blocking the Outpost Road while the best ale in the Territories soaks into the ground for the earthworms to carouse on? Is that correct?"

"Yes . . . yes. But—"

*"Morgan is coming by the Outpost Road!"* Osmond screamed. *"Morgan is coming and you know how he drives his horses!* If his diligence comes around a bend and upon that mess, his driver may not have time to stop! *He could be overturned! He could be killed!"*

"Dear-God," Stephen said, all as one word. His pallid face went two shades whiter.

Osmond nodded slowly. "I think, if Morgan's diligence were to overturn, we would all do better to pray for his death than for his recovery."

"But—but—"

Osmond turned from him and almost ran back to where the Captain of the Outer Guards stood with his "son." Behind Osmond, the hapless carter still writhed in the mud, bubbling *My Lords.*

Osmond's eyes touched Jack and then swept over him as if he weren't there. "Captain Farren," he said. "Have you followed the events of the last five minutes?"

"Yes, Osmond."

"Have you followed them closely? Have you *gleaned* them? Have you gleaned them most closely?"

"Yes. I think so."

"Do you think so? What an excellent Captain you are, Captain! We will talk more, I think, about how such an excellent Captain could produce such a frog's testicle of a son."

His eyes touched Jack's face briefly, coldly.

"But there's no time for that now, is there? No. I suggest that you summon a dozen of your brawniest men and that you double-time them—no, *triple*-time them—out to the Outpost Road. You'll be able to follow your nose, to the site of the accident, won't you?"

"Yes, Osmond."

Osmond glanced quickly at the sky. "Morgan is expected at six of the clock—perhaps a little sooner. It is now—two. I would say two. Would you say two, Captain?"

"Yes, Osmond."

"And what would you say, you little turd? Thirteen? Twenty-three? Eighty-one of the clock?"

Jack gaped. Osmond grimaced contemptuously, and Jack felt the clear tide of his hate rise again.

*You hurt me, and if I get the chance—!*

Osmond looked back at the Captain. "Until five of the clock, I suggest that you be at pains to save whatever barrels may still be whole. After five, I suggest you simply clear the road as rapidly as you can. Do you understand?"

"Yes, Osmond."

"Then get out of here."

Captain Farren brought a fist to his forehead and bowed. Gaping stupidly, still hating Osmond so fiercely that his brains seemed to pulse, Jack did the same. Osmond had whirled away from them before the salute was even fairly begun. He was striding back toward the carter, popping his whip, making it cough out those Daisy air rifle sounds.

The carter heard Osmond's approach and began to scream.

"Come on," the Captain said, pulling Jack's arm for the last time. "You don't want to see this."

"No," Jack managed. "God, no."

But as Captain Farren pushed the right-hand gate open and they finally left the pavillion, Jack heard it—and he heard it in his dreams that night: one whistling carbine-crack after another, each followed by a scream from the doomed carter. And Osmond was making a sound. The man was panting, out of breath, and so it was hard to tell exactly what that sound was, without turning around to look at his face—something Jack did not want to do.

He was pretty sure he knew, though.

He thought Osmond was laughing.

### 5

They were in the public area of the pavillion grounds now. The strollers glanced at Captain Farren from the corners of their eyes . . . and gave him a wide berth. The Captain strode swiftly, his face tight and dark with thought. Jack had to trot in order to catch up.

"We were lucky," the Captain said suddenly. "Damned lucky. I think he meant to kill you."

Jack gaped at him, his mouth dry and hot.

"He's mad, you know. Mad as the man who chased the cake."

Jack had no idea what that might mean, but he agreed that Osmond was mad.

"What—"

"Wait," the Captain said. They had come back around to the small tent where the Captain had taken Jack after seeing the shark's tooth. "Stand right here and wait for me. Speak to no one."

The Captain entered the tent. Jack stood watching and waiting. A juggler passed him, glancing at Jack but never losing his rhythm as he tossed half a dozen balls in a complex and airy pattern. A straggle of dirty children followed him as the children followed the Piper out of Hamelin. A young woman with a dirty baby at one huge breast told him she could teach him something to do with his little man besides let piss out of it, if he had a coin or two. Jack looked uncomfortably away, his face hot.

The girl cawed laughter. *"Oooooo, this pretty young man's SHY! Come over here, pretty! Come—"*

"Get out, slut, or you'll finish the day in the under-kitchens."

It was the Captain. He had come out of the tent with another man. This second fellow was old and fat, but he shared one characteristic with Farren—he looked like a real soldier rather than one from Gilbert and Sullivan. He was trying to fasten the front of his uniform over his bulging gut while holding a curly, French horn–like instrument at the same time.

The girl with the dirty baby scurried away with never another look at Jack. The Captain took the fat man's horn so he could finish buttoning, and passed another word with him. The fat man nodded, finished with his shirt, took his horn back, and then strode off, blowing it. It was not like the sound Jack had heard on his first flip into the Territories; that had been many horns, and their sound had been somehow showy:

the sound of heralds. This was like a factory whistle, announcing work to be done.

The Captain returned to Jack.

"Come with me," he said.

"Where?"

"Outpost Road," Captain Farren said, and then he cast a wondering, half-fearful eye down on Jack Sawyer. "What my father's father called Western Road. It goes west through smaller and smaller villages until it reaches the Outposts. Beyond the Outposts it goes into nowhere . . . or hell. If you're going west, you'll need God with you, boy. But I've heard it said He Himself never ventures beyond the Outposts. Come on."

Questions crowded Jack's mind—a million of them—but the Captain set a killer pace and he didn't have the spare breath to ask them. They breasted the rise south of the great pavillion and passed the spot where he had first flipped back out of the Territories. The rustic fun-fair was now close—Jack could hear a barker cajoling patrons to try their luck on Wonder the Devil-Donkey; to stay on two minutes was to win a prize, the barker cried. His voice came on the sea-breeze with perfect clarity, as did the mouthwatering smell of hot food—roast corn as well as meat this time. Jack's stomach rumbled. Now safely away from Osmond the Great and Terrible, he was ravenous.

Before they quite reached the fair, they turned right on a road much wider than the one which led toward the great pavillion. *Outpost Road*, Jack thought, and then, with a little chill of fear and anticipation in his belly, he corrected himself: *No . . . Western Road. The way to the Talisman.*

Then he was hurrying after Captain Farren again.

6

Osmond had been right; they could have followed their noses, if necessary. They were still a mile outside the village with that odd name when the first sour tang of spilled ale came to them on the breeze.

Eastward-bearing traffic on the road was heavy. Most of it was wagons drawn by lathered teams of horses (none with two heads, however). The wagons were, Jack supposed, the Diamond Reos and Peterbilts of this world. Some were piled high with bags and bales and sacks, some with raw meat, some with clacking cages of chickens. On the outskirts of All-Hands' Village, an open wagon filled with women swept by them at an alarming pace. The women were laughing and shrieking. One got to her feet, raised her skirt all the way to her hairy crotch, and did a tipsy bump and grind. She would have tumbled over the side of the wagon and into the ditch—probably breaking her neck—if one of her colleagues hadn't grabbed her by the back of the skirt and pulled her rudely back down.

Jack blushed again: he saw the girl's white breast, its nipple in the dirty baby's working mouth. *Oooooo, this pretty young man's SHY!*

"God!" Farren muttered, walking faster than ever. "They were all drunk! Drunk on spilled Kingsland! Whores and driver both! He's apt to wreck them on the road or drive them right off the sea-cliffs—no great loss. Diseased sluts!"

"At least," Jack panted, "the road must be fairly clear, if all this traffic can get through. Mustn't it?"

They were in All-Hands' Village now. The wide Western Road had been oiled here to lay the dust. Wagons came and went, groups of people crossed the street, and everyone seemed to be talking too loudly. Jack saw two men arguing outside what might have been a restaurant. Abruptly, one of them threw a punch. A moment later, both men were rolling on the ground. *Those whores aren't the only ones drunk on Kingsland*, Jack thought. *I think everyone in this town's had a share.*

"All of the big wagons that passed us came from here," Captain Farren said. "Some of the smaller ones may be getting through, but Morgan's diligence isn't small, boy."

"Morgan—"

"Never mind Morgan now."

The smell of the ale grew steadily sharper as they passed through the center of the village and out the other side. Jack's legs ached as he struggled to keep up with the Captain. He guessed they had now come perhaps three miles. *How far is that in my world?* he thought, and that thought made him think of Speedy's magic juice. He groped frantically in his jerkin, convinced it was no longer there—but it was, held securely within whatever Territories undergarment had replaced his Jockey shorts.

Once they were on the western side of the village, the wagon-traffic decreased, but the pedestrian traffic headed east increased dramatically. Most of the pedestrians were weaving, staggering, laughing. They all reeked of ale. In some cases, their clothes were dripping, as if they had lain full-length in it and drunk of it like dogs. Jack supposed they had. He saw a laughing man leading a laughing boy of perhaps eight by the hand. The man bore a nightmarish resemblance to the hateful desk clerk at the Alhambra, and Jack understood with perfect clarity that this man was that man's Twinner. Both he and the boy he led by the hand were drunk, and as Jack turned to look after them, the little boy began to vomit. His father—or so Jack supposed him to be—jerked him hard by the arm as the boy attempted to flounder his way into the brushy ditch, where he could be sick in relative privacy. The kid reeled back to his father like a cur-dog on a short leash, spraying puke on an elderly man who had collapsed by the side of the road and was snoring there.

Captain Farren's face grew blacker and blacker. "God pound them all," he said.

Even those furthest into their cups gave the scarred Captain a wide and prudent berth. While in the guard-post outside the pavillion, he had belted a short, businesslike leather scabbard around his waist. Jack assumed (not unreasonably) that it contained a short, businesslike sword. When any of the sots came too close, the Captain touched the sword and the sot detoured quickly away.

Ten minutes later—as Jack was becoming sure he could no longer keep up—they arrived at the site of the accident. The driver had been coming out of the turn on the inside when the wagon had tilted and gone over. As a result, the kegs had sprayed all the way across the road. Many of them were smashed, and the road was a quagmire for twenty feet. One horse lay dead beneath the wagon, only its hindquarters visible. Another lay in the ditch, a shattered chunk of barrel-stave protruding from its ear. Jack didn't think that could have happened by accident. He supposed the horse had been badly hurt and someone had put it out of its misery by the closest means at hand. The other horses were nowhere to be seen.

Between the horse under the wagon and the one in the ditch lay the carter's son, spreadeagled on the road. Half of his face stared up at the bright blue Territories sky with an expression of stupid amazement. Where the other half had been was now only red pulp and splinters of white bone like flecks of plaster.

Jack saw that his pockets had been turned out.

Wandering around the scene of the accident were perhaps a dozen people. They walked slowly, often bending over to scoop ale two-handed from a hoofprint or to dip a handkerchief or a torn-off piece of singlet into another puddle. Most of them were staggering. Voices were raised in laughter and in quarrelsome shouts. After a good deal of pestering, Jack's mother had allowed him to go with Richard to see a midnight double feature of *Night of the Living Dead* and *Dawn of the Dead* at one of Westwood's dozen or so movie theaters. The shuffling, drunken people here reminded him of the zombies in those two films.

Captain Farren drew his sword. It was as short and businesslike as Jack had imagined, the very antithesis of a sword in a romance. It was little more than a long butcher's knife, pitted and nicked and scarred, the handle wrapped in old leather that had been sweated dark. The blade itself was dark . . . except for the cutting edge. That looked bright and keen and *very* sharp.

"Make away, then!" Farren bawled. "Make away from the Queen's ale, God-pounders! Make away and keep your guts where they belong!"

Growls of displeasure met this, but they moved away from Captain Farren—all except one hulk of a man with tufts of hair growing at wildly random points from his otherwise bald skull. Jack guessed his weight at close to three hundred pounds, his height at just shy of seven feet.

"D'you like the idea of taking on all of us, sojer?" this hulk asked, and waved one grimy hand at the knot of villagers who had stepped away from the swamp of ale and the litter of barrels at Farren's order.

"Sure," Captain Farren said, and grinned at the big man. "I like it fine, just as long as you're first, you great drunken clot of shit." Farren's grin widened, and the big man faltered away from its dangerous power. "Come for me, if you like. Carving you will be the first good thing that's happened to me all day."

Muttering, the drunken giant slouched away.

"Now, all of you!" Farren shouted. "Make away! There's a dozen of my men just setting out from the Queen's pavillion! They'll not be happy with this duty and I don't blame them and I can't be responsible for them! I think you've just got time to get back to the village and hide in your cellars before they arrive there! It would be prudent to do so! Make away!"

They were already streaming back toward the village of All-Hands', the big man who had challenged the Captain in their van. Farren grunted and then turned back to the scene of the accident. He removed his jacket and covered the face of the carter's son with it.

"I wonder which of them robbed the lad's pockets as he lay dead or dying in the roadstead," Farren said meditatively. "If I knew, I'd have them hung on a cross by nightfall."

Jack made no answer.

The Captain stood looking down at the dead boy for a long time, one hand rubbing at the smooth, ridged flesh of the scar on his face. When he looked up at Jack, it was as if he had just come to.

"You've got to leave now, boy. Right away. Before Osmond decides he'd like to investigate my idiot son further."

"How bad is it going to be with you?" Jack asked.

The Captain smiled a little. "If you're gone, I'll have no trouble. I can say that I sent you back to your mother, or that I was overcome with rage and hit you with a chunk of wood and killed you. Osmond would believe either. He's distracted. They all are. They're waiting for her to die. It will be soon. Unless . . ."

He didn't finish.

"Go," Farren said. "Don't tarry. And when you hear Morgan's diligence coming, get off the road and get deep into the woods. *Deep.* Or he'll smell you like a cat smells a rat. He knows instantly if something is out of order. *His* order. He's a devil."

"Will I hear it coming? His diligence?" Jack asked timidly. He looked at the road beyond the litter of barrels. It rose steadily upward, toward the edge of a piney forest. It would be dark in there, he thought . . . and Morgan would be coming the other way. Fear and loneliness combined in the sharpest, most disheartening wave of unhappiness he had ever known. *Speedy, I can't do this! Don't you know that? I'm just a kid!*

"Morgan's diligence is drawn by six pairs of horses and a thirteenth to lead," Farren said. "At the full gallop, that damned hearse sounds like thunder rolling along the earth. You'll hear it, all right. Plenty of time to burrow down. Just make sure you do."

Jack whispered something.

"What?" Farren asked sharply.

"I said I don't want to go," Jack said, only a little louder. Tears were close and he knew that once they began to fall he was going to lose it, just blow his cool entirely and ask Captain Farren to get him out of it, protect him, *something*—

"I think it's too late for your wants to enter into the question," Captain Farren said. "I don't know your tale, boy, and I don't want to. I don't even want to know your name."

Jack stood looking at him, shoulders slumped, eyes burning, his lips trembling.

"Get your shoulders up!" Farren shouted at him with sudden fury. "Who are you going to save? Where are you going? Not ten feet, looking like that! You're too young to be a man, but you can at least *pretend*, can't you? You look like a kicked dog!"

Stung, Jack straightened his shoulders and blinked his tears back. His eyes fell on the remains of the carter's son and he thought: *At least I'm not like that, not yet. He's right. Being sorry for myself is a luxury I can't afford.* It was true. All the same, he could not help hating the scarred Captain a little for reaching inside him and pushing the right buttons so easily.

"Better," Farren said dryly. "Not much, but a little."

"Thanks," Jack said sarcastically.

"You can't cry off, boy. Osmond's behind you. Morgan will soon be behind you as well. And perhaps . . . perhaps there are problems wherever you came from, too. But take this. If Parkus sent you to me, he'd want me to give you this. So take it, and then go."

He was holding out a coin. Jack hesitated, then took it. It was the size of a Kennedy half-dollar, but much heavier—as heavy as gold, he guessed, although its color was dull silver. What he was looking at was the face of Laura DeLoessian in profile—he was struck again, briefly but forcibly, by her resemblance to his mother. No, not just resemblance—in spite of such physical dissimilarities as the thinner nose and rounder chin, she *was* his mother. Jack knew it. He turned the coin over and saw an animal with the head and wings of an eagle and the body of a lion. It seemed to be looking at Jack. It made him a little nervous, and he put the coin inside his jerkin, where it joined the bottle of Speedy's magic juice.

"What's it for?" he asked Farren.

"You'll know when the time comes," the Captain replied. "Or perhaps you won't. Either way, I've done my duty by you. Tell Parkus so, when you see him."

Jack felt wild unreality wash over him again.

"Go, son," Farren said. His voice was lower, but not necessarily more gentle. "Do your job . . . or as much of it as you can."

In the end, it was that feeling of unreality—the pervasive sense that he was no more than a figment of someone else's hallucination—that got him moving. Left foot, right foot, hay foot, straw foot. He kicked aside a splinter of ale-soaked wood. Stepped over the shattered remnants of a wheel. Detoured around the end of the wagon, not impressed by the blood drying there or the buzzing flies. What was blood or buzzing flies in a dream?

He reached the end of the muddy, wood- and barrel-littered stretch of road, and looked back . . . but Captain Farren had turned the other way, perhaps to look for his men, perhaps so he would not have to look at Jack. Either way, Jack reckoned, it came to the same thing. A back was a back. Nothing to look at.

He reached inside his jerkin, tentatively touched the coin Farren had given him, and then gripped it firmly. It seemed to make him feel a little better. Holding it as a child might hold a quarter given him to buy a treat at the candy store, Jack went on.

### 7

It might have been as little as two hours later when Jack heard the sound Captain Farren had described as "thunder rolling along the earth"—or it might have been as long as four. Once the sun passed below the western rim of the forest (and it did that not long after Jack had entered it), it became difficult to judge the time.

On a number of occasions vehicles came out of the west, presumably bound for the Queen's pavillion. Hearing each one come (and vehicles could be heard a long way away here; the clarity with which sound carried made Jack think of what Speedy had said about one man pulling a radish out of the ground and another smelling it half a mile away) made him think of Morgan, and each time he hurried first down into the ditch and then up the other side, and so into the woods. He didn't *like* being in these dark woods—not even a little way in, where he could still peer around the trunk of a tree and see the road; it was no rest-cure for the nerves, but he liked the idea of Uncle Morgan (for so he still believed Osmond's superior to be, in spite of what Captain Farren had said) catching him out on the road even less.

So each time he heard a wagon or carriage approaching he got out of sight, and each time the vehicle passed he went back to the road. Once, while he was crossing the damp and weedy right-hand ditch, something ran—or slithered—over his foot, and Jack cried out.

The traffic was a pain in the tail, and it wasn't exactly helping him to make better time, but there was also something comforting about the irregular passage of wagons—they served notice that he wasn't alone, at least.

He wanted to get the hell out of the Territories altogether.

Speedy's magic juice was the worst medicine he'd ever had in his life, but he would gladly have taken a belly-choking swig of it if someone—Speedy himself, for example—had just happened to appear in front of him and assure him that, when he opened his eyes again, the first thing he would see would be a set of McDonald's golden arches—what his mother called The Great Tits of America. A sense of oppressive danger was growing in him—a feeling that the forest was indeed dangerous, that there were things in it aware of his passage, that perhaps the forest *itself* was aware of his passage. The trees had gotten closer to the road, hadn't they? Yes. Before, they had stopped at the ditches. Now they infested those as well. Before, the forest had seemed composed solely of pines and spruces. Now other sorts of trees had crept in, some with black boles that twisted together like gnarls of rotted strings, some that looked like weird hybrids of firs and ferns—these latter had nasty-looking gray roots that gripped at the ground like pasty fingers. *Our boy?* these nasty things seemed to whisper inside of Jack's head. *OUR boy?*

*All in your mind, Jack-O. You're just freaking out a little.*

Thing was, he didn't really believe that.

The trees *were* changing. That sense of thick oppression in the air—that sense of being *watched*—was all too real. And he had begun to think that his mind's obsessive return to monstrous thoughts was almost something he was picking up from the forest . . . as if the trees themselves were sending to him on some horrible shortwave.

But Speedy's bottle of magic juice was only half-full. Somehow that had to last him all the way across the United States. It wouldn't last until he was out of New England if he sipped a little every time he got the willies.

His mind also kept returning to the amazing distance he had travelled in his world when he had flipped back from the Territories. A hundred and fifty feet over here had equalled half a mile over there. At that rate—unless the ratio of distance travelled were somehow variable, and Jack recognized that it might be—he could walk ten miles over here and be damn near out of New Hampshire over there. It was like wearing seven-league boots.

Still, the trees . . . those gray, pasty roots . . .

*When it starts to get really dark—when the sky goes from blue to purple—I'm flipping back. That's it; that's all she wrote. I'm not walking through these woods after dark. And if I run out of magic juice in Indiana or something, ole Speedy can just send me another bottle by UPS, or something.*

Still thinking these thoughts—and thinking how much better it made him feel to have a plan (even if the plan only encompassed the next two hours or so)—Jack suddenly realized he could hear another vehicle and a great many horses.

Cocking his head, he stopped in the middle of the road. His eyes widened, and two pictures suddenly unspooled behind his eyes with shutterlike speed: the big car the two men had been in—the car that had not been a Mercedes—and then the WILD CHILD van, speeding down the street and away from Uncle Tommy's corpse, blood dripping from the broken plastic fangs of its grille. He saw the hands on the van's steering wheel . . . but they weren't hands. They were weird, articulated hooves.

*At the full gallop, that damned hearse sounds like thunder rolling along the earth.*

Now, hearing it—the sound still distant but perfectly clear in the pure air—Jack wondered how he could have even thought those other approaching wagons might be Morgan's diligence. He would certainly never make such a mistake again. The sound he heard now was perfectly ominous, thick with a potential for evil—the sound of a hearse, yes, a hearse driven by a devil.

He stood frozen in the road, almost hypnotized, as a rabbit is hypnotized by headlights. The sound grew steadily louder—the thunder of the wheels and hooves, the creak of leather rigging. Now he could hear the driver's voice: *"Hee-yah! Heee-yahhh! HEEEEE-YAHHHH!"*

He stood in the road, stood there, his head drumming with horror. *Can't move, oh dear God oh dear Christ I can't move Mom Mom Muhhhhhmeeeee—!*

He stood in the road and the eye of his imagination saw a huge black thing like a stagecoach tearing up the road, pulled by black animals that looked more like pumas than horses; he saw black curtains flapping in and out of the coach's windows; he saw the driver standing on the teeterboard, his hair blown back, his eyes as wild and crazed as those of a psycho with a switchblade.

He saw it coming toward him, never slowing.

He saw it run him down.

That broke the paralysis. He ran to the right, skidding down the side of the road, catching his foot under one of those gnarled roots, falling, rolling. His back, relatively quiet for the last couple of hours, flared with fresh pain, and Jack drew his lips back with a grimace.

He got to his feet and scurried into the woods, hunched over.

He slipped first behind one of the black trees, but the touch of the gnarly trunk—it was a bit like the banyans he had seen while on vacation on Hawaii year before last—was oily and unpleasant. Jack moved to the left and behind the trunk of a pine.

The thunder of the coach and its outriders grew steadily louder. At every second Jack expected the company to flash by toward All-Hands' Village. Jack's fingers squeezed and relaxed on the pine's gummy back. He bit at his lips.

Directly ahead was a narrow but perfectly clear sightline back to the road, a tunnel with sides of leaf and fern and pine needles. And just when Jack had begun to think that Morgan's party would never arrive, a dozen or more mounted soldiers passed heading east, riding at a gallop. The one in the lead carried a banner, but Jack could not make out its device . . . nor was he sure he wanted to. Then the diligence flashed across Jack's narrow sightline.

The moment of its passage was brief—no more than a second, perhaps less than that—but Jack's recall of it was total. The diligence was a gigantic vehicle, surely a dozen feet high. The trunks and bundles lashed with stout cord to the top added another three feet. Each horse in the team which pulled it wore a black plume on its head—these plumes were blown back almost flat in a speed-generated wind. Jack thought later that Morgan must need a new team for every run, because these looked close to the end of their endurance. Foam and blood sprayed back from their working mouths in curds; their eyes rolled crazily, showing arcs of white.

As in his imagining—or his vision—black crepe curtains flew and fluttered through glassless windows. Suddenly a white face appeared in one of those black oblongs, a white face framed in strange, twisted carving-work. The sudden appearance of that face was as shocking as the face of a ghost in the ruined window of a haunted house. It was not the face of Morgan Sloat . . . but it *was*.

And the owner of that face knew that Jack—or some other danger, just as hated and just as *personal*—was out there. Jack saw this in the widening of the eyes and the sudden vicious downtwist of the mouth.

Captain Farren had said *He'll smell you like a rat*, and now Jack thought dismally: *I've been smelled, all right. He knows I'm here, and what happens now? He'll stop the whole bunch of them, I bet, and send the soldiers into the woods after me.*

Another band of soldiers—these protecting Morgan's diligence from the rear—swept by. Jack waited, his hands frozen to the bark of the pine, sure that Morgan would call a halt. But no halt came; soon the heavy thunder of the diligence and its outriders began to fade.

*His eyes. That's what's the same. Those dark eyes in that white face. And—*

*Our boy? YESSSS!*

Something slithered over his foot . . . and up his ankle. Jack screamed and floundered backward, thinking it must be a snake. But when he looked down he saw that one of those gray roots had slipped up his foot . . . and now it ringed his calf.

*That's impossible*, he thought stupidly. *Roots don't* move—

He pulled back sharply, yanking his leg out of the rough gray manacle the root had formed. There was thin pain in his calf, like the pain of a rope-burn. He raised his eyes and felt sick fear slip into his heart. He thought he knew now why Morgan had sensed him and gone on anyway; Morgan knew that walking in this forest was like walking into a jungle stream infested with piranhas. Why hadn't Captain Farren warned him? All Jack could think was that the scarred Captain must not have known; must never have been this far west.

The grayish roots of those fir-fern hybrids were all moving now—rising, falling, scuttling along the mulchy ground toward him. *Ents and Entwives*, Jack thought crazily. *BAD Ents and Entwives.* One particularly thick root, its last six inches dark with earth and damp, rose and wavered in front of him like a cobra piped up from a fakir's basket. *OUR boy! YESS!*

It darted toward him and Jack backed away from it, aware that the roots had now formed a living screen between him and the safety of the road. He backed into a tree . . . and then lurched away from it, screaming, as its bark began to ripple and twitch against his back—it was like feeling a muscle which has begun to spasm wildly. Jack looked around and saw one of those black trees with the gnarly trunks. Now the trunk was moving, writhing. Those twisted knots of bark formed something like a dreadful runnelled face, one eye widely, blackly open, the other drawn down in a hideous wink. The tree split open lower down with a grinding, rending sound, and whitish-yellow sap began to drool out. *OURS! Oh, yesssss!*

Roots like fingers slipped between Jack's upper arm and ribcage, as if to tickle.

He tore away, holding on to the last of his rationality with a huge act of will, groping in his jerkin for Speedy's bottle. He was aware—faintly—of a series of gigantic ripping sounds. He supposed the trees were tearing themselves right out of the ground. Tolkien had never been like this.

He got the bottle by the neck and pulled it out. He scrabbled at the cap, and then one of those gray roots slid easily around his neck. A moment later it pulled as bitterly tight as a hangman's noose.

Jack's breath stopped. The bottle tumbled from his fingers as he grappled with the thing that was choking him. He managed to work his fingers under the root. It was not cold and stiff but warm and limber and fleshlike. He struggled with it, aware of the choked gargling sound coming from him and the slick of spittle on his chin.

With a final convulsive effort he tore the root free. It tried to circle his wrist then, and Jack whipped his arm away from it with a cry. He looked down and saw the bottle twisting and bumping away, one of those gray roots coiled about its neck.

Jack leaped for it. Roots grabbed his legs, circled them. He fell heavily to the earth, stretching, reaching, the tips of his fingers digging at the thick black forest soil for an extra inch—

He touched the bottle's slick green side . . . and seized it. He pulled as hard as he could, dimly aware that the roots were all over his legs now, crisscrossing like bonds, holding him firmly. He spun the cap off the bottle. Another root floated down, cobweb-light, and tried to snatch the bottle away from him. Jack pushed it away and raised the bottle to his lips. That smell of sickish fruit suddenly seemed everywhere, a living membrane.

*Speedy, please let it work!*

As more roots slid over his back and around his waist, turning him helplessly this way and that, Jack drank, cheap wine splattering both of his cheeks. He swallowed, groaning, praying, and it was no good, *it wasn't working,* his eyes were still closed but he could feel the roots entangling his arms and legs, could feel

### 8

the water soaking into his jeans and his shirt, could smell

*Water?* mud and damp, could hear

*Jeans? Shirt?* the steady croak of frogs and

Jack opened his eyes and saw the orange light of the setting sun reflected from a wide river. Unbroken forest grew on the east side of this river; on the western side, the side that he was on, a long field, now partially obscured with evening ground-mist, rolled down to the water's edge. The ground here was wet and squelchy. Jack was lying at the edge of the water, in the boggiest area of all. Thick weeds still grew here—the hard frosts that would kill them were still a month or more away—and Jack had gotten entangled in them, the way a man awakening from a nightmare may entangle himself in the bedclothes.

He scrambled and stumbled to his feet, wet and slimed with the fragrant mud, the straps of his pack pulling under his arms. He pushed the weedy fragments from his arms and face with horror. He started away from the water, then looked back and saw Speedy's bottle lying in the mud, the cap beside it. Some of the "magic juice" had either run out or been spilled in his struggle with the malignant Territories trees. Now the bottle was no more than a third full.

He stood there a moment, his caked sneakers planted in the oozy muck, looking out at the river. This was his world; this was the good old United States of America. He didn't see the golden arches he had hoped for, or a skyscraper, or an earth satellite blinking overhead in the darkening sky, but he knew where he was as well as he knew his own name. The question was, had he ever been in that other world at all?

He looked around at the unfamiliar river, the likewise unfamiliar countryside, and listened to the distant mellow mooing of cows. He thought: *You're somewhere different. This sure isn't Arcadia Beach anymore, Jack-O.*

No, it wasn't Arcadia Beach, but he didn't know the area surrounding Arcadia Beach well enough to say for sure that he was more than four or five miles away—just enough inland, say, to no longer be able to smell the Atlantic. He had come back as if waking from a nightmare—was it not possible that was all it had been, the whole thing, from the carter with his load of fly-crawling meat to the living trees? A sort of waking nightmare in which sleepwalking had played a part? It made sense. His mother was dying, and he now thought he had known that for quite a while—the signs had been there, and his subconscious had drawn the correct conclusion even while his conscious mind denied it. That would have contributed the correct atmosphere for an act of self-hypnosis, and that crazy wino Speedy Parker had gotten him in gear. Sure. It all hung together.

Uncle Morgan would have loved it.

Jack shivered and swallowed hard. The swallow hurt. Not the way a sore throat hurts, but the way an abused muscle hurts.

He raised his left hand, the one not holding the bottle, and rubbed his palm gently against his throat. For a moment he looked absurdly like a woman checking for dewlaps or wrinkles. He found a welted abrasion just above his adam's apple. It hadn't bled much, but it was almost too painful to touch. The root that had closed about his throat had done that.

"True," Jack whispered, looking out at the orange water, listening to the *twank* of the bullfrogs and the mooing, distant cows. "All true."

## 9

Jack began walking up the slope of the field, setting the river—and the east—at his back. After he had gone half a mile, the steady rub and shift of the pack against his throbbing back (the strokes Osmond had laid on were still there, too, the shifting pack reminded him) triggered a memory. He had refused Speedy's enormous sandwich, but hadn't Speedy slipped the remains into his pack anyway, while Jack was examining the guitar-pick?

His stomach pounced on the idea.

Jack unshipped the pack then and there, standing in a curdle of ground-mist beneath the evening star. He unbuckled one of the flaps, and there was the sandwich, not just a piece or a half, but the whole thing, wrapped up in a sheet of newspaper. Jack's eyes filled with a warmth of tears and he wished that Speedy were here so he could hug him.

*Ten minutes ago you were calling him a crazy old wino.*

His face flamed at that, but his shame didn't stop him from gobbling the sandwich in half a dozen big bites. He rebuckled his pack and reshouldered it. He went on, feeling better—with that whistling hole in his gut stopped up for the time being, Jack felt himself again.

Not long after, lights twinkled up out of the growing darkness. A farmhouse. A dog began to bark—the heavy bark of a really big fellow—and Jack froze for a moment.

*Inside*, he thought. *Or chained up. I hope.*

He bore to the right, and after a while the dog stopped barking. Keeping the lights of the farmhouse as a guide, Jack soon came out on a narrow blacktop road. He stood looking from right to left, having no idea which way to go.

*Well, folks, here's Jack Sawyer, halfway between hoot and holler, wet through to the skin and sneakers packed with mud. Way to go, Jack!*

The loneliness and homesickness rose in him again. Jack fought them off. He put a drop of spit on his left index finger, then spanked the drop sharply. The larger of the two halves flew off to the right—or so it seemed to Jack—and so he turned that way and began to walk. Forty minutes later, drooping with weariness (and hungry again, which was somehow worse), he saw a gravel-pit with a shed of some sort standing beyond a chained-off access road.

Jack ducked under the chain and went to the shed. The door was padlocked shut, but he saw that the earth had eroded under one side of the small outbuilding. It was the work of a minute to remove his pack, wriggle under the shed's side, and then pull the pack in after him. The lock on the door actually made him feel safer.

He looked around and saw that he was in with some very old tools—this place hadn't been used in a long time, apparently, and that suited Jack just fine. He stripped to the skin, not liking the feel of his clammy, muddy clothes. He felt the coin Captain Farren had given him in one of his pants pockets, resting there like a giant amid his little bit of more ordinary change. Jack took it out and saw that Farren's coin, with the Queen's head on one side and the winged lion on the other—had become a 1921 silver dollar. He looked fixedly at the profile of Lady Liberty on the cartwheel for some time, and then slipped it back into the pocket of his jeans.

He rooted out fresh clothes, thinking he would put the dirty ones in his pack in the morning—they would be dry then—and perhaps clean them along the way, maybe in a Laundromat, maybe just in a handy stream.

While searching for socks, his hand encountered something slim and hard. Jack pulled it out and saw it was his tooth-brush. At once, images of home and safety and rationality—all the things a toothbrush could represent—rose up and over-whelmed him. There was no way that he could beat these emo-tions down or turn them aside this time. A toothbrush was a thing meant to be seen in a well-lighted bathroom, a thing to be used with cotton pajamas on the body and warm slippers on the feet. It was nothing to come upon in the bottom of your knapsack in a cold, dark toolshed on the edge of a gravel-pit in a deserted rural town whose name you did not even know.

Loneliness raged through him; his realization of his out-cast status was now complete. Jack began to cry. He did not weep hysterically or shriek as people do when they mask rage with tears; he cried in the steady sobs of one who has discovered just how alone he is, and is apt to remain for a long time yet. He cried because all safety and reason seemed to have departed from the world. Loneliness was here, a real-ity; but in this situation, insanity was also too much of a pos-sibility.

Jack fell asleep before the sobs had entirely run their course. He slept curled around his pack, naked except for clean underpants and socks. The tears had cut clean courses down his dirty cheeks, and he held his toothbrush loosely in one hand.

8

# The Oatley Tunnel

## 1

Six days later, Jack had climbed nearly all the way out of his despair. By the end of his first days on the road, he seemed to himself to have grown from childhood right through adoles-cence into adulthood—into competence. It was true that he had not returned to the Territories since he had awakened on the western bank of the river, but he could rationalize that, and the slower travelling it involved, by telling himself that he was saving Speedy's juice for when he really needed it.

And anyhow, hadn't Speedy told him to travel mainly on the roads in this world? Just following orders, pal.

When the sun was up and the cars whirled by him thirty, forty miles west and his stomach was full, the Territories seemed unbelievably distant and dreamlike: they were like a movie he was beginning to forget, a temporary fantasy. Sometimes, when Jack leaned back into the passenger seat of some schoolteacher's car and answered the usual questions about the Story, he actually did forget. The Territories left him, and he was again—or nearly so—the boy he had been at the start of the summer.

Especially on the big state highways, when a ride dropped him off near the exit ramp, he usually saw the next car pulling off to the side ten or fifteen minutes after he stuck his thumb into the air. Now he was somewhere near Batavia, way over in the western part of New York State, walking backward down the breakdown lane of I-90, his thumb out again, working his way toward Buffalo—after Buffalo, he would start to swing south. It was a matter, Jack thought, of working out the best way to accomplish something and then just doing it. Rand McNally and the Story had gotten him this far; all he needed was enough luck to find a driver going all the way to Chicago or Denver (or Los Angeles, if we're going to daydream about luck, Jacky-baby), and he could be on his way home again before the middle of October.

He was suntanned, he had fifteen dollars in his pocket from his last job—dishwasher at the Golden Spoon Diner in Auburn—and his muscles felt stretched and toughened. Though sometimes he wanted to cry, he had not given in to his tears since that first miserable night. He was in control, that was the difference. Now that he knew how to proceed, had worked it out so painstakingly, he was on top of what was happening to him; he thought he could see the end of his journey already, though it was so far ahead of him. If he travelled mainly in this world, as Speedy had told him, he could move as quickly as he had to and get back to New Hampshire with the Talisman in plenty of time. It was going to work, and he was going to have many fewer problems than he had expected.

That, at least, was what Jack Sawyer was imagining as a dusty blue Ford Fairlane swerved off to the shoulder of the road and waited for him to run up to it, squinting into the lowering sun. *Thirty or forty miles*, he thought to himself. He pictured the page from Rand McNally he had studied that morning, and decided: *Oatley*. It sounded dull, small, and safe—he was on his way, and nothing could hurt him now.

## 2

Jack bent down and looked in the window before opening the Fairlane's door. Fat sample books and printed fliers lay messily over the back seat; two oversize briefcases occupied the passenger seat. The slightly paunchy black-haired man who now seemed almost to be mimicking Jack's posture, bending over the wheel and peering through the open window at the boy, was a salesman. The jacket to his blue suit hung from the hook behind him; his tie was at half-mast, his sleeves were rolled. A salesman in his mid-thirties, tooling comfortably through his territory. He would love to talk, like all salesmen. The man smiled at him and picked up first one of the outsize briefcases, hoisting it over the top of the seat and onto the litter of papers behind, then the other. "Let's create a little room," he said.

Jack knew that the first thing the man would ask him was why he was not at school.

He opened the door, said, "Hey, thanks," and climbed in.

"Going far?" the salesman asked, checking the rear-view mirror as he slid the gear-lever down into drive and swung back out onto the road.

"Oatley," Jack said. "I think it's about thirty miles."

"You just flunked geography," the salesman said. "Oatley's more like forty-five miles." He turned his head to look at Jack, and surprised the boy by winking at him. "No offense," he said, "but I hate to see young kids hitching. That's why I always pick em up when I see em. At least I know they're safe with me. No touchie-feelie, know what I mean? Too many crazies out there, kid. You read the papers? I mean, I'm talking carnivores. You could turn yourself into an endangered species."

"I guess you're right," Jack said. "But I try to be pretty careful."

"You live somewhere back there, I take it?"

The man was still looking at him, snatching little birdlike peeks ahead down the road, and Jack frantically searched his memory for the name of a town back down the road. "Palmyra. I'm from Palmyra."

The salesman nodded, said, "Nice enough old place," and turned back to the highway. Jack relaxed back into the comfortable plush of the seat. Then the man finally said, "I guess you're not actually playing hooky, are you?" and it was time yet again for the Story.

He had told it so often, varying the names of the towns involved as he worked westward, that it had a slick, monologue-like feel in his mouth. "No, sir. It's just that I have to go over to Oatley to live with my Aunt Helen for a little while. Helen Vaughan? That's my mom's sister. She's a schoolteacher. My dad died last winter, see, and things have been pretty tough—then two weeks ago my mom's cough got a lot worse and she could hardly get up the stairs and the doctor said she had to stay in bed for as long as she could and she asked her sister if I could come stay with her for a while. Her being a teacher and all, I guess I'll be in Oatley school for sure. Aunt Helen wouldn't let any kid play hooky, you bet."

"You mean your mother told you to hitchhike all the way from Palmyra to *Oatley*?" the man asked.

"Oh no, not at all—she'd never do that. No, she gave me bus money but I decided to save it. There won't be much money from home for a long time, I guess, and Aunt Helen doesn't really have any money. My mom would hate it if she knew I was thumbing it. But it seemed like a waste of money to me. I mean, five bucks is five bucks, and why give it to a bus driver?"

The man looked sideways at him. "How long do you think you'll be in Oatley?"

"Hard to say. I sure hope my mom gets well pretty soon."

"Well, don't hitch back, okay?"

"We don't have a car anymore," Jack said, adding to the Story. He was beginning to enjoy himself. "Can you believe this? They came out in the middle of the night and repossessed it. Dirty cowards. They knew everybody would be asleep. They just came out in the middle of the night and stole the car right out of the garage. Mister, I would have fought for that car—and not so I could get a ride to my aunt's house. When my mom goes to the doctor, she has to walk all the way down the hill and then go about another five blocks just to get to the bus stop. They shouldn't be able to do that, should they? Just come in and steal your own car? As soon as we could, we were going to start making the payments again. I mean, wouldn't you call that stealing?"

"If it happened to me, I suppose I would," the man said. "Well, I hope your mother gets better in a hurry."

"You and me both," Jack said with perfect honesty.

And that held them until the signs for the Oatley exit began to appear. The salesman pulled back into the breakdown lane just after the exit ramp, smiled again at Jack and said, "Good luck, kid."

Jack nodded and opened the door.

"I hope you don't have to spend much time in Oatley, anyhow."

Jack looked at him questioningly.

"Well, you know the place, don't you?"

"A little. Not really."

"Ah, it's a real pit. Sort of place where they eat what they run over on the road. Gorillaville. You eat the beer, then you drink the glass. Like that."

"Thanks for the warning," Jack said and got out of the car. The salesman waved and dropped the Fairlane into drive. In moments it was only a dark shape speeding toward the low orange sun.

### 3

For a mile or so the road took him through flat dull countryside—far off, Jack saw small two-story frame houses perched on the edges of fields. The fields were brown and bare, and the houses were not farmhouses. Widely separated, the houses overlooking the desolate fields existed in a gray moveless quiet broken only by the whine of traffic moving along I-90. No cows lowed, no horses whinnied—there were no animals, and no farm equipment. Outside one of the little houses squatted half a dozen junked and rusting cars. These were the houses of men who disliked their own species so thoroughly that even Oatley was too crowded for them. The empty fields gave them the moats they needed around their peeling frame castles.

At length he came to a crossroads. It looked like a crossroads in a cartoon, two narrow empty roads bisecting each other in an absolute nowhere, then stretching on toward another kind of nowhere. Jack had begun to feel insecure about his sense of direction, and he adjusted the pack on his back and moved up toward the tall rusted iron pipe supporting the black rectangles, themselves rusting, of the street names. Should he have turned left instead of right off the exit ramp? The sign pointing down the road running parallel to the highway read DOGTOWN ROAD. Dogtown? Jack looked down this road and saw only endless flatness, fields full of weeds and the black streak of asphalt rolling on. His own particular streak of asphalt was called MILL ROAD, according to the sign. About a mile ahead it slipped into a tunnel nearly overgrown by leaning trees and an oddly pubic mat of ivy. A white sign hung in the thickness of ivy, seemingly supported by it. The words were too small to be read. Jack put his right hand in his pocket and clutched the coin Captain Farren had given him.

His stomach talked to him. He was going to need dinner soon, so he had to move off this spot and find a town where he could earn his meals. Mill Road it was—at least he could go far enough to see what was on the other side of the tunnel. Jack pushed himself toward it, and the dark opening in the bank of trees enlarged with every step.

Cool and damp and smelling of brick dust and overturned earth, the tunnel seemed to take the boy in and then tighten down around him. For a moment Jack feared that he was being led underground—no circle of light ahead showed the tunnel's end—but then realized that the asphalt floor was level. TURN ON LIGHTS, the sign outside the tunnel had read. Jack bumped into a brick wall and felt grainy powder crumble onto his hands. "Lights," he said to himself, wishing he had one to turn on. The tunnel must, he realized, bend somewhere along its length. He had cautiously, slowly, carefully, walked straight into the wall, like a blind man with his hands extended. Jack groped his way along the wall. When the coyote in the Roadrunner cartoons did something like this, he usually wound up splashed across the front of a truck.

Something rattled busily along the floor of the tunnel, and Jack froze.

A rat, he thought. Maybe a rabbit out taking a shortcut between fields. But it had sounded bigger than that.

He heard it again, farther away in the dark, and took another blind step forward. Ahead of him, just once, he heard an intake of breath. And stopped, wondering: *Was that an animal?* Jack held his fingertips against the damp brick wall, waiting for the exhalation. It had not sounded like an animal—certainly no rat or rabbit inhaled so deeply. He crept a few inches forward, almost unwilling to admit to himself that whatever was up there had frightened him.

Jack froze again, hearing a quiet little sound like a raspy chuckle come out of the blackness before him. In the next second a familiar but unidentifiable smell, coarse, strong, and musky, drifted toward him out of the tunnel.

Jack looked back over his shoulder. The entrance was now only half-visible, half-obscured by the curve of the wall, a long way off and looking about the size of a rabbit-hole.

"What's in here?" he called out. "Hey! Anything in here with me? Anybody?"

He thought he heard something whisper deeper into the tunnel.

He was not in the Territories, he reminded himself—at the worst he might have startled some imbecilic dog who had come into the cool dark for a nap. In that case, he'd be saving its life by waking it up before a car came along. "Hey, dog!" he yelled. *"Dog!"*

And was rewarded instantly by the sound of paws trotting through the tunnel. But were they . . . going out or coming in? He could not tell, listening to the soft *pad pad pad*, whether the animal was leaving or approaching. Then it occurred to him that maybe the noise was coming toward him from behind, and he twisted his neck and looked back and saw that he had moved far enough along so that he could not see that entrance, either.

"Where are you, dog?" he said.

Something scratched the ground only a foot or two behind him, and Jack jumped forward and struck his shoulder, hard, against the curve of the wall.

He sensed a shape—doglike, perhaps—in the darkness.

Jack stepped forward—and was stopped short by a sense of dislocation so great that he imagined himself back in the Territories. The tunnel was filled with that musky, acrid zoo-odor, and whatever was coming toward him was not a dog.

A gust of cold air smelling of grease and alcohol pushed toward him. He sensed that shape getting nearer.

Only for an instant he had a glimpse of a face hanging in the dark, glowing as if with its own sick and fading interior light, a long, bitter face that should have been almost youthful but was not. Sweat, grease, a stink of alcohol on the breath that came from it. Jack flattened himself against the wall, raising his fists, even as the face faded back into the dark.

In the midst of his terror he thought he heard footfalls softly, quickly covering the ground toward the tunnel's entrance, and turned his face from the square foot of darkness which had spoken to him to look back. Darkness, silence. The tunnel was empty now. Jack squeezed his hands under his armpits and gently fell back against the brick, taking the blow on his knapsack. A moment later he began to edge forward again.

As soon as Jack was out of the tunnel, he turned around to face it. No sounds emerged, no weird creatures slunk toward him. He took three steps forward, peered in. And then his heart nearly stopped, because coming toward him were two huge orange eyes. They halved the distance between themselves and Jack in seconds. He could not move—his feet were past the ankles in asphalt. Finally he managed to extend his hands, palm-out, in the instinctive gesture of warding-off. The eyes continued toward him, and a horn blasted. Seconds before the car burst out of the tunnel, revealing a red-faced man waving a fist, Jack threw himself out of the way.

"SHIIITHEEAAA . . ." came from the contorted mouth.

Still dazed, Jack turned and watched the car speed downhill toward a village that had to be Oatley.

## 4

Situated in a long depression in the land, Oatley spread itself out meagerly from two principal streets. One, the continuation of Mill Road, dipped past an immense and shabby building set in the midst of a vast parking lot—a factory, Jack thought—to become a strip of used-car lots (sagging pennants), fast-food franchises (The Great Tits of America), a bowling alley with a huge neon sign (BOWL-A-RAMA!), grocery stores, gas stations. Past all this, Mill Road became Oatley's five or six blocks of downtown, a strip of old two-story buildings before which cars were parked nose-in. The other street was obviously the location of Oatley's most important houses—large frame buildings with porches and long slanting lawns. Where these streets intersected stood a traffic light winking its red eye in the late afternoon. Another light perhaps eight blocks down changed to green before a high dingy many-windowed building that looked like a mental hospital, and so was probably the high school. Fanning out from the two streets was a jumble of little houses interspersed with anonymous buildings fenced in behind tall wire mesh.

Many of the windows in the factory were broken, and some of the windows in the strip of downtown had been boarded over. Heaps of garbage and fluttering papers littered the fenced-in concrete yards. Even the important houses seemed neglected, with their sagging porches and bleached-out paint jobs. These people would own the used-car lots filled with unsaleable automobiles.

For a moment Jack considered turning his back on Oatley and making the hike to Dogtown, wherever that was. But that would mean walking through the Mill Road tunnel again. From down in the middle of the shopping district a car horn blatted, and the sound unfurled toward Jack full of an inexpressible loneliness and nostalgia.

He could not relax until he was all the way to the gates of the factory, the Mill Road tunnel far up behind him. Nearly a third of the windows along the dirty-brick facade had been broken in, and many of the others showed blank brown squares of cardboard. Even out on the road, Jack could smell machine oil, grease, smouldering fanbelts, and clashing gears. He put his hands in his pockets and walked downhill as quickly as he could.

## 5

Seen close up, the town was even more depressed than it had looked from the hill. The salesmen at the car lots leaned against the windows in their offices, too bored to come outside. Their pennants hung tattered and joyless, the once-optimistic signs propped along the cracked sidewalk fronting the rows of cars—ONE OWNER! FANTASTIC BUY! CAR OF THE WEEK!—had yellowed. The ink had feathered and run on some of the signs, as if they had been left out in the rain. Very few people moved along the streets. As Jack went toward the center of town, he saw an old man with sunken cheeks and gray skin trying to wrestle an empty shopping cart up onto a curb. When he approached, the old man screeched something hostile and frightened and bared gums as black as a badger's. He thought Jack was going to steal his cart! "Sorry," Jack said, his heart pounding again. The old man was trying to hug the whole cumbersome body of the cart, protecting it, all the while showing those blackened gums to his enemy. "Sorry," Jack repeated. "I was just going to . . ."

"Fusshhingfeef! FusshhingFEEEFF!" the old man screeched, and tears crawled into the wrinkles on his cheeks.

Jack hurried off.

Twenty years before, during the sixties, Oatley must have prospered. The relative brightness of the strip of Mill Road leading out of town was the product of that era when stocks went go-go and gas was still cheap and nobody had heard the term "discretionary income" because they had plenty of it. People had sunk their money into franchise operations and little shops and for a time had, if not actually flourished, held their heads above the waves. This short series of blocks still had that superficial hopefulness—but only a few bored teenagers sat in the franchise restaurants, nursing medium Cokes, and in the plate-glass windows of too many of the little shops placards as faded as those in the used-car lots announced EVERYTHING MUST GO! CLOSING SALE. Jack saw no signs advertising for help, and kept on walking.

Downtown Oatley showed the reality beneath the happy clown's colors left behind by the sixties. As Jack trudged along these blocks of baked-looking brick buildings, his pack grew heavier, his feet more tender. He would have walked to Dogtown after all, if it were not for his feet and the necessity of going through the Mill Road tunnel again. Of course there was no snarling man-wolf lurking in the dark there—he'd worked that out by now. No one could have spoken to him in the tunnel. The Territories had shaken him. First the sight of the Queen, then that dead boy beneath the cart with half his face gone. Then Morgan; the trees. But that was *there*, where such things could be—were, perhaps, even normal. *Here*, normality did not admit such gaudiness.

He was before a long, dirty window above which the flaking slogan FURNITURE DEPOSITORY was barely legible on the brickwork. He put his hands to his eyes and stared in. A couch and a chair, each covered by a white sheet, sat fifteen feet apart on a wide wooden floor. Jack moved farther down the block, wondering if he was going to have to beg for food.

Four men sat in a car before a boarded-up shop a little way down the block. It took Jack a moment to see that the car, an ancient black DeSoto that looked as though Broderick Crawford should come bustling out of it, had no tires. Taped to the windshield was a yellow five-by-eight card which read FAIR WEATHER CLUB. The men inside, two in front and two in back, were playing cards. Jack stepped up to the front passenger window.

"Excuse me," he said, and the cardplayer closest to him rolled a fishy gray eye toward him. "Do you know where—"

"Get lost," the man said. His voice sounded squashed and phlegmy, unfamiliar with speech. The face half-turned to Jack was deeply pitted with acne scars and oddly flattened out, as if someone had stepped on it when the man was an infant.

"I just wondered if you knew somewhere I could get a couple days' work."

"Try Texas," said the man in the driver's seat, and the pair in the back seat cracked up, spitting beer out over their hands of cards.

"I told you, kid, get lost," said the flat-faced gray-eyed man closest to Jack. "Or I'll personally pound the shit out of you."

It was just the truth, Jack understood—if he stayed there a moment longer, this man's rage would boil over and he would get out of the car and beat him senseless. Then the man would get back in the car and open another beer. Cans of Rolling Rock covered the floor, the opened ones tipped every which way, the fresh ones linked by white plastic nooses. Jack stepped backward, and the fish-eye rolled away from him.

"Guess I'll try Texas after all," he said. He listened for the sound of the DeSoto's door creaking open as he walked away, but all he heard being opened was another Rolling Rock.

*Crack! Hiss!*

He kept moving.

He got to the end of the block and found himself looking across the town's other main street at a dying lawn filled with yellow weeds from which peeked fiberglass statues of Disney-like fawns. A shapeless old woman gripping a fly-swatter stared at him from a porch swing.

Jack turned away from her suspicious gaze and saw before him the last of the lifeless brick buildings on Mill Road. Three concrete steps led up to a propped-open screen door. A long, dark window contained a glowing BUDWEISER sign and, a foot to the right of that, the painted legend UPDIKE'S OATLEY TAP. And several inches beneath that, handwritten on a yellow five-by-eight card like the one on the DeSoto, were the miraculous words HELP WANTED. Jack pulled the knapsack off his back, bunched it under one arm, and went up the steps. For no more than an instant, moving from the tired sunlight into the darkness of the bar, he was reminded of stepping past the thick fringe of ivy into the Mill Road tunnel.

# 9

# Jack in the Pitcher Plant

### 1

Not quite sixty hours later a Jack Sawyer who was in a very different frame of mind from that of the Jack Sawyer who had ventured into the Oatley tunnel on Wednesday was in the chilly storeroom of the Oatley Tap, hiding his pack behind the kegs of Busch which sat in the room's far corner like aluminum bowling pins in a giant's alley. In less than two hours, when the Tap finally shut down for the night, Jack meant to

run away. That he should even think of it in such a fashion—
not *leaving*, not moving on, but *running away*—showed how
desperate he now believed his situation to be.

*I was six, six, John B. Sawyer was six, Jacky was six. Six.*

This thought, apparently nonsensical, had fallen into his
mind this evening and had begun to repeat there. He supposed
it went a long way toward showing just how scared he was
now, how certain he was that things were beginning to close
in on him. He had no idea what the thought meant; it just circled and circled, like a wooden horse bolted to a carousel.

*Six. I was six. Jacky Sawyer was six.*

Over and over, round and round she goes.

The storeroom shared a wall in common with the taproom
itself, and tonight that wall was actually vibrating with noise;
it throbbed like a drumhead. Until twenty minutes before, it
had been Friday night, and both Oatley Textiles and Weaving
and Dogtown Custom Rubber paid on Friday. Now the Oatley
Tap was full to the overflow point . . . and past. A big poster to
the left of the bar read OCCUPANCY BY MORE THAN 220 PER-
SONS IS IN VIOLATION OF GENESEE COUNTY FIRE CODE 331. Apparently fire code 331 was suspended on the weekends,
because Jack guessed there were more than three hundred
people out there now, boogying away to a country-western
band which called itself The Genny Valley Boys. It was a terrible band, but they had a pedal-steel guitar. "There's guys
around here that'd fuck a pedal-steel, Jack," Smokey had said.

*"Jack!"* Lori yelled over the wall of sound.

Lori was Smokey's woman. Jack still didn't know what her
last name was. He could barely hear her over the juke, which
was playing at full volume while the band was on break. All
five of them were standing at the far end of the bar, Jack
knew, tanking up on half-price Black Russians. She stuck her
head through the storeroom door. Tired blond hair, held back
with childish white plastic barrettes, glittered in the overhead
fluorescent.

"Jack, if you don't run that keg out real quick, I guess he'll
give your arm a try."

"Okay," Jack said. "Tell him I'll be right there."

He felt gooseflesh on his arms, and it didn't come entirely
from the storeroom's damp chill. Smokey Updike was no one
to fool with—Smokey who wore a succession of paper fry-

cook's hats on his narrow head, Smokey with his large plastic mail-order dentures, grisly and somehow funereal in their perfect evenness, Smokey with his violent brown eyes, the scleras an ancient, dirty yellow. Smokey Updike who in some way still unknown to Jack—and who was all the more frightening for that—had somehow managed to take him prisoner.

The jukebox fell temporarily silent, but the steady roar of the crowd actually seemed to go up a notch to make up for it. Some Lake Ontario cowboy raised his voice in a big, drunken *"Yeeeee-HAW!"* A woman screamed. A glass broke. Then the jukebox took off again, sounding a little like a Saturn rocket achieving escape velocity.

*Sort of place where they eat what they run over on the road.*

Raw.

Jack bent over one of the aluminum kegs and dragged it out about three feet, his mouth screwed down in a painful wince, sweat standing out on his forehead in spite of the air-conditioned chill, his back protesting. The keg gritted and squealed on the unadorned cement. He stopped, breathing hard, his ears ringing.

He wheeled the hand-truck over to the keg of Busch, stood it up, then went around to the keg again. He managed to rock it up on its rim and walk it forward, toward where the hand-truck stood. As he was setting it down he lost control of it— the big bar-keg weighed only a few pounds less than Jack did himself. It landed hard on the foot of the hand-truck, which had been padded with a remnant of carpet so as to soften just such landings. Jack tried to both steer it and get his hands out of the way in time. He was slow. The keg mashed his fingers against the back of the hand-truck. There was an agonizing thud, and he somehow managed to get his throbbing, pulsing fingers out of there. Jack stuck all the fingers of his left hand in his mouth and sucked on them, tears standing in his eyes.

Worse than jamming his fingers, he could hear the slow sigh of gases escaping through the breather-cap on top of the keg. If Smokey hooked up the keg and it came out foamy . . . or, worse yet, if he popped the cap and the beer went a gusher in his face . . .

Best not to think of those things.

Last night, Thursday night, when he'd tried to "run

Smokey out a keg," the keg had gone right over on its side. The breather-cap had shot clear across the room. Beer foamed white-gold across the storeroom floor and ran down the drain. Jack had stood there, sick and frozen, oblivious to Smokey's shouts. It wasn't Busch, it was Kingsland. Not beer but ale— the Queen's Own.

That was when Smokey hit him for the first time—a quick looping blow that drove Jack into one of the storeroom's splintery walls.

"There goes your pay for today," Smokey had said. "And you never want to do that again, Jack."

What chilled Jack most about that phrase *you never want to do that again* was what it assumed: that there would be lots of opportunities for him to do that again; as if Smokey Updike expected him to be here a long, long time.

*"Jack, hurry it up!"*

*"Coming."* Jack puffed. He pulled the hand-truck across the room to the door, felt behind himself for the knob, turned it, and pushed the door open. He hit something large and soft and yielding.

"Christ, watch it!"

"Whoops, sorry," Jack said.

"I'll whoops you, asshole," the voice replied.

Jack waited until he heard heavy steps moving on down the hall outside the storeroom and then tried the door again.

The hall was narrow and painted a bilious green. It stank of shit and piss and TidyBowl. Holes had been punched through both plaster and lath here and there; graffiti lurched and staggered everywhere, written by bored drunks waiting to use either POINTERS or SETTERS. The largest of them all had been slashed across the green paint with a black Magic Marker, and it seemed to scream out all of Oatley's dull and objectless fury. SEND ALL AMERICAN NIGGERS AND JEWS TO IRAN, it read.

The noise from the taproom was loud in the storeroom; out here it was a great wave of sound which never seemed to break. Jack took one glance back into the storeroom over the top of the keg tilted on the hand-truck, trying to make sure his pack wasn't visible.

He had to get out. *Had* to. The dead phone that had finally spoken, seeming to encase him in a capsule of dark ice . . .

that had been bad. Randolph Scott was worse. The guy wasn't *really* Randolph Scott; he only looked the way Scott had looked in his fifties films. Smokey Updike was perhaps worse still . . . although Jack was no longer sure of that. Not since he had seen (or thought he had seen) the eyes of the man who looked like Randolph Scott change color.

But that Oatley itself was worst of all . . . he was sure of that.

Oatley, New York, deep in the heart of Genny County, seemed now to be a horrible trap that had been laid for him . . . a kind of municipal pitcher plant. One of nature's real marvels, the pitcher plant. Easy to get in. Almost impossible to get out.

## 2

A tall man with a great swinging gut porched in front of him stood waiting to use the men's room. He was rolling a plastic toothpick from one side of his mouth to the other and glaring at Jack. Jack supposed that it was the big man's gut that he had hit with the door.

"Asshole," the fat man repeated, and then the men's-room door jerked open. A man strode out. For a heart-stopping moment his eyes and Jack's eyes met. It was the man who looked like Randolph Scott. But this was no movie-star; this was just an Oatley millhand drinking up his week's pay. Later on he would leave in a half-paid-for doorsucker Mustang or maybe on a three-quarters-paid-for motorcycle—a big old Harley with a BUY AMERICAN sticker plastered on the nacelle, probably.

*His eyes turned yellow.*

*No, your imagination, Jack, just your imagination. He's just—*

—just a millhand who was giving him the eye because he was new. He had probably gone to high school here in town, played football, knocked up a Catholic cheerleader and married her, and the cheerleader had gotten fat on chocolates and Stouffer's frozen dinners; just another Oatley oaf, just—

*But his eyes turned yellow.*

*Stop it! They did not!*

Yet there was something about him that made Jack think of

what had happened when he was coming into town . . . what had happened in the dark.

The fat man who had called Jack an asshole shrank back from the rangy man in the Levi's and the clean white T-shirt. Randolph Scott started toward Jack. His big, veined hands swung at his sides.

His eyes sparkled an icy blue . . . and then began to change, to moil and lighten.

"Kid," he said, and Jack fled with clumsy haste, butting the swinging door open with his fanny, not caring who he hit.

Noise pounced on him. Kenny Rogers was bellowing an enthusiastic redneck paean to someone named Reuben James. "*You allus turned your other CHEEK*," Kenny testified to this room of shuffling, sullen-faced drunks, "*and said there's a better world waitin for the MEEK!*" Jack saw no one here who looked particularly meek. The Genny Valley Boys were trooping back onto the bandstand and picking up their instruments. All of them but the pedal steel player looked drunk and confused . . . perhaps not really sure of where they were. The pedal steel player only looked bored.

To Jack's left, a woman was talking earnestly on the Tap's pay phone—a phone Jack would never touch again if he had his way about it, not for a thousand dollars. As she talked, her drunken companion probed and felt inside her half-open cowboy shirt. On the big dancefloor, perhaps seventy couples groped and shuffled, oblivious of the current song's bright up-tempo, simply squeezing and grinding, hands gripping buttocks, lips spit-sealed together, sweat running down cheeks and making large circles under the armpits.

"Well thank *Gawd*," Lori said, and flipped up the hinged partition at the side of the bar for him. Smokey was halfway down the bar, filling up Gloria's tray with gin-and-tonics, vodka sours, and what seemed to be beer's only competition for the Oatley Town Drink: Black Russians.

Jack saw Randolph Scott come out through the swinging door. He glanced toward Jack, his blue eyes catching Jack's again at once. He nodded slightly, as if to say: *We'll talk. Yessirree. Maybe we'll talk about what might or might not be in the Oatley tunnel. Or about bullwhips. Or sick mothers. Maybe we'll talk about how you're gonna be in Genny County for a long, long time . . . maybe until you're an old man crying over a shopping cart. What do you think, Jacky?*

Jack shuddered.

Randolph Scott smiled, as if he had seen the shudder . . . or felt it. Then he moved off into the crowd and the thick air.

A moment later Smokey's thin, powerful fingers bit into Jack's shoulder—hunting for the most painful place and, as always, finding it. They were educated, nerve-seeking fingers.

"Jack, you just got to move faster," Smokey said. His voice sounded almost sympathetic, but his fingers dug and moved and probed. His breath smelled of the pink Canada Mints he sucked almost constantly. His mail-order false teeth clicked and clacked. Sometimes there was an obscene slurping as they slipped a little and he sucked them back into place. "You got to move faster or I'm going to have to light a fire under your ass. You understand what I'm saying?"

"Y-yeah," Jack said. Trying not to moan.

"All right. That's good then." For an excruciating second Smokey's fingers dug even deeper, grinding with a bitter enthusiasm at the neat little nest of nerves there. Jack *did* moan. That was good enough for Smokey. He let up.

"Help me hook this keg up, Jack. And let's make it fast. Friday night, people got to drink."

"Saturday morning," Jack said stupidly.

"Then, too. Come on."

Jack somehow managed to help Smokey lift the keg into the square compartment under the bar. Smokey's thin, ropey muscles bulged and writhed under his Oatley Tap T-shirt. The paper fry-cook's hat on his narrow weasel's head stayed in place, its leading edge almost touching his left eyebrow, in apparent defiance of gravity. Jack watched, holding his breath, as Smokey flicked off the red plastic breather-cap on the keg. The keg breathed more gustily than it should have done . . . but it didn't foam. Jack let his breath out in a silent gust.

Smokey spun the empty toward him. "Get that back in the storeroom. And then swamp out the bathroom. Remember what I told you this afternoon."

Jack remembered. At three o'clock a whistle like an air-raid siren had gone off, almost making him jump out of his skin. Lori had laughed, had said: *Check out Jack, Smokey—I think he just went wee-wee in his Tuffskins.* Smokey had given her a narrow, unsmiling look and motioned Jack over. Told Jack that was the payday whistle at the Oatley T & W. Told Jack that a whistle very much like it was going off at Dogtown Rubber, a company that made beach-toys, inflatable rubber dolls, and condoms with names like Ribs of Delight. Soon, he said, the Oatley Tap would begin filling up.

"And you and me and Lori and Gloria are going to move just as fast as lightning," Smokey said, "because when the eagle screams on Friday, we got to make up for what this place don't make every Sunday, Monday, Tuesday, Wednesday, and Thursday. When I tell you to run me out a keg, you want to have it out to me before I finish yelling. And you're in the men's room every half an hour with your mop. On Friday nights, a guy blows his groceries every fifteen minutes or so."

"I got the women's," Lori said, coming over. Her hair was thin, wavy gold, her complexion as white as a comic-book vampire's. She either had a cold or a bad coke habit; she kept sniffing. Jack guessed it was a cold. He doubted if anyone in Oatley could afford a bad coke habit. "Women ain't as bad as men, though. Almost, but not quite."

"Shut up, Lori."

"Up yours," she said, and Smokey's hand flickered out like lightning. There was a crack and suddenly the imprint of Smokey's palm was printed red on one of Lori's pallid cheeks like a child's Tattoodle. She began to snivel . . . but Jack was sickened and bewildered to see an expression in her eyes that was almost happy. It was the look of a woman who believed such treatment was a sign of caring.

"You just keep hustling and we'll have no problem," Smokey said. "Remember to move fast when I yell for you to run me out a keg. And remember to get in the men's can with your mop every half an hour and clean up the puke."

And then he had told Smokey again that he wanted to leave and Smokey had reiterated his false promise about Sunday afternoon . . . but what good did it do to think of that?

There were louder screams now, and harsh caws of laughter. The crunch of a breaking chair and a wavering yell of pain. A fistfight—the third of the night—had broken out on the dance floor. Smokey uttered a curse and shoved past Jack. "Get rid of that keg," he said.

Jack got the empty onto the dolly and trundled it back toward the swinging door, looking around uneasily for Randolph Scott as he went. He saw the man standing in the crowd that was watching the fight, and relaxed a little.

In the storeroom he put the empty keg with the others by the loading-bay—Updike's Oatley Tap had already gone through six kegs tonight. That done, he checked his pack again. For one panicky moment he thought it was gone, and his heart began to hammer in his chest—the magic juice was in there, and so was the Territories coin that had become a silver dollar in this world. He moved to the right, sweat now standing out on his forehead, and felt between two more kegs. There it was—he could trace the curve of Speedy's bottle through the green nylon of the pack. His heartbeat began to slow down, but he felt shaky and rubber-legged—the way you feel after a narrow escape.

The men's toilet was a horror. Earlier in the evening Jack might have vomited in sympathy, but now he actually seemed to be getting used to the stench . . . and that was somehow the worst thing of all. He drew hot water, dumped in Comet, and began to run his soapy mop back and forth through the unspeakable mess on the floor. His mind began to go back over the last couple of days, worrying at them the way an animal in a trap will worry at a limb that has been caught.

### 3

The Oatley Tap had been dark, and dingy, and apparently dead empty when Jack first walked into it. The plugs on the juke, the pinball machine, and the Space Invaders game were all pulled. The only light in the place came from the Busch display over the bar—a digital clock caught between the peaks of two mountains, looking like the weirdest UFO ever imagined.

Smiling a little, Jack walked toward the bar. He was almost there when a flat voice said from behind him, "This is a bar. No minors. What are you, stupid? Get out."

Jack almost jumped out of his skin. He had been touching the money in his pocket, thinking it would go just as it had at the Golden Spoon: he would sit on a stool, order something, and then ask for the job. It was of course illegal to hire a kid like him—at least without a work permit signed by his parents or a guardian—and that meant they could get him for under the minimum wage. Way under. So the negotiations would start, usually beginning with Story #2—Jack and the Evil Stepfather.

He whirled around and saw a man sitting alone in one of the booths, looking at him with chilly, contemptuous alertness. The man was thin, but ropes of muscles moved under his white undershirt and along the sides of his neck. He wore baggy white cook's pants. A paper cap was cocked forward over his left eyebrow. His head was narrow, weasellike. His hair was cut short, graying at the edges. Between his big hands were a stack of invoices and a Texas Instruments calculator.

"I saw your Help Wanted sign," Jack said, but now without much hope. This man was not going to hire him, and Jack was not sure he would want to work for him anyway. This guy looked mean.

"You did, huh?" the man in the booth said. "You must have learned to read on one of the days you weren't playing hooky." There was a package of Phillies Cheroots on the table. He shook one out.

"Well, I didn't know it was a bar," Jack said, taking a step back toward the door. The sunlight seemed to come through the dirty glass and then just fall dead on the floor, as if the Oatley Tap were located in a slightly different dimension. "I guess I thought it was . . . you know, a bar and grill. Something like that. I'll just be going."

"Come here." The man's brown eyes were looking at him steadily now.

"No, hey, that's all right," Jack said nervously. "I'll just—"

"Come here. Sit down." The man popped a wooden match alight with his thumbnail and lit the cigar. A fly which had been preening on his paper hat buzzed away into the darkness. His eyes remained on Jack. "I ain't gonna bite you."

Jack came slowly over to the booth, and after a moment he slipped in on the other side and folded his hands in front of him neatly. Some sixty hours later, swamping out the men's toilet at twelve-thirty in the morning with his sweaty hair hanging in his eyes, Jack thought—no, he *knew*—that it was his own stupid confidence that had allowed the trap to spring shut (and it had shut the moment he sat down opposite Smokey Updike, although he had not known it then). The Venus flytrap is able to close on its hapless, insectile victims; the pitcher plant, with its delicious smell and its deadly, glassy-smooth sides, only waits for some flying asshole of a bug to buzz on down and inside . . . where it finally drowns in the rainwater the pitcher collects. In Oatley the pitcher was full of beer instead of rainwater—that was the only difference.

*If he had run—*

But he hadn't run. And maybe, Jack thought, doing his best to meet that cold brown stare, there would be a job here after all. Minette Banberry, the woman who owned and operated the Golden Spoon in Auburn, had been pleasant enough to Jack, had even given him a little hug and a peck of a kiss as well as three thick sandwiches when he left, but he had not been fooled. Pleasantness and even a remote sort of kindness did not preclude a cold interest in profits, or even something very close to outright greed.

The minimum wage in New York was three dollars and forty cents an hour—that information had been posted in the Golden Spoon's kitchen by law, on a bright pink piece of paper almost the size of a movie poster. But the short-order cook was a Haitian who spoke little English and was almost surely in the country illegally, Jack thought. The guy cooked like a whiz, though, never allowing the spuds or the fried clams to spend a moment too long in the Fryolaters. The girl who helped Mrs. Banberry with the waitressing was pretty but vacant and on a work-release program for the retarded in Rome. In such cases, the minimum wage did not apply, and the lisping, retarded girl told Jack with unfeigned awe that she was getting a dollar and twenty-five cents *each hour*, and *all for her*.

Jack himself was getting a dollar-fifty. He had bargained for that, and he knew that if Mrs. Banberry hadn't been strapped—her old dishwasher had quit just that morning, had gone on his coffee-break and just never came back—she would not have bargained at all; would have simply told him take the buck and a quarter, kid, or see what's down the road. It's a free country.

Now, he thought, with the unknowing cynicism that was also a part of his new self-confidence, here was another Mrs. Banberry. Male instead of female, rope-skinny instead of fat and grandmotherly, sour instead of smiling, but almost surely a Mrs. Banberry for a' that and a' that.

"Looking for a job, huh?" The man in the white pants and the paper hat put his cigar down in an old tin ashtray with the word CAMELS embossed on the bottom. The fly stopped washing its legs and took off.

"Yes, sir, but like you say, this is a bar and all—"

The unease stirred in him again. Those brown eyes and yellowed scleras troubled him—they were the eyes of some old hunting cat that had seen plenty of errant mice like him before.

"Yeah, it's my place," the man said. "Smokey Updike." He held his hand out. Surprised, Jack shook it. It squeezed Jack's hand once, hard, almost to the point of pain. Then it relaxed . . . but Smokey didn't let go. "Well?" he said.

"Huh?" Jack said, aware he sounded stupid and a little afraid—he *felt* stupid and a little afraid. And he wanted Updike to let go of his hand.

"Didn't your folks ever teach you to innerduce yourself?"

This was so unexpected that Jack came close to gabbling out his real name instead of the one he had used at the Golden Spoon, the name he also used if the people who picked him up asked for his handle. That name—what he was coming to think of as his "road-name"—was Lewis Farren.

"Jack Saw—ah—Sawtelle," he said.

Updike held his hand yet a moment longer, those brown eyes never moving. Then he let it go. "Jack Saw-ah-Sawtelle," he said. "Must be the longest fucking name in the phonebook, huh, kid?"

Jack flushed but said nothing.

"You ain't very big," Updike said. "You think you could manage to rock a ninety-pound keg of beer up on its side and walk it onto a hand-dolly?"

"I think so," Jack said, not knowing if he could or not. It didn't look as if it would be much of a problem, anyway—in a place as dead as this, the guy probably only had to change kegs when the one hooked up to the taps went flat.

As if reading his mind, Updike said, "Yeah, nobody here now. But we get pretty busy by four, five o'clock. And on weekends the place really fills up. That's when you'd earn your keep, Jack."

"Well, I don't know," Jack said. "How much would the job pay?"

"Dollar an hour," Updike said. "Wish I could pay you more, but—" He shrugged and tapped the stack of bills. He even smiled a little, as if to say *You see how it is, kid, everything in Oatley is running down like a cheap pocket-watch someone forgot to wind—ever since about 1971 it's been running down.* But his eyes did not smile. His eyes were watching Jack's face with still, catlike concentration.

"Gee, that's not very much," Jack said. He spoke slowly but he was thinking as fast as he could.

The Oatley Tap was a tomb—there wasn't even a single bombed-out old alky at the bar nursing a beer and watching General Hospital on the tube. In Oatley you apparently drank in your car and called it a club. A dollar-fifty an hour was a hard wage when you were busting your buns; in a place like this, a buck an hour might be an easy one.

"Nope," Updike agreed, going back to his calculator, "it ain't." His voice said Jack could take it or leave it; there would be no negotiations.

"Might be all right," Jack said.

"Well, that's good," Updike said. "We ought to get one other thing straight, though. Who you running from and who's looking for you?" The brown eyes were on him again, and they drilled hard. "If you got someone on your backtrail, I don't want him fucking up my life."

This did not shake Jack's confidence much. He wasn't the world's brightest kid, maybe, but bright enough to know he wouldn't last long on the road without a second cover story for prospective employers. This was a Story #2—The Wicked Stepfather.

"I'm from a little town in Vermont," he said. "Fenderville. My mom and dad got divorced two years ago. My dad tried to get custody of me, but the judge gave me to my mom. That's what they do most of the time."

"Fucking-A they do." He had gone back to his bills and was bent so far over the pocket calculator that his nose was almost touching the keys. But Jack thought he was listening all the same.

"Well, my dad went out to Chicago and he got a job in a plant out there," Jack said. "He writes to me just about every week, I guess, but he quit coming back last year, when Aubrey beat him up. Aubrey's—"

"Your stepfather," Updike said, and for just a moment Jack's eyes narrowed and his original distrust came back. There was no sympathy in Updike's voice. Instead, Updike seemed almost to be laughing at him, as if he knew the whole tale was nothing but a great big swatch of whole cloth.

"Yeah," he said. "My mom married him a year and a half ago. He beats on me a lot."

"Sad, Jack. Very sad." Now Updike did look up, his eyes sardonic and unbelieving. "So now you're off to Shytown, where you and Dads will live happily ever after."

"Well, I hope so," Jack said, and he had a sudden inspiration. "All I know is that my *real* dad never hung me up by the neck in my closet." He pulled down the neck of his T-shirt, baring the mark there. It was fading now; during his stint at the Golden Spoon it had still been a vivid, ugly red-purple—like a brand. But at the Golden Spoon he'd never had occasion to uncover it. It was, of course, the mark left by the root that had nearly choked the life from him in that other world.

He was gratified to see Smokey Updike's eyes widen in surprise and what might almost have been shock. He leaned forward, scattering some of his pink and yellow pages. "Holy *Jesus*, kid," he said. "Your stepfather did that?"

"That's when I decided I had to split."

"Is he going to show up here, looking for his car or his motorcycle or his wallet or his fucking dope-stash?"

Jack shook his head.

Smokey looked at Jack for a moment longer, and then pushed the OFF button on the calculator. "Come on back to the storeroom with me, kid," he said.

"Why?"

"I want to see if you can really rock one of those kegs up on its side. If you can run me out a keg when I need one, you can have the job."

### 4

Jack demonstrated to Smokey Updike's satisfaction that he could get one of the big aluminum kegs up on its rim and walk it forward just enough to get it on the foot of the dolly. He even made it look fairly easy—dropping a keg and getting punched in the nose was still a day away.

"Well, that ain't too bad," Updike said. "You ain't big enough for the job and you'll probably give yourself a fucking rupture, but that's your nevermind."

He told Jack he could start at noon and work through until one in the morning ("For as long as you can hack it, anyway"). Jack would be paid, Updike said, at closing time each night. Cash on the nail.

They went back out front and there was Lori, dressed in dark blue basketball shorts so brief that the edges of her rayon panties showed, and a sleeveless blouse that had almost surely come from Mammoth Mart in Batavia. Her thin blond hair was held back with plastic barrettes and she was smoking a Pall Mall, its end wet and heavily marked with lipstick. A large silver crucifix dangled between her breasts.

"This is Jack," Smokey said. "You can take the Help Wanted sign out of the window."

"Run, kid," Lori said. "There's still time."

"Shut the fuck up."

"Make me."

Updike slapped her butt, not in a loving way but hard enough to send her against the padded edge of the bar. Jack blinked and thought of the sound Osmond's whip had made.

"Big man," Lori said. Her eyes brimmed with tears . . . and yet they also looked contented, as if this was just the way things were supposed to be.

Jack's earlier unease was now clearer, sharper . . . now it was almost fright.

"Don't let us get on your case, kid," Lori said, headed past him to the sign in the window. "You'll be okay."

"Name's Jack, not *kid*," Smokey said. He had gone back to the booth where he had "interviewed" Jack and began gathering up his bills. "A kid's a fucking baby goat. Didn't they teach you that in school? Make the kid a couple of burgers. He's got to go to work at noon."

She got the HELP WANTED sign out of the window and put it behind the jukebox with the air of one who has done this a good many times before. Passing Jack, she winked at him.

The telephone rang.

All three of them looked toward it, startled by its abrupt shrilling. To Jack it looked for a moment like a black slug stuck to the wall. It was an odd moment, almost timeless. He had time to notice how pale Lori was—the only color in her cheeks came from the reddish pocks of her fading adolescent acne. He had time to study the cruel, rather secretive planes of Smokey Updike's face and to see the way the veins stood out on the man's long hands. Time to see the yellowed sign over the phone reading PLEASE LIMIT YOUR CALLS TO THREE MINUTES.

The phone rang and rang in the silence.

Jack thought, suddenly terrified: *It's for me. Long distance . . . long, LONG distance.*

"Answer that, Lori," Updike said, "what are you, simple?"

Lori went to the phone.

"Oatley Tap," she said in a trembling, faint voice. She listened. "Hello? Hello? . . . Oh, fuck off."

She hung up with a bang.

"No one there. Kids. Sometimes they want to know if we got Prince Albert in a can. How do you like your burgers, kid?"

*"Jack!"* Updike roared.

"Jack, okay, okay, *Jack.* How do you like your burgers, Jack?"

Jack told her and they came medium, just right, hot with brown mustard and Bermuda onions. He gobbled them and drank a glass of milk. His unease abated with his hunger. Kids, as she had said. Still, his eyes drifted back to the phone every once in a while, and he wondered.

## 5

Four o'clock came, and as if the Tap's total emptiness had been only a clever piece of stage setting to lure him in—like the pitcher plant with its innocent look and its tasty smell— the door opened and nearly a dozen men in work-clothes came sauntering in. Lori plugged in the juke, the pinball machine, and Space Invaders game. Several of the men bellowed greetings at Smokey, who grinned his narrow grin, exposing the big set of mail-order dentures. Most ordered beer. Two or three ordered Black Russians. One of them—a member of the Fair Weather Club, Jack was almost sure—dropped quarters into the jukebox, summoning up the voices of Mickey Gilley, Eddie Rabbit, Waylon Jennings, others. Smokey told him to get the mop-bucket and squeegee out of the storeroom and swab down the dancefloor in front of the bandstand, which waited, deserted, for Friday night and The Genny Valley Boys. He told Jack when it was dry he wanted him to put the Pledge right to it. "You'll know it's done when you can see your own face grinnin up at you," Smokey said.

## 6

So his time of service at Updike's Oatley Tap began.

*We get pretty busy by four, five o'clock.*

Well, he couldn't very well say that Smokey had lied to him. Up until the very moment Jack pushed away his plate and began making his wage, the Tap had been deserted. But by six o'clock there were maybe fifty people in the Tap, and the brawny waitress—Gloria—came on duty to yells and hooraws from some of the patrons. Gloria joined Lori, serving a few carafes of wine, a lot of Black Russians, and oceans of beer.

Besides the kegs of Busch, Jack lugged out case after case of bottled beer—Budweiser, of course, but also such local favorites as Genesee, Utica Club, and Rolling Rock. His hands began to blister, his back to ache.

Between trips to the storeroom for cases of bottled beer and trips to the storeroom to "run me out a keg, Jack" (a phrase for which he was already coming to feel an elemental dread), he went back to the dancefloor, the mop-bucket, and the big bottle of Pledge. Once an empty beer-bottle flew past his head, missing him by inches. He ducked, heart racing, as it shattered against the wall. Smokey ran the drunken perpetrator out, his dentures bared in a great false alligator grin. Looking out the window, Jack saw the drunk hit a parking-meter hard enough to pop the red VIOLATION flag up.

"Come on, Jack," Smokey called impatiently from the bar, "it missed you, didn't it? Clean that mess up!"

Smokey sent him into the men's can half an hour later. A middle-aged man with a Joe Pyne haircut was standing woozily at one of the two ice-choked urinals, one hand braced against the wall, the other brandishing a huge uncircumcised penis. A puddle of puke steamed between his spraddled workboots.

"Clean her up, kid," the man said, weaving his way back toward the door and clapping Jack on the back almost hard enough to knock him over. "Man's gotta make room any way he can, right?"

Jack was able to wait until the door closed, and then he could control his gorge no longer.

He managed to make it into the Tap's only stall, where he was faced with the unflushed and sickeningly fragrant spoor of the last customer. Jack vomited up whatever remained of his dinner, took a couple of hitching breaths, and then vomited again. He groped for the flush with a shaking hand and pushed it. Waylon and Willie thudded dully through the walls, singing about Luckenbach, Texas.

Suddenly his mother's face was before him, more beautiful than it had ever been on any movie screen, her eyes large and dark and sorrowing. He saw her alone in their rooms at the Alhambra, a cigarette smouldering forgotten in the ashtray beside her. She was crying. Crying for him. His heart seemed to hurt so badly that he thought he would die from love for her and want of her—for a life where there were no things in tunnels, no women who somehow wanted to be slapped and made to cry, no men who vomited between their own feet while taking a piss. He wanted to be with her and hated Speedy Parker with a black completeness for ever having set his feet on this awful road west.

In that moment whatever might have remained of his self-confidence was demolished—it was demolished utterly and forever. Conscious thought was overmastered by a deep, elemental, wailing, childish cry: *I want my mother please God I want my MOTHER—*

He trembled his way out of the stall on watery legs, thinking *Okay that's it everybody out of the pool fuck you Speedy this kid's going home. Or whatever you want to call it.* In that moment he didn't care if his mother might be dying. In that moment of inarticulate pain he became totally Jack's Jack, as unconsciously self-serving as an animal on which any carnivore may prey: deer, rabbit, squirrel, chipmunk. In that moment he would have been perfectly willing to let her die of the cancer metastasizing wildly outward from her lungs if only she would hold him and then kiss him goodnight and tell him not to play his goddam transistor in bed or read with a flashlight under the covers for half the night.

He put his hand against the wall and little by little managed to get hold of himself. This taking-hold was no conscious thing but a simple tightening of the mind, something that was very much Phil Sawyer and Lily Cavanaugh. He'd made a mistake, yeah, but he wasn't going back. The Territories were real and so the Talisman might also be real; he was not going to murder his mother with faintheartedness.

Jack filled his mop-bucket with hot water from the spigot in the storeroom and cleaned up the mess.

When he came out again, it was half past ten and the crowd in the Tap began to thin out—Oatley was a working town, and its working drinkers went home early on weeknights.

Lori said, "You look as pale as pastry, Jack. You okay?"

"Do you think I could have a gingerale?" he asked.

She brought him one and Jack drank it while he finished waxing the dancefloor. At quarter to twelve Smokey ordered him back to the storeroom to "run out a keg." Jack managed the keg—barely. At quarter to one Smokey started bawling for people to finish up. Lori unplugged the juke—Dick Curless died with a long, unwinding groan—to a few halfhearted cries of protest. Gloria unplugged the games, donned her sweater (it was as pink as the Canada Mints Smokey ate regularly, as pink as the false gums of his dentures), and left. Smokey began to turn out the lights and to urge the last four or five drinkers out the door.

"Okay, Jack," he said when they were gone. "You did good. There's room for improvement, but you got a start, anyway. You can doss down in the storeroom."

Instead of asking for his pay (which Smokey did not offer

anyway), Jack stumbled off toward the storeroom, so tired that he looked like a slightly smaller version of the drunks so lately ushered out.

In the storeroom he saw Lori squatting down in one corner—the squat caused her basketball shorts to ride up to a point that was nearly alarming—and for a moment Jack thought with dull alarm that she was going through his knapsack. Then he saw that she had spread a couple of blankets on a layer of burlap apple-sacks. Lori had also put down a small satin pillow which said NEW YORK WORLD'S FAIR on one side.

"Thought I'd make you a little nest, kid," she said.

"Thanks," he said. It was a simple, almost offhand act of kindness, but Jack found himself having to struggle from bursting into tears. He managed a smile instead. "Thanks a lot, Lori."

"No problem. You'll be all right here, Jack. Smokey ain't so bad. Once you get to know him, he ain't half bad." She said this with an unconscious wistfulness, as if wishing it were so.

"Probably not," Jack said, and then he added impulsively, "but I'm moving on tomorrow. Oatley's just not for me, I guess."

She said: "Maybe you'll go, Jack . . . and maybe you'll decide to stay awhile. Why don't you sleep on it?" There was something forced and unnatural about this little speech—it had none of the genuineness of her grin when she'd said *Thought I'd make you a little nest*. Jack noticed it, but was too tired to do more than that.

"Well, we'll see," he said.

"Sure we will," Lori agreed, going to the door. She blew a kiss toward him from the palm of one dirty hand. "Good night, Jack."

"Good night."

He started to pull off his shirt . . . and then left it on, deciding he would just take off his sneakers. The storeroom was cold and chilly. He sat down on the apple-sacks, pulled the knots, pushed off first one and then the other. He was about to lie back on Lori's New York World's Fair souvenir—and he might well have been sound asleep before his head ever touched it—when the telephone began to ring out in the bar, shrilling into the silence, *drilling* into it, making him think of wavering, pasty-gray roots and bullwhips and two-headed ponies.

Ring, ring, ring, into the silence, into the dead silence.

Ring, ring, ring, long after the kids who call up to ask about Prince Albert in a can have gone to bed. Ring, ring, ring, *Hello, Jacky it's Morgan and I felt you in my woods, you smart little shit I SMELLED you in my woods, and how did you ever get the idea that you were safe in your world? My woods are there, too. Last chance, Jacky. Get home or we send out the troops. You won't have a chance. You won't—*

Jack got up and ran across the storeroom floor in his stocking feet. A light sweat that felt freezing cold, seemed to cover his entire body.

He opened the door a crack.

Ring, ring, ring, ring.

Then finally: "Hello, Oatley Tap. And this better be good." Smokey's voice. A pause. "Hello?" Another pause. "Fuck *off!*" Smokey hung up with a bang, and Jack heard him re-cross the floor and then start up the stairs to the small overhead apartment he and Lori shared.

### 7

Jack looked unbelievingly from the green slip of paper in his left hand to the small pile of bills—all ones—and change by his right. It was eleven o'clock the next morning. Thursday morning, and he had asked for his pay.

"What *is* this?" he asked, still unable to believe it.

"You can read," Smokey said, "and you can count. You don't move as fast as I'd like, Jack—at least not yet—but you're bright enough."

Now he sat with the green slip in one hand and the money by the other. Dull anger began to pulse in the middle of his forehead like a vein. GUEST CHECK, the green slip was headed. It was the exact same form Mrs. Banberry had used in the Golden Spoon. It read:

| 1 hmbrg | $1.35 |
|---------|-------|
| 1 hmbrg | $1.35 |
| 1 lrg mk | .55 |
| 1 gin-ale | .55 |
| Tx | .30 |

At the bottom the figure $4.10 was written in large numbers and circled. Jack had made nine dollars for his four-to-one stint. Smokey had charged off nearly half of it; what he had left by his right hand was four dollars and ninety cents.

He looked up, furious—first at Lori, who looked away as if vaguely embarrassed, and then at Smokey, who simply looked back.

"This is a cheat," he said thinly.

"Jack, that's not true. Look at the menu prices—"

"That's not what I mean and you know it!"

Lori flinched a little, as if expecting Smokey to clout him one . . . but Smokey only looked at Jack with a kind of terrible patience.

"I didn't charge you for your bed, did I?"

"Bed!" Jack shouted, feeling the hot blood boil up into his cheeks. "Some *bed!* Cut-open burlap bags on a concrete floor! Some *bed!* I'd like to see you try to charge me for it, you dirty *cheat!*"

Lori made a scared sound and shot a look at Smokey . . . but Smokey only sat across from Jack in the booth, the thick blue smoke of a Cheroot curling up between them. A fresh paper fry-cook's hat was cocked forward on Smokey's narrow head.

"We talked about you dossing down back there," Smokey said. "You asked if it came with the job. I said it did. No mention was made of your meals. If it had been brought up, maybe something could have been done. Maybe not. Point is, you never brought it up, so now you got to deal with that."

Jack sat shaking, tears of anger standing in his eyes. He tried to talk and nothing came out but a small strangled groan. He was literally too furious to speak.

"Of course, if you wanted to discuss an employees' discount on your meals now—"

"Go to *hell!*" Jack managed finally, snatching up the four singles and the little strew of change. "Teach the next kid who comes in here how to look out for number one! I'm *going!*"

He crossed the floor toward the door, and in spite of his anger he knew—did not just think but flat-out *knew*—that he wasn't going to make the sidewalk.

"Jack."

He touched the doorknob, thought of grasping it and turning it—but that voice was undeniable and full of a certain threat. He dropped his hand and turned around, his anger leaving him. He suddenly felt shrunken and old. Lori had gone behind the bar, where she was sweeping and humming. She had apparently decided that Smokey wasn't going to work Jack over with his fists, and since nothing else really mattered, everything was all right.

"You don't want to leave me in the lurch with my weekend crowd coming up."

"I want to get out of here. You cheated me."

"No sir," Smokey said, "I explained that. If anyone blotted your copybook, Jack, it was you. Now we could discuss your meals—fifty percent off the food, maybe, and even free sodas. I never went that far before with the younger help I hire from time to time, but this weekened's going to be especially hairy, what with all the migrant labor in the county for the applepicking. And I *like* you, Jack. That's why I didn't clout you one when you raised your voice to me, although maybe I should have. But I need you over the weekend."

Jack felt his rage return briefly, and then die away again.

"What if I go anyhow?" he asked. "I'm five dollars to the good, anyway, and being out of this shitty little town might be just as good as a bonus."

Looking at Jack, still smiling his narrow smile, Smokey said, "You remember going into the men's last night to clean after some guy who whoopsed his cookies?"

Jack nodded.

"You remember what he looked like?"

"Crewcut. Khakis. So what?"

"That's Digger Atwell. His real name's Carlton, but he spent ten years taking care of the town cemeteries, so everyone got calling him Digger. That was—oh, twenty or thirty years ago. He went on the town cops back around the time Nixon got elected President. Now he's Chief of Police."

Smokey picked up his cheroot, puffed at it, and looked at Jack.

"Digger and me go back," Smokey said. "And if you was to just walk out of here now, Jack, I couldn't guarantee that you wouldn't have some trouble with Digger. Might end up getting sent home. Might end up picking the apples on the town's land—Oatley Township's got . . . oh, I guess forty acres of good trees. Might end up getting beat up. Or . . . I've heard that ole Digger's got a taste for kids on the road. Boys, mostly."

Jack thought of that clublike penis. He felt both sick and cold.

"In here, you're under my wing, so to speak," Smokey said. "Once you hit the street, who can say? Digger's apt to be cruising anyplace. You might get over the town line with no sweat. On the other hand, you might just see him pulling up beside you in that big Plymouth he drives. Digger ain't totally bright, but he does have a nose, sometimes, Or . . . someone might give him a call."

Behind the bar, Lori was doing dishes. She dried her hands, turned on the radio, and began to sing along with an old Steppenwolf song.

"Tell you what," Smokey said. "Hang in there, Jack. Work the weekend. Then I'll pack you into my pick-up and drive you over the town line myself. How would that be? You'll go out of here Sunday noon with damn near thirty bucks in your poke that you didn't have coming in. You'll go out thinking that Oatley's not such a bad place after all. So what do you say?"

Jack looked into those brown eyes, noted the yellow scleras and the small flecks of red; he noted Smokey's big, sincere smile lined with false teeth; he even saw with a weird and terrifying sense of *déjà vu* that the fly was back on the paper frycook's hat, preening and washing its hair-thin forelegs.

He suspected Smokey *knew* that *he* knew that everything Updike had said was a lie, and didn't even care. After working into the early hours of Saturday morning and then Sunday morning, Jack would sleep until maybe two Sunday afternoon. Smokey would tell him he couldn't give him that ride because Jack had woken up too late; now he, Smokey, was too busy watching the Colts and the Patriots. And Jack would not only be too tired to walk, he would be too afraid that Smokey might lose interest in the Colts and Patriots just long enough to call his good friend Digger Atwell and say, "He's walking down Mill Road right now, Digger old boy, why don't you pick him up? Then get over here for the second half. Free beer, but don't you go puking in my urinal until I get the kid back here."

That was one scenario. There were others that he could think of, each a little different, each really the same at bottom.

Smokey Updike's smile widened a little.

# 10

# Elroy

## 1

*When I was six . . .*

The Tap, which had begun to wind down by this time on his previous two nights, was roaring along as if the patrons expected to greet the dawn. He saw two tables had vanished—victims of the fistfight that had broken out just before his last expedition into the john. Now people were dancing where the tables had been.

"About time," Smokey said as Jack staggered the length of the bar on the inside and put the case down by the refrigerator compartments. "You get those in there and go back for the fucking Bud. You should have brought that first, anyway."

"Lori didn't say—"

Hot, incredible pain exploded in his foot as Smokey drove one heavy shoe down on Jack's sneaker. Jack uttered a muffled scream and felt tears sting his eyes.

"Shut up," Smokey said. "Lori don't know shit from Shinola, and you are smart enough to know it. Get back in there and run me out a case of Bud."

He went back to the storeroom, limping on the foot Smokey had stomped, wondering if the bones in some of his toes might be broken. It seemed all too possible. His head roared with smoke and noise and the jagged ripsaw rhythm of The Genny Valley Boys, two of them now noticeably weaving on the bandstand. One thought stood out clearly: it might not be possible to wait until closing. He really might not be able to last that long. If Oatley was a prison and the Oatley Tap was his cell, then surely exhaustion was as much his warder as Smokey Updike—maybe even more so.

In spite of his worries about what the Territories might be like at this place, the magic juice seemed more and more to promise him his only sure way out. He could drink some and flip over . . . and if he could manage to walk a mile west over there, two at the most, he could drink a bit more and flip back into the U.S.A. well over the town line of this horrible little place, perhaps as far west as Bushville or even Pembroke.

*When I was six, when Jack-O was six, when—*

He got the Bud and stumble-staggered out through the door again . . . and the tall, rangy cowboy with the big hands, the one who looked like Randolph Scott, was standing there, looking at him.

"Hello, Jack," he said, and Jack saw with rising terror that the irises of the man's eyes were as yellow as chicken-claws. "Didn't somebody tell you to get gone? You don't listen very good, do you?"

Jack stood with the case of Bud dragging at the ends of his arms, staring into those yellow eyes, and suddenly a horrid idea hammered into his mind: that *this* had been the lurker in the tunnel—this man-thing with its dead yellow eyes.

"Leave me alone," he said—the words came out in a wintery little whisper.

He crowded closer. "You were supposed to get *gone.*"

Jack tried to back up . . . but now he was against the wall, and as the cowboy who looked like Randolph Scott leaned toward him, Jack could smell dead meat on its breath.

## 2

Between the time Jack started work on Thursday at noon and four o'clock, when the Tap's usual after-work crowd started to come in, the pay phone with the PLEASE LIMIT YOUR CALLS TO THREE MINUTES sign over it rang twice.

The first time it rang, Jack felt no fear at all—and it turned out to be only a solicitor for the United Fund.

Two hours later, as Jack was bagging up the last of the previous night's bottles, the telephone began to shrill again. This time his head snapped up like an animal which scents fire in a dry forest . . . except it wasn't fire he sensed, but ice. He turned toward the telephone, which was only four feet from where he was working, hearing the tendons in his neck creak. He thought he must see the pay phone caked with ice, ice that was sweating through the phone's black plastic case, extruding from the holes in the earpiece and the mouthpiece in lines of blue ice as thin as pencil-leads, hanging from the rotary dial and the coin return in icicle beards.

But it was just the phone, and all the coldness and death was on the inside.

He stared at it, hypnotized.

"Jack!" Smokey yelled. "Answer the goddam phone! What the fuck am I paying you for?"

Jack looked toward Smokey, as desperate as a cornered animal . . . but Smokey was staring back with the thin-lipped, out-of-patience expression that he got on his face just before he popped Lori one. He started toward the phone, barely aware that his feet were moving; he stepped deeper and deeper into that capsule of coldness, feeling the gooseflesh run up his arms, feeling the moisture crackle in his nose.

He reached out and grasped the phone. His hand went numb.

He put it to his ear. His ear went numb.

"Oatley Tap," he said into that deadly blackness, and his mouth went numb.

The voice that came out of the phone was the cracked, rasping croak of something long dead, some creature which could never be seen by the living: the sight of it would drive a living person insane, or strike him dead with frost-etchings on his lips and staring eyes blinded by cataracts of ice. *"Jack,"* this scabrous, rattling voice whispered up out of the earpiece, and his face went numb, the way it did when you needed to spend a heavy day in the dentist's chair and the guy needled you up with a little too much Novocain. *"You get your ass back home, Jack."*

From far away, a distance of light-years, it seemed, he could hear his voice repeating: "Oatley Tap, is anyone there? Hello? . . . Hello? . . ."

Cold, so cold.

His throat was numb. He drew breath and his lungs seemed to freeze. Soon the chambers of his heart would ice up and he would simply drop dead.

That chilly voice whispered, *"Bad things can happen to a boy alone on the road, Jack. Ask anybody."*

He hung the phone up with a quick, clumsy reaching gesture. He pulled his hand back and then stood looking at the phone.

"Was it the asshole, Jack?" Lori asked, and her voice was distant . . . but a little closer than his own voice had seemed a few moments ago. The world was coming back. On the handset of the pay phone he could see the shape of his hand, outlined in a glittering rime of frost. As he looked, the frost began to melt and run down the black plastic.

### 3

That was the night—Thursday night—that Jack first saw Genny County's answer to Randolph Scott. The crowd was a little smaller than it had been Wednesday night—very much a day-before-payday crowd—but there were still enough men present to fill the bar and spill over into the tables and booths.

They were town men from a rural area where the plows were now probably rusting forgotten in back sheds, men who perhaps wanted to be farmers but had forgotten how. There were a lot of John Deere caps in evidence, but to Jack, very few of these men looked as if they would be at home riding a tractor. These were men in gray chinos and brown chinos and green chinos; men with their names stitched on blue shirts in gold thread; men in square-toed Dingo Boots and men in great big clumping Survivors. These men carried their keys on their belts. These men had wrinkles but no laugh-lines; their mouths were dour. These men wore cowboy hats and when Jack looked at the bar from in back of the stools, there were as many as eight who looked like Charlie Daniels in the chewing-tobacco ads. But these men didn't chew; these men smoked cigarettes, and a lot of them.

Jack was cleaning the bubble front of the jukebox when Digger Atwell came in. The juke was turned off; the Yankees were on the cable, and the men at the bar were watching intently. The night before, Atwell had been in the Oatley male's

version of sports clothes (chinos, khaki shirt with a lot of
pens in one of the two big pockets, steel-toed workboots).
Tonight he was wearing a blue cop's uniform. A large gun
with wood grips hung in a holster on his creaking leather belt.

He glanced at Jack, who thought of Smokey saying *I've
heard that ole Digger's got a taste for kids on the road. Boys,
mostly,* and flinched back as if guilty of something. Digger
Atwell grinned a wide, slow grin. "Decided to stick around
for a while, boy?"

"Yes, sir," Jack muttered, and squirted more Windex onto
the juke's bubble front, although it was already as clean as it
was going to get. He was only waiting for Atwell to go away.
After a while, Atwell did. Jack turned to watch the beefy cop
cross to the bar . . . and that was when the man at the far left
end of the bar turned around and looked at him.

*Randolph Scott,* Jack thought at once, *that's just who he
looks like.*

But in spite of the rangy and uncompromising lines of his
face, the real Randolph Scott had had an undeniable look of
heroism; if his good looks had been harsh, they had also been
part of a face that could smile. This man looked both bored
and somehow crazy.

And with real fright, Jack realized the man was looking at
him, at *Jack.* Nor had he simply turned around during the
commercial to see who might be in the bar; he had turned
around to look at Jack. Jack knew this was so.

The phone. The ringing phone.

With a tremendous effort, Jack pulled his gaze away. He
looked back into the bubble front of the juke and saw his own
frightened face hovering, ghostlike, over the records inside.

The telephone began to shriek on the wall.

The man at the left end of the bar looked at it . . . and then
looked back at Jack, who stood frozen by the jukebox with his
bottle of Windex in one hand and a rag in the other, his hair
stiffening, his skin freezing.

"If it's that asshole again, I'm gonna get me a whistle to
start blowing down the phone when he calls, Smokey," Lori
was saying as she walked toward it. "I swear to God I am."

She might have been an actress in a play, and all the customers extras paid the standard SAG rate of thirty-five dollars
a day. The only two real people in the world were him and this

dreadful cowboy with the big hands and the eyes Jack could not . . . quite . . . see.

Suddenly, shockingly, the cowboy mouthed these words: *Get your ass home.* And winked.

The phone stopped ringing even as Lori stretched out her hand to it.

Randolph Scott turned around, drained his glass, and yelled, "Bring me another tapper, okay?"

"I'll be damned," Lori said. "That phone's got the ghosts."

## 4

Later on, in the storeroom, Jack asked Lori who the guy was who looked like Randolph Scott.

"Who looks like *who?*" she asked.

"An old cowboy actor. He was sitting down at the end of the bar."

She shrugged. "They all look the same to me, Jack. Just a bunch of swinging dicks out for a good time. On Thursday nights they usually pay for it with the little woman's Beano money."

"He calls beers 'tappers.' "

Her eyes lit. "Oh yeah! Him. He looks mean." She said this last with actual appreciation . . . as if admiring the straightness of his nose or the whiteness of his smile.

"Who is he?"

"I don't know his name," Lori said. "He's only been around the last week or two. I guess the mill must be hiring again. It—"

*"For Christ's sake, Jack, did I tell you to run me out a keg or not?"*

Jack had been in the process of walking one of the big kegs of Busch onto the foot of the hand-dolly. Because his weight and the keg's weight were so close, it was an act requiring a good deal of careful balancing. When Smokey shouted from the doorway, Lori screamed and Jack jumped. He lost control of the keg and it went over on its side, the cap shooting out like a champagne cork, beer following in a white-gold jet. Smokey was still shouting at him but Jack could only stare at the beer, frozen . . . until Smokey popped him one.

When he got back out to the taproom perhaps twenty minutes later, holding a Kleenex against his swelling nose, Randolph Scott had been gone.

## 5

*I'm six.*

*John Benjamin Sawyer is six.*

*Six—*

Jack shook his head, trying to clear this steady, repeating thought out as the rangy millhand who was not a millhand leaned closer and closer. His eyes . . . yellow and somehow scaly. He—*it*—blinked, a rapid, milky, swimming blink, and Jack realized it had nictitating membranes over its eyeballs.

"You were supposed to get *gone*," it whispered again, and reached toward Jack with hands that were beginning to twist and plate and harden.

The door banged open, letting in a raucous flood of the Oak Ridge Boys.

"Jack, if you don't quit lollygagging, I'm going to have to make you sorry," Smokey said from behind Randolph Scott. Scott stepped backward. No melting, hardening hooves here; his hands were just hands again—big and powerful, their backs crisscrossed with prominent ridged veins. There was another milky, swirling sort of blink that didn't involve the eyelids at all . . . and then the man's eyes were not yellow but a simple faded blue. He gave Jack a final glance and then headed toward the men's room.

Smokey came toward Jack now, his paper cap tipped forward, his narrow weasel's head slightly inclined, his lips parted to show his alligator teeth.

"Don't make me speak to you again," Smokey said. "This is your last warning, and don't you think I don't mean it."

As it had against Osmond, Jack's fury suddenly rose up— that sort of fury, closely linked as it is to a sense of hopeless injustice, is perhaps never as strong as it is at twelve—college students sometimes think they feel it, but it is usually little more than an intellectual echo.

This time it boiled over.

"I'm not your dog, so don't you treat me like I am," Jack said, and took a step toward Smokey Updike on legs that were still rubbery with fear.

Surprised—possibly even flabbergasted—by Jack's totally unexpected anger, Smokey backed up a step.

"Jack, I'm warning you—"

"No, man, I'm warning *you*," Jack heard himself say. "I'm not Lori. I don't want to be hit. And if you hit me, I'm going to hit you back, or something."

Smokey Updike's discomposure was only momentary. He had most assuredly not seen everything—not living in Oatley, he hadn't—but he *thought* he had, and even for a minor leaguer, sometimes assurance can be enough.

He reached out to grab Jack's collar.

"Don't you smart off to me, Jack," he said, drawing Jack close. "As long as you're in Oatley, my dog is just what you are. As long as you're in Oatley I'll pet you when I want and I'll beat you when I want."

He adminstered a single neck-snapping shake. Jack bit his tongue and cried out. Hectic spots of anger now glowed in Smokey's pale cheeks like cheap rouge.

"You may not think that is so right now, but Jack, it is. As long as you're in Oatley you're my dog, and you'll be in Oatley until I decide to let you go. And we might as well start getting that learned right now."

He pulled his fist back. For a moment the three naked sixty-watt bulbs which hung in this narrow hallway sparkled crazily on the diamond chips of the horseshoe-shaped pinky ring he wore. Then the fist pistoned forward and slammed into the side of Jack's face. He was driven backward into the graffiti-covered wall, the side of his face first flaring and then going numb. The taste of his own blood washed into his mouth.

Smokey looked at him—the close, judgmental stare of a man who might be thinking about buying a heifer or a lottery number. He must not have seen the expression he wanted to see in Jack's eye, because he grabbed the dazed boy again, presumably the better to center him for a second shot.

At that moment a woman shrieked, from the Tap, "*No, Glen! No!*" There was a tangle of bellowing male voices, most of them alarmed. Another woman screamed—a high, drilling sound. Then a gunshot.

"Shit on *toast!*" Smokey cried, enunciating each word as carefully as an actor on a Broadway stage. He threw Jack back against the wall, whirled, and slammed out through the swinging door. The gun went off again and there was a scream of pain.

Jack was sure of only one thing—the time had come to get out. Not at the end of tonight's shift, or tomorrow's, or on Sunday morning. Right *now*.

The uproar seemed to be quieting down. There were no sirens, so maybe nobody had gotten shot . . . but, Jack remembered, cold, the millhand who looked like Randolph Scott was still down in the men's can.

Jack went into the chilly, beer-smelling storeroom, knelt by the kegs, and felt around for his pack. Again there was that suffocating certainty, as his fingers encountered nothing but thin air and the dirty concrete floor, that one of them— Smokey or Lori—had seen him hide the pack and had taken it. *All the better to keep you in Oatley, my dear.* Then relief, almost as suffocating as the fear, when his fingers touched the nylon. Jack donned the pack and looked longingly toward the loading door at the back of the storeroom. He would much rather use that door—he didn't want to go down to the fire-door at the end of the hall. That was too close to the men's bathroom. But if he opened the loading door, a red light would go on at the bar. Even if Smokey was still sorting out the ruckus on the floor, Lori would see that light and tell him. So . . .

He went to the door which gave on the back corridor. He eased it open a crack and applied one eye. The corridor was empty. All right, that was cool. Randolph Scott had tapped a kidney and gone back to where the action was while Jack was getting his backpack. Great.

*Yeah, except maybe he's still in there. You want to meet him in the hall, Jacky? Want to watch his eyes turn yellow again? Wait until you're sure.*

But he couldn't do that. Because Smokey would see he wasn't out in the Tap, helping Lori and Gloria swab tables, or behind the bar, unloading the dishwasher. He would come back here to finish teaching Jack what his place was in the great scheme of things. So—

*So what? Get going!*

*Maybe he's in there waiting for you, Jacky . . . maybe he's going to jump out just like a big bad Jack-in-the-Box . . .*

The lady or the tiger? Smokey or the millhand? Jack hesitated a moment longer in an agony of indecision. That the man with the yellow eyes was still in the bathroom was a possibility; that Smokey would be back was a certainty.

Jack opened the door and stepped out into the narrow hallway. The pack on his back seemed to gain weight—an eloquent accusation of his planned escape to anyone who might see it. He started down the hallway, moving grotesquely on tiptoe in spite of the thundering music and the roar of the crowd, his heart hammering in his chest.

*I was six, Jacky was six.*

So what? Why did that keep coming back?

*Six.*

The corridor seemed longer. It was like walking on a treadmill. The fire-door at the far end seemed to draw closer only by agonizing degrees. Sweat now coated his brow and his upper lip. His gaze flicked steadily toward the door to the right, with the black outline of a dog on it. Beneath this outline was the word POINTERS. And at the end of the corridor, a door of fading, peeling red. The sign on the door said EMERGENCY USE ONLY! ALARM WILL SOUND! In fact, the alarm bell had been broken for two years. Lori had told him so when Jack had hesitated about using the door to take out the trash.

Finally almost there. Directly opposite POINTERS.

*He's in there, I know he is . . . and if he jumps out I'll scream . . . I . . . I'll . . .*

Jack put out a trembling right hand and touched the crash-bar of the emergency door. It felt blessedly cool to his touch. For one moment he really believed he would simply fly out of the pitcher plant and into the night . . . free.

Then the door *behind* him suddenly banged open, the door to SETTERS, and a hand grabbed his backpack. Jack uttered a high-pitched, despairing shriek of a trapped animal and lunged at the emergency door, heedless of the pack and the magic juice inside it. If the straps had broken he would have simply gone fleeing through the trashy, weedy vacant lot behind the Tap, and never mind anything else.

But the straps were tough nylon and didn't break. The door opened a little way, revealing a brief dark wedge of the night, and then thumped shut again. Jack was pulled into the women's room. He was whirled around and then thrown backward. If he had hit the wall dead on, the bottle of magic juice would undoubtedly have shattered in the pack, drenching his few clothes and good old Rand McNally with the odor of rotting grapes. Instead, he hit the room's one wash-basin with the small of his back. The pain was giant, excruciating.

The millhand was walking toward him slowly, hitching up his jeans with hands that had begun to twist and thicken.

"You were supposed to be gone, kid," he said, his voice roughening, becoming at every moment more like the snarl of an animal.

Jack began to edge to his left, his eyes never leaving the man's face. His eyes now seemed almost transparent, not just yellow but lighted from within . . . the eyes of a hideous Halloween jack-o'-lantern.

"But you can trust old Elroy," the cowboy-thing said, and now it grinned to reveal a mouthful of curving teeth, some of them jaggedly broken off, some black with rot. Jack screamed. "Oh, you can trust Elroy," it said, its words now hardly discernible from a doglike growl. "He ain't gonna hurt you *too* bad.

"You'll be all right," it growled, moving toward Jack, "you'll be all right, oh yeah, you'll . . ." It continued to talk, but Jack could no longer tell what it was saying. Now it was only snarling.

Jack's foot hit the tall wastecan by the door. As the cowboy thing reached for him with its hooflike hands, Jack grabbed the can and threw it. The can bounced off the Elroy-thing's chest. Jack tore open the bathroom door and lunged to the left, toward the emergency door. He slammed into the crash-bar, aware that Elroy was right behind him. He lurched into the dark behind the Oatley Tap.

There was a colony of overloaded garbage cans to the right of the door. Jack blindly swept three of them behind him, heard them clash and rattle—and then a howl of fury as Elroy stumbled into them.

He whirled in time to see the thing go down. There was even a moment to realize—*Oh dear Jesus a tail it's got something like a tail*—that the thing was now almost entirely an animal. Golden light fell from its eyes in weird rays, like bright light falling through twin keyholes.

Jack backed away from it, pulling the pack from his back, trying to undo the catches with fingers which felt like blocks of wood, his mind a roaring confusion—

—*Jacky was six God help me Speedy Jacky was SIX God please*—

—of thoughts and incoherent pleas. The thing snarled and flailed at the garbage cans. Jack saw one hoof-hand go up and then come whistling down, splitting the side of one corrugated metal can in a jagged slash a yard long. It got up again, stumbled, almost fell, and then began to lurch toward Jack, its snarling, rippling face now almost at chest level. And somehow, through its barking growls, he was able to make out what it was saying. "Now I'm not just gonna ream you, little chicken. Now I'm gonna kill you . . . *after*."

Hearing it with his *ears*? Or in his *head*?

It didn't matter. The space between this world and that had shrunk from a universe to a mere membrane.

The Elroy-thing snarled and came toward him, now unsteady and awkward on its rear feet, its clothes bulging in all the wrong places, its tongue swinging from its fanged mouth. Here was the vacant lot behind Smokey Updike's Oatley Tap, yes, here it was at last, choked with weeds and blown trash— a rusty bedspring here, the grille of a 1957 Ford over there, and a ghastly sickle moon like a bent bone in the sky overhead, turning every shard of broken glass into a dead and staring eye, and this hadn't begun in New Hampshire, had it? No. It hadn't begun when his mother got sick, or with the appearance of Lester Parker. It had begun when—

*Jacky was six. When we all lived in California and no one lived anywhere else and Jacky was*—

He fumbled at the straps of his pack.

It came again, seeming almost to dance, for a moment reminding him of some animated Disney cartoon-figure in the chancy moonlight. Crazily, Jack began to laugh. The thing snarled and leaped at him. The swipe of those heavy hoof-claws again missed him by barest inches as he danced back through the weeds and litter. The Elroy-thing came down on the bedspring and somehow became entangled in it. Howling, snapping white gobbets of foam into the air, it pulled and twisted and lunged, one foot buried deep in the rusty coils.

Jack groped inside his pack for the bottle. He dug past socks and dirty undershorts and a wadded, fragrant pair of jeans. He seized the neck of the bottle and yanked it out.

The Elroy-thing split the air with a howl of rage, finally pulling free of the bedspring.

Jack hit the cindery, weedy, scruffy ground and rolled over, the last two fingers of his left hand hooked around one pack-strap, his right hand holding the bottle. He worked at the cap with the thumb and forefinger of his left hand, the pack dangling and swinging. The cap spun off.

*Can it follow me?* he wondered incoherently, tipping the bottle to his lips. *When I go, do I punch some kind of hole through the middle of things? Can it follow me through and finish me on the other side?*

Jack's mouth filled with that rotten dead-grape taste. He gagged, his throat closing, seeming to actually reverse direction. Now that awful taste filled his sinuses and nasal passages as well and he uttered a deep, shaking groan. He could hear the Elroy-thing screaming now, but the scream seemed far away, as if it were on one end of the Oatley tunnel and he, Jack, were falling rapidly toward the other end. And this time there was a sense of falling and he thought: *Oh my God what if I just flipped my stupid self over a cliff or off a mountain over there?*

He held on to the pack and the bottle, his eyes screwed desperately shut, waiting for whatever might happen next—Elroy-thing or no Elroy-thing. Territories or oblivion—and the thought which had haunted him all night came swinging back like a dancing carousel horse—Silver Lady, maybe Ella Speed. He caught it and rode it down in a cloud of the magic juice's awful smell, holding it, waiting for whatever would happen next; feeling his clothes change on his body.

*Six oh yes when we were all six and nobody was anything else and it was California who blows that sax daddy is it Dexter Gordon or is it is it what does Mom mean when she says we're living on a fault-line and where where oh where do you go Daddy you and Uncle Morgan oh Daddy sometimes he looks at you like like oh like there is a fault-line in his head and an earthquake going on behind his eyes and you're dying in it oh Daddy!*

Falling, twisting, turning in the middle of limbo, in the middle of a smell like a purple cloud, Jack Sawyer, John Benjamin Sawyer, Jacky, Jacky

*—was six when it started to happen, and who blew that sax Daddy? Who blew it when I was six, when Jacky was six, when Jacky—*

# 11

# The Death of Jerry Bledsoe

## 1

*was six . . .* when it really started, Daddy, when the engines that eventually pulled him to Oatley and beyond began to chug away. There had been loud saxophone music. *Six. Jacky was six.* At first his attention had been entirely on the toy his father had given him, a scale model of a London taxi—the toy car was heavy as a brick, and on the smooth wooden floors of the new office a good push sent it rumbling straight across the room. Late afternoon, first grade all the way on the other side of August, a neat new car that rolled like a tank on the strip of bare wood behind the couch, a contented, relaxed feeling in the air-conditioned office . . . no more work to do, no more phone calls that couldn't wait until the next day. Jack pushed the heavy toy taxi down the strip of bare wood, barely able to hear the rumbling of the solid rubber tires under the soloing of a saxophone. The black car struck one of the legs of the couch, spun sideways, and stopped. Jack crawled down and Uncle Morgan had parked himself in one of the chairs on the other side of the couch. Each man nursed a drink; soon they would put down their glasses, switch off the turntable and the amplifier, and go downstairs to their cars.

*when we were all six and nobody was anything else and it was California*

"Who's playing that sax?" he heard Uncle Morgan ask,

and, half in a reverie, heard that familiar voice in a new way: something whispery and hidden in Morgan Sloat's voice coiled into Jacky's ear. He touched the top of the toy taxi and his fingers were as cold as if it were of ice, not English steel.

"That's Dexter Gordon, is who that is," his father answered. His voice was as lazy and friendly as it always was, and Jack slipped his hand around the heavy taxi.

"Good record."

"*Daddy Plays the Horn*. It is a nice old record, isn't it?"

"I'll have to look for it." And then Jack thought he knew what that strangeness in Uncle Morgan's voice was all about—Uncle Morgan didn't really like jazz at all, he just pretended to in front of Jack's father. Jack had known this fact about Morgan Sloat for most of his childhood, and he thought it was silly that his father couldn't see it too. Uncle Morgan was never going to look for a record called *Daddy Plays the Horn,* he was just flattering Phil Sawyer—and maybe the reason Phil Sawyer didn't see it was that like everyone else he never paid quite enough attention to Morgan Sloat. Uncle Morgan, smart and ambitious ("smart as a wolverine, sneaky as a courthouse lawyer," Lily said), good old Uncle Morgan deflected observation—your eye just sort of naturally slid off him. When he was a kid, Jacky would have bet, his teachers would have had trouble even remembering his name.

"Imagine what this guy would be like over there," Uncle Morgan said, for once fully claiming Jack's attention. That falsity still played through his voice, but it was not Sloat's hypocrisy that jerked up Jacky's head and tightened his fingers on his heavy toy—the words *over there* had sailed straight into his brain and now were gonging like chimes. Because *over there* was the country of Jack's Daydreams. He had known that immediately. His father and Uncle Morgan had forgotten that he was behind the couch, and they were going to talk about the Daydreams.

His father knew about the Daydream-country. Jack could never have mentioned the Daydreams to either his father or his mother, but his father knew about the Daydreams because he had to—simple as that. And the next step, felt along Jack's emotions more than consciously expressed, was that his dad helped keep the Daydreams safe.

But for some reason, equally difficult to translate from emotion into language, the conjunction of Morgan Sloat and the Daydreams made the boy uneasy.

"Hey?" Uncle Morgan said. "This guy would really turn em around, wouldn't he? They'd probably make him Duke of the Blasted Lands, or something."

"Well, probably not that," Phil Sawyer said. "Not if they liked him as much as we do."

*But Uncle Morgan doesn't like him, Dad,* Jacky thought, suddenly clear that this was important. *He doesn't like him at all, not really, he thinks that music is too* loud, *he thinks it takes something from him. . . .*

"Oh, you know a lot more about it than I do," Uncle Morgan said in a voice that sounded easy and relaxed.

"Well, I've been there more often. But you're doing a good job of catching up." Jacky heard that his father was smiling.

"Oh, I've learned a few things, Phil. But really, you know—I'll never get over being grateful to you for showing all that to me." The two syllables of *grateful* filled with smoke and the sound of breaking glass.

But all of these little warnings could not do more than dent Jack's intense, almost blissful satisfaction. They were talking about the Daydreams. It was magical, that such a thing was possible. What they said was beyond him, their terms and vocabulary were too adult, but six-year-old Jack experienced again the wonder and joy of the Daydreams, and was at least old enough to understand the direction of their conversation. The Daydreams were real, and Jacky somehow shared them with his father. That was half his joy.

## 2

"Let me just get some things straight," Uncle Morgan said, and Jacky saw the word *straight* as a pair of lines knotting around each other like snakes. "They have magic like we have physics, right? We're talking about an agrarian monarchy, using magic instead of science."

"Sure," Phil Sawyer said.

"And presumably they've gone on like that for centuries. Their lives have never changed very much."

"Except for political upheavals, that's right."

Then Uncle Morgan's voice tightened, and the excitement he tried to conceal cracked little whips within his consonants. "Well, forget about the political stuff. Suppose we think about us for a change. You'll say—and I'd agree with you, Phil— that we've done pretty well out of the Territories already, and that we'd have to be careful about how we introduce changes there. I have no problems at all with that position. I feel the same way myself."

Jacky could feel his father's silence.

"Okay," Sloat continued. "Let's go with the concept that, within a situation basically advantageous to ourselves, we can spread the benefits around to anybody on our side. We don't sacrifice the advantage, but we're not greedy about the bounty it brings. We owe these people, Phil. Look what they've done for us. I think we could put ourselves into a really synergistic situation over there. Our energy can feed their energy and come up with stuff we've never even thought of, Phil. And we end up looking generous, which we are—but which also doesn't hurt us." He would be frowning forward, the palms of his hands pressed together. "Of course I don't have a total window on this situation, you know that, but I think the synergy alone is worth the price of admission, to tell you the truth. But Phil—can you imagine how much fucking clout we'd swing if we gave them electricity? If we got modern weapons to the right guys over there? Do you have any idea? I think it'd be awesome. *Awesome.*" The damp, squashy sound of his clapping hands. "I don't want to catch you unprepared or anything, but I thought it might be time for us to think along those lines—to think, Territories-wise, about increasing our involvement."

Phil Sawyer still said nothing. Uncle Morgan slapped his hands together again. Finally Phil Sawyer said, in a noncommittal voice, "You want to think about increasing our involvement."

"I think it's the way to go. And I can give you chapter and verse, Phil, but I shouldn't have to. You can probably remember as well I can what it was like before we started going there together. Hey, maybe we could have made it all on our own, and maybe we would have, but as for me, I'm grateful not to be representing a couple of broken-down strippers and Little Timmy Tiptoe anymore."

"Hold on," Jack's father said.

"Airplanes," Uncle Morgan said. "Think airplanes."

"Hold on, hold on there, Morgan, I have a lot of ideas that apparently have yet to occur to you."

"I'm always ready for new ideas," Morgan said, and his voice was smoky again.

"Okay. I think we have to be careful about what we do over there, partner. I think anything major—any real changes we bring about—just might turn around and bite our asses back here. Everything has consequences, and some of those consequences might be on the uncomfortable side."

"Like what?" Uncle Morgan asked.

"Like war."

"That's nuts, Phil. We've never seen anything . . . unless you mean Bledsoe. . . ."

"I do mean Bledsoe. Was that a coincidence?"

*Bledsoe?* Jack wondered. He had heard the name before; but it was vague.

"Well, that's a long way from war, to put it mildly, and I don't concede the connection anyhow."

"All right. Do you remember hearing about how a Stranger assassinated the old King over there—a long time ago? You ever hear about that?"

"Yeah, I suppose," Uncle Morgan said, and Jack heard again the falseness in his voice.

His father's chair squeaked—he was taking his feet off his desk, leaning forward. "The assassination touched off a minor war over there. The followers of the old King had to put down a rebellion led by a couple of disgruntled nobles. These guys saw their chance to take over and run things—seize lands, impound property, throw their enemies in jail, make themselves rich."

"Hey, be fair," Morgan broke in. "I heard about this stuff, too. They also wanted to bring some kind of political order to a crazy inefficient system—sometimes you have to be tough, starting out. I can see that."

"And it's not for us to make judgments about their politics, I agree. But here's my point. That little war over there lasted about three weeks. When it was over, maybe a hundred people had been killed. Fewer, probably. Did anyone ever tell you when that war began? What year it was? What day?"

"No," Uncle Morgan muttered in a sulky voice.

"It was the first of September, 1939. Over here, it was the day Germany invaded Poland." His father stopped talking, and Jacky, clutching his black toy taxi behind the couch, yawned silently but hugely.

"That's screwball," Uncle Morgan finally said. "*Their* war started *ours?* Do you really believe that?"

"I do believe that," Jack's father said. "I believe a three-week squabble over there in some way sparked off a war here that lasted six years and killed millions of people. Yes."

"Well . . ." Uncle Morgan said, and Jack could see him beginning to huff and blow.

"There's more. I've talked to lots of people over there about this, and the feeling I get is that the stranger who assassinated the King was a *real* Stranger, if you see what I mean. Those who saw him got the feeling that he was uncomfortable with Territories clothes. He acted like he was unsure of local customs—he didn't understand the money right away."

"Ah."

"Yes. If they hadn't torn him to pieces right after he stuck a knife into the King, we could be sure about this, but I'm sure anyhow that he was—"

"Like us."

"Like us. That's right. A visitor. Morgan, I don't think we can mess around too much over there. Because we simply don't know what the effects will be. To tell you the truth, I think we're affected all the time by things that go on in the Territories. And should I tell you another crazy thing?"

"Why not?" Sloat answered.

"That's not the only other world out there."

## 3

"Bullshit," Sloat said.

"I mean it. I've had the feeling, once or twice when I was there, that I was near to somewhere *else*—the Territories' Territories."

*Yes*, Jack thought, *that's right, it has to be, the Daydreams' Daydreams, someplace even more beautiful, and on the other side of that is the Daydreams' Daydreams' Daydreams, and on the other side of that is another place, another world nicer still. . . .* He realized for the first time that he had become very sleepy.

*The Daydreams' Daydreams*

And then he was almost immediately asleep, the heavy little taxi in his lap, his whole body simultaneously weighty with sleep, anchored to the strip of wooden floor, and so blissfully light.

The conversation must have continued—there must have been much that Jacky missed. He rose and fell, heavy and light, through the second whole side of *Daddy Plays the Horn*, and during that time Morgan Sloat must at first have argued—gently, but with what squeezings of his fists, what contortions of his forehead!—for his plan; then he must have allowed himself to seem persuadable, then finally persuaded by his partner's doubts. At the end of this conversation, which returned to the twelve-year-old Jacky Sawyer in the dangerous borderland between Oatley, New York, and a nameless Territories village, Morgan Sloat had allowed himself to seem not only *persuaded* but positively grateful for the lessons. When Jack woke up, the first thing he heard was his father asking, "Hey, did Jack disappear or something?" and the second thing was Uncle Morgan saying, "Hell, I guess you're right, Phil. You have a way of seeing right to the heart of things, you're great the way you do that."

"Where the hell is Jack?" his father said, and Jack stirred behind the couch, really waking up now. The black taxi thudded to the floor.

"Aha," Uncle Morgan said. "Little pitchers and big ears, *peut-être?*"

"You behind there, kiddo?" his father said. Noises of chairs pushing back across the wooden floor, of men standing up.

He said, "*Oooh*," and slowly lifted the taxi back into his lap. His legs felt stiff and uncomfortable—when he stood, they would tingle.

His father laughed. Footsteps came toward him. Morgan Sloat's red, puffy face appeared over the top of the couch. Jack yawned and pushed his knees into the back of the couch. His father's face appeared beside Sloat's. His father was smiling. For a moment, both of those grown-up adult male heads seemed to be floating over the top of the couch. "Let's move

on home, sleepyhead," his father said. When the boy looked
into Uncle Morgan's face, he saw calculation sink into his
skin, slide underneath his jolly-fat-man's cheeks like a snake
beneath a rock. He looked like Richard Sloat's daddy again,
like good old Uncle Morgan who always gave spectacular
Christmas and birthday presents, like good old sweaty Uncle
Morgan, so easy not to notice. But what had he looked like
before? *Like a human earthquake, like a man crumbling
apart over the fault-line behind his eyes, like something all
wound up and waiting to explode. . . .*

"How about a little ice cream on the way home, Jack?"
Uncle Morgan said to him. "That sound good to you?"

"Uh," Jack said.

"Yeah, we can stop off at that place in the lobby," his father
said.

"Yummy-yummy-yum," Uncle Morgan said. "Now we're
really talking about synergy," and smiled at Jack once more.

This happened when he was six, and in the midst of his
weightless tumble through limbo, it happened again—the
horrible purple taste of Speedy's juice backed up into his
mouth, into the passages behind his nose, and all of that lan-
guid afternoon of six years before replayed itself out in his
mind. He saw it just as if the magic juice brought total recall,
and so speedily that he lived through that afternoon in the
same few seconds which told him that this time the magic
juice really was going to make him vomit.

Uncle Morgan's eyes smoking, and inside Jack, a question
smoking too, demanding to finally come out . . .

*Who played*
*What changes what changes*
*Who plays those changes, daddy?*
*Who*

killed Jerry Bledsoe? The magic juice forced itself into the
boy's mouth, stinging threads of it nauseatingly trickled into
his nose, and just as Jack felt loose earth beneath his hands he
gave up and vomited rather than drown. *What* killed Jerry
Bledsoe? Foul purple stuff shot from Jack's mouth, choking
him, and he blindly pushed himself backward—his feet and
legs snagged in tall stiff weeds. Jack pushed himself up on his

hands and knees and waited, patient as a mule, his mouth drooping open, for the second attack. His stomach clenched, and he did not have time to groan before more of the stinking juice burned up through his chest and throat and spattered out of his mouth. Ropey pink strings of saliva hung from his lips, and Jack feebly brushed them away. He wiped his hand on his pants. Jerry Bledsoe, yes. *Jerry*—who'd always had his name spelled out on his shirt, like a gas-station attendant. Jerry, who had died when— The boy shook his head and wiped his hands across his mouth again. He spat into a nest of saw-toothed wild grass sprouting like a giant's corsage out of the gray-brown earth. Some dim animal instinct he did not understand made him push loose earth over the pinkish pool of vomit. Another reflex made him brush the palms of his hands against his trousers. Finally he looked up.

He was kneeling, in the last of the evening light, on the edge of a dirt lane. No horrible Elroy-thing pursued him—he had known that immediately. Dogs penned in a wooden, cage-like enclosure barked and snarled at him, thrusting their snouts through the cracks of their jail. On the other side of the fenced-in dogs was a rambling wooden structure and from here too doggy noises rose up into the immense sky. These were unmistakably similar to the noises Jack had just been hearing from the other side of a wall in the Oatley Tap: the sounds of drunken men bellowing at each other. A bar—here it would be an inn or a public house, Jack imagined. Now that he was no longer sickened by Speedy's juice, he could smell the pervasive, yeasty odors of malt and hops. He could not let the men from the inn discover him.

For a moment he imagined himself running from all those dogs yipping and growling through the cracks in their enclosure, and then he stood up. The sky seemed to tilt over his head, to darken. And back home, in *his* world, what was happening? A nice little disaster in the middle of Oatley? Maybe a nice little flood, a sweet little fire? Jack slipped quietly backward away from the inn, then began to move sideways through the tall grass. Perhaps sixty yards away, thick candles burned in the windows of the only other building he could see. From somewhere not far off to his right drifted the odor of pigs. When Jack had gone half the distance between the inn and the house, the dogs ceased growling and snapping, and he slowly began walking forward toward the Western Road. The night was dark and moonless.

*Jerry Bledsoe.*

4

There were other houses, though Jack did not see them until he was nearly before them. Except for the noisy drinkers behind him at the inn, here in the country Territories people went to bed when the sun did. No candles burned in these small square windows. Themselves squarish and dark, the houses on either side of the Western Road sat in a puzzling isolation—something was wrong, as in a visual game from a child's magazine, but Jack could not identify it. Nothing hung upside-down, nothing burned, nothing seemed extravagantly out of place. Most of the houses had thick fuzzy roofs which resembled haystacks with crewcuts, but Jack assumed that these were thatch—he had heard of it, but never seen it before. *Morgan*, he thought with a sudden thrill of panic, *Morgan of Orris*, and saw the two of them, the man with long hair and a built-up boot and his father's sweaty workaholic partner, for a moment jumbled up together—Morgan Sloat with pirate's hair and a hitch in his walk. But Morgan—this world's Morgan—was not what was Wrong with This Picture.

Jack was just now passing a short squat one-story building like an inflated rabbit hutch, crazily half-timbered with wide black wooden X's. A fuzzy crewcut thatch capped this building too. If he were walking out of Oatley—or even running out of Oatley, to be closer to the truth—what would he expect to see in the single dark window of this hutch for giant rabbits? He knew: the dancing glimmer of a television screen. But of course Territories houses did not have television sets inside them, and the absence of that colorful glimmer was not what had puzzled him. It was something else, something so much an aspect of any grouping of houses along a road that its absence left a hole in the landscape. You noticed the hole even if you could not quite identify what was absent.

Television, television sets . . . Jack continued past the half-timbered little building and saw ahead of him, its front door set only inches back from the verge of the road, another gnomishly small dwelling. This one seemed to have a sod, not a thatched, roof, and Jack smiled to himself—this tiny village had reminded him of Hobbiton. Would a Hobbit cable-stringer pull up here and say to the lady of the . . . shack? doghouse? . . . anyhow, would he say, "Ma'am, we're installing cable in your area, and for a small monthly fee—hitch you up right now—you get fifteen new channels, you get *Midnight Blue*, you get the all-sports and all-weather channels, you get . . ."?

And that, he suddenly realized, was it. In front of these houses were no poles. No wiring! No TV antennas complicated the sky, no tall wooden poles marched the length of the Western Road, because in the Territories there was no electricity. Which was why he had not permitted himself to identify the absent element. Jerry Bledsoe had been, at least part of the time, Sawyer & Sloat's electrician and handyman.

## 5

When his father and Morgan Sloat used that name, *Bledsoe*, he thought he had never heard it before—though, having remembered it, he must have heard the handyman's last name once or twice. But Jerry Bledsoe was almost always just *Jerry*, as it said above the pocket on his workshirt. "Can't Jerry do something about the air-conditioning?" "Get Jerry to oil the hinges on that door, will you? The squeaks are driving me batshit." And Jerry would appear, his work-clothes clean and pressed, his thinning rust-red hair combed flat, his glasses round and earnest, and quietly fix whatever was wrong. There was a Mrs. Jerry, who kept the creases sharp and clean in the tan workpants, and several small Jerrys, whom Sawyer & Sloat invariably remembered at Christmas. Jack had been small enough to associate the name *Jerry* with Tom Cat's eternal adversary, and so imagined that the handyman and Mrs. Jerry and the little Jerrys lived in a giant mouse-hole, accessible by a curved arch cut into a baseboard.

But who had killed Jerry Bledsoe? His father and Morgan Sloat, always so sweet to the Bledsoe children at Christmastime?

Jack stepped forward into the darkness of the Western Road, wishing that he had forgotten completely about Sawyer & Sloat's handyman, that he had fallen asleep as soon as he had crawled behind the couch. Sleep was what he wanted now—wanted it far more than the uncomfortable thoughts which that six-years-dead conversation had aroused in him. Jack promised himself that as soon as he was sure he was at least a couple of miles past the last house, he would find someplace to sleep. A field would do, even a ditch. His legs did not want to move anymore; all his muscles, even his bones, seemed twice their weight.

It had been just after one of those times when Jack had wandered into some enclosed place after his father and found that Phil Sawyer had somehow contrived a disappearance. Later, his father would manage to vanish from his bedroom, from the dining room, from the conference room at Sawyer & Sloat. On this occasion he executed his mystifying trick in the garage beside the house on Rodeo Drive.

Jack, sitting unobserved on the little knob of raised land which was the closest thing to a hill offered by this section of Beverly Hills, saw his father leave their house by the front door, cross the lawn while digging in his pockets for money or keys, and let himself into the garage by the side door. The white door on the right side should have swung up seconds later; but it remained stubbornly closed. Then Jack realized that his father's car was where it had been all this Saturday morning, parked at the curb directly in front of the house. Lily's car was gone—she'd plugged a cigarette into her mouth and announced that she was taking herself off to a screening of *Dirt Track*, the latest film by the director of *Death's Darling*, and nobody by God had better try to stop her—and so the garage was empty. For minutes, Jack waited for something to happen. Neither the side door nor the big front doors opened. Eventually Jack slid down off the grassy elevation, went to the garage, and let himself in. The wide familiar space was entirely empty. Dark oil stains patterned the gray cement floor. Tools hung from silver hooks set into the walls. Jack grunted in astonishment, called out, "Dad?" and looked at everything again, just to make sure. This time he saw a cricket hop toward the shadowy protection of a wall, and for a second *almost* could have believed that magic was real and some malign wizard had happened along and . . . the cricket reached the wall and slipped into an invisible crack. No, his father had not been turned into a cricket. Of course he had not. "Hey," the boy said—to himself it seemed. He walked backward to the side door and left the garage. Sunlight fell on the lush, springy lawns of Rodeo Drive. He would have called someone, but whom? The police? *My daddy walked into the garage and I couldn't find him in there and now I'm scared. . . .*

Two hours later Phil Sawyer came walking up from the Beverly Wilshire end of the street. He carried his jacket over his shoulder, had pulled down the knot of his tie—to Jack, he looked like a man returning from a journey around the world. Jack jumped down from his anxious elevation and tore toward his father. "You sure cover the ground," his father said, smiling, and Jack flattened himself against his legs. "I thought you were taking a nap, Travelling Jack."

They heard the telephone ringing as they came up the walk, and some instinct—perhaps the instinct to keep his father close—made Jacky pray that it had already rung a dozen times, that whoever was calling would hang up before they reached the front door. His father ruffled the hair on his crown, put his big warm hand on the back of his neck, then pulled open the door and made it to the phone in five long strides. "Yes, Morgan," Jacky heard his father say. "Oh? Bad news? You'd better tell me, yes." After a long moment of silence in which the boy could hear the tinny, rasping sound of Morgan Sloat's voice stealing through the telephone wires: "Oh, Jerry. My God. Poor Jerry. I'll be right over." Then his father looked straight at him, not smiling, not winking, not doing anything but taking him in. "I'll come over, Morgan. I'll have to bring Jack, but he can wait in the car." Jack felt his muscles relax, and was so relieved that he did not ask why he had to wait in the car, as he would have at any other time.

Phil drove up Rodeo Drive to the Beverly Hills Hotel, turned left onto Sunset, and pointed the car toward the office building. He said nothing.

His father zipped through the oncoming traffic and swung the car into the parking lot beside the office building. Already in the lot were two police cars, a fire truck, Uncle Morgan's pocket-size white Mercedes convertible, the rusted old Plymouth two-door that had been the handyman's car. Just inside the entrance Uncle Morgan was talking to a policeman, who shook his head slowly, slowly, in evident sympathy. Morgan

Sloat's right arm squeezed the shoulders of a slim young woman in a dress too large for her who had twisted her face into his chest. Mrs. Jerry, Jack knew, seeing that most of her face was obscured by a white handkerchief she had pressed to her eyes. A behatted, raincoated fireman pushed a mess of twisted metal and plastic, ashes and broken glass into a disorderly heap far past them down the hall. Phil said, "Just sit here for a minute or two, okay, Jacky?" and sprinted toward the entrance. A young Chinese woman sat talking to a policeman on a concrete abutment at the end of the parking lot. Before her lay a crumpled object it took Jack a moment to recognize as a bike. When Jack inhaled, he smelled bitter smoke.

Twenty minutes later, both his father and Uncle Morgan left the building. Still gripping Mrs. Jerry, Uncle Morgan waved goodbye to the Sawyers. He led the woman around to the passenger door of his tiny car. Jack's father twirled his own car out of the lot and back into the traffic on Sunset.

"Is Jerry hurt?" Jack asked.

"Some kind of freak accident," his father said. "Electricity—the whole building could've gone up in smoke."

"Is Jerry hurt?" Jack repeated.

"Poor son of a bitch got hurt so bad he's dead," said his father.

Jack and Richard Sloat needed two months to really put the story together out of the conversations they overheard. Jack's mother and Richard's housekeeper supplied other details—the housekeeper, the goriest.

Jerry Bledsoe had come in on a Saturday to try to iron out some of the kinks in the building's security system. If he tampered with the delicate system on a weekday, he was sure to confuse or irritate the tenants with the Klaxon alarm whenever he accidentally set it off. The security system was wired into the building's main electrical board, set behind two large removable walnut panels on the ground floor. Jerry had set down his tools and lifted off the panels, having already seen that the lot was empty and nobody would jump out of his skin when the alarm went off. Then he went downstairs to the telephone in his basement cubicle and told the local precinct house to ignore any signals from the Sawyer & Sloat address until his next telephone call. When he went back upstairs to tackle the mare's nest of wires coming into the board from all the contact points, a twenty-three-year-old woman named Lorette Chang was just riding her bicycle into the building's lot—she was distributing a leaflet advertising a restaurant which was due to open down the street in fifteen days.

Miss Chang later told the police that she looked through the glass front door and saw a workman enter the hall from the basement. Just before the workman picked up his screwdriver and touched the wiring panel, she felt the parking lot wobble beneath her feet. It was, she assumed, a mini-earthquake: a lifelong resident of Los Angeles, Lorette Chang was untroubled by any seismic event that did not actually knock anything down. She saw Jerry Bledsoe set his feet (so he felt it, too, though no one else did), shake his head, then gently insert the tip of the screwdriver into a hive of wires.

And then the entry and downstairs corridor of the Sawyer & Sloat building turned into a holocaust.

The entire wiring panel turned instantly to a solid rectangular body of flame; bluish-yellow arcs of what looked like lightning shot out and encased the workman. Electronic horns bawled and bawled: KA-WHAAAAM! KA-WHAAAM! A ball of fire six feet high fell right out of the wall, slammed the already dead Jerry Bledsoe aside, and rolled down the corridor toward the lobby. The transparent front door blew into flying glass and smoking, twisted pieces of frame. Lorette Chang dropped her bike and sprinted toward the pay telephone across the street. As she told the fire department the building's address and noticed that her bicycle had been twisted neatly in half by whatever force had burst through the door, Jerry Bledsoe's roasted corpse still swayed upright back and forth before the devastated panel. Thousands of volts poured through his body, twitching it with regular surges, snapping it back and forth in a steady pulse. All the handyman's body hair and most of his clothes had fried off, and his skin had become a cooked blotchy gray. His eyeglasses, a solidifying lump of brown plastic, covered his nose like a poultice.

Jerry Bledsoe. *Who plays those changes, daddy?* Jack made his feet move until he had gone half an hour without seeing another of the little thatched cottages. Unfamiliar stars in unfamiliar patterns lay all over the sky above him—messages in a language he could not read.

# 12

# Jack Goes to the Market

## 1

He slept that night in a sweetly fragrant Territories haystack, first burrowing his way in and then turning around so the fresh air could reach him along the tunnel he had made. He listened apprehensively for small scuttering sounds—he had heard or read somewhere that fieldmice were great haystack fans. If they were in this one, then a great big mouse named Jack Sawyer had scared them into silence. He relaxed little by little, his left hand tracing the shape of Speedy's bottle—he had plugged the top with a piece of springy moss from a small stream where he had stopped to drink. He supposed it was entirely possible that some of the moss would fall into the bottle, or already had. What a pity, it would spoil the piquant flavor and the delicate bouquet.

As he lay in here, warm at last, heavily sleepy, the feeling he was most aware of was relief . . . as if there had been a dozen ten-pound weights strapped to his back and some kind soul had undone the buckles and allowed them to fall to the ground. He was in the Territories again, the place which such charming folks as Morgan of Orris, Osmond the Bullwhipper, and Elroy the Amazing Goat-Man all called home, the Territories, where anything could happen.

But the Territories could be good, too. He remembered that from his earliest childhood, when everyone had lived in California and no one had lived anyplace else. The Territories could be good, and it seemed he felt that goodness around him now, as calmly, inarguably sweet as the smell of the haystack, as clear as the smell of the Territories air.

Does a fly or a ladybug feel relief if an unexpected gust of wind comes along and tilts the pitcher plant just enough to allow the drowning insect to fly out? Jack didn't know . . . but he knew that he was out of Oatley, away from Fair Weather Clubs and old men who wept over their stolen shopping carts, away from the smell of beer and the smell of puke . . . most important of all, he was away from Smokey Updike and the Oatley Tap.

He thought he might travel in the Territories for a while, after all.

And so thinking, fell asleep.

## 2

He had walked two, perhaps three miles along the Western Road the following morning, enjoying the sunshine and the good, earthy smell of fields almost ready for the harvests of summer's end, when a cart pulled over and a whiskery farmer in what looked like a toga with rough breeches under it pulled up and shouted:

"Are you for market-town, boy?"

Jack gaped at him, half in a panic, realizing that the man was not speaking English—never mind "prithee" or "Dost thou go cross-gartered, varlet," it wasn't English *at all*.

There was a woman in a voluminous dress sitting beside the whiskery farmer; she held a boy of perhaps three on her lap. She smiled pleasantly enough at Jack and rolled her eyes at her husband. "He's a simpleton, Henry."

*They're not speaking English . . . but whatever it is they're speaking, I understand it. I'm actually thinking in that language . . . and that's not all—I'm seeing in it, or with it, or whatever it is I mean.*

Jack realized he had been doing it the last time he had been in the Territories, too—only then he had been too confused to realize it; things had moved too fast, and *everything* had seemed strange.

The farmer leaned forward. He smiled, showing teeth which were absolutely horrid. "Are you a simpleton, laddie?" he asked, not unkindly.

"No," he said, smiling back as best he could, aware that he had not said *no* but some Territories word which meant *no*— when he had flipped, he had changed his speech and his way of thinking (his way of *imaging*, anyway—he did not have that word in his vocabulary, but understood what he meant just the same), just as he had changed his clothes. "I'm not simple. It's just that my mother told me to be careful of people I might meet along the road."

Now the farmer's wife smiled. "Your mother was right," she said. "Are you for the market?"

"Yes," Jack said. "That is, I'm headed up the road—west."

"Climb up in the back, then," Henry the farmer said. "Daylight's wasting. I want to sell what I have if I can and be home again before sunset. Corn's poor but it's the last of the season. Lucky to have corn in ninemonth at all. Someone may buy it."

"Thank you," Jack said, climbing into the back of the low wagon. Here, dozens of corn ears were bound with rough hanks of rope and stacked like cordwood. If the corn was poor, then Jack could not imagine what would constitute good corn over here—they were the biggest ears he had ever seen in his life. There were also small stacks of squashes and gourds and things that looked like pumpkins—but they were reddish instead of orange. Jack didn't know what they were, but he suspected they would taste wonderful. His stomach rumbled busily. Since going on the road, he had discovered what hunger was—not as a passing acquaintance, something you felt dimly after school and which could be assuaged with a few cookies and a glass of milk souped up with Nestlé's Quik, but as an intimate friend, one that sometimes moved away to a distance but who rarely left entirely.

He was sitting with his back to the front of the wagon, his sandal-clad feet dangling down, almost touching the hard-packed dirt of the Western Road. There was a lot of traffic this morning, most of it bound for the market, Jack assumed. Every now and then Henry bawled a greeting to someone he knew.

Jack was still wondering how those apple-colored pumpkins might taste—and just where his next meal was going to come from, anyway—when small hands twined in his hair and gave a brisk tug—brisk enough to make his eyes water.

He turned and saw the three-year-old standing there in his bare feet, a big grin on his face and a few strands of Jack's hair in each of his hands.

"Jason!" his mother cried—but it was, in its way, an indulgent cry *(Did you see the way he pulled that hair? My, isn't he strong!)*—"Jason, that's not *nice!*"

Jason grinned, unabashed. It was a big, dopey, sunshiney grin, as sweet in its way as the smell of the haystack in which Jack had spent the night. He couldn't help returning it . . . and while there had been no politics of calculation in his returning grin, he saw he had made a friend of Henry's wife.

"Sit," Jason said, swaying back and forth with the unconscious movement of a veteran sailor. He was still grinning at Jack.

"Huh?"

"Yap."

"I'm not getting you, Jason."

"Sit-yap."

"I'm not—"

And then Jason, who was husky for a three-year-old, plopped into Jack's lap, still grinning.

*Sit-yap, oh yeah, I get it*, Jack thought, feeling the dull ache from his testicles spreading up into the pit of his stomach.

"Jason *bad!*" his mother called back in that same indulgent, but-isn't-he-cute voice . . . and Jason, who knew who ruled the roost, grinned his dopey, sweetly charming grin.

Jack realized that Jason was wet. Very, extremely, indubitably wet.

*Welcome back to the Territories, Jack-O.*

And sitting there with the child in his arms and warm wetness slowly soaking through his clothes, Jack began to laugh, his face turned up to the blue, blue sky.

### 3

A few minutes later Henry's wife worked her way to where Jack was sitting with the child on his lap and took Jason back.

"Oooh, wet, bad baby," she said in her indulgent voice. *Doesn't my Jason wet big!* Jack thought, and laughed again. That made Jason laugh, and Mrs. Henry laughed with them.

As she changed Jason, she asked Jack a number of questions—ones he had heard often enough in his own world. But here he would have to be careful. He was a stranger, and there might be hidden trapdoors. He heard his father telling Morgan, . . . *a real Stranger, if you see what I mean.*

Jack sensed that the woman's husband was listening

closely. He answered her questions with a careful variation of the Story—not the one he told when he was applying for a job but the one he told when someone who had picked him up thumbing got curious.

He said he had come from the village of All-Hands'—Jason's mother had a vague recollection of hearing of the place, but that was all. Had he really come so far? she wanted to know. Jack told her that he had. And where was he going? He told her (and the silently listening Henry) that he was bound for the village of California. That one she had not heard of, even vaguely, in such stories as the occasional peddler told. Jack was not exactly very surprised . . . but he was grateful that neither of them exclaimed "California? Whoever heard of a village named California? Who are you trying to shuck and jive, boy?" In the Territories there had to be lots of places—whole areas as well as villages—of which people who lived in their own little areas had never heard. No power poles. No electricity. No movies. No cable TV to tell them how wonderful things were in Malibu or Sarasota. No Territories version of Ma Bell, advertising that a three-minute call to the Outposts after five p.m. cost only $5.83, plus tax, rates may be higher on God-Pounders' Eve and some other holidays. *They live in a mystery*, he thought. *When you live in a mystery, you don't question a village simply because you never heard of it. California doesn't sound any wilder than a place named All-Hands'.*

Nor did they question. He told them that his father had died the year before, and that his mother was quite ill (he thought of adding that the Queen's repossession men had come in the middle of the night and taken away their donkey, grinned, and decided that maybe he ought to leave that part out). His mother had given him what money she could (except the word that came out in the strange language wasn't really *money*—it was something like *sticks*) and had sent him off to the village of California, to stay with his Aunt Helen.

"These are hard times," Mrs. Henry said, holding Jason, now changed, more closely to her.

"All-Hands' is near the summer palace, isn't it, boy?" It was the first time Henry had spoken since inviting Jack aboard.

"Yes," Jack said. "That is, fairly near. I mean—"

"You never said what your father died of."

Now he had turned his head. His gaze was narrow and assessing, the former kindness gone; it had been blown out of his eyes like candle-flames in a wind. Yes, there were trapdoors here.

"Was he ill?" Mrs. Henry asked. "So much illness these days—pox, plague—hard times . . ."

For a wild moment Jack thought of saying, *No, he wasn't ill, Mrs. Henry. He took a lot of volts, my dad. You see he went off one Saturday to do some work, and he left Mrs. Jerry and all the little Jerrys—including me—back at home. This was when we all lived in a hole in the baseboard and nobody lived anywhere else, you see. And do you know what? He stuck his screwdriver into a bunch of wires and Mrs. Feeny, she works over at Richard Sloat's house, she heard Uncle Morgan talking on the phone and he said the electricity came out, all of the electricity, and it cooked him, it cooked him so bad that his glasses melted all over his nose, only you don't know about glasses because you don't have them here. No glasses . . . no electricity . . . no* Midnight Blue *. . . no airplanes. Don't end up like Mrs. Jerry, Mrs. Henry. Don't—*

"Never mind was he ill," the whiskered farmer said. "Was he *political*?"

Jack looked at him. His mouth was working but no sounds came out. He didn't know what to say. There were too many trapdoors.

Henry nodded, as if he had answered. "Jump down, laddie. Market's just over the next rise. I reckon you can ankle it from here, can't you?"

"Yes," Jack said. "I reckon I can."

Mrs. Henry looked confused . . . but she was now holding Jason away from Jack, as if he might have some contagious disease.

The farmer, still looking back over his shoulder, smiled a bit ruefully. "I'm sorry. You seem a nice enough lad, but we're simple people here—whatever's going on back yonder by the sea is something for great lords to settle. Either the Queen will die or she won't . . . and of course, someday she must. God pounds all His nails sooner or later. And what happens to little people when they meddle into the affairs of the great is that they get hurt."

"My father—"

"I don't want to know about your father!" Henry said sharply. His wife scrambled away from Jack, still holding Jason to her bosom. "Good man or bad, I don't know and I don't *want* to know—all I know is that he's a dead man, I don't think you lied about that, and that his son has been sleeping rough and has all the smell of being on the dodge. The son doesn't talk as if he comes from any of these parts. So climb down. I've a son of my own, as you see."

Jack got down, sorry for the fear in the young woman's face—fear he had put there. The farmer was right—little people had no business meddling in the affairs of the great. Not if they were smart.

# 13

# The Men in the Sky

## 1

It was a shock to discover that the money he had worked so hard to get literally *had* turned into sticks—they looked like toy snakes made by an inept craftsman. The shock lasted only for a moment, however, and he laughed ruefully at himself. The sticks *were* money, of course. When he came over here, *everything* changed. Silver dollar to gryphon-coin, shirt to jerkin, English to Territories speech, and good old American money to—well, to jointed sticks. He had flipped over with about twenty-two dollars in all, and he guessed that he had exactly the same amount in Territories money, although he had counted fourteen joints on one of the money-sticks and better than twenty on the other.

The problem wasn't so much money as cost—he had very little idea of what was cheap and what was dear, and as he walked through the market, Jack felt like a contestant on *The New Price Is Right*—only, if he flubbed it here, there wouldn't be any consolation prize and a clap on the back from Bob

Barker; if he flubbed it here, they might . . . well, he didn't know for sure *what* they might do. Run him out for sure. Hurt him, rough him up? Maybe. Kill him? Probably not, but it was impossible to be absolutely certain. They were little people. They were not political. And he was a stranger.

Jack walked slowly from one end of the loud and busy market-day throng to the other, wrestling with the problem. It now centered mostly in his stomach—he was dreadfully hungry. Once he saw Henry, dickering with a man who had goats to sell. Mrs. Henry stood near him, but a bit behind, giving the men room to trade. Her back was to Jack, but she had the baby hoisted in her arms—*Jason, one of the little Henrys*, Jack thought—but Jason saw him. The baby waved one chubby hand at Jack and Jack turned away quickly, putting as much crowd as he could between himself and the Henrys.

Everywhere was the smell of roasting meat, it seemed. He saw vendors slowly turning joints of beef over charcoal fires both small and ambitious; he saw 'prentices laying thick slices of what looked like pork on slabs of homemade bread and taking them to the buyers. They looked like runners at an auction. Most of the buyers were farmers like Henry, and it appeared that they also called for food the way people entered a bid at an auction—they simply raised one of their hands imperiously, the fingers splayed out. Jack watched several of these transactions closely, and in every case the medium of exchange was the jointed sticks . . . but how many knuckles would be enough? he wondered. Not that it mattered. He had to eat, whether the transaction marked him as a stranger or not.

He passed a mime-show, barely giving it a glance although the large audience that had gathered—women and children, most of them—roared with appreciative laughter and applauded. He moved toward a stall with canvas sides where a big man with tattoos on his slabbed biceps stood on one side of a trench of smouldering charcoal in the earth. An iron spit about seven feet long ran over the charcoal. A sweating, dirty boy stood at each end. Five large roasts were impaled along the length of the spit, and the boys were turning them in unison.

"Fine meats!" the big man was droning. "Fine meats! *Fiiine* meats! Buy my fine meats! Fine meats here! Fine meats right here!" In an aside to the boy closest to him: "Put your back into it, God pound you." Then back to his droning, huckstering cry.

A farmer passing with his adolescent daughter raised his hand, and then pointed at the joint of meat second from the left. The boys stopped turning the spit long enough for their boss to hack a slab from the roast and put in on a chunk of bread. One of them ran with it to the farmer, who produced one of the jointed sticks. Watching closely, Jack saw him break off two knuckles of wood and hand them to the boy. As the boy ran back to the stall the customer pocketed his money-stick with the absent but careful gesture of any man repocketing his change, took a gigantic bite of his open-faced sandwich, and handed the rest to his daughter, whose first chomp was almost as enthusiastic aṣ her father's.

Jack's stomach boinged and goinged. He had seen what he had to see . . . he hoped.

"Fine meats! Fine meats! Fine—" The big man broke off and looked down at Jack, his beetling brows drawing together over eyes that were small but not entirely stupid. "I hear the song your stomach is singing, friend. If you have money, I'll take your trade and bless you to God in my prayers tonight. If you haven't, then get your stupid sheep's face out of here and go to the devil."

Both boys laughed, although they were obviously tired— they laughed as if they had no control over the sounds they were making.

But the maddening smell of the slowly cooking meat would not let him leave. He held out the shorter of his jointed sticks and pointed to the roast which was second from the left. He didn't speak. It seemed safer not to. The vendor grunted, produced his crude knife from his wide belt again, and cut a slice—it was a smaller slice than the one he had cut the farmer, Jack observed, but his stomach had no business with such matters; it was rumbling crazily in anticipation.

The vendor slapped the meat on bread and brought it over himself instead of handing it to either of the boys. He took Jack's money-stick. Instead of two knuckles, he broke off three.

His mother's voice, sourly amused, spoke up in his mind:
*Congratulations, Jack-O . . . you've just been screwed.*

The vendor was looking at him, grinning around a mouthful of wretched blackish teeth, daring him to say anything, to protest in any way. *You just ought to be grateful I only took three knuckles instead of all fourteen of them. I could have, you know. You might as well have a sign hung around your neck, boy: I AM A STRANGER HERE, AND ON MY OWN. So tell me, Sheep's-Face: do you want to make an issue of it?*

What he wanted didn't matter—he obviously *couldn't* make an issue of it. But he felt that thin, impotent anger again.

"Go on," the vendor said, tiring of him. He flapped a big hand in Jack's face. His fingers were scarred, and there was blood under his nails. "You got your food. Now get out of here."

Jack thought, *I could show you a flashlight and you'd run like all the devils of hell were after you. Show you an airplane and you'd probably go crazy. You're maybe not as tough as you think, chum.*

He smiled, perhaps there was something in his smile that the meat-vendor didn't like, because he drew away from Jack, his face momentarily uneasy. Then his brows beetled together again.

"Get out, I said!" he roared. "Get out, God pound you!"
And this time Jack went.

### 2

The meat was delicious. Jack gobbled it and the bread it sat on, and then unselfconsciously licked the juice from his palms as he strolled along. The meat *did* taste like pork . . . and yet it didn't. It was somehow richer, tangier than pork. Whatever it was, it filled the hole in the middle of him with authority. Jack thought he could take it to school in bag lunches for a thousand years.

Now that he had managed to shut his belly up—for a little while, anyway—he was able to look about himself with more interest . . . and although he didn't know it, he had finally begun to blend into the crowd. Now he was only one more rube from the country come to the market-town, walking slowly between the stalls, trying to gawk in every direction at once. Hucksters recognized him, but only as one more potential mark among many. They yelled and beckoned at him, and as he passed by they yelled and beckoned at whoever happened to be behind him—man, woman, or child. Jack gaped frankly at the wares scattered all around him, wares both wonderful and strange, and amidst all the others staring at them he ceased to be a stranger himself—perhaps because he had given up his effort to seem blasé in a place where *no one acted blasé*. They laughed, they argued, they haggled . . . but no one seemed bored.

The market-town reminded him of the Queen's pavillion without the air of strained tension and too-hectic gaiety—there was the same absurdly rich mingle of smells (dominated by roasting meat and animal ordure), the same brightly dressed crowds (although even the most brightly dressed people Jack saw couldn't hold a candle to some of the dandies he had seen inside the pavillion), the same unsettling but somehow exhilarating juxtaposition of the perfectly normal, cheek by jowl with the extravagantly strange.

He stopped at a stall where a man was selling carpets with the Queen's portrait woven into them. Jack suddenly thought of Hank Scoffler's mom and smiled. Hank was one of the kids Jack and Richard Sloat had hung around with in L.A. Mrs. Scoffler had a thing for the most garish decorations Jack had ever seen. And God, wouldn't she have loved these rugs, with the image of Laura DeLoessian, her hair done up in a high, regal coronet of braids, woven into them! Better than her velvet paintings of Alaskan stags or the ceramic diorama of the Last Supper behind the bar in the Scoffler living room. . . .

Then the face woven into the rugs seemed to change even as he looked at it. The face of the Queen was gone and it was his mother's face he saw, repeated over and over and over, her eyes too dark, her skin much too white.

Homesickness surprised Jack again. It rushed through his mind in a wave and he called out for her in his heart—*Mom! Hey Mom! Jesus, what am I doing here? Mom!!*—wondering with a lover's longing intensity what she was doing now, right this minute. Sitting at the window, smoking, looking out at the ocean, a book open beside her? Watching TV? At a movie? Sleeping? Dying?

*Dead?* an evil voice added before he could stop it. *Dead, Jack? Already dead?*

*Stop it.*

He felt the burning sting of tears.

"Why so sad, my little lad?"

He looked up, startled, and saw the rug salesman looking at him. He was as big as the meat-vendor, and his arms were also tattooed, but his smile was open and sunny. There was no meanness in it. That was a big difference.

"It's nothing," Jack said.

"If it's nothing makes you look like that, you ought to be thinking of *something*, my son, my son."

"I looked that bad, did I?" Jack asked, smiling a little. He had also grown unselfconscious about his speech—at least for the moment—and perhaps that was why the rug salesman heard nothing odd or off-rhythm in it.

"Laddie, you looked as if you only had one friend left on this side o' the moon and you just saw the Wild White Wolf come out o' the north an' gobble him down with a silver spoon."

Jack smiled a little. The rug salesman turned away and took something from a smaller display to the right of the largest rug—it was oval and had a short handle. As he turned it over the sun flashed across it—it was a mirror. To Jack it looked small and cheap, the sort of thing you might get for knocking over all three wooden milk-bottles in a carnival game.

"Here, laddie," the rug salesman said. "Take a look and see if I'm not right."

Jack looked into the mirror and gaped, for a moment so stunned he thought his heart must have forgotten to beat. It was him, but he looked like something from Pleasure Island in the Disney version of *Pinocchio*, where too much pool-shooting and cigar-smoking had turned boys into donkeys. His eyes, normally as blue and round as an Anglo-Saxon heritage could make them, had gone brown and almond-shaped. His hair, coarsely matted and falling across the middle of his forehead, had a definite manelike look. He raised one hand to brush it away, and touched only bare skin—in the mirror, his fingers seemed to fade right through the hair. He heard the vendor laugh, pleased. Most amazing of all, long jackass-ears dangled down to below his jawline. As he stared, one of them twitched.

He thought suddenly: *I HAD one of these!*

And on the heels of that: *In the* Daydreams *I had one of these. Back in the regular world it was . . . was . . .*

He could have been no more than four. In the regular world (he had stopped thinking of it as the *real* world without even noticing) it had been a great big glass marble with a rosy center. One day while he was playing with it, it had rolled down the cement path in front of their house and before he could catch it, it had fallen down a sewer grate. It had been gone—forever, he had thought then, sitting on the curb with his face propped on his dirty hands and weeping. But it wasn't; here was that old toy rediscovered, just as wonderful now as it had been when he was three or four. He grinned, delighted. The image changed and Jack the Jackass became Jack the Cat, his face wise and secret with amusement. His eyes went from donkey-brown to tomcat-green. Now pert little gray-furred ears cocked alertly where the droopy donkey-ears had dangled.

"Better," the vendor said. "Better, my son. I like to see a happy boy. A happy boy is a healthy boy, and a healthy boy finds his way in the world. *Book of Good Farming* says that, and if it doesn't, it should. I may just scratch it in my copy, if I ever scratch up enough scratch from my pumpkin-patch to buy a copy someday. Want the glass?"

"Yes!" Jack cried. "Yeah, great!" He groped for his sticks. Frugality was forgotten. "How much?"

The vendor frowned and looked around swiftly to see if they were being watched. "Put it away, my son. Tuck it down deep, that's the way. You show your scratch, you're apt to lose the batch. Dips abound on market-ground."

"What?"

"Never mind. No charge. Take it. Half of em get broken in the back of my wagon when I drag em back to my store come tenmonth. Mothers bring their little 'uns over and they try it but they don't buy it."

"Well, at least you don't deny it," Jack said.

The vendor looked at him with some surprise and then they both burst out laughing.

"A happy boy with a snappy mouth," the vendor said. "Come see me when you're older and bolder, my son. We'll take your mouth and head south and treble what we peddle."

Jack giggled. This guy was better than a rap record by the Sugarhill Gang.

"Thanks," he said (a large, improbable grin had appeared on the chops of the cat in the mirror). "Thanks very much!"

"Thank me to God," the vendor said . . . then, as an afterthought: "And watch your wad!"

Jack moved on, tucking the mirror-toy carefully into his jerkin, next to Speedy's bottle.

And every few minutes he checked to make sure his sticks were still there.

He guessed he knew what dips were, after all.

### 3

Two stalls down from the booth of the rhyming rug-vendor, a depraved-looking man with a patch askew over one eye and the smell of strong drink about him was trying to sell a farmer a large rooster. He was telling the farmer that if he bought this rooster and put it in with his hens, the farmer would have nothing but double-yolkers for the next twelve-month.

Jack, however, had neither eyes for the rooster nor ears for the salesman's pitch. He joined a crowd of children who were staring at the one-eyed man's star attraction. This was a parrot in a large wicker cage. It was almost as tall as the youngest children in the group, and it was as smoothly, darkly green as a Heineken beer-bottle. Its eyes were a brilliant gold . . . its four eyes. Like the pony he had seen in the pavillion stables, the parrot had two heads. It gripped its perch with its big yellow feet and looked placidly in two directions at once, its two tufted crowns almost touching.

The parrot was talking to itself, to the amusement of the children—but even in his amazement Jack noted that, while they were paying close attention to the parrot, they seemed neither stunned nor even very wondering. They weren't like kids seeing their first movie, sitting stupefied in their seats and all eyes; they were more like kids getting their regular Saturday-morning cartoon-fix. This was a wonder, yes, but not a wholly new one. And to whom do wonders pall more rapidly than the very young?

"*Bawwwrk!* How high is up?" East-Head enquired.

"As low as low," West-Head responded, and the children giggled.

"*Graaak!* What's the great truth of noblemen?" East-Head now asked.

"That a king will be a king all his life, but once a knight's enough for any man!" West-Head replied pertly. Jack smiled and several of the older children laughed, but the younger ones only looked puzzled.

"And what's in Mrs. Spratt's cupboard?" East-Head now posed.

"A sight no man shall see!" West-Head rejoined, and although Jack was mystified, the children went into gales of laughter.

The parrot solemnly shifted its talons on its perch and made droppings into the straw below it.

"And what frightened Alan Destry to death in the night?"

"He saw his wife—*growwwwk!*—getting out of the bath!"

The farmer was now walking away and the one-eyed salesman still had charge of the rooster. He rounded furiously on the children. "Get out of here! Get out of here before I kick your asses square!"

The children scattered. Jack went with them, sparing a last bemused look over his shoulder at the wonderful parrot.

### 4

At another stall he gave up two knuckles of wood for an apple and a dipper of milk—the sweetest, richest milk he had ever tasted. Jack thought that if they had milk like that back at home, Nestlé's and Hershey's would go bankrupt in a week.

He was just finishing the milk when he saw the Henry family moving slowly in his direction. He handed the dipper back to the woman in the stall, who poured the lees thriftily back into the large wooden cask beside her. Jack hurried on, wiping a milk moustache from his upper lip and hoping uneasily that no one who had drunk from the dipper before him had had leprosy or herpes or anything like that. But he somehow didn't think such awful things even existed over here.

He walked up the market-town's main thoroughfare, past the mimers, past two fat women selling pots and pans (*Terri-*

*tories Tupperware*, Jack thought, and grinned), past that wonderful two-headed parrot (its one-eyed owner was now drinking quite openly from a clay bottle, reeling wildly from one end of his booth to the other, holding the dazed-looking rooster by the neck and yelling truculently at passersby—Jack saw the man's scrawny right arm was caked with yellowish-white guano, and grimaced), past an open area where farmers were gathered. He paused there for a moment, curious. Many of the farmers were smoking clay pipes, and Jack saw several clay bottles, much the same as the one the bird-salesman had been brandishing, go from hand to hand. In a long, grassy field, men were hitching stones behind large shaggy horses with lowered heads and mild, stupid eyes.

Jack passed the rug-stall. The vendor saw him and raised a hand. Jack raised one in turn and thought of calling *Use it, my man, but don't abuse it!* He decided he better not. He was suddenly aware that he felt blue. That feeling of strangeness, of being an outsider, had fallen over him again.

He reached the crossroads. The way going north and south was little more than a country lane. The Western Road was much wider.

*Old Travelling Jack*, he thought, and tried to smile. He straightened his shoulders and heard Speedy's bottle clink lightly against the mirror. *Here goes old Travelling Jack along the Territories version of Interstate 90*. Feets don't fail me now!

He set off again, and soon that great dreaming land swallowed him.

### 5

About four hours later, in the middle of the afternoon, Jack sat down in the tall grass by the side of the road and watched as a number of men—from this distance they looked little bigger than bugs—climbed a tall, rickety-looking tower. He had chosen this place to rest and eat his apple because it was here that the Western Road seemed to make its closest approach to that tower. It was still at least three miles away (and perhaps much more than that—the almost supernatural clarity of the air made distances extremely hard to judge), but it had been in Jack's view for an hour or more.

Jack ate his apple, rested his tired feet, and wondered what that tower could be, standing out there all by itself in a field of rolling grass. And, of course, he wondered why those men should be climbing it. The wind had blown quite steadily ever since he had left the market-town, and the tower was downwind of Jack, but whenever it died away for a minute, Jack could hear them calling to each other . . . and laughing. There was a lot of laughing going on.

Some five miles west of the market, Jack had walked through a village—if your definition of a village stretched to cover five tiny houses and one store that had obviously been closed for a long time. Those had been the last human habitations he had seen between then and now. Just before glimpsing the tower, he had been wondering if he had already come to the Outposts without even knowing it. He remembered well enough what Captain Farren had said: *Beyond the Outposts the Western Road goes into nowhere . . . or into hell. I've heard it said that God Himself never ventures beyond the Outposts. . . .*

Jack shivered a little.

But he didn't really believe he had come so far. Certainly there was none of the steadily deepening unease he had been feeling before he floundered into the living trees in his effort to get away from Morgan's diligence . . . the living trees which now seemed like a hideous prologue to all the time he had spent in Oatley.

Indeed, the good emotions he had felt from the time he woke up warm and rested inside the haystack until the time Henry the farmer had invited him to jump down from his wagon had now resurfaced: that feeling that the Territories, in spite of whatever evil they might harbor, were fundamentally good, and that he could be a part of this place anytime he wanted . . . that he was really no Stranger at all.

He had come to realize that he *was* part of the Territories for long periods of time. A strange thought had come to him as he swung easily along the Western Road, a thought which came half in English and half in whatever the Territories language was: *When I'm having a dream, the only time I really KNOW it's a dream is when I'm starting to wake up. If I'm dreaming and just wake up all at once—if the alarm clock goes off, or something—then I'm the most surprised guy alive. At first it's the waking that seems like a dream. And I'm no stranger over here when the dream gets deep—is that what I mean? No, but it's getting close. I bet my dad dreamed deep a lot. And I'll bet Uncle Morgan almost never does.*

He had decided he would take a swig out of Speedy's bottle and flip back the first time he saw anything that might be dangerous . . . even if he saw anything scary. Otherwise he would walk all day over here before returning to New York. In fact, he might have been tempted to spend the night in the Territories, if he'd had anything to eat beyond the one apple. But he didn't, and along the wide, deserted dirt track of the Western Road there was not a 7-Eleven or a Stop-'n-Go in sight.

The old trees which had surrounded the crossroads and the market-town had given way to open grassland on either side once Jack got past the final small settlement. He began to feel that he was walking along an endless causeway which crossed the middle of a limitless ocean. He travelled the Western Road alone that day under a sky that was bright and sunny but cool *(late September now, of course it's cool,* he thought, except the word which came to mind was not *September* but a Territories word which really did translate better as *ninemonth).* No pedestrians passed him, no wagons either loaded or empty. The wind blew pretty steadily, sighing through the ocean of grasses with a low sound that was both autumnal and lonely. Great ripples ran across the grasses before that wind.

If asked "How do you feel, Jack?," the boy would have responded: "Pretty good, thanks. Cheerful." *Cheerful* is the word which would have come into his mind as he hiked through those empty grasslands; *rapture* was a word he associated most easily with the pop hit of the same name by the rock group Blondie. And he would have been astounded if told he had wept several times as he stood watching those great ripples chase each other toward the horizon, drinking in a sight that only a very few American children of his time had ever seen—huge empty tracts of land under a blue sky of dizzying width and breadth and, yes, even depth. It was a sky unmarked by either jet contrails across its dome or smutty bands of smog at any of its lower edges.

Jack was having an experience of remarkable sensory impact, seeing and hearing and smelling things which were brand-new to him, while other sensory input to which he had grown utterly accustomed was missing for the first time. In many ways he was a remarkably sophisticated child—brought up in a Los Angeles family where his father had been an agent and his mother a movie actress, it would have been odder if he had been naive—but he was still just a child, sophisticated or not, and that was undeniably his gain . . . at least in a situation such as this. That lonely day's journey across the grasslands would surely have produced sensory overload, perhaps even a pervasive sense of madness and hallucination, in an adult. An adult would have been scrabbling for Speedy's bottle—probably with fingers too shaky to grasp it very successfully—an hour west of the market-town, maybe less.

In Jack's case, the wallop passed almost completely through his conscious mind and into his subconscious. So when he blissed out entirely and began to weep, he was really unaware of the tears (except as a momentary doubling of vision which he attributed to sweat) and thought only: *Jeez, I feel good . . . it should feel spooky out here with no one around, but it doesn't.*

That was how Jack came to think of his rapture as no more than a good, cheerful feeling as he walked alone up the Western Road with his shadow gradually growing longer behind him. It did not occur to him that part of his emotional radiance might stem from the fact that hardly less than twelve hours before he had been a prisoner of Updike's Oatley Tap (the blood-blisters from the last keg to land on his fingers were still fresh); that hardly less than twelve hours ago he had escaped— barely!—some sort of murdering beast that he had begun to think of as a were-goat; that for the first time in his life he was on a wide, open road that was utterly deserted except for him; there was not a Coca-Cola sign anywhere in view, or a Budweiser billboard showing the World-Famous Clydesdales; no ubiquitous wires ran beside the road on either side or crisscrossed above it, as had been the case *on every road Jack Sawyer had ever travelled in his entire life*; there was not so much as even the distant rolling sound of an airplane, let alone the rolling thunder of the 747s on their final approaches to LAX, or the F-111s that were always blasting off from the

Portsmouth Naval Air Station and then cracking the air over the Alhambra like Osmond's whip as they headed out over the Atlantic; there was only the sound of his feet on the road and the clean ebb and flow of his own respiration.

*Jeez, I feel good*, Jack thought, wiping absently at his eyes, and defined it all as "cheerful."

### 6

Now there was this tower to look at and wonder about.

*Boy, you'd never get me up on that thing*, Jack thought. He had gnawed the apple right down to the core, and without thinking about what he was doing or even taking his eyes off the tower, he dug a hole in the tough, springy earth with his fingers and buried the apple-core in it.

The tower seemed made of barn-boards, and Jack guessed it had to be at least five hundred feet high. It appeared to be a big hollow square, the boards rising on all sides in X after X. There was a platform on top, and Jack, squinting, could see a number of men strolling around up there.

Wind pushed by him in a gentle gust as he sat at the side of the road, his knees against his chest and his arms wrapped around them. Another of those grassy ripples ran away in the direction of the tower. Jack imagined the way that rickety thing must be swaying and felt his stomach turn over.

*NEVER get me up there*, he thought, *not for a million bucks*.

And then the thing he had been afraid might happen since the moment he had observed that there were men on the tower now *did* happen: one of them fell.

Jack came to his feet. His face wore the dismayed, slack-jawed expression of anyone who has ever been present at a circus performance where some dangerous trick has gone wrong—the tumbler who falls badly and lies in a huddled heap, the aerialist who misses her grip and bounces off the net with a thud, the human pyramid that unexpectedly collapses, spilling bodies into a heap.

*Oh shit, oh cripes, oh—*

Jack's eyes suddenly widened. For a moment his jaw sagged even farther—until it was almost lying on his breast-bone, in fact—and then it came up and his mouth spread in a dazed, unbelieving grin. The man hadn't fallen from the tower, nor had he been blown off it. There were tonguelike protrusions on two sides of the platform—they looked like diving boards—and the man had simply walked out to the end of one of these and jumped off. Halfway down something began to unfurl—a parachute, Jack thought, but it would never have time to open.

Only it hadn't been a parachute.

It was wings.

The man's fall slowed and then stopped completely while he was still some fifty feet above the high fieldgrass. Then it reversed itself. The man was now flying upward and outward, the wings going up so high they almost touched—like the crowns on the heads of that Henny Youngman parrot—and then driving downward again with immense power, like the arms of a swimmer in a finishing sprint.

*Oh wow,* Jack thought, driven back to the dumbest cliché he knew by his total, utter amazement. This topped everything; this was an utter pisser. *Oh wow, look at that, oh wow.*

Now a second man leaped from the diving board at the top of the tower; now a third; now a fourth. In less than five minutes there must have been fifty men in the air, flying complicated but discernible patterns: out from the tower, describe a figure-eight, back over the tower and out to the other side, another figure-eight, back to the tower, alight on the platform, do it all again.

They spun and danced and crisscrossed in the air. Jack began to laugh with delight. It was a little like watching the water ballets in those corny old Esther Williams movies. Those swimmers—Esther Williams herself most of all, of course—always made it look easy, as if you yourself could dip and swirl like that, or as if you and a few of your friends could easily come off the opposite sides of the diving board in timed choreography, making a kind of human fountain.

But there was a difference. The men flying out there did not give that sense of effortlessness; they seemed to be expending prodigious amounts of energy to stay in the air, and Jack felt with sudden certainty that it hurt, the way some of the calisthenics in phys ed—leg-lifts, or halfway sit-ups, for instance—hurt. *No pain, no gain!* Coach would roar if someone had the nerve to complain.

And now something else occurred to him—the time his mother had taken him with her to see her friend Myrna, who was a *real* ballet dancer, practicing in the loft of a dance studio on lower Wilshire Boulevard. Myrna was part of a ballet troupe and Jack had seen her and the other dancers perform— his mother often made him go with her and it was mostly boring stuff, like church or *Sunrise Semester* on TV. But he had never seen Myrna in practice . . . never that close up. He had been impressed and a little frightened by the contrast between seeing ballet on stage, where everyone seemed to either glide or mince effortlessly on the tips of their *pointes*, and seeing it from less than five feet away, with harsh daylight pouring in the floor-to-ceiling windows and no music—only the choreographer rhythmically clapping his hands and yelling harsh criticisms. No praise; only criticisms. Their faces ran with sweat. Their leotards were wet with sweat. The room, as large and airy as it was, stank of sweat. Sleek muscles trembled and fluttered on the nervous edge of exhaustion. Corded tendons stood out like insulated cables. Throbbing veins popped out on foreheads and necks. Except for the choreographer's clapping and angry, hectoring shouts, the only sounds were the *thrup-thud* of ballet dancers on *pointe* moving across the floor and harsh, agonized panting for breath. Jack had suddenly realized that these dancers were not just earning a living; they were killing themselves. Most of all he remembered their expressions—all that exhausted concentration, all that pain . . . but transcending the pain, or at least creeping around its edges, he had seen joy. Joy was unmistakably what that look was, and it had scared Jack because it had seemed inexplicable. What kind of person could get off by subjecting himself or herself to such steady, throbbing, excruciating pain?

And pain that he was seeing here, he thought. Were they actual winged men, like the bird-people in the old *Flash Gordon* serials, or were the wings more in the Icarus and Daedalus line, something that you strapped on? Jack found that it didn't really matter . . . at least, not to him.

*Joy.*
*They live in a mystery, these people live in a mystery.*
*It's joy that holds them up.*

That was what mattered. It was joy that held them up, no matter if the wings grew out of their backs or were somehow held on with buckles and clamps. Because what he saw, even from this distance, was the same sort of effort he had seen in the loft on lower Wilshire that day. All that profligate investment of energy to effect a splendid, momentary reversal of natural law. That such a reversal should demand so much and last such a short time was terrible; that people would go for it anyway was both terrible and wonderful.

*And it's all just a game*, he thought and suddenly felt sure of it. A game, or maybe not even that—maybe it was only *practice* for a game, the way that all the sweat and trembling exhaustion in the Wilshire loft that day had just been practice. Practice for a show that only a few people would probably care to attend and which would probably close quickly.

*Joy*, he thought again, standing now, his face turned up to look at the flying men in the distance, the wind spilling his hair across his forehead. His time of innocence was fast approaching its end (and, if pressed, even Jack would have reluctantly agreed that he felt such an end approaching—a boy couldn't go on the road for long, couldn't go through many experiences such as the one he had gone through in Oatley, and expect to remain an innocent), but in those moments as he stood looking into the sky, innocence seemed to surrounded him, like the young fisherman during his brief moment of epiphany in the Elizabeth Bishop poem, everything was rainbow, rainbow, rainbow.

*Joy—damn, but that's a cheerful little word.*

Feeling better than he had since all of this began—and only God knew just how long ago *that* had been—Jack set off along the Western Road again, his step light, his face wreathed in that same silly, splendid grin. Every now and then he looked back over his shoulder, and he was able to see the fliers for a very long time. The Territories air was so clear it almost seemed to magnify. And even after he could no longer see them, that feeling of joy remained, like a rainbow inside his head.

## 7

When the sun began to go down, Jack realized he was putting off his return to the other world—to the *American* Territories—and not just because of how terrible the magic juice tasted, either. He was putting it off because he didn't want to leave here.

A streamlet had flowed out of the grasslands (where small groves of trees had again begun to appear—billowy trees with oddly flat tops, like eucalyptus trees) and had hooked a right so that it flowed along beside the road. Farther off, to the right and ahead, was a huge body of water. It was *so* huge, in fact, that until the last hour or so Jack had thought it was a patch of sky that somehow had a slightly bluer color than the rest. But it wasn't sky; it was a lake. A *great lake*, he thought, smiling at the pun. He guessed that in the other world that would be Lake Ontario.

He felt good. He was headed in the right direction—maybe a little too far north, but he had no doubt that the Western Road would bend away from that direction soon enough. That feeling of almost manic joy—what he had defined as cheerfulness—had mellowed to a lovely sort of calm serenity, a feeling that seemed as clear as the Territories air. Only one thing marred his good feeling, and that was the memory

*(six, is six, Jack was six)*

of Jerry Bledsoe. Why had his mind given him such a hard time about coughing that memory up?

*No—not the memory . . . the two memories. First me and Richard hearing Mrs. Feeny telling her sister that the electricity came out and cooked him, that it melted his glasses all over his nose, that she heard Mr. Sloat talking on the phone and he said so . . . and then being behind the couch, not really meaning to snoop or eavesdrop, and hearing my dad say "Everything has consequences, and some of those consequences might be on the uncomfortable side." And something surely made Jerry Bledsoe uncomfortable, didn't it? When your glasses end up melted all over your nose, I'd say you'd been through something mildly uncomfortable, yes. . . .*

Jack stopped. Stopped dead.

*What are you trying to say?*

*You know what I'm trying to say, Jack. Your father was gone that day—he and Morgan both. They were over here. Where, over here? I think they were at the same spot over here where their building is in California, over in the American Territories. And they did something, or one of them did. Maybe something big, maybe no more than tossing a rock . . .*

*or burying an apple core in the dirt. And it somehow . . . it echoed over there. It echoed over there and it killed Jerry Bledsoe.*

Jack shivered. Oh yes, he supposed he knew why it had taken his mind so long to cough up the memory—the toy taxi, the murmur of the men's voices, Dexter Gordon blowing his horn. It hadn't wanted to cough it up. Because

*(who plays those changes daddy)*

it suggested that just by being over here he could be doing something terrible in the other world. Starting World War III? No, probably not. He hadn't assassinated any kings lately, young or old. But how much had it taken to set up the echo which had fried Jerry Bledsoe? Had Uncle Morgan shot Jerry's Twinner (if Jerry had had one)? Tried to sell some Territories bigwig on the concept of electricity? Or had it been just some little thing . . . something no more earth-shattering than buying a chunk of meat in a rural market-town? Who played those changes? *What* played those changes?

*A nice flood, a sweet fire.*

Suddenly Jack's mouth was as dry as salt.

He crossed to the little stream by the side of the road, dropped to his knees, and put a hand down to scoop up water. His hand froze suddenly. The smooth-running stream had taken on the colors of the coming sunset . . . but these colors suddenly suffused with red, so that it seemed to be a stream of blood rather than water running beside the road. Then it went black. A moment later it had become transparent and Jack saw—

A little mewling sound escaped him as he saw Morgan's diligence roaring along the Western Road, pulled by its foaming baker's dozen of black-plumed horses. Jack saw with almost swooning terror that the driver sitting up high in the peak-seat, his booted feet on the splashboard and a ceaselessly cracking whip in one hand, was Elroy. But it was not a hand at all that held that whip. It was some sort of hoof. Elroy was driving that nightmare coach, Elroy grinning with a mouth that was filled with dead fangs, Elroy who just couldn't wait to find Jack Sawyer again and split open Jack Sawyer's belly and pull out Jack Sawyer's intestines.

Jack knelt before the stream, eyes bulging, mouth quivering with dismay and horror. He had seen one final thing in this vision, not a large thing, no, but by implication it was the most frightful thing of all: the eyes of the horses seemed to glow. They seemed to glow because they were full of light—full of the sunset.

*The diligence was travelling west along this same road . . . and it was after him.*

Crawling, not sure he could stand even if he had to, Jack retreated from the stream and lurched clumsily out into the road. He fell flat in the dust, Speedy's bottle and the mirror the rug salesman had given him digging into his guts. He turned his head sideways so that his right cheek and ear were pressed tightly against the surface of the Western Road.

He could feel the steady rumble in the hard, dry earth. It was distant . . . but coming closer.

Elroy up on top . . . Morgan inside. Morgan Sloat? Morgan of Orris? Didn't matter. Both were one.

He broke the hypnotic effect of that rumbling in the earth with an effort and got up again. He took Speedy's bottle—the same over here in the Territories as in the U.S.A.—out of his jerkin and pulled as much of the moss-plug out of the neck as he could, never minding the shower of particles into the little bit of liquid remaining—no more than a couple of inches now. He looked nervously to his left, as if expecting to see the black diligence appear at the horizon, the sunset-filled eyes of the horses glowing like weird lanterns. Of course he saw nothing. Horizons were closer over here in the Territories, as he had already noticed, and sounds travelled farther. Morgan's diligence had to be ten miles to the east, maybe as much as twenty.

*Still right on top of me*, Jack thought, and raised the bottle to his lips. A bare second before he drank from it, his mind shouted, *Hey, wait a minute! Wait a minute, dummy, you want to get killed?* He would look cute, wouldn't he, standing in the middle of the Western Road and then flipping back into the other world in the middle of some road over there, maybe getting run down by a highballing semi or a UPS truck.

Jack shambled over to the side of the road . . . and then walked ten or twenty paces into the thigh-high grass for good measure. He took one final deep breath, inhaling the sweet smell of this place, groping for that feeling of serenity . . . that feeling of rainbow.

*Got to try and remember how that felt*, he thought. *I may need it . . . and I may not get back here for a long time.*

He looked out at the grasslands, darkening now as night stole over them from the east. The wind gusted, chilly now but still fragrant, tossing his hair—it was getting shaggy now—as it tossed the grass.

*You ready, Jack-O?*

Jack closed his eyes and steeled himself against the awful taste and the vomiting that was apt to follow.

"Banzai," he whispered, and drank.

# 14

# Buddy Parkins

## 1

He vomited up a thin purple drool, his face only inches from the grass covering the long slope down to a four-lane highway; shook his head and rocked backward onto his knees, so that only his back was exposed to the heavy gray sky. The world, this world, stank. Jack pushed himself backward, away from the threads of puke settling over the blades of grass, and the stench altered but did not diminish. Gasoline, other nameless poisons floated in the air; and the air itself stank of exhaustion, fatigue—even the noises roaring up from the highway punished this dying air. The back end of a roadsign reared like a gigantic television screen over his head. Jack wobbled to his feet. Far down the other side of the highway glinted an endless body of water only slightly less gray than the sky. A sort of malignant luminescence darted across the surface. From here, too, rose an odor of metal filings and tired breath. Lake Ontario: and the snug little city down there might be Olcott or Kendall. He'd gone miles out of his way— lost a hundred miles or more and just about four and a half days. Jack stepped under the sign, hoping it was no worse than that. He looked up at the black letters. Wiped his mouth. ANGOLA. Angola? Where was that? He peered down at the smoky little city through the already nearly tolerable air.

• • •

And Rand McNally, that invaluable companion, told him that the acres of water way down there were Lake Erie—instead of losing days of travel time, he had gained them.

But before the boy could decide that he'd be smarter after all if he jumped back into the Territories as soon as he thought it might be safe—which is to say, as soon as Morgan's diligence had roared long past the place he had been—before he could do that, before he could even begin to think about doing that, he had to go down into the smokey little city of Angola and see if this time Jack Sawyer, Jack-O, had played any of those changes, Daddy. He began to make his way down the slope, a twelve-year-old boy in jeans and a plaid shirt, tall for his age, already beginning to look uncared-for, with suddenly too much worry in his face.

Halfway down the long slope, he realized that he was thinking in English again.

## 2

Many days later, and a long way west: the man, Buddy Parkins by name, who, just out of Cambridge, Ohio, on U.S. 40, had picked up a tall boy calling himself Lewis Farren, would have recognized that look of worry—this kid Lewis looked like worry was about to sink into his face for good. *Lighten up, son, for your own sake if no one else's;* Buddy wanted to tell the boy. But the boy had troubles enough for ten, according to his story. Mother sick, father dead, sent off to some schoolteacher aunt in Buckeye Lake . . . Lewis Farren had plenty to trouble him. He looked as though he had not seen as much as five dollars all together since the previous Christmas. Still . . . Buddy thought that somewhere along the line this Farren kid was jiving him.

For one thing, he smelled like farm, not town. Buddy Parkins and his brothers ran three hundred acres not far from Amanda, about thirty miles southeast of Columbus, and Buddy knew that he could not be wrong about this. This boy smelled like Cambridge, and Cambridge was country. Buddy had grown up with the smell of farmland and barnyard, of manure and growing corn and pea vineries, and the unwashed clothes of this boy beside him had absorbed all these familiar odors.

And there were the clothes themselves. Mrs. Farren must have been awful sick, Buddy thought, if she sent her boy off down the road in ripped jeans so stiff with dirt the wrinkles seemed bronzed. And the shoes! Lewis Farren's sneakers were about to fall off his feet, the laces all spliced together and the fabric split or worn through in a couple of places on each shoe.

"So they got yore daddy's car, did they, Lewis?" Buddy asked.

"Just like I said, that's right—the lousy cowards came out after midnight and just stole it right out of the garage. I don't think they should be allowed to do that. Not from people who work hard and really are going to start making their payments as soon as they can. I mean, do you? You don't, do you?"

The boy's honest, sunburned face was turned toward him as if this were the most serious question since the Nixon Pardon or maybe the Bay of Pigs, and all Buddy's instincts were to agree—he would be inclined to agree with any generally good-hearted opinion uttered by a boy so redolent of farm work. "I guess there's two sides to everything when you come down to it," Buddy Parkins said, not very happily. The boy blinked, and then turned away to face forward again. Again Buddy felt his anxiety, the cloud of worry that seemed to hang over the boy, and was almost sorry he had not given Lewis Farren the agreement he seemed to need.

"I suppose yore aunt's in the grade school there in Buckeye Lake," Buddy said, at least in part hoping to lighten the boy's misery. Point to the future, not the past.

"Yes, sir, that's right. She teaches in the grade school. Helen Vaughan." His expression did not change.

But Buddy had heard it again—he didn't consider himself any Henry Higgins, the professor guy in that musical, but he knew for certain sure that young Lewis Farren didn't talk like anyone who had been raised in Ohio. The kid's voice was all wrong, too pushed-together and full of the wrong ups and downs. It wasn't an Ohio voice at all. It especially was not a rural Ohioan's voice. It was an *accent*.

Or was it possible that some boy from Cambridge, Ohio, could learn to talk like that? Whatever his crazy reason might be? Buddy supposed it was.

On the other hand, the newspaper this Lewis Farren had never once unclamped from beneath his left elbow seemed to validate Buddy Parkins's deepest and worst suspicion, that his fragrant young companion was a runaway and his every word a lie. The name of the paper, visible to Buddy with only the slightest tilt of his head, was *The Angola Herald*. There was that Angola in Africa that a lot of Englishmen had rushed off to as mercenaries, and there was Angola, New York—right up there on Lake Erie. He'd seen pictures of it on the news not long ago, but could not quite remember why.

"I'd like to ask you a question, Lewis," he said, and cleared his throat.

"Yes?" the boy said.

"How come a boy from a nice little burg on U.S. Forty is carrying around a paper from Angola, New York? Which is one hell of a long way away. I'm just curious, son."

The boy looked down at the paper flattened under his arm and hugged it even closer to him, as if he were afraid it might squirm away. "Oh," he said. "I found it."

"Oh, hell," Buddy said.

"Yes, sir. It was on a bench at the bus station back home."

"You went to the bus station this morning?"

"Right before I decided to save the money and hitch. Mr. Parkins, if you can get me to the turnoff at Zanesville, I'll only have a short ride left. Could probably get to my aunt's house before dinner."

"Could be," Buddy said, and drove in an uncomfortable silence for several miles. Finally he could bear it no longer, and he said, very quietly and while looking straight ahead, "Son, are you running away from home?"

Lewis Farren astonished him by smiling—not grinning and not faking it, but actually smiling. He thought the whole notion of running away from home was funny. It tickled him. The boy glanced at him a fraction of a second after Buddy had looked sideways, and their eyes met.

For a second, for two seconds, three . . . for however long that moment lasted, Buddy Parkins saw that this unwashed boy sitting beside him was beautiful. He would have thought himself incapable of using that word to describe any male human being above the age of nine months, but underneath the road-grime this Lewis Farren was beautiful. His sense of humor had momentarily murdered his worries, and what shone out of him at Buddy—who was fifty-two years old and had three teenage sons—was a kind of straightforward goodness that had only been dented by a host of unusual experiences. This Lewis Farren, twelve years old by his own account, had somehow gone farther and seen more than Buddy Parkins, and what he had seen and done had made him beautiful.

"No, I'm not a runaway, Mr. Parkins," the boy said.

Then he blinked, and his eyes went inward again and lost their brightness, their light, and the boy slumped back again against his seat. He pulled up a knee, rested it on the dashboard, and snugged the newspaper up under his bicep.

"No, I guess not," Buddy Parkins said, snapping his eyes back to the highway. He felt relieved, though he was not quite sure why. "I guess yore not a runaway, Lewis. Yore something, though."

The boy did not respond.

"Been workin on a farm, haven't you?"

Lewis looked up at him, surprised. "I did, yeah. The past three days. Two dollars an hour."

*And yore mommy didn't even take the time out from bein sick to wash yore clothes before she sent you to her sister, is that right?* Buddy thought. But what he said was "Lewis, I'd like you to think about coming home with me. I'm not saying yore on the run or anything, but if yore from anywhere around Cambridge I'll eat this beat-up old car, tires and all, and I got three boys myself and the youngest one, Billy, he's only about three years older'n you, and we know how to feed *boys* around my house. You can stay about as long as you like, depending on how many questions you want to answer. 'Cuz I'll be asking em, at least after the first time we break bread together."

He rubbed one palm over his gray crewcut and glanced across the seat. Lewis Farren was looking more like a boy and less like a revelation. "You'll be welcome, son."

Smiling, the boy said, "That's really nice of you, Mr. Parkins, but I can't. I have to go see my, ah, aunt in . . ."

"Buckeye Lake," Buddy supplied.

The boy swallowed and looked forward again.

"I'll give you help, if you want help," Buddy repeated.

Lewis patted his forearm, sunburned and thick. "This ride is a big help, honest."

Ten nearly silent minutes later he was watching the boy's forlorn figure trudge down the exit ramp outside Zanesville.

Emmie would probably have brained him if he'd come home with a strange dirty boy to feed, but once she'd seen him and talked to him, Emmie would have brought out the good glasses and the plates her mother had given her. Buddy Parkins didn't believe that there was any woman named Helen Vaughan in Buckeye Lake, and he wasn't so sure this mysterious Lewis Farren even had a mother—the boy seemed such an orphan, off on a vast errand. Buddy watched until the boy was taken by the curve of the off-ramp, and he was staring out at space and the enormous yellow-and-purple sign of a shopping mall.

For a second he thought of jumping out of the car and running after the kid, trying to get him back . . . and then he had a moment of recall of a crowded, smokey scene on the six-o'clock news. Angola, New York. Some disaster too small to be reported more than once, that was what had happened in Angola; one of those little tragedies the world shovels under a mountain of newsprint. All Buddy could catch, in this short, probably flawed moment of memory, was a picture of girders strewn like giant straws over battered cars, jutting up out of a fuming hole in the ground—a hole that might lead down into hell. Buddy Parkins looked once more at the empty place on the road where the boy had been, and then stamped on his clutch and dropped the old car into low.

## 3

Buddy Parkins's memory was more accurate than he imagined. If he could have seen the first page of the month-old *Angola Herald* "Lewis Farren," that enigmatic boy, had been holding so protectively yet fearfully beneath his arm, these are the words he would have read:

### FREAK EARTHQUAKE KILLS 5
by Herald staff reporter Joseph Gargan

Work on the Rainbird Towers, intended to be Angola's tallest and most luxurious condominium development and still six months from completion, was tragically halted yesterday as an unprecedented earth tremor collapsed the structure of the building, burying many construction workers beneath the rubble. Five bodies have been retrieved from the ruins of the proposed condominium, and two other workers have not yet been found but are presumed dead. All seven workers were welders and fitters in the employ of Speiser Construction, and all were on the girders of the building's top two floors at the time of the incident.

Yesterday's tremor was the first earthquake in Angola's recorded history. Armin Van Pelt of New York University's Geology Department, contacted today by telephone, described the fatal quake as a "seismic bubble." Representatives of the State Safety Commission are continuing their examinations of the site, as is a team of . . .

The dead men were Robert Heidel, twenty-three; Thomas Thielke, thirty-four; Jerome Wild, forty-eight; Michael Hagen, twenty-nine; and Bruce Davey, thirty-nine. The two men still missing were Arnold Schulkamp, fifty-four, and Theodore Rasmussen, forty-three. Jack no longer had to look at the newspaper's front page to remember their names. The first earthquake in the history of Angola, New York, had occurred on the day he had flipped away from the Western Road and landed on the town's border. Part of Jack Sawyer wished that he could have gone home with big kindly Buddy Parkins, eaten dinner around the table in the kitchen with the Parkins family—boiled beef and deep-dish apple pie—and then snuggled into the Parkinses' guest bed and pulled the homemade quilt up over his head. And not moved, except toward the table, for four or five days. But part of the trouble was that he saw that knotty-pine kitchen table heaped with crumbly cheese, and on the other side of the table a mouse-hole was cut into a giant baseboard; and from holes in the jeans of the three Parkins boys protruded thin long tails. Who plays these Jerry Bledsoe changes, Daddy? *Heidel, Thielke, Wild, Hagen, Davey; Schulkamp and Rasmussen*. Those Jerry changes? He knew who played them.

## 4

The huge yellow-and-purple sign reading BUCKEYE MALL floated ahead of Jack as he came around the final curve of the off-ramp, drifted past his shoulder and reappeared on his other side, at which point he could finally see that it was erected on a tripod of tall yellow poles in the shopping-center parking lot. The mall itself was a futuristic assemblage of ochre-colored buildings that seemed to be windowless—a second later, Jack realized that the mall was covered, and what he was seeing was only the illusion of separate buildings. He put his hand in his pocket and fingered the tight roll of twenty-three single dollar bills which was his earthly fortune.

In the cool sunlight of an early autumn afternoon, Jack sprinted across the street toward the mall's parking lot.

If it had not been for his conversation with Buddy Parkins, Jack would very likely have stayed on U.S. 40 and tried to cover another fifty miles—he wanted to get to Illinois, where Richard Sloat was, in the next two or three days. The thought of seeing his friend Richard again had kept him going during the weary days of nonstop work on Elbert Palamountain's farm: the image of spectacled, serious-faced Richard Sloat in his room at Thayer School, in Springfield, Illinois, had fueled him as much as Mrs. Palamountain's generous meals. Jack still wanted to see Richard, and as soon as he could: but Buddy Parkins's inviting him home had somehow unstrung him. He could not just climb into another car and begin all over again on the Story. (In any case, Jack reminded himself, the Story seemed to be losing its potency.) The shopping mall gave him a perfect chance to drop out for an hour or two, especially if there was a movie theater somewhere in there—right now, Jack could have watched the dullest, soppiest *Love Story* of a movie.

And before the movie, were he lucky enough to find a theater, he would be able to take care of two things he had been putting off for at least a week. Jack had seen Buddy Parkins looking at his disintegrating Nikes. Not only were the running shoes falling apart, the soles, once spongy and elastic, had mysteriously become hard as asphalt. On days when he had to walk great distances—or when he had to work standing up all day—his feet stung as if they'd been burned.

The second task, calling his mother, was so loaded with guilt and other fearful emotions that Jack could not quite allow it to become conscious. He did not know if he could keep from weeping, once he'd heard his mother's voice. What if she sounded weak—what if she sounded really sick? Could he really keep going west if Lily hoarsely begged him to come back to New Hampshire? So he could not admit to himself that he was probably going to call his mother. His mind gave him the suddenly very clear image of a bank of pay telephones beneath their hairdryer plastic bubbles, and almost immediately bucked away from it—as if Elroy or some other Territories creature could reach right out of the receiver and clamp a hand around his throat.

Just then three girls a year or two older than Jack bounced out of the back of a Subaru Brat which had swung recklessly into a parking spot near the mall's main entrance. For a second they had the look of models contorted into awkwardly elegant poses of delight and astonishment. When they had adjusted into more conventional postures the girls glanced incuriously at Jack and began to flip their hair expertly back into place. They were leggy in their tight jeans, these confident little princesses of the tenth grade, and when they laughed they put their hands over their mouths in a fashion which suggested that laughter itself was laughable. Jack slowed his walk into a kind of sleepwalker's stroll. One of the princesses glanced at him and muttered something to the brown-haired girl beside her.

*I'm different now*, Jack thought: *I'm not like them anymore*. The recognition pierced him with loneliness.

A thickset blond boy in a blue sleeveless down vest climbed out of the driver's seat and gathered the girls around him by the simple expedient of pretending to ignore them. The boy, who must have been a senior and at the very least in the varsity backfield, glanced once at Jack and then looked appraisingly at the facade of the mall. "Timmy?" said the tall brown-haired girl. "Yeah, yeah," the boy said. "I was just wondering what smells like shit out here." He rewarded the girls with a superior little smile. The brown-haired girl looked smirkingly toward Jack, then swung herself across the asphalt with her friends. The three girls followed Timmy's arrogant body through the glass doors into the mall.

Jack waited until the figures of Timmy and his court, visible through the glass, had shrunk to the size of puppies far down the long mall before he stepped on the plate which opened the doors.

Cold predigested air embraced him.

Water trickled down over a fountain two stories high set in a wide pool surrounded by benches. Open-fronted shops on both levels faced the fountain. Bland Muzak drifted down from the ochre ceiling, as did the peculiar bronzy light; the smell of popcorn, which had struck Jack the moment the glass doors had whooshed shut behind him, emanated from an antique popcorn wagon, painted fire-engine red and stationed outside a Waldenbooks to the left of the fountain on the ground level. Jack had seen immediately that there was no movie theater in the Buckeye Mall. Timmy and his leggy princesses were floating up the escalator at the mall's other end, making, Jack thought, for a fast-food restaurant called The Captain's Table right at the top of the escalator. Jack put his hand in his pants pocket again and touched his roll of bills. Speedy's guitar-pick and Captain Farren's coin nested at the bottom of the pocket, along with a handful of dimes and quarters.

On Jack's level, sandwiched between a Mr. Chips cookie shop and a liquor store advertising NEW LOW PRICES for Hiram Walker bourbon and Inglenook Chablis, a Fayva shoe store drew him toward its long table of running shoes. The clerk at the cash register leaned forward and watched Jack pick over the shoes, clearly suspicious that he might try to steal something. Jack recognized none of the brands on the table. There were no Nikes or Pumas here—they were called Speedster or Bullseye or Zooms, and the laces of each pair were tied together. These were sneakers, not true running shoes. They were good enough, Jack supposed.

He bought the cheapest pair the store had in his size, blue canvas with red zigzag stripes down the sides. No brand name was visible anywhere on the shoes. They seemed indistinguishable from most of the other shoes on the table. At the register he counted out six limp one-dollar bills and told the clerk that he did not need a bag.

Jack sat on one of the benches before the tall fountain and toed off the battered Nikes without bothering to unlace them.

When he slipped on the new sneakers, his feet fairly sighed with gratitude. Jack left the bench and dropped his old shoes in a tall black wastebasket with DON'T BE A LITTERBUG stencilled on it in white. Beneath that, in smaller letters, the wastebasket read *The earth is our only home.*

Jack began to move aimlessly through the long lower arcade of the mall, searching for the telephones. At the popcorn wagon he parted with fifty cents and was handed a quart-size tub of fresh popcorn glistening with grease. The middle-aged man in a bowler hat, a walrus moustache, and sleeve garters who sold him the popcorn told him that the pay phones were around a corner next to 31 Flavors, upstairs. The man gestured vaguely toward the nearest escalator.

Scooping the popcorn into his mouth, Jack rode up behind a woman in her twenties and an older woman with hips so wide they nearly covered the entire width of the escalator, both of them in pants suits.

If Jack were to flip inside the Buckeye Mall—or even a mile or two from it—would the walls shake and the ceiling crumble down, dropping bricks and beams and Muzak speakers and light fixtures down on everybody unlucky enough to be inside? And would the tenth-grade princesses, and even arrogant Timmy, and most of the others, too, wind up with skull fractures and severed limbs and mangled chests and . . . for a second just before he reached the top of the escalator Jack saw giant chunks of plaster and metal girders showering down, heard the terrible cracking of the mezzanine floor, the screams, too—inaudible, they were still printed in the air.

Angola. The Rainbird Towers.

Jack felt his palms begin to itch and sweat, and he wiped them on his jeans.

THIRTY-ONE FLAVORS, gleamed out a chilly incandescent white light to his left, and when he turned that way he saw a curving hallway on its other side. Shiny brown tiles on the walls and floor; as soon as the curve of the hallway took him out of sight of anyone on the mezzanine level, Jack saw three telephones, which were indeed under transparent plastic bubbles. Across the hall from the telephones were doors to MEN and LADIES.

Beneath the middle bubble, Jack dialed 0, followed by the area code and the number for the Alhambra Inn and Gardens.

"Billing?" asked the operator, and Jack said, "This is a collect call for Mrs. Sawyer in four-oh-seven and four-oh-eight. From Jack."

The hotel operator answered, and Jack's chest tightened. She transferred the call to the suite. The telephone rang once, twice, three times.

Then his mother said "Jesus, kid, I'm glad to hear from you! This absentee-mother business is hard on an old girl like me. I kind of miss you when you're not moping around and telling me how to act with waiters."

"You're just too classy for most waiters, that's all," Jack said, and thought that he might begin to cry with relief.

"Are you all right, Jack? Tell me the truth."

"I'm fine, sure," he said. "Yeah, I'm fine. I just had to make sure that you . . . you know."

The phone whispered electronically, a skirl of static that sounded like sand blowing across a beach.

"I'm okay," Lily said. "I'm great. I'm not any worse, anyhow, if that's what you're worried about. I suppose I'd like to know where you are."

Jack paused, and the static whispered and hissed for a moment. "I'm in Ohio now. Pretty soon I'm going to be able to see Richard."

"When are you coming home, Jack-O?"

"I can't say. I wish I could."

"You can't say. I swear, kid, if your father hadn't called you that silly name—and if you'd asked me about this ten minutes earlier or ten minutes later . . ."

A rising tide of static took her voice, and Jack remembered how she'd looked in the tea shop, haggard and feeble, an old woman. When the static receded he asked, "Are you having any trouble with Uncle Morgan? Is he bothering you?"

"I sent your Uncle Morgan away from here with a flea in his ear," she said.

"He was there? He did come? Is he still bothering you?"

"I got rid of the Stoat about two days after you left, baby. Don't waste time worrying about him."

"Did he say where he was going?" Jack asked her, but as soon as the words were out of his mouth the telephone uttered a tortured electronic squeal that seemed to bore right into his head. Jack grimaced and jerked the receiver away from his ear. The awful whining noise of static was so loud that anyone stepping into the corridor would have heard it. "MOM!" Jack shouted, putting the phone as close to his head as he dared. The squeal of static increased, as if a radio between stations had been turned up to full volume.

The line abruptly fell silent. Jack clamped the receiver to his ear and heard only the flat black silence of dead air. "Hey," he said, and jiggled the hook. The flat silence in the phone seemed to press up against his ear.

Just as abruptly, and as if his jiggling the hook had caused it, the dial tone—an oasis of sanity, of regularity, now—resumed. Jack jammed his right hand in his pocket, looking for another coin.

He was holding the receiver, awkwardly, in his left hand as he dug in his pocket; he froze when he heard the dial tone suddenly slot off into outer space.

Morgan Sloat's voice spoke to him as clearly as if good old Uncle Morgan were standing at the next telephone. "Get your ass back home, Jack." Sloat's voice carved the air like a scalpel. "You just get your ass back home before we have to take you back ourselves."

"Wait," Jack said, as if he were begging for time: in fact, he was too terrified to know quite what he was saying.

"Can't wait any longer, little pal. You're a murderer now. That's right, isn't it? You're a murderer. So we're not able to give you any more chances. You just get your can back to that resort in New Hampshire. Now. Or maybe you'll go home in a bag."

Jack heard the click of the receiver. He dropped it. The telephone Jack had used shuddered forward, then sagged off the wall. For a second it drooped on a network of wires; then crashed heavily to the floor.

The door to the men's room banged open behind Jack, and a voice yelled, "Holy SHIT!"

Jack turned to see a thin crewcut boy of about twenty staring at the telephones. He was wearing a white apron and a bow tie: a clerk at one of the shops.

"I didn't do it," Jack said. "It just happened."

"Holy shit." The crewcut clerk goggled at Jack for a split-second, jerked as if to run, and then ran his hands over the crown of his head.

Jack backed away down the hall. When he was halfway down the escalator he finally heard the clerk yelling, "Mr. Olafson! The phone, Mr. Olafson!" Jack fled.

Outside, the air was bright, surprisingly humid. Dazed, Jack wandered across the sidewalk. A half-mile away across the parking lot, a black-and-white police car swung in toward the mall. Jack turned sideways and began to walk down the pavement. Some way ahead, a family of six struggled to get a lawn chair in through the next entrance to the mall. Jack slowed down and watched the husband and wife tilt the long chair diagonally, hindered by the attempts of the smaller children to either sit on the chair or to assist them. At last, nearly in the posture of the flag-raisers in the famous photograph of Iwo Jima, the family staggered through the door. The police car lazily circled through the big parking lot.

Just past the door where the disorderly family had succeeded in planting their chair, an old black man sat on a wooden crate, cradling a guitar in his lap. As Jack slowly drew nearer, he saw the metal cup beside the man's feet. The man's face was hidden behind big dirty sunglasses and beneath the brim of a stained felt hat. The sleeves of his denim jacket were as wrinkled as an elephant's hide.

Jack swerved out to the edge of the pavement to give the man all the room he seemed to warrant, and noticed that around the man's neck hung a sign handwritten in big shaky capital letters on discolored white cardboard. A few steps later he could read the letters.

BLIND SINCE BIRTH
WILL PLAY ANY SONG
GOD BLESS YOU

He had nearly walked past the man holding the beat-up old guitar when he heard him utter, his voice a cracked and juicy whisper, "Yeah-bob."

# 15

# Snowball Sings

### 1

Jack swung back toward the black man, his heart hammering in his chest.

*Speedy?*

The black man groped for his cup, held it up, shook it. A few coins rattled in the bottom.

It *is* Speedy. Behind those dark glasses, it *is* Speedy.

Jack was sure of it. But a moment later he was just as sure that it *wasn't* Speedy. Speedy wasn't built square in the shoulders and broad across the chest; Speedy's shoulders were rounded, a little slumped over, and his chest consequently had a slightly caved-in look. Mississippi John Hurt, not Ray Charles.

*But I could tell one way or the other for sure if he'd take off those shades.*

He opened his mouth to speak Speedy's name aloud, and suddenly the old man began to play, his wrinkled fingers, as dully dark as old walnut that has been faithfully oiled but never polished, moving with limber speed and grace on both strings and frets. He played well, finger-picking the melody. And after a moment, Jack recognized the tune. It had been on one of his father's older records. A Vanguard album called *Mississippi John Hurt Today*. And although the blind man didn't sing, Jack knew the words:

> *O kindly friends, tell me, ain't it hard?*
> *To see ole Lewis in a new graveyard,*
> *The angels laid him away. . . .*

The blond football player and his three princesses came out of the mall's main doors. Each of the princesses had an ice

cream cone. Mr. All-America had a chili-dog in each hand.
They sauntered toward where Jack stood. Jack, whose whole
attention was taken up by the old black man, had not even noticed them. He had been transfixed by the idea that it was
Speedy, and Speedy had somehow read his mind. How else
could it be that this man had begun to play a Mississippi John
Hurt composition just as Jack happened to think Speedy
looked like that very man? And a song containing his own
road-name, as well?

The blond football player transferred both chili-dogs to his
left hand and slapped Jack on the back with his right as hard
as he could. Jack's teeth snapped on his own tongue like a
bear-trap. The pain was sudden and excruciating.

"You just shake her easy, urine-breath," he said. The
princesses giggled and shrieked.

Jack stumbled forward and kicked over the blind man's
cup. Coins spilled and rolled. The gentle lilt of the blues tune
came to a jangling halt.

Mr. All-America and the Three Little Princesses were already moving on. Jack stared after them and felt the now-
familiar impotent hate. This was how it felt to be on your
own, just young enough to be at everyone's mercy and to be
anyone's meat—anyone from a psychotic like Osmond to a
humorless old Lutheran like Elbert Palamountain, whose idea
of a pretty fair work-day was to slog and squelch through
gluey fields for twelve hours during a steady cold downpour
of October rain, and to sit bolt-upright in the cab of his International Harvester truck during lunch hour, eating onion
sandwiches and reading from the Book of Job.

Jack had no urge to "get" them, although he had a strange
idea that if he wanted to, he could—that he was gaining some
sort of power, almost like an electrical charge. It sometimes
seemed to him that other people knew that, too—that it was in
their faces when they looked at him. But he didn't *want* to get
them; he only wanted to be left alone. He—

The blind man was feeling around himself for the spilled
money, his pudgy hands moving gently over the pavement, almost seeming to read it. He happened on a dime, set his cup
back up again, and dropped the dime in. *Plink!*

Faintly, Jack heard one of the princesses: "Why do they let
him stay there, he's so *gross*, you know?"

Even more faintly still: "Yeah, *rilly!*"

Jack got down on his knees and began to help, picking up coins and putting them into the blind man's cup. Down here, close to the old man, he could smell sour sweat, mildew, and some sweet bland smell like corn. Smartly dressed mall shoppers gave them a wide berth.

"Thankya, thankya," the blind man croaked monotonously. Jack could smell dead chili on his breath. "Thankya, blessya, God blessya, thankya."

He *is* Speedy.

He's *not* Speedy.

What finally forced him to speak—and this was not really so odd—was remembering just how little of the magic juice he had left. Barely two swallows now. He did not know if, after what had happened in Angola, he could ever bring himself to travel in the Territories again, but he was still determined to save his mother's life, and that meant he might have to.

And, whatever the Talisman was, he might have to flip into the other world to get it.

"Speedy?"

"Blessya, thankya, God blessya, didn't I hear one go over there?" He pointed.

*"Speedy!* It's Jack!"

"Ain't nothin speedy round here, boy, No *sir*." His hands began to whisper-walk along the concrete in the direction he had just pointed. One of them found a nickel and he dropped it into the cup. His other happened to touch the shoe of a smartly dressed young woman who was passing by. Her pretty, empty face wrinkled in almost painful disgust as she drew away from him.

Jack picked the last coin out of the gutter. It was a silver dollar—a big old cartwheel with Lady Liberty on one side.

Tears began to spill out of his eyes. They ran down his dirty face and he wiped them away with an arm that shook. He was crying for Thielke, Wild, Hagen, Davey, and Heidel. For his mother. For Laura DeLoessian. For the carter's son lying dead in the road with his pockets turned out. But most of all for himself. He was tired of being on the road. Maybe when you rode it in a Cadillac it was a road of dreams, but when you had to hitch it, riding on your thumb and a story that was just about worn out, when you were at everybody's mercy and anyone's meat, it was nothing but a road of trials. Jack felt that he had been tried enough . . . but there was no way to cry it off. If he cried it off, the cancer would take his mother, and Uncle Morgan might well take *him*.

"I don't think I can do it, Speedy," he wept. "I don't think so, man."

Now the blind man groped for Jack instead of the spilled coins. Those gentle, reading fingers found his arm and closed around it. Jack could feel the hard pad of callus in the tip of each finger. He drew Jack to him, into those odors of sweat and heat and old chili. Jack pressed his face against Speedy's chest.

"Hoo, boy. I don't know no Speedy, but it sounds like you puttin an awful lot on him. You—"

"I miss my mom, Speedy," Jack wept, "and Sloat's after me. It was him on the phone inside the mall, *him*. And that's not the worst thing. The worst thing was in Angola . . . the Rainbird Towers . . . earthquake . . . five men . . . *me, I did it, Speedy, I killed those men when I flipped into this world, I killed them just like my dad and Morgan Sloat killed Jerry Bledsoe that time!*"

Now it was out, the worst of it. He had sicked up the stone of guilt that had been in his throat, threatening to choke him, and a storm of weeping seized him—but this time it was relief rather than fear. It was said. It had been confessed. He was a murderer.

"Hooo-*eeee!*" the black man cried. He sounded perversely delighted. He held Jack with one thin, strong arm, rocked him. "You tryin to carry you one heavy load, boy. You sure am. Maybe you ought to put some of it down."

"I killed em," Jack whispered. "Thielke, Wild, Hagen, Davey . . ."

"Well, if yo friend Speedy was here," the black man said, "*whoever* he might be, or *wherever* he might be in this wide old world, he might tell you that you cain't carry the world on yo shoulders, son. You cain't do that. No one can. Try to carry the world on yo shoulders, why, first it's gonna break yo *back*, and then it's gonna break you *sperrit*."

"I killed—"

"Put a gun to their heads and shot somebodies, didya?"

"No . . . the earthquake . . . I flipped. . . ."

"Don't know nothin bout *dat*," the black man said. Jack had pulled away from him a bit and was staring up into the black man's seamed face with wondering curiosity, but the black man had turned his head toward the parking lot. If he *was* blind, then he had picked out the smoother, slightly more powerful beat of the police car's engine from the others as it approached, because he was looking right at it. "All I know is you seem to have this idear of 'moider' a little broad. Prolly if some fella dropped dead of a heart-attack goin around us as we sit here, you'd think you killed him. 'Oh look, I done moidered that fella on account of where I was sittin, oh woe, oh *dooom*, oh *gloooooom*, oh *this* . . . oh *that!*' " As he spoke *this* and *that*, the blind man punctuated it with a quick change from G to C and back to G again. He laughed, pleased with himself.

"Speedy—"

"Nothin speedy round here," the black man reiterated, and then showed yellow teeth in a crooked grin. " 'Cept maybe how speedy some folks are to put the blame on themselves for things others might have got started. Maybe you runnin, boy, and maybe you bein *chased*."

G-chord.

"Maybe you be just a little off-*base*."

C-chord, with a nifty little run in the middle that made Jack grin in spite of himself.

"Might be somebody else gettin on yo *case*."

Back down to G again, and the blind man laid his guitar aside (while, in the police car, the two cops were flipping to see which of them would actually have to touch Old Snowball if he wouldn't get into the back of the cruiser peaceably).

"Maybe dooom and maybe gloooooom and maybe *this* and maybe *that* . . ." He laughed again, as if Jack's fears were the funniest thing he'd ever heard.

"But I don't know what could happen if I—"

"No one ever knows what could happen if they do anything, do dey?" the black man who might or might not be Speedy Parker broke in. "No. Dey do *not*. If you thought about it, you'd stay in yo house all day, ascairt to come out! I don't know yo problems, boy. Don't want to know em. Could be crazy, talkin bout earthquakes and all. But bein as how you helped me pick up my money and didn't steal none—I counted every *plinkety-plink*, so I know—I'll give you some advice. Some things you cain't help. Sometimes people get killed because somebody does somethin . . . but if somebody *didn't* do that somethin, a whole lot of more people would have got killed. Do you see where I'm pushin, son?"

The dirty sunglasses inclined down toward him.

Jack felt a deep, shuddery relief. He saw, all right. The blind man was talking about hard choices. He was suggesting that maybe there was a difference between hard choices and criminal behavior. And that maybe the criminal wasn't here.

The criminal might have been the guy who had told him five minutes ago to get his ass home.

"Could even be," the blind man remarked, hitting a dark D-minor chord on his box, "that all things soive the Lord, just like my momma tole me and your momma might have tole you, if she was a Christian lady. Could be we think we doin one thing but are really doin another. Good Book says all things, even those that seem evil, soive the Lord. What you think, boy?"

"I don't know," Jack said honestly. He was all mixed up. He only had to close his eyes and he could see the telephone tearing off the wall, hanging from its wires like a weird puppet.

"Well, it *smells* like you lettin it drive you to drink."

"What?" Jack asked, astonished. Then he thought, *I thought that Speedy looked like Mississippi John Hurt, and this guy started playing a John Hurt blues . . . and now he's talking about the magic juice. He's being careful, but I swear that's what he's talking about—it's got to be!*

"You're a mind-reader," Jack said in a low voice. "Aren't you? Did you learn it in the Territories, Speedy?"

"Don't know nothin bout readin minds," the blind man said, "but my lamps have been out forty-two year come November, and in forty-two year your nose and ears take up some of the slack. I can smell cheap wine on you, son. Smell it *all over you*. It's almost like you washed yo hair widdit!"

Jack felt an odd, dreamy guilt—it was the way he always felt when accused of doing something wrong when he was in fact innocent—mostly innocent, anyway. He had done no more than touch the almost-empty bottle since flipping back into this world. Just touching it filled him with dread—he had come to feel about it the way a fourteenth-century European peasant might have felt about a splinter of the One True Cross or the fingerbone of a saint. It was magic, all right. *Powerful* magic. And sometimes it got people killed.

"I haven't been drinking it, honest," he finally managed. "What I started with is almost gone. It . . . I . . . man, I don't even *like* it!" His stomach had begun to clench nervously; just thinking about the magic juice was making him feel nauseated. "But I need to get some more. Just in case."

"More Poiple Jesus? Boy your age?" The blind man laughed and made a shooing gesture with one hand. "Hell, you don't need *dat.* No boy needs *dat* poison to travel with."

"But—"

"Here. I'll sing you a song to cheer you up. Sounds like you could use it."

He began to sing, and his singing voice was nothing at all like his speaking voice. It was deep and powerful and thrilling, without the Nigger Jim "My-Huck-dat-sure-is-*gay!*" cadences of his talk. It was, Jack thought, awed, almost the trained, cultured voice of an opera singer, now amusing itself with a little piece of popular fluff. Jack felt goosebumps rise on his arms and back at that rich, full voice. Along the sidewalk which ran along the dull, ochre flank of the mall, heads turned.

*"When the red, red robin goes bob-bob-bobbin along, ALONG, there'll be no more sobbin when he starts throbbin his old . . . sweet SONG—"*

Jack was struck by a sweet and terrible familiarity, a sense that he had heard this before, or something very like it, and as the blind man bridged, grinning his crooked, yellowing smile, Jack realized where the feeling was coming from. He knew what had made all those heads turn, as they would have turned if a unicorn had gone galloping across the mall's parking lot. There was a beautiful, alien clarity in the man's voice. It was the clarity of, say, air so pure that you could smell a radish when a man pulled one out of the ground half a mile away. It was a good old Tin Pan Alley song . . . but the voice was pure Territories.

*"Get up . . . get up, you sleepyhead . . . get out . . . get out, get outta bed . . . live, love, laugh and be ha—"*

Both guitar and voice came to a sudden halt. Jack, who

had been concentrating fiercely on the blind man's face (trying subconsciously to peer right through those dark glasses, perhaps, and see if Speedy Parker's eyes were behind them), now widened his focus and saw two cops standing beside the blind man.

"You know, I don't *hear* nothin," the blind guitarist said, almost coyly, "but I b'lieve I *smell* somethin blue."

"Goddammit, Snowball, you know you're not supposed to work the mall!" one of the cops cried. "What did Judge Hallas tell you the last time he had you in chambers? Downtown between Center Street and Mural Street. No place else. Damn, boy, how senile have you got? Your pecker rotted off yet from that whatall your woman gave you before she took off? Christ, I just don't—"

His partner put a hand on his arm and nodded toward Jack in a little-pitchers-have-big-ears gesture.

"Go tell your mother she wants you, kid," the first cop said curtly.

Jack started walking down the sidewalk. He couldn't stay. Even if there was something he could do, he couldn't stay. He was lucky the cops' attention had been taken up by the man they called Snowball. If they had given him a second glance, Jack had no doubt he would have been asked to produce his bona fides. New sneakers or not, the rest of him looked used and battered. It doesn't take cops long to get good at spotting road-kids, and Jack was a boy on the road if there ever had been one.

He imagined being tossed into the Zanesville pokey while the Zanesville cops, fine upstanding boys in blue who listened to Paul Harvey every day and supported President Reagan, tried to find out whose little boy *he* was.

No, he didn't want the Zanesville cops giving him more than the one passing glance.

A motor, throbbing smoothly, coming up behind him.

Jack hunched his pack a little higher on his back and looked down at his new sneakers as if they interested him tremendously. From the corners of his eyes he saw the police cruiser slide slowly by.

The blind man was in the back seat, the neck of his guitar poking up beside him.

As the cruiser swung into one of the outbound lanes, the blind man abruptly turned his head and looked out the back window, looked directly at Jack . . .

. . . and although Jack could not see through the dirty dark glasses, he knew perfectly well that Lester "Speedy" Parker had winked at him.

## 2

Jack managed to keep further thought at bay until he reached the turnpike ramps again. He stood looking at the signs, which seemed the only clear-cut things left in a world

*(worlds?)*

where all else was a maddening gray swirl. He felt a dark depression swirling all around him, sinking into him, trying to destroy his resolve. He recognized that homesickness played a part in this depression, but this feeling made his former homesickness seem boyish and callow indeed. He felt utterly adrift, without a single firm thing to hold on to.

Standing by the signs, watching the traffic on the turnpike, Jack realized he felt damn near suicidal. For quite a while he had been able to keep himself going with the thought that he would see Richard Sloat soon (and, although he had hardly admitted the thought to himself, the idea that Richard might head west with him had done more than cross Jack's mind— after all, it would not be the first time that a Sawyer and a Sloat had made strange journeys together, would it?), but the hard work at the Palamountain farm and the peculiar happenings at the Buckeye Mall had given even that the false glitter of fool's gold.

*Go home, Jacky, you're beaten*, a voice whispered. *If you keep on, you're going to end up getting the living shit kicked out of you . . . and next time it may be fifty people that die. Or five hundred.*

I-70 East.

I-70 West.

Abruptly he fished in his pocket for the coin—the coin that was a silver dollar in this world. Let whatever gods there were decide this, once and for all. He was too beaten to do it for himself. His back still smarted where Mr. All-America had whacked him. Come up tails, and he would go down the east-bound ramp and head home. Come up heads, he would go on . . . and there would be no more looking back.

He stood in the dust of the soft shoulder and flicked the coin into the chilly October air. It rose, turning over and over, kicking up glints of sun. Jack craned his head to follow its course.

A family passing in an old station-wagon stopped squabbling long enough to look at him curiously. The man driving the wagon, a balding C.P.A. who sometimes awoke in the middle of the night fancying that he could feel shooting pains in his chest and down his left arm, had a sudden and absurd series of thoughts: Adventure. Danger. A quest of some noble purpose. Dreams of fear and glory. He shook his head, as if to clear it, and glanced at the boy in the wagon's rear-view mirror just as the kid leaned over to look at something. *Christ,* the balding C.P.A. thought. *Get it out of your head, Larry, you sound like a fucking boys' adventure book.*

Larry shot into traffic, quickly getting the wagon up to seventy, forgetting about the kid in the dirty jeans by the side of the road. If he could get home by three, he'd be in good time to watch the middleweight title fight on ESPN.

The coin came down. Jack bent over it. It was heads . . . but that was not all.

The lady on the coin wasn't Lady Liberty. It was Laura DeLoessian, Queen of the Territories. But God, what a difference here from the pale, still, sleeping face he had glimpsed for a moment in the pavillion, surrounded by anxious nurses in their billowing white wimples! This face was alert and aware, eager and beautiful. It was not a classic beauty; the line of the jaw was not clear enough for that, and the cheekbone which showed in profile was a little soft. Her beauty was in the regal set of her head combined with the clear sense that she was kind as well as capable.

And oh it was so like the face of his mother.

Jack's eyes blurred with tears and he blinked them hard, not wanting the tears to fall. He had cried enough for one day. He had his answer, and it was not for crying over.

When he opened his eyes again, Laura DeLoessian was gone; the woman on the coin was Lady Liberty again.

He had his answer all the same.

Jack bent over, picked up the coin out of the dust, put it in his pocket, and headed down the westbound ramp of Interstate 70.

### 3

A day later; white overcast in the air that tasted of chilly rain on its way; the Ohio-Indiana border not much more than a lick and a promise from here.

"Here" was in a scrub of woods beyond the Lewisburg rest area on I-70. Jack was standing concealed—he hoped—among the trees, patiently waiting for the large bald man with the large bald voice to get back into his Chevy Nova and drive away. Jack hoped he would go soon, before it started to rain. He was cold enough without getting wet, and all morning his sinuses had been plugged, his voice foggy. He thought he must finally be getting a cold.

The large bald man with the large bald voice had given his name as Emory W. Light. He had picked Jack up around eleven o'clock, north of Dayton, and Jack had felt a tired sinking sensation in the pit of his belly almost at once. He had gotten rides with Emory W. Light before. In Vermont Light had called himself Tom Ferguson, and said he was a shoeshop foreman; in Pennsylvania the alias had been Bob Darrent ("Almost like that fellow who sang 'Splish-Splash,' ah-ha-hah-hah"), and the job had changed to District High School Superintendent; this time Light said he was President of the First Mercantile Bank of Paradise Falls, in the town of Paradise Falls, Ohio. Ferguson had been lean and dark, Darrent as portly and pink as a freshly tubbed baby, and this Emory W. Light was large and owlish, with eyes like boiled eggs behind his rimless glasses.

Yet all of these differences were only superficial, Jack had found. They all listened to the Story with the same breathless interest. They all asked him if he had had any girlfriends back home. Sooner or later he would find a hand (a large bald hand) lying on his thigh, and when he looked at

Ferguson/Darrent/Light, he would see an expression of half-mad hope in the eyes (mixed with half-mad guilt) and a stipple of sweat on the upper lip (in the case of Darrent, the sweat had gleamed through a dark moustache like tiny white eyes peering through scant underbrush).

Ferguson had asked him if he would like to make ten dollars.

Darrent had upped that to twenty.

Light, in a large bald voice that nonetheless cracked and quivered through several registers, asked him if he couldn't use fifty dollars—he always kept a fifty in the heel of his left shoe, he said, and he'd just love to give it to Master Lewis Farren. There was a place they could go near Randolph. An empty barn.

Jack did not make any correlation between the steadily increasing monetary offers from Light in his various incarnations and any changes his adventures might be working on him—he was not introspective by nature and had little interest in self-analysis.

He had learned quickly enough how to deal with fellows like Emory W. Light. His first experience with Light, when Light had been calling himself Tom Ferguson, had taught him that discretion was by far the better part of valor. When Ferguson put his hand on Jack's thigh, Jack had responded automatically out of a California sensibility in which gays had been merely part of the scenery: "No thanks, mister. I'm strictly A.C."

He had been groped before, certainly—in movie theaters, mostly, but there had been the men's-shop clerk in North Hollywood who had cheerfully offered to blow him in a changing booth (and when Jack told him no thanks, the clerk said, "Fine, now try on the blue blazer, okay?").

These were annoyances a good-looking twelve-year-old boy in Los Angeles simply learned to put up with, the way a pretty woman learns to put up with being groped occasionally on the subway. You eventually find a way to cope without letting it spoil your whole day. The deliberate passes, such as the one this Ferguson was making, were less of a problem than the sudden gropes from ambush. They could simply be shunted aside.

At least in California they could. Eastern gays—especially

out here in the sticks—apparently had a different way of dealing with rejection.

Ferguson had come to a screeching, sliding halt, leaving forty yards of rubber behind his Pontiac and throwing a cloud of shoulder-dust into the air.

"Who you' calling *D.C.?*" he screamed. "Who you calling *queer?* I'm not *queer!* Jesus! Give a kid a fucking ride and he calls you a fucking *queer!*"

Jack was looking at him, dazed. Unprepared for the sudden stop, he had thumped his head a damned good one on the padded dash. Ferguson, who had only a moment before been looking at him with melting brown eyes, now looked ready to kill him.

"*Get out!*" Ferguson yelled. "*You're the queer, not me! You're the queer! Get out, you little queerboy! Get out! I've got a wife! I've got kids! I've probably got bastards scattered all over New England! I'm not queer! You're the queer, not me, SO GET OUT OF MY CAR!*"

More terrified than he had been since his encounter with Osmond, Jack had done just that. Ferguson tore out, spraying him with gravel, still raving. Jack staggered over to a rock wall, sat down, and began to giggle. The giggles became shrieks of laughter, and he decided right then and there that he would have to develop A POLICY, at least until he got out of the boondocks. "Any serious problem demands A POLICY," his father had said once. Morgan had agreed vigorously, but Jack decided he shouldn't let that hold him back.

His POLICY had worked well enough with Bob Darrent, and he had no reason to believe it wouldn't also work with Emory Light . . . but in the meantime he was cold and his nose was running. He wished Light would head em up and move em out. Standing in the trees, Jack could see him down there, walking back and forth with his hands in his pockets, his large bald head gleaming mellowly under the white-out sky. On the turnpike, big semis droned by, filling the air with the stink of burned diesel fuel. The woods here were trashed-out, the way the woods bordering any interstate rest area always were. Empty Dorito bags. Squashed Big Mac boxes. Crimped Pepsi and Budweiser cans with pop-tops that rattled inside if you kicked them. Smashed bottles of Wild Irish Rose and Five O'Clock gin. A pair of shredded nylon panties over there, with a mouldering sanitary napkin still glued to the crotch. A rubber poked over a broken branch. Plenty of nifty stuff, all right, hey-hey. And lots of graffiti jotted on the walls of the men's room, almost all of it the sort a fellow like Emory W. Light could really relate to: I LIKE TO SUK BIG FAT COX. BE HERE AT 4 FOR THE BEST BLOJOB YOU EVER HAD. REEM OUT MY BUTT. And here was a gay poet with large aspirations: LET THE HOLE HUMAN RACE/JERK OFF ON MY SMILING FACE.

*I'm homesick for the Territories*, Jack thought, and there was no surprise at all in the realization. Here he stood behind two brick outhouses off I-70 somewhere in western Ohio, shivering in a ragged sweater he had bought in a thrift store for a buck and a half, waiting for that large bald man down there to get back on his horse and ride.

Jack's POLICY was simplicity itself: don't antagonize a man with large bald hands and a large bald voice.

Jack sighed with relief. Now it was starting to work. An expression that was half-anger, half-disgust, had settled over Emory W. Light's large bald face. He went back to his car, got in, backed up so fast he almost hit the pick-up truck passing behind him (there was a brief blare of horns and the passenger in the truck shot Emory W. Light the finger), and then left.

Now it was only a matter of standing on the ramp where the rest-area traffic rejoined the turnpike traffic with his thumb out . . . and, he hoped, catching a ride before it started to rain.

Jack spared another look around. *Ugly, wretched.* These words came quite naturally to mind as he looked around at the littery desolation here on the rest area's pimply backside. It occurred to Jack that there was a feeling of death here—not just at this rest area or on the interstate roads but pressed deep into all the country he had travelled. Jack thought that some-times he could even see it, a desperate shade of hot dark brown, like the exhaust from the shortstack of a fast-moving Jimmy-Pete.

The new homesickness came back—the wanting to go to the Territories and see that dark blue sky, the slight curve at the edge of the horizon. . . .

*But it plays those Jerry Bledsoe changes.*

*Don't know nothin bout* dat . . . *All I know is you seem to have this idear of "moider" a little broad. . . .*

Walking down to the rest area—now he really did have to urinate—Jack sneezed three times, quickly. He swallowed and winced at the hot prickle in his throat. Getting sick, oh yeah. Great. Not even into Indiana yet, fifty degrees, rain in the forecast, no ride, and now I'm—

The thought broke off cleanly. He stared at the parking lot, his mouth falling wide open. For one awful moment he thought he was going to wet his pants as everything below his breastbone seemed to cramp and squeeze.

Sitting in one of the twenty or so slant parking spaces, its deep green surface now dulled with road-dirt, was Uncle Morgan's BMW. No chance of a mistake; no chance at all. California vanity plates MLS, standing for Morgan Luther Sloat. It looked as if it had been driven fast and hard.

*But if he flew to New Hampshire, how can his car be here?* Jack's mind yammered. *It's a coincidence, Jack, just a—*

Then he saw the man standing with his back to him at the pay telephone and knew it was no coincidence. He was wearing a bulky Army-style anorak, fur-lined, a garment more suited to five below than to fifty degrees. Back-to or not, there was no mistaking those broad shoulders and that big, loose, hulking frame.

The man at the phone started to turn around, crooking the phone between his ear and shoulder.

Jack drew back against the brick side of the men's toilet.

*Did he see me?*

*No,* he answered himself. *No, I don't think so. But—*

But Captain Farren had said that Morgan—that *other* Morgan—would smell him like a cat smells a rat, and so he had. From his hiding place in that dangerous forest, Jack had seen the hideous white face in the window of the diligence change.

This Morgan would smell him, too. If given the time.

Footfalls around the corner, approaching.

Face numb and twisted with fear, Jack fumbled off his pack and then dropped it, knowing he was too late, too slow, that Morgan would come around the corner and seize him by the neck, smiling. *Hi, Jacky! Allee-allee-in-free! Game's over now, isn't it, you little prick?*

A tall man in a houndstooth-check jacket passed the corner of the rest-room, gave Jack a disinterested glance, and went to the drinking fountain.

Going back. He was going back. There was no guilt, at least not now; only that terrible trapped fear mingling oddly with feelings of relief and pleasure. Jack fumbled his pack open. Here was Speedy's bottle, with less than an inch of the purple liquid now left

*(no boy needs dat poison to travel with but I do Speedy I do!)*

sloshing around in the bottom. No matter. He was going back. His heart leaped at the thought. A big Saturday-night grin dawned on his face, denying both the gray day and the fear in his heart. *Going back, oh yeah, dig it.*

More footsteps approaching, and this was Uncle Morgan, no doubt about that heavy yet somehow mincing step. But the fear was gone. Uncle Morgan had smelled something, but when he turned the corner he would see nothing but empty Dorito bags and crimped beercans.

Jack pulled in breath—pulled in the greasy stink of diesel fumes and car exhausts and cold autumn air. Tipped the bottle up to his lips. Took one of the two swallows left. And even with his eyes shut he squinted as—

# 16

# Wolf

### 1

—the strong sunlight struck his closed lids.

Through the gagging-sweet odor of the magic juice he could smell something else . . . the warm smell of animals. He could hear them, too, moving all about him.

Frightened, Jack opened his eyes but at first could see nothing—the difference in the light was so sudden and abrupt that it was as if someone had suddenly turned on a cluster of two-hundred-watt bulbs in a black room.

A warm, hide-covered flank brushed him, not in a threatening way (or so Jack hoped), but most definitely in an I'm-in-a-hurry-to-be-gone-thank-you-very-much way. Jack, who had been getting up, thumped back to the ground again.

*"Hey! Hey! Get away from im! Right here and right now!"* A loud, healthy whack followed by a disgruntled animal sound somewhere between a moo and a baa. *"God's nails! Got no sense! Get away from im fore I bite your God-pounding eyes out!"*

Now his eyes had adjusted enough to the brightness of this almost flawless Territories autumn day to make out a young giant standing in the middle of a herd of milling animals, whacking their sides and slightly humped backs with what appeared to be great gusto and very little real force. Jack sat up, automatically finding Speedy's bottle with its one precious swallow left and putting it away. He never took his eyes from the young man who stood with his back to him.

Tall he was—six-five at least, Jack guessed—and with shoulders so broad that his across still looked slightly out of proportion to his high. Long, greasy black hair shagged down his back to the shoulder blades. Muscles bulged and rippled as he moved amid the animals, which looked like pygmy cows. He was driving them away from Jack and toward the Western Road.

He was a striking figure, even when seen from behind, but what amazed Jack was his dress. Everyone he had seen in the Territories (including himself) had been wearing tunics, jerkins, or rough breeches.

This fellow appeared to be wearing Oshkosh bib overalls.

Then he turned around and Jack felt a horrible shocked dismay well up in his throat. He shot to his feet.

It was the Elroy-thing.

The herdsman was the Elroy-thing.

## 2

Except it wasn't.

Jack perhaps would not have lingered to see that, and everything that happened thereafter—the movie theater, the shed, and the hell of the Sunlight Home—would not have happened (or would, at the very least, have happened in some

completely different way), but in the extremity of his terror he
froze completely after getting up. He was no more able to run
than a deer is when it is frozen in a hunter's jacklight.

As the figure in the bib overalls approached, he thought:
*Elroy wasn't that tall or that broad. And his eyes were
yellow*—The eyes of this creature were a bright, impossible
shade of orange. Looking into them was like looking into the
eyes of a Halloween pumpkin. And while Elroy's grin had
promised madness and murder, the smile on this fellow's face
was large and cheerful and harmless.

His feet were bare, huge, and spatulate, the toes clumped
into groups of three and two, barely visible through curls
of wiry hair. Not hooflike, as Elroy's had been, Jack realized,
half-crazed with surprise, fear, a dawning amusement, but
padlike-pawlike.

As he closed the distance between himself and Jack,
*(his? its?)*
eyes flared an even brighter orange, going for a moment to
the Day-Glo shade favored by hunters and flagmen on road-
repair jobs. The color faded to a muddy hazel. As it did, Jack
saw that his smile was puzzled as well as friendly, and understood two things at once: first, that there was no harm in this
fellow, not an ounce of it, and second, that he was slow. Not
feeble, perhaps, but slow.

"Wolf!" the big, hairy boy-beast cried, grinning. His
tongue was long and pointed, and Jack thought with a shudder
that a wolf was exactly what he looked like. Not a goat but a
wolf. He hoped he was right about there not being any harm
in him. *But if I made a mistake about that, at least I won't
have to worry about making any more mistakes . . . ever
again.* "Wolf! Wolf!" He stuck out one hand, and Jack saw
that, like his feet, his hands were covered with hair, although
this hair was finer and more luxuriant—actually quite handsome. It grew especially thick in the palms, where it was the
soft white of a blaze on a horse's forehead.

*My God I think he wants to shake hands with me!*

Gingerly, thinking of Uncle Tommy, who had told him he
must never refuse a handshake, not even with his worst enemy
("Fight him to the death afterward if you must, but shake his
hand first," Uncle Tommy had said), Jack put his own hand

out, wondering if it was about to be crushed . . . or perhaps eaten.

"Wolf! Wolf! Shakin hands right here and now!" the boy-thing in the Oshkosh biballs cried, delighted. "Right here and now! Good old Wolf! God-pound it! Right here and now! *Wolf!*"

In spite of this enthusiasm, Wolf's grip was gentle enough, cushioned by the crisp, furry growth of hair on his hand. *Bib overalls and a big handshake from a guy who looks like an overgrown Siberian husky and smells a little bit like a hayloft after a heavy rain*, Jack thought. *What next? An offer to come to his church this Sunday?*

"Good old Wolf, you bet! Good old Wolf right here and now!" Wolf wrapped his arms around his huge chest and laughed, delighted with himself. Then he grabbed Jack's hand again.

This time his hand was pumped vigorously up and down. Something seemed required of him at his point, Jack reflected. Otherwise, this pleasant if rather simple young man might go on shaking his hand until sundown.

"Good old Wolf," he said. It seemed to be a phrase of which his new acquaintance was particularly fond.

Wolf laughed like a child and dropped Jack's hand. This was something of a relief. The hand had been neither crushed nor eaten, but it did feel a bit seasick. Wolf had a faster pump than a slot-machine player on a hot streak.

"Stranger, ain'tcha?" Wolf asked. He stuffed his hairy hands into the slit sides of his biballs and began playing pocket-pool with a complete lack of self-consciousness.

"Yes," Jack said, thinking of what that word meant over here. It had a very specific meaning over here. "Yes, I guess that's just what I am. A stranger."

"God-pounding right! I can smell it on you! Right here and now, oh yeah, oh boy! Got it! Doesn't smell bad, you know, but it sure is *funny*. Wolf! That's me. Wolf! Wolf! Wolf!" He threw back his head and laughed. The sound ended being something that was disconcertingly like a howl.

"Jack," Jack said. "Jack Saw—"

His hand was seized again and pumped with abandon.

"Sawyer," he finished, when he was released again. He

smiled, feeling very much as though someone had hit him with a great big goofystick. Five minutes ago he had been standing scrunched against the cold brick side of a shithouse on I-70. Now he was standing here talking to a young fellow who seemed to be more animal than man.

And damned if his cold wasn't completely gone.

### 3

"Wolf meet Jack! Jack meet Wolf! Here and now! Okay! Good! Oh, Jason! Cows in the road! Ain't they stupid! Wolf! Wolf!"

Yelling, Wolf loped down the hill to the road, where about half of his herd was standing, looking around with expressions of bland surprise, as if to ask where the grass had gone. They really did look like some strange cross between cows and sheep, Jack saw, and wondered what you would call such a crossbreed. The only word to come immediately to mind was *creeps*—or perhaps, he thought, the singular would be more proper in this case, as in *Here's Wolf taking care of his flock of creep. Oh yeah. Right here and now.*

The goofystick came down on Jack's head again. He sat down and began to giggle, his hands crisscrossed over his mouth to stifle the sounds.

Even the biggest creep stood no more than four feet high. Their fur was woolly, but of a muddy shade that was similar to Wolf's eyes—at least, when Wolf's eyes weren't blazing like Halloween jack-o'-lanterns. Their heads were topped with short, squiggly horns that looked good for absolutely nothing. Wolf herded them back out of the road. They went obediently, with no sign of fear. *If a cow or a sheep on my side of the jump got a whiff of that guy*, Jack thought, *it'd kill itself trying to get out of his way.*

But Jack liked Wolf—liked him on sight, just as he had feared and disliked Elroy on sight. And that contrast was particularly apt, because the comparison between the two was undeniable. Except that Elroy had been goatish while Wolf was . . . well, wolfish.

Jack walked slowly toward where Wolf had set his herd to graze. He remembered tiptoeing down the stinking back hall of the Oatley Tap toward the fire-door, sensing Elroy somewhere near, smelling him, perhaps, as a cow on the other side would undoubtedly smell Wolf. He remembered the way Elroy's hands had begun to twist and thicken, the way his neck had swelled, the way his teeth had become a mouthful of blackening fangs.

"Wolf?"

Wolf turned and looked at him, smiling. His eyes flared a bright orange and looked for a moment both savage and intelligent. Then the glow faded and they were only that muddy, perpetually puzzled hazel again.

"Are you . . . sort of a werewolf?"

"Sure am," Wolf said, smiling. "You pounded that nail, Jack. Wolf!"

Jack sat down on a rock, looking at Wolf thoughtfully. He believed it would be impossible for him to be further surprised than he had already been, but Wolf managed the trick quite nicely.

"How's your father, Jack?" he asked, in that casual, by-the-way tone reserved for enquiring after the relatives of others. "How's Phil doing these days? Wolf!"

### 4

Jack made a queerly apt cross-association: he felt as if all the wind had been knocked out of his mind. For a moment it just sat there in his head, not a thought in it, like a radio station broadcasting nothing but a carrier wave. Then he saw Wolf's face change. The expression of happiness and childish curiosity was replaced by one of sorrow. Jack saw that Wolf's nostrils were flaring rapidly.

"He's dead, isn't he? Wolf! I'm sorry, Jack. God pound me! I'm stupid! *Stupid!*" Wolf crashed a hand into his forehead and this time he really *did* howl. It was a sound that chilled Jack's blood. The herd of creep looked around uneasily.

"That's all right," Jack said. He heard his voice more in his ears than in his head, as if someone else had spoken. "But . . . how did you know?"

"Your smell changed," Wolf said simply. "I knew he was

dead because it was in your smell. Poor Phil! What a good guy! Tell you that right here and now, Jack! Your father was a good guy! Wolf!"

"Yes," Jack said, "he was. But how did you know him? And how did you know he was my father?"

Wolf looked at Jack as though he had asked a question so simple it barely needed answering. "I remember his smell, of course. Wolfs remember all smells. You smell just like him."

*Whack!* The goofystick came down on his head again. Jack felt an urge to just roll back and forth on the tough, springy turf, holding his gut and howling. People had told him he had his father's eyes and his father's mouth, even his father's knack for quick-sketching, but never before had he been told that he smelled like his father. Yet he supposed the idea had a certain crazy logic, at that.

"How did you know him?" Jack asked again.

Wolf looked at a loss. "He came with the other one," he said at last. "The one from Orris. I was just little. The other one was bad. The other one stole some of us. Your father didn't know," he added hastily, as if Jack had shown anger. "Wolf! No! He was good, your father. Phil. The other one . . ."

Wolf shook his head slowly. On his face was an expression even more simple than his pleasure. It was the memory of some childhood nightmare.

"Bad," Wolf said. "He made himself a place in this world, my father says. Mostly he was in his Twinner, but he was from your world. We knew he was bad, we could tell, but who listens to Wolfs? No one. Your father knew he was bad, but he couldn't smell him as good as we could. He knew he was bad, but not *how* bad."

And Wolf threw his head back and howled again, a long, chilly ululation of sorrow that resounded against the deep blue sky.

# Interlude

# Sloat in This World (II)

From the pocket of his bulky parka (he had bought it convinced that from the Rockies east, America was a frigid wasteland after October 1st or so—now he was sweating rivers), Morgan Sloat took a small steel box. Below the latch were ten small buttons and an oblong of cloudy yellow glass a quarter of an inch high and two inches long. He pushed several of the buttons carefully with the fingernail of his left-hand pinky, and a series of numbers appeared briefly in the readout window. Sloat had bought this gadget, billed as the world's smallest safe, in Zurich. According to the man who had sold it to him, not even a week in a crematory oven would breach its carbon-steel integrity.

Now it clicked open.

Sloat folded back two tiny wings of ebony jeweler's velvet, revealing something he had had for well over twenty years—since long before the odious little brat who was causing all this trouble had been born. It was a tarnished tin key, and once it had gone into the back of a mechanical toy soldier. Sloat had seen the toy soldier in the window of a junkshop in the odd little town of Point Venuti, California—a town in which he had great interest. Acting under a compulsion much too strong to deny (he hadn't even wanted to deny it, not really; he had always made a virtue of compulsion, had Morgan Sloat), he had gone in and paid five dollars for the dusty, dented soldier . . . and it wasn't the soldier he had wanted, anyway. It was the key that had caught his eye and then whispered to him. He had removed the key from the soldier's back and pocketed it as soon as he was outside the junkshop door. The soldier itself he threw in a litter-basket outside the Dangerous Planet Bookstore.

Now, as Sloat stood beside his car in the Lewisburg rest area, he held the key up and looked at it. Like Jack's croaker, the tin key became something else in the Territories. Once, when coming back, he had dropped that key in the lobby of the old office building. And there must have been some Territories magic left in it, because that idiot Jerry Bledsoe had gotten himself fried not an hour later. Had Jerry picked it up? Stepped on it, perhaps? Sloat didn't know and didn't care. Nor had he cared a tinker's damn about Jerry—and considering the handyman had had an insurance policy specifying double indemnity for accidental death (the building's super, with whom Sloat sometimes shared a hashpipe, had passed this little tidbit on to him), Sloat imagined that Nita Bledsoe had done nipups—but he had been nearly frantic about the loss of his key. It was Phil Sawyer who had found it, giving it back to him with no comment other than "Here, Morg. Your lucky charm, isn't it? Must have a hole in your pocket. I found it in the lobby after they took poor old Jerry away."

Yes, in the lobby. In the lobby where everything smelled like the motor of a Waring Blender that had been running continuously on Hi Speed for about nine hours. In the lobby where everything had been blackened and twisted and fused.

Except for this humble tin key.

Which, in the other world, was a queer kind of lightning-rod—and which Sloat now hung around his neck on a fine silver chain.

"Coming for you, Jacky," said Sloat in a voice that was almost tender. "Time to bring this entire ridiculous business to a crashing halt."

# 17

# Wolf and the Herd

**1**

Wolf talked of many things, getting up occasionally to shoo his cattle out of the road and once to move them to a stream about half a mile to the west. When Jack asked him where he lived, Wolf only waved his arm vaguely northward. He lived, he said, with his family. When Jack asked for clarification a few minutes later, Wolf looked surprised and said he had no mate and no children—that he would not come into what he called the "big rut-moon" for another year or two. That he looked forward to the "big rut-moon" was quite obvious from the innocently lewd grin that overspread his face.

"But you said you lived with your family."

"Oh, family! Them! Wolf!" Wolf laughed. "Sure. *Them!* We all live together. Have to keep the cattle, you know. *Her* cattle."

"The Queen's?"

"Yes. May she never, never die." And Wolf made an absurdly touching salute, bending briefly forward with his right hand touching his forehead.

Further questioning straightened the matter out somewhat in Jack's mind . . . at least, he thought it did. Wolf was a bachelor (although that word barely fit, somehow). The family of which he spoke was a hugely extended one—literally, the Wolf family. They were a nomadic but fiercely loyal race that moved back and forth in the great empty areas east of the Outposts but west of "The Settlements," by which Wolf seemed to mean the towns and villages of the east.

Wolfs (never Wolves—when Jack once used the proper plural, Wolf had laughed until tears spurted from the corners of his eyes) were solid, dependable workers, for the most part. Their strength was legendary, their courage unquestioned.

Some of them had gone east into The Settlements, where they served the Queen as guards, soldiers, even as personal bodyguards. Their lives, Wolf explained to Jack, had only two great touchstones: the Lady and the family. Most of the Wolfs, he said, served the Lady as he did—watching the herds.

The cow-sheep were the Territories' primary source of meat, cloth, tallow, and lamp-oil (Wolf did not tell Jack this, but Jack inferred it from what he said). All the cattle belonged to the Queen, and the Wolf family had been watching over them since time out of mind. It was their job. In this Jack found an oddly persuasive correlative to the relationship that had existed between the buffalo and the Indians of the American Plains . . . at least until the white man had come into those territories and upset the balance.

"Behold, and the lion shall lie down with the lamb, and the Wolf with the creep," Jack murmured, and smiled. He was lying on his back with his hands laced behind his head. The most marvellous feeling of peace and ease had stolen over him.

"What, Jack?"

"Nothing," he said. "Wolf, do you really change into an animal when the moon gets full?"

" 'Course I do!" Wolf said. He looked astounded, as if Jack had asked him something like *Wolf, do you really pull up your pants after you finish taking a crap?* "Strangers don't, do they? Phil told me *that*."

"The, ah, herd," Jack said. "When you change, do they—"

"Oh, we don't go *near* the herd when we change," Wolf said seriously. "Good Jason, no! We'd eat them, don't you know that? And a Wolf who eats of his herd must be put to death. *The Book of Good Farming* says so. Wolf! Wolf! We have places to go when the moon is full. So does the herd. They're stupid, but they know they have to go away at the time of the big moon. Wolf! They better know, God pound them!"

"But you *do* eat meat, don't you?" Jack asked.

"Full of questions, just like your father," Wolf said. "Wolf! I don't mind. Yeah, we eat meat. Of course we do. We're Wolfs, aren't we?"

"But if you don't eat from the herds, what do you eat?"

"We eat well," Wolf said, and would say no more on that subject.

Like everything else in the Territories, Wolf was a mystery—a mystery that was both gorgeous and frightening. The fact that he had known both Jack's father and Morgan Sloat—had, at least, met their Twinners on more than one occasion—contributed to Wolf's particular aura of mystery, but did not define it completely. Everything Wolf told him led Jack to a dozen more questions, most of which Wolf couldn't—or wouldn't—answer.

The matter of Philip Sawtelle's and Orris's visits was a case in point. They had first appeared when Wolf was in the "little moon" and living with his mother and two "litter-sisters." They were apparently just passing through, as Jack himself was now doing, only they had been heading east instead of west ("Tell you the truth, you're just about the only human I've ever seen this far west who was still *going* west," Wolf said).

They had been jolly enough company, both of them. It was only later that there had been trouble . . . trouble with Orris. That had been after the partner of Jack's father had "made himself a place in this world," Wolf told Jack again and again—only now he seemed to mean Sloat, in the physical guise of Orris. Wolf said that Morgan had stolen one of his litter-sisters ("My mother bit her hands and toes for a month after she knew for certain that he took her," Wolf told Jack matter-of-factly) and had taken other Wolfs from time to time. Wolf dropped his voice and, with an expression of fear and superstitious awe on his face, told Jack that the "limping man" had taken some of these Wolfs into the other world, the Place of the Strangers, and had taught them to eat of the herd.

"That's very bad for guys like you, isn't it?" Jack asked.

"They're damned," Wolf replied simply.

Jack had thought at first that Wolf was speaking of kidnapping—the verb Wolf had used in connection with his litter-sister, after all, was the Territories version of *take*. He began to see now that kidnapping wasn't what was going on at all—unless Wolf, with unconscious poetry, had been trying to say that Morgan had kidnapped the minds of some of the Wolf family. Jack now thought that Wolf was really talking about werewolves who had thrown over their ancient allegiance to the Crown and the herd and had given it to Morgan instead . . . Morgan Sloat and Morgan of Orris.

Which led naturally enough to thoughts of Elroy.

*A Wolf who eats of his herd must be put to death.*

To thoughts of the men in the green car who had stopped to ask him directions, and offered him a Tootsie Roll, and who had then tried to pull him into their car. The eyes. *The eyes had changed.*

*They're damned.*

*He made himself a place in this world.*

Until now he had felt both safe and delighted: delighted to be back in the Territories where there was a nip in the air but nothing like the dull, cold gray bite of western Ohio, safe with big, friendly Wolf beside him, way out in the country, miles from anything or anyone.

*Made himself a place in this world.*

He asked Wolf about his father—Philip Sawtelle in this world—but Wolf only shook his head. He had been a God-pounding good guy, and a Twinner—thus obviously a Stranger—but that was all Wolf seemed to know. Twinners, he said, was something that had something to do with litters of *people*, and about such business he could not presume to say. Nor could he describe Philip Sawtelle—he didn't remember. He only remembered the smell. All *he* knew, he told Jack, was that, while both of the Strangers had *seemed* nice, only Phil Sawyer had really *been* nice. Once he had brought presents for Wolf and his litter-sisters and litter-brothers. One of the presents, unchanged from the world of the Strangers, had been a set of bib overalls for Wolf.

"I wore em all the time," Wolf said. "My mother wanted to throw em away after I'd wore em for five years or so. Said they were worn out! Said I was too big for them! Wolf! Said they were only patches holding more patches together. I wouldn't give em up, though. Finally, she bought some cloth from a drummer headed out toward the Outposts. I don't know how much she paid, and Wolf! I'll tell you the truth, Jack, I'm afraid to ask. She dyed it blue and made me six pairs. The ones your father brought me, I sleep on them now. Wolf! Wolf! It's my God-pounding pillow, I guess." Wolf smiled so openly—and yet so wistfully—that Jack was moved to take his hand. It was something he never could have done in his old life, no matter what the circumstances, but that now seemed like his loss. He was glad to take Wolf's warm, strong hand.

"I'm glad you liked my dad, Wolf," he said.

"I did! I did! Wolf! Wolf!"

And then all hell broke loose.

## 2

Wolf stopped talking and looked around, startled.

"Wolf? What's wr—"

"Shhhh!"

Then Jack heard it. Wolf's more sensitive ears had picked the sound up first, but it swelled quickly; before long, a deaf man would have heard it, Jack thought. The cattle looked around and then began to move away from the source of the sound in a rough, uneasy clot. It was like a radio sound-effect where someone is supposed to be ripping a bedsheet down the middle, very slowly. Only the volume kept going up and up and up until Jack thought he was going to go crazy.

Wolf leaped to his feet, looking stunned and confused and frightened. That ripping sound, a low, ragged purr, continued to grow. The bleating of the cattle became louder. Some were backing into the stream, and as Jack looked that way he saw one go down with a splash and a clumsy flailing of legs. It had been pushed over by its milling, retreating comrades. It let out a shrill, *baaa*-ing cry. Another cow-sheep stumbled over it and was likewise trampled into the water by the slow retreat. The far side of the stream was low and wet, green with reeds, muddy-marshy. The cow-sheep who first reached this muck quickly became mired in it.

*"Oh you God-pounding good-for-nothing cattle!"* Wolf bellowed, and charged down the hill toward the stream, where the first animal to fall over now looked as if it were in its death-throes.

"Wolf!" Jack shouted, but Wolf couldn't hear him. Jack could barely hear himself over that ragged ripping sound. He looked a little to the right, on this side of the stream, and gaped with amazement. Something was happening to the air. A patch of it about three feet off the ground was rippling and blistering, seeming to twist and pull at itself. Jack could see the Western Road through this patch of air, but the road seemed blurry and shimmery, as if seen through the heated, rippling air over an incinerator.

*Something's pulling the air open like a wound—something's coming through—from our side? Oh Jason, is that what I do when I come through?* But even in his own panic and confusion he knew it was not.

Jack had a good idea who *would* come through like this, like a rape in progress.

Jack began to run down the hill.

### 3

The ripping sound went on and on and on. Wolf was down on his knees in the stream, trying to help the second downed animal to its feet. The first floated limply downstream, its body tattered and mangled.

*"Get up! God pound you, get up! Wolf!"*

Wolf shoved and slapped as best he could at the cow-sheep who milled and backed into him, then got both arms around the drowning animal's midriff and pulled upward. *"WOLF! HERE AND NOW!"* he screamed. The sleeves of his shirt split wide open along the biceps, reminding Jack of David Banner having one of the gamma-ray-inspired tantrums that turned him into The Incredible Hulk. Water sprayed everywhere and Wolf lurched to his feet, eyes blazing orange, blue overalls now soaked black. Water streamed from the nostrils of the animal, which Wolf held clutched against his chest as if it were an overgrown puppy. Its eyes were turned up to sticky whites.

"Wolf!" Jack screamed. "It's Morgan! It's—"

*"The herd!"* Wolf screamed back. *"Wolf! Wolf! My God-pounding herd! Jack! Don't try—"*

The rest was drowned out by a grinding clap of thunder that shook the earth. For a moment the thunder even covered that maddening, monotonous ripping sound. Almost as confused as Wolf's cattle, Jack looked up and saw a clear blue sky, innocent of clouds save for a few puffy white ones that were miles away.

The thunder ignited outright panic in Wolf's herd. They tried to bolt, but in their exquisite stupidity, many of them tried to do it by backing up. They crashed and splashed and were rolled underwater. Jack heard the bitter snap of a breaking bone, followed by the *baaaa*-ing scream of an animal in pain. Wolf bellowed in rage, dropped the cow-sheep he had been trying to save, and floundered toward the muddy far bank of the stream.

Before he could get there, half a dozen cattle struck him and bore him down. Water splashed and flew in thin, bright sprays. Now, Jack saw, Wolf was the one in danger of being simultaneously trampled and drowned by the stupid, fleeing animals.

Jack pushed into the stream, which was now dark with roiling mud. The current tried continually to push him off-balance. A bleating cow-sheep, its eyes rolling madly, splashed past him, almost knocking him down. Water sprayed into his face and Jack tried to wipe it out of his eyes.

Now that sound seemed to fill the whole world: *RRRRRII-IPPPP—*

Wolf. Never mind Morgan, at least not for the moment. Wolf was in trouble.

His shaggy, drenched head was momentarily visible above the water, and then three of the animals ran right over him and Jack could only see one waving, fur-covered hand. He pushed forward again, trying to weave through the cattle, some still up, others floundering and drowning underfoot.

*"Jack!"* a voice bellowed over that ripping noise. It was a voice Jack knew. Uncle Morgan's voice.

*"Jack!"*

There was another clap of thunder, this one a huge oaken thud that rolled through the sky like an artillery shell.

Panting, his soaked hair hanging in his eyes, Jack looked over his shoulder . . . and directly into the rest area on I-70 near Lewisburg, Ohio. He was seeing it as if through ripply, badly made glass . . . but he was *seeing* it. The edge of the brick toilet was on the left side of that blistered, tortured patch of air. The snout of what looked like a Chevrolet pick-up truck was on the right, floating three feet above the field where he and Wolf had been sitting peacefully and talking not five minutes ago. And in the center, looking like an extra in a film about Admiral Byrd's assault on the South Pole, was

Morgan Sloat, his thick red face twisted with murderous rage. Rage, and something else. Triumph? Yes. Jack thought that was what it was.

He stood at midstream in water that was crotch-deep, cattle passing on either side of him, *baa*-ing and bleating, staring at that window which had been torn in the very fabric of reality, his eyes wide, his mouth wider.

*He's found me, oh dear God, he's found me.*

*"There you are, you little shithead!"* Morgan bellowed at him. His voice carried, but it had a muffled, dead quality as it came from the reality of that world into the reality of this one. It was like listening to a man shout inside a telephone booth. *"Now we'll see, won't we? Won't we?"*

Morgan started forward, his face swimming and rippling as if made of limp plastic, and Jack had time to see there was something clutched in his hand, something hung around his neck, something small and silvery.

Jack stood, paralyzed, as Sloat bulled his way through the hole between the two universes. As he came he did his own werewolf number, changing from Morgan Sloat, investor, land speculator, and sometime Hollywood agent, into Morgan of Orris, pretender to the throne of a dying Queen. His flushed, hanging jowls thinned. The color faded out of them. His hair renewed itself, growing forward, first tinting the rondure of his skull, as if some invisible being were coloring Uncle Morgan's head, then covering it. The hair of Sloat's Twinner was long, black, flapping, somehow dead-looking. It had been tied at the nape of his neck, Jack saw, but most of it had come loose.

The parka wavered, disappeared for a moment, then came back as a cloak and hood.

Morgan Sloat's suede boots became dark leather knee-boots, their tops turned down, what might have been the hilt of a knife poking out of one.

And the small silver thing in his hand had turned to a small rod tipped with crawling blue fire.

*It's a lightning-rod. Oh Jesus, it's a—*

"Jack!"

The cry was low, gargling, full of water.

Jack whirled clumsily around in the stream, barely avoiding another cow-sheep, this one floating on its side, dead in the water. He saw Wolf's head going down again, both hands waving. Jack fought his way toward those hands, still dodging the cattle as best he could. One of them bunted his hip hard and Jack went over, inhaling water. He got up again quick, coughing and choking, one hand feeling inside his jerkin for the bottle, afraid it might have washed away. It was still there.

*"Boy! Turn around and look at me, boy!"*

*No time just now, Morgan. Sorry, but I've got to see if I can avoid getting drowned by Wolf's herd before I see if I can avoid getting fried by your doomstick there. I—*

Blue fire arched over Jack's shoulder, sizzling—it was like a deadly electric rainbow. It struck one of the cow-sheep caught in the reedy muck on the other side of the stream and the unfortunate beast simply exploded, as if it had swallowed dynamite. Blood flew in a needle-spray of droplets. Gobbets of flesh began to rain down around Jack.

*"Turn and look at me, boy!"*

He could feel the *force* of that command, gripping his face with invisible hands, trying to turn it.

Wolf struggled up again, his hair plastered against his face, his dazed eyes peering through a curtain of it like the eyes of an English sheepdog. He was coughing and staggering, seemingly no longer aware of where he was.

*"Wolf!"* Jack screamed, but thunder exploded across the blue sky again, drowning him out.

Wolf bent over and retched up a great muddy sheet of water. A moment later another of the terrified cow-sheep struck him and bore him under again.

*That's it*, Jack thought despairingly. *That's it, he's gone, must be, let him go, get out of here—*

But he struggled on toward Wolf, pushing a dying, weakly convulsing cow-sheep out of his way to get there.

*"Jason!"* Morgan of Orris screamed, and Jack realized that Morgan was not cursing in the Territories argot; he was calling his, Jack's, name. Only here he was not Jack. Here he was Jason.

*But the Queen's son died an infant, died, he—*

The wet, sizzling zap of electricity again, seeming almost to part his hair. Again it struck the other bank, this time vaporizing one of Wolf's cattle. No, Jack saw, at least not utterly. The animal's legs were still there, mired in the mud like shake-poles. As he watched, they began to sag tiredly outward in four different directions.

*"TURN AND LOOK AT ME, GOD POUND YOU!"*

*The water, why doesn't he throw it at the water, fry me, Wolf, all these animals at the same time?*

Then his fifth-grade science came back to him. Once electricity went to water, it could go anywhere . . . including back to the generator of the current.

Wolf's dazed face, floating underwater, drove these thoughts from Jack's flying mind. Wolf was still alive, but partially pinned under a cow-sheep, which, although apparently unhurt, had frozen in panic. Wolf's hands waved with pathetic, flagging energy. As Jack closed the last of the distance, one of those hands dropped and simply floated, limp as a water-lily.

Without slowing, Jack lowered his left shoulder and hit the cow-sheep like Jack Armstrong in a boy's sports story.

If it had been a full-sized cow instead of a Territories compact model, Jack would probably not have budged it, not with the stream's fairly stiff current working against him. But it was smaller than a cow, and Jack was pumped up. It bawled when Jack hit it, floundered backward, sat briefly on its haunches, and then lunged for the far bank. Jack grabbed Wolf's hands and pulled with all of his might.

Wolf came up as reluctantly as a waterlogged tree-trunk, his eyes now glazed and half-closed, water streaming from his ears and nose and mouth. His lips were blue.

Twin forks of lightning blazed to the right and left of where Jack stood holding Wolf, the two of them looking like a pair of drunks trying to waltz in a swimming pool. On the far bank, another cow-sheep flew in all directions, its severed head still bawling. Hot rips of fire zigzagged through the marshy area, lighting the reeds on the tussocks and then finding the drier grass of the field where the land began to rise again.

*"Wolf!"* Jack screamed. *"Wolf, for Christ's sake!"*

"Auh," Wolf moaned, and vomited warm muddy water over Jack's shoulder. *"Auhhhhhhhhhhh . . ."*

Now Jack saw Morgan standing on the other bank, a tall, Puritanical figure in his black cloak. His hood framed his pallid, vampirelike face with a kind of cheerless romance. Jack had time to think that the Territories had worked their magic even here, on behalf of his dreadful uncle. Over here, Morgan was not an overweight, hypertensive actuarial toad with piracy in his heart and murder in his mind; over here, his face had narrowed and found a frigid masculine beauty. He pointed the silver rod like a toy magic wand, and blue fire tore the air open.

*"Now you and your dumb friend!"* Morgan screamed. His thin lips split in a triumphant grin, revealing sunken yellow teeth that spoiled Jack's blurred impression of beauty once and forever.

Wolf screamed and jerked in Jack's aching arms. He was staring at Morgan, his eyes orange and bulging with hate and fear.

*"You, devil!"* Wolf screamed. *"You, devil! My sister! My litter-sister! Wolf! Wolf! You, devil!"*

Jack pulled the bottle out of his jerkin. There was a single swallow left anyway. He couldn't hold Wolf up with his one arm; he was losing him, and Wolf seemed unable to support himself. Didn't matter. Couldn't take him back through into the other world anyway . . . or could he?

*"You, devil!"* Wolf screamed, weeping, his wet face sliding down Jack's arm. The back of his bib overalls floated and belled in the water.

Smell of burning grass and burning animals.

Thunder, exploding.

This time the river of fire in the air rushed by Jack so close that the hairs in his nostrils singed and curled.

*"OH YES, BOTH OF YOU, BOTH OF YOU!"* Morgan howled. *"I'LL TEACH YOU TO GET IN MY WAY, YOU LITTLE BASTARD! I'LL BURN BOTH OF YOU! I'LL POUND YOU DOWN!"*

"Wolf, hold on!" Jack yelled. He gave up his effort to hold Wolf up; instead, he snatched Wolf's hand in his own and held it as tightly as he could. "Hold on to me, do you hear?"

*"Wolf!"*

He tipped the bottle up, and the awful cold taste of rotted grapes filled his mouth for the last time. The bottle was empty. As he swallowed, he heard it shatter as one of Morgan's bolts of lightning struck it. But the sound of the breaking glass was faint . . . the tingle of electricity . . . even Morgan's screams of rage.

He felt as if he were falling over backward into a hole. A grave, maybe. Then Wolf's hand squeezed down on Jack's so hard that Jack groaned. That feeling of vertigo, of having done a complete dipsy-doodle, began to fade . . . and then the sunlight faded, too, and became the sad purplish gray of an October twilight in the heartland of America. Cold rain struck Jack in the face, and he was faintly aware that the water he was standing in seemed much colder than it had only seconds ago. Somewhere not far away he could hear the familiar snoring drone of the big rigs on the interstate . . . except that now they seemed to be coming from directly overhead.

*Impossible*, he thought, but was it? The bounds of that word seemed to be stretching with plastic ease. For one dizzy moment he had an image of flying Territories trucks driven by flying Territories men with big canvas wings strapped to their backs.

Back, he thought. Back again, same time, same turnpike.

He sneezed.

Same cold, too.

But two things were not the same now.

No rest area here. They were standing thigh-deep in the icy water of a stream beneath a turnpike overpass.

Wolf was with him. That was the other change.

And Wolf was screaming.

# 18

# Wolf Goes to the Movies

## 1

Overhead, another truck pounded across the overpass, big diesel engine bellowing. The overpass shook. Wolf wailed and clutched at Jack, almost knocking them both into the water.

"Quit it!" Jack shouted. "Let go of me, Wolf! It's just a truck! Let *go!*"

He slapped at Wolf, not wanting to do it—Wolf's terror was pathetic. But, pathetic or not, Wolf had the best part of a foot and maybe a hundred and fifty pounds on Jack, and if he overbore him, they would both go into this freezing water and it would be pneumonia for sure.

*"Wolf! Don't like it! Wolf! Don't like it! Wolf! Wolf!"*

But his hold slackened. A moment later his arms dropped to his sides. When another truck snored by overhead, Wolf cringed but managed to keep from grabbing Jack again. But he looked at Jack with a mute, trembling appeal that said *Get me out of this, please get me out of this, I'd rather be dead than in this world.*

*Nothing I'd like better, Wolf, but Morgan's over there. Even if he weren't, I don't have the magic juice anymore.*

He looked down at his left hand and saw he was holding the jagged neck of Speedy's bottle, like a man getting ready to do some serious barroom brawling. Just dumb luck Wolf hadn't gotten a bad cut when he grabbed Jack in his terror.

Jack tossed it away. *Splash.*

Two trucks this time—the noise was doubled. Wolf howled in terror and plastered his hands over his ears. Jack could see that most of the hair had disappeared from Wolf's hands in the flip—most, but not all. And, he saw, the first two fingers of each of Wolf's hands were exactly the same length.

"Come on, Wolf," Jack said when the racket of the trucks

had faded a little. "Let's get out of here. We look like a couple of guys waiting to get baptized on a *PTL Club* special."

He took Wolf's hand, and then winced at the panicky way Wolf's grip closed down. Wolf saw his expression and loosened up . . . a little.

"Don't leave me, Jack," Wolf said. "Please, please don't leave me."

"No, Wolf, I won't," Jack said. He thought: *How do you get into these things, you asshole? Here you are, standing under a turnpike overpass somewhere in Ohio with your pet werewolf. How do you do it? Do you practice? And, oh, by the way, what's happening with the moon, Jack-O? Do you remember?*

He didn't, and with clouds blanketing the sky and a cold rain falling, there was no way to tell.

What did that make the odds? Thirty to one in his favor? Twenty-eight to two?

Whatever the odds were, they weren't good enough. Not the way things were going.

"No, I won't leave you," he repeated, and then led Wolf toward the far bank of the stream. In the shallows, the decayed remains of some child's dolly floated belly-up, her glassy blue eyes staring into the growing dark. The muscles of Jack's arm ached from the strain of pulling Wolf through into this world, and the joint in his shoulder throbbed like a rotted tooth.

As they came out of the water onto the weedy, trashy bank, Jack began to sneeze again.

### 2

This time, Jack's total progress in the Territories had been half a mile west—the distance Wolf had moved his herd so they could drink in the stream where Wolf himself had later almost been drowned. Over here, he found himself ten miles farther west, as best he could figure. They struggled up the bank— Wolf actually ended up pulling Jack most of the way—and in the last of the daylight Jack could see an exit-ramp splitting off to the right some fifty yards up the road. A reflectorized sign read: ARCANUM  LAST EXIT IN OHIO  STATE LINE 15 MILES.

"We've got to hitch," Jack said.

"Hitch?" Wolf said doubtfully.

"Let's have a look at you."

He thought Wolf would do, at least in the dark. He was still wearing the bib overalls, which now had an actual OSHKOSH label on them. His homespun shirt had become a machine-produced blue chambray that looked like an Army-Navy Surplus special. His formerly bare feet were clad in a huge pair of dripping penny loafers and white socks.

Oddest of all, a pair of round steel-rimmed spectacles of the sort John Lennon used to wear sat in the middle of Wolf's big face.

"Wolf, did you have trouble seeing? Over in the Territories?"

"I didn't know I did," Wolf said. "I guess so. Wolf! I sure see better over here, with these glass eyes. Wolf, right here and now!" He looked out at the roaring turnpike traffic, and for just a moment Jack saw what he must be seeing: great steel beasts with huge yellow-white eyes, snarling through the night at unimaginable speeds, rubber wheels blistering the road. "I see better than I want to," Wolf finished forlornly.

### 3

Two days later a pair of tired, footsore boys limped past the MUNICIPAL TOWN LIMITS sign on one side of Highway 32 and the 10-4 Diner on the other side, and thus into the city of Muncie, Indiana. Jack was running a fever of a hundred and two degrees and coughing pretty steadily. Wolf's face was swollen and discolored. He looked like a pug that has come out on the short end in a grudge match. The day before, he had tried to get them some late apples from a tree growing in the shade of an abandoned barn beside the road. He had actually been in the tree and dropping shrivelled autumn apples into the front of his overalls when the wall-wasps, which had built their nest somewhere in the eaves of the old barn, had found him. Wolf had come back down the tree as fast as he could, with a brown cloud around his head. He was howling. And still, with one eye completely closed and his nose beginning to resemble a large purple turnip, he had insisted that Jack have the best of the apples. None of them was very good—small and sour and wormy—and Jack didn't feel much like eating anyway, but after what Wolf had gone through to get them, he hadn't had the heart to refuse.

A big old Camaro, jacked in the back so that the nose

pointed at the road, blasted by them. *"Heyyyyy, assholes!"* someone yelled, and there was a burst of loud, beer-fueled laughter. Wolf howled and clutched at Jack. Jack had thought that Wolf would eventually get over his terror of cars, but now he was really beginning to wonder.

"It's all right, Wolf," he said wearily, peeling Wolf's arms off for the twentieth or thirtieth time that day. "They're gone."

"So *loud!*" Wolf moaned. "Wolf! Wolf! Wolf! So *loud,* Jack, my *ears,* my *ears!*"

"Glasspack muffler," Jack said, thinking wearily: *You'd love the California freeways, Wolf. We'll check those out if we're still travelling together, okay? Then we'll try a few stock-car races and motorcycle scrambles. You'll be nuts about them.* "Some guys like the sound, you know. They—" But he went into another coughing fit that doubled him over. For a moment the world swam away in gray shades. It came back very, very slowly.

*"Like it,"* Wolf muttered. "Jason! How could anyone *like* it, Jack? And the *smells . . ."*

Jack knew that, for Wolf, the smells were the worst. They hadn't been over here four hours before Wolf began to call it the Country of Bad Smells. That first night Wolf had retched half a dozen times, at first throwing up muddy water from a stream which existed in another universe onto the Ohio ground, then simply dry-heaving. It was the smells, he explained miserably. He didn't know how Jack could stand them, how anyone could stand them.

Jack knew—coming back from the Territories, you were bowled over by odors you barely noticed when you were living with them. Diesel fuel, car exhausts, industrial wastes, garbage, bad water, ripe chemicals. Then you got used to them again. Got used to them or just went numb. Only that wasn't happening to Wolf. He hated the cars, he hated the smells, he hated this world. Jack didn't think he was ever going to get used to it. If he didn't get Wolf back into the Territories fairly soon, Jack thought he might go crazy. *He'll probably drive* me *crazy while he's at it,* Jack thought. *Not that I've got far to go anymore.*

A clattering farm-truck loaded with chickens ground by them, followed by an impatient line of cars, some of them honking. Wolf almost jumped into Jack's arms. Weakened by

the fever, Jack reeled into the brushy, trash-littered ditch and
sat down so hard his teeth clicked together.

"I'm sorry, Jack," Wolf said miserably. "God pound me!"

"Not your fault," Jack said. "Fall out. Time to take five."

Wolf sat down beside Jack, remaining silent, looking at Jack
anxiously. He knew how hard he was making it for Jack; he
knew that Jack was in a fever to move faster, partly to outdis-
tance Morgan, but mostly for some other reason. He knew that
Jack moaned about his mother in his sleep, and sometimes
cried. But the only time he had cried when awake was after Wolf
went a little crazy on the Arcanum turnpike ramp. That was
when he realized what Jack meant by "hitching." When Wolf
told Jack he didn't think he could hitch rides—at least not for a
while and maybe not ever—Jack had sat down on the top strand
of guardrail cable and had wept into his hands. And then he had
stopped, which was good . . . but when he took his face out of
his hands, he had looked at Wolf in a way that made Wolf feel
sure that Jack would leave him in this horrible Country of Bad
Smells . . . and without Jack, Wolf would soon go quite mad.


4

They had walked up to the Arcanum exit in the breakdown
lane, Wolf cringing and pawing at Jack each time a car or
truck passed in the deepening dusk. Jack had heard a mocking voice drift back on the slipstream: "Where's your car, fag-
gots?" He shook it off like a dog shaking water out of his
eyes, and had simply kept going, taking Wolf's hand and
pulling him after when Wolf showed signs of lagging or drifting toward the woods. The important thing was to get off the
turnpike proper, where hitchhiking was forbidden, and onto
the westbound Arcanum entrance ramp. Some states had le-
galized hitching from the ramps (or so a road-bum with
whom Jack had shared a barn one night had told him), and
even in states where thumbing was technically a crime, the
cops would usually wink if you were on a ramp.

So first, get to the ramp. Hope no state patrol happened
along while you were getting there. What a state trooper
might make of Wolf Jack didn't want to think about. He
would probably think he had caught an eighties incarnation of
Charles Manson in Lennon glasses.

They made the ramp and crossed over to the westbound lane. Ten minutes later a battered old Chrysler had pulled up. The driver, a burly man with a bull neck and a cap which read CASE FARM EQUIPMENT tipped back on his head, leaned over and opened the door.

"Hop in, boys! Dirty night, ain't it?"

"Thanks, mister, it sure is," Jack said cheerfully. His mind was in overdrive, trying to figure out how he could work Wolf into the Story, and he barely noticed Wolf's expression.

The man noticed it, however.

His face hardened.

"You smell anything bad, son?"

Jack was snapped back to reality by the man's tone, which was as hard as his face. All cordiality had departed it, and he looked as if he might have just wandered into the Oatley Tap to eat a few beers and drink a few glasses.

Jack whipped around and looked at Wolf.

Wolf's nostrils were flaring like the nostrils of a bear which smells a blown skunk. His lips were not just pulled back from his teeth; they were *wrinkled* back from them, the flesh below his nose stacked in little ridges.

"What is he, retarded?" the man in the CASE FARM EQUIPMENT hat asked Jack in a low voice.

"No, ah, he just—"

Wolf began to growl.

That was it.

"Oh, Christ," the man said in the tones of one who simply cannot believe this is happening. He stepped on the gas and roared down the exit ramp, the passenger door flopping shut. His taillights dot-dashed briefly in the rainy dark at the foot of the ramp, sending reflections in smeary red arrows up the pavement toward where they stood.

"Boy, that's *great*," Jack said, and turned to Wolf, who shrank back from his anger. "That's just *great*! If he'd had a CB radio, he'd be on Channel Nineteen right now, yelling for a cop, telling anyone and everyone that there are a couple of loonies trying to hitch a ride out of Arcanum! Jason! Or Jesus! Or Whoever, I don't care! You want to see some fucking nails get pounded, Wolf? You do that a few more times and you'll *feel* them get pounded! Us! *We'll* get pounded!"

Exhausted, bewildered, frustrated, almost used up, Jack advanced on the cringing Wolf, who could have torn his head from his shoulders with one hard, swinging blow if he had wanted to, and Wolf backed up before him.

"Don't shout, Jack," he moaned. "The smells . . . to be in there . . . shut up in there with those *smells* . . ."

"I didn't smell *anything!*" Jack shouted. His voice broke, his sore throat hurt more than ever, but he couldn't seem to stop; it was shout or go mad. His wet hair had fallen in his eyes. He shook it away and then slapped Wolf on the shoulder. There was a smart crack and his hand began to hurt at once. It was as if he had slapped a stone. Wolf howled abjectly, and this made Jack angrier. The fact that he was lying made him angrier still. He had been in the Territories less than six hours this time, but that man's car had smelled like a wild animal's den. Harsh aromas of old coffee and fresh beer (there had been an open can of Stroh's between his legs), an air-freshener hanging from the rear-view mirror that smelled like dry sweet powder on the cheek of a corpse. And there had been something else, something darker, something wetter . . .

"Not *anything!*" he shouted, his voice breaking hoarsely. He slapped Wolf's other shoulder. Wolf howled again and turned around, hunching like a child who is being beaten by an angry father. Jack began to slap at his back, his smarting hands spatting up little sprays of water from Wolf's overalls. Each time Jack's hand descended, Wolf howled. "So you better get *used* to it *(Slap!)* because the *next* car to come along might be a *cop (Slap!)* or it might be Mr. Morgan Bloat in his puke-green BMW *(Slap!)* and if all you can be is a big *baby,* we're going to be in one big fucking *world of hurt! (Slap!)* Do you understand that?"

Wolf said nothing. He stood hunched in the rain, his back to Jack, quivering. Crying. Jack felt a lump rise in his own throat, felt his eyes grow hot and stinging. All of this only increased his fury. Some terrible part of him wanted most of all to hurt himself, and knew that hurting Wolf was a wonderful way to do it.

*"Turn around!"*

Wolf did. Tears ran from his muddy brown eyes behind the round spectacles. Snot ran from his nose.

*"Do you understand me?"*

"Yes," Wolf moaned. "Yes, I understand, but I couldn't ride with him, Jack."

"Why not?" Jack looked at him angrily, fisted hands on his hips. Oh, his head was aching.

"Because he was dying," Wolf said in a low voice.

Jack stared at him, all his anger draining away.

"Jack, didn't you know?" Wolf asked softly. "Wolf! You couldn't *smell* it?"

"No," Jack said in a small, whistling, out-of-breath voice. Because he had smelled *something*, hadn't he? Something he had never smelled before. Something like a mixture of . . .

It came to him, and suddenly his strength was gone. He sat down heavily on the guardrail cable and looked at Wolf.

Shit and rotting grapes. That was what that smell had been like. That wasn't it a hundred percent, but it was too hideously close.

Shit and rotting grapes.

"It's the worst smell," Wolf said. "It's when people forget how to be healthy. We call it—*Wolf!*—the Black Disease. I don't even think he knew he had it. And . . . these Strangers can't smell it, can they, Jack?"

"No," he whispered. If he were to be suddenly teleported back to New Hampshire, to his mother's room in the Alhambra, would he smell that stink on *her?*

Yes. He would smell it on his mother, drifting out of her pores, the smell of shit and rotting grapes, the Black Disease.

"We call it cancer," Jack whispered. *We call it cancer and my mother has it.*

"I just don't know if I can hitch," Wolf said. "I'll try again if you want, Jack, but the smells . . . inside . . . they're bad enough in the outside air, *Wolf!* but inside . . ."

That was when Jack put his face in his hands and wept, partly out of desperation, mostly out of simple exhaustion. And, yes, the expression Wolf believed he had seen on Jack's face really had been there; for an instant the temptation to leave Wolf was more than a temptation, it was a maddening imperative. The odds against his ever making it to California and finding the Talisman—whatever it might be—had been long before; now they were so long they dwind'ed to a point on the horizon. Wolf would do more than slow him down; Wolf would sooner or later get both of them thrown in jail.

Probably sooner. And how could he ever explain Wolf to Rational Richard Sloat?

What Wolf saw on Jack's face in that moment was a look of cold speculation that unhinged his knees. He fell on them and held his clasped hands up to Jack like a suitor in a bad Victorian melodrama.

"Don't go away an' leave me, Jack," he wept. "Don't leave old Wolf, don't leave me here, *you* brought me here, please, please don't leave me alone. . . ."

Beyond this, conscious words were lost; Wolf was perhaps trying to talk but all he really seemed able to do was sob. Jack felt a great weariness fall over him. It fit well, like a jacket that one has worn often. *Don't leave me here,* you *brought me here . . .*

There it was. Wolf was his responsibility, wasn't he? Yes. Oh yes indeed. He had taken Wolf by the hand and dragged him out of the Territories and into Ohio and he had the throbbing shoulder to prove it. He had had no choice, of course; Wolf had been drowning, and even if he hadn't drowned, Morgan would have crisped him with whatever that lightning-rod thing had been. So he could have turned on Wolf again, could have said: *Which would you prefer, Wolf old buddy? To be here and scared, or there and dead?*

He could, yes, and Wolf would have no answer because Wolf wasn't too swift in the brains department. But Uncle Tommy had been fond of quoting a Chinese proverb that went: *The man whose life you save is your responsibility for the rest of your life.*

Never mind the ducking, never mind the fancy footwork; Wolf was his responsibility.

"Don't leave me, Jack," Wolf wept. "Wolf-Wolf! Please don't leave good old Wolf, I'll help you, I'll stand guard at night, I can do lots, only don't don't—"

"Quit bawling and get up," Jack said quietly. "I won't leave you. But we've got to get out of here in case that guy does send a cop back to check on us. Let's move it."

### 5

"Did you figure out what to do next, Jack?" Wolf asked timidly. They had been sitting in the brushy ditch just over the

Muncie town line for more than half an hour, and when Jack turned toward Wolf, Wolf was relieved to see he was smiling. It was a weary smile, and Wolf didn't like the dark, tired circles under Jack's eyes (he liked Jack's smell even less—it was a sick smell), but it was a smile.

"I think I see what we should do next right over there," Jack said. "I was thinking about it just a few days ago, when I got my new sneakers."

He bowed his feet. He and Wolf regarded the sneakers in depressed silence. They were scuffed, battered, and dirty. The left sole was bidding a fond adieu to the left upper. Jack had owned them for . . . he wrinkled his forehead and thought. The fever made it hard to think. Three days. Only three days since he had picked them out of the bargain bin of the Fayva store. Now they looked old. Old.

"Anyway . . ." Jack sighed. Then he brightened. "See that building over there, Wolf?"

The building, an explosion of uninteresting angles in gray brick, stood like an island in the middle of a giant parking lot. Wolf knew what the asphalt in that parking lot would smell like: dead, decomposing animals. That smell would almost suffocate him, and Jack would barely notice it.

"For your information, the sign there said Town Line Sixplex," Jack said. "It sounds like a coffee pot, but actually it's a movie with six shows. There ought to be one we like." *And in the afternoon, there won't be many people there and that's good because you have this distressing habit of going Section Eight, Wolf.* "Come on." He got unsteadily to his feet.

"What's a movie, Jack?" Wolf asked. He had been a dreadful problem to Jack, he knew—such a dreadful problem that he now hesitated to protest about anything, or even express unease. But a frightening intuition had come to him: that *going to a movie* and *hitching a ride* might be the same thing. Jack called the roaring carts and carriages "cars," and "Chevys," and "Jartrans," and "station-wagons" (these latter, Wolf thought, must be like the coaches in the Territories which carried passengers from one coach-station to the next). Might the bellowing, stinking carriages also be called "movies"? It sounded very possible.

"Well," Jack said, "it's easier to show you than to tell you. I think you'll like it. Come on."

Jack stumbled coming out of the ditch and went briefly to his knees. "Jack, are you okay?" Wolf asked anxiously.

Jack nodded. They started across the parking lot, which smelled just as bad as Wolf had known it would.

## 6

Jack had come a good part of the thirty-five miles between Arcanum, Ohio, and Muncie, Indiana, on Wolf's broad back. Wolf was frightened of cars, terrified of trucks, nauseated by the smells of almost everything, apt to howl and run at sudden loud noises. But he was also almost tireless. *As far as that goes, you can strike the "almost,"* Jack thought now. *So far as I know, he* is *tireless.*

Jack had moved them away from the Arcanum ramp as fast as he could, forcing his wet, aching legs into a rusty trot. His head had been throbbing like a slick, flexing fist inside his skull, waves of heat and cold rushing through him. Wolf moved easily to his left, his stride so long that he was keeping up with Jack easily by doing no more than a moderately fast walk. Jack knew that he had maybe gotten paranoid about the cops, but the man in the CASE FARM EQUIPMENT hat had looked really scared. And pissed.

They hadn't gone even a quarter of a mile when a deep, burning stitch settled into his side and he asked Wolf if he could give him a piggyback for a while.

"Huh?" Wolf asked.

"You know," Jack said, and pantomimed.

A big grin had overspread Wolf's face. Here at last was something he understood; here was something he could *do.*

"You want a *horsey*back!" he cried, delighted.

"Yeah, I guess . . ."

"Oh, yeah! Wolf! Here and now! Used to give em to my litter-brothers! Jump up, Jack!" Wolf bent down, holding his curved hands ready, stirrups for Jack's thighs.

"Now when I get too heavy, just put me d—"

Before he could finish, Wolf had swept him up and was running lightly down the road with him into the dark—really running. The cold, rainy air flipped Jack's hair back from his hot brow.

"Wolf, you'll wear yourself out!" Jack shouted.

"Not me! Wolf! Wolf! Runnin here and now!" For the first
time since they had come over, Wolf sounded actually happy.
He ran for the next two hours, until they were west of Arcanum and travelling along a dark, unmarked stretch of two-
lane black-top. Jack saw a deserted barn standing slumped in
a shaggy, untended field, and they slept there that night.

Wolf wanted nothing to do with downtown areas where the
traffic was a roaring flood and the stinks rose up to heaven in
a noxious cloud, and Jack didn't want anything to do with
them, either. Wolf stuck out too much. But he had forced one
stop, at a roadside store just across the Indiana line, near Har-
risville. While Wolf waited nervously out by the road, hunkering down, digging at the dirt, getting up, walking around in a
stiff little circle, then hunkering again, Jack bought a newspaper and checked the weather page carefully. The next full
moon was on October 31st—Halloween, that was fitting
enough. Jack turned back to the front page so he could see
what day it was today . . . yesterday, that had been now. It had
been October 26th.

### 7

Jack pulled open one of the glass doors and stepped inside the
lobby of the Town Line Sixplex. He looked around sharply at
Wolf, but Wolf looked—for the moment, at least—pretty
much okay. Wolf was, in fact, cautiously optimistic . . . at
least for the moment. He didn't like being inside a building,
but at least it wasn't a car. There was a good smell in here—
light and sort of tasty. Or would have been, except for a bitter,
almost rancid undersmell. Wolf looked left and saw a glass
box full of white stuff. That was the source of the good light
smell.

"Jack," he whispered.

"Huh?"

"I want some of that white stuff, please. But none of the
pee."

"Pee? What are you talking about?"

Wolf searched for a more formal word and found it.
"Urine." He pointed at a thing with a light going off and on
inside it. BUTTERY FLAVORING, it read. "That's some kind of
urine, isn't it? It's got to be, the way it smells."

Jack smiled tiredly. "A popcorn without the fake butter, right," he said. "Now pipe down, okay?"

"Sure, Jack," Wolf said humbly. "Right here and now."

The ticket-girl had been chewing a big wad of grape-flavored bubble gum. Now she stopped. She looked at Jack, then at Jack's big, hulking companion. The gum sat on her tongue inside her half-open mouth like a large purple tumor. She rolled her eyes at the guy behind the counter.

"Two, please," Jack said. He took out his roll of bills, dirty, tag-eared ones with an orphan five hiding in the middle.

"Which show?" Her eyes moved back and forth, back and forth, Jack to Wolf and Wolf to Jack. She looked like a woman watching a hot table-tennis match.

"What's just starting?" Jack asked her.

"Well . . ." She glanced down at the paper Scotch-taped beside her. "There's *The Flying Dragon* in Cinema Four. It's a kung-fu movie with Chuck Norris." Back and forth went her eyes, back and forth, back and forth. "Then, in Cinema Six, there's a double feature. Two Ralph Bakshi cartoons. *Wizards* and *The Lord of the Rings*."

Jack felt relieved. Wolf was nothing but a big, overgrown kid, and kids loved cartoons. This could work out after all. Wolf would maybe find at least one thing in the Country of Bad Smells that would amuse him, and Jack could sleep for three hours.

"That one," he said. "The cartoons."

"That'll be four dollars," she said. "Bargain Matinee prices end at two." She pushed a button and two tickets poked out of a slot with a mechanical ratcheting noise. Wolf flinched backward with a small cry.

The girl looked at him, eyebrows raised.

"You jumpy, mister?"

"No, I'm Wolf," Wolf said. He smiled, showing a great many teeth. Jack would have sworn that Wolf showed more teeth now when he smiled than he had a day or two ago. The girl looked at all those teeth. She wet her lips.

"He's okay. He just—" Jack shrugged. "He doesn't get off the farm much. You know." He gave her the orphan five. She handled it as if she wished she had a pair of tongs to do it with.

"Come on, Wolf."

As they turned away to the candy-stand, Jack stuffing the
one into the pocket of his grimy jeans, the ticket-girl mouthed
to the counterman: *Look at his nose!*

Jack looked at Wolf and saw Wolf's nose flaring rhythmically.

"Stop that," he muttered.

"Stop what, Jack?"

"Doing that thing with your nose."

"Oh. I'll try, Jack, but—"

"Shh."

"Help you, son?" the counterman asked.

"Yes, please. A Junior Mints, a Reese's Pieces, and an
extra-large popcorn without the grease."

The counterman got the stuff and pushed it across to them.
Wolf got the tub of popcorn in both hands and immediately
began to snaffle it up in great jaw-cracking chomps.

The counterman looked at this silently.

"Doesn't get off the farm much," Jack repeated. Part of
him was already wondering if these two had seen enough of
sufficient oddness to get them thinking that a call to the police
might be in order. He thought—not for the first time—that
there was a real irony in all this. In New York or L.A., probably no one would have given Wolf a second look . . . or if a
second look, certainly not a third. Apparently the weirdness-
toleration level was a lot lower out in the middle of the country. But, of course, Wolf would have flipped out of his gourd
long since if they had been in New York or L.A.

"I'll bet he don't," the counterman said. "That'll be two-
eighty."

Jack paid it with an inward wince, realizing he had just
laid out a quarter of his cash for their afternoon at the movies.

Wolf was grinning at the counterman through a mouthful
of popcorn. Jack recognized it as Wolf's A #1 Friendly Smile,
but he somehow doubted that the counterman was seeing it
that way. There were all those teeth in that smile . . . hundreds
of them, it seemed.

And Wolf was flaring his nostrils again.

*Screw it, let them call the cops, if that's what they want to
do,* he thought with a weariness that was more adult than
child. *It can't slow us down much more than we're slowed
down already. He can't ride in the new cars because he can't*

*stand the smell of the catalytic convertors and he can't ride in
old cars because they smell like exhaust and sweat and oil
and beer and he probably can't ride in any cars because he's
so goddam claustrophobic. Tell the truth, Jack-O, even if it's
only to yourself. You're going along telling yourself he's going
to get over it pretty soon, but it's probably not going to happen. So what are we going to do? Walk across Indiana, I
guess. Correction,* Wolf *is going to walk across Indiana. Me,
I'm going to cross Indiana riding horseyback. But first I'm
going to take Wolf into this damn movie theater and sleep either until both pictures are over or until the cops arrive. And
that is the end of my tale, sir.*

"Well, enjoy the show," the counterman said.

"You bet," Jack replied. He started away and then realized
Wolf wasn't with him. Wolf was staring at something over the
counterman's head with vacant, almost superstitious wonder.
Jack looked up and saw a mobile advertising the re-issue of
Steven Spielberg's *Close Encounters* floating around on drafts
of convection.

"Come on, Wolf," he said.

## 8

Wolf knew it wasn't going to work as soon as they went
through the door.

The room was small, dim, and dank. The smells in here
were terrible. A poet, smelling what Wolf was smelling at that
moment, might have called it the stink of sour dreams. Wolf
was no poet. He only knew that the smell of the popcorn-
urine predominated, and that he felt suddenly like throwing up.

Then the lights began to dim even further, turning the
room into a cave.

"Jack," he moaned, clutching at Jack's arm. "Jack, we
oughtta get out of here, okay?"

"You'll like it, Wolf," Jack muttered, aware of Wolf's distress but not of its depth. Wolf was, after all, always distressed
to some degree. In this world, the word *distress* defined him.
"Try it."

"Okay," Wolf said, and Jack heard the agreement but not
the thin waver that meant Wolf was holding on to the last

thread of his control with both hands. They sat down with
Wolf on the aisle, his knees accordioned up uncomfortably,
the tub of popcorn (which he no longer wanted) clutched to
his chest.

In front of them a match flared briefly yellow. Jack smelled
the dry tang of pot, so familiar in the movies that it could be
dismissed as soon as identified. Wolf smelled a forest-fire.

"Jack—!"

"Shhh, picture's starting."

*And I'm dozing off.*

Jack would never know of Wolf's heroism in the next few
minutes; Wolf did not really know of it himself. He only knew
that he had to try to stick this nightmare out for Jack's sake. *It
must be all right,* he thought, *look, Wolf, Jack's going right to
sleep, right to sleep right here and now. And you know Jack
wouldn't take you to a Hurt-Place, so just stick it out . . . just
wait . . . Wolf! . . . it'll be all right . . .*

But Wolf was a cyclic creature, and his cycle was approaching its monthly climax. His instincts had become exquisitely refined, almost undeniable. His rational mind told
him that he would be all right in here, that Jack wouldn't have
brought him otherwise. But that was like a man with an itchy
nose telling himself not to sneeze in church because it was
impolite.

He sat there smelling forest-fire in a dark, stinking cave,
twitching each time a shadow passed down the aisle, waiting
numbly for something to fall on him from the shadows overhead. And then a magic window opened at the front of the
cave and he sat there in the acrid stink of his own terror-
sweat, eyes wide, face a mask of horror, as cars crashed and
overturned, as buildings burned, as one man chased another.

"Previews," Jack mumbled. "Told you you'd like it. . . ."

There were Voices. One said *nosmoking*. One said *don't
litter*. One said *groupratesavailable*. One said *Bargain
Matinee-priceseveryweekdayuntilfourp.m.*

"Wolf, we got screwed," Jack mumbled. He started to say
something else, but it turned into a snore.

A final voice said *andnowourfeaturepresentation* and that
was when Wolf lost control. Bakshi's *The Lord of the Rings*
was in Dolby sound, and the projectionist had orders to really

crank it in the afternoons, because that's when the heads drifted in, and the heads really liked loud Dolby.

There was a screeching, discordant crash of brass. The magic window opened again and now Wolf could *see* the fire—shifting oranges and reds.

He howled and leaped to his feet, pulling with him a Jack who was more asleep than awake.

*"Jack!"* he screamed. *"Get out! Got to get out! Wolf! See the fire! Wolf! Wolf!"*

"Down in front!" someone shouted.

"Shut up, hoser!" someone else yelled.

The door at the back of Cinema 6 opened. "What's going on in here?"

"Wolf, shut up!" Jack hissed. "For God's sake—"

*"OWWWWWW-OOOOOOOOOOOOOOOOOOOOO!"*
Wolf howled.

A woman got a good look at Wolf as the white light from the lobby fell on him. She screamed and began dragging her little boy out by one arm. Literally *dragging* him; the kid had fallen to his knees and was skidding up the popcorn-littered carpet of the center aisle. One of his sneakers had come off.

*"OWWWWWWWW-OOOOOOOOOOOOOOOOOHH-HHH-HHOOOOOOHHHHOOOOOO!"*

The pothead three rows down had turned around and was looking at them with bleary interest. He held a smouldering joint in one hand; a spare was cocked behind his ear. "Far . . . out," he pronounced. "Fucking werewolves of London strike again, right?"

"Okay," Jack said. "Okay, we'll get out. No problem. Just . . . just don't do that anymore, okay? Okay?"

He started leading Wolf out. The weariness had fallen over him again.

The light of the lobby hit his eyes sharply, needling them. The woman who had dragged the little boy out of the theater was backed into a corner with her arms around the kid. When she saw Jack lead the still-howling Wolf through the double doors of Cinema 6, she swept the kid up and made a break for it.

The counterman, the ticket-girl, the projectionist, and a tall man in a sportcoat that looked as if it belonged on the back of a racetrack tout were clustered together in a tight little group. Jack supposed the guy in the checkered sportcoat and white shoes was the manager.

The doors of the other cinemas in the hive had opened partway. Faces peered out of the darkness to see what all the hooraw was. To Jack, they all looked like badgers peering out of their holes.

"Get out!" the man in the checkered sportcoat said. "Get out, I've called the police already, they'll be here in five minutes."

*Bullshit you did,* Jack thought, feeling a ray of hope. *You didn't have time. And if we blow right away, maybe—just maybe—you won't bother.*

"We're going," he said. "Look, I'm sorry. It's just that . . . my big brother's an epileptic and he just had a seizure. We . . . we forgot his medicine."

At the word *epileptic*, the ticket-girl and the counterman recoiled. It was as if Jack had said *leper*.

"Come on, Wolf."

He saw the manager's eyes drop, saw his lip curl with distaste. Jack followed the glance and saw the wide dark stain on the front of Wolf's Oshkosh biballs. He had wet himself.

Wolf also saw. Much in Jack's world was foreign to him, but he apparently knew well enough what that look of contempt meant. He burst into loud, braying, heartbroken sobs.

*"Jack, I'm sorry, Wolf is so SORRY!"*

"Get him out of here," the manager said contemptuously, and turned away.

Jack put an arm around Wolf and got him started toward the door. "Come on, Wolf," he said. He spoke quietly, and with an honest tenderness. He had never felt quite so keenly for Wolf as he did now. "Come on, it was my fault, not yours. Let's go."

"Sorry." Wolf wept brokenly. "I'm no good, God pound me, just no good."

"You're plenty good," Jack said. "Come on."

He pushed open the door and they went out into the thin, late-October warmth.

The woman with the child was easily twenty yards away, but when she saw Jack and Wolf, she retreated backward toward her car, holding her kid in front of her like a cornered gangster with a hostage.

"Don't let him come near me!" she screamed. "Don't let that monster come near my baby! Do you hear? *Don't let him come near me!*"

Jack thought he should say something to calm her down, but he couldn't think what it might be. He was too tired.

He and Wolf started away, heading across the parking lot at an angle. Halfway back to the road, Jack staggered. The world went briefly gray.

He was vaguely aware of Wolf sweeping him up in his arms and carrying him that way, like a baby. Vaguely aware that Wolf was crying.

"Jack, I'm so sorry, please don't hate Wolf, I can be a good old Wolf, you wait, you'll see . . ."

"I don't hate you," Jack said. "I know you're . . . you're a good old—"

But before he could finish, he had fallen asleep. When he woke up it was evening and Muncie was behind them. Wolf had gotten off the main roads and on to a web of farm roads and dirt tracks. Totally unconfused by the lack of signs and the multitude of choices, he had continued west with all the unerring instinct of a migrating bird.

They slept that night in an empty house north of Cammack, and Jack thought in the morning that his fever had gone down a little.

It was midmorning—midmorning of October 28th—when Jack realized that the hair was back on Wolf's palms.

# 19

# Jack in the Box

### 1

They camped that night in the ruins of a burned-out house with a wide field on one side and a copse of woods on another. There was a farmhouse on the far side of the field, but Jack thought that he and Wolf would be safe enough if they were quiet and stayed in most of the time. After the sun went down, Wolf went off into the woods. He was moving slowly, his face close to the ground. Before Jack lost sight of him, he thought that Wolf looked like a nearsighted man hunting for his dropped spectacles. Jack became quite nervous (visions of Wolf caught in a steel-jawed trap had begun to come to him, Wolf caught and grimly not howling as he gnawed at his own leg . . .) before Wolf returned, walking almost upright this time, and carrying plants in both hands, the roots dangling out of his fists.

"What have you got there, Wolf?" Jack asked.

"Medicine," Wolf said morosely. "But it's not very good, Jack. *Wolf! Nothing's* much good in your world!"

"Medicine? What do you mean?"

But Wolf would say no more. He produced two wooden matches from the bib pocket of his overalls and started a smokeless fire and asked Jack if he could find a can. Jack found a beer can in the ditch. Wolf smelled it and wrinkled his nose.

"More bad smells. Need water, Jack. Clean water. I'll go, if you're too tired."

"Wolf, I want to know what you're up to."

"I'll go," Wolf said. "There's a farm right across that field. *Wolf!* There'll be water there. You rest."

Jack had a vision of some farmer's wife looking out the kitchen window as she did the supper dishes and seeing Wolf skulking around in the dooryard with a beer can in one hairy paw and a bunch of roots and herbs in the other.

"*I'll* go," he said.

The farm was not five hundred feet away from where they had camped; the warm yellow lights were clearly visible across the field. Jack went, filled the beer can at a shed faucet without incident, and started back. Halfway across the field he realized he could see his shadow, and looked up at the sky.

The moon, now almost full, rode the eastern horizon.

Troubled, Jack went back to Wolf and gave him the can of water. Wolf sniffed, winced again, but said nothing. He put the can over the fire and began to sift crumbled bits of the things he had picked in through the pop-top hole. Five minutes or so later, a terrible smell—a reek, not to put too fine a point on it—began to rise on the steam. Jack winced. He had no doubt at all that Wolf would want him to drink that stuff, and Jack also had no doubt it would kill him. Slowly and horribly, probably.

He closed his eyes and began snoring loudly and theatrically. If Wolf thought he was sleeping, he wouldn't wake him up. No one woke up sick people, did they? And Jack *was* sick; his fever had come back at dark, raging through him, punishing him with chills even while he oozed sweat from every pore.

Looking through his lashes, he saw Wolf set the can aside to cool. Wolf sat back and looked skyward, his hairy hands locked around his knees, his face dreamy and somehow beautiful.

*He's looking at the moon,* Jack thought, and felt a thread of fear.

*We don't go near the herd when we change. Good Jason, no! We'd eat them!*

*Wolf, tell me something: am I the herd now?*

Jack shivered.

Five minutes later—Jack almost *had* gone to sleep by then—Wolf leaned over the can, sniffed, nodded, picked it up, and came over to where Jack was leaning against a fallen, fire-blackened beam with an extra shirt behind his neck to pad the angle. Jack closed his eyes tightly and resumed snoring.

"Come on, Jack," Wolf said jovially. "I know you're awake. You can't fool Wolf."

Jack opened his eyes and looked at Wolf with bleary resentment. "How did you know?"

"People have a sleep-smell and a wake-smell," Wolf said. "Even Strangers must know that, don't they?"

"I guess we don't," Jack said.

"Anyway, you have to drink this. It's medicine. Drink it up, Jack, right here and now."

"I don't want it," Jack said. The smell coming from the can was swampy and rancid.

"Jack," Wolf said, "you've got a sick-smell, too."

Jack looked at him, saying nothing.

"Yes," Wolf said. "And it keeps getting worse. It's not really bad, not yet, but—*Wolf!*—it's going to *get* bad if you don't take some medicine."

"Wolf, I'll bet you're great at sniffing out herbs and things back in the Territories, but this is the Country of Bad Smells, remember? You've probably got ragweed in there, and poison oak, and bitter vetch, and—"

"They're good things," Wolf said. "Just not very strong, God pound them." Wolf looked wistful. "Not everything smells bad here, Jack. There are good smells, too. But the good smells are like the medicine plants. Weak. I think they were stronger, once."

Wolf was looking dreamily up at the moon again, and Jack felt a recurrence of his earlier unease.

"I'll bet this was a good place once," Wolf said. "Clean and full of power . . ."

"Wolf?" Jack asked in a low voice. "Wolf, the hair's come back on your palms."

Wolf started and looked at Jack. For a moment—it might have been his feverish imagination, and even if not, it was only for a moment—Wolf looked at Jack with a flat, greedy hunger. Then he seemed to shake himself, as if out of a bad dream.

"Yes," he said. "But I don't want to talk about that, and I don't want you to talk about that. It doesn't matter, not yet. *Wolf!* Just drink your medicine, Jack, that's all *you* have to do."

Wolf was obviously not going to take no for an answer; if Jack didn't drink the medicine, then Wolf might feel duty-bound to simply pull open his jaws and pour it down his throat.

"Remember, if this kills me, you'll be alone," Jack said grimly, taking the can. It was still warm.

A look of terrible distress spread over Wolf's face. He pushed the round glasses up on his nose. "Don't want to hurt you, Jack—Wolf never wants to hurt Jack." The expression was so large and so full of misery that it would have been ludicrous had it not been so obviously genuine.

Jack gave in and drank the contents of the can. There was no way he could stand against that expression of hurt dismay. The taste was as awful as he had imagined it would be . . . *and for a moment didn't the world waver? Didn't it waver as if he were about to flip back into the Territories?*

"*Wolf!*" he yelled. "*Wolf, grab my hand!*"

Wolf did, looking both concerned and excited. "Jack? Jacky? What is it?"

The taste of the medicine began to leave his mouth. At the same time, a warm glow—the sort of glow he got from a small sip of brandy on the few occasions his mother had allowed him to have one—began to spread in his stomach. And the world grew solid around him again. That brief wavering might also have been imagination . . . but Jack didn't think so.

*We almost went. For a moment there it was very close. Maybe I can do it without the magic juice . . . maybe I can!*

"Jack? What is it?"

"I feel better," he said, and managed a smile. "I feel better, that's all." He discovered that he did, too.

"You smell better, too," Wolf said cheerfully. "*Wolf! Wolf!*"

### 2

He continued to improve the next day, but he was weak. Wolf carried him "horseyback" and they made slow progress west. Around dusk they started looking for a place to lie up for the night. Jack spotted a woodshed in a dirty little gully. It was surrounded by trash and bald tires. Wolf agreed without saying much. He had been quiet and morose all day long.

Jack fell asleep almost at once and woke up around eleven needing to urinate. He looked beside him and saw that Wolf's place was empty. Jack thought he had probably gone in search of more herbs in order to administer the equivalent of a booster shot. Jack wrinkled his nose, but if Wolf wanted him to drink more of the stuff, he would. It surely had made him feel one hell of a lot better.

He went around to the side of the shed, a straight slim boy wearing Jockey shorts, unlaced sneakers, and an open shirt. He peed for what seemed like a very long time indeed, looking up at the sky as he did so. It was one of those misleading nights which sometimes comes to the midwest in October and early November, not so long before winter comes down with a cruel, iron snap. It was almost tropically warm, and the mild breeze was like a caress.

Overhead floated the moon, white and round and lovely. It cast a clear and yet eerily misleading glow over everything, seeming to simultaneously enhance and obscure. Jack stared at it, aware that he was almost hypnotized, not really caring.

*We don't go* near *the herd when we change. Good Jason, no!*

*Am I the herd now, Wolf?*

There was a face on the moon. Jack saw with no surprise that it was Wolf's face . . . except it was not wide and open and a little surprised, a face of goodness and simplicity. This face was narrow, ah yes, and dark; it was dark with hair, but the hair didn't matter. It was dark with intent.

*We don't go* near *them, we'd eat them, eat them, we'd eat them, Jack, when we change we'd—*

The face in the moon, a chiaroscuro carved in bone, was the face of a snarling beast, its head cocked in that final moment before the lunge, the mouth open and filled with teeth.

*We'd eat we'd kill we'd kill, kill, KILL KILL*

A finger touched Jack's shoulder and ran slowly down to his waist.

Jack had only been standing there with his penis in his hand, the foreskin pinched lightly between thumb and forefinger, looking at the moon. Now a fresh, hard jet of urine spurted out of him.

"I scared you," Wolf said from behind him. "I'm sorry, Jack. God pound me."

But for a moment Jack didn't think Wolf was sorry.

For a moment it sounded as if Wolf were grinning.

And Jack was suddenly sure he was going to be eaten up.

*House of bricks?* he thought incoherently. *I don't even have a house of straw that I can run to.*

*Now* the fear came, dry terror in his veins hotter than any fever.

*Who's afraid of the big bad Wolf the big bad Wolf the big
bad—*

"Jack?"

*I am, I am, oh God I am afraid of the big bad Wolf—*

He turned around slowly.

Wolf's face, which had been lightly scruffed with stubble
when the two of them crossed to the shed and lay down, was
now heavily bearded from a point so high on his cheekbones
that the hair almost seemed to begin at his temples. His eyes
glared a bright red-orange.

"Wolf, are you all right?" Jack asked in a husky, breathy
whisper. It was as loud as he could talk.

"Yes," Wolf said. "I've been running with the moon. It's
beautiful. I ran . . . and ran . . . and ran. But I'm all right,
Jack." Wolf smiled to show how all right he was, and revealed
a mouthful of giant, rending teeth. Jack recoiled in numb horror. It was like looking into the mouth of that *Alien* thing in
the movies.

Wolf saw his expression, and dismay crossed his rough-
ened, thickening features. But under the dismay—and not far
under, either—was something else. Something that capered
and grinned and showed its teeth. Something that would
chase prey until blood flew from the prey's nose in its terror,
until it moaned and begged. Something that would laugh as it
tore the screaming prey open.

It would laugh even if *he* were the prey.

*Especially* if he were the prey.

"Jack, I'm sorry," he said. "The time . . . it's coming. We'll
have to do something. We'll . . . tomorrow. We'll have to . . .
have to . . ." He looked up and that hypnotized expression
spread over his face as he looked into the sky.

He raised his head and howled.

And Jack thought he heard—very faintly—the Wolf in the
moon howl back.

Horror stole through him, quietly and completely. Jack
slept no more that night.

### 3

The next day Wolf was better. A little better, anyway, but he
was almost sick with tension. As he was trying to tell Jack

what to do—as well as he could, anyway—a jet plane passed high overhead. Wolf jumped to his feet, rushed out, and howled at it, shaking his fists at the sky. His hairy feet were bare again. They had swelled and split the cheap penny loafers wide open.

He tried to tell Jack what to do, but he had little to go on except old tales and rumors. He knew what the change was in his own world, but he sensed it might be much worse—more powerful and more dangerous—in the land of the Strangers. And he felt that now. He felt that power sweeping through him, and tonight when the moon rose he felt sure it would sweep him away.

Over and over again he reiterated that he didn't want to hurt Jack, that he would rather kill himself than hurt Jack.

### 4

Daleville was the closest small town. Jack got there shortly after the courthouse clock struck noon, and went into the True Value hardware store. One hand was stuffed into his pants pocket, touching his depleted roll of bills.

"Help you, son?"

"Yes sir," Jack said. "I want to buy a padlock."

"Well, step over here and let's us have a look. We've got Yales, and Mosslers, and Lok-Tites, and you name it. What kind of padlock you want?"

"A big one," Jack said, looking at the clerk with his shadowed, somehow disquieting eyes. His face was gaunt but still persuasive in its odd beauty.

"A big one," the clerk mused. "And what would you be wanting it for, might I ask?"

"My dog," Jack said steadily. A Story. Always they wanted a Story. He had gotten this one ready on the way in from the shed where they had spent the last two nights. "I need it for my dog. I have to lock him up. He bites."

### 5

The padlock he picked out cost ten dollars, leaving Jack with about ten dollars to his name. It hurt him to spend that much, and he almost went for a cheaper item . . . and then he had a memory of how Wolf had looked the night before, howling at the moon with orange fire spilling from his eyes.

He paid the ten dollars.

He stuck out his thumb at every passing car as he hurried back to the shed, but of course none of them stopped. Perhaps he looked too wild-eyed, too frantic. He certainly *felt* wild-eyed and frantic. The newspaper the hardware store clerk had let him look at promised sunset at six o'clock P.M. on the dot. Moonrise was not listed, but Jack guessed seven, at the latest. It was already one p.m., and he had no idea where he was going to put Wolf for the night.

*You have to lock me up, Jack,* Wolf had said. *Have to lock me up good. Because if I get out, I'll hurt anything I can run down and catch hold of. Even you, Jack. Even you. So you have to lock me up and keep me locked up, no matter what I do or what I say. Three days, Jack, until the moon starts to get thin again. Three days . . . even four, if you're not completely sure.*

Yes, but where? It had to be someplace away from people, so no one would hear Wolf if—*when*, he amended reluctantly—he began to howl. And it had to be someplace a lot stronger than the shed they had been staying in. If Jack used his fine new ten-dollar padlock on the door of that place, Wolf would bust right out through the back.

*Where?*

He didn't know, but he knew he had only six hours to find a place . . . maybe less.

Jack began to hurry along even faster.

### 6

They had passed several empty houses to come this far, had even spent the night in one, and Jack watched all the way back from Daleville for the signs of lack of occupancy: for blank uncovered windows and FOR SALE signs, for grass grown as high as the second porch step and the sense of life-lessness common to empty houses. It was not that he hoped he could lock Wolf into some farmer's bedroom for the three days of his Change. Wolf would be able to knock down the door of the shed. But one farmhouse had a root cellar; that would have worked.

A stout oaken door set into a grassy mound like a door in a fairy tale, and behind it a room without walls or ceiling—an underground room, a cave no creature could dig its way out of in less than a month. The cellar would have held Wolf, and the earthen floor and walls would have kept him from injuring himself.

But the empty farmhouse, and the root cellar, must have been at least thirty or forty miles behind them. They would never make it back there in the time remaining before moonrise. And would Wolf still be willing to run forty miles, especially for the purpose of putting himself in a foodless solitary confinement, so close to the time of his Change?

Suppose, in fact, that too much time had passed. Suppose that Wolf had come too close to the edge and would refuse any sort of imprisonment? What if that capering, greedy underside of his character had climbed up out of the pit and was beginning to look around this odd new world, wondering where the food was hiding? The big padlock threatening to rip the seams out of Jack's pocket would be useless.

He could turn around, Jack realized. He could walk back to Daleville and keep on going. In a day or two he'd be nearly to Lapel or Cicero, and maybe he would work an afternoon at a feed store or get in some hours as a farmhand, make a few dollars or scrounge a meal or two, and then push all the way to the Illinois border in the next few days. Illinois would be easy, Jack thought—he didn't know how he was going to do this, exactly, but he was pretty sure he could get to Springfield and the Thayer School only a day or two after he made it into Illinois.

And, Jack puzzled as he hesitated a quarter-mile down the road from the shed, how would he explain Wolf to Richard Sloat? His old buddy Richard, in his round glasses and ties and laced cordovans? Richard Sloat was thoroughly rational and, though very intelligent, hard-headed. If you couldn't see it, it probably didn't exist. Richard had never been interested in fairy tales as a child; he had remained unexcited by Disney films about fairy godmothers who turned pumpkins into coaches, about wicked queens who owned speaking mirrors. Such conceits were too absurd to snare Richard's six-year-old (or eight-year-old, or ten-year-old) fancy—unlike, say, a photograph of an electron microscope. Richard's enthusiasm had embraced Rubik's Cube, which he could solve in less than ninety seconds, but Jack did not think it would go so far as to accept a six-foot-five, sixteen-year-old werewolf.

For a moment Jack twisted helplessly on the road—for a moment he almost thought that he would be able to leave Wolf behind and get on with his journey toward Richard and then the Talisman.

*What if I'm the herd?* he asked himself silently. And what he thought of was Wolf scrambling down the bank after his poor terrified animals, throwing himself into the water to rescue them.

## 7

The shed was empty. As soon as Jack saw the door leaning open he knew that Wolf had taken himself off somewhere, but he scrambled down the side of the gully and picked his way through the trash almost in disbelief. Wolf could not have gone farther than a dozen feet by himself, yet he had done so. "I'm back," Jack called. "Hey, Wolf? I got the lock." He knew he was talking to himself, and a glance into the shed confirmed this. His pack lay on a little wooden bench; a stack of pulpy magazines dated 1973 stood beside it. In one corner of the windowless wooden shed odd lengths of deadwood had been carelessly heaped, as if someone had once half-heartedly made a stab at squirreling away firewood. Otherwise the shed was bare. Jack turned around from the gaping door and looked helplessly up the banks of the gully.

Old tires scattered here and there among the weeds, a bundle of faded and rotting political pamphlets still bearing the name LUGAR, one dented blue-and-white Connecticut license plate, beer-bottles with labels so faded they were white . . . no Wolf. Jack raised his hands to cup his mouth. "Hey, Wolf! I'm back!" He expected no reply, and got none. Wolf was gone.

"Shit," Jack said, and put his hands on his hips. Conflicting emotions, exasperation and relief and anxiety, surged through him. Wolf had left in order to save Jack's life—that had to be the meaning of his disappearance. As soon as Jack had set off for Daleville, his partner had skipped out. He had run away on those tireless legs and by now was miles away, waiting for the moon to come up. By now, Wolf could be anywhere.

This realization was part of Jack's anxiety. Wolf could have taken himself into the woods visible at the end of the long field bordered by the gully, and in the woods gorged himself on rabbits and fieldmice and whatever else might live there, moles and badgers and the whole cast of *The Wind in the Willows*. Which would have been dandy. But Wolf just might sniff out the livestock, wherever it was, and put himself in real danger. He might also, Jack realized, sniff out the farmer and his family. Or, even worse, Wolf might have worked his way close to one of the towns north of them. Jack couldn't be sure, but he thought that a transformed Wolf would probably be capable of slaughtering at least half a dozen people before somebody finally killed him.

"Damn, damn, damn," Jack said, and began to climb up the far side of the gully. He had no real hopes of seeing Wolf—he would probably never see Wolf again, he realized. In some small-town paper, a few days down the road, he'd find a horrified description of the carnage caused by an enormous wolf which had apparently wandered into Main Street looking for food. And there would be more names. More names like Thielke, Heidel, Hagen . . .

At first he looked toward the road, hoping even now to see Wolf's giant form skulking away to the east—he wouldn't want to meet Jack returning from Daleville. The long road was as deserted as the shed.

Of course.

The sun, as good a clock as the one he wore on his wrist, had slipped well below its meridian.

Jack turned despairingly toward the long field and the edge of the woods behind it. Nothing moved but the tips of the stubble, which bent before a chill wandering breeze.

HUNT CONTINUES FOR KILLER WOLF, a headline would read, a few days down the road.

Then a large brown boulder at the edge of the woods did move, and Jack realized that the boulder was Wolf. He had hunkered down on his heels and was staring at Jack.

"Oh, you inconvenient son of a bitch," Jack said, and in the midst of his relief knew that a part of him had been secretly delighted by Wolf's departure. He stepped toward him.

Wolf did not move, but his posture somehow intensified,

became more electric and aware. Jack's next step required more courage than the first.

Twenty yards farther, he saw that Wolf had continued to change. His hair had become even thicker, more luxuriant, as if it had been washed and blow-dried; and now Wolf's beard really did seem to begin just beneath his eyes. He entire body, hunkered down as it was, seemed to have become wider and more powerful. His eyes, filled with liquid fire, blazed Halloween orange.

Jack made himself go nearer. He nearly stopped when he thought he saw that Wolf now had paws instead of hands, but a moment later realized that his hands and fingers were completely covered by a thatch of coarse dark hair. Wolf continued to gaze at him with his blazing eyes. Jack again halved the distance between them, then paused. For the first time since he had come upon Wolf tending his flock beside a Territories stream, he could not read his expression. Maybe Wolf had become too alien for that already, or maybe all the hair simply concealed too much of his face. What he was sure of was that some strong emotion had gripped Wolf.

A dozen feet away he stopped for good and forced himself to look into the werewolf's eyes.

"Soon now, Jacky," Wolf said, and his mouth dropped open in a fearsome parody of a smile.

"I thought you ran away," Jack said.

"Sat here to see you coming. Wolf!"

Jack did not know what to make of this declaration. Obscurely, it reminded him of Little Red Riding Hood. Wolf's teeth did look particularly crowded, sharp, and strong. "I got the lock," he said. He pulled it out of his pocket and held it up. "You have any ideas while I was gone, Wolf?"

Wolf's whole face—eyes, teeth, everything—blazed out at Jack.

"You're the herd now, Jacky," Wolf said. And lifted his head and released a long unfurling howl.

### 8

A less frightened Jack Sawyer might have said, "Can that stuff, willya?" or "We'll have every dog in the county around here if you keep that up," but both of these statements died in his throat. He was too scared to utter a word. Wolf gave him his A #1 smile again, his mouth looking like a television commercial for Ginsu knives, and rose effortlessly to his feet. The John Lennon glasses seemed to be receding back into the bristly top of his beard and the thick hair falling over his temples. He looked at least seven feet tall to Jack, and as burly as the beer barrels in the back room of the Oatley Tap.

"You have good smells in this world, Jacky," Wolf said.

And Jack finally recognized his mood. Wolf was exultant. He was like a man who against steep odds had just won a particularly difficult contest. At the bottom of this triumphant emotion percolated that joyful and feral quality Jack had seen once before.

"Good smells! Wolf! Wolf!"

Jack took a delicate step backward, wondering if he was upwind of Wolf. "You never said anything good about it before," he said, not quite coherently.

"Before is before and now is now," Wolf said. "Good things. Many good things—all around. Wolf will find them, you bet."

That made it worse, for now Jack could see—could nearly feel—a flat, confident greed, a wholly amoral hunger shining in the reddish eyes. I'll eat anything I catch and kill, it said. Catch and kill.

"I hope none of those good things are people, Wolf," Jack said quietly.

Wolf lifted his chin and uttered a bubbling series of noises half-howl, half-laughter.

"Wolfs need to eat," he said, and his voice, too, was joyous. "Oh, Jacky, how Wolfs do need to eat. EAT! Wolf!"

"I'm going to have to put you in that shed," Jack said. "Remember, Wolf? I got the lock? We'll just have to hope it'll hold you. Let's start over there now, Wolf. You're scaring the shit out of me."

This time the bubbling laughter ballooned out of Wolf's chest. "Scared! Wolf knows! Wolf knows, Jacky! You have the fear-smell."

"I'm not surprised," Jack said. "Let's get over to that shed now, okay?"

"Oh, I'm not going in the shed," Wolf said, and a long

pointed tongue curled out from between his jaws. "No, not me, Jacky. Not Wolf. Wolf can't go in the shed." The jaws widened, and the crowded teeth shone. "Wolf remembered, Jacky. Wolf! Right here and now! Wolf remembered!"

Jack stepped backward.

"More fear-smell. Even on your shoes. Shoes, Jacky! Wolf!"

Shoes that smelled of fear were evidently deeply comic.

"You have to go in the shed, that's what you should remember."

"Wrong! Wolf! *You* go in the shed, Jacky! Jacky goes in shed! I remembered! Wolf!"

The werewolf's eyes slid from blazing reddish-orange to a mellow, satisfied shade of purple. "From *The Book of Good Farming*, Jacky. The story of the Wolf Who Would Not Injure His Herd. Remember it, Jacky? The herd goes in the barn. Remember? The lock goes on the door. When the Wolf knows his Change is coming on him, the herd goes in the barn and the lock goes on the door. He Would Not Injure His Herd." The jaws split and widened again, and the long dark tongue curled up at the tip in a perfect image of delight. "Not! Not! Not Injure His Herd! Wolf! Right here and now!"

"You want me to stay locked up in the shed for three days?" Jack said.

"I have to eat, Jacky," Wolf said simply, and the boy saw something dark, quick, and sinister slide toward him from Wolf's changing eyes. "When the moon takes me with her, I have to eat. Good smells here, Jacky. Plenty of food for Wolf. When the moon lets me go, Jacky comes out of the shed."

"What happens if I don't want to be locked up for three days?"

"Then Wolf will kill Jacky. And then Wolf will be damned."

"This is all in *The Book of Good Farming*, is it?"

Wolf nodded his head. "I remembered. I remembered in time, Jacky. When I was waiting for you."

Jack was still trying to adjust himself to Wolf's idea. He would have to go three days without food. Wolf would be free to wander. He would be in prison, and Wolf would have the world. Yet it was probably the only way he would survive Wolf's transformation. Given the choice of a three-day fast or death, he'd choose an empty stomach. And then it suddenly seemed to Jack that this reversal was really no reversal at all—he would still be free, locked in the shed, and Wolf out in the world would still be imprisoned. His cage would just be larger than Jack's. "Then God bless *The Book of Good Farming*, because I would never have thought of it myself."

Wolf gleamed at him again, and then looked up at the sky with a blank, yearning expression. "Not long now, Jacky. You're the herd. I have to put you inside."

"Okay," Jack said. "I guess you do have to."

And this too struck Wolf as uproariously funny. As he laughed his howling laugh, he threw an arm around Jack's waist and picked him up and carried him all the way across the field. "Wolf will take care of you, Jacky," he said when he had nearly howled himself inside-out. He set the boy gently on the ground at the top of the gully.

"Wolf," Jack said.

Wolf widened his jaws and began rubbing his crotch.

"You can't kill any people, Wolf," Jack said. "Remember that—if you remembered that story, then you can remember not to kill any people. Because if you do, they'll hunt you down for sure. If you kill any people, if you kill even one person, then a lot of people will come to kill you. And they'd get you, Wolf. I promise you. They'd nail your hide to a board."

"No people, Jacky. Animals smell better than people. No people. Wolf!"

They walked down the slope into the gully. Jack removed the lock from his pocket and several times clipped it through the metal ring that would hold it, showing Wolf how to use the key. "Then you slide the key under the door, okay?" he asked. "When you've changed back, I'll push it back to you." Jack glanced down at the bottom of the door—there was a two-inch gap between it and the ground.

"Sure, Jacky. You'll push it back to me."

"Well, what do we do now?" Jack said. "Should I go in the shed right now?"

"Sit there," Wolf said, pointing to a spot on the floor of the shed a foot from the door.

Jack looked at him curiously, then stepped inside the shed and sat down. Wolf hunkered back down just outside the shed's open door, and without even looking at Jack, held out his hand toward the boy. Jack took Wolf's hand. It was like holding a hairy creature about the size of a rabbit. Wolf squeezed so hard that Jack nearly cried out—but even if he had, he didn't think that Wolf would have heard him. Wolf was staring upward again, his face dreamy and peaceful and rapt. After a second or two Jack was able to shift his hand into a more comfortable position inside Wolf's grasp.

"Are we going to stay like this a long time?" he asked.

Wolf took nearly a minute to answer. "Until," he said, and squeezed Jack's hand again.

### 9

They sat like that, on either side of the doorframe, for hours, wordlessly, and finally the light began to fade. Wolf had been almost imperceptibly trembling for the previous twenty minutes, and when the air grew darker the tremor in his hand intensified. It was, Jack thought, the way a thoroughbred horse might tremble in its stall at the beginning of a race, waiting for the sound of a gun and the gate to be thrown open.

"She's beginning to take me with her," Wolf said softly. "Soon we'll be running, Jack. I wish you could, too."

He turned his head to look at Jack, and the boy saw that while Wolf meant what he had just said, there was a significant part of him that was silently saying: *I could run after you as well as beside you, little friend.*

"We have to close the door now, I guess," Jack said. He tried to pull his hand from Wolf's grasp, but could not free himself until Wolf almost disdainfully released him.

"Lock Jacky in, lock Wolf out." Wolf's eyes flared for a moment, becoming red molten Elroy-eyes.

"Remember, you're keeping the herd safe," Jack said. He stepped backward into the middle of the shed.

"The herd goes in the barn, and the lock goes on the door. He Would Not Injure His Herd." Wolf's eyes ceased to drip fire, shaded toward orange.

"Put the lock on the door."

"God pound it, that's what I'm doing now," Wolf said. "I'm putting the God-pounding lock on the God-pounding door, see?" He banged the door shut, immediately sealing Jack up in the darkness. "Hear that, Jacky? That's the God-pounding lock." Jack heard the lock click against the metal loop, then heard its ratchets catch as Wolf slid it home.

"Now the key," Jack said.

"God-pounding key, right here and now," Wolf said, and a key rattled into a slot, rattled out. A second later the key bounced off the dusty ground beneath the door high enough to skitter onto the shed's floorboards.

"Thanks," Jack breathed. He bent down and brushed his fingers along the boards until he touched the key. For a moment he clamped it so hard into his palm that he almost drove it through his skin—the bruise, shaped like the state of Florida, would endure nearly five days, when in the excitement of being arrested he would fail to notice that it had left him. Then Jack carefully slid the key into his pocket. Outside, Wolf was panting in hot regular agitated-sounding spurts.

"Are you angry with me, Wolf?" he whispered through the door.

A fist thumped the door, hard. "Not! Not angry! Wolf!"

"All right," Jack said. "No people, Wolf. Remember that. Or they'll hunt you down and kill you."

No peopOOOWWW-OOOOOOOOOHHHOOOO!" The word turned into a long, liquid howl. Wolf's body bumped against the door, and his long black-furred feet slid into the opening beneath it. Jack knew that Wolf had flattened himself out against the shed door. "Not angry, Jack," Wolf whispered, as if his howl had embarrassed him. "Wolf isn't angry. Wolf is *wanting*, Jacky. It's so soon now, so God-pounding *soon*."

"I know," Jack said, now suddenly feeling as if he had to cry—he wished he could have hugged Wolf. More painfully, he wished that they had stayed the extra days at the farmhouse, and that he were now standing outside a root cellar where Wolf was safely jailed.

The odd, disturbing thought came to him again that Wolf *was* safely jailed.

Wolf's feet slid back under the door, and Jack thought he had a glimpse of them becoming more concentrated, slimmer, narrower.

Wolf grunted, panted, grunted again. He had moved well back from the door. He uttered a noise very like "Aaah."

"Wolf?" Jack said.

An earsplitting howl lifted up from above Jack: Wolf had moved to the top of the gully.

"Be careful," Jack said, knowing that Wolf would not hear him, and fearing that he would not understand him even if he were close enough to hear.

A series of howls followed soon after—the sound of a creature set free, or the despairing sound of one who wakes to find himself still confined, Jack could not tell which. Mournful and feral and oddly beautiful, the cries of poor Wolf flew up into the moonlit air like scarves flung into the night. Jack did not know he was trembling until he wrapped his arms around himself and felt his arms vibrating against his chest, which seemed to vibrate, too.

The howls diminished, retreating. Wolf was running with the moon.

## 10

For three days and three nights, Wolf was engaged in a nearly ceaseless search for food. He slept from each dawn until just past noon, in a hollow he had discovered beneath the fallen trunk of an oak. Certainly Wolf did not feel himself imprisoned, despite Jack's forebodings. The woods on the other side of the field were extensive, and full of a wolf's natural diet. Mice, rabbits, cats, dogs, squirrels—all these he found easily. He could have contained himself in the woods and eaten more than enough to carry him through to his next Change.

But Wolf was riding with the moon, and he could no more confine himself to the woods than he could have halted his transformation in the first place. He roamed, led by the moon, through barnyards and pastures, past isolated suburban houses and down unfinished roads where bulldozers and giant asymmetrical rollers sat like sleeping dinosaurs on the banks. Half of his intelligence was in his sense of smell, and it is not exaggerating to suggest that Wolf's nose, always acute, had attained a condition of genius. He could not only smell a coop full of chickens five miles away and distinguish their odors from those of the cows and pigs and horses on the same farm—that was elementary—he could smell when the chickens moved. He could smell that one of the sleeping pigs had an injured foot, and one of the cows in the barn an ulcerated udder.

And this world—for was it not this world's moon which led him?—no longer stank of chemicals and death. An older, more primitive order of being met him on his travels. He inhaled whatever remained of the earth's original sweetness and power, whatever was left of qualities we might once have shared with the Territories. Even when he approached some human dwelling, even while he snapped the backbone of the family mutt and tore the dog into gristly rags he swallowed whole, Wolf was aware of pure cool streams moving far beneath the ground, of bright snow on a mountain somewhere a long way west. This seemed a perfect place for a transmogrified Wolf, and if he had killed any human being he would have been damned.

He killed no people.

He saw none, and perhaps that is why. During the three days of his Change, Wolf did kill and devour representatives of most other forms of life to be found in eastern Indiana, including one skunk and an entire family of bobcats living in limestone caves on a hillside two valleys away. On his first night in the woods he caught a low-flying bat in his jaws, bit off its head, and swallowed the rest while it was still jerking. Whole squadrons of domestic cats went down his throat, platoons of dogs. With a wild, concentrated glee he one night slaughtered every pig in a pen the size of a city block.

But twice Wolf found that he was mysteriously forbidden from killing his prey, and this too made him feel at home in the world through which he prowled. It was a question of place, not of any abstract moral concern—and on the surface, the places were merely ordinary. One was a clearing in the woods into which he had chased a rabbit, the other the scruffy back yard of a farmhouse where a whimpering dog lay chained to a stake. The instant he set a paw down in these places, his hackles rose and an electric tingling traversed the entire distance of his spine. These were sacred places, and in a sacred place a Wolf could not kill. That was all. Like all hallowed sites, they had been set apart a long time ago, so long ago that the word *ancient* could have been used to describe them—*ancient* is probably as close as we can come to representing the vast well of time Wolf sensed about him in the farmer's back yard and the little clearing, a dense envelope of years packed together in a small, highly charged location. Wolf simply backed off the sacred ground and took himself elsewhere. Like the wing-men Jack had seen, Wolf lived in a mystery and so was comfortable with all such things.

And he did not forget his obligations to Jack Sawyer.

## 11

In the locked shed, Jack found himself thrown upon the properties of his own mind and character more starkly than at any other time in his life.

The only furniture in the shed was the little wooden bench, the only distraction the nearly decade-old magazines. And these he could not actually read. Since there were no windows, except in very early morning when light came streaming under the door he had trouble just working out the pictures on the pages. The words were streams of gray worms, indecipherable. He could not imagine how he would get through the next three days. Jack went toward the bench, struck it painfully with his knee, and sat down to think.

One of the first things he realized was that shed-time was different from time on the outside. Beyond the shed, seconds marched quickly past, melted into minutes which melted into hours. Whole days ticked along like metronomes, whole weeks. In shed-time, the seconds obstinately refused to move—they stretched into grotesque monster-seconds, Plasticman-seconds. Outside, an hour might go by while four or five seconds swelled and bloated inside the shed.

The second thing Jack realized was that thinking about the slowness of time made it worse. Once you started concentrating on the passing of seconds, they more or less refused to move at all. So he tried to pace off the dimensions of his cell just to take his mind off the eternity of seconds it took to make up three days. Putting one foot in front of another and counting his steps, he worked out that the shed was approximately seven feet by nine feet. At least there would be enough room for him to stretch out at night.

If he walked all the way around the inside of the shed, he'd walk about thirty-two feet.

If he walked around the inside of the shed a hundred and sixty-five times, he'd cover a mile.

He might not be able to eat, but he sure could walk. Jack took off his watch and put it in his pocket, promising himself that he would look at it only when he absolutely had to.

He was about one-fourth of the way through his first mile when he remembered that there was no water in the shed. No food and no water. He supposed that it took longer than three or four days to die of thirst. As long as Wolf came back for him, he'd be all right—well, maybe not all right, but at least alive. And if Wolf didn't come back? He would have to break the door down.

In that case, he thought, he'd better try it now, while he still had some strength.

Jack went to the door and pushed it with both hands. He pushed it harder, and the hinges squeaked. Experimentally, Jack threw his shoulder at the edge of the door, opposite the hinges. He hurt his shoulder, but he didn't think he had done anything to the door. He banged his shoulder against the door more forcefully. The hinges squealed but did not move a millimeter. Wolf could have torn the door off with one hand, but Jack did not think that he could move it if he turned his shoulders into hamburger by running into it. He would just have to wait for Wolf.

By the middle of the night, Jack had walked seven or eight miles—he'd lost count of the number of times he had reached one hundred and sixty-five, but it was something like seven or eight. He was parched, and his stomach was rumbling. The shed stank of urine, for Jack had been forced to pee against the far wall, where a crack in the boards meant that at least some of it went outside. His body was tired, but he did not think he could sleep. According to clock-time, Jack had been in the shed barely five hours; in shed-time it was more like twenty-four. He was afraid to lie down.

His mind would not let him go—that was how it felt. He had tried making lists of all the books he'd read in the past year, of every teacher he'd had, of every player on the Los Angeles Dodgers . . . but disturbing, disorderly images kept breaking in. He kept seeing Morgan Sloat tearing a hole in the air. Wolf's face floated underwater, and his hands drifted down like heavy weeds. Jerry Bledsoe twitched and rocked before the electrical panel, his glasses smeared over his nose. A man's eyes turned yellow, and his hand became a claw-hoof. Uncle Tommy's false teeth coruscated in the Sunset Strip gutter. Morgan Sloat came toward his mother, not himself.

"Songs by Fats Waller," he said, sending himself around another circuit in the dark. " 'Your Feets Too Big.' 'Ain't Misbehavin.' 'Jitterbug Waltz.' 'Keepin Out of Mischief Now.' "

The Elroy-thing reached out toward his mother, whispering lewdly, and clamped a hand down over her hip.

"Countries in Central America. Nicaragua. Honduras. Guatemala. Costa Rica . . ."

Even when he was so tired he finally had to lie down and curl into a ball on the floor, using his knapsack as a pillow, Elroy and Morgan Sloat rampaged through his mind. Osmond flicked his bullwhip across Lily Cavanaugh's back, and his eyes danced. Wolf reared up, massive, absolutely inhuman, and caught a rifle bullet directly in the heart.

The first light woke him, and he smelled blood. His whole body begged for water, then for food. Jack groaned. Three more nights of this would be impossible to survive. The low angle of the sunlight allowed him dimly to see the walls and roof of the shed. It all looked larger than he had felt it to be last night. He had to pee again, though he could scarcely believe that his body could afford to give up any moisture. Finally he realized that the shed seemed larger because he was lying on the floor.

Then he smelled blood again, and looked sideways, toward the door. The skinned hindquarters of a rabbit had been thrust through the gap. They lay sprawled on the rough boards, leaking blood, glistening. Smudges of dirt and a long ragged scrape showed that they had been forced into the shed. Wolf was trying to feed him.

"Oh, Jeez," Jack groaned. The rabbit's stripped legs were disconcertingly human. Jack's stomach folded into itself. But instead of vomiting, he laughed, startled by an absurd comparison. Wolf was like the family pet who each morning presents his owners with a dead bird, an eviscerated mouse.

With two fingers Jack delicately picked up the horrible offering and deposited it under the bench. He still felt like laughing, but his eyes were wet. Wolf had survived the first night of his transformation, and so had Jack.

The next morning brought an absolutely anonymous, almost ovoid knuckle of meat around a startingly white bone splintered at both ends.

## 12

On the morning of the fourth day Jack heard someone sliding down into the gully. A startled bird squawked, then noisily lifted itself off the roof of the shed. Heavy footsteps advanced toward the door. Jack raised himself onto his elbows and blinked into the darkness.

A large body thudded against the door and stayed there. A pair of split and stained penny loafers was visible through the gap.

"Wolf?" Jack asked softly. "That's you, isn't it?"

"Give me the key, Jack."

Jack slipped his hand into his pocket, brought out the key, and pushed it directly between the penny loafers. A large brown hand dropped into view and picked up the key.

"Bring any water?" Jack asked. Despite what he had been able to extract from Wolf's gruesome presents, he had come close to serious dehydration—his lips were puffy and cracked, and his tongue felt swollen, baked. The key slid into the lock, and Jack heard it click open.

Then the lock came away from the door.

"A little," Wolf said. "Close your eyes, Jacky. You have night-eyes now."

Jack clasped his hands over his eyes as the door opened, but the light which boomed and thundered into the shed still managed to trickle through his fingers and stab his eyes. He hissed with the pain. "Better soon," Wolf said, very close to him. Wolf's arms circled and lifted him. "Eyes closed," Wolf warned, and stepped backward out of the shed.

Even as Jack said, "Water," and felt the rusty lip of an old cup meet his own lips, he knew why Wolf had not lingered in the shed. The air outside seemed unbelievably fresh and sweet—it might have been imported directly from the Territories. He sucked in a double tablespoon of water that tasted like the best meal on earth and wound down through him like a sparkling little river, reviving everything it touched. He felt as though he were being irrigated.

Wolf removed the cup from his lips long before Jack considered he was through with it. "If I give you more you'll just sick it up," Wolf said. "Open your eyes, Jack—but only a little bit."

Jack followed directions. A million particles of light stormed into his eyes. He cried out.

Wolf sat down, cradling Jack in his arms. "Sip," he said, and put the cup once more to Jack's lips. "Eyes open, little more."

Now the sunlight hurt much less. Jack peered out through the screen of his eyelashes at a flaring dazzle while another miraculous trickle of water slipped down his throat.

"Ah," Jack said. "What makes water so delicious?"

"The western wind," Wolf promptly replied.

Jack opened his eyes wider. The swarm and dazzle resolved into the weathered brown of the shed and the mixed green and lighter brown of the gully. His head rested against Wolf's shoulder. The bulge of Wolf's stomach pressed into his backbone.

"Are you okay, Wolf?" he asked. "Did you get enough to eat?"

"Wolfs always get enough to eat," Wolf said simply. He patted the boy's thigh.

"Thanks for bringing me those pieces of meat."

"I promised. You were the herd. Remember?"

"Oh, yes, I remember," Jack said. "Can I have some more of that water?" He slid off Wolf's huge lap and sat on the ground, where he could face him.

Wolf handed him the cup. The John Lennon glasses were back; Wolf's beard was now little more than a scurf covering his cheeks; his black hair, though still long and greasy, fell well short of his shoulders. Wolf's face was friendly and peaceful, almost tired-looking. Over the bib overalls he wore a gray sweatshirt, about two sizes too small, with INDIANA UNIVERSITY ATHLETIC DEPARTMENT stenciled on the front.

He looked more like an ordinary human being than at any other time since he and Jack had met. He did not look as if he

could have made it through the simplest college course, but
he could have been a great high-school football player.

Jack sipped again—Wolf's hand hovered above the rusty
tin cup, ready to snatch it away if Jack gulped. "You're really
okay?"

"Right here and now," Wolf said. He rubbed his other hand
over his belly, so distended that it stretched the fabric at the
bottom of the sweatshirt as taut as a hand would a rubber
glove. "Just tired. Little sleep, Jack. Right here and now."

"Where'd you get the sweatshirt?"

"It was hanging on a line," Wolf said. "Cold here, Jacky."

"You didn't hurt any people, did you?"

"No people. Wolf! Drink that water slow, now." His eyes
disconcertingly shaded into happy Halloween orange for a
second, and Jack saw that Wolf could never really be said to
resemble an ordinary human being. Then Wolf opened his
wide mouth and yawned. "Little sleep." He hitched himself
into a more comfortable position on the slope and put down
his head. He was almost immediately asleep.

# THREE

# A COLLISION OF WORLDS

# 20

# Taken by the Law

## 1

By two o'clock that afternoon they were a hundred miles west, and Jack Sawyer felt as if he too had been running with the moon—it had gone that easily. In spite of his extreme hunger, Jack sipped slowly at the water in the rusty can and waited for Wolf to awaken. Finally Wolf stirred, said, "Ready now, Jack," hitched the boy up onto his back, and trotted into Daleville.

While Wolf sat outside on the curb and tried to look inconspicuous, Jack entered the Daleville Burger King. He made himself go first to the men's room and strip to the waist. Even in the bathroom, the maddening smell of grilling meat caused the saliva to spill into his mouth. He washed his hands, arms, chest, face. Then he stuck his head under the tap and washed his hair with liquid soap. Crumpled paper towels fell, one after the other, to the floor.

At last he was ready to go to the counter. The uniformed girl there stared at him while he gave his order—his wet hair, he thought. While she waited for the order to come through, the girl stepped back and leaned against the service hatch, still unabashedly looking at him.

He was biting into the first Whopper as he turned away toward the glass doors. Juice ran down his chin. He was so hungry he could scarcely bother to chew. Three enormous bites took most of the big sandwich. He had just worked his mouth far enough around the remainder to take a fourth when he saw through the doors that Wolf had attracted a crowd of children. The meat congealed in his mouth, and his stomach slammed shut.

Jack hurried outside, still trying to swallow his mouthful of ground chuck, limp bread, pickles, lettuce, tomatoes, and

sauce. The kids stood in the street on three sides of Wolf, staring at him every bit as frankly as the waitress had stared at
Jack. Wolf had hunched down on the curb as far as he was
able, bowing his back and pulling in his neck like a turtle. His
ears seemed flattened against his head. The wad of food stuck
in Jack's throat like a golfball, and when he swallowed convulsively, it dropped down another notch.

Wolf glanced at him out of the side of his eye, and visibly
relaxed. A tall blue-jeaned man in his twenties opened the
door of a battered red pick-up five or six feet away down the
curb, leaned against the cab, and watched, smiling. "Have a
burger, Wolf," Jack said as carelessly as he could. He handed
Wolf the box, which Wolf sniffed. Then Wolf lifted his head
and took a huge bite out of the box. He began methodically to
chew. The children, astounded and fascinated, stepped nearer.
A few of them were giggling. "What is he?" asked a little girl
with blond pigtails tied with fuzzy pink gift-wrapping yarn.
"Is he a monster?" A crewcut boy of seven or eight shoved
himself in front of the girl and said, "He's the Hulk, isn't he?
He's really the Hulk. Hey? Hey? Huh? Right?"

Wolf had managed to extract what was left of his Whopper
from its cardboard container. He pushed the whole thing into
his mouth with his palm. Shreds of lettuce fell between his
upraised knees, mayonnaise and meat juices smeared over his
chin, his cheek. Everything else became a brownish pulp
smacked to death between Wolf's enormous teeth. When he
swallowed he started to lick the inside of the box.

Jack gently took the container out of his hands. "No, he's
just my cousin. He's not a monster, and he's not the Hulk.
Why don't you kids get away and leave us alone, huh? Go on.
Leave us alone."

They continued to stare. Wolf was now licking his fingers.

"If you keep on gawping at him like that, you might make
him mad. I don't know what he'd do if he got mad."

The boy with the crewcut had seen David Banner's transformation often enough to have an idea of what anger might
do to this monstrous Burger King carnivore. He stepped back.
Most of the others moved back with him.

"Go on, please," Jack said, but the children had frozen
again.

Wolf rose up mountainously, his fists clenched. "GOD

POUND YOU, DON'T LOOK AT ME!" he bellowed. "DON'T MAKE ME FEEL FUNNY! EVERYBODY MAKES ME FEEL FUNNY!"

The children scattered. Breathing hard, red-faced, Wolf stood and watched them disappear up Daleville's Main Street and around the corner. When they were gone, he wrapped his arms around his chest and looked dartingly at Jack. He was miserable with embarrassment. "Wolf shouldn't have yelled," he said. "They were just little ones."

"Big fat scare'll do them a lot of good," a voice said, and Jack saw that the young man from the red pick-up was still leaning against his cab, smiling at them. "Never saw anything like that before myself. Cousins, are you?"

Jack nodded suspiciously.

"Hey, I didn't mean to get personal or anything." He stepped forward, an easy, dark-haired young man in a sleeveless down vest and a plaid shirt. "I especially don't want to make anybody feel funny now, ya know." He paused, lifted his hands, palm-out. "Really. I was just thinking that you guys look like you've been on the road awhile."

Jack glanced at Wolf, who was still hugging himself in embarrassment but also glowering through his round glasses at this figure.

"I've been there myself," the man said. "Hey, dig it—the year I got out of good old DHS—Daleville High, you know—I hitched all the way to northern California and all the way back. Anyhow, if you're sort of going west, I can give you a lift."

"Can't, Jacky." Wolf spoke in a thunderous stage whisper.

"How far west?" Jack asked. "We're trying to make it to Springfield. I have a friend in Springfield."

"Hey, no probleema, seenyor." He raised his hands again. "I'm going just this side of Cayuga, right next to the Illinois border. You let me scarf a burger, we gone. Straight shot. An hour and a half, maybe less—you'll be about halfway to Springfield."

*"Can't,"* Wolf rasped again.

"There's one problem, okay? I got some stuff on the front seat. One of you guys'll have to ride behind. It's gonna be windy back there."

"You don't know how great that is," Jack said, speaking

nothing more than the truth. "We'll see you when you come back out." Wolf began to dance in agitation. "Honest. We'll be out here, mister. And thanks."

He turned to whisper to Wolf as soon as the man went through the doors.

And so when the young man—Bill "Buck" Thompson, for that was his name—returned to his pick-up carrying the containers for two more Whoppers, he found a sedate-looking Wolf kneeling in the open back, his arms resting on the side panel, mouth open, nose already lifting. Jack was in the passenger seat, crowded by a stack of bulky plastic bags which had been taped, then stapled shut, and then sprayed extensively with room freshener, to judge by the smell. Through the translucent sides the bags were visible long frondlike cuttings, medium green. Clusters of buds grew on these amputated fronds.

"I reckoned you still looked a little hungry," he said, and tossed another Whopper to Wolf. Then he let himself in on the driver's side, across the pile of plastic bags from Jack. "Thought he might catch it in his teeth, no reflection on your cousin. Here, take this one, he already pulverized his."

And a hundred miles west they went, Wolf delirious with joy to have the wind whipping past his head, half-hypnotized by the speed and variety of the odors which his nose caught in flight. Eyes blazing and glowing, registering every nuance of the wind, Wolf twitched from side to side behind the cab, shoving his nose into the speeding air.

Buck Thompson spoke of himself as a farmer. He talked nonstop during the seventy-five minutes he kept his foot near the floor, and never once asked Jack any questions. And when he swung off onto a narrow dirt road just outside the Cayuga town line and stopped the car beside a cornfield that seemed to run for miles, he dug in his shirt pocket and brought out a faintly irregular cigarette rolled in almost tissuelike white paper. "I've heard of red-eye," he said. "But your cousin's ridiculous." He dropped the cigarette into Jack's hand. "Have him take some of this when he gets excited, willya? Doctor's orders."

Jack absently stuffed the joint into his shirt pocket and climbed out of the cab. "Thanks, Buck," he called up to the driver.

"Man, I thought I'd seen something when I saw him eat," Buck said. "How do you get him to go places? Yell *mush! mush!* at him?"

Once Wolf realized that the ride was over, he bounded off the back of the truck.

The red pick-up rolled off, leaving a long plume of dust behind it.

"Let's do that again!" Wolf sang out. "Jacky! Let's do that again!"

"Boy, I wish we could," Jack said. "Come on, let's walk for a while. Someone will probably come along."

He was thinking that his luck had turned, that in no time at all he and Wolf would be over the border into Illinois—and he'd always been certain that things would go smoothly once he got to Springfield and Thayer School and Richard. But Jack's mind was still partially in shed-time, where what is unreal bloats and distorts whatever is real, and when the bad things started to happen again, they happened so quickly that he was unable to control them. It was a long time before Jack saw Illinois, and during that time he found himself back in the shed.

## 2

The bewilderingly rapid series of events which led to the Sunlight Home began ten minutes after the two boys had walked past the stark little roadsign telling them that they were now in Cayuga, pop. 23,568. Cayuga itself was nowhere visible. To their right the endless cornfield rolled across the land; to their left a bare field allowed them to see how the road bent, then arrowed straight toward the flat horizon. Just after Jack had realized that they would probably have to walk all the way into town to get their next ride, a car appeared on this road, travelling fast toward them.

"Ride in back?" Wolf yelled, joyfully raising his arms up over his head. "Wolf ride in back! Right here and now!"

"It's going the wrong way," Jack said. "Just be calm and let it pass us, Wolf. Get your arms down or he'll think you're signalling him."

Reluctantly Wolf lowered his arms. The car had come nearly to the bend in the road which would take it directly past Jack and Wolf. "No ride in the back now?" Wolf asked, pouting almost childishly.

Jack shook his head. He was staring at an oval medallion painted on the car's dusty white doorpanel. County Parks Commission, this might have said, or State Wildlife Board. It might have been anything from the vehicle of the state agricultural agent to the property of the Cayuga Maintenance Department. But when it turned into the bend, Jack saw it was a police car.

"That's a cop, Wolf. A policeman. Just keep walking and stay nice and loose. We don't want him to stop."

"What's a coppiceman?" Wolf's voice had dropped into a dark brown range; he had seen that the speeding car was now coming straight toward him. "Does a coppiceman kill Wolfs?"

"No," Jack said, "they absolutely never kill Wolfs," but it did no good. Wolf captured Jack's hand in his own, which trembled.

"Let go of me, please, Wolf," Jack pleaded. "He'll think it's funny."

Wolf's hand dropped away.

As the police car advanced toward them, Jack glanced at the figure behind the wheel, and then turned around and walked back a few paces so that he could watch Wolf. What he had seen was not encouraging. The policeman driving the car had a wide doughy domineering face with livid slabs of fat where he'd once had cheekbones. And Wolf's terror was plain on his face. Eyes, nostrils flared; he was showing his teeth.

"You really liked riding in the back of that truck, didn't you?" Jack asked him.

Some of the terror disappeared, and Wolf nearly managed a smile. The police car roared past—Jack was conscious of the driver turning his head to inspect them. "All right," Jack said. "He's on his way. We're okay, Wolf."

He had turned around again when he heard the sound of the police car suddenly begin to grow louder again.

"Coppiceman's coming back!"

"Probably just going back to Cayuga," Jack said. "Turn around and just act like me. Don't stare at him."

Wolf and Jack trudged along, pretending to ignore the car,

which seemed to hang behind them deliberately. Wolf uttered a sound that was half-moan, half-howl.

The police car swung out into the road, passed them, flashed its brake lights, and then cut in diagonally before them. The officer pushed open his door and got his feet planted on the ground. Then he hoisted himself out of the seat. He was roughly Jack's height, and all his weight was in his face and his stomach—his legs were twig-skinny, his arms and shoulders those of a normally developed man. His gut, trussed in the brown uniform like a fifteen-pound turkey, bulged out on both sides of the wide brown belt.

"I can't wait for it," he said, and cocked an arm and leaned on the open door. "What's your story, anyhow? Give."

Wolf padded up behind Jack and hunched his shoulders, his hands shoved deep into the pockets of his overalls.

"We're going to Springfield, officer," Jack said. "We've been hitching—I guess maybe we shouldn't've."

"You guess maybe you shouldn't've. Hol-eee shit. What's this guy tryinna disappear behind you, a Wookie?"

"He's my cousin." Jack thought frantically for a moment—the Story had to be bent far enough to accommodate Wolf. "I'm supposed to be taking him home. He lives in Springfield with his Aunt Helen, I mean my Aunt Helen, the one who's a schoolteacher. In Springfield."

"What'd he do, escape from somewhere?"

"No, no, nothing like that. It was just that—"

The cop looked at him neutrally, his face sizzling. "Names."

Now the boy met a dilemma: Wolf was certain to call him Jack, no matter what name he gave the cop. "I'm Jack Parker," he said. "And he's—"

"Hold it. I want the feeb to tell me himself. Come on, you. You remember your name, basket case?"

Wolf squirmed behind Jack, digging his chin into the top of his overalls. He muttered something.

"I couldn't hear you, sonny."

"Wolf," he whispered.

"Wolf. Prob'ly I should have guessed. What's your first name, or did they just give you a number?"

Wolf had squeezed his eyes shut, and was twisting his legs together.

"Come on, Phil," Jack said, thinking that it was one of the few names Wolf might remember.

But he had just finished it when Wolf pulled up his head and straightened his back and yelled, "JACK! JACK! JACK WOLF!"

"We call him Jack sometimes," the boy put in, knowing it was already too late. "It's because he likes me so much, sometimes I'm the only one who can do anything with him. I might even stay there in Springfield a few days after I get him home, just to make sure he settles down okay."

"I sure am sick of the sound of your voice, Jack boy. Why don't you and good old Phil-Jack get in the back seat here and we'll go into town and straighten everything out?" When Jack did not move, the policeman put a hand on the butt of the enormous pistol which hung from his straining belt. "Get in the car. Him first. I want to find out why you're a hundred miles from home on a school day. In the car. Right now."

"Ah, officer," Jack began, and behind him Wolf rasped, "No. Can't."

"My cousin has this problem," Jack said. "He's claustrophobic. Small spaces, especially the insides of cars, drive him crazy. We can only get rides in pick-ups, so he can be in the back."

*"Get in the car,"* the policeman said. He stepped forward and opened the back door.

"CAN'T!" Wolf wailed. "Wolf CAN'T! Stinks, Jacky, it *stinks* in there." His nose and lip had wrinkled into corrugations.

"You get him in the car or I will," the cop said to Jack.

"Wolf, it won't be for long," Jack said, reaching for Wolf's hand. Reluctantly, Wolf allowed him to take it. Jack pulled him toward the back seat of the police car, Wolf literally dragging his feet across the surface of the road.

For a couple of seconds it looked as though it would work. Wolf got close enough to the police car to touch the doorframe. Then his entire body shook. He clamped both hands onto the top of the doorframe. It looked as though he were going to try to rip the top of the car in half, as a circus strongman tears a telephone book in two.

"Please," Jack said quietly. "We have to."

But Wolf was terrified, and too disgusted by whatever he

had smelled. He shook his head violently. Slobber ran from his mouth and dripped onto the top of the car.

The policeman stepped around Jack and released something from a catch on his belt. Jack had time only to see that it was not his pistol before the cop expertly whapped his black-jack into the base of Wolf's skull. Wolf's upper body dropped onto the top of the car, and then all of Wolf slid gracefully down onto the dusty road.

"You get on his other side," the cop said, fastening the sap to his belt. "We're gonna finally get this big bag of shit into the vehicle."

Two or three minutes later, after they had twice dropped Wolf's heavy unconscious body back onto the road, they were speeding toward Cayuga. "I already know what's gonna happen to you and your feeb cousin, if he is your cousin, which I doubt." The cop looked up at Jack in his rear-view mirror, and his eyes were raisins dipped in fresh tar.

All the blood in Jack's body seemed to swing down, down in his veins, and his heart jumped in his chest. He had remembered the cigarette in his shirt pocket. He clapped his hand over it, then jerked his hand away before the cop could say anything.

"I gotta put his shoes back on," Jack said. "They sort of fell off."

"Forget it," the cop said, but did not object further when Jack bent over. Out of sight of the mirror, he first shoved one of the split-seamed loafers back up on Wolf's bare heel, then quickly snatched the joint out of his pocket and popped it in his mouth. He bit into it, and dry crumbly particles with a oddly herbal taste spilled over his tongue. Jack began to grind them between his teeth. Something scratched down into his throat, and he convulsively jerked upright, put his hand in front of his mouth, and tried to cough with his lips together. When his throat was clear, he hurriedly swallowed all of the dampened, now rather sludgy marijuana. Jack ran his tongue over his teeth, collecting all the flecks and traces.

"You got a few surprises ahead of you," the policeman said. "You're gonna get a little sunlight in your soul."

"Sunlight in my soul?" Jack asked, thinking that the cop had seen him stuff the joint into his mouth.

"A few blisters on your hands, too," the cop said, and glared happily at Jack's guilty image in the rear-view mirror.

The Cayuga Municipal Building was a shadowy maze of unlighted hallways and narrow staircases that seemed to wind unexpectedly upward alongside equally narrow rooms. Water sang and rumbled in the pipes. "Let me explain something to you kids," the policeman said, ushering them toward the last staircase to their right. "You're not under arrest. Got that? You are being detained for questioning. I don't want to hear any bullshit about one phone call. You're in limbo until you tell us who you are and what you're up to," the cop went on. "You hear me? Limbo. Nowhere. We're gonna see Judge Fairchild, he's the magistrate, and if you don't tell us the truth, you're gonna pay some big fuckin consequences. Upstairs. Move it!"

At the top of the stairs the policeman pushed a door open. A middle-aged woman in wire glasses and a black dress looked up from a typewriter placed sideways against the far wall. "Two more runaways," the policeman said. "Tell him we're here."

She nodded, picked up her telephone, and spoke a few words. "You may go in," the secretary said to them, her eyes wandering from Wolf to Jack and back again.

The cop pushed them across the anteroom and opened the door to a room twice as large, lined with books on one long wall, framed photographs and diplomas and certificates on another. Blinds had been lowered across the long windows opposite. A tall skinny man in a dark suit, a wrinkled white shirt, and a narrow tie of no discernible pattern stood up behind a chipped wooden desk that must have been six feet long. The man's face was a relief map of wrinkles, and his hair was so black it must have been dyed. Stale cigarette smoke hung visibly in the air. "Well, what have we got here, Franky?" His voice was startlingly deep, almost theatrical.

"Kids I picked up on French Lick Road, over by Thompson's place."

Judge Fairchild's wrinkles contorted into a smile as he looked at Jack. "You have any identification papers on you, son?"

"No sir," Jack said.

"Have you told Officer Williams here the truth about

everything? He doesn't think you have, or you wouldn't be here."

"Yes sir," Jack said.

"Then tell me your story." He walked around his desk, disturbing the flat layers of smoke just over his head, and half-sat, half-leaned on the front corner nearest Jack. Squinting, he lit a cigarette—Jack saw the Judge's recessed pale eyes peering at him through the smoke and knew there was no charity in them.

It was the pitcher plant again.

Jack drew in a large breath. "My name is Jack Parker. He's my cousin, and he's called Jack, too. Jack Wolf. But his real name is Philip. He was staying with us in Daleville because his dad's dead and his mother got sick. I was just taking him back to Springfield."

"Simple-minded, is he?"

"A little slow," Jack said, and glanced up at Wolf. His friend seemed barely conscious.

"What's your mother's name?" the Judge asked Wolf. Wolf did not respond in any way. His eyes were clamped shut and his hands stuffed into his pockets.

"She's named Helen," Jack said. "Helen Vaughan."

The Judge eased himself off the desk and walked slowly over to Jack. "Have you been drinking, son? You're a little unsteady."

"No."

Judge Fairchild came to within a foot of Jack and bent down. "Let me smell your breath."

Jack opened his mouth and exhaled.

"Nope. No booze." The Judge straightened up again. "But that's the only thing you were telling the truth about, isn't it? You're trying to string me along, boy."

"I'm sorry we were hitching," Jack said, aware that he had to speak with great caution now. Not only might what he said determine whether he and Wolf were to be let free, but he was having a little trouble forming the words themselves—everything seemed to be happening with great slowness. As in the shed, the seconds had wandered off the metronome. "In fact, we hardly ever hitch because Wolf—Jack, that is—hates being in cars. We'll never do it again. We haven't done anything wrong, sir, and that really is the truth."

"You don't understand, sonny," the Judge said, and his far-off eyes gleamed again. *He's enjoying this,* Jack understood. Judge Fairchild moved slowly back behind his desk. "Hitching rides isn't the issue. You two boys are out on the road by yourself, coming from nowhere, going nowhere—real targets for trouble." His voice was like dark honey. "Now we have here in this country what we think is a most unusual facility—state-approved and state-funded, by the way—which might have been set up expressly for the benefit of boys like yourselves. It's called the Sunlight Gardener Scripture Home for Wayward Boys. Mr. Gardener's work with young fellows in trouble has been nothing short of miraculous. We've sent him some tough cases, and in no time at all he has those boys on their knees begging Jesus for forgiveness. Now I'd say that was pretty special, wouldn't you?"

Jack swallowed. His mouth felt drier than it had been in the shed. "Ah, sir, it's really urgent that we get to Springfield. Everybody's going to wonder—"

"I very much doubt that," said the Judge, smiling with all his wrinkles. "But I'll tell you what. As soon as you two wags are on your way to the Sunlight Home, I'll telephone Springfield and try to get the number of this Helen . . . Wolf, is it? Or is it Helen Vaughan?"

"Vaughan," Jack said, and a red-hot blush covered his face like a fever.

"Yes," the Judge said.

Wolf shook his head, blinking, and then put a hand on Jack's shoulder.

"Coming around are you, son?" the Judge asked. "Could you tell me your age?"

Wolf blinked again, and looked at Jack.

"Sixteen," Jack said.

"And you?"

"Twelve."

"Oh. I would have taken you for several years older. All the more reason for seeing you get help now before you get in real deep trouble, wouldn't you say, Franky?"

"Amen," the policeman said.

"You boys come back here in a month," said the Judge. "Then we'll see if your memory is any better. Why are your eyes so bloodshot?"

"They feel kind of funny," Jack said, and the policeman barked. He had laughed, Jack realized a second later.

"Take them away, Franky," the Judge said. He was already picking up the telephone. "You're going to be different boys thirty days from now. Depend on it."

While they walked down the steps of the redbrick Municipal Building, Jack asked Franky Williams why the Judge had asked for their ages. The cop paused on the bottom step and half-turned to glare up at Jack out of his blazing face. "Old Sunlight generally takes em in at twelve and turns em loose at nineteen." He grinned. "You tellin me you never heard him on the radio? He's about the most famous thing we got around here. I'm pretty sure they heard of old Sunlight Gardener even way over in Daleville." His teeth were small discolored pegs, irregularly spaced.

### 3

Twenty minutes later they were in farmland again.

Wolf had climbed into the back seat of the police car with surprisingly little fuss. Franky Williams had pulled his sap from his belt and said, "You want this again, you fuckin freak? Who knows, it might make you smart." Wolf had trembled, Wolf's nose had wrinkled up, but he had followed Jack into the car. He had immediately clapped his hand over his nose and begun breathing through his mouth. "We'll get away from this place, Wolf," Jack had whispered into his ear. "A couple of days, that's all, and we'll see how to do it." "No chatter" came from the front seat.

Jack was strangely relaxed. He was certain that they would find a way to escape. He leaned back against the plastic seat, Wolf's hand wrapped around his, and watched the fields go by.

"There she is," Franky Williams called from the front seat. "Your future home."

Jack saw a meeting of tall brick walls planted surrealistically amidst the fields. Too tall to see over, the walls around the Sunlight Home were topped with three strands of barbed wire and shards of broken glass set in cement. The car was now driving past exhausted fields bordered with fences in which strands of barbed and smooth wire alternated.

"Got sixty acres out here," Williams said. "And all of it is either walled or fenced—you better believe it. Boys did it themselves."

A wide iron gate interrupted the expanse of wall where the drive turned into the Home's property. As soon as the police car turned into the drive the gates swung open, triggered by some electronic signal. "TV camera," the policeman explained. "They're a-waitin for you two fresh fish."

Jack leaned forward and put his face to the window. Boys in denim jackets worked in the long fields to either side, hoeing and raking, pushing wheelbarrows.

"You two shitheads just earned me twenty bucks," Williams said. "Plus another twenty for Judge Fairchild. Ain't that great?"

# 21

# The Sunlight Home

## 1

The Home looked like something made from a child's blocks, Jack thought—it had grown randomly as more space was needed. Then he saw that the numerous windows were barred, and the sprawling building immediately seemed penal, rather than childish.

Most of the boys in the fields had put down their tools to watch the progress of the police car.

Franky Williams pulled up into the wide, rounded end of the drive. As soon as he had cut off his engine, a tall figure stepped through the front door and stood regarding them from the top of the steps, his hands knitted together before him. Beneath a full head of longish wavy white hair, the man's face seemed unrealistically youthful—as if these chipped, vitally masculine features had been created or at least assisted by plastic surgery. It was the face of a man who could sell anything, anywhere, to anybody. His clothes were as white as his hair: white suit, white shoes, white shirt, and a trailing white silk scarf around his neck. As Jack and Wolf got out of the back seat, the man in white pulled a pair of dark green sunglasses from his suitpocket, put them on, and appeared to examine the two boys for a moment before smiling—long creases split his cheeks. Then he removed the sunglasses and put them back in his pocket.

"Well," he said. "Well, well, well. Where would we all be without you, Officer Williams?"

"Afternoon, Reverend Gardener," the policeman said.

"Is it the usual sort of thing, or were these two bold fellows actually engaged in criminal activity?"

"Vagrants," said the cop. Hands on hips, he squinted up at Gardener as if all that whiteness hurt his eyes. "Refused to give Fairchild their right names. This one, the big one," he said, pointing a thumb at Wolf, "he wouldn't talk at all. I had to nail him in the head just to get him in the car."

Gardener shook his head tragically. "Why don't you bring them up here so they can introduce themselves, and then we'll take care of the various formalities. Is there any reason why the two of them should look so, ah, shall we say, 'befuddled'?"

"Just that I cracked that big one behind the ears."

"Ummmmm." Gardener stepped backward, steepling his fingers before his chest.

As Williams prodded the boys up the steps to the long porch, Gardener cocked his head and regarded his new arrivals. Jack and Wolf reached the top of the steps and moved tentatively onto the surface of the porch. Franky Williams wiped his forehead and huffed himself up beside them. Gardener was smiling mistily, but his eyes switched back and forth between the boys. The second after something hard, cold, and familiar jumped out of his eyes at Jack, the Reverend again twitched the sunglasses out of his pocket and put them on. The smile remained misty and delicate, but even wrapped as he was in a sense of false security, Jack felt frozen by that glance—because he had seen it before.

Reverend Gardener pulled the sunglasses below the bridge of his nose and peered playfully over the tops of the frames. "Names? Names? Might we have some names from you two gentlemen?"

"I'm Jack," the boy said, and then stopped—he did not

want to say one more word until he had to. Reality seemed to fold and buckle about Jack for a moment: he felt that he had been jerked back into the Territories, but that now the Territories were evil and threatening, and that foul smoke, jumping flames, the screams of tortured bodies filled the air.

A powerful hand closed over his elbow and held him upright. Instead of the foulness and smoke, Jack smelled some heavy sweet cologne, applied too liberally. A pair of melancholy gray eyes were looking directly into his.

"And have you been a bad boy, Jack? Have you been a very bad boy?"

"No, we were just hitching, and—"

"I think you're a trifle stoned," said the Reverend Gardener. "We'll have to see that you get some special attention, won't we?" The hand released his elbow; Gardener stepped neatly away, and pushed the sunglasses up over his eyes again. "You do possess a last name, I imagine."

"Parker," Jack said.

"Yesss." Gardener whipped the glasses off his head, executed a dancing little half-turn, and was scrutinizing Wolf. He had given no indication whether he believed Jack or not.

"My," he said. "You're a healthy specimen, aren't you? Positively strapping. We'll certainly be able to find a use for a big strong boy like you around here, praise the Lord. And might I ask you to emulate Mr. Jack Parker here, and give me your name?"

Jack looked uneasily at Wolf. His head was bowed, and he was breathing heavily. A glistening line of slobber went from the corner of his mouth to his chin. A black smudge, half-dirt, half-grease, covered the front of the stolen Athletic Department sweatshirt. Wolf shook his head, but the gesture seemed to have no content—he might have been shaking away a fly.

"Name, son? Name? Name? Are you called Bill? Paul? Art? Sammy? No—something exceedingly foursquare, I'm sure. George, perhaps?"

"Wolf," said Wolf.

"Ah, that *is* nice." Gardener beamed at both of them. "Mr. Parker and Mr. Wolf. Perhaps you'll escort them inside, Officer Williams? And aren't we happy that Mr. Bast is in residence already? For the presence of Mr. Hector Bast—one of our stewards, by the way—means that we shall probably be able to outfit Mr. Wolf." He peered at the two boys over the frames of his sunglasses. "One of our beliefs here at the Scripture Home is that the soldiers of the Lord march best when they march in uniform. And Heck Bast is nearly as large as your friend Wolf, young Jack Parker. So from the points of view of both clothing and discipline you shall be very well served indeed. A comfort, yes?"

"Jack," Wolf said in a low voice.

"Yes."

"My head hurts, Jack. Hurts bad."

"Your little head pains you, Mr. Wolf?" Reverend Sunlight Gardener half-danced toward Wolf and gently patted his arm. Wolf snatched his arm away, his face working into an exaggerated reflex of disgust. The cologne, Jack knew—that heavy cloying odor would have been like ammonia in Wolf's sensitive nostrils.

"Never mind, son," said Gardener, seemingly unaffected by Wolf's withdrawal from him. "Mr. Bast or Mr. Singer, our other steward, will see to that inside. Frank, I thought I told you to get them into the Home."

Officer Williams reacted as if he had been jabbed in the back with a pin. His face grew more feverish, and he jerked his peculiar body across the porch to the front door.

Sunlight Gardener twinkled at Jack again, and the boy saw that all his dandified animation was only a kind of sterile self-amusement: the man in white was cold and crazy within. A heavy gold chain rattled out of Gardener's sleeve and came to rest against the base of his thumb. Jack heard the whistle of a whip cutting through the air, and this time he recognized Gardener's dark gray eyes.

Gardener was Osmond's Twinner.

"Inside, young fellows," Gardener said, half-bowing and indicating the open door.

## 2

"By the way, Mr. Parker," Gardener said, once they had gone in, "is it possible that we've met before? There must be some reason you look so familiar to me, mustn't there?"

"I don't know," Jack said, looking carefully around the odd interior of the Scripture Home.

Long couches covered with a dark blue fabric sat against the wall on the forest-green carpet; two massive leather-topped desks had been placed against the opposite wall. At one of the desks a pimply teenager glanced at them dully, then returned to the video screen before him, where a TV preacher was inveighing against rock and roll. The teenage boy seated at the adjoining desk straightened up and fixed Jack with an aggressive stare. He was slim and black-haired and his narrow face looked clever and bad-tempered. To the pocket of his white turtleneck sweater was pinned a rectangular nameplate of the sort worn by soldiers: SINGER.

"But I do think we have met each other somewhere, don't you, my lad? I assure you, we must have—I don't forget, I am literally incapable of forgetting, the face of a boy I have encountered. Have you ever been in trouble before this, Jack?"

Jack said, "I never saw you before."

Across the room, a massive boy had lifted himself off one of the blue couches and was now standing at attention. He too wore a white turtleneck sweater and a military nameplate. His hands wandered nervously from his sides to his belt, into the pockets of his blue jeans, back to his sides. He was at least six-three and seemed to weigh nearly three hundred pounds. Acne burned across his cheeks and forehead. This, clearly, was Bast.

"Well, perhaps it will come to me later," Sunlight Gardener said. "Heck, come up here and help our new arrivals at the desk, will you?"

Bast lumbered forward, scowling. He made a point of coming up very close to Wolf before he sidestepped past him, scowling more fiercely all the while—if Wolf had opened his eyes, which he did not, he would have seen no more than the ravaged moonscape of Bast's forehead and the mean small eyes, like a bear's eyes, bulging up at him from beneath crusty brows. Bast switched his gaze to Jack, muttered, "C'mon," and flapped a hand toward the desk.

"Registration, then take them up to the laundry for clothes," Gardener said in a flat voice. He smiled with chromelike brilliance at Jack. "Jack Parker," he said softly. "I wonder who you really are, Jack Parker. Bast, make sure everything is out of his pockets."

Bast grinned.

Sunlight Gardener drifted across the room toward an obviously impatient Franky Williams and languidly withdrew a long leather wallet from his jacket's inside pocket. Jack saw him begin to count money out into the policeman's hands.

"Pay attention, snotface," said the boy behind the desk, and Jack snapped around to face him. The boy was playing with a pencil, the smirk on his face an utterly inadequate disguise for what seemed to Jack's keyed-up perceptions his characteristic anger—a rage that bubbled far down within him, eternally stoked. "Can he write?"

"Jeez, I don't think so," Jack said.

"Then you'll have to sign in for him." Singer shoved two legal-sized sheets of paper at him. "Print on the top line, write on the bottom one. Where the X's are." He fell back into his chair, raising the pencil to his lips, and slumped eloquently into its corner. Jack supposed that was a trick learned from the very Reverend Sunlight Gardener.

JACK PARKER, he printed, and scrawled something like that at the bottom of the sheet. PHILIP JACK WOLF. Another scrawl, even less like his real handwriting.

"Now you're wards of the State of Indiana, and that's what you'll be for the next thirty days, unless you decide to stay longer." Singer twitched the papers back toward himself. "You'll be—"

"Decide?" Jack asked. "What do you mean, decide?"

A trifle of red grew smooth beneath Singer's cheeks. He jerked his head to one side and seemed to smile. "I guess you don't know that over sixty percent of our kids are here voluntarily. It's possible, yeah. You could decide to stay here."

Jack tried to keep his face expressionless.

Singer's mouth twitched violently, as if a fishhook had snagged it. "This is a pretty good place, and if I ever hear you ranking it I'll pound the shit out of you—it's the best place you've ever been in, I'm sure. I'll tell you another thing: you got no choice. You have to respect the Sunlight Home. You understand?"

Jack nodded his head.

"How about him? Does he?"

Jack looked up at Wolf, who was blinking slowly and breathing through his mouth.

"I think so."

"All right. The two of you will be bunkmates. The day starts at five in the morning, when we have chapel. Fieldwork until seven, then breakfast in the dining hall. Back to the field until noon, when we get lunch plus Bible readings—everybody gets a crack at this, so you better start thinking about what you'll read. None of that sexy stuff from the Song of Songs, either, unless you want to find out what discipline means. More work after lunch."

He looked sharply up at Jack. "Hey, don't think that you work for nothing at the Sunlight Home. Part of our arrangement with the state is that everybody gets a fair hourly wage, which is set against the cost of keeping you here—clothes and food, electricity, heating, stuff like that. You are credited fifty cents an hour. That means that you earn five dollars a day for the hours you put in—thirty dollars a week. Sundays are spent in the Sunlight Chapel, except for the hour when we actually put on the *Sunlight Gardener Gospel Hour*."

The red smoothed itself out under the surface of his skin again, and Jack nodded in recognition, being more or less obliged to.

"If you turn out right and if you can talk like a human being, which most people can't, then you might get a shot at OS—Outside Staff. We've got two squads of OS, one that works the streets, selling hymn sheets and flowers and Reverend Gardener's pamphlets, and the other one on duty at the airport. Anyhow, we got thirty days to turn you two scumbags around and make you see how dirty and filthy and diseased your crummy lives were before you came here, and this is where we start, right now exactly."

Singer stood up, his face the color of a blazing autumn leaf, and delicately set the tips of his fingers atop his desk. "Empty your pockets. Right now."

"Right here and now," Wolf mumbled, as if by rote.

"TURN EM OUT!" Singer shouted. "I WANT TO SEE IT ALL!"

Bast stepped up beside Wolf. Reverend Gardener, having

seen Franky Williams to his car, drifted expressively into Jack's vicinity.

"Personal possessions tend to tie our boys too much to the past, we've found," Gardener purred to Jack. "Destructive. We find this a very helpful tool."

"EMPTY YOUR POCKETS!" Singer bawled, now nearly in a straightforward rage.

Jack pulled from his pockets the random detritus of his time on the road. A red handkerchief Elbert Palamountain's wife had given him when she'd seen him wipe his nose on his sleeve, two matchbooks, the few dollars and scattered change that was all of his money—a total of six dollars and forty-two cents—the key to room 407 of the Alhambra Inn and Gardens. He closed his fingers over the three objects he intended to keep. "I guess you want my pack, too," he said.

"Sure, you sorry little fart," Singer ranted, "of course we want your foul backpack, but first we want whatever you're trying to hide. Get it out—right now."

Reluctantly Jack took Speedy's guitar-pick, the croaker marble, and the big wheel of the silver dollar from his pocket and put them in the nest of the handkerchief. "They're just good-luck stuff."

Singer snatched up the pick. "Hey, what's this? I mean, what is it?"

"Fingerpick."

"Yeah, sure." Singer turned it over in his fingers, sniffed it. If he had bitten it, Jack would have slugged him in the face. "Fingerpick. You tellin me the truth?"

"A friend of mine gave it to me," Jack said, and suddenly felt as lonely and adrift as he ever had during these weeks of travelling. He thought of Snowball outside the shopping mall, who had looked at him with Speedy's eyes, who in some fashion Jack did not understand had actually been Speedy Parker. Whose name he had just adopted for his own.

"Bet he stole it," Singer said to no one in particular, and dropped the pick back into the handkerchief beside the coin and the marble. "Now the knapsack." When Jack had unshouldered the backpack, handed it over, Singer pawed through it for some minutes in growing distaste and frustration. The distaste was caused by the condition of the few clothes Jack had left, the frustration by the reluctance of the pack to yield up any drugs.

*Speedy, where are you now?*

"He's not holding," Singer complained. "You think we should do a skin search?"

Gardener shook his head. "Let us see what we can learn from Mr. Wolf."

Bast shouldered up even closer. Singer said, "Well?"

"He doesn't have anything in his pockets," Jack said.

"I want those pockets EMPTY! EMPTY!" Singer yelled. "ON THE TABLE!"

Wolf tucked his chin into his chest and clamped his eyes shut.

"You don't have anything in your pockets, do you?" Jack asked.

Wolf nodded once, very slowly.

"He's holding! The dummy's holding!" Singer crowed. "Come on, you big dumb idiot, get the stuff out on the table." He clapped his hands sharply together twice. "Oh wow, Williams never searched him! Fairchild never did! This is incredible—they're going to look like such morons."

Bast shoved his face up to Wolf's and snarled, "If you don't empty your pockets onto that table in a hurry, I'm going to tear your face off."

Jack softly said, "Do it, Wolf."

Wolf groaned. Then he removed his balled right hand from its overall pocket. He leaned over the desk, brought his hand forward, and opened his fingers. Three wooden matches and two small water-polished stones, grained and straited and colorful, fell out onto the leather. When his left hand opened, two more pretty little stones rolled alongside the others.

"Pills!" Singer snatched at them.

"Don't be an idiot, Sonny," Gardener said.

"You made me look like a jerk," Singer said in low but vehement tones to Jack as soon as they were on the staircase to the upper floors. These stairs were covered with a shabby rose-patterned carpet. Only the principal downstairs rooms of the Sunlight Scripture Home had been decorated, dressed up— the rest of it looked rundown and ill cared for. "You're gonna be sorry, I promise you that—in this place, *nobody* makes

Sonny Singer into a jackass. I practically run this place, you two idiots. Christ!" He pushed his burning narrow face into Jack's. "That was a great stunt back there, the dummy and his fuckin stones. It'll be a long time before you get over that one."

"I didn't know he had anything in his pockets," Jack said.

A step ahead of Jack and Wolf, Singer abruptly stopped moving. His eyes narrowed; his entire face seemed to contract. Jack understood what was going to happen a second before Singer's hand slapped stingingly over the side of his face.

"Jack?" Wolf whispered.

"I'm okay," he said.

"When you hurt me, I'll hurt you back twice as bad," Singer said to Jack. "When you hurt me in front of Reverend Gardener, I'll hurt you four times as bad, you got that?"

"Yeah," Jack said. "I think I got it. Aren't we supposed to get some clothes?"

Singer whirled around and marched upward, and for a second Jack stood still and watched the other boy's thin intense back go up the stairs. *You, too,* he said to himself. *You and Osmond. Someday.* Then he followed, and Wolf trudged after.

In a long room stacked with boxes Singer fidgeted at the door while a tall boy with a passionless bland face and the demeanor of a sleepwalker researched the shelves for their clothes.

"Shoes, too. You get him into regulation shoes or you're gonna be holding a shovel all day," Singer said from the doorway, conspicuously not looking at the clerk. Weary disgust— it would have been another of Sunlight Gardener's lessons.

The boy finally located a size thirteen pair of the heavy square black lace-ups in a corner of the storeroom, and Jack got them on Wolf's feet. Then Singer took them up another flight to the dormitory floor. Here there was no attempt to disguise the real nature of the Sunlight Home. A narrow corridor ran the entire length of the top of the house—it might have been fifty feet long. Rows of narrow doors with inset eye-level windows marched down either side of the long corridor. To Jack, the so-called dormitory looked like a prison.

Singer took them a short way up the narrow hall and paused before one of the doors. "On their first day, nobody works. You start the full schedule tomorrow. So get in here for now and look at your Bibles or something until five. I'll come back and let you out in time for the confession period. And change into the Sunlight clothes, hey?"

"You mean you're going to lock us in there for the next three hours?" Jack asked.

"You want me to hold your hand?" Singer exploded, his face reddening again. "Look. If you were a voluntary, I could let you walk around, get a look at the place. But since you're a ward of the state on a referral from a local police department, you're one step up from being a convicted criminal. Maybe in thirty days you'll be voluntaries, if you're lucky. In the meantime, get in your room and start acting like a human being made in God's image instead of like an animal." He impatiently fitted a key into the lock, swung the door open, and stood beside it. "Get in there. I got work to do."

"What happens to all our stuff?"

Singer theatrically sighed. "You little creep, do you think we'd be interested in stealing anything you could have?"

Jack kept himself from responding.

Singer sighed again. "Okay. We keep it all for you, in a folder with your name on it. In Reverend Gardener's office downstairs—that's where we keep your money, too, right up until the time you get released. Okay? Get in there now before I report you for disobedience. I mean it."

Wolf and Jack went into the little room. When Singer slammed the door, the overhead light automatically went on, revealing a windowless cubicle with a metal bunkbed, a small corner sink, and a metal chair. Nothing more. On the white Sheetrock walls yellowing tape marks showed where pictures had been put up by the room's previous inhabitants. The lock clicked shut. Jack and Wolf turned to see Singer's driven face in the small rectangular window. "Be good, now," he said, grinning, and disappeared.

"No, Jacky," Wolf said. The ceiling was no more than an inch from the top of his head. "Wolf can't stay here."

"You'd better sit down," Jack said. "You want the top or the bottom bunk?"

"Huh?"

"Take the bottom one and sit down. We're in trouble here."

"Wolf knows, Jacky. Wolf knows. This is a bad bad place. Can't stay."

"Why is it a bad place? How do you know it, I mean?"

Wolf sat heavily on the lower bunk, dropped his new clothes on the floor, and idly picked up the book and two pamphlets set out there. The book was a Bible bound in some artificial fabric that looked like blue skin; the pamphlets, Jack saw by looking at those on his own bunk, were entitled *The High Road to Everlasting Grace* and *God Loves You!* "Wolf knows. You know, too, Jacky." Wolf looked up at him, almost scowling. Then he glanced back down at the books in his hands, began turning them over, almost shuffling them. They were, Jack supposed, the first books Wolf had ever seen.

"The white man," Wolf said, almost too softly for Jack to hear.

"White man?"

Wolf held up one of the pamphlets, its back cover showing. The whole rear cover was a black-and-white photograph of Sunlight Gardener, his beautiful hair lifting in a breeze, his arms outstretched—a man of everlasting grace, beloved of God.

"Him," Wolf said. "He kills, Jacky. With whips. This is one of *his* places. No Wolf should ever be in one of *his* places. No Jack Sawyer, either. Never. We have to get away from here, Jacky."

"We'll get out," Jack said. "I promise you. Not today, not tomorrow—we have to work it out. But soon."

Wolf's feet protruded far past the edge of his bunk. "Soon."

### 3

*Soon,* he had promised, and Wolf had required the promise. Wolf was terrified. Jack could not tell if Wolf had ever seen Osmond in the Territories, but he had certainly heard of him. Osmond's reputation in the Territories, at least among members of the Wolf family, appeared to be even worse than Morgan's. But though both Wolf and Jack had recognized Osmond in Sunlight Gardener, Gardener had not recognized them—which brought up two possibilities. Either Gardener was just having fun with them, pretending ignorance; or he was a Twinner like Jack's mother, profoundly connected to a Territories figure but unaware of the connection at any but the deepest level.

And if that was true, as Jack thought it was, then he and Wolf could wait for the really right moment to escape. They had time to watch, time to learn.

Jack put on the scratchy new clothes. The square black shoes seemed to weigh several pounds apiece, and to be suited to either foot. With difficulty, he persuaded Wolf to put on the Sunlight Home uniform. Then the two of them lay down. Jack heard Wolf begin to snore, and after a while, he drifted off himself. In his dreams his mother was somewhere in the dark, calling for him to help her, help her.

# 22

# The Sermon

## 1

At five that afternoon, an electric bell went off in the hallway, a long, toneless blare of sound. Wolf leaped from his bunk, thudding the metal frame of the upper with the side of his head hard enough to wake up Jack, who had been dozing, with a jolt.

The bell stopped shrieking after fifteen seconds or so; Wolf went right on.

He staggered over into the corner of the room, his hands wrapped around his head.

"*Bad place, Jack!*" he screamed. "*Bad place right here and now! Gotta get outta here! Gotta get outta here RIGHT HERE AND NOW!*"

Pounding on the wall.

"Shut the dummy up!"

From the other side, a shrieking, whinnying, horsey laugh. "You gittin some sunlight in you souls now, boys! And from de way dat big fella soun, it sho feel *fine!*" The giggling, whinnying laugh, too much like a horrified scream, came again.

"*Bad, Jack! Wolf! Jason! Bad! Bad, bad—*"

Doors were opening all up and down the hall. Jack could hear the rumble of many feet dressed in blocky Sunlight Home shoes.

He got down from the top bunk, forcing himself to move. He felt cross-grained to reality—not awake, not really asleep, either. Moving across the mean little room to Wolf was like moving through Karo syrup instead of air.

He felt so tired now . . . so very tired.

"Wolf," he said. "Wolf, stop it."

"Can't, Jacky!" Wolf sobbed. His arms were still wrapped around his head, as if to keep it from exploding.

"You got to, Wolf. We have to go out in the hall now."

"Can't, Jacky," Wolf sobbed, "it's a bad place, bad smells. . . ."

From the hallway, someone—Jack thought it was Heck Bast—yelled, "Out for confession!"

"Out for confession!" someone else yelled, and they all took up the chant: *Out for confession! Out for confession!* It was like some weird football cheer.

"If we're going to get out of here with our skins on, we've got to stay cool."

"Can't, Jacky, can't stay cool, bad. . . ."

Their door was going to open in a minute and Bast or Sonny Singer would be there . . . maybe both. They were not "out for confession," whatever that was, and while newcomers to the Sunlight Home might be allowed a few screw-ups during their orientation period, Jack thought their chances for escape would be better if they blended in as completely as they could as soon as they could. With Wolf, that wasn't going to be easy. *Christ, I'm sorry I got you into this, big guy,* Jack thought. *But the situation is what the situation is. And if we can't ride it, it's gonna ride us down. So if I'm hard with you, it's for your own good.* He added miserably to himself, *I hope.*

"Wolf," he whispered, "do you want Singer to start beating on me again?"

"No, Jack, no. . . ."

"Then you better come out in the hall with me," Jack said. "You have to remember that what you do is going to have a lot to do with how Singer and that guy Bast treat me. Singer slapped me around because of your stones—"

"Someone might slap *him* around," Wolf said. His voice was low and mild, but his eyes suddenly narrowed, flared orange. For a moment Jack saw the gleam of white teeth between Wolf's lips—not as if Wolf had grinned, but as if his teeth had grown.

"Don't even think of that," Jack said grimly. "It'll only makes things worse."

Wolf's arms fell away from his head. "Jack, I don't know. . . ."

"Will you try?" Jack asked. He threw another urgent glance at the door.

"I'll try," Wolf whispered shakily. Tears shone in his eyes.


## 2

The upstairs corridor should have been bright with late-afternoon light, but it wasn't. It was as if some sort of filtering device had been fitted over the windows at the end of the corridor so that the boys could see out—out to where the *real* sunlight was—but that the light itself wasn't allowed to enter. It seemed to drop dead on the narrow inner sills of those high Victorian windows.

There were forty boys standing in front of twenty doors, ten on each side. Jack and Wolf were by far the last to appear, but their lateness was not noticed. Singer, Bast, and two other boys had found someone to rag and could not be bothered with taking attendance.

Their victim was a narrow-chested, bespectacled kid of maybe fifteen. He was standing at a sorry approximation of attention with his chinos puddled around his black shoes. He wore no underpants.

"Have you stopped it yet?" Singer asked.

"I—"

*"Shut up!"* One of the other boys with Singer and Bast yelled this last. The four of them wore blue jeans instead of chinos, and clean white turtleneck sweaters. Jack learned soon enough that the fellow who had just shouted was Warwick. The fat fourth was Casey.

"When we want you to talk, we'll ask you!" Warwick shouted now. "You still whipping your weasel, Morton?"

Morton trembled and said nothing.

*"ANSWER HIM!"* Casey shrieked. He was a tubby boy who looked a little bit like a malevolent Tweedledum.

"No," Morton whispered.

*"WHAT? SPEAK UP!"* Singer yelled.

"No!" Morton moaned.

"If you can stop for a whole week, you'll get your underpants back," Singer said with the air of one conferring a great favor on an undeserving subject. "Now pull up your pants, you little creep."

Morton, sniffling, bent over and pulled up his trousers.

The boys went down to confession and supper.

### 3

Confession was held in a large bare-walled room across the way from the dining hall. The maddening smells of baked beans and hotdogs drifted across, and Jack could see Wolf's nostrils flaring rhythmically. For the first time that day the dull expression left his eyes and he began to look interested.

Jack was more wary of "confession" than he had let on to Wolf. Lying in his upper bunk with his hands behind his head, he had seen a black something in the upper corner of the room. He had thought for a moment or two that it was some sort of a dead beetle, or the husk of its shell—he thought if he got closer he would perhaps see the spider's web the thing was caught in. It had been a bug, all right, but not the organic kind. It was a small, old-fashioned-looking microphone gadget, screwed into the wall with an eyebolt. A cord snaked from the back of it and through a ragged hole in the plaster. There had been no real effort to conceal it. Just part of the service, boys. Sunlight Gardener Listens Better.

After seeing the bug, after the ugly little scene with Morton in the hall, he had expected confession to be an angry, perhaps scary, adversary situation. Someone, possibly Sunlight Gardener himself, more probably Sonny Singer or Hector Bast, would try to get him to admit that he had used drugs on the road, that he had broken into places in the middle of the night and robbed while on the road, that he had spit on every sidewalk he could find while on the road, and played with himself after a hard day on the road. If he hadn't done any of those things, they would keep after him until he admit-

ted them, anyway. They would try to break him. Jack thought
he could hold up under such treatment, but he wasn't sure
Wolf could.

But what was most disturbing about confession was the eagerness with which the boys in the Home greeted it.

The inner cadre—the boys in the white turtlenecks—sat
down near the front of the room. Jack looked around and saw
the others looking toward the open door with a sort of witless
anticipation. He thought it must be supper they were antici-
pating—it smelled very damn good, all right, especially after
all those weeks of pick-up hamburgers interspersed with large
helpings of nothing at all. Then Sunlight Gardener walked
briskly in and Jack saw the expressions of anticipation change
to looks of gratification. Apparently it hadn't been dinner they
had been looking forward to, after all. Morton, who had been
cowering in the upper hallway with his pants puddled around
his ankles only fifteen minutes ago, looked almost exalted.

The boys got to their feet. Wolf sat, nostrils flaring, looking puzzled and frightened, until Jack grabbed a fistful of
shirt and pulled him up.

"Do what they do, Wolf," he muttered.

"Sit down, boys," Gardener said, smiling. "Sit down,
please."

They sat. Gardener was wearing faded blue jeans overtopped with an open-throated shirt of blinding white silk. He
looked at them, smiling benignly. The boys looked back worshipfully, for the most part. Jack saw one boy—wavy brown
hair that came to a deep widow's peak on his brow, receding
chin, delicate little hands as pale as Uncle Tommy's Delftware—turn aside and cup his mouth to hide a sneer, and he,
Jack, felt some encouragement. Apparently not everyone's
head had been blown by whatever was going on here . . . but a
lot of heads *had* been. Wide-open they had been blown, from
the way things looked. The fellow with the great buck teeth
was looking at Sunlight Gardener adoringly.

"Let us pray. Heck, will you lead us?"

Heck did. He prayed fast and mechanically. It was like listening to a Dial-a-Prayer recorded by a dyslexic. After asking
God to favor them in the days and weeks ahead, to forgive
them their trespasses and to help them become better people,
Heck Bast rapped out, "For-Jesussakeamen," and sat down.

"Thank you, Heck," Gardener said. He had taken an armless chair, had turned it around backward, and was sitting on it like a range-ridin cowpoke in a John Ford Western. He was at his most charming tonight; the sterile, self-referring craziness Jack had seen that morning was almost gone. "Let us have a dozen confessions, please. No more than that. Will you lead us, Andy?"

Warwick, an expression of ludicrous piety on his face, took Heck's place.

"Thank you, Reverend Gardener," he said, and then looked at the boys. "Confession," he said. "Who will start?"

There was a rustling stir . . . and then hands began to go up. Two . . . six . . . nine of them.

"Roy Owdersfelt," Warwick said.

Roy Owdersfelt, a tall boy with a pimple the size of a tumor on the end of his nose, stood up, twisting his rawboned hands in front of him. "I stole ten bucks from my momma's purse last year!" he announced in a high, screamy voice. One scabbed, grimy hand wandered up to his face, settled on the pimple, and gave it a fearful tweak. "I took it down to The Wizard of Odds and I turned it into quarters and I played all these different games like Pac-Man and Laser Strike until it was gone! That was money she had put away against the gas bill, and that's how come for a while they turned off our heat!" He blinked around at them. "And my brother got sick and had to go in the hospital up in Indianapolis with pneumonia! Because I stole that money!

"That's my confession."

Roy Owdersfelt sat down.

Sunlight Gardener said, "Can Roy be forgiven?"

In unison the boys replied, *"Roy can be forgiven."*

"Can anyone here forgive him, boys?"

*"No one here."*

"Who can forgive him?"

*"God through the power of His only begotten Son, Jesus."*

"Will you pray to Jesus to intercede for you?" Gardener asked Roy Owdersfelt.

"Sure am gonna!" Roy Owdersfelt cried in an unsteady voice, and tweaked the pimple again. Jack saw that Roy Owdersfelt was weeping.

"And the next time your momma comes here are you going

to tell your momma that you know you sinned against her and
your little brother and against the face of God and you're just
as sorry a boy as ever there was?"

"You bet!"

Sunlight Gardener nodded to Andy Warwick.

"Confession," Warwick said.

Before confession was over at six o'clock, almost everyone except Jack and Wolf had his hand up, hoping to relate
some sin to those gathered. Several confessed petty theft.
Others told of stealing liquor and drinking until they threw
up. There were, of course, many tales of drugs.

Warwick called on them, but it was Sunlight Gardener
they looked to for approval as they told . . . and told . . . and
told.

*He's got them* liking *their sins*, Jack thought, troubled.
*They love him, they want his approval, and I guess they only
get it if they confess. Some of these sad sacks probably even
make their crimes up.*

The smells from the dining hall had been getting stronger.
Wolf's stomach rumbled furiously and constantly next to
Jack. Once, during one boy's tearful confession of having
hooked a *Penthouse* magazine so he could look at those filthy
pictures of what he called "sexed-out women," Wolf's stomach rumbled so loudly that Jack elbowed him.

Following the last confession of the evening, Sunlight Gardener offered a short, melodious prayer. Then he stood in the
doorway, informal and yet resplendent in his jeans and white
silk shirt, as the boys filed out. As Jack and Wolf passed, he
closed one of his hands around Jack's wrist.

"I've met you before." *Confess*, Sunlight Gardener's eyes
demanded.

And Jack felt an urge to do just that.

*Oh yes, we know each other, yes. You whipped my back
bloody.*

"No," he said.

"Oh yes," Gardener said. "Oh yes. I've met you before. In
California? In Maine? Oklahoma? Where?"

*Confess.*

"I don't know you," Jack said.

Gardener giggled. Inside his own head, Jack suddenly
knew, Sunlight Gardener was jigging and dancing and snap-

ping a bullwhip. "So Peter said when he was asked to identify Jesus Christ," he said. "But Peter lied. So do you, I think. Was it in Texas, Jack? El Paso? Was it in Jerusalem in another life? On Golgotha, the place of the skull?"

"I tell you—"

"Yes, yes, I know, we've only just met." Another giggle. Wolf, Jack saw, had shied as far away from Sunlight Gardener as the doorway would allow. It was the smell. The gagging, cloying smell of the man's cologne. And under it, the smell of craziness.

"I never forget a face, Jack. I never forget a face or a place. I'll remember where we met."

His eyes flicked from Jack to Wolf—Wolf whined a little and pulled back—and then back to Jack again.

"Enjoy your dinner, Jack," he said. "Enjoy your dinner, Wolf. Your real life at the Sunlight Home begins tomorrow."

Halfway to the stairs, he turned and looked back.

"I never forget a place or a face, Jack. I'll remember."

Coldly, Jack thought, *God, I hope not. Not until I'm about two thousand miles away from this fucking pris—*

Something slammed into him hard. Jack flew out into the hall, pinwheeling his arms madly for balance. He hit his head on the bare concrete floor and saw a tangled shower of stars.

When he was able to sit up, he saw Singer and Bast standing together, grinning. Behind them was Casey, his gut pouching out his white turtleneck. Wolf was looking at Singer and Bast, and something in his tensed-down posture alarmed Jack.

"No, Wolf!" he said sharply.

Wolf slumped.

"No, go ahead, dummy," Heck Bast said, laughing a little. "Don't listen to him. Go on and try me, if you want. I always liked a little warmup before dinner."

Singer glanced at Wolf and said, "Leave the dummy alone, Heck. He's just the body." He nodded at Jack. "There's the *head*. There's the *head* we got to change." He looked down at Jack, hands on his knees, like an adult bending to pass a pleasant word or two with a very small child. "And we will change it, Mr. Jack Parker. You can believe it."

Deliberately, Jack said, "Piss off, you bullying asshole."

Singer recoiled as if slapped, a flush rising out of his collar, up his neck, and into his face. With a growl, Heck Bast stepped forward.

Singer grabbed Bast's arm. Still looking at Jack, he said, "Not now. Later."

Jack got to his feet. "You want to watch out for me," he said quietly to them both, and although Hector Bast only glowered, Sonny Singer looked almost scared. For a moment he seemed to see something in Jack Sawyer's face that was both strong and forbidding—something that had not been there almost two months ago, when a much younger boy had set the small seafront town of Arcadia Beach to his back and had begun walking west.

### 4

Jack thought that Uncle Tommy might have described dinner—not unkindly—as consisting of American Grange Hall Cuisine. The boys sat at long tables and were served by four of their number, who had changed into clean mess-whites following the confession period.

Following another prayer, chow was duly brought on. Big glass bowls full of home-baked beans were passed up and down the four tables, steaming platters of cheap red hotdogs, tureens of canned pineapple chunks, lots of milk in plain cartons marked DONATED COMMODITIES and INDIANA STATE DAIRY COMMISSION.

Wolf ate with grim concentration, his head down, a piece of bread always in one hand to serve as a combination pusher and mopper. As Jack watched, he gobbled five hotdogs and three helpings of the bullet-hard beans. Thinking of the small room with its closed window, Jack wondered if he were going to need a gas-mask tonight. He supposed so—not that he was likely to be issued one. He watched dismally as Wolf slopped a fourth helping of beans onto his plate.

Following dinner, all the boys rose, formed lines, and cleared the tables. As Jack took his dishes, a Wolf-decimated loaf of bread, and two milk-pitchers out into the kitchen, he kept his eyes wide open. The stark labels on the milk cartons had given him an idea.

This place wasn't a prison, and it wasn't a workhouse. It

was probably classed as a boarding school or something, and the law would demand that some sort of state inspectors must keep an eye on it. The kitchen would be a place where the State of Indiana's eye would fall most often. Bars on the windows upstairs, okay. Bars on the kitchen windows? Jack didn't think so. They would raise too many questions.

The kitchen might make a good jumping-off point for an escape attempt, so Jack studied it carefully.

It looked a lot like the cafeteria kitchen at his school in California. The floor and walls were tiled, the big sinks and counters stainless steel. The cupboards were nearly the size of vegetable bins. An old conveyor-belt dishwasher stood against one wall. Three boys were already operating this hoary antique under the supervision of a man in cook's whites. The man was narrow, pallid, and possessed of a ratlike little face. An unfiltered cigarette was pasted to his upper lip, and that identified him in Jack's mind as a possible ally. He doubted if Sunlight Gardener would let any of his own people smoke cigarettes.

On the wall, he saw a framed certificate which announced that this public kitchen had been rated acceptable under standards set by the State of Indiana and the U.S. Government.

And no, there were no bars on the frosted-glass windows.

The ratlike man looked over at Jack, peeled his cigarette off his lower lip, and tossed it into one of the sinks.

"New fish, you and your buddy, huh?" he asked. "Well, you'll be old fish soon enough. The fish get old real quick here in the Sunlight Home, don't they, Sonny?"

He grinned insolently at Sonny Singer. It was quite obvious that Singer did not know how to cope with such a smile; he looked confused and unsure, just a kid again.

"You know you're not supposed to talk to the boys, Rudolph," he said.

"You can just cram it up your ass anytime you can't roll it down the alley or kick it in the air, buddy-roo," Rudolph said, flicking his eyes lazily over Singer. "You know that, don't you?"

Singer looked at him, lips first trembling, then writhing, then pushing together hard.

He suddenly turned around. "Night-chapel!" he shouted

furiously. "Night-chapel, come on, let's go, get those tables cleared and let's get up the hall, we're late! Night-chapel!"

## 5

The boys trooped down a narrow staircase lit by naked bulbs enclosed in wire mesh. The walls were dank plaster, and Jack didn't like the way Wolf's eyeballs were rolling.

After that, the cellar chapel was a surprise. Most of the downstairs area—which was considerable—had been converted into a spare, modern chapel. The air down here was good—not too warm, not too cold. And fresh. Jack could hear the whispering of convection units somewhere near. There were five pews split by a central aisle, leading up to a dais with a lectern and a simple wooden cross hung on a purple velvet backdrop.

Somewhere, an organ was playing.

The boys filed quietly into the pews. The microphone on the lectern had a large, professional-looking baffle on the end of it. Jack had been in plenty of studio sound-rooms with his mother, often sitting patiently by and reading a book or doing his homework assignments while she did TV overdubs or looped unclear dialogue, and he knew that sort of baffle was meant to keep the speaker from "popping" the mike. He thought it a strange thing to see in the chapel of a religious boarding home for wayward boys. Two video cameras stood at either side of the lectern, one to catch Sunlight Gardener's right profile, the other to catch his left. Neither was turned on this evening. There were heavy purple drapes on the walls. On the right, they were unbroken. Set into the left wall, however, was a glass rectangle. Jack could see Casey crouched over an extremely professional-looking sound-board, reel-to-reel tape recorder close to his right hand. As Jack watched, Casey grabbed a pair of cans from the board and slipped them over his ears.

Jack looked up and saw hardwood beams rising in a series of six modest arches. Between them was drilled white composition board . . . soundproofing. The place looked like a chapel, but it was a very efficient combination TV-and-radio studio. Jack suddenly thought of Jimmy Swaggart, Rex Humbard, Jack Van Impe.

*Folks, just lay yo hand on yo television set, and you gone be HEALED!!!*

He suddenly felt like screaming with laughter.

A small door to the left of the podium opened, and Sunlight Gardener stepped out. He was dressed in white from head to toe, and Jack saw expressions varying from exaltation to outright adoration on the faces of many of the boys, but Jack again had to restrain himself from a wild laughing-spree. The vision in white approaching the lectern reminded him of a series of commercials he had seen as a very young child.

He thought Sunlight Gardener looked like the Man from Glad.

Wolf turned toward him and whispered hoarsely, "What's the matter, Jack? You smell like something's really funny."

Jack snorted so hard into the hand cupped over his mouth that he blew colorless snot all over his fingers.

Sunlight Gardener, his face glowing with ruddy good health, turned the pages of the great Bible on the lectern, apparently lost in deepest meditation. Jack saw the glowering scorched-earth landscape of Heck Bast's face, the narrow, suspicious face of Sonny Singer. He sobered up in a hurry.

In the glass booth, Casey was sitting up, watching Gardener alertly. And as Gardener raised his handsome face from his Bible and fastened his cloudy, dreaming, and utterly insane eyes upon his congregation, Casey flipped a switch. The reels of the big tape recorder began to turn.

### 6

*"Fret not thyself because of evildoers,"*

said Sunlight Gardener. His voice was low, musical, thoughtful.

> *"Neither be thou envious against*
> *the workers of iniquity.*
> *For they shall soon be cut down like the grass,*
> *and wither as the green herb.*
> *Trust in the Lord, and do good;*
> *so shalt thou dwell in the Territories—"*

(Jack Sawyer felt his heart take a nasty, leaping turn in his chest)

> *"—and verily thou shalt be fed.*
> *Delight thyself also in the Lord;*
> *and he shall give thee the desires of thine heart.*
> *Commit thy way unto the Lord;*
> *trust also in him;*
> *and he shall bring it to pass. . . .*
> *Cease from anger, and forsake wrath;*
> *fret not thyself in any wise to do evil.*
> *For evildoers shall be cut off:*
> *but those that wait upon the Lord,*
> *they shall inherit his Territory."*

Sunlight Gardener closed the Book.

"May God," he said, "add His Blessing to the reading of His Holy Word."

He looked down at his hands for a long, long time. In Casey's glass booth, the wheels of the tape recorder turned. Then he looked up again, and in his mind Jack suddenly heard this man scream: *Not the Kingsland? You don't mean to tell me you've overturned a full wagonload of Kingsland Ale, you stupid goat's penis? You don't mean to tell me that, do yoooooouuuuuuuu?*

Sunlight Gardener studied his young male congregation closely and earnestly. Their faces looked back at him—round faces, lean faces, bruised faces, faces flaring with acne, faces that were sly, and faces that were open and youthful and lovely.

"What does it *mean*, boys? Do you understand Psalm Thirty-seven? Do you understand this lovely, lovely song?"

*No*, their faces said—sly and open, clear and sweet, pitted and poxed. *Not too much, only got as far as the fifth grade, been on the road, been on the bum, been in trouble . . . tell me . . . tell me. . . .*

Suddenly, shockingly, Gardener shrieked into the mike, "It means *DON'T SWEAT IT!*"

Wolf recoiled, moaning a little.

"Now you know what that means, don't you? You boys have heard that one, haven't you?"

*"Yeah!"* someone shouted from behind Jack.

*"OH-YEAH!"* Sunlight Gardener echoed, beaming. "DON'T SWEAT IT! NEGATIVE PERSPIRATION! They are good words, aren't they, boys? Those are some kind of *gooooood* words, *OH-YEAH!"*

*"Yeah! . . . YEAH!"*

"This Psalm says you don't have to WORRY about the evildoers! *NO SWEAT! OH-YEAH!* It says you don't have to WORRY about the workers of sin and iniquity! *NEGATIVE PERSPIRATION!* This Psalm here says that if you WALK the Lord and TALK the Lord, *EVERYTHING'S GONNA BE SO COOL!* Do you understand that, boys? Do you have an understanding ear for that?"

"Yeah!"

*"Hallelujah!"* Heck Bast cried, grinning divinely.

*"Amen!"* a boy with a great lazy eye behind his magnifying spectacles returned.

Sunlight Gardener took the mike with practiced ease, and Jack was again reminded of a Las Vegas lounge performer. Gardener began to walk back and forth with nervous, mincing rapidity. He sometimes did a jigging little half-step in his clean white leather shoes; now he was Dizzy Gillespie, now Jerry Lee Lewis, now Stan Kenton, now Gene Vincent; he was in a fever of jive Godhead testimony.

*"Naw, you don't have to fear! Ah, naw! You don't have to fear that kid who wants to show you dirty-book pictures! You don't have to fear that boy who says just one toke on just one joint won't hurt you and you'll be a sissy if you don't take it! Ah, naw! 'CAUSE WHEN YOU GOT THE LORD YOU GONNA WALK WITH THE LORD, AM I RIGHT?"*

*"YEAH!!!"*

*"OH-YEAH! AND WHEN YOU GOT THE LORD YOU GONNA TALK WITH THE LORD, AM I RIGHT?"*

*"YEAH!"*

*"I CAN'T HEAR YOU, AM I RIGHT?"*

*"YEAH!!!"* They screamed it out, many of them rocking back and forth in a frenzy now.

*"IF I'M RIGHT SAY HALLELUJAH!"*

*"HALLELUJAH!"*

*"IF I'M RIGHT SAY OH-YEAH!"*

*"OH-YEAH!"*

They rocked back and forth; Jack and Wolf were rocked with them, helplessly. Jack saw that some of the boys were actually weeping.

"Now tell me this," Gardener said, looking toward them warmly and confidentially. "Is there any place for the evildoer here in the Sunlight Home? Huh? What do you think?"

"No *sir!*" cried out the thin boy with the buck teeth.

"That's right," Sunlight Gardener said, approaching the podium again. He gave the mike a quick, professional flick to clear the cord out from under his feet and then he slipped it back into the clamp again. "That's the ticket. No room here for tattletale liars and workers of iniquity, say hallelujah."

"Hallelujah," the boys replied.

"Amen," Sunlight Gardener agreed. "The Lord says—in the Book of Isaiah he says it—that if you lean on the Lord, you're gonna mount up—oh-yeah!—with wings as eagles, and your strength shall be the strength of ten and I say to you, boys, *THAT THE SUNLIGHT HOME IS A NEST FOR EAGLES, CAN YOU SAY OH-YEAH!"*

*"OH-YEAH!"*

There was another caesura. Sunlight Gardener gripped the sides of the podium, head down as if in prayer, gorgeous white hair hanging in disciplined waves. When he spoke again, his voice was low and brooding. He did not look up. The boys listened breathlessly.

"But we have enemies," Sunlight Gardener said at last. This was little more than a whisper, but the mike picked it up and transmitted it perfectly.

The boys sighed—a rustle of wind through autumn leaves.

Heck Bast was looking around truculently, eyes rolling, pimples glowing such a deep red that he looked like a boy in the grip of a tropical illness. *Show me an enemy,* Heck Bast's face said. *Yeah, you go on, show me an enemy and just see what happens to him!*

Gardener looked up. Now his mad eyes appeared filled with tears.

"Yes, we have enemies," he repeated. "Twice now the State of Indiana has tried to shut me down. Do you know what? The radical humanists can barely stand to think of me down here at the Sunlight Home, teaching my boys to love Jesus and their country. It makes em mad, and do you want to know something, boys? Do you want to know a deep old dark secret?"

They leaned forward, eyes on Sunlight Gardener.

"We don't just make em mad," Gardener said in a hoarse conspirator's whisper. "We make em *scaaaaaared.*"

"Hallelujah!"

"Oh-yeah!"

"Amen!"

In a flash, Sunlight Gardener grabbed the mike again, and he was off! Up and down! back and forth! sometimes he jigged a two-step neat as a minstrel in a 1910 cakewalk! He bopped the word to them, pumping one arm first at the boys, then up toward heaven, where God had presumably dragged up His armchair to listen.

*"We scare em, oh-yeah! Scare em so bad they got to have another cocktail, or another joint, or another sniff of cocaine! We scare em, because even smart old God-denying, Jesus-hating radical humanists like them can smell righteousness and the love of God, and when they smell that they can smell the brimstone coming out of their own pores, and they don't like that smell, oh no!*

"So they send down an extra inspector or two to plant garbage under the kitchen counters, or to let loose some cock-a-roaches in the flour! They start a lot of vile rumors about how my boys are beaten. *Are you beaten?*"

*"NO!"* they roared indignantly, and Jack was dumbfounded to see Morton roaring the negative out as enthusiastically as all the rest, even though a bruise was already beginning to form on Morton's cheek.

"Why, they sent down a bunch of smart news reporters from some smart radical humanist news show!" Sunlight Gardener cried in a kind of disgusted wonder. "They came down here and they said, 'Okay, who are we supposed to do the hatchet-job on? We've done a hundred and fifty already, we're experts at smearing the righteous, don't worry about us, just give us a few joints and a few cocktails and point us in the right direction.'

"But we fooled em, didn't we, boys?"

Rumbling, almost vicious assent.

"They didn't find no one chained to a beam in the barn, did they? Didn't find no boys in strait-jackets, like they heard down in town from some of these hellbound School Board jackals, did they? Didn't find no boys getting their fingernails pulled, or all their hair shaved off, or nothing like that! Most they could find was some boys who said they got spanked, and they DID get spanked, oh-yeah, they was spanked and I'd testify on that matter myself before the Throne of Almighty God, with a lie-detector strapped to each arm, because the book says if you SPARE that rod, you gonna SPOIL that child, and if you believe that, boys, you gimme hallelujah!"

*"HALLELUJAH!"*

"Even the Indiana Board of Education, much as they'd like to get rid of me and leave a clear field for the devil, even *they* had to admit that when it comes to spanking, God's law and the State of Indiana's law runs just about the same: that if you SPARE that rod, you gonna SPOIL that child!

"They found HAPPY boys! They found HEALTHY boys! They found boys who were willing to WALK the Lord and TALK the Lord, oh can you say hallelujah?"

They could.

"Can you say oh-yeah?"

They could do that, too.

Sunlight Gardener came back to the podium.

"The Lord protects those that love Him, and the Lord is not gonna see a bunch of dope-smoking, communist-loving radical humanists take away this resting place for tired, confused boys.

"There were a few boys who told tattletale lies to those so-called news-people," Gardener said. "I heard the lies repeated on that TV news show, and although the boys slinging that mud were too cowardly to show their own faces on the screen, I knew—oh-yeah!—I knew those voices. When you've fed a boy, when you've held his head tenderly against your breast when he cries for his momma in the night, why, I guess then you know his voice.

"Those boys are gone now. God may forgive them—I hope He does, oh-yeah—but Sunlight Gardener is just a man."

He hung his head to show what a shameful admission this was. But when he raised it again, his eyes were still hot, sparkling with fury.

"Sunlight Gardener cannot forgive them. So Sunlight Gardener set them out on the road again. They have been sent out into the Territories, but there they shall not be fed; there even the trees may eat them up, like beasts which walk in the night."

Terrified silence in the room. Behind the glass panel, even Casey looked pallid and strange.

"The Book says that God sent Cain out to the East of Eden, into the land of Nod. Being cast out onto the road is like that, my boys. You have a safe haven here."

He surveyed them.

"But if you weaken . . . if you lie . . . then woe unto you! Hell awaits the backslider just as it awaits the boy or man who dives into it on purpose.

"Remember, boys.

"Remember.

"Let us pray."

# 23

# Ferd Janklow

## 1

It took Jack less than a week to decide that a detour into the Territories was the only way they could possibly escape the Sunlight Home. He was willing to try that, but he found he would do almost anything, run any risk, if only he could avoid flipping from the Sunlight Home itself.

There was no concrete reason for this, only the voice of his undermind whispering that what was bad here would be worse over there. This was, perhaps, a bad place in all worlds . . . like a bad spot in an apple which goes all the way to the core. Anyway, the Sunlight Home was bad enough; he had no urge to see what its Territories counterpart looked like unless he had to.

But there might be a way.

Wolf and Jack and the other boys not lucky enough to be on the Outside Staff—and that was most of them—spent their days in what the long-timers called Far Field. It was about a mile and half down the road, at the edge of Gardener's property, and there the boys spent their days picking rocks. There was no other field-work to be done at this time of year. The last of the crops had been harvested in mid-October, but as Sunlight Gardener had pointed out each morning in Chapel Devotions, rocks were always in season.

Sitting in the back of one of the Home's two dilapidated farm-trucks each morning, Jack surveyed Far Field while Wolf sat beside him, head down, like a boy with a hangover. It had been a rainy fall in the midwest, and Far Field was a gluey, sticky, muddy mess. Day before yesterday one of the boys had cursed it under his breath and called it a "real bootsucker."

*Suppose we just take off?* Jack thought for the fortieth time. *Suppose I just yell "Go for it!" at Wolf and we start busting our buns? Where? North end, where those trees are, and the rock wall. That's where his land ends.*

There might be a fence.

*We'll climb over it. For that matter, Wolf can throw me over it, if he has to.*

Might be barbed wire.

*Wiggle under it. Or—*

Or Wolf could tear it apart with his bare hands. Jack didn't like to think of it, but he knew Wolf had the strength . . . and if he asked, Wolf would do it. It would rip up the big guy's hands, but he was getting ripped up in worse ways right now.

And then what?

Flip, of course. That was what. If they could just get off the land that belonged to the Sunlight Home, that undervoice whispered, they would have a fighting chance all the way clear.

And Singer and Bast (whom Jack had come to think of as the Thuggsy Twins) would not be able to use one of the trucks to run them down; the first truck to turn wheels into Far Field before the deep frosts of December would mire itself rocker-panel deep.

*It'd be a footrace, pure and simple. Got to try it. Better than trying it back there, at the Home. And—*

And it wasn't just Wolf's growing distress that was driving him; he was now nearly frantic about Lily, who was back in

New Hampshire dying by inches while Jack said hallelujah under duress.

*Go for it. Magic juice or no magic juice. Got to try.*

But before Jack was quite ready, Ferd Janklow tried.

Great minds run in the same channel, can you say amen.

## 2

When it happened, it happened fast. At one moment Jack was listening to Ferd Janklow's usual line of cynical, amusing bullshit. At the next, Ferd was pelting north across the murky field toward the stone wall. Until Ferd went for it, the day had seemed as drearily ordinary as any other at the Sunlight Home. It was cold and overcast; there was a smell of rain, possibly even snow in the air. Jack looked up to ease his aching back, and also to see if Sonny Singer was around. Sonny enjoyed harassing Jack. Most of the harassment was of the nuisance variety. Jack had his feet stepped on, he was pushed on the stairs, his plate had been knocked out of his hands for three meals running—until he had learned to simultaneously cradle it on the inner side of his body and hold it in a death-grip.

Jack wasn't completely sure why Sonny hadn't organized a mass stomping. Jack thought maybe it was because Sunlight Gardener was interested in the new boy. He didn't *want* to think that, it scared him to think that, but it made sense. Sonny Singer was holding off because Sunlight Gardener had told him to, and that was another reason to get out of here in a hurry.

He looked to his right. Wolf was about twenty yards away, grubbing rocks with his hair in his face. Closer by was a gantry-thin boy with buck teeth—Donald Keegan, his name was. Donny grinned at him worshipfully, baring those amazing buck teeth. Spit dribbled from the end of his lolling tongue. Jack looked away quickly.

Ferd Janklow was on his left—the boy with the narrow Delftware hands and the deep widow's peak. In the week since Jack and Wolf had been incarcerated in the Sunlight Home, he and Ferd had become good friends.

Ferd was grinning cynically.

"Donny's in love with you," he said.

"Blow it out," Jack said uncomfortably, feeling a flush rise in his cheeks.

"I bet *Donny'd* blow it out if you let him," Ferd said. "Wouldn't you, Donny?"

Donny Keegan laughed his big, rusty yuck-yuck, not having the slightest idea of what they were talking about.

"I wish you'd quit it," Jack said. He felt more uncomfortable than ever.

*Donny's in love with you.*

The bloody hell of it was, he thought that maybe poor, retarded Donny Keegan really *was* in love with him . . . and Donny was maybe not the only one. Oddly, Jack found himself thinking of the nice man who had offered to take him home and who had then settled for dropping him off at the mall exit near Zanesville. *He saw it first,* Jack thought. *Whatever's new about me, that man saw it first.*

Ferd said, "You've gotten very popular around here, Jack. Why, I think even old Heck Bast would blow it out for you, if you asked him."

"Man, that's sick," Jack said, flushing. "I mean—"

Abruptly, Ferd dropped the rock he had been working at and stood up. He looked swiftly around, saw none of the white turtlenecks were looking at him, and then turned back to Jack. "And now, my darling," he said, "it's been a *very* dull party, and I really must be going."

Ferd made kissing noises at Jack, and then a grin of amazing radiance lit and broadened Ferd's narrow, pale face. A moment later he was in full flight, running for the rock wall at the end of Far Field, running in big gangling storklike strides.

He did indeed catch the guards napping—at least to a degree. Pedersen was talking about girls with Warwick and a horse-faced boy named Peabody, an Outside Staffer who had been rotated back to the Home for a while. Heck Bast had been granted the supreme pleasure of accompanying Sunlight Gardener to Muncie on some errand. Ferd got a good headstart before a startled cry went up:

*"Hey! Hey, someone's takin off!"*

Jack gaped after Ferd, who was already six rows over and humping like hell. In spite of seeing his own plan co-opted, Jack felt a moment of triumphant excitement, and in his heart he wished him nothing but well. *Go! Go, you sarcastic son of a bitch! Go, for Jason's sake!*

"It's Ferd Janklow," Donny Keegan gurgled, and then laughed his big, whooping laugh.

## 3

The boys gathered for confession in the common room that night as they always did, but confession was cancelled. Andy Warwick strode in, announced the cancellation with abrupt baldness, and told them they could have an hour of "fellowship" before dinner. Then he strode out.

Jack thought Warwick had looked, under his patina of goose-stepping authority, frightened.

And Ferd Janklow was not here.

Jack looked around the room and thought with glum humor that if this was "fellowship one with the other," he would hate to see what would happen if Warwick had told them to have "a quiet hour." They sat around the big long room, thirty-nine boys between age twelve and age seventeen, looking at their hands, picking at scabs, morosely biting their nails. They all shared a common look—junkies robbed of their fix. They wanted to hear confessions; even more, they wanted to *make* confessions.

No one mentioned Ferd Janklow. It was as though Ferd, with his grimaces at Sunlight Gardener's sermons and his pale Delftware hands, had never existed.

Jack found himself barely able to restrain an impulse to stand and scream at them. Instead, he began to think as hard as he ever had in his life.

*He's not here because they killed him. They're all mad. You think madness isn't catching? Just look what happened at that nutty place down in South America—when the man in the reflector sunglasses told them to drink the purple grape drink, they said yassuh, boss, and drank it.*

Jack looked around at the dreary, indrawn, tired, blank faces—and thought how they would light, how they would kindle, if Sunlight Gardener strode in here—if he strode in here right here and now.

*They'd do it, too, if Sunlight Gardener asked them to.*

*They'd drink it, and then they'd hold me and Wolf, and they'd*
*pour it down our throats as well. Ferd was right—they see*
*something on my face, or in it, something that came into me*
*in the Territories, and maybe they do love me a little . . . I*
*guess that's what pulled Heck Bast's bell-rope anyway. That*
*slob isn't used to loving anything or anyone. So, yeah, maybe*
*they do love me a little . . . but they love him a lot more.*
*They'd do it. They're mad.*

Ferd could have told him that, and, sitting there in the common room, Jack supposed that Ferd *had* told him.

He told Jack he had been committed to the Sunlight Home
by his parents, born-again Christians who fell down on their
knees in the living room whenever anyone on *The 700 Club*
began to say a prayer. Neither of them had understood Ferd,
who was cut from an entirely different bolt of cloth. They
thought Ferd must be a child of the devil—a communistic,
radical humanist changeling. When he ran away for the fourth
time and was bagged by none other than Franky Williams, his
parents came to the Sunlight Home—where Ferd had of
course been stashed—and fell in love with Sunlight Gardener
on sight. Here was the answer to all the problems their bright,
troublesome, rebellious son had caused them. Sunlight Gardener would educate their son toward the Lord. Sunlight
Gardener would show him the error of his ways. Sunlight
Gardener would take him off their hands and get him off the
streets of Anderson.

"They saw that story about the Sunlight Home on *Sunday*
*Report*," Ferd told Jack. "They sent me a postcard saying God
would punish liars and false prophets in a lake of fire. I wrote
them back—Rudolph in the kitchen smuggled the letter out
for me. Dolph's a pretty good guy." He paused. "You know
what the Ferd Janklow definition of a good guy is, Jack?"

"No."

"One who stays bought," Ferd said, and laughed a cynical,
hurt laugh. "Two bucks buys Dolph's mailman services. So I
wrote them a letter and said that if God punished liars the way
they said, then I hoped Sunlight Gardener could find a set of
asbestos longjohns in the other world, because he was lying
about what goes on here faster than a horse can trot. Everything they had on *Sunday Report*—the rumors about the
strait-jackets and about the Box—it was all true. Oh, they

couldn't prove it. The guy's a nut, Jack, but he's a *smart* nut. If you ever make a mistake about that, he'll put a real hurt on you and on Phil the Fearless Wolf-Boy for good measure."

Jack said, "Those *Sunday Report* guys are usually pretty good at catching people with their hands in the pork barrel. At least, that's what my mom says."

"Oh, he was scared. He got real shrill and shrieky. Ever see Humphrey Bogart in *The Caine Mutiny?* He was like that for a week before they showed up. When they finally got here he was all sweetness and reason, but the week before was a living hell. Mr. Ice Cream was shitting in his pants. That was the week he kicked Benny Woodruff down the stairs from the third floor because he caught him with a Superman comic. Benny was out cold for three hours, and he couldn't quite get it straight who he was or where he was until that night."

Ferd paused.

"He knew they were coming. Same as he always knows when the state inspectors are going to pull a surprise inspection. He hid the strait-jackets in the attic and made believe the Box was a hay-drying shed."

Ferd's cynical, hurt laugh again.

"Know what my folks did, Jack? They sent Sunny Gardener a Xerox of my letter to them. 'For my own good,' my pop says in his next letter to me. And guess what? It's Ferd's turn in the Box, courtesy of my own folks!"

The hurt laugh again.

"Tell you one other thing. He wasn't kidding at night-chapel. The kids that talked to the *Sunday Report* people all disappeared—the ones he could get hold of, anyway."

*The way Ferd himself has disappeared now,* Jack thought, watching Wolf brood across the room. He shivered. His hands felt very, very cold.

*Your friend Phil the Fearless Wolf-Boy.*

Was Wolf starting to look hairier again? So soon? Surely not. But that was coming of course—it was as relentless as the tides.

*And by the way, Jack, while we're just sitting around here worrying about the dangers of just sitting around here, how's your mother? How's Darling Lil, Queen of the Bs? Losing weight? Having pain? Is she finally starting to feel it eat into her with its sharp, ratty little teeth as you sit here growing*

*roots in this weird prison? Is Morgan maybe getting ready to
wind up the lightning and give the cancer a hand?*

He had been shocked at the idea of strait-jackets, and although he had seen the Box—a big ugly iron thing which sat
in the Home's back yard like a weird abandoned refrigerator—he couldn't believe that Gardener actually put boys in it.
Ferd had slowly convinced him, talking in a low voice as they
harvested rocks in Far Field.

"He's got a great setup here," Ferd had said. "It's a license
to coin money. His religious shows play all over the midwest
on the radio and over most of the country on cable TV and the
indy stations. We're his captive audience. We sound great on
the radio and we look great on the tube—when Roy Owdersfelt isn't milking that fucking pimple on the end of his nose,
that is. He's got Casey, his pet radio and TV producer—Casey
videotapes every morning-chapel and audiotapes every night-
chapel. He cuts all the sound and picture together and hypes
everything until Gardener looks like Billy Graham and us
guys sound like the crowd in Yankee Stadium during the seventh game of the World Series. That isn't all Casey does, either. He's the house genius. You see the bug in your room?
Casey set up the bugs. Everything feeds into his control
room, and the only way into that control room is through Gardener's private office. The bugs are voice-actuated, so he
doesn't waste any tape. Anything juicy he saves for Sunlight
Gardener. I've heard Casey put a blue box on Gardener's
phone so he can make long-distance phone calls free, and I
know damned well he's spliced a line into the pay-TV cable
that goes by out front. You like the idea of Mr. Ice Cream settling back and watching a big double feature on Cinemax after a hard day of selling Jesus to the masses? I like it. This guy
is as American as spinner hubcaps, Jack, and here in Indiana
they love him almost as much as they love high-school basketball."

Ferd hawked back snot, grimaced, twisted his head, and
spat into the dirt.

"You're kidding," Jack said.

"Ferd Janklow never kids about the Marching Morons of
the Sunlight Home," Ferd said solemnly. "He's rich, he
doesn't have to declare any of it to the Internal Revenue, he's

got the local school board buffaloed—I mean, they're scared to death of him; there's this one woman who practically *skitters* every time she's out here, looks like she'd like to give him the sign against the evil eye, or something—and like I said, he always seems to know when someone from the State Education Board is going to pay us a surprise visit. We clean this place from top to bottom, Bast the Bastard takes the canvas overcoats up to the attic, and the Box gets filled with hay from the barn. And when they come, we're always in class. How many classes you been in since you landed here in Indiana's version of the *Love Boat*, Jack?"

"None," Jack said.

"None!" Ferd agreed, delighted. He laughed his cynical, hurt laugh again—that laugh said, *Guess what I found out when I turned eight or so? I found out that I was getting a royal fucking from life, and that things weren't going to change in a hurry. Or maybe they were never going to change. And although it bums me out, it also has its funny side. You know what I mean, jellybean?*

## 4

Such was the run of Jack's thoughts when hard fingers suddenly grasped the back of his neck at the pressure-points below the ears and lifted him out of his chair. He was turned around into a cloud of foul breath and treated—if that was the word—to the sterile moonscape of Heck Bast's face.

"Me and the Reverend was still in Muncie when they brought your queer troublemaker friend into the hospital," he said. His fingers pulsed and squeezed, pulsed and squeezed. The pain was excruciating. Jack moaned and Heck grinned. The grin allowed bad breath to escape his mouth in even greater quantities. "Reverend got the news on his beeper. Janklow looked like a taco that spent about forty-five minutes in a microwave oven. It's gonna be a while before they put *that* boy back together again."

*He's not talking to me,* Jack thought. *He's talking to the whole room. We're supposed to get the message that Ferd's still alive.*

"You're a stinking liar," he said. "Ferd's—"

Heck Bast hit him. Jack went sprawling on the floor. Boys scattered away from him. From somewhere, Donny Keegan hee-hawed.

There was a roar of rage. Jack looked up, dazed, and shook his head in an effort to clear it. Heck turned and saw Wolf standing protectively over Jack, his upper lip pulled back, the overhead lights sending weird orange glints off his round glasses.

"So the dumbhead finally wants to dance," Heck said, beginning to grin. "Hey, all right! I *love* to dance. Come on, snotface. Come on over here and let's dance."

Still growling, saliva now coating his lower lip, Wolf began to move forward. Heck moved to meet him. Chairs scraped across linoleum as people moved back hurriedly to give them room.

"What's going on h—"

From the door. Sonny Singer. No need to finish his question; he saw what was going on here. Smiling, he pulled the door shut and leaned against it, watching, arms crossed over his narrow chest, his dark narrow face now alight.

Jack switched his gaze back to Wolf and Heck.

"Wolf, be careful!" he shouted.

"I'll be careful, Jack," Wolf said, his voice little more than a growl. "I'll—"

"Let's *dance*, asshole," Heck Bast grunted, and threw a whistling, country-boy roundhouse. It hit Wolf high on the right cheekbone, driving him backward three or four steps. Donny Keegan laughed his high, whinnying laugh, which Jack now knew was as often a signal of dismay as of glee.

The roundhouse was a good, heavy blow. Under other circumstances, the fight would probably have ended right there. Unfortunately for Hector Bast, it was also the only blow he landed.

He advanced confidently, big fists up at chest height, and drove the roundhouse again. This time Wolf's arm moved upward and outward to meet it. Wolf caught Heck's fist.

Heck's hand was big. Wolf's hand was bigger.

Wolf's fist swallowed Heck's.

Wolf's fist clenched.

From within it came a sound like small dry sticks first cracking, then breaking.

Heck's confident smile first curdled, then froze solid. A moment later he began to shriek.

"Shouldn't have hurt the herd, you bastard," Wolf whispered. "Oh your Bible this and oh your Bible that—*Wolf!*—and all you have to do is hear six verses of *The Book of Good Farming* to know you never . . ."

*Crackle!*

". . . *never* . . ."

*Crunch!*

"*NEVER* hurt the herd."

Heck Bast fell to his knees, howling and weeping. Wolf still held Heck's fist in his own, and Heck's arm angled up. Heck looked like a Fascist giving a *Heil Hitler* salute on his knees. Wolf's arm was as rigid as stone, but his face showed no real effort; it was, except for the blazing eyes, almost serene.

Blood began to drip out of Wolf's fist.

"Wolf, stop! That's enough!"

Jack looked around swiftly and saw that Sonny was gone, the door standing open. Almost all of the boys were on their feet now. They had drawn away from Wolf as far as the room's walls would allow, their faces awed and fearful. And still the tableau held in the center of the room: Heck Bast on his knees, arms up and out, his fist swallowed in Wolf's, blood pouring onto the floor from Wolf's fist.

People crowded back into the doorway. Casey, Warwick, Sonny Singer, three more big guys. And Sunlight Gardener, with a small black case, like a glasses-case, in one hand.

"*That's enough, I said!*" Jack took one look at the newcomers and raced toward Wolf. "*Right here and now! Right here and now!*"

"All right," Wolf said quietly. He let go of Heck's hand, and Jack saw a horrible crushed thing that looked like a mangled pinwheel. Heck's fingers stuck off at jagged angles. Heck mewled and held his destroyed hand against his chest.

"All right, Jack."

The six of them grabbed Wolf. Wolf made a half-turn, slipped one arm free, pushed, and suddenly Warwick went rattling against the wall. Someone screamed.

"Hold him!" Gardener yelled. "Hold him! Hold him, for Jesus' sake!" He was opening the flat black case.

*"No, Wolf!"* Jack shouted. *"Quit it!"*

For a moment Wolf went on struggling, and then he slumped back, allowing them to push him to the wall. To Jack they looked like Lilliputians clinging to Gulliver. Sonny looked afraid of Wolf at last.

"Hold him," Gardener repeated, taking a glittering hypodermic out of the flat case. That mincing, almost coy smile had come onto his face. "Hold him, praise Jesus!"

"You don't need that," Jack said.

"Jack?" Wolf looked suddenly frightened. "Jack? *Jack?*"

Gardener, headed for Wolf, pushed Jack as he went by. There was good whipcord muscle in that push. Jack went reeling into Morton, who squealed and shrank away as if Jack were contaminated. Belatedly, Wolf began to struggle again—but they were six, and that was too many. Perhaps, when the Change was on him, it wouldn't have been.

*"Jack!"* he howled. *"Jack! Jack!"*

"Hold him, praise God," Gardener whispered, his lips skinned back brutally from his teeth, and plunged the hypodermic into Wolf's arm.

Wolf went rigid, threw his head back, and howled.

*Kill you, you bastard*, Jack thought incoherently. *Kill you, kill you, kill you.*

Wolf struggled and thrashed. Gardener stood back, watching coldly. Wolf got a knee up into Casey's expansive gut. Casey *whoofed* air out, staggered backward, then came back. A minute or two later, Wolf began first to flag . . . then to sag.

Jack got to his feet, weeping with rage. He tried to plunge toward the knot of white turtlenecks holding his friend—as he watched he saw Casey swing a fist into Wolf's drooping face, and saw blood begin to pour from Wolf's nose.

Hands held him back. He struggled, then looked around and saw the frightened faces of the boys he picked rocks with in Far Field.

"I want him in the Box," Gardener said as Wolf's knees finally buckled. He looked slowly around at Jack. "Unless . . . perhaps you'd like to tell me where we've met before, Mr. Parker?"

Jack stood looking down at his feet, saying nothing. His eyes stung and burned with hot, hateful tears.

"The Box, then," Gardener said. "You may feel different when he starts to vocalize, Mr. Parker."

Gardener strode out.

## 5

Wolf was still screaming in the Box when Jack and the other boys were marched down to morning-chapel. Sunlight Gardener's eyes seemed to dwell ironically on Jack's pale, strained face. *Perhaps now, Mr. Parker?*

*Wolf, it's my mother, my mother—*

Wolf was still screaming when Jack and the other boys scheduled for field-work were split into two groups and marched out to the trucks. As he passed near the Box, Jack had to suppress an urge to jam his hands over his ears. Those growls, those gibbering sobs.

All at once Sonny Singer was at his shoulder.

"Reverend Gardener's in his office waiting to take your confession right this minute, snotface," he said. "Told me to tell you he'll let the dummy out of the Box the minute you tell him what he wants to know." Sonny's voice was silky, his face dangerous.

Wolf, screaming and howling to be let out, pounding the home-riveted iron sides of the Box with a fury of blows.

*Ah, Wolf, she's my MOTHER—*

"I can't tell him what he wants to know," Jack said. He turned suddenly toward Sonny, turning the force of whatever had come into him in the Territories upon Sonny. Sonny took two giant steps backward, his face dismayed and sickly scared. He tripped over his own feet and stumbled into the side of one of the idling trucks. If it hadn't been there, he would have fallen down.

"All right," Sonny said . . . the words came out in a breathy rush that was close to a whine. "All right, all right, forget it." His thin face grew arrogant again. "Reverend Gardener told me if you said no that I should tell you that your friend's screaming for you. Do you get it?"

"I know who he's screaming for."

"Get in the truck!" Pedersen said grimly, barely looking at them as he passed by . . . but when he passed Sonny, Pedersen grimaced as though he had smelled something rotten.

Jack could hear Wolf screaming even after the trucks got rolling, though the mufflers on both were little more than scallops of iron lace and the engines blatted stridently. Nor did Wolf's screams fade. He had made some sort of connection with Wolf's mind now, and he could hear Wolf screaming even after the work parties had reached Far Field. The understanding that these screams were only in his mind did nothing at all to improve matters.

Around lunchtime, Wolf fell silent, and Jack knew, suddenly and with no doubt at all, that Gardener had ordered him taken out of the Box before his screams and howls attracted the wrong sort of attention. After what had happened to Ferd, he wouldn't want any attention at all focused on the Sunlight Home.

When the work parties returned that late afternoon, the door of the Box was standing open and the Box was empty. Upstairs in the room they shared, Wolf was lying on the lower bunk. He smiled wanly as Jack came in.

"How's your head, Jack? Bruise looks a little better. Wolf!"

"Wolf, are you all right?"

"Screamed, didn't I? Couldn't help it."

"Wolf, I'm sorry," Jack said. Wolf looked strange—too white, somehow diminished.

*He's dying*, Jack thought. No, his mind corrected; Wolf had been dying ever since they had flipped into this world to escape Morgan. But now he was dying faster. Too white . . . diminished . . . but . . .

Jack felt a creeping chill.

Wolf's bare legs and arms weren't really bare; they were downed with a fine pelt of hair. It hadn't been there two nights ago, he was sure of that.

He felt an urge to rush over to the window and stare out, searching for the moon, trying to make sure he hadn't somehow misplaced about seventeen days.

"It's not the time of the Change, Jacky," Wolf said. His voice was dry, somehow husked-out. The voice of an invalid. "But I started to change in that dark smelly place they put me in. Wolf! I did. Because I was so mad and scared. Because I was yelling and screaming. Yelling and screaming can make the Change all by themselves, if a Wolf does it long enough." Wolf brushed at the hair on his legs. "It'll go away."

"Gardener set a price for letting you out," Jack said, "but I couldn't pay it. I wanted to, but . . . Wolf . . . my mother . . ."

His voice blurred and wavered toward tears.

"Shhh, Jacky. Wolf knows. Right here and now." Wolf smiled his terrible wan smile again, and took Jack's hand.

# 24

# Jack Names the Planets

## 1

Another week in the Sunlight Home, praise God. The moon put on weight.

On Monday, a smiling Sunlight Gardener asked the boys to bow their heads and give thanks to God for the conversion of their brother Ferdinand Janklow. Ferd had made a soul-decision for Christ while recuperating in Parkland Hospital, Sunlight said, his smile radiant. Ferd had made a collect call to his parents and told them he wanted to be a soul-winner for the Lord, and they prayed for guidance right there over the long-distance line, and his parents had come to pick him up that very day. *Dead and buried under some frosty Indiana field . . . or over in the Territories, perhaps, where the Indiana State Patrol could never go.*

Tuesday was too coldly rainy for field-work. Most of the boys had been allowed to stay in their rooms and sleep or read, but for Jack and Wolf, the period of harassment had begun. Wolf was lugging load after load of garbage from the barn and the sheds out to the side of the road in the driving rain. Jack had been set to work cleaning toilets. He supposed that Warwick and Casey, who had assigned him this duty, thought they were giving him a really nasty job to do. It was obvious that they'd never seen the men's room of the world-famous Oatley Tap.

Just another week at the Sunlight Home, can you say oh-yeah.

Hector Bast returned on Wednesday, his right arm in a cast up to the elbow, his big, doughy face so pallid that the pimples on it stood out like garish dots of rouge.

"Doctor says I may never get the use of it back," Heck Bast said. "You and your numbnuts buddy have got a lot to answer for, Parker."

"You aiming to have the same thing happen to your other hand?" Jack asked him . . . but he was afraid. It was not just a desire for revenge he saw in Heck's eyes; it was a desire to commit murder.

"I'm not afraid of him," Heck said. "Sonny says they took most of the mean out of him in the Box. Sonny says he'll do anything to keep from going back in. As for you—"

Heck's left fist flashed out. He was even clumsier with his left hand than with his right, but Jack, stunned by the big boy's pallid rage, never saw it coming. His lips spread into a weird smile under Heck's fist and broke open. He reeled back against the wall.

A door opened and Billy Adams looked out.

*"Shut that door or I'll see you get a helping!"* Heck screamed, and Adams, not anxious for a dose of assault and battery, complied in a hurry.

Heck started toward Jack. Jack pushed groggily away from the wall and raised his fists. Heck stopped.

"You'd like that, wouldn't you," Heck said. "Fighting with a guy that's only got one good hand." Color rushed up into his face.

Footsteps rattled on the third floor, heading toward the stairs. Heck looked at Jack. "That's Sonny. Go on. Get out of here. We're gonna get you, my friend. You and the dummy both. Reverend Gardener says we can, unless you tell him whatever it is he wants to know."

Heck grinned.

"Do me a favor, snotface. Don't tell him."

## 2

They had taken *something* out of Wolf in the Box, all right, Jack thought. Six hours had passed since his hallway confrontation with Heck Bast. The bell for confession would ring soon, but for now Wolf was sleeping heavily in the bunk below him. Outside, rain continued to rattle off the sides of the Sunlight Home.

It wasn't meanness, and Jack knew it wasn't just the Box that had taken it. Not even just the Sunlight Home. It was this whole world. Wolf was, simply, pining for home. He had lost most of his vitality. He smiled rarely and laughed not at all. When Warwick yelled at him at lunch for eating with his fingers, Wolf cringed.

*It has to be soon, Jacky. Because I'm dying. Wolf's dying.*

Heck Bast said he wasn't afraid of Wolf, and indeed there seemed nothing left to be afraid of; it seemed that crushing Heck's hand had been the last strong act of which Wolf was capable.

The confession bell rang.

That night, after confession and dinner and chapel, Jack and Wolf came back to their room to find both of their beds dripping wet and reeking of urine. Jack went to the door, yanked it open, and saw Sonny, Warwick, and a big lunk named Van Zandt standing in the hall, grinning.

"Guess we got the wrong room, snotface," Sonny said. "Thought it had to be the toilet, on account of the turds we always see floating around in there."

Van Zandt almost ruptured himself laughing at this sally.

Jack stared at them for a long moment, and Van Zandt stopped laughing.

"Who you looking at, turd? You want your fucking nose broke off?"

Jack closed the door, looked around, and saw Wolf asleep in his wet bunk with all his clothes on. Wolf's beard was coming back, but still his face looked pale, the skin stretched and shiny. It was an invalid's face.

*Leave him alone, then,* Jack thought wearily. *If he's that tired, let him sleep in it.*

*No. You will not leave him alone to sleep in that fouled bed. You will not!*

Tiredly, Jack went to Wolf, shook him half-awake, got him off the wet, stinking mattress, and out of his biballs. They slept curled up together on the floor.

At four in the morning, the door opened and Sonny and Heck marched in. They yanked Jack up and half-carried him down to Sunlight Gardener's basement office.

Gardener was sitting with his feet up on the corner of his desk. He was fully dressed in spite of the hour. Behind him was a picture of Jesus walking on the Sea of Galilee while his disciples gawped in wonder. To his right was a glass window looking into the darkened studio where Casey worked his idiot-savant wonders. There was a heavy keychain attached to one of Gardener's belt-loops. The keys, a heavy bunch of them, lay in the palm of his hand. He played with them while he spoke.

"You haven't given us a single confession since you got here, Jack," Sunlight Gardener said, his tone one of mild reproof. "Confession is good for the soul. Without confession we cannot be saved. Oh, I don't mean the idolatrous, heathenish confession of the Catholics. I mean confession before your brothers and your Saviour."

"I'll keep it between me and my Saviour, if it's all the same to you," Jack said evenly, and in spite of his fear and disorientation, he could not help relishing the expression of fury which overspread Gardener's face.

"It's *not* all the same to me!" Gardener screamed. Pain exploded in Jack's kidneys. He fell to his knees.

"Watch what you say to Reverend Gardener, snotface," Sonny said. "Some of us around here stand up for him."

"God bless you for your trust and your love, Sonny," Gardener said gravely, and turned his attention to Jack again.

"Get up, son."

Jack managed to get up, holding on to the edge of Sunlight Gardener's expensive blondewood desk.

"What's your real name?"

"Jack Parker."

He saw Gardener nod imperceptibly, and tried to turn, but it was a moment too late. Fresh pain exploded in his kidneys. He screamed and went down again, knocking the fading bruise on his forehead against the edge of Gardener's desk.

"Where are you from, you lying, impudent, devil's spawn of a boy?"

"Pennsylvania."

Pain exploded in the meaty upper part of his left thigh. He rolled into a fetal position on the white Karastan carpet, huddled with his knees against his chest.

"Get him up."

Sonny and Heck got him up.

Gardener reached into the pocket of his white jacket and took out a Zippo lighter. He flicked the wheel, produced a big yellow flame, and brought the flame slowly toward Jack's face. Nine inches. He could smell the sweet, pungent reek of lighter fluid. Six inches. Now he could feel heat. Three inches. Another inch—maybe just half that—and discomfort would turn to pain. Sunlight Gardener's eyes were hazy-happy. His lips trembled on the edge of a smile.

"Yeah!" Heck's breath was hot, and it smelled like mouldy pepperoni. "Yeah, do it!"

"Where do I know you from?"

"I never met you before!" Jack gasped.

The flame moved closer. Jack's eyes began to water, and he could feel his skin beginning to sear. He tried to pull his head back. Sonny Singer pushed it forward.

"Where have I met you?" Gardener rasped. The lighter's flame danced deep in his black pupils, each deep spark a twinner of the other. "Last chance!"

*Tell him, for God's sake tell him!*

"If we ever met I don't remember it," Jack gasped. "Maybe California—"

The Zippo clicked closed. Jack sobbed with relief.

"Take him back," Gardener said.

They yanked Jack toward the door.

"It won't do you any good, you know," Sunlight Gardener said. He had turned around and appeared to be meditating on the picture of Christ walking on water. "I'll get it out of you. If not tonight, then tomorrow night. If not tomorrow night, then the night after. Why not make it easy on yourself, Jack?"

Jack said nothing. A moment later he felt his arm twisted up to his shoulder blades. He moaned.

*"Tell him!"* Sonny whispered.

And part of Jack wanted to, not because he was hurt but because—*because confession was good for the soul.*

He remembered the muddy courtyard, he remembered this same man in a different envelope of skin asking who he was, he remembered thinking: *I'll tell you anything you want to know if only you'll stop looking at me with those freaked-out eyes of yours, sure, because I'm only a kid, and that's what kids do, they tell, they tell everything—*

Then he remembered his mother's voice, that tough voice, asking him if he was going to spill his guts to this guy.

"I can't tell you what I don't know," he said.

Gardener's lips parted in a small, dry smile. "Take him back to his room," he said.

### 3

Just another week in the Sunlight Home, can you say amen, brothers and sisters. Just another long, long week.

Jack lingered in the kitchen after the others had taken in their breakfast dishes and left. He knew perfectly well that he was risking another beating, more harassment . . . but by this time, that seemed a minor consideration. Only three hours before, Sunlight Gardener had come within an ace of burning his lips off. He had seen it in the man's crazy eyes, and felt it in the man's crazy heart. After something like that, the risk of a beating seemed a very minor consideration indeed.

Rudolph's cook's whites were as gray as the lowering November sky outside. When Jack spoke his name in a near-whisper, Rudolph turned a bloodshot, cynical gaze on him. Cheap whiskey was strong on his breath.

"You better get outta here, new fish. They're keepin an eye on you pretty good."

*Tell me something I don't know.*

Jack glanced nervously toward the antique dishwasher, which thumped and hissed and gasped its steamy dragon's breath at the boys loading it. They seemed not to be looking at Jack and Rudolph, but Jack knew that *seemed* was really the operant word. Tales would be carried. Oh yes. At the Sunlight Home they took away your dough, and carried tales became a kind of replacement currency.

"I need to get out of here," Jack said. "Me and my big friend. How much would you take to look the other way while we went out that back door?"

"More than you could pay me even if you could get your hands on what they took from you when they ho'd you in here, buddy-roo," Rudolph said. His words were hard but he looked at Jack with a bleary sort of kindness.

Yes, of course—it was all gone, everything. The guitar-pick, the silver dollar, the big croaker marble, his six

dollars . . . all gone. Sealed in an envelope and held somewhere, probably in Gardener's office downstairs. But—

"Look, I'd give you an IOU."

Rudolph grinned. "Comin from someone in this den of
thieves and dope-addicts, that's almost funny," he said. "Piss
on your fuckin IOU, old hoss."

Jack turned all the new force that was in him upon
Rudolph. There was a way to hide that force, that new
beauty—to a degree, at least—but now he let it all come out,
and saw Rudolph step back from it, his face momentarily
confused and amazed.

"My IOU would be good and I think you know it," Jack
said quietly. "Give me an address and I'll mail you the cash.
How much? Ferd Janklow said that for two bucks you'd mail a
letter for someone. Would ten be enough to look the other
way just long enough for us to take a walk?"

"Not ten, not twenty, not a hundred," Rudolph said quietly.
He now looked at the boy with a sadness that scared Jack
badly. It was that look as much as anything else—maybe
more—that told him just how badly he and Wolf were caught.
"Yeah, I've done it before. Sometimes for five bucks. Sometimes, believe it or not, for free. I would have done it free for
Ferdie Janklow. He was a good kid. These *fuckers*—"

Rudolph raised one water- and detergent-reddened fist and
shook it toward the green-tiled wall. He saw Morton, the accused pud-puller, looking at him, and Rudolph glared horribly at him. Morton looked away in a hurry.

"Then why *not?*" Jack asked desperately.

"Because I'm scared, hoss," Rudolph said.

"What do you mean? The night I came here, when Sonny
started to give you some trouble—"

"Singer!" Rudolph flapped one hand contemptuously. "I
ain't scared of Singer, and I ain't scared of Bast, no matter
how big he is. It's *him* I'm afraid of."

"Gardener?"

"He's a devil from hell," Rudolph said. He hesitated and
then added, "I'll tell you something I never told nobody else.
One week he was late givin me my pay envelope and I went
downstairs to his office. Most times I don't, I don't like to go
down there, but this time I had to . . . well, I had to see a man.
I needed my money in a hurry, you know what I mean? And I

seen him go down the hall and into his office, so I knew he was there. I went down and knocked on the door, and it swung open when I did, because it hadn't completely latched. And you know what, kid? *He wasn't there.*"

Rudolph's voice had lowered steadily as he told this story, until Jack could barely hear the cook over the thump and wheeze of the dishwasher. At the same time, his eyes had widened like the eyes of a child reliving a scary dream.

"I thought maybe he was in that recordin-studio thing they got, but he wasn't. And he hadn't gone into the chapel because there's no direct connectin door. There's a door to the outside from his office, but it was locked and bolted *on the inside*. So where did he go, buddy-roo? *Where did he go?*"

Jack, who knew, could only look at Rudolph numbly.

"I think he's a devil from hell and he took some weird elevator down to report to fuckin HQ," Rudolph said. "I'd like to help you but I can't. There ain't enough money in Fort Knox for me to cross the Sunlight Man. Now you get out of here. Maybe they ain't noticed you're missin."

But they had, of course. As he came out through the swinging doors, Warwick stepped up behind him and clubbed Jack in the middle of the back with hands interlaced to form one gigantic fist. As he went stumbling forward through the deserted cafeteria, Casey appeared from nowhere like an evil jack-in-the-box and stuck out a foot. Jack couldn't stop. He tripped over Casey's foot, his own feet went out from under him, and he sprawled in a tangle of chairs. He got up, fighting back tears of rage and shame.

"You don't want to be so slow taking in your dishes, snot-face," Casey said. "You could get hurt."

Warwick grinned. "Yeah. Now get on upstairs. The trucks are waiting to leave."

### 4

At four the next morning he was awakened and taken down to Sunlight Gardener's office again.

Gardener looked up from his Bible as if surprised to see him.

"Ready to confess, Jack Parker?"

"I have nothing—"

The lighter again. The flame, dancing a bare inch from the tip of his nose.

"Confess. Where have we met?" The flame danced a little closer yet. "I mean to have it out of you, Jack. Where? *Where?*"

*"Saturn!"* Jack screamed. It was all he could think of. *"Uranus! Mercury! Somewhere in the asteroid belt! Io! Ganymede! Dei—"*

Pain, thick and leaden and excruciating, exploded in his lower belly as Hector Bast reached between his legs with his good hand and squeezed Jack's testes.

"There," Heck Bast said, smiling cheerfully. "Didn't you just have that coming, you hellbound mocker."

Jack collapsed slowly to the floor, sobbing.

Sunlight Gardener leaned slowly down, his face patient—almost beatific. "Next time, it will be your friend down here," Sunlight Gardener said gently. "And with him I will not hesitate. Think about it, Jack. Until tomorrow night."

But tomorrow night, Jack decided, he and Wolf would not be here. If only the Territories were left, then the Territories it would be . . .

. . . if he could get them back there.

# 25

# Jack and Wolf Go to Hell

## 1

They had to flip from downstairs. He concentrated on that rather than on the question of whether or not they would be able to flip at all. It would be simpler to go from the room, but the miserable little cubicle he and Wolf shared was on the third floor, forty feet above the ground. Jack didn't know how exactly the Territories geography and topography corresponded to the geography and topography of Indiana, but he wasn't going to take a chance that could get their necks broken.

He explained to Wolf what they would do.

"You understand?"

"Yes," Wolf said listlessly.

"Give it back to me, anyway, pal."

"After breakfast, I go into the bathroom across from the common room. I go into the first stall. If no one notices I'm gone, you'll come in. And we'll go back to the Territories. Is that right, Jacky?"

"That's it," Jack said. He put a hand on Wolf's shoulder and squeezed it. Wolf smiled wanly. Jack hesitated and said, "I'm sorry I got you into this. It's all my fault."

"No, Jack," Wolf said kindly. "We'll try this. Maybe . . ." A small, wistful hope seemed to glimmer briefly in Wolf's eyes.

"Yes," Jack said. "Maybe."

## 2

Jack was too scared and excited to want breakfast, but he thought he might attract attention by not eating. So he shovelled in eggs and potatoes that tasted like sawdust, and even managed one fatty piece of bacon.

The weather had finally cleared. There had been frost the night before, and the rocks in Far Field would be like chunks of slag embedded in hardened plastic.

Plates taken out to the kitchen.

Boys allowed to go back to the common room while Sonny Singer, Hector Bast, and Andy Warwick got their day-rosters.

They sat around, looking blank. Pedersen had a fresh copy of the magazine the Gardener organization published, *The Sunlight of Jesus*. He turned the pages idly, glancing up every once in a while to look at the boys.

Wolf looked a question at Jack. Jack nodded. Wolf got up and lumbered from the room. Pedersen glanced up, saw Wolf cross the hall and go into the long, narrow bathroom across the way, and then went back to his magazine.

Jack counted to sixty, then forced himself to count to sixty again. They were the two longest minutes of his life. He was dreadfully afraid that Sonny and Heck would come back into the common room and order all the boys out to the trucks, and he wanted to get into the bathroom before that happened. But Pedersen wasn't stupid. If Jack followed Wolf too closely, Pedersen might suspect something.

At last Jack got up and walked across the room toward the door. It seemed impossibly far away, and his heavy feet seemed to bring him no closer; it was like an optical illusion.

Pederson looked up. "Where are you going, snotface?"

"Bathroom," Jack said. His tongue was dry. He had heard of people's *mouths* getting dry when they were afraid, but their *tongues?*

"They'll be upstairs in a minute," Pedersen said, nodding toward the end of the hall, where the stairs led down to the chapel, the studio, and Gardener's office. "You better hold it and water Far Field."

"I got to take a crap," Jack said desperately.

*Sure. And maybe you and your big stupid friend like to pull each other's dorks a little before you start the day. Just to sort of perk yourselves up. Go sit down.*

"Well, go on, then," Pedersen said crossly. "Don't just stand there and whine about it."

He looked back at his magazine. Jack crossed the hall and stepped into the bathroom.

### 3

Wolf had picked the wrong stall—he was halfway down the line, his big, clunky workshoes unmistakable under the door. Jack pushed in. It was cramped with the two of them, and he was very aware of Wolf's strong, clearly animal odor.

"Okay," Jack said. "Let's try it."

"Jack, I'm scared."

Jack laughed shakily. "I'm scared, too."

"How do we—"

"I don't know. Give me your hands." That seemed like a good start.

Wolf put his hairy hands—paws, almost—in Jack's hands, and Jack felt an eerie strength flow from them into him. Wolf's strength wasn't gone after all, then. It had simply gone underground, as a spring will sometimes go underground in a savagely hot season.

Jack closed his eyes.

"*Want* to get back," he said. "*Want* to get back, Wolf, *Help* me!"

"I do," Wolf breathed. "I will if I can! Wolf!"

"Here and now."

"Right here and now!"

Jack squeezed Wolf's paw-hands tighter. He could smell Lysol. Somewhere he could hear a car passing. A phone rang. He thought, *I am drinking the magic juice. In my mind I'm drinking it, right here and now I'm drinking it, I can smell it, so purple and so thick and new, I can taste it, I can feel my throat closing on it—*

As the taste filled his throat, the world swayed under them, around them. Wolf cried out, "Jacky, it's working!"

It startled him out of his fierce concentration and for a moment he became aware that it was only a trick, like trying to get to sleep by counting sheep, and the world steadied again. The smell of the Lysol flooded back. Faintly he heard someone answer the phone querulously: "Yes, hello, who is it?"

*Never mind, it's not a trick, not a trick at all—it's magic. It's magic and I did it before when I was little and I can do it again, Speedy said so that blind singer Snowball said so, too, THE MAGIC JUICE IS IN MY MIND—*

He bore down with all his force, all his effort of will . . . and the ease with which they flipped was stupefying, as if a punch aimed at something which looked like granite hit a cleverly painted papier-mâché shell instead, so that the blow you thought would break all your knuckles instead encountered no resistance at all.

## 4

To Jack, with his eyes screwed tightly shut, it felt as if the floor had first crumbled under his feet . . . and then disappeared completely.

*Oh shit we're going to fall anyway,* he thought dismally.

But it wasn't really a fall, only a minor sideslip. A moment later he and Wolf were standing firmly, not on hard bathroom tile but on dirt.

A reek of sulphur mingled with what smelled like raw sewage flooded in. It was a deathly smell, and Jack thought it meant the end of all hope.

"Jason! What's that *smell*?" Wolf groaned. "Oh Jason that *smell*, can't stay here, Jacky, can't stay—"

Jack's eyes snapped open. At the same moment Wolf let go of Jack's hands and blundered forward, his own eyes still tightly shut. Jack saw that Wolf's ill-fitting chinos and checked shirt had been replaced by the Oshkosh biballs in which Jack had originally seen the big herdsman. The John Lennon glasses were gone. And—

—and Wolf was blundering toward the edge of a precipice less than four feet away.

*"Wolf!"* He lunged at Wolf and wrapped his arms around Wolf's waist. *"Wolf, no!"*

"Jacky, can't stay," Wolf moaned. "It's a Pit, one of the Pits, Morgan made these places, oh I heard that Morgan made them, I can smell it—"

*"Wolf, there's a cliff, you'll fall!"*

Wolf's eyes opened. His jaw dropped as he saw the smokey chasm which spread at their feet. In its deepest, cloudy depths, red fire winked like infected eyes.

"A Pit," Wolf moaned. "Oh Jacky, it's a Pit. Furnaces of the Black Heart down there. Black Heart at the middle of the world. Can't stay, Jacky, it's the worst bad there is."

Jack's first cold thought as he and Wolf stood at the edge of the Pit, looking down into hell, or the Black Heart at the middle of the world, was that Territories geography and Indiana geography *weren't* the same. There was no corresponding place in the Sunlight Home to this cliff, this hideous Pit.

*Four feet to the right,* Jack thought with sudden, sickening horror. *That's all it would have taken—just four feet to the right. And if Wolf had done what I told him—*

If Wolf had done just what Jack had told him, they would have flipped from that first stall. And if they had done that, they would have come into the Territories just over this cliff's edge.

The strength ran out of his legs. He groped at Wolf again, this time for support.

Wolf held him absently, his eyes wide and glowing a steady orange. His face was a grue of dismay and fear. "It's a Pit, Jacky."

It looked like the huge open-pit molybdenum mine he had visited with his mother when they had vacationed in Colorado three winters ago—they had gone to Vail to ski but one day it had been too bitterly cold for that and so they had taken a bus tour to the Continental Minerals molybdenum mine outside the little town of Sidewinder. "It looks like Gehenna to me, Jack-O," she had said, and her face as she looked out the frost-bordered bus window had been dreamy and sad. "I wish they'd shut those places down, every one of them. They're pulling fire and destruction out of the earth. It's Gehenna, all right."

Thick, choking vines of smoke rose from the depths of the Pit. Its sides were veined with thick lodes of some poisonous green metal. It was perhaps half a mile across. A road leading downward spiraled its inner circumference. Jack could see figures toiling both upward and downward upon this road.

It was a prison of some kind, just as the Sunlight Home was a prison, and these were the prisoners and their keepers. The prisoners were naked, harnessed in pairs to carts like rickshaws—carts filled with huge chunks of that green, greasy-looking ore. Their faces were drawn in rough wood-cuts of pain. Their faces were blackened with soot. Their faces ran with thick red sores.

The guards toiled beside them, and Jack saw with numb dismay that they were not human; in no sense at all could they be called human. They were twisted and humped, their hands were claws, their ears pointed like Mr. Spock's. *Why, they're gargoyles!* he thought. *All those nightmare monsters on those cathedrals in France—Mom had a book and I thought we were going to have to see every one in the whole country but she stopped when I had a bad dream and wet the bed—did they come from here? Did somebody see them here? Some-body from the Middle Ages who flipped over, saw this place, and thought he'd had a vision of hell?*

But this was no vision.

The gargoyles had whips, and over the rumble of the wheels and the sounds of rock cracking steadily under some steady, baking heat, Jack heard their pop and whistle. As he and Wolf watched, one team of men paused near the very top of the spiral road, their heads down, tendons on their necks standing out in harsh relief, their legs trembling with exhaustion.

The monstrosity who was guarding them—a twisted creature with a breechclout twisted around its legs and a patchy line of stiff hair growing from the scant flesh over the knobs of its spine—brought its whip down first on one and then on the other, howling at them in a high, screeching language that seemed to drive silver nails of pain into Jack's head. Jack saw the same silver beads of metal that had decorated Osmond's whip, and before he could blink, the arm of one prisoner had been torn open and the nape of the other's neck lay in ruined flaps.

The men wailed and leaned forward even farther, their blood the deepest color in the yellowish murk. The thing screeched and gibbered and its grayish, plated right arm flexed as it whirled the whip over the slaves' heads. With a final staggering jerk, they yanked the cart up and onto the level. One of them fell forward onto his knees, exhausted, and the forward motion of the cart knocked him sprawling. One of the wheels rolled over his back. Jack heard the sound of the downed prisoner's spine as it broke. It sounded like a track referee's starter-gun.

The gargoyle shrieked with rage as the cart tottered and then fell over, dumping its load onto the split, cracked, arid ground at the top of the Pit. He reached the fallen prisoner in two lunging steps and raised his whip. As he did, the dying man turned his head and looked into Jack Sawyer's eyes.

It was Ferd Janklow.

Wolf saw, too.

They groped for each other.

And flipped back.

### 5

They were in a tight, closed place—a bathroom stall, in fact—and Jack could barely breathe because Wolf's arms were wrapped around him in a crushing embrace. And one of his feet was sopping wet. He had somehow managed to flip back with one foot in a toilet-bowl. Oh, great. *Things like this never happen to Conan the Barbarian,* Jack thought dismally.

"Jack *no*, Jack *no*, the Pit, it was the Pit, *no*, Jack—"

"Quit it! Quit it, Wolf! We're back!"

"No, no, n—"

Wolf broke off. He opened his eyes slowly.

"Back?"

"You bet, right here and now, so let go of me, you're break-ing my ribs, and besides, my foot's stuck in the damn—"

The door between the bathroom and the hall burst open with a bang. It struck the inner tile wall with enough force to shatter the frosted-glass panel.

The stall door was torn open. Andy Warwick took one look and spoke three furious, contemptuous words:

*"You fucking queers."*

He grabbed the dazed Wolf by the front of his checked shirt and pulled him out. Wolf's pants caught on the steel hood over the toilet-paper dispenser and pulled the whole works off the wall. It went flying. The toilet-paper roll broke free and went unspooling across the floor. Warwick sent Wolf crashing into the sinks, which were just the right height to catch him in the privates. Wolf fell to the floor, holding him-self.

Warwick turned to Jack, and Sonny Singer appeared at the stall door. He reached in and grabbed Jack by the front of his shirt.

"All right, you fag—" Sonny began, and that was as far as he got. Ever since he and Wolf had been dragooned into this place, Sonny Singer had been in Jack's face. Sonny Singer with his sly dark face that wanted to look just like Sunlight Gardener's face (and as soon as it could). Sonny Singer who had coined the charming endearment *snotface*. Sonny Singer whose idea it had undoubtedly been to piss in their beds.

Jack pistoned his right fist out, not swinging wildly in the Heck Bast style but driving strong and smooth from the el-bow. His fist connected with Sonny's nose. There was an audi-ble crunch. Jack felt a moment of satisfaction so perfect it was sublime.

"There," Jack cried. He pulled his foot out of the john. A great grin suffused his face, and he shot a thought at Wolf just as hard as he could:

*We ain't doing that bad, Wolf—you broke one bastard's hand, and I broke one bastard's nose.*

Sonny stumbled backward, screaming, blood spouting through his fingers.

Jack came out of the stall, his fists held up in front of him in a pretty fair imitation of John L. Sullivan. "I told you to watch out for me, Sonny. Now I'm gonna teach you to say hallelujah."

"Heck!" Sonny screamed. "Andy! Casey! Somebody!"

"Sonny, you sound scared," Jack said. "I don't know why—"

And then something—something that felt like a full hod of bricks—fell on the back of his neck, driving him forward into one of the mirrors over the sinks. If it had been glass, it would have broken and cut Jack badly. But all the mirrors here were polished steel. There were to be no suicides in the Sunlight Home.

Jack was able to get one arm up and cushion the blow a little, but he still felt woozy as he turned around and saw Heck Bast grinning at him. Heck Bast had hit him with the cast on his right hand.

As he looked at Heck, an enormous, sickening realization suddenly dawned on Jack. *It was you!*

"That hurt like hell," Heck said, holding his plastered right hand in his left, "but it was worth it, snotface." He started forward.

*It was you! It was you standing over Ferd in that other world, whipping him to death. It was you, you were the gargoyle, it was your Twinner!*

A rage so hot it was like shame swept through Jack. As Heck came in range, Jack leaned back against the sink, grasped its edge tightly in both hands, and shot both of his feet out. They caught Heck Bast squarely in the chest and sent him reeling back into the open stall. The shoe that had come back to Indiana planted in a toilet-bowl left a clear wet print on Heck's white turtleneck sweater. Heck sat down in the toilet with a splash, looking stunned. His cast clunked on porcelain.

Others were bursting in now. Wolf was trying to get up. His hair hung in his face. Sonny was advancing on him, one hand still clapped over his squirting nose, obviously meaning to kick Wolf back down.

"Yeah, you go ahead and touch him, Sonny," Jack said softly, and Sonny cringed away.

Jack caught one of Wolf's arms and helped him up. He saw as if in a dream that Wolf had come back hairier than ever. *It's putting him under too much stress, all of this. It's bringing on*

*his Change and Christ this is never going to end, never . . .
never. . . .*

He and Wolf backed away from the others—Warwick,
Casey, Pedersen, Peabody, Singer—and toward the rear of the
bathroom. Heck was coming out of the stall Jack had kicked
him into, and Jack saw something else. They had flipped from
the fourth stall down the line. Heck Bast was coming out of
the fifth. They had moved just far enough in that other world
to come back into a different stall.

"They was buggering each other in there!" Sonny cried,
his words muffled and nasal. "The retard and the pretty boy!
Warwick and me caught em with their dicks out!"

Jack's buttocks touched cold tile. Nowhere else to run. He
let go of Wolf, who slumped, dazed and pitiful, and put up his
fists.

"Come on," he said. "Who's first?"

"You gonna take us all on?" Pedersen asked.

"If I have to, I will," Jack said. "What are you going to do,
put me in traction for Jesus? Come on!"

A flicker of unease on Pedersen's face; a cramp of outright
fear on Casey's. They stopped . . . they actually stopped. Jack
felt a moment of wild, stupid hope. The boys stared at him
with the unease of men looking at a mad dog which can be
brought down . . . but which may bite someone badly first.

"Stand aside, boys," a powerful, mellow voice said, and
they moved aside willingly, relief lighting their faces. It was
Reverend Gardener. Reverend Gardener would know how to
handle this.

He came toward the cornered boys, dressed this morning
in charcoal slacks and a white satin shirt with full, almost By-
ronic, sleeves. In his hand he held that black hypodermic
case.

He looked at Jack and sighed. "Do you know what the
Bible says about homosexuality, Jack?"

Jack bared his teeth at him.

Gardener nodded sadly, as if this were no more than he had
expected.

"Well, all boys are bad," he said. "It's axiomatic."

He opened the case. The hypo glittered.

"I think that you and your friend have been doing something even worse than sodomy, however," Gardener went on

in his mellow, regretful voice. "Going to places better left to your elders and betters, perhaps."

Sonny Singer and Hector Bast exchanged a startled, uneasy look.

"I think that some of this evil . . . this perversity . . . has been my own fault." He took the hypo out, glanced at it, and then took out a vial. He handed the case to Warwick and filled the hypo. "I have never believed in forcing my boys to confess, but without confession there can be no decision for Christ, and with no decision for Christ, evil continues to grow. So, although I regret it deeply, I believe that the time to ask has ended and the time to demand in God's name has come. Pedersen. Peabody. Warwick. Casey. Hold them!"

The boys surged forward on his command like trained dogs. Jack got in one blow at Peabody, and then his hands were grabbed and pinned.

*"Led me hid imb!"* Sonny cried in his new, muffled voice. He elbowed through the crowd of goggling boys, his eyes glittering with hate. *"I wand to hid imb!"*

"Not now," Gardener said. "Later, perhaps. We'll pray on it, won't we, Sonny?"

"Yeah." The glitter in Sonny's eyes had become positively feverish. "I'mb going to bray on id all day."

Like a man who is finally waking up after a very long sleep, Wolf grunted and looked around. He saw Jack being held, saw the hypodermic needle, and peeled Pedersen's arm off Jack as if it had been the arm of a child. A surprisingly strong roar came from his throat.

*"No! Let him GO!"*

Gardener danced in toward Wolf's blind side with a fluid grace that reminded Jack of Osmond turning on the carter in that muddy stableyard. The needle flashed and plunged. Wolf wheeled, bellowing as if he had been stung . . . which, in a way, was just what had happened to him. He swept a hand at the hypo, but Gardener avoided the sweep neatly.

The boys, who had been looking on in their dazed Sunlight Home way, now began to stampede for the door, looking alarmed. They wanted no part of big, simple Wolf in such a rage.

*"Let him GO!* Let . . . him . . . let him . . ."

*"Wolf!"*

"Jack . . . Jacky . . ."

Wolf looked at him with puzzled eyes that shifted like strange kaleidoscopes from hazel to orange to a muddy red. He held his hairy hands out to Jack, and then Hector Bast stepped up behind him and clubbed him to the floor.

*"Wolf! Wolf!"* Jack stared at him with wet, furious eyes. *"If you killed him, you son of a bitch—"*

"Shhh, Mr. Jack Parker," Gardener whispered in his ear, and Jack felt the needle sting his upper arm. "Just be quiet now. We're going to get a little sunlight in your soul. And maybe then we'll see how you like pulling a loaded wagon up the spiral road. Can you say hallelujah?"

That one word followed him down into dark oblivion.

*Hallelujah . . . hallelujah . . . hallelujah . . .*

# 26

# Wolf in the Box

## 1

Jack was awake for quite a long time before they knew he was awake, but he became aware of who he was and what had happened and what his situation was now only by degrees—he was, in a way, like the soldier who has survived a fierce and prolonged artillery barrage. His arm throbbed where Gardener had punched the hypodermic into it. His head ached so badly that his very eyeballs seemed to pulse. He was ragingly thirsty.

He advanced a step up the ladder of awareness when he tried to touch the hurt place on his upper right arm with his left hand. He couldn't do it. And the reason he couldn't do it was that his arms were somehow wrapped around himself. He could smell old, mouldy canvas—it was the smell of a Boy Scout tent found in an attic after many dark years. It was only then (although he had been looking at it stupidly through his mostly lidded eyes for the last ten minutes) that he understood what he was wearing. It was a strait-jacket.

*Ferd would have figured that out quicker, Jack-O,* he thought, and thinking of Ferd had a focusing effect on his mind in spite of the crushing headache. He stirred a little and the bolts of pain in his head and the throb in his arm made him moan. He couldn't help it.

Heck Bast: "He's waking up."

Sunlight Gardener: "No, he's not. I gave him a shot big enough to paralyze a bull alligator. He'll be out until nine tonight at the earliest. He's just dreaming a little. Heck, I want you to go up and hear the boys' confessions tonight. Tell them there will be no night chapel; I've got a plane to meet, and that's just the start of what's probably going to be a very long night. Sonny, you stay and help me do the bookwork."

Heck: "It sure *sounded* like he was waking up."

Sunlight: "Go on, Heck. And have Bobby Peabody check on Wolf."

Sonny (snickering): "He doesn't like it in there much, does he?"

*Ah, Wolf, they put you back in the Box,* Jack mourned. *I'm sorry . . . my fault . . . all of this is my fault. . . .*

"The hellbound rarely care much for the machinery of salvation," Jack heard Sunlight Gardener say. "When the devils inside them start to die, they go out screaming. Go on now, Heck."

"Yes sir, Reverend Gardener."

Jack heard but did not see Heck as he lumbered out. He did not as yet dare to look up.

## 2

Stuffed into the crudely made, home-welded and home-bolted Box like a victim of premature burial in an iron coffin, Wolf had howled the day away, battering his fists bloody against the sides of the Box, kicking with his feet at the double-bolted, Dutch-oven-type door at the coffin's foot until the jolts of pain travelling up his legs made his crotch ache. He wasn't going to get out battering with his fists or kicking with his feet, he knew that, just as he knew they weren't going to let him out just because he screamed to be let out. But he couldn't help it. Wolfs hated being shut up above all things.

His screams carried through the Sunlight Home's immediate grounds and even into the near fields. The boys who heard them glanced at each other nervously and said nothing.

"I seen him in the bathroom this morning, and he turned mean," Roy Owdersfelt confided to Morton in a low, nervous voice.

"Was they queerin off, like Sonny said?" Morton asked.

Another Wolf-howl rose from the squat iron Box, and both boys glanced toward it.

"And how!" Roy said eagerly. "I didn't exactly see it because I'm short, but Buster Oates was right up front and he said that big retarded boy had him a whanger the size of a Akron fire-plug. That's what he said."

"Jesus!" Morton said respectfully, thinking perhaps of his own substandard whanger.

Wolf howled all day, but as the sun began to go down, he stopped. The boys found the new silence ominous. They looked at one another often, and even more often, and with more unease, toward that rectangle of iron standing in the center of a bald patch in the Home's back yard. The Box was six feet long and three feet high—except for the crude square cut in the west side and covered with heavy-gauge steel mesh, an iron coffin was exactly what it looked like. What was going on in there? they wondered. And even during confession, during which time the boys were usually held rapt, every other consideration forgotten, eyes turned toward the common room's one window, even though that window looked on the side of the house directly opposite the Box.

*What's going on in there?*

Hector Bast knew that their minds were not on confession and it exasperated him, but he was unable to bring them around because he did not know what precisely was wrong. A feeling of chilly expectation had gripped the boys in the Home. Their faces were paler than ever; their eyes glittered like the eyes of dope-fiends.

*What's going on in there?*

What was going on was simple enough.

Wolf was going with the moon.

He felt it happen as the patch of sun coming in through the ventilation square began to rise higher and higher, as the quality of the light became reddish. It was too early to go with the moon; she was not fully pregnant yet and it would hurt him.

Yet it would happen, as it always happened to Wolfs eventually, in season or out of it, when they were pressed too long and too hard. Wolf had held himself in check for a long time because it was what Jacky wanted. He had performed great heroisms for Jack in this world. Jack would dimly suspect some of them, yet never come close to apprehending their incredible depth and breadth.

But now he was dying, and he was going with the moon, and because the latter made the former seem more than bearable—almost holy, and surely ordained—Wolf went in relief, and in gladness. It was wonderful not to have to struggle anymore.

His mouth, suddenly deep with teeth.

## 3

After Heck left, there were office sounds: the soft scrape of chairs being moved, a jingle of the keys on Sunlight Gardener's belt, a file-cabinet door running open and then closed.

"Abelson. Two hundred and forty dollars and thirty-six cents."

Sounds of keys being punched. Peter Abelson was one of the boys on OS. Like all of the OS boys, he was bright, personable, and had no physical defects. Jack had seen him only a few times, but he thought Abelson looked·like Dondi, that homeless waif with the big eyes in the comic strips.

"Clark. Sixty-two dollars and seventeen cents."

Keys being punched. The machine rumbled as Sonny hit the TOTAL key.

"That's a real fall-off," Sonny remarked.

"I'll talk to him, never fear. Now please don't chatter at me, Sonny. Mr. Sloat arrives in Muncie at ten-fifteen and it's a long drive. I don't want to be late."

"Sorry, Reverend Gardener."

Gardener made some reply Jack didn't even hear. At the name *Sloat*, a great shock had walloped him—and yet part of him was unsurprised. Part of him had known this might be in the cards. Gardener had been suspicious from the first. He had not wanted to bother his boss with trivialities, Jack figured. Or maybe he had not wanted to admit he couldn't get the truth out of Jack without help. But at last he had called—

where? East? West? Jack would have given a great lot just then to know. Had Morgan been in Los Angeles, or New Hampshire?

*Hello, Mr. Sloat. I hope I'm not disturbing you, but the local police have brought me a boy—two boys, actually, but it's only the intelligent one I'm concerned with. I seem to know him. Or perhaps it's my . . . ah, my other self who knows him. He gives his name as Jack Parker, but . . . what? Describe him? All right. . . .*

And the balloon had gone up.

*Please don't chatter at me, Sonny. Mr. Sloat arrives in Muncie at ten-fifteen . . .*

Time had almost run out.

*I told you to get your ass home, Jack . . . too late now.*

*All boys are bad. It's axiomatic.*

Jack raised his head a tiny bit and looked across the room. Gardener and Sonny Singer sat together on the far side of the desk in Gardener's basement office. Sonny was punching the keys of an adding machine as Gardener gave him set after set of figures, each figure following the name of an Outside Staffer, each name neatly set in alphabetical order. In front of Sunlight Gardener was a ledger, a long steel file-box, and an untidy stack of envelopes. As Gardener held one of these envelopes up to read the amount scribbled on the front, Jack was able to see the back. There was a drawing of two happy children, each carrying a Bible, skipping down the road toward a church, hand-in-hand. Written below them was I'LL BE A SUNBEAM FOR JESUS.

"Temkin. A hundred and six dollars even." The envelope went into the steel file-box with the others that had been recorded.

"I think he's been skimming again," Sonny said.

"God sees the truth but waits," Gardener said mildly. "Victor's all right. Now shut up and let's get this done before six."

Sonny punched the keys.

The picture of Jesus walking on the water had been swung outward, revealing a safe behind it. The safe was open.

Jack saw that there were other things of interest on Sunlight Gardener's desk: two envelopes, one marked JACK PARKER and the other PHILIP JACK WOLFE. And his good old pack.

The third thing was Sunlight Gardener's bunch of keys.

From the keys, Jack's eyes moved to the locked door on the left-hand side of the room—Gardener's private exit to the outside, he knew. If only there was a way—

"Yellin. Sixty-two dollars and nineteen cents."

Gardener sighed, put the last envelope into the long steel tray, and closed his ledger. "Apparently Heck was right. I believe our dear friend Mr. Jack Parker has awakened." He got up, came around the desk, and walked toward Jack. His mad, hazy eyes glittered. He reached into his pocket and came out with a lighter. Jack felt a panic rise inside him at the sight of it. "Only your name isn't really Parker at all, is it, my dear boy? Your real name is Sawyer, isn't it? Oh yes, Sawyer. And someone with a great interest in you is going to arrive very, very soon. And we'll have all sorts of interesting things to tell him, won't we?"

Sunlight Gardener tittered and flicked back the Zippo's hood, revealing the blackened wheel, the smoke-darkened wick.

"Confession is so good for the soul," he whispered, and struck a light.

## 4

*Thud.*

"What was that?" Rudolph asked, looking up from his bank of double-ovens. Supper—fifteen large turkey pies—was coming along nicely.

"What was what?" George Irwinson asked.

At the sink, where he was peeling potatoes, Donny Keegan uttered his loud yuck-yuck of a laugh.

"I didn't hear anything," Irwinson said.

Donny laughed again.

Rudolph looked at him, irritated. "You gonna peel those goddam potatoes down to nothing, you idiot?"

*"Hyuck-hyuck-hyuck!"*

*Thud!*

"There, you heard it that time, didn't you?"

Irwinson only shook his head.

Rudolph was suddenly afraid. Those sounds were coming from the Box—which, of course, he was supposed to believe was a hay-drying shed. Some fat chance. That big boy was in the Box—the one they were saying had been caught in

sodomy that morning with his friend, the one who had tried to
bribe their way out only the day before. They said the big boy
had shown a mean streak before Bast whopped him one . . .
and some of them were also saying that the big boy hadn't just
broken Bast's hand; they were saying he had *squeezed* it to a
pulp. That was a lie, of course, had to be, but—

*THUD!*

This time Irwinson looked around. And suddenly Rudolph
decided he needed to go to the bathroom. And that maybe he
would go all the way up to the third floor to do his business.
And not come out for two, maybe three hours. He felt the approach of black work—very black work.

*THUD-THUD!*

Fuck the turkey pies.

Rudolph took off his apron, tossed it on the counter over
the salt cod he had been freshening for tomorrow night's supper, and started out of the room.

"Where are you going?" Irwinson asked. His voice was
suddenly too high. It trembled. Donny Keegan went right on
furiously peeling potatoes the size of Nerf footballs down to
potatoes the size of Spalding golfballs, his dank hair hanging
in his face.

*THUD! THUD! THUD- THUD-THUD!*

Rudolph didn't answer Irwinson's question, and by the
time he hit the second-floor stairs, he was nearly running. It
was hard times in Indiana, work was scarce, and Sunlight
Gardener paid cash.

All the same, Rudolph had begun to wonder if the time to
look for a new job had not come, could you say get me outta
here.

## 5

*THUD!*

The bolt at the top of the Box's Dutch-oven-type door
snapped in two. For a moment there was a dark gap between
the Box and the door.

Silence for a time. Then:

*THUD!*

The bottom bolt creaked, bent.

*THUD!*

It snapped.

The door of the box creaked open on its big, clumsy home-made hinges. Two huge, heavily pelted feet poked out, soles up. Long claws dug into the dust.

Wolf started to work his way out.

6

Back and forth the flame went in front of Jack's eyes; back and forth, back and forth. Sunlight Gardener looked like a cross between a stage hypnotist and some old-time actor playing the lead in the biography of a Great Scientist on *The Late Late Show*. Paul Muni, maybe. It was funny—if he hadn't been so terrified, Jack would have laughed. And maybe he would laugh, anyway.

"Now I have a few questions for you, and you are going to answer them," Gardener said. "Mr. Morgan could get the answers out of you himself—oh, easily, indubitably!—but I prefer not to put him to the trouble. So . . . how long have you been able to Migrate?"

"I don't know what you mean."

"How long have you been able to Migrate to the Territories?"

"I don't know what you're talking about."

The flame came closer.

"Where's the nigger?"

"Who?"

"The nigger, the nigger!" Gardener shrieked. "Parker, Parkus, whatever he calls himself! Where is he?"

"I don't know who you're talking about."

"Sonny! Andy!" Gardener screamed. "Unlace his left hand. Hold it out to me."

Warwick bent over Jack's shoulder and did something. A moment later they were peeling Jack's hand away from the small of his back. It tingled with pins and needles, waking up. Jack tried to struggle, but it was useless. They held his hand out.

"Now spread his fingers open."

Sonny pulled Jack's ring finger and his pinky in one direction; Warwick pulled his pointer and middle finger in the other. A moment later, Gardener had applied the Zippo's flame to the webbing at the base of the V they had created. The pain was exquisite, bolting up his left arm and from there seeming to fill his whole body. A sweet, charring smell drifted up. Himself. Burning. Himself.

After an eternity, Gardener pulled the Zippo back and snapped it shut. Fine beads of sweat covered his forehead. He was panting.

"Devils scream before they come out," he said. "Oh yes indeed they do. Don't they, boys?"

"Yes, praise God," Warwick said.

"You pounded that nail," Sonny said.

"Oh yes, I know it. Yes indeed I do. I know the secrets of both boys and devils." Gardener tittered, then leaned forward until his face was an inch from Jack's. The cloying scent of cologne filled Jack's nose. Terrible as it was, he thought it was quite a lot better than his own burning flesh. "Now, Jack. How long have you been Migrating? Where is the nigger? How much does your mother know? Who have you told? What has the nigger told you? We'll start with those."

"I don't know what you're talking about."

Gardener bared his teeth in a grin.

"Boys," he said, "we're going to get sunlight in this boy's soul yet. Lace up his left arm again and unlace his right."

Sunlight Gardener opened his lighter again and waited for them to do it, his thumb resting lightly on the striker wheel.

# 7

George Irwinson and Donny Keegan were still in the kitchen.

"Someone's out there," George said nervously.

Donny said nothing. He had finished peeling the potatoes and now stood by the ovens for their warmth. He didn't know what to do next. Confession was being held just down the hall, he knew, and that's where he wanted to be—confession was safe, and here in the kitchen he felt very, very nervous—but Rudolph hadn't dismissed them. Best to stay right here.

"I heard someone," George said.

Donny laughed: *"Hyuck! Hyuck! Hyuck!"*

"Jesus, that laugh of yours barfs me out," George said. "I got a new Captain America funnybook under my mattress. If you take a look out there, I'll let you read it."

Donny shook his head and honked his donkey-laugh again.

George looked toward the door. Sounds. Scratching. That's

what it sounded like. Scratching at the door. Like a dog that wanted to be let in. A lost, homeless pup. Except what sort of lost, homeless pup scratched near the top of a door that was nearly seven feet tall?

George went to the window and looked out. He could see almost nothing in the gloom. The Box was just a darker shadow amid shadows.

George moved toward the door.

## 8

Jack shrieked so loud and so hard he thought that surely his throat would rupture. Now Casey had also joined them, Casey with his big swinging gut, and that was a good thing for them, because now it took three of them—Casey, Warwick, and Sonny Singer—to grapple with Jack's arm and keep his hand applied to the flame.

When Gardener drew it away this time, there was a black, bubbling, blistered patch the size of a quarter on the side of Jack's hand.

Gardener got up, took the envelope marked JACK PARKER from his desk, and brought it back. He brought out the guitar-pick.

"What's this?"

"A guitar-pick," Jack managed. His hands were burning agony.

"What is it in the Territories?"

"I don't know what you mean."

"What's this?"

"A marble. What are you, blind?"

"Is it a toy in the Territories?"

"I don't—"

"Is it a mirror?"

"—know—"

"Is it a top that disappears when you spin it fast?"

"—what you're—"

*"YOU DO! YOU DO TOO, YOU FAGGOT HELLBOUND WHELP!"*

"—talking about."

Gardener drove a hand across Jack's face.

He brought out the silver dollar. His eyes gleamed.

"What's this?"

"It's a lucky piece from my Aunt Helen."

"What is it in the Territories?"

"Box of Rice Krispies."

Gardener held up the lighter. "Your last chance, boy."

"It turns into a vibraphone and plays 'Crazy Rhythm.'"

"Hold out his right hand again," Gardener said.

Jack struggled, but at last they got his hand out.

## 9

In the oven, the turkey pies had begun to burn.

George Irwinson had been standing by the door for almost five minutes, trying to get up nerve enough to open it. That scratching noise had not been repeated.

"Well, I'll show you there's nothing to be afraid of, chicken-guts," George said heartily. "When you're strong in the Lord, there's never any need to be afraid!"

With this grand statement, he threw open the door. A huge, shaggy, shadowy thing stood on the threshold, its eyes blazing red from deep sockets. George's eyes tracked one paw as it rose in the windy autumn dark and whickered down. Six-inch claws gleamed in the kitchen's light. They tore George Irwinson's head from his neck and his head flew across the room, spraying blood, to strike the shoes of the laughing Donny Keegan, the madly laughing Donny Keegan.

Wolf leaped into the kitchen, dropping down to all fours. He passed Donny Keegan with hardly a look and ran into the hall.

## 10

*Wolf! Wolf! Right here and now!*

It was Wolf's voice in his mind, all right, but it was deeper, richer, more commanding than Jack had ever heard it. It cut through the haze of pain in his mind like a fine Swedish knife.

He thought, *Wolf is riding with the moon.* The thought brought a mixture of triumph and sorrow.

Sunlight Gardener was looking upward, his eyes narrowed. In that moment he looked very much like a beast himself—a beast who has scented danger downwind.

"Reverend?" Sonny asked. Sonny was panting slightly, and

the pupils of his eyes were very large. *He's been enjoying himself,* Jack thought. *If I start to talk, Sonny's going to be disappointed.*

"I heard something," Gardener said. "Casey. Go and listen to the kitchen and the common room."

"Right." Casey took off.

Gardener looked back at Jack. "I'm going to have to leave for Muncie soon," he said, "and when I meet Mr. Morgan, I want to be able to give him some information immediately. So you had better talk to me, Jack. Spare yourself further pain."

Jack looked at him, hoping the jackhammer beat of his heart didn't show either in his face or as a faster, more noticeable pulse in his neck. If Wolf was out of the Box—

Gardener held up the pick Speedy had given him in one hand, the coin Captain Farren had given him in the other. "What are they?"

"When I flip, they turn into tortoise testicles," Jack said, and laughed wildly, hysterically.

Gardener's face darkened with angry blood.

"Lace up his arms again," he said to Sonny and Andy. "Lace up his arms and then pull down this hellbound bastard's pants. Let's see what happens when we heat up *his* testicles."

## 11

Heck Bast was deathly bored with confession. He had heard them all before, these paltry mail-order sins. *I hooked money from my mother's purse, I used to blow joints in the school-yard, we usta put glue in a paper bag and sniff it, I did this, I did that.* Little kids' stuff. No excitement. Nothing to take his mind off the steady drone of pain in his hand. Heck wanted to be downstairs, working on that kid Sawyer. And then they could get started on the big retard who had somehow surprised him and destroyed his good right hand. Yes, getting to work on the big retard would be a real pleasure. Preferably with a set of bolt-cutters.

A boy named Vernon Skarda was currently droning away.

"... so me and him, we seen the keys was in her, know what I mean. So he goes, 'Let's jump in the whore, and drive her around the block,' he goes. But I knew it was wrong, and I said it was, so he goes, 'You ain't nothin but a chickenshit.' So

I go, 'I ain't no chickenshit.' Like that. So he goes, 'Prove it, prove it.' 'I ain't doin no joy-ride,' I go, so he goes . . .''

*Oh dear Christ,* Heck thought. His hand was really starting to yell at him, and his pain-pills were up in his room. On the far side of the room, he saw Peabody stretch his jaws in a bone-cracking yawn.

"So we went around the block, and then he goes to me, he goes—"

The door suddenly slammed inward so hard it tore off its hinges. It hit the wall, bounced, struck a boy named Tom Cassidy, drove him to the floor, and pinned him there. Something leaped into the common room—at first Heck Bast thought it was the biggest motherfucking dog he had ever seen. Boys screamed and bolted up from their chairs . . . and then froze, eyes wide and unbelieving, as the gray-black beast that was Wolf stood upright, shreds of chinos and checked shirt still clinging to him.

Vernon Skarda stared, eyes bulging, jaws hanging.

Wolf bellowed, eyes glaring around as the boys fell back from him. Pedersen made for the door. Wolf, towering so high his head almost brushed the ceiling, moved with liquid speed. He swung an arm as thick as a barn-beam. Claws tore a channel through Pedersen's back. For a moment his spine was clearly visible—it looked like a bloody extension cord. Gore splashed the walls. Pedersen took one great, shambling step out into the hall and then collapsed.

Wolf turned back . . . and his blazing eyes fastened on Heck Bast. Heck got up suddenly on nerveless legs, staring at this shaggy, red-eyed horror. He knew who it was . . . or, at least, who it had been.

Heck would have given anything in the world just then to be bored again.

### 12

Jack was sitting in the chair again, his burned and throbbing hands once more pressed against the small of his back—Sonny had laced the strait-jacket cruelly tight and then unbuttoned Jack's chinos and pushed them down.

"Now," Gardener said, holding his Zippo up where Jack

could see it. "You listen to me, Jack, and listen well. I'm going to begin asking you questions again. And if you don't answer them well and truly, then buggery is one temptation you will never have to worry about being led into again."

Sonny Singer giggled wildly at this. That muddy, half-dead look of lust was back in his eyes again. He stared at Jack's face with a kind of sickly greed.

"Reverend Gardener! Reverend Gardener!" It was Casey, and Casey sounded distressed. Jack opened his eyes again. "Some kind of hooraw going on upstairs!"

"I don't want to be bothered now."

"Donny Keegan's laughing like a loon in the kitchen! And—"

"He said he didn't want to be bothered now," Sonny said. "Didn't you hear him?"

But Casey was too dismayed to stop. "—and it sounds like there's a riot going on in the common room! Yelling! Screaming! And it sounds like—"

Suddenly, Jack's mind filled with a bellow of incredible force and vitality:

*Jacky! Where are you? Wolf! Where are you right here and now?*

"—there's a dog-pack or something loose up there!"

Gardener was looking at Casey now, eyes narrow, lips pressed tightly together.

*Gardener's office! Downstairs! Where we were before!*
*DOWN-side, Jacky?*
*Stairs! Down-STAIRS, Wolf!*
*Right here and now!*

That was it; Wolf was gone from his head. From upstairs, Jack heard a thump and a scream.

"Reverend Gardener?" Casey asked. His normally flushed face was deeply pale. "Reverend Gardener, what is it? What—"

"Shut up!" Gardener said, and Casey recoiled as if slapped, eyes wide and hurt, considerable jowls trembling. Gardener brushed past him and went to the safe. From it he took an outsized pistol which he stuck in his belt. For the first time, the Reverend Sunlight Gardener looked scared and baffled.

Upstairs, there was a dim shattering sound, followed by a

screech. The eyes of Singer, Warwick, and Casey all turned
nervously upward—they looked like nervous bomb-shelter
occupants listening to a growing whistle above them.

Gardener looked at Jack. A grin surfaced on his face, the
corners of his mouth twitching irregularly, as if strings were
attached to them, strings that were being pulled by a pup-
peteer who wasn't particularly good at his job.

"He'll come here, won't he?" Sunlight Gardener said. He
nodded as if Jack had answered. "He'll come . . . but I don't
think he'll leave."

## 13

Wolf leaped. Heck Bast was able to get his right hand in its
plaster cast up in front of his throat. There was a hot flash of
pain, a brittle crunch, and a puff of plaster-dust as Wolf bit the
cast—and what was left of the hand inside it—off. Heck
looked stupidly down at where it had been. Blood jetted from
his wrist. It soaked his white turtleneck with bright, hot
warmth.

"Please," Heck whined. "Please, please, don't—"

Wolf spat out the hand. His head moved forward with the
speed of a striking snake. Heck felt a dim pulling sensation as
Wolf tore his throat open, and then he knew no more.

## 14

As he bolted out of the common room, Peabody skidded in
Pedersen's blood, went down to one knee, got up, and then ran
down the first-floor hall as fast as he could go, vomiting all
over himself as he went. Kids were running everywhere,
shrieking in panic. Peabody's own panic was not quite that
complete. He remembered what he was supposed to do in extreme situations—although he didn't think anyone had ever
envisioned a situation as extreme as *this*; he had an idea that
Reverend Gardener had been thinking in terms of a kid going
bugfuck and cutting another kid up, something like that.

Beyond the parlor where new boys were brought when
they first came to the Sunlight Home was a small upstairs office used only by the thugs Gardener referred to as his "student aides."

Peabody locked himself in this room, picked up the phone, and dialled an emergency number. A moment later he was talking to Franky Williams.

"Peabody, at the Sunlight Home," he said. "You ought to get up here with as many police as you can get, Officer Williams. All hell has—"

Outside he heard a wailing shriek followed by a crash of breaking wood. There was a snarling, barking roar, and the shriek was cut off.

"—has busted loose up here," he finished.

"What kind of hell?" Williams asked impatiently. "Lemme talk to Gardener."

"I don't know where the Reverend is, but he'd want you up here. There's people dead. *Kids* dead."

*"What?"*

"Just get up here with a lot of men," Peabody said. "And a lot of guns."

Another scream. The crash-thud of something heavy—the old highboy in the front hall, probably—being overturned.

"Machine-guns, if you can find them."

A crystalline jangle as the big chandelier in the hall came down. Peabody cringed. It sounded like that monster was tearing the whole place apart with its bare hands.

"Hell, bring a nuke if you can," Peabody said, beginning to blubber.

"What—"

Peabody hung up before Williams could finish. He crawled into the kneehole under the desk. Wrapped his arms around his head. And began to pray assiduously that all of this should prove to be only a dream—the worst fucking nightmare he had ever had.

### 15

Wolf raged along the first-floor hall between the common room and the front door, pausing only to overturn the highboy, then to leap easily up and grab the chandelier. He swung on it like Tarzan until it tore out of the ceiling and spilled diamonds of crystal all over the hallway runner.

*DOWN-side. Jacky was on the DOWN-side.* Now . . . which side was that?

A boy who was no longer able to stand the agonizing tension of waiting for the thing to be gone jerked open the door of the closet where he had been hiding and bolted for the stairs. Wolf grabbed him and threw him the length of the hall. The boy struck the closed kitchen door with a bone-breaking thud and fell in a heap.

Wolf's head swam with the intoxicating odor of fresh-spilled blood. His hair hung in bloody dreadlocks around his jaw and muzzle. He tried to hold on to thought, but it was hard—hard. He had to find Jacky very quickly now, before he lost the ability to think completely.

He raced back toward the kitchen, where he had come in, dropping to all fours again because movement was faster and easier that way . . . and suddenly, passing a closed door, he remembered. The narrow place. It had been like going down into a grave. The smell, wet and heavy in his throat—

*DOWN-side. Behind that door. Right here and now!*

*"Wolf!"* he cried, although the boys cringing in their hiding places on the first and second floors heard only a rising, triumphant howl. He raised both of the heavily muscled battering rams that had been his arms and drove them into the door. It burst open in the middle, vomiting splinters down the stairwell. Wolf drove his way through, and yes, here was the narrow place, like a throat; here was the way to the place where the White Man had told his lies while Jack and the Weaker Wolf had to sit and listen.

Jack was down there now. Wolf could smell him.

But he also smelled the White Man . . . and gunpowder.

*Careful . . .*

Oh yes. Wolfs knew careful. Wolfs could run and tear and kill, but when they had to be . . . Wolfs knew careful.

He went down the stairs on all fours, silent as oiled smoke, eyes as red as brake lights.

## 16

Gardener was becoming steadily more nervous; to Jack he looked like a man who was entering the freakout zone. His eyes moved jerkily in a triple play, from the studio where Casey was frantically listening to Jack, and then to the closed door which gave on the hall.

Most of the noises from upstairs had stopped some time ago.

Now Sonny Singer started for the door. "I'll go up and see what's—"

*"You're not going anywhere! Come back here!"*

Sonny winced as if Gardener had struck him.

"What the matter, Reverend Gardener?" Jack asked. "You look a little nervous."

Sonny rocked him with a slap. "You want to watch the way you talk, snotface! You just want to watch it!"

"You look nervous, too, Sonny. And you, Warwick. And Casey in there—"

*"Shut him up!"* Gardener suddenly screamed. *"Can't you do anything? Do I have to do everything around here myself?"*

Sonny slapped Jack again, much harder. Jack's nose began to bleed, but he smiled. Wolf was very close now . . . and Wolf was being careful. Jack had begun to have a crazy hope that they might get out of this alive.

Casey suddenly straightened up and then tore the cans off his head and flicked the intercom switch.

"Reverend Gardener! I hear sirens on the outside mikes!"

Gardener's eyes, now too wide, skidded back to Casey.

"What? How many? How far away?"

"Sounds like a lot," Casey said. "Not close yet. But they're coming here. No doubt about that."

Gardener's nerve broke then; Jack saw it happen. The man sat, indecisive, for a moment, and then he wiped his mouth delicately with the side of his hand.

*It isn't whatever happened upstairs, not just the sirens, either. He knows that Wolf is close, too. In his own way he smells him . . . and he doesn't like it. Wolf, we might have a chance! We just might!*

Gardener handed the pistol to Sonny Singer. "I haven't time to deal with the police, or whatever mess there might be upstairs, right now," he said. "The important thing is Morgan Sloat. I'm going to Muncie. You and Andy are coming with me, Sonny. You keep this gun on our friend Jack here while I get the car out of the garage. When you hear the horn, come on out."

"What about Casey?" Andy Warwick rumbled.

"Yes, yes, all right, Casey, too," Gardener agreed at once, and Jack thought, *He's running out on you, you stupid assholes. He's running out on you, it's so obvious that he might as well take out a billboard on the Sunset Strip and advertise the fact, and your brains are too blown to even know it. You'd go on sitting down here for ten years waiting to hear that horn blow, if the food and toilet paper held out that long.*

Gardener got up. Sonny Singer, his face flushed with new importance, sat down behind his desk and pointed the gun at Jack. "If his retarded friend shows up," Gardener said, "shoot him."

"How could *he* show up?" Sonny asked. "He's in the Box."

"Never mind," Gardener said. "He's evil, they're both evil, it's indubitable, it's axiomatic, if the retard shows up, shoot him, shoot them both."

He fumbled through the keys on his ring and selected one. "When you hear the horn," he said. He opened the door and went out. Jack strained his ears for the sound of sirens but heard nothing.

The door closed behind Sunlight Gardener.

## 17

Time, stretching out.

A minute that felt like two; two that felt like ten; four that felt like an hour. The three of Gardener's "student aides" who had been left with Jack looked like boys who had been caught in a game of Statue Tag. Sonny sat bolt-upright behind Sunlight Gardener's desk—a place he both relished and coveted. The gun pointed steadily at Jack's face. Warwick stood by the door to the hall. Casey sat in the brightly lighted booth with the cans on his ears again, staring blankly out through the other glass square, into the darkness of the chapel, seeing nothing, only listening.

"He's not going to take you with him, you know," Jack said suddenly. The sound of his voice surprised him a little. It was even and unafraid.

"Shut up, snotface," Sonny snapped.

"Don't hold your breath until you hear him honk that horn," Jack said. "You'll turn pretty blue."

"Next thing he says, Andy, break his nose," Sonny said.

"That's right," Jack said. "Break my nose, Andy. Shoot me, Sonny. The cops are coming, Gardener's gone, and they're going to find the three of you standing over a corpse in a strait-jacket." He paused, and amended: "A corpse in a strait-jacket with a broken nose."

"Hit him, Andy," Sonny said.

Andy Warwick moved from the door to where Jack sat, strait-jacketed, his pants and underpants puddled around his ankles.

Jack turned his face openly up to Warwick's.

"That's right, Andy," he said. "Hit me. I'll hold still. Hell of a target."

Andy Warwick balled up his fist, drew it back . . . and then hesitated. Uncertainty flickered in his eyes.

There was a digital clock on Gardener's desk. Jack's eyes shifted to it for a moment, and then back to Warwick's face. "It's been four minutes, Andy. How long does it take a guy to back a car out of the garage? Especially when he's in a hurry?"

Sonny Singer bolted out of Sunlight Gardener's chair, came around the desk, and charged at Jack. His narrow, secretive face was furious. His fists were balled up. He made as if to hit Jack. Warwick, who was bigger, restrained him. There was trouble on Warwick's face now—deep trouble.

"Wait," he said.

"I don't have to listen to this! I don't—"

"Why don't you ask Casey how close those sirens are getting?" Jack asked, and Warwick's frown deepened. "You've been left in the lurch, don't you know that? Do I have to draw you a picture? It's going bad here. He knew it—he *smelled* it! He's leaving you with a bag. From the sounds upstairs—"

Singer broke free of Warwick's half-hearted hold and clouted Jack on the side of the face. His head rocked to one side, then came slowly back.

"—it's a big, messy bag," Jack finished.

"You shut up or I'll kill you," Sonny hissed.

The digits on the clock had changed.

"Five minutes now," Jack said.

"Sonny," Warwick said with a catch in his voice. "Let's get him out of that thing."

"No!" Sonny's cry was wounded, furious . . . ultimately frightened.

"You know what the Rev'rend said," Warwick said rapidly. "Before. When the TV people came. Nobody can see the strait-jackets. They wouldn't understand. They—"

*Click!* The intercom.

"Sonny! Andy!" Casey sounded panicky. "They're closer! The sirens! Christ! What are we supposed to do?"

"Let him out *now!*" Warwick's face was pallid, except for two red spots high on his cheekbones.

"Reverend Gardener *also* said—"

"I don't give a fuck *what* he also said!" Warwick's voice dropped, and now he voiced the child's deepest fear: "We're gonna get *caught*, Sonny! We're gonna get *caught*!"

And Jack thought that now he could hear sirens, or perhaps it was only his imagination.

Sonny's eyes rolled toward Jack with horrible, trapped indecision. He half-raised the gun and for one moment Jack believed Sonny was really going to shoot him.

But it was six minutes now, and still no honk from the Godhead, announcing that the *deus ex machina* was now boarding for Muncie.

"You let him loose," Sonny said sulkily to Andy Warwick. "I don't even want to touch him. He's a sinner. And he's a queer."

Sonny retreated to the desk as Andy Warwick's fingers fumbled with the strait-jacket's lacings.

"You better not say anything," he panted. "You better not say anything or I'll kill you myself."

Right arm free.

Left arm free.

They collapsed bonelessly into his lap. Pins and needles coming back.

Warwick hauled the hateful restraint off him, a horror of dun-colored canvas and rawhide lacings. Warwick looked at it in his hands and grimaced. He darted across the room and began to stuff it into Sunlight Gardener's safe.

"Pull up your pants," Sonny said. "You think I want to look at your works?"

Jack fumbled up his shorts, got the waistband of his pants, dropped them, and managed to pull them up.

*Click!* The intercom.

"Sonny! Andy!" Casey's voice, panicked. "I *hear* something!"

"Are they turning in?" Sonny almost screamed. Warwick redoubled his efforts to stuff the strait-jacket into the safe. "Are they turning in the front—"

*"No! In the chapel! I can't see nothing but I can hear something in the—"*

There was an explosion of shattering glass as Wolf leaped from the darkness of the chapel and into the studio.

## 18

Casey's screams as he pushed back from the control board in his wheel-footed chair were hideously amplified.

Inside the studio there was a brief storm of glass. Wolf landed four-footed on the slanted control board and half-climbed, half-slid down it, his eyes throwing a red glare. His long claws turned dials and flicked switches at random. The big reel-to-reel Sony tape recorder started to turn.

"—*COMMUNISTS!*" the voice of Sunlight Gardener bellowed. He was cranked to maximum volume, drowning out Casey's shrieks and Warwick's screams to shoot it, Sonny, shoot it, *shoot* it! But the voice of Gardener was not alone. In the background, like music from hell, came the mingled warble of many sirens as Casey's mikes picked up a caravan of police cruisers turning into the Sunlight Home's drive.

*"OH, THEY'RE GONNA TELL YOU IT'S ALL RIGHT TO LOOK AT THOSE DIRTY BOOKS! THEY'RE GONNA TELL YOU IT DON'T MATTER THAT IT'S AGAINST THE LAW TO PRAY IN THE PUBLIC SCHOOLS! THEY'RE GONNA TELL YOU IT DON'T EVEN MATTER THAT THERE ARE SIXTEEN U.S. REPRESENTATIVES AND TWO U.S. GOVERNORS WHO ARE AVOWED HOMOSEXUALS! THEY'RE GONNA TELL YOU—"*

Casey's chair rolled back against the glass wall between the studio and Sunlight Gardener's office. His head turned, and for one moment they could all see his agonized, bulging eyes. Then Wolf leaped from the edge of the control panel. His head struck Casey's gut . . . and plowed into it. His jaws began to open and close with the speed of a cane-cutting machine. Blood flew up and splattered the window as Casey began to convulse.

*"Shoot it, Sonny, shoot the fucking thing!"* Warwick whooped.

"Think I'm gonna shoot him instead," Sonny said, looking around at Jack. He spoke with the air of a man who has finally arrived at a great conclusion. He nodded, began to grin.

*"—DAY IS COMING, BOYS! OH YES, A MIGHTY DAY, AND ON THAT DAY THOSE COMMUNIST HUMANIST HELLBOUND ATHEISTS ARE GONNA FIND OUT THAT THE ROCK WILL NOT SHIELD THEM, THE DEAD TREE WILL NOT GIVE THEM SHELTER! THEY'RE GONNA, OH SAY HALLELUJAH, THEY'RE GONNA—"*

Wolf, snarling and ripping.

Sunlight Gardener, ranting about communism and humanism, the hellbound dope-pushers who wanted to see that prayer never made it back into the public schools.

Sirens from outside; slamming car doors; someone telling someone else to take it slow, the kid had sounded scared.

"Yes, you're the one, you made all this trouble."

He raised the .45. The muzzle of the .45 looked as big as the mouth of the Oatley tunnel.

The glass wall between the studio and the office blew inward with a loud, coughing roar. A gray-black shaggy shape exploded into the room, its muzzle torn nearly in two by a jag of glass, its feet bleeding. It bellowed an almost human sound, and the thought came to Jack so powerfully that it sent him reeling backward:

*YOU WILL NOT HARM THE HERD!*

*"Wolf!"* he wailed. "Look out! Look out, he got a g—"

Sonny pulled the trigger of the .45 twice. The reports were defeaning in the closed space. The bullets were not aimed at Wolf; they were aimed at Jack. But they tore into Wolf instead, because at that instant he was between the two boys, in midleap. Jack saw huge, ragged, bloody holes open in Wolf's side as the bullets exited. The paths of both slugs were deflected as they pulverized Wolf's ribs, and neither touched Jack, although he felt one whiff past his left cheek.

*"Wolf!"*

Wolf's dextrous, limber leap had turned awkward. His

right shoulder rolled forward and he crashed into the wall, splattering blood and knocking down a framed photograph of Sunlight Gardener in a Shriner's fez.

Laughing, Sonny Singer turned toward Wolf, and shot him again. He held the gun in both hands and his shoulders jerked with the recoil. Gunsmoke hung in a thick, noxious, unmoving rafter. Wolf struggled up on all fours and then rose somehow to his feet. A shattering, wounded bellow of pain and rage overtopped Sunlight Gardener's thundering recorded voice.

Sonny shot Wolf a fourth time. The slug tore a gaping hole in his left arm. Blood and gristle flew.

*JACKY! JACKY! OH JACKY, HURTS, THAT HURTS ME—*

Jacky shambled forward and grabbed Gardener's digital clock; it was simply the first thing that came to hand.

*"Sonny, look out!"* Warwick shouted. "Look—" Then Wolf, his entire midsection now a gory tangle of blood-matted hair, pounced on him. Warwick grappled with Wolf and for a moment they appeared almost to be dancing.

*"—IN A LAKE OF FIRE FOREVER! FOR THE BIBLE SAYS—"*

Jack brought the digital radio down on Sonny's head with all the force he could muster as Sonny began to turn around. Plastic crunched. The numbers on the front of the clock began to blink randomly.

Sonny reeled around, trying to bring the gun up. Jack swung the radio in a flat, rising arc that ended at Sonny's mouth. Sonny's lips flew back in a great funhouse grin. There was a brittle crunch as his teeth broke. His finger jerked the trigger of the gun again. The bullet went between his feet.

He hit the wall, rebounded, and grinned at Jack from his bloody mouth. Swaying on his feet, he raised the gun.

"Hellbound—"

Wolf threw Warwick. Warwick flew through the air with the greatest of ease and struck Sonny in the back as Sonny fired. The bullet went wild, hitting one of the turning tapereels in the sound-studio and pulverizing it. The ranting, screaming voice of Sunlight Gardener ceased. A great bass hum of feedback began to rise from the speakers.

Roaring, staggering, Wolf advanced on Sonny Singer. Sonny pointed the .45 at him and pulled the trigger. There was a dry, impotent click. Sonny's wet grin faltered.

"No," he said mildly, and pulled the trigger again . . . and again . . . and again. As Wolf reached for him, he threw the gun and tried to run around Gardener's big desk. The pistol bounced off Wolf's skull, and with a final, failing burst of strength, Wolf leaped across Sunlight Gardener's desk after Sonny, scattering everything that had been there. Sonny backed away, but Wolf was able to grab his arm.

*"No!"* Sonny screamed. *"No, you better not, you'll go back in the Box, I'm a big man around here, I . . . I . . . IYYYYYYYYYYYYY—!"*

Wolf twisted Sonny's arm. There was a ripping sound, the sound of a turkey drumstick being torn from the cooked bird by an overenthusiastic child. Suddenly Sonny's arm was in Wolf's big front paw. Sonny staggered away, blood jetting from his shoulder. Jack saw a wet white knob of bone. He turned away and was violently sick.

For a moment the whole world swam into grayness.

### 19

When he looked around again, Wolf was swaying in the middle of the carnage that had been Gardener's office. His eyes guttered pale yellow, like dying candles. Something was happening to his face, to his arms and legs—he was becoming Wolf again, Jack saw . . . and then understood fully what that meant. The old legends had lied about how only silver bullets could destroy a werewolf, but apparently about some things they did not lie. Wolf was changing back because he was dying.

*"Wolf, no!"* he wailed, and managed to get to his feet. He got halfway to Wolf, slipped in a puddle of blood, went to one knee, got up again. *"No!"*

"Jacky—" The voice was low, guttural, little more than a growl . . . but understandable.

And, incredibly, Wolf was trying to smile.

Warwick had gotten Gardener's door open. He was backing slowly up the steps, his eyes wide and shocked.

*"Go on!"* Jack screamed. *"Go on, get outta here!"*

Andy Warwick fled like a scared rabbit.

A voice from the intercom—Franky Williams's voice—cut through the droning buzz of feedback. It was horrified, but filled with a terrible, sickly excitement. "Christ, lookit this! Looks like somebody went bullshit with a meat-cleaver! Some of you guys check the kitchen!"

"Jacky—"

Wolf collapsed like a falling tree.

Jack knelt, turned him over. The hair was melting away from Wolf's cheeks with the eerie speed of time-lapse photography. His eyes had gone hazel again. And to Jack he looked horribly tired.

"Jacky—" Wolf raised a bloody hand and touched Jack's cheek. "Shoot . . . you? Did he . . ."

"No," Jack said, cradling his friend's head. "No, Wolf, never got me. Never did."

"I . . ." Wolf's eyes closed and then opened slowly again. He smiled with incredible sweetness and spoke carefully, enunciating each word, obviously needing to convey this if nothing else. "I . . . kept . . . my herd . . . safe."

"Yes, you did," Jack said, and his tears began to flow. They hurt. He cradled Wolf's shaggy, tired head and wept. "You sure did, good old Wolf—"

"Good . . . good old Jacky."

"Wolf, I'm gonna go upstairs . . . there are cops . . . an ambulance . . ."

"No!" Wolf once again seemed to rouse himself to a great effort. "Go on . . . you go on . . ."

*"Not without you, Wolf!"* All the lights had blurred double, treble. He held Wolf's head in his burned hands. "Not without you, huh-uh, no way—"

"Wolf . . . doesn't want to live in this world." He pulled a great, shuddering breath into his broad, shattered chest and tried another smile. "Smells . . . smells too bad."

"Wolf . . . listen, Wolf—"

Wolf took his hands gently; as he held them, Jack could feel the hair melting from Wolf's palms. It was a ghostly, terrible sensation.

"I love you, Jacky."

"I love you, too, Wolf," Jack said. "Right here and now."

Wolf smiled.

"Going back, Jacky . . . I can feel it. Going back . . ."

Suddenly Wolf's very hands felt insubstantial in Jack's grip.

*"Wolf!"* he screamed.

"Going back home . . ."

*"Wolf, no!"* He felt his heart stagger and wrench in his chest. It would break, oh yes, hearts could break, he felt that. *"Wolf, come back, I love you!"* There was a sensation of lightness in Wolf now, a feeling that he was turning into something like a milkweed pod . . . or a shimmer of illusion. A Daydream.

". . . goodbye . . ."

Wolf was fading glass. Fading . . . fading . . .

*"Wolf!"*

" . . .love you J . . ."

Wolf was gone. There was only a bloody outline on the floor where he had been.

"Oh God," Jack moaned. "Oh God, oh God."

He hugged himself and began to rock back and forth in the demolished office, moaning.

# 27

# Jack Lights Out Again

## 1

Time passed. Jack had no idea how much or how little. He sat with his arms wrapped around himself as if he were in the strait-jacket again, rocking back and forth, moaning, wondering if Wolf could really be gone.

*He's gone. Oh yes, he's gone. And guess who killed him, Jack? Guess who?*

At some point the feedback hum took on a rasping note. A moment later there was a high-gain crackle of static and everything shorted out—feedback hum, upstairs chatter, idling engines out front. Jack barely noticed.

*Go on. Wolf said to go on.*

*I can't. I can't. I'm tired, and whatever I do is the wrong thing. People get killed—*

*Quit it, you self-pitying jerk! Think about your mother, Jack.*

*No! I'm tired. Let me be.*

*And the Queen.*

*Please, just leave me alone—*

At last he heard the door at the top of the stairs open, and that roused him. He did not want to be found here. Let them take him outside, in the back yard, but not in this stinking, blood-spattered, smokey room where he had been tortured and his friend killed.

Barely thinking about what he was doing, Jack took up the envelope with JACK PARKER written across the front. He looked inside and saw the guitar-pick, the silver dollar, his beat-up wallet, the Rand McNally road atlas. He tilted the envelope and saw the marble. He stuck everything in the pack and slipped it on, feeling like a boy in a state of hypnosis.

Footfalls on the stairs, slow and cautious.

"—where's the damn lights—"

"—funny smell, like a zoo—"

"—watch it, boys—"

Jack's eyes happened on the steel file-tray, neatly stacked with envelopes reading I'LL BE A SUNBEAM FOR JESUS. He helped himself to two of them.

*Now when they grab you coming out, they can get you for robbery as well as murder.*

Didn't matter. He was moving now for the simple sake of movement, no more than that.

The back yard appeared completely deserted. Jack stood at the top of the stairs that exited through a bulkhead and looked around, hardly able to believe it. There were voices from the front, and pulses of light, and occasional smears of static and dispatchers' voices from police radios that had been cranked up all the way to high gain, but the back yard was empty. It made no sense. But he supposed if they were confused enough, rattled enough by what they had found inside . . .

Then a voice, muffled, less than twenty feet away on Jack's left, said, "Christ! Do you believe this?"

Jack's head snapped around. There, squatting on the beaten

dirt like a crude Iron Age coffin, was the Box. A flashlight was moving around inside. Jack could see shoe-soles sticking out. A dim figure was crouching by the mouth of the Box, examining the door.

"Looks like this thing was ripped right off'n its hinges," the fellow looking at the door called into the Box. "I don't know how anyone coulda done it, though. Hinges are steel. But they're just . . . *twisted.*"

"Never mind the damn hinges," the muffled voice came back. "This goddam thing . . . they kept *kids* in here, Paulie! I really think they did! *Kids!* There's initials on the walls . . ."

The light moved.

". . . and Bible verses . . ."

The light moved again.

". . . and pictures. Little pictures. Little stick-men and -women, like kids draw . . . Christ, do you think Williams knew about this?"

"Must have," Paulie said, still examining the torn and twisted steel hinges on the Box's door.

Paulie was bending in; his colleague was backing out. Making no special attempt at concealment, Jack walked across the open yard behind them. He went along the side of the garage and came out on the shoulder of the road. From here he had an angle on the careless jam of police cars in the Sunlight Home's front yard. As Jack stood watching, an ambulance came tearing up the road, flashers whirling, siren warbling.

"Loved you, Wolf," Jack muttered, and wiped an arm across his wet eyes. He set off down the road into darkness, thinking he would most likely be picked up before he got a mile west of the Sunlight Home. But three hours later he was still walking; apparently the cops had more than enough to occupy them back there.

## 2

There was a highway up ahead, over the next rise or the rise after that. Jack could see the orangey glow of high-intensity sodium arcs on the horizon, could hear the whine of the big rigs.

He stopped in a trash-littered ravine and washed his face and hands in the trickle of water coming out of a culvert. The water was almost paralyzing cold, but at least it silenced the throbbing in his hands for a while. The old cautions were coming back almost unbidden.

Jack stood for a moment where he was, under the dark night sky of Indiana, listening to the whine of the big trucks.

The wind, murmuring in the trees, lifted his hair. His heart was heavy with the loss of Wolf, but even that could not change how good, how very good it was to be free.

An hour later a trucker slowed for the tired, pallid boy standing in the breakdown lane with his thumb cocked. Jack climbed in.

"Where you headed, kiddo?" the trucker asked.

Jack was too tired and too sick at heart to bother with the Story—he barely remembered it, anyway. He supposed it would come back to him.

"West," he said. "Far as you're going."

"That'd be Midstate."

"Fine," Jack said, and fell asleep.

The big Diamond Reo rolled through the chilly Indiana night; Charlie Daniels on the tape-player, it rolled west, chasing its own headlights toward Illinois.

# 28

# Jack's Dream

## 1

Of course he carried Wolf with him. Wolf had gone home, but a big loyal shadow rode beside Jack in all the trucks and Volkswagen vans and dusty cars pounding along the Illinois highways. This smiling ghost pierced Jack's heart. Sometimes he could see—could almost see—Wolf's huge hairy form bounding alongside, romping through the stripped fields. Free, Wolf beamed at him with pumpkin-colored eyes. When he jerked his eyes away, Jack felt the absence of a Wolf-hand folding itself around his. Now that he missed his friend so completely, the memory of his impatience with Wolf shamed him, brought the blood to his face. He had thought about abandoning Wolf more times than he could count. Shameful, shameful. Wolf had been . . . it took Jack a long time to take it in, but the word was *noble*. And this noble being, so out of place in this world, had died for him.

*I kept my herd safe.* Jack Sawyer was the herd no longer. *I kept my herd safe.* There were times when the truckdrivers or insurance salesmen who had picked up this strange, compelling boy on the side of the road—picked him up even though the boy was road-dirty and shaggy, even though they might never have taken on a hitchhiker before in their lives—looked over and saw him blinking back tears.

Jack mourned Wolf as he sped across Illinois. He had somehow known that he would have no trouble getting rides once in that state, and it was true that often all he had to do was stick out his thumb and look an oncoming driver in the eye—instant ride. Most of the drivers did not even demand the Story. All he had to do was give some minimal explanation for travelling alone. "I'm going to see a friend in Springfield." "I have to pick up a car and drive it back home." "Great, great," the drivers said—had they even heard? Jack could not tell. His mind riffled through a mile-high stack of images of Wolf splashing into a stream to rescue his Territories creatures, Wolf nosing into a fragrant box that had held a hamburger, Wolf pushing food into his shed, bursting into the recording studio, taking the bullets, melting away. . . . Jack did not want to see these things again and again, but he had to and they made his eyes burn with tears.

Not far out of Danville, a short, fiftyish man with iron-gray hair and the amused but stern expression of one who has taught fifth grade for two decades kept darting sly looks at him from behind the wheel, then finally said, "Aren't you cold, buster? You ought to have more than that little jacket."

"Maybe a little," Jack said. Sunlight Gardener had thought the denim jackets warm enough for field-work right through the winter, but now the weather licked and stabbed right through its pores.

"I have a coat on the back seat," the man said. "Take it. No, don't even try to talk your way out of it. That coat's yours now. Believe me, I won't freeze."

"But—"

"You have no choice at all in the matter. That is now your coat. Try it on."

Jack reached over the back of the seat and dragged a heavy length of material onto his lap. At first it was shapeless, anonymous. A big patch pocket surfaced, then a toggle button. It was a loden coat, fragrant with pipe tobacco.

"My old one," the man said. "I just keep it in the car because I don't know what to do with it—last year, the kids gave me this goosedown thing. So you have it."

Jack struggled into the big coat, putting it on right over the denim jacket. "Oh boy," he said. It was like being embraced by a bear with a taste for Borkum Riff.

"Good," the man said. "Now if you ever find yourself standing out on a cold and windy road again, you can thank Myles P. Kiger of Ogden, Illinois, for saving your skin. Your—" Myles P. Kiger looked as though he were going to say more: the word hung in the air for a second, the man was still smiling; then the smile warped into goofy embarrassment and Kiger snapped his head forward. In the gray morning light, Jack saw a mottled red pattern spread out across the man's cheeks.

*Your (something) skin?*

Oh, no.

Your beautiful skin. Your touchable, kissable, adorable . . . Jack pushed his hands deep into the loden coat's pockets and pulled the coat tightly around him. Myles P. Kiger of Ogden, Illinois, stared straight ahead.

"Ahem," Kiger said, exactly like a man in a comic book.

"Thanks for the coat," Jack said. "Really. I'll be grateful to you whenever I wear it."

"Sure, okay," Kiger said, "forget it." But for a second his face was oddly like poor Donny Keegan's, back in the Sunlight Home. "There's a place up ahead," Kiger said. His voice was choppy, abrupt, full of phony calm. "We can get some lunch, if you like."

"I don't have any money left," Jack said, a statement exactly two dollars and thirty-eight cents shy of the truth.

"Don't worry about it." Kiger had already snapped on his turn indicator.

They drove into a windswept, nearly empty parking lot before a low gray structure that looked like a railway car. A neon sign above the central door flashed EMPIRE DINER. Kiger pulled up before one of the diner's long windows and they left the car. This coat would keep him warm, Jack realized. His chest and arms seemed protected by woolen armor. Jack began to move toward the door under the flashing sign, but turned around when he realized that Kiger was still standing beside the car. The gray-haired man, only an inch or two taller than Jack, was looking at him over the car's top.

"Say," Kiger said.

"Look, I'd be happy to give you your coat back," Jack said.

"No, that's yours now. I was just thinking I'm not really hungry after all, and if I keep on going I can make pretty good time, get home a little earlier."

"Sure," Jack said.

"You'll get another ride here. Easy. I promise. I wouldn't drop you here if you were going to be stranded."

"Fine."

"Hold on. I said I'd get you lunch, and I will." He put his hand in his trouser pocket, then held a bill out across the top of the car to Jack. The chill wind ruffled his hair and flattened it against his forehead. "Take it."

"No, honest," Jack said. "It's okay. I have a couple dollars."

"Get yourself a good steak," Kiger said, and was leaning across the top of the car holding out the bill as if offering a life preserver, or reaching for one.

Jack reluctantly came forward and took the bill from Kiger's extended fingers. It was a ten. "Thanks a lot. I mean it."

"Here, why don't you take the paper, too, have something to read? You know, if you have to wait a little or something." Kiger had already opened his door, and leaned inside to pluck a folded tabloid newspaper off the back seat. "I've already read it." He tossed it over to Jack.

The pockets of the loden coat were so roomy that Jack could slip the folded paper into one of them.

Myles P. Kiger stood for a moment beside his open car door, squinting at Jack. "If you don't mind my saying so, you're going to have an interesting life," he said.

"It's pretty interesting already," Jack said truthfully.

Salisbury steak was five dollars and forty cents, and it came with french fries. Jack sat at the end of the counter and opened the newspaper. The story was on the second page—the day before, he had seen it on the first page of an Indiana newspaper. ARRESTS MADE, RELATED TO SHOCK HORROR DEATHS. Local Magistrate Ernest Fairchild and Police Officer Frank B. Williams of Cayuga, Indiana, had been charged with misuse of public monies and acceptance of bribes in the course of the investigation of the deaths of six boys at the Sunlight Gardener Scripture Home for Wayward Boys. The popular evangelist Robert "Sunlight" Gardener had apparently escaped from the grounds of the Home shortly before the arrival of the police, and while no warrants had as yet been issued for his arrest he was urgently being sought for questioning. WAS HE ANOTHER JIM JONES? asked a caption beneath a picture of Gardener at his most gorgeous, arms outspread, hair falling in perfect waves. Dogs had led the State Police to an area near the electrified fences where boy's bodies had been buried without ceremony—five bodies, it appeared, most of them so decomposed that identification was not possible. They would probably be able to identify Ferd Janklow. His parents would be able to give him a real burial, all the while wondering what they had done wrong, exactly; all the while wondering just *how* their love for Jesus had condemned their brilliant, rebellious son.

When the Salisbury steak came, it tasted both salty and woolly, but Jack ate every scrap. And soaked up all the thick gravy with the Empire Diner's underdone fries. He had just about finished his meal when a bearded trucker with a Detroit Tigers cap shoved down over long black hair, a parka that seemed to be made from wolfskins, and a thick cigar in his mouth paused beside him and asked, "You need a ride west, kid? I'm going to Decatur." Halfway to Springfield, just like that.

## 2

That night, in a three-dollar-a-night hotel the trucker had told him about, Jack had two distinct dreams: or he later remembered these two out of many that deluged his bed, or the two were actually one long joined dream. He had locked his door, peed into the stained and cracked sink in the corner, put his knapsack under his pillow, and fallen asleep holding the big marble that in the other world was a Territories mirror. There had been a suggestion of music, an almost cinematic touch—fiery alert bebop, at a volume so low Jack could just pick out that the lead instruments were a trumpet and an alto saxophone. *Richard,* Jack drowsily thought, *tomorrow I should be seeing Richard Sloat,* and fell down the slope of the rhythm into brimming unconsciousness.

Wolf was trotting toward him across a blasted, smoking landscape. Strings of barbed wire, now and then coiling up into fantastic and careless barbed-wire intricacies, separated them. Deep trenches, too, divided the spoiled land, one of which Wolf vaulted easily before nearly tumbling into one of the ranks of wire.

—Watch out, Jack called.

Wolf caught himself before falling into the triple strands of wire. He waved one big paw to show Jack that he was unhurt, and then cautiously stepped over the wires.

Jack felt an amazing surge of happiness and relief pass through him. Wolf had not died; Wolf would join him again.

Wolf made it over the barbed wire and began trotting forward again. The land between Jack and Wolf seemed mysteriously to double in length—gray smoke hanging over the many trenches almost obscured the big shaggy figure coming forward.

—Jason! Wolf shouted. Jason! Jason!

—I'm still here, Jack shouted back.

—Can't make it, Jason! Wolf can't make it!

—Keep trying, Jack bawled. Damn it, don't give up!

Wolf paused before an impenetrable tangle of wire, and through the smoke Jack saw him slip down to all fours and trot back and forth, nosing for an open place. From side to side Wolf trotted, each time going out a greater distance, with every second becoming more evidently disturbed. Finally Wolf stood up again and placed his hands on the thick tangle of wire and forced a space he could shout through. —Wolf can't! Jason, Wolf can't!

—I love you, Wolf, Jack shouted across the smouldering plain.

—JASON! Wolf bawled back. BE CAREFUL! They are COMING for you! There are MORE of them!

—More what, Jack wanted to shout, but could not. He knew.

Then either the whole character of the dream changed or another dream began. He was back in the ruined recording studio and office at the Sunlight Home, and the smells of gunpowder and burned flesh crowded the air. Singer's mutilated body lay slumped on the floor, and Casey's dead form drooped through the shattered glass panel. Jack sat on the floor cradling Wolf in his arms, and knew again that Wolf was dying. Only Wolf was not Wolf.

Jack was holding Richard Sloat's trembling body, and it was Richard who was dying. Behind the lenses of his sensible black plastic eyeglasses, Richard's eyes skittered aimlessly, painfully. —Oh no, oh no, Jack breathed out in horror. Richard's arm had been shattered, and his chest was a pulp of ruined flesh and bloodstained white shirt. Fractured bones glinted whitely here and there like teeth.

—I don't want to die, Richard said, every word a superhuman effort. Jason, you should not . . . you should not have . . .

—You can't die, too, Jack pleaded, not you, too.

Richard's upper body lurched against Jack's arms, and a long, liquid sound escaped Richard's throat, and then Richard found Jack's eyes with his own suddenly clear and quiet eyes. —Jason. The sound of the name, which was almost appropriate, hung softly in the stinking air. —You killed me, Richard breathed out, or *you killed 'e,* since his lips could not meet to form one of the letters. Richard's eyes swam out of focus again, and his body seemed to grow instantly heavier in Jack's arms. There was no longer life in that body. Jason De-Loessian stared up in shock—

### 3

—and Jack Sawyer snapped upright in the cold, unfamiliar bed of a flophouse in Decatur, Illinois, and in the yellowish murk shed by a streetlamp outside saw his breath plume out as luxuriantly as if exhaled from two mouths at once. He kept himself from screaming only by clasping his hands, his own two hands, and squeezing them together hard enough to crack a walnut. Another enormous white feather of air steamed out of his lungs.

Richard.

Wolf running across that dead world, calling out . . . what? *Jason*.

The boy's heart executed a quick, decided leap, with the kick of a horse clearing a fence.

# 29

# Richard at Thayer

## 1

At eleven o'clock the next morning an exhausted Jack Sawyer unshouldered his pack at the end of a long playing field covered with crisp brown dead grass. Far away, two men in plaid jackets and baseball caps labored with leaf-blower and rake down on the stretch of lawn surrounding the most distant group of buildings. To Jack's left, directly behind the red-brick backside of the Thayer library, was the faculty parking lot. In the front of Thayer School a great gate opened onto a tree-lined drive which circled around a large quad criss-crossed with narrow paths. If anything stood out on the campus, it was the library—a Bauhaus steamship of glass and steel and brick.

Jack had already seen that a secondary gate opened onto another access road before the library. This ran two-thirds the length of the school and ended at the garbage Dumpsters nested in the round cul-de-sac just before the land climbed up to form the plateau of the football field.

Jack began to move across the top of the field toward the rear of the classroom buildings. When the Thayerites began to go to dining hall, he could find Richard's room—Entry 5, Nelson House.

The dry winter grass crunched beneath his feet. Jack pulled Myles P. Kiger's excellent coat tightly about him—the coat at least looked preppy, if Jack did not. He walked between Thayer Hall and an Upper School dormitory named

Spence House, in the direction of the quad. Lazy preluncheon voices came through the Spence House windows.

## 2

Jack glanced toward the quad and saw an elderly man, slightly stooped and of a greenish-bronze, standing on a plinth the height of a carpenter's bench and examining the cover of a heavy book. Elder Thayer, Jack surmised. He was dressed in the stiff collar, flowing tie, and frock coat of a New England Transcendentalist. Elder Thayer's brass head inclined over the volume, pointed generally in the direction of the classroom buildings.

Jack took the right-angle at the end of the path. Sudden noise erupted from an upstairs window ahead—boys shouting out the syllables of a name that sounded like "Etheridge! Etheridge!" Then an irruption of wordless screams and shouts, accompanied by the sounds of heavy furniture moving across a wooden floor. *"Etheridge!"*

Jack heard a door closing behind his back, and looked over his shoulder to see a tall boy with dirty-blond hair rushing down the steps of Spence House. He wore a tweed sport jacket and a tie and a pair of L. L. Bean Maine hunting shoes. Only a long yellow-and-blue scarf wound several times around his neck protected him from the cold. His long face looked both haggard and arrogant, and just now was the face of a senior in a self-righteous rage. Jack pushed the hood of the loden coat over his head and moved down the path.

"I don't want anybody to move!" the tall boy shouted up at the closed window. "You freshmen just stay put!"

Jack drifted toward the next building.

"You're moving the chairs!" the tall boy screamed behind him. "I can hear you doing it! STOP!" Then Jack heard the furious senior call out to him.

Jack turned around, his heart beating loudly.

"Get over to Nelson House right now, whoever you are, on the double, post-haste, immediately. Or I'll go to your house master."

"Yes sir," Jack said, and quickly turned away to move in the direction the prefect had pointed.

*"You're at least seven minutes late!"* Etheridge screeched

at him, and Jack was startled into jogging. *"On the double, I said!"* Jack turned the jog into a run.

When he started downhill (he hoped it was the right way; it was, anyway, the direction in which Etheridge had seemed to be looking), he saw a long black car—a limousine—just beginning to swing through the main front gates and whisper up the long drive to the quad. He thought that maybe whatever sat behind the tinted windows of the limousine was nothing so ordinary as the parent of a Thayer School sophomore.

The long black car eased forward, insolently slow.

No, Jack thought, I'm spooking myself.

Still he could not move. Jack watched the limousine pull up to the bottom of the quad and stop, its motor running. A black chauffeur with the shoulders of a running back got out of the front seat and opened the rear passenger door. An old white-haired man, a stranger, effortlully got out of the limousine's back seat. He wore a black topcoat which revealed an immaculate white shirtfront and a solid dark tie. The man nodded to his chauffeur and began to toil across the quad in the direction of the main building. He never even looked in Jack's direction. The chauffeur elaborately craned his neck and looked upward, as if speculating about the possibility of snow. Jack stepped backward and watched while the old man made it to the steps of Thayer Hall. The chauffeur continued his specious examination of the sky. Jack melted backward down the path until the side of the building shielded him, and then he turned around and began to trot.

Nelson House was a three-story brick building on the other side of the quadrangle. Two windows on the ground floor showed him a dozen seniors exercising their privileges: reading while sprawled on couches, playing a desultory game of cards on a coffee table; others stared lazily at what must have been a television set parked beneath the windows.

An unseen door slammed shut a little farther up the hill, and Jack caught a glimpse of the tall blond senior, Etheridge, stalking back to his own building after dealing with the freshmen's crimes.

Jack cut across the front of the building and a gust of cold wind smacked up against him as soon as he reached its side. And around the corner was a narrow door and a plaque (wooden this time, white with Gothic black lettering) saying ENTRY 5. A series of windows stretched down to the next corner.

And here, at the third window—relief. For here was Richard Sloat, his eyeglasses firmly hooked around his ears, his necktie knotted, his hands only slightly stained with ink, sitting erect at his desk and reading some fat book as if for dear life. He was positioned sideways to Jack, who had time to take in Richard's dear, well-known profile before he rapped on the glass.

Richard's head jerked up from the book. He stared wildly about him, frightened and surprised by the sudden noise.

"Richard," Jack said softly, and was rewarded by the sight of his friend's astonished face turning toward him. Richard looked almost moronic with surprise.

"Open the window," Jack said, mouthing the words with exaggerated care so that his friend could read his lips.

Richard stood up from his desk, still moving with the slowness of shock. Jack mimed pushing the window up. When Richard reached the window he put his hands on the frame and looked down severely at Jack for a moment—in that short and critical glance was a judgment about Jack's dirty face and unwashed, lank hair, his unorthodox arrival, much else. *What on earth are you up to now?* Finally he pushed up the window.

"Well," Richard said. "Most people use the door."

"Great," Jack said, almost laughing. "When I'm like most people, I probably will, too. Stand back, okay?"

Looking very much as though he had been caught off-guard, Richard stepped a few paces back.

Jack hoisted himself up onto the sill and slid through the window head-first. "Oof."

"Okay, hi," Richard said. "I suppose it's even sort of nice to see you. But I have to go to lunch pretty soon. You could take a shower, I guess. Everybody else'll be down in the dining room." He stopped talking, as if startled that he had said so much.

Richard, Jack saw, would require delicate handling. "Could you bring some food back for me? I'm really starving."

"Great," Richard said. "First you get everybody crazy, including my dad, by running away, then you break in here like a burglar, and now you want me to steal food for you. Fine, sure. Okay. Great."

"We have a lot to talk about," Jack said.

"*If,*" Richard said, leaning slightly forward with his hands in his pockets, "*if* you'll start going back to New Hampshire today, or *if* you'll let me call my dad and get him here to take you back, I'll try to grab some extra food for you."

"I'm willing to talk about anything with you, Richie-boy. Anything. I'll talk about going back, sure."

Richard nodded. "Where in the world have you been, anyhow?" His eyes burned beneath their thick lenses. Then a big, surprising blink. "And *how* in the world can you justify the way you and your mother are treating my father? Shit, Jack. I really think you ought to go back to that place in New Hampshire."

"I will go back," Jack said. "That's a promise. But I have to get something first. Is there anyplace I can sit down? I'm sort of dead tired."

Richard nodded at his bed, then—typically—flapped one hand at his desk chair, which was nearer Jack.

Doors slammed in the hallway. Loud voices passed by Richard's door, a crowd's shuffling feet.

"You ever read about the Sunlight Home?" Jack asked. "I was there. Two of my friends died at the Sunlight Home, and get this, Richard, the second one was a werewolf."

Richard's face tightened. "Well, that's an amazing coincidence, because—"

"I really was at the Sunlight Home, Richard."

"So I gather," said Richard. "Okay. I'll be back with some food in about half an hour. Then I'll have to tell you who lives next door. But this is Seabrook Island stuff, isn't it? Tell me the truth."

"Yeah, I guess it is." Jack let Myles P. Kiger's coat slip off his shoulders and fold itself over the back of the chair.

"I'll be back," Richard said. He waved uncertainly to Jack on his way out the door.

Jack kicked off his shoes and closed his eyes.

### 3

The conversation to which Richard had alluded as "Seabrook Island stuff," and which Jack remembered as well as his friend, took place in the last week of their final visit to the resort of that name.

The two families had taken joint vacations nearly every year while Phil Sawyer was alive. The summer after his death, Morgan Sloat and Lily Sawyer had tried to keep the tradition going, and booked the four of them into the vast old hotel on Seabrook Island, South Carolina, which had been the site of some of their happiest summers. The experiment had not worked.

The boys were accustomed to being in each other's company. They were also accustomed to places like Seabrook Island. Richard Sloat and Jack Sawyer had scampered through resort hotels and down vast tanned beaches all through their childhood—but now the climate had mysteriously altered. An unexpected seriousness had entered their lives, an awkwardness.

The death of Phil Sawyer had changed the very color of the future. Jack began to feel that final summer at Seabrook that he might not want to sit in the chair behind his father's desk—that he wanted more in his life. More what? He knew—this was one of the few things he did truly know—that this powerful "moreness" was connected to the Daydreams. When he had begun to see this in himself, he became aware of something else: that his friend Richard was not only incapable of sensing this quality of "moreness," but that in fact he quite clearly wanted its opposite. Richard wanted less. Richard did not want anything he could not respect.

Jack and Richard had sloped off by themselves in that slow-breathing time composed at good resorts by the hours between lunch and cocktails. In fact they had not gone far—only up at the side of a pine-tree-covered hill overlooking the rear of the inn. Beneath them sparkled the water of the inn's huge rectangular pool, through which Lily Cavanaugh Sawyer smoothly and efficiently swam length after length. At one of the tables set back from the pool sat Richard's father, wrapped in a bulging, fuzzy terrycloth robe, flip-flops on his white feet, simultaneously eating a club sandwich and wheeling and dealing on the plug-in telephone in his other hand.

"Is this sort of stuff what you want?" he asked Richard, who was seated neatly beside his own sprawl and held—no surprise—a book. *The Life of Thomas Edison.*

"What I want? When I grow up, you mean?" Richard

seemed a little nonplussed by the question: "It's pretty nice, I guess. I don't know if I want it or not."

"Do you know what you want, Richard? You always say you want to be a research chemist," Jack said. "Why do you say that? What does it mean?"

"It means that I want to be a research chemist." Richard smiled.

"You know what I mean, don't you? What's the *point* of being a research chemist? Do you think that would be fun? Do you think you'll cure cancer and save millions of people's lives?"

Richard looked at him very openly, his eyes slightly magnified by the glasses he had begun to wear four months earlier. "I don't think I'll ever cure cancer, no. But that's not even the point. The point is finding out how things work. The point is that things actually really do work in an orderly way, in spite of how it looks, and you can find out about it."

"Order."

"Yeah, so why are you smiling?"

Jack grinned. "You're going to think I'm crazy. I'd like to find something that makes all this—all these rich guys chasing golfballs and yelling into telephones—that makes all this look sick."

"It already looks sick," Richard said, with no intention of being funny.

"Don't you sometimes think there's more to life than order?" He looked over at Richard's innocent, skeptical face. "Don't you want just a little magic, Richard?"

"You know, sometimes I think you just want chaos," Richard said, flushing a bit. "I think you're making fun of me. If you want magic, you completely wreck everything I believe in. In fact you wreck reality."

"Maybe there isn't just one reality."

"In *Alice in Wonderland*, sure!" Richard was losing his temper.

He stomped off through the pines, and Jack realized for the first time that the talk released by his feelings about the Daydreams had infuriated his friend. Jack's longer legs brought him alongside Richard in seconds. "I wasn't making fun of you," he said. "It's just, I was sort of curious about why you always say you want to be a chemist."

Richard stopped short and looked soberly up at Jack.

"Just stop driving me crazy with that kind of stuff," Richard said. "That's just Seabrook Island talk. It's hard enough being one of the six or seven sane people in America without having my best friend flip out totally."

From then on, Richard Sloat bristled at any signs of fancifulness in Jack, and immediately dismissed it as "Seabrook Island stuff."

### 4

By the time Richard returned from the dining room, Jack, freshly showered and with his wet hair adhering to his scalp, was idly turning over books at Richard's desk. Jack was wondering, as Richard swung through the door carrying a grease-stained paper napkin clearly wrapped around a substantial quantity of food, whether the conversation to come might be easier if the books on the desk were *The Lord of the Rings* and *Watership Down* instead of *Organic Chemistry* and *Mathematical Puzzles*.

"What was lunch?" Jack asked.

"You got lucky. Southern fried chicken—one of the few things they serve here that don't make you sorry for the animal who died to become part of the food chain." He handed the greasy napkin over to Jack. Four thick, richly battered sections of chicken sent up an aroma of almost unbelievable goodness and density. Jack waded in.

"How long have you been eating as though you oinked?" Richard pushed his glasses up on his nose and sat down on his narrow bed. Beneath his tweed jacket he wore a patterned brown V-neck sweater, the bottom of which had been tucked into the waistband of his trousers.

Jack had an uneasy moment, wondering if it were really possible to talk about the Territories with someone so tightly buttoned that he tucked his sweaters beneath his belts.

"The last time I ate," he said mildly, "was yesterday, around noon. I'm a little hungry, Richard. Thanks for bringing me the chicken. It's great. It's the best chicken I ever ate. You're a great guy, risking expulsion like this."

"You think that's a joke, do you?" Richard yanked at the sweater, frowning. "If anybody finds you in here, I probably *will* get expelled. So don't get too funny. We have to figure out how we're going to get you back to New Hampshire."

Silence then, for a moment: an appraising look from Jack, a stern look from Richard.

"I know you want me to explain what I'm doing, Richard," Jack said around a mouthful of chicken, "and believe me, it's not going to be easy."

"You don't look the same, you know," Richard said. "You look . . . older. But that's not all. You're changed."

"I know I've changed. You'd be a little different, too, if you'd been with me since September." Jack smiled, looked at scowling Richard in his good-boy clothes, and knew that he would never be able to tell Richard about his father. He simply was not capable of that. If events did it for him, so be it; but he himself did not possess the assassin's heart required for that particular disclosure.

His friend continued to frown at Jack, clearly waiting for the story to begin.

Perhaps to stall the moment when he would have to try to convince Rational Richard of the unbelievable, Jack asked, "Is the kid in the next room quitting school? I saw his suitcases on his bed from outside."

"Well, yes, that's interesting," Richard said. "I mean, interesting in the light of what you said. He *is* leaving—in fact, he's already gone. Someone is supposed to come for his things, I guess. God knows what kind of a fairy tale you'll make of this, but the kid next door was Reuel Gardener. The son of that preacher who ran that home you claim you escaped from." Richard ignored Jack's sudden fit of coughing. "In most senses, I should say, Reuel was anything but the normal kid next door, and probably nobody here was too sorry to see him go. Just when the story came out about kids dying at that place his father ran, he got a telegram ordering him to leave Thayer."

Jack had gotten down the wad of chicken that had tried to choke him. "Sunlight Gardener's son? That guy had a son? And he was *here?*"

"He came at the start of the term," Richard said simply. "That's what I was trying to tell you before."

Suddenly Thayer School was menacing to Jack in a way

that Richard could not begin to comprehend. "What was he *like?*"

"A sadist," Richard said. "Sometimes I heard really peculiar noises coming out of Reuel's room. And once I saw a dead cat on the garbage thing out in back that didn't have any eyes or ears. When you saw him, you'd think he was the kind of person who might torture a cat. And he sort of smelled like rancid English Leather, I thought." Richard was silent for a carefully timed moment, and then asked, "Were you really in the Sunlight Home?"

"For thirty days. It was hell, or hell's next-door neighbor." He inhaled, looking at Richard's scowling but now at least half-convinced face. "This is hard for you to swallow, Richard, and I know that, but the guy with me was a werewolf. And if he hadn't been killed while he was saving my life he'd be here right now."

"A werewolf. Hair on the palms of his hands. Changes into a blood-thirsty monster every full moon." Richard looked musingly around the little room.

Jack waited until Richard's gaze returned to him. "Do you want to know what I'm doing? Do you want me to tell you why I'm hitchhiking all the way across the country?"

"I'm going to start screaming if you don't," Richard said.

"Well," Jack said, "I'm trying to save my mother's life." As he uttered it, this sentence seemed to him filled with a wondrous clarity.

"How the hell are you going to do that?" Richard exploded. "Your mother probably has cancer. As my father has been pointing out to you, she needs doctors and science . . . and you hit the road? What are you going to use to save your mother, Jack? Magic?"

Jack's eyes began to burn. "You got it, Richard old chum." He raised his arm and pressed his already damp eyes into the fabric at the crook of his elbow.

"Oh hey, calm down, hey really . . ." Richard said, tugging frantically at his sweater. "Don't cry, Jack, come on, please, I know it's a terrible thing, I didn't mean to . . . it was just that—" Richard had crossed the room instantly and without noise, and was now awkwardly patting Jack's arm and shoulder.

"I'm okay," Jack said. He lowered his arm. "It's not some crazy fantasy, Richard, no matter how it looks to you." He sat up straight. "My father called me Travelling Jack, and so did an old man in Arcadia Beach." Jack hoped he was right about Richard's sympathy opening internal doors; when he looked at Richard's face, he saw that it was true. His friend looked worried, tender, four-square.

Jack began his story.

## 5

Around the two boys the life of Nelson House went on, both calm and boisterous in the manner of boarding schools, punctuated with shouts and roars and laughter. Footsteps padded past the door but did not stop. From the room above came regular thumps and an occasional drift of music Jack finally recognized as a record by Blue Oyster Cult. He began by telling Richard about the Daydreams. From the Daydreams he went to Speedy Parker. He described the voice speaking to him from the whirling funnel in the sand. And then he told Richard of how he had taken Speedy's "magic juice" and first flipped into the Territories.

"But I think it was just cheap wine, wino wine," Jack said. "Later, after it was all gone, I found out that I didn't need it to flip. I could just do it by myself."

"Okay," Richard said noncommittally.

He tried to truly represent the Territories to Richard: the cart-track, the sight of the summer palace, the timelessness and specificity of it. Captain Farren; the dying Queen, which brought him to Twinners; Osmond. The scene at All-Hands' Village; the Outpost Road which was the Western Road. He showed Richard his little collection of sacred objects, the guitar-pick and marble and coin. Richard merely turned these over in his fingers and gave them back without comment. Then Jack relived his wretched time in Oatley. Richard listened to Jack's tales of Oatley silent but wide-eyed.

Jack carefully omitted Morgan Sloat and Morgan of Orris from his account of the scene at the Lewisburg rest area on I-70 in western Ohio.

Then Jack had to describe Wolf as he had first seen him,

that beaming giant in Oshkosh B'Gosh bib overalls, and he felt his tears building again behind his eyes. He did actually startle Richard by weeping while he told about trying to get Wolf into cars, and confessed his impatience with his companion, fighting not to weep again, and was fine for a long time—he managed to get through the story of Wolf's first Change without tears or a constricted throat. Then he struck trouble again. His rage kept him talking freely until he got to Ferd Janklow, and then his eyes grew hot again.

Richard said nothing for a long time. Then he stood up and fetched a clean handkerchief from a bureau drawer. Jack noisily, wetly blew his nose.

"That's what happened," Jack said. "Most of it, anyhow."

"What have you been reading? What movies have you been seeing?"

"Fuck you," Jack said. He stood up and walked across the room to get his pack, but Richard reached out and put his hand around Jack's wrist. "I don't think you made it all up. I don't think you made any of it up."

"Don't you?"

"No. I don't know what I do think, actually, but I'm sure you're not telling me deliberate lies." He dropped his hand. "I believe you were in the Sunlight Home, I believe that, all right. And I believe that you had a friend named Wolf, who died there. I'm sorry, but I cannot take the Territories seriously, and I cannot accept that your friend was a werewolf."

"So you think I'm nuts," Jack said.

"I think you're in trouble. But I'm not going to call my father, and I'm not going to make you leave now. You'll have to sleep in the bed here tonight. If we hear Mr. Haywood coming around to do bed checks, you'll be able to hide under the bed."

Richard had taken on a faintly executive air, and he put his hands on his hips and glanced critically around his room. "You have to get some rest. I'm sure that's part of the problem. They worked you half to death in that horrible place, and your mind got twisted, and now you need to rest."

"I do," Jack admitted.

Richard rolled his eyes upward. "I have to go to intramural basketball pretty soon, but you can hide in here, and I'll bring some more food back from the dining room later on. The important thing is, you need rest and you need to get back home."

Jack said, "New Hampshire isn't home."

# 30

# Thayer Gets Weird

## 1

Through the window Jack could see boys in coats, hunched against the cold, crossing to and fro between the library and the rest of the school. Etheridge, the senior who had spoken to Jack that morning, bustled by, his scarf flying out behind him.

Richard took a tweed sport jacket from the narrow closet beside the bed. "Nothing is going to make me think that you should do anything but go back to New Hampshire. I have to go to basketball now, because if I don't Coach Frazer'll make me do ten punishment laps as soon as he comes back. Some other coach is taking our practice today, and Frazer said he'd run us into the ground if we cut out. Do you want to borrow some clean clothes? I at least have a shirt that'll fit you—my father sent it to me from New York, and Brooks Brothers got the size wrong."

"Let's see it," Jack said. His clothes had become definitely disreputable, so stiff with filth that whenever he noticed it Jack felt like Pigpen, the "Peanuts" character who lived in a mist of dirt and disapproval. Richard gave him a white button-down still in its plastic bag. "Great, thanks," Jack said. He took it out of the bag and began removing the pins. It would almost fit.

"There's a jacket you might try on, too," Richard said. "The blazer hanging at the end of the closet. Try it on, okay? And you might as well use one of my ties, too. Just in case anyone comes in. Say you're from Saint Louis Country Day, and you're on a Newspaper Exchange. We do two or three of those a year—kids from here go there, kids from there come here, to work on the other school's paper." He went toward the door. "I'll come back before dinner and see how you are."

Two ballpoints were clipped to a plastic insert in his jacket pocket, Jack noticed, and all the buttons of the jacket were buttoned.

Nelson House grew perfectly quiet within minutes. From Richard's window Jack saw boys seated at desks in the big library windows. Nobody moved on the paths or over the crisp brown grass. An insistent bell rang, marking the beginning of fourth period. Jack stretched his arms out and yawned. A feeling of security returned to him—a school around him, with all those familiar rituals of bells and classes and basketball practices. Maybe he would be able to stay another day; maybe he would even be able to call his mother from one of the Nelson House phones. He would certainly be able to catch up on his sleep.

Jack went to the closet and found the blazer hanging where Richard had said it would be. A tag still hung from one of the sleeves: Sloat had sent it from New York, but Richard had never worn it. Like the shirt, the blazer was one size too small for Jack and clung too tightly to his shoulders, but the cut was roomy and the sleeves allowed the white shirt cuffs to peek out half an inch.

Jack lifted a necktie from the hook just inside the closet—red, with a pattern of blue anchors. Jack slipped the tie around his neck and laboriously knotted it. Then he examined himself in the mirror and laughed out loud. Jack saw that he had made it at last. He looked at the beautiful new blazer, the club tie, his snowy shirt, his rumpled jeans. He was there. He was a preppy.

## 2

Richard had become, Jack saw, an admirer of John McPhee and Lewis Thomas and Stephen Jay Gould. He picked *The Panda's Thumb* from the row of books on Richard's shelves because he liked the title and returned to the bed.

Richard did not return from his basketball practice for what seemed an impossibly long time. Jack paced back and forth in the little room. He could not imagine what would keep Richard from returning to his room, but his imagination gave him one calamity after another.

After the fifth or sixth time Jack checked his watch, he noticed that he could see no students on the grounds.

Whatever had happened to Richard had happened to the entire school.

The afternoon died. Richard too, he thought, was dead. Perhaps all Thayer School was dead—and he was a plague-bearer, a carrier of death. He had eaten nothing all day since the chicken Richard had brought him from the dining room, but he wasn't hungry. Jack sat in numb misery. He brought destruction wherever he went.

### 3

Then there were footfalls in the corridor once more.

From the floor above, Jack now dimly heard the *thud thud thud* of a bass pattern, and then again recognized it as being from a record by Blue Oyster Cult. The footsteps paused outside the door. Jack hurried to the door.

Richard stood in the doorway. Two boys with cornsilk hair and half-mast ties glanced in and kept moving down the corridor. The rock music was much more audible in the corridor.

"Where were you all afternoon?" Jack demanded.

"Well, it was sort of freaky," Richard said. "They cancelled all the afternoon classes. Mr. Dufrey wouldn't even let kids go back to their lockers. And then we all had to go to basketball practice, and that was even weirder."

"Who's Mr. Dufrey?"

Richard looked at him as if he'd just tumbled out of a bassinette. "Who's Mr. Dufrey? He's the headmaster. Don't you know anything at all about this school?"

"No, but I'm getting a few ideas," Jack said. "What was so weird about practice?"

"Remember I told you that Coach Frazer got some friend of his to handle it today? Well, he said we'd all get punishment laps if we tried to cut out, so I thought his friend would be some Al Maguire type, you know, some real hotshot. Thayer School doesn't have a very good athletic tradition. Anyhow, I thought his replacement must be somebody really special."

"Let me guess. The new guy didn't look like he had anything to do with sports."

Richard lifted his chin, startled. "No," he said. "No, he didn't." He gave Jack a considering look. "He smoked all the time. And his hair was really long and greasy—he didn't look anything like a coach. He looked like somebody most coaches would like to step on, to tell you the truth. Even his eyes looked funny. I bet you he smokes pot." Richard tugged at his sweater. "I don't think he knew anything about basketball. He didn't even make us practice our patterns—that's what we usually do, after the warm-up period. We sort of ran around and threw baskets and he shouted at us. Laughing. Like kids playing basketball was the most ridiculous thing he'd seen in his whole life. You ever see a coach who thought sports was funny? Even the warm-up period was strange. He just said, 'Okay, do push-ups,' and smoked his cigarette. No count, no cadence, everybody just doing them by themselves. After that it was 'Okay, run around a little bit.' He looked . . . really wild. I think I'm going to complain to Coach Frazer tomorrow."

"I wouldn't complain to him or the headmaster either," Jack said.

"Oh, I get it," Richard said. "Mr. *Dufrey's* one of them. One of the Territories people."

"Or he works for them," Jack said.

"Don't you see that you could fit *anything* into that pattern? *Anything* that goes wrong? It's too easy—you could explain everything that way. That's how craziness works. You make connections that aren't real."

"And see things that aren't there."

Richard shrugged, and despite the insouciance of the gesture, his face was miserable. "You said it."

"Wait a minute," Jack said. "You remember me telling you about the building that collapsed in Angola, New York?"

"The Rainbird Towers."

"What a memory. I think that accident was my fault."

"Jack, you're—"

Jack said: "Crazy, I know. Look, would anyone blow the whistle on me if we went out and watched the evening news?"

"I doubt it. Most kids are studying now, anyway. Why?"

*Because I want to know what's been happening around* here,

Jack thought but did not say. *Sweet little fires, nifty little earth-quakes—signs that they're coming through. For me. For us.*

"I need a change of scenery, Richard old chum," Jack said, and followed Richard down the watery green corridor.

# 31

# Thayer Goes to Hell

## 1

Jack became aware of the change first and recognized what had happened; it had happened before, while Richard was out, and he was sensitized to it.

The screaming heavy metal of Blue Oyster Cult's "Tattoo Vampire" was gone. The TV in the common room, which had been cackling out an episode of *Hogan's Heroes* instead of the news, had fallen dormant.

Richard turned toward Jack, opening his mouth to speak.

"I don't like it, Gridley," Jack said first. "The native tom-toms have stopped. It's too quiet."

"Ha-ha," Richard said thinly.

"Richard, can I ask you something?"

"Yes, of course."

"Are you scared?"

Richard's face said that he wanted more than anything to say *No, of course not—it always gets quiet around Nelson House this time of the evening*. Unfortunately, Richard was utterly incapable of telling a lie. Dear old Richard. Jack felt a wave of affection.

"Yes," Richard said. "I'm a little scared."

"Can I ask you something else?"

"I guess so."

"Why are we both whispering?"

Richard looked at him for a long time without saying anything. Then he started down the green corridor again.

The doors of the other rooms on the other corridor were either open or ajar. Jack smelled a very familiar odor wafting through the half-open door of Suite 4, and pushed the door all the way open with tented fingers.

"Which one of them is the pothead?" Jack asked.

"What?" Richard replied uncertainly.

Jack sniffed loudly. "Smell it?"

Richard came back and looked into the room. Both study lamps were on. There was an open history text on one desk, an issue of *Heavy Metal* on the other. Posters decorated the walls: the Costa del Sol, Frodo and Sam trudging across the cracked and smoking plains of Mordor toward Sauron's castle, Eddie Van Halen. Earphones lay on the open issue of *Heavy Metal*, giving out little tinny squeaks of music.

"If you can get expelled for letting a friend sleep under your bed, I doubt if they just slap your wrist for smoking pot, do they?" Jack said.

"They expel you for it, of course." Richard was looking at the joint as if mesmerized, and Jack thought he looked more shocked and bewildered than he had at any other time, even when Jack had shown him the healing burns between his fingers.

"Nelson House is empty," Jack said.

"Don't be ridiculous!" Richard's voice was sharp.

"It is, though." Jack gestured down the hall. "We're the only ones left. And you don't get thirty-some boys out of a dorm without a sound. They didn't just leave; they disappeared."

"Over into the Territories, I suppose."

"I don't know," Jack said. "Maybe they're still here, but on a slightly different level. Maybe they're there. Maybe they're in Cleveland. But they're not where we are."

"Close that door," Richard said abruptly, and when Jack didn't move quickly enough to suit him, Richard closed it himself.

"Do you want to put out the—"

"I don't even want to touch it," Richard said. "I ought to report them, you know. I ought to report them both to Mr. Haywood."

"Would you do that?" Jack asked, fascinated.

Richard looked chagrined. "No . . . probably not," he said. "But I don't like it."

"Not orderly," Jack said.

"Yeah." Richard's eyes flashed at him from behind his spectacles, telling him that was exactly right, he had hit the nail on the head, and if Jack didn't like it, he could lump it. He started down the hall again. "I want to know what's going *on* around here," he said, "and believe me, I'm going to find out."

*That might be a lot more hazardous to your health than marijuana, Richie-boy,* Jack thought, and followed his friend.

## 2

They stood in the lounge, looking out. Richard pointed toward the quad. In the last of the dying light, Jack saw a bunch of boys grouped loosely around the greenish-bronze statue of Elder Thayer.

"They're smoking!" Richard cried angrily. "Right on the quad, they're *smoking!*"

Jack thought immediately of the pot-smell in Richard's hall.

"They're smoking, all right," he said to Richard, "and not the kind of cigarettes you get out of a cigarette machine, either."

Richard rapped his knuckles angrily on the glass. For him, Jack saw, the weirdly deserted dorm was forgotten; the leather-jacketed, chain-smoking substitute coach was forgotten; Jack's apparent mental aberration was forgotten. That look of outraged propriety on Richard's face said *When a bunch of boys stand around like that, smoking joints within touching distance of the statue of the founder of this school, it's as if someone were trying to tell me that the earth is flat, or that prime numbers may sometimes be divisible by two, or something equally ridiculous.*

Jack's heart was full of pity for his friend, but it was also full of admiration for an attitude which must seem so reactionary and even eccentric to his school-mates. He wondered again if Richard could stand the shocks which might be on the way.

"Richard," he said, "those boys aren't from Thayer, are they?"

"God, you really *have* gone crazy, Jack. They're Uppers. I

recognize every last one of them. The guy wearing that stupid leather flying hat is Norrington. The one in the green sweat-pants is Buckley. I see Garson . . . Littlefield . . . the one with the scarf is Etheridge," he finished.

"Are you *sure* it's Etheridge?"

*"Of course it's him!"* Richard shouted. He suddenly turned the catch on the window, rammed it up, and leaned out into the cold air.

Jack pulled Richard back. "Richard, please, just listen—"

Richard didn't want to. He turned and leaned out into the cold twilight.

*"Hey!"*

*No, don't attract their attention, Richard, for Christ's sake—*

*"Hey, you guys! Etheridge! Norrington! Littlefield! What in the hell is going on out there?"*

The talk and rough laughter broke off. The fellow who was wearing Etheridge's scarf turned toward the sound of Richard's voice. He tilted his head slightly to look up at them. The lights from the library and the sullen furnace afterglow of the winter sunset fell on his face. Richard's hands flew to his mouth.

The right half of the face disclosed was actually a bit like Etheridge's—an older Etheridge, an Etheridge who had been in a lot of places nice prep-school boys didn't go and who had done a lot of things nice prep-school boys didn't do. The other half was a twisted mass of scars. A glittery crescent that might have been an eye peered from a crater in the lumpy mess of flesh below the forehead. It looked like a marble that had been shoved deeply into a puddle of half-melted tallow. A single long fang hooked out of the left corner of the mouth.

*It's his Twinner,* Jack thought with utter calm certainty. *That's Etheridge's Twinner down there. Are they all Twinners? A Littlefield Twinner and a Norrington Twinner and a Buckley Twinner and so on and so on? That can't be, can it?*

"Sloat!" the Etheridge-thing cried. It shambled two steps toward Nelson House. The glow from the streetlights on the drive now fell directly onto its ruined face.

"Shut the window," Richard whispered. "Shut the window. I was wrong. It sort of looks like Etheridge but it's not, maybe it's his older brother, maybe someone threw battery acid or something in Etheridge's brother's face and now he's crazy, but it's not Etheridge so *close the window Jack close it right n—*"

Below, the Etheridge-thing shambled yet another step toward them. It grinned. Its tongue, hideously long, fell out of its mouth like an unrolling party favor.

"Sloat!" it cried. "Give us your passenger!"

Jack and Richard both jerked around, looking at each other with strained faces.

A howl shivered in the night . . . for it *was* night now; twilight was done.

Richard looked at Jack, and for a moment Jack saw something like real hate in the other boy's eyes—a flash of his father. *Why did you have to come here, Jack? Huh? Why did you have to bring me this mess? Why did you have to bring me all this goddam Seabrook Island stuff?*

"Do you want me to go?" Jack asked softly.

For a moment that look of harried anger remained in Richard's eyes, and then it was replaced by Richard's old kindness.

"No," he said, running distracted hands through his hair. "No, you're not going anywhere. There are . . . there are wild dogs out there. Wild dogs, Jack, on the Thayer campus! I mean . . . did you see them?"

"Yeah, I saw em, Richie-boy," Jack said softly, as Richard ran his hands through his formerly neat hair again, mussing it into ever wilder tangles. Jack's neat and orderly friend was starting to look a little bit like Donald Duck's amiably mad inventor cousin, Gyro Gearloose.

"Call Boynton, he's Security, that's what I have to do," Richard said. "Call Boynton, or the town police, or—"

A howl rose from the trees on the far side of the quad, from the gathered shadows there—a rising, wavering howl that was really almost human. Richard looked toward it, mouth trembling in an infirm old person's way, and then he looked pleadingly at Jack.

"Close the window, Jack, okay? I feel feverish. I think maybe I've gotten a chill."

"You bet, Richard," Jack said, and closed it, shutting the howl out as best he could.

# 32

# "Send Out Your Passenger!"

## 1

"Help me with this, Richard," Jack grunted.

"I don't want to move the bureau, Jack," Richard said in a childish, lecturing voice. Those dark circles under his eyes were even more pronounced now than they had been in the lounge. "That's not where it belongs."

Out on the quad, that howl rose in the air again.

The bed was in front of the door. Richard's room was now pulled entirely out of shape. Richard stood looking around at this, blinking. Then he went to his bed and pulled off the blankets. He handed one to Jack without speaking, then took his and spread it on the floor. He took his change and his billfold out of his pockets, and put them neatly on the bureau. Then he lay down in the middle of his blanket, folded the sides over himself and then just lay there on the floor, his glasses still on, his face a picture of silent misery.

The silence outside was thick and dreamlike, broken only by the distant growls of the big rigs on the turnpike. Nelson House itself was eerily silent.

"I don't want to talk about what's outside," Richard said. "I just want that up front."

"Okay, Richard," Jack said soothingly. "We won't talk about it."

"Good night, Jack."

"Good night, Richard."

Richard gave him a smile that was wan, and terribly tired; yet there was enough sweet friendliness in it to both warm Jack's heart and wrench it. "I'm still glad you came," Richard said, "and we'll talk about all of this in the morning. I'm sure it will make more sense then. This little fever I have will be gone then."

Richard rolled over on his right side and closed his eyes. Five minutes later, in spite of the hard floor, he was deeply asleep.

Jack sat up for a long time, looking out into the darkness. Sometimes he could see the lights of passing cars on Springfield Avenue; at other times both the headlights and the streetlamps themselves seemed to be gone, as if the entire Thayer School kept sideslipping out of reality and hanging in limbo for a while before slipping back in again.

A wind was rising. Jack could hear it rattling the last frozen leaves from the trees on the quad; could hear it knocking the branches together like bones, could hear it shrieking coldly in the spaces between the buildings.

## 2

"That guy's coming," Jack said tensely. It was an hour or so later. "Etheridge's Twinner."

"Huzzzat?"

"Never mind," Jack said. "Go back to sleep. You don't want to see."

But Richard was sitting up. Before his eye could fix on the slumped, somehow twisted form walking toward Nelson House, it was abducted by the campus itself. He was profoundly shocked, deeply frightened.

The ivy on the Monkson Field House, which had that morning been skeletal but still faintly green, had now gone an ugly, blighted yellow. "*Sloat! Give us your passenger!*"

Suddenly all Richard wanted to do was to go back to sleep—go to sleep until his flu was all gone (he had awakened deciding it *must* be the flu; not just a chill or fever but a real case of the flu); the flu and the fever that was giving him such horrid, twisted hallucinations. He should never have stood by that open window . . . or, earlier, allowed Jack through the window of his room. Richard thought this, and was then deeply and immediately ashamed.

## 3

Jack shot a quick sideways glance at Richard—but his pallid face and bulging eyes suggested to Jack that Richard was edging farther and farther into The Magical Land of Overload.

The thing out there was short. It stood on the frost-whitened grass like a troll that had crawled out from under some bridge, its long-clawed hands hanging almost to its knees. It wore an Army duffel coat with ETHERIDGE stencilled above the left pocket. The jacket hung unzipped and open. Beneath it, Jack could see a torn and rumpled Pendleton shirt. A dark stain which might have been either blood or vomit was splashed over one side. It was wearing a rumpled blue tie with tiny gold upper-case $E$'s woven into the rep fabric; a couple of burrs were stuck on it like grotesque tie-tacks.

Only half of this new Etheridge's face worked right. There was dirt in its hair and leaves on its clothes.

*"Sloat! Give us your passenger!"*

Jack looked down at Etheridge's freakish Twinner again. He was caught and held by its eyes, which were somehow vibrating in their sockets, like tuning forks moving rapidly in their lab-mounts. He had to work to drag his eyes away.

"Richard!" he grunted. "Don't look in its eyes."

Richard didn't reply; he was staring down at the grinning troll-version of Etheridge with drugged and pallid interest.

Scared, Jack butted his friend with his shoulder.

"Oh," Richard said. Abruptly he snatched up Jack's hand and pressed it against his forehead. "How hot do I feel?" he demanded.

Jack pulled his hand away from Richard's forehead, which was a bit warm but no more.

"Pretty hot," he lied.

"I knew it," Richard said with real relief. "I'm going to the infirmary pretty soon, Jack. I think I need an antibiotic."

*"Give him to us, Sloat!"*

"Let's get the bureau in front of the window," Jack said.

*"You're in no danger, Sloat!"* Etheridge called. It grinned reassuringly—the right half of its face grinned reassuringly, anyway; the left half only continued its corpselike gape.

"How can it look so much like Etheridge?" Richard asked with unsettling, eerie calmness. "How can its voice come through the glass so clearly? What's wrong with its face?" His voice sharpened a little and recovered some of its earlier dismay as he asked a final question, one which seemed to be at that moment the most vital question of all, at least to Richard Sloat: *"Where did it get Etheridge's tie, Jack?"*

"I don't know," Jack said. *We're back on Seabrook Island for sure, Richie-boy, and I think we're gonna boogy till you puke.*

*"Give him to us, Sloat, or we'll come in and get him!"*

The Etheridge-thing showed its single fang in a ferocious cannibal's grin.

*"Send your passenger out, Sloat, he's dead! He's dead and if you don't send him out soon, you'll smell him when he starts to stink!"*

"Help me move the frigging bureau!" Jack hissed.

"Yes," Richard said. "Yes, okay. We'll move the bureau and then I'll lie down, and maybe later I'll go over to the infirmary. What do you think, Jack? What do you say? Is that a good plan?" His face begged Jack to say it was a good plan.

"We'll see," Jack said. "First things first. The bureau. They might throw stones."

### 4

Soon after, Richard began to mutter and moan in the sleep which had overtaken him again. That was bad enough; then tears began to squeeze from the corners of his eyes and that was worse.

"I can't give him up," Richard moaned in the weepy, bewildered voice of a five-year-old. Jack stared at him, his skin cold. "I can't give him up, I want my daddy, please someone tell me where my daddy is, he went into the closet but he's not in the closet now, I want my daddy, he'll tell me what to do, please—"

A rock came crashing through the window. Jack screamed.

It boomed against the back of the bureau in front of the window. A few splinters of glass flew through the gaps to the left and right of the bureau and shattered into smaller pieces on the floor.

*"Give us your passenger, Sloat!"*

"Can't," Richard moaned, writhing inside the blanket.

*"Give him to us!"* another laughing, howling voice from outside screamed. *"We'll take him back to Seabrook Island, Richard! Back to Seabrook Island, where he belongs!"*

Another rock. Jack ducked instinctively, although this rock also bounced off the back of the bureau. Dogs howled and yapped and snarled.

"No Seabrook Island," Richard was muttering in his sleep. "Where's my daddy? I want him to come out of that closet! Please, *please, no Seabrook Island stuff, PLEASE—*"

Then Jack was on his knees, shaking Richard as hard as he dared, telling him to wake up, it was just a dream, wake up, for Christ's sake, *wake up!*

"Pleeze-pleeze-pleeze." A hoarse, inhuman chorus of voices rose outside. The voices sounded like a chorus of manimals from Wells's *Island of Dr. Moreau.*

*"Way-gup, way-gup, way-gup!"* a second chorus responded.

Dogs howled.

A flurry of stones flew, knocking more glass from the window, bonking against the back of the bureau, making it rock.

"*DADDY'S IN THE CLOSET!*" Richard screamed. "*DADDY, COME OUT, PLEASE COME OUT, I'M AFRAID!*"

*"Pleeze-pleeze-pleeze!"*

*"Way-gup, way-gup, way-gup!"*

Richard's hands waving in the air.

Stones flying, striking the bureau; soon a rock big enough to either punch straight through the cheap piece of furniture or to simply knock it over on top of them would come through the window, Jack thought.

Outside, they laughed and bellowed and chanted in their hideous troll-voices. Dogs—packs of them now, it seemed—howled and growled.

*"DADEEEEEEEEEE—!!"* Richard screamed in a chilling, rising voice.

Jack slapped him.

Richard's eyes jerked open. He stared up at Jack for a moment with a dreadful lack of recognition, as if the dream he'd been having had burned away his sanity. Then he pulled in a long, shaking breath and let it out in a sigh.

"Nightmare," he said. "Part of the fever, I guess. Horrible. But I don't remember exactly what it was!" he added sharply, as if Jack might ask him this at any moment.

"Richard, I want us to get out of this room," Jack said.

"Out of this—?" Richard looked at Jack as though he must

be crazy. "I can't do that, Jack. I'm running a fever of . . . it
must be a hundred and three at least, might be a hundred and
four or five. I can't—"

"You've got a degree of fever at most, Richard," Jack said
calmly. "Probably not even that—"

"I'm burning up!" Richard protested.

"They're throwing stones, Richard."

"Hallucinations can't throw stones, Jack," Richard said, as
if explaining some simple but vital fact to a mental defective.
"That's Seabrook Island stuff. It's—"

Another volley of rocks flew through the window.

*"Send out your passenger, Sloat!"*

"Come on, Richard," Jack said, getting the other boy to his
feet. He led him to the door and outside. He felt enormously
sorry for Richard now—perhaps not as sorry as he had felt
for Wolf . . . but he was getting there.

"No . . . sick . . . fever . . . I can't . . ."

More rocks thudded against the bureau behind them.

Richard shrieked and clutched at Jack like a boy who is
drowning.

Wild, cackling laughter from outside. Dogs howled and
fought with each other.

Jack saw Richard's white face grow whiter still, saw him
sway, and got up in a hurry. But he was not quite in time to
catch Richard before he collapsed in Reuel Gardener's doorway.

### 5

It was a simple fainting spell, and Richard came around
quickly enough when Jack pinched the delicate webbings between his thumbs and forefingers. He would not talk about
what was outside—affected, in fact, not to know what Jack
was talking about.

They moved cautiously down the hallway toward the stairs.
At the common room Jack poked his head in and whistled.
"Richard, look at this!"

Richard looked reluctantly in. The common room was a
shambles. Chairs were overturned. The cushions on the couch
had been slashed open. The oil portrait of Elder Thayer on the
far wall had been defaced—someone had crayoned a pair of

devil's horns poking out of his neat white hair, someone else had added a moustache under his nose, and a third had used a nail-file or similar implement to scratch a crude phallus on his crotch. The glass of the trophy case was shattered.

Jack didn't much care for the look of drugged, unbelieving horror on Richard's face. In some ways, elves trooping up and down the halls in glowing, unearthly platoons or dragons over the quad would have been easier for Richard to take than this constant erosion of the Thayer School he had come to know and love . . . the Thayer School Richard undoubtedly believed to be noble and good, an undisputed bulwark against a world where nothing could be counted on for long . . . not even, Jack thought, that fathers would come back out of the closets they had gone into.

"Who did this?" Richard asked angrily. "Those freaks did it," he answered himself. "That's who." He looked at Jack, a great, cloudy suspicion beginning to dawn on his face. "They might be Colombians," he said suddenly. "They might be Colombians, and this might be some sort of drug-war, Jack. Has that occurred to you?"

Jack had to throttle an urge to bellow out mad gusts of laughter. Here was an explanation which perhaps only Richard Sloat could have conceived. It was the Colombians. The cocaine range-wars had come to Thayer School in Springfield, Illinois. Elementary, my dear Watson; this problem has a seven and a half percent solution.

"I guess anything's possible," Jack said. "Let's take a look upstairs."

"What in God's name for?"

"Well . . . maybe we'll find someone else," Jack said. He didn't really believe this, but it was something to say. "Maybe someone's hiding out up there. Someone normal like us."

Richard looked at Jack, then back at the shambles of the common room. That look of haunted pain came back into his face again, the look that said *I don't really want to look at this, but for some reason it seems to be all I DO want to look at right now; it's bitterly compulsive, like biting a lemon, or scratching your fingernails across a blackboard, or scraping the tines of a fork on the porcelain of a sink.*

"Dope is rampant in the country," Richard said in eerie lecture-hall tones. "I read an article on drug proliferation in

*The New Republic* just last week. Jack, all those people out there could be doped up! They could be freebasing! They could be—"

"Come on, Richard," Jack said quietly.

"I'm not sure I can climb the stairs," Richard said, weakly querulous. "My fever may be too bad for me to climb stairs."

"Well, give it the good old Thayer try," Jack said, and continued to lead him in that direction.

### 6

As they reached the second-floor landing, sound bled back into the smooth, almost breathless silence that had held inside Nelson House.

Dogs snarled and barked outside—it sounded as if there were not just dozens or scores of them now, but hundreds. The bells in the chapel burst into a wild jangle of sound.

The bells were driving the mongrel dogs racing back and forth across the quad absolutely nuts. They turned on each other, rolled over and over on the grass—which was beginning to look ragged, weedy, and unkempt—and savaged anything within mouthshot. As Jack watched, one of them attacked an elm tree. Another launched itself at the statue of Elder Thayer. As its biting, snapping muzzle collided with the solid bronze, blood splashed and sprayed.

Jack turned away, sickened. "Come on, Richard," Jack said.

Richard came willingly enough.

### 7

The second floor was a jumbled confusion of overturned furniture, shattered windows, fistfuls of stuffing, records that had apparently been thrown like Frisbees, clothes that had been tossed everywhere.

The third floor was cloudy with steam and as warmly moist as a tropical rain-forest. As they got closer to the door marked SHOWERS, the heat went up to sauna levels. The mist they had first encountered creeping down the stairs in thin tendrils grew foglike and opaque.

"Stay here," Jack said. "Wait for me."

"Sure, Jack," Richard said serenely, raising his voice enough to be heard over the drumming showers. His glasses had fogged up, but he made no effort to wipe them off.

Jack pushed the door open and went in. The heat was soggy and thick. His clothes were soaked at once from sweat and the hot, foggy moisture. The tile-lined room roared and drummed with water. All twenty of the showers had been turned on, and the driving needle-spray from all twenty had been focused on a pile of sports equipment in the middle of the tiled room. The water was able to drain through this crazy pile, but only slowly, and the room was awash. Jack took off his shoes and circled the room, sliding under the showers to keep himself as dry as possible, and also to keep himself from being scalded—whoever had turned on the showers hadn't bothered with the cold faucets, apparently. He turned all of them off, one by one. There was no reason for him to do this, no reason at all, and he scolded himself for wasting time in such a way, when he should be trying to think of a way for them to get out of here—out of Nelson House and off the Thayer School grounds—before the axe fell.

No reason for it, except that maybe Richard wasn't the only one with a need to create order out of chaos . . . to create order and to maintain it.

He went back into the hall and Richard was gone.

"Richard?" He could feel his heartbeat picking up in his chest.

There was no answer. "Richard!"

Spilled cologne hung on the air, noxiously heavy.

*"Richard, where the hell are you!"*

Richard's hand fell on Jack's shoulder, and Jack shrieked.

## 8

"I don't know why you had to yell like that," Richard said later. "It was only me."

"I'm just nervous," Jack said wanly.

They were sitting in the third-floor room of a boy with the strangely harmonious name of Albert Humbert. Richard told him that Albert Humbert, whose nickname was Albert the Blob, was the fattest boy in school, and Jack could believe it; his room contained an amazing variety of junk food—it was the stash of a kid whose worst nightmare isn't getting cut from the basketball team or flunking a trig test but rather waking up in the night and not being able to find a Ring-Ding or a Reese's Peanut Butter Cup. A lot of the stuff had been thrown around. The glass jar containing the Marshmallow Fluff had been broken, but Jack had never been very wild about Marshmallow Fluff, anyway. He also passed on the licorice whips—Albert the Blob had a whole carton of them stashed on the upper shelf of his closet. Written across one of the carton-flaps was *Happy birthday, dear, from Your Loving Mom.*

*Some Loving Moms send cartons of licorice whips, and some Loving Dads send blazers from Brooks Brothers*, Jack thought wearily, *and if there's any difference, Jason alone knows what it is.*

They found enough food in the room of Albert the Blob to make a crazy sort of meal—Slim Jims, pepperoni slices, Salt 'n Vinegar potato chips. Now they were finishing up with a package of cookies. Jack had retrieved Albert's chair from the hall and was sitting by the window. Richard was sitting on Albert's bed.

"Well, you sure *are* nervous," Richard agreed, shaking his head in refusal when Jack offered him the last cookie. "Paranoid, actually. It comes from spending the last couple of months on the road. You'll be okay once you get home to your mother, Jack."

"Richard," Jack said, tossing away the empty Famous Amos bag, "let's cut the shit. Do you *see* what's going on outside on your campus?"

Richard wet his lips. "I *explained* that," he said. "I have a fever. Probably none of this is happening at all, and if it is, then perfectly ordinary things are going on and my mind is twisting them, heightening them. That's one possibility. The other is . . . well . . . drug-pushers."

Richard sat forward on Albert the Blob's bed.

"*You* haven't been experimenting with drugs, have you, Jack? While you were on the road?" The old intelligent, incisive light had suddenly rekindled in Richard's eyes. *Here's a possible explanation, a possible way out of this madness*, his eyes said. *Jack has gotten involved in some crazy drug-scam, and all these people have followed him here.*

"No," Jack said wearily. "I always used to think of you as

the master of reality, Richard," Jack said. "I never thought I'd live to see you—*you!*—using your brains to twist the facts."

"Jack, that's just a . . . a crock, and you know it!"

"Drug-wars in Springfield, Illinois?" Jack asked. "Who's talking Seabrook Island stuff now?"

And that was when a rock suddenly crashed in through Albert Humbert's window, spraying glass across the floor.

## 33

# Richard in the Dark

### 1

Richard screamed and threw an arm up to shield his face. Glass flew.

*"Send him out, Sloat!"*

Jack got up. Dull fury filled him.

Richard grabbed his arm. "Jack, no! Stay away from the window!"

"Fuck that," Jack almost snarled. "I'm tired of being talked about like I was a pizza."

The Etheridge-thing stood across the road. It was on the sidewalk at the edge of the quad, looking up at them.

"Get out of here!" Jack shouted at it. A sudden inspiration burst in his head like a sunflare. He hesitated, then bellowed: *"I order you out of here! All of you! I order you to leave in the name of my mother, the Queen!"*

The Etheridge-thing flinched as if someone had used a whip to lay a stripe across its face.

Then the look of pained surprise passed and the Etheridge-thing began to grin. "She's dead, Sawyer!" it shouted up—but Jack's eyes had grown sharper, somehow, in his time on the road, and he saw the expression of twitchy unease under the manufactured triumph. "Queen Laura's dead and your mother's dead, too . . . dead back in New Hampshire . . . dead and *stinking*."

*"Begone!"* Jack bellowed, and he thought that the Etheridge-thing flinched back in baffled fury again.

Richard had joined him at the window, pallid and distracted. "What are you two yelling about?" he asked. He looked fixedly at the grinning travesty below them and across the way. "How does Etheridge know your mother's in New Hampshire?"

*"Sloat!"* the Etheridge-thing yelled up. *"Where's your tie?"*

A spasm of guilt contracted Richard's face; his hands jerked toward the open neck of his shirt.

*"We'll let it go this time, if you send out your passenger, Sloat!"* the Etheridge-thing yelled up. *"If you send him out, everything can go back to the way it was! You want that, don't you?"*

Richard was staring down at the Etheridge-thing, nodding—Jack was sure of it—quite unconsciously. His face was a knotted rag of misery, his eyes bright with unshed tears. He wanted everything to go back to the way it had been, oh yes.

*"Don't you love this school, Sloat?"* the Etheridge-thing bellowed up at Albert's window.

"Yes," Richard muttered, and gulped down a sob. "Yes, of *course* I love it."

"You know what we do to little punks who don't love this school? Give him to us! It'll be like he was never here!"

Richard turned slowly and looked at Jack with dreadfully blank eyes.

"You decide, Richie-boy," Jack said softly.

"He's carrying drugs, Richard!" the Etheridge-thing called up. "Four or five different kinds! Coke, hash, angel-dust! He's been selling all of that stuff to finance his trip west! Where do you think he got that nice coat he was wearing when he showed up on your doorstep?"

"Drugs," Richard said with great, shuddery relief. "I knew it."

"But you don't believe it," Jack said. "Drugs didn't change your school, Richard. And the dogs—"

"Send him out, Sl . . ." the Etheridge-thing's voice was fading, fading.

When the two boys looked down again, it was gone.

"Where did your father go, do you think?" Jack asked

softly. "Where do you think he went when he didn't come out of the closet, Richard?"

Richard turned slowly to look at him, and Richard's face, usually so calm and intelligent and serene, now began to shiver into pieces. His chest began to hitch irregularly. Richard suddenly fell into Jack's arms, clutching at him with a blind, panicky urgency. *"It t-t-touched muh-me-eeee!"* he screamed at Jack. His body trembled under Jack's hands like a winchwire under a near-breaking strain. *"It touched me, it t-touched m-me, something in there t-t-touched me AND I DON'T NUH-NUH-KNOW WHAT IT WAS!"*

## 2

With his burning forehead pressed against Jack's shoulder, Richard coughed out the story he had held inside him all these years. It came in hard little chunks, like deformed bullets. As he listened, Jack found himself remembering the time his own father had gone into the garage . . . and had come back two hours later, from around the block. That had been bad, but what had happened to Richard had been a lot worse. It explained Richard's iron, no-compromise insistence on reality, the whole reality, and nothing *but* the reality. It explained his rejection of any sort of fantasy, even science fiction . . . and, Jack knew from his own school experience, techies like Richard usually ate and drank sf . . . as long as it was the hard stuff, that was, your basic Heinlein, Asimov, Arthur C. Clarke, Larry Niven—spare us the metaphysical bullshit of the Robert Silverbergs and Barry Malzbergs, please, but we'll read the stuff where they get all the stellar quadrants and logarithms right until it's running out of our ears. Not Richard, though. Richard's dislike of fantasy ran so deep that he would not pick up *any* novel unless it was an assignment—as a kid, he had let Jack pick out the books he read for free-choice book reports, not caring what they were, chewing them up as if they were cereal. It became a challenge to Jack to find a story—*any* story— which would please Richard, divert Richard, carry Richard away as good novels and stories sometimes carried Jack away . . . the good ones, he thought, were almost as good as the Daydreams, and each mapped out its own version of the Territories. But he was never able to produce any *frisson*, any spark, any reaction at all. Whether it was *The Red Pony, Dragstrip Demon, The Catcher in the Rye,* or *I Am Legend,* the reaction was always the same—frowning, dull-eyed concentration, followed by a frowning, dull-eyed book report that would earn either a hook or, if his English teacher was feeling particularly generous that day, a B–. Richard's Cs in English were what kept him off the honor roll during the few marking periods when he missed it.

Jack had finished William Golding's *Lord of the Flies,* feeling hot and cold and trembly all over—both exalted and frightened, most of all wishing what he always wished when the story was most particularly good—that it didn't have to stop, that it could just roll on and on, the way that life did (only life was always so much more boring and so much more pointless than stories). He knew Richard had a book report due and so he had given him the lap-eared paperback, thinking that this must surely do it, this would turn the trick, Richard must react to the story of these lost boys and their descent into savagery. But Richard had plodded through *Lord of the Flies* as he had plodded through all the other novels before it, and wrote another book report which contained all the zeal and fire of a hungover pathologist's post-mortem on a traffic accident victim. *What is it with you?* Jack had burst out, exasperated. *What in God's name have you got against a good story, Richard?* And Richard had looked at him, flabbergasted, apparently really not understanding Jack's anger. *Well, there's really no such thing as a good made-up story, is there?* Richard had responded.

Jack had gone away that day sorely puzzled by Richard's total rejection of make-believe, but he thought he understood better now—better than he really wanted to, perhaps. Perhaps to Richard each opening storybook cover had looked a little like an opening closet door; perhaps each bright paperback cover, illustrating people who never were as if they were perfectly real, reminded Richard of the morning when he had Had Enough, Forever.

### 3

*Richard sees his father go into the closet in the big front bedroom, pulling the folding door shut behind him. He is five, maybe . . . or six . . . surely not as old as seven. He waits five minutes, then ten, and when his father still hasn't come out of the closet he begins to be a little frightened. He calls. He calls*

*(for his pipe he calls for his bowl he calls for his)*

*father and when his father doesn't answer he calls in a louder and louder voice and he goes closer and closer to the closet as he calls and finally, when fifteen minutes have gone by and his father still hasn't come out, Richard pulls the folding door open and goes in. He goes into darkness like a cave.*

*And something happens.*

*After pushing through the rough tweeds and the smooth cottons and the occasional slick silks of his father's coats and suits and sport jackets, the smell of cloth and mothballs and closed-up dark closet air begins to give way to another smell— a hot, fiery smell. Richard begins to blunder forward, screaming his father's name, he thinking there must be a fire back here and his father may be burning in it, because it smells like a fire . . . and suddenly he realizes that the boards are gone under his feet, and he is standing in black dirt. Weird black insects with clustered eyes on the ends of long stalks are hopping all around his fuzzy slippers. Daddy! he screams. The coats and suits are gone, the floor is gone, but it isn't crisp white snow underfoot; it's stinking black dirt which is apparently the birthing ground for these unpleasant black jumping insects; this place is by no stretch of the imagination Narnia. Other screams answer Richard's scream—screams and mad, demented laughter. Smoke drifts around him on a dark idiot wind and Richard turns, stumbling back the way he came, hands outstretched like the hands of a blind man, feeling frantically for the coats, smelling for the faint, acrid reek of mothballs—*

*And suddenly a hand slithers around his wrist.*

Daddy? *he asks, but when he looks down he sees not a human hand but a scaly green thing covered with writhing suckers, a green thing attached to a long, rubbery arm which stretches off into the darkness and toward a pair of yellow, upslanted eyes that stare at him with flat hunger.*

*Screeching, he tears free and flings himself blindly into the black . . . and just as his groping fingers find his father's sport coats and suits again, as he hears the blessed, rational sound of jangling coathangers, that green, sucker-lined hand waltzes dryly across the back of his neck again . . . and is gone.*

He waits, trembling, as pallid as day-old ashes in a cold stove, for three hours outside that damned closet, afraid to go back in, afraid of the green hand and the yellow eyes, more and more sure that his father must be dead. And when his father comes back into the room near the end of the fourth hour, not from the closet but from the door which communicates between the bedroom and the upstairs hall—the door BEHIND Richard—when that happens, Richard rejects fantasy for good and all; Richard negates fantasy; Richard refuses to deal with fantasy, or treat with it, or compromise with it. He has, quite simply, Had Enough, Forever. He jumps up, runs to his father, to the beloved Morgan Sloat, and hugs him so tightly that his arms will be sore all that week. Morgan lifts him up, laughs, and asks him why he looks so pale. Richard smiles, and tells him that it was probably something he ate for breakfast, but he feels better now, and he kisses his father's cheek, and smells the beloved smell of mingled sweat and Raj cologne. And later that day, he takes all of his storybooks— the Little Golden Books, the pop-up books, the I-Can-Read books, the Dr. Seuss books, the Green Fairy Book for Young Folks, and he puts them in a carton, and he puts the carton down in the basement, and he thinks: "I would not care if an earthquake came now and opened a crack in the floor and swallowed up every one of those books. In fact, it would be a relief. In fact, it would be such a relief that I would probably laugh all day and most of the weekend." This does not happen, but Richard feels a great relief when the books are shut in double darkness—the darkness of the carton and the darkness of the cellar. He never looks at them again, just as he never goes in his father's closet with the folding door again, and although he sometimes dreams that there is something under his bed or in his closet, something with flat yellow eyes, he never thinks about that green, sucker-covered hand again until the strange time comes to Thayer School and he bursts into unaccustomed tears in his friend Jack Sawyer's arms.

He has Had Enough, Forever.

### 4

Jack had hoped that with the telling of his story and the passing of his tears, Richard would return—more or less—to his normal, sharply rational self. Jack didn't really care if Richard bought the whole nine yards or not; if Richard could just reconcile himself to accepting the leading edge of this craziness, he could turn his formidable mind to helping Jack find a way out . . . a way off the Thayer campus, anyway, and out of Richard's life before Richard went totally bananas.

But it didn't work that way. When Jack tried to talk to him—to tell Richard about the time his own father, Phil, had gone into the garage and hadn't come out—Richard refused to listen. The old secret of what had happened that day in the closet was out (sort of; Richard still clung stubbornly to the idea that it had been a hallucination), but Richard had still Had Enough, Forever.

The next morning, Jack went downstairs. He got all of his own things and those things he thought Richard might want—toothbrush, textbooks, notebooks, a fresh change of clothes. They would spend that day in Albert the Blob's room, he decided. They could keep an eye on the quad and the gate from up there. When night fell again, maybe they could get away.

## 5

Jack hunted through Albert's desk and found a bottle of baby aspirin. He looked at this for a moment, thinking that these little orange pills said almost as much about the departed Albert's Loving Mom as the carton of licorice whips on the closet shelf. Jack shook out half a dozen pills. He gave them to Richard and Richard took them absently. "Come on over here and lie down," Jack said.

"No," Richard answered—his tone was cross and restless and terribly unhappy. He returned to the window. "I ought to keep a watch. So a full report can be made to . . . to . . . to the trustees. Later."

Jack touched Richard's brow lightly. And although it was cool—almost chilly—he said: "Your fever's worse, Richard. Better lie down until that aspirin goes to work."

"Worse?" Richard looked at him with pathetic gratitude. "Is it?"

"It is," Jack said gravely. "Come on and lie down."

Richard was asleep five minutes after he lay down. Jack sat in Albert the Blob's easy chair, its seat nearly as sprung as the

middle of Albert's mattress. Richard's pale face glowed wax-
ily in the growing daylight.

## 6

Somehow the day passed, and around four o'clock, Jack fell
asleep. He awoke to darkness, not knowing how long he had
been out. He only knew there had been no dreams, and for
that he was grateful. Richard was stirring uneasily and Jack
guessed he would be up soon. He stood and stretched, wincing at the stiffness in his back. He went to the window, looked
out, and stood motionless, eyes wide. His first thought was *I
don't want Richard to see this. Not if I can help it.*

*O God, we've got to get out of here, and just as soon as we
can,* Jack thought, frightened. *Even if, for whatever reasons,
they're afraid to come straight at us.*

But was he really going to take Richard out of here? They
didn't think he would do it, he knew that—they were counting
on his refusing to expose his friend to any more of this craziness.

*Flip, Jack-O. You've got to flip over, and you know it. And
you've got to take Richard with you because this place is going to hell.*

*I can't. Flipping into the Territories would blow Richard's
wheels completely.*

*Doesn't matter. You have to do it. It's the best thing, any-
way—maybe the only thing—because they won't be expecting it.*

"Jack?" Richard was sitting up. His face had a strange,
naked look without his glasses. "Jack, is it over? Was it a
dream?"

Jack sat down on the bed and put an arm around Richard's
shoulders. "No," he said, his voice low and soothing. "It's not
over yet, Richard."

"I think my fever's worse," Richard announced, pulling
away from Jack. He drifted over to the window, one of the
bows of his glasses pinched delicately between the thumb
and forefinger of his right hand. He put his spectacles on
and looked out. Shapes with glowing eyes roamed back and
forth. He stood there for a long time, and then he did some-

thing so un-Richardlike that Jack could barely credit it. He took his glasses off again and deliberately dropped them. There was a frigid little crunch as one lens cracked. Then he stepped deliberately back on them, shattering both lenses to powder.

He picked them up, looked at them, and then tossed them unconcernedly toward Albert the Blob's wastebasket. He missed by a wide margin. There was now something softly stubborn in Richard's face, too—something that said *I don't want to see any more, so I won't see any more, and I have taken care of the problem. I have Had Enough, Forever.*

"Look at that," he said in a flat, unsurprised voice. "I broke my glasses. I had another pair, but I broke them in gym two weeks ago. I'm almost blind without them."

Jack knew this wasn't true, but he was too flabbergasted to say anything. He could think of absolutely no appropriate response to the radical action Richard had just taken—it had been too much like a calculated last-ditch stand against madness.

"I think my fever's worse too," Richard said. "Have you got any more of those aspirin, Jack?"

Jack opened the desk drawer and wordlessly handed Richard the bottle. Richard swallowed six or eight of them, then lay down again.

## 7

As the night deepened, Richard, who repeatedly promised to discuss their situation, repeatedly went back on his word. He couldn't discuss leaving, he said, couldn't discuss *any* of this, not now, his fever had come back and it felt much, much worse, he thought it might be as high as a hundred and five, possibly a hundred and six. He said he needed to go back to sleep.

"Richard, for Christ's sake!" Jack roared. "You're punking out on me! Of all the things I never expected from you—"

"Don't be silly," Richard said, falling back onto Albert's bed. "I'm just sick, Jack. You can't expect me to talk about all these crazy things when I'm sick."

"Richard, do you want me to go away and leave you?"

Richard looked back over his shoulder at Jack for a moment, blinking slowly. "You won't," he said, and then went back to sleep.

## 8

Around nine o'clock, the campus entered another of those mysterious quiet periods, and Richard, perhaps sensing that there would be less strain put on his tottering sanity now, woke up and swung his legs over the bed. Brown spots had appeared on the walls, and he stared at them until he saw Jack coming toward him.

"I feel a lot better, Jack," he said hastily, "but it really won't do us any good to talk about leaving, it's dark, and—"

"We have to leave tonight," Jack said grimly. "All they have to do is wait us out. There's fungus growing on the walls, and don't tell me you don't see *that*."

Richard smiled with a blind tolerance that nearly drove Jack mad. He loved Richard, but he could cheerfully have pounded him through the nearest fungus-rotted wall.

At that precise moment, long, fat white bugs began to squirm into Albert the Blob's room. They came pushing out of the brown fungoid spots on the wall as if the fungus were in some unknown way giving birth to them. They twisted and writhed half in and half out of the soft brown spots, then plopped to the floor and began squirming blindly toward the bed.

Jack had begun to wonder if Richard's sight weren't really a lot worse than he remembered, or if it had degenerated badly since he had last seen Richard. Now he saw that he had been right the first time. Richard could see quite well. He certainly wasn't having any trouble picking up the gelatinous things that were coming out of the walls, anyway. He screamed and pressed against Jack, his face frantic with revulsion.

*"Bugs, Jack! Oh, Jesus! Bugs! Bugs!"*

"We'll be all right—right, Richard?" Jack said. He held Richard in place with a strength he didn't know he had. "We'll just wait for the morning, right? No problem, right?"

They were squirming out in dozens, in hundreds, plump,

waxy-white things like overgrown maggots. Some burst open
when they struck the floor. The rest humped sluggishly across
the floor toward them.

*"Bugs, Jesus, we have to get out, we have to—"*

"Thank God, this kid finally sees the light," Jack said.

He slung his knapsack over his left arm and grabbed
Richard's elbow in his right hand. He hustled Richard to the
door. White bugs squashed and splattered under their shoes.
Now they were pouring out of the brown patches in a flood;
an obscene, ongoing multiple birth that was happening all
over Albert's room. A stream of the white bugs fell from a
patch on the ceiling and landed, squirming, on Jack's hair and
shoulders; he brushed them away as best he could and hauled
the screaming, flailing Richard out the door.

*I think we're on our way,* Jack thought. *God help us, I
really think we are.*

# 9

They were in the common room again. Richard, it turned out,
had even less idea of how to sneak off the Thayer campus than
Jack did himself. Jack knew one thing very well: he was not
going to trust that deceptive quiet and go out any of Nelson
House's Entry doors.

Looking hard to the left out of the wide common-room
window, Jack could see a squat octagonal brick building.

"What's that, Richard?"

"Huh?" Richard was looking at the gluey, sluggish torrents
of mud flowing over the darkening quad.

"Little squatty brick building. You can just barely see it
from here."

"Oh. The Depot."

"What's a Depot?"

"The name itself doesn't mean anything anymore,"
Richard said, still looking uneasily out at the mud-drenched
quad. "Like our infirmary. It's called The Creamery because
there used to be a real dairy barn and milk-bottling plant over
there. Until 1910 or so there was, anyway. Tradition, Jack. It's
very important. It's one of the reason I like Thayer."

Richard looked forlornly out at the muddy campus again.

"One of the reasons I always did, anyway."

"The Creamery, okay. How come The Depot?"

Richard was slowly warming to the twin ideas of Thayer and Tradition.

"This whole area of Springfield used to be a railhead," he said. "In fact, in the old days—"

"Which old days are we talking about, Richard?"

"Oh. The eighteen-eighties. Eighteen-nineties. You see . . ."

Richard trailed off. His nearsighted eyes began moving around the common room—looking for more bugs, Jack supposed. There weren't any . . . at least not yet. But he could already see a few brown patches beginning to form on the walls. The bugs weren't here yet, but they would be along.

"Come on, Richard," Jack prompted. "No one used to have to prime you to get you to run your mouth."

Richard smiled a little. His eyes returned to Jack. "Springfield was one of the three or four biggest American railheads during the last two decades of the nineteenth century. It was geographically handy to all the points of the compass." He raised his right hand toward his face, forefinger extended to push his glasses up on his nose in a scholarly gesture, realized they were no longer there, and lowered the hand again, looking a bit embarrassed. "There were main rail routes leaving Springfield for everywhere. This school exists because Andrew Thayer saw the possibilities. He made a fortune in rail shippage. Mostly to the west coast. He was the first one to see the potential in shipping west as well as east."

A bright light suddenly went on in Jack's head, bathing all of his thoughts in its harsh glare.

"West coast?" His stomach lurched. He could not yet identify the new shape that bright light had shown him, but the word that leaped into his mind was fiery and utterly clear!

*Talisman!*

"*West* coast, did you say?"

"Of course I did." Richard looked at Jack strangely. "Jack, are you going deaf?"

"No," Jack said. *Springfield was one of the three or four biggest American railheads . . .* "No, I'm fine." *He was the first one to see the potential in shipping west . . .*

"Well, you looked damn funny for a minute."

*He was, you might say, the first one to see the potential of shipping stuff by rail to the Outposts.*

Jack knew, utterly *knew*, that Springfield was still a pressure point of some kind, perhaps still a shipping point. That was, perhaps, why Morgan's magic worked so well here.

"There were coal-piles and switching yards and roundhouses and boxcar sheds and about a billion miles of tracks and sidings," Richard was saying. "It covered this whole area where Thayer School is now. If you dig down a few feet under this turf anywhere, you find cinders and pieces of rail and all sorts of stuff. But all that's left now is that little building. The Depot. Of course it never was a real depot; it's too small, anyone could see that. It was the main railyard office, where the stationmaster and the rail-boss did their respective things."

"You know a hell of a lot about it," Jack said, speaking almost automatically—his head was still filled with that savage new light.

"It's part of the Thayer tradition," Richard said simply.

"What's it used for now?"

"There's a little theater in there. It's for Dramatics Club productions, but the Dramatics Club hasn't been very active over the last couple of years."

"Do you think it's locked?"

"Why would anyone lock The Depot?" Richard asked. "Unless you think someone would be interested in stealing a few flats from the 1979 production of *The Fantasticks*."

"So we could get in there?"

"I think so, yes. But why—"

Jack pointed to a door just beyond the Ping-Pong tables. "What's in there?"

"Vending machines. And a coin-op microwave to heat up snacks and frozen dinners. Jack—"

"Come on."

"Jack, I think my fever's coming back again." Richard smiled weakly. "Maybe we should just stay here for a while. We could rack out on the sofas for the night—"

"See those brown patches on the walls?" Jack said grimly, pointing.

"No, not without my glasses, of course not!"

"Well, they're there. And in about an hour, those white bugs are going to hatch out of—"

"All right," Richard said hastily.

## 10

The vending machines stank.

It looked to Jack as if all the stuff inside them had spoiled. Blue mould coated the cheese crackers and Doritos and Jax and fried pork-rinds. Sluggish creeks of melted ice cream were oozing out of the panels in the front of the Hav-a-Kone machine.

Jack pulled Richard toward the window. He looked out. From here Jack could make out The Depot quite well. Beyond it he could see the chain-link fence and the service road leading off-campus.

"We'll be out in a few seconds," Jack whispered back. He unlocked the window and ran it up.

*This school exists because Andrew Thayer saw the possibilities . . . do you see the possibilities, Jack-O?*

He thought maybe he did.

"Are there any of those people out there?" Richard asked nervously.

"No," Jack said, taking only the most cursory of glances. It didn't really matter if there were or not, anymore.

*One of the three or four biggest American railheads . . . a fortune in rail shippage . . . mostly to the west coast . . . he was the first one to see the potential in shipping west . . . west . . . west . . .*

A thick, mucky mixture of tidal-flat aroma and garbage stench drifted in the window. Jack threw one leg over the sill and grabbed for Richard's hand. "Come on," he said.

Richard drew back, his face long and miserable with fright.

"Jack . . . I don't know . . ."

"The place is falling apart," Jack said, "and pretty soon it's going to be crawling with bugs as well. Now come on. Someone's going to see me sitting here in this window and we'll lose our chance to scurry out of here like a couple of mice."

"I don't understand any of this!" Richard wailed. "I don't understand what in the goddam hell is going on here!"

"Shut up and come on," Jack said. "Or I will leave you, Richard. Swear to God I will. I love you, but my mother is dying. I'll leave you to fend for yourself."

Richard looked at Jack's face and saw—even without his glasses—that Jack was telling the truth. He took Jack's hand. "God, I'm scared," he whispered.

"Join the club," Jack said, and pushed him off. His feet hit the mucky lawn a second later. Richard jumped down beside him.

"We're going to cross to The Depot," Jack whispered. "I make it about fifty yards. We'll go in if it's unlocked, try to hide as well as we can on the Nelson House side of it if it isn't. Once we're sure no one's seen us and the place is still quiet—"

"We go for the fence."

"Right." Or maybe we'll have to flip, but never mind that just now. "The service road. I've got an idea that if we can get off the Thayer grounds, everything will be okay again. Once we get a quarter of a mile down the road, you may look back over your shoulder and see the lights in the dorms and the library just as usual, Richard."

"That'd be *so* great," Richard said with a wistfulness that was heartbreaking.

"Okay, you ready?"

"I guess so," Richard said.

"Run to The Depot. Freeze against the wall on this side. Low, so those bushes screen you. See them?"

"Yes."

"Okay . . . go for it!"

They broke away from Nelson House and ran for The Depot side by side.

## 11

They were less than halfway there, breath puffing out of their mouths in clear white vapor, feet pounding the mucky ground, when the bells in the chapel broke into a hideous, grinding jangle of sound. A howling chorus of dogs answered the bells.

They were back, all these were-prefects. Jack groped for Richard and found Richard groping for him. Their hands linked together.

Richard screamed and tried to pull him off to the left. His hand tightened down on Jack's until the fingerbones grated together paralyzingly. A lean white wolf, a Board Chairman of Wolves, came around The Depot and was now racing toward them. That was the old man from the limousine, Jack thought. Other wolves and dogs followed . . . and then Jack realized with sick surety that some of them were not dogs; some of them were half-transformed boys, some grown men—teachers, he supposed.

*"Mr Dufrey!"* Richard shrieked, pointing with his free hand (*Gee, you see pretty well for someone who's lost his glasses, Richie-boy,* Jack thought crazily). *"Mr. Dufrey! Oh God, it's Mr. Dufrey! Mr. Dufrey! Mr. Dufrey!"*

So Jack got his first and only look at Thayer School's headmaster—a tiny old man with gray hair, a big, bent nose, and the wizened, hairy body of an organ grinder's monkey. He ran swiftly along on all fours with the dogs and the boys, a mortarboard bobbing crazily up and down on his head and somehow refusing to fall off. He grinned at Jack and Richard, and his tongue, long and lolling and stained yellow with nicotine, fell out through the middle of his grin.

*"Mr. Dufrey! Oh God! Oh dear God! Mr. Dufrey! Mr. Du—"*

He was yanking Jack harder and harder toward the left. Jack was bigger, but Richard was in the grip of panic. Explosions rocked the air. That foul, garbagey smell grew thicker and thicker. Jack could hear the soft *flupping* and *plupping* of mud squeezing out of the earth. The white wolf which led the pack was closing the distance and Richard was trying to pull them away from it, trying to pull them toward the fence, and that was right, but it was wrong, too, it was wrong because it was The Depot they had to get to, not the fence. That was the spot, that was the spot because this had been one of the three or four biggest American railheads, because Andrew Thayer had been the first one to see the potential in shipping west, because Andrew Thayer had seen the potential and now he, Jack Sawyer, saw the potential, as well. All of this was of course only intuition, but Jack had come to believe that, in these universal matters, his intuition was the only thing he could trust.

*"Let go of your passenger, Sloat!"* Dufrey was gobbling. *"Let go of your passenger, he's too pretty for you!"*

*But what's a passenger?* Jack thought in those last few seconds, as Richard tried blindly to pull them off-course and Jack yanked him back on, toward the mixed bunch of mongrels and boys and teachers that ran behind the big white wolf, toward The Depot. *I'll tell you what a passenger is; a passenger is one who rides. And where does a passenger begin to ride? Why, at a depot . . .*

"Jack, it'll bite!" Richard screamed.

The wolf outran Dufrey and leaped at them, its jaws dropping open like a loaded trap. From behind them there was a thick, crunching thud as Nelson House split open like a rotten cantaloupe.

Now it was Jack who was bearing down on Richard's fingerbones, clamping tight and tighter and tightest as the night rang with crazy bells and flared with gasoline bombs and rattled with firecrackers.

"Hold on!" he screamed. "Hold on, Richard, here we go!"

He had time to think: *Now the shoe is on the other foot; now it's Richard who is the herd, who is my passenger. God help us both.*

"Jack, what's happening?" Richard shrieked. "What are you doing? Stop it! STOP IT! STOP—"

Richard was still shrieking, but Jack no longer heard him—suddenly, triumphantly, that feeling of creeping doom cracked open like a black egg and his brain filled up with light—light and a sweet purity of air; air so pure that you could smell the radish a man pulled out of his garden half a mile away. Suddenly Jack felt as if he could simply push off and jump all the way across the quad . . . or fly, like those men with the wings strapped to their backs.

Oh, there was light and clear air replacing that foul, garbagey stench and a sensation of crossing voids of darkness, and for a moment everything in him seemed clear and full of radiance; for a moment everything was rainbow, rainbow, rainbow.

So Jack Sawyer flipped into the Territories again, this time while running headlong across the degenerating Thayer campus, with the sound of cracked bells and snarling dogs filling the air.

And this time he dragged Morgan Sloat's son Richard with him.

# Interlude

# Sloat in This World/Orris in the Territories (III)

Shortly after seven a.m. on the morning following Jack and Richard's flip out from Thayer, Morgan Sloat drew up to the curb just outside the main gates of Thayer School. He parked. The space was marked with a HANDICAPPED ONLY sign. Sloat glanced at it indifferently, then reached into his pocket, drew out a vial of cocaine, and used some of it. In a few moments the world seemed to gain color and vitality. It was wonderful stuff. He wondered if it would grow in the Territories, and if it would be more potent over there.

Gardener himself had awakened Sloat in his Beverly Hills home at two in the morning to tell him what had happened— it had been midnight in Springfield. Gardener's voice had been trembling. He was obviously terrified that Morgan would fly into a rage, and furious that he had missed Jack Sawyer by less than an hour.

"That boy . . . that bad, bad boy . . ."

Sloat had not flown into a rage. Indeed, he had felt extraordinary calm. He felt a sense of predestination which he suspected came from that other part of him—what he thought of as "his Orris-ness" in a half-understood pun on royalty.

"Be calm," Sloat had soothed. "I'll be there as soon as I can. Hang in there, baby."

He had broken the connection before Gardener could say any more, and lain back on the bed. He had crossed his hands on his stomach and closed his eyes. There was a moment of weightlessness . . . just a moment . . . and then he felt a sensation of movement beneath him. He heard the creak of leather traces, the groan and thump of rough iron springs, the curses of his driver.

He had opened his eyes as Morgan of Orris.

As always, his first reaction was pure delight: this made coke seem like baby aspirin. His chest was narrower, his weight less. Morgan Sloat's heartbeat ran anywhere from eighty-five beats a minute to a hundred and twenty when he was pissed off; Orris's rarely went higher than sixty-five or so. Morgan Sloat's eyesight was tested at 20/20, but Morgan of Orris nonetheless saw better. He could see and trace the course of every minute crack in the sidewall of the diligence, could marvel over the fineness of the mesh curtains which blew through the windows. Cocaine had clogged Sloat's nose, dulling his sense of smell; Orris's nose was totally clear and he could smell dust and earth and air with perfect fidelity—it was as if he could sense and appreciate every molecule.

Behind him he had left an empty double bed still marked with the shape of his large body. Here he was sitting on a bench seat plusher than the seat in any Rolls-Royce ever made, riding west toward the end of the Outposts, toward a place which was called Outpost Depot. Toward a man named Anders. He knew these things, knew exactly where he was, because Orris was still here, inside his head—speaking to him the way the right side of the brain may speak to the rational left during daydreams, in a low but perfectly clear voice. Sloat had spoken to Orris in this same low undervoice on the few occasions when Orris had Migrated to what Jack had come to think of as the American Territories. When one Migrated and entered the body of one's Twinner, the result was a kind of benign possession. Sloat had read of more violent cases of possession, and although the subject did not greatly interest him, he guessed that the poor, unlucky slobs so afflicted had been taken over by mad hitchhikers from other worlds—or perhaps it was the American world itself which had driven them mad. That seemed more than possible; it had certainly done a number on poor old Orris's head the first two or three times he had popped over, although he had been wildly excited as well as terrified.

The diligence took a mighty bounce—in the Outposts, you took the roads as you found them and thanked God they were there at all. Orris shifted in his seat and his clubfoot muttered dull pain.

"Hold on steady, God pound you," the driver muttered up above. His whip whistled and popped. "Roll, you sons of dead whores! Roll on!"

Sloat grinned with the pleasure of being here, even though it would only be for moments. He already knew what he needed to know; Orris's voice had muttered it to him. The diligence would arrive at Outpost Depot—Thayer School in the other world—well before morning. It might be possible to take them there if they had lingered; if not, the Blasted Lands awaited them. It hurt and enraged him to think that Richard was now with the Sawyer brat, but if a sacrifice was demanded . . . well, Orris had lost *his* son and survived.

The only thing that had kept Jack alive this long was the maddening fact of his single nature—when the whelp flipped to a place, he was always in the analogue of the place he had left. Sloat, however, always ended up where Orris was, which might be miles away from where he needed to be . . . as was the case now. He had been lucky at the rest area, but Sawyer had been luckier.

"Your luck will run out soon enough, my little friend," Orris said. The diligence took another terrific bounce. He grimaced, then grinned. If nothing else, the situation was simplifying itself even as the final confrontation took on wider and deeper implications.

Enough.

He closed his eyes and crossed his arms. For just a moment he felt another dull thud of pain in the deformed foot . . . and when he opened his eyes, Sloat was looking up at the ceiling of his apartment. As always, there was a moment when the extra pounds fell into him with sickening weight, when his heart reacted with a surprised double-beat and then sped up.

He had gotten to his feet then and had called West Coast Business Jet. Seventy minutes later he had been leaving LAX. The Lear's steep and abrupt takeoff stance made him feel as it always did—it was as if a blowtorch had been strapped to his ass. They had touched down in Springfield at five-fifty central time, just as Orris would be approaching Outpost Depot in the

Territories. Sloat had rented a Hertz sedan and here he was. American travel *did* have its advantages.

He got out of the car and, just as the morning bells began to ring, he walked onto the Thayer campus his own son had so lately quitted.

Everything was the essence of an early Thayer weekday morning. The chapel bells were playing a normal morning tune, something classical but not quite recognizable which sounded a bit like "Te Deum" but wasn't. Students passed Sloat on their way to the dining hall or to morning workouts. They were perhaps a little more silent than usual, and they shared a look—pale and slightly dazed, as if they had all shared a disquieting dream.

Which, of course, they had, Sloat thought. He stopped for a moment in front of Nelson House, looking at it thoughtfully. They simply didn't know how fundamentally unreal they all were, as all creatures who live near the thin places between worlds must be. He walked around to the side and watched a maintenance man picking up broken glass that lay on the ground like trumpery diamonds. Beyond his bent back Sloat could see into the Nelson House lounge, where an unusually quiet Albert the Blob was sitting and looking blankly at a Bugs Bunny cartoon.

Sloat started across toward The Depot, his thoughts turning to the first time that Orris had flipped over into this world. He found himself thinking of that time with a nostalgia that was, when one really stopped to think about it, damned near grotesque—after all, he had nearly died. *Both* of them had nearly died. But it had been in the middle fifties, and now he was in *his* middle fifties—it made all the difference in the world.

He had been coming back from the office and the sun had been going down in a Los Angeles haze of smudged purples and smokey yellows—this had been in the days before the L.A. smog had really begun to thicken up. He had been on Sunset Boulevard and looking at a billboard advertising a new Peggy Lee record when he had felt a coldness in his mind. It had been as if a wellspring had suddenly opened somewhere in his subconscious, spilling out some alien weirdness that was like . . . like . . .

*(like semen)*

. . . well, he didn't know exactly *what* it had been like. Except that it had quickly become warm, gained cognizance, and he had just had time to realize it was *he*, Orris, and then everything had turned topsy-turvy like a secret door on its gimbal—a bookcase on one side, a Chippendale dresser on the other, both fitting the ambience of the room perfectly—and it had been Orris sitting behind the wheel of a 1952 bullet-nosed Ford, Orris wearing the brown double-breasted suit and the John Penske tie, Orris who was reaching down toward his crotch, not in pain but in slightly disgusted curiosity—Orris who had, of course, never worn undershorts.

There had been a moment, he remembered, when the Ford had nearly driven up onto the sidewalk, and then Morgan Sloat—now very much the undermind—had taken over that part of the operation and Orris had been free to go along his way, goggling at everything, nearly half-mad with delight. And what remained of Morgan Sloat had also been delighted; he had been delighted the way a man is delighted when he shows a friend around his new home for the first time and finds that his friend likes it as much as he likes it himself.

Orris had cruised into a Fat Boy Drive-in, and after some fumbling with Morgan's unfamiliar paper money, he had ordered a hamburger and french fries and a chocolate thickshake, the words coming easily out of his mouth—welling up from that undermind as water wells up from a spring. Orris's first bite of the hamburger had been tentative . . . and then he had gobbled the rest with the speed of Wolf gobbling his first Whopper. He had crammed the fries into his mouth with one hand while dialling the radio with the other, picking up an enticing babble of bop and Perry Como and some big band and early rhythm and blues. He had sucked down the shake and then had ordered more of everything.

Halfway through the second burger he—Sloat as well as Orris—began to feel sick. Suddenly the fried onions had seemed too strong, too cloying; suddenly the smell of car exhaust was everywhere. His arms had suddenly begun to itch madly. He pulled off the coat of the double-breasted suit (the second thick-shake, this one mocha, fell unheeded to one side, dribbling ice cream across the Ford's seat) and looked at his arms. Ugly red blotches with red centers were growing there, and spreading. His stomach lurched, he leaned out the window, and even as he puked into the tray that was fixed there, he had felt Orris fleeing from him, going back into his own world. . . .

"Can I help you, sir?"

"Hmmmm?" Startled out of his reverie, Sloat looked around. A tall blond boy, obviously an upperclassman, was standing there. He was dressed prep—an impeccable blue flannel blazer worn over an open-collared shirt and a pair of faded Levi's.

He brushed hair out of his eyes which had that same dazed, dreaming look. "I'm Etheridge, sir. I just wondered if I could help you. You looked . . . lost."

Sloat smiled. He thought of saying—but did not—*No, that's how you look, my friend*. Everything was all right. The Sawyer brat was still on the loose, but Sloat knew where he was going and that meant that Jacky was on a chain. It was invisible, but it was still a chain.

"Lost in the past, that's all," he said. "Old times. I'm not a stranger here, Mr. Etheridge, if that's what you're worried about. My son's a student. Richard Sloat."

Etheridge's eyes grew even dreamier for a moment—puzzled, lost. Then they cleared. "Sure. Richard!" he exclaimed.

"I'll be going up to see the headmaster in a bit. I just wanted to have a poke around first."

"Well, I guess that's fine." Etheridge looked at his watch. "I have table-duty this morning, so if you're sure you're okay . . ."

"I'm sure."

Etheridge gave him a nod, a rather vague smile, and started off.

Sloat watched him go, and then he surveyed the ground between Nelson House and here. Noted the broken window again. A straight shot. It was fair—more than fair—to assume that, somewhere between Nelson House and this octagonal brick building, the two boys had Migrated into the Territories. If he liked, he could follow them. Just step inside—there was no lock on the door—and disappear. Reappear wherever Orris's body happened to be at this moment. It would be somewhere close; perhaps even, in fact, in front of the depot-keeper himself. No nonsense about Migrating to a spot which might be a hundred miles away from the point of interest in Territories geography and no way to cover the intervening distance but by wagon or, worse, what his father had called shanks' mare.

The boys would already have gone on, in all likelihood. Into the Blasted Lands. If so, the Blasted Lands would finish them. And Sunlight Gardener's Twinner, Osmond, would be more than capable of squeezing out all the information that Anders knew. Osmond and his horrid son. No need to Migrate at all.

Except maybe for a look-see. For the pleasure and refreshment of becoming Orris again, if only for a few seconds.

And to Make Sure, of course. His entire life, from childhood onward, had been an exercise in Making Sure.

He looked around once to assure himself that Etheridge had not lingered; then he opened the door of The Depot and went inside.

The smell was stale, dark, and incredibly nostalgic—the smell of old makeup and canvas flats. For a moment he had the crazy idea that he had done something even more incredible than Migrating; he felt that he might have travelled back through time to those undergraduate days when he and Phil Sawyer had been theater-mad college students.

Then his eyes adjusted to the dimness and he saw the unfamiliar, almost mawkish props—a plaster bust of Pallas for a production of *The Raven*, an extravagantly gilt birdcage, a bookcase full of false bindings—and remembered that he was in the Thayer School excuse for a "little theater."

He paused for a moment, breathing deeply of the dust; he turned his eyes up to one dusty sunray falling through a small window. The light wavered and was suddenly a deeper gold, the color of lamplight. He was in the Territories. Just like that, he was in the Territories. There was a moment of almost staggering exhilaration at the speed of the change. Usually there was a pause, a sense of sideslipping from one place to another. This caesura seemed to be in direct proportion to the distance between the physical bodies of his two selves, Sloat and Orris. Once, when he had Migrated from Japan, where he was negotiating a deal with the Shaw brothers for a terrible novel about Hollywood stars menaced by a crazed ninja, the pause had gone on so long that he had feared he might be lost forever somewhere in the empty, senseless purgatory that exists between the worlds. But this time they had been close . . . so close! It was like those few times, he thought

*(Orris thought)*

when a man and woman achieve orgasm at the exact same instant and die in sex together.

The smell of dried paint and canvas was replaced with the light, pleasant smell of Territories burning-oil. The lamp on the table was guttering low, sending out dark membranes of smoke. To his left a table was set, the remains of a meal congealing on the rough plates. Three plates.

Orris stepped forward, dragging his clubfoot a little as always. He tipped one of the plates up, let the guttering lamplight skate queasily across the grease. *Who ate from this one? Was it Anders, or Jason, or Richard . . . the boy who would also have been Rushton if my son had lived?*

Rushton had drowned while swimming in a pond not far from the Great House. There had been a picnic. Orris and his wife had drunk a quantity of wine. The sun had been hot. The boy, little more than an infant, had been napping. Orris and his wife had made love and then they had also fallen asleep in the sweet afternoon sunshine. He had been awakened by the child's cries. Rushton had awakened and gone down to the water. He had been able to dog-paddle a little, just enough to get well out beyond his depth before panicking. Orris had limped to the water, dived in, and swum as fast as he could out to where the boy floundered. It was his foot, his damned foot, that had hampered him and perhaps cost his son his life. When he reached the boy, he had been sinking. Orris had managed to catch him by the hair and pull him to shore . . . but by then Rushton had been blue and dead.

Margaret had died by her own hand less than six weeks later.

Seven months after that, Morgan Sloat's own young son had nearly drowned in a Westwood YMCA pool during a Young Paddlers class. He had been pulled from the pool as blue and dead as Rushton . . . but the lifeguard had applied mouth-to-mouth resuscitation, and Richard Sloat had responded.

*God pounds His nails,* Orris thought, and then a deep, blurry snore snapped his head around.

Anders, the depot-keeper, lay on a pallet in the corner with his kilt rudely pulled up to his breeks. An earthen jug of wine lay overturned nearby. Much of the wine had flowed into his hair.

He snored again, then moaned, as if with bad dreams.

*No dream you might have could be as bad as your future now is,* Orris thought grimly. He took a step closer, his cloak flapping around him. He looked down on Anders with no pity.

Sloat was able to plan murder, but it had been Orris, time and time again, who had Migrated to carry out the act itself. It had been Orris in Sloat's body who had attempted to smother the infant Jack Sawyer with a pillow while a wrestling announcer droned on and on in the background. Orris who had overseen the assassination of Phil Sawyer in Utah (just as he had overseen the assassination of Phil Sawyer's counterpart, the commoner Prince Philip Sawtelle, in the Territories).

Sloat had a taste for blood, but ultimately he was as allergic to it as Orris was to American food and American air. It was Morgan of Orris, once derided as Morgan Thudfoot, who had always done the deeds Sloat had planned.

*My son died; his still lives. Sawtelle's son died. Sawyer's still lives. But these things can be remedied.* Will *be remedied. No Talisman for you, my sweet little friends. You are bound for a radioactive version of Oatley, and you each owe the balance-scales a death. God pounds His nails.*

"And if God doesn't, you may be sure I will," he said aloud.

The man on the floor moaned again, as if he had heard. Orris took another step toward him, perhaps meaning to kick him awake, and then cocked his head. In the distance he heard hoofbeats, the faint creak and jingle of harness, the hoarse cries of drovers.

That would be Osmond, then. Good. Let Osmond take care of business here—he himself had little interest in questioning a man with a hangover when he knew well enough what the man would have to say.

Orris clumped across to the door, opened it, and looked out on a gorgeous peach-colored Territories sunrise. It was from this direction—the direction of the sunrise—that the sounds of approaching riders came. He allowed himself to drink in that lovely glow for a moment and then turned toward the west again, where the sky was still the color of a fresh bruise. The land was dark . . . except for where the first sunlight bounced off a pair of bright parallel lines.

*Boys, you have gone to your deaths,* Orris thought with satisfaction . . . and then a thought occurred which brought even more satisfaction: their deaths might already have happened.

"Good," Orris said, and closed his eyes.

A moment later Morgan Sloat was gripping the handle of the door of Thayer School's little theater, opening his own eyes, and planning his trip back to the west coast.

It might be time to take a little trip down memory lane, he thought. To a town in California called Point Venuti. A trip back east first, perhaps—a visit to the Queen—and then . . .

"The sea air," he said to the bust of Pallas, "will do me good."

He ducked back inside, had another jolt from the small vial in his pocket (hardly noticing the smells of canvas and makeup now), and, thus refreshed, he started back downhill toward his car.

# FOUR

# THE TALISMAN

# 34

# Anders

## 1

Jack suddenly realized that, although he was still running, he was running on thin air, like a cartoon character who has time for one surprised double-take before plunging two thousand feet straight down. But it wasn't two thousand feet. He had time—just—to realize that the ground wasn't there anymore, and then he dropped four or five feet, still running. He wobbled and might have remained upright, but then Richard came piling into him and they both went tumbling.

*"Look out, Jack!"* Richard was screaming—he was apparently not interested in taking his own advice, because his eyes were squeezed tightly shut. *"Look out for the wolf! Look out for Mr. Dufrey! Look out—"*

"Stop it, Richard!" These breathless screams frightened him more than anything else had done. Richard sounded mad, absolutely mad. "Stop it, we're all right! They're gone!"

*"Look out for Etheridge! Look out for the bugs! Look out, Jack!"*

"Richard, they're *gone!* Look around you, for Jason's sake!" Jack hadn't had a chance to do this himself, but he knew they had made it—the air was still and sweet, the night perfectly silent except for a slim breeze that was blessedly warm.

*"Look out, Jack! Look out, Jack! Look out, look out—"*

Like a bad echo inside his head, he heard a memory of the dog-boys outside Nelson House chorusing *Way-gup, way-gup, way-gup! Pleeze, pleeze, pleeze!*

*"Look out, Jack!"* Richard wailed. His face was slammed into the earth and he looked like an overenthusiastic Moslem determined to get in good with Allah. *"LOOK OUT! THE WOLF! PREFECTS! THE HEADMASTER! LOOK O—"*

Panicked by the idea that Richard actually *had* gone crazy,

Jack yanked his friend's head up by the back of his collar and slapped his face.

Richard's words were cut cleanly off. He gaped at Jack, and Jack saw the shape of his own hand rising on Richard's pale cheek, a dim red tattoo. His shame was replaced by an urgent curiosity to know just where they were. There was light; otherwise he wouldn't have been able to see that mark.

A partial answer to the question came from inside him—it was certain and unquestionable . . . at least, as far as it went.

*The Outposts, Jack-O. You're in the Outposts now.*

But before he could spend any time mulling that over, he had to try to get Richard shipshape.

"Are you all right, Richie?"

He was looking at Jack with numb, hurt surprise. "You hit me, Jack."

"I slapped you. That's what you're supposed to do with hysterical people."

"I wasn't hysterical! I've never been hysterical in my l—" Richard broke off and jumped to his feet, looking around wildly. "The wolf! We have to look out for the wolf, Jack! If we can get over the fence he won't be able to get us!"

He would have gone sprinting off into the darkness right then, making for a cyclone fence which was now in another world, if Jack hadn't grabbed him and held him back.

"The wolf is gone, Richard."

"Huh?"

"We made it."

":What are you talking about—"

"The Territories, Richard! We're in the Territories! We flipped over!" *And you almost pulled my damn arm out of its socket, you unbeliever,* Jack thought, rubbing his throbbing shoulder. *The next time I try to haul someone across, I'm going to find myself a real little kid, one who still believes in Santa Claus and the Easter Bunny.*

"That's ridiculous," Richard said slowly. "There's no such thing as the Territories, Jack."

"If there isn't," Jack said grimly, "then how come that great big white wolf isn't biting your ass? Or your own damn headmaster?"

Richard looked at Jack, opened his mouth to say something, then closed it again. He looked around, this time with a bit more attention (at least Jack hoped so). Jack did the same, enjoying the warmth and the clarity of the air as he did so. Morgan and his crowd of snake-pit crazies might come bursting through at any second, but for now it was impossible not to luxuriate in the pure animal joy of being back here again.

They were in a field. High, yellowish grass with bearded heads—not wheat, but something like wheat; some edible grain, anyway—stretched off into the night in every direction. The warm breeze rippled it in mysterious but rather lovely waves. To the right was a wooden building standing on a slight knoll, a lamp mounted on a pole in front of it. A yellow flame almost too bright to look at burned clearly inside the lamp's glass globe. Jack saw that the building was octagonal. The two boys had come into the Territories on the outermost edge of the circle of light that lamp threw—and there was something on the far side of the circle, something metallic that threw back the lamplight in broken glimmers. Jack squinted at the faint, silvery glow . . . and then understood. What he felt was not so much wonder as a sense of fulfilled expection. It was as if two very large jigsaw-puzzle pieces, one in the American Territories and one over here, had just come neatly together.

Those were railroad tracks. And although it was impossible to tell direction in the darkness, Jack thought he knew in which direction those tracks would travel:

West.

## 2

"Come on," Jack said.

"I don't want to go up there," Richard said.

"Why not?"

"Too much crazy stuff going on." Richard wet his lips. "Could be anything up there in that building. Dogs. Crazy people." He wet his lips again. "Bugs."

"I told you, we're in the Territories now. The craziness has all blown away—it's clean here. Hell, Richard, can't you *smell* it?"

"There are no such things as *Territories*," Richard said thinly.

"Look around you."

"No," Richard said. His voice was thinner than ever, the voice of an infuriatingly stubborn child.

Jack snatched up a handful of the heavily bearded grass. "Look at this!"

Richard turned his head.

Jack had to actively restrain an urge to shake him.

Instead of doing that, he tossed the grass away, counted mentally to ten, and then started up the hill. He looked down and saw that he was now wearing something like leather chaps. Richard was dressed in much the same way, and he had a red bandanna around his neck that looked like something out of a Frederic Remington painting. Jack reached up to his own neck and felt a similar bandanna. He ran his hands down along his body and discovered that Myles P. Kiger's wonderfully warm coat was now something very like a Mexican serape. *I bet I look like an advertisement for Taco Bell,* he thought, and grinned.

An expression of utter panic came over Richard's face when Jack started up the hill, leaving him alone at the bottom.

"Where are you going?"

Jack looked at Richard and came back. He put his hands on Richard's shoulders and looked soberly into Richard's eyes.

"We can't stay here," he said. "Some of them must have seen us flip. It may be that they can't come right after us, or it may be that they can. I don't know. I know as much about the laws governing all of this as a kid of five knows about magnetism—and all a kid of five knows on the subject is that sometimes magnets attract and sometimes they repel. But for the time being, that's all I have to know. We have to get out of here. End of story."

"I'm dreaming all this, I know I am."

Jack nodded toward the ramshackle wooden building. "You can come or you can stay here. If you want to stay here, I'll come back for you after I check the place out."

"None of this is happening," Richard said. His naked, glassesless eyes were wide and flat and somehow dusty. He looked for a moment up at the black Territories sky with its strange and unfamiliar sprawl of stars, shuddered, and looked away. "I have a fever. It's the flu. There's been a lot of flu around. This is a delirium. You're guest-starring in my delirium, Jack."

"Well, I'll send somebody around to the Delirium Actors' Guild with my AFTRA card when I get a chance," Jack said. "In the meantime, why don't you just stay here, Richard? If none of this is happening, then you have nothing to worry about."

He started away again, thinking that it would take only a few more of these Alice-at-the-tea-party conversations with Richard to convince him that *he* was crazy, as well.

He was halfway up the hill when Richard joined him.

"I would have come back for you," Jack said.

"I know," Richard said. "I just thought that I might as well come along. As long as all of this is a dream, anyway."

"Well, keep your mouth shut if there's anyone up there," Jack said. "I think there is—I think I saw someone looking out that front window at me."

"What are you going to do?" Richard asked.

Jack smiled. "Play it by ear, Richie-boy," he said. "That's what I've been doing ever since I left New Hampshire. Playing it by ear."

### 3

They reached the porch. Richard clutched Jack's shoulder with panicky strength. Jack turned toward him wearily; Richard's patented Kansas City Clutch was something else that was getting old in a big hurry.

"What?" Jack asked.

"This is a dream, all right," Richard said, "and I can prove it."

"How?"

*"We're not talking English anymore, Jack! We're talking some language, and we're speaking it perfectly, but it's not English!"*

"Yeah," Jack said. "Weird, isn't it?"

He started up the steps again, leaving Richard standing below him, gape-mouthed.

### 4

After a moment or two, Richard recovered and scrambled up the steps after Jack. The boards were warped and loose and splintery. Stalks of that richly bearded grain-grass grew up through some of them. Off in the deep darkness, both boys could hear the sleepy hum of insects—it was not the reedy scratch of crickets but a sweeter sound—so much was sweeter over here, Jack thought.

The outside lamp was now behind them; their shadows ran ahead of them across the porch and then made right-angles to climb the door. There was an old, faded sign on that door. For a moment it seemed to Jack to be written in strange Cyrillic letters, as indecipherable as Russian. Then they came clear, and the word was no surprise. DEPOT.

Jack raised his hand to knock, then shook his head a little. No. He would not knock. This was not a private dwelling; the sign said DEPOT, and that was a word he associated with public buildings—places to wait for Greyhound buses and Amtrak trains, loading zones for the Friendly Skies.

He pushed the door open. Friendly lamplight and a decidedly unfriendly voice came out onto the porch together.

*"Get away, ye devil!"* the cracked voice screeched. *"Get away, I'm going in the morning! I swear! The train's in the shed! Go away! I swore I'd go and I will go, s'now YE go . . . go and leave me some peace!"*

Jack frowned. Richard gaped. The room was clean but very old. The boards were so warped that the walls seemed almost to ripple. A picture of a stagecoach which looked almost as big as a whaling ship hung on one wall. An ancient counter, its flat surface almost as ripply as the walls, ran across the middle of the room, splitting it in two. Behind it, on the far wall, was a slate board with STAGE ARRIVES written above one column and STAGE LEAVES written above the other. Looking at the ancient board, Jack guessed it had been a good long time since any information had been written there; he thought that if someone tried to write on it with even a piece of soft chalk, the slate would crack in pieces and fall to the weathered floor.

Standing on one side of the counter was the biggest hourglass Jack had ever seen—it was as big as a magnum of champagne and filled with green sand.

*"Leave me alone, can't you? I've promised ye I'd go, and I will! Please, Morgan! For yer mercy! I've promised, and if ye don't believe me, look in the shed! The train is ready, I swear the train is ready!"*

There was a good deal more gabble and gobble in this same vein. The large, elderly man spouting it was cringing in the far right-hand corner of the room. Jack guessed the oldster's height at six-three at least—even in his present servile posture, The Depot's low ceiling was only four inches or so above his head. He might have been seventy; he might have been a fairly well-preserved eighty. A snowy white beard began under his eyes and cascaded down over his breast in a spray of baby fine hair. His shoulders were broad, although now so slumped that they looked as if someone had broken them by forcing him to carry heavy weights over the course of many long years. Deep crow's-feet radiated out from the corners of his eyes; deep fissures undulated on his forehead. His complexion was waxy-yellow. He was wearing a white kilt shot through with bright scarlet threads, and he was obviously scared almost to death. He was brandishing a stout staff, but with no authority at all.

Jack glanced sharply around at Richard when the old man mentioned the name of Richard's father, but Richard was currently beyond noticing such fine points.

"I am not who you think I am," Jack said, advancing toward the old man.

*"Get away!"* he shrieked. *"None of yer guff! I guess the devil can put on a pleasing face! Get away! I'll do it! She's ready to go, first thing in the morning! I said I'd do it and I mean to, now get away, can't ye?"*

The knapsack was now a haversack hanging from Jack's arm. As Jack reached the counter, he rummaged in it, pushing aside the mirror and a number of the jointed money-sticks. His fingers closed around what he wanted and brought it out. It was the coin Captain Farren had given him so long ago, the coin with the Queen on one side and the gryphon on the other. He slammed it down on the counter, and the room's mellow light caught the lovely profile of Laura DeLoessian—again he was struck with wonder by the similarity of that profile to the profile of his mother. *Did they look that much alike at the beginning? Is it just that I see the similarities more as I think about them more? Or am I actually bringing them together somehow, making them one?*

The old man cringed back even farther as Jack came forward to the counter; it began to seem as though he might push himself right through the back of the building. His words began to pour out in a hysterical flood. When Jack slammed the coin down on the counter like a badman in a Western movie demanding a drink, he suddenly stopped talking. He stared at the coin, his eyes widening, the spit-shiny corners of his mouth twitching. His widening eyes rose to Jack's face and really saw him for the first time.

"Jason," he whispered in a trembling voice. Its former weak bluster was gone. It trembled now not with fear but with awe. "Jason!"

"No," he said. "My name is—" Then he stopped, realizing that the word which would come out in this strange language was not *Jack* but—

*"Jason!"* the old man cried, and fell on his knees. "Jason, ye've come! Ye've come and a' wi' be well, aye, a' wi' be well, a' wi' be well, and a' manner a' things wi' be well!"

"Hey," Jack said. "Hey, really—"

*"Jason! Jason's come and the Queen'll be well, aye, a' manner a' things wi' be well!"*

Jack, less prepared to cope with this weepy adoration than he had been to deal with the old depot-keeper's terrified truculence, turned toward Richard . . . but there was no help there. Richard had stretched out on the floor to the left of the door and had either gone to sleep or was giving a damned good facsimile thereof.

"Oh *shit,*" Jack groaned.

The old man was on his knees, babbling and weeping. The situation was rapidly passing from the realms of the merely ridiculous into those of the cosmically comic. Jack found a flip-up partition and went behind the counter.

"Ah, rise, you good and faithful servant," Jack said. He wondered blackly if Christ or Buddha had ever had problems like this. "On your feet, fella."

*"Jason! Jason!"* the old man sobbed. His white hair obscured Jack's sandaled feet as he bent over them and began to kiss them—they weren't little kisses, either, but good old spooning-in-the-hayloft smackers. Jack began to giggle helplessly. He had managed to get them out of Illinois, and here they were in a ramshackle depot at the center of a great field of grain which wasn't quite wheat, somewhere

in the Outposts, and Richard was sleeping by the door, and this strange old man was kissing his feet and his beard tickled.

"*Rise!*" Jack yelled, giggling. He tried to step back but hit the counter. "*Rise up, O good servant! Get on your frigging feet, get up, that's enough!*"

"*Jason!*" Smack! "*A' wi' be well!*" Smack-smack!

*And a' manner a' things wi' be well,* Jack thought crazily, giggling as the old man kissed his toes through the sandals. *I didn't know they read Robert Burns over here in the Territories, but I guess they must—*

*Smack-smack-smack.*

*Oh, no more of this, I really can't stand it.*

"*RISE!*" he bellowed at the top of his voice, and the old man finally stood before him, trembling and weeping, unable to meet Jack's eye. But his amazingly broad shoulders had come up a bit, had lost that broken look, and Jack was obscurely glad of that.

5

It was an hour or better before Jack could manage a coherent run of conversation with the old man. They would *begin* talking, and then Anders, who was a liveryman by trade, would go off on another of his O-Jason-my-Jason-how-great-thou-art jags and Jack would have to quiet him down as quickly as he could . . . certainly before the feet-kissing started again. Jack liked the old man, however, and sympathized. In order to sympathize, all he had to do was imagine how he would feel if Jesus or Buddha turned up at the local car-wash or in the school lunch line. And he had to acknowledge one other clear and present fact: there was a part of him which was not entirely surprised by Anders's attitude. Although he felt like Jack, he was coming more and more to also feel like . . . the other one.

*But he'd died.*

That was true; undeniably true. Jason had died, and Morgan of Orris had probably had something to do with his death. But guys like Jason had a way of coming back, didn't they?

Jack considered the time it took to get Anders talking well spent if only because it allowed him to be sure that Richard wasn't shamming; that he really had gone back to sleep again. This was good, because Anders had a lot to say about Morgan.

Once, he said, this had been the last stage depot in the known world—it went by the euphonious name of Outpost Depot. Beyond here, he said, the world became a monstrous place.

"Monstrous how?" Jack asked.

"I don't know," Anders said, lighting his pipe. He looked out into the darkness, and his face was bleak. "There are stories about the Blasted Lands, but each is apt to be different from each, and they always begin something like 'I know a man who met a man who was lost on the edge of the Blasted Lands for three days and he said . . .' But I never heard a story that begun '*I* was lost on the edge of the Blasted Lands for three days and *I* say . . .' Ye ken the difference, Jason my Lord?"

"I ken it," Jack said slowly. *The Blasted Lands.* Just the sound of that had raised the hairs on his arms and the nape of his neck. "No one knows what they are, then?"

"Not for sure," Anders said. "But if even a quarter of what I've heard is true—"

"What have you heard?"

"That there are monstrosities out there that makes the things in Orris's ore-pits look almost normal. That there are balls of fire that go rolling across the hills and empty places, leaving long black trails behind them—the trails are black in the daytime, anyway, but I've heard they glow at night. And if a man gets too close to one of those fireballs, he gets turrible sick. He loses his hair, and sores're apt to raise all over his body, and then he begins to vomit; and mayhap he gets better, but more often he only vomits and vomits until his stomach ruptures and his throat bursts and then . . ."

Anders rose.

"My Lord! Why d'ye look so? Have y'seen something out the window? Have y'seen a spook along those double-damned tracks?"

Anders looked wildly toward the window.

*Radiation poisoning,* Jack thought. *He doesn't know it, but he's described the symptoms of radiation poisoning almost to a* T.

They had studied both nuclear weapons and the consequences of exposure to radiation in a physical science mod the year before—because his mother was at least casually involved in both the nuclear-freeze movement and the movement to prevent the proliferation of nuclear power plants, Jack had paid very close attention.

How well, he thought, how well radiation poisoning fit with the whole idea of the Blasted Lands! And then he realized something else, as well: the west was where the first tests had been carried out—where the prototype of the Hiroshima bomb had been hung from a tower and then exploded, where any number of suburbs inhabited only by department-store mannequins had been destroyed so the Army could get a more or less accurate idea of what a nuclear explosion and the resulting firestorm would really do. And in the end they had returned to Utah and Nevada, among the last of the *real* American Territories, and had simply resumed testing underground. There was, he knew, a lot of government land out there in those great wastes, those tangles of buttes and mesas and crenellated badlands, and bombs were not all they were testing out there.

How much of that shit would Sloat bring over here if the Queen died? How much of that shit had he *already* brought? Was this stageline-*cum*-railhead part of the shipping system for it?

"Ye don't look good, my Lord, not at all. Ye look as white as a sheet; I'll take an oath that ye do!"

"I'm fine," Jack said slowly. "Sit down. Go on with your story. And light your pipe, it's gone out."

Anders took his pipe from his mouth, relit it, and looked from Jack to the window again . . . and now his face was not just bleak; it was haggard with fright. "But I'll know soon enough if the stories are true, I suppose."

"Why is that?"

"Because I start through the Blasted Lands tomorrow morning, at first light," Anders said. "I start through the Blasted Lands, driving Morgan of Orris's devil-machine in yon shed, and carrying God alone knows what sort of hideous devil's work."

Jack stared at him, his heart pumping hard, the blood humming in his head.

"Where? How far? To the ocean? The big water?"

Anders nodded slowly. "Aye," he said. "To the water. And—" His voice dropped, became a strengthless whisper. His eyes rolled toward the dark windows, as if he feared some nameless thing might be peering in, watching, eavesdropping.

"And there Morgan will meet me, and we're to take his goods on."

"On to where?" Jack asked.

"To the black hotel," Anders finished in a low, trembling voice.

## 6

Jack felt the urge to break into wild cackles of laughter again. *The Black Hotel*—it sounded like the title of a lurid mystery novel. And yet . . . and yet . . . all of this had begun at a hotel, hadn't it? The Alhambra in New Hampshire, on the Atlantic coast. Was there some other hotel, perhaps even another rambling old Victorian monstrosity of a hotel, on the Pacific coast? Was that where his long, strange adventure was supposed to end? In some analogue of the Alhambra and with a seedy amusement park close at hand? This idea was terribly persuasive; in an odd, yet precise way, it even seemed to pick up the idea of Twinners and Twinning . . .

"Why do ye look at me so, my Lord?"

Anders sounded agitated and upset. Jack shifted his gaze away quickly. "I'm sorry," he said. "I was just thinking."

He smiled reassuringly, and the liveryman smiled tentatively back at him.

"And I wish you'd stop calling me that."

"Calling ye what, my Lord?"

"My Lord."

"My Lord?" Anders looked puzzled. He was not echoing what Jack had said but asking for clarification. Jack had a feeling that if he tried to push on with this, he would end up in the middle of a "Who's on first, What's on second" sort of sketch.

"Never mind," Jack said. He leaned forward. "I want you to tell me everything. Can you do that?"

"I'll try, my Lord," Anders said.

## 7

His words came slowly at first. He was a single man who had spent his entire life in the Outposts and he was not used to talking much at the best of times. Now he had been commanded to speak by a boy whom he considered to be at least royalty, and perhaps even something like a god. But, little by little, his words began to come faster, and by the end of his inconclusive but terribly provocative tale, the words were nearly pouring out. Jack had no trouble following the tale he told in spite of the man's accent, which his mind kept translating into a sort of ersatz Robert Burns burr.

Anders knew Morgan because Morgan was, quite simply, Lord of the Outposts. His real title, Morgan of Orris, was not so grand, but as a practical matter, the two came to nearly the same. Orris was the easternmost cantonment of the Outposts, and the only really organized part of that large, grassy area. Because he ruled Orris utterly and completely, Morgan ruled the rest of the Outposts by default. Also, the bad Wolfs had begun to gravitate to Morgan in the last fifteen years or so. At first that meant little, because there were only a few bad (except the word Anders used also sounded a bit like *rabid* to Jack's ear) Wolfs. But in later years there had been more and more of them, and Anders said he had heard tales that, since the Queen had fallen ill, more than half the tribe of skin-turning shepherds were rotten with the sickness. Nor were these the only creatures at Morgan of Orris's command, Anders said; there were others, even worse—some, it was told, could drive a man mad at a single look.

Jack thought of Elroy, the bogeyman of the Oatley Tap, and shuddered.

"Does this part of the Outposts we're in have a name?" Jack asked.

"My Lord?"

"This part we're in now."

"No real name, my Lord, but I've heard people call it Ellis-Breaks."

"Ellis-Breaks," Jack said. A picture of Territories geography, vague and probably in many ways incorrect, was finally beginning to take shape in Jack's mind. There were the Territories, which corresponded to the American east; the Outposts, which corresponded to the American midwest and great plains (Ellis-Breaks? Illinois? Nebraska?); and the Blasted Lands, which corresponded to the American west.

He looked at Anders so long and so fixedly that at last the liveryman began to stir uneasily again. "I'm sorry," Jack said. "Go on."

His father, Anders said, had been the last stage driver who "drove out east" from Outpost Depot. Anders had been his 'prentice. But even in those days, he said, there were great confusions and upheavals in the east; the murder of the old King and the short war which had followed it had seen the beginning of those upheavals, and although the war had ended with the installation of Good Queen Laura, the upheavals had gone on ever since, seeming to work their way steadily eastward, out of the spoiled and twisted Blasted Lands. There were some, Anders said, who believed the evil had begun all the way west.

"I'm not sure I understand you," Jack said, although in his heart he thought he did.

"At land's end," Anders said. "At the edge of the big water, where I am bound to go."

*In other words, it began in the same place my father came from . . . my father, and me, and Richard . . . and Morgan. Old Bloat.*

The troubles, Anders said, had come to the Outposts, and now the Wolf tribe was partly rotten—just how rotten none could say, but the liveryman told Jack he was afraid that the rot would be the end of them if it didn't stop soon. The upheavals had come here, and now they had even reached the east, where, he had heard, the Queen lay ill and near death.

"That's not true, is it, my Lord?" Anders asked . . . almost begged.

Jack looked at him. "Should I know how to answer that?" he asked.

"Of course," Anders said. "Are ye not her son?"

For a moment, the entire world seemed to become very

quiet. The sweet hum of the bugs outside stilled. Richard seemed to pause between heavy, sluggish breaths.

Even his own heart seemed to pause . . . perhaps that most of all.

Then, his voice perfectly even, he said, "Yes . . . I am her son. And it's true . . . she's very ill."

"But dying?" Anders persisted, his eyes nakedly pleading now. "Is she dying, my Lord?"

Jack smiled a little and said: "That remains to be seen."

## 8

Anders said that until the troubles began, Morgan of Orris had been a little-known frontier lord and no more; he had inherited his comic-opera title from a father who had been a greasy, evil-smelling buffoon. Morgan's father had been something of a laughing-stock while alive, Anders went on, and had even been a laughing-stock in his manner of dying.

"He was taken with the squitters after a day of drinking peach-fruit wine and died while on the trots."

People had been prepared to make the old man's son a laughing-stock as well, but the laughing had stopped soon after the hangings in Orris began. And when the troubles began in the years after the death of the old King, Morgan had risen in importance as a star of evil omen rises in the sky.

All of this meant little this far out in the Outposts—these great empty spaces, Anders said, made politics seem unimportant. Only the deadly change in the Wolf tribe made a practical difference to them, and since most of the bad Wolfs went to the Other Place, even that didn't make much difference to them ("It fashes us little, my Lord" was what Jack's ears insisted they had heard).

Then, not long after the news of the Queen's illness had reached this far west, Morgan had sent out a crew of grotesque, twisted slaves from the ore-pits back east; these slaves were tended by stolen Wolfs and other, stranger creatures. Their foreman was a terrible man who carried a whip; he had been here almost constantly when the work began, but then he had disappeared. Anders, who had spent most of those terrible weeks and months cowering in his house, which was some five miles south of here, had been delighted to see him go. He had heard rumors that Morgan had called the man with the whip back east, where affairs were reaching some great point of climax; Anders didn't know if this was true or not, and didn't care. He was simply glad that the man, who was sometimes accompanied by a scrawny, somehow gruesome-looking little boy, was gone.

"His name," Jack demanded. "What was his name?"

"My Lord, I don't know. The Wolfs called him He of the Lashes. The slaves just called him the devil. I'd say they were both right."

"Did he dress like a dandy? Velvet coats? Shoes with buckles on the tops, maybe?"

Anders was nodding.

"Did he wear a lot of strong perfume?"

"Aye! Aye, he did!"

"And the whip had little rawhide strings with metal caps on them."

"Aye, my Lord. An evil whip. And he was fearsome good with it, aye, he was."

*It was Osmond. It was Sunlight Gardener. He was here, overseeing some project for Morgan . . . then the Queen got sick and Osmond was called back to the summer palace, where I first made his cheerful acquaintance.*

"His son," Jack said. "What did his son look like?"

"Skinny," Anders said slowly. "One eye was afloat. That's all I can remember. He . . . my Lord, the Whipman's son was hard to see. The Wolfs seemed more afraid of him than of his father, although the son carried no whip. They said he was *dim*."

"Dim," Jack mused.

"Yes. It is their word for one who is hard to see, no matter how hard ye look for that one. Invisibility is impossible—so the Wolfs say—but one can make himself *dim* if only he knows the trick of it. Most Wolfs do, and this little whoreson knew it, too. So all I remember is how thin he was, and that floating eye, and that he was as ugly as black, syphilitic sin."

Anders paused.

"He liked to hurt things. Little things. He used to take them under the porch and I'd hear the most awful screams. . . ." Anders shuddered. "That was one of the reasons I kept to my house, you know. I don't like to hear wee animals in pain. Makes me feel turrible bad, it does."

Everything Anders said raised a hundred fresh questions in Jack's mind. He would particularly have liked to know all that Anders knew about the Wolfs—just hearing of them woke simultaneous pleasure and a deep, dully painful longing for *his* Wolf in his heart.

But time was short; this man was scheduled to drive west into the Blasted Lands in the morning, a horde of crazy scholars led by Morgan himself might burst through from what the liveryman called the Other Place at any moment, Richard might wake up and want to know who this Morgan was they were discussing, and who this *dim* fellow was—this *dim* fellow who sounded suspiciously like the fellow who had lived next door to him in Nelson House.

"They came," he prompted, "this crew came, and Osmond was their foreman—at least until he was called away or whenever he had to lead the devotions at night-chapel back in Indiana—"

"My Lord?" Anders's face was again ponderous with puzzlement.

"They came, and they built . . . what?" He was sure he already knew the answer to this, but he wanted to hear Anders himself say it.

"Why, the tracks," Anders said. "The tracks going west into the Blasted Lands. The tracks I must travel myself tomorrow." He shuddered.

"No," Jack said. A hot, terrible excitement exploded in his chest like a sun, and he rose to his feet. Again there was that click in his head, that terrible, persuasive feeling of great things coming together.

Anders fell on his knees with a crash as a terrible, beautiful light filled Jack's face. Richard stirred at the sound and sat sleepily up.

"Not you," Jack said. "Me. And him." He pointed at Richard.

"Jack?" Richard looked at him with sleepy, nearsighted confusion. "What are you talking about? And why is that man sniffing the floor?"

"My Lord . . . yer will, of course . . . but I don't understand. . . ."

"Not you," Jack said, "us. We'll take the train for you."

"But my Lord, why?" Anders managed, not yet daring to look up.

Jack Sawyer looked out into the darkness.

"Because," he said, "I think there's something at the end of the tracks—at the end of the tracks or near the end—that I have to get."

Interlude

# Sloat in This World (IV)

On the tenth of December, a bundled-up Morgan Sloat was sitting on the uncomfortable little wooden chair beside Lily Sawyer's bed—he was cold, so he had his heavy cashmere coat wrapped around him and his hands thrust deep into its pockets, but he was having a much better time than his appearance suggested. Lily was dying. She was going out, away, to that place from which you never came back, not even if you were a Queen in a football field–sized bed.

Lily's bed was not so grand, and she did not in the least resemble a Queen. Illness had subtracted her good looks, had skinned down her face and aged her a quick twenty years. Sloat let his eyes roam appreciatively over the prominent ridges of bone about her eyes, the tortoiselike shell of her forehead. Her ravaged body barely made a lump beneath the sheets and blankets. Sloat knew that the Alhambra had been well paid to leave Lily Cavanaugh Sawyer alone, for it was he who had paid them. They no longer bothered to send heat up to her room. She was the hotel's only guest. Besides the desk clerk and cook, the only employees still in the Alhambra were three Portuguese maids who spent all their time cleaning the lobby—it must have been the maids who kept Lily piled high with blankets. Sloat himself had commandeered the suite across the hall, and ordered the desk clerk and the maids to keep a close eye on Lily.

To see if she would open her eyes, he said, "You're looking better, Lily. I really think I see signs of improvement."

Without moving anything but her mouth, Lily said, "I don't know why you pretend to be human, Sloat."

"I'm the best friend you have," Sloat responded.

Now she did open her eyes, and they were not dull enough to suit him. "Get out of here," she whispered. "You're obscene."

"I'm trying to help you, and I wish you'd remember that. I have all the papers, Lily. All you have to do is sign them. Once you do, you and your son are taken care of for life." Sloat regarded Lily with an expression of satisfied gloom. "I haven't had much luck in locating Jack, by the way. Spoken to him lately?"

"You know I haven't," she said. And did not weep, as he had hoped.

"I really do think the boy ought to be here, don't you?"

"Piss up a stick," Lily said.

"I think I *will* use your bathroom, if you don't mind," he said, and stood up. Lily closed her eyes again, ignoring him. "I hope he's staying out of trouble, anyhow," Sloat said, slowly walking down the side of the bed. "Terrible things happen to boys on the road." Lily still did not respond. "Things I hate to think about." He reached the end of the bed and continued on to the bathroom door. Lily lay under her sheets and blankets like a crumpled piece of tissue paper. Sloat went into the bathroom.

He rubbed his hands together, gently closed the door, and turned on both taps over the sink. From the pocket of his suitcoat he extracted a small brown two-gram vial, from his inner jacket pocket a small case containing a mirror, a razor blade, and a short brass straw. Onto the mirror he tapped about an eighth of a gram of the purest Peruvian Flake cocaine he'd been able to find. Then he chopped it ritualistically with his blade, forming it into two stubby lines. He snorted the lines through the brass straw, gasped, inhaled sharply, and held his breath for a second or two. "Aah." His nasal passages opened up as wide as tunnels. Way back there, a drip began to deliver the goodies.

Sloat ran his hands under the water, then for the sake of his nose drew a little of the moisture on his thumb and index finger up into his nostrils. He dried his hands and his face.

*That lovely train,* he allowed himself to think, *that lovely lovely train, I bet I'm prouder of it than I am of my own son.*

Morgan Sloat revelled in the vision of his precious train, which was the same in both worlds and the first concrete manifestation of his long-held plan to import modern technology into the Territories, arriving in Point Venuti loaded with its useful cargo. Point Venuti! Sloat smiled as the coke blasted through his brain, bringing its usual message that all would be well, all would be well. Little Jacky Sawyer would be a very lucky boy *ever* to leave the odd little town of Point Venuti. In fact, he'd be lucky ever to get there in the first place, considering that he'd have to make his way across the Blasted Lands. But the drug reminded Sloat that in some ways he'd prefer Jack to make it to dangerous, warped little Point Venuti, he'd even prefer Jack to survive his exposure to the black hotel, which was not merely boards and nails, bricks and stone, but was also somehow alive . . . because it was possible that he might walk out with the Talisman in his thieving little hands. And if that were to happen . . .

Yes, if that absolutely wonderful event were to take place, all would indeed be well.

And both Jack Sawyer and the Talisman would be broken in half.

And he, Morgan Sloat, would finally have the canvas his talents deserved. For a second he saw himself spreading his arms over starry vastnesses, over worlds folded together like lovers on a bed, over all that the Talisman protected, and all that he had coveted so when he'd bought the Agincourt, years back. Jack could get all that for him. Sweetness. Glory.

To celebrate this thought, Sloat brought the vial out of his pocket again and did not bother with the ritual of razor and mirror, but simply used the attached little spoon to raise the medicinal white powder to first one nostril, then the other. Sweetness, yes.

Sniffing, he came back into the bedroom. Lily appeared slightly more animated, but his mood now was so good that even this evidence of her continuing life did not darken it.

Bright and oddly hollow within their circles of bone, her eyes followed him. "Uncle Bloat has a new loathsome habit," she said.

"And you're dying," he said. "Which one would you choose?"

"Do enough of that stuff, and you'll be dying, too."

Undeterred by her hostility, Sloat returned to the rickety wooden chair. "For God's sake, Lily, grow up," he said. "Everybody does coke now. You're out of touch—you've been out of touch for years. You wanna try some?" He lifted the vial from his pocket and swung it by the chain attached to the little spoon.

"Get out of here."

Sloat waggled the vial closer to her face.

Lily sat up in bed as smartly as a striking snake and spat in his face.

"Bitch!" He recoiled, grabbing for his handkerchief as the wad of spittle slid down his cheek.

"If that crap is so wonderful, why do you have to sneak into the toilet to take it? Don't answer, just leave me alone. I don't want to see you again, Bloat. Take your fat ass out of here."

"You're going to die alone, Lily," he said, now perversely filled with a cold, hard joy. "You're going to die alone, and this comic little town is going to give you a pauper's burial, and your son is going to be killed because he can't possibly handle what's lying in wait for him, and no one will ever hear of either one of you again." He grinned at her. His plump hands were balled into white hairy fists. "Remember Asher Dondorf, Lily? Our client? The sidekick on that series *Flanagan and Flanagan?* I was reading about him in *The Hollywood Reporter*— some issue a few weeks ago. Shot himself in his living room, but his aim wasn't too cool, because instead of killing himself he just blew away the roof of his mouth and put himself in a coma. Might hang on for years, I hear, just rotting away." He leaned toward her, his forehead corrugating. "You and good old Asher have a lot in common, it seems to me."

She stonily looked back. Her eyes seemed to have crawled back inside her head, and at that moment she resembled some hard-bitten old frontier woman with a squirrel rifle in one hand and Scripture in the other. "My son is going to save my life," she said. "Jack is going to save my life, and you won't be able to stop him."

"Well, we'll see, won't we?" Sloat answered. "We'll just see about that."

# 35

# The Blasted Lands

### 1

"But will ye be safe, my Lord?" Anders asked, kneeling down before Jack with his white-and-red kilt pooled out around him like a skirt.

"Jack?" Richard asked, his voice a whiny, irrelevant skirl of sound.

"Would you be safe yourself?" Jack asked.

Anders twisted his big white head sideways and squinted up at Jack as if he had just asked a riddle. He looked like a huge puzzled dog.

"I mean, I'll be about as safe as you would be yourself. That's all I mean."

"But my Lord . . ."

"Jack?" came Richard's querulous voice again. "I fell asleep, and now I should be awake, but we're still in this weird place, so I'm still dreaming . . . but I want to be awake, Jack, I don't want to have this dream anymore. No. I don't want to."

*And that's why you busted your damn glasses,* Jack said to himself. Aloud, he said, "This isn't a dream, Richie-boy. We're about to hit the road. We're gonna take a train ride."

"Huh?" Richard said, rubbing his face and sitting up. If Anders resembled a big white dog in skirts, Richard looked like nothing so much as a newly awakened baby.

"My Lord Jason," Anders said. Now he seemed as if he might weep—with relief, Jack thought. "It is yer will? It is yer will to drive that devil-machine through the Blasted Lands?"

"It sure is," Jack said.

"Where are we?" Richard said. "Are you sure they're not following us?"

Jack turned toward him. Richard was sitting up on the undulating yellow floor, blinking stupidly, terror still drifting about him like a fog. "Okay," he said. "I'll answer your question. We're in a section of the Territories called Ellis-Breaks—"

"My head hurts," Richard said. He had closed his eyes.

"And," Jack went on, "we're going to take this man's train all the way through the Blasted Lands to the black hotel, or as close to it as we can get. That's it, Richard. Believe it or not. And the sooner we do it, the sooner we'll get away from whatever just might be trying to find us."

"Etheridge," Richard whispered. "Mr. Dufrey." He looked around the mellow interior of The Depot as if he expected all their pursuers to suddenly pour through the walls. "It's a brain tumor, you know," he said to Jack in a tone of perfect reasonableness. "That's what it is—my headache."

"My Lord Jason," old Anders was saying, bowing so low that his hair settled down on the rippling floorboards. "How good ye are, O High One, how good to yer lowliest servant, how good to those who do not deserve yer blessed presence. . . ." He crawled forward, and Jack saw with horror that he was about to begin that moony foot-kissing all over again.

"Pretty far advanced, too, I'd say," Richard offered.

"Get up, please, Anders," Jack said, stepping back. "Get up, come on, that's enough." The old man continued to crawl forward, babbling with his relief at not having to endure the Blasted Lands. "ARISE!" Jack bellowed.

Anders looked up, his forehead wrinkled. "Yes, my Lord." He slowly got up.

"Bring your brain tumor over here, Richard," Jack said "We're going to see if we can figure out how to drive this damn train."

## 2

Anders had moved over behind the long, rippling counter, and was rooting in a drawer. "I believe it works on devils, my

Lord," he said. "Strange devils, all hurtled down together. They do not appear to live, yet they do. Aye." He fetched out of the drawer the longest, fattest candle that Jack had ever seen. From a box atop the counter Anders selected a foot-long, narrow softwood strip, then lowered one of its ends into a glowing lamp. The strip of wood ignited, and Anders used it to light his enormous candle. Then he waved the "match" back and forth until the flame expired in a curl of smoke.

"Devils?" Jack asked.

"Strange square things—I believe the devils are contained therein. Sometimes how they spit and spark! I shall show this to ye, Lord Jason."

Without another word he swept toward the door, the warm glow of the candle momentarily erasing the wrinkles from his face. Jack followed him outside into the sweetness and ampli-tude of the deep Territories. He remembered a photograph on the wall of Speedy Parker's office, a photograph even then filled with an inexplicable power, and realized that he was ac-tually near the site of that photograph. Far off rose a familiar-looking mountain. Down the little knoll the fields of grain rolled away in all directions, waving in smooth, wide patterns. Richard Sloat moved hesitantly beside Jack, rubbing his fore-head. The silvery bands of metal, out of key with the rest of the landscape, stretched inexorably west.

"The shed is in back, my Lord," Anders said softly, and al-most shyly turned away toward the side of The Depot. Jack took another glance at the far-off mountain. Now it looked less like the mountain in Speedy's photograph—newer—a western, not an eastern, mountain.

"What's with that Lord Jason business?" Richard whis-pered right into his ear. "He thinks he knows you."

"It's hard to explain," Jack said.

Richard tugged at his bandanna, then clamped a hand on Jack's biceps. The old Kansas City Clutch. "What happened to the school, Jack? What happened to the dogs? Where are we?"

"Just come along," Jack said. "You're probably still dream-ing."

"Yes," Richard said in the tone of purest relief. "Yes, that's it, isn't it? I'm still asleep. You told me all that crazy stuff about the Territories, and now I'm dreaming about it."

"Yeah," Jack said, and set off after Anders. The old man was holding up the enormous candle like a torch and drifting down the rear side of the knoll toward another, slightly larger, octagonal wooden building. The two boys followed him through the tall yellow grass. Light spilled from another of the transparent globes, revealing that this second building was open at opposite ends, as if two matching faces of the octagon had been neatly sliced away. The silvery train tracks ran through these open ends. Anders reached the large shed and turned around to wait for the boys. With the flaring, sputtering, upheld candle, his long beard and odd clothes, Anders resembled a creature from legend or faery, a sorcerer or wizard.

"It sits here, as it has since it came, and may the demons drive it hence." Anders scowled at the boys, and all his wrinkles deepened. "Invention of hell. A foul thing, d'ye ken." He looked over his shoulder when the boys were before him. Jack saw that Anders did not even like being in the shed with the train. "Half its cargo is aboard, and it, too, stinks of hell."

Jack stepped into the open end of the shed, forcing Anders to follow him. Richard stumbled after, rubbing his eyes. The little train sat pointing west on the tracks—an odd-looking engine, a boxcar, a flatcar covered with a straining tarp. From this last car came the smell Anders so disliked. It was a wrong smell, not of the Territories, both metallic and greasy.

Richard immediately went to one of the interior angles of the shed, sat down on the floor with his back to the wall, and closed his eyes.

"D'ye ken its workings, my Lord?" Anders asked in a low voice.

Jack shook his head and walked up along the tracks to the head of the train. Yes, there were Anders's "demons." They were box batteries, just as Jack had supposed. Sixteen of them, in two rows strung together in a metal container supported by the cab's first four wheels. The entire front part of the train looked like a more sophisticated version of a deliveryboy's bicycle-cart—but where the bicycle itself should have been was a little cab which reminded Jack of something else . . . something he could not immediately identify.

"The demons talk to the upright stick," Anders said from behind him.

Jack hoisted himself up into the little cab. The "stick" Anders had mentioned was a gearshift set in a slot with three notches. Then Jack knew what the little cab resembled. The whole train ran on the same principle as a golf cart. Battery-powered, it had only three gears: forward, neutral, and reverse. It was the only sort of train that might possibly work in the Territories, and Morgan Sloat must have had it specially constructed for him.

"The demons in the boxes spit and spark, and talk to the stick, and the stick moves the train, my Lord." Anders hovered anxiously beside the cab, his face contorting into an astonishing display of wrinkles.

"You were going to leave in the morning?" Jack asked the old man.

"Aye."

"But the train is ready now?"

"Yes, my Lord."

Jack nodded, and jumped down. "What's the cargo?"

"Devil-things," Anders said grimly. "For the bad Wolfs. To take to the black hotel."

I'd be a jump ahead of Morgan Sloat if I left now, Jack thought. And looked uneasily over at Richard, who had managed to put himself asleep again. If it weren't for pig-headed, hypochondriacal Rational Richard, he would never have stumbled onto Sloat's choo-choo; and Sloat would have been able to use the "devil-things"—weapons of some kind, surely—against him as soon as he got near the black hotel. For the hotel was the end of his quest, he was sure of that now. And all of that seemed to argue that Richard, as helpless and annoying as he now was, was going to be more important to his quest than Jack had ever imagined. The son of Sawyer and the son of Sloat: the son of Prince Philip Sawtelle and the son of Morgan of Orris. For an instant the world wheeled above Jack and he snagged a second's insight that Richard might just be essential to whatever he was going to have to do in the black hotel. Then Richard snuffled and let his mouth drop open, and the feeling of momentary comprehension slipped away from Jack.

"Let's have a look at those devil-things," he said. He whirled around and marched back down the length of the train, along the way noticing for the first time that the floor of the octagonal shed was in two sections—most of it was one round circular mass, like an enormous dinner plate. Then there was a break in the wood, and what was beyond the perimeter of the circle extended to the walls. Jack had never heard of a roundhouse, but he understood the concept: the circular part of the floor could turn a hundred and eighty degrees. Normally, trains or coaches came in from the east, and returned in the same direction.

The tarpaulin had been tied down over the cargo with thick brown cord so hairy it looked like steel wool. Jack strained to lift an edge, peered under, saw only blackness. "Help me," he said, turning to Anders.

The old man stepped forward, frowning, and with one strong, deft motion released a knot. The tarpaulin loosened and sagged. Now when Jack lifted its edge, he saw that half of the flatcar held a row of wooden boxes stencilled MACHINE PARTS. *Guns,* he thought: Morgan is arming his rebel Wolfs. The other half of the space beneath the tarp was occupied by bulky rectangular packages of a squashy-looking substance wrapped in layers of clear plastic sheeting. Jack had no idea what this substance might be, but he was pretty sure it wasn't Wonder Bread. He dropped the tarpaulin and stepped back, and Anders pulled at the thick rope and knotted it again.

"We're going tonight," Jack said, having just decided this.

"But my Lord Jason . . . the Blasted Lands . . . at night . . . d'ye ken—"

"I ken, all right," Jack said. "I ken that I'll need all the surprise I can whip up. Morgan and that man the Wolfs call He of the Lashes are going to be looking for me, and if I show up twelve hours before anybody is expecting this train, Richard and I might get away alive."

Anders nodded gloomily, and again looked like an oversize dog accommodating itself to unhappy knowledge.

Jack looked at Richard again—asleep, sitting up with his mouth open. As if he knew what was in Jack's mind, Anders, too, looked toward sleeping Richard. "Did Morgan of Orris have a son?" Jack asked.

"He did, my Lord. Morgan's brief marriage had issue—a boy child named Rushton."

"And what became of Rushton? As if I couldn't guess."

"He died," Anders said simply. "Morgan of Orris was not meant to be a father."

Jack shuddered, remembering how his enemy had torn his way through the air and nearly killed Wolf's entire herd.

"We're going," he said. "Will you please help me get Richard into the cab, Anders?"

"My Lord . . ." Anders hung his head, then lifted it and gave Jack a look of almost parental concern. "The journey will require at least two days, perhaps three, before ye reach the western shore. Have ye any food? Would ye share my evening meal?"

Jack shook his head, impatient to begin this last leg of his journey to the Talisman, but then his stomach abruptly growled, reminding him of how long it had been since he had eaten anything but the Ring-Dings and stale Famous Amos cookies in Albert the Blob's room. "Well," he said, "I suppose another half hour won't make any difference. Thank you, Anders. Help me get Richard up on his feet, will you?" And maybe, he thought, he wasn't so eager to cross the Blasted Lands after all.

The two of them jerked Richard to his feet. Like the Dormouse, he opened his eyes, smiled, and sagged back to sleep again. "Food," Jack said. "Real food. You up for that, chum?"

"I never eat in dreams," Richard answered with surreal rationality. He yawned, then wiped his eyes. He gradually had found his feet, and no longer leaned against Anders and Jack. "I am pretty hungry, though, to tell you the truth. I'm having a long dream, aren't I, Jack?" He seemed almost proud of it.

"Yep," said Jack.

"Say, is that the train we're going to take? It looks like a cartoon."

"Yep."

"Can you drive that thing, Jack? It's my dream, I know, but—"

"It's about as hard to operate as my old electric train set," Jack said. "I can drive it, and so can you."

"I don't want to," Richard said, and that cringing, whining tone came back into his voice again. "I don't want to get on that train at all. I want to go back to my room."

"Come and have some food instead," Jack said, and found

himself leading Richard out of the shed. "Then we're on our way to California."

And so the Territories showed one of its best faces to the boys immediately before they entered the Blasted Lands. Anders gave them thick sweet slices of bread clearly made from the grain growing around The Depot, kebabs of tender sections of meat and plump juicy unfamiliar vegetables, a spicy pink juice that Jack for some reason thought of as papaya though he knew it was not. Richard chewed in a happy trance, the juice running down his chin until Jack wiped it off for him. "California," he said once. "I should have known." Assuming that he was alluding to that state's reputation for craziness, Jack did not question him. He was more concerned about what the two of them were doing to Anders's presumably limited stock of food, but the old man kept nipping behind the counter, where he or his father before him had installed a small wood-burning stove, and returning with yet more food. Corn muffins, calf's-foot jelly, things that looked like chicken legs but tasted of . . . what? Frankincense and myrrh? Flowers? The taste fairly exploded over his tongue, and he thought that he, too, might begin to drool.

The three of them sat around a little table in the warm and mellow room. At the end of the meal Anders almost shyly brought forth a heavy beaker half-filled with red wine. Feeling as if he were following someone else's script, Jack drank a small glassful.

### 3

Two hours later, beginning to feel drowsy, Jack wondered if that enormous meal had been an equally enormous error. First of all, there had been the departure from Ellis-Breaks and The Depot, which had not gone easily; secondly, there was Richard, who threatened to go seriously crazy; and thirdly, and above all else, there were the Blasted Lands. Which were far crazier than Richard would ever be, and which absolutely demanded concentrated attention.

After the meal the three of them had returned to the shed, and the trouble had started. Jack knew that he was fearful of

whatever might be ahead—and, he now knew, that fear was
perfectly justified—and perhaps his trepidation had made him
behave less well than he should have. The first difficulty had
come when he tried to pay old Anders with the coin Captain
Farren had given him. Anders responded as if his beloved Jason had just stabbed him in the back. Sacrilege! Outrage! By
offering the coin, Jack had done more than merely insult the
old liveryman; he had metaphorically smeared mud on his religion. Supernaturally restored divine beings apparently were
not supposed to offer coins to their followers. Anders had
been upset enough to smash his hand into the "devil-box," as
he called the metal container for the rank of batteries, and
Jack knew that Anders had been mightily tempted to strike
another target besides the train. Jack had managed only a
semi-truce: Anders did not want his apologies any more than
he wanted his money. The old man had finally calmed down
once he realized the extent of the boy's dismay, but he did not
really return to his normal behavior until Jack speculated out
loud that the Captain Farren coin might have other functions,
other roles for him. "Ye're not Jason entire," the old man
gloomed, "yet the Queen's coin may aid ye toward yer destiny." He shook his head heavily. His farewell wave had been
distinctly half-hearted.

But a good portion of that had been due to Richard. What
had begun as a sort of childish panic had quickly blossomed
into full-blown terror. Richard had refused to get in the cab.
Up until that moment he had mooned around the shed, not
looking at the train, seemingly in an uncaring daze. Then he
had realized that Jack was serious about getting him on that
thing, and he had freaked—and, strangely, it had been the idea
of ending up in California which had disturbed him most.
"NO! NO! CAN'T!" Richard had yelled when Jack urged
him toward the train. "I WANT TO GO BACK TO MY
ROOM!"

"They might be following us, Richard," Jack said wearily.
"We have to get going." He reached out and took Richard's
arm. "This is all a dream, remember?"

"Oh my Lord, oh my Lord," Anders had said, moving aimlessly around in the big shed, and Jack understood that for
once the liveryman was not addressing him.

"I HAVE TO GO BACK TO MY ROOM!" Richard

squalled. His eyes were clamped shut so tightly that a single painful crease ran from temple to temple.

Echoes of Wolf again. Jack had tried to pull Richard toward the train, but Richard had stuck fast, like a mule. "I CAN'T GO THERE!" he yelled.

"Well, you can't stay here, either," Jack said. He made another futile effort at yanking Richard toward the train, and this time actually budged him a foot or two. "Richard," he said, "this is ridiculous. Do you want to be here alone? Do you want to be left alone in the Territories?" Richard shook his head. "Then come with me. It's time. In two days we'll be in California."

"Bad business," Anders muttered to himself, watching the boys. Richard simply continued to shake his head, offering a single comprehensive negative. "I can't go there," he repeated. "I can't get on that train and I can't go there."

"California?"

Richard bit his mouth into a lipless seam and closed his eyes again. "Oh hell," Jack said. "Can you help me, Anders?" The huge old man gave him a dismayed, almost disgusted look, then marched across the room and scooped up Richard in his arms—as if Richard were the size of a puppy. The boy let out a distinctly puppyish squeal. Anders dropped him onto the padded bench in the cab. "Jack!" Richard called, afraid that he somehow was going to wind up in the Blasted Lands all by himself. "I'm here," Jack said, and was in fact already climbing into the other side of the cab. "Thank you, Anders," he said to the old liveryman, who nodded gloomily and retreated back into a corner of the shed. "Take care." Richard had begun to weep, and Anders looked at him without pity.

Jack pushed the ignition button, and two enormous blue sparks shot out from the "devil-box" just as the engine whirred into life. "Here goes," Jack said, and eased the lever forward. The train began to glide out of the shed. Richard whimpered and drew up his knees. Saying something like "Nonsense" or "Impossible"—Jack chiefly heard the hiss of the sibilants—he buried his face between his knees. He looked as though he were trying to become a circle. Jack waved to Anders, who waved back, and then they were out of the lighted shed and were covered only by the vast dark sky. Anders's silhouette appeared in the opening through which they had gone, as if he had decided to run after them. The train was not capable of going more than thirty miles an hour, Jack thought, and at present was doing no better than eight or nine. This seemed excruciatingly slow. West, Jack said to himself, west, west, west. Anders stepped back inside the shed, and his beard lay against his massive chest like a covering of frost. The train lurched forward—another sizzling blue spark snapped upward—and Jack turned around on the padded seat to see what was coming.

"NO!" Richard screamed, almost making Jack fall out of the cab. "I CAN'T! CAN'T GO THERE!" He had drawn his head up from his knees, but he wasn't seeing anything—his eyes were still clamped shut, and his whole face looked like a knuckle.

"Be quiet," Jack said. Ahead the tracks arrowed through the endless fields of waving grain; dim mountains, old teeth, floated in the western clouds. Jack glanced one last time over his shoulder and saw the little oasis of warmth and light which was The Depot and the octagonal shed, slipping slowly backward behind him. Anders was a tall shadow in a lighted doorway. Jack gave a final wave, and the tall shadow waved, too. Jack turned around again and looked over the immensity of grain, all that lyric distance. If this was what the Blasted Lands were like, the next two days were going to be positively restful.

Of course they were not, not like that at all. Even in the moonlit dark he could tell that the grain was thinning out, becoming scrubby—about half an hour out of The Depot the change had begun. Even the color seemed wrong now, almost artificial, no longer the beautiful organic yellow he had seen before, but the yellow of something left too near a powerful heat source—the yellow of something with most of the life bleached out of it. Richard now had a similar quality. For a time he had hyperventilated, then he had wept as silently and shamelessly as a jilted girl, then he had fallen into a twitchy sleep. "Can't go back," he had muttered in his sleep, or such were the words Jack thought he had heard. In sleep he seemed to dwindle.

The whole character of the landscape had begun to alter. From the broad sweep of the plains in Ellis-Breaks, the land had mutated to secretive little hollows and dark little valleys crowded with black trees. Huge boulders lay everywhere, skulls, eggs, giant teeth. The ground itself had changed, become much sandier. Twice the walls of the valleys grew up right alongside the tracks, and all Jack could see on either side were scrubby reddish cliffs covered with low creeping plants. Now and then he thought he saw an animal scurrying for cover, but the light was too weak, and the animal too quick, for him to identify it. But Jack had the eerie feeling that if the animal had frozen absolutely still in the middle of Rodeo Drive at high noon, he would still have been unable to identify it—a suggestion that the head was twice the size it should be, that this animal was better off hiding from human sight.

By the time ninety minutes had elapsed, Richard was moaning in his sleep and the landscape had passed into utter strangeness. The second time they had emerged from one of the claustrophobic valleys, Jack had been surprised by a sense of sudden openness—at first it was like being back in the Territories again, the Daydreams-land. Then he had noticed, even in the dark, how the trees were stunted and bent; then he had noticed the smell. Probably this had been slowly growing in his consciousness, but it was only after he had seen how the few trees scattered on the black plain had coiled themselves up like tortured beasts that he finally noticed the faint but unmistakable odor of corruption in the air. Corruption, hellfire. Here the Territories stank, or nearly.

The odor of long-dead flowers overlaid the land; and beneath it, as with Osmond, was a coarser, more potent odor. If Morgan, in either of his roles, had caused this, then he had in some sense brought death to the Territories, or so Jack thought.

Now there were no more intricate valleys and hollows; now the land seemed a vast red desert. The queerly stunted trees dotted the sloping sides of this great desert. Before Jack, the twin silver rails of the tracks rolled on through darkened reddish emptiness; to his side, empty desert also rolled away through the dark.

The red land seemed empty, anyhow. For several hours Jack never actually caught sight of anything larger than the deformed little animals concealing themselves on the slopes of the railway cuttings—but there were times when he thought he caught a sudden sliding movement in the corner of one eye, turned to see it, and it was gone. At first he thought he was being followed. Then, for a hectic time, no longer than twenty or thirty minutes, he imagined that he was being tracked by the dog-things from Thayer School. Wherever he looked, something had just ceased to move—had nipped behind one of the coiled-up trees or slipped into the sand. During this time the wide desert of the Blasted Lands did not seem empty or dead, but full of slithery, hidden life. Jack pushed forward on the train's gearshift (as if that could help) and urged the little train to go faster, faster. Richard slumped in the ell of his seat, whimpering. Jack imagined all those beings, those things neither canine nor human, rushing toward them, and prayed that Richard's eyes would stay closed.

"NO!" Richard yelled, still sleeping.

Jack nearly fell out of the cab. He could *see* Etheridge and Mr. Dufrey loping after them. They gained ground, their tongues lolling, their shoulders working. In the next second, he realized that he had seen only shadows travelling beside the train. The loping schoolboys and their headmaster had winked out like birthday candles.

"NOT THERE!" Richard bawled. Jack inhaled carefully. He, they, were safe. The dangers of the Blasted Lands were overrated, mainly literary. In not very many hours the sun would lift itself up again. Jack raised his watch to the level of his eyes and saw that they had been on the train just under two hours. His mouth opened in a huge yawn, and he found himself regretting that he had eaten so much back in The Depot.

A piece of cake, he thought, this is going to be—

And just as he was about to complete his paraphrase of the Burns lines old Anders had rather startlingly quoted, he saw the first of the fireballs, which destroyed his complacency forever.

## 4

A ball of light at least ten feet in diameter tumbled over the edge of the horizon, sizzling hot, and at first arrowed straight toward the train. "Holy shit," Jack muttered to himself, remembering what Anders had said about the balls of fire. *If a*

*man gets too close to one of those fireballs, he gets turrible
sick . . . loses his hair . . . sores're apt to raise all over his
body . . . he begins to vomit . . . vomits and vomits until his
stomach ruptures and his throat bursts. . . .* He swallowed,
hard—it was like swallowing a pound of nails. "Please, God,"
he said aloud. The giant ball of light sped straight toward him,
as though it owned a mind and had decided to erase Jack
Sawyer and Richard Sloat from the earth. Radiation poisoning. Jack's stomach contracted, and his testicles froze up under his body. *Radiation poisoning. Vomits and vomits until his
stomach ruptures . . .*

The excellent dinner Anders had given him nearly leaped
out of his stomach. The fireball continued to roll straight toward the train, shooting out sparks and sizzling with its own
fiery energy. Behind it lengthened a glowing golden trail
which seemed magically to instigate other snapping, burning
lines in the red earth. Just when the fireball bounced up off
the earth and took a zagging bounce like a giant tennis ball,
wandering harmlessly off to the left, Jack had his first clear
glimpse of the creatures he had all along thought were following them. The reddish-golden light of the wandering fireball,
and the residual glow of the old trails in the earth, illuminated
a group of deformed-looking beasts which had evidently been
following the train. They were dogs, or once had been dogs,
or their ancestors had been dogs, and Jack glanced uneasily at
Richard to make sure that he was still sleeping.

The creatures falling behind the train flattened out on the
ground like snakes. Their heads were doglike, Jack saw, but
their bodies had only vestigial hind legs and were, as far as he
could see, hairless and tailless. They looked wet—the pink
hairless skin glistened like that of newborn mice. They
snarled, hating to be seen. It had been these awful mutant
dogs that Jack had seen on the banks of the railway cutting.
Exposed, flattened out like reptiles, they hissed and snarled
and began creeping away—they, too, feared the fireballs and
the trails the fireballs left on the earth. Then Jack caught the
odor of the fireball, now moving swiftly, somehow almost angrily, toward the horizon again, igniting an entire row of the
stunted trees. Hellfire, corruption.

Another of the fireballs came cruising over the horizon and

blazed away off to the boys' left. The stink of missed connections, of blasted hopes and evil desires—Jack, with his heart
lodged just under his tongue, imagined he found all this in the
foul smell broadcast by the fireball. Mewing, the crowd of
mutant dogs had dispersed into the threat of glinting teeth, a
whisper of surreptitious movement, the *hushushush* of heavy
legless bodies dragged through red dust. How many of them
were there? From the base of a burning tree which tried to
hide its head in its trunk two of the deformed dogs bared long
teeth at him.

Then another fireball lurched over the wide horizon, spinning off a wide glowing track a distance from the train, and
Jack momentarily glimpsed what looked like a ramshackle
little shed set just below the curve of the desert wall. Before it
stood a large humanoid figure, male, looking toward him. An
impression of size, hairiness, force, malice . . .

Jack was indelibly conscious of the slowness of Anders's
little train, of his and Richard's exposure to anything that
might want to investigate them a little more closely. The first
fireball had dispatched the horrible dog-things, but human
residents of the Blasted Lands might prove more difficult to
overcome. Before the light diminished into the glowing trail,
Jack saw that the figure before the shed was following his
progress, turning a great shaggy head as the train passed by. If
what he had seen were dogs, then what would the people be
like? In the last of the flaring light from the ball of fire, the
manlike being scuttled around the side of its dwelling. A thick
reptilian tail swung from its hindquarters, and then the thing
had slipped around the side of the building, and then it was
dark again and nothing—dogs, man-beast, shed—was visible.
Jack could not even be sure that he had really seen it.

Richard jerked in his sleep, and Jack pushed his hand
against the simple gearshift, vainly trying for more speed. The
dog-noises gradually faded behind them. Sweating, Jack
raised his left wrist again to the level of his eyes and saw that
only fifteen minutes had passed since the last time he'd
checked his watch. He astonished himself by yawning again,
and again regretted eating so much at The Depot.

"NO!" Richard screamed. "NO! I CAN'T GO THERE!"

There? Jack wondered. Where was "there"? California? Or
was it anywhere threatening, anywhere Richard's precarious

control, as insecure as an unbroken horse, might slip away
from him?

## 5

All night Jack stood at the gearshift while Richard slept,
watching the trails of the departed fireballs flicker along the
reddish surface of the earth. Their odor, of dead flowers and
hidden corruption, filled the air. From time to time he heard
the chatter of the mutant dogs, or of other poor creatures, rising from the roots of the stunted, ingrown trees which still
dotted the landscape. The ranks of batteries occasionally sent
up snapping arcs of blue. Richard was in a state beyond mere
sleep, wrapped in an unconsciousness he both required and
had willed. He made no more tortured outcries—in fact he
did nothing but slump into his corner of the cab and breathe
shallowly, as if even respiration took more energy than he
had. Jack half-prayed for, half-feared the coming of the light.
When morning came, he would be able to see the animals; but
what else might he have to see?

From time to time he glanced over at Richard. His friend's
skin seemed oddly pale, an almost ghostly shade of gray.

## 6

Morning came with a relaxation of the darkness. A band of
pink appeared along the bowllike edge of the eastern horizon,
and soon a rosy stripe grew up beneath it, pushing the optimistic pinkness higher in the sky. Jack's eyes felt almost as
red as that stripe, and his legs ached. Richard lay across the
whole of the cab's little seat, still breathing in a restricted, almost reluctant way. It was true, Jack saw—Richard's face did
seem peculiarly gray. His eyelids fluttered in a dream, and
Jack hoped that his friend was not about to erupt in another
of his screams. Richard's mouth dropped open, but what
emerged was the tip of his tongue, not a loud outcry. Richard
passed his tongue along his upper lip, snorted, then fell back
into his stupefied coma.

Although Jack wished desperately to sit down and close
his own eyes, he did not disturb Richard. For the more Jack
saw as the new light filled in the details of the Blasted Lands,

the more he hoped Richard's unconsciousness would endure as long as he himself could endure the conditions of Anders's cranky little train. He was anything but eager to witness the response of Richard Sloat to the idiosyncrasies of the Blasted Lands. A small amount of pain, a quantity of exhaustion—these were a minimal price to pay for what he knew must be a temporary peace.

What he saw through his squinting eyes was a landscape in which nothing seemed to have escaped withering, crippling damage. By moonlight, it had seemed a vast desert, though a desert furnished with trees. Now Jack took in that his "desert" was actually nothing of the sort. What he had taken for a reddish variety of sand was a loose, powdery soil—it looked as though a man would sink in it up to his ankles, if not his knees. From this starved dry soil grew the wretched trees. Looked at directly, these were much as they had appeared by night, so stunted they seemed to be straining over in an attempt to flee back under their own coiling roots. This was bad enough—bad enough for Rational Richard, anyhow. But when you saw one of these trees obliquely, out of the side of your eye, then you saw a living creature in torment—the straining branches were arms thrown up over an agonized face caught in a frozen scream. As long as Jack was not looking directly at the trees, he saw their tortured faces in perfect detail, the open O of the mouth, the staring eyes and the drooping nose, the long, agonized wrinkles running down the cheeks. They were cursing, pleading, howling at him—their unheard voices hung in the air like smoke. Jack groaned. Like all the Blasted Lands, these trees had been poisoned.

The reddish land stretched out for miles on either side, dotted here and there with patches of acrid-looking yellow grass bright as urine or new paint. If it had not been for the hideous coloration of the long grass, these areas would have resembled oases, for each lay beside a small round body of water. The water was black, and oily patches floated on its skin. Thicker than water, somehow; itself oily, poisonous. The second of these false oases that Jack saw began to ripple sluggishly as the train went past, and at first Jack thought with horror that the black water itself was alive, a being as tormented as the trees he no longer wished to see. Then he momentarily saw something break the surface of the thick fluid, a

broad black back or side which rolled over before a wide, ravenous mouth appeared, biting down on nothing. A suggestion
of scales that would have been iridescent if the creature had
not been discolored by the pool. *Holy cow,* Jack thought, *was
that a fish?* It seemed to him to have been nearly twenty feet
long, too big to inhabit the little pool. A long tail roiled the
water before the entire enormous creature slipped back down
into what must have been the pool's considerable depth.

Jack looked up sharply at the horizon, imagining that he
had momentarily seen the round shape of a head peering over
it. And then he had another of those shocks of a sudden dis-
placement, similar to that the Loch Ness monster, or whatever
it was, had given him. How could a head peer over the *horizon,* for God's sake?

Because the horizon wasn't the real horizon, he finally
understood—all night, and for as long as it took him to really
see what lay at the end of his vision, he had drastically underestimated the size of the Blasted Lands. Jack finally understood, as the sun began to force its way up into the world
again, that he was in a broad valley, and the rim far off to either side was not the edge of the world but the craggy top of a
range of hills. Anybody or anything could be tracking him,
keeping just out of sight past the rim of the surrounding hills.
He remembered the humanoid being with the crocodile's tail
that had slipped around the side of the little shed. Could he
have been following Jack all night, waiting for him to fall
asleep?

The train *poop-pooped* through the lurid valley, moving
with a suddenly maddening lack of speed.

He scanned the entire rim of hills about him, seeing nothing but new morning sunlight gild the upright rocks far above
him. Jack turned around completely in the cab, fear and tension for the moment completely negating his tiredness.
Richard threw one arm over his eyes, and slept on. Anything,
anybody might have been keeping pace with them, waiting
them out.

A slow, almost hidden movement off to his left made him
catch his breath. A movement huge, slithery . . . Jack had a
vision of a half-dozen of the crocodile-men crawling over the
rim of the hills toward him, and he shielded his eyes with his
hands and stared at the place where he thought he had seen

them. The rocks were stained the same red as the powdery soil, and between them a deep trail wound its way over the crest of the hills through a cleft in the high-standing rocks. What was moving between two of the standing rocks was a shape not even vaguely human. It was a snake—at least, Jack thought it was . . . It had slipped into a concealed section of the trail, and Jack saw only a huge sleek round reptilian body disappearing behind the rocks. The skin of the creature seemed oddly ridged; burned, too—a suggestion, just before it disappeared, of ragged black holes in its side . . . Jack craned to see the place where it would emerge, and in seconds witnessed the wholly unnerving spectacle of the head of a giant worm, one-quarter buried in the thick red dust, swivelling toward him. It had hooded, filmy eyes, but it was the head of a worm.

Some other animal bolted from under a rock, heavy head and dragging body, and as the worm's big head darted toward it, Jack saw that the fleeing creature was one of the mutant dogs. The worm opened a mouth like the slot of a corner mailbox and neatly scooped up the frantic dog-thing. Jack clearly heard the snapping of bones. The dog's wailing ceased. The huge worm swallowed the dog as neatly as if it were a pill. Now, immediately before the worm's monstrous form, lay one of the black trails left by the fireballs, and as Jack watched, the long creature burrowed into the dust like a cruise ship sinking beneath the surface of the ocean. It apparently understood that the traces of the fireballs could do it damage and, wormlike, it would dig beneath them. Jack watched as the ugly thing completely disappeared into the red powder. And then cast his eyes uneasily over the whole of the long red slope dotted with pubic outpatches of the shiny yellow grass, wondering where it would surface again.

When he could be at least reasonably certain that the worm was not going to try to ingest the train, Jack went back to inspecting the ridge of rocky hills about him.


7


Before Richard woke up late that afternoon, Jack saw:

at least one unmistakable head peering over the rim of the hills;

two more jouncing and deadly fireballs careering down at him;

the headless skeleton of what he at first took to be a large rabbit, then sickeningly knew was a human baby, picked shining clean, lying beside the tracks and closely followed by:

the round babyish gleaming skull of the same baby, half-sunk in the loose soil. And he saw:

a pack of the big-headed dogs, more damaged than the others he had seen, pathetically come crawling after the train, drooling with hunger;

three board shacks, human habitations, propped up over the thick dust on stilts, promising that somewhere out in that stinking poisoned wilderness which was the Blasted Lands other people schemed and hunted for food;

a small leathery bird, featherless, with—this a real Territories touch—a bearded monkeylike face, and clearly delineated fingers protruding from the tips of its wings;

and worst of all (apart from what he *thought* he saw), two completely unrecognizable animals drinking from one of the black pools—animals with long teeth and human eyes and forequarters like those of pigs, hindquarters like those of big cats. Their faces were matted with hair. As the train pulled past the animals, Jack saw that the testicles of the male had swollen to the size of pillows and sagged onto the ground. What had made such monstrosities? Nuclear damage, Jack supposed, since scarcely anything else had such power to deform nature. The creatures, themselves poisoned from birth, snuffled up the equally poisoned water and snarled at the little train as it passed.

Our world could look like this someday, Jack thought. What a treat.

## 8

Then there were the things he *thought* he saw. His skin began to feel hot and itchy—he had already dumped the serapelike overgarment which had replaced Myles P. Kiger's coat onto the floor of the cab. Before noon he stripped off his homespun shirt, too. There was a terrible taste in his mouth, an acidic combination of rusty metal and rotten fruit. Sweat ran from his hairline into his eyes. He was so tired he began to dream standing up, eyes open and stinging with sweat. He saw great packs of the obscene dogs scuttling over the hills; he saw the reddish clouds overhead open up and reach down for Richard and himself with long flaming arms, devil's arms. When at last his eyes finally did close, he saw Morgan of Orris, twelve feet tall and dressed in black, shooting thunderbolts all around him, tearing the earth into great dusty spouts and craters.

Richard groaned and muttered, "No, no, no."

Morgan of Orris blew apart like a wisp of fog, and Jack's painful eyes flew open.

"Jack?" Richard said.

The red land ahead of the train was empty but for the blackened trails of the fireballs. Jack wiped his eyes and looked at Richard, feebly stretching. "Yeah," he said. "How are you?"

Richard lay back against the stiff seat, blinking out of his drawn gray face.

"Sorry I asked," Jack said.

"No," Richard said, "I'm better, really," and Jack felt at least a portion of his tension leave him. "I still have a headache, but I'm better."

"You were making a lot of noise in your . . . um . . ." Jack said, unsure of how much reality his friend could stand.

"In my sleep. Yeah, I guess I probably did." Richard's face worked, but for once Jack did not brace himself against a scream. "I know I'm not dreaming now, Jack. And I know I don't have a brain tumor."

"Do you know where you are?"

"On that train. That old man's train. In what he called the Blasted Lands."

"Well, I'll be double-damned," Jack said, smiling.

Richard blushed beneath his gray pallor.

"What brought this on?" Jack asked, still not quite sure that he could trust Richard's transformation.

"Well, I knew I wasn't dreaming," Richard said, and his cheeks grew even redder. "I guess I . . . I guess it was just time to stop fighting it. If we're in the Territories, then we're in the Territories, no matter how impossible it is." His eyes found Jack's, and the trace of humor in them startled his friend. "You remember that gigantic hourglass back in The

Depot?" When Jack nodded, Richard said, "Well, that was it, really . . . when I saw that thing, I knew I wasn't just making everything up. Because I knew I *couldn't* have made up that thing. Couldn't. Just . . . couldn't. If I were going to invent a primitive clock, it'd have all sorts of wheels, and big pulleys . . . it wouldn't be so simple. So I didn't make it up. Therefore it was real. Therefore everything else was real, too."

"Well, how do you feel now?" Jack asked. "You've been asleep for a long time."

"I'm still so tired I can hardly hold my head up. I don't feel very good in general, I'm afraid."

"Richard, I have to ask you this. Is there some reason why you'd be afraid to go to California?"

Richard looked down and shook his head.

"Have you ever heard of a place called the black hotel?"

Richard continued to shake his head. He was not telling the truth, but as Jack recognized, he was facing as much of it as he could. Anything more—for Jack was suddenly sure that there was more, quite a lot of it—would have to wait. Until they actually reached the black hotel, maybe. Rushton's Twinner, Jason's Twinner: yes, together they would reach the Talisman's home and prison.

"Well, all right," he said. "Can you walk okay?"

"I guess so."

"Good, because there's something I want to do now—since you're not dying of a brain tumor anymore, I mean. And I need your help."

"What's that?" Richard asked. He wiped his face with a trembling hand.

"I want to open up one or two of those cases on the flatcar and see if we can get ourselves some weapons."

"I hate and detest guns," Richard said. "You should, too. If nobody had any guns, your father—"

"Yeah, and if pigs had wings they'd fly," Jack said. "I'm pretty sure somebody's following us."

"Well, maybe it's my dad," Richard said in a hopeful voice.

Jack grunted, and eased the little gearshift out of the first slot. The train appreciably began to lose power. When it had coasted to a halt, Jack put the shift in neutral. "Can you climb down okay, do you think?"

"Oh sure," Richard said, and stood up too quickly. His legs bowed out at the knees, and he sat down hard on the bench. His face now seemed even grayer than it had been, and moisture shone on his forehead and upper lip. "Ah, maybe not," he whispered.

"Just take it easy," Jack said, and moved beside him and placed one hand on the crook of his elbow, the other on Richard's damp, warm forehead. "Relax." Richard closed his eyes briefly, then looked into Jack's own eyes with an expression of perfect trust.

"I tried to do it too fast," he said. "I'm all pins and needles from staying in the same position for so long."

"Nice and easy, then," Jack said, and helped a hissing Richard get to his feet.

"Hurts."

"Only for a little while. I need your help, Richard."

Richard experimentally stepped forward, and hissed in air again. "Ooch." He moved the other leg forward. Then he leaned forward slightly and slapped his palms against his thighs and calves. As Jack watched, Richard's face altered, but this time not with pain—a look of almost rubbery astonishment had printed itself there.

Jack followed the direction of his friend's eyes and saw one of the featherless, monkey-faced birds gliding past the front of the train.

"Yeah, there're a lot of funny things out here," Jack said. "I'm going to feel a lot better if we can find some guns under that tarp."

"What do you suppose is on the other side of those hills?" Richard asked. "More of the same?"

"No, I think there are more people over there," Jack said. "If you can call them people. I've caught somebody watching us twice."

At the expression of quick panic which flooded into Richard's face, Jack said, "I don't think it was anybody from your school. But it could be something just as bad—I'm not trying to scare you, buddy, but I've seen a little more of the Blasted Lands than you have."

"The Blasted Lands," Richard said dubiously. He squinted out at the red dusty valley with its scabrous patches of piss-colored grass. "Oh—that tree—ah . . ."

"I know," Jack said. "You have to just sort of learn to ignore it."

"Who on *earth* would create this kind of devastation?" Richard asked. "This isn't natural, you know."

"Maybe we'll find out someday." Jack helped Richard leave the cab, so that both stood on a narrow running board that covered the tops of the wheels. "Don't get down in that dust," he warned Richard. "We don't know how deep it is. I don't want to have to pull you out of it."

Richard shuddered—but it may have been because he had just noticed out of the side of his eye another of the screaming, anguished trees. Together the two boys edged along the side of the stationary train until they could swing onto the coupling of the empty boxcar. From there a narrow metal ladder led to the roof of the car. On the boxcar's far end another ladder let them descend to the flatcar.

Jack pulled at the thick hairy rope, trying to remember how Anders had loosened it so easily. "I think it's here," Richard said, holding up a twisted loop like a hangman's noose. "Jack?"

"Give it a try."

Richard was not strong enough to loosen the knot by himself, but when Jack helped him tug on the protruding cord, the "noose" smoothly disappeared, and the tarpaulin collapsed over the nest of boxes. Jack pulled the edge back over those closest—MACHINE PARTS—and over a smaller set of boxes Jack had not seen before, marked LENSES. "There they are," he said. "I just wish we had a crowbar." He glanced up toward the rim of the valley, and a tortured tree opened its mouth and silently yowled. Was that another head up there, peering over? It might have been one of the enormous worms, sliding toward them. "Come on, let's try to push the top off one of these boxes," he said, and Richard meekly came toward him.

After six mighty heaves against the top of one of the crates, Jack finally felt movement and heard the nails creak. Richard continued to strain at his side of the box. "That's all right," Jack said to him. Richard seemed even grayer and less healthy than he had before exerting himself. "I'll get it, next push." Richard stepped back and almost collapsed over one of the smaller boxes. He straightened himself and began to probe further under the loose tarpaulin.

Jack set himself before the tall box and clamped his jaw shut. He placed his hands on the corner of the lid. After taking in a long breath, he pushed up until his muscles began to shake. Just before he was going to have to ease up, the nails creaked again and began to slide out of the wood. Jack yelled "AAAGH!" and heaved the top off the box.

Stacked inside the carton, slimy with grease, were half a dozen guns of a sort Jack had never seen before—like grease-guns metamorphosing into butterflies, half-mechanical, half-insectile. He pulled one out and looked at it more closely, trying to see if he could figure out how it worked. It was an automatic weapon, so it would need a clip. He bent down and used the barrel of the weapon to pry off the top of one of the LENSES cartons. As he had expected, in the second, smaller box stood a little pile of heavily greased clips packed in plastic beads.

"It's an Uzi," Richard said behind him. "Israeli machine-gun. Pretty fashionable weapon, I gather. The terrorists' favorite toy."

"How do you know that?" Jack asked, reaching in for another of the guns.

"I watch television. How do you think?"

Jack experimented with the clip, at first trying to fit it into the cavity upside-down, then finding the correct position. Next he found the safety and clicked it off, then on again.

"Those things are so damn ugly," Richard said.

"You get one, too, so don't complain." Jack took a second clip for Richard, and after a moment's consideration took all the clips out of the box, put two in his pockets, tossed two to Richard, who managed to catch them both, and slid the remaining clips into his haversack.

"Ugh," Richard said.

"I guess it's insurance," Jack said.

### 9

Richard collapsed on the seat as soon as they got back to the cab—the trips up and down the two ladders and inching along the narrow strip of metal above the wheels had taken nearly all of his energy. But he made room for Jack to sit down and watched with heavy-lidded eyes while his friend started the train rolling again. Jack picked up his serape and began massaging his gun with it.

"What are you doing?"

"Rubbing the grease off. You'd better do it, too, when I'm done."

For the rest of the day the two boys sat in the open cab of the train, sweating, trying not to take into account the wailing trees, the corrupt stink of the passing landscape, their hunger. Jack noticed that a little garden of open sores had bloomed around Richard's mouth. Finally Jack took Richard's Uzi from his hand, wiped it free of grease, and pushed in the clip. Sweat burned saltily in cracks on his lips.

Jack closed his eyes. Maybe he had not seen those heads peering over the rim of the valley; maybe they were not being followed after all. He heard the batteries sizzle and send off a big snapping spark, and felt Richard jump at it. An instant later he was asleep, dreaming of food.

## 10

When Richard shook Jack's shoulder, bringing him up out of a world in which he had been eating a pizza the size of a truck tire, the shadows were just beginning to spread across the valley, softening the agony of the wailing trees. Even they, bending low and spreading their hands across their faces, seemed beautiful in the low, receding light. The deep red dust shimmered and glowed. The shadows printed themselves out along it, almost perceptibly lengthening. The terrible yellow grass was melting toward an almost mellow orange. Fading red sunlight painted itself slantingly along the rocks at the valley's rim. "I just thought you might want to see this," Richard said. A few more small sores seemed to have appeared about his mouth. Richard grinned weakly. "It seemed sort of special— the spectrum, I mean."

Jack feared that Richard was going to launch into a scientific explanation of the color shift at sunset, but his friend was too tired or sick for physics. In silence the two boys watched the twilight deepen all the colors about them, turning the western sky into purple glory.

"You know what else you're carrying on this thing?" Richard asked.

"What else?" Jack asked. In truth, he hardly cared. It could be nothing good. He hoped he might live to see another sunset as rich as this one, as large with feeling.

"Plastic explosive. All wrapped up in two-pound packages—I think two pounds, anyhow. You've got enough to blow up a whole city. If one of these guns goes off accidentally, or if someone else puts a bullet into those bags, this train is going to be nothing but a hole in the ground."

"I won't if you won't," Jack said. And let himself be taken by the sunset—it seemed oddly premonitory, a dream of accomplishment, and led him into memories of all he had undergone since leaving the Alhambra Inn and Gardens. He saw his mother drinking tea in the little shop, suddenly a tired old woman; Speedy Parker sitting at the base of a tree; Wolf tending his herd; Smokey and Lori from Oatley's horrible Tap; all the hated faces from the Sunlight Home: Heck Bast, Sonny Singer, and the others. He missed Wolf with a particular and sharp poignancy, for the unfolding and deepening sunset summoned him up wholly, though Jack could not have explained why. He wished he could take Richard's hand. Then he thought, *Well, why not?* and moved his hand along the bench until he encountered his friend's rather grubby, clammy paw. He closed his fingers around it.

"I feel so sick," Richard said. "This isn't like—before. My stomach feels terrible, and my whole face is tingling."

"I think you'll get better once we finally get out of this place," Jack said. *But what proof do you have of that, doctor?* he wondered. *What proof do you have that you're not just poisoning him?* He had none. He consoled himself with his newly invented (newly discovered?) idea that Richard was an essential part of whatever was going to happen at the black hotel. He was going to need Richard Sloat, and not just because Richard Sloat could tell plastic explosive from bags of fertilizer.

Had Richard ever been to the black hotel before? Had he actually been in the Talisman's vicinity? He glanced over at his friend, who was breathing shallowly and laboriously. Richard's hand lay in his own like a cold waxen sculpture.

"I don't want this gun anymore," Richard said, pushing it off his lap. "The smell is making me sick."

"Okay," Jack said, taking it onto his own lap with his free hand. One of the trees crept into his peripheral vision and howled soundlessly in torment. Soon the mutant dogs would begin foraging. Jack glanced up toward the hills to his left—Richard's side—and saw a manlike figure slipping through the rocks.

## 11

"Hey," he said, almost not believing. Indifferent to his shock, the lurid sunset continued to beautify the unbeautifiable. "Hey, Richard."

"What? You sick, too?"

"I think I saw somebody up there. On your side." He peered up at the tall rocks again, but saw no movement.

"I don't care," Richard said.

"You'd better care. See how they're timing it? They want to get to us just when it's too dark for us to see them."

Richard cracked his left eye open and made a half-hearted inspection. "Don't see anybody."

"Neither do I, now, but I'm glad we went back and got these guns. Sit up straight and pay attention, Richard, if you want to get out of here alive."

"You're such a cornball. Jeez." But Richard did pull himself up straight and open both his eyes. "I really don't see anything up there, Jack. It's getting too dark. You probably imagined—"

"Hush," Jack said. He thought he had seen another body easing itself between the rocks at the valley's top. "There's two. I wonder if there'll be another one?"

"I wonder if there'll be anything at all," Richard said. "Why would anyone want to hurt us, anyhow? I mean, it's not—"

Jack turned his head and looked down the tracks ahead of the train. Something moved behind the trunk of one of the screaming trees. Something larger than a dog, Jack recorded.

"Uh-oh," Jack said. "I think another guy is up there waiting for us." For a moment, fear castrated him—he could not think of what to do to protect himself from the three assailants. His stomach froze. He picked up the Uzi from his lap and looked at it dumbly, wondering if he really would be able to use this weapon. Could Blasted Lands hijackers have guns, too?

"Richard, I'm sorry," he said, "but this time I think the shit is really going to hit the fan, and I'm going to need your help."

"What can I do?" Richard asked, his voice squeaky.

"Take your gun," Jack said, handing it to him. "And I think we ought to kneel down so we don't give them so much of a target."

He got on his knees and Richard imitated him in a slow-moving, underwater fashion. From behind them came a long cry, from above them another. "They know we saw them," Richard said. "But where are they?"

The question was almost immediately answered. Still visible in the dark purplish twilight, a man—or what looked like a man—burst out of cover and began running down the slope toward the train. Rags fluttered out behind him. He was screaming like an Indian and raising something in his hands. It appeared to be a flexible pole, and Jack was still trying to work out its function when he heard—more than saw—a narrow shape slice through the air beside his head. "Holy mackerel! They've got bows and arrows!" he said.

Richard groaned, and Jack feared that he would vomit all over both of them.

"I have to shoot him," he said.

Richard gulped and made some noise that wasn't quite a word.

"Oh, hell," Jack said, and flicked off the safety on his Uzi. He raised his head and saw the ragged being behind him just loosing off another arrow. If the shot had been accurate, he would never have seen another thing, but the arrow whanged harmlessly into the side of the cab. Jack jerked up the Uzi and depressed the trigger.

He expected none of what happened. He had thought that the gun would remain still in his hands and obediently expel a few shells. Instead, the Uzi jumped in his hands like an animal, making a series of noises loud enough to damage his eardrums. The stink of powder burned in his nose. The ragged man behind the train threw out his arms, but in amazement, not because he had been wounded. Jack finally thought to take his finger off the trigger. He had no idea of how many shots he had just wasted, or how many bullets remained in the clip.

"Didja get him, didja get him?" Richard asked.

The man was now running up the side of the valley, huge flat feet flapping. Then Jack saw that they were not feet—the man was walking on huge platelike constructions, the Blasted Lands equivalent of snowshoes. He was trying to make it to one of the trees for cover.

He raised the Uzi with both hands and sighted down the short barrel. Then he gently squeezed the trigger. The gun bucked in his hands, but less than the first time. Bullets sprayed out in a wide arc, and at least one of them found its intended target, for the man lurched over sideways as though a truck had just smacked into him. His feet flew out of the snowshoes.

"Give me your gun," Jack said, and took the second Uzi from Richard. Still kneeling, he fired half a clip into the shadowy dark in front of the train and hoped he had killed the creature waiting up there.

Another arrow rattled against the train, and another thunked solidly into the side of the boxcar.

Richard was shaking and crying in the bottom of the cab. "Load mine," Jack said, and jammed a clip from his pocket under Richard's nose. He peered up the side of the valley for the second attacker. In less than a minute it would be too dark to see anything beneath the rim of the valley.

"I see him," Richard shouted. "I saw him—right there!" He pointed toward a shadow moving silently, urgently, among the rocks, and Jack spent the rest of the second Uzi's clip noisily blasting at it. When he was done, Richard took the machine-gun from him and placed the other in his hands.

"Nize boyz, goot boyz," came a voice from the right side— how far ahead of them it was impossible to tell. "You stop now, I stop now, too, geddit? All done now, dis bizness. You nize boys, maybe you zell me dat gun. You kill plenty goot dat way, I zee."

*"Jack!"* Richard whispered frantically, warning him.

"Throw away the bow and arrows," Jack yelled, still crouching beside Richard.

"Jack, you can't!" Richard whispered.

"I t'row dem 'way now," the voice came, still ahead of them. Something light puffed into the dust. "You boyz stop going, zell me gun, geddit?"

"Okay," Jack said. "Come up here where we can see you."

"Geddit," the voice said.

Jack pulled back on the gearshift, letting the train coast to a halt. "When I holler," he whispered to Richard, "jam it forward as fast as you can, okay?"

"Oh, Jesus," Richard breathed.

Jack checked that the safety was off on the gun Richard had just given him. A trickle of sweat ran from his forehead directly into his right eye.

"All goot now, yaz," the voice said. "Boyz can siddup, yaz. Siddup, boys."

*Way-gup, way-gup, pleeze, pleeze.*

The train coasted toward the speaker. "Put your hand on the shift," Jack whispered. "It's coming soon."

Richard's trembling hand, looking too small and childlike to accomplish anything even slightly important, touched the gear lever.

Jack had a sudden, vivid memory of old Anders kneeling before him on a rippling wooden floor, asking, *But will you be safe, my Lord?* He had answered flippantly, hardly taking the question seriously. What were the Blasted Lands to a boy who had humped out kegs for Smokey Updike?

Now he was a lot more afraid that he was going to soil his pants than that Richard was going to lose his lunch all over the Territories version of Myles P. Kiger's loden coat.

A shout of laughter erupted in the darkness beside the cab, and Jack pulled himself upright, bringing up the gun, and yelled just as a heavy body hit the side of the cab and clung there. Richard shoved the gearshift forward, and the train jerked forward.

A naked hairy arm clamped itself on the side of the cab. *So much for the wild west,* Jack thought, and then the man's entire trunk reared up over them. Richard screeched, and Jack very nearly did evacuate his bowels into his underwear.

The face was nearly all teeth—it was a face as instinctively evil as that of a rattler baring its fangs, and a drop of what Jack as instinctively assumed to be venom fell off one of the long, curved teeth. Except for the tiny nose, the creature looming over the boys looked very like a man with the head of a snake. In one webbed hand he raised a knife. Jack squeezed off an aimless, panicky shot.

Then the creature altered and wavered back for a moment, and it took Jack a fraction of a second to see that the webbed hand and the knife were gone. The creature swung forward a bloody stump and left a smear of red on Jack's shirt. Jack's mind conveniently left him, and his fingers were able to point the Uzi straight at the creature's chest and pull the trigger back.

A great hole opened redly in the middle of the mottled chest, and the dripping teeth snapped together. Jack kept the trigger depressed, and the Uzi raised its barrel by itself and destroyed the creature's head in a second or two of total carnage. Then it was gone. Only a large bloodstain on the side of the cab, and the smear of blood on Jack's shirt, showed that the two boys had not dreamed the entire encounter.

"Watch out!" Richard yelled.

"I got him," Jack breathed.

"Where'd he go?"

"He fell off," Jack said. "He's dead."

"You shot his *hand* off," Richard whispered. "How'd you do that?"

Jack held up his hands before him and saw how they shook. The stink of gunpowder encased them. "I just sort of imitated someone with good aim." He put his hands down and licked his lips.

Twelve hours later, as the sun came up again over the Blasted Lands, neither boy had slept—they had spent the entire night as rigid as soldiers, holding their guns in their laps and straining to hear the smallest of noises. Remembering how much ammunition the train was carrying, every now and then Jack randomly aimed a few rounds at the lip of the valley. And that second entire day, if there were people or monsters in this far sector of the Blasted Lands, they let the boys pass unmolested. Which could mean, Jack tiredly thought, that they knew about the guns. Or that out here, so near to the western shore, nobody wanted to mess with Morgan's train. He said

none of this to Richard, whose eyes were filmy and unfocused, and who seemed feverish much of the time.

## 12

By evening of that day, Jack began to smell saltwater in the
acrid air.

## 36

# Jack and Richard Go to War

### 1

The sunset that night was wider—the land had begun to open
out again as they approached the ocean—but not so spectacular. Jack stopped the train at the top of an eroded hill and
climbed back to the flatcar again. He poked about for nearly
an hour—until the sullen colors had faded from the sky and a
quarter moon had risen in the east—and brought back six
boxes, all marked LENSES.

"Open those," he told Richard. "Get a count. You're appointed Keeper of the Clips."

"Marvelous," Richard said in a wan voice. "I knew I was
getting all that education for something."

Jack went back to the flatcar again and pried up the lid of
one of the crates marked MACHINE PARTS. While he was doing
this he heard a harsh, hoarse cry somewhere off in the darkness, followed by a shrill scream of pain.

"Jack? Jack, you back there?"

"Right here!" Jack called. He thought it very unwise for
the two of them to be yelling back and forth like a couple of
washerwomen over a back fence, but Richard's voice suggested that he was close to panicking.

"You coming back pretty soon?"

"Be right there!" Jack called, levering faster and harder

with the Uzi's barrel. They were leaving the Blasted Lands behind, but Jack still didn't want to stand at a stop for too long. It would have been simpler if he could have just carried the box of machine-guns back to the engine, but it was too heavy.

*They ain't heavy, they're my Uzis,* Jack thought, and giggled a little in the dark.

"*Jack?*" Richard's voice was high-pitched, frantic.

"Hold your water, chum," he said.

"Don't call me chum," Richard said.

Nails shrieked out of the crate's lid, and it came up enough for Jack to be able to pull it off. He grabbed two of the grease-guns and was starting back when he saw another box—it was about the size of a portable-TV carton. A fold of the tarp had covered it previously.

Jack went skittering across the top of the boxcar under the faint moonlight, feeling the breeze blow into his face. It was clean—no taint of rotted perfume, no feeling of corruption, just clean dampness and the unmistakable scent of salt.

"What were you doing?" Richard scolded. "Jack, we *have* guns! And we *have* bullets! Why did you want to go back and get more? Something could have climbed up here while you were playing around!"

"More guns because machine-guns have a tendency to overheat," Jack said. "More bullets because we may have to shoot a lot. *I* watch TV, too, you see." He started back toward the flatcar again. He wanted to see what was in that square box.

Richard grabbed him. Panic turned his hand into a birdlike talon.

"Richard, it's going to be all right—"

"Something might grab you off!"

"I think we're almost out of the Bl—"

"Something might grab *me* off! Jack, don't leave me *alone!*"

Richard burst into tears. He did not turn away from Jack or put his hands to his face; he only stood there, his face twisted, his eyes spouting tears. He looked cruelly naked to Jack just then. Jack folded him into his arms and held him.

"If something gets you and kills you, what happens to

me?" Richard sobbed. "How would I ever, ever, get out of this place?"

*I don't know,* Jack thought. *I really don't know.*

## 2

So Richard came with him on Jack's last trip to the travelling ammo dump on the flatcar. This meant boosting him up the ladder and then supporting him along the top of the boxcar and helping him carefully down, as one might help a crippled old lady across a street. Rational Richard was making a mental comeback—but physically he was growing steadily worse.

Although preservative grease was bleeding out between its boards, the square box was marked FRUIT. Nor was that completely inaccurate, Jack discovered when they got it open. The box was full of pineapples. The exploding kind.

"Holy Hannah," Richard whispered.

"Whoever *she* is," Jack agreed. "Help me. I think we can each get four or five down our shirts."

"Why do you want all this firepower?" Richard asked. "Are you expecting to fight an army?"

"Something like that."

## 3

Richard looked up into the sky as he and Jack were recrossing the top of the boxcar, and a wave of faintness overtook him. Richard tottered and Jack had to grab him to keep him from toppling over the side. He had realized that he could recognize constellations of neither the Northern Hemisphere nor the Southern. Those were alien stars up there . . . but there *were* patterns, and somewhere in this unknown, unbelievable world, sailors might be navigating by them. It was that thought which brought the reality of all this home to Richard—brought it home with a final, undeniable thud.

Then Jack's voice was calling him back from far away: "Hey, Richie! Jason! You almost fell over the side!"

Finally they were in the cab again.

Jack pushed the lever into the forward gear, pressed down on the accelerator bar, and Morgan of Orris's oversized flashlight started to move forward again. Jack glanced down at the floor of the cab: four Uzi machine-guns, almost twenty piles of clips, ten to a pile, and ten hand grenades with pull-pins that looked like the pop-tops of beercans.

"If we haven't got enough stuff now," Jack said, "we might as well forget it."

"What are you expecting, Jack?"

Jack only shook his head.

"Guess you must think I'm a real jerk, huh?" Richard asked.

Jack grinned. "Always have, chum."

"Don't call me chum!"

"Chum-chum-*chum!*"

This time the old joke raised a small smile. Not much, and it rather highlighted the growing line of lip-blisters on Richard's mouth . . . but better than nothing.

"Will you be okay if I go back to sleep?" Richard asked, brushing machine-gun clips aside and settling in a corner of the cab with Jack's serape over him. "All that climbing and carrying . . . I think I really must be sick because I feel really bushed."

"I'll be fine," Jack said. Indeed, he seemed to be getting a second wind. He supposed he would need it before long.

"I can smell the ocean," Richard said, and in his voice Jack heard an amazing mixture of love, loathing, nostalgia, and fear. Richard's eyes slipped closed.

Jack pushed the accelerator bar all the way down. His feeling that the end—some sort of end—was now close had never been stronger.

## 4

The last mean and miserable vestiges of the Blasted Lands were gone before the moon set. The grain had reappeared. It was coarser here than it had been in Ellis-Breaks, but it still radiated a feeling of cleanness and health. Jack heard the faint calling of birds which sounded like gulls. It was an inexpressibly lonely sound, in these great open rolling fields which smelled faintly of fruit and more pervasively of ocean salt.

After midnight the train began to hum through stands of trees—most of them were evergreens, and their piney scent, mixed with the salty tang in the air, seemed to cement the connection between this place he was coming to and the place from which he had set out. He and his mother had never spent a great deal of time in northern California—perhaps because Bloat vacationed there often—but he remembered Lily's telling him that the land around Mendocino and Sausalito looked very much like New England, right down to the salt-boxes and Cape Cods. Film companies in need of New England settings usually just went upstate rather than travelling all the way across the country, and most audiences never knew the difference.

*This is how it should be. In a weird way, I'm coming back to the place I left behind.*

Richard: *Are you expecting to fight an army?*

He was glad Richard had gone to sleep, so he wouldn't have to answer that question—at least, not yet.

Anders: *Devil-things. For the bad Wolfs. To take to the black hotel.*

The devil-things were Uzi machine-guns, plastic explosive, grenades. The devil-things were here. The bad Wolfs were not. The boxcar, however, was empty, and Jack found that fact terribly persuasive.

*Here's a story for you, Richie-boy, and I'm very glad you're asleep so I don't have to tell it to you. Morgan knows I'm coming, and he's planning a surprise party. Only it's werewolves instead of naked girls who are going to jump out of the cake, and they're supposed to have Uzi machine-guns and grenades as party-favors. Well, we sort of hijacked his train, and we're running ten or twelve hours ahead of schedule, but if we're heading into an encampment full of Wolfs waiting to catch the Territories choo-choo—and I think that's just what we're doing—we're going to need all the surprise we can get.*

Jack ran a hand up the side of his face.

It would be easier to stop the train well away from wherever Morgan's hit-squad was, and make a big circle around the encampment. Easier and safer, too.

*But that would leave the bad Wolfs around, Richie, can you dig it?*

He looked down at the arsenal on the floor of the cab and wondered if he could really be planning a commando raid on Morgan's Wolf Brigade. Some commandos. Good old Jack Sawyer, King of the Vagabond Dishwashers, and His Co-

matose Sidekick, Richard. Jack wondered if he had gone
crazy. He supposed he had, because that was exactly what he
was planning—it would be the last thing any of them would
expect . . . and there had been too much, too much, too goddam much. He had been whipped; Wolf had been killed. They
had destroyed Richard's school and most of Richard's sanity,
and, for all he knew, Morgan Sloat was back in New Hampshire, harrying his mother.

Crazy or not, payback time had come.

Jack bent over, picked up one of the loaded Uzis, and held
it over his arm as the tracks unrolled in front of him and the
smell of salt grew steadily stronger.


## 5

During the small hours of the morning Jack slept awhile,
leaning against the accelerator bar. It would not have comforted him much to know such a device was called a dead-
man's switch. When dawn came, it was Richard who woke
him up.

"Something up ahead."

Before looking at that, Jack took a good look at Richard.
He had hoped that Richard would look better in daylight, but
not even the cosmetic of dawn could disguise the fact that
Richard was sick. The color of the new day had changed the
dominant color in his skin-tone from gray to yellow . . . that
was all.

*"Hey! Train! Hello you big fuckin train!"* This shout was
guttural, little more than an animal roar. Jack looked forward
again.

They were closing in on a narrow little pillbox of a building.

Standing outside the guardhouse was a Wolf—but any resemblance to Jack's Wolf ended with the flaring orange eyes.
This Wolf's head looked dreadfully flattened, as if a great
hand had scythed off the curve of skull at the top. His face
seemed to jut over his underslung jaw like a boulder teetering
over a long drop. Even the present surprised joy on that face
could not conceal its thick, brutal stupidity. Braided pigtails
of hair hung from his cheeks. A scar in the shape of an X rode
his forehead.

The Wolf was wearing something like a mercenary's uniform—or what he imagined a mercenary's uniform would look like. Baggy green pants were bloused out over black boots—but the toes of the boots had been cut off, Jack saw, to allow the Wolf's long-nailed, hairy toes to protrude.

*"Train!"* he bark-growled as the engine closed the last fifty yards. He began to jump up and down, grinning savagely. He was snapping his fingers like Cab Calloway. Foam flew from his jaws in unlovely clots. *"Train! Train! Fuckin train RIGHT HERE AND NOW!"* His mouth yawned open in a great and alarming grin, showing a mouthful of broken yellow spears. *"You guys some kinda fuckin early, okay, okay!"*

"Jack, what is it?" Richard asked. His hand was clutching Jack's shoulder with panicky tightness, but to his credit, his voice was fairly even.

"It's a Wolf. One of Morgan's."

*There, Jack, you said his name. Asshole!*

But there was no time to worry about that now. They were coming abreast of the guardhouse, and the Wolf obviously meant to swing aboard. As Jack watched, he cut a clumsy caper in the dust, cut-off boots thumping. He had a knife in the leather belt he wore across his naked chest like a bandoleer, but no gun.

Jack flicked the control on the Uzi to single-fire.

"Morgan? Who's Morgan? *Which* Morgan?"

"Not now," Jack said.

His concentration narrowed down to a fine point—the Wolf. He manufactured a big, plastic grin for his benefit, holding the Uzi down and well out of sight.

*"Anders-train! All-fuckin-right! Here and now!"*

A handle like a big staple stuck off from the right side of the engine, above a wide step like a running board. Grinning wildly, drizzling foam over his chin and obviously insane, the Wolf grabbed the handle and leaped lightly up onto the step.

"Hey, where's the old man? Wolf! Where's—"

Jack raised the Uzi and put a bullet into the Wolf's left eye.

The glaring orange light puffed out like a candle-flame in a strong gust of wind. The Wolf fell backward off the step like a man doing a rather stupid dive. He thudded loosely on the ground.

"Jack!" Richard pulled him around. His face looked as

wild as the Wolf's face had been—only it was terror, not joy, that distorted it. *"Did you mean my father? Is my father involved in this?"*

"Richard, do you trust me?"

"Yes, but—"

"Then let it go. *Let it go.* This is not the time."

"But—"

"Get a gun."

"Jack—"

"Richard, *get a gun!*"

Richard bent over and got one of the Uzis. "I hate guns," he said again.

"Yeah, I know. I'm not particularly keen on them myself, Richie-boy. But it's payback time."

## 6

The tracks were now approaching a high stockade wall. From behind it came grunts and yells, cheers, rhythmic clapping, the sound of bootheels punching down on bare earth in steady rhythms. There were other, less identifiable sounds as well, but all of them fell into a vague set for Jack—*military training operation.* The area between the guardhouse and the approaching stockade wall was half a mile wide, and with all this other stuff going on, Jack doubted that anyone had heard his single shot. The train, being electric, was almost silent. The advantage of surprise should still be on their side.

The tracks disappeared beneath a closed double gate in the side of the stockade wall. Jack could see chinks of daylight between the rough-peeled logs.

"Jack, you better slow down." They were now a hundred and fifty yards from the gate. From behind it, bellowing voices chanted, *"Sound-HOFF! Hun-too! Hree-FO! Sound-HOFF!"* Jack thought again of H. G. Wells's manimals and shivered.

"No way, chum. We're through the gate. You got just about time to do the Fish Cheer."

"Jack, you're crazy!"

"I know."

A hundred yards. The batteries hummed. A blue spark jumped, sizzling. Bare earth flowed past them on either side.

*No grain here,* Jack thought. *If Noël Coward had written a play about Morgan Sloat, I guess he would have called it* Blight Spirit.

"Jack, what if this creepy little train jumps its tracks?"

"Well, it might, I guess," Jack said.

"Or what if it breaks through the gate and the tracks just *end?*"

"That'd be one on us, wouldn't it?"

Fifty yards.

"Jack, you really have lost your mind, haven't you?"

"I guess so. Take your gun off safety, Richard."

Richard flicked the safety.

Thuds . . . grunts . . . marching men . . . the creak of leather . . . yells . . . an inhuman, laughing shriek that made Richard cringe. And yet Jack saw a clear resolution in Richard's face that made Jack grin with pride. *He means to stick by me—old Rational Richard or not, he really means to stick by me.*

Twenty-five yards.

Shrieks . . . squeals . . . shouted commands . . . and a thick, reptilian cry—*Groooo-OOOO!*—that made the hair stand up on the back of Jack's neck.

"If we get out of this," Jack said, "I'll buy you a chili-dog at Dairy Queen."

*"Barf me out!"* Richard yelled, and, incredibly, he began to laugh. In that instant the unhealthy yellow seemed to fade a bit from his face.

Five yards—and the peeled posts which made up the gate looked solid, yes, very solid, and Jack just had time to wonder if he hadn't made a great big fat mistake.

"Get down, chum!"

"Don't call m—"

The train hit the stockade gate, throwing them both forward.

### 7

The gate was really quite strong, and in addition it was double-barred across the inside with two large logs. Morgan's train was not terribly big, and the batteries were nearly flat after its long run across the Blasted Lands. The collision surely would have derailed it, and both boys might well have been killed in the wreck, but the gate had an Achilles' heel. New hinges, forged according to modern American processes, were on order. They had not yet arrived, however, and the old iron hinges snapped when the engine hit the gate.

The train came rolling into the stockade at twenty-five miles an hour, pushing the amputated gate in front of it. An obstacle course had been built around the stockade's perimeter, and the gate, acting like a snowplow, began shoving makeshift wooden hurdles in front of it, turning them, rolling them, snapping them into splinters.

It also struck a Wolf who had been doing punishment laps. His feet disappeared under the bottom of the moving gate and were chewed off, customized boots and all. Shrieking and growling, his Change beginning, the Wolf began to claw-climb his way up the gate with fingernails which were growing rapidly to the length and sharpness of a telephone-lineman's spikes. The gate was now forty feet inside the stockade. Amazingly, he got almost to the top before Jack dropped the gear-lever into neutral. The train stopped. The gate fell over, puffing up big dust and crushing the unfortunate Wolf beneath it. Underneath the last car of the train, the Wolf's severed feet continued to grow hair, and would for several more minutes.

The situation inside the camp was better than Jack had dared hope. The place apparently woke up early, as military installations have a way of doing, and most of the troops seemed to be out, going through a bizarre menu of drills and body-building exercises.

*"On the right!"* he shouted at Richard.

*"Do what?"* Richard shouted back.

Jack opened his mouth and cried out: for Uncle Tommy Woodbine, run down in the street; for an unknown carter, whipped to death in a muddy courtyard; for Ferd Janklow; for Wolf, dead in Sunlight Gardener's filthy office; for his mother; but most of all, he discovered, for Queen Laura De-Loessian, who was also his mother, and for the crime that was being carried out on the body of the Territories. He cried out as Jason, and his voice was thunder.

*"TEAR THEM UP!"* Jack Sawyer/Jason DeLoessian bellowed, and opened fire on the left.

### 8

There was a rough parade ground on Jack's side, a long log building on Richard's. The log building looked like the bunkhouse in a Roy Rogers movie, but Richard guessed that it was a barracks. In fact, this whole place looked more familiar to Richard than anything he had seen so far in this weird world Jack had taken him into. He had seen places like it on the TV news. CIA-supported rebels training for takeovers of South and Central American countries trained in places like this. Only, the training camps were usually in Florida, and those weren't *cubanos* pouring out of the barracks—Richard didn't know *what* they were.

Some of them looked a bit like medieval paintings of devils and satyrs. Some looked like degenerate human beings—cave-people, almost. And one of the things lurching into the early-morning sunlight had scaly skin and nictitating eyelids . . . it looked to Richard Sloat like an alligator that was somehow walking upright. As he looked, the thing lifted its snout and uttered that cry he and Jack had heard earlier: *Grooo-OOOOO!* He just had time to see that most of these hellish creatures looked totally bewildered, and then Jack's Uzi split the world with thunder.

On Jack's side, roughly two dozen Wolfs had been doing callies on the parade ground. Like the guardhouse Wolf, most wore green fatigue pants, boots with cut-off toes, and bandoleer belts. Like the guard, they looked stupid, flatheaded, and essentially evil.

They had paused in the middle of a spastic set of jumping jacks to watch the train come roaring in, the gate and the unfortunate fellow who had been running laps at the wrong place and time plastered to the front. At Jack's cry they began to move, but by then they were too late.

Most of Morgan's carefully culled Wolf Brigade, handpicked over a period of five years for their strength and brutality, their fear of and loyalty to Morgan, were wiped out in one spitting, raking burst of the machine-gun in Jack's hands.

They went stumbling and reeling backward, chests blown open, heads bleeding. There were growls of bewildered anger and howls of pain . . . but not many. Most of them simply died.

Jack popped the clip, grabbed another one, slammed it in. On the left side of the parade ground, four of the Wolfs had escaped; in the center two more had dropped below the line of fire. Both of these had been wounded but now both were coming at him, long-nailed toes digging divots in the packed dust, faces sprouting hair, eyes flaring. As they ran at the engine, Jack saw fangs grow out of their mouths and push through fresh, wiry hair growing from their chins.

He pulled the trigger on the Uzi, now holding the hot barrel down only with an effort; the heavy recoil was trying to force the muzzle up. Both of the attacking Wolfs were thrown back so violently that they flipped through the air head-over-heels like acrobats. The other four Wolfs did not pause; they headed for the place where the gate had been two minutes before.

The assorted creatures which had spilled out of the bunk-house-style barracks building seemed to be finally getting the idea that, although the newcomers were driving Morgan's train, they were a good deal less than friendly. There was no concentrated charge, but they began to move forward in a muttering clot. Richard laid the Uzi's barrel on the chest-high side of the engine cab and opened fire. The slugs tore them open, drove them backward. Two of the things which looked like goats dropped to hands and knees—or hooves—and scurried back inside. Richard saw three others spin and drop under the force of the slugs. A joy so savage that it made him feel faint swept through him.

Bullets also tore open the whitish-green belly of the alligator-thing, and a blackish fluid—ichor, not blood—began to pour out of it. It fell backward, but its tail seemed to cushion it. It sprang back up and leaped at Richard's side of the train. It uttered its rough, powerful cry again . . . and this time it seemed to Richard that there was something hideously feminine in that cry.

He pulled the trigger of the Uzi. Nothing happened. The clip was spent.

The alligator-thing ran with slow, clumsy, thudding determination. Its eyes sparkled with murderous fury . . . and intelligence. The vestiges of breasts bounced on its scaly chest.

He bent, groped, without taking his eyes off the were-alligator, and found one of the grenades.

*Seabrook Island,* Richard thought dreamily. *Jack calls this place the Territories, but it's really Seabrook Island, and there is no need to be afraid, really no need; this is all a dream and if that thing's scaly claws settle around my neck I will surely wake up, and even if it's not all a dream, Jack will save me somehow—I know he will, I know it, because over here Jack is some kind of a god.*

He pulled the pin on the grenade, restrained the strong urge he felt to simply chuck it in a panicky frenzy, and lobbed it gently, underhand. *"Jack, get down!"*

Jack dropped below the level of the engine cab's sides at once, without looking. Richard did, too, but not before he had seen an incredible, blackly comic thing: the alligator-creature had caught the grenade . . . and was trying to eat it.

The explosion was not the dull crump Richard had expected but a loud, braying roar that drilled into his ears, hurting them badly. He heard a splash, as if someone had thrown a bucket of water against his side of the train.

He looked up and saw that the engine, boxcar and flatcar were covered with hot guts, black blood, and shreds of the alligator-creature's flesh. The entire front of the barracks building had been blown away. Much of the splintered rubble was bloody. In the midst of it he saw a hairy foot in a boot with a cut-off toe.

The jackstraw blowdown of logs was thrown aside as he watched, and two of the goatlike creatures began to pull themselves out. Richard bent, found a fresh clip, and slammed it into his gun. It was getting hot, just as Jack had said it would.

*Whoopee!* Richard thought faintly, and opened fire again.

### 9

When Jack popped up after the grenade explosion, he saw that the four Wolfs who had escaped his first two fusillades were just running through the hole where the gate had been. They were howling with terror. They were running side by

side, and Jack had a clear shot at them. He raised the Uzi—
then lowered it again, knowing he would see them later, probably at the black hotel, knowing he was a fool . . . but, fool or
not, he was unable to just let them have it in the back.

Now a high, womanish shrieking began from behind the
barracks. *"Get out there! Get out there, I say! Move! Move!"*
There was the whistling crack of a whip.

Jack knew that sound, and he knew that voice. He had been
wrapped up in a strait-jacket when he had last heard it. Jack
would have known that voice anywhere.

*—If his retarded friend shows up, shoot him.*

*Well, you managed that, but maybe now it's payback time—
and maybe, from the way your voice sounds, you know it.*

*"Get them, what's the matter with you cowards? Get them,
do I have to show you how to do everything? Follow us, follow us!"*

Three creatures came from behind what remained of the
barracks, and only one of them was clearly human—Osmond.
He carried his whip in one hand, a Sten gun in the other. He
wore a red cloak and black boots and white silk pants with
wide, flowing legs. They were splattered with fresh blood. To
his left was a shaggy goat-creature wearing jeans and West-
ernstyle boots. This creature and Jack looked at each other
and shared a moment of complete recognition. It was the
dreadful barroom cowboy from the Oatley Tap. It was Randolph Scott. It was Elroy. It grinned at Jack; its long tongue
snaked out and lapped its wide upper lip.

*"Get him!"* Osmond screamed at Elroy.

Jack tried to lift the Uzi, but it suddenly seemed very
heavy in his arms. Osmond was bad, the reappearance of Elroy was worse, but the thing between the two of them was a
nightmare. It was the Territories version of Reuel Gardener,
of course; the son of Osmond, the son of Sunlight. And it did
indeed look a bit like a child—a child as drawn by a bright
kindergarten student with a cruel turn of mind.

It was curdy-white and skinny; one of its arms ended in a
wormy tentacle that somehow reminded Jack of Osmond's
whip. Its eyes, one of them adrift, were on different levels. Fat
red sores covered its cheeks.

*Some of it's radiation sickness . . . Jason, I think Osmond's
boy might have gotten a little too close to one of those fire-*

*balls . . . but the rest of it . . . Jason . . . Jesus . . . what was its mother? In the name of all the worlds, WHAT WAS ITS MOTHER?*

"*Get the Pretender!*" Osmond was shrieking. "*Save Morgan's son but get the Pretender! Get the false Jason! Get out here, you cowards! They're out of bullets!*"

Roars, bellows. In a moment, Jack knew, a fresh contingent of Wolfs, supported by Assorted Geeks and Freaks, was going to appear from the back end of the long barracks, where they would have been shielded from the explosion, where they had probably been cowering with their heads down, and where they would have remained . . . except for Osmond.

"Should have stayed off the road, little chicken," Elroy grunted, and ran at the train. His tail was swishing through the air. Reuel Gardener—or whatever Reuel was in this world—made a thick mewling sound and attempted to follow. Osmond reached out and hauled him back; his fingers, Jack saw, appeared to slide right into the monster-boy's slatlike, repulsive neck.

Then he raised the Uzi and fired an entire clip, point-blank, into Elroy's face. It tore the goat-thing's entire head off, and yet Elroy, headless, continued to climb for a moment, and one of his hands, the fingers melted together in two clumps to make a parody of a cloven hoof, pawed blindly for Jack's head before it tumbled backward.

Jack stared at it, stunned—he had dreamed that final nightmarish confrontation at the Oatley Tap over and over again, trying to stumble away from the monster through what seemed to be a dark jungle filled with bedsprings and broken glass. Now here was that creature, and he had somehow killed it. It was hard to get his mind around the fact. It was as if he had killed childhood's bogeyman.

Richard was screaming—and his machine-gun roared, nearly deafening Jack.

"*It's Reuel! Oh Jack oh my God oh Jason it's Reuel, it's Reuel—*"

The Uzi in Richard's hands coughed out another short burst before falling silent, its clip spent. Reuel shook free of his father. He lurched and hopped toward the train, mewling. His upper lip curled back, revealing long teeth that looked false and flimsy, like the wax teeth children don at Halloween.

Richard's final burst took him in the chest and neck, punching holes in the brown kilt-*cum*-jumper he wore, ripping open flesh in long, ragged furrows. Sluggish rills of dark blood flowed from these wounds, but no more. Reuel might once have been human—Jack supposed it was just possible. If so, he was not human now; the bullets did not even slow him down. The thing which leaped clumsily over Elroy's body was a demon. It smelled like a wet toadstool.

Something was growing warm against Jack's leg. Just warm at first . . . then hot. What was it? Felt like he had a teakettle in his pocket. But he didn't have time to think. Things were unfolding in front of him. In Technicolor.

Richard dropped his Uzi and staggered back, clapping his hands to his face. His horrified eyes stared out at the Reuel-thing through the bars of his fingers.

*"Don't let him get me, Jack! Don't let him get meeeee. . . ."*

Reuel bubbled and mewled. His hands slapped against the side of the engine and the sound was like large fins slapping down on thick mud.

Jack saw there were indeed thick, yellowish webs between the fingers.

*"Come back!"* Osmond was yelling at his son, and the fear in his voice was unmistakable. *"Come back, he's bad, he'll hurt you, all boys are bad, it's axiomatic, come back, come back!"*

Reuel burbled and grunted enthusiastically. He pulled himself up and Richard screamed insanely, backing into the far corner of the cab.

*"DON'T LET HIM GET MEEEEEEE—"*

More Wolfs, more strange freaks charging around the corner. One of them, a creature with curly ram's horns jutting from the sides of its head and wearing only a pair of patched L'il Abner britches, fell down and was trampled by the others.

Heat against Jack's leg in a circle.

Reuel, now throwing one reedy leg over the side of the cab. It was slobbering, reaching for him, and the leg was writhing, it wasn't a leg at all, it was a tentacle. Jack raised the Uzi and fired.

Half of the Reuel-thing's face sheered away like pudding. A flood of worms began to fall out of what was left.

Reuel was still coming.

Reaching for him with those webbed fingers.

Richard's shrieks, Osmond's shrieks merging, melting together into one.

Heat like a branding iron against his leg and suddenly he knew what it was, even as Reuel's hands squashed down on his shoulders he knew—it was the coin Captain Farren had given him, the coin Anders had refused to take.

He drove his hand into his pocket. The coin was like a chunk of ore in his hand—he made a fist around it, and felt power ram through him in big volts. Reuel felt it, too. His triumphant slobberings and grunts became mewlings of fear. He tried to back away, his one remaining eye rolling wildly.

Jack brought the coin out. It glowed red-hot in his hand. He felt the heat clearly—but it was not burning him.

The profile of the Queen glowed like the sun.

*"In her name, you filthy, aborted thing!"* Jack shouted. *"Get you off the skin of this world!"* He opened his fist and slammed his hand into Reuel's forehead.

Reuel and his father shrieked in harmony—Osmond a tenor-verging-on-soprano, Reuel a buzzing, insectile bass. The coin slid into Reuel's forehead like the tip of a hot poker into a tub of butter. A vile dark fluid, the color of overbrewed tea, ran out of Reuel's head and over Jack's wrist. The fluid was hot. There were tiny worms in it. They twisted and writhed on Jack's skin. He felt them biting. Nevertheless, he pressed the first two fingers of his right hand harder, driving the coin farther into the monster's head.

*"Get you off the skin of this world, vileness! In the name of the Queen and in the name of her son, get you off the skin of this world!"*

It shrieked and wailed; Osmond shrieked and wailed with it. The reinforcements had stopped and were milling behind Osmond, their faces full of superstitious terror. To them Jack seemed to have grown; he seemed to be giving off a bright light.

Reuel jerked. Uttered one more bubbling screech. The black stuff running out of his head turned yellow. A final worm, long and thickly white, wriggled out of the hole the coin had made. It fell to the floor of the engine compartment. Jack stepped on it. It broke open under his heel and splattered. Reuel fell in a wet heap.

Now such a screaming wail of grief and fury arose in the

dusty stockade yard that Jack thought his skull might actually split open with it. Richard had curled into a fetal ball with his arms wrapped around his head.

Osmond was wailing. He had dropped his whip and the machine-pistol.

*"Oh, filthy!"* he cried, shaking his fists at Jack. *"Look what you've done! Oh, you filthy, bad boy! I hate you, hate you forever and beyond forever! Oh, filthy Pretender! I'll kill you! Morgan will kill you! Oh my darling only son! FILTHY! MORGAN WILL KILL YOU FOR WHAT YOU'VE DONE! MORGAN—"*

The others took up the cry in a whispering voice, reminding Jack of the boys in the Sunlight Home: *can you gimme hallelujah*. And then they fell silent, because there was the other sound.

Jack was tumbled back instantly to the pleasant afternoon he had spent with Wolf, the two of them sitting by the stream, watching the herd graze and drink as Wolf talked about his family. It had been pleasant enough . . . pleasant enough, that is, until Morgan came.

And now Morgan was coming again—not flipping over but bludgeoning his way through, raping his way in.

"Morgan! It's—"

"—Morgan, Lord—"

"Lord of Orris—"

"Morgan . . . Morgan . . . Morgan . . ."

The ripping sound grew louder and louder. The Wolfs were abasing themselves in the dust. Osmond danced a shuffling jig, his black boots trampling the steel-tipped rawhide thongs woven into his whip.

"Bad boy! Filthy boy! Now you'll pay! Morgan's coming! Morgan's coming!"

The air about twenty feet to Osmond's right began to blur and shimmer, like the air over a burning incinerator.

Jack looked around, saw Richard curled up in the litter of machine-guns and ammunition and grenades like a very small boy who has fallen asleep while playing war. Only Richard wasn't asleep, he knew, and this was no game, and if Richard saw his father stepping through a hole between the worlds, he feared, Richard would go insane.

Jack sprawled beside his friend and wrapped his arms

tightly around him. That ripping-bedsheet sound grew louder, and suddenly he heard Morgan's voice bellow in terrible rage:

*"What is the train doing here NOW, you fools?"*

He heard Osmond wail, *"The filthy Pretender has killed my son!"*

"Here we go, Richie," Jack muttered, and tightened his grip around Richard's wasted upper body. "Time to jump ship."

He closed his eyes, concentrated . . . and there was that brief moment of spinning vertigo as the two of them flipped.

# 37

# Richard Remembers

## 1

There was a sensation of rolling sideways and down, as if there were a short ramp between the two worlds. Dimly, fading, at last wavering into nothingness, Jack heard Osmond screaming, *"Bad! All boys! Axiomatic! All boys! Filthy! Filthy!"*

For a moment they were in thin air. Richard cried out. Then Jack thudded to the ground on one shoulder. Richard's head bounced against his chest. Jack did not open his eyes but only lay there on the ground hugging Richard, listening, smelling.

Silence. Not utter and complete, but large—its size counterpointed by two or three singing birds.

The smell was cool and salty. A good smell . . . but not as good as the world could smell in the Territories. Even here—wherever *here* was—Jack could smell a faint underodor, like the smell of old oil ground into the concrete floors of gas-station garage bays. It was the smell of too many people running too many motors, and it had polluted the entire atmosphere. His nose had been sensitized to it and he could smell it even here, in a place where he could hear no cars.

"Jack? Are we okay?"

"Sure," Jack said, and opened his eyes to see whether he was telling the truth.

His first glance brought a terrifying idea: somehow, in his frantic need to get out of there, to get away before Morgan could arrive, he had not flipped them into the American Territories but pushed them somehow forward in time. This seemed to be the same place, but older, now abandoned, as if a century or two had gone by. The train still sat on the tracks, and the train looked just as it had. Nothing else did. The tracks, which crossed the weedy exercise yard they were standing in and went on to God knew where, were old and thick with rust. The crossties looked spongy and rotted. High weeds grew up between them.

He tightened his hold on Richard, who squirmed weakly in his grasp and opened his eyes.

"Where are we?" he asked Jack, looking around. There was a long Quonset hut with a rust-splotched corrugated-tin roof where the bunkhouse-style barracks had been. The roof was all either of them could see clearly; the rest was buried in rambling woods ivy and wild weeds. There were a couple of poles in front of it which had perhaps once supported a sign. If so, it was long gone now.

"I don't know," Jack said, and then, looking at where the obstacle course had been—it was now a barely glimpsed dirt rut overgrown with the remains of wild phlox and goldenrod— he brought out his worst fear: "I may have pushed us forward in time."

To his amazement, Richard laughed. "It's good to know nothing much is going to change in the future, then," he said, and pointed to a sheet of paper nailed to one of the posts standing in front of the Quonset/barracks. It was somewhat weather-faded but still perfectly readable:

NO TRESPASSING!
By Order of the Mendocino County Sheriff's Department
By Order of the California State Police
VIOLATORS WILL BE PROSECUTED!

## 2

"Well, if you *knew* where we were," Jack said, feeling simultaneously foolish and very relieved, "why did you ask?"

"I just saw it," Richard replied, and any urge Jack might

have had to chaff Richard anymore over it blew away. Richard
looked awful; he looked as if he had developed some weird
tuberculosis which was working on his mind instead of on his
lungs. Nor was it just his sanity-shaking round trip to the Territories and back—he had actually seemed to be adapting to
that. But now he knew something else as well. It wasn't just a
reality which was radically different from all of his carefully
developed notions; *that* he might have been able to adapt to, if
given world enough and time. But finding out that your dad is
one of the guys in the black hats, Jack reflected, can hardly be
one of life's groovier moments.

"Okay," he said, trying to sound cheerful—he actually *did*
feel a little cheerful. Getting away from such a monstrosity as
Reuel would have made even a kid dying of terminal cancer
feel a little cheerful, he figured. "Up you go and up you get,
Richie-boy. We've got promises we must keep, miles to go before we sleep, and you are still an utter creep."

Richard winced. "Whoever gave you the idea you had a
sense of humor should be shot, chum."

*"Bitez mon crank, mon ami."*

"Where are we going?"

"I don't know," Jack said, "but it's somewhere around here.
I can feel it. It's like a fishhook in my mind."

"Point Venuti?"

Jack turned his head and looked at Richard for a long time.
Richard's tired eyes were unreadable.

"Why did you ask that, chum?"

"Is that where we're going?"

Jack shrugged. *Maybe. Maybe not.*

They began walking slowly across the weed-grown parade
ground and Richard changed the subject. "Was all of that
real?" They were approaching the rusty double gate. A lane of
faded blue sky showed above the green. "Was *any* of it real?"

"We spent a couple of days on an electric train that ran at
about twenty-five miles an hour, thirty tops," Jack said, "and
somehow we got from Springfield, Illinois, into northern California, near the coast. Now *you* tell *me* if it was real."

"Yes . . . yes, but . . ."

Jack held out his arms. The wrists were covered with angry red weals that itched and smarted.

"Bites," Jack said. "From the worms. The worms that fell out of Reuel Gardener's head."

Richard turned away and was noisily sick.

Jack held him. Otherwise, he thought, Richard simply would have fallen sprawling. He was appalled at how thin Richard had become, at how hot his flesh felt through his preppy shirt.

"I'm sorry I said that," Jack said when Richard seemed a little better. "It was pretty crude."

"Yeah, it was. But I guess maybe it's the only thing that could have . . . you know . . ."

"Convinced you?"

"Yeah. Maybe." Richard looked at him with his naked, wounded eyes. There were now pimples all across his forehead. Sores surrounded his mouth. "Jack, I have to ask you something, and I want you to answer me . . . you know, straight. I want to ask you—"

*Oh, I know what you want to ask me, Richie-boy.*

"In a few minutes," Jack said. "We'll get to all the questions and as many of the answers as I know in a few minutes. But we've got a piece of business to take care of first."

"What business?"

Instead of answering, Jack went over to the little train. He stood there for a moment, looking at it: stubby engine, empty boxcar, flatcar. Had he somehow managed to flip this whole thing into northern California? He didn't think so. Flipping with Wolf had been a chore, dragging Richard into the Territories from the Thayer campus had nearly torn his arm out of its socket, and doing both had been a conscious effort on his part. So far as he could remember, he hadn't been thinking of the train at all when he flipped—only getting Richard out of the Wolfs' paramilitary training camp before he saw his old man. Everything else had taken a slightly different form when it went from one world into the other—the act of Migrating seemed to demand an act of translation, as well. Shirts might become jerkins; jeans might become woolen trousers; money might become jointed sticks. But this train looked exactly the same here as it had over there. Morgan had succeeded in creating something which lost nothing in the Migration.

*Also, they were wearing blue jeans over there, Jack-O.*

*Yeah. And although Osmond had his trusty whip, he also
had a machine-pistol.*

*Morgan's machine-pistol. Morgan's train.*

Chilly gooseflesh rippled up his back. He heard Anders
muttering, *A bad business.*

It was that, all right. A very bad business. Anders was
right; it was devils all hurtled down together. Jack reached
into the engine compartment, got one of the Uzis, slapped a
fresh clip into it, and started back toward where Richard stood
looking around with pallid, contemplative interest.

"This looks like an old survivalist camp," he said.

"You mean the kind of place where soldier-of-fortune
types get ready for World War Three?"

"Yes, sort of. There are quite a few places like that in
northern California . . . they spring up and thrive for a while,
and then the people lose interest when World War Three
doesn't start right away, or they get busted for illegal guns or
dope, or something. My . . . my father told me that."

Jack said nothing.

"What are you going to do with the gun, Jack?"

"I'm going to try and get rid of that train. Any objections?"

Richard shuddered; his mouth pulled down in a grimace of
distaste. "None whatever."

"Will the Uzi do it, do you think? If I shoot into that plastic
junk?"

"One bullet wouldn't. A whole clip might."

"Let's see." Jack pushed off the safety.

Richard grabbed his arm. "It might be wise to remove ourselves to the fence before making the experiment," he said.

"Okay."

At the ivy-covered fence, Jack trained the Uzi on the flat
and squashy packages of *plastique*. He pulled the trigger, and
the Uzi bellowed the silence into rags. Fire hung mystically
from the end of the barrel for a moment. The gunfire was
shockingly loud in the chapellike silence of the deserted camp.
Birds squawked in surprised fear and headed out for quieter
parts of the forest. Richard winced and pressed his palms
against his ears. The tarpaulin flirted and danced. Then, although he was still pulling the trigger, the gun stopped firing.
The clip was exhausted, and the train just sat there on the track.

"Well," Jack said, "that was great. Have you got any other i—"

The flatcar erupted in a sheet of blue fire and a bellowing roar. Jack saw the flatcar actually starting to rise from the track, as if it were taking off. He grabbed Richard around the neck, shoved him down.

The explosions went on for a long time. Metal whistled and flew overhead. It made a steady metallic rain-shower on the roof of the Quonset hut. Occasionally a larger piece made a sound like a Chinese gong, or a crunch as something *really* big just punched on through. Then something slammed through the fence just above Jack's head, leaving a hole bigger than both of his fists laced together, and Jack decided it was time to cut out. He grabbed Richard and started pulling him toward the gates.

*"No!"* Richard shouted. *"The tracks!"*

*"What?"*

*"The tr—"*

Something whickered over them and both boys ducked. Their heads knocked together.

*"The tracks!"* Richard shouted, rubbing his skull with one pale hand. *"Not the road! Go for the tracks!"*

*"Gotcha!"* Jack was mystified but unquestioning. They had to go *somewhere*.

The two boys began to crawl along the rusting chain-link fence like soldiers crossing no-man's-land. Richard was slightly ahead, leading them toward the hole in the fence where the tracks exited the far side of the compound.

Jack looked back over his shoulder as they went—he could see as much as he needed to, or wanted to, through the partially open gates. Most of the train seemed to have been simply vaporized. Twisted chunks of metal, some recognizable, most not, lay in a wide circle around the place where it had come back to America, where it had been built, bought, and paid for. That they had not been killed by flying shrapnel was amazing; that they had not been even so much as scratched seemed well-nigh impossible.

The worst was over now. They were outside the gate, standing up (but ready to duck and run if there were residual explosions).

"My father's not going to like it that you blew up his train, Jack," Richard said.

His voice was perfectly calm, but when Jack looked at him, he saw that Richard was weeping.

"Richard—"

"No, he won't like it at all," Richard said, as if answering himself.

### 3

A thick and luxuriant stripe of weeds, knee-high, grew up the center of the railroad tracks leading away from the camp, leading away in a direction Jack believed to be roughly south. The tracks themselves were rusty and long unused; in places they had twisted strangely—rippled.

*Earthquakes did that,* Jack thought with queasy awe.

Behind them, the plastic explosive continued to explode. Jack would think it was finally over, and then there would be another long, hoarse BREEE-APPP!—it was, he thought, the sound of a giant clearing its throat. Or breaking wind. He glanced back once and saw a black pall of smoke hanging in the sky. He listened for the thick, heavy crackle of fire—like anyone who has lived for any length of time on the California coast, he was afraid of fire—but heard none. Even the woods here seemed New Englandy, thick and heavy with moisture. Certainly it was the antithesis of the pale-brown country around Baja, with its clear, bone-dry air. The woods were almost smug with life; the railway itself was a slowly closing lane between the encroaching trees, shrubs, and ubiquitous ivy (*poison* ivy, I bet, Jack thought, scratching unconsciously at the bites on his hands), with the faded blue sky an almost matching lane overhead. Even the cinders on the railroad bed were mossy. This place seemed secret, a place for secrets.

He set a hard pace, and not only to get the two of them off his track before the cops or the firemen showed up. The pace also assured Richard's silence. He was toiling too hard to keep up to talk . . . or ask questions.

They had gone perhaps two miles and Jack was still congratulating himself on this conversion-strangling ploy when Richard called out in a tiny, whistling voice, "Hey Jack—"

Jack turned just in time to see Richard, who had fallen a bit behind, toppling forward. The blemishes stood out on his paper-white skin like birthmarks.

Jack caught him—barely. Richard seemed to weigh no more than a paper bag.

"Oh, Christ, Richard!"

"Felt okay until a second or two ago," Richard said in that same tiny, whistling voice. His respiration was very fast, very dry. His eyes were half-closed. Jack could only see whites and tiny arcs of blue irises. "Just got . . . faint. Sorry."

From behind them came another heavy, belching explosion, followed by the rattling sound of train-debris falling on the tin roof of the Quonset hut. Jack glanced that way, then anxiously up the tracks.

"Can you hang on to me? I'll piggyback you a ways." *Shades of Wolf,* he thought.

"I can hang on."

"If you can't, say so."

"Jack," Richard said with a heartening trace of that old fussy Richard-irritation, "if I couldn't hang on, I wouldn't say I could."

Jack set Richard on his feet. Richard stood there, swaying, looking as if someone could blow once in his face and topple him over backward. Jack turned and squatted, the soles of his sneakers on one of the old rotted ties. He made his arms into thigh-stirrups, and Richard put his own arms around Jack's neck. Jack got to his feet and started to shag along the crossties at a fast walk that was very nearly a jog. Carrying Richard seemed to be no problem at all, and not just because Richard had lost weight. Jack had been running kegs of beer, carrying cartons, picking apples. He had spent time picking rocks in Sunlight Gardener's Far Field, can you gimme hallelujah. It had toughened him, all of that. But the toughening went deeper into the fiber of his essential self than something as simple and mindless as physical exercise could go. Nor was all of it a simple function of flipping back and forth between the two worlds like an acrobat, or of that other world—gorgeous as it could be—rubbing off on him like wet paint. Jack recognized in a dim sort of way that he had been trying to do more than simply save his mother's life; from the very beginning he had been trying to do something greater than that. He had been trying to do a good work, and his dim realization now was that such mad enterprises must always be toughening.

He *did* begin to jog.

"If you make me seasick," Richard said, his voice jiggling in time with Jack's footfalls, "I'll just vomit on your head."

"I knew I could count on you, Richie-boy," Jack panted, grinning.

"I feel . . . extremely foolish up here. Like a human pogo stick."

"Probably just how you look, chum."

"Don't . . . call me chum," Richard whispered, and Jack's grin widened. He thought, *Oh Richard, you bastard, live forever*.

## 4

"I knew that man," Richard whispered from above Jack.

It startled him, as if out of a doze. He had picked Richard up ten minutes ago, they had covered another mile, and there was still no sign of civilization of any kind. Just the tracks, and that smell of salt in the air.

*The tracks,* Jack wondered. *Do they go where I think they go?*

"What man?"

"The man with the whip and the machine-pistol. I knew him. I used to see him around."

"When?" Jack panted.

"A long time ago. When I was a little kid." Richard then added with great reluctance, "Around the time that I had that . . . that funny dream in the closet." He paused. "Except I guess it wasn't a dream, was it?"

"No. I guess it wasn't."

"Yes. Was the man with the whip Reuel's dad?"

"What do you think?"

"It was," Richard said glumly. "Sure it was."

Jack stopped.

"Richard, where do these tracks go?"

"You know where they go," Richard said with a strange, empty serenity.

"Yeah—I think I do. But I want to hear you say it." Jack paused. "I guess I *need* to hear you say it. Where do they go?"

"They go to a town called Point Venuti," Richard said, and he sounded near tears again. "There's a big hotel there. I don't know if it's the place you're looking for or not, but I think it probably is."

"So do I," Jack said. He set off once more, Richard's legs in his arms, a growing ache in his back, following the tracks that would take him—both of them—to the place where his mother's salvation might be found.

### 5

As they walked, Richard talked. He did not come on to the subject of his father's involvement in this mad business all at once, but began to circle slowly in toward it.

"I knew that man from before," Richard said. "I'm pretty sure I did. He came to the house. Always to the back of the house. He didn't ring the bell, or knock. He kind of ... scratched on the door. It gave me the creeps. Scared me so bad I felt like peeing my pants. He was a tall man—oh, all grown men seem tall to little kids, but this guy was *very* tall—and he had white hair. He wore dark glasses most of the time. Or sometimes the kind of sunglasses that have the mirror lenses. When I saw that story on him they had on *Sunday Report*, I knew I'd seen him *somewhere* before. My father was upstairs doing some paperwork the night that show was on. I was sitting in front of the tube, and when my father came in and saw what was on, he almost dropped the drink he was holding. Then he changed the station to a *Star Trek* rerun.

"Only the guy wasn't calling himself Sunlight Gardener when he used to come and see my father. His name ... I can't quite remember. But it was something like Banlon ... or Orlon ..."

"Osmond?"

Richard brightened. "*That* was it. I never heard his first name. But he used to come once every month or two. Sometimes more often. Once he came almost every other night, for a week, and then he was gone for almost half a year. I used to lock myself in my room when he came. I didn't like his smell. He wore some kind of scent ... cologne, I suppose, but it really smelled stronger than that. Like perfume. Cheap dimestore perfume. But underneath it—"

"Underneath it he smelled like he hadn't had a bath for about ten years."

Richard looked at him, wide-eyed.

"I met him as Osmond, too," Jack explained. He had explained before—at least some of this—but Richard had not been listening then. He was listening now. "In the Territories version of New Hampshire, before I met him as Sunlight Gardener in Indiana."

"Then you must have seen that . . . that *thing*."

"Reuel?" Jack shook his head. "Reuel must have been out in the Blasted Lands then, having a few more radical cobalt treatments." Jack thought of the running sores on the creature's face, thought of the worms. He looked at his red, puffy wrists where the worms had bitten, and shuddered. "I never saw Reuel until the end, and I never saw his American Twinner at all. How old were you when Osmond started showing up?"

"I must have been four. The thing about the . . . you know, the closet . . . that hadn't happened yet. I remember I was more afraid of him after that."

"After the thing touched you in the closet."

"Yes."

"And that happened when you were five."

"Yes."

"When we were *both* five."

"Yes. You can put me down. I can walk for a while."

Jack did. They walked in silence, heads down, not looking at each other. At five, something had reached out of the dark and touched Richard. When they were both six

*(six, Jacky was six)*

Jack had overheard his father and Morgan Sloat talking about a place they went to, a place that Jacky called the Daydream-country. And later that year, something had reached out of the dark and had touched him and his mother. It had been nothing more or less than Morgan Sloat's voice. Morgan Sloat calling from Green River, Utah. Sobbing. He, Phil Sawyer, and Tommy Woodbine had left three days before on their yearly November hunting trip—another college chum, Randy Glover, owned a luxurious hunting lodge in Blessington, Utah. Glover usually hunted with them, but that year he had been cruising in the Caribbean. Morgan called to say that

Phil had been shot, apparently by another hunter. He and Tommy Woodbine had packed him out of the wilderness on a lashed-together stretcher. Phil had regained consciousness in the back of Glover's Jeep Cherokee, Morgan said, and had asked that Morgan send his love to Lily and Jack. He died fifteen minutes later, as Morgan drove wildly toward Green River and the nearest hospital.

Morgan had not killed Phil; there was Tommy to testify that the three of them had been together when the shot rang out, if any testimony had ever been required (and, of course, none ever was).

But that was not to say he couldn't have hired it done, Jack thought now. And it was not to say that Uncle Tommy might not have harbored his own long doubts about what had happened. If so, maybe Uncle Tommy hadn't been killed just so that Jack and his dying mother would be totally unprotected from Morgan's depredations. Maybe he had died because Morgan was tired of wondering if the old faggot might finally hint to the surviving son that there might have been more to Phil Sawyer's death than an accident. Jack felt his skin crawl with dismay and revulsion.

"Was that man around before your father and my father went hunting together that last time?" Jack asked fiercely.

"Jack, I was four years old—"

"No, you weren't, you were *six*. You were four when he started coming, you were six when my father got killed in Utah. And you don't forget much, Richard. Did he come around before my father died?"

"That was the time he came almost every night for a week," Richard said, his voice barely audible. "Just before that last hunting trip."

Although none of this was precisely Richard's fault, Jack was unable to contain his bitterness. "My dad dead in a hunting accident in Utah, Uncle Tommy run down in L.A. The death-rate among your father's friends is very fucking high, Richard."

"Jack—" Richard began in a small, trembling voice.

"I mean it's all water over the dam, or spilled milk, or pick your cliché," Jack said. "But when I showed up at your school, Richard, you called me crazy."

"Jack, you don't under—"

"No, I guess I don't. I was tired and you gave me a place to sleep. Fine. I was hungry and you got me some food. Great. But what I needed most was for you to *believe* me. I knew it was too much to expect, but jeepers! You *knew* the guy I was talking about! You *knew* he'd been in your father's life before! And you just said something like 'Good old Jack's been spending too much time in the hot sun out there on Seabrook Island and blah-blah-blah!' Jesus, Richard, I thought we were better friends than that."

"You still don't understand."

"What? That you were too afraid of Seabrook Island stuff to believe in me a little?" Jack's voice wavered with tired indignation.

"No. I was afraid of more than that."

"Oh yeah?" Jack stopped and looked at Richard's pale, miserable face truculently. "What could be more than that for Rational Richard?"

"I was afraid," Richard said in a perfectly calm voice. "I was afraid that if I knew any more about those secret pockets . . . that man Osmond, or what was in the closet that time, I wouldn't be able to love my father anymore. And I was right."

Richard covered his face with his thin, dirty fingers and began to cry.

### 6

Jack stood watching Richard cry and damned himself for twenty kinds of fool. No matter what else Morgan was, he was still Richard Sloat's father; Morgan's ghost lurked in the shape of Richard's hands and in the bones of Richard's face. Had he forgotten those things? No—but for a moment his bitter disappointment in Richard had covered them up. And his increasing nervousness had played a part. The Talisman was very, very close now, and he felt it in his nerve-endings the way a horse smells water in the desert or a distant grass-fire in the plains. That nerviness was coming out in a kind of prancy skittishness.

*Yeah, well, this guy's supposed to be your best buddy, Jack-O—get a little funky if you have to, but don't trample Richard. The kid's sick, just in case you hadn't noticed.*

He reached for Richard. Richard tried to push him away. Jack was having none of that. He held Richard. The two of them stood that way in the middle of the deserted railroad bed for a while, Richard's head on Jack's shoulder.

"Listen," Jack said awkwardly, "try not to worry too much about . . . you know . . . everything . . . just yet, Richard. Just kind of try to roll with the changes, you know?" Boy, that sounded really stupid. Like telling somebody they had cancer but don't worry because pretty soon we're going to put *Star Wars* on the VCR and it'll cheer you right up.

"Sure," Richard said. He pushed away from Jack. The tears had cut clean tracks on his dirty face. He wiped an arm across his eyes and tried to smile. "A' wi' be well an' a' wi' be well—"

"An' a' manner a' things wi' be well," Jack chimed in— they finished together, then laughed together, and that was all right.

"Come on," Richard said. "Let's go."

"Where?"

"To get your Talisman," Richard said. "The way you're talking, it must be in Point Venuti. It's the next town up the line. Come on, Jack. Let's get going. But walk slow—I'm not done talking yet."

Jack looked at him curiously, and then they started walking again—but slowly.

### 7

Now that the dam had broken and Richard had allowed himself to begin remembering things, he was an unexpected fountain of information. Jack began to feel as if he had been working a jigsaw puzzle without knowing that several of the most important pieces were missing. It was Richard who had had most of those pieces all along. Richard had been in the survivalist camp before; that was the first piece. His father had owned it.

"Are you sure it was the same place, Richard?" Jack asked doubtfully.

"I'm sure," Richard said. "It even looked a little familiar to me on the other side, there. When we got back over . . . over here . . . I was sure."

Jack nodded, unsure what else to do.

"We used to stay in Point Venuti. That's where we always stayed before we came here. The train was a big treat. I mean, how many dads have their own private train?"

"Not many," Jack said. "I guess Diamond Jim Brady and some of those guys had private trains, but I don't know if they were dads or not."

"Oh, my dad wasn't in their league," Richard said, laughing a little, and Jack thought: *Richard, you might be surprised.*

"We'd drive up to Point Venuti from L.A. in a rental car. There was a motel we stayed at. Just the two of us." Richard stopped. His eyes had gone misty with love and remembering. "Then—after we hung out there for a while—we'd take my dad's train up to Camp Readiness. It was just a little train." He looked at Jack, startled. "Like the one we came on, I guess."

"Camp Readiness?"

But Richard appeared not to have heard him. He was looking at the rusted tracks. They were whole here, but Jack thought Richard might be remembering the twisted ripples they had passed some way back. In a couple of places the ends of rail-sections actually curved up into the air, like broken guitar-strings. Jack guessed that in the Territories those tracks would be in fine shape, neatly and lovingly maintained.

"See, there used to be a trolley line here," Richard said. "This was back in the thirties, my father said. The Mendocino County Red Line. Only it wasn't owned by the county, it was owned by a private company, and they went broke, because in California . . . you know . . ."

Jack nodded. In California, everyone used cars. "Richard, why didn't you ever tell me about this place?"

"That was the one thing my dad said never to tell you. You and your parents knew we sometimes took vacations in northern California and he said that was all right, but I wasn't to tell you about the train, or Camp Readiness. He said if I told, Phil would be mad because it was a secret."

Richard paused.

"He said if I told, he'd never take me again. I thought it was because they were supposed to be partners. I guess it was more than that.

"The trolley line went broke because of the cars and the

freeways." He paused thoughtfully. "That was one thing about the place you took me to, Jack. Weird as it was, it didn't stink of hydrocarbons. I could get into that."

Jack nodded again, saying nothing.

"The trolley company finally sold the whole line—grandfather clause and all—to a development company. *They* thought people would start to move inland, too. Except it didn't happen."

"Then your father bought it."

"Yes, I guess so. I don't really know. He never talked much about buying the line . . . or how he replaced the trolley tracks with these railroad tracks."

That would have taken a lot of work, Jack thought, and then he thought of the ore-pits, and Morgan of Orris's apparently unlimited supply of slave labor.

"I know he replaced them, but only because I got a book on railroads and found out there's a difference in gauge. Trolleys run on ten-gauge track. This is sixteen-gauge."

Jack knelt, and yes, he could see a very faint double indentation inside the existing tracks—that was where the trolley tracks had been.

"He had a little red train," Richard said dreamily. "Just an engine and two cars. It ran on diesel fuel. He used to laugh about it and say that the only thing that separated the men from the boys was the price of their toys. There was an old trolley station on the hill above Point Venuti, and we'd go up there in the rental car and park and go on in. I remember how that station smelled—kind of old, but nice . . . full of old sunlight, sort of. And the train would be there. And my dad . . . he'd say, 'All aboard for Camp Readiness, Richard! You got your ticket?' And there'd be lemonade . . . or iced tea . . . and we sat up in the cab . . . sometimes he'd have stuff . . . supplies . . . behind . . . but we'd sit up front . . . and . . . and . . ."

Richard swallowed hard and swiped a hand across his eyes.

"And it was a nice time," he finished. "Just him and me. It was pretty cool."

He looked around, his eyes shiny with unshed tears.

"There was a plate to turn the train around at Camp Readiness," he said. "Back in those days. The old days."

Richard uttered a terrible strangled sob.

"Richard—"

Jack tried to touch him.

Richard shook him off and stepped away, brushing tears from his cheeks with the backs of his hands.

"Wasn't so grown-up then," he said, smiling. Trying to. "*Nothing* was so grown-up then, was it, Jack?"

"No," Jack said, and now he found he was crying himself. *Oh Richard. Oh my dear one.*

"No," Richard said, smiling, looking around at the encroaching woods and brushing the tears away with the dirty backs of his hands, "nothing was so grown-up back then. In the old days, when we were just kids. Back when we all lived in California and nobody lived anywhere else."

He looked at Jack, trying to smile.

"Jack, help me," he said. "I feel like my leg is caught in some stuh-stupid truh-truh-hap and I . . . I . . ."

Then Richard fell on his knees with his hair in his tired face, and Jack got down there with him, and I can bear to tell you no more—only that they comforted each other as well as they could, and, as you probably know from your own bitter experience, that is never quite good enough.

## 8

"The fence was new back then," Richard said when he could continue speaking. They had walked on a ways. A whippoorwill sang from a tall sturdy oak. The smell of salt in the air was 'stronger. "I remember that. And the sign—CAMP READINESS, that's what it said. There was an obstacle course, and ropes to climb, and other ropes that you hung on to and then swung over big puddles of water. It looked sort of like bootcamp in a World War Two movie about the Marines. But the guys using the equipment didn't look much like Marines. They were fat, and they were all dressed the same—gray sweat-suits with CAMP READINESS written on the chest in small letters, and red piping on the sides of the sweat-pants. They all looked like they were going to have heart-attacks or strokes any minute. Maybe both at the same time. Sometimes we stayed overnight. A couple of times we stayed the whole weekend. Not in the Quonset hut; that was like a barracks for the guys who were paying to get in shape."

"If that's what they were doing."

"Yeah, right. If that's what they were doing. Anyway, we stayed in a big tent and slept on cots. It was a blast." Again, Richard smiled wistfully. "But you're right, Jack—not all the guys shagging around the place looked like businessmen trying to get in shape. The others—"

"What about the others?" Jack asked quietly.

"Some of them—a lot of them—looked like those big hairy creatures in the other world," Richard said in a low voice Jack had to strain to hear. "The Wolfs. I mean, they looked *sort* of like regular people, but not too much. They looked . . . rough. You know?"

Jack nodded. He knew.

"I remember I was a little afraid to look into their eyes very closely. Every now and then there'd be these funny flashes of light in them . . . like their brains were on fire. Some of the others . . ." A light of realization dawned in Richard's eyes. "Some of the others looked like that substitute basketball coach I told you about. The one who wore the leather jacket and smoked."

"How far is this Point Venuti, Richard?"

"I don't know, exactly. But we used to do it in a couple of hours, and the train never went very fast. Running speed, maybe, but not much more. It can't be much more than twenty miles from Camp Readiness, all told. Probably a little less."

"Then we're maybe fifteen miles or less from it. From—" *(from the Talisman)*

"Yeah. Right."

Jack looked up as the day darkened. As if to show that the pathetic fallacy wasn't so pathetic after all, the sun now sailed behind a deck of clouds. The temperature seemed to drop ten degrees and the day seemed to grow dull—the whippoorwill fell silent.

## 9

Richard saw the sign first—a simple whitewashed square of wood painted with black letters. It stood on the left side of the tracks, and ivy had grown up its post, as if it had been here for a very long time. The sentiment, however, was quite current.

It read: GOOD BIRDS MAY FLY; BAD BOYS MUST DIE. THIS IS YOUR
LAST CHANCE: GO HOME.

"You can go, Richie," Jack said quietly. "It's okay by me.
They'll let you go, no sweat. None of this is your business."

"I think maybe it is," Richard said.

"I dragged you into it."

"No," Richard said. "My father dragged me into it. Or fate
dragged me into it. Or God. Or Jason. Whoever it was, I'm
sticking."

"All right," Jack said. "Let's go."

As they passed the sign, Jack lashed out with one foot in a
passably good kung-fu kick and knocked it over.

"Way to go, chum," Richard said, smiling a little.

"Thanks. But don't call me chum."

## 10

Although he had begun to look wan and tired again, Richard
talked for the next hour as they walked down the tracks and
into the steadily strengthening smell of the Pacific Ocean. He
spilled out a flood of reminiscences that had been bottled up
inside of him for years. Although his face didn't reveal it,
Jack was stunned with amazement . . . and a deep, welling
pity for the lonely child, eager for the last scrap of his father's
affection, that Richard was revealing to him, inadvertently or
otherwise.

He looked at Richard's pallor, the sores on his cheeks and
forehead and around his mouth; listened to that tentative, almost whispering voice that nevertheless did not hesitate or
falter now that the chance to tell all these things had finally
come; and was glad once more that Morgan Sloat had never
been *his* father.

He told Jack that he remembered landmarks all along this
part of the railroad. They could see the roof of a barn over the
trees at one point, with a faded ad for Chesterfield Kings
on it.

" 'Twenty great tobaccos make twenty wonderful smokes,' "
Richard said, smiling. "Only, in those days you could see the
whole barn."

He pointed out a big pine with a double top, and fifteen
minutes later told Jack, "There used to be a rock on the other

side of this hill that looked just like a frog. Let's see if it's still there."

It was, and Jack supposed it did look like a frog. A little. If you stretched your imagination. *And maybe it helps to be three. Or four. Or seven. Or however old he was.*

Richard had loved the railroad, and had thought Camp Readiness was really neat, with its track to run on and its hurdles to jump over and its ropes to climb. But he hadn't liked Point Venuti itself. After some self-prodding, Richard even remembered the name of the motel at which he and his father had stayed during their time in the little coastal town. The Kingsland Motel, he said . . . and Jack found that name did not surprise him much at all.

The Kingsland Motel, Richard said, was just down the road from the old hotel his father always seemed interested in. Richard could see the hotel from his window, and he didn't like it. It was a huge, rambling place with turrets and gables and gambrels and cupolas and towers; brass weathervanes in strange shapes twirled from all of the latter. They twirled even when there was no wind, Richard said—he could clearly remember standing at the window of his room and watching them go around and around and around, strange brass creations shaped like crescent moons and scarab beetles and Chinese ideograms, winking in the sun while the ocean foamed and roared below.

*Ah yes, doc, it all comes back to me now,* Jack thought.

"It was deserted?" Jack asked.

"Yes. For sale."

"What was its name?"

"The Agincourt." Richard paused, then added another child's color—the one most small children are apt to leave in the box. "It was black. It was made of wood, but the wood looked like stone. Old black stone. And that's what my father and his friends called it. The Black Hotel."

## 11

It was partly—but not entirely—to divert Richard that Jack asked, "Did your father buy that hotel? Like he did Camp Readiness?"

Richard thought about it awhile and then nodded. "Yes," he

said. "I think he did. After a while. There was a For Sale sign on the gates in front of the place when he first started taking me there, but one time when we went there it was just gone."

"But you never stayed there?"

"God, no!" Richard shuddered. "The only way he could have gotten me in there would have been with a towing chain . . . even then I might not have gone."

"Never even went in?"

"No. Never did, never will."

*Ah, Richie-boy, didn't anyone ever teach you to never say never?*

"That goes for your father as well? He never even went in?"

"Not to my knowledge," Richard said in his best professorial voice. His forefinger went to the bridge of his nose, as if to push up the glasses that weren't there. "I'd be willing to bet he never went in. He was as scared of it as I was. But with me, that's all I felt . . . just scared. For my father, there was something more. He was . . ."

"Was what?"

Reluctantly, Richard said, "He was obsessed with the place, I think."

Richard paused, eyes vague, thinking back. "He'd go and stand in front of it every day we were in Point Venuti. And I don't mean just for a couple of minutes, or something like that—he'd stand in front of it for, like, three hours. Sometimes more. He was alone most of those times. But not always. He had . . . strange friends."

"Wolfs?"

"I guess so," Richard said, almost angrily. "Yeah, I guess some of them could have been Wolfs, or whatever you call them. They looked uncomfortable in their clothes—they were always scratching themselves, usually in those places where nice people aren't supposed to scratch. Others looked like the substitute coach. Kind of hard and mean. Some of those guys I used to see out at Camp Readiness, too. I'll tell you one thing, Jack—those guys were even more scared of that place than my father was. They just about cringed when they got near it."

"Sunlight Gardener? Was he ever there?"

"Uh-huh," Richard said. "But in Point Venuti he looked more like the man we saw over there. . . ."

"Like Osmond."

"Yes. But those people didn't come very often. Mostly it was just my father, by himself. Sometimes he'd get the restaurant at our motel to pack him some sandwiches, and he'd sit on a sidewalk bench and eat his lunch looking at the hotel. I stood at the window in the lobby of the Kingsland and looked at my father looking at the hotel. I never liked his face at those times. He looked afraid, but he also looked like . . . like he was gloating."

"Gloating," Jack mused.

"Sometimes he asked me if I wanted to come with him, and I always said no. He'd nod and I remember once he said, 'There'll be time. You'll understand everything, Rich . . . in time.' I remember thinking that if it was about that black hotel, I didn't want to understand.

"Once," Richard said, "when he was drunk, he said there was something inside that place. He said it had been there for a long time. We were lying in our beds, I remember. The wind was high that night. I could hear the waves hitting the beach, and the squeaky sound of those weathervanes turning on top of the Agincourt's towers. It was a scary sound. I thought about that place, all those rooms, all of them empty—"

"Except for the ghosts," Jack muttered. He thought he heard footsteps and looked quickly behind them. Nothing; no one. The roadbed was deserted for as far as he could see.

"That's right; except for the ghosts," Richard agreed. "So I said, 'Is it valuable, Daddy?'

" 'It's the most valuable thing there is,' he said.

" 'Then some junkie will probably break in and steal it,' I said. It wasn't—how can I say this?—it wasn't a subject I wanted to pursue, but I didn't want him to go to sleep, either. Not with that wind blowing outside, and the sound of those vanes squeaking in the night.

"He laughed, and I heard a clink as he poured himself a little more bourbon from the bottle on the floor.

" 'Nobody is going to steal it, Rich,' he said. 'And any junkie who went into the Agincourt would see things he *never* saw before.' He drank his drink, and I could tell he was getting sleepy. 'Only one person in the whole world could ever touch that thing, and he'll never even get close to it, Rich. I can guarantee that. One thing that interests me is that it's the same over there as over here. It doesn't change—at least, as far as I can tell, it doesn't change. I'd like to have it, but I'm not even going to try, at least not now, and maybe not ever. I could do things with it—you bet!—but on the whole, I think I like the thing best right where it is.'

"I was getting sleepy myself by then, but I asked him what *it* was that he kept talking about."

"What did he say?" Jack asked, dry-mouthed.

"He called it—" Richard hesitated, frowning in thought. "He called it 'the axle of all possible worlds.' Then he laughed. Then he called it something else. Something you wouldn't like."

"What was that?"

"It'll make you mad."

"Come on, Richard, spill it."

"He called it . . . well . . . he called it 'Phil Sawyer's folly.' "

It was not anger he felt but a burst of hot, dizzying excitement. That was it, all right; that was the Talisman. The axle of all possible worlds. How many worlds? God alone knew. The American Territories; the Territories themselves; the hypothetical Territories' Territories; and on and on, like the stripes coming ceaselessly up and out of a turning barber pole. A universe of worlds, a dimensional macrocosm of worlds—and in all of them one thing that was always the same; one unifying force that was undeniably good, even if it now happened to be imprisoned in an evil place; the Talisman, axle of all possible worlds. And was it also Phil Sawyer's folly? Probably so. Phil's folly . . . Jack's folly . . . Morgan Sloat's . . . Gardener's . . . and the hope, of course, of two Queens.

"It's more than Twinners," he said in a low voice.

Richard had been plodding along, watching the rotted ties disappear beneath his feet. Now he looked nervously up at Jack.

"It's more than Twinners, because there are more than two worlds. There are triplets . . . quadruplets . . . who knows? Morgan Sloat here; Morgan of Orris over there; maybe Morgan, Duke of Azreel, somewhere else. *But he never went inside the hotel!*"

"I don't know what you're talking about," Richard said in a resigned voice. *But I'm sure you'll go right on, anyway,* that resigned tone said, *progressing from nonsense to outright insanity. All aboard for Seabrook Island!*

"He *can't* go inside. That is, Morgan of California can't—and do you know why? Because Morgan of *Orris* can't. And Morgan of Orris can't because Morgan of *California* can't. If one of them can't go into *his* version of the black hotel, then *none* of them can. Do you see?"

"No."

Jack, feverish with discovery, didn't hear what Richard said at all.

"Two Morgans, or dozens. It doesn't matter. Two Lilys, or dozens—dozens of Queens in dozens of worlds, Richard, think of that! How does that mess your mind? Dozens of black hotels—only in some worlds it might be a black amusement park . . . or a black trailer court . . . or I don't know what. But Richard—"

He stopped, turned Richard by the shoulders, and stared at him, his eyes blazing. Richard tried to draw away from him for a moment, and then stopped, entranced by the fiery beauty on Jack's face. Suddenly, briefly, Richard believed that all things might be possible. Suddenly, briefly, he felt *healed.*

"What?" he whispered.

"*Some* things are not excluded. Some *people* are not excluded. They are . . . well . . . *single-natured.* That's the only way I can think of to say it. They are like *it*—the Talisman. Single-natured. Me. I'm single-natured. I had a Twinner, but he died. Not just in the Territories world, but in *all* worlds but this one. I know that—I feel that. My dad knew it, too. I think that's why he called me Travelling Jack. When I'm here, I'm not there. When I'm there, I'm not here. And Richard, *neither are you!*"

Richard stared at him, speechless.

"You don't remember; you were mostly in Freakout City while I was talking to Anders. But he said Morgan of Orris had a boy-child. Rushton. Do you know what he was?"

"Yes," Richard whispered. He was still unable to pull his eyes away from Jack's. "He was my Twinner."

"That's right. The little boy died, Anders said. The Talisman is single-natured. *We're* single-natured. Your father isn't. I've seen Morgan of Orris in that other world, and he's *like* your father, but he's *not* your father. He couldn't go into the black hotel, Richard. He can't now. But he knew you were single-natured, just as he knows I am. He'd like me dead. He needs you on his side.

"Because then, if he decided he *did* want the Talisman, he could always send *you* in to get it, couldn't he?"

Richard began to tremble.

"Never mind," Jack said grimly. "He won't have to worry about it. We're going to bring it out, but *he's* not going to have it."

"Jack, I don't think I can go into that place," Richard said, but he spoke in a low, strengthless whisper, and Jack, who was already walking on, didn't hear him.

Richard trotted to catch up.

## 12

Conversation lapsed. Noon came and went. The woods had become very silent, and twice Jack had seen trees with strange, gnarly trunks and tangled roots growing quite close to the tracks. He did not much like the looks of these trees. They looked familiar.

Richard, staring at the ties as they disappeared beneath his feet, at last stumbled and fell over, hitting his head. After that, Jack piggybacked him again.

"There, Jack!" Richard called, after what seemed an eternity.

Up ahead, the tracks disappeared into an old car-barn. The doors hung open on a shadowy darkness that looked dull and moth-eaten. Beyond the car-barn (which might once have been as pleasant as Richard had said, but which only looked spooky to Jack now) was a highway—101, Jack guessed.

Beyond that, the ocean—he could hear the pounding waves.

"I guess we're here," he said in a dry voice.

"Almost," Richard said. "Point Venuti's a mile or so down the road. God, I wish we didn't have to go there, Jack . . . Jack? Where are you going?"

But Jack didn't look around. He stepped off the tracks, detoured around one of those strange-looking trees (this one not even shrub-high), and headed for the road. High grasses and weeds brushed his road-battered jeans. Something inside the

trolley-barn—Morgan Sloat's private train-station of yore—
moved with a nasty slithering bump, but Jack didn't even look
toward it.

He reached the road, crossed it, and walked to the edge.

## 13

*Near the middle of December in the year 1981, a boy named
Jack Sawyer stood where the water and the land came together, hands in the pockets of his jeans, looking out at the
steady Pacific. He was twelve years old and extraordinarily
beautiful for his age. His brown hair was long—probably too
long—but the sea-breeze swept it back from a fine, clear brow.
He stood thinking of his mother, who was dying, and of
friends, both absent and present, and worlds within worlds,
turning in their courses.*

*I've come the distance,* he thought, and shivered. *Coast to
coast with Travelling Jack Sawyer.* His eyes abruptly filled
with tears. He breathed deeply of the salt. Here he was—and
the Talisman was close by.

"Jack!"

Jack didn't look at him at first; his gaze was held by the
Pacific, by the sunlight gleaming gold on top of the waves. He
was here; he had made it. He—

*"Jack!"* Richard struck his shoulder, bringing him out of
his daze.

"Huh?"

"Look!" Richard was gaping, pointing at something down
the road, in the direction in which Point Venuti presumably
lay. "Look there!"

Jack looked. He understood Richard's surprise, but he felt
none himself—or no more than he had felt when Richard had
told him the name of the motel where he and his father had
stayed in Point Venuti. No, not much surprise, but—

But it was damned good to see his mother again.

Her face was twenty feet high, and it was a younger face
than Jack could remember. It was Lily as she had looked at
the height of her career. Her hair, a glorious be-bop shade of
brassy blond, was pulled back in a Tuesday Weld ponytail.
Her insouciant go-to-hell grin was, however, all her own. No
one else in films had ever smiled that way—she had invented

it, and she still held the patent. She was looking back over one
bare shoulder. At Jack . . . at Richard . . . at the blue Pacific.

It was his mother . . . but when he blinked, the face changed
the slightest bit. The line of chin and jaw grew rounder, the
cheekbones less pronounced, the hair darker, the eyes an even
deeper blue. Now it was the face of Laura DeLoessian, mother
of Jason. Jack blinked again, and it was his mother again—his
mother at twenty-eight, grinning her cheerful *fuckya*-if-you-
can't-take-a-joke defiance at the world.

It was a billboard. Across the top of it ran this legend:

THIRD ANNUAL KILLER B FILM FESTIVAL
POINT VENUTI, CALIFORNIA
BITKER THEATER
DECEMBER 10TH–DECEMBER 20TH
THIS YEAR FEATURING LILY CAVANAUGH
"QUEEN OF THE B'S"

"Jack, it's your *mother*," Richard said. His voice was hoarse
with awe. "Is it just a coincidence? It *can't* be, can it?"

Jack shook his head. No, not a coincidence.

The word his eyes kept fixing on, of course, was QUEEN.

"Come on," he said to Richard. "I think we're almost
there."

The two of them walked side by side down the road toward
Point Venuti.

# 38

# The End of the Road

## 1

Jack inspected Richard's drooping posture and glistening face
carefully as they walked along. Richard now looked as though
he were dragging himself along on will power alone. A few
more wet-looking pimples had blossomed on his face.

"Are you okay, Richie?"

"No. I don't feel too good. But I can still walk, Jack. You don't have to carry me." He bent his head and plodded glumly on. Jack saw that his friend, who had so many memories of that peculiar little railway and that peculiar little station, was suffering far more than he from the reality that now existed—rusty, broken ties, weeds, poison ivy . . . and at the end, a ramshackle building from which all the bright, remembered paint had faded, a building where something slithered uneasily in the dark.

*I feel like my leg is caught in some stupid trap,* Richard had said, and Jack thought he could understand that well enough . . . but not with the *depth* of Richard's understanding. That was more understanding than he was sure he could bear. A slice of Richard's childhood had been burned out of him, turned inside-out. The railway and the dead station with its staring glassless windows must have seemed like dreadful parodies of themselves to Richard—yet more bits of the past destroyed in the wake of everything he was learning or admitting about his father. Richard's entire life, as much as Jack's, had begun to fold into the pattern of the Territories, and Richard had been given much less preparation for this transformation.

### 2

As for what he had told Richard about the Talisman, Jack would have sworn it was the truth—the Talisman knew they were coming. He had begun feeling it just about when he had seen the billboard shining out with his mother's picture; now the feeling was urgent and powerful. It was as if a great animal had awakened some miles away, and its purring made the earth resonate . . . or as if every single bulb inside a hundred-story building just over the horizon had just gone on, making a blaze of light strong enough to conceal the stars . . . or as if someone had switched on the biggest magnet in the world, which was tugging at Jack's belt buckle, at the change in his pockets and the fillings in his teeth, and would not be satisfied until it had pulled him into its heart. That great animal purring, that sudden and drastic illumination, that magnetic yearning—all these echoed in Jack's chest. Something out there, something in the direction of Point Venuti, wanted Jack Sawyer, and what Jack Sawyer chiefly knew of the object calling him so viscerally was that it was big. Big. No small thing could own such power. It was elephant-sized, city-sized.

And Jack wondered about his capacity to handle something so monumental. The Talisman had been imprisoned in a magical and sinister old hotel; presumably it had been put there not only to keep it from evil hands but at least in part because it was hard for anybody to handle it, whatever his intentions. Maybe, Jack wondered, Jason had been the only being capable of handling it—capable of dealing with it without doing harm either to himself or to the Talisman itself. Feeling the strength and urgency of its call to him, Jack could only hope that he would not weaken before the Talisman.

" 'You'll understand, Rich,' " Richard surprised him by saying. His voice was dull and low. "My father said that. He said I'd understand. *'You'll understand, Rich.'* "

"Yeah," Jack said, looking worriedly at his friend. "How are you feeling, Richard?"

In addition to the sores surrounding his mouth, Richard now had a collection of angry-looking raised red dots or bumps across his pimply forehead and his temples. It was as though a swarm of insects had managed to burrow just under the surface of his protesting skin. For a moment Jack had a flash of Richard Sloat on the morning he had climbed in his window at Nelson House, Thayer School; Richard Sloat with his glasses riding firmly on the bridge of his nose and his sweater tucked neatly into his pants. Would that maddeningly correct, unbudgeable boy ever return?

"I can still walk," Richard said. "But is this what he meant? Is *this* the understanding I was supposed to get, or have, or whatever the hell . . . ?"

"You've got something new on your face," Jack said. "You want to rest for a while?"

"Naw," Richard said, still speaking from the bottom of a muddy barrel. "And I can feel that rash. It itches. I think I got it all over my back, too."

"Let me see," Jack said. Richard stopped in the middle of the road, obedient as a dog. He closed his eyes and breathed through his mouth. The red spots blazed on his forehead and temples. Jack stepped behind him, raised his jacket, and lifted the back of his stained and dirty blue button-down shirt. The spots were smaller here, not as raised or as angry-looking; they spread from Richard's thin shoulder blades to the small of his back, no larger than ticks.

Richard let out a big dispirited unconscious sigh.

"You got em there, but it's not so bad," Jack said.

"Thanks," Richard said. He inhaled, lifted his head. Overhead the gray sky seemed heavy enough to come crashing to earth. The ocean seethed against the rocks, far down the rough slope. "It's only a couple of miles, really," Richard said. "I'll make it."

"I'll piggyback you when you need it," Jack said, unwittingly exposing his conviction that before long Richard would need to be carried again.

Richard shook his head and made an inefficient stab at shoving his shirt back in his trousers. "Sometimes I think I . . . sometimes I think I can't—"

"We're going to go into that hotel, Richard," Jack said, putting his arm through Richard's and half-forcing him to step forward. "You and me. Together. I don't have the faintest idea of what happens once we get in there, but you and I are going in. No matter who tries to stop us. Just remember that."

Richard gave him a look half-fearful, half-grateful. Now Jack could see the irregular outlines of future bumps crowding beneath the surface of Richard's cheeks. Again he was conscious of a powerful force pulling at him, forcing him along as he had forced Richard.

"You mean my father," Richard said. He blinked, and Jack thought he was trying not to cry—exhaustion had magnified Richard's emotions.

"I mean everything," Jack said, not quite truthfully. "Let's get going, old pal."

"But what am I supposed to understand? I don't get—" Richard looked around, blinking his unprotected eyes. Most of the world, Jack remembered, was a blur to Richard.

"You understand a lot more already, Richie," Jack pointed out.

And then for a moment a disconcertingly bitter smile twisted Richard's mouth. He had been made to understand a great deal more than he had ever wished to know, and his friend found himself momentarily wishing that he had run away from Thayer School in the middle of the night by him-self. But the moment in which he might have preserved Richard's innocence was far behind him, if it had ever really existed—Richard was a necessary part of Jack's mission. He felt strong hands fold around his heart: Jason's hands, the Tal-isman's hands.

"We're on our way," he said, and Richard settled back into the rhythm of his strides.

"We're going to see my dad down there in Point Venuti, aren't we?" he asked.

Jack said, "I'm going to take care of you, Richard. You're the herd now."

"What?"

"Nobody's going to hurt you, not unless you scratch your-self to death."

Richard muttered to himself as they plodded along. His hands slid over his inflamed temples, rubbing and rubbing. Now and then he dug his fingers in his hair, scratched himself like a dog, and grunted in an only partially fulfilled satisfac-tion.

### 3

Shortly after Richard lifted his shirt, revealing the red blotches on his back, they saw the first of the Territories trees. It grew on the inland side of the highway, its tangle of dark branches and column of thick, irregular bark emerging from a reddish, waxy tangle of poison ivy. Knotholes in the bark gaped, mouths or eyes, at the boys. Down in the thick mat of poison ivy a rustling, rustling of unsatisfied roots agitated the waxy leaves above them, as if a breeze blew through them. Jack said, "Let's cross the road," and hoped that Richard had not seen the tree. Behind him he could still hear the thick, rubbery roots prowling through the stems of the ivy.

*Is that a BOY? Could that be a BOY up there? A SPECIAL boy perhaps?*

Richard's hands flew from his sides to his shoulders to his temples to his scalp. On his cheeks, the second wave of raised bumps resembled horror-movie makeup—he could have been a juvenile monster from one of Lily Cavanaugh's old films.

Jack saw that on the backs of Richard's hands the red bumps of the rash had begun to grow together into great red welts.

"Can you really keep going, Richard?" he asked.

Richard nodded. "Sure. For a while." He squinted back across the road. "That wasn't a regular tree, was it? I never saw a tree like that before, not even in a book. It was a Territories tree, wasn't it?"

" 'Fraid so," Jack said.

"That means the Territories are really close, doesn't it?"

"I guess it does."

"So there'll be more of those trees up ahead, won't there?"

"If you know the answers, why ask the questions?" Jack asked. "Oh Jason, what a dumb thing to say. I'm sorry, Richie—I guess I was hoping that you didn't see it. Yeah, I suppose there'll be more of them up there. Let's just not get too close to them."

In any case, Jack thought, "up there" was hardly an accurate way to describe where they were going: the highway slid resolutely down a steady grade, and every hundred feet seemed to take it farther from the light. Everything seemed invaded by the Territories.

"Could you take a look at my back?" Richard asked.

"Sure." Jack again lifted Richard's shirt. He kept himself from saying anything, though his instinct was to groan. Richard's back was now covered with raised red blotches which seemed almost to radiate heat. "It's a little worse," he said.

"I thought it had to be. Only a little, huh?"

"Only a little."

Before long, Jack thought, Richard was going to look one hell of a lot like an alligator suitcase—Alligator Boy, son of Elephant Man.

Two of the trees grew together a short way ahead, their warty trunks twisted around each other in a way that suggested violence more than love. As Jack stared at them while they hurried past, he thought he saw the black holes in the bark mouthing at them, blowing curses or kisses: and he knew that he heard the roots gnashing together at the base of the joined trees. *(BOY! A BOY's out there! OUR boy's out there!)*

Though it was only mid-afternoon, the air was dark, oddly
grainy, like an old newspaper photograph. Where grass had
grown on the inland side of the highway, where Queen Anne's
lace had bloomed delicately and whitely, low unrecognizable
weeds blanketed the earth. With no blossoms and few leaves,
they resembled snakes coiled together and smelled faintly of
diesel oil. Occasionally the sun flared through the granular
murk like a dim orange fire. Jack was reminded of a photograph he had once seen of Gary, Indiana, at night—hellish
flames feeding on poison in a black, poisoned sky. From
down there the Talisman pulled at him as surely as if it were a
giant with its hands on his clothes. The nexus of all possible
worlds. He would take Richard into that hell—and fight for
his life with all his strength—if he had to haul him along by
the ankles. And Richard must have seen this determination in
Jack, for, scratching at his sides and shoulders, he toiled
along beside him.

*I'm going to do this,* Jack said to himself, and tried to ignore how greatly he was merely trying to bolster his courage.
*If I have to go through a dozen different worlds, I'm going to
do it.*

### 4

Three hundred yards farther down the road a stand of the ugly
Territories trees hovered by the side of the highway like mug-
gers. As he passed by on the other side of the road, Jack
glanced at their coiling roots and saw half-embedded in the
earth through which they wove a small bleached skeleton,
once a boy of eight or nine, still wearing a moldering green-
and-black plaid shirt. Jack swallowed and hurried on, trailing
Richard behind like a pet on a leash.

### 5

A few minutes later Jack Sawyer beheld Point Venuti for the
first time.

# 39

# Point Venuti

## 1

Point Venuti hung low in the landscape, clinging to the sides of the cliff leading down to the ocean. Behind it, another range of cliffs rose massively but raggedly into the dark air. They looked like ancient elephants, hugely wrinkled. The road led down past high wooden walls until it turned a corner by a long brown metal building that was a factory or warehouse, where it disappeared into a descending series of terraces, the dull roofs of other warehouses. From Jack's perspective, the road did not reappear again until it began to mount the rise opposite, going uphill and south toward San Francisco. He saw only the stairlike descent of the warehouse roofs, the fenced-in parking lots, and, way off to the right, the wintry gray of the water. No people moved on any portion of the road visible to him; nobody appeared in the row of little windows at the back of the nearest factory. Dust swirled through the empty parking lots. Point Venuti looked deserted, but Jack knew that it was not. Morgan Sloat and his cohorts—those who had survived the surprise arrival of the Territories choo-choo, anyway—would be waiting for the arrival of Travelling Jack and Rational Richard. The Talisman boomed out to Jack, urging him forward, and he said, "Well, this is it, kiddo," and stepped forward.

Two new facets of Point Venuti immediately came into view. The first was the appearance of approximately nine inches of the rear of a Cadillac limousine—Jack saw the glossy black paint, the shiny bumper, part of the right taillight. Jack wished fervently that the renegade Wolf behind the wheel had been one of the Camp Readiness casualties. Then he looked out toward the ocean again. Gray water lathered toward the shore. A slow movement up above the factory and warehouse roofs took his attention in the middle of his next step. COME HERE, the Talisman called in that urgent, magnetic manner. Point Venuti seemed somehow to contract like a hand into a fist. Up above the roofs, and only now visible, a dark but colorless weathervane shaped like the head of a wolf spun erratically back and forth, obeying no wind.

When Jack saw the lawless weathervane tracking left-right, then right–left, and continuing around in a complete circle, he knew that he had just had his first sight of the black hotel—at least a portion of it. From the roofs of the warehouses, from the road ahead, from all of the unseen town, rose an unmistakable feeling of enmity as palpable as a slap in the face. The Territories were bleeding through into Point Venuti, Jack realized; here, reality had been sanded thin. The wolf's head whirled meaninglessly in mid-air, and the Talisman continued to pull at Jack. COME HERE COME HERE COME NOW COME NOW NOW . . . Jack realized that along with its incredible and increasing pull, the Talisman was singing to him. Wordlessly, tunelessly, but singing, a curving rise and fall of whale's melody that would be inaudible to anyone else.

The Talisman knew he had just seen the hotel's weathervane.

Point Venuti might be the most depraved and dangerous place in all North and South America, Jack thought, suddenly bolder by half, but it could not keep him from going into the Agincourt Hotel. He turned to Richard, feeling now as if he had been doing nothing but resting and exercising for a month, and tried not to let his dismay at his friend's condition show in his face. Richard could not stop him, either—if he had to, he'd shove Richard right through the walls of the damned hotel. He saw tormented Richard drag his fingernails through his hair and down the hivelike rash on his temples and cheeks.

"We're going to do this, Richard," he said. "I know we are. I don't care how much crazy bullshit they throw at us. We are going to do this."

"Our troubles are going to have troubles with us," said Richard, quoting—surely unconsciously—from Dr. Seuss. He paused. "I don't know if I can make it. That's the truth. I'm dead on my feet." He gave Jack a look of utterly naked anguish. "What's *happening* to me, Jack?"

"I don't know, but I know how to stop it." And hoped that that was true.

"Is my father doing this to me?" Richard asked miserably. He ran his hands experimentally over his puffy face. Then he lifted his shirt out of his trousers and examined the red coalescing rash on his stomach. The bumps, shaped vaguely like the state of Oklahoma, began at his waistline and extended around both sides and up nearly to his neck. "It looks like a virus or something. Did my father give it to me?"

"I don't think he did it on purpose, Richie," Jack said. "If that means anything."

"It doesn't," Richard said.

"It's all going to stop. The Seabrook Island Express is coming to the end of the line."

Richard right beside him, Jack stepped forward—and saw the taillights of the Cadillac flash on, then off, before the car slipped forward out of his sight.

There would be no surprise attack this time, no wonderful slam-bang arrival through a fence with a trainful of guns and ammunition, but even if everybody in Point Venuti knew they were coming, Jack was on his way. He felt suddenly as if he had strapped on armor, as if he held a magic sword. Nobody in Point Venuti had the power to harm him, at least not until he got to the Agincourt Hotel. He was on his way, Rational Richard beside him, and all would be well. And before he had taken three more steps, his muscles singing along with the Talisman, he had a better, more accurate image of himself than of a knight going out to do battle. The image came straight from one of his mother's movies, delivered by celestial telegram. It was as if he were on a horse, a broadbrimmed hat on his head and a gun tied to his hip, riding in to clean up Deadwood Gulch.

*Last Train to Hangtown,* he remembered: Lily Cavanaugh, Clint Walker, and Will Hutchins, 1960. So be it.

## 2

Four or five of the Territories trees struggled out of the hard brown soil beside the first of the abandoned buildings. Maybe they had been there all along, snaking their branches over the road nearly to the white line, maybe not; Jack could not remember seeing them when he first looked down toward the concealed town. It was scarcely more conceivable, though, that he could overlook the trees than he could a pack of wild dogs. He could hear their roots rustling along the surface of the ground as he and Richard approached the warehouse.

*(OUR boy? OUR boy?)*

"Let's get on the other side of the road," he said to Richard, and took his lumpy hand to lead him across.

As soon as they reached the opposite side of the road, one of the Territories trees visibly stretched out, root and branch, for them. If trees had stomachs, they could have heard its stomach growl. The gnarly branch and the smooth snakelike root whipped across the yellow line, then across half the remaining distance to the boys. Jack prodded gasping Richard in the side with his elbow, then grasped his arm and pulled him along.

*(MY MY MY MY BOY! YESSS!!)*

A tearing, ripping sound suddenly filled the air, and for a moment Jack thought that Morgan of Orris was raping a passage through the worlds again, becoming Morgan Sloat . . . Morgan Sloat with a final, not-to-be-refused offer involving a machine-gun, a blowtorch, a pair of red-hot pincers . . . but instead of Richard's furious father, the crown of the Territories tree struck the middle of the road, bounced once in a snapping of branches, then rolled over on its side like a dead animal.

"Oh my God," Richard said. "It came right out of the ground after us."

Which was precisely what Jack had been thinking. "Kamikaze tree," he said. "I think things are going to be a little wild here in Point Venuti."

"Because of the black hotel?"

"Sure—but also because of the Talisman." He looked down the road and saw another clump of the carnivorous trees about ten yards down the hill. "The vibes or the atmosphere or whatever the ding-dong you want to call it are all screwed up—because everything's evil and good, black and white, all mixed up."

Jack was keeping his eye on the clump of trees they now slowly approached as he talked, and saw the nearest tree twitch its crown toward them, as if it had heard his voice.

Maybe this whole town is a big Oatley, Jack was thinking,

and maybe he would come through after all—but if there was a tunnel up ahead, the last thing Jack Sawyer was going to do was enter it. He really did not want to meet the Point Venuti version of Elroy.

"I'm afraid," Richard said behind him. "Jack, what if more of those trees can jump out of the ground like that?"

"You know," Jack said, "I've noticed that even when trees are mobile, they can't actually get very far. Even a turkey iike you ought to be able to outrun a tree."

He was rounding the last curve in the road, going downhill past the final warehouses. The Talisman called and called, as vocal as the giant's singing harp in "Jack and the Beanstalk." At last Jack came around the curve, and the rest of Point Venuti lay beneath him.

His Jason-side kept him going. Point Venuti might once have been a pleasant little resort town, but those days had passed long ago. Now Point Venuti itself was the Oatley tunnel, and he would have to walk through all of it. The cracked, broken surface of the road dipped toward an area of burned-out houses surrounded by Territories trees—the workers in the empty factories and warehouses would have lived in these small frame houses. Enough was left of one or two of them to show what they had been. The twisted hulks of burned cars lay here and there about the houses, entwined with thick weeds. Through the wasted foundations of the little houses, the roots of the Territories trees slowly prowled. Blackened bricks and boards, upended and smashed bathtubs, twisted pipes littered the burned-out lots. A flash of white caught Jack's eye, but he looked away as soon as he saw that it was the white bone of a disarranged skeleton hooked beneath the tangle of roots. Once children had piloted bikes through these streets, housewives had gathered in kitchens to complain about wages and unemployment, men had waxed their cars in their driveways—all gone, now. A tipped-over swingset, powdery with rust, poked its limbs through rubble and weeds.

Reddish little flares winked on and off in the murky sky.

Below the two-block-square area of burned houses and feeding trees, a dead stoplight hung over an empty intersection. Across the intersection, the side of a charred building still showed letters reading UH OH! BETTER GET MAA over a pocked, blistered picture of the front end of a car protruding through a plate-glass window. The fire had gone no farther, but Jack wished that it had. Point Venuti was a blighted town; and fire was better than rot. The building with the half-destroyed advertisement for Maaco paint stood first in a row of shops. The Dangerous Planet Bookstore, Tea & Sympathy, Ferdy's Wholefood Healthstore, Neon Village: Jack could read only a few of the names of the shops, for above most of them the paint had long ago flaked and curdled off the facades. These shops appeared to be closed, as abandoned as the factories and warehouses up the hill. Even from where he stood, Jack could see that the plate-glass windows had been broken so long ago they were like empty eyeglass frames, blank idiot eyes. Smears of paint decorated the fronts of the shops, red and black and yellow, oddly bright and scarlike in the dull gray air. A naked woman, so starved Jack could have counted her ribs, twisted slowly and ceremoniously as a weathervane in the littered street before the shops. Above her pale body with its drooping breasts and mop of pubic hair, her face had been painted blazing orange. Orange, too, was her hair. Jack stopped moving and watched the insane woman with the painted face and dyed hair raise her arms, twist her upper body as deliberately as one doing a Tai Chi movement, kick her left foot out over the flyblown corpse of a dog, and freeze into position like a statue. An emblem of all Point Venuti, the madwoman held her posture. Slowly the foot came down, and the skinny body revolved.

Past the woman, past the row of empty shops, Main Street turned residential—at least Jack supposed that it had once been residential. Here, too, bright scars of paint defaced the buildings, tiny two-story houses once bright white, now covered with the slashes of paint and graffiti. One slogan jumped out at him: YOU'RE DEAD NOW, scrawled up the side of an isolated peeling building that had surely once been a boarding house. The words had been there a long time.

JASON, I NEED YOU, the Talisman boomed out at him in a language both above and beneath speech.

"I can't," Richard whispered beside him. "Jack, I know I can't."

After the row of peeling, hopeless-looking houses, the road dipped again, and Jack could see only the backs of a pair of black Cadillac limousines, one on either side of Main

Street, parked with their noses pointed downhill, motors running. Like a trick photograph, looking impossibly large, impossibly sinister, the top—half? third?—of the black hotel reared up over the back ends of the Cadillacs and the despairing little houses. It seemed to float, cut off by the curve of the final hill. "I can't go in there," Richard repeated.

"I'm not even sure we can get past those trees," Jack said. "Hold your water, Richie."

Richard uttered an odd, snuffling noise which it took Jack a second to recognize as the sound of crying. He put his arm over Richard's shoulder. The hotel owned the landscape—that much was obvious. The black hotel owned Point Venuti, the air above it, the ground beneath. Looking at it, Jack saw the weathervanes spin in contradictory directions, the turrets and gambrels rise like warts into the gray air. The Agincourt did look as if it were made of stone—thousand-year-old stone, black as tar. In one of the upper windows, a light suddenly flashed—to Jack, it was as if the hotel had winked at him, secretly amused to find him at last so near. A dim figure seemed to glide away from the window: a second later the reflection of a cloud swam across the glass.

From somewhere inside, the Talisman trilled out its song only Jack could hear.

## 3

"I think it grew," Richard breathed. He had forgotten to scratch since he had seen the hotel floating past the final hill. Tears ran over and through the raised red bumps on his cheeks, and Jack saw that his eyes were now completely encased by the raised rash—Richard didn't have to squint to squint anymore. "It's impossible, but the hotel used to be smaller, Jack. I'm sure of it."

"Right now, nothing's impossible," Jack said, almost unnecessarily—they had long ago passed into the realm of the impossible. And the Agincourt was so large, so dominating, that it was wildly out of scale with the rest of the town.

The architectural extravagance of the black hotel, all the turrets and brass weathervanes attached to fluted towers, the cupolas and gambrels which should have made it a playful fantasy, instead made it menacing, nightmarish. It looked as

though it belonged in some kind of anti-Disneyland where
Donald Duck had strangled Huey, Dewey, and Louie and
Mickey shot Minnie Mouse full of heroin.

"I'm afraid," Richard said; and JASON COME NOW, sang
out the Talisman.

"Just stick close to me, pal, and we'll go through that place
like grease through a goose."

JASON COME NOW!

The clump of Territories trees just ahead rustled as Jack
stepped forward.

Richard, frightened, hung back—it might have been, Jack
realized, that Richard was nearly blind by now, deprived of his
glasses and with his eyes gradually being squeezed shut. He
reached behind him and pulled Richard forward, feeling as he
did so how thin Richard's hand and wrist had become.

Richard came stumbling along. His skinny wrist burned in
Jack's hand. "Whatever you do, don't slow down," Jack said.
"All we have to do is get by them."

"I can't," Richard sobbed.

"Do you want me to carry you? I'm being serious,
Richard. I mean, this could be a lot worse. I bet if we hadn't
blown so many of his troops away back there, he'd have
guards every fifty feet."

"You couldn't move fast enough if you carried me. I'd slow
you down."

*What in the Sam Hill do you think you're doing now?* went
through Jack's mind, but he said, "Stay on my far side and go
like hell, Richie. When I say three. Got it? One . . . two . . .
three!"

He jerked Richard's arm and began sprinting past the trees.
Richard stumbled, gasped, then managed to right himself and
keep on moving without falling down. Geysers of dust appeared at the base of the trees, a commotion of shredding
earth and scrambling things that looked like enormous beetles, shiny as shoe polish. A small brown bird took off out of
the weeds near the clump of conspiring trees, and a limber
root like an elephant's trunk whipped out of the dust and
snatched it from the air.

Another root snaked toward Jack's left ankle, but fell short.
The mouths in the coarse bark howled and screamed.

*(LOVERRR? LOVER BOYYY?)*

Jack clenched his teeth together and tried to force Richard Sloat to fly. The heads of the complicated trees had begun to sway and bow. Whole nests and families of roots were slithering toward the white line, moving as though they had independent wills. Richard faltered, then unambiguously slowed as he turned his head to look past Jack toward the reaching trees.

"Move!" Jack yelled, and yanked at Richard's arm. The red lumps felt like hot stones buried beneath the skin. He hauled away at Richard, seeing too many of the whickering roots crawl gleefully toward them across the white line.

Jack put his arm around Richard's waist at the same instant that a long root whistled through the air and wrapped itself around Richard's arm.

"Jesus!" Richard yelled. "Jason! It got me! It got me!"

In horror Jack saw the tip of the root, a blind worm's head, lift up and stare at him. It twitched almost lazily in the air, then wound itself once again around Richard's burning arm. Other roots came sliding toward them across the road.

Jack yanked Richard back as hard as he could, and gained another six inches. The root around Richard's arm grew taut. Jack locked his arms around Richard's waist and hauled him mercilessly backward. Richard let out an unearthly, floating scream. For a second, Jack was afraid that Richard's shoulder had separated, but a voice large within him said *PULL!* and he dug in his heels and pulled back even harder.

Then they both nearly went tumbling into a nest of crawling roots, for the single tendril around Richard's arm had neatly snapped. Jack stayed on his feet only by back-pedalling frantically, bending over at the waist to keep Richard, too, off the road. In this way they got past the last of the trees just as they heard the rending, snapping sounds they had heard once before. This time, Jack did not have to tell Richard to run for it.

The nearest tree came roaring up out of the ground and fell with a ground-shaking thud only three or four feet behind Richard. The others crashed to the surface of the road behind it, waving their roots like wild hair.

"You saved my life," Richard said. He was crying again, more from weakness and exhaustion and shock than from fear.

"From now on, my old pal, you ride piggyback," Jack said, panting, and bent down to help Richard get on his back.

## 4

"I should have told you," Richard was whispering. His face burned against Jack's neck, his mouth against Jack's ear. "I don't want you to hate me, but I wouldn't blame you if you did, really I wouldn't. I know I should have told you." He seemed to weigh no more than the husk of himself, as if nothing were left inside him.

"About what?" Jack settled Richard squarely in the center of his back, and again had the unsettling feeling that he was carrying only an empty sack of flesh.

"The man who came to visit my father . . . and Camp Readiness . . . and the closet." Richard's hollow-seeming body trembled against his friend's back. "I should have told you. But I couldn't even tell *myself*." His breath, hot as his skin, blew agitatedly into Jack's ear.

Jack thought, *The Talisman is doing this to him.* An instant later he corrected himself. *No. The black hotel is doing this to him.*

The two limousines which had been parked nose-down at the brow of the next hill had disappeared sometime during the fight with the Territories trees, but the hotel endured, growing larger with every forward step Jack took. The skinny naked woman, another of the hotel's victims, still performed her mad slow dance before the bleak row of shops. The little red flares danced, winked out, danced in the murky air. It was no time at all, neither morning nor afternoon nor night—it was time's Blasted Lands. The Agincourt Hotel did seem made of stone, though Jack knew it was not—the wood seemed to have calcified and thickened, to have blackened of itself, from the inside out. The brass weathervanes, wolf and crow and snake and circular cryptic designs Jack did not recognize, swung about to contradictory winds. Several of the windows flashed a warning at Jack; but that might have been merely a reflection of one of the red flares. He still could not see the bottom of the hill and the Agincourt's ground floor, and would not be able to see them until he had gone past the bookstore, tea shop, and other stores that had escaped the fire. Where was Morgan Sloat?

Where, for that matter, was the whole god-forsaken reception committee? Jack tightened his grip on Richard's sticklike legs, hearing the Talisman call him again, and felt a tougher, stronger being rear up within him.

"Don't hate me because I couldn't . . ." Richard said, his voice trailing off at the end.

JASON, COME NOW COME NOW!

Jack gripped Richard's thin legs and walked down past the burned-over area where so many houses had once stood. The Territories trees which used these wasted blocks as their own private lunch counter whispered and stirred, but they were too far away to trouble Jack.

The woman in the midst of the empty littered street slowly swivelled around as she became aware of the boys' progress down the hill. She was in the midst of a complex exercise, but all suggestion of Tai Chi Chuan left her when she dropped her arms and one outstretched leg and stood stockstill beside a dead dog, watching burdened Jack come down the hill toward her. For a moment she seemed to be a mirage, too hallucinatory to be real, this starved woman with her stick-out hair and face the same brilliant orange; then she awkwardly bolted across the street and into one of the shops without a name. Jack grinned, without knowing he was going to do it—the sense of triumph and of something he could only describe as armored virtue took him so much by surprise.

"Can you really make it there?" Richard gasped, and Jack said, "Right now I can do anything."

He could have carried Richard all the way back to Illinois if the great singing object imprisoned in the hotel had ordered him to do it. Again Jack felt that sense of coming resolution, and thought, *It's so dark here because all those worlds are crowded together, jammed up like a triple exposure on film.*

## 5

He sensed the people of Point Venuti before he saw them. They would not attack him—Jack had known that with absolute certainty ever since the madwoman had fled into one of the shops. They were watching him. From beneath porches, through lattices, from the backs of empty rooms, they peered out at him, whether with fear, rage, or frustration he could not tell.

Richard had fallen asleep or passed out on his back, and was breathing in heated harsh little puffs.

Jack skirted the body of the dog and glanced sideways into the hole where the window of the Dangerous Planet Bookstore should have been. At first he saw only the messy macaroni of used hypodermic needles which covered the floor, atop and beside the splayed books spread here and there. On the walls, the tall shelves stood empty as yawns. Then a convulsive movement in the dim back of the store caught his eye, and two pale figures coalesced out of the gloom. Both had beards and long naked bodies in which the tendons stood out like cords. The whites of four mad eyes flashed at him. One of the naked men had only one hand and was grinning. His erection waved before him, a thick pale club. He couldn't have seen that, he told himself. Where was the man's other hand? He glanced back. Now he saw only a tangle of skinny white limbs.

Jack did not look into the windows of any of the other shops, but eyes tracked him as he passed.

Soon he was walking past the tiny two-story houses. YOU'RE DEAD NOW splayed itself on a side wall. He would not look in the windows, he promised himself, he could not.

Orange faces topped with orange hair wagged through a downstairs window.

"Baby," a woman whispered from the next house. "Sweet baby Jason." This time he did look. *You're dead now.* She stood just on the other side of a broken little window, twiddling the chains that had been inserted in her nipples, smiling at him lopsidedly. Jack stared at her vacant eyes, and the woman dropped her hands and hesitantly backed away from the window. The length of chain drooped between her breasts.

Eyes watched Jack from the backs of dark rooms, between lattices, from crawl spaces beneath porches.

The hotel loomed before him, but no longer straight ahead. The road must have delicately angled, for now the Agincourt stood decidedly off to his left. And did it, in fact, actually *loom* as commandingly as it had? His Jason-side, or Jason himself, blazed up within Jack, and saw that the black hotel, though still very large, was nothing like mountainous.

COME I NEED YOU NOW, sang out the Talisman. YOU ARE RIGHT IT IS NOT AS GREAT AS IT WANTS YOU TO BELIEVE.

• • •

At the top of the last hill he stopped and looked down. There they were, all right, all of them. And there was the black hotel, all of *it*. Main Street descended to the beach, which was white sand interrupted by big outcroppings of rocks like jagged discolored teeth. The Agincourt reared up a short distance off to his left, flanked on the ocean side by a massive stone breakwater running far out into the water. Before it, stretching out in a line, a dozen long black limousines, some dusty, others as polished as mirrors, sat, their motors running. Streamers of white exhaust, low-flying clouds whiter than the air, drifted out from many of the cars. Men in FBI-agent black suits patrolled along the fence, holding their hands up to their eyes. When Jack saw two red flashes of light stab out before one of the men's faces, he reflexively dodged sideways around the side of the little houses, moving before he was actually conscious that the men carried binoculars.

For a second or two, he must have looked like a beacon, standing upright at the brow of a hill. Knowing that a momentary carelessness had nearly led to his capture, Jack breathed hard for a moment and rested his shoulder against the peeling gray shingles of the house. Jack hitched Richard up to a more comfortable position on his back.

Anyhow, now he knew that he would somehow have to approach the black hotel from its sea side, which meant getting across the beach unseen.

When he straightened up again, he peeked around the side of the house and looked downhill. Morgan Sloat's reduced army sat in its limousines or, random as ants, milled before the high black fence. For a crazy moment Jack recalled with total precision his first sight of the Queen's summer palace. Then, too, he had stood above a scene crowded with people moving back and forth with apparent randomness. What was it like there, now? On that day—which seemed to have taken place in prehistory, so far must he look back—the crowds before the pavillion, the entire scene, had in spite of all an undeniable aura of peace, of order. That would be gone now, Jack knew. Now Osmond would rule the scene before the great tentlike structure, and those people brave enough to enter the pavillion would scurry in, heads averted. And what of the Queen? Jack wondered. He could not help remembering that shockingly familiar face cradled in the whiteness of bed linen.

And then Jack's heart nearly froze, and the vision of the pavillion and the sick Queen dropped back into a slot in Jack's memory. Sunlight Gardener strolled into Jack's line of vision, a bullhorn in his hand. Wind from the sea blew a thick strand of white hair across his sunglasses. For a second Jack was sure that he could smell his odor of sweet cologne and jungle rot. Jack forgot to breathe for perhaps five seconds, and just stood beside the cracked and peeling shingle wall, staring down as a madman yelled orders to black-suited men, pirouetted, pointed at something hidden from Jack, and made an expressive move of disapproval.

He remembered to breathe.

"Well, we've got an interesting situation here, Richard," Jack said. "We got a hotel that can double its size whenever it wants to, I guess, and down there we also have the world's craziest man."

Richard, who Jack had thought was asleep, surprised him by mumbling something audible only as *guffuf*.

"What?"

"Go for it," Richard whispered weakly. "Move it, chum."

Jack actually laughed. A second later, he was carefully moving downhill past the backs of houses, going through tall horsetail grass toward the beach.

# 40

# Speedy on the Beach

## 1

At the bottom of the hill, Jack flattened out in the grass and crawled, carrying Richard as he had once carried his backpack. When he reached the border of high yellow weeds alongside the edge of the road, he inched forward on his belly

and looked out. Directly ahead of him, on the other side of the
road, the beach began. Tall weatherbeaten rocks jutted out of
the grayish sand; grayish water foamed onto the shore. Jack
looked leftward down the street. A short distance past the hotel, on the inland side of the beach road, stood a long crumbling structure like a sliced-off wedding cake. Above it a
wooden sign with a great hole in it read KINGSLAND MOTEL.
The Kingsland Motel, Jack remembered, where Morgan Sloat
had installed himself and his little boy during his obsessive
inspections of the black hotel. A flash of white that was Sunlight Gardener roamed farther up the street, clearly berating
several of the black-suited men and flapping his hand toward
the hill. *He doesn't know I'm down here already,* Jack realized as one of the men began to trudge across the beach road,
looking from side to side. Gardener made another abrupt,
commanding gesture, and the limousine parked at the foot of
Main Street wheeled away from the hotel and began to coast
alongside the man in the black suit. He unbuttoned his jacket
as soon as he hit the sidewalk of Main Street and took out a
pistol from a shoulder holster.

In the limousines the drivers turned their heads and stared
up the hill. Jack blessed his luck—five minutes later, and a
renegade Wolf with an oversized gun would have ended his
quest for that great singing thing in the hotel.

He could see only the top two floors of the hotel, and the
madly spinning devices attached to the architectural extrava-
gances on the roof. Because of his worm's-eye angle, the
break-water bisecting the beach on the right side of the hotel
seemed to rear up twenty feet or more, marching down the
sand and on into the water.

COME NOW COME NOW, called the Talisman in words
that were not words, but almost physical expressions of urgency.

The man with the gun was now out of sight, but the drivers
still stared after him as he went uphill toward Point Venuti's
lunatics. Sunlight Gardener lifted his bullhorn and roared,
"Root him out! I want him rooted out!" He jabbed the bullhorn at another black-suited man, just raising his binoculars
to look down the street in Jack's direction. "You! Pig-brains!
Take the other side of the street . . . and *root that bad boy out,*

oh yes, that baddest baddest boy, *baddest...*" His voice trailed away as the second man trotted across the street to the opposite sidewalk, his pistol already lengthening his fist.

It was the best chance he'd ever get, Jack realized— nobody was facing down the length of the beach road. "Hang on tight," he whispered to Richard, who did not move. "Time to boogie." He got his feet up under him, and knew that Richard's back was probably visible above the yellow weeds and tall grass. Bending over, he burst out of the weeds and set his feet on the beach road.

In seconds Jack Sawyer was flat on his stomach in the gritty sand. He pushed himself forward with his feet. One of Richard's hands tightened on his shoulder. Jack wiggled forward across the sand until he had made it behind the first tall outcropping of rock; then he simply stopped moving and lay with his head on his hands, Richard light as a leaf on his back, breathing hard. The water, no more than twenty feet away, beat against the edge of the beach. Jack could still hear Sunlight Gardener screeching about imbeciles and incompetents, his crazy voice drifting down from uphill on Main Street. The Talisman urged him forward, urged him on, on, on. . . .

Richard fell off his back.

"You okay?"

Richard raised a thin hand and touched his forehead with his fingers, his cheekbone with his thumb. "I guess. You see my father?"

Jack shook his head. "Not yet."

"But he's here."

"I guess. He has to be." The Kingsland, Jack remembered, seeing in his mind the dingy facade, the broken wooden sign. Morgan Sloat would have holed up in the hotel he had used so often six or seven years ago. Jack immediately felt the furious presence of Morgan Sloat near him, as if knowing where Sloat was had summoned him up.

"Well, don't worry about him." Richard's voice was paper-thin. "I mean, don't worry about me worrying about him. I think he's dead, Jack."

Jack looked at his friend with a fresh anxiety: could Richard actually be losing his mind? Certainly Richard was feverish. Up on the hill, Sunlight Gardener bawled "SPREAD OUT!" through his bullhorn.

"You think——"

And then Jack heard another voice, one that had first whispered beneath Gardener's angry command. It was a half-familiar voice, and Jack recognized its timbre and cadence before he had truly identified it. And, oddly, he recognized that the sound of this particular voice made him feel relaxed—almost as if he could stop scheming and fretting now, for everything would be taken care of—before he could name its owner.

"Jack Sawyer," the voice repeated. "Over here, sonny."

The voice was Speedy Parker's.

"I do," Richard said, and closed his puffy eyes again and looked like a corpse washed up by the tide.

*I do think my father is dead,* Richard meant, but Jack's mind was far from the ravings of his friend. "Over here, Jacky," Speedy called again, and the boy saw that the sound came from the largest group of tall rocks, three joined vertical piles only a few feet from the edge of the water. A dark line, the high-tide mark, cut across the rocks a quarter of the way up.

"Speedy," Jack whispered.

"Yeah-bob," came the reply. "Get yourself over here without them zombies seein you, can you? And bring your frien' along, too."

Richard still lay face-up on the sand, his hand over his face. "Come on, Richie," Jack whispered into his ear. "We have to move a little bit down the beach. Speedy's here."

"Speedy?" Richard whispered back, so quietly Jack had trouble hearing the word.

"A friend. See the rocks down there?" He lifted Richard's head on the reedlike neck. "He's behind them. He'll help us, Richie. Right now, we could use a little help."

"I can't really see," Richard complained. "And I'm so *tired* . . ."

"Get on my back again." He turned around and nearly flattened out on the sand. Richard's arms came over his shoulders and feebly joined.

Jack peered around the edge of the rock. Down the beach road, Sunlight Gardener stroked his hair into place as he strode toward the front door of the Kingsland Motel. The black hotel reared up awesomely. The Talisman opened its

throat and called for Jack Sawyer. Gardener hesitated outside
the door of the motel, swept both hands over his hair, shook
his head, and turned smartly about and began walking much
more rapidly back up the long line of limousines. The bullhorn lifted. "REPORTS EVERY FIFTEEN MINUTES!" he
screeched. "YOU POINT MEN—TELL ME IF YOU SEE A
BUG MOVE! I MEAN IT, YES I DO!"

Gardener was walking away; everybody else watched him.
It was time. Jack kicked off away from his shelter of rock and,
bending over while he clasped Richard's skimpy forearms,
raced down the beach. His feet kicked up scallops of damp
sand. The three joined pillars of rocks, which had seemed so
close while he talked to Speedy, now appeared to be half a
mile away—the open space between himself and them would
not close. It was as if the rocks receded while he ran. Jack expected to hear the crack of a shot. Would he feel the bullet
first, or would he hear the report before the bullet knocked
him down? At last the three rocks grew larger and larger in
his vision, and then he was there, falling onto his chest and
skidding behind their protection.

"Speedy!" he said, almost laughing in spite of everything.
But the sight of Speedy, who was sitting down beside a colorful little blanket and leaning against the middle pillar of rock,
killed the laughter in his throat—killed at least half of his
hope, too.

## 2

For Speedy Parker looked worse than Richard. Much worse.
His cracked, leaking face gave Jack a weary nod, and the boy
thought that Speedy was confirming his hopelessness. Speedy
wore only a pair of old brown shorts, and all of his skin
seemed horribly diseased, as if with leprosy.

"Settle down now, ole Travellin Jack," Speedy whispered
in a hoarse, crackling voice. "There's lots you got to hear, so
open your ears up good."

"How are you?" Jack asked. "I mean . . . Jesus, Speedy . . .
is there anything I can do for you?"

He gently placed Richard down on the sand.

"Open your ears, like I said. Don't you go worryin bout

Speedy. I ain't too com'fable, the way you see me now, but I can be com'fable again, if you does the right thing. Your little friend's dad put this hurtin on me—on his own boy, too, looks like. Old Bloat don't want his child in that hotel, no sir. But you got to take him there, son. There ain't but one way about it. You got to do it."

Speedy seemed to be fading in and out as he talked to Jack, who wanted to scream or wail more than he had at any time since the death of Wolf. His eyes smarted, and he knew he wanted to cry. "I know, Speedy," he said. "I figured that out."

"You a good boy," the old man said. He cocked his head back and regarded Jack carefully. "You the one, all right. The road laid its mark on you, I see. You the one. You gonna do it."

"How's my mom, Speedy?" Jack asked. "Please tell me. She's still alive, isn't she?"

"You can call her soon's you can, find out she's okay," Speedy answered. "But first you got to get it, Jack. Because if you *don't* get it, she be dead. And so be Laura, the Queen. She be dead, too." Speedy hitched himself up, wincing, to straighten his back. "Let me tell you. Most everybody at the court gave up on her—gave her up for dead already." His face expressed his disgust. "They all afraid of Morgan. Because they know Morgan'll take they skin off they backs if they don't swear allegiance to him now. While Laura still got a few breaths in her. But out in the far Territories, two-legged snakes like Osmond and his gang been goin around, tellin folks she already dead. And if she dies, Travellin Jack, if she dies . . ." He levelled his ruined face at the boy. "Then we got black horror in both worlds. Black horror. And you can call your momma. But first you has to get it. You has to. It's all that's left, now."

Jack did not have to ask him what he meant.

"I'm glad you understand, son." Speedy closed his eyes and leaned his head back against the stone.

A second later his eyes slowly opened again. "Destinies. That's what all this is about. More destinies, more lives, than you know. You ever hear the name Rushton? I suspect you might have, all this time gone by."

Jack nodded.

"All those destinies be the reason your momma brought you all the way to the Alhambra Hotel, Travellin Jack. I was just sittin and waitin, knowin you'd show up. The Talisman pulled you here, boy. Jason. That's a name you heard, too, I spect."

"It's *me*," Jack said.

"Then get the Talisman. I brought this l'il thing along, he'p you out some." He wearily picked up the blanket, which, Jack saw, was of rubber and therefore not a blanket after all.

Jack took the bundle of rubber from Speedy's charred-looking hand. "How can I get into the hotel, though?" he asked. "I can't get over the fence, and I can't swim in with Richard."

"Blow it up." Speedy's eyes had closed again.

Jack unfolded the object. It was an inflatable raft in the shape of a legless horse.

"Recognize her?" Speedy's voice, ruined as it was, bore a nostalgic lightness. "You and me picked her up, sometime back. I explained about the names."

Jack suddenly remembered coming to Speedy, that day that seemed filled with slashes of black and white, and finding him sitting inside a round shed, repairing the merry-go-round horses. *You be takin liberties with the Lady, but I guess she ain't gonna mind if you're helpin me get her back where she belongs.* Now that, too, had a larger meaning. Another piece of the world locked into place for Jack. "Silver Lady," he said.

Speedy winked at him, and again Jack had the eerie sense that everything in his life had conspired to get him to precisely this point. "Your friend here all right?" It was—almost—a deflection.

"I think so." Jack looked uneasily at Richard who had rolled on his side and was breathing shallowly, his eyes shut.

"Then long's you think so, blow up ole Silver Lady here. You gotta bring that boy in with you no matter what. He's a part of it, too."

Speedy's skin seemed to be getting worse as they sat on the beach—it had a sickly ash-gray tinge. Before Jack put the air nozzle to his mouth he asked, "Can't I do anything for you, Speedy?"

"Sure. Go to the Point Venuti drugstore and fetch me a bottle of Lydia Pinkham's ointment." Speedy shook his head.

"You know how to he'p Speedy Parker, boy. Get the Talisman. That's all the he'p I need."

Jack blew into the nozzle.

### 3

A very short time later he was pushing in the stopper located beside the tail of a raft shaped like a four-foot-long rubber horse with an abnormally broad back.

"I don't know if I'll be able to get Richard on this thing," he said, not complaining but merely thinking out loud.

"He be able to follow orders, ole Travellin Jack. Just sit behind him, kind of he'p hold him on. That's all he needs."

And in fact Richard had pulled himself into the lee of the standing rocks and was breathing smoothly and regularly through his open mouth. He might have been either asleep or awake, Jack could not tell which.

"All right," Jack said. "Is there a pier or something out behind that place?"

"Better than a pier, Jacky. Once you gets out beyond the break-water, you'll see big pilins—they built part of the hotel right out over the water. You'll see a ladder down in them pilins. Get Richard there up the ladder and you be on the big deck out back. Big windows right there—the kind of windows that be doors, you know? Open up one of them window-doors and you be in the dinin room." He managed to smile. "Once you in the dinin room, I reckon you'll be able to sniff out the Talisman. And don't be afraid of her, sonny. She's been waitin for you—she'll come to your hand like a good hound."

"What's to stop all these guys from coming in after me?"

"Shoo, *they* can't go in the black hotel." Disgust with Jack's stupidity was printed in every line on Speedy's face.

"I know. I mean in the water. Why wouldn't they come after me with a boat or something?"

Now Speedy managed a painful but genuine smile. "I think you gonna see why, Travellin Jack. Ole Bloat and his boys gotta steer clear of the water, hee hee. Don't worry bout that now—just remember what I told you and get to gettin, hear?"

"I'm already there," Jack said, and edged toward the rocks

to peer around at the beach road and the hotel. He had managed to get across the road and to Speedy's cover without being seen: surely he could drag Richard the few feet down to the water and get him on the raft. With any luck at all, he should be able to make it unseen all the way to the pilings—Gardener and the men with binoculars were concentrating on the town and the hillside.

Jack peeked around the side of one of the tall columns. The limousines still stood before the hotel. Jack put his head out an inch or two farther to look across the street. A man in a black suit was just stepping through the door of the wreck of the Kingsland Motel—he was trying, Jack saw, to keep from looking at the black hotel.

A whistle began to shrill, as high and insistent as a woman's scream.

"Move!" Speedy whispered hoarsely.

Jack jerked his head up and saw at the top of the grassy rise behind the crumbling houses a black-suited man blasting away at the whistle and pointing straight downhill at him. The man's dark hair swayed around his shoulders—hair, black suit, and sunglasses, he looked like the Angel of Death.

"FOUND HIM! FOUND HIM!" Gardener bawled. "SHOOT HIM! A THOUSAND DOLLARS TO THE BROTHER WHO BRINGS ME HIS BALLS!"

Jack recoiled back into the safety of the rocks. A half-second later a bullet spanged off the front of the middle pillar just before the sound of the shot reached them. *So now I know,* Jack thought as he grabbed Richard's arm and pulled him toward the raft. *First you get knocked down, then you hear the gun go off.*

"You gotta go now," Speedy said in a breathless rush of words. "In thirty seconds, there's gonna be a lot more shootin. Stay behind the breakwater as long's you can and then cut over. Get her, Jack."

Jack gave Speedy a frantic, driven look as a second bullet smacked into the sand before their little redoubt. Then he pushed Richard down in the front of the raft and saw with some satisfaction that Richard had enough presence of mind to grasp and hang on to the separate rubbery tufts of the mane. Speedy lifted his right hand in a gesture both wave and blessing. On his knees Jack gave the raft a shove which sent it almost to the edge of the water. He heard another trilling blast of the whistle. Then he scrambled to his feet. He was still running when the raft hit the water, and was wet to the waist when he pulled himself into it.

Jack paddled steadily out to the break-water. When he reached the end, he turned into unprotected open water and began paddling.

4

After that, Jack concentrated on his paddling, firmly putting out of his mind any considerations of what he would do if Morgan's men had killed Speedy. He had to get under the pilings, and that was that. A bullet hit the water, causing a tiny eruption of droplets about six feet to his left. He heard another ricochet off the breakwater with a *ping*. Jack paddled forward with his whole strength.

Some time, he knew not how long, went by. At last he rolled off the side of the raft and swam to the back, so that he could push it even faster by scissoring his legs. An almost imperceptible current swept him nearer his goal. At last the pilings began, high crusty columns of wood as thick around as telephone poles. Jack raised his chin out of the water and saw the immensity of the hotel lifting itself above the wide black deck, leaning out over him. He glanced back and to his right, but Speedy had not moved. Or had he? Speedy's arms looked different. Maybe—

There was a flurry of movement on the long grassy descent behind the row of falling-down houses. Jack looked up and saw four of the men in black suits racing down toward the beach. A wave slapped the raft, almost taking it from his grasp. Richard moaned. Two of the men pointed toward him. Their mouths moved.

Another high wave rocked the raft and threatened to push both raft and Jack Sawyer back toward the beach.

Wave, Jack thought, what wave?

He looked up over the front of the raft as soon as it dipped again into a trough. The broad gray back of something surely too large to be a mere fish was sinking beneath the surface. A shark? Jack was uneasily conscious of his two legs fluttering out behind him in the water. He ducked his head under, afraid he'd see a long cigar-shaped stomach with teeth sweeping toward him.

He did not see that shape, not exactly, but what he saw astounded him.

The water, which appeared now to be very deep, was as full as an aquarium, though one containing no fish of normal size or description. In this aquarium only monsters swam. Beneath Jack's legs moved a zoo of outsize, sometimes horrendously ugly animals. They must have been beneath him and the raft ever since the water had grown deep enough to accommodate them, for the water was crowded everywhere. The thing that had frightened the renegade Wolfs glided by ten feet down, long as a southbound freight train. It moved upward as he watched. A film over its eyes blinked. Long whiskers trailed back from its cavernous mouth—it had a mouth like an elevator door, Jack thought. The creature glided past him, pushing Jack closer to the hotel with the weight of the water it displaced, and raised its dripping snout above the surface. Its furry profile resembled Neanderthal Man's.

*Ole Bloat and his boys gotta steer clear of the water,* Speedy had told him, and laughed.

Whatever force had sealed the Talisman in the black hotel had set these creatures in the waters off Point Venuti to make sure that the wrong people kept away; and Speedy had known it. The great bodies of the creatures in the water delicately nudged the raft nearer and nearer the pilings, but the waves they made kept Jack from getting all but the most fragmentary view of what was happening on shore.

He rode up a crest and saw Sunlight Gardener, his hair flowing out behind him, standing beside the black fence levelling a long heavy hunting rifle at his head. The raft sank into the trough; the shell sizzled past far overhead with the noise of a hummingbird's passing; the report came. When Gardener shot next, a fishlike thing ten feet long with a great sail of a dorsal fin rose straight up out of the water and stopped the bullet. In one motion, the creature rolled back down and sliced into the water again. Jack saw a great ragged hole in its side. The next time he rode up a crest, Gardener was trotting off across the beach, clearly on his way to the Kingsland Mo-

tel. The giant fish continued to wash him diagonally forward
toward the pilings.

### 5

A ladder, Speedy had said, and as soon as Jack was under the
wide deck he peered through the gloom to try to find it. The
thick pilings, encrusted with algae and barnacles and dripping
with seaweed, stood in four rows. If the ladder had been installed at the time the deck was built it might easily be useless
now—at the least a wooden ladder would be hard to see, overgrown with weed and barnacles. The big shaggy pilings were
now much thicker than they had been originally. Jack got his
forearms over the back of the raft and used the thick rubbery
tail to lever himself back inside. Then, shivering, he unbuttoned his sodden shirt—the same white button-down, at least
one size too small, Richard had given him on the other side of
the Blasted Lands—and dropped it squashily in the bottom of
the raft. His shoes had fallen off in the water, and he peeled
off the wet socks and tossed them on top of the shirt. Richard
sat in the bow of the raft, slouching forward over his knees,
his eyes shut and his mouth closed.

"We're looking for a ladder," Jack said.

Richard acknowledged this with a barely perceptible
movement of his head.

"Do you think you could get up a ladder, Richie?"

"Maybe," Richard whispered.

"Well, it's around here somewhere. Probably attached to
one of these pilings."

Jack paddled with both hands, bringing the raft between
two of the pilings in the first row. The Talisman's call was continuous now, and seemed nearly strong enough to pick him up
out of the raft and deposit him on the deck. They were drifting
between the first and second rows of pilings, already under
the heavy black line of the deck above; here as well as outside, little red flares ignited in the air, twisted, winked out.
Jack counted: four rows of pilings, five pilings in each row.
Twenty places where the ladder might be. With the darkness
beneath the deck and the endless refinements of corridors
suggested by the pilings, being here was like taking a tour of
the Catacombs.

"They didn't shoot us," Richard said without affect. In the same tone of voice he might have said, "The store is out of bread."

"We had some help." He looked at Richard, slumped over his knees. Richard would never be able to get up a ladder unless he were somehow galvanized.

"We're coming up to a piling," Jack said. "Lean forward and shove us off, will you?"

"What?"

"Keep us from bumping into the piling," Jack repeated. "Come on, Richard. I need your help."

It seemed to work. Richard cracked open his left eye and put his right hand on the edge of the raft. As they drifted nearer to the thick piling he held out his left hand to deflect them. Then something on the pillar made a smacking sound, as of lips pulled wetly apart.

Richard grunted and retracted his hand.

"What was it?" Jack said, and Richard did not have to answer—now both boys saw the sluglike creatures clinging to the pilings. Their eyes had been closed, too, and their mouths. Agitated, they began to shift positions on their pillars, clattering their teeth. Jack put his hands in the water and swung the bow of the raft around the piling.

"Oh God," Richard said. Those lipless tiny mouths held a quantity of teeth. "God, I can't take—"

"You have to take it, Richard," Jack said. "Didn't you hear Speedy back there on the beach? He might even be dead now, Richard, and if he is, he died so he could be certain that I knew you had to go in the hotel."

Richard had closed his eyes again.

"And I don't care how many slugs we have to kill to get up the ladder, you are going up the ladder, Richard. That's all. That's it."

"Shit on you," Richard said. "You don't have to talk to me like that. I'm sick of you being so high and mighty. I know I'm going up the ladder, wherever it is. I probably have a fever of a hundred and five, but I know I'm going up that ladder. I just don't know if I can take it. So to hell with you." Richard had uttered this entire speech with his eyes shut. He effortfully forced both eyes open again. "Nuts."

"I need you," Jack said.

"Nuts. I'll get up the ladder, you asshole."

"In that case, I'd better find it," Jack said, pushed the raft forward toward the next row of pilings, and saw it.

## 6

The ladder hung straight down between the two inner rows of pilings, ending some four feet above the surface of the water. A dim rectangle at the top of the ladder indicated that a trap-door opened onto the deck. In the darkness it was only the ghost of a ladder, half-visible.

"We're in business, Richie," Jack said. He guided the raft carefully past the next piling, making sure not to scrape against it. The hundreds of sluglike creatures clinging to the piling bared their teeth. In seconds the horse's head at the front of the raft was gliding beneath the bottom of the ladder, and then Jack could reach up to grab the bottom rung. "Okay," he said. First he tied one sleeve of his sodden shirt around the rung, the other around the stiff rubbery tail next to him. At least the raft would still be there—if they ever got out of the hotel. Jack's mouth abruptly dried. The Talisman sang out, calling to him. He stood up carefully in the raft and hung on to the ladder. "You first," he said. "It's not going to be easy, but I'll help you."

"Don't need your help," Richard said. Standing up, he nearly pitched forward and threw both of them out of the raft.

"Easy now."

"Don't easy me." Richard extended both arms and steadied himself. His mouth was pinched. He looked afraid to breathe. He stepped forward.

"Good."

"Asshole." Richard moved his left foot forward, raised his right arm, brought his right foot forward. Now he could find the bottom of the ladder with his hands, as he fiercely squinted through his right eye. "See?"

"Okay," Jack said, holding both hands palm-out before him, fingers extended, indicating that he would not insult Richard with the offer of physical aid.

Richard pulled on the ladder with his hands, and his feet

slid irresistibly forward, pushing the raft with them. In a second he was suspended half over the water—only Jack's shirt kept the raft from zooming out from under Richard's feet.

"Help!"

"Pull your feet back."

Richard did so, and stood upright again, breathing hard.

"Let me give you a hand, okay?"

"Okay."

Jack crawled along the raft until he was immediately before Richard. He stood up with great care. Richard gripped the bottom rung with both hands, trembling. Jack put his hands on Richard's skinny hips. "I'm going to help lift you. Try not to kick out with your feet—just pull yourself up high enough to get your knee on the rung. First put your hands up on the next one." Richard cracked open an eye and did so.

"You ready?"

"Go."

The raft slid forward, but Jack yanked Richard upright so high that he could easily place his right knee on the bottom rung. Then Jack grabbed the sides of the ladder and used the strength in his arms and legs to stabilize the raft. Richard was grunting, trying to get his other knee on the rung; in a second he had done it. In another two seconds, Richard Sloat stood upright on the ladder.

"I can't go any farther," he said. "I think I'm going to fall off. I feel so sick, Jack."

"Just go up one more, please. Please. Then I can help you."

Richard wearily moved his hands up a rung. Jack, looking toward the deck, saw that the ladder must be thirty feet long. "Now move your feet. Please, Richard."

Richard slowly placed one foot, then the next, on the second rung.

Jack placed his hands on the outsides of Richard's feet and pulled himself up. The raft swung out in a looping half-circle, but he raised his knees and got both legs securely on the lowest rung. Held by Jack's outstretched shirt, the raft swung back around like a dog on a leash.

A third of the way up the ladder, Jack had to put one arm around Richard's waist to keep him from falling into the black water.

At last the rectangular square of the trapdoor floated in the black wood directly above Jack's head. He clamped Richard to himself—his unconscious head fell against Jack's chest—by reaching around both Richard and ladder with his left hand, and tried the trapdoor with his right. Suppose it had been nailed shut? But it swung up immediately and banged flat against the top of the deck. Jack got his left arm firmly under Richard's armpits and hauled him up out of the blackness and through the hole in the deck.

Interlude

# Sloat in This World (V)

The Kingsland Motel had been empty for nearly six years, and it had the mouldy yellow-newspaper smell of buildings that have been deserted for a long time. This smell had disturbed Sloat at first. His maternal grandmother had died at home when Sloat was a boy—it had taken her four years, but she had finally made the grade—and the smell of her dying had been like this. He did not want such a smell, or such memories, at a moment which was supposed to be his greatest triumph.

Now, however, it didn't matter. Not even the infuriating losses inflicted on him by Jack's early arrival at Camp Readiness mattered. His earlier feelings of dismay and fury had turned into a frenzy of nervous excitement. Head down, lips twitching, eyes bright, he strode back and forth through the room where he and Richard had stayed in the old days. Sometimes he locked his hands behind his back, sometimes he slammed one fist into the other palm, sometimes he stroked his bald pate. Mostly, however, he paced as he had in college, with his hands clenched into tight and somehow anal little fists, the hidden nails digging viciously into his palms. His stomach was by turns sour and giddily light.

Things were coming to a head.

No; no. Right idea, wrong phrase.

Things were coming *together*.

*Richard is dead by now. My son is dead. Got to be. He survived the Blasted Lands—barely—but he'll never survive the Agincourt. He's dead. Hold out no false hope for yourself on that score. Jack Sawyer killed him, and I'll gouge the eyes out of his living head for it.*

"But *I* killed him, too," Morgan whispered, stopping for a moment.

Suddenly he thought of his father.

Gordon Sloat had been a dour Lutheran minister in Ohio—Morgan had spent his whole boyhood trying to flee that harsh and frightening man. Finally he had escaped to Yale. He had set his entire mind and spirit on Yale in his sophomore year of high school for one reason above all others, unadmitted by his conscious mind but as deep as bedrock: it was a place where his rude, rural father would never dare to come. If his father ever tried to set foot on the Yale campus, *something* would happen to him. Just what that *something* might be, the high-school-age Sloat was not sure . . . but it would be roughly akin, he felt, to what had happened to the Wicked Witch when Dorothy threw the bucket of water over her. And this insight seemed to have been true: his father never *had* set foot on the Yale campus. From Morgan's first day there, Gordon Sloat's power over his son had begun to wane—that alone made all the striving and effort seem worthwhile.

But now, as he stood with his fists clenched and his nails digging into his soft palms, his father spoke up: *What does it profit a man to gain the whole world, if he should lose his own son?*

For a moment that wet yellow smell—the empty-motel-smell, the grandmother-smell, the death-smell—filled his nostrils, seeming to choke him, and Morgan Sloat/Morgan of Orris was afraid.

*What does it profit a man—*

*For it says in* The Book of Good Farming *that a man shall not bring the get of his seed to any place of sacrifice, for what—*

*What does it profit—*

*That man shall be damned, and damned, and damned*

*—a man to gain the whole world, if he should lose his own son?*

Stinking plaster. The dry smell of vintage mouseturds turning to powder in the dark spaces behind the walls. Crazies. There were crazies in the streets.

*What does it profit a man?*

Dead. One son dead in that world, one son dead in this.

*What does it profit a man?*

Your son is dead, Morgan. Must be. Dead in the water, or dead under the pilings and floating around under there, or dead—for sure!—topside. Couldn't take it. Couldn't—

*What does it profit—*

And suddenly the answer came to him.

*"It profits a man the world!"* Morgan shouted in the decaying room. He began to laugh and pace again. "It profits a man the *world*, and by Jason, the world is enough!"

Laughing, he began to pace faster and faster, and before long, blood had begun to drip out of his clenched fists.

A car pulled up out front about ten minutes later. Morgan went to the window and saw Sunlight Gardener come bursting out of the Cadillac.

Seconds later he was hammering on the door with both fists, like a tantrumy three-year-old hammering on the floor. Morgan saw that the man had gone utterly crazy, and wondered if this was good or bad.

"Morgan!" Gardener bellowed. "Open for me, my Lord! News! I have news!"

*I saw all your news through my binoculars, I think. Hammer on that door awhile longer, Gardener, while I make up my mind on this. Is it good that you should be crazy, or is it bad?*

Good, Morgan decided. In Indiana, Gardener had turned Sunlight Yellow at the crucial moment and had fled without taking care of Jack once and for all. But now his wild grief had made him trustworthy again. If Morgan needed a kamikaze pilot, Sunlight Gardener would be the first one to the planes.

"Open for me, my Lord! News! News! N—"

Morgan opened the door. Although he himself was wildly excited, the face he presented to Gardener was almost eerily serene.

"Easy," he said. "Easy, Gard. You'll pop a blood vessel."

"They've gone to the hotel . . . the beach . . . shot at them while they were on the beach . . . stupid assholes missed . . . in the water, I thought . . . we'll get them in the water . . . then the deep-creatures rose up . . . I had him in my sights . . . I had that bad bad boy RIGHT IN MY SIGHTS . . . and then . . . the creatures . . . they . . . they . . ."

"Slow down," Morgan said soothingly. He closed the door and took a flask out of his inside pocket. He handed it to Gardener, who spun the cap off and took two huge gulps. Morgan waited. His face was benign, serene, but a vein pulsed in the center of his forehead and his hands opened and closed, opened and closed.

Gone to the hotel, yes. Morgan had seen the ridiculous raft with its painted horse's head and its rubber tail bobbing its way out there.

"My son," he said to Gardener. "Do your men say he was alive or dead when Jack put him in the raft?"

Gardener shook his head—but his eyes said what he believed. "No one knows for sure, my Lord. Some say they saw him move. Some say not."

*Doesn't matter. If he wasn't dead then, he's dead now. One breath of the air in that place and his lungs will explode.*

Gardener's cheeks were full of whiskey-color and his eyes were watering. He didn't give the flask back but stood holding it. That was fine with Sloat. He wanted neither whiskey nor cocaine. He was on what those sixties slobs had called a natural high.

"Start over," Morgan said, "and this time be coherent."

The only thing Gardener had to tell that Morgan hadn't gleaned from the man's first broken outburst was the fact of the old nigger's presence down on the beach, and he almost could have guessed that. Still, he let Gardener go on. Gardener's voice was soothing, his rage invigorating.

As Gardener talked, Morgan ran over his options one final time, dismissing his son from the equation with a brief throb of regret.

*What does it profit a man? It profits a man the world, and the world is enough . . . or, in this case, worlds. Two to start with, and more when and if they play out. I can rule them all if I like—I can be something like the God of the Universe.*

*The Talisman. The Talisman is—*

*The key?*

No; oh no.

Not a key but a door; a locked door standing between him and his destiny. He did not want to open that door but to destroy it, destroy it utterly and completely and eternally, so it could never be shut again, let alone locked.

When the Talisman was smashed, all those worlds would be *his* worlds.

"Gard!" he said, and began to pace jerkily again.

Gardener looked at Morgan questioningly.

"What does it profit a man?" Morgan chirruped brightly.

"My Lord? I don't underst—"

Morgan stopped in front of Gardener, his eyes feverish and sparkling. His face rippled. Became the face of Morgan of Orris. Became the face of Morgan Sloat again.

"It profits a man the *world*," Morgan said, putting his hands on Osmond's shoulders. When he took them away a second later, Osmond was Gardener again. "It profits a man the *world*, and the world is enough."

"My Lord, you don't understand," Gardener said, looking at Morgan as if he might be crazy. "I think they've gone *inside*. Inside where *IT* is. We tried to shoot them, but the creatures . . . the deep-creatures . . . rose up and protected them, just as *The Book of Good Farming* said they would . . . and if they're *inside* . . ." Gardener's voice was rising. Osmond's eyes rolled with mingled hate and dismay.

"I understand," Morgan said comfortingly. His face and voice were calm again, but his fists worked and worked, and blood dribbled down onto the mildewy carpet. "Yessirree-bob, yes-indeedy-doo, rooty-patootie. They've gone in, and my son is never going to come out. You've lost yours, Gard, and now I've lost mine."

*"Sawyer!"* Gardener barked. "Jack *Sawyer! Jason!* That—"

Gardener lapsed into a horrible bout of cursing that went on for nearly five minutes. He cursed Jack in two languages; his voice racketed and perspired with grief and insane rage. Morgan stood there and let him get it all out of his system.

When Gardener paused, panting, and took another swallow from the flask, Morgan said:

"Right! Doubled in brass! Now listen, Gard—are you listening?"

"Yes, my Lord."

Gardener/Osmond's eyes were bright with bitter attention.

"My son is never going to come out of the black hotel, and I don't think Sawyer ever will, either. There's a very good chance that he isn't *Jason* enough yet to deal with what's in there. *IT* will probably kill him, or drive him mad, or send him a hundred worlds away. But he *may* come out, Gard. Yes, he *may*."

"He's the baddest baddest bitch's bastard to ever draw breath," Gardener whispered. His hand tightened on the flask . . . tightened . . . tightened . . . and now his fingers actually began to make dents in the steel shell.

"You say the old nigger man is down on the beach?"

"Yes."

"Parker," Morgan said, and at the same moment Osmond said, "Parkus."

"Dead?" Morgan asked this without much interest.

"I don't know. I think so. Shall I send men down to pick him up?"

"*No!*" Morgan said sharply. "No—but we're going down near where he is, aren't we, Gard?"

"We are?"

Morgan began to grin.

"Yes. You . . . me . . . all of us. Because if Jack comes out of the hotel, he'll go there first. He won't leave his old night-fighting buddy on the beach, will he?"

Now Gardener also began to grin. "No," he said. "No."

For the first time Morgan became aware of dull and throbbing pain in his hands. He opened them and looked thoughtfully at the blood which flowed out of the deep semi-circular wounds in his palms. His grin did not falter. Indeed, it widened.

Gardener was staring at him solemnly. A great sense of power filled Morgan. He reached up to his neck and closed one bloody hand over the key that brought the lightning.

"It profits a man the *world*," he whispered. "Can you gimme *hallelujah*."

His lips pulled even farther back. He grinned the sick yellow grin of a rogue wolf—a wolf that is old but still sly and tenacious and powerful.

"Come on, Gard," he said. "Let's go to the beach."

# 41

# The Black Hotel

### 1

Richard Sloat wasn't dead, but when Jack picked his old friend up in his arms, he was unconscious.

*Who's the herd now?* Wolf asked in his head. *Be careful, Jacky! Wolf! Be—*

*COME TO ME! COME NOW!* the Talisman sang in its powerful, soundless voice. *COME TO ME, BRING THE HERD, AND ALL WILL BE WELL AND ALL WILL BE WELL AND—*

"—a' manner a' things wi' be well," Jack croaked.

He started forward and came within an inch of stepping right back through the trapdoor, like a kid participating in some bizarre double execution by hanging. *Swing with a Friend,* Jack thought crazily. His heart was hammering in his ears, and for a moment he thought he might vomit straight down into the gray water slapping at the pilings. Then he caught hold of himself and closed the trapdoor with his foot. Now there was only the sound of the weathervanes—cabalistic brass designs spinning restlessly in the sky.

Jack turned toward the Agincourt.

He was on a wide deck like an elevated verandah, he saw. Once, fashionable twenties and thirties folk had sat out here at the cocktail hour under the shade of umbrellas, drinking gin rickeys and sidecars, perhaps reading the latest Edgar Wallace or Ellery Queen novel, perhaps only looking out toward where Los Cavernes Island could be dimly glimpsed—a blue-gray whale's hump dreaming on the horizon. The men in whites, the women in pastels.

Once, maybe.

Now the boards were warped and twisted and splintered. Jack didn't know what color the deck had been painted before, but now it had gone black, like the rest of the hotel—the color of this place was the color he imagined the malignant tumors in his mother's lungs must be.

Twenty feet away were Speedy's "window-doors," through which guests would have passed back and forth in those dim old days. They had been soaped over in wide white strokes so that they looked like blind eyes.

Written on one was:

YOUR LAST CHANCE TO GO HOME

Sound of the waves. Sound of the twirling ironmongery on the angled roofs. Stink of sea-salt and old spilled drinks— drinks spilled long ago by beautiful people who were now wrinkled and dead. Stink of the hotel itself. He looked at the soaped window again and saw with no real surprise that the message had already changed.

SHE'S ALREADY DEAD JACK SO WHY BOTHER?

*(now who's the herd?)*

"You are, Richie," Jack said, "but you ain't alone."

Richard made a snoring, protesting sound in Jack's arms. "Come on," Jack said, and began to walk. "One more mile. Give or take."

## 2

The soaped-over windows actually seemed to *widen* as Jack walked toward the Agincourt, as if the black hotel were now regarding him with blind but contemptuous surprise.

*Do you really think, little boy, that you can come in here and really hope to ever come out? Do you think there's really that much Jason in you?*

Red sparks, like those he had seen in the air, flashed and twisted across the soaped glass. For a moment they took form. Jack watched, wondering, as they became tiny fire-imps. They skated down to the brass handles of the doors and converged there. The handles began to glow dully, like a smith's iron in the forge.

*Go on, little boy. Touch one. Try.*

Once, as a kid of six, Jack had put his finger on the cold coil of an electric range and had then turned the control knob onto the HIGH setting. He had simply been curious about how fast the burner would heat up. A second later he had pulled his finger, already blistering, away with a yell of pain. Phil Sawyer had come running, taken a look, and had asked Jack when he had started to feel this weird compulsion to burn himself alive.

Jack stood with Richard in his arms, looking at the dully glowing handles.

*Go on, little boy. Remember how the stove burned? You thought you'd have plenty of time to pull your finger off—* *"Hell," you thought, "the thing doesn't even start to get red for almost a minute"—but it burned right away, didn't it? Now, how do you think this is going to feel, Jack?*

More red sparks skated liquidly down the glass to the handles of the French doors. The handles began to take on the delicate red-edged-with-white look of metal which is no more than six degrees from turning molten and starting to drip. If he touched one of those handles it would sink into his flesh, charring tissue and boiling blood. The agony would be like nothing he had ever felt before.

He waited for a moment with Richard in his arms, hoping the Talisman would call him again, or that the "Jason-side" of him would surface. But it was his mother's voice that rasped in his head.

*Has something or someone always got to push you, Jack-O? Come on, big guy—you set this going by yourself; you can keep going if you really want to. Has that other guy got to do everything for you?*

"Okay, Mom," Jack said. He was smiling a little, but his voice was trembling with fright. "Here's one for you. I just hope someone remembered to pack the Solarcaine."

He reached out and grasped one of the red-hot handles.

Except it wasn't; the whole thing had been an illusion. The handle was warm, but that was all. As Jack turned it, the red glow died from all the handles. And as he pushed the glass door inward, the Talisman sang out again, bringing gooseflesh out all over his body:

*WELL DONE! JASON! TO ME! COME TO ME!*

With Richard in his arms, Jack stepped into the dining room of the black hotel.

### 3

As he crossed the threshold, he felt an inanimate force— something like a dead hand—try to shove him back out. Jack pushed against it, and a second or two later, that feeling of being repelled ceased.

The room was not particularly dark—but the soaped windows gave it a monochrome whiteness Jack did not like. He felt fogged in, blind. Here were yellow smells of decay inside walls where the plaster was slowly turning to a vile soup: the smells of empty age and sour darkness. But there was more here, and Jack knew it and feared it.

*Because this place was not empty.*

Exactly what manner of things might be here he did not know—but he knew that Sloat had never dared to come in, and he guessed that no one else would, either. The air was heavy and unpleasant in his lungs, as if filled with a slow poison. He felt the strange levels and canted passageways and secret rooms and dead ends above him pressing down like the walls of a great and complex crypt. There was madness here, and walking death, and gibbering irrationality. Jack might not have had the words to express these things, but he felt them, all the same . . . he knew them for what they were. Just as he knew that all the Talismans in the cosmos could not protect him from those things. He had entered a strange, dancing ritual whose conclusion, he felt, was not at all pre-ordained.

He was on his own.

Something tickled against the back of his neck. Jack swept his hand at it and skittered to one side. Richard moaned thickly in his arms.

It was a large black spider hanging on a thread. Jack looked up and saw its web in one of the stilled overhead fans, tangled in a dirty snarl between the hardwood blades. The spider's body was bloated. Jack could see its eyes. He couldn't remember ever having seen a spider's *eyes* before. Jack began to edge around the hanging spider toward the tables. The spider turned at the end of its thread, following him.

"Fushing *feef!*" it suddenly squealed at him.

Jack screamed and clutched Richard against him with panicky, galvanic force. His scream echoed across the high-ceilinged dining room. Somewhere in the shadows beyond, there was a hollow metallic clank, and something laughed.

*"Fushing feef, fushing FEEF!"* the spider squealed, and then suddenly it scuttled back up into its web below the scrolled tin ceiling.

Heart thumping, Jack crossed the dining room and put Richard on one of the tables. The boy moaned again, very faintly. Jack could feel the twisted bumps under Richard's clothes.

"Got to leave you for a little while, buddy," Jack said.

From the shadows high above: *". . . I'll take . . . take good . . . good care of him you fushing . . . fushing feef . . ."* There was a dark, buzzing little giggle.

There was a pile of linen underneath the table where Jack had laid Richard down. The top two or three tablecloths were slimy with mildew, but halfway through the pile he found one that wasn't too bad. He spread it out and covered Richard with it to the neck. He started away.

The voice of the spider whispered thinly down from the angle of the fan-blades, down from a darkness that stank of decaying flies and silk-wrapped wasps. ". . . I'll take care of him, you fushing feef . . ."

Jack looked up, cold, but he couldn't see the spider. He could imagine those cold little eyes, but imagination was all it was. A tormenting, sickening picture came to him: that spider scuttling onto Richard's face, burrowing its way between Richard's slack lips and into Richard's mouth, crooning all the while *fushing feef, fushing feef, fushing feef . . .*

He thought of pulling the tablecloth up over Richard's mouth as well, and discovered he could not bring himself to turn Richard into something that would look so much like a corpse—it was almost like an invitation.

He went back to Richard and stood there, indecisive, knowing that his very indecision must make whatever forces there were here very happy indeed—anything to keep him away from the Talisman.

He reached into his pocket and came out with the large dark green marble. The magic mirror in the other world. Jack had no reason to believe it contained any special power against evil forces, but it came from the Territories . . . and, Blasted Lands aside, the Territories were innately good. And innate goodness, Jack reasoned, must have its own power over evil.

He folded the marble into Richard's hand. Richard's hand closed, then fell slowly open again as soon as Jack removed his own hand.

From somewhere overhead, the spider chuffed dirty laughter.

Jack bent low over Richard, trying to ignore the smell of disease—so like the smell of this place—and murmured, "Hold it in your hand, Richie. Hold it tight, chum."

"Don't . . . chum," Richard muttered, but his hand closed weakly on the marble.

"Thanks, Richie-boy," Jack said. He kissed Richard's cheek gently and then started across the dining room toward the closed double doors at the far end. *It's like the Alhambra,* he thought. *Dining room giving on the gardens there, dining room giving on a deck over the water here. Double doors in both places, opening on the rest of the hotel.*

As he crossed the room, he felt that dead hand pushing against him again—it was the hotel repelling him, trying to push him back out.

*Forget it,* Jack thought, and kept going.

The force seemed to fade almost at once.

*We have other ways,* the double doors whispered as he approached them. Again, Jack heard the dim, hollow clank of metal.

*You're worried about Sloat,* the double doors whispered; only now it wasn't just *them*—now the voice Jack was hearing was the voice of the entire hotel. *You're worried about Sloat, and bad Wolfs, and things that look like goats, and basketball coaches who aren't really basketball coaches; you're worried about guns and plastic explosive and magic keys. We in here don't worry about any of those things, little one. They are nothing to us. Morgan Sloat is no more than a scurrying ant. He has only twenty years to live, and that is less than the space between breaths to us. We in the Black Hotel care only for the Talisman— the nexus of all possible worlds. You've come as a burglar to rob us of what is ours, and we tell you once more: we have other ways of dealing with fushing feeves like you. And if you persist, you'll find out what they are—you'll find out for yourself.*

### 4

Jack pushed open first one of the double doors, then the other. The casters squealed unpleasantly as they rolled along their recessed tracks for the first time in years.

Beyond the doors was a dark hallway. *That'll go to the lobby,* Jack thought. *And then, if this place really is the same as the Alhambra, I'll have to go up the main staircase one flight.*

On the second floor he would find the grand ballroom. And in the grand ballroom, he would find the thing he had come for.

Jack took one look back, saw that Richard hadn't moved, and stepped into the hallway. He closed the doors behind him.

He began to move slowly along the corridor, his frayed and dirty sneakers whispering over the rotting carpet.

A little farther down, Jack could see another set of double doors, with birds painted on them.

Closer by were a number of meeting-rooms. Here was the Golden State Room, directly opposite the Forty-Niner Room. Five paces farther up toward the double doors with the painted birds was the Mendocino Room (hacked into a lower panel of the mahogany door: YOUR MOTHER DIED SCREAMING!). Far down the corridor—impossibly far!—was watery light. The lobby.

*Clank.*

Jack wheeled around fast, and caught a glimmer of movement just beyond one of the peaked doorways in the stone throat of this corridor—

*(?stones?) (?peaked doorways?)*

Jack blinked uneasily. The corridor was lined with dark mahogany panelling which had now begun to rot in the oceanside damp. No stone. And the doors giving on the Golden State Room and the Forty-Niner Room and the Mendocino Room were just doors, sensibly rectangular and with no peaks. Yet for one moment he had seemed to see openings like modified cathedral arches. Filling these openings had been iron drop-gates—the sort that could be raised or lowered by turning a windlass. Drop-gates with hungry-looking iron spikes at the bottom. When the gate was lowered to block the entrance, the spikes fitted neatly into holes in the floor.

*No stone archways, Jack-O. See for yourself. Just doorways. You saw drop-gates like that in the Tower of London, on that tour you went on with Mom and Uncle Tommy, three years ago. You're just freaking a little, that's all . . .*

But the feeling in the pit of his stomach was unmistakable.

*They were there, all right. I flipped—for just a second I was in the Territories.*

*Clank.*

Jack whirled back the other way, sweat breaking out on his cheeks and forehead, hair beginning to stiffen on the nape of his neck.

He saw it again—a flash of something metallic in the shadows of one of those rooms. He saw huge stones as black as sin, their rough surfaces splotched with green moss. Nasty, soft-looking albino bugs squirmed in and out of the large pores of the decaying mortar between the stones. Empty sconces stood at fifteen- or twenty-foot intervals. The torches that the sconces had once held were long since gone.

*Clank.*

This time he didn't even blink. The world sideslipped before his eyes, wavering like an object seen through clear running water. The walls were blackish mahogany again instead of stone blocks. The doors were *doors* and not latticed-iron drop-gates. The two worlds, which had been separated by a membrane as thin as a lady's silk stocking, had now actually begun to overlap.

And, Jack realized dimly, his Jason-side had begun to overlap with his Jack-side—some third being which was an amalgamation of both was emerging.

*I don't know what that combination is, exactly, but I hope it's strong—because there are things behind those doors . . . behind all of them.*

Jack began to sidle up the hallway again toward the lobby.

*Clank.*

This time the worlds didn't change; solid doors remained solid doors and he saw no movement.

*Right behind there, though. Right behind—*

Now he heard something behind the painted double doors—written in the sky above the marsh scene were the words HERON BAR. It was the sound of some large rusty machine that had been set in motion. Jack swung toward

*(Jason swung toward)*

toward that opening door

*(that rising drop-gate)*

his hand plunging into

*(the poke)*

the pocket
*(he wore on the belt of his jerkin)*
of his jeans and closing around the guitar-pick Speedy had
given him so long ago.
*(and closing arouind the shark's tooth)*
He waited to see what would come out of the Heron Bar,
and the walls of the hotel whispered dimly: *We have ways of
dealing with fushing feeves like you. You should have left
while there was still time . . .*

   *. . .because now, little boy, your time is up.*

### 5

*Clank . . . THUD!*
   *Clank . . . THUD!*
   *Clank . . . THUD!*

The noise was large and clumsy and metallic. There was
something relentless and inhuman about it which frightened
Jack more badly than a more human sound would have done.

It moved and shuffled its way forward with its own slow
idiot rhythm:
*Clank . . . THUD!*
   *Clank . . . THUD!*

There was a long pause. Jack waited, pressed against the
far wall a few feet to the right of the painted doors, his nerves
so tightly wound they seemed to hum. Nothing at all happened for a long time. Jack began to hope the clanker had
fallen back through some interdimensional trapdoor and into
the world it had come from. He became aware that his back
ached from his artificially still and tautly erect posture. He
slumped.

Then there was a splintering crash, and a huge mailed fist
with blunt two-inch spikes sprouting from the knuckles
slammed through the peeling blue sky on the door. Jack
shrank back against the wall again, gaping.

And, helplessly, flipped into the Territories.

### 6

Standing on the other side of the drop-gate was a figure in
blackish, rusty armor. Its cylindrical helmet was broken only

by a black horizontal eye-slit no more than an inch wide. The helmet was topped by a frowzy red plume—white bugs squirmed in and out of it. They were the same sort, Jason saw, as those which had come out of the walls first in Albert the Blob's room and then all over Thayer School. The helmet ended in a coif of mail which draped the rusty knight's shoulders like a lady's stole. The upper arms and forearms were plated with heavy steel brassards. They were joined at the elbows with cubitieres. These were crusted with layers of ancient filth, and when the knight moved, the cubitieres squealed like the high, demanding voices of unpleasant children.

Its armored fists were crazy with spikes.

Jason stood against the stone wall, looking at it, unable in fact to look away; his mouth was dry as fever and his eyeballs seemed to be swelling rhythmically in their sockets in time to his heartbeat.

In the knight's right hand was *le martel de fer*—a battle-hammer with a rusty thirty-pound forged-steel head, as mute as murder.

*The drop-gate; remember that the drop-gate is between you and it—*

But then, although no human hand was near it, the windlass began to turn; the iron chain, each link as long as Jack's forearm, began to wind around the drum, and the gate began to rise.

## 7

The mailed fist was withdrawn from the door, leaving a splintered hole that changed the mural at once from faded pastoral romantic to surrealist bar-sinister: it now looked as if some apocalyptic hunter, disappointed by his day in the marshes, had put a load of birdshot through the sky itself in a fit of pique. Then the head of the battle-hammer exploded through the door in a huge blunt swipe, obliterating one of the two herons struggling to achieve liftoff. Jack raised his hand in front of his face to protect it from splinters. The *martel de fer* was withdrawn. There was another brief pause, almost long enough for Jack to think about running again. Then the spiked fist tore through again. It twisted first one way and then the other, widening the hole, then withdrew. A second later the hammer slammed through the middle of a reed-bed and a large chunk of the right-hand door fell to the carpet.

Jack could now see the hulking armored figure in the shadows of the Heron Bar. The armor was not the same as that worn by the figure confronting Jason in the black castle; that one wore a helmet which was nearly cylindrical, with a red plume. This one wore a helmet that looked like the polished head of a steel bird. Horns rose from either side, sprouting from the helmet at roughly ear level. Jack saw a breastplate, a kilt of plate-mail, a hemming of chain-mail below that. The hammer was the same in both worlds, and in both worlds the knight-Twinners dropped them at the same instant, as if in contempt—who would need a battle-hammer to deal with such a puny opponent as this?

*Run! Jack, run!*

*That's right,* the hotel whispered. *Run! That's what fushing feeves are supposed to do! Run! RUN!*

But he would not run. He might die, but he would not run—because that sly, whispering voice was right. Running was exactly what fushing feeves did.

*But I'm no thief,* Jack thought grimly. *That thing may kill me, but I won't run. Because I'm no thief.*

"*I won't run!*" Jack shouted at the blank, polished-steel bird-face. "*I'm no thief! Do you hear me? I've come for what's mine and I'M NO THIEF!*"

A groaning scream came from the breathing-holes at the bottom of the bird-helmet. The knight raised its spiked fists and brought them down, one on the sagging left door, one on the sagging right. The pastoral marsh-world painted there was destroyed. The hinges snapped . . . and as the doors fell toward him, Jack actually saw the one painted heron who remained go flying away like a bird in a Walt Disney cartoon, its eyes bright and terrified.

The suit of armor came toward him like a killer robot, its feet rising and then crashing down. It was more than seven feet tall, and when it came through the door the horns rising from its helmet tore a set of ragged slashes into the upper jamb. They looked like quotation marks.

*Run!* a yammering voice in his mind screamed.

*Run, you feef,* the hotel whispered.

*No,* Jack answered. He stared up at the advancing knight, and his hand wrapped itself tightly around the guitar-pick in his pocket. The spike-studded gauntlets came up toward the visor of its bird-helmet. They raised it. Jack gaped.

The inside of the helmet was empty.

Then those studded hands were reaching for Jack.

### 8

The spike-studded hands came up and grasped either side of the cylindrical helmet. They lifted it slowly off, disclosing the livid, haggard face of a man who looked at least three hundred years old. One side of this ancient's head had been bashed in. Splinters of bone like broken eggshell poked out through the skin, and the wound was caked with some black goop which Jason supposed was decayed brains. It was not breathing, but the red-rimmed eyes which regarded Jason were sparkling and hellishly avid. It grinned, and Jason saw the needle-sharp teeth with which this horror would rip him to pieces.

It clanked unsteadily forward . . . but that wasn't the only sound.

He looked to his left, toward the main hall.

*(lobby)*

of the castle

*(hotel)*

and saw a second knight, this one wearing the shallow, bowl-shaped head-guard known as the Great Helm. Behind it were a third . . . and a fourth. They came slowly down the corridor, moving suits of ancient armor which now housed vampires of some sort.

Then the hands seized him by the shoulders. The blunt spikes on the gloves slid into his shoulders and arms. Warm blood flowed and the livid, wrinkled face drew into a horrid hungry grin. The cubitieres at the elbows screeched and wailed as the dead knight drew the boy toward itself.

### 9

Jack howled with the pain—the short blunt-tipped spikes on its hands were *in* him, *in* him, and he understood once and for all that this was real, and in another moment this thing was going to kill him.

He was yanked toward the yawning, empty blackness inside that helmet—

*But was it really empty?*

Jack caught a blurred, faded impression of a double red glow in the darkness . . . something like eyes. And as the armored hands drew him up and up, he felt freezing cold, as if all the winters that ever were had somehow combined, had somehow become one winter . . . and that river of frigid air was now pouring out of that empty helmet.

*It's really going to kill me and my mother will die, Richard will die, Sloat will win, going to kill me, going to*

*(tear me apart rip me open with its teeth)*

*freeze me solid—*

*JACK!* Speedy's voice cried.

*(JASON! Parkus's voice cried.)*

*The pick, boy! Use the pick! Before it's too late! FOR JASON'S SAKE USE THE PICK BEFORE IT'S TOO LATE!*

Jack's hand closed around it. It was as hot as the coin had been, and the numbing cold was replaced with a sudden sense of brain-busting triumph. He brought it out of his pocket, crying out in pain as his punctured muscles flexed against the spikes driven into him, but not losing that sense of triumph—that lovely sensation of Territories *heat*, that clear feeling of *rainbow*.

The pick, for it was a pick again, was in his fingers, a strong and heavy triangle of ivory, filigreed and inlaid with strange designs—and in that moment Jack

*(and Jason)*

saw those designs come together in a face—the face of Laura DeLoessian.

*(the face of Lily Cavanaugh Sawyer.)*

## 10

*"In her name, you filthy, aborted thing!"* they shouted together—but it was one shout only: the shout of that single nature, Jack/Jason. *"Get you off the skin of this world! In the name of the Queen and in the name of her son, get you off the skin of this world!"*

Jason brought the guitar-pick down into the white, scrawny face of the old vampire-thing in the suit of armor; at the same instant he sideslipped without blinking into Jack and saw the pick whistle down into a freezing black emptiness. There was another moment as Jason when he saw the vampire-thing's red eyes bulge outward in disbelief as the tip of the pick plunged into the center of its deeply wrinkled forehead. A moment later the eyes themselves, already filming over, exploded, and a black, steaming inchor ran over his hand and wrist. It was full of tiny biting worms.

## 11

Jack was flung against the wall. He hit his head. In spite of that and of the deep, throbbing pain in his shoulders and upper arms, he held on to the pick.

The suit of armor was rattling like a scarecrow made out of tin cans. Jack had time to see it was *swelling* somehow, and he threw a hand up to shield his eyes.

The suit of armor self-destructed. It did not spray shrapnel everywhere, but simply fell apart—Jack thought if he had seen it in a movie instead of as he saw it now, huddled in a lower hallway of this stinking hotel with blood trickling into his armpits, he would have laughed. The polished-steel helmet, so like the face of a bird, fell onto the floor with a muffled thump. The curved gorget, meant to keep the knight's enemy from running a blade or a spear-point through the knight's throat, fell directly inside it with a jingle of tightly meshed rings of mail. The cuirasses fell like curved steel bookends. The greaves split apart. Metal rained down on the mouldy carpet for two seconds, and then there was only a pile of something that looked like scrap-heap leftovers.

Jack pushed himself up the wall, staring with wide eyes as if he expected the suit of armor to suddenly fly back together. In fact, he really did expect something like that. But when nothing happened he turned left, toward the lobby . . . and saw three more suits of armor moving slowly toward him. One held a cheesy, mould-caked banner, and on it was a symbol Jack recognized: he had seen it fluttering from guidons held by Morgan of Orris's soldiers as they escorted Morgan's black diligence down the Outpost Road and toward Queen

Laura's pavillion. Morgan's sign—but these were not Morgan's creatures, he understood dimly; they carried his banner as a kind of morbid joke on this frightened interloper who presumed to steal away their only reason for being.

"No more," Jack whispered hoarsely. The pick trembled between his fingers. Something had happened to it; it had been damaged somehow when he used it to destroy the suit of armor which had come from the Heron Bar. The ivory, formerly the color of fresh cream, had yellowed noticeably. Fine cracks now crisscrossed it.

The suits of armor clanked steadily toward him. One slowly drew a long sword which ended in a cruel-looking double point.

"No more," Jack moaned. "Oh God please, no more, I'm tired, I can't, please, no more, no more—"

*Travellin Jack, ole Travellin Jack—*

"*Speedy, I can't!*" he screamed. Tears cut through the dirt on his face. The suits of armor approached with all the inevitability of steel auto parts on an assembly line. He heard an Arctic wind whistling inside their cold black spaces.

*—you be here in California to bring her back.*

"*Please, Speedy, no more!*"

Reaching for him—black-metal robot-faces, rusty greaves, mail splotched and smeared with moss and mould.

*Got to do your best, Travellin Jack,* Speedy whispered, exhausted, and then he was gone and Jack was left to stand or fall on his own.

# 42

# Jack and the Talisman

## 1

*You made a mistake*—a ghostly voice in Jack Sawyer's head spoke up as he stood outside the Heron Bar and watched these other suits of armor bear down on him. In his mind an eye opened wide and he saw an angry man—a man who was really not much more than an overgrown boy—striding up a Western street toward the camera, buckling on first one gunbelt and then another, so that they crisscrossed his belly. *You made a mistake—you shoulda killed both of the Ellis brothers!*

## 2

Of all his mother's movies, the one Jack had always liked the best was *Last Train to Hangtown*, made in 1960 and released in 1961. It had been a Warner Brothers picture, and the major parts—as in many of the lower-budget pictures Warners made during that period—were filled by actors from the half-dozen Warner Brothers TV series which were in constant production. Jack Kelly from the *Maverick* show had been in *Last Train* (the Suave Gambler), and Andrew Duggan from *Bourbon Street Beat* (the Evil Cattle-Baron). Clint Walker, who played a character called Cheyenne Bodie on TV, starred as Rafe Ellis (the Retired Sheriff Who Must Strap on His Guns One Last Time). Inger Stevens had been originally slated to play the part of the Dance Hall Girl with Willing Arms and a Heart of Gold, but Miss Stevens had come down with a bad case of bronchitis and Lily Cavanaugh had stepped into the part. It was of a sort she could have done competently in a coma. Once, when his parents thought he was asleep and were talking in the living room downstairs, Jack overheard his mother say something striking as he padded barefoot to the bathroom to get a glass of water . . . it was striking enough, at any rate, so that Jack never forgot it. "All the women I played knew how to fuck, but not one of them knew how to fart," she told Phil.

Will Hutchins, who starred in *another* Warner Brothers program (this one was called *Sugarfoot*), had also been in the film. *Last Train to Hangtown* was Jack's favorite chiefly because of the character Hutchins played. It was this character—Andy Ellis, by name—who came to his tired, tottering, overtaxed mind now as he watched the suits of armor marching down the dark hallway toward him.

Andy Ellis had been the Cowardly Kid Brother Who Gets Mad in the Last Reel. After skulking and cowering through the entire movie, he had gone out to face Duggan's evil minions after the Chief Minion (played by sinister, stubbly, walleyed Jack Elam, who played Chief Minions in all sorts of Warner epics, both theatrical and televisional) had shot his brother Rafe in the back.

Hutchins had gone striding down the dusty wide-screen street, strapping on his brother's gunbelts with clumsy fingers, shouting, "Come on! Come on, I'm ready for ya! You made a mistake! You shoulda killed *both* of the Ellis brothers!"

Will Hutchins had not been one of the greatest actors of all time, but in that moment he had achieved—at least in Jack's eyes—a moment of clear truth and real brilliance. There was a sense that the kid was going to his death, and knew it, *but meant to go on, anyway.* And although he was frightened, he was not striding up that street toward the showdown with the slightest reluctance; he went eagerly, sure of what he meant to do, even though he had to fumble again and again with the buckles of the gunbelts.

The suits of armor came on, closing the distance, rocking from side to side like toy robots. *They should have keys sticking out of their backs,* Jack thought.

He turned to face them, the yellowed pick held between the thumb and forefinger of his right hand, as if to strum a tune.

They seemed to hesitate, as if sensing his fearlessness. The hotel itself seemed to suddenly hesitate, or to open its eyes to a danger that was deeper than it had at first thought; floors

groaned their boards, somewhere a series of doors clapped
shut one after the other, and on the roofs, the brass ornaments
ceased turning for a moment.

Then the suits of armor clanked forward again. They now
made a single moving wall of plate- and chain-mail, of
greaves and helmets and sparkling gorgets. One held a spiked
iron ball on a wooden haft; one a *martel de fer;* the one in the
center held the double-pointed sword.

Jack suddenly began to walk toward them. His eyes lit up;
he held the guitar-pick out before him. His face filled with
that radiant Jason-glow. He
                              sideslipped
                                        momentarily into the Territories and
*became* Jason; here the shark's tooth which had been a pick
seemed to be aflame. As he approached the three knights, one
pulled off its helmet, revealing another of those old, pale
faces—this one was thick with jowls, and the neck hung with
waxy wattles that looked like melting candlewax. It heaved its
helmet at him. Jason dodged it easily
                                     and
                                        slipped back
into his Jack-self as a helmet crashed off a panelled wall behind him. Standing in front of him was a headless suit of
armor.

*You think that scares me?* he thought contemptuously. *I've
seen that trick before. It doesn't scare me, you don't scare me,
and I'm going to get it, that's all.*

This time he did not just feel the hotel *listening;* this time
it seemed to recoil all around him, as the tissue of a digestive
organ might recoil from a poisoned bit of flesh. Upstairs, in
the five rooms where the five Guardian Knights had died, five
windows blew out like gunshots. Jack bore down on the suits
of armor.

The Talisman sang out from somewhere above in its clear
and sweetly triumphant voice:

*JASON! TO ME!*

*"Come on!"* Jack shouted at the suits of armor, and began
to laugh. He couldn't help himself. Never had laughter
seemed so strong to him, so potent, so good as this—it was
like water from a spring, or from some deep river. *"Come on,
I'm ready for ya! I don't know what fucked-up Round Table*

*you guys came from, but you shoulda stayed there! You made a mistake!"*

Laughing harder than ever but as grimly determined inside as Wotan on the Valkyries' rock, Jack leaped at the headless, swaying figure in the center.

*"You shoulda killed* both *of the Ellis brothers!"* he shouted, and as Speedy's guitar-pick passed into the zone of freezing air where the knight's head should have been, the suit of armor fell apart.

### 3

In her bedroom at the Alhambra, Lily Cavanaugh Sawyer suddenly looked up from the book she had been reading. She thought she had heard someone—no, not just someone, *Jack!*—call out from far down the deserted corridor, perhaps even from the lobby. She listened, eyes wide, lips pursed, heart hoping . . . but there was nothing. Jack-O was still gone, the cancer was still eating her up a bite at a time, and it was still an hour and a half before she could take another of the big brown horse-pills that damped down the pain a little bit.

She had begun to think more and more often of taking all the big brown horse-pills at once. That would do more than damp the pain for a bit; that would finish it off forever. *They say we can't cure cancer, but don't you believe that bullshit, Mr. C—try eating about two dozen of these. What do you say? Want to go for it?*

What kept her from doing it was Jack—she wanted so badly to see him again that now she was imagining his voice . . . not just doing a simple albeit corny sort of thing like calling her name, either, but quoting from one of her old pictures.

"You are one crazy old bitch, Lily," she croaked, and lit a Herbert Tarrytoon with thin, shaking fingers. She took two puffs and then put it out. Any more than two puffs started the coughing these days, and the coughing tore her apart. "One crazy old bitch." She picked up her book again but couldn't read because the tears were coursing down her face and her guts hurt, they hurt, oh they hurt, and she wanted to take all the brown pills but she wanted to see him again first, her dear son with his clear handsome forehead and his shining eyes.

*Come home, Jack-O,* she thought, *please come home soon or the next time I talk to you it'll be by Ouija board. Please, Jack, please come home.*

She closed her eyes and tried to sleep.

## 4

The knight which had held the spike-ball swayed a moment longer, displaying its vacant middle, and then it also exploded. The one remaining raised its battle-hammer . . . and then simply fell apart in a heap. Jack stood amid the wreckage for a moment, still laughing, and then stopped as he looked at Speedy's pick.

It was a deep and ancient yellow now; the crack-glaze had become a snarl of fissures.

*Never mind, Travellin Jack. You get on. I think there may be one more o' those walkin Maxwell House cans around someplace. If so, you'll take it on, won't you?*

"If I have to, I will," Jack muttered aloud.

Jack kicked aside a greave, a helmet, a breastplate. He strode down the middle of the hall, the carpet squelching under his sneakers. He reached the lobby and looked around briefly.

*JACK! COME TO ME! JASON! COME TO ME!* the Talisman sang.

Jack started up the staircase. Halfway up he looked at the landing and saw the last of the knights, standing and looking down at him. It was a gigantic figure, better than eleven feet tall; its armor and its plume were black, and a baleful red glare fell through the eye-slit in its helmet.

One mailed fist gripped a huge mace.

For a moment, Jack stood frozen on the staircase, and then he began to climb again.

## 5

*They saved the worst for last,* Jack thought, and as he advanced steadily upward toward the black knight he

        slipped

                through

                        again

into Jason. The knight still wore black armor, but of a different sort; its visor was tilted up to reveal a face that had been almost obliterated by old dried sores. Jason recognized them. This fellow had gotten a little too close to one of those rolling balls of fire in the Blasted Lands for his own good.

Other figures were passing him on the stairs, figures he could not quite see as his fingers trailed over a wide bannister that was not mahogany from the West Indies but ironwood from the Territories. Figures in doublets, figures in blouses of silk-sack, women in great belling gowns with gleaming white cowls thrown back from their gorgeously dressed hair; these people were beautiful but doomed—and so, perhaps, ghosts always seem to the living. Why else would even the idea of ghosts inspire such terror?

*JASON! TO ME!* the Talisman sang, and for a moment all partitioned reality seemed to break down; he did not flip but seemed to *fall* through worlds like a man crashing through the rotted floors of an ancient wooden tower, one after the other. He felt no fear. The idea that he might never be able to get back—that he might just go on falling through a chain of realities forever, or become lost, as in a great wood—occurred to him, but he dismissed it out of hand. All of this was happening to Jason

*(and Jack)*

in an eyeblink; less time than it would take for his foot to go from one riser on the broad stairs to the next. He would come back; he was single-natured, and he did not believe it was possible for such a person to become lost, because he had a place in all of these worlds. *But I do not exist simultaneously in all of them,* Jason

*(Jack)*

thought. *That's the important thing, that's the difference; I'm flickering through each of them, probably too fast to see, and leaving a sound like a handclap or a sonic boom behind me as the air closes on the vacancy where, for a millisecond, I took up space.*

In many of these worlds, the black hotel was a black ruin—these were worlds, he thought dimly, where the great evil that now impended on the tightwire drawn between California and the Territories had already happened. In one of them the sea which roared and snarled at the shore was a dead, sickly green; the sky had a similar gangrenous look. In another he saw a flying creature as big as a Conestoga wagon fold its wings and plummet earthward like a hawk. It grabbed a creature like a sheep and swooped up again, holding the bloody hindquarters in its beak.

*Flip . . . flip . . . flip.* Worlds passed by his eyes like cards shuffled by a riverboat gambler.

Here was the hotel again, and there were half a dozen different versions of the black knight above him, but the intent in each was the same, and the differences were as unimportant as the stylings of rival automobiles. Here was a black tent filled with the thick dry smell of rotting canvas—it was torn in many places so that the sun shone through in dusty, conflicting rays. In this world Jack/Jason was on some sort of rope rigging, and the black knight stood inside a wooden basket like a crow's nest, and as he climbed he flipped again . . . and again . . . and again.

Here the entire ocean was on fire; here the hotel was much as it was in Point Venuti, except it had been half-sunk into the ocean. For a moment he seemed to be in an elevator car, the knight standing on top of it and peering down at him through the trapdoor. Then he was on a rampway, the top of which was guarded by a huge snake, its long, muscular body armored with gleaming black scales.

*And when do I get to the end of everything? When do I stop crashing through floors and just smash my way into the blackness?*

*JACK! JASON!* the Talisman called, and it called in all the worlds. *TO ME!*

And Jack came to it, and it was like coming home.

### 6

He was right, he saw; he had come up only a single stair. But reality had solidified again. The black knight—*his* black knight, Jack Sawyer's black knight—stood blocking the stair-landing. It raised its mace.

Jack was afraid, but he kept climbing, Speedy's pick held out in front of him.

"I'm not going to mess with you," Jack said. "You better get out of my—"

The black figure swung the mace. It came down with incredible force. Jack dodged aside. The mace crashed into the stair where he had been standing and splintered the entire riser down into hollow blackness.

The figure wrenched the mace free. Jack lunged up two more stairs, Speedy's pick still held between his thumb and forefinger . . . and suddenly it simply disintegrated, falling in a little eggshell rain of yellowed ivory fragments. Most of these sprinkled the tops of Jack's sneakers. He stared stupidly at them.

The sound of dead laughter.

The mace, tiny splinters of wood and chews of old dank stair-runner still clinging to it, was upraised in the knight's two armored gloves. The specter's hot glare fell through the slit in its helmet. It seemed to slice blood from Jack's upturned face in a horizontal line across the bridge of his nose.

That chuffing sound of laughter again—not heard with his ears, because he knew this suit of armor was as empty as the rest, nothing but a steel jacket for an undead spirit, but heard inside his head. *You've lost, boy—did you really think that puny little thing could get you past me?*

The mace whistled down again, this time slicing on a diagonal, and Jack tore his eyes away from that red gaze just in time to duck low—he felt the head of the mace pass through the upper layer of his long hair a second before it ripped away a four-foot section of bannister and sent it sailing out into space.

A scraping clack of metal as the knight leaned toward him, its cocked helmet somehow a hideous and sarcastic parody of solicitude—then the mace drew back and up again for another of those portentous swings.

*Jack, you didn't need no magic juice to git ovah, and you don't need no magic pick to pull the chain on this here coffee can, neither!*

The mace came blasting through the air again—*wheeee-ossshhhh!* Jack lurched backward, sucking in his stomach; the web of muscles in his shoulders screamed as they pulled around the punctures the spiked gloves had left.

The mace missed the skin of his chest by less than an inch before passing beyond him and swiping through a line of thick mahogany balusters as if they had been toothpicks. Jack

tottered on emptiness, feeling Buster Keatonish and absurd.
He snatched at the ragged ruins of the bannister on his left
and got splinters under two of his fingernails instead. The
pain was so wire-thin excruciating that he thought for a moment that his eyeballs would explode with it. Then he got a
good hold with his right hand and was able to stabilize himself and move away from the drop.

*All the magic's in YOU, Jack! Don't you know that by now?*

For a moment he only stood there, panting, and then he
started up the stairs again, staring at the blank iron face above
him.

"Better get thee gone, Sir Gawain."

The knight cocked its great helmet again in that strangely
delicate gesture—*Pardon, my boy . . . can you actually be
speaking to me?* Then it swung the mace again.

Perhaps blinded by his fear, Jack hadn't noticed until now
how slow its setup for those swings was, how clearly it
telegraphed the trajectory of each portentous blow. Maybe its
joints were rusted, he thought. At any rate, it was easy enough
for him to dive inside the circle of its swing now that his head
was clear again.

He stood on his toes, reached up, and seized the black helmet in both hands. The metal was sickeningly warm—like
hard skin that carried a fever.

"Get you off the skin of this world," he said in a voice that
was low and calm, almost conversational. "In *her* name I
command you."

The red light in the helmet puffed out like the candle inside a carved pumpkin, and suddenly the weight of the
helmet—fifteen pounds at least—was all in Jack's hands, because there was nothing else supporting it; beneath the helmet, the suit of armor had collapsed.

"You shoulda killed *both* of the Ellis brothers," Jack said,
and threw the empty helmet over the landing. It hit the floor
far below with a hard *bang* and rolled away like a toy. The hotel seemed to cringe.

Jack turned toward the broad second-floor corridor, and
here, at last, was light: clean, clear light, like that on the day
he had seen the flying men in the sky. The hallway ended in
another set of double doors and the doors were closed, but
enough light came from above and below them, as well as

through the vertical crack where they were latched together, to tell him that the light inside must be very bright indeed.

He wanted very badly to see that light, and the source of that light; he had come far to see it, and through much bitter darkness.

The doors were heavy and inlaid with delicate scrollwork. Written above them in gold leaf which had flaked a bit but which was still perfectly readable for a' that an' a' that, were the words TERRITORIES BALLROOM.

"Hey, Mom," Jack Sawyer said in a soft, wondering voice as he walked into that glow. Happiness lit his heart—that feeling was rainbow, rainbow, rainbow. "Hey, Mom, I think I'm here, I really think I'm here."

Gently then, and with awe, Jack grasped a handle with each hand, and pressed them down. He opened the doors, and as he did, a widening bar of clean white light fell on his up-turned, wondering face.

## 7

Sunlight Gardener happened to be looking back up the beach at the exact moment Jack dispatched the last of the five Guardian Knights. He heard a dull boom, as if a low charge of dynamite had gone off somewhere inside the hotel. At the same moment, bright light flashed from all of the Agincourt's second-floor windows, and all of the carved brass symbols—moons and stars and planetoids and weird crooked arrows—came to a simultaneous stop.

Gardener was decked out like some sort of goony Los Angeles SWAT squad cop. He had donned a puffy black flak-vest over his white shirt and carried a radio pack-set on a canvas strap over one shoulder. Its thick, stubby antenna wavered back and forth as he moved. Over his other shoulder was slung a Weatherbee .360. This was a hunting rifle almost as big as an anti-aircraft gun; it would have made Robert Ruark himself drool with envy. Gardener had bought it six years ago, after circumstances had dictated that he must get rid of his old hunting rifle. The Weatherbee's genuine zebra-skin case was in the trunk of a black Cadillac, along with his son's body.

"Morgan!"

Morgan did not turn around. He was standing behind and slightly to the left of a leaning grove of rocks that jutted out of the sand like black fangs. Twenty feet beyond this rock and only five feet above the high-tide line lay Speedy Parker, aka Parker. As Parkus, he had once ordered Morgan of Orris marked—there were livid scars down the insides of that Morgan's large white thighs, the marks by which a traitor is known in the Territories. It had only been through the intercession of Queen Laura herself that those scars had not been made to run down his cheeks instead of his inner thighs, where they were almost always hidden by his clothes. Morgan—this one as well as that one—had not loved the Queen any better for her intercession . . . but his hatred for Parkus, who had sniffed out that earlier plot, had grown exponentially.

Now Parkus/Parker lay face-down on the beach, his skull covered with festering sores. Blood dribbled listlessly from his ears.

Morgan wanted to believe that Parker was still alive, still suffering, but the last discernible rise and fall of his back had been just after he and Gardener arrived down here at these rocks, some five minutes ago.

When Gardener called, Morgan didn't turn because he was rapt in his study of his old enemy, now fallen. Whoever had claimed revenge wasn't sweet had been so wrong.

*"Morgan!"* Gardener hissed again.

Morgan turned this time, frowning. "Well? What?"

"Look! The roof of the hotel!"

Morgan saw that all of the weathercocks and roof ornaments—beaten brass shapes which spun at exactly the same speed whether the wind was perfectly calm or howling up a hurricane—had stopped moving. At the same instant the earth rippled briefly under their feet and then was still again. It was as if a subterranean beast of enormous size had shrugged in its hibernal sleep. Morgan would almost have believed he had imagined it if it had not been for the widening of Gardener's bloodshot eyes. *I'll bet you wish you never left Indiana, Gard,* Morgan thought. *No earthquakes in Indiana, right?*

Silent light flashed in all of the Agincourt's windows again.

"What does it mean, Morgan?" Gardener asked hoarsely.

His insane fury over the loss of his son had for the first time moderated into fear for himself, Morgan saw. That was a bore, but he could be whipped back into his previous frenzy again, if necessary. It was just that Morgan hated to have to waste energy on anything at this point that didn't bear directly on the problem of ridding the world—*all the worlds*—of Jack Sawyer, who had begun as a pest and who had developed into the most monstrous problem of Sloat's life.

Gardener's pack-set squawked.

"Red Squad Leader Four to the Sunlight Man! Come in, Sunlight Man!"

"Sunlight Man here, Red Squad Leader Four," Gardener snapped. "What's up?"

In quick succession Gardener took four gabbling, excited reports that were all exactly the same. There was no intelligence the two of them hadn't seen and felt for themselves— flashes of light, weathercocks at a standstill, something that might have been a ground-tremblor or possibly an earthquake preshock—but Gardener labored with sharp-eyed enthusiasm over each report just the same, asking sharp questions, snapping *"Over!"* at the end of each transmission, sometimes breaking in with "Say again" or "Roger." Sloat thought he was acting like a bit player in a disaster movie.

But if it eased him, that was fine with Sloat. It saved him from having to answer Gardener's question . . . and now that he thought about it, he supposed it was just possible that Gardener didn't *want* his question answered, and that was why he was going through this rigmarole with the radio.

The Guardians were dead, or out of commission. That was why the weathercocks had stopped, and that's what the flashes of light meant. Jack didn't have the Talisman . . . at least, not yet. If he got that, things in Point Venuti would *really* shake, rattle, and roll. And Sloat now thought that Jack *would* get it . . . that he had always been *meant* to get it. This did not frighten him, however.

His hand reached up and touched the key around his neck.

Gardener had run out of *overs* and *rogers* and *ten-fours*. He reshouldered the pack-set and looked at Morgan with wide, frightened eyes. Before he could say a word, Morgan put gentle hands on Gardener's shoulders. If he could feel love for anyone other than his poor dead son, he felt love—of a twisted variety, most certainly—for this man. They went back a long way, both as Morgan of Orris and Osmond and as Morgan Sloat and Robert "Sunlight" Gardener.

It had been with a rifle much like the one now slung over Gardener's shoulder that Gardener had shot Phil Sawyer in Utah.

"Listen, Gard," he said calmly. "We are going to win."

"Are you sure of that?" Gardener whispered. "I think he's killed the Guardians, Morgan. I know that sounds crazy, but I realy think—" He stopped, mouth trembling infirmly, lips sheened with a thin membrane of spittle.

"We are going to win," Morgan repeated in that same calm voice, and he meant it. There was a sense of clear predestination in him. He had waited many years for this; his resolve had been true; it remained true now. Jack would come out with the Talisman in his arms. It was a thing of immense power . . . but it was fragile.

He looked at the scoped Weatherbee, which could drop a charging rhino, and then he touched the key that brought the lightning.

"We're well equipped to deal with him when he comes out," Morgan said, and added, "In either world. Just as long as you keep your courage, Gard. As long as you stick right by me."

The trembling lips firmed a bit. "Morgan, of course I'll—"

"Remember who killed your son," Morgan said softly.

At the same instant that Jack Sawyer had jammed the burning coin into the forehead of a monstrosity in the Territories, Reuel Gardener, who had been afflicted with relatively harmless petit mal epileptic seizures ever since the age of six (the same age at which Osmond's son had begun to show signs of what was called Blasted Lands Sickness), apparently suffered a grand mal seizure in the back of a Wolf-driven Cadillac on I-70, westbound to California from Illinois.

He had died, purple and strangling, in Sunlight Gardener's arms.

Gardener's eyes now began to bulge.

"Remember," Morgan repeated softly.

"Bad," Gardener whispered. "All boys. Axiomatic. That boy in particular."

"Right!" Morgan agreed. "Hold that thought! We can stop him, but I want to make damn sure that he can only come out of the hotel on dry land."

He led Gardener down to the rock where he had been watching Parker. Flies—bloated albino flies—had begun to light on the dead nigger, Morgan observed. That was just as fine as paint with him. If there had been a *Variety* magazine for flies, Morgan would gladly have bought space, advertising Parker's location. Come one, come all. They would lay their eggs in the folds of his decaying flesh, and the man who had scarred his Twinner's thighs would give birth to maggots. That was fine indeed.

He pointed out toward the dock.

"The raft's under there," he said. "It looks like a horse, Christ knows why. It's in the shadows, I know. But you were always a hell of a shot. If you can pick it up, Gard, put a couple of bullets in it. Sink the fucking thing."

Gardener unshouldered the rifle and peered into the scope. For a long time the muzzle of the big gun wandered minutely back and forth.

"I see it," Gardener whispered in a gloating voice, and triggered the gun. The echo pealed off across the water in a long curl that at last Dopplered away into nothing. The barrel of the gun rose, then came back down. Gardener fired again. And again.

"I got it," Gardener said, lowering the gun. He'd got his courage back; his pecker was up again. He was smiling the way he had been smiling when he had come back from that errand in Utah. "It's just a dead skin on the water now. You want a look in the scope?" He offered the rifle to Sloat.

"No," Sloat said. "If you say you got it, you got it. Now he has to come out by land, and we know what direction he'll be coming in. I think he'll have what's been in our way for so many years."

Gardener looked at him, shiny-eyed.

"I suggest that we move up there." He pointed to the old boardwalk. It was just inside the fence where he had spent so many hours watching the hotel and thinking about what was in the ballroom.

"All r—"

That was when the earth began to groan and heave under their feet—that subterranean creature had awakened; it was shaking itself and roaring.

At the same instant, dazzling white light filled every window of the Agincourt—the light of a thousand suns. The windows blew out all at once. Glass flew in diamond showers.

*"REMEMBER YOUR SON AND FOLLOW ME!"* Sloat roared. That sense of predestination was clear in him now, clear and undeniable. *He was meant to win, after all.*

The two of them began to run up the heaving beach toward the boardwalk.

## 8

Jack moved slowly, filled with wonder, across the hardwood ballroom floor. He was looking up, his eyes sparkling. His face was bathed in a clear white radiance that was all colors— sunrise colors, sunset colors, *rainbow* colors. The Talisman hung in the air high above him, slowly revolving.

It was a crystal globe perhaps three feet in circumference—the corona of its glow was so brilliant it was impossible to tell exactly how big it was. Gracefully curving lines seemed to groove its surface, like lines of longitude and latitude . . . *and why not?* Jack thought, still in a deep daze of awe and amazement. *It is the world—ALL worlds—in microcosm. More; it is the axis of all possible worlds.*

Singing; turning; *blazing.*

He stood beneath it, bathed in its warmth and clear sense of well-meant force; he stood in a dream, feeling that force flow into him like the clear spring rain which awakens the hidden power in a billion tiny seeds. He felt a terrible joy lift through his conscious mind like a rocket, and Jack Sawyer lifted both hands over his upturned face, laughing, both in response to that joy and in imitation of its rise.

*"Come to me, then!"* he shouted,
                    and slipped
                         *(through? across?)*
                              into
Jason.

*"Come to me, then!"* he shouted again in the sweetly liq-

uid and slightly slippery tongue of the Territories—he cried it laughing, but tears coursed down his cheeks. And he understood that the quest had begun with the other boy and thus must end with him; so he let go and

slipped

back

into

Jack Sawyer.

Above him, the Talisman trembled in the air, slowly turning, throwing off light and heat and a sensation of true goodness, of *whiteness*.

*"Come to me!"*

It began to descend through the air.


## 9


So, after many weeks, and hard adventuring, and darkness and despair; after friends found and friends lost again; after days of toil, and nights spent sleeping in damp haystacks; after facing the demons of dark places (not the least of which lived in the cleft of his own soul)—after all these things, it was in this wise that the Talisman came to Jack Sawyer:

He watched it come down, and while there was no desire to flee, he had an overwhelming sense of worlds at risk, worlds in the balance. Was the Jason-part of him real? Queen Laura's son had been killed; he was a ghost whose name the people of the Territories swore by. Yet Jack decided he was. Jack's quest for the Talisman, a quest that had been meant for Jason to fulfill, had made Jason live again for a little while—Jack really *had* a Twinner, at least of a sort. If Jason was a ghost, just as the knights had been ghosts, he might well disappear when that radiant, twirling globe touched his upstretched fingers. Jack would be killing him again.

*Don't worry, Jack,* a voice whispered. That voice was warm and clear.

Down it came, a globe, a world, *all* worlds—it was glory and warmth, it was goodness, it was the coming-again of the white. And, as has always been with the white and must always be, it was dreadfully fragile.

As it came down, worlds reeled about his head. He did not seem to be crashing through layers of reality now but seeing an entire cosmos of realities, all overlapping one another, linked like a shirt of

*(reality)*

chain-mail.

*You're reaching up to hold a universe of worlds, a cosmos of good, Jack*—this voice was his father's. *Don't drop it, son. For Jason's sake, don't drop it.*

Worlds upon worlds upon worlds, some gorgeous, some hellish, all of them for a moment illumined in the warm white light of this star that was a crystal globe chased with fine engraved lines. It came slowly down through the air toward Jack Sawyer's trembling, outstretched fingers.

*"Come to me!"* he shouted to it as it had sung to him. *"Come to me now!"*

It was three feet above his hands, branding them with its soft, healing heat; now two; now one. It hesitated for a moment, rotating slowly, its axis slightly canted, and Jack could see the brilliant, shifting outlines of continents and oceans and ice-caps on its surface. It hesitated . . . and then slowly slipped down into the boy's reaching hands.

43

# News From Everywhere

## 1

Lily Cavanaugh, who had fallen into a fitful doze after imagining Jack's voice somewhere below her, now sat bolt-upright in bed. For the first time in weeks bright color suffused her waxy yellow cheeks. Her eyes shone with a wild hope.

"Jason?" she gasped, and then frowned; that was not her son's name. But in the dream from which she had just been startled awake she had had a son by such a name, and in that dream she had been someone else. It was the dope, of course. The dope had queered her dreams to a fare-thee-well.

"Jack?" she tried again. "Jack, where *are* you?"

No answer . . . but she *sensed* him, knew for sure that he was alive. For the first time in a long time—six months, maybe—she felt really good.

"Jack-O," she said, and grabbed her cigarettes. She looked at them for a moment and then heaved them all the way across the room, where they landed in the fireplace on top of the rest of the shit she meant to burn later in the day. "I think I just quit smoking for the second and last time in my life, Jack-O," she said. "Hang in there, kid. Your momma loves you."

And she found herself for no reason grinning a large idiotic grin.

## 2

Donny Keegan, who had been pulling Sunlight Home kitchen duty when Wolf escaped from the box, had survived that terrible night—George Irwinson, the fellow who had been pulling the duty with him, had not been so lucky. Now Donny was in a more conventional orphans' home in Muncie, Indiana. Unlike some of the other boys at the Sunlight Home, Donny had been a real orphan; Gardener had needed to take a token few to satisfy the state.

Now, mopping a dark upstairs hall in a dim daze, Donny looked up suddenly, his muddy eyes widening. Outside, clouds which had been spitting light snow into the used-up fields of December suddenly pulled open in the west, letting out a single broad ray of sunshine that was terrible and exalting in its isolated beauty.

*"You're right, I DO love him!"* Donny shouted triumphantly. It was Ferd Janklow that Donny was shouting to, although Donny, who had too many toys in his attic to accommodate many brains, had already forgotten his name. *"He's beautiful and I DO love him!"*

Donny honked his idiot laugh, only now even his *laugh* was nearly beautiful. Some of the other boys came to their doors and stared at Donny in wonder. His face was bathed in the sunlight from that one clear, ephemeral ray, and one of the other boys would whisper to a close friend that night that for a moment Donny Keegan had looked like Jesus.

The moment passed; the clouds moved over that weird clear place in the sky, and by evening the snow had intensified into the first big winter storm of the season. Donny had known—for one brief moment he had known—what that feeling of love and triumph actually meant. That passed quickly, the way dreams do upon waking . . . but he never forgot the feeling itself, that almost swooning sensation of grace for once fulfilled and delivered instead of promised and then denied; that feeling of clarity and sweet, marvellous love; that feeling of ecstasy at the coming once more of the white.

### 3

Judge Fairchild, who had sent Jack and Wolf to the Sunlight Home, was no longer a judge of any kind, and as soon as his final appeals ran out, he would be going to jail. There no longer seemed any question that jail was where he would fetch up, and that he would do hard time there. Might never come out at all. He was an old man, and not very healthy. If they hadn't found the damned *bodies* . . .

He had remained as cheerful as possible under the circumstances, but now, as he sat cleaning his fingernails with the long blade of his pocketknife in his study at home, a great gray wave of depression crashed over him. Suddenly he pulled the knife away from his thick nails, looked at it thoughtfully for a moment, and then inserted the tip of the blade into his right nostril. He held it there for a moment and then whispered, "Oh shit. Why not?" He jerked his fist upward, sending the six-inch blade on a short, lethal trip, skewering first his sinuses and then his brain.

### 4

Smokey Updike sat in a booth at the Oatley Tap, going over invoices and totting up numbers on his Texas Instruments calculator, just as he had been doing on the day Jack had met him. Only now it was early evening and Lori was serving the evening's first customers. The jukebox was playing "I'd

Rather Have a Bottle in Front of Me (Than a Frontal Lobotomy)."

At one moment everything was normal. At the next Smokey sat bolt-upright, his little paper cap tumbling backward off his head. He clutched his white T-shirt over the left side of his chest, where a hammering bolt of pain had just struck like a silver spike. *God pounds his nails,* Wolf would have said.

At the same instant the grill suddenly exploded into the air with a loud bang. It hit a Busch display sign and tore it from the ceiling. It landed with a crash. A rich smell of LP gas filled the area in back of the bar almost at once. Lori screamed.

The jukebox speeded up: 45 rpms, 78, 150, 400! The woman's seriocomic lament became the speedy gabble of deranged chipmunks on a rocket-sled. A moment later the top blew off the juke. Colored glass flew everywhere.

Smokey looked down at his calculator and saw a single word blinking on and off in the red window:

TALISMAN-TALISMAN-TALISMAN-TALISMAN

Then his eyes exploded.

*"Lori, turn off the gas!"* one of the customers screamed. He got down off his stool, and turned toward Smokey. "Smokey, tell her—" The man wailed with fright as he saw blood gushing from the holes where Smokey Updike's eyes had been.

A moment later the entire Oatley Tap blew sky-high, and before the fire-trucks could arrive from Dogtown and Elmira, most of downtown was in flames.

No great loss, children, can you say amen.

## 5

At Thayer School, where normality now reigned as it always had (with one brief interlude which those on campus remembered only as a series of vague, related dreams), the last classes of the day had just begun. What was light snow in Indiana was a cold drizzle here in Illinois. Students sat dreaming and thoughtful in their classes.

Suddenly the bells in the chapel began to peal. Heads came up. Eyes widened. All over the Thayer campus, fading dreams suddenly seemed to renew themselves.

## 6

Etheridge had been sitting in advanced-math class and pressing his hand rhythmically up and down against a raging hard-on while he stared unseeingly at the logarithms old Mr. Hunkins was piling up on the blackboard. He was thinking about the cute little townie waitress he would be boffing later on. She wore garter-belts instead of pantyhose, and was more than willing to leave her stockings on while they fucked. Now Etheridge stared around at the windows, forgetting his erection, forgetting the waitress with her long legs and smooth nylons—suddenly, for no reason at all, Sloat was on his mind. Prissy little Richard Sloat, who should have been safely classifiable as a wimp but who somehow wasn't. He thought about Sloat and wondered if he was all right. Somehow he thought that maybe Sloat, who had left school unexcused four days ago and who hadn't been heard from since, wasn't doing so good.

In the headmaster's office, Mr. Dufrey had been discussing the expulsion of a boy named George Hatfield for cheating with his furious—and rich—father when the bells began to jingle out their unscheduled little tune. When it ended, Mr. Dufrey found himself on his hands and knees with his gray hair hanging in his eyes and his tongue lolling over his lips. Hatfield the Elder was standing by the door—cringing against it, actually—his eyes wide and his jaw agape, his anger forgotten in wonder and fear. Mr. Dufrey had been crawling around on his rug barking like a dog.

Albert the Blob had just been getting himself a snack when the bells began to ring. He looked toward the window for a moment, frowning the way a person frowns when he is trying to remember something that is right on the tip of his tongue. He shrugged and went back to opening a bag of nacho chips—his mother had just sent him a whole case. His eyes widened. He thought—just for a moment, but a moment was long enough—that the bag was full of plump, squirming white bugs.

He fainted dead away.

When he awoke and worked up enough courage to peer into the bag again, he saw it had been nothing but a hallucination. Of course! What else? All the same, it was a hallucination which exercised a strange power over him in the future; whenever he opened a bag of chips, or a candy bar, or a Slim Jim, or a package of Big Jerk beef jerky, he saw those bugs in his mind's eye. By spring, Albert had lost thirty-five pounds, was playing on the Thayer tennis team, and had gotten laid. Albert was delirious with ecstasy. For the first time in his life he felt that he might survive his mother's love.


## 7

They all looked around when the bells began to ring. Some laughed, some frowned, a few burst into tears. A pair of dogs howled from somewhere, and that was passing strange because no dogs were allowed on campus.

The tune the bells rang was not in the computerized schedule of tunes—the disgruntled head custodian later verified it. A campus wag suggested in that week's issue of the school paper that some eager beaver had programmed the tune with Christmas vacation in mind.

It had been "Happy Days Are Here Again."


## 8

Although she had believed herself far too old to catch pregnant, no blood had come to the mother of Jack Sawyer's Wolf at the time of the Change some twelve months ago. Three months ago she had given birth to triplets—two litter-sisters and one litter-brother. Her labor had been hard, and the foreknowledge that one of her older children was about to die had been upon her. That child, she knew, had gone into the Other Place to protect the herd, and he would die in that Other Place, and she would never see him anymore. This was very hard, and she had wept in more than the pain of her delivery.

Yet now, as she slept with her new young beneath a full moon, all of them safely away from the herd for the time being, she rolled over with a smile on her face and pulled the newest litter-brother to her and began to lick him. Still sleep-

ing himself, the Wolfling put his arms around his mother's
shaggy neck and pressed his cheek against her downy breast,
and now they both smiled; in her alien sleep a human thought
arose: *God pounds his nails well and true.* And the moonlight
of that lovely world where all smells were good shone down
on the two of them as they slept in each other's arms with the
litter-sisters nearby.

## 9

In the town of Goslin, Ohio (not far from Amanda, and some
thirty miles south of Columbus), a man named Buddy Parkins
was shovelling chickenshit in a henhouse at dusk. A cheese-
cloth mask was tied over his mouth and nose to keep the
choking white cloud of powdered guano he was raising from
getting up his nose and into his mouth. The air reeked of ammonia. The stink had given him a headache. He also had a
backache, because he was tall and the henhouse wasn't. All
things considered, he would have to say that this was one
bitch-kitty of a job. He had three sons, and every damned one
of them seemed to be unavailable when the henhouse needed
to be swamped out. Only thing to be said about it was that he
was almost done, and—

*The kid! Jesus Christ! That kid!*

He suddenly remembered the boy who had called himself
Lewis Farren with total clarity and a stunned kind of love.
The boy who had claimed to be going to his aunt, Helen
Vaughan, in the town of Buckeye Lake; the boy who had
turned to Buddy when Buddy had asked him if he was running away and had in that turning, revealed a face filled with
honest goodness and an unexpected, amazing beauty—a
beauty that had made Buddy think of rainbows glimpsed at
the end of storms, and sunsets at the end of days that have
groaned and sweated with work that has been well done and
not scamped.

He straightened up with a gasp and bonked his head on the
henhouse beams hard enough to make his eyes water . . . but
he was grinning crazily all the same. *Oh my God, that boy is
THERE, he's THERE,* Buddy Parkins thought, and although
he had no idea of where "there" was, he was suddenly overtaken by a sweet, violent feeling of absolute adventure; never,

since reading *Treasure Island* at the age of twelve and cupping a girl's breast in his hand for the first time at fourteen, had he felt so staggered, so excited, so full of warm joy. He began to laugh. He dropped his shovel, and while the hens stared at him with stupid amazement, Buddy Parkins danced a shuffling jig in the chickenshit, laughing behind his mask and snapping his fingers.

"He's there!" Buddy Parkins yelled to the chickens, laughing. "By diddly-damn, he's there, he made it after all, he's there *and he's got it!*"

Later, he almost thought—almost, but never quite—that he must have somehow gotten high on the stench of the chickendust. That *wasn't* all, dammit, that *wasn't*. He had had some kind of revelation, but he could no longer remember what it had been . . . he supposed it was like that British poet some high-school English teacher had told them about: the guy had taken a big dose of opium and had started to write some poems about a make-believe Chink whorehouse while he was stoned . . . except when he came down to earth again he couldn't finish it.

*Like that,* he thought, but somehow he knew it wasn't; and although he couldn't remember exactly what had caused the joy, he, like Donny Keegan, never forgot the way the joy had come, all deliciously unbidden—he never forgot that sweet, violent feeling of having touched some great adventure, of having looked for a moment at some beautiful white light that was, in fact, every color of the rainbow.

## 10

There's an old Bobby Darin song which goes: *"And the ground coughs up some roots/wearing denim shirts and boots,/haul em away . . . haul em away."* This was a song the children in the area of Cayuga, Indiana, could have related to enthusiastically, if it hadn't been popular quite a bit before their time. The Sunlight Home had been empty for only a little more than a week, and already it had gotten a reputation with the local kids as a haunted house. Considering the grisly remains the payloaders had found near the rock wall at the back of Far Field, this was not surprising. The local Realtor's FOR SALE sign looked as if it had been standing on the lawn for a year instead of just nine days, and the Realtor had already dropped the price once and was thinking about doing it again.

As it happened, he would not have to. As the first snow began to spit down from the leaden skies over Cayuga (and as Jack Sawyer was touching the Talisman some two thousand miles away), the LP tanks behind the kitchen exploded. A workman from Eastern Indiana Gas and Electric had come the week before and had sucked all the gas back into his truck, and he would have sworn you could have crawled right inside one of those tanks and lit up a cigarette, but they exploded anyway—they exploded at the exact moment the windows of the Oatley Tap were exploding out into the street (along with a number of patrons wearing denim shirts and boots . . . and Elmira rescue units hauled em away).

The Sunlight Home burned to the ground in almost no time at all.

Can you gimme hallelujah?

## 11

In all worlds, something shifted and settled into a slightly new position like a great beast . . . but in Point Venuti the beast was in the earth; it had been awakened and was roaring. It did not go to sleep for the next seventy-nine seconds, according to the Institute of Seismology at CalTech.

The earthquake had begun.

# 44

# The Earthquake

## 1

It was some time before Jack became aware that the Agincourt was shaking itself to pieces around him, and this was not surprising. He was transported with wonder. In one sense he was not in the Agincourt at all, not in Point Venuti, not in

Mendocino County, not in California, not in the American Territories, not in those other Territories; but he *was* in them, and in an infinite number of other worlds as well, and all at the same time. Nor was he simply in one place in all those worlds; he was in them everywhere because he *was* those worlds. The Talisman, it seemed, was much more than even his father had believed. It was not just the axle of all possible worlds, but the worlds themselves—the worlds, and the spaces between those worlds.

Here was enough transcendentalism to drive even a cave-dwelling Tibetan holy man insane. Jack Sawyer was everywhere; Jack Sawyer was everything. A blade of grass on a world fifty thousand worlds down the chain from earth died of thirst on an inconsequential plain somewhere in the center of a continent which roughly corresponded in position to Africa; Jack died with that blade of grass. In another world, dragons were copulating in the center of a cloud high above the planet, and the fiery breath of their ecstasy mixed with the cold air and precipitated rain and floods on the ground below. Jack was the he-dragon; Jack was the she-dragon; Jack was the sperm; Jack was the egg. Far out in the ether a million universes away, three specks of dust floated near one another in interstellar space. Jack was the dust, and Jack was the space between. Galaxies unreeled around his head like long spools of paper, and fate punched each in random patterns, turning them into macrocosmic player-piano tapes which would play everything from ragtime to funeral dirges. Jack's happy teeth bit an orange: Jack's unhappy flesh screamed as the teeth tore him open. He was a trillion dust-kitties under a billion beds. He was a joey dreaming of its previous life in its mother's pouch as the mother bounced over a purple plain where rabbits the size of deer ran and gambolled. He was ham on a hock in Peru and eggs in a nest under one of the hens in the Ohio henhouse Buddy Parkins was cleaning. He was the powdered henshit in Buddy Parkins's nose; he was the trembling hairs that would soon cause Buddy Parkins to sneeze; he was the sneeze; he was the germs in the sneeze; he was the atoms in the germs; he was the tachyons in the atoms travelling backward through time toward the big bang at the start of creation.

His heart skipped and a thousand suns flashed up in novas.

He saw a googolplex of sparrows in a googolplex of worlds and marked the fall or the well-being of each.

He died in the Gehenna of Territories ore-pit mines.

He lived as a flu-virus in Etheridge's tie.

He ran in a wind over far places.

He was . . .

Oh he was . . .

*He was God. God, or something so close as to make no difference.*

*No!* Jack screamed in terror. *No, I don't want to be God! Please! Please, I don't want to be God, I ONLY WANT TO SAVE MY MOTHER'S LIFE!*

And suddenly infinitude closed up like a losing hand folding in a cardsharp's grasp. It narrowed down to a beam of blinding white light, and this he followed back to the Territories Ballroom, where only seconds had passed. He still held the Talisman in his hands.

## 2

Outside, the ground had begun to do a carny kooch dancer's bump and grind. The tide, which had been coming in, rethought itself and began to run backward, exposing sand as deeply tanned as a starlet's thighs. Flopping on this uncovered sand were strange fish, some which seemed to be no more than gelatinous clots of eyes.

The cliffs behind the town were nominally of sedimentary rock, but any geologist would have taken one look and told you at once that these rocks were to the sedimentary classification as the nouveau riche were to the Four Hundred. The Point Venuti Highlands were really nothing but mud with a hard-on and now they cracked and split in a thousand crazy directions. For a moment they held, the new cracks opening and closing like gasping mouths, and then they began to collapse in landslides on the town. Showers of dirt came sifting down. Amid the dirt were boulders as big as Toledo tire-factories.

Morgan's Wolf Brigade had been decimated by Jack and Richard's surprise attack on Camp Readiness. Now the number was even further reduced as many of them ran screaming and wailing in superstitious fear. Some catapulated back into their own world. Some of these got away, but most were swallowed by the upheavals that were happening there. A core of similar cataclysms ran from this place through all the worlds, as if punched through by a surveyor's hollow sampling rod. One group of three Wolfs dressed in Fresno Demons motorcycle jackets gained their car—a horny old Lincoln Mark IV—and managed to drive a block and a half with Harry James bellowing brass out of the tapedeck before a chunk of stone fell from the sky and crushed the Connie flat.

Others simply ran shrieking in the streets, their Change beginning. The woman with the chains in her nipples strolled serenely in front of one of these. She was serenely ripping her hair out in great chunks. She held one of these chunks out to the Wolf. The bloody roots wavered like the tips of sea-grass as she waltzed in place on the unsteady earth.

"Here!" she cried, smiling serenely. "A bouquet! For you!"

The Wolf, not a bit serene, tore her head off with a single snap of his jaws and ran on, on, on.

### 3

Jack studied what he had captured, as breathless as a child who has a shy woodland creature come out of the grass and eat from his hand.

It glowed between his palms, waxing and waning, waxing and waning.

*With my heartbeat,* he thought.

It seemed to be glass, but it had a faintly yielding feeling in his hands. He pressed and it gave a little. Color shot inward from the points of his pressure in enchanting billows: inky blue from his left hand, deepest carmine from the right. He smiled . . . and then the smile faded.

*You may be killing a billion people doing that—fires, floods, God knows what. Remember the building that collapsed in Angola, New York, after—*

*No, Jack,* the Talisman whispered, and he understood why it had yielded to the gentle pressure of his hands. It was alive; of course it was. *No, Jack: All will be well . . . all will be well . . . and all manner of things will be well. Only believe; be true; stand; do not falter now.*

Peace in him—oh such deep peace.

*Rainbow, rainbow, rainbow,* Jack thought, and wondered if he could ever bring himself to let this wondrous bauble go.

### 4

On the beach below the wooden walk, Gardener had fallen flat on his belly in terror. His fingers hooked into the loose sand. He was mewling.

Morgan reeled toward him like a drunk and ripped the pack-set from Gardener's shoulder.

*"Stay outside!"* he roared into it, and then realized he had forgotten to press the SEND button. He did it now. *"STAY OUTSIDE! IF YOU TRY TO GET OUT OF TOWN THE MOTHERFUCKING CLIFFS WILL FALL ON YOU! GET DOWN HERE! COME TO ME! THIS IS NOTHING BUT A BUNCH OF GODDAM SPECIAL EFFECTS! GET DOWN HERE! FORM A RING AROUND THE BEACH! THOSE OF YOU WHO COME WILL BE REWARDED! THOSE OF YOU WHO DON'T WILL DIE IN THE PITS AND IN THE BLASTED LANDS! GET DOWN HERE! IT'S OPEN! GET DOWN HERE WHERE NOTHING CAN FALL ON YOU! GET DOWN HERE, DAMMIT!"*

He threw the pack-set aside. It split open. Beetles with long feelers began to squirm out by the dozens.

He bent down and yanked the howling, whey-faced Gardener up. "On your feet, beautiful," he said.

### 5

Richard cried out in his unconsciousness as the table he was lying on bucked him off onto the floor. Jack heard the cry, and it dragged him out of his fascinated contemplation of the Talisman.

He became aware that the Agincourt was groaning like a ship in a high gale. As he looked around, boards snapped up, revealing dusty beamwork beneath. The beams were sawing back and forth like shuttles in a loom. Albino bugs scuttered and squirmed away from the Talisman's clear light.

*"I'm coming, Richard!"* he shouted, and began to work his way back across the floor. He was thrown over once and he went down holding the glowing sphere high, knowing it was vulnerable—if it was hit hard enough, it would break. What then, God knew. He got to one knee, was thrown back down on his butt, and lurched to his feet again.

From below, Richard screamed again.

*"Richard! Coming!"*

From overhead, a sound like sleigh-bells. He looked up and saw the chandelier penduluming back and forth, faster and faster. Its crystal pendants were making that sound. As Jack watched, the chain parted and it hit the unravelling floor like a bomb with diamonds instead of high explosive in its nose. Glass flew.

He turned and exited the room in big, larruping strides— he looked like a burlesque comic doing a turn as a drunken sailor.

Down the hall. He was thrown against first one wall and then the other as the floor seesawed and split open. Each time he crashed into a wall he held the Talisman out from him, his arms like tongs in which it glowed like a white-hot coal.

*You'll never make it down the stairs.*

*Gotta. Gotta.*

He reached the landing where he had faced the black knight. The world heaved a new way; Jack staggered and saw the helmet on the floor below roll crazily away.

Jack continued to look down. The stairs were moving in great tortured waves that made him feel like puking. A stair-level snapped upward, leaving a writhing black hole.

*"Jack!"*

*"Coming, Richard!"*

*No way you can make it down those stairs. No way, baby.*

*Gotta. Gotta.*

Holding the precious, fragile Talisman in his hands, Jack started down a flight of stairs that now looked like an Arabian flying carpet caught in a tornado.

The stairs heaved and he was flung toward the same gap through which the black knight's helmet had fallen. Jack screamed and staggered backward toward the drop, holding the Talisman against his chest with his right hand and flailing behind him with his left. Flailing at nothing. His heels hit the drop and tilted backward over oblivion.

## • 6

Fifty seconds had passed since the earthquake began. Only fifty seconds—but earthquake survivors will tell you that objective time, clock-time, loses all meaning in an earthquake. Three days after the '64 earthquake in Los Angeles, a television news reporter asked a survivor who had been near the epicenter how long the quake had lasted.

"It's still going on," the survivor said calmly.

Sixty-two seconds after the quake began, almost all of the Point Venuti Highlands decided to give in to destiny and become the Point Venuti Lowlands. They fell on the town with a muddy *kurrummmmp*, leaving only a single jut of slightly harder rock, which pointed at the Agincourt like an accusing finger. From one of the new slumped hills a dirty smokestack pointed like a randy penis.

## 7

On the beach, Morgan Sloat and Sunlight Gardener stood supporting each other, appearing to hula. Gardener had unslung the Weatherbee. A few Wolfs, their eyes alternately bulging with terror and glaring with hellacious rage, had joined them. More were coming. They were all Changed or Changing. Their clothes hung from them in tatters. Morgan saw one of them dive at the ground and begin to bite at it, as if the uneasy earth were an enemy that could be killed. Morgan glanced at this madness and dismissed it. A van with the words WILD CHILD written on the sides in psychedelic lettering plowed hell-for-leather across Point Venuti Square, where children had once begged their parents for ice creams and pennants emblazoned with the Agincourt's likeness. The van made it to the far side, jumped across the sidewalk, and then roared toward the beach, plowing through boarded-up concessions as it came. One final fissure opened in the earth and the WILD CHILD that had killed Tommy Woodbine disappeared forever, nose first. A jet of flame burst up as its gas-tank exploded. Watching, Sloat thought dimly of his father preaching about the Pentecostal Fire. Then the earth snapped shut.

"Hold steady," he shouted at Gardener. "I think the place is going to fall on top of him and crush him flat, but if he gets out, you're going to shoot him, earthquake or no earthquake."

"Will we know if IT breaks?" Gardener squealed.

Morgan Sloat grinned like a boar in a canebrake.

"We'll know," he said. "The sun will turn black."

Seventy-four seconds.

## 8

Jack's left hand scrabbled a grip on the ragged remains of the bannister. The Talisman glowed fiercely against his chest, the lines of latitude and longitude which girdled it shining as brightly as the wire filaments in a lightbulb. His heels tilted and his soles began to slide.

*Falling! Speedy! I'm going to—*

Seventy-nine seconds.

It stopped.

Suddenly, it just stopped.

Only, for Jack, as for that survivor of the '64 quake, it was still going on, at least in part of his brain. In part of his brain the earth would continue to shake like a church-picnic Jell-O forever.

He pulled himself back from the drop and staggered to the middle of the twisted stair. He stood, gasping, his face shiny with sweat, hugging the bright round star of the Talisman against his chest. He stood and listened to the silence.

Somewhere something heavy—a bureau or a wardrobe, perhaps—which had been tottering on the edge of balance now fell over with an echoing crash.

*"Jack! Please! I think I'm dying!"* Richard's groaning, helpless voice did indeed sound like that of a boy in his last extremity.

*"Richard! Coming!"*

He began to work his way down the stairs, which were now twisted and bent and tottery. Many of the stair-levels were gone, and he had to step over these spaces. In one place four in a row were gone and he leaped, holding the Talisman to his chest with one hand and sliding his hand along the warped bannister with the other.

Things were still falling. Glass crashed and tinkled. Somewhere a toilet was flushing manically, again and again.

The redwood registration desk in the lobby had split down the middle. The double doors were ajar, however, and a bright wedge of sunlight came through them—the old dank carpet seemed to sizzle and steam in protest at that light.

*The clouds have broken,* Jack thought. *Sun's shining outside.* And then: *Going out those doors, Richie-boy. You and me. Big as life and twice as proud.*

The corridor which led past the Heron Bar and down to the dining room reminded him of sets in some of the old *Twilight Zone* shows, where everything was askew and out of kilter. Here the floor tilted left; here to the right; here it was like the twin humps of a camel. He negotiated the dimness with the Talisman lighting his way like the world's biggest flashlight.

He shoved into the dining room and saw Richard lying on the floor in a tangle of tablecloth. Blood was running from his nose. When he got closer he saw that some of those hard red bumps had split open and white bugs were working their way out of Richard's flesh and crawling sluggishly over Richard's cheeks. As he watched, one birthed itself from Richard's nose.

Richard screamed, a weak, bubbling, wretched scream, and clawed at it. It was the scream of someone who is dying in agony.

His shirt humped and writhed with the things.

Jack stumbled across the distorted floor toward him . . . and the spider swung down from the dimness, squirting its poison blindly into the air.

"*Flushing feef!*" it gibbered in its whining, droning insect's voice. "*Oh you fushing feef, put it back put it back!*"

Without thinking, Jack raised the Talisman. It flashed clean white fire—rainbow fire—and the spider shrivelled and turned black. In only a second it was a tiny lump of smoking coal penduluming slowly to a dead stop in the air.

No time to gawp at this wonder. Richard was dying.

Jack reached him, fell on his knees beside him, and stripped back the tablecloth as if it were a sheet.

"Finally made it, chum," he whispered, trying not to see the bugs crawling out of Richard's flesh. He raised the Talisman, considered, and then placed it on Richard's forehead. Richard shrieked miserably and tried to writhe away. Jack placed an arm on Richard's scrawny chest and held him—it wasn't hard to do. There was a stench as the bugs beneath the Talisman fried away.

*Now what? There's more, but what?*

He looked across the room and his eye happened to fix upon the green croaker marble that he had left with Richard—the marble that was a magic mirror in that other world. As he looked, it rolled six feet of its own volition, and then stopped. It rolled, yes. It rolled because it was a marble, and it was a marble's job to roll. Marbles were round. Marbles were round and so was the Talisman.

Light broke in his reeling mind.

Holding Richard, Jack slowly rolled the Talisman down the length of his body. After he reached Richard's chest, Richard stopped struggling. Jack thought he had probably fainted, but a quick glance showed him this wasn't so. Richard was staring at him with dawning wonder . . .

. . . *and the pimples on his face were gone! The hard red bumps were fading!*

"Richard!" he yelled, laughing like a crazy loon. "Hey, Richard, look at this! Bwana make juju!"

He rolled the Talisman slowly down over Richard's belly, using his palm. The Talisman glowed brightly, singing a clear, wordless harmonic of health and healing. Down over Richard's crotch. Jack moved Richard's thin legs together and rolled it down the groove between them to Richard's ankles. The Talisman glowed bright blue . . . deep red . . . yellow . . . the green of June meadow-grass.

Then it was white again.

"Jack," Richard whispered. "Is that what we came for?"

"Yes."

"It's beautiful," Richard said. He hesitated. "May I hold it?"

Jack felt a sudden twist of Scrooge-miserliness. He snatched the Talisman close to himself for a moment. *No! You might break it! Besides, it's mine! I crossed the country for it! I fought the knights for it! You can't have it! Mine! Mine! Mi—*

In his hands the Talisman suddenly radiated a terrible chill,

and for a moment—a moment more frightening to Jack than
all the earthquakes in all the worlds that ever had been or ever
would be—it turned a Gothic black. Its white light was extin-
guished. In its rich, thundery, thanatropic interior he saw the
black hotel. On turrets and gambrels and gables, on the roofs
of cupolas which bulged like warts stuffed with thick malig-
nancies, the cabalistic symbols turned—wolf and crow and
twisted genital star.

*Would you be the new Agincourt, then?* the Talisman whispered. *Even a boy can be a hotel . . . if he would be.*

His mother's voice, clear in his head: *If you don't want to
share it, Jack-O, if you can't bring yourself to risk it for your
friend, then you might as well stay where you are. If you can't
bring yourself to share the prize—risk the prize—don't even
bother to come home. Kids hear that shit all their lives, but
when it comes time to put up or shut up, it's never quite the
same, is it? If you can't share it, let me die, chum, because I
don't want to live at that price.*

The weight of the Talisman suddenly seemed immense, the
weight of dead bodies. Yet somehow Jack lifted it, and put it
in Richard's hands. His hands were white and skeletal . . . but
Richard held it easily, and Jack realized that sensation of
weight had been only his own imagination, his own twisted
and sickly wanting. As the Talisman flashed into glorious
white light again, Jack felt his own interior darkness pass
from him. It occurred to him dimly that you could only express your ownership of a thing in terms of how freely you
could give it up . . . and then that thought passed.

Richard smiled, and the smile made his face beautiful.
Jack had seen Richard smile many times, but there was a
peace in this smile he had never seen before; it was a peace
which passed his understanding. In the Talisman's white,
healing light, he saw that Richard's face, although still ravaged and haggard and sickly, was healing. He hugged the Talisman against his chest as if it were a baby, and smiled at Jack
with shining eyes.

"If *this* is the Seabrook Island Express," he said, "I may
just buy a season ticket. *If* we ever get out of this."

"You feel better?"

Richard's smile shone like the Talisman's light. "*Worlds*
better," he said. "Now help me up, Jack."

Jack moved to take his shoulder. Richard held out the Talisman.

"Better take this first," he said. "I'm still weak, and it wants to go back with you. I feel that."

Jack took it and helped Richard up. Richard put an arm around Jack's neck.

"You ready . . . *chum?*"

"Yeah," Richard said. "Ready. But I somehow think the seagoing route's out, Jack. I think I heard the deck out there collapse during the Big Rumble."

"We're going out the front door," Jack said. "Even if God put down a gangway over the ocean from the windows back there to the beach, I'd still go out the front door. We ain't ditching this place, Richie. We're going out like paying guests. I feel like I've paid plenty. What do you think?"

Richard held out one thin hand, palm-up. Healing red blemishes still glared on it.

"I think we ought to go for it," he said. "Gimme some skin, Jacky."

Jack slapped his palm down on Richard's, and then the two of them started back toward the hallway, Richard with one arm around Jack's neck.

Halfway down the hall, Richard stared at the litter of dead metal. "What in heck?"

"Coffee cans," Jack said, and smiled. "Maxwell House."

"Jack, what in the world are you t—"

"Never mind, Richard," Jack said. He was grinning, and he still felt good, but wires of tension were working into his body again just the same. The earthquake was over . . . but it wasn't over. Morgan would be waiting for them now. And Gardener.

*Never mind. Let it come down the way it will.*

They reached the lobby and Richard looked around wonderingly at the stairs, the broken registration desk, the tumbled trophies and flagstands. The stuffed head of a black bear had its nose in one of the pigeonholes of the mail depository, as if smelling something good—honey, perhaps.

"Wow," Richard said. "Whole place just about fell down."

Jack got Richard over to the double doors, and observed Richard's almost greedy appreciation of that little spray of sunlight.

"Are you really ready for this, Richard?"

"Yes."

"Your father's out there."

"No, he's not. He's dead. All that's out there is his . . . what do you call it? His Twinner."

"Oh."

Richard nodded. In spite of the Talisman's proximity, he was beginning to look exhausted again. "Yes."

"There's apt to be a hell of a fight."

"Well, I'll do what I can."

"I love you, Richard."

Richard smiled wanly. "I love you, too, Jack. Now let's go for it before I lose my nerve."

### 9

Sloat really believed he had everything under control—the situation, of course, but more important, himself. He went right on believing this until he saw his son, obviously weak, obviously sick, but still very much alive, come out of the black hotel with his arm around Jack Sawyer's neck and his head leaning against Jack's shoulder.

Sloat had also believed he finally had his feelings about Phil Sawyer's brat under control—it was his previous rage that had caused him to miss Jack, first at the Queen's pavillion, then in the midwest. Christ, he had crossed Ohio unscathed—and Ohio was only an eyeblink from Orris, that other Morgan's stronghold. But his fury had led to uncontrolled behavior, and so the boy had slipped through. He had suppressed his rage—but now it flared up with wicked and unbridled freedom. It was as if someone had hosed kerosene on a well-banked fire.

*His son, still alive. And his beloved son, to whom he had meant to turn over the kingship of worlds and universes, was leaning on Sawyer for support.*

Nor was that all. Glimmering and flashing in Sawyer's hands like a star which had fallen to earth was the Talisman. Even from here Sloat could feel it—it was as if the planet's gravitational field had suddenly gotten stronger, pulling him down, making his heart labor; as if time were speeding up, drying out his flesh, dimming his eyes.

*"It hurts!"* Gardener wailed beside him.

Most of the Wolfs who had stood up to the quake and rallied to Morgan were now reeling away, hands before their faces. A couple of them were vomiting helplessly.

Morgan felt a moment of swooning fear . . . and then his rage, his excitement, and the lunacy that had been feeding on his increasingly grandiose dreams of overlordship—these things burst apart the webbing of his self-control.

He raised his thumbs to his ears and slammed them deep inside, so deep it hurt. Then he stuck out his tongue and waggled his fingers at Mr. Jack Dirty Motherfuck and Soon-to-be-Dead Sawyer. A moment later his upper teeth descended like a drop-gate and seered the tip of his wagging tongue. Sloat didn't even notice it. He seized Gardener by the flak-vest.

Gardener's face was moony with fear. "They're out, he's got IT, Morgan . . . my Lord . . . we ought to run, we *must* run—"

*"SHOOT HIM!"* Morgan screamed into Gardener's face. Blood from his severed tongue flew in a fine spray. *"SHOOT HIM, YOU ETHIOPIAN JUG-FUCKER, HE KILLED YOUR BOY! SHOOT HIM AND SHOOT THE FUCKING TALISMAN! SHOOT RIGHT THROUGH HIS ARMS AND BREAK IT!"*

Sloat now began to dance slowly up and down before Gardener, his face working horribly, his thumbs back in his ears, his fingers waggling beside his head, his amputated tongue popping in and out of his mouth like one of those New Year's Eve party favors that unroll with a tooting sound. He looked like a murderous child—hilarious, and at the same time awful.

*"HE KILLED YOUR SON! AVENGE YOUR SON! SHOOT HIM! SHOOT IT! YOU SHOT HIS FATHER, NOW SHOOT HIM!"*

"Reuel," Gardener said thoughtfully. "Yes. He killed Reuel. He's the baddest bitch's bastard to ever draw a breath. *All* boys. Axiomatic. But he . . . *he* . . ."

He turned toward the black hotel and raised the Weatherbee to his shoulder. Jack and Richard had reached the bottom of the twisted front steps and were beginning to move down the broad walkway, which had been flat a few minutes ago and which was now crazy-paved. In the Judkins scope, the two boys were as big as house-trailers.

*"SHOOT HIM!"* Morgan bellowed. He ran out his bleeding tongue again and made a hideously triumphant nursery-school sound: *Yadda-yadda-yadda-yah!* His feet, clad in dirty Gucci loafers, bumped up and down. One of them landed squarely on the severed tip of his tongue and tromped it deeper into the sand.

*"SHOOT HIM! SHOOT IT!"* Morgan howled.

The muzzle of the Weatherbee circled minutely as it had when Gardener was preparing to shoot the rubber horse. Then it settled. Jack was carrying the Talisman against his chest. The crosshairs were over its flashing, circular light. The .360 slug would pass right through it, shattering it, and the sun would turn black . . . *but before it does,* Gardener thought, *I will see that baddest bad boy's chest explode.*

"He's dead meat," Gardener whispered, and began to settle pressure against the Weatherbee's trigger.

## 10

Richard raised his head with great effort and his eyes were sizzled by reflected sunlight.

Two men. One with his head slightly cocked, the other seeming to dance. That flash of sunlight again, and Richard understood. He understood . . . and Jack was looking in the wrong place. Jack was looking down toward the rocks where Speedy lay.

*"Jack look out!"* he screamed.

Jack looked around, surprised. "What—"

It happened fast. Jack missed it almost entirely. Richard saw it and understood it, but could never quite explain what had happened to Jack. The sunlight flashed off the shooter's riflescope again. The ray of reflected light this time struck the Talisman. And the Talisman reflected it back directly at the shooter. This was what Richard later told Jack, but that was like saying the Empire State Building is a few stories high.

The Talisman did not just reflect the sunflash; it *boosted* it somehow. It sent back a thick ribbon of light like a deathray in a space movie. It was there only for a second, but it imprinted Richard's retinas for almost an hour afterward, first white, then green, then blue, and finally, as it faded, the lemony yellow of sunshine.

## 11

"He's dead meat," Gardener whispered, and then the scope was full of living fire. Its thick glass lenses shattered. Smoking fused glass was driven backward into Gardener's right eye. The shells in the Weatherbee's magazine exploded, tearing its mid-section apart. One of the whickers of flying metal amputated most of Gardener's right cheek. Other hooks and twists of steel flew around Sloat in a storm, leaving him incredibly untouched. Three Wolfs had remained through everything. Now two of them took to their heels. The third lay dead on his back, glaring into the sky. The Weatherbee's trigger was planted squarely between his eyes.

"What?" Morgan bellowed. His bloody mouth hung open. "What? What?"

Gardener looked weirdly like Wile E. Coyote in the Road-runner cartoons after one of his devices from the Acme Company has misfired.

He cast the gun aside, and Sloat saw that all the fingers had been torn from Gard's left hand.

Gardener's right hand pulled out his shirt with effeminate tweezing delicacy. There was a knife-case clipped to the inner waistband of his pants—a narrow sleeve of fine-grained kid leather. From it Gardener took a piece of chrome-banded ivory. He pushed a button, and a slim blade seven inches long shot out.

"Bad," he whispered. "Bad!" His voice began to rise. "All boys! *Bad! It's axiomatic! IT'S AXIOMATIC!*" He began to run up the beach toward the Agincourt's walk, where Jack and Richard stood. His voice continued to rise until it was a thin febrile shriek.

*"BAD! EVIL! BAD! EEVIL! BAAAD! EEEEEEEEEEEE-EEEEE—"*

Morgan stood a moment longer, then grasped the key around his neck. By grasping it, he seemed also to grasp his own panicked, flying thoughts.

*He'll go to the old nigger. And that's where I'll take him.*

*"EEEEEEEEEEEEEEEE—"* Gardener shrieked, his killer knife held out before him as he ran.

Morgan turned and ran down the beach. He was vaguely aware that the Wolfs, all of them, had fled. That was all right.

He would take care of Jack Sawyer—and the Talisman—all by himself.

# 45

# In Which Many Things are Resolved on the Beach

## 1

Sunlight Gardener ran dementedly toward Jack, blood streaming down his mutilated face. He was the center of a devastated madness. Under bright blistering sunshine for the first time in what must have been decades, Point Venuti was a ruin of collapsed buildings and broken pipes and sidewalks heaved up like books tilting and leaning on a shelf. Actual books lay here and there, their ripped jackets fluttering in raw seams of earth. Behind Jack the Agincourt Hotel uttered a sound uncannily like a groan; then Jack heard the sound of a thousand boards collapsing in on themselves, of walls tipping over in a shower of snapped lath and plaster-dust. The boy was faintly conscious of the beelike figure of Morgan Sloat slipping down the beach and realized with a stab of unease that his adversary was going toward Speedy Parker—or Speedy's corpse.

"He's got a knife, Jack," Richard whispered.

Gardener's ruined hand carelessly smeared blood on his once-spotless white silk shirt. "EEEEEEVIL!" he screeched, his voice still faint over the constant pounding of the water on the beach and the continuing, though intermittent, noises of destruction. "EEEEEEEEEEE . . ."

"What are you going to do?" Richard asked.

"How should I know?" Jack answered—it was the best,

truest answer he could give. He had no idea of how he could defeat this madman. Yet he would defeat him. He was certain of that. "You shoulda killed *both* of the Ellis brothers," Jack said to himself.

Gardener, still shrieking, came racing across the sand. He was even now a good distance away, about halfway between the end of the fence and the front of the hotel. A red mask covered half his face. His useless left hand leaked a steady spattering stream of blood onto the sandy ground. The distance between the madman and the boys seemed to halve in a second. Was Morgan Sloat on the beach by now? Jack felt an urgency like the Talisman's, pushing him forward; pushing him on.

"Evil! Axiomatic! Evil!" Gardener screamed.

"Flip!" Richard loudly said—

and Jack

        sidestepped

as he had inside the black hotel.

And then found himself standing in front of Osmond in blistering Territories sunlight. Most of his certainty abruptly left him. Everything was the same but everything was different. Without looking, he knew that behind him was something much worse than the Agincourt—he had never seen the exterior of the castle the hotel became in the Territories, but he suddenly *knew* that through the great front doors a tongue was coiling out for him . . . and that Osmond was going to drive him and Richard back toward it.

Osmond wore a patch over his right eye and a stained glove on his left hand. The complicated tendrils of his whip came slithering off his shoulder. "Oh, yes," he half-hissed, half-whispered. "*This* boy. Captain Farren's boy." Jack pulled the Talisman protectively into his belly. The intricacies of the whip slid over the ground, as responsive to Osmond's minute movements of hand and wrist as is a racehorse to the hand of the jockey. "What does it profit a boy to gain a glass bauble if he loses the world?" The whip seemed almost to lift itself off the ground. "NOTHING! NAUGHT!" Osmond's true smell, that of rot and filth and hidden corruption, boomed out, and his lean crazy face somehow rippled, as if a lightning-bolt had cracked beneath it. He smiled brightly, emptily, and raised the coiling whip above his shoulder.

"Goat's-penis," Osmond said, almost lovingly. The thongs of the whip came singing down toward Jack, who stepped backward, though not far enough, in a sudden sparkling panic.

Richard's hand gripped his shoulder as he flipped again, and the horrible, somehow laughing noise of the whip instantly erased itself from the air.

*Knife!* he heard Speedy say.

Fighting his instincts, Jack stepped inside the space where the whip had been, not backward as almost all of him wished to do. Richard's hand fell away from the ridge of his shoulder, and Speedy's voice went wailing and lost. Jack clutched the glowing Talisman into his belly with his left hand and reached up with his right. His fingers closed magically around a bony wrist.

Sunlight Gardener giggled.

"JACK!" Richard bellowed behind him.

He was standing in this world again, under streaming cleansing light, and Sunlight Gardener's knife hand was straining down toward him. Gardener's ruined face hung only inches from his own. A smell as of garbage and long-dead animals left on the road blanketed them. "Naught," Gardener said. "Can you give me hallelujah?" He pushed down with the elegant lethal knife, and Jack managed to hold it back.

"JACK!" Richard yelled again.

Sunlight Gardener stared at him with a bright birdlike air. He continued to push down with his knife.

*Don't you know what Sunlight done?* said Speedy's voice. *Don't you yet?*

Jack looked straight into Gardener's crazily dancing eye. Yes.

Richard rushed in and kicked Gardener in the ankle, then clouted a weak fist into his temple.

"You killed my father," Jack said.

Gardener's single eye sparkled back. "You killed my boy, baddest bastard!"

"Morgan Sloat told you to kill my father and you did."

Gardener pushed the knife down a full two inches. A knot of yellow gristly stuff and a bubble of blood squeezed out of the hole that had been his right eye.

Jack screamed—with horror, rage, and all the long-hidden

feelings of abandonment and helplessness which had followed his father's death. He found that he had pushed Gardener's knife hand all the way back up. He screamed again. Gardener's fingerless left hand battered against Jack's own left arm. Jack was just managing to twist Gardener's wrist back when he felt that dripping pad of flesh insinuate itself between his chest and his arm. Richard continued to skirmish about Gardener, but Gardener was managing to get his fingerless hand very near the Talisman.

Gardener tilted his face right up to Jack's.

*"Hallelujah,"* he whispered.

Jack twisted his entire body around, using more strength than he'd known he had. He hauled down on Gardener's knife hand. The other, fingerless hand flew to the side. Jack *squeezed* the wrist of the knife hand. Corded tendons wriggled in his grasp. Then the knife dropped, as harmless now as the fingerless cushion of skin which struck repeatedly at Jack's ribs. Jack rolled his whole body into the off-center Gardener and sent him lurching away.

He shoved the Talisman toward Gardener. Richard squawked, *What are you doing?* This was right, right, right. Jack moved in toward Gardener, who was still gleaming at him, though with less assurance, and thrust the Talisman out toward him. Gardener grinned, another bubble of blood bulging fatly in the empty eye-socket, and swung wildly at the Talisman. Then he ducked for the knife. Jack rushed in and touched the Talisman's grooved warm skin against Gardener's own skin. Like Reuel, like Sunlight. He jumped back.

Gardener howled like a lost, wounded animal. Where the Talisman had brushed against him, the skin had blackened, then turned to a slowly sliding fluid, skimming away from the skull. Jack retreated another step. Gardener fell to his knees. All the skin on his head turned waxy. Within half a second, only a gleaming skull protruded through the collar of the ruined shirt.

*That's you taken care of,* Jack thought, *and good riddance!*

## 2

"All right," Jack said. He felt full of crazy confidence. "Let's go get him, Richie. Let's—"

He looked at Richard and saw that his friend was on the verge of collapsing again. He stood swaying on the sand, his eyes half-lidded and dopey.

"Maybe you better just sit this one out, on second thought," Jack said.

Richard shook his head. "Coming, Jack. Seabrook Island. All the way . . . to the end of the line."

"I'm going to have to kill him," Jack said. "That is, if I can."

Richard shook his head with dogged, stubborn persistence. "Not my father. Told you. Father's dead. If you leave me I'll crawl. Crawl right through the muck *that* guy left behind, if I have to."

Jack looked toward the rocks. He couldn't see Morgan, but he didn't think there was much question that Morgan was there. And if Speedy was still alive, Morgan might at this moment be taking steps to remedy that situation.

Jack tried to smile but couldn't make it. "Think of the germs you might pick up." He hesitated a moment longer, then held the Talisman reluctantly out to Richard. "I'll carry you, but you'll have to carry this. Don't drop the ball, Richard. If you drop it—"

What was it Speedy had said?

"If you drop it, all be lost."

"I won't drop it."

Jack put the Talisman into Richard's hands, and again Richard seemed to improve at its touch . . . but not so much. His face was terribly wan. Washed in the Talisman's bright glow, it looked like the face of a dead child caught in the glare of a police photographer's flash.

*It's the hotel. It's poisoning him.*

But it wasn't the hotel; not entirely. It was Morgan. *Morgan* was poisoning him.

Jack turned around, discovering he was loath to look away from the Talisman even for a moment. He bent his back and curved his hands into stirrups.

Richard climbed on. He held to the Talisman with one hand and curled the other around Jack's neck. Jack grabbed Richard's thighs.

*He is as light as a thistle. He has his own cancer. He's had*

*it all his life. Morgan Sloat is radioactive with evil and
Richard is dying of the fallout.*

He started to jog down toward the rocks behind which
Speedy lay, conscious of the light and heat of the Talisman
just above him.

### 3

He ran around the left side of the clump of rocks with Richard
on his back, still full of that crazy assurance . . . and that it
*was* crazy was brought home to him with rude suddenness. A
plumpish leg clad in light brown wool (and just below the
pulled-back cuff Jack caught a blurred glimpse of a perfectly
proper brown nylon sock) suddenly stuck straight out from
behind the last rock like a toll-gate.

*Shit!* Jack's mind screamed. *He was waiting for you! You
total nerd!*

Richard cried out. Jack tried to pull up and couldn't.

Morgan tripped him up as easily as a schoolyard bully trips
up a younger boy in the play-yard. After Smokey Updike, and
Osmond, and Gardener, and Elroy, and something that looked
like a cross between an alligator and a Sherman tank, all it
really took to bring him down was overweight, hypertensive
Morgan Sloat crouched behind a rock, watching and waiting
for an overconfident boy named Jack Sawyer to come boogying right down on top of him.

*"Yiyyy!"* Richard cried as Jack stumbled forward. He was
dimly aware of their combined shadow tracking out to his
left—it seemed to have as many arms as a Hindu idol. He felt
the psychic weight of the Talisman shift . . . and then over-
shift.

*"WATCH OUT FOR IT, RICHARD!"* Jack screamed.

Richard fell over the top of Jack's head, his eyes huge and
dismayed. The cords on his neck stood out like piano wire. He
held the Talisman up as he went down. His mouth was pulled
down at the corners in a desperate snarl. He hit the ground
face-first like the nosecone of a defective rocket. The sand
here around the place where Speedy had gone to earth was
not precisely sand at all but a rough-textured scree stubbly
with smaller rocks and shells. Richard came down on a rock

that had been burped up by the earthquake. There was a compact thudding sound. For a moment Richard looked like an ostrich with its head buried in the sand. His butt, clad in dirty polished-cotton slacks, wagged drunkenly back and forth in the air. In other circumstances—circumstances unattended by that dreadful compact thudding sound, for instance—it would have been a comic pose, worthy of a Kodachrome: "Rational Richard Acts Wild and Crazy at the Beach." But it wasn't funny at all. Richard's hands opened slowly . . . and the Talisman rolled three feet down the gentle slope of the beach and stopped there, reflecting sky and clouds, not on its surface but in its gently lighted interior.

*"Richard!"* Jack bellowed again.

Morgan was somewhere behind him, but Jack had momentarily forgotten him. All his reassurance was gone; it had left him at the moment when that leg, clad in light brown wool, had stuck out in front of him like a toll-gate. Fooled like a kid in a nursery-school play-yard, and Richard . . . Richard was . . .

*"Rich—"*

Richard rolled over and Jack saw that Richard's poor, tired face was covered with running blood. A flap of his scalp hung down almost to one eye in a triangular shape like a ragged sail. Jack could see hair sticking out of the underside and brushing Richard's cheek like sand-colored grass . . . and where that hair-covered skin had come from he could see the naked gleam of Richard Sloat's skull.

"Did it break?" Richard asked. His voice cracked toward a scream. *"Jack, did it break when I fell?"*

"It's okay, Richie—it's—"

Richard's blood-rimmed eyes bulged widely at something behind him. *"Jack! Jack, look o—!"*

Something that felt like a leather brick—one of Morgan Sloat's Gucci loafers—crashed up between Jack's legs and into his testicles. It was a dead-center hit, and Jack crumpled forward, suddenly living with the greatest pain of his life—a physical agony greater than any he had ever imagined. He couldn't even scream.

*"It's* okay," Morgan Sloat said, "but *you* don't look so good. Jacky-boy. Not

at

all."

And now the man slowly advancing on Jack—advancing slowly because he was savoring this—was a man to whom Jack had never been properly introduced. He had been a white face in the window of a great black coach for a space of moments, a face with dark eyes that somehow sensed his presence; he had been a rippling, changing shape bludgeoning itself into the reality of the field where he and Wolf had been talking of such wonders as litter-brothers and the big rut-moon; he had been a shadow in Anders's eyes.

*But I've never really seen Morgan of Orris until now,* Jack thought. And he still *was* Jack—Jack in a pair of faded, dirty cotton pants of a sort you might expect to see an Asian coolie wearing, and sandals with rawhide thongs, but not Jason—Jack. His crotch was a great frozen scream of pain.

Ten yards away was the Talisman, throwing its effulgent glow along a beach of black sand. Richard was not there, but this fact did not impress itself on Jack's conscious mind until a bit later.

Morgan was wearing a dark blue cape held at the neck with a catch of beaten silver. His pants were the same light wool as Sloat's pants, only here they were bloused into black boots.

This Morgan walked with a slight limp, his deformed left foot leaving a line of short hyphens in the sand. The silver catch on his cloak swung loose and low as he moved, and Jack saw that the silver thing had nothing at all to do with the cape, which was held by a simple unadorned dark cord. This was some sort of pendant. He thought for a moment that it was a tiny golf-club, the sort of thing a woman might take off her charm-bracelet and wear around her neck, just for the fun of it. But as Sloat got closer, he saw it was too slim—it did not end in a club-head but came to a point.

It looked like a lightning-rod.

"No, you don't look well at all, boy," Morgan of Orris said. He stepped over to where Jack lay, moaning, holding his crotch, legs drawn up. He bent forward, hands planted just above his knees, and studied Jack as a man might study an animal his car has run over. A rather uninteresting animal like a woodchuck or a squirrel. "Not a *bit* well."

Morgan leaned even closer.

"You've been quite a problem for me," Morgan of Orris said, bending lower. "You've caused a great deal of damage. But in the end—"

"I think I'm dying," Jack whispered.

"Not yet. Oh, I know it feels like that, but believe me, you're not dying yet. In five minutes, or so, you'll know what dying *really* feels like."

"No . . . really . . . I'm broken . . . inside," Jack moaned. "Lean down . . . I want to tell . . . to ask . . . beg . . ."

Morgan's dark eyes gleamed in his pallid face. It was the thought of Jack begging, perhaps. He leaned down until his face was almost touching Jack's. Jack's legs had drawn up in response to the pain. Now he pistoned them out and up. For a moment it felt as if a rusty blade were ripping up from his genitals and into his stomach, but the sound of his sandals striking Morgan's face, splitting his lips and crunching his nose to one side, more than made up for the pain.

Morgan of Orris flailed backward, roaring in pain and surprise, his cape flapping like the wings of a great bat.

Jack got to his feet. For a moment he saw the black castle—it was much larger than the Agincourt had been; seemed, in fact, to cover acres—and then he was lunging spastically past the unconscious *(or dead!)* Parkus. He lunged for the Talisman, which lay peacefully glowing on the sand, and as he ran he

flipped back

to the American Territories.

*"Oh you bastard!"* Morgan Sloat bellowed. *"You rotten little bastard, my face, my face, you hurt my face!"*

There was a crackling sizzle and a smell like ozone. A brilliant blue-white branch of lightning passed just to Jack's right, fusing sand like glass.

Then he had the Talisman—*had it again!* The torn, throbbing ache in his crotch began to diminish at once. He turned to Morgan with the glass ball raised in his hands.

Morgan Sloat was bleeding from the lip and holding one hand up to his cheek—Jack hoped that he had cracked a few of Sloat's teeth while he was at it. In Sloat's other hand, outstretched in a curious echo of Jack's own posture, was the keylike thing which had just sent a lightning-bolt snapping into the sand beside Jack.

Jack moved sideways, his arms straight out before him and the Talisman shifting internal colors like a rainbow machine. It seemed to understand that Sloat was near, for the great grooved glass ball had begun a kind of subtonal *humming* that Jack felt—more than heard—as a tingle in his hands. A band of clear bright white opened in the Talisman, like a shaft of light right through its center, and Sloat jerked himself sideways and pointed the key at Jack's head.

He wiped a smear of blood away from his lower lip. "You hurt me, you stinking little bastard," he said. "Don't think that glass ball can help you now. Its future is a little shorter than your own."

"Then why are you afraid of it?" the boy asked, thrusting it forward again.

Sloat dodged sideways, as if the Talisman, too, could shoot out bolts of lightning. *He doesn't know* what *it can do,* Jack realized: *he doesn't really know anything about it, he just knows he wants it.*

"Drop it right now," Sloat said. "Let go of it, you little fraud. Or I'll take the top of your head off right now. Drop it."

"You're afraid," Jack said. "Now that the Talisman is right in front of you, you're afraid to come and get it."

"I don't have to come and get it," Sloat said. "You goddam Pretender. Drop it. Let's see you break it by yourself, Jacky."

"Come for it, Bloat," Jack said, feeling a blast of wholly bracing anger shoot through him. *Jacky.* He *hated* hearing his mother's nickname for him in Sloat's wet mouth. "I'm not the black hotel, Bloat. I'm just a kid. Can't you take a glass ball away from a kid?" Because it was clear to him that they were in stalemate as long as Jack held the Talisman in his hands. A deep blue spark, as vibrant as one of the sparks from Anders's "demons," flared up and died in the Talisman's center. Another immediately followed. Jack could still feel that powerful *humming* emanating from the heart of the grooved glass ball. He had been destined to get the Talisman—he was *supposed to get it.* The Talisman had known of his existence since his birth, Jack now thought, and ever since had awaited him to set it free. It needed Jack Sawyer and no one else. "Come on and try for it," Jack taunted.

Sloat pushed the key toward him, snarling. Blood drooled down his chin. For a moment Sloat appeared baffled, as frustrated and enraged as a bull in a pen, and Jack actually smiled at him. Then Jack glanced sideways to where Richard lay on the sand, and the smile disappeared from his face. Richard's face was literally covered with blood, his dark hair was matted with it.

"You bast—" he began, but it had been a mistake to look away. A searing blast of blue and yellow light smacked into the beach directly beside him.

He turned to Sloat, who was just firing off another lightning-bolt at his feet. Jack danced back, and the shaft of destructive light melted the sand at his feet into molten yellow liquid, which almost instantly cooled into a long straight slick of glass.

"Your son is going to die," Jack said.

"Your mother is going to die," Sloat snarled back at him. "Drop that damned thing before I cut your head off. Now. Let go of it."

Jack said, "Why don't you go hump a weasel?"

Morgan Sloat opened his mouth and screeched, revealing a row of square bloodstained teeth. "I'll hump your *corpse!*" The pointing key wavered toward Jack's head, wavered away. Sloat's eyes glittered, and he jerked his hand up so that the key pointed at the sky. A long skein of lightning seemed to erupt upward from Sloat's fist, widening out as it ascended. The sky blackened. Both the Talisman and Morgan Sloat's face shone in the sudden dark, Sloat's face because the Talisman shed its light upon it. Jack realized that his face, too, must be picked out by the Talisman's fierce illumination. And as soon as he brandished the glowing Talisman toward Sloat, trying God knew what—to get him to drop the key, to anger him, to rub his nose in the fact that he was powerless—Jack was made to understand that he had not yet reached the end of Morgan Sloat's capabilities. Fat snowflakes spun down out of the dark sky. Sloat disappeared behind the thickening curtain of snow; Jack heard his wet laughter.

## 4

She struggled out of her invalid's bed and crossed to the window. She looked out at the dead December beach, which was lit by a single streetlight on the boardwalk. Suddenly a gull alighted on the sill outside the window. A string of gristle hung from one side of its beak, and in that moment she thought of Sloat. The gull looked like Sloat.

Lily first recoiled, and then came back. She felt a wholly ridiculous anger. A gull couldn't look like Sloat, and a gull couldn't invade her territory . . . it wasn't *right*. She tapped the cold glass. The bird fluffed its wings briefly but did not fly. And she heard a thought come from its cold mind, heard it as clearly as a radio wave:

*Jack's dying, Lily . . . Jack's dyyyyyinn . . .*

It bent its head forward. Tapped on the glass as deliberately as Poe's raven.

*Dyyyyyyinnnn . . .*

"*NO!*" she shrieked at it. "*FUCK OFF, SLOAT!*" She did not simply tap this time but slammed her fist forward, driving it through the glass. The gull fluttered backward, squawking, almost falling. Frigid air funnelled in through the hole in the window.

Blood was dripping from Lily's hand—no; no, not just dripping. It was *running*. She had cut herself quite badly in two places. She picked shards of glass out of the pad on the side of her palm and then wiped her hand against the bodice of her nightdress.

"*DIDN'T EXPECT THAT, DID YOU, FUCKHEAD?*" she screamed at the bird, which was circling restlessly over the gardens. She burst into tears. "*Now leave him alone! Leave him alone! LEAVE MY SON ALONE!*"

She was covered all over in blood. Cold air blew in the pane she had shattered. And outside she saw the first flakes of snow come swirling down from the sky and into the white glow of that streetlight.

### 5

"Look out, Jacky."

Soft. On the left.

Jack pivoted that way, holding the Talisman up like a searchlight. It sent out a beam of light filled with falling snow.

Nothing else. Darkness . . . snow . . . the sound of the ocean.

"Wrong side, Jacky."

He spun to the right, feet slipping in the icing of snow. Closer. He had been closer.

Jack held up the Talisman. "Come and get it, Bloat!"

"You haven't got a chance, Jack. I can take you anytime I want to."

Behind him . . . and closer still. But when he raised the blazing Talisman, there was no Sloat to be seen. Snow roared into his face. He inhaled it and began to cough on the cold.

Sloat tittered from directly in front of him.

Jack recoiled and almost tripped over Speedy.

"Hoo-hoo, Jacky!"

A hand came out of the darkness on his left and tore at Jack's ear. He turned in that direction, heart pumping wildly, eyes bulging. He slipped and went to one knee.

Richard uttered a thick, snoring moan somewhere close by.

Overhead, a cannonade of thunder went off in the darkness Sloat had somehow brought down.

"Throw it at me!" Sloat taunted. He danced forward out of that stormy, exposures-all-jammed-up-together dark. He was snapping the fingers of his right hand and wagging the tin key at Jack with the left. The gestures had a jerky, eccentric syncopation. To Jack, Sloat looked crazily like some old-time Latin bandleader—Xavier Cugat, perhaps. "Throw it at me, why don't you? Shooting gallery, Jack! Clay pigeon! Big old Uncle Morgan! What do you say, Jack? Have a go? Throw the ball and win a Kewpie doll!"

And Jack discovered he had pulled the Talisman back to his right shoulder, apparently intending to do just that. *He's spooking you, trying to panic you, trying to get you to cough it up, to—*

Sloat faded back into the murk. Snow flew in dust-devils.

Jack wheeled nervously around but could see Sloat nowhere. *Maybe he's taken off. Maybe—*

"Wassa matta, Jacky?"

No, he was still here. Somewhere. On the left.

"I laughed when your dear old daddy died, Jacky. I laughed in his face. When his motor finally quit I felt—"

The voice warbled. Faded for a moment. Came back. On the right. Jack whirled that way, not understanding what was going on, his nerves increasingly frayed.

"—my heart flew like a bird on the wing. It flew like *this*, Jacky-boy."

A rock came out of the dark—aimed not at Jack but at the glass ball. He dodged. Got a murky glimpse of Sloat. Gone again.

A pause . . . then Sloat was back, and playing a new record.

"Fucked your mother, Jacky," the voice teased from behind him. A fat hot hand snatched at the seat of his pants.

Jack whirled around, this time almost stumbling over Richard. Tears—hot, painful, outraged—began to squeeze out of his eyes. He hated them, but here they were, and nothing in the world would deny them. The wind screamed like a dragon in a wind-tunnel. *The magic's in you,* Speedy had said, but where was the magic now? Where oh where oh where?

*"You shut up about my mom!"*

"Fucked her a lot," Sloat added with smug cheeriness.

On the right again. A fat, dancing shape in the dark.

"Fucked her by *invitation*, Jacky!"

Behind him! *Close!*

Jack spun. Held up the Talisman. It flashed a white slice of light. Sloat danced back out of it, but not before Jack had seen a grimace of pain and anger. That light had touched Sloat, had hurt him.

*Never mind what he's saying—it's all lies and you know it is. But how can he do that? He's like Edgar Bergen. No . . . he's like Indians in the dark, closing in on the wagon train. How can he do it?*

"Singed my whiskers a little that time, Jacky," Sloat said, and chuckled fruitily. He sounded a bit out of breath, but not enough. Not nearly enough. Jack was panting like a dog on a hot summer day, his eyes frantic as he searched the stormy blackness for Sloat. "But I'll not hold it against you, Jacky Now, let's see. What were we talking about? Oh yes. Your mother . . ."

A little warble . . . a little fade . . . and then a stone came whistling out of the darkness on the right and struck Jack's temple. He whirled, but Sloat was gone again, skipping nimbly back into the snow.

"She'd wrap those long legs around me until I *howled* for

mercy!" Sloat declared from behind Jack and to the right
*"OWWWWWOOOOOO!"*

*Don't let him get you don't let him psych you out don't—*

But he couldn't help it. It was his *mother* this dirty man
was talking about; his *mother.*

*"You stop it! You shut up!"*

Sloat was in front of him now—so close Jack should have
been able to see him clearly in spite of the swirling snow, but
there was only a glimmer, like a face seen underwater at night.
Another stone zoomed out of the dark and struck Jack in the
back of the head. He staggered forward and nearly tripped
over Richard again—a Richard who was rapidly disappearing
under a mantle of snow.

He saw stars . . . and understood what was happening.

*Sloat's flipping! Flipping . . . moving . . . flipping back!*

Jack turned in an unsteady circle, like a man beset with a
hundred enemies instead of just one. Lightning-fire licked out
of the dark in a narrow greenish-blue ray. He reached toward
it with the Talisman, hoping to deflect it back at Sloat. Too
late. It winked out.

*Then how come I don't see him over there? Over there in
the Territories?*

The answer came to him in a dazzling flash . . . and as if in
response, the Talisman flashed a gorgeous fan of white
light—it cut the snowy light like the headlamp of a locomo-
tive.

*I don't see him over there, don't respond to him over there,
because I'm NOT over there! Jason's gone . . . and I'm single-
natured! Sloat's flipping onto a beach where there's no one
but Morgan of Orris and a dead or dying man named
Parkus—Richard isn't there either, because Morgan of Orris's
son, Rushton, died a long time ago and Richard's single-
natured, too! When I flipped before, the Talisman was
there . . . but Richard wasn't! Morgan's flipping . . . moving . . . flipping back . . . trying to freak me out. . . .*

*"Hoo-hoo! Jacky-boy!"*

The left.

*"Over here!"*

The right.

But Jack wasn't listening for the place anymore. He was

looking into the Talisman, waiting for the downbeat. The most important downbeat of his life.

From behind. This time he would come from behind.

The Talisman flashed out, a strong lamp in the snow.

Jack pivoted . . . and as he pivoted he flipped into the Territories, into bright sunlight. And there was Morgan of Orris, big as life and twice as ugly. For a moment he didn't realize Jack had tumbled to the trick; he was limping rapidly around to a place which would be behind Jack when he flipped back into the American Territories. There was a nasty little-boy grin on his face. His cloak popped and billowed behind him. His left boot dragged, and Jack saw the sand was covered with those dragging hashmarks all around him. Morgan had been running around him in a harrying circle, all the while goading Jack with obscene lies about his mother, throwing stones, and flipping back and forth.

Jack shouted:

*"I SEE YOU!"* at the top of his lungs.

Morgan stared around at him in utter stunned shock, one hand curled around that silver rod.

"SEE YOU!" Jack shouted again. "Should we go around one more time, Bloat?"

Morgan of Orris flicked the end of the rod at him, his face altering in a second from that rubbery simple-minded expression of shock to a much more characteristic look of craft—of a clever man quickly seeing all the possibilities in a situation. His eyes narrowed. Jack almost, in that second when Morgan of Orris looked down his lethal silver rod at him and narrowed his eyes into gunsights, flipped back into the American Territories, and that would have killed him. But an instant before prudence or panic caused him in effect to jump in front of a moving truck, the same insight that had told him that Morgan was flipping between worlds saved him again—Jack had learned the ways of his adversary. He held his ground, again waiting for that almost mystical downbeat. For a fraction of a second Jack Sawyer held his breath. If Morgan had been a shade less proud of his deviousness, he might well have murdered Jack Sawyer, which he so dearly wished to do, at that moment.

But instead, just as Jack had thought it would, Morgan's

image abruptly departed the Territories. Jack inhaled.
Speedy's body *(Parkus's* body, Jack realized) lay motionless a
short distance away. The downbeat came. Jack exhaled and
*flipped* back.

A new streak of glass divided the sand on the Point Venuti
beach, glimmeringly reflecting the sudden beam of white
light which emanated from the Talisman.

"Missed one, did you?" Morgan Sloat whispered out of the
darkness. Snow pelted Jack, cold wind froze his limbs, his
throat, his forehead. A car's length away, Sloat's face hung before him, the forehead drawn up into its familiar corrugations,
the bloody mouth open. He was extending the key toward
Jack in the storm, and a ridge of powdery snow adhered to the
brown sleeve of his suit. Jack saw a black trail of blood oozing from the left nostril of the incongruously small nose.
Sloat's eyes, bloodshot with pain, shone through the dark air.

## 6

Richard Sloat confusedly opened his eyes. Every part of him
was cold. At first he thought, quite without emotion of any
kind, that he was dead. He had fallen down somewhere, probably down those steep, tricky steps at the back of the Thayer
School grandstand. Now he was cold and dead and nothing
more could happen to him. He experienced a second of dizzying relief.

His head offered him a fresh surge of pain, and he felt
warm blood ooze out over his cold hand—both of these sensations evidence that, whatever he might welcome at the moment, Richard Llewellyn Sloat was not yet dead. He was only
a wounded suffering creature. The whole top of his head
seemed to have been sliced off. He had no proper idea of
where he was. It was cold. His eyes focused long enough to
report to him that he was lying down in the snow. Winter had
happened. More snow dumped on him from out of the sky.
Then he heard his father's voice, and everything returned
to him.

Richard kept his hand on top of his head, but very slowly
tilted his chin so that he could look in the direction of his father's voice.

Jack Sawyer was holding the Talisman—that was the next

thing Richard took in. The Talisman was unbroken. He felt
the return of a portion of that relief he had experienced when
he'd thought he was dead. Even without his glasses, Richard
could see that Jack had an undefeated, *unbowed* look that
moved him very deeply. Jack looked like . . . like a hero. That
was all. He looked like a dirty, dishevelled, outrageously
youthful hero, wrong for the role on almost every count, but
undeniably still a hero.

Jack was just Jack now, Richard now saw. That extraordinary *extra* quality, as of a movie star deigning to walk around
as a shabbily dressed twelve-year-old, had gone. This made
his heroism all the more impressive to Richard.

His father smiled rapaciously. But that was not his father.
His father had been hollowed out a long time ago—hollowed
out by his envy of Phil Sawyer, by the greed of his ambitions.

"We can keep on going around like this forever," Jack said.
"I'm never going to give you the Talisman, and you're never
going to be able to destroy it with that gadget of yours.
Give up."

The point of the key in his father's hand slowly moved
across and down, and it, like his father's greedy needful face,
pointed straight at him.

"First I'll blow Richard apart," his father said. "Do you
really want to see your pal Richard turned into bacon? Hmmmm? Do you? And of course I won't hesitate to do the same
favor for that pest beside him."

Jack and Sloat exchanged short glances. His father was not
kidding, Richard knew. He would kill him if Jack did not surrender the Talisman. And then he would kill the old black
man, Speedy.

"Don't do it," he managed to whisper. "Stuff him, Jack.
Tell him to screw himself."

Jack almost deranged Richard by winking at him.

"Just drop the Talisman," he heard his father say.

Richard watched in horror as Jack tilted the palms of his
hands and let the Talisman tumble out.

7

*"Jack, no!"*

Jack didn't look around at Richard. *You don't own a thing*

*unless you can give it up,* his mind hammered at him. *You don't own a thing unless you can give it up, what does it profit a man, it profits him nothing, it profits him zilch, and you don't learn that in school, you learn it on the road, you learn it from Ferd Janklow, and Wolf, and Richard going head-first into the rocks like a Titan II that didn't fire off right.*

You learned these things, or you died somewhere out in the world where there was no clear light.

"No more killing," he said in the snow-filled darkness of this California beach afternoon. He should have felt utterly exhausted—it had been, all told, a four-day run of horrors, and now, at the end, he had coughed up the ball like a freshman quarterback with a lot to learn. Had thrown it all away. Yet it was the sure voice of Anders he heard, Anders who had knelt before Jack/Jason with his kilt spread out around him and his head bowed: Anders saying *A' wi' be well, a' wi' be well, and a' manner a' things wi' be well.*

The Talisman glowed on the beach, snow melting down one sweetly gravid side in droplets, and in each droplet was a rainbow, and in that moment Jack knew the staggering cleanliness of *giving up the thing which was required.*

"No more *slaughter.* Go on and break it if you can," he said. "I'm sorry for you."

It was that last which surely destroyed Morgan Sloat. If he had retained a shred of rational thought, he would have unearthed a stone from the unearthly snow and smashed the Talisman . . . as it *could* have been smashed, in its simple unjacketed vulnerability.

Instead, he turned the key on it.

As he did so, his mind was filled with loving, hateful memories of Jerry Bledsoe, and Jerry Bledsoe's wife. Jerry Bledsoe, whom he had killed, and Nita Bledsoe, who should have been Lily Cavanaugh . . . Lily, who had slapped him so hard his nose bled the one time when, drunk, he had tried to touch her.

Fire sang out—green-blue fire spanning out from the cheapjack barrel of the tin key. It arrowed out at the Talisman, struck it, spread over it, turning it into a burning sun. Every color was there for a moment . . . for a moment every *world* was there. Then it was gone.

The Talisman swallowed the fire from Morgan's key.

Ate it whole.

Darkness came back. Jack's feet slid out from under him and he sat down with a thud on Speedy Parker's limply splayed calves. Speedy made a grunting noise and twitched.

There was a two-second lag when everything held static . . . and then fire suddenly blew back out of the Talisman in a flood. Jack's eyes opened wide in spite of his frantic, tortured thought

*(it'll blind you! Jack! it'll)*

and the altered geography of Point Venuti was lit up as if the God of All Universes had bent forward to snap a picture. Jack saw the Agincourt, slumped and half-destroyed; he saw the collapsed Highlands that were now the Lowlands; he saw Richard on his back; he saw Speedy lying on his belly with his face turned to one side. Speedy was smiling.

Then Morgan Sloat was driven backward and enveloped in a field of fire from his own key—fire that had been absorbed inside the Talisman as the flashes of light from Sunlight Gardener's telescopic sight had been absorbed—and which was returned to him a thousandfold.

A hole opened between the worlds—a hole the size of the tunnel leading into Oatley—and Jack saw Sloat, his handsome brown suit burning, one skeletal, tallowy hand still clutching the key, driven through that hole. Sloat's eyes were boiling in their sockets, but they were wide . . . they were *aware*.

And as he passed, Jack saw him change—saw the cloak appear like the wings of a bat that has swooped through the flame of a torch, saw his burning boots, his burning hair. Saw the key become a thing like a miniature lightning-rod.

Saw . . . *daylight!*

8

It came back in a flood. Jack rolled away from it on the snowy beach, dazzled. In his ears—ears deep inside his head—he heard Morgan Sloat's dying scream as he was driven back through all the worlds that were, into oblivion.

"Jack?" Richard was sitting up woozily, holding his head. "Jack, what happened? I think I fell down the stadium steps."

Speedy was twitching in the snow, and now he did a sort of

girl's pushup and looked toward Jack. His eyes were exhausted . . . but his face was clear of blemishes.

"Good job, Jack," he said, and grinned. "Good—" He fell partway forward again, panting.

*Rainbow,* Jack thought woozily. He stood up and then fell down again. Freezing snow coated his face and then began to melt like tears. He pushed himself to his knees, then stood up again. The field of his vision was filled with spots . . . but he saw the enormous burned swatch in the snow where Morgan had stood. It tailed away like a teardrop.

*"Rainbow!"* Jack Sawyer shouted, and raised his hands to the sky, weeping and laughing. *"Rainbow! Rainbow!"*

He went to the Talisman, and picked it up, still weeping.

He took it to Richard Sloat, who had been Rushton; to Speedy Parker, who was what he was.

He healed them.

*Rainbow, rainbow, rainbow!*

# 46

# Another Journey

## 1

He healed them, but he was never able to recall exactly how that had gone, or any of the specific details—for a while the Talisman had blazed and sung in his hands, and he had the vaguest possible memory of its fire's actually seeming to *flow out over them* until they glowed in a bath of light. That was all he could bring back.

At the end of it, the glorious light in the Talisman faded . . . faded . . . went out.

Jack, thinking of his mother, uttered a hoarse, wailing cry.

Speedy staggered over to him through the melting snow and put an arm around Jack's shoulders.

"It be back, Travellin Jack," Speedy said. He smiled, but he looked twice as tired as Jack. Speedy had been healed . . . but he was still not well. *This world is killing him,* Jack thought dimly. *At least, it's killing the part of him that's Speedy Parker. The Talisman healed him . . . but he is still dying.*

"You did for *it,*" Speedy said, "and you wanna believe that *it's* gonna do for *you.* Don't worry. Come on over here, Jack. Come on over to where your frien' be layin'."

Jack did. Richard was sleeping in the melting snow. That horrid loose flap of skin was gone, but there was a long white streak of scalp showing in his hair now—a streak of scalp from which no hair would ever grow.

"Take his han'."

"Why? What for?"

"We're gonna flip."

Jack looked at Speedy questioningly, but Speedy offered no explanation. He only nodded, as if to say *Yes; you heard me right.*

*Well,* Jack thought, *I trusted him this far—*

He reached down and took Richard's hand. Speedy held Jack's other hand.

With hardly a tug at all, the three of them went over.

## 2

It was as Jack had intuited—the figure standing beside him over here, on this black sand that was stitched everywhere by Morgan of Orris's dragging foot, looked hale and hearty and healthy.

Jack stared with awe—and some unease—at this stranger who looked a bit like Speedy Parker's younger brother.

"Speedy—Mr. Parkus, I mean—what are you—"

"You boys need rest," Parkus said. "You for sure, this other young squire even more. He came closer to dying than anyone will ever know but himself . . . and I don't think he's the type to do much admitting, even *to* himself."

"Yeah," Jack said. "You got *that* right."

"He'll rest better over here," Parkus told Jack, and struck off up the beach, away from the castle, carrying Richard. Jack stumbled along as best he could, but gradually found himself falling behind. He was quickly out of breath, his legs rubbery. His head ached with reaction from the final battle—shock hangover, he supposed.

"Why . . . where . . ." That was all he could pant. He held

the Talisman against his chest. It was dull now, its exterior sooty and opaque and uninteresting.

"Just up a little way," Parkus said. "You and your friend don't want to rest where *he* was, do you?"

And, exhausted as he was, Jack shook his head.

Parkus glanced back over his shoulder, then looked sadly at Jack.

"It stinks of his evil back there," he said, "and it stinks of your world, Jack.

"To me, they smell too much alike for comfort."

He set off again, Richard in his arms.

### 3

Forty yards up the beach he stopped. Here the black sand had moderated to a lighter color—not white, but a medium gray. Parkus set Richard down gently. Jack sprawled beside him. The sand was warm—blessedly warm. No snow here.

Parkus sat beside him, cross-legged.

"You're going to have a sleep now," he said. "Might be to-morrow before you wake up. Won't anybody bother you, if so. Take a look."

Parkus waved his arm toward the place where Point Venuti had been in the American Territories. Jack first saw the black castle, one entire side of it crumbled and burst, as if there had been a tremendous explosion inside. Now the castle looked almost pedestrian. Its menace was burnt out, its illicit treasure borne away. It was only stones piled up in patterns.

Looking farther, Jack saw that the earthquake had not been so violent over here—and there had been less to destroy. He saw a few overturned huts that looked as if they had been built mostly of driftwood; he saw a number of burst coaches that might or might not have been Cadillacs back in the American Territories; here and there he could see a fallen, shaggy body.

"Those who were here and survived have now gone," Parkus said. "They know what has happened, they know Orris is dead, and they'll not trouble you more. The evil that was here has gone. Do you know that? Can you *feel* it?"

"Yes," Jack whispered. "But . . . Mr. Parkus . . . you're not . . . not . . ."

"Going? Yes. Very soon. You and your friend are going to have a good sleep, but you and I must have a bit of a talk first. It won't take long, so I want you to try and get your head up off your chest, at least for the moment."

With some effort, Jack got his head up and his eyes all—well, *most*—of the way open again. Parkus nodded.

"When you wake up, strike east . . . but don't flip! You stay right here for a while. Stay in the Territories. There's going to be too much going on over there on your side—rescue units, news crews, Jason knows what else. At least the snow will melt before anybody knows it's there, except for a few people who'll be dismissed as crackpots—"

"Why do you have to go?"

"I just got to ramble some now, Jack. There's a lot of work to be done over here. News of Morgan's death will already be travelling east. Travelling fast. I'm behind that news right now, and I've got to get ahead of it if I can. I want to get back to the Outposts . . . and the east . . . before a lot of pretty bad folks start to head out for other places." He looked out at the ocean, his eyes as cold and gray as flint. "When the bill comes due, people have to pay. Morgan's gone, but there's still a debt owing."

"You're something like a policeman over here, aren't you?"

Parkus nodded. "I am what you'd call the Judge General and Lord High Executioner all rolled into one. Over here, that is." He put a strong, warm hand on Jack's head. "Over there, I'm just this fella who goes around from place to place, does a few odd jobs, strums a few tunes. And sometimes, believe me, I like that a lot better."

He smiled again, and this time he *was* Speedy.

"And you be seein that guy from time to time, Jacky. Yeah, from time to time and place to place. In a shoppin center, maybe, or a park."

He winked at Jack.

"But Speedy's . . . not well," Jack said. "Whatever was wrong with him, it was something the Talisman couldn't touch."

"Speedy's *old*," Parkus said. "He's my age, but your world made him older than me. Just the same, he's still got a few years left in him. Maybe quite a few. Feel no fret, Jack."

"You promise?" Jack asked.

Parkus grinned. "Yeah-bob."

Jack grinned tiredly back.

"You and your friend head out to the east. Go until you reckon you've done five miles. You get over those low hills and then you'll be fine—easy walking. Look for a big tree— biggest damn tree you've ever seen. You get to that big old tree, Jack, and you take Richard's hand, and you flip back. You'll come out next to a giant redwood with a tunnel cut through the bottom of it to let the road through. The road's Route Seventeen, and you'll be on the outskirts of a little town in northern California called Storyville. Walk into town. There's a Mobil station at the blinker-light."

"And then?"

Parkus shrugged. "Don't know, not for sure. Could be, Jack, you'll meet someone you'll recognize."

"But how will we get h—"

"Shhh," Parkus said, and put a hand on Jack's forehead exactly as his mother had done when he was

*(baby-bunting, daddy's gone a-hunting, and all that good shit, la-la, go to sleep, Jacky, all's well and all's well and)*

very small. "Enough questions. All will be well with you and Richard now, I think."

Jack lay down. He cradled the dark ball in the crook of one arm. Each of his eyelids now seemed to have a cinderblock attached to it.

"You have been brave and true, Jack," Parkus said with calm gravity. "I wish you were my own son . . . and I salute you for your courage. And your faith. There are people in many worlds who owe you a great debt of gratitude. And in some way or other, I think most of them sense that."

Jack managed a smile.

"Stay a little while," he managed to say.

"All right," Parkus said. "Until you sleep. Feel no fret, Jack. Nothing will harm you here."

"My mom always said—"

But before he finished the thought, sleep had claimed him.

### 4

And sleep continued to claim him, in some mysterious wise, the next day when he was technically awake—or if not sleep, then a protective numbing faculty of the mind which turned most of that day slow and dreamlike. He and Richard, who was similarly slow-moving and tentative, stood beneath the tallest tree in the world. All about them spangles of light lay across the floor of the forest. Ten grown men holding hands could not have reached around it. The tree soared up, massive and apart: in a forest of tall trees it was a leviathan, a pure example of Territories exuberance.

*Feel no fret,* Parkus had said, even while he threatened to fade hazily away like the Cheshire Cat. Jack tilted his head to stare up toward the top of the tree. He did not quite know this, but he was emotionally exhausted. The immensity of the tree aroused only a flicker of wonder in him. Jack rested a hand against the surprisingly smooth bark. *I killed the man who killed my father,* he said to himself. He clutched the dark, seemingly dead ball of the Talisman in his other hand. Richard was staring upward at the giant head of the tree, a skyscraper's height above them. Morgan was dead, Gardener too, and the snow must have melted from the beach by now. Yet not all of it was gone. Jack felt as though a whole beachful of snow filled his head. He had thought once—a thousand years ago, it seemed now—that if he could ever actually get his hands around the Talisman, he would be so inundated with triumph and excitement and awe that he'd have to fizz over. Instead he now felt only the tiniest hint of all that. It was snowing in his head, and he could see no farther than Parkus's instructions. He realized that the enormous tree was holding him up.

"Take my hand," he said to Richard.

"But how are we going to get home?" Richard asked.

"Feel no fret," he said, and closed his hand around Richard's. Jack Sawyer didn't need a tree to hold him up. Jack Sawyer had been to the Blasted Lands, he had vanquished the black hotel, Jack Sawyer was *brave and true.* Jack Sawyer was a played-out twelve-year-old boy with snow falling in his brain. He flipped effortlessly back into his own world, and Richard slid through whatever barriers there were right beside him.

### 5

The forest had contracted; now it was an American forest. The roof of gently moving boughs was noticeably lower, the trees about them conspicuously smaller than in the part of the Territories forest to which Parkus had directed them. Jack was dimly conscious of this alteration in the scale of everything about him before he saw the two-lane blacktop road in front of him: but twentieth-century reality kicked him almost immediately in the shins, for as soon as he saw the road he heard the eggbeater sound of a small motor and instinctively drew himself and Richard back just before a white little Renault Le Car zipped by him. The car sped past and went through the tunnel cut into the trunk of the redwood (which was slightly more than half the size of its Territories counterpart). But at least one adult and two children in the Renault were not looking at the redwoods they had come to see all the way from New Hampshire ("Live Free or Die!"). The woman and the two small children in the back seat had swivelled around to gawp at Jack and Richard. Their mouths were small black caves, open wide. They had just seen two boys appear beside the road like ghosts, miraculously and instantaneously forming out of nothing, like Captain Kirk and Mr. Spock after beaming down from the *Enterprise*.

"You okay to walk for a little while?"

"Sure," Richard said.

Jack stepped onto the surface of Route 17 and walked through the huge hole in the tree.

He might be dreaming all this, he thought. He might be still on the Territories beach, Richard knocked out beside him, both of them under Parkus's kindly gaze. *My mom always said . . . My mom always said . . .*

## 6

Moving as if through thick fog (though that day in that part of northern California was in fact sunny and dry), Jack Sawyer led Richard Sloat out of the redwood forest and down a sloping road past dry December meadows.

*. . . that the most important person in any movie is usually the cameraman . . .*

His body needed more sleep. His mind needed a vacation.

*. . . that vermouth is the ruination of a good martini . . .*

Richard followed silently along, brooding. He was so much slower that Jack had to stop still on the side of the road and wait for Richard to catch up with him. A little town that must have been Storyville was visible a half-mile or so ahead. A few low white buildings sat on either side of the road. AN-TIQUES, read the sign atop one of them. Past the buildings a blinking stoplight hung over an empty intersection. Jack could see the corner of the MOBIL sign outside the gas station. Richard trudged along, his head so far down his chin nearly rested on his chest. When Richard drew nearer, Jack finally saw that his friend was weeping.

Jack put his arm around Richard's shoulders. "I want you to know something," he said.

"What?" Richard's small face was tear-streaked but defiant.

"I love you," Jack said.

Richard's eyes snapped back to the surface of the road. Jack kept his arm over his friend's shoulders. In a moment Richard looked up—looked straight at Jack—and nodded. And that was like something Lily Cavanaugh Sawyer once or twice really had said to her son: *Jack-O, there are times you don't have to spill your guts out of your mouth*.

"We're on our way, Richie," Jack said. He waited for Richard to wipe his eyes. "I guess somebody's supposed to meet us up there at the Mobil station."

"Hitler, maybe?" Richard pressed the heels of his hands to his eyes. In a moment he was ready again, and the two boys walked into Storyville together.

## 7

It was a Cadillac, parked on the shady side of the Mobil station—an El Dorado with a boomerang TV antenna on the back. It looked as big as a house-trailer and as dark as death.

"Oh, Jack, *baaaad* shit," Richard moaned, and grabbed at Jack's shoulder. His eyes were wide, his mouth trembling.

Jack felt adrenaline whippet into his system again. It didn't pump him up any longer. It only made him feel tired. There had been too much, too much, too much.

Clasping the dark junk-shop crystal ball that the Talisman had become, Jack started down the hill toward the Mobil station.

*"Jack!"* Richard screamed weakly from behind him.

*"What the hell are you doing? It's one of THEM! Same cars as at Thayer! Same cars as in Point Venuti!"*

"Parkus told us to come here," Jack said.

"You're crazy, chum," Richard whispered.

"I know it. But this'll be all right. You'll see. And don't call me chum."

The Caddy's door swung open and a heavily muscled leg clad in faded blue denim swung out. Unease became active terror when he saw that the toe of the driver's black engineer boot had been cut off so long, hairy toes could stick out.

Richard squeaked beside him like a fieldmouse.

It was a Wolf, all right—Jack knew that even before the guy turned around. He stood almost seven feet tall. His hair was long, shaggy, and not very clean. It hung in tangles to his collar. There were a couple of burdocks in it. Then the big figure turned, Jack saw a flash of orange eyes—and suddenly terror became joy.

Jack sprinted toward the big figure down there, heedless of the gas station attendant who had come out to stare at him, and the idlers in front of the general store. His hair flew back from his forehead; his battered sneakers thumped and flapped; his face was split by a dizzy grin; his eyes shone like the Talisman itself.

Bib overalls: Oshkosh, by gosh. Round rimless spectacles: John Lennon glasses. And a wide, welcoming grin.

*"Wolf!"* Jack Sawyer screamed. *"Wolf, you're alive! Wolf, you're alive!"*

He was still five feet from Wolf when he leaped. And Wolf caught him with neat, casual ease, grinning delightedly.

"Jack Sawyer! Wolf! Look at this! Just like Parkus said! I'm here at this God-pounding place that smells like shit in a swamp, and you're here, too! Jack and his friend! Wolf! Good! Great! Wolf!"

It was the Wolf's *smell* that told Jack this wasn't *his* Wolf, just as it was the smell that told him this Wolf was some sort of relation . . . surely a very close one.

"I knew your litter-brother," Jack said, still in the Wolf's shaggy, strong arms. Now, looking at this face, he could see it was older and wiser. But still kind.

"My brother Wolf," Wolf said, and put Jack down. He reached out one hand and touched the Talisman with the tip of one finger. His face was full of awed reverence. When he touched it, one bright spark appeared and shot deep into the globe's dull depths like a tumbling comet.

He drew in a breath, looked at Jack, and grinned. Jack grinned back.

Richard now arrived, staring at both of them with wonder and caution.

"There are good Wolfs as well as bad in the Territories—" Jack began.

"*Lots* of good Wolfs," Wolf interjected.

He stuck out his hand to Richard. Richard pulled back for a second and then shook it. The set of his mouth as his hand was swallowed made Jack believe Richard expected the sort of treatment Wolf had accorded Heck Bast a long time ago.

"This is *my* Wolf's litter-brother," Jack said proudly. He cleared his throat, not knowing exactly how to express his feelings for this being's brother. Did Wolfs understand condolence? Was it part of their ritual?

"I loved your brother," he said. "He saved my life. Except for Richard here, he was just about the best friend I ever had, I guess. I'm sorry he died."

"He's in the moon now," Wolf's brother said. "He'll be back. Everything goes away, Jack Sawyer, like the moon. Everything comes back, like the moon. Come on. Want to get away from this stinking place."

Richard looked puzzled, but Jack understood and more than sympathized—the Mobil station seemed surrounded with a hot, oily aroma of fried hydrocarbons. It was like a brown shroud you could see through.

The Wolf went to the Cadillac and opened the rear door like a chauffeur—which was, Jack supposed, exactly what he was.

"Jack?" Richard looked frightened.

"It's okay," Jack said.

"But where—"

"To my mother, I think," Jack said. "All the way across the country to Arcadia Beach, New Hampshire. Going first class. Come on, Richie."

They walked to the car. Shoved over to one side of the wide back seat was a scruffy old guitar case. Jack felt his heart leap up again.

"Speedy!" He turned to Wolf's litter-brother. "Is Speedy coming with us?"

"Don't know anyone speedy," the Wolf said. "Had an uncle who was sort of speedy, then he pulled up lame—Wolf!—and couldn't even keep up with the herd anymore."

Jack pointed at the guitar case.

"Where did that come from?"

Wolf grinned, showing many big teeth. "Parkus," he said. "Left this for you, too. Almost forgot."

From his back pocket he took a very old postcard. On the front was a carousel filled with a great many familiar horses—Ella Speed and Silver Lady among them—but the ladies in the foreground were wearing bustles, the boys knickers, many of the men derby hats and Rollie Fingers moustaches. The card felt silky with age.

He turned it over, first reading the print up the middle: ARCADIA BEACH CAROUSEL, JULY 4TH, 1894.

It was Speedy—not Parkus—who had scratched two sentences in the message space. His hand was sprawling, not very literate; he had written with a soft, blunt pencil.

*You done great wonders, Jack. Use what you need of what's in the case—keep the rest or throw it away.*

Jack put the postcard in his hip pocket and got into the back of the Cadillac, sliding across the plush seat. One of the catches on the old guitar case was broken. He unsnapped the other three.

Richard had gotten in after Jack. "Holy crow!" he whispered.

The guitar case was stuffed with twenty-dollar bills.

## 8

Wolf took them home, and although Jack grew hazy about many of that autumn's events in a very short time, each moment of that trip was emblazoned on his mind for the rest of his life. He and Richard sat in the back of the El Dorado and Wolf drove them east and east and east. Wolf knew the roads and Wolf drove them. He sometimes played Creedence Clearwater Revival tapes—"Run Through the Jungle" seemed to be his favorite—at a volume just short of ear-shattering. Then he would spend long periods of time listening to the tonal varia-

tions in the wind as he worked the button that controlled his
wing window. This seemed to fascinate him completely.

East, east, east—into the sunrise each morning, into the
mysterious deepening blue dusk of each coming night, listening first to John Fogerty and then to the wind, John Fogerty
again and then the wind again.

They ate at Stuckeys'. They ate at Burger Kings. They
stopped at Kentucky Fried Chicken. At the latter, Jack and
Richard got dinners; Wolf got a Family-Style Bucket and ate
all twenty-one pieces. From the sounds, he ate most of the
bones as well. This made Jack think of Wolf and the popcorn.
Where had that been? Muncie. The outskirts of Muncie—the
Town Line Sixplex. Just before they had gotten their asses
slammed into the Sunlight Home. He grinned . . . and then
felt something like an arrow slip into his heart. He looked out
the window so Richard wouldn't see the gleam of his tears.

They stopped on the second night in Julesburg, Colorado,
and Wolf cooked them a huge picnic supper on a portable barbecue he produced from the trunk. They ate in a snowy field
by starlight, bundled up in heavy parkas bought out of the
guitar-case stash. A meteor-shower flashed overhead, and
Wolf danced in the snow like a child.

"I love that guy," Richard said thoughtfully.

"Yeah, me too. You should have met his brother."

"I wish I had." Richard began to gather up the trash. What
he said next flummoxed Jack almost completely. "I'm forgetting a lot of stuff, Jack."

"What do you mean?"

"Just that. Every mile I remember a little less about what
happened. It's all getting misty. And I think . . . I think that's
the way I want it. Look, are you really sure your mother's
okay?"

Three times Jack had tried to call his mother. There was no
answer. He was not too worried about this. Things were okay.
He hoped. When he got there, she would be there. Sick . . .
but still alive. He hoped.

"Yes."

"Then how come she doesn't answer the phone?"

"Sloat played some tricks with the phones," Jack said. "He
played some tricks with the help at the Alhambra, too, I bet.
She's still okay. Sick . . . but okay. Still there. I can feel her."

"And if this healing thing works—" Richard grimaced a little, then plunged. "You still . . . I mean, you still think she'd let me . . . you know, stay with you guys?"

"No," Jack said, helping Richard pick up the remains of supper. "She'll want to see you in an orphanage, probably. Or maybe in jail. Don't be a dork, Richard, of course you can stay with us."

"Well . . . after all my father did . . ."

"That was your dad, Richie," Jack said simply. "Not you."

"And you won't always be reminding me? You know . . . jogging my memory?"

"Not if you want to forget."

"I do, Jack. I really do."

Wolf was coming back.

"You guys ready? Wolf!"

"All ready," Jack said. "Listen, Wolf, how about that Scott Hamilton tape I got in Cheyenne?"

"Sure, Jack. Then how about some Creedence?"

" 'Run Through the Jungle,' right?"

"Good tune, Jack! Heavy! *Wolf!* God-pounding *heavy* tune!"

"You bet, Wolf." He rolled his eyes at Richard. Richard rolled his back, and grinned.

The next day they rolled across Nebraska and Iowa; a day later they tooled past the gutted ruin of the Sunlight Home. Jack thought Wolf had taken them past it on purpose, that he perhaps wanted to see the place where his brother had died. He turned up the Creedence tape in the cassette player as loud as it would go, but Jack still thought he heard the sound of Wolf sobbing.

Time—suspended swatches of time. Jack seemed almost to be floating, and there was a feeling of suspension, triumph, valediction. Work honorably discharged.

Around sunset of the fifth day, they crossed into New England.

# 47

# Journey's End

## 1

The whole long drive from California to New England seemed, once they had got so far, to have taken place in a single long afternoon and evening. An afternoon that lasted days, an evening perhaps life-long, bulging with sunsets and music and emotions. *Great humping balls of fire,* Jack thought, *I'm really out of it,* when he happened for the second time in what he assumed to be about an hour to look at the discreet little clock set in the dashboard—and discovered that three hours had winked past him. Was it even the same day? "Run Through the Jungle" pumped through the air; Wolf bobbed his head in time, grinning unstoppably, infallibly finding the best roads; the rear window showing the whole sky opening in great bands of twilight color, purple and blue and that particular deep plangent red of the down-going sun. Jack could remember every detail of this long long journey, every word, every meal, every nuance of the music, Zoot Sims or John Fogerty or simply Wolf delighting himself with the noises of the air, but the true span of time had warped itself in his mind to a concentration like a diamond's. He slept in the cushiony backseat and opened his eyes on light or darkness, on sunlight or stars. Among the things he remembered with particular sharpness, once they had crossed into New England and the Talisman began to glow again, signalling the return of normal time—or perhaps the return of time itself to Jack Sawyer—were the faces of people peering into the back seat of the El Dorado (people in parking lots, a sailor and an ox-faced girl in a convertible at a stoplight in a sunny little town in Iowa, a skinny Ohio kid wearing *Breaking Away*–style bicycle gear) in order to see if maybe Mick Jagger or Frank Sinatra had decided to pay them a call. Nope, just us, folks. Sleep kept stealing him away. Once he awoke (Colorado? Illinois?) to the thumping of rock music, Wolf snapping his fingers while keeping the big car rolling smoothly, a bursting sky of orange and purple and blue, and saw that Richard had somewhere acquired a book and was reading it with the aid of the El Dorado's recessed passenger light. The book was *Broca's Brain*. Richard always knew what time it was. Jack rolled his eyes upward and let the music, the evening colors, take him. They had *done it*, they had done *everything* . . . everything except what they would have to do in an empty little resort town in New Hampshire.

Five days, or one long, dreaming twilight? "Run Through the Jungle." Zoot Sims's tenor saxophone saying *Here's a story for you, do you like this story?* Richard was his brother, his brother.

Time returned to him about when the Talisman came back to life, during the magical sunset of the fifth day. *Oatley,* Jack thought on the sixth day. *I could have shown Richard the Oatley tunnel, and whatever's left of the Tap,* I could have shown Wolf which way to go . . . but he did not want to see Oatley again, there was no satisfaction or pleasure in that. And he was conscious now of how close they had come, of how far they had travelled while he drifted through time like a whistle. Wolf had brought them to the great broad artery of I-95, now that they were in Connecticut, and Arcadia Beach lay only a few states away, up the indented New England coast. From now on Jack counted the miles, and the minutes, too.

## 2

At quarter past five on the evening of December 21st, some three months after Jack Sawyer had set his face—and his hopes—on the west, a black El Dorado Cadillac swung into the crushed-gravel driveway of the Alhambra Inn and Gardens in the town of Arcadia Beach, New Hampshire. In the west, the sunset was a mellow valediction of reds and oranges fading to yellow . . . and blue . . . and royal purple. In the gardens themselves, naked branches clattered together in a bitter winter wind. Amid them, until a day not quite a week ago, had been a tree which caught and ate small animals—chipmunks, birds, the desk clerk's starveling, slat-sided cat. This small tree had died very suddenly. The other growing things in the garden, though skeletal now, still bided with dormant life.

The El Dorado's steel-belted radials popped and cracked over the gravel. From inside, muffled behind the polarized glass, came the sound of Creedence Clearwater Revival. *"The people who know my magic,"* John Fogerty sang, *"have filled the land with smoke."*

The Cadillac stopped in front of the wide double doors. There was only darkness beyond them. The double headlights went out and the long car stood in shadow, tailpipe idling white exhaust, orange parking lights gleaming.

Here at the end of day; here at sunset with color fanning up from the western sky in glory.

*Here:*

*Right here and now.*


### 3

The back of the Caddy was lit with faint, uncertain light. The Talisman flickered . . . but its glow was weak, little more than the glow of a dying firefly.

Richard turned slowly toward Jack. His face was wan and frightened. He was clutching Carl Sagan with both hands, wringing the paperback the way a washerwoman might wring a sheet.

*Richard's Talisman,* Jack thought, and smiled.

"Jack, do you want—"

"No," Jack said. "Wait until I call."

He opened the rear right door, started to get out of the car, then looked back at Richard. Richard sat small and shrunken in his seat, wringing his paperback in his hand. He looked miserable.

Not thinking, Jack came back in for a moment and kissed Richard's cheek. Richard put his arms around Jack's neck for a moment, and hugged fiercely. Then he let Jack go. Neither of them said anything.


### 4

Jack started for the stairs leading up to the lobby-level . . . and then turned right and walked for a moment to the edge of the driveway instead. There was an iron railing here. Below it, cracked and tiered rock fell to the beach. Farther to his right, standing against the darkling sky, was the Arcadia Funworld roller coaster.

Jack lifted his face to the east. The wind that was harrying through the formal gardens lifted his hair away from his forehead and blew it back.

He lifted the globe in his hands, as if as an offering to the ocean.

## 5

*On December 21st, 1981, a boy named Jack Sawyer stood near the place where the water and the land came together, hands cradling an object of some worth, looking out at the night-steady Atlantic. He had turned thirteen years old that day, although he did not know it, and he was extraordinarily beautiful. His brown hair was long—probably too long—but the sea-breeze swept it back from a fine, clear brow. He stood there thinking about his mother, and about the rooms in this place which they had shared. Was she going to turn on a light up there? He rather suspected she was.*

Jack turned, eyes flashing wildly in the Talisman's light.

## 6

Lily felt along the wall with one trembling, skeletal hand, groping for the light-switch. She found it and turned it on. Anyone who had seen her in that moment might well have turned away. In the last week or so, the cancer had begun to sprint inside her, as if sensing that something might be on the way which would spoil all its fun. Lily Cavanaugh now weighed seventy-eight pounds. Her skin was sallow, stretched over her skull like parchment. The brown circles under her eyes had turned a dead and final black; the eyes themselves stared from their sockets with fevered, exhausted intelligence. Her bosom was gone. The flesh on her arms was gone. On her buttocks and the backs of her thighs, bedsores had begun to flower.

Nor was that all. In the course of the last week, she had contracted pneumonia.

In her wasted condition she was, of course, a prime candidate for that or any other respiratory disease. It might have come under the best of circumstances . . . and these were definitely not those. The radiators in the Alhambra had ceased their nightly clankings some time ago. She wasn't sure just how long—time had become as fuzzy and indefinable to her as it had been for Jack in the El Dorado. She only knew the heat had gone out on the same night she had punched her fist through the window, making the gull that had looked like Sloat fly away.

In the time since that night the Alhambra had become a deserted coldbox. A crypt in which she would soon die.

If Sloat was responsible for what had happened at the Alhambra, he had done one hell of a good job. Everyone was gone. *Everyone.* No more maids in the halls trundling their squeaky carts. No more whistling maintenance man. No more mealy-mouthed desk clerk. Sloat had put them all in his pocket and taken them away.

Four days ago—when she could not find enough in the room to satisfy even her birdlike appetite—she had gotten out of bed and had worked her way slowly down the hall to the elevator. She brought a chair with her on this expedition, alternately sitting on it, her head hanging in exhaustion, and using it as a walker. It took her forty minutes to traverse forty feet of corridor to the elevator shaft.

She had pushed the button for the car repeatedly, but the car did not come. The buttons did not even light.

"Fuck a duck," Lily muttered hoarsely, and then slowly worked herself another twenty feet down the hall to the stairwell.

*"Hey!"* she shouted downstairs, and then broke into a fit of coughing, bent over the back of the chair.

*Maybe they couldn't hear the yell but they sure as shit must have been able to hear me coughing out whatever's left of my lungs,* she thought.

But no one came.

She yelled again, twice, had another coughing fit, and then started back down the hallway, which looked as long as a stretch of Nebraska turnpike on a clear day. She didn't dare go down those stairs. She would never get back up them. And there was no one down there; not in the lobby, not in The Sad-

dle of Lamb, not in the coffee shop, not *anywhere*. And the
phones were out. At least, the phone in *her* room was out; and
she hadn't heard a single ring anywhere else in this old mau-
soleum. Not worth it. A bad gamble. She didn't want to freeze
to death in the lobby.

"Jack-O," she muttered, "where the hell are y—"

Then she began to cough again and this one was really bad
and in the middle of it she collapsed to one side in a faint,
pulling the ugly sitting-room chair over on top of her, and she
lay there on the cold floor for nearly an hour, and that was
probably when the pneumonia moved into the rapidly declin-
ing neighborhood that was Lily Cavanaugh's body. *Hey there,
big C! I'm the new kid on the block! You can call me big P!
Race you to the finish line!*

Somehow she had made it back to her room, and since
then she had existed in a deepening spiral of fever, listening
to her respiration grow louder and louder until her fevered
mind began to imagine her lungs as two organic aquariums in
which a number of submerged chains were rattling. And yet
she held on—held on because part of her mind insisted with
crazy, failing certainty that Jack was on his way back from
wherever he had been.

## 7

The beginning of her final coma had been like a dimple in the
sand—a dimple that begins to spin like a whirlpool. The
sound of submerged chains in her chest became a long, dry
exhalation—*Hahhhhhhhh* . . .

Then something had brought her out of that deepening spiral and started her feeling along the wall in the cold darkness
for the light-switch. She got out of bed. She did not have
strength enough left to do this; a doctor would have laughed
at the idea. And yet she did. She fell back twice, then finally
made it to her feet, mouth turned down in a snarl of effort.
She groped for the chair, found it, and began to lurch her way
across the room to the window.

Lily Cavanaugh, Queen of the Bs, was gone. This was a
walking horror, eaten by cancer, burned by rising fever.

She reached the window and looked out.

Saw a human shape down there—and a glowing globe.

*"Jack!"* she tried to scream. Nothing came out but a gravelly whisper. She raised a hand, tried to wave. Faintness
*(Haahhhhhhhhh . . . )*
washed over her. She clutched at the windowsill.
*"Jack!"*
Suddenly the lighted ball in the figure's hands flashed up brightly, illuminating his face, and it *was* Jack's face, it was Jack, oh thank God, it was Jack. Jack had come home.
The figure broke into a run.
*Jack!*
Those sunken, dying eyes grew yet more brilliant. Tears spilled down her yellow, stretched cheeks.

### 8

*"Mom!"*
Jack ran across the lobby, seeing that the old-fashioned telephone switchboard was fused and blackened, as if from an electrical fire, and instantly dismissing it. He had seen her and she looked *awful*—it had been like looking at the silhouette of a scarecrow propped in the window.
*"Mom!"*
He pounded up the stairs, first by twos, then by threes, the Talisman stuttering one burst of pink-red light and then falling dark in his hands.
*"Mom!"*
Down the hallway to their rooms, feet flying, and now, at last, he heard her voice—no brassy bellow or slightly throaty chuckle now; this was the dusty croak of a creature on the outer edge of death.
"Jacky?"
*"Mom!"*
He burst into the room.

### 9

Down in the car, a nervous Richard Sloat stared upward through his polarized window. What was he doing here, what was *Jack* doing here? Richard's eyes hurt. He strained to see the upper windows in the murky evening. As he bent sideways and stared upward, a blinding white flash erupted from several of the upstairs windows, sending a momentary, almost palpable sheet of dazzling light over the entire front of the hotel. Richard put his head between his knees and moaned.

## 10

She was on the floor beneath the window—he saw her there finally. The rumpled, somehow dusty-looking bed was empty, the whole bedroom, as disordered as a child's room, seemed empty . . . Jack's stomach had frozen and words backed up in his throat. Then the Talisman had shot out another of its great illuminating flashes, in and for an instant turning everything in the room a pure colorless white. She croaked, *"Jacky?"* once more, and he bellowed, *"MOM!"* seeing her crumpled like a candy wrapper under the window. Thin and lank, her hair trailed on the room's dirty carpet. Her hands seemed like tiny animal paws, pale and scrabbling. "Oh Jesus, Mom, oh jeepers, oh holy moe," he babbled, and somehow moved across the room without taking a step, he *floated*, he *swam* across Lily's crowded frozen bedroom in an instant that seemed as sharp to him as an image on a photographic plate. Her hair puddled on the grimy carpet, her small knotty hands.

He inhaled the thick odor of illness, of close death. Jack was no doctor, and he was ignorant of most of the things so wrong with Lily's body. But he knew one thing—his mother was dying, her life was falling away through invisible cracks, and she had very little time left. She had uttered his name twice, and that was about all the life left in her would permit. Already beginning to weep, he put his hand on her unconscious head, and set the Talisman on the floor beside her.

Her hair felt full of sand and her head was burning. "Oh Mom, Mom," he said, and got his hands under her. He still could not see her face. Through her flimsy nightgown her hip felt as hot as the door of a stove. Against his other palm, her left shoulder blade pulsed with an equal warmth. She had no comfortable pads of flesh over her bones—for a mad second of stopped time it was as though she were a small dirty child somehow left ill and alone. Sudden unbidden tears squirted out of his eyes. He lifted her, and it was like picking up a bundle of clothes. Jack moaned. Lily's arms sprawled loosely, gracelessly.

*(Richard)*

Richard had felt . . . not as bad as this, not even when Richard had felt like a dried husk on his back, coming down the final hill into poisoned Point Venuti. There had been little but pimples and a rash left of Richard at that point, but he, too, had burned with fever. But Jack realized with a sort of unthinking horror that there had been more actual life, more *substance*, to Richard than his mother now possessed. Still, she had called his name.

*(and Richard had nearly died)*

She had called his name. He clung to that. She had *made it to the window*. She had *called his name*. It was impossible, unthinkable, immoral to imagine that she could die. One of her arms dangled before him like a reed meant to be cut in half by a scythe . . . her wedding ring had fallen off her finger. He was crying steadily, unstoppably, unconsciously. "Okay, Mom," he said, "okay, it's okay now, okay, it's okay."

From the limp body in his arms came a vibration that might have been assent.

He gently placed her on the bed, and she rolled weightlessly sideways. Jack put a knee on the bed and leaned over her. The tired hair fell away from her face.

## 11

Once, at the very beginning of his journey, he had for a shameful moment seen his mother as an old woman—a spent, exhausted old woman in a tea shop. As soon as he had recognized her, the illusion had dissipated, and Lily Cavanaugh Sawyer had been restored to her unaging self. For the real, the true Lily Cavanaugh could never have aged—she was eternally a blonde with a quick switchblade of a smile and a go-to-hell amusement in her face. This had been the Lily Cavanaugh whose picture on a billboard had strengthened her son's heart.

The woman on the bed looked very little like the actress on the billboard. Jack's tears momentarily blinded him. "Oh don't don't don't," he said, and laid one palm across her yellowed cheek.

She did not look as though she had enough strength to lift her hand. He took her tight dry discolored claw of a hand into his own hand. "Please please please don't—" He could not even allow himself to say it.

And then he realized how much an effort this shrunken woman had made. She had been looking for him, he understood in a great giddy rush of comprehension. His mother had known he was coming. She had trusted him to return and in a way that must have been connected to the fact of the Talisman itself, she had known the moment of his return.

"I'm here, Mom," he whispered. A wad of wet stuff bubbled from his nostrils. He unceremoniously wiped his nose with the sleeve of his coat.

He realized for the first time that his entire body was trembling.

"I brought it back," he said. He experienced a moment of absolute radiant pride, of pure accomplishment. "I brought back the Talisman," he said.

Gently he set her nutlike hand down on the counterpane.

Beside the chair, where he had placed it (every bit as gently) on the floor, the Talisman continued to glow. But its light was faint, hesitant, cloudy. He had healed Richard by simply rolling the globe down the length of his friend's body; he had done the same for Speedy. But this was to be something else. He knew that, but not what "it" was to be . . . unless it was a question of knowing and not wanting to believe.

He could not possibly break the Talisman, not even to save his mother's life—that much he *did* know.

Now the interior of the Talisman slowly filled with a cloudy whiteness. The pulses faded into one another and became a single steady light. Jack placed his hands on it, and the Talisman shot forth a blinding wall of light, *rainbow!* which seemed nearly to speak. AT LAST!

Jack went back across the room toward the bed, the Talisman bouncing and spraying light from floor to wall to ceiling, illuminating the bed fitfully, garishly.

As soon as he stood beside his mother's bed, the texture of the Talisman seemed to Jack to subtly alter beneath his fingers. Its glassy hardness *shifted* somehow, became less slippery, more porous. The tips of his fingers seemed almost to sink into the Talisman. The cloudiness filling it boiled and darkened.

And at this moment Jack experienced a strong—in fact,

passionate—feeling he would have thought was impossible, that day long ago when he had set off for his first day's walk in the Territories. He knew that in some unforeseen way the Talisman, the object of so much blood and trouble, was going to alter. It was going to change forever, and he was going to lose it. The Talisman would *no longer be his*. Its clear skin was clouding over, too, and the entire beautiful grooved gravid surface was softening. The feeling now was not glass but warming plastic.

Jack hurriedly set the altering Talisman down in his mother's hands. It knew its job; it had been made for this moment; in some fabulous smithy it had been created to answer the requirements of this particular moment and of none other.

He did not know what he expected to happen. An explosion of light? A smell of medicine? Creation's big bang?

Nothing happened. His mother continued visibly but motionlessly to die.

"Oh please," Jack blurted, "please—Mom—please—"

His breath solidified in the middle of his chest. A seam, once one of the vertical grooves in the Talisman, had soundlessly opened. Light slowly poured out and pooled over his mother's hands. From the cloudy interior of the loose, emptying ball, more light spilled through the open seam.

From outside came a sudden and loud music of birds celebrating their existence.

## 12

But of that Jack was only distractedly conscious. He leaned breathlessly forward and watched the Talisman pour itself out onto his mother's bed. Cloudy brightness welled up within it. Seams and sparks of light enlivened it. His mother's eyes twitched. "Oh Mom," he whispered. "Oh . . ."

Gray-golden light flooded through the opening in the Talisman and cloudily drifted up his mother's arms. Her sallow, wizened face very slightly frowned.

Jack inhaled unconsciously.

*(What?)*

*(Music?)*

The gray-golden cloud from the heart of the Talisman was lengthening over his mother's body, coating her in a translucent but slightly opaque, delicately moving membrane. Jack watched this fluid fabric slide across Lily's pitiful chest, down her wasted legs. From the open seam in the Talisman a wondrous odor spilled out with the gray-golden cloud, an odor sweet and unsweet, of flowers and earth, wholly good, yeasty; a smell of birth, Jack thought, though he had never attended an actual birth. Jack drew it into his lungs and in the midst of his wonder was gifted with the thought that he himself, Jack-O Sawyer, was being born at this minute—and then he imagined, with a barely perceptible shock of recognition, that the opening in the Talisman was like a vagina. (He had of course never seen a vagina and had only the most rudimentary idea of its structure.) Jack looked directly into the opening in the distended loosened Talisman.

Now he became conscious for the first time of the incredible racket, in some way all mixed up with faint music, of the birds outside the dark windows.

*(Music? What . . . ?)*

A small colored ball full of light shot past his vision, flashing in the open seam for a moment, then continued beneath the Talisman's cloudy surface as it dove into the shifting moving gaseous interior. Jack blinked. It had resembled—Another followed, and this time he had time to see the demarcation of blue and brown and green on the tiny globe, the coastal shorelines and tiny mountain ranges. On that tiny world, it occurred to him, stood a paralyzed Jack Sawyer looking down at an even tinier colored speck, and on that speck stood a Jack-O the height of a dust mote staring at a little world the size of an atom. Another world followed the first two, spinning in, out, in, out of the widening cloud within the Talisman.

His mother moved her right hand and moaned.

Jack began openly to weep. She would live. He knew it now. All had worked as Speedy had said, and the Talisman was forcing life back into his mother's exhausted, disease-ridden body, killing the evil that was killing her. He bent forward, for a moment almost giving in to the image of himself kissing the Talisman which filled his mind. The odors of jasmine and hibiscus and freshly overturned earth filled his nostrils. A tear rolled off the end of his nose and sparkled like a jewel in the shafts of light from the Talisman. He saw a belt of stars drift past the open seam, a beaming yellow sun swimming in vast black space. Music seemed to fill the Talisman, the room, the whole world outside. A woman's face, the face of a stranger, moved across the open seam. Children's faces, too, then the faces of other women. . . . Tears rolled down his own face, for he had seen swimming in the Talisman his mother's own face, the confident wise-cracking tender features of the Queen of half a hundred quick movies. When he saw his own face drifting among all the worlds and lives falling toward birth within the Talisman, he thought he would burst with feeling. He *expanded*. He breathed in light. And became at last aware of the astonishment of noises taking place all about him when he saw his mother's eyes stay open as long, at least, as a blessed two seconds . . .

(for alive as birds, as alive as the worlds contained within the Talisman, there came to him the sounds of trombones and trumpets, the cries of saxophones; the joined voices of frogs and turtles and gray doves singing, *The people who know my magic have filled the land with smoke;* there came to him the voices of Wolfs making Wolfmusic at the moon. Water spanked against the bow of a ship and a fish spanked the surface of a lake with the side of its body and a rainbow spanked the ground and a travelling boy spanked a drop of spittle to tell him which way to go and a spanked baby squinched its face and opened its throat; and there came the huge voice of an orchestra singing with its whole massive heart; and the room filled with the smoky trail of a single voice rising and rising and rising over all these forays of sound. Trucks jammed gears and factory whistles blew and somewhere a tire exploded and somewhere a firecracker loudly spent itself and a lover whispered *again* and a child squalled and the voice rose and rose and for a short time Jack was unaware that he could not see; but then he could again).

Lily's eyes opened wide. They stared up into Jack's face with a startled where-am-I expression. It was the expression of a newborn infant who has just been spanked into the world. Then she jerked in a startled breath—

—and a river of worlds and tilted galaxies and universes were pulled up and out of the Talisman as she did. They were pulled up in a stream of rainbow colors. They streamed into her mouth and nose . . . they settled, gleaming, on her sallow skin like droplets of dew, and melted inward. For a moment his mother was all clothed in radiance—

*—for a moment his mother was the Talisman.*

All the disease fled from her face. It did not happen in the manner of a time-lapse sequence in a movie. It happened *all at once*. It happened *instantly*. She was sick . . . and then she was well. Rosy good health bloomed in her cheeks. Wispy, sparse hair was suddenly full and smooth and rich, the color of dark honey.

Jack stared at her as she looked up into his face.

*"Oh . . . oh . . . my GOD . . ."* Lily whispered.

That rainbow radiance was fading now—but the health remained.

"Mom?" He bent forward. Something crumpled like cellophane under his fingers. It was the brittle husk of the Talisman. He put it aside on the nighttable. He pushed several of her medicine bottles out of the way to do it. Some crashed on the floor, and it didn't matter. She would not be needing the medicines anymore. He put the husk down with gentle reverence, suspecting—no, *knowing*—that even that would be gone very soon.

His mother smiled. It was a lovely, fulfilled, somewhat surprised smile—*Hello, world, here I am again! What do you know about that?*

"Jack, you came home," she said at last, and rubbed her eyes as if to make sure it was no mirage.

"Sure," he said. He tried to smile. It was a pretty good smile in spite of the tears that were pouring down his face. "Sure, you bet."

"I feel . . . a lot better, Jack-O."

"Yeah?" He smiled, rubbed his wet eyes with the heels of his palms. "That's good, Mom."

Her eyes were radiant.

"Hug me, Jacky."

In a room on the fourth floor of a deserted resort hotel on the minuscule New Hampshire seacoast, a thirteen-year-old boy named Jack Sawyer leaned forward, closed his eyes, and hugged his mother tightly, smiling. His ordinary life of school and friends and games and music, a life where there were schools to go to and crisp sheets to slide between at night, the ordinary life of a thirteen-year-old boy (if the life of such a creature can ever, in its color and riot, be considered ordinary) had been returned to him, he realized. The Talisman had done that for him, too. When he remembered to turn and look for it, the Talisman was gone.

# Epilogue

In a billowing white bedroom filled with anxious women, Laura DeLoessian, Queen of the Territories, opened her eyes.

# Conclusion

So endeth this chronicle. It being strictly the history of a *boy*, it must stop here; the story could not go much further without becoming the history of a *man*. When one writes a novel about grown people, he knows exactly where to stop—that is, with a marriage; but when he writes of juveniles, he must stop where he best can.

Most of the characters who perform in this book still live, and are prosperous and happy. Some day it may seem worthwhile to take up the story again and see what . . . they turned out to be; therefore, it will be wisest not to reveal any of that part of their lives at present.

—Mark Twain, Tom Sawyer

Are you ready to continue the magnificent adventure
that began with *The Talisman*?

Here is Chapter 1 of the *New York Times* bestseller

# BLACK HOUSE,
the long-awaited sequel to *The Talisman*,
by Stephen King and Peter Straub.

Available from Ballantine Books wherever books are sold.

# 1

*Right here and now,* as an old friend used to say, we are in the
fluid present, where clear-sightedness never guarantees perfect vision. *Here:* about two hundred feet, the height of a gliding eagle, above Wisconsin's far western edge, where the
vagaries of the Mississippi River declare a natural border.
*Now:* an early Friday morning in mid-July a few years into
both a new century and a new millennium, their wayward
courses so hidden that a blind man has a better chance of seeing what lies ahead than you or I. Right here and now, the
hour is just past 6 A.M., and the sun stands low in the cloudless eastern sky, a fat, confident yellow-white ball advancing
as ever for the first time toward the future and leaving in its
wake the steadily accumulating past, which darkens as it recedes, making blind men of us all.

Below, the early sun touches the river's wide, soft ripples
with molten highlights. Sunlight glints from the tracks of the
Burlington Northern Santa Fe Railroad running between the
riverbank and the backs of the shabby two-story houses along
County Road Oo, known as Nailhouse Row, the lowest point
of the comfortable-looking little town extending uphill and
eastward beneath us. At this moment in the Coulee Country,
life seems to be holding its breath. The motionless air around

us carries such remarkable purity and sweetness that you might imagine a man could smell a radish pulled out of the ground a mile away.

Moving toward the sun, we glide away from the river and over the shining tracks, the backyards and roofs of Nailhouse Row, then a line of Harley-Davidson motorcycles tilted on their kickstands. These unprepossessing little houses were built, early in the century recently vanished, for the metal pourers, mold makers, and crate men employed by the Pederson Nail factory. On the grounds that working stiffs would be unlikely to complain about the flaws in their subsidized accommodations, they were constructed as cheaply as possible. (Pederson Nail, which had suffered multiple hemorrhages during the fifties, finally bled to death in 1963.) The waiting Harleys suggest that the factory hands have been replaced by a motorcycle gang. The uniformly ferocious appearance of the Harleys' owners, wild-haired, bushy-bearded, swag-bellied men sporting earrings, black leather jackets, and less than the full complement of teeth, would seem to support this assumption. Like most assumptions, this one embodies an uneasy half-truth.

The current residents of Nailhouse Row, whom suspicious locals dubbed the Thunder Five soon after they took over the houses along the river, cannot so easily be categorized. They have skilled jobs in the Kingsland Brewing Company, located just out of town to the south and one block east of the Mississippi. If we look to our right, we can see "the world's largest six-pack," storage tanks painted over with gigantic Kingsland Old-Time Lager labels. The men who live on Nailhouse Row met one another on the Urbana-Champaign campus of the University of Illinois, where all but one were undergraduates majoring in English or philosophy. (The exception was a resident in surgery at the UI-UC university hospital.) They get an ironic pleasure from being called the Thunder Five: the name strikes them as sweetly cartoonish. What they call themselves is "the Hegelian Scum." These gentlemen form an interesting crew, and we will make their acquaintance later on. For now, we have time only to note the hand-painted posters taped to the fronts of several houses, two lamp poles, and a couple of abandoned buildings. The posters say: FISHERMEN, YOU BET-

TER PRAY TO YOUR STINKING GOD WE DON'T CATCH YOU FIRST!
REMEMBER AMY!

From Nailhouse Row, Chase Street runs steeply uphill between listing buildings with worn, unpainted facades the
color of fog: the old Nelson Hotel, where a few impoverished
residents lie sleeping, a blank-faced tavern, a tired shoe store
displaying Red Wing workboots behind its filmy picture window, a few other dim buildings that bear no indication of their
function and seem oddly dreamlike and vaporous. These
structures have the air of failed resurrections, of having been
rescued from the dark westward territory although they were
still dead. In a way, that is precisely what happened to them.
An ocher horizontal stripe, ten feet above the sidewalk on the
facade of the Nelson Hotel and two feet from the rising
ground on the opposed, ashen faces of the last two buildings,
represents the high-water mark left behind by the flood of
1965, when the Mississippi rolled over its banks, drowned the
railroad tracks and Nailhouse Row, and mounted nearly to the
top of Chase Street.

Where Chase rises above the flood line and levels out, it
widens and undergoes a transformation into the main street of
French Landing, the town beneath us. The Agincourt Theater,
the Taproom Bar & Grille, the First Farmer State Bank, the
Samuel Stutz Photography Studio (which does a steady business in graduation photos, wedding pictures, and children's
portraits), and shops, not the ghostly relics of shops, line its
blunt sidewalks: Benton's Rexall drugstore, Reliable Hardware, Saturday Night Video, Regal Clothing, Schmitt's Allsorts Emporium, stores selling electronic equipment,
magazines and greeting cards, toys, and athletic clothing featuring the logos of the Brewers, the Twins, the Packers, the
Vikings, and the University of Wisconsin. After a few blocks,
the name of the street changes to Lyall Road, and the buildings separate and shrink into one-story wooden structures
fronted with signs advertising insurance offices and travel
agencies; after that, the street becomes a highway that glides
eastward past a 7-Eleven, the Reinhold T. Grauerhammer
VFW Hall, a big farm-implement dealership known locally as
Goltz's, and into a landscape of flat, unbroken fields. If we
rise another hundred feet into the immaculate air and scan

what lies beneath and ahead, we see kettle moraines, coulees, blunted hills furry with pines, loam-rich valleys invisible from ground level until you have come upon them, meandering rivers, miles-long patchwork fields, and little towns—one of them, Centralia, no more than a scattering of buildings around the intersection of two narrow highways, 35 and 93.

Directly below us, French Landing looks as though it had been evacuated in the middle of the night. No one moves along the sidewalks or bends to insert a key into one of the locks of the shop fronts along Chase Street. The angled spaces before the shops are empty of the cars and pickup trucks that will begin to appear, first by ones and twos, then in a mannerly little stream, an hour or two later. No lights burn behind the windows in the commercial buildings or the unpretentious houses lining the surrounding streets. A block north of Chase on Sumner Street, four matching redbrick buildings of two stories each house, in west-east order, the French Landing Public Library; the offices of Patrick J. Skarda, M.D., the local general practitioner; and Bell & Holland, a two-man law firm now run by Garland Bell and Julius Holland, the sons of its founders; the Heartfield & Son Funeral Home, now owned by a vast, funereal empire centered in St. Louis; and the French Landing Post Office.

Separated from these by a wide driveway into a good-sized parking lot at the rear, the building at the end of the block, where Sumner intersects with Third Street, is also of redbrick and only two stories high but longer than its immediate neighbors. Unpainted iron bars block the rear second-floor windows, and two of the four vehicles in the parking lot are patrol cars with light bars across their tops and the letters FLPD on their sides. The presence of police cars and barred windows seem incongruous in this rural vastness—what sort of crime can happen here? Nothing serious, surely; surely, nothing worse than shoplifting, drunk driving, and an occasional bar fight.

As if in testimony to the peacefulness and regularity of small-town life, a red van with the words LA RIVIERE HERALD on its side panels drifts slowly down Third Street, pausing at nearly all of the mailbox stands for its driver to insert copies of the day's newspaper, wrapped in a blue plastic bag, into gray metal cylinders bearing the same words. When the van turns onto Sumner, where the buildings have mail slots instead of boxes, the route man simply throws the wrapped papers at the front doors. Blue parcels thwack against the doors of the police station, the funeral home, and the office buildings. The post office does not get a paper.

What do you know, lights *are* burning behind the front downstairs windows of the police station. The door opens. A tall, dark-haired young man in a pale blue short-sleeved uniform shirt, a Sam Browne belt, and navy trousers steps outside. The wide belt and the gold badge on Bobby Dulac's chest gleam in the fresh sunlight, and everything he is wearing, including the 9mm pistol strapped to his hip, seems as newly made as Bobby Dulac himself. He watches the red van turn left onto Second Street, and frowns at the rolled newspaper. He nudges it with the tip of a black, highly polished shoe, bending over just far enough to suggest that he is trying to read the headlines through the plastic. Evidently this technique does not work all that well. Still frowning, Bobby tilts all the way over and picks up the newspaper with unexpected delicacy, the way a mother cat picks up a kitten in need of relocation. Holding it a little distance away from his body, he gives a quick glance up and down Sumner Street, about-faces smartly, and steps back into the station. We, who in our curiosity have been steadily descending toward the interesting spectacle presented by Officer Dulac, go inside behind him.

A gray corridor leads past a blank door and a bulletin board with very little on it to two sets of metal stairs, one going down to a small locker room, shower stalls, and a firing range, the other upward to an interrogation room and two facing rows of cells, none presently occupied. Somewhere nearby, a radio talk show is playing at a level that seems too loud for a peaceful morning.

Bobby Dulac opens the unmarked door and enters, with us on his shiny heels, the ready room he has just left. A rank of filing cabinets stands against the wall to our right, beside them a beat-up wooden table on which sit neat stacks of papers in folders and a transistor radio, the source of the discordant noise. From the nearby studio of KDCU-AM, Your Talk Voice in the Coulee Country, the entertainingly rabid George Rathbun has settled into *Badger Barrage*, his popular morning broadcast. Good old George sounds too loud for the occasion no matter how low you dial the volume; the guy is just flat-out *noisy*—that's part of his appeal.

Set in the middle of the wall directly opposite us is a closed door with a dark pebble-glass window on which has been painted DALE GILBERTSON, CHIEF OF POLICE. Dale will not be in for another half hour or so.

Two metal desks sit at right angles to each other in the corner to our left, and from the one that faces us, Tom Lund, a fair-haired officer of roughly his partner's age but without his appearance of having been struck gleaming from the mint five minutes before, regards the bag tweezed between two fingers of Bobby Dulac's right hand.

"All right," Lund says. "Okay. The latest installment."

"You thought maybe the Thunder Five was paying us another social call? Here. I don't want to read the damn thing."

Not deigning to look at the newspaper, Bobby sends the new day's issue of *La Riviere Herald* sailing in a flat, fast arc across ten feet of wooden floor with an athletic snap of his wrist, spins rightward, takes a long stride, and positions himself in front of the wooden table a moment before Tom Lund fields his throw. Bobby glares at the two names and various details scrawled on the long chalkboard hanging on the wall behind the table. He is not pleased, Bobby Dulac; he looks as though he might burst out of his uniform through the sheer force of his anger.

Fat and happy in the KDCU studio, George Rathbun yells, "Caller, gimme a break, willya, and get your prescription fixed! Are we talking about the same game here? Caller—"

"Maybe Wendell got some sense and decided to lay off," Tom Lund says.

*"Wendell,"* Bobby says. Because Lund can see only the sleek, dark back of his head, the little sneering thing he does with his lip wastes motion, but he does it anyway.

"Caller, let me ask you this one question, and in all sincerity, I want you to be honest with me. Did you actually *see* last night's game?"

"I didn't know *Wendell* was a big buddy of yours," Bobby says. "I didn't know you ever got as far south as La Riviere. Here I was thinking your idea of a big night out was a pitcher of beer and trying to break a hundred at the Arden Bowl-A-

Drome, and now I find out you hang out with newspaper reporters in college towns. Probably get down and dirty with the Wisconsin Rat, too, that guy on KWLA. Do you pick up a lot of punk babes that way?"

The caller says he missed the first inning on account of he had to pick up his kid after a special counseling session at Mount Hebron, but he sure saw everything after that.

"Did I say Wendell Green was a friend of mine?" asks Tom Lund. Over Bobby's left shoulder he can see the first of the names on the chalkboard. His gaze helplessly focuses on it. "It's just, I met him after the Kinderling case, and the guy didn't seem so bad. Actually, I kind of liked him. *Actually,* I wound up feeling sorry for him. He wanted to do an interview with Hollywood, and Hollywood turned him down flat."

Well, naturally he saw the extra innings, the hapless caller says, that's how he knows Pokey Reese was safe.

"And as for the Wisconsin Rat, I wouldn't know him if I saw him, and I think that so-called music he plays sounds like the worst bunch of crap I ever heard in my life. How did that scrawny pasty-face creep get a radio show in the first place? On the *college station*? What does that tell you about our wonderful UW-La Riviere, Bobby? What does it say about our whole society? Oh, I forgot, you like that shit."

"No, I like 311 and Korn, and you're so out of it you can't tell the difference between Jonathan Davis and Dee Dee Ramone, but forget about that, all right?" Slowly, Bobby Dulac turns around and smiles at his partner. "Stop stalling." His smile is none too pleasant.

"*I'm* stalling?" Tom Lund widens his eyes in a parody of wounded innocence. "Gee, was it me who fired the paper across the room? No, I guess not."

"If you never laid eyes on the Wisconsin Rat, how come you know what he looks like?"

"Same way I know he has funny-colored hair and a pierced nose. Same way I know he wears a beat-to-shit black leather jacket day in, day out, rain or shine."

Bobby waited.

"By the way he sounds. People's voices are full of *information*. A guy says, Looks like it'll turn out to be a nice day, he tells you his whole life story. Want to know something else about Rat Boy? He hasn't been to the dentist in six, seven years. His teeth look like shit."

From within KDCU's ugly cement-block structure next to the brewery on Peninsula Drive, via the radio Dale Gilbertson donated to the station house long before either Tom Lund or Bobby Dulac first put on their uniforms, comes good old dependable George Rathbun's patented bellow of genial outrage, a passionate, inclusive uproar that for a hundred miles around causes breakfasting farmers to smile across their tables at their wives and passing truckers to laugh out loud:

"I swear, caller, and this goes for my last caller, too, and every single one of you out there, I love you *dearly*, that is the honest truth, I love you like my momma loved her *turnip patch*, but sometimes you people DRIVE ME CRAZY! Oh, boy. *Bottom of the eleventh inning, two outs!* Six–seven, *Brewers*! Men on second and third. Batter lines to short center field, Reese takes off from third, good throw to the plate, clean tag, *clean tag*. A BLIND MAN COULDA MADE THAT CALL!"

"Hey, I thought it was a good tag, and I only heard it on the radio," says Tom Lund.

Both men are stalling, and they know it.

"In fact," shouts the hands-down most popular Talk Voice of the Coulee Country, "let me go out on a *limb* here, boys and girls, let me make the following *recommendation*, okay? Let's replace every umpire at Miller Park, hey, every umpire in the *National League*, with BLIND MEN! You know what, my friends? I *guarantee* a sixty to seventy percent *improvement* in the accuracy of their calls. GIVE THE JOB TO THOSE WHO CAN HANDLE IT—THE BLIND!"

Mirth suffuses Tom Lund's bland face. That George Rathbun, man, he's a hoot. Bobby says, "Come on, okay?"

Grinning, Lund pulls the folded newspaper out of its wrapper and flattens it on his desk. His face hardens; without altering its shape, his grin turns stony. "Oh, no. Oh, hell."

"What?"

Lund utters a shapeless groan and shakes his head.

"Jesus. I don't even want to know." Bobby rams his hands into his pockets, then pulls himself perfectly upright, jerks his right hand free, and clamps it over his eyes. "I'm a blind guy, all right? Make me an umpire—I don't wanna be a cop anymore."

Lund says nothing.

"It's a headline? Like a banner headline? How bad is it?" Bobby pulls his hand away from his eyes and holds it suspended in midair.

"Well," Lund tells him, "it looks like Wendell didn't get some sense, after all, and he sure as hell didn't decide to lay off. I can't believe I said I liked the dipshit."

"Wake up," Bobby says. "Nobody ever told you law enforcement officers and journalists are on opposite sides of the fence?"

Tom Lund's ample torso tilts over his desk. A thick lateral crease like a scar divides his forehead, and his stolid cheeks burn crimson. He aims his finger at Bobby Dulac. "This is one thing that really *gets* me about you, Bobby. How long have you been here? Five, six months? Dale hired me four years ago, and when him and Hollywood put the cuffs on Mr. Thornberg *Kinderling*, which was the biggest case in this county for maybe thirty years, I can't claim any credit, but at least I pulled my weight. I helped put some of the pieces together."

"One of the pieces," Bobby says.

"I reminded Dale about the girl bartender at the Taproom, and Dale told Hollywood, and Hollywood talked to the girl, and that was a big, big piece. It helped get him. So don't you talk to me that way."

Bobby Dulac assumes a look of completely hypothetical contrition. "Sorry, Tom. I guess I'm kind of wound up and beat to shit at the same time." What he thinks is: *So you got a couple years on me and you once gave Dale this crappy little bit of information. So what? I'm a better cop than you'll ever be. How heroic were you last night, anyhow?*

At 11:15 the previous night, Armand "Beezer" St. Pierre and his fellow travelers in the Thunder Five had roared up from Nailhouse Row to surge into the police station and demand of its three occupants, each of whom had worked an eighteen-hour shift, exact details of the progress they were making on the issue that most concerned them all. What the hell was going on here? What about the third one, huh, what about Irma Freneau? Had they found her yet? Did these clowns have *anything,* or were they still just blowing smoke? You need help? Beezer roared. Then deputize us, we'll give you all the goddamn help you need and then some. A giant named Mouse had strolled smirking up to Bobby Dulac and kept on strolling, jumbo belly to six-pack belly, until Bobby was backed up against a filing cabinet, whereupon the giant Mouse mysteriously inquired, in a cloud of beer and marijuana, whether Bobby had ever dipped into the works of a gentleman named Jacques Derrida. When Bobby replied that he had never heard of the gentleman, Mouse said, "No shit, Sherlock," and stepped aside to glare at the names on the chalkboard. Half an hour later, Beezer, Mouse, and their companions were sent away unsatisfied, undeputized, but pacified, and Dale Gilbertson said he had to go home and get some sleep, but Tom ought to remain, just in case. The regular night men had both found excuses not to come in. Bobby said he would stay, too, no problem, Chief, which is why we find these two men in the station so early in the morning.

"Give it to me," says Bobby Dulac.

Lund picks up the paper, turns it around, and holds it out for Bobby to see: FISHERMAN STILL AT LARGE IN FRENCH LANDING AREA, reads the headline over an article that takes up three columns on the top left-hand side of the front page. The columns of type have been printed against a background of pale blue, and a black border separates them from the remainder of the page. Beneath the head, in smaller print, runs the line *Identity of Psycho Killer Baffles Police.* Underneath the subhead, a line in even smaller print attributes the article to *Wendell Green, with the support of the editorial staff.*

"The Fisherman," Bobby says. "Right from the start, your *friend* has his thumb up his butt. The Fisherman, the Fisherman, the Fisherman. If I all of a sudden turned into a fifty-foot ape and started stomping on buildings, would you call me King Kong?" Lund lowers the newspaper and smiles. "Okay," Bobby allows, "bad example. Say I held up a couple banks. Would you call me John Dillinger?"

"Well," says Lund, smiling even more broadly, "they say Dillinger's tool was so humungous, they put it in a jar in the Smithsonian. So . . ."

Tom Lund looks down and reads: " 'As the police in French Landing fail to discover any leads to the identity of the fiendish double murderer and sex criminal this reporter has dubbed "the Fisherman," the grim specters of fear, despair, and suspicion run increasingly rampant through the streets of that little town, and from there out into the farms and villages throughout French County, darkening by their touch every portion of the Coulee Country.' "

"Just what we need," Bobby says, "Jee-*zus*!" and in an instant has crossed the room and is leaning over Tom Lund's shoulder, reading the *Herald*'s front page with his hand resting on the butt of his Glock, as if ready to drill a hole in the article right here and now.

" 'Our traditions of trust and good neighborliness, our habit of extending warmth and generosity to all [*writes Wendell Green, editorializing like crazy*] are eroding daily under the corrosive onslaught of these dread emotions. Fear, despair, and suspicion are poisonous to the soul of communities large and small, for they turn neighbor against neighbor and make a mockery of civility.

" 'Two children have been foully murdered and their remains partially consumed. Now a third child has disappeared. Eight-year-old Amy St. Pierre and seven-year-old Johnny Irkenham fell victim to the passions of a monster in human form. Neither will know the happiness of adolescence or the satisfactions of adulthood. Their grieving parents will never know the grandchildren they would have cherished. The parents of Amy and Johnny's playmates shelter their children within the safety of their own homes, as do parents whose children never knew the deceased. As a result, summer play-groups and other programs for young children have been canceled in virtually every township and municipality in French County.

" 'With the disappearance of ten-year-old Irma Freneau seven days after the death of Amy St. Pierre and only three after that of Johnny Irkenham, public patience has grown dangerously thin. As this correspondent has already reported, Merlin Graasheimer, fifty-two, an unemployed farm laborer of no fixed abode, was set upon and beaten by an unidentified group of men in a Fountain side street late Tuesday evening. Another such epidose occurred in the early hours of Thursday morning, when Elvar Praetorious, thirty-six, a Swedish tourist traveling alone, was assaulted by three men, again unidentified, while asleep in La Riviere's Leif Eriksson Park. Graasheimer and Praetorious required only routine medical attention, but future incidents of vigilantism will almost certainly end more seriously.' "

Tom Lund looks down at the next paragraph, which describes the Freneau girl's abrupt disappearance from a Chase Street sidewalk, and pushes himself away from his desk.

Bobby Dulac reads silently for a time, then says, "You gotta hear this shit, Tom. This is how he winds up:

" 'When will the Fisherman strike again?

" 'For he will strike again, my friends, make no mistake.

" 'And when will French Landing's chief of police, Dale Gilbertson, do his duty and rescue the citizens of this county from the obscene savagery of the Fisherman and the understandable violence produced by his own inaction?' "

Bobby Dulac stamps to the middle of the room. His color has heightened. He inhales, then exhales, a magnificent quantity of oxygen. "How about the next time the Fisherman *strikes*," Bobby says, "how about he goes right up Wendell Green's flabby rear end?"

"I'm with you," says Tom Lund. "Can you believe that shinola? 'Understandable violence'? He's telling people it's okay to mess with anyone who looks suspicious!"

Bobby levels an index finger at Lund. "I personally am going to nail this guy. That *is* a promise. I'll bring him down, alive or dead." In case Lund may have missed the point, he repeats, "Personally."

Wisely choosing not to speak the words that first come to his mind, Tom Lund nods his head. The finger is still pointing. He says, "If you want some help with that, maybe you should talk to Hollywood. Dale didn't have no luck, but could be you'd do better."

Bobby waves this notion away. "No need. Dale and me . . . and you, too, of course, we got it covered. But I personally am going to get this guy. That is a guarantee." He pauses for a second. "Besides, Hollywood retired when he moved here, or did you forget?"

"Hollywood's too young to retire," Lund says. "Even in cop years, the guy is practically a baby. So you must be the next thing to a fetus."

And on their cackle of shared laughter, we float away and

out of the ready room and back into the sky, where we glide one block farther north, to Queen Street.

Moving a few blocks east we find, beneath us, a low, rambling structure that branches out from a central hub occupies, with its wide, rising breadth of lawn dotted here and there with tall oaks and maples, the whole of a block lined with bushy hedges in need of a good trim. Obviously an institution of some kind, the structure at first resembles a progressive elementary school in which the various wings represent classrooms without walls, the square central hub the dining room and administrative offices. When we drift downward, we hear George Rathbun's genial bellow rising toward us from several windows. The big glass front door swings open, and a trim woman in cat's-eye glasses comes out into the bright morning, holding a poster in one hand and a roll of tape in the other. She immmediately turns around and, with quick, efficient gestures, fixes the poster to the door. Sunlight reflects from a smoky gemstone the size of a hazlenut on the third finger of her right hand.

While she takes a moment to admire her work, we can peer over her crisp shoulder and see that the poster announces, in a cheerful burst of hand-drawn balloons, that TODAY IS STRAWBERRY FEST!!!, when the woman walks back inside, we take in the presence, in the portion of the entry visible just beneath the giddy poster, of two or three folded wheelchairs. Beyond the wheelchairs, the woman, whose chestnut hair has been pinned back into an architectural whorl, strides on her high-heeled pumps through a pleasant lobby with blond wooden chairs and matching tables strewn artfully with magazines, marches past a kind of unmanned guardpost or reception desk before a handsome fieldstone wall, and vanishes, with the trace of a skip, through a burnished door marked WILLIAM MAXTON, DiRECTOR.

What kind of school is this? Why is it open for business? Why is it putting on festivals, in the middle of July?

We could call it a graduate school, for those who reside here have graduated from every stage of their existences but the last, which they live out, day after day, under the careless stewardship of Mr. William "Chipper" Maxton, Director. This is the Maxton Elder Care Facility, once—in a more innocent time, and before the cosmetic renovations done in the mid-eighties—known as the Maxton Nursing Home, which was owned and managed by its founder, Herbert Maxton, Chipper's father. Herbert was a decent if wishy-washy man who, it is safe to say, would be appalled by some of the things the sole fruit of his loins gets up to. Chipper never wanted to take over "the family playpen," as he calls it, with its freight of "gummers," "zombies," "bed wetters," and "droolies," and after getting an accounting degree at UW–La Riviere (with hard-earned minors in promiscuity, gambling, and beer drinking), our boy accepted a position with the Madison, Wisconsin, office of the Internal Revenue Service, largely for the purpose of learning how to steal from the government undetected. Five years with the IRS taught him much that was useful, but when his subsequent career as a freelancer failed to match his ambitions, he yielded to his father's increasingly frail entreaties and threw in his lot with the undead and the droolies. With a certain grim relish, Chipper acknowledged that despite a woeful shortage of glamour, his father's business would at least provide him with the opportunity to steal from the clients and the government alike.

Let us flow in through the big glass doors, cross the handsome lobby (noting, as we do so, the mingled odors of air freshener and ammonia that pervade even the public areas of all such institutions), pass through the door bearing Chipper's name, and find out what that well-arranged young woman is doing here so early.

Beyond Chipper's door lies a windowless cubicle equipped with a desk, a coatrack, and a small bookshelf crowded with computer printouts, pamphlets, and flyers. A door stands open beside the desk. Through the opening, we see a much larger office, paneled in the same burnished wood as the director's door and containing leather chairs, a glass-topped coffee table, and an oatmeal-colored sofa. At its far end looms a vast desk untidily heaped with papers and so deeply polished it seems nearly to glow.

Our young woman, whose name is Rebecca Vilas, sits perched on the edge of this desk, her legs crossed in a particularly architectural fashion. One knee folds over the other, and the calves form two nicely molded, roughly parallel lines running down to the triangular tips of the black high-heeled pumps, one of which points to four o'clock and the other to six. Rebecca Vilas, we gather, has arranged herself to be seen, has struck a pose intended to be appreciated, though certainly not by us. Behind the cat's-eye glasses, her eyes look skeptical and amused, but we cannot see what has aroused these emotions. We assume that she is Chipper's secretary, and this assumption, too, expresses only half of the truth: as the ease and irony of her attitude imply, Ms. Vilas's duties have long extended beyond the purely secretarial. (We might speculate about the source of that nice ring she is wearing; as long as our minds are in the gutter, we will be right on the money.)

We float through the open door, follow the direction of Rebecca's increasingly impatient gaze, and find ourselves staring at the sturdy, khaki-clad rump of her kneeling employer, who has thrust his head and shoulders into a good-sized safe, in which we glimpse stacks of record books and a number of manila envelopes apparently stuffed with currency. A few bills flop out of these envelopes as Chipper pulls them from the safe.

"You did the sign, the poster thing?" he asks without turning around.

"Aye, aye, *mon capitaine*," says Rebecca Vilas. "And a splendid day it is we shall be havin' for the great occasion, too, as is only roight and proper." Her Irish accent is surprisingly good, if a bit generic. She has never been anywhere more exotic than Atlantic City, where Chipper used his frequent flier miles to escort her for five enchanted days two years before. She learned the accent from old movies.

"I hate Strawberry Fest," Chipper says, dredging the last of the envelopes from the safe. "The zombies' wives and children mill around all afternoon, cranking them up so we have to sedate them into comas just to get some peace. And if you want to know the truth, I *hate* balloons." He dumps the money onto the carpet and begins to sort the bills into stacks of various denominations.

"Only Oi was wonderin', in my simple country manner," says Rebecca, "why Oi should be requested to appear at the crack o' dawn on the grand day."

"Know what else I hate? The whole music thing. Singing zombies and that stupid deejay. Symphonic Stan with his big-band records, whoo boy, talk about thrills."

"I assume," Rebecca says, dropping the stage-Irish accent, "you want me to do something with that money before the action begins."

"Time for another journey to Miller." An account under a fictitious name in the State Provident Bank in Miller, forty miles away, receives regular deposits of cash skimmed from patients' funds intended to pay for extra goods and services. Chipper turns around on his knees with his hands full of money and looks up at Rebecca. He sinks back down to his heels and lets his hands fall into his lap. "Boy, do you have great legs. Legs like that, you ought to be famous."

"I thought you'd never notice," Rebecca says.

Chipper Maxton is forty-two years old. He has good teeth, all his hair, a wide, sincere face, and narrow brown eyes that always look a little damp. He also has two kids, Trey, nine, and Ashley, seven and recently diagnosed with ADD, a matter Chipper figures is going to cost him maybe two thousand a year in pills alone. And of course he has a wife, his life-partner, Marion, thirty-nine years of age, five foot five, and somewhere in the neighborhood of 190 pounds. In addition to these blessings, as of last night Chipper owes his bookie $13,000, the result of an unwise investment in the Brewers game George Rathbun is still bellowing about. He has noticed, oh, yes he has, Chipper has noticed Ms. Vilas's splendidly cantilevered legs.

"Before you go over there," he says, "I was thinking we could kind of stretch out on the sofa and fool around."

"Ah," Rebecca says. "Fool around how, exactly?"

"Gobble, gobble, gobble," Chipper says, grinning like a satyr.

"You romantic devil, you," says Rebecca, a remark that utterly escapes her employer. Chipper thinks he actually is being romantic.

She slides elegantly down from her perch, and Chipper pushes himself inelegantly upright and closes the safe door with his foot. Eyes shining damply, he takes a couple of thuggish, strutting strides across the carpet, wraps one arm around Rebecca Vilas's slender waist and with the other slides the fat manila envelopes onto the desk. He is yanking at his belt before he begins to pull Rebecca toward the sofa.

"So I can see him?" says clever Rebecca, who understands exactly how to turn her lover's brains to porridge . . .

. . . and before Chipper obliges her, we do the sensible thing and float out into the lobby, which is still empty. A corridor to the left of the reception desk takes us to two large, blond, glass-inset doors marked DAISY and BLUEBELL, the names of the wings to which they give entrance. Far down the gray length of BLUEBELL, a man in baggy coveralls dribbles ash from his cigarette onto the tiles over which he is dragging with exquisite slowness, a filthy mop. We move into DAISY.

The functional parts of Maxton's are a great deal less attractive than the public areas. Numbered doors line both sides of the corridor. Hand-lettered cards in plastic holders beneath the numerals give the names of the residents. Four doors along, a desk, at which a burly male attendant in an unclean white uniform sits dozing upright, faces the entrance to the men's and women's bathrooms—at Maxton's, only the most expensive rooms, those on the other side of the lobby, in Asphodel, provide anything but a sink. Dirty mop-swirls harden and dry all up and down the tiled floor, which stretches out before us to improbable length. Here, too, the walls and the air seem the same shade of gray. If we look closely at the edges of the hallway, at the juncture of the walls and the ceiling, we see spiderwebs, old stains, accumulations of grime. Pine-Sol, ammonia, urine, and worse scent the atmosphere. As an elderly lady in Bluebell Wing likes to say, when you live with a bunch of people who are old and incontinent, you never get far from the smell of caca.

The rooms themselves vary according to the conditions and capacities of their inhabitants. Since nearly everyone is asleep, we can glance into a few of these quarters. Here in D10, a single room two doors past the dozing aide, old Alice Weathers lies (snoring gently, dreaming of dancing in perfect partnership with Fred Astaire across a white marble floor) surrounded by so much of her former life that she must navigate past the chairs and end tables to maneuver from the door to her bed. Alice still possesses even more of her wits than she does her old furniture, and she cleans her room herself, immaculately. Next door in D12, two old farmers named Thorvaldson and Jesperson, who have not spoken to each other in years, sleep, separated by a thin curtain, in a bright clutter of family photographs and grandchildren's drawings.

Farther down the hallway, D18 presents a spectacle completely opposite to the clean, crowded jumble of D10, just as its inhabitant, a man known as Charles Burnside, could be considered the polar opposite of Alice Weathers. In D18, there are no end tables, hutches, overstuffed chairs, gilded mirrors, lamps, woven rugs, or velvet curtains: this barren room contains only a metal bed, a plastic chair, and a chest of drawers. No photographs of children and grandchildren stand atop the chest, and no crayon drawings of blocky houses and stick figures decorate the walls. Mr. Burnside has no interest in housekeeping, and a thin layer of dust covers the floor, the window sill, and the chest's bare top. D18 is bereft of history, empty of personality; it seems as brutal and soulless as a prison cell. A powerful smell of excrement contaminates the air.

For all the entertainment offered by Chipper Maxton and all the charm of Alice Weathers, it is Charles Burnside, "Burny," we have most come to see.

Now that you've read *The Talisman*, don't miss the #1 *New York Times* bestselling sequel:

# BLACK HOUSE

**"EXTRAORDINARY. . .
HARD TO PUT DOWN."
—*People* (Page-turner of the Week)**

Jack Sawyer is a retired Los Angeles homicide detective living in the small hamlet of Tamarak, Wisconsin. He has no recollection of the events twenty years ago that led him to a parallel universe called the Territories to save his mother from certain death. When a series of gruesome murders occur in western Wisconsin, Jack's buddy, the local chief of police, begs Jack to help the inexperienced force find the killer. As cryptic messages in Jack's waking dreams become increasingly impossible to ignore, he is drawn back to the Territories and to his own hidden past, where he must find the soul-strength to enter a terrifying house at the end of a deserted tract of forest—and to encounter the obscene and ferocious evils sheltered within it.

**"HUGELY PLEASURABLE. . .
*Black House* allows us to see two master craftsmen, each at the top of his game."
—*The Washington Post Book World***

# Murder on the Internet

# "A DARKLY ABSORBING READ . . .

*Black House* may open the door to a hellish world of madness, but essentially it's a story of heroes and their response to tragedy, not a story of tragedy itself. In that respect, it could be a tonic for the times."

—*Houston Chronicle*

"*Black House* has an ending that almost ensures yet another sequel. And I find myself sitting on the edge of my seat looking forward to taking on a sequel. Which is a fine testament to the literary skills of King and Straub, and the relentless narrative of *Black House*, surely one of the finest novels yet."

—*The Denver Post*

"Delightfully creepy . . . A thrilling epic packed with horrifying monsters and a surprisingly potent emotional payoff."

—*Entertainment Weekly*

"A dark and disturbing book. I loved it. . . . In addition to an addictive plot, the authors treat us to a unique narrative device that makes the reader part of the story. . . . The 'Territories' [is] a fantasy land that has become as real to lovers of the genre as Frank Baum's Oz and J.R.R. Tolkien's Middle Earth."

—MARK GRAHAM
*Rocky Mountain News*

*Please turn the page for more reviews. . . .*

## "IF YOU'RE A FAN OF EITHER AUTHOR'S HERNIA-INDUCING CHILLERS, THEN ROCK THIS <u>HOUSE</u>."
—*Maxim*

"The book's vivid, carefully detailed depiction of small-town life, its folksy, common-man characters confronted by supernatural evil, and even the plot's structure, which follows a group of characters as they band together for a life-and-death showdown against larger-than-life monsters, are all familiar tropes of King's novels. Straub's influence is felt mostly in the writing, which takes the kind of elegant, stylistic chances for which the author is known. . . . *Black House* reminds you that although King and Straub are best known for their abilities to tap into our collective nightmares, their true strength, and the quality that makes this novel so engrossing, lies in depicting ordinary situations with uncommon perception and understanding."
—*The Miami Herald*

"Fine fiction, elegantly crafted and exceptionally unnerving . . . What's left at the end is a profound hope that King and Straub won't take seventeen more years before thrilling us with the further adventures of Jack Sawyer."
—*The San Diego Union-Tribune*

# "ENGROSSING AND ENJOYABLE ... THE WRITING CRACKLES WITH LIFE."
—*Detroit Free Press*

"A brilliant and challenging dark fantasy that fans of both authors are going to love.... There's so much here to revel in, from expertly executed sequences of terror, awe, or passion, to some of the most wonderful characters to spring from a page in years, to a story whose energy is so high and craft so accomplished that most readers will wish it ran twice its great length. What is probably the most anticipated novel of the year turns out to be its most memorable to date, a high point in both the King and Straub canons."
—*Publishers Weekly* (boxed and starred review)

"From its foundation on up, [*Black House*] is a solid piece of popular storytelling."
—*San Francisco Chronicle*

"The kind of book you can get lost in, only to look up at 5 A.M. and realize you only have a couple of hours to sleep—that is, if you can get to sleep after some of the scenes."
—*The News-Star*

# BLACK
# HOUSE

# Stephen King
# Peter Straub

BALLANTINE BOOKS • NEW YORK

A Ballantine Book
Published by The Ballantine Publishing Group
Copyright © 2001 by Stephen King and Peter Straub

Permission Acknowledgments

*I CAN'T GET STARTED*, by Ira Gershwin and Vernon Duke
© 1935 (Renewed) Ira Gershwin Music and Chappell & Co.
All Rights o/b/o Ira Gershwin Music administered by WB Music Corp.
All Rights Reserved. Used by permission.
WARNER BROS. PUBLICATIONS U.S. INC., Miami, FL 33014

*QUEEN OF THE WORLD*, by Gary Louris, Tim O'Reagan, Bob Ezrin
© 2000 Warner-Tamerlane Publishing Corp. (BMI), Absinthe Music (BMI) & Under-Cut-
Music Publ. Co. (PRS)
All Rights o/b/o Absinthe Music administered by Warner-Tamerlane Publishing Corp.
All Rights Reserved. Used by permission.
WARNER BROS. PUBLICATIONS U.S. INC., Miami, FL 33014

*WHEN THE RED, RED ROBIN COMES BOB, BOB, BOBBIN' ALONG*
Written by Harry Woods © 1926, renewed
All rights controlled by Callicoon Music.
Used by permission. All rights reserved.

www.ballantinebooks.com

ISBN 0-345-44103-6

This edition published by arrangement with Random House, Inc.

Manufactured in the United States of America

First Ballantine Mass Market International Edition: May 2002

First Ballantine Mass Market Domestic Edition: September 2002

OPM  10  9  8  7  6  5  4  3  2  1

*For David Gernert and Ralph Vicinanza*

You take me to a place I never go,
You send me kisses made of gold,
I'll place a crown upon your curls,
All hail the Queen of the World!
                    —The Jayhawks

# RIGHT HERE
# AND NOW . . .

# PART ONE

# WELCOME TO
# COULEE COUNTY

# 1

Right here and now, as an old friend used to say, we are in the fluid present, where clear-sightedness never guarantees perfect vision. Here: about two hundred feet, the height of a gliding eagle, above Wisconsin's far western edge, where the vagaries of the Mississippi River declare a natural border. Now: an early Friday morning in mid-July a few years into both a new century and a new millennium, their wayward courses so hidden that a blind man has a better chance of seeing what lies ahead than you or I. Right here and now, the hour is just past six A.M., and the sun stands low in the cloudless eastern sky, a fat, confident yellow-white ball advancing as ever for the first time toward the future and leaving in its wake the steadily accumulating past, which darkens as it recedes, making blind men of us all.

Below, the early sun touches the river's wide, soft ripples with molten highlights. Sunlight glints from the tracks of the Burlington Northern Santa Fe Railroad running between the riverbank and the backs of the shabby two-story houses along County Road Oo, known as Nailhouse Row, the lowest point of the comfortable-looking little town extending uphill and eastward beneath us. At this moment in the Coulee Country, life seems to be holding its breath. The motionless air around us carries such remarkable purity and sweetness that you might imagine a man could smell a radish pulled out of the ground a mile away.

Moving toward the sun, we glide away from the river and over the shining tracks, the backyards and roofs of Nailhouse Row, then a line of Harley-Davidson motorcycles tilted on their kick-stands. These unprepossessing little houses were built, early in the century recently vanished, for the metal pourers, mold makers, and crate men employed by the Pederson Nail factory. On the grounds that working stiffs would be unlikely to complain about the flaws in their subsidized accommodations, they were constructed as cheaply as possible. (Pederson Nail, which had suffered multiple hemorrhages during the fifties, finally bled to death in 1963.) The waiting Harleys suggest that the factory hands have been replaced by a motorcycle gang. The uniformly ferocious appearance of the Harleys' owners, wild-haired, bushy-bearded, swag-bellied men sporting earrings, black leather jackets, and less than the full complement of teeth, would seem to support this assumption. Like most assumptions, this one embodies an uneasy half-truth.

The current residents of Nailhouse Row, whom suspicious locals dubbed the Thunder Five soon after they took over the houses along the river, cannot so easily be categorized. They have skilled jobs in the Kingsland Brewing Company, located just out of town to the south and one block east of the Mississippi. If we look to our right, we can see "the world's largest six-pack," storage tanks painted over with gigantic Kingsland Old-Time Lager labels. The men who live on Nailhouse Row met one another on the Urbana-Champaign campus of the University of Illinois, where all but one were undergraduates majoring in English or philosophy. (The exception was a resident in surgery at the UI-UC university hospital.) They get an ironic pleasure from being called the Thunder Five: the name strikes them as sweetly cartoonish. What they call themselves is "the Hegelian Scum." These gentlemen form an interesting crew, and we will make their acquaintance later on. For now, we have time only to note the hand-painted posters taped to the fronts of several houses, two lamp poles, and a couple of abandoned buildings. The posters say: FISHERMAN, YOU BETTER PRAY TO YOUR STINKING GOD WE DON'T CATCH YOU FIRST! REMEMBER AMY!

From Nailhouse Row, Chase Street runs steeply uphill between listing buildings with worn, unpainted facades the color of fog: the old Nelson Hotel, where a few impoverished residents lie sleeping, a blank-faced tavern, a tired shoe store displaying Red Wing workboots behind its filmy picture window, a few other dim buildings that bear no indication of their function and seem oddly dreamlike and vaporous. These structures have the air of failed resurrections, of having been rescued from the dark westward territory although they were still dead. In a way, that is precisely what happened to them. An ocher horizontal stripe, ten feet above the sidewalk on the facade of the Nelson Hotel and two feet from the rising ground on the opposed, ashen faces of the last two buildings, represents the high-water mark left behind by the flood of 1965, when the Mississippi rolled over its banks, drowned the railroad tracks and Nailhouse Row, and mounted nearly to the top of Chase Street.

Where Chase rises above the flood line and levels out, it widens and undergoes a transformation into the main street of French Landing, the town beneath us. The Agincourt Theater, the Taproom Bar & Grille, the First Farmer State Bank, the Samuel Stutz Photography Studio (which does a steady business in graduation photos, wedding pictures, and children's portraits) and shops, not the ghostly relics of shops, line its blunt sidewalks: Benton's Rexall drugstore, Reliable Hardware, Saturday Night Video, Regal Clothing, Schmitt's Allsorts Emporium, stores selling electronic equipment, magazines and greeting cards, toys, and athletic clothing featuring the logos of the Brewers, the Twins, the Packers, the Vikings, and the University of Wisconsin. After a few blocks, the name of the street changes to Lyall Road, and the buildings separate and shrink into one-story wooden structures fronted with signs advertising insurance offices and travel agencies; after that, the street becomes a highway that glides eastward past a 7-Eleven, the Reinhold T. Grauerhammer VFW Hall, a big farm-implement dealership known locally as Goltz's, and into a landscape of flat, unbroken fields. If we rise another hundred feet into the immaculate air and scan what lies beneath and ahead, we see kettle moraines, coulees, blunted hills furry with pines, loam-rich valleys invisible from ground level until you have come upon them, meandering rivers, miles-long patchwork fields, and little towns—one of them, Centralia, no more than a scattering of buildings around the intersection of two narrow highways, 35 and 93.

Directly below us, French Landing looks as though it had been evacuated in the middle of the night. No one moves along the sidewalks or bends to insert a key into one of the locks of the shop fronts along Chase Street. The angled spaces before the shops are empty of the cars and pickup trucks that will begin to appear, first by ones and twos, then in a mannerly little stream, an hour or two later. No lights burn behind the windows in the commercial buildings or the unpretentious houses lining the surrounding streets. A block north of Chase on Sumner Street, four matching red-brick buildings of two stories each house, in west-east order, the French Landing Public Library; the offices of Patrick J. Skarda, M.D., the local general practitioner, and Bell & Holland, a two-man law firm now run by Garland Bell and Julius Holland, the sons of its founders; the Heartfield & Son Funeral Home, now owned by a vast, funereal empire centered in St. Louis; and the French Landing Post Office.

Separated from these by a wide driveway into a good-sized parking lot at the rear, the building at the end of the block, where Sumner intersects with Third Street, is also of red brick and two stories high but longer than its immediate neighbors. Unpainted iron bars block the rear second-floor windows, and two of the four vehicles in the parking lot are patrol cars with light bars across their tops and the letters FLPD on their sides. The presence of police cars and barred windows seems incongruous in this rural fastness—what sort of crime can happen here? Nothing serious, surely; surely nothing worse than a little shoplifting, drunken driving, and an occasional bar fight.

As if in testimony to the peacefulness and regularity of small-town life, a red van with the words LA RIVIERE HERALD on its side panels drifts slowly down Third Street, pausing at nearly all of the mailbox stands for its driver to insert copies of the day's newspaper, wrapped in a blue plastic bag, into gray metal cylinders bearing the same words. When the van turns onto Sumner, where the buildings have mail slots instead of boxes, the route man simply throws the wrapped papers at the front doors. Blue parcels thwack against the doors of the police station, the funeral home, and the office buildings. The post office does not get a paper.

What do you know, lights *are* burning behind the front downstairs windows of the police station. The door opens. A tall, dark-haired young man in a pale blue short-sleeved uniform shirt, a Sam Browne belt, and navy trousers steps outside. The wide belt and the gold badge on Bobby Dulac's chest gleam in the fresh sunlight, and everything he is wearing, including the 9mm pistol strapped to his hip, seems as newly made as Bobby Dulac himself. He watches the red van turn left onto Second Street, and frowns at the rolled newspaper. He nudges it with the tip of a black, highly polished shoe, bending over just far enough to suggest that he is trying to read the headlines through the plastic. Evidently this technique does not work all that well. Still frowning, Bobby tilts all the way over and picks up the newspaper with unexpected delicacy, the way a mother cat picks up a kitten in need of relocation. Holding it a little distance away from his body, he gives a quick glance up and down Sumner Street, about-faces smartly, and steps back into the station. We, who in our curiosity have been steadily descending toward the interesting spectacle presented by Officer Dulac, go inside behind him.

A gray corridor leads past a blank door and a bulletin board with very little on it to two sets of metal stairs, one going down to a small locker room, shower stalls, and a firing range, the other upward to an interrogation room and two facing rows of cells, none presently occupied. Somewhere near, a radio talk show is playing at a level that seems too loud for a peaceful morning.

Bobby Dulac opens the unmarked door and enters, with us on his shiny heels, the ready room he has just left. A rank of filing cabinets stands against the wall to our right, beside them a beat-up wooden table on which sit neat stacks of papers in folders and a transistor radio, the source of the discordant noise. From the nearby studio of KDCU-AM, Your Talk Voice in the Coulee Country, the entertainingly rabid George Rathbun has settled into *Badger Barrage,* his popular morning broadcast. Good old George sounds too loud for the occasion no matter how low you dial the volume; the guy is just flat-out *noisy*—that's part of his appeal.

Set in the middle of the wall directly opposite us is a closed door with a dark pebble-glass window on which has been painted DALE GILBERTSON, CHIEF OF POLICE. Dale will not be in for another half hour or so.

Two metal desks sit at right angles to each other in the corner to our left, and from the one that faces us, Tom Lund, a fair-haired officer of roughly his partner's age but without his appearance of having been struck gleaming from the mint five minutes before, regards the bag tweezed between two fingers of Bobby Dulac's right hand.

"All right," Lund says. "Okay. The latest installment."

"You thought maybe the Thunder Five was paying us another social call? Here. I don't want to read the damn thing."

Not deigning to look at the newspaper, Bobby sends the new day's issue of the *La Riviere Herald* sailing in a flat, fast arc across ten feet of wooden floor with an athletic snap of his wrist, spins rightward, takes a long stride, and positions himself in front of the wooden table a moment before Tom Lund fields his throw. Bobby glares at the two names and various details scrawled on the long chalkboard hanging on the wall behind the table. He is not pleased, Bobby Dulac; he looks as though he might burst out of his uniform through the sheer force of his anger.

Fat and happy in the KDCU studio, George Rathbun yells, "Caller, gimme a break, willya, and get your prescription fixed! Are we talking about the same game here? Caller—"

"Maybe Wendell got some sense and decided to lay off," Tom Lund says.

*"Wendell,"* Bobby says. Because Lund can see only the sleek, dark back of his head, the little sneering thing he does with his lip wastes motion, but he does it anyway.

"Caller, let me ask you this one question, and in all sincerity, I want you to be honest with me. Did you actually *see* last night's game?"

"I didn't know *Wendell* was a big buddy of yours," Bobby says. "I didn't know you ever got as far south as La Riviere. Here I was thinking your idea of a big night out was a pitcher of beer and trying to break one hundred at the Arden Bowl-A-Drome, and now I find out you hang out with newspaper reporters in college towns. Probably get down and dirty with the Wisconsin Rat, too, that guy on KWLA. Do you pick up a lot of punk babes that way?"

The caller says he missed the first inning on account of he

had to pick up his kid after a special counseling session at Mount Hebron, but he sure saw everything after that.

"Did I say Wendell Green was a friend of mine?" asks Tom Lund. Over Bobby's left shoulder he can see the first of the names on the chalkboard. His gaze helplessly focuses on it. "It's just, I met him after the Kinderling case, and the guy didn't seem so bad. Actually, I kind of liked him. *Actually,* I wound up feeling sorry for him. He wanted to do an interview with Hollywood, and Hollywood turned him down flat."

Well, naturally he saw the extra innings, the hapless caller says, that's how he knows Pokey Reese was safe.

"And as for the Wisconsin Rat, I wouldn't know him if I saw him, and I think that so-called music he plays sounds like the worst bunch of crap I ever heard in my life. How did that scrawny pasty-face creep get a radio show in the first place? On the *college station*? What does that tell you about our wonderful UW–La Riviere, Bobby? What does it say about our whole society? Oh, I forgot, you like that shit."

"No, I like 311 and Korn, and you're so out of it you can't tell the difference between Jonathan Davis and Dee Dee Ramone, but forget about that, all right?" Slowly, Bobby Dulac turns around and smiles at his partner. "Stop stalling." His smile is none too pleasant.

"*I'm* stalling?" Tom Lund widens his eyes in a parody of wounded innocence. "Gee, was it me who fired the paper across the room? No, I guess not."

"If you never laid eyes on the Wisconsin Rat, how come you know what he looks like?"

"Same way I know he has funny-colored hair and a pierced nose. Same way I know he wears a beat-to-shit black leather jacket day in, day out, rain or shine."

Bobby waited.

"By the way he sounds. People's voices are full of *information.* A guy says, Looks like it'll turn out to be a nice day, he tells you his whole life story. Want to know something else about Rat Boy? He hasn't been to the dentist in six, seven years. His teeth look like shit."

From within KDCU's ugly cement-block structure next to the brewery on Peninsula Drive, via the radio Dale Gilbertson

donated to the station house long before either Tom Lund or
Bobby Dulac first put on their uniforms, comes good old dependable George Rathbun's patented bellow of genial outrage,
a passionate, inclusive uproar that for a hundred miles around
causes breakfasting farmers to smile across their tables at their
wives and passing truckers to laugh out loud:

"I swear, caller, and this goes for my last last caller, too, and
every single one of you out there, I love you *dearly,* that is the
honest truth, I love you like my momma loved her *turnip patch,*
but sometimes you people DRIVE ME CRAZY! Oh, boy. *Top
of the eleventh inning, two outs!* Six–seven, *Reds!* Men on second and third. Batter lines to short center field, Reese takes off
from third, good throw to the plate, clean tag, *clean tag.* A
BLIND MAN COULDA MADE THAT CALL!"

"Hey, I thought it was a good tag, and I only heard it on the
radio," says Tom Lund.

Both men are stalling, and they know it.

"In fact," shouts the hands-down most popular Talk Voice of
the Coulee Country, "let me go out on a *limb* here, boys and
girls, let me make the following *recommendation,* okay? Let's
replace every umpire at Miller Park, hey, every umpire in the
*National League,* with BLIND MEN! You know what, my
friends? I *guarantee* a sixty to seventy percent *improvement* in
the accuracy of their calls. GIVE THE JOB TO THOSE WHO
CAN HANDLE IT—THE BLIND!"

Mirth suffuses Tom Lund's bland face. That George Rathbun, man, he's a hoot. Bobby says, "Come on, okay?"

Grinning, Lund pulls the folded newspaper out of its
wrapper and flattens it on his desk. His face hardens; without
altering its shape, his grin turns stony. "Oh, no. Oh, hell."

"What?"

Lund utters a shapeless groan and shakes his head.

"Jesus. I don't even want to know." Bobby rams his hands
into his pockets, then pulls himself perfectly upright, jerks his
right hand free, and clamps it over his eyes. "I'm a blind guy,
all right? Make me an umpire—I don't wanna be a cop anymore."

Lund says nothing.

"It's a headline? Like a banner headline? How bad is it?"

Bobby pulls his hand away from his eyes and holds it suspended in midair.

"Well," Lund tells him, "it looks like Wendell didn't get some sense, after all, and he sure as hell didn't decide to lay off. I can't believe I said I liked the dipshit."

"Wake up," Bobby says. "Nobody ever told you law enforcement officers and journalists are on opposite sides of the fence?"

Tom Lund's ample torso tilts over his desk. A thick lateral crease like a scar divides his forehead, and his stolid cheeks burn crimson. He aims a finger at Bobby Dulac. "This is one thing that really *gets* me about you, Bobby. How long have you been here? Five, six months? Dale hired me four years ago, and when him and Hollywood put the cuffs on Mr. Thornberg *Kinderling,* which was the biggest case in this county for maybe thirty years, I can't claim any credit, but at least I pulled my weight. I helped put some of the pieces together."

"One of the pieces," Bobby says.

"I reminded Dale about the girl bartender at the Taproom, and Dale told Hollywood, and Hollywood talked to the girl, and that was a big, big piece. It helped get him. So don't you talk to me that way."

Bobby Dulac assumes a look of completely hypothetical contrition. "Sorry, Tom. I guess I'm kind of wound up and beat to shit at the same time." What he thinks is: *So you got a couple years on me and you once gave Dale this crappy little bit of information, so what, I'm a better cop than you'll ever be. How heroic were you last night, anyhow?*

At 11:15 the previous night, Armand "Beezer" St. Pierre and his fellow travelers in the Thunder Five had roared up from Nailhouse Row to surge into the police station and demand of its three occupants, each of whom had worked an eighteen-hour shift, exact details of the progress they were making on the issue that most concerned them all. What the hell was going on here? What about the third one, huh, what about Irma Freneau? Had they found her yet? Did these clowns have *anything,* or were they still just blowing smoke? You need help? Beezer roared, Then deputize us, we'll give you all the goddamn help you need and then some. A giant named Mouse had strolled smirking up to Bobby Dulac and kept on strolling, jumbo belly to six-pack belly, until Bobby was backed up against a filing cabinet, whereupon the giant Mouse had mysteriously inquired, in a cloud of beer and marijuana, whether Bobby had ever dipped into the works of a gentleman named Jacques Derrida. When Bobby replied that he had never heard of the gentleman, Mouse said, "No shit, Sherlock," and stepped aside to glare at the names on the chalkboard. Half an hour later, Beezer, Mouse, and their companions were sent away unsatisfied, un-deputized, but pacified, and Dale Gilbertson said he had to go home and get some sleep, but Tom ought to remain, just in case. The regular night men had both found excuses not to come in. Bobby said he would stay, too, no problem, Chief, which is why we find these two men in the station so early in the morning.

"Give it to me," says Bobby Dulac.

Lund picks up the paper, turns it around, and holds it out for Bobby to see: FISHERMAN STILL AT LARGE IN FRENCH LANDING AREA, reads the headline over an article that takes up three columns on the top left-hand side of the front page. The columns of type have been printed against a background of pale blue, and a black border separates them from the remainder of the page. Beneath the head, in smaller print, runs the line *Identity of Psycho Killer Baffles Police.* Underneath the subhead, a line in even smaller print attributes the article to *Wendell Green, with the support of the editorial staff.*

"The Fisherman," Bobby says. "Right from the start, your *friend* has his thumb up his butt. The Fisherman, the Fisher-man, the Fisherman. If I all of a sudden turned into a fifty-foot ape and started stomping on buildings, would you call me King Kong?" Lund lowers the newspaper and smiles. "Okay," Bobby allows, "bad example. Say I held up a couple banks. Would you call me John Dillinger?"

"Well," says Lund, smiling even more broadly, "they say Dillinger's tool was so humongous, they put it in a jar in the Smithsonian. So . . ."

"Read me the first sentence," Bobby says.

Tom Lund looks down and reads: " 'As the police in French Landing fail to discover any leads to the identity of the fiendish double murderer and sex criminal this reporter has dubbed "the Fisherman," the grim specters of fear, despair, and suspicion run increasingly rampant through the streets of that little town, and from there out into the farms and villages throughout French County, darkening by their touch every portion of the Coulee Country.' "

"Just what we need," Bobby says. "Jee-*zus!*" And in an instant has crossed the room and is leaning over Tom Lund's shoulder, reading the *Herald*'s front page with his hand resting on the butt of his Glock, as if ready to drill a hole in the article right here and now.

" 'Our traditions of trust and good neighborliness, our habit of extending warmth and generosity to all [writes Wendell Green, editorializing like crazy], are eroding daily under the corrosive onslaught of these dread emotions. Fear, despair, and suspicion are poisonous to the soul of communities large and small, for they turn neighbor against neighbor and make a mockery of civility.

" 'Two children have been foully murdered and their remains partially consumed. Now a third child has disappeared. Eight-year-old Amy St. Pierre and seven-year-old Johnny Irkenham fell victim to the passions of a monster in human form. Neither will know the happiness of adolescence or the satisfactions of adulthood. Their grieving parents will never know the grandchildren they would have cherished. The parents of Amy and Johnny's playmates shelter their children within the safety of their own homes, as do parents whose children never knew the deceased. As a result, summer playgroups and other programs for young children have been canceled in virtually every township and municipality in French County.

" 'With the disappearance of ten-year-old Irma Freneau seven days after the death of Amy St. Pierre and only three after that of Johnny Irkenham, public patience has grown dangerously thin. As this correspondent has already reported, Merlin Graasheimer, fifty-two, an unemployed farm laborer of no fixed abode, was set upon and beaten by an unidentified group of men in a Grainger side street late Tuesday evening. Another such episode occurred in the early hours of Thursday morning, when Elvar Praetorious, thirty-six, a Swedish tourist traveling alone, was assaulted by three men, again unidentified, while asleep in La Riviere's Leif Eriksson Park. Graasheimer and Praetorious required only routine medical attention, but future incidents of vigilantism will almost certainly end more seriously.' "

Tom Lund looks down at the next paragraph, which describes the Freneau girl's abrupt disappearance from a Chase Street sidewalk, and pushes himself away from his desk.

Bobby Dulac reads silently for a time, then says, "You gotta hear this shit, Tom. This is how he winds up:

" 'When will the Fisherman strike again?

" 'For he will strike again, my friends, make no mistake.

" 'And when will French Landing's chief of police, Dale Gilbertson, do his duty and rescue the citizens of this county from the obscene savagery of the Fisherman and the understandable violence produced by his own inaction?' "

Bobby Dulac stamps to the middle of the room. His color has heightened. He inhales, then exhales a magnificent quantity of oxygen. "How about the next time the Fisherman *strikes,*" Bobby says, "how about he goes right up Wendell Green's flabby rear end?"

"I'm with you," says Tom Lund. "Can you believe that shinola? 'Understandable violence'? He's telling people it's okay to mess with anyone who looks suspicious!"

Bobby levels an index finger at Lund. "I personally am going to nail this guy. That *is* a promise. I'll bring him down, alive or dead." In case Lund may have missed the point, he repeats, "Personally."

Wisely choosing not to speak the words that first come to his mind, Tom Lund nods his head. The finger is still pointing. He says, "If you want some help with that, maybe you should talk to Hollywood. Dale didn't have no luck, but could be you'd do better."

Bobby waves this notion away. "No need. Dale and me . . . and you, too, of course, we got it covered. But I personally am going to get this guy. That is a guarantee." He pauses for a second. "Besides, Hollywood retired when he moved here, or did you forget?"

"Hollywood's too young to retire," Lund says. "Even in cop years, the guy is practically a baby. So you must be the next thing to a fetus."

And on their cackle of shared laughter, we float away and out of the ready room and back into the sky, where we glide one block farther north, to Queen Street.

• • •

Moving a few blocks east we find, beneath us, a low, rambling structure branching out from a central hub that occupies, with its wide, rising breadth of lawn dotted here and there with tall oaks and maples, the whole of a block lined with bushy hedges in need of a good trim. Obviously an institution of some kind, the structure at first resembles a progressive elementary school in which the various wings represent classrooms without walls, the square central hub the dining room and administrative offices. When we drift downward, we hear George Rathbun's genial bellow rising toward us from several windows. The big glass front door swings open, and a trim woman in cat's-eye glasses comes out into the bright morning, holding a poster in one hand and a roll of tape in the other. She immediately turns around and, with quick, efficient gestures, fixes the poster to the door. Sunlight reflects from a smoky gemstone the size of a hazelnut on the third finger of her right hand.

While she takes a moment to admire her work, we can peer over her crisp shoulder and see that the poster announces, in a cheerful burst of hand-drawn balloons, that TODAY IS STRAWBERRY FEST!!!; when the woman walks back inside, we take in the presence, in the portion of the entry visible just beneath the giddy poster, of two or three folded wheelchairs. Beyond the wheelchairs, the woman, whose chestnut hair has been pinned back into an architectural whorl, strides on her high-heeled pumps through a pleasant lobby with blond wooden chairs and matching tables strewn artfully with magazines, marches past a kind of unmanned guardpost or reception desk before a handsome fieldstone wall, and vanishes, with the trace of a skip, through a burnished door marked WILLIAM MAXTON, DIRECTOR.

What kind of school is this? Why is it open for business, why is it putting on festivals, in the middle of July?

We could call it a graduate school, for those who reside here have graduated from every stage of their existences but the last, which they live out, day after day, under the careless stewardship of Mr. William "Chipper" Maxton, Director. This is the Maxton Elder Care Facility, once—in a more innocent time, and before the cosmetic renovations done in the mid-eighties—known as the Maxton Nursing Home, which was owned and managed by its founder, Herbert Maxton, Chipper's father. Herbert was a decent if wishy-washy man who, it is safe to say, would be appalled by some of the things the sole fruit of his loins gets up to. Chipper never wanted to take over "the family playpen," as he calls it, with its freight of "gummers," "zombies," "bed wetters," and "droolies," and after getting an accounting degree at UW–La Riviere (with hard-earned minors in promiscuity, gambling, and beer drinking), our boy accepted a position with the Madison, Wisconsin, office of the Internal Revenue Service, largely for the purpose of learning how to steal from the government undetected. Five years with the IRS taught him much that was useful, but when his subsequent career as a freelancer failed to match his ambitions, he yielded to his father's increasingly frail entreaties and threw in his lot with the undead and the droolies. With a certain grim relish, Chipper acknowledged that despite a woeful shortage of glamour, his father's business would at least provide him with the opportunity to steal from the clients and the government alike.

Let us flow in through the big glass doors, cross the handsome lobby (noting, as we do so, the mingled odors of air freshener and ammonia that pervade even the public areas of all such institutions), pass through the door bearing Chipper's name, and find out what that well-arranged young woman is doing here so early.

Beyond Chipper's door lies a windowless cubicle equipped with a desk, a coatrack, and a small bookshelf crowded with computer printouts, pamphlets, and flyers. A door stands open beside the desk. Through the opening, we see a much larger office, paneled in the same burnished wood as the director's door and containing leather chairs, a glass-topped coffee table, and an oatmeal-colored sofa. At its far end looms a vast desk untidily heaped with papers and so deeply polished it seems nearly to glow.

Our young woman, whose name is Rebecca Vilas, sits perched on the edge of this desk, her legs crossed in a particularly architectural fashion. One knee folds over the other, and the calves form two nicely molded, roughly parallel lines running down to the triangular tips of the black high-heeled pumps, one of which points to four o'clock and the other to six. Rebecca Vilas, we gather, has arranged herself to be seen, has struck a pose intended to be appreciated, though certainly not by us. Behind the cat's-eye glasses, her eyes look skeptical and amused, but we cannot see what has aroused these emotions. We assume that she is Chipper's secretary, and this assumption, too, expresses only half of the truth: as the ease and irony of her attitude imply, Ms. Vilas's duties have long extended beyond the purely secretarial. (We might speculate about the source of that nice ring she is wearing; as long as our minds are in the gutter, we will be right on the money.)

We float through the open door, follow the direction of Rebecca's increasingly impatient gaze, and find ourselves staring at the sturdy, khaki-clad rump of her kneeling employer, who has thrust his head and shoulders into a good-sized safe, in which we glimpse stacks of record books and a number of manila envelopes apparently stuffed with currency. A few bills flop out of these envelopes as Chipper pulls them from the safe.

"You did the sign, the poster thing?" he asks without turning around.

"Aye, aye," says Rebecca Vilas. "And a splendid day it is we shall be havin' for the great occasion, too, as is only roight and proper." Her Irish accent is surprisingly good, if a bit generic. She has never been anywhere more exotic than Atlantic City, where Chipper used his frequent-flier miles to escort her for five enchanted days two years before. She learned the accent from old movies.

"I hate Strawberry Fest," Chipper says, dredging the last of the envelopes from the safe. "The zombies' wives and children mill around all afternoon, cranking them up so we have to sedate them into comas just to get some peace. And if you want to know the truth, I *hate* balloons." He dumps the money onto the carpet and begins to sort the bills into stacks of various denominations.

"Only Oi was wonderin', in me simple country manner," says Rebecca, "why Oi should be requested to appear at the crack o' dawn on the grand day."

"Know what else I hate? The whole music thing. Singing zombies and that stupid deejay. Symphonic Stan with his big-band records, whoo boy, talk about thrills."

"I assume," Rebecca says, dropping the stage-Irish accent,

"you want me to do something with that money before the action begins."

"Time for another journey to Miller." An account under a fictitious name in the State Provident Bank in Miller, forty miles away, receives regular deposits of cash skimmed from patients' funds intended to pay for extra goods and services. Chipper turns around on his knees with his hands full of money and looks up at Rebecca. He sinks back down to his heels and lets his hands fall into his lap. "Boy, do you have great legs. Legs like that, you ought to be famous."

"I thought you'd never notice," Rebecca says.

Chipper Maxton is forty-two years old. He has good teeth, all his hair, a wide, sincere face, and narrow brown eyes that always look a little damp. He also has two kids, Trey, nine, and Ashley, seven and recently diagnosed with ADD, a matter Chipper figures is going to cost him maybe two thousand a year in pills alone. And of course he has a wife, his life's partner, Marion, thirty-nine years of age, five foot five, and somewhere in the neighborhood of 190 pounds. In addition to these blessings, as of last night Chipper owes his bookie $13,000, the result of an unwise investment in the Brewers game George Rathbun is still bellowing about. He has noticed, oh, yes he has, Chipper has noticed Ms. Vilas's splendidly cantilevered legs.

"Before you go over there," he says, "I was thinking we could kind of stretch out on the sofa and fool around."

"Ah," Rebecca says. "Fool around how, exactly?"

"Gobble, gobble, gobble," Chipper says, grinning like a satyr.

"You romantic devil, you," says Rebecca, a remark that utterly escapes her employer. Chipper thinks he actually is being romantic.

She slides elegantly down from her perch, and Chipper pushes himself inelegantly upright and closes the safe door with his foot. Eyes shining damply, he takes a couple of thuggish, strutting strides across the carpet, wraps one arm around Rebecca Vilas's slender waist and with the other slides the fat manila envelopes onto the desk. He is yanking at his belt even before he begins to pull Rebecca toward the sofa.

"So can I see him?" says clever Rebecca, who understands exactly how to turn her lover's brains to porridge . . .

. . . and before Chipper obliges her, we do the sensible thing and float out into the lobby, which is still empty. A corridor to the left of the reception desk takes us to two large, blond, glass-inset doors marked DAISY and BLUEBELL, the names of the wings to which they give entrance. Far down the gray length of Bluebell, a man in baggy coveralls dribbles ash from his cigarette onto the tiles over which he is dragging, with exquisite slowness, a filthy mop. We move into Daisy.

The functional parts of Maxton's are a great deal less attractive than the public areas. Numbered doors line both sides of the corridor. Hand-lettered cards in plastic holders beneath the numerals give the names of the residents. Four doors along, a desk at which a burly male attendant in an unclean white uniform sits dozing upright faces the entrances to the men's and women's bathrooms—at Maxton's, only the most expensive rooms, those on the other side of the lobby, in Asphodel, provide anything but a sink. Dirty mop-swirls harden and dry all up and down the tiled floor, which stretches out before us to improbable length. Here, too, the walls and air seem the same shade of gray. If we look closely at the edges of the hallway, at the juncture of the walls and the ceiling, we see spiderwebs, old stains, accumulations of grime. Pine-Sol, ammonia, urine, and worse scent the atmosphere. As an elderly lady in Bluebell wing likes to say, when you live with a bunch of people who are old and incontinent, you never get far from the smell of caca.

The rooms themselves vary according to the conditions and capacities of their inhabitants. Since nearly everyone is asleep, we can glance into a few of these quarters. Here in D10, a single room two doors past the dozing aide, old Alice Weathers lies (snoring gently, dreaming of dancing in perfect partnership with Fred Astaire across a white marble floor) surrounded by so much of her former life that she must navigate past the chairs and end tables to maneuver from the door to her bed. Alice still possesses even more of her wits than she does her old furniture, and she cleans her room herself, immaculately. Next door in D12, two old farmers named Thorvaldson and Jesperson, who have not spoken to each other in years, sleep, separated by a thin curtain, in a bright clutter of family photographs and grandchildren's drawings.

Farther down the hallway, D18 presents a spectacle completely opposite to the clean, crowded jumble of D10, just as its inhabitant, a man known as Charles Burnside, could be considered the polar opposite of Alice Weathers. In D18, there are no end tables, hutches, overstuffed chairs, gilded mirrors, lamps, woven rugs, or velvet curtains: this barren room contains only a metal bed, a plastic chair, and a chest of drawers. No photographs of children and grandchildren stand atop the chest, and no crayon drawings of blocky houses and stick figures decorate the walls. Mr. Burnside has no interest in housekeeping, and a thin layer of dust covers the floor, the windowsill, and the chest's bare top. D18 is bereft of history, empty of personality; it seems as brutal and soulless as a prison cell. A powerful smell of excrement contaminates the air.

For all the entertainment offered by Chipper Maxton and all the charm of Alice Weathers, it is Charles Burnside, "Burny," we have most come to see.

# 2

Chipper's background we know. Alice arrived at Maxton's from a big house on Gale Street, the old part of Gale Street, where she outlived two husbands, raised five sons, and taught piano to four generations of French Landing children, none of whom ever became professional pianists but who all remember her fondly and think of her with affection. Alice came to this place as most people do, in a car driven by one of her children and with a mixture of reluctance and surrender. She had become too old to live alone in the big house in the old section of Gale Street; she had two grown, married sons who were kind enough, but she could not tolerate adding to their cares. Alice Weathers had spent her entire life in French Landing, and she had no desire to live anywhere else; in a way, she had always known that she would end her days in Maxton's, which though not at all luxurious was agreeable enough. On the day her son Martin had driven her over to inspect the place, she had realized that she knew at least half the people there.

Unlike Alice, Charles Burnside, the tall, skinny old man lying covered by a sheet before us in his metal bed, is not in full possession of his wits, nor is he dreaming of Fred Astaire. The veiny expanse of his bald, narrow head curves down to eyebrows like tangles of gray wire, beneath which, on either side of the fleshy hook of his nose, two narrow eyes shine at his north-facing window and the expanse of woods beyond Maxton's. Alone of all the residents of Daisy wing, Burny is not asleep. His eyes gleam, and his lips are wormed into a bizarre smile—but these details mean nothing, for Charles Burnside's mind may be as empty as his room. Burny has suffered from Alzheimer's disease for many years, and what looks like an aggressive form of pleasure could be no more than physical satisfaction of a very basic kind. If we had failed to guess that he was the origin of the stench in this room, the stains rising into the sheet that covers him make it clear. He has just evacuated, massively, into his bed, and the very least we can say about his response to the situation is that he does not mind a bit; no sir, shame is not a part of this picture.

But if—unlike delightful Alice—Burny no longer has a firm grasp on all of his marbles, neither is he a typical Alzheimer's patient. He might spend a day or two mumbling into his oatmeal like the rest of Chipper's zombies, then revitalize himself and join the living again. When not undead, he usually manages to get down the hall to the bathroom as necessary, and he spends hours either sneaking off on his own or patrolling the grounds, being unpleasant—in fact, offensive—to all and sundry. Restored from zombiehood, he is sly, secretive, rude, caustic, stubborn, foul-tongued, mean-spirited, and resentful, in other words—in the world according to Chipper—a blood brother to the other old men who reside at Maxton's. Some of the nurses, aides, and attendants doubt that Burny really does have Alzheimer's. They think he is faking it, opting out, lying low, deliberately making them work harder while he rests up and gathers his strength for yet another episode of unpleasantness. We can hardly blame them for their suspicion. If Burny has not been misdiagnosed, he is probably the only advanced Alzheimer's patient in the world to experience prolonged spells of remission.

In 1996, his seventy-eighth year, the man known as Charles Burnside arrived at Maxton's in an ambulance from La Riviere General Hospital, not in a vehicle driven by a helpful relative. He had appeared in the emergency room one morning, carrying two heavy suitcases filled with dirty clothing and loudly demanding medical attention. His demands were not coherent, but they were clear. He claimed to have walked a considerable distance to reach the hospital, and he wanted the hospital to take care of him. The distance varied from telling to telling— ten miles, fifteen miles, twenty-five. He either had or had not spent some nights sleeping in fields or by the side of the road. His general condition and the way he smelled suggested that he had been wandering the countryside and sleeping rough for perhaps a week. If he had once had a wallet, he had lost it on his journey. La Riviere General cleaned him up, fed him, gave him a bed, and tried to extract a history. Most of his statements trailed off into disjointed babble, but in the absence of any documents, at least these facts seemed reliable: Burnside had been a carpenter, framer, and plasterer in the area for many years, working for himself and general contractors. An aunt who lived in the town of Blair had given him a room.

*He had walked the eighteen miles from Blair to La Riviere, then?* No, he had started his walk somewhere else, he could not remember where, but it was ten miles away, no, twenty-five miles away, some town, and the people in that town were no-good jackass asswipes. *What was the name of his aunt?* Althea Burnside. *What were her address and telephone number?* No idea, couldn't remember. *Did his aunt have a job of any kind?* Yes, she was a full-time jackass asswipe. *But she had permitted him to live in her house?* Who? Permitted what? Charles Burnside needed no one's permission, he did what he damn well wanted. *Had his aunt ordered him out of her house?* Who are you talking about, you jackass asshole?

The admitting M.D. entered an initial diagnosis of Alzheimer's disease, pending the results of various tests, and the social worker got on the telephone and requested the address and telephone number of an Althea Burnside currently residing in Blair. The telephone company reported no listing for a person of that name in Blair, nor was she listed in Ettrick, Cochrane, Fountain, Sparta, Onalaska, Arden, La Riviere, or any other of the towns and cities within a fifty-mile radius. Widening her net, the social worker consulted the Records Office and the departments of Social Security, Motor Vehicle License, and Taxation for information about Althea and Charles Burnside. Of the two Altheas that popped up out of the system, one owned a diner in Butternut, far to the north of the state, and the other was a black woman who worked in a Milwaukee day-care center. Neither had any connection to the man in La Riviere General. The Charles Burnsides located by the records search were not the social worker's Charles Burnside. Althea seemed not to exist. Charles, it seemed, was one of those elusive people who go through life without ever paying taxes, registering to vote, applying for a Social Security card, opening a bank account, joining the armed forces, getting a driver's license, or spending a couple of seasons at the state farm.

Another round of telephone calls resulted in the elusive Charles Burnside's classification as a ward of the county and his admission to the Maxton Elder Care Facility until accommodation could be found at the state hospital in Whitehall. The ambulance conveyed Burnside to Maxton's at the expense of the generous public, and grumpy Chipper slammed him into Daisy wing. Six weeks later, a bed opened up in a ward at the state hospital. Chipper received the telephone call a few minutes after the day's mail brought him a check, drawn by an Althea Burnside on a bank in De Pere, for Charles Burnside's maintenance at his facility. Althea Burnside's address was a De Pere post office box. When the state hospital called, Chipper announced that in the spirit of civic duty he would be happy to continue Mr. Burnside's status at Maxton Elder Care. The old fellow had just become his favorite patient. Without putting Chipper through any of the usual shenanigans, Burny had doubled his contribution to the income stream.

For the next six years, the old man slid relentlessly into the darkness of Alzheimer's. If he was faking, he gave a brilliant performance. Down he went, through the descending way stations of incontinence, incoherence, frequent outbursts of anger, loss of memory, loss of the ability to feed himself, loss of personality. He dwindled into infancy, then into vacuity, and spent his days strapped into a wheelchair. Chipper mourned the inevitable loss of a uniquely cooperative patient. Then, in the summer of the year before these events, the amazing resuscitation occurred. Animation returned to Burny's slack face, and he began to utter vehement nonsense syllables. *Abbalah! Gorg! Munshun! Gorg!* He wanted to feed himself, he wanted to exercise his legs, to stagger around and reacquaint himself with his surroundings. Within a week, he was using English words to insist on wearing his own clothes and going to the bathroom by himself. He put on weight, gained strength, once again became a nuisance. Now, often in the same day, he passes back and forth between late-stage Alzheimer's lifelessness and a guarded, gleaming surliness so healthy in a man of eighty-five it might be called robust. Burny is like a man who went to Lourdes and experienced a cure but left before it was complete.

For Chipper, a miracle is a miracle. As long as the old creep stays alive, who cares if he is wandering the grounds or drooping against the restraining strap in his wheelchair?

We move closer. We try to ignore the stench. We want to see what we can glean from the face of this curious fellow. It was never a pretty face, and now the skin is gray and the cheeks are sunken potholes. Prominent blue veins wind over the gray scalp, spotted as a plover's egg. The rubbery-looking nose hooks slightly to the right, which adds to the impression of slyness and concealment. The wormy lips curl in a disquieting smile—the smile of an arsonist contemplating a burning building—that may after all be merely a grimace.

Here is a true American loner, an internal vagrant, a creature of shabby rooms and cheap diners, of aimless journeys resentfully taken, a collector of wounds and injuries lovingly fingered and refingered. Here is a spy with no cause higher than himself. Burny's real name is Carl Bierstone, and under this name he conducted, in Chicago, from his mid-twenties until the age of forty-six, a secret rampage, an unofficial war, during which he committed wretched deeds for the sake of the pleasures they afforded him. Carl Bierstone is Burny's great secret, for he cannot allow anyone to know that this former incarnation, this earlier self, still lives inside his skin. Carl Bierstone's awful pleasures, his foul toys, are also Burny's, and he must keep them hidden in the darkness, where only he can find them.

So is that the answer to Chipper's miracle? That Carl Bierstone found a way to creep out through a seam in Burny's zombiedom and assume control of the foundering ship? The human soul contains an infinity of rooms, after all, some of them vast, some no bigger than a broom closet, some locked, some few imbued with a radiant light. We bow closer to the veiny scalp, the wandering nose, the wire-brush eyebrows; we lean deeper into the stink to examine those interesting eyes. They are like black neon; they glitter like moonlight on a sodden riverbank. All in all, they look unsettlingly gleeful, but not particularly human. Not much help here.

Burny's lips move: he is still smiling, if you can call that rictus a smile, but he has begun to whisper. What is he saying?

*. . . dey are gowering in their bloody holes and govering their eyes, dey are whimbering in derror, my boor loss bab-*

*bies. . . . No, no, dat won't help, will it? Ah, zee de engynes, yezz, oh dose beeyoodiful beeyoodiful engynes, whad a zight, the beeyoodiful engynes againzt de vire, how they churrn, how dey churrn and burrn. . . . I zee a hole, yez yez dere id iz oho zo brighd around de etches zo folded back . . .*

Carl Bierstone may be reporting in, but his babble is not of much help. Let us follow the direction of Burny's mud-glitter gaze in hopes that it might give us a hint as to what has so excited the old boy. Aroused, too, as we observe from the shape beneath the sheet. He and Chipper seem to be in sync here, since both are standing at the ready, except that instead of the benefit of Rebecca Vilas's expert attentions, Burny's only stimulation is the view through his window.

The view hardly measures up to Ms. Vilas. Head slightly elevated upon a pillow, Charles Burnside looks raptly out over a brief expanse of lawn to a row of maple trees at the beginning of an extensive woods. Farther back tower the great, leafy heads of oaks. A few birch trunks shine candlelike in the inner darkness. From the height of the oaks and the variety of the trees, we know that we are regarding a remnant of the great climax forest that once blanketed this entire part of the country. Like all of the ancient forest's traces, the woods extending north and east from Maxton's speak of profound mysteries in a voice nearly too deep to be heard. Beneath its green canopy, time and serenity embrace bloodshed and death; violence roils on unseen, constantly, absorbed into every aspect of a hushed landscape that never pauses but moves with glacial lack of haste. The spangled, yielding floor covers millions of scattered bones in layer upon layer; all that grows and thrives here thrives on rot. Worlds within worlds churn, and great, systematic universes hum side by side, each ignorantly bringing abundance and catastrophe upon its unguessed-at neighbors.

Does Burny contemplate these woods, is he enlivened by what he sees in them? Or, for that matter, is he in fact still asleep, and does Carl Bierstone caper behind Charles Burnside's peculiar eyes?

Burny whispers, *Fogzes down fogzhulls, radz in radhulls, hyenaz over embdy stomachs wail, oho aha dis iz mozt-mozt gladzome my frenz, more an more de liddle wunz drudge drudge drudge oho on bledding foodzies . . .*

Let's blow this pop stand, okay?

Let's sail away from old Burny's ugly mouth—enough is enough. Let us seek the fresh air and fly north, over the woods. Foxes down foxholes and rats in ratholes may be wailing, true, that's how it works, but we are not about to find any starving hyenas in western Wisconsin. Hyenas are always hungry anyhow. No one feels sorry for them, either. You'd have to be a real bleeding heart to pity a creature that does nothing but skulk around the periphery of other species until the moment when, grinning and chuckling, it can plunder their leftovers. Out we go, right through the roof.

East of Maxton's, the woods carpet the ground for something like a mile or two before a narrow dirt road curves in from Highway 35 like a careless parting in a thick head of hair. The woods continue for another hundred yards or so, then yield to a thirty-year-old housing development consisting of two streets. Basketball hoops, backyard swing sets, tricycles, bicycles, and vehicles by Fisher-Price clutter the driveways of the modest houses on Schubert and Gale. The children who will make use of them lie abed, dreaming of cotton candy, puppy dogs, home runs, excursions to distant territories, and other delightful infinitudes; also asleep are their anxious parents, doomed to become even more so after reading Wendell Green's contribution to the front page of the day's *Herald*.

Something catches our eye—that narrow dirt road curving into the woods from Highway 35's straightaway. More a lane than an actual road, its air of privacy seems at odds with its apparent uselessness. The lane loops off into the woods and, three-fourths of a mile later, comes to an end. What is its point, what is it for? From our height above the earth, the track resembles a faint line sketched by a No. 4 pencil—you practically need an eagle's eye to see it at all—but someone went to considerable effort to draw this line through the woods. Trees had to be cut and cleared, stumps to be pried from the ground. If one man did it, the work would have taken months of sweaty, muscle-straining labor. The result of all that inhuman effort has the remarkable property of *concealing* itself, of evading the eye, so that it fades away if attention wanders, and must be located again. We might think of dwarfs and secret dwarf mines, the path to a dragon's hidden cache of gold—a treasure so safe-guarded that access to it has been camouflaged by a magic spell. No, dwarf mines, dragon treasures, and magic spells are too childish, but when we drop down for a closer examination, we see that a weathered NO TRESPASSING sign stands at the beginning of the lane, proof that something is being guarded, even if it is merely privacy.

Having noticed the sign, we look again at the end of the lane. In the darkness under the trees down there, one area seems murkier than the rest. Even as it shrinks back into the gloom, this area possesses an unnatural solidity that distinguishes it from the surrounding trees. Aha oho, we say to ourselves in an echo of Burny's gibberish, what have we here, a wall of some kind? It seems that featureless. When we reach the midpoint in the curve of the lane, a triangular section of darkness all but obscured by the treetops abruptly defines itself as a peaked roof. Not until we are nearly upon it does the entire structure move into definition as a three-story wooden house, oddly shambling in structure, with a sagging front porch. This house has clearly stood empty for a long time, and after taking in its eccentricity, the first thing we notice is its inhospitability to new tenants. A second NO TRESPASSING sign, leaning sideways at an improbable angle against a newel post, merely underlines the impression given by the building itself.

The peaked roof covers only the central section. To the left, a two-story extension retreats back into the woods. On the right, the building sprouts additions like outsized sheds, more like growths than afterthoughts. In both senses of the word, the building looks unbalanced: an off-kilter mind conceived it, then relentlessly brought it into off-center being. The intractable result deflects inquiry and resists interpretation. An odd, mono-lithic invulnerability emanates from the bricks and boards, despite the damage done by time and weather. Obviously built in search of seclusion, if not isolation, the house seems still to demand them.

Oddest of all, from our vantage point the house appears to have been painted a uniform black—not only the boards, but every inch of the exterior, the porch, the trim, the rain gutters, even the windows. Black, from top to bottom. And that cannot be possible; in this guileless, good-hearted corner of the world, not even the most crazily misanthropic builder would turn his house into its own shadow. We float down to just above ground level and move nearer along the narrow lane . . .

When we come close enough for reliable judgment, which is uncomfortably close, we find that misanthropy can go further than we had supposed. The house is not black now, but it used to be. What it has faded into makes us feel that we might have been too critical about the original color. The house has become the leaden gray-black of thunderheads and dismal seas and the hulls of wrecked ships. Black would be preferable to this utter lifelessness.

We may be certain that very few of the adults who live in the nearby development, or any adults in French Landing or the surrounding towns, have defied the admonition on 35 and ventured up the narrow lane. Almost none so much as notice the sign anymore; none of them know of the existence of the black house. We can be just as certain, however, that a number of their children have explored the lane, and that some of those children wandered far enough to come upon the house. They would have seen it in a way their parents could not, and what they saw would have sent them racing back toward the highway.

The black house seems as out of place in western Wisconsin as a skyscraper or a moated palace. In fact, the black house would be an anomaly anywhere in our world, except perhaps as a "Haunted Mansion," a "Castle of Terrors," in an amusement park, where its capacity to repel ticket buyers would put it out of business within a week. Yet in one specific way it might remind us of the dim buildings along the ascent of Chase Street into respectability from the riverbank and Nailhouse Row. The shabby Nelson Hotel, the obscure tavern, the shoe store, and the others, marked with the horizontal stripe drawn by the river's grease pencil, share the same eerie, dreamlike, half-unreal flavor that saturates the black house.

At this moment in our progress—and through everything that follows—we would do well to remember that this strange flavor of the dreamlike and slightly unnatural is characteristic of borderlands. It can be detected in every seam between one specific territory and another, however significant or insignificant the border in question. Borderlands places are different from other places; they are *borderish*.

Say you happen to be driving for the first time through a semirural section of Oostler County in your home state, on your way to visit a recently divorced friend of the opposite sex who has abruptly and, you think, unwisely decamped to a small town in adjacent Orelost County. On the passenger seat beside you, atop a picnic basket containing two bottles of a superior white Bordeaux held tightly in place by various gourmet goodies in exquisite little containers, lies a map carefully folded to expose the relevant area. You may not know your exact location, but you are on the right road and making good time.

Gradually, the landscape alters. The road veers around a nonexistent berm, then begins winding through inexplicable curves; on either side, the trees slouch; beneath their twisted boughs, the intermittent houses grow smaller and seedier. Ahead, a three-legged dog squirms through a hedge and barrels snarling toward your right front tire. A crone wearing a teensy straw hat and what appears to be a shroud glances up red-eyed from a listing porch swing. Two front yards along, a little girl costumed in dirty pink gauze and a foil crown flaps a glittery, star-headed wand over a heap of burning tires. Then a rectangular placard bearing the legend WELCOME TO ORELOST COUNTY glides into view. Soon the trees improve their posture and the road straightens out. Released from anxieties barely noticed until they were gone, you nudge the accelerator and hasten toward your needy friend.

Borderlands taste of unruliness and distortion. The grotesque, the unpredictable, and the lawless take root in them and luxuriate. The central borderlands flavor is of *slippage*. And while we are in a setting of wondrous natural beauty, we have also been traveling over a natural borderland, delineated by a great river and defined by other, lesser rivers, wide glacial moraines, limestone cliffs, and valleys that remain invisible, like the black house, until you turn the right corner and meet them face to face.

Have you ever seen a furious old wreck in worn-out clothes who pushes an empty shopping cart down deserted streets and

rants about a "fushing feef"? Sometimes he wears a baseball
cap, sometimes a pair of sunglasses with one cracked lens.

Have you ever moved frightened into a doorway and
watched a soldierly man with a zigzag lightning-bolt scar on
one side of his face storm into a drunken mob and discover,
lying spread-eagled in death on the ground, a boy, his head
smashed and his pockets turned out? Have you seen the anger
and the pity blaze in that man's mutilated face?

These are signs of *slippage.*

Another lies concealed below us on the outskirts of French
Landing, and despite the terror and heartbreak that surround
this sign, we have no choice but to stand in witness before it.
By our witness, we shall do it honor, to the measure of our individual capabilities; by being witnessed, by offering its testimony to our mute gaze, it will repay us in measure far greater.

We are back in midair, and spread out—we could say,
*spread-eagled* out—beneath us French County sprawls like a
topographical map. The morning sunlight, stronger now, glows
on green rectangular fields and dazzles off the lightning rods
rising from the tops of barns. The roads look clean. Molten
pools of light shine from the tops of the few cars drifting toward
town along the edges of the fields. Holsteins nudge pasture
gates, ready for the confinement of their stanchions and the
morning's date with the milking machine.

At a safe distance from the black house, which has already
given us an excellent example of slippage, we are gliding eastward, crossing the long straight ribbon of Eleventh Street and
beginning a journey into a transitional area of scattered houses
and small businesses before Highway 35 cuts through actual
farmland. The 7-Eleven slips by, and the VFW hall, where the
flagpole will not display Old Glory for another forty-five minutes. In one of the houses set back from the road, a woman
named Wanda Kinderling, the wife of Thornberg Kinderling, a
wicked and foolish man serving a life sentence in a California
prison, awakens, eyes the level of the vodka in the bottle on
her bedside table, and decides to postpone breakfast for another hour. Fifty yards along, gleaming tractors in military
rows face the giant steel-and-glass bubble of Ted Goltz's farm-
implement dealership, French County Farm Equipment, where
a decent, troubled husband and father named Fred Marshall,

whom we shall be meeting before long, will soon report for
work.

Beyond the showy glass bubble and the asphalt sea of
Goltz's parking lot, a half mile of stony, long-neglected field
eventually degenerates into bare earth and spindly weeds. At
the end of a long, overgrown turn-in, what seems to be a pile of
rotting lumber stands between an old shed and an antique gas
pump. This is our destination. We glide toward the earth. The
heap of lumber resolves into a leaning, dilapidated structure on
the verge of collapse. An old tin Coca-Cola sign pocked with
bullet holes tilts against the front of the building. Beer cans and
the milkweed of old cigarette filters litter the scrubby ground.
From within comes the steady, somnolent buzz of a great many
flies. We wish to retreat into the cleansing air and depart. The
black house was pretty bad; in fact, it was terrible, but
this . . . this is going to be worse.

One secondary definition of *slippage* is: the feeling that
things in general have just gotten, or very shortly will get,
worse.

The ruined boxcar-shaped shack before us used to house a
comically ill-run and unsanitary establishment called Ed's Eats
& Dawgs. From behind an eternally messy counter, a chortling
350-pound mass of blubber named Ed Gilbertson once served
up greasy, overdone hamburgers, baloney-and-mayonnaise
sandwiches ornamented with black thumbprints, and oozing
ice-cream cones to a small, undiscriminating clientele, mostly
local children who arrived on bicycles. Now long deceased, Ed
was one of the numerous uncles of French Landing's chief of
police, Dale Gilbertson, and a good-hearted slob and dimwit of
great local renown. His cook's apron was of an indescribable
filthiness; the state of his hands and fingernails would have
brought any visiting health inspector to the verge of nausea; his
utensils might as well have been cleaned by cats. Immediately
behind the counter, tubs of melting ice cream cooked in the heat
from the crusted griddle. Overhead, limp flypaper ribbons hung
invisible within the fur of a thousand fly corpses. The unlovely
truth is that for decades Ed's Eats permitted generation upon
generation of microbes and germs to multiply unchecked,
swarming from floor, counter, and griddle—not hesitating to
colonize Ed himself!—to spatula, fork, and the unwashed ice-

cream scoop, thence into the horrible food, finally into the mouths and guts of the kids who ate that stuff, plus those of the occasional mother.

Remarkably, no one ever died from eating at Ed's, and after a long-overdue heart attack felled its proprietor one day when he mounted a stool for the purpose of finally tacking up a dozen new strips of flypaper, nobody had the heart to raze his little shack and clear away the rubble. For twenty-five years, under the shelter of darkness its rotting shell has welcomed romantic teenage couples, as well as gatherings of boys and girls in need of a secluded place to investigate for the first time in recorded history, or so it seemed to them, the liberation of drunkenness.

The rapt buzzing of the flies tells us that whatever we might be about to witness within this ruin will be neither a pair of spent young lovers nor a few silly, passed-out kids. That soft, greedy uproar, inaudible from the road, declares the presence of ultimate things. We could say that it represents a kind of portal.

We enter. Mild sunlight filtering in through gaps in the eastern wall and the battered roof paints luminous streaks across the gritty floor. Feathers, dust, eddy and stir over animal tracks and the dim impressions left by many long-gone shoes. Threadbare army-surplus blankets speckled with mold lie crumpled against the wall to our left; a few feet away, discarded beer cans and flattened cigarette ends surround a kerosene-burning hurricane lamp with a cracked glass housing. The sunlight lays warm stripes over crisp footprints advancing in a wide curve around the remains of Ed's appalling counter and into the vacancy formerly occupied by the stove, a sink, and a rank of storage shelves. There, in what once was Ed's sacred domain, the footprints vanish. Some ferocious activity has scattered the dust and grit, and something that is not an old army blanket, though we wish it were, lies disarrayed against the rear wall, half in, half out of a dark, irregular pool of tacky liquid. Delirious flies hover and settle upon the dark pool. In the far corner, a rust-colored mongrel with quill-like hair gets its teeth into the knuckle of meat and bone protruding from the white object held between its front paws. The white object is a running shoe, a sneaker. A New Balance sneaker, to be exact. To be more exact, a child's New Balance sneaker, size 5.

We want to invoke our capacity for flight and get the hell out of here. We want to float through the unresisting roof, to regain the harmless air, but we cannot, we must bear witness. An ugly dog is chewing on a child's severed foot while making every effort to extract the foot from the white New Balance sneaker. The mongrel's scrawny back arches down and extends, the quilled shoulders and narrow head drop, the bony front legs rigidly clamp the prize, tug tug tug, but the sneaker's laces are tied—too bad for the mutt.

As for the something that is not an old army-surplus blanket, beyond a swirl of dusty tracks and furrows, at the floor's far edge, its pale form lies flattened and face-up on the floor, its top half extending out of the dark pool. One arm stretches limply out into the grit; the other props upright against the wall. The fingers of both hands curl palmward. Blunt, strawberry-blond hair flops back from the small face. If the eyes and mouth display any recognizable expression, it is that of mild surprise. This is an accident of structure; it means nothing, for the configuration of this child's face caused her to look faintly surprised even while she was asleep. Bruises like ink stains and eraser smudges lie upon her cheekbones, her temple, her neck. A white T-shirt bearing the logo of the Milwaukee Brewers and smeared with dirt and dried blood covers her torso from neck to navel. The lower half of her body, pale as smoke except where drizzled with blood, lengthens into the dark pool, where the ecstatic flies hover and settle. Her bare, slender left leg incorporates a scabby knee and concludes with the uptick of a bloodstained New Balance sneaker, size 5, laces double-knotted, toe pointed to the ceiling. Where the partner to this leg should be is a vacancy, for her right hip ends, abruptly, at a ragged stump.

We are in the presence of the Fisherman's third victim, ten-year-old Irma Freneau. The shock waves aroused by her disappearance yesterday afternoon from the sidewalk outside the video store will increase in force and number after Dale Gilbertson comes upon her body, a little over a day from now.

The Fisherman gathered her up on Chase Street and transported her—we cannot say how—up the length of Chase Street and Lyall Road, past the 7-Eleven and the VFW hall, past the house where Wanda Kinderling seethes and drinks, past the shiny glass spaceship of Goltz's, and across the border between town and farmland.

She was alive when the Fisherman moved her through the doorway next to the pockmarked Coca-Cola sign. She must have struggled, she must have screamed. The Fisherman brought her to the rear wall and silenced her with blows to the face. Very likely, he strangled her. He lowered her body to the floor and arranged her limbs. Except for the white New Balance sneakers, he removed all the clothing from her waist down, underwear, jeans, shorts, whatever Irma had been wearing when he abducted her. After that, the Fisherman amputated her right leg. Using some sort of long, heavy-bladed knife, and without the assistance of cleaver or saw, he parted flesh and bone until he had managed to detach the leg from the rest of the body. Then, perhaps with no more than two or three downward chops to the ankle, he severed the foot. He tossed it, still contained within the white sneaker, aside. Irma's foot was not important to the Fisherman—all he wanted was her leg.

Here, my friends, we have true *slippage*.

Irma Freneau's small, inert body seems to flatten out as if it intends to melt through the rotting floorboards. The drunken flies sing on. The dog keeps trying to yank the whole of its juicy prize out of the sneaker. Were we to bring simpleminded Ed Gilbertson back to life and stand him beside us, he would sink to his knees and weep. We, on the other hand . . .

We are not here to weep. Not like Ed, anyhow, in horrified shame and disbelief. A tremendous mystery has inhabited this hovel, and its effects and traces hover everywhere about us. We have come to observe, register, and record the impressions, the afterimages, left in the comet trail of the mystery. It speaks from their details, therefore it lingers in its own wake, therefore it surrounds us. A deep, deep gravity flows outward from the scene, and this gravity humbles us. Humility is our best, most accurate first response. Without it, we would miss the point; the great mystery would escape us, and we would go on deaf and blind, ignorant as pigs. Let us not go on like pigs. We must honor this scene—the flies, the dog worrying the severed foot, the poor, pale body of Irma Freneau, the magnitude of what befell Irma Freneau—by acknowledging our littleness. In comparison, we are no more than vapors.

A fat bee wanders in through the empty window frame in the side wall six feet from Irma's body and makes a slow, exploratory circuit around the rear of the shack. Suspended beneath its blurred wings, the bee looks nearly too heavy for flight, but it proceeds with easy, unhurried deliberation, moving well above the bloody floor in a wide curve. The flies, the mongrel, and Irma pay it no attention.

For us, though, the bee, which continues to drift contentedly about the rear of the horror chamber, has ceased to be a welcome distraction and has been absorbed into the surrounding mystery. It is a detail within the scene, and it, too, commands our humility and speaks. The weighty, burrowing rumble of its wings seems to define the exact center of the undulating sound waves, higher in pitch, produced by the greedy flies: Like a singer at a microphone in front of a chorus, the bee controls the aural background. The sound gathers and comes to a serious point. When the bee ambles into a shaft of yellow light streaming through the eastern wall, its stripes glow black and gold, the wings coalesce into a fan, and the insect becomes an intricate, airborne wonder. The slaughtered girl flattens into the bloody floorboards. Our humility, our sense of littleness, our appreciation of the gravity deeply embedded in this scene grant us the sense of forces and powers beyond our understanding, of a kind of grandeur always present and at work but perceptible only during moments like this.

We have been honored, but the honor is unbearable. The speaking bee circles back to the window and passes into another world, and, following his lead, we move on, out the window, into the sun, and into the upper air.

Smells of shit and urine at Maxton Elder Care; the fragile, slick feel of *slippage* at the off-kilter house north of Highway 35; the sound of the flies and the sight of the blood at the former Ed's Eats. Ag! Yuck! Is there no place here in French Landing, we may ask, where there is something nice under the skin? Where what we see is what we get, so to speak?

The short answer: no. French Landing should be marked

with big road signs at every point of ingress: WARNING! SLIPPAGE
IN PROGRESS! PASS AT YOUR OWN RISK!

The magic at work here is Fishermagic. It has rendered
"nice" at least temporarily obsolete. But we can go someplace
nice-*er,* and if we can we probably should, because we need a
break. We may not be able to escape *slippage,* but we can at
least visit where no one shits the bed or bleeds on the floor (at
least not yet).

So the bee goes its way and we go ours; ours takes us southwest, over more woods exhaling their fragrance of life and oxygen—there is no air like this air, at least not in this world—and
then back to the works of man again.

This section of town is called Libertyville, so named by the
French Landing Town Council in 1976. You won't believe this,
but big-bellied Ed Gilbertson, the Hot Dog King himself, was
a member of that bicentennial band of town fathers; those were
strange days, pretty mama, strange days indeed. Not as strange
as these, however; in French Landing, these are the Fisherdays,
the slippery slippage days.

The streets of Libertyville have names that adults find colorful and children find painful. Some of the latter have been
known to call this area of town Faggotyville. Let us descend
now, down through the sweet morning air (it's warming up already; this will be a Strawberry Fest kind of day for sure). We
cruise silently over Camelot Street, past the intersection of
Camelot and Avalon, and travel on down Avalon to Maid Marian Way. From Maid Marian we progress to—is it any surprise?—Robin Hood Lane.

Here, at No. 16, a sweet little Cape Cod honey of a home that
looks just right for The Decent Hardworking Family On Its Way
Up, we find a kitchen window open. There is the smell of coffee and toast, a wonderful combined odor that denies slippage
(if only we did not know better; if only we had not seen the dog
at work, eating a foot out of a sneaker as a child might eat the
hot dog right out of its bun), and we follow the aroma in. It's
nice to be invisible, isn't it? To watch in our godlike silence. If
only what our godlike eyes saw was just a little less goddamn
upsetting! But that is by the way. We're in it now, for better or

for worse, and we had better get on about our business. Daylight's a-wasting, as they say in this part of the world.

Here in the kitchen of No. 16 is Fred Marshall, whose picture currently graces the Salesman of the Month easel in the
showroom of French County Farm Equipment. Fred has also
been named Employee of the Year three years out of the last
four (two years ago Ted Goltz gave the award to Otto Eisman,
just to break the monotony), and when he is on the job no one
radiates more charm, personality, or all around *niceness.* You
wanted nice? Ladies and gentlemen, presenting Fred Marshall!

Only now his confident smile is not in evidence, and his hair,
always carefully combed on the job, hasn't yet seen the brush.
He's wearing Nike shorts and a tee with cutoff sleeves instead
of his usual pressed khakis and sport shirt. On the counter is the
Marshall copy of the *La Riviere Herald,* open to an inside page.

Fred has his share of problems just lately—or, rather, his
wife, Judy, has problems, and what's hers is his, so said the
minister when he joined them in holy wedlock—and what he's
reading isn't making him feel any better. Far from it. It's a sidebar to the lead story on the front page, and of course the author
is everyone's favorite muckraker, Wendell "FISHERMAN STILL AT
LARGE" Green.

The sidebar is your basic recap of the first two murders
(*Gruesome and Gruesomer* is how Fred thinks of them), and as
he reads, Fred bends first his left leg up behind him and then his
right, stretching those all-important thigh muscles and preparing for his morning run. What could be more antislippage than
a morning run? What could be *nicer*? What could possibly spoil
such a lovely start to such a beautiful Wisconsin day?

Well, how about this:

*Johnny Irkenham's dreams were simple enough, according
to his grief-stricken father.* [*Grief-stricken father,* Fred thinks,
stretching and imagining his son asleep upstairs. *Dear God,
save me from ever being a grief-stricken father.* Not knowing,
of course, how soon he must assume this role.] *"Johnny wanted
to be an astronaut," George Irkenham said, a smile briefly
lighting his exhausted face. "When he wasn't putting out fires
for the French Landing F.D. or fighting crime with the Justice
League of America, that is."*

*These innocent dreams ended in a nightmare we cannot*

*imagine.* [*But I'm sure you'll try,* Fred thinks, now beginning his toe raises.] *Earlier this week, his dismembered body was discovered by Spencer Hovdahl of Centralia. Hovdahl, a First Farmer State Bank loan officer, was inspecting an abandoned French Landing farm owned by John Ellison, who lives in a neighboring county, with an eye to initiating repossession proceedings. "I didn't want to be there in the first place,"* Hovdahl *told this reporter. "If there's anything I hate, it's the repo stuff.* [Knowing Spence Hovdahl as he does, Fred very much doubts if "stuff " was the word he used.] *I wanted to be there even less after I went into the henhouse. It's all rickety and falling down, and I would have stayed out except for the sound of the bees. I thought there might be a hive in there. Bees are an interest of mine, and I was curious. God help me, I was curious. I hope I'll never be curious again."*

*What he found in the henhouse was the body of seven-year-old John Wesley Irkenham. The corpse had been dismembered, the pieces hung from the henhouse's decaying rafters by chains. Although Police Chief Dale Gilbertson would neither confirm nor deny it, reliable police sources in La Riviere say that the thighs, torso, and buttocks had been bitten—*

Okay, that's enough for Fred, everybody out of the pool. He sweeps the newspaper closed and shoves it all the way down the counter to the Mr. Coffee. By God, they never put stuff like that in the paper when *he* was a kid. And why the Fisherman, for heaven's sake? Why did they have to tag every monster with a catchy nickname, turn a guy like whoever did this into the Celebrity Sicko of the Month?

Of course, nothing like this had ever happened when he was Tyler's age, but the principle . . . the goddamned *principle* of the matter . . .

Fred finishes his toe raises, reminding himself to have a talk with Tyler. It will be harder than their little talk about why his thing sometimes gets hard, but it absolutely must be done. *Buddy system,* Fred will say. *You've got to stick with your buddies now, Ty. No more rambling around on your own for a while, okay?*

Yet the idea of Ty actually being murdered seems remote to Fred; it is the stuff of TV docudramas or maybe a Wes Craven movie. Call it *Scream 4: The Fisherman.* In fact, wasn't there a movie sort of like that? A guy in a fisherman's slicker wandering around and killing teenagers with a hook? Maybe, but not little kids, not *babies* like Amy St. Pierre and Johnny Irkenham. Jesus, the world was disintegrating right in front of him.

Body parts hanging from chains in a crumbling henhouse, that is the part which haunts him. Can that really be? Can it be *here,* right here and now in Tom Sawyer–Becky Thatcher country?

Well, let it go. It's time to run.

*But maybe the paper kind of got lost this morning,* Fred thinks, picking it up from the counter and folding it until it looks like a thick paperback book (but part of the headline accuses him even so: FISHERMAN STILL AT L). *Maybe the paper just kind of, I don't know, migrated straight to the old garbage can beside the house.*

Yes, good idea. Because Judy has been strange lately, and Wendell Green's pulsating stories about the Fisherman are not helping (*Thighs and torso bitten,* Fred thinks as he glides through the early-morning-quiet house toward the door, *and while you're at it, waiter, have them cut me a nice rare chunk of butt*). She reads the press accounts obsessively, making no comment, but Fred doesn't like the way her eyes jump around, or some of the other tics she's picked up: the obsessive touching of her tongue to her upper lip, for instance . . . and sometimes, this in the last two or three days, he has seen her tongue reach all the way up and pet at her philtrum just below her nose, a feat he would have thought impossible if he had not seen it again last night, during the local news. She goes to bed earlier and earlier, and sometimes she talks in her sleep—strange, slurry words that don't sound like English. Sometimes when Fred speaks to her, she doesn't respond, simply stares off into space, eyes wide, lips moving slightly, hands kneading together (cuts and scratches have begun to show up on the backs of them, even though she keeps her nails cropped sensibly short).

Ty has noticed his mother's encroaching oddities, too. On Saturday, while father and son were having lunch together— Judy was upstairs taking one of her long naps, another new wrinkle—the boy suddenly asked, right out of a blue clear sky, "What's wrong with Mom?"

"Ty, nothing's wrong with—"

"There *is*! Tommy Erbter says she's a Coke short of a Happy Meal these days."

And had he almost reached across the tomato soup and toasted-cheese sandwiches and clouted his son? His only child? Good old Ty, who was nothing but concerned? God help him, he had.

Outside the door, at the head of the concrete path leading down to the street, Fred begins to jog slowly in place, taking deep breath after deep breath, depositing the oxygen he will soon withdraw. It is usually the best part of his day (assuming he and Judy don't make love, that is, and lately there has been precious little of that). He likes the feeling—the *knowledge*— that his path might be the beginning of the road to anywhere, that he could start out here in the Libertyville section of French Landing and wind up in New York . . . San Francisco . . . Bombay . . . the mountain passes of Nepal. Every step outside one's own door invites the world (perhaps even the universe), and this is something Fred Marshall intuitively understands. He sells John Deere tractors and Case cultivators, yes, all *right,* already, but he is not devoid of imagination. When he and Judy were students at UW-Madison, their first dates were at the coffeehouse just off campus, an espresso-jazz-and-poetry haven called the Chocolate Watchband. It would not be entirely unfair to say that they had fallen in love to the sound of angry drunks declaiming the works of Allen Ginsberg and Gary Snyder into the Chocolate Watchband's cheap but exquisitely loud sound system.

Fred draws one more deep breath and begins to run. Down Robin Hood Lane to Maid Marian Way, where he gives Deke Purvis a wave. Deke, in his robe and slippers, is just picking Wendell Green's daily dose of doom up off his own stoop. Then he wheels onto Avalon Street, picking it up a little now, showing his heels to the morning.

He cannot outrun his worries, however.

*Judy, Judy, Judy,* he thinks in the voice of Cary Grant (a little joke that has long since worn thin with the love of his life).

There is the gibberish when she sleeps. There's the way her eyes dart hither and yon. And let's not forget the time (just three days ago) when he followed her into the kitchen and she wasn't there—she'd turned out to be *behind* him, coming down the stairs, and *how* she had done that seems less important to him than *why* she had done it, gone sneaking up the back stairs and then come tromping down the front ones (because that is what she must have done; it's the only solution he can think of). There's the constant tapping and petting she does with her tongue. Fred knows what it all adds up to: Judy has been acting like a woman in terror. This has been going on since *before* the murder of Amy St. Pierre, so it can't be the Fisherman, or not *entirely* the Fisherman.

And there is a larger issue. Before the last couple of weeks, Fred would have told you that his wife doesn't have a fearful bone in her body. She might be just five foot two ("Why, you're no bigger than a minute" was his grandmother's comment when she first met Fred's intended), but Judy has the heart of a lion, of a Viking warrior. This isn't bullshit, or hype, or poetic license; it is the simple truth as Fred sees it, and it is the contrast between what he has always known and what he sees now that scares him the most.

From Avalon he races onto Camelot, crossing the intersection without looking for traffic, going much faster than usual, almost sprinting instead of jogging. He is remembering something that happened about a month after they started going out.

It was the Chocolate Watchband they had gone to, as usual, only this time during the afternoon, to listen to a jazz quartet that had actually been pretty good. Not that they had listened very much, as Fred now recalls it; mostly he had talked to Judy about how little he liked being in the College of Agricultural and Life Sciences (Moo U, the Letters and Science snooties called it), and how little he liked the unspoken family assumption that when he graduated he would come on back home and help Phil run the family farm in French Landing. The idea of spending his life in harness with Phil gave Fred a severe case of the glooms.

*What do you want, then?* Judy had asked. Holding his hand on the table, a candle burning inside a jelly glass, the combo onstage working a sweet little number called "I'll Be There for You."

*I don't know,* he'd said, *but I tell you what, Jude, I should be*

*in Business Admin, not Moo U. I'm a hell of a lot better at sell-
ing than at planting.*

*Then why don't you switch?*

*Because my family thinks—*

*Your family isn't going to have to live your life, Fred—you are.*

Talk is cheap, he remembers thinking, but then something
had happened on the way back to campus, something so amazing and out of his understanding of how life was supposed to
work that it fills him with wonder even now, some thirteen years
later.

Still talking about his future and their future together (*I
could be a farm wife,* Judy had said, *but only if my husband
really wants to be a farmer*). Deep into that. Letting their feet
carry them along without much interest in exactly where they
were. And then, at the intersection of State Street and Gorham,
a scream of brakes and a hearty metallic bang had interrupted
the conversation. Fred and Judy had looked around and seen a
Dodge pickup that had just tangled bumpers with an elderly
Ford station wagon.

Getting out of the wagon, which had pretty clearly run the
stop sign at the end of Gorham Street, was a middle-aged man
in a middle-aged brown suit. He looked scared as well as
shaken up, and Fred thought there was good reason for that; the
man advancing toward him from the pickup truck was young,
heavyset (Fred particularly remembered the belly bulging over
the waist of his jeans), and carrying a tire iron. *You goddamn
careless asshole!* Young and Heavyset cried. *Look what you
done to my truck! This my dad's truck, you goddamn asshole!*

Middle-Aged Suit backing up, eyes wide, hands raised, Fred
watching fascinated from in front of Rickman's Hardware, thinking *Oh no, mister, bad idea. You don't back away from a guy like
this, you go toward him, even as mad as he is. You're provoking
him—can't you see that you're provoking him?* So fascinated he
didn't realize that Judy's hand was no longer in his, listening with
a kind of sick foreknowledge as Mr. Middle-Aged Suit, still backing up, blathered about how he was sorry . . . entirely his fault,
wasn't looking, wasn't thinking . . . insurance papers . . . State
Farm . . . draw a diagram . . . get a policeman to take
statements . . .

And all the time Young and Heavyset was advancing, thwocking the end of the tire iron into the palm of his hand, not listening. This wasn't about insurance or compensation; this was about how Mr. Middle-Aged Suit had scared the shit out of him while he was just driving along and minding his own business and listening to Johnny Paycheck sing "Take This Job and Shove It." Young and Heavyset intended to take a little payback paycheck of his own for getting the shit scared out of him and all jounced around behind the wheel . . . had to take a little, because the other man's smell was inciting him, that piss-yellow smell of fear and innate defenselessness. It was a case of rabbit and farmyard dog, and all at once the rabbit was clean out of backing room; Mr. Middle-Aged Suit was pressed against the side of his station wagon, and in a moment the tire iron was going to start swinging and the blood was going to start flying.

Except there *was* no blood and not a single swing, because all at once Judy DeLois was there, no bigger than a minute but standing between them, looking fearlessly up into Young and Heavyset's burning face.

Fred blinked, wondering how in the name of God she'd gotten there so damned fast. (Much later he would feel the same way when he followed her into the kitchen, only to hear the steady thump of her feet descending the front stairs.) And then? Then Judy slapped Young and Heavyset's arm! *Whack,* right on the meaty bicep she slapped him, leaving a white palm print on the sunburned freckled flesh below the sleeve of the guy's torn blue T-shirt. Fred saw it but couldn't believe it.

*Quit it!* Judy shouted up into Young and Heavyset's surprised, beginning-to-be-bewildered face. *Put it down, quit it! Don't be dumb! You want to go to jail over seven hundred dollars' worth of bodywork? Put it down! Get it together, big boy! Put . . . that . . . thing . . . DOWN!*

There'd been one second when Fred was quite sure Young and Heavyset was going to bring the tire iron down anyway, and right on his pretty little girlfriend's head. But Judy never flinched; her eyes never left the eyes of the young man with the tire iron, who towered at least a foot over her and must have outweighed her by a couple of hundred pounds. There was certainly no pissy yellow fear smell coming off her that day; her tongue did no nervous patting at her upper lip or her philtrum; her blazing eyes were steadfast.

And, after another moment, Young and Heavyset put the tire iron down.

Fred wasn't aware that a crowd had gathered until he heard the spontaneous applause from perhaps thirty onlookers. He joined in, never more proud of her than he was at that moment. And for the first time, Judy looked startled. She hung in there, though, startled or not. She got the two of them together, tugging Mr. Middle-Aged Suit forward by one arm, and actually hectored them into shaking hands. By the time the cops arrived, Young and Heavyset and Mr. Middle-Aged Suit were sitting side by side on the curb, studying each other's insurance papers. Case closed.

Fred and Judy walked on toward the campus, holding hands again. For two blocks Fred didn't speak. Was he in awe of her? He supposes now that he was. At last he said: *That was amazing.*

She gave him an uncomfortable little look, an uncomfortable little smile. *No it wasn't,* she said. *If you want to call it something, call it good citizenship. I could see that guy getting ready to send himself to jail. I didn't want that to happen. Or the other guy to be hurt.*

Yet she said that last almost as an afterthought, and Fred for the first time sensed not only her courage but her unflinching Viking's heart. She was on the side of Young and Heavyset because . . . well, because the other fellow had been afraid.

*Weren't you worried, though?* he asked her. He had still been so stunned by what he'd seen that it hadn't crossed his mind—yet—to think he should be a little ashamed; after all, it was his girlfriend who'd stepped in instead of him, and that wasn't the Gospel According to Hollywood. *Weren't you afraid that in the heat of the moment the guy with the tire iron would take a swing at you?*

Judy's eyes had grown puzzled. *It never crossed my mind,* she said.

Camelot eventually debouches into Chase Street, where there is a pleasant little gleam of the Mississippi on clear days like this one, but Fred doesn't go that far. He turns at the top of Liberty Heights and starts back the way he came, his shirt now soaked with sweat. Usually the run makes him feel better, but not today, at least not yet. The fearless Judy of that afternoon on the corner of State and Gorham is so unlike the shifty-eyed, sometimes disconnected Judy who now lives in his house—the naptaking, hand-wringing Judy—that Fred has actually spoken to Pat Skarda about it. Yesterday, this was, when the doc was in Goltz's, looking at riding lawn mowers.

Fred had shown him a couple, a Deere and a Honda, inquired after his family, and then asked (casually, he hoped), *Hey, Doc, tell me something—do you think it's possible for a person to just go crazy? Without any warning, like?*

Skarda had given him a sharper look than Fred had really liked. *Are we talking about an adult or an adolescent, Fred?*

*Well, we're not talking about* anyone, *actually.* Big, hearty laugh—unconvincing to Fred's own ears, and judging from Pat Skarda's look, not very convincing to him, either. *Not anyone* real, *anyway. But as a hypothetical case, let's say an adult.*

Skarda had thought about it, then shook his head. *There are few absolutes in medicine, even fewer in* psychiatric *medicine. That said, I have to tell you that I think it's very unlikely for a person to "just go crazy." It may be a fairly rapid process, but it is a process. We hear people say "So-and-so snapped," but that's rarely the case. Mental dysfunction—neurotic or psychotic behavior—takes time to develop, and there are usually signs. How's your mom these days, Fred?*

*Mom? Oh hey, she's fine. Right in the pink.*

*And Judy?*

It had taken him a moment to get a smile started, but once he did, he managed a big one. Big and guileless. *Judy? She's in the pink, too, Doc. Of course she is. Steady as she goes.*

Sure. Steady as she goes. Just showing a few *signs,* that was all.

*Maybe they'll pass,* he thinks. Those good old endorphins are finally kicking in, and all at once this seems plausible. Optimism is a more normal state for Fred, who does not believe in *slippage,* and a little smile breaks on his face—the day's first. *Maybe the signs will pass. Maybe whatever's wrong with her will blow out as fast as it blew in. Maybe it's even, you know, a menstrual thing. Like PMS.*

God, if that was all it was, what a *relief*! In the meantime, there's Ty to think about. He has to have a talk with Tyler about the buddy system, because while Fred doesn't believe what Wendell Green is apparently trying to insinuate, that the ghost of a fabulous turn-of-the-century cannibal and all-around boogerman named Albert Fish has for some reason turned up here in Coulee Country, *someone* is certainly out there, and this someone has murdered two little children and done unspeakable (at least unless you're Wendell Green, it seems) things to the bodies.

*Thighs, torso, and buttocks bitten,* Fred thinks, and runs faster, although now he's getting a stitch in his side. Yet this bears repeating: he does not believe that these horrors can actually touch his son, nor does he see how they can have caused Judy's condition, since her oddities started while Amy St. Pierre was still alive, Johnny Irkenham, too, both of them presumably playing happily in their respective backyards.

Maybe this, maybe that . . . but enough of Fred and his worries, all right? Let us rise from the environs of his troubled head and precede him back to No. 16, Robin Hood Lane—let's go directly to the source of his troubles.

The upstairs window of the connubial bedroom is open, and the screen is certainly no problem; we strain ourselves right through, entering with the breeze and the first sounds of the awakening day.

The sounds of French Landing awakening do not awaken Judy Marshall. Nope, she has been starey-eyed since three, conning the shadows for she doesn't know what, fleeing dreams too horrible to remember. Yet she does remember *some* things, little as she wants to.

"Saw the eye again," she remarks to the empty room. Her tongue comes out and with no Fred around to watch her (she knows he's watching, she is beset but not *stupid* ), it does not just pet at her philtrum but *slathers* it in a great big wipe, like a dog licking its chops after a bowl of scraps. "It's a red eye. *His* eye. Eye of the King."

She looks up at the shadows of the trees outside. They dance on the ceiling, making shapes and faces, shapes and faces.

"Eye of the King," she repeats, and now it starts with the hands: kneading and twisting and squeezing and digging. "Abbalah! Foxes down foxholes! Abbalah-doon, the Crimson King! Rats in their ratholes! Abbalah Munshun! The King is in his Tower, eating bread and honey! The Breakers in the basement, making all the money!"

She shakes her head from side to side. Oh, these voices, out of the darkness they come, and sometimes she awakens with a vision burning behind her eyes, a vision of a vast slaty tower standing in a field of roses. A field of blood. Then the talking begins, the speaking in tongues, testification, words she can't understand let alone control, a mixed stream of English and gibberish.

"Trudge, trudge, trudge," she says. "The little ones are trudging on their bleeding footsies . . . oh for Christ's sake, won't this ever stop?"

Her tongue yawns out and licks across the tip of her nose; for a moment her nostrils are plugged with her own spit, and her head roars

*—Abbalah, Abbalah-doon, Can-tah Abbalah—*

with those terrible foreign words, those terrible impacted images of the Tower and the burning caves beneath, caves through which little ones trudge on bleeding feet. Her mind strains with them, and there is only one thing that will make them stop, only one way to get relief.

Judy Marshall sits up. On the table beside her there is a lamp, a copy of the latest John Grisham novel, a little pad of paper (a birthday present from Ty, each sheet headed HERE'S ANOTHER GREAT IDEA I HAD!), and a ballpoint pen with LA RIVIERE SHERATON printed on the side.

Judy seizes the pen and scribbles on the pad.

*No Abbalah no Abbalah-doon no Tower no Breakers no Crimson King only dreams these are just my dreams*

It is enough, but pens are also roads to anywhere, and before she can divorce the tip of this one from the birthday pad, it writes one more line:

*The Black House is the doorway to Abbalah the entrance to hell Sheol Munshun all these worlds and spirits*

No more! Good merciful God, no more! And the worst thing: What if it all begins to make sense?

She throws the pen back on the table, where it rolls to the base of the lamp and lies still. Then she tears the page from the pad, crumples it, and sticks it in her mouth. She chews furiously, not tearing it but at least mashing it sodden, then swallows. There is an awful moment when it sticks in her throat, but then it goes down. Words and worlds recede and Judy falls back against the pillows, exhausted. Her face is pale and sweaty, her eyes huge with unshed tears, but the moving shadows on the ceiling no longer look like faces to her—the faces of trudging children, of rats in their ratholes, foxes in foxholes, eye of the King, Abbalah-Abbalah-doon! Now they are just the shadows of the trees again. She is Judy DeLois Marshall, wife of Fred, mother of Ty. This is Libertyville, this is French Landing, this is French County, this is Wisconsin, this is America, this is the Northern Hemisphere, this is the world, and there is no other world than this. Let it be so.

Ah, let it be so.

Her eyes close, and as she finally slips back to sleep we slip across the room to the door, but just before we get there, Judy Marshall says one other thing—says it as she crosses over the border and into sleep.

"Burnside is not your name. Where is your hole?"

The bedroom door is closed and so we use the keyhole, passing through it like a sigh. Down the hall we go, past pictures of Judy's family and Fred's, including one photo of the Marshall family farm where Fred and Judy spent a horrible but blessedly short period not long after their marriage. Want some good advice? Don't talk to Judy Marshall about Fred's brother, Phil. Just don't get her started, as George Rathbun would undoubtedly say.

No keyhole in the door at the end of the hall and so we slide underneath like a telegram and into a room we immediately know is a boy's room: we can tell from the mingled smells of dirty athletic socks and neat's-foot oil. It's small, this room, but it seems bigger than Fred and Judy's down the hall, very likely because the odor of anxiety is missing. On the walls are pictures of Shaquille O'Neal, Jeromy Burnitz, last year's Milwaukee Bucks team . . . and Tyler Marshall's idol, Mark McGwire. McGwire plays for the Cards, and the Cards are the enemy, but hell, it's not as if the Milwaukee Brewers are actually competition for anything. The Brew Crew were doormats in the American League, and they are likewise doormats in the National. And McGwire . . . well, he's a hero, isn't he? He's strong, he's modest, and he can hit the baseball a country mile. Even Tyler's dad, who roots strictly for Wisconsin teams, thinks McGwire is something special. "The greatest hitter in the history of the game," he called him after the seventy-home-run season, and Tyler, although little more than an infant in that fabled year, has never forgotten this.

Also on the wall of this little boy who will soon be the Fisherman's fourth victim (yes, there has already been a third, as we have seen), holding pride of place directly over his bed, is a travel poster showing a great dark castle at the end of a long and misty meadow. At the bottom of the poster, which he has Scotch-taped to the wall (his mom absolutely forbids pushpins), it says COME BACK TO THE AULD SOD in big green letters. Ty is considering taking the poster down long enough to cut this part off. He doesn't like the poster because he has any interest in Ireland; to him the picture whispers of somewhere else, somewhere Entirely Else. It is like a photograph of some splendid mythical kingdom where there might be unicorns in the forests and dragons in the caves. Never mind Ireland; never mind Harry Potter, either. Hogwarts is fine enough for summer afternoons, but this is a castle in the Kingdom of Entirely Else. It's the first thing Tyler Marshall sees in the morning, the last thing he sees at night, and that's just the way he likes it.

He lies curled on his side in his underwear shorts, a human comma with tousled dark blond hair and a thumb that is close to his mouth, really just an inch or so away from being sucked. He is dreaming—we can see his eyeballs moving back and forth behind his closed lids. His lips move . . . he's whispering something . . . Abbalah? Is he whispering his mother's word? Surely not, but . . .

We lean closer to listen, but before we can hear anything, a circuit in Tyler's jazzy red clock-radio goes hot, and all at once the voice of George Rathbun fills the room, calling Tyler hence from whatever dreams have been playing themselves out under that tousled thatch.

"Fans, you gotta listen to me now, how many times have I told you this? If you don't know Henreid Brothers Furniture of French Landing and Centralia, then you don't know furniture. That's right, I'm talking Henreid Brothers, home of the Colonial Blowout. Living-room sets dining-room sets bedroom sets, famous names you know and trust like La-Z-Boy, Breton Woods and Moosehead, EVEN A BLIND MAN CAN SEE THAT HENREID BROTHERS MEANS QUALITY!"

Ty Marshall is laughing even before he's got both eyes fully open. He loves George Rathbun; George is absolutely fly.

And now, without even changing gears from the commercial: "You guys are all ready for the Brewer Bash, ain'tcha? Sent me those postcards with your name, address, and *el teléfono* on 'em? Hope so, because the contest closed at midnight. If you missed out . . . so solly, Cholly!"

Ty closes his eyes again and mouths the same word over three times: *Shit, shit, shit.* He *did* forget to enter, and now he can only hope that his dad (who knows how forgetful his son can be) remembered and entered the contest for him.

"Grand prize?" George is saying. "ONLY the chance for you or the fav-o-rite young person of your acquaintance to be the Brew Crew's batboy or batgirl for the entire Cincinnati series. ONLY the chance to win an aut-o-graphed Richie Sexson bat, the LUMBER that holds the LIGHTNING! Not to mention fifty free seats on the first-base side with me, George Rathbun, Coulee Country's Traveling College of Baseball Knowledge. BUT WHY AM I TELLING YOU THIS? If you missed out, you're too late. Case closed, game over, zip up your fly! Oh, I know why I brought it up—to make sure you tune in next Friday to see if I speak YOUR NAME over the radio!"

Ty groans. There are only two chances that George will speak his name over the radio: slim and none. Not that he cared so much about being a batboy, dressed in a baggy Brewers uni and running around in front of all those people at Miller Park, but to own Richie Sexson's *own bat,* the lumber with the lightning . . . how boss would that've been?

Tyler rolls out of bed, sniffs the armpits of yesterday's

T-shirt, tosses it aside, gets another out of the drawer. His dad sometimes asks him why he sets his alarm so *early*—it's summer vacation, after all—and Tyler can't seem to make him understand that every day is important, especially those filled with warmth and sunlight and no particular responsibilities. It's as if there's some little voice deep inside him, warning him not to waste a minute, not a single one, because time is short.

What George Rathbun says next drives the remaining sleep-fog from Tyler's brain—it's like a dash of cold water. "Say there, Coulee, want to talk about the Fisherman?"

Tyler stops what he's doing, an odd little chill running up his back and then down his arms. The Fisherman. Some crazy guy killing kids . . . and *eating* them? Well, he's heard that rumor, mostly from the bigger kids down at the baseball field or at the French Landing Rec Center, but who would do something so gross? Cannibalism, ack!

George's voice drops. "Now I'm going to tell you a little secret, so listen close to your Uncle George." Tyler sits on his bed, holding his sneakers by the laces and listening closely to his Uncle George, as bidden. It seems odd to hear George Rathbun talking about a subject so . . . so *unsporty,* but Tyler trusts him. Didn't George Rathbun predict that the Badgers would go to at least the Elite Eight two years ago, when everyone else said they'd get blown out in the first round of the Big Dance? Yeah, he did. Case closed, game over, zip up your fly.

George's voice drops further, to what is almost a confidential whisper. "The original Fisherman, boys and girls, Albert Fish, has been dead and gone for sixty-seven years, and s'far's I know, he never got much west of New Jersey. *Furthermore,* he was probably a DAMYANKEE FAN! SO COOL IT, COULEE COUNTRY! JUST CAAAALM DOWN!"

Tyler relaxes, smiling, and starts putting on his sneakers. Calm down, you got that right. The day is new, and yeah, okay, his mom's been a little on the Tinky Winky side lately, but she'll pull out of it.

Let us leave on this optimistic note—make like an amoeba and split, as the redoubtable George Rathbun might say. And speaking of George, that ubiquitous voice of the Coulee Country morning, should we not seek him out? Not a bad idea. Let us do so immediately.

# 3

Out Tyler's window we go, away from Libertyville, flying southwest on a diagonal, not lingering now but really flapping those old wings, flying with a purpose. We're headed toward the heliograph flash of early-morning sun on the Father of Waters, also toward the world's largest six-pack. Between it and County Road Oo (we can call it Nailhouse Row if we want; we're practically honorary citizens of French Landing now) is a radio tower, the warning beacon on top now invisible in the bright sunshine of this newborn July day. We smell grass and trees and warming earth, and as we draw closer to the tower, we also smell the yeasty, fecund aroma of beer.

Next to the radio tower, in the industrial park on the east side of Peninsula Drive, is a little cinder-block building with a parking lot just big enough for half a dozen cars and the Coulee patrol van, an aging Ford Econoline painted candy-apple pink. As the day winds down and afternoon wears into evening, the cylindrical shadows of the six-pack will fall first over the sign on the balding lawn facing the drive, then the building, then the parking lot. KDCU-AM, this sign reads, YOUR TALK VOICE IN COULEE COUNTRY. Spray-painted across it, in a pink that almost matches the patrol van, is a fervent declaration: TROY LUVS MARYANN! YES! Later on, Howie Soule, the U-Crew engineer, will clean this off (probably during the Rush Limbaugh show, which is satellite fed and totally automated), but for now it stays, telling us all we need to know about small-town luv in middle America. Looks like we found something nice after all.

Coming out of the station's side door as we arrive is a slender man dressed in pleated khaki Dockers, a tieless white shirt of Egyptian cotton buttoned all the way to the neck, and ma-

roon braces (they are as slim as he is, those braces, and far too
cool to be called suspenders; suspenders are vulgar things worn
by such creatures as Chipper Maxton and Sonny Heartfield,
down at the funeral home). This silver-haired fellow is also
wearing a *very* sharp straw fedora, antique but beautifully kept.
The maroon hatband matches his braces. Aviator-style sunglasses cover his eyes. He takes a position on the grass to the
left of the door, beneath a battered speaker that is amping
KDCU's current broadcast: the local news. This will be followed by the Chicago farm report, which gives him ten minutes
before he has to settle in behind the mike again.

We watch in growing puzzlement as he produces a pack of
American Spirit cigarettes from his shirt pocket and fires one up
with a gold lighter. Surely this elegant fellow in the braces,
Dockers, and Bass Weejuns cannot be George Rathbun. In our
minds we have already built up a picture of George, and it is one
of a fellow very different from this. In our mind's eye we see a
guy with a huge belly hanging over the white belt of his checked
pants (all those ballpark bratwursts), a brick-red complexion (all
those ballpark beers, not to mention all that bellowing at the das-
tardly umps), and a squat, broad neck (perfect for housing those
asbestos vocal cords). The George Rathbun of our imagination—and all of Coulee Country's, it almost goes without saying—is a pop-eyed, broad-assed, wild-haired, leather-lunged,
Rolaids-popping, Chevy-driving, Republican-voting heart attack waiting to happen, a churning urn of sports trivia, mad en-
thusiasms, crazy prejudices, and high cholesterol.

This fellow is not that fellow. This fellow moves like a
dancer. This fellow is iced tea on a hot day, cool as the king of
spades.

But say, that's the joke of it, isn't it? Uh-huh. The joke of the
fat deejay with the skinny voice, only turned inside out. In a
very real sense, George Rathbun does not exist at all. He is a
hobby in action, a fiction in the flesh, and only one of the slim
man's multiple personalities. The people at KDCU know his
real name and think they're in on the joke (the punch line of
course being George's trademark line, the even-a-blind-man
thing), but they don't know the half of it. Nor is this a
metaphorical statement. They know exactly one-third of it, be-

cause the man in the Dockers and the straw fedora is actually four people.

In any case, George Rathbun has been the saving of KDCU, the last surviving AM station in a predatory FM market. For five mornings a week, week in and week out, he has been a drive-time bonanza. The U-Crew (as they call themselves) love him just about to death.

Above him, the loudspeaker cackles on: "—still no leads, according to Chief Dale Gilbertson, who has called *Herald* reporter Wendell Green 'an out-of-town fearmonger who is more interested in selling papers than in how we do things in French Landing.'

"Meanwhile, in Arden, a house fire has taken the lives of an elderly farmer and his wife. Horst P. Lepplemier and his wife, Gertrude, both eighty-two . . ."

"Horst P. Lepplemier," says the slim man, drawing on his cigarette with what appears to be great enjoyment. "Try saying that one ten times fast, you moke."

Behind him and to his right, the door opens again, and although the smoker is still standing directly beneath the speaker, he hears the door perfectly well. The eyes behind the aviator shades have been dead his whole life, but his hearing is exquisite.

The newcomer is pasty-faced and comes blinking into the morning sun like a baby mole that has just been turned out of its burrow by the blade of a passing plow. His head has been shaved except for the Mohawk strip up the center of his skull and the pigtail that starts just above the nape of his neck and hangs to his shoulder blades. The Mohawk has been dyed bright red; the 'tail is electric blue. Dangling from one earlobe is a lightning-bolt earring that looks suspiciously like the Nazi S.S. insignia. He is wearing a torn black T-shirt with a logo that reads SNIVELLING SHITS '97: THE WE GET HARD FOR JESUS TOUR. In one hand this colorful fellow has a CD jewel box.

"Hello, Morris," says the slim man in the fedora, still without turning.

Morris pulls in a little gasp, and in his surprise looks like the nice Jewish boy that he actually is. Morris Rosen is the U-Crew's summer intern from the Oshkosh branch of UW.

"Man, I love that unpaid grunt labor!" station manager Tom Wiggins has been heard to say, usually while rubbing his hands together fiendishly. Never has a checkbook been guarded so righteously as the Wigger guards the KDCU checkbook. He is like Smaug the Dragon reclining on his heaps of gold (not that there are heaps of anything in the 'DCU accounts; it bears repeating to say that, as an AM talker, the station is lucky just to be alive).

Morris's look of surprise—it might be fair to call it *uneasy* surprise—dissolves into a smile. "Wow, Mr. Leyden! Good grab! What a pair of ears!"

Then he frowns. Even if Mr. Leyden—who's standing directly beneath the outside honker, can't forget that—heard *someone* come out, how in God's name did he know *which* someone it was?

"How'd you know it was me?" he asks.

"Only two people around here smell like marijuana in the morning," Henry Leyden says. "One of them follows his morning smoke with Scope; the other—that's you, Morris—just lets her rip."

"Wow," Morris says respectfully. "That is totally bitchrod."

"I *am* totally bitchrod," Henry agrees. He speaks softly and thoughtfully. "It's a tough job, but somebody has to do it. In regard to your morning rendezvous with the undeniably tasty Thai stick, may I offer an Appalachian aphorism?"

"Go, dude." This is Morris's first real discussion with Henry Leyden, who is every bit the head Morris has been told to expect. Every bit and more. It is no longer so hard to believe that he could have another identity . . . a *secret* identity, like Bruce Wayne. But still . . . this is just so *pimp*.

"What we do in our childhood forms as a habit," Henry says in the same soft, totally un–George Rathbun voice. "That is my advice to you, Morris."

"Yeah, totally," Morris says. He has no clue what Mr. Leyden is talking about. But he slowly, shyly, extends the CD jewel box in his hand. For a moment, when Henry makes no move to take it, Morris feels crushed, all at once seven years old again and trying to wow his always-too-busy father with a picture he has spent all afternoon drawing in his room. Then he thinks,

*He's* blind, *dickweed. He may be able to smell pot on your breath and he may have ears like a bat, but how's he supposed to know you're holding out a fucking CD?*

Hesitantly, a bit frightened by his own temerity, Morris takes Henry's wrist. He feels the man start a little, but then Leyden allows his hand to be guided to the slender box.

"Ah, a CD," Henry says. "And what is it, pray tell?"

"You gotta play the seventh track tonight on your show," Morris says. *"Please."*

For the first time, Henry looks alarmed. He takes a drag on his cigarette, then drops it (without even looking—of course, ha ha) into the sand-filled plastic bucket by the door.

"What show could you possibly mean?" he asks.

Instead of answering directly, Morris makes a rapid little smacking noise with his lips, the sound of a small but voracious carnivore eating something tasty. And, to make things worse, he follows it with the Wisconsin Rat's trademark line, as well known to the folks in Morris's age group as George Rathbun's hoarse "Even a blind man" cry is known to their elders: "Chew it up, eat it up, wash it down, *it aaallll comes out the same place!"*

He doesn't do it very well, but there's no question *who* he's doing: the one and only Wisconsin Rat, whose evening drive-time program on KWLA-FM is famous in Coulee Country (except the word we probably want is "infamous"). KWLA is the tiny college FM station in La Riviere, hardly more than a smudge on the wallpaper of Wisconsin radio, but the Rat's audience is huge.

And if anyone found out that the comfortable Brew Crew–rooting, Republican-voting, AM-broadcasting George Rathbun was also the Rat—who had once narrated a gleeful on-air evacuation of his bowels onto a Backstreet Boys CD—there could be trouble. Quite serious, possibly, resounding well beyond the tight-knit little radio community.

"What in God's name would ever make you think that I'm the Wisconsin Rat, Morris?" Henry asks. "I barely know who you're talking about. Who put such a weird idea in your head?"

"An informed source," Morris says craftily.

He won't give Howie Soule up, not even if they pull out his

fingernails with red-hot tongs. Besides, Howie only found out by accident: went into the station crapper one day after Henry left and discovered that Henry's wallet had fallen out of his back pocket while he was sitting on the throne. You'd have thought a fellow whose other senses were so obviously tightwired would have sensed the absence, but probably Henry's mind had been on other things—he was obviously a heavy dude who undoubtedly spent his days getting through some heavy thoughts. In any case, there was a KWLA I.D. card in Henry's wallet (which Howie had thumbed through "in the spirit of friendly curiosity," as he put it), and on the line marked NAME, someone had stamped a little inkpad drawing of a rat. Case closed, game over, zip up your fly.

"I have never in my life so much as stepped through the door of KWLA," Henry says, and this is the absolute truth. He makes the Wisconsin Rat tapes (among others) in his studio at home, then sends them in to the station from the downtown Mail Boxes Etc., where he rents under the name of Joe Strummer. The card with the rat stamped on it was more in the nature of an invitation from the KWLA staff than anything else, one he's never taken up . . . but he kept the card.

"Have you become anyone else's informed source, Morris?"

"Huh?"

"Have you told anyone that you think I'm the Wisconsin Rat?"

"No! Course not!" Which, as we all know, is what people always *say*. Luckily for Henry, in this case it happens to be true. So far, at least, but the day is still young.

"And you won't, will you? Because rumors have a way of taking root. Just like certain bad habits." Henry mimes puffing, pulling in smoke.

"I know how to keep my mouth shut," Morris declares, with perhaps misplaced pride.

"I hope so. Because if you bruited this about, I'd have to kill you."

*Bruited,* Morris thinks. *Oh man, this guy is complete.*

"Kill me, yeah," Morris says, laughing.

"And eat you," Henry says. *He* is not laughing; not even smiling.

"Yeah, right." Morris laughs again, but this time the laugh

sounds strangely forced to his own ears. "Like you're Hannibal Lecture."

"No, like I'm the Fisherman," Henry says. He slowly turns his aviator sunglasses toward Morris. The sun reflects off them, for a moment turning them into rufous eyes of fire. Morris takes a step back without even realizing that he has done so. "Albert Fish liked to start with the ass, did you know that?"

"N—"

"Yes indeed. He claimed that a good piece of young ass was as sweet as a veal cutlet. His exact words. Written in a letter to the mother of one of his victims."

"Far out," Morris says. His voice sounds faint to his own ears, the voice of a plump little pig denying entrance to the big bad wolf. "But I'm not exactly, like, worried that you're the Fisherman."

"No? Why not?"

"Man, you're *blind,* for one thing!"

Henry says nothing, only stares at the now vastly uneasy Morris with his fiery glass eyes. And Morris thinks: *But is he blind? He gets around pretty good for a blind guy . . . and the way he tabbed me as soon as I came out here, how weird was that?*

"I'll keep quiet," he says. "Honest to God."

"That's all I want," Henry says mildly. "Now that we've got that straight, what exactly have you brought me?" He holds up the CD—but not as if he's *looking* at it, Morris observes with vast relief.

"It's, um, this Racine group. Dirtysperm? And they've got this cover of 'Where Did Our Love Go'? The old Supremes thing? Only they do it at like a hundred and fifty beats a minute? It's fuckin' hilarious. I mean, it destroys the whole pop thing, man, *blitzes* it!"

"Dirtysperm," Henry says. "Didn't they used to be Jane Wyatt's Clit?"

Morris looks at Henry with awe that could easily become love. "Dirtysperm's lead guitarist, like, *formed* JWC, man. Then him and the bass guy had this political falling-out, something about Dean Kissinger and Henry Acheson, and Ucky Ducky—he's the guitarist—went off to form Dirtysperm."

" 'Where Did Our Love Go'?" Henry muses, then hands the CD back. And, as if he sees the way Morris's face falls: "I can't be seen with something like that—use your head. Stick it in my locker."

Morris's gloom disappears and he breaks into a sunny smile. "Yeah, okay! You got it, Mr. Leyden!"

"And don't let anyone see you doing it. Especially not Howie Soule. Howie's a bit of a snoop. You'd do well not to emulate him."

"No way, baby!" Still smiling, delighted at how all this has gone, Morris reaches for the door handle.

"And Morris?"

"Yeah?"

"Since you know my secret, perhaps you'd better call me Henry."

"Henry! Yeah!" Is this the best morning of the summer for Morris Rosen? You better believe it.

"And something else."

"Yeah? *Henry?*" Morris dares imagine a day when they will progress to Hank and Morrie.

*"Keep your mouth shut about the Rat."*

"I already told you—"

"Yes, and I believe you. But temptation comes creeping, Morris; temptation comes creeping like a thief in the night, or like a killer in search of prey. If you give in to temptation, I'll know. I'll smell it on your skin like bad cologne. Do you believe me?"

"Uh . . . yeah." And he does. Later, when he has time to kick back and reflect, Morris will think what a ridiculous idea that is, but yes, at the time, he believes it. Believes *him*. It's like being hypnotized.

"Very good. Now off you go. I want Ace Hardware, Zaglat Chevy, and Mr. Tastee Ribs all cued up for the first seg."

"Gotcha."

"Also, last night's game—"

"Wickman striking out the side in the eighth? That was pimp. Totally, like, un-Brewers."

"No, I think we want the Mark Loretta home run in the fifth. Loretta doesn't hit many, and the fans like him. I can't think why. Even a blind man can see he has no range, especially from deep in the hole. Go on, son. Put the CD in my locker, and if I see the Rat, I'll give it to him. I'm sure he'll give it a spin."

"The track—"

"Seven, seven, rhymes with heaven. I won't forget and neither will he. Go on, now."

Morris gives him a final grateful look and goes back inside. Henry Leyden, alias George Rathbun, alias the Wisconsin Rat, also alias Henry Shake (we'll get to that one, but not now; the hour draweth late), lights another cigarette and drags deep. He won't have time to finish it; the farm report is already in full flight (hog bellies up, wheat futures down, and the corn as high as an elephant's eye), but he needs a couple of drags just now to steady himself. A long, long day stretches out ahead of him, ending with the Strawberry Fest Hop at Maxton Elder Care, that house of antiquarian horrors. God save him from the clutches of William "Chipper" Maxton, he has often thought. Given a choice between ending his days at MEC and burning his face off with a blowtorch, he would reach for the blowtorch every time. Later, if he's not totally exhausted, perhaps his friend from up the road will come over and they can begin the long-promised reading of *Bleak House*. That would be a treat.

How long, he wonders, can Morris Rosen hold on to his momentous secret? Well, Henry supposes he will find that out. He likes the Rat too much to give him up unless he absolutely has to; that much is an undeniable fact.

"Dean Kissinger," he murmurs. "Henry Acheson. Ucky Ducky. God save us."

He takes another drag on his cigarette, then drops it into the bucket of sand. It is time to go back inside, time to replay last night's Mark Loretta home run, time to start taking more calls from the Coulee Country's dedicated sports fans.

And time for us to be off. Seven o'clock has rung from the Lutheran church steeple.

In French Landing, things are getting into high gear. No one lies abed long in this part of the world, and we must speed along to the end of our tour. Things are going to start happening soon, and they may happen fast. Still, we have done well, and we have only one more stop to make before arriving at our final destination.

We rise on the warm summer updrafts and hover for a moment by the KDCU tower (we are close enough to hear the tik-tik-tik of the beacon and the low, rather sinister hum of electricity), looking north and taking our bearings. Eight miles upriver is the town of Great Bluff, named for the limestone outcropping that rises there. The outcropping is reputed to be haunted, because in 1888 a chief of the Fox Indian tribe (Far Eyes was his name) assembled all his warriors, shamans, squaws, and children and told them to leap to their deaths, thereby escaping some hideous fate he had glimpsed in his dreams. Far Eyes's followers, like Jim Jones's, did as they were bidden.

We won't go that far upriver, however; we have enough ghosts to deal with right here in French Landing. Let us instead fly over Nailhouse Row once more (the Harleys are gone; Beezer St. Pierre has led the Thunder Five off to their day's work at the brewery), over Queen Street and Maxton Elder Care (Burny's down there, still looking out his window—ugh), to Bluff Street. This is almost the countryside again. Even now, in the twenty-first century, the towns in Coulee Country give up quickly to the woods and the fields.

Herman Street is a left turn from Bluff Street, in an area that is not quite town and not quite city. Here, in a sturdy brick house sitting at the end of a half-mile meadow as yet undiscovered by the developers (even here there are a few developers, unknowing agents of *slippage*), lives Dale Gilbertson with his wife, Sarah, and his six-year-old son, David.

We can't stay long, but let us at least drift in through the kitchen window for a moment. It's open, after all, and there is room for us to perch right here on the counter, between the Silex and the toaster. Sitting at the kitchen table, reading the newspaper and shoveling Special K into his mouth without tasting it (he has forgotten both the sugar and the sliced banana in his distress at seeing yet another Wendell Green byline on the front page of the *Herald*), is Chief Gilbertson himself. This morning he is without doubt the unhappiest man in French Landing. We will meet his only competition for that booby prize soon, but for the moment, let us stick with Dale.

*The Fisherman,* he thinks mournfully, his reflections on this subject very similar to those of Bobby Dulac and Tom Lund.

*Why didn't you name him something a little more turn-of-the-century, you troublesome scribbling fuck? Something a little bit local? Dahmerboy, maybe, that'd be good.*

Ah, but Dale knows why. The similarities between Albert Fish, who did his work in New York, and their boy here in French Landing are just too good—too *tasty*—to be ignored. Fish strangled his victims, as both Amy St. Pierre and Johnny Irkenham were apparently strangled; Fish dined on his victims, as both the girl and the boy were apparently dined upon; both Fish and the current fellow showed an especial liking for the . . . well, for the posterior regions of the anatomy.

Dale looks at his cereal, then drops his spoon into the mush and pushes the bowl away with the side of his hand.

And the letters. Can't forget the letters.

Dale glances down at his briefcase, crouched at the side of his chair like a faithful dog. The file is in there, and it draws him like a rotted, achy tooth draws the tongue. Maybe he can keep his *hands* off it, at least while he's here at home, where he plays toss with his son and makes love to his wife, but keeping his *mind* off it . . . that's a whole 'nother thing, as they also say in these parts.

Albert Fish wrote a long and horribly explicit letter to the mother of Grace Budd, the victim who finally earned the old cannibal a trip to the electric chair. ("What a thrill electrocution will be!" Fish reputedly told his jailers. "The only one I haven't tried!") The current doer has written similar letters, one addressed to Helen Irkenham, the other to Amy's father, the awful (but genuinely grief-stricken, in Dale's estimation) Armand "Beezer" St. Pierre. It would be good if Dale could believe these letters were written by some troublemaker not otherwise connected to the murders, but both contain information that has been withheld from the press, information that presumably only the killer could know.

Dale at last gives in to temptation (how well Henry Leyden would understand) and hauls up his briefcase. He opens it and puts a thick file where his cereal bowl lately rested. He returns the briefcase to its place by his chair, then opens the file (it is marked ST. PIERRE/IRKENHAM rather than FISHERMAN). He leafs past heartbreaking school photos of two smiling, gap-toothed children, past state medical examiner reports too horrible to read and crime-scene photos too horrible to look at (ah, but he must look at them, again and again he must look at them—the blood-slicked chains, the flies, the open eyes). There are also various transcripts, the longest being the interview with Spencer Hovdahl, who found the Irkenham boy and who was, very briefly, considered a suspect.

Next come Xerox copies of three letters. One had been sent to George and Helen Irkenham (addressed to Helen alone, if it made any difference). One went to Armand "Beezer" St. Pierre (addressed just that way, too, nickname and all). The third had been sent to the mother of Grace Budd, of New York City, following the murder of her daughter in the late spring of 1928.

Dale lays the three of them out, side by side.

*Grace sat in my lap and kissed me. I made up my mind to eat her.* So Fish had written to Mrs. Budd.

*Amy sat in my lap and hugged me. I made up my mind to eat her.* So had Beezer St. Pierre's correspondent written, and was it any wonder the man had threatened to burn the French Landing police station to the ground? Dale doesn't like the son of a bitch, but has to admit he might feel the same way in Beezer's shoes.

*I went upstairs and stripped all my clothes off. I knew if I did not I would get her blood on them.* Fish, to Mrs. Budd.

*I went around back of the hen-house and stripped all my cloes off. New if I did not I would get his blood on them.* Anonymous, to Helen Irkenham. And here was a question: How could a mother receive a letter like that and retain her sanity? Was that possible? Dale thought not. Helen answered questions coherently, had even offered him tea the last time he was out there, but she had a glassy, poleaxed look in her eye that suggested she was running entirely on instruments.

Three letters, two new, one almost seventy-five years old. And yet all three are so similar. The St. Pierre letter and the Irkenham letter had been hand-printed by someone who was left-handed, according to the state experts. The paper was plain white Hammermill mimeo, available in every Office Depot and Staples in America. The pen used had probably been a Bic—now, *there* was a lead.

Fish to Mrs. Budd, back in '28: *I did not fuck her tho I could of had I wished. She died a virgin.*

Anonymous to Beezer St. Pierre: *I did NOT fuck her tho I could of had I wished. She died a VIRGIN.*

Anonymous to Helen Irkenham: *This may comfort you I did NOT fuck him tho I could of had I wished. He died a VIRGIN.*

Dale's out of his depth here and knows it, but he hopes he isn't a complete fool. This doer, although he did not sign his letters with the old cannibal's name, clearly *wanted* the connection to be made. He had done everything but leave a few dead trout at the dumping sites.

Sighing bitterly, Dale puts the letters back into the file, the file back into the briefcase.

"Dale? Honey?" Sarah's sleepy voice, from the head of the stairs.

Dale gives the guilty jump of a man who has almost been caught doing something nasty and latches his briefcase. "I'm in the kitchen," he calls back. No need to worry about waking Davey; he sleeps like the dead until at least seven-thirty every morning.

"Going in late?"

"Uh-huh." He often goes in late, then makes up for it by working until seven or eight or even nine in the evening. Wendell Green hasn't made a big deal of *that* . . . at least not so far, but give him time. Talk about your cannibals!

"Give the flowers a drink before you go, would you? It's been so dry."

"You bet." Watering Sarah's flowers is a chore Dale likes. He gets some of his best thinking done with the garden hose in his hand.

A pause from upstairs . . . but he hasn't heard her slippers shuffling back toward the bedroom. He waits. And at last: "You okay, hon?"

"Fine," he calls back, pumping what he hopes will be the right degree of heartiness into his voice.

"Because you were still tossing around when I dropped off."

"No, I'm fine."

"Do you know what Davey asked me last night while I was washing his hair?"

Dale rolls his eyes. He hates these long-distance conversations. Sarah seems to love them. He gets up and pours himself another cup of coffee. "No, what?"

"He asked, 'Is Daddy going to lose his job?' "

Dale pauses with the cup halfway to his lips. "What did you say?"

"I said no. Of course."

"Then you said the right thing."

He waits, but there is no more. Having injected him with one more dram of poisonous worry—David's fragile psyche, as well as what a certain party might do to the boy, should David be so unlucky as to run afoul of him—Sarah shuffles back to their room and, presumably, to the shower beyond.

Dale goes back to the table, sips his coffee, then puts his hand to his forehead and closes his eyes. In this moment we can see precisely how frightened and miserable he is. Dale is just forty-two and a man of abstemious habits, but in the cruel morning light coming through the window by which we entered, he looks, for the moment, anyway, a sickly sixty.

He *is* concerned about his job, knows that if the fellow who killed Amy and Johnny keeps it up, he will almost certainly be turned out of office the following year. He is also concerned about Davey . . . although Davey isn't his chief concern, for, like Fred Marshall, he cannot actually conceive that the Fisherman could take his and Sarah's own child. No, it is the *other* children of French Landing he is more worried about, possibly the children of Centralia and Arden as well.

His worst fear is that he is simply not good enough to catch the son of a bitch. That he will kill a third, a fourth, perhaps an eleventh and twelfth.

God knows he has requested help. And gotten it . . . sort of. There are two State Police detectives assigned to the case, and the FBI guy from Madison keeps checking in (on an informal basis, though; the FBI is not officially part of the investigation). Even his outside help has a surreal quality for Dale, one that has been partially caused by an odd coincidence of their names. The FBI guy is Agent John P. Redding. The state detectives are Perry Brown and Jeffrey Black. So he has Brown, Black, and Redding on his team. The Color Posse, Sarah calls them. All three making it clear that they are strictly working support, at least for the time being. Making it clear that Dale Gilbertson is the man standing on ground zero.

*Christ, but I wish Jack would sign on to help me with this,*

Dale thinks. *I'd deputize him in a second, just like in one of those corny old Western movies.*

Yes indeed. In a second.

When Jack had first come to French Landing, almost four years ago, Dale hadn't known what to make of the man his officers immediately dubbed Hollywood. By the time the two of them had nailed Thornberg Kinderling—yes, inoffensive little Thornberg Kinderling, hard to believe but absolutely true—he knew *exactly* what to make of him. The guy was the finest natural detective Dale had ever met in his life.

*The* only *natural detective, that's what you mean.*

Yes, all right. The *only* one. And although they had shared the collar (at the L.A. newcomer's absolute insistence), it had been Jack's detective work that had turned the trick. He was almost like one of those storybook detectives . . . Hercule Poirot, Ellery Queen, one of those. Except that Jack didn't exactly deduct, nor did he go around tapping his temple and talking about his "little gray cells." He . . .

"He listens," Dale mutters, and gets up. He heads for the back door, then returns for his briefcase. He'll put it in the back seat of his cruiser before he waters the flower beds. He doesn't want those awful pictures in his house any longer than strictly necessary.

*He listens.*

Like the way he'd listened to Janna Massengale, the bartender at the Taproom. Dale had had no idea why Jack was spending so much time with the little chippy; it had even crossed his mind that Mr. Los Angeles Linen Slacks was trying to hustle her into bed so he could go back home and tell all his friends on Rodeo Drive that he'd gotten himself a little piece of the cheese up there in Wisconsin, where the air was rare and the legs were long and strong. But that hadn't been it at all. He had been *listening,* and finally she had told him what he needed to hear.

*Yeah, shurr, people get funny ticks when they're drinking,* Janna had said. *There's this one guy who starts doing this after a couple of belts.* She had pinched her nostrils together with the tips of her fingers . . . only with her hand turned around so the palm pointed out.

Jack, still smiling easily, still sipping a club soda: *Always with the palm out? Like this?* And mimicked the gesture.

Janna, smiling, half in love: *That's it, doll—you're a quick study.*

Jack: *Sometimes, I guess. What's this fella's name, darlin'?*

Janna: *Kinderling. Thornberg Kinderling.* She giggled. *Only, after a drink or two—once he's started up with that pinchy thing—he wants everyone to call him Thorny.*

Jack, still with his own smile: *And does he drink Bombay gin, darlin'? One ice cube, little trace of bitters?*

Janna's smile starting to fade, now looking at him as if he might be some kind of wizard: *How'd you know that?*

But how he knew it didn't matter, because that was really the whole package, done up in a neat bow. Case closed, game over, zip up your fly.

Eventually, Jack had flown back to Los Angeles with Thornberg Kinderling in custody—Thornberg Kinderling, just an inoffensive, bespectacled farm-insurance salesman from Centralia, wouldn't say boo to a goose, wouldn't say shit if he had a mouthful, wouldn't dare ask your mamma for a drink of water on a hot day, but he had killed two prostitutes in the City of Angels. No strangulation for Thorny; he had done his work with a Buck knife, which Dale himself had eventually traced to Lapham Sporting Goods, the nasty little trading post a door down from the Sand Bar, Centralia's grungiest drinking establishment.

By then DNA testing had nailed Kinderling's ass to the barn door, but Jack had been glad to have the provenance of the murder weapon anyway. He had called Dale personally to thank him, and Dale, who'd never been west of Denver in his life, had been almost absurdly touched by the courtesy. Jack had said several times during the course of the investigation that you could never have enough evidence when the doer was a genuine bad guy, and Thorny Kinderling had turned out to be about as bad as you could want. He'd gone the insanity route, of course, and Dale—who had privately hoped he might be called upon to testify—was delighted when the jury rejected the plea and sentenced him to consecutive life terms.

And what made all that happen? What had been the first cause? Why, a man listening. That was all. Listening to a lady bartender who was used to having her breasts stared at while her words most commonly went in one ear of the man doing the staring and out the other. And who had Hollywood Jack listened to before he had listened to Janna Massengale? Some Sunset Strip hooker, it seemed . . . or more likely a whole bunch of them. (*What would you call that, anyway?* Dale wonders absently as he goes out to the garage to get his trusty hose. *A shimmy of streetwalkers? A strut of hookers?*) None of them could have picked Thornberg Kinderling out of a lineup, because the Thornberg who visited L.A. surely hadn't looked much like the Thornberg who traveled around to the farm-supply companies in the Coulee and over in Minnesota. L.A. Thorny had worn a wig, contacts instead of specs, and a little false mustache.

"The most brilliant thing was the skin darkener," Jack had said. "Just a little, just enough to make him look like a native."

"Dramatics all four years at French Landing High School," Dale had replied grimly. "I looked it up. The little bastard played Don Juan his junior year, do you believe it?"

A lot of sly little changes (too many for a jury to swallow an insanity plea, it seemed), but Thorny had forgotten that one revelatory little signature, that trick of pinching his nostrils together with the palm of his hand turned outward. Some prostitute had remembered it, though, and when she mentioned it—only in passing, Dale has no doubt, just as Janna Massengale did—Jack heard it.

Because he listened.

*Called to thank me for tracing the knife, and again to tell me how the jury came back,* Dale thinks, *but that second time he wanted something, too. And I knew what it was. Even before he opened his mouth I knew.*

Because, while he is no genius detective like his friend from the Golden State, Dale had not missed the younger man's unexpected, immediate response to the landscape of western Wisconsin. Jack had fallen in love with the Coulee Country, and Dale would have wagered a good sum that it had been love at first look. It had been impossible to mistake the expression on his face as they drove from French Landing to Centralia, from Centralia to Arden, from Arden to Miller: wonder, pleasure, almost a kind of rapture. To Dale, Jack had looked like a man who has come to a place he has never been before only to discover he is back home.

"Man, I can't get over this," he'd said once to Dale. The two of them had been riding in Dale's old Caprice cruiser, the one that just wouldn't stay aligned (and sometimes the horn stuck, which could be embarrassing). "Do you realize how lucky you are to live here, Dale? It must be one of the most beautiful places in the world."

Dale, who had lived in the Coulee his entire life, had not disagreed.

Toward the end of their final conversation concerning Thornberg Kinderling, Jack had reminded Dale of how he'd once asked (not quite kidding, not quite serious, either) for Dale to let him know if a nice little place ever came on the market in Dale's part of the world, something out of town. And Dale had known at once from Jack's tone—the almost anxious drop in his voice—that the kidding was over.

"So you owe me," Dale murmurs, shouldering the hose. "You *owe* me, you bastard."

Of course he has asked Jack to lend an unofficial hand with the Fisherman investigation, but Jack has refused . . . almost with a kind of fear. *I'm retired,* he'd said brusquely. *If you don't know what that word means, Dale, we can look it up in the dictionary together.*

But it's ridiculous, isn't it? Of course it is. How can a man not yet thirty-five be retired? Especially one who is so infernally good at the job?

"You *owe* me, baby," he says again, now walking along the side of the house toward the bib faucet. The sky above is cloudless; the well-watered lawn is green; there is nary a sign of *slippage,* not out here on Herman Street. Yet perhaps there is, and perhaps we feel it. A kind of discordant hum, like the sound of all those lethal volts coursing through the steel struts of the KDCU tower.

But we have stayed here too long. We must take wing again and proceed to our final destination of this early morning. We don't know everything yet, but we know three important things: first, that French Landing is a town in terrible distress; second, that a few people (Judy Marshall, for one; Charles Burnside, for another) understand on some deep level that the town's ills go far beyond the depredations of a single sick pedophile-murderer; third, that we have met no one capable of consciously recognizing the force—the slippage—that has now come to bear on this quiet town hard by Tom and Huck's river. Each person we've met is, in his own way, as blind as Henry Leyden. This is as true of the folks we haven't so far encountered— Beezer St. Pierre, Wendell Green, the Color Posse—as it is of those we have.

Our hearts groan for a hero. And while we may not find one (this is the twenty-first century, after all, the days not of d'Artagnan and Jack Aubrey but of George W. Bush and Dirtysperm), we can perhaps find a man who *was* a hero once upon a time. Let us therefore search out an old friend, one we last glimpsed a thousand and more miles east of here, on the shore of the steady Atlantic. Years have passed and they have in some ways lessened the boy who was; he has forgotten much and has spent a good part of his adult life maintaining that state of amnesia. But he is French Landing's only hope, so let us take wing and fly almost due east, back over the woods and fields and gentle hills.

Mostly, we see miles of unbroken farmland: regimental cornfields, luxuriant hay fields, fat yellow swaths of alfalfa. Dusty, narrow drives lead to white farmhouses and their arrays of tall barns, granaries, cylindrical cement-block silos, and long metal equipment sheds. Men in denim jackets are moving along the well-worn paths between the houses and the barns. We can already smell the sunlight. Its odor, richly compacted of butter, yeast, earth, growth, and decay, will intensify as the sun ascends and the light grows stronger.

Below us, Highway 93 intersects Highway 35 at the center of tiny Centralia. The empty parking lot behind the Sand Bar awaits the noisy arrival of the Thunder Five, who customarily spend their Saturday afternoons, evenings, and nights in the enjoyment of the Sand Bar's pool tables, hamburgers, and pitchers of that ambrosia to the creation of which they have devoted their eccentric lives, Kingsland Brewing Company's finest product and a beer that can hold up its creamy head among anything made in a specialty microbrewery or a Belgian monastery, Kingsland Ale. If Beezer St. Pierre, Mouse, and company say it is the greatest beer in the world, why should we doubt them? Not only do they know much more about beer than we do, they called upon every bit of the knowledge, skill, expertise, and seat-of-the-pants inspiration at their disposal to make Kingsland Ale a benchmark of the brewer's art. In fact, they moved to French Landing because the brewery, which they had selected after careful deliberation, was willing to work with them.

To invoke Kingsland Ale is to wish for a good-sized mouthful of the stuff, but we put temptation behind us; 7:30 A.M. is far too early for drinking anything but fruit juice, coffee, and milk (except for the likes of Wanda Kinderling, and Wanda thinks of beer, even Kingsland Ale, as a dietary supplement to Aristocrat vodka); and we are in search of our old friend and the closest we can come to a hero, whom we last saw as a boy on the shore of the Atlantic Ocean. We are not about to waste time; we are on the move, right here and now. The miles fly past beneath us, and along Highway 93 the fields narrow as the hills rise up on both sides.

For all our haste, we must *take this in,* we must *see where we are.*

# 4

Three years ago, our old friend traveled down this stretch of 93 in the passenger seat of Dale Gilbertson's old Caprice, his heart going crazy in his chest, his throat constricting, and his mouth dry, as friendly Dale, in those days little more than a small-town cop whom he had impressed beyond rational measure simply by doing his job more or less as well as he could, piloted him toward a farmhouse and five acres left Dale by his deceased father. "The nice little place" could be purchased for next to nothing, since Dale's cousins did not particularly want it and it had no value to anyone else. Dale had been holding on to the property for sentimental reasons, but he had no particular interest in it, either. Dale had scarcely known what to do with a second house, apart from spending a great deal of time keeping it up, a task he had found oddly enjoyable but did not at all mind turning over to someone else. And at this point in their relationship, Dale was so in awe of our friend that, far from resenting the prospect of this man occupying his father's old house, he considered it an honor.

As for the man in the passenger seat, he was too caught up in his response to the landscape—too caught up *by* the landscape—to be embarrassed by Dale's awe. Under ordinary circumstances, our friend would have urged his admirer into a quiet bar, bought him a beer and said, "Look, I know you were impressed by what I did, but after all, Dale, I'm just another cop, like you. That's all. And in all honesty, I'm a lot luckier than I deserve to be." (It would be the truth, too: ever since we last saw him, our friend has been blessed, if it is a blessing, with such extravagantly good luck that he no longer dares to play cards or bet on sporting events. When you win almost all the time, winning tastes like spoiled grape juice.) But these were not ordinary circumstances, and in the swarm of emotion that had been threatening to undo him since they left Centralia on the flat straightaway of Highway 93, Dale's adulation barely registered. This short drive to a place he had never seen before felt like a long-delayed journey home: everything he saw seemed charged with remembered meaning, a part of him, essential. Everything seemed sacred. He knew he was going to buy the nice little place, no matter what it looked like or how much it cost, not that price could in any way have been an obstacle. He was going to buy it, that was all. Dale's hero-worship affected him only to the extent that he realized he would be forced to keep his admirer from undercharging him. In the meantime, he struggled against the tears that wanted to fill his eyes.

From above, we see the glacial valleys dividing the landscape to the right of 93 like the imprint of a giant's fingers. He saw only the sudden narrow roads that split off the highway and slipped into mingled sunshine and darkness. Each road said, *Nearly there.* The highway said, *This is the way.* Gazing down, we can observe a roadside parking area, two gasoline pumps, and a long gray roof bearing the fading legend ROY'S STORE; when he looked to his right and saw, past the gas pumps, the wooden stairs rising to a wide, inviting porch and the store's entrance, he felt as though he had already mounted those stairs a hundred times before and gone inside to pick up bread, milk, beer, cold cuts, work gloves, a screwdriver, a bag of tenpenny nails, whatever he needed from the practical cornucopia crowded onto the shelves, as after that day he would do, a hundred times and more.

Fifty yards down the highway the blue-gray sliver of Tamarack Creek comes winding into Norway Valley. When Dale's car rolled across the rusting little metal bridge, the bridge said, *This is it!,* and the casually but expensively dressed man in the passenger seat, who looked as though all he knew of farmland had been learned through the windows next to first-class seats on transcontinental flights and in fact was incapable of telling wheat from hay, felt his heart shiver. On the other side of the bridge, a road sign read NORWAY VALLEY ROAD.

"This is it," said Dale, and made the right turn into the val-

ley. Our friend covered his mouth with his hand, stifling whatever sounds his shivering heart might cause him to utter.

Here and there, wildflowers bloomed and nodded on the
roadside, some of them audacious and bright, others half-hidden
in a blanket of vibrant green. "Driving up this road always
makes me feel good," Dale said.

"No wonder," our friend managed to say.

Most of what Dale said failed to penetrate the whirlwind of
emotion roaring through his passenger's mind and body. That's
the old Lund farm—cousins of my mother. The one-room
schoolhouse where my great-grandmother taught used to be
right over there, only they tore it down way back. This here is
Duane Updahl's place, he's no relation, thank goodness. Buzz
blur mumble. Blur mumble buzz. They once again drove over
Tamarack Creek, its glittering blue-gray water laughing and
calling out, *Here we are!* Around a bend in the road they went,
and a wealth of luxuriant wildflowers leaned carousing toward
the car. In their midst, the blind, attentive faces of tiger lilies
tilted to meet our friend's face. A ripple of feeling distinct from
the whirlwind, quieter but no less potent, brought dazzled tears
to the surface of his eyes.

Tiger lilies, why? Tiger lilies meant nothing to him. He used
the pretense of a yawn to wipe his eyes and hoped that Dale had
not noticed.

"Here we are," Dale said, having noticed or not, and swerved
into a long, overgrown drive, hedged with wildflowers and tall
grasses, which appeared to lead nowhere except into a great expanse of meadow and banks of waist-high flowers. Beyond the
meadow, striped fields sloped upward to the wooded hillside.
"You'll see my dad's old place in a second. The meadow goes
with the house, and my cousins Randy and Kent own the field."

Our friend could not see the white two-story farmhouse that
stands at the end of the last curve of the drive until the moment
Dale Gilbertson swung halfway into the curve, and he did not
speak until Dale had pulled up in front of the house, switched
off the engine, and both men had left the car. Here was "the nice
little place," sturdy, newly painted, lovingly maintained, modest
yet beautiful in its proportions, removed from the road, removed from the world, at the edge of a green and yellow
meadow profuse with flowers.

"My God, Dale," he said, "it's perfection."

Here we will find our former traveling companion, who in his own boyhood knew a boy named Richard Sloat and, once, too briefly, knew yet another whose name was, simply, Wolf. In this sturdy, comely, removed white farmhouse we will find our old friend, who once in his boyhood journeyed cross-country from ocean to ocean in pursuit of a certain crucial thing, a necessary object, a great talisman, and who, despite horrendous obstacles and fearful perils, succeeded in finding the object of his search and used it wisely and well. Who, we could say, accomplished a number of miracles, heroically. And who remembers none of this. Here, making breakfast for himself in his kitchen while listening to George Rathbun on KDCU, we at last find the former Los Angeles County lieutenant of police, Homicide Division, Jack Sawyer.

Our Jack. Jacky-boy, as his mother, the late Lily Cavanaugh Sawyer, used to say.

He had followed Dale through the empty house, upstairs and down, into the basement, dutifully admiring the new furnace and water heater Gilbertson had installed the year before his father's death, the quality of the repairs he had made since then, the shining grain of the wooden floors, the thickness of the insulation in the attic, the solidity of the windows, the many craftsmanlike touches that met his eye.

"Yeah, I did a lot of work on the place," Dale told him. "It was pretty shipshape to begin with, but I like working with my hands. After a while it turned into sort of a hobby. Whenever I had a couple of hours free, weekends and such, I got in the habit of driving over here and puttering around. I don't know, maybe it helped me feel like I was staying in touch with my dad. He was a really good guy, my dad. He wanted me to be a farmer, but when I said I was thinking of getting into law enforcement, he supported me straight down the line. Know what he said? 'Go into farming halfhearted, it'll kick you in the tail sunrise to sundown. You'd wind up feeling no better than a mule. Your mom and I didn't bring you into this world to turn you into a mule.' "

"What did she think?" Jack had asked.

"My mom came from a long line of farmers," Dale had said. "She thought I might find out that being a mule wasn't so bad after all. By the time she passed away, which was four years before my dad, she'd gotten used to my being a cop. Let's go out the kitchen door and take a gander at the meadow, okay?"

While they were standing outside and taking their gander, Jack had asked Dale how much he wanted for the house. Dale, who had been waiting for this question, had knocked five thousand off the most he and Sarah had ever thought he could get. Who was he kidding? Dale had wanted Jack Sawyer to buy the house where he had grown up—he'd wanted Jack to live near him for at least a couple of weeks during the year. And if Jack did not buy the place, no one else would.

"Are you serious?" Jack had asked.

More dismayed than he wished to admit, Dale had said, "Sounds like a fair deal to me."

"It isn't fair to *you*," Jack had said. "I'm not going to let you give this place away just because you like me. Raise the asking price, or I walk."

"You big-city hotshots sure know how to negotiate. All right, make it three thousand more."

"Five," Jack said. "Or I'm outta here."

"Done. But you're breaking my heart."

"I hope this is the last time I buy property off one of you low-down Norwegians," Jack said.

He had purchased the house long-distance, sending a down payment from L.A., exchanging signatures by fax, no mortgage, cash up front. Whatever Jack Sawyer's background might have been, Dale had thought, it was a lot wealthier than the usual police officer's. Some weeks later, Jack had reappeared at the center of a self-created tornado, arranging for the telephone to be connected and the electricity billed in his name, scooping up what looked like half the contents of Roy's Store, zipping off to Arden and La Riviere to buy a new bed, linens, tableware, cast-iron pots and pans and a set of French knives, a compact microwave and a giant television, and a stack of sound equipment so sleek, black, and resplendent that Dale, who had been invited over for a companionable drink, figured it must have cost more than his own annual salary. Much else, besides, had Jack reeled in, some of the much else consisting of items Dale had been surprised to learn could be obtained in French County, Wisconsin. Why would anyone need a sixty-five-dollar cork-screw called a WineMaster? Who was this guy, what kind of family had produced him?

He'd noticed a bag bearing an unfamiliar logo filled with compact discs—at fifteen, sixteen dollars a pop, he was looking at a couple hundred dollars' worth of CDs. Whatever else might have been true of Jack Sawyer, he was into music in a big way. Curious, Dale bent down, pulled out a handful of jewel boxes, and regarded images of people, generally black, generally with instruments pressed to or in their mouths. Clifford Brown, Lester Young, Tommy Flanagan, Paul Desmond. "I never heard of these guys," he said. "What is this, jazz, I guess?"

"You guess right," Jack said. "Could I ask you to help me move furniture around and hang pictures, stuff like that, in a month or two? I'm going to have a lot of stuff shipped here."

"Anytime." A splendid idea bloomed in Dale's mind. "Hey, you have to meet my uncle Henry! He's even a neighbor of yours, lives about a quarter mile down the road. He was mar-ried to my aunt Rhoda, my father's sister, who died three years ago. Henry's like an encyclopedia of weird music."

Jack did not take up the assumption that jazz was weird. Maybe it was. Anyhow, it probably sounded weird to Dale. "I wouldn't have thought farmers had much time to listen to music."

Dale opened his mouth and uttered a bray of laughter. "Henry isn't a farmer. Henry . . ." Grinning, Dale raised his hands, palms up and fingers spread, and looked into the middle dis-tance, searching for the right phrase. "He's like the *reverse* of a farmer. When you get back, I'll introduce you to him. You're going to be crazy about the guy."

Six weeks later, Jack returned to greet the moving van and tell the men where to put the furniture and other things he had shipped; a few days afterward, when he had unpacked most of the boxes, he telephoned Dale and asked if he was still willing to give him a hand. It was 5:00 on a day so slow that Tom Lund had fallen asleep at his desk, and Dale drove over without even bothering to change out of his uniform.

His first response, after Jack had shaken his hand and ush-ered him in, was undiluted shock. Having taken a single step past the doorway, Dale froze in his tracks, unable to move any farther. Two or three seconds passed before he realized that it was a *good* shock, a shock of pleasure. His old house had been transformed: it was as if Jack Sawyer had tricked him and opened the familiar front door upon the interior of another house altogether. The sweep from the living room into the kitchen looked nothing like either the space he remembered from childhood or the clean, bare progression of the recent past. Jack had decorated the house with the wave of a wand, it seemed to Dale, in the process somehow turning it into he hardly knew what—a villa on the Riviera, a Park Avenue apartment. (Dale had never been to New York or the south of France.) Then it struck him that, instead of transforming the old place into something it was not, Jack had simply seen more in it than Dale ever had. The leather sofas and chairs, the glowing rugs, the wide tables and discreet lamps, had come from another world but fit in perfectly, as if they had been made specifically for this house. Everything he saw beckoned him in, and he found that he could move again.

"Wow," he said. "Did I ever sell this place to the right guy."

"I'm glad you like it," Jack said. "I have to admit, I do, too. It looks even better than I expected."

"What am I supposed to do? The place is already organized."

"We're going to hang some pictures," Jack said. "*Then* it'll be organized."

Dale supposed Jack was talking about family photographs. He did not understand why anyone would need help to hang up a bunch of framed photos, but if Jack wanted his assistance, he would assist. Besides that, the pictures would tell him a considerable amount about Jack's family, still a subject of great interest to him. However, when Jack led him to a stack of flat wooden crates leaning against the kitchen counter, Dale once again got the feeling that he was out of his depth here, that he had entered an unknown world. The crates had been made by hand; they were serious objects built to provide industrial-strength protection. Some of them were five or six feet tall and nearly as wide. These monsters did not have pictures of Mom and Dad inside them. He and Jack had to pry up the corners and loosen the nails along the edges before they could get the crates open. It took a surprising amount of effort to lever the tops off

the crates. Dale regretted not stopping at his house long enough
to take off his uniform, which was damp with sweat by the time
he and Jack had pulled from their cocoons five heavy, rectangular objects thickly swaddled in layers of tissue. Many crates
remained.

An hour later, they carried the empty crates down to the
basement and came back upstairs to have a beer. Then they
sliced open the layers of tissue, exposing paintings and graph-
ics in a variety of frames, including a few that looked as if the
artist had nailed them together himself out of barn siding.
Jack's pictures occupied a category Dale vaguely thought of as
"modern art." He did not grasp what some of these things were
supposed to be about, although he actually liked almost all of
them, especially a couple of landscapes. He knew that he had
never heard of the artists, but their names, he thought, would be
recognized by the kind of people who lived in big cities and
hung out in museums and galleries. All this art—all of these
images large and small now lined up on the kitchen floor—
stunned him, not altogether pleasantly. He really had entered
another world, and he knew none of its landmarks. Then he remembered that he and Jack Sawyer were going to hang these
pictures on the walls of his parents' old house. Immediately, unexpected warmth flooded into this notion and filled it to the
brim. Why shouldn't adjoining worlds mingle now and then?
And wasn't this other world Jack's?

"All right," he said. "I wish Henry, that uncle I was telling
you about? Who lives right down the road? I wish he could see
this stuff. Henry, he'd know how to appreciate it."

"Why won't he be able to see them? I'll invite him over."

"Didn't I say?" Dale asked. "Henry's blind."

Paintings went up on the living-room walls, ascended the
stairwell, moved into the bedrooms. Jack put up a couple of
small pictures in the upstairs bathroom and the little half bath
on the ground floor. Dale's arms began to ache from holding the
frames while Jack marked the places where the nails would go
in. After the first three paintings, he had removed his necktie
and rolled up his sleeves, and he could feel sweat trickling out
of his hair and sliding down his face. His unbuttoned collar had
soaked through. Jack Sawyer had worked as hard or harder than

he, but looked as if he had done nothing more strenuous than think about dinner.

"You're like an art collector, huh?" Dale said. "Did it take a long time to get all these paintings?"

"I don't know enough to be a collector," Jack said. "My father picked up most of this work back in the fifties and sixties. My mother bought a few things, too, when she saw something that turned her on. Like that little Fairfield Porter over there, with the front porch and a lawn and the flowers."

The little Fairfield Porter, which name Dale assumed to be that of its painter, had appealed to him as soon as he and Jack had pulled it out of its crate. You could hang a picture like that in your own living room. You could almost step into a picture like that. The funny thing was, Dale thought, if you hung it in your living room, most of the people who came in would never really notice it at all.

Jack had said something about being glad to get the paintings out of storage. "So," Dale said, "your mom and dad *gave* them to you?"

"I inherited them after my mother's death," Jack said. "My father died when I was a kid."

"Oh, darn, I'm sorry," Dale said, snapped abruptly out of the world into which Mr. Fairfield Porter had welcomed him. "Had to be tough on you, losing your dad so young." He thought Jack had given him the explanation for the aura of apartness and isolation that seemed always to envelop him. A second before Jack could respond, Dale told himself he was bullshitting. He had no idea how someone wound up being like Jack Sawyer.

"Yeah," Jack said. "Fortunately, my mother was even tougher."

Dale seized his opportunity with both hands. "What did your folks do? Were you brought up in California?"

"Born and raised in Los Angeles," Jack said. "My parents were in the entertainment industry, but don't hold that against them. They were great people."

Jack did not invite him to stay for supper—that was what stuck with Dale. Over the hour and a half it took them to hang the rest of the pictures, Jack Sawyer remained friendly and good-humored, but Dale, who was not a cop for nothing,

sensed something evasive and adamant in his friend's affability:
a door had opened a tiny crack, then slammed shut. The phrase
"great people" had placed Jack's parents out of bounds. When
the two men broke for another beer, Dale noticed a pair of bags
from a Centralia grocery next to the microwave. It was then
nearly 8:00, at least two hours past French County's suppertime. Jack might reasonably have assumed that Dale had already eaten, were his uniform not evidence to the contrary.

He tossed Jack a softball about the hardest case he had ever
solved and sidled up to the counter. The marbled red tips of two
sirloin steaks protruded from the nearest bag. His stomach
emitted a reverberant clamor. Jack ignored the thunder roll and
said, "Thornberg Kinderling was right up there with anything I
handled in L.A. I was really grateful for your help." Dale got
the picture. Here was another locked door. This one had declined to open by as much as a crack. History was not spoken
here; the past had been nailed shut.

They finished their beers and installed the last of the pictures. Over the next few hours, they spoke of a hundred things,
but always within the boundaries Jack Sawyer had established.
Dale was sure that his question about Jack's parents had short-
ened the evening, but why should that be true? What was the
guy hiding? And from whom was he hiding it? After their work
was done, Jack thanked him warmly and walked him outside to
his car, thereby cutting off any hope of a last-minute reprieve.
Case closed, game over, zip up your fly, in the words of the immortal George Rathbun. While they stood in the fragrant darkness beneath the millions of stars arrayed above them, Jack
sighed with pleasure and said, "I hope you know how grateful
I am. Honestly, I'm sorry I have to go back to L.A. Would you
*look* at how beautiful this is?"

Driving back to French Landing, his the only headlights on
the long stretch of Highway 93, Dale wondered if Jack's parents
had been involved in some aspect of the entertainment business
embarrassing to their adult son, like pornography. Maybe Dad
directed skin flicks, and Mom starred in them. The people who
made dirty movies probably raked in the dough, especially if
they kept it in the family. Before his odometer ticked off another tenth of a mile, the memory of the little Fairfield Porter
turned Dale's satisfaction to dust. No woman who earned her

keep having on-camera sex with strangers would spend actual money on a painting like that.

Let us enter Jack Sawyer's kitchen. The morning's *Herald* lies unfolded on the dining table; a black frying pan recently sprayed with Pam heats atop the circle of blue flames from the gas stove's front left-hand burner. A tall, fit, distracted-looking man wearing an old USC sweatshirt, jeans, and Italian loafers the color of molasses is swirling a whisk around the interior of a stainless steel bowl containing a large number of raw eggs.

Looking at him as he frowns at a vacant section of air well above the shiny bowl, we observe that the beautiful twelve-year-old boy last seen in a fourth-floor room of a deserted New Hampshire hotel has aged into a man whose good looks contribute only the smallest portion to what makes him interesting. For that Jack Sawyer *is* interesting declares itself instantly. Even when troubled to distraction by some private concern, some *enigma,* we might as well say in the face of that contemplative frown, Jack Sawyer cannot help but radiate a persuasive authority. Just by looking at him, you know that he is one of those persons to whom others turn when they feel stumped, threatened, or thwarted by circumstance. Intelligence, resolve, and dependability have shaped the cast of his features so deeply that their attractiveness is irrelevant to their meaning. This man never pauses to admire himself in mirrors—vanity plays no part in his character. It makes perfect sense that he should have been a rising star in the Los Angeles Police Department, that his file bulged with commendations, and that he had been selected for several FBI-sponsored programs and training courses designed to aid the progress of rising stars. (A number of Jack's colleagues and superiors had privately concluded that he would become the police commissioner of a city like San Diego or Seattle around the time he turned forty and, ten to fifteen years later, if all went well, step up to San Francisco or New York.)

More strikingly, Jack's age seems no more relevant than his attractiveness: he has the air of having passed through lifetimes before this one, of having gone places and seen things beyond the scope of most other people. No wonder Dale Gilbertson admires him; no wonder Dale yearns for Jack's assistance. In his place, we would want it, too, but our luck would be no better than his. This man has *retired,* he is out of the game, sorry, damn shame and all that, but a man's gotta whisk eggs when he's gotta have omelettes, as John Wayne said to Dean Martin in *Rio Bravo.*

"And as my momma told me," Jack says out loud to himself, "she said, 'Sonny boy,' said she, 'when the Duke *spoke* up, everdangbody *lissened* up, lessen he was a-grindin' one of his numerous political axes,' yes, she did, them were her same exack words, just as she said 'em to me." A half second later, he adds, "On that fine morning in Beverly Hills," and finally takes in what he is doing.

What we have here is a spectacularly lonely man. Loneliness has been Jack Sawyer's familiar for so long that he takes it for granted, but what you can't fix eventually turns into wallpaper, all right? Plenty of things, such as cerebral palsy and Lou Gehrig's disease, to name but two, are worse than loneliness. Loneliness is just part of the program, that's all. Even Dale noticed this aspect of his friend's character, and despite his many virtues, our chief of police cannot be described as a particularly psychological human being.

Jack glances at the clock above the stove and sees he has another forty-five minutes before he must drive to French Landing and pick up Henry Leyden at the end of his shift. That's good; he has plenty of time, he's keeping it together, the subtext to which is *Everything is all right, and nothing's wrong with me, thank you very much.*

When Jack woke up this morning, a small voice in his head announced *I am a coppiceman.* Like hell I am, he thought, and told the voice to leave him alone. The little voice could go to hell. He had given up on the coppiceman business, he had walked away from the homicide trade . . .

. . . *the lights of a carousel reflected on the bald head of a black man lying dead on the Santa Monica Pier . . .*

No. Don't go there. Just . . . just don't, that's all.

Jack should not have been in Santa Monica, anyhow. Santa Monica had its own coppicemen. As far as he knew, they were a swell bunch of guys, though perhaps not quite up to the standard set by that ace boy, whizbang, and youngest-ever lieutenant of LAPD's Homicide Division, himself. The only reason the ace boy and whizbang had been on their turf in the first place was that he had just broken up with this extremely nice, or at least moderately nice, resident of Malibu, Ms. Brooke Greer, a screenwriter greatly esteemed within her genre, the action adventure–romantic comedy, also a person of remarkable wit, insight, and bodily charm, and as he sped homeward down the handsome stretch of the Pacific Coast Highway below the Malibu Canyon exit he yielded to an uncharacteristically edgy spell of gloom.

A few seconds after swinging up the California Incline into Santa Monica, he saw the bright ring of the Ferris wheel revolving above the strings of lights and the lively crowd on the pier. A tawdry enchantment, or an enchanted tawdriness, spoke to him from the heart of this scene. On a whim, Jack parked his car and walked down to the array of brilliant lights glowing in the darkness. The last time he had visited the Santa Monica Pier, he had been an excited six-year-old boy pulling on Lily Cavanaugh Sawyer's hand like a dog straining at a leash.

What happened was accidental. It was too meaningless to be called coincidence. Coincidence brings together two previously unrelated elements of a larger story. Here nothing connected, and there was no larger story.

He came to the pier's gaudy entrance and noticed that, after all, the Ferris wheel was not revolving. A circle of stationary lights hung over empty gondolas. For a moment, the giant machine looked like an alien invader, cleverly disguised and biding its time until it could do the maximum amount of damage. Jack could almost hear it purring to itself. *Right,* he thought, *an evil Ferris wheel—get a grip. You're shaken up more than you want to admit.* Then he looked back down at the scene before him, and finally took in that his fantasy of the pier had hidden a real-life evil rendered far too familiar by his profession. He had stumbled onto the initial stages of a homicide investigation.

Some of the brilliant lights he had seen flashed not from the Ferris wheel but from the tops of Santa Monica patrol cars. Out on the pier, four uniforms were discouraging a crowd of civilians from breaching the circle of crime-scene tape around a brightly illuminated carousel. Jack told himself to leave it alone. He had no role here. Besides that, the carousel aroused some smoky, indistinct feeling, an entire set of unwelcome feelings, in him. The carousel was creepier than the stalled Ferris wheel. Carousels had always spooked him, hadn't they? Painted midget horses frozen into place with their teeth bared and steel poles rammed through their guts—sadistic kitsch.

*Walk away,* Jack told himself. *Your girlfriend dumped you and you're in a rotten mood.*

*And as for carousels . . .*

The abrupt descent of a mental lead curtain ended the debate about carousels. Feeling as though pushed from within, Jack stepped onto the pier and began moving through the crowd. He was half conscious of taking the most unprofessional action of his career.

When he had pushed his way to the front of the crowd, he ducked under the tape and flashed his badge at a babyfaced cop who tried to order him back. Somewhere nearby, a guitarist began playing a blues melody Jack could almost identify; the title swam to the surface of his mind, then dove out of sight. The infant cop gave him a puzzled look and walked away to consult one of the detectives standing over a long shape Jack did not quite feel like looking at just then. The music annoyed him. It annoyed him a lot. In fact, it bugged the hell out of him. His irritation was out of proportion to its cause, but what kind of idiot thought homicides needed a sound track?

A painted horse reared, frozen in the garish light.

Jack's stomach tightened, and deep in his chest something fierce and insistent, something at all costs not to be named, flexed itself and threw out its arms. Or extended its wings. The terrible something wished to break free and make itself known. Briefly, Jack feared he would have to throw up. The passing of this sensation bought him a moment of uncomfortable clarity.

Voluntarily, idly, he had walked into craziness, and now he was crazy. You could put it no other way. Marching toward him with an expression nicely combining disbelief and fury was a detective named Angelo Leone, before his expedient transfer to Santa Monica a colleague of Jack's distinguished by his gross appetites, his capacity for violence and corruption, his contempt for all civilians regardless of color, race, creed, or social status, and, to be fair, his fearlessness and utter loyalty to all police officers who went with the program and did the same things he did, which meant anything they could get away with. Angelo Leone's disdain for Jack Sawyer, who had not gone with the program, had equaled his resentment at the younger man's success. In a few seconds, this brutal caveman would be in his face. Instead of trying to figure out how to explain himself to the caveman, he was obsessing about carousels and guitars, attending to the details of going crazy. He had no way of explaining himself. Explanation was impossible. The internal necessity that had pushed him into this position hummed on, but Jack could hardly speak to Angelo Leone of internal necessities. Nor could he offer a rational explanation to his captain, if Leone filed a complaint.

*Well, you see, it was like someone else was pulling my strings, like another person was doing the driving . . .*

The first words out of Angelo Leone's fleshy mouth rescued him from disaster.

—Don't tell me you're here for a reason, you ambitious little prick.

A piratical career like Leone's inevitably exposed the pirate to the danger of an official investigation. A strategic sidestep to a neighboring force offered little protection from the covert archaeological digs police officials mounted into records and reputations when the press gave them no other choice. Every decade or two, do-gooders, whistle-blowers, whiners, snitches, pissed-off civilians, and cops too stupid to accept the time-honored program got together, rammed a cherry bomb up the press's collective anus, and set off an orgy of bloodletting. Leone's essential, guilt-inspired paranoia had instantly suggested to him that L.A. Homicide's ace boy might be gilding his résumé.

As Jack had known it would, his claim of having been pulled toward the scene like a fire hose to a fire magnified Leone's suspicions.

—Okay, you *happened* to walk into my investigation. Fine. Now listen to me. If I *happen* to hear your name in some connection I don't like anytime during the next six months, make that ever, you'll be pissing through a tube for the rest of your life. Now get the fuck out of here and let me do my job.

—I'm gone, Angelo.

Leone's partner started to come forward across the gleaming pier. Leone grimaced and waved him back. Without intending to do so, without thinking about it, Jack let his eyes drift past the detective and down to the corpse in front of the carousel. Far more powerfully than it had the first time, the ferocious creature at the center of his chest flexed itself, unfurled, and extended its wings, its arms, its talons, whatever they were, and by means of a tremendous upward surge attempted to rip free of its moorings.

The wings, the arms, the talons crushed Jack's lungs. Hideous claws splayed through his stomach.

There is one act a homicide detective, especially a homicide lieutenant, must never commit, and it is this: confronted with a dead body, he must not puke. Jack struggled to remain on the respectable side of the Forbidden. Bile seared the back of his throat, and he closed his eyes. A constellation of glowing dots wavered across his eyelids. The creature, molten and foul, battered against its restraints.

*Lights reflected on the scalp of a bald, black man lying dead beside a carousel . . .*

Not you. No, not you. Knock all you like, but you can't come in.

The wings, arms, talons retracted; the creature dwindled to a dozing speck. Having succeeded in avoiding the Forbidden Act, Jack found himself capable of opening his eyes. He had no idea how much time had passed. Angelo Leone's corrugated forehead, murky eyes, and carnivorous mouth heaved into view and, from a distance of six inches, occupied all the available space.

—What are we doing here? Reviewing our situation?

—I wish that idiot would put his guitar back in its case.

And that was one of the oddest turns of the evening.

—Guitar? I don't hear no guitar.

Neither, Jack realized, did he.

Wouldn't any rational person attempt to put such an episode out of mind? To throw this garbage overboard? You couldn't *do* anything with it, you couldn't *use* it, so why hold on to it? The incident on the pier meant nothing. It connected to nothing beyond itself, and it led to nothing. It was literally inconsequential, for it had had no consequences. After his lover had sandbagged him Jack had lost his bearings, suffered a momentary aberration, and trespassed upon another jurisdiction's crime scene. It was no more than an embarrassing mistake.

Fifty-six days and eleven hours later, the ace boy slipped into his captain's office, laid down his shield and his gun, and announced, much to the captain's astonishment, his immediate retirement. Knowing nothing of the confrontation with Detective Leone on the Santa Monica Pier, the captain did not inquire as to the possible influence upon his lieutenant's decision of a stalled carousel and a dead black man; if he had, Jack would have told him he was being ridiculous.

*Don't go there,* he advises himself, and does an excellent job of not going there. He receives a few involuntary flashes, no more, strobe-lit snapshots of a wooden pony's rearing head, of Angelo Leone's distempered mug, also of one other thing, the object occupying the dead center of the scene in every sense, that which above all must not be witnessed . . . the instant these imagistic lightning bolts appear, he *sends them away.* It feels like a magical performance. He is doing magic, good magic. He knows perfectly well that these feats of image banishment represent a form of self-protection, and if the motives behind his need for this protective magic remain unclear, the need is motive enough. When you gotta have an omelette, you gotta whisk eggs, to quote that unimpeachable authority, Duke Wayne.

Jack Sawyer has more on his mind than the irrelevancies suggested by a dream voice's having uttered the word "policeman" in baby talk. These matters, too, he wishes he could *send away* by the execution of a magic trick, but the wretched matters refuse banishment; they zoom about him like a tribe of wasps.

All in all, he is not doing so well, our Jack. He is marking time and staring at the eggs, which no longer look quite right, though he could not say why. The eggs resist interpretation. The eggs are the least of it. In the periphery of his vision, the banner across the front page of the *La Riviere Herald* seems to rise off the sheet of newsprint and float toward him. FISHERMAN STILL AT LARGE IN. . . . Nope, that's enough; he turns away with the terrible knowledge of having brought on this Fisherman business by himself. How about IN STATEN ISLAND or IN BROOKLYN, where the real Albert Fish, a tormented piece of work if there ever was one, found two of his victims?

This stuff is making him sick. Two dead kids, the Freneau girl missing and probably dead, body parts eaten, a lunatic who plagiarized from Albert Fish. . . . Dale insisted on assaulting him with information. The details enter his system like a contaminant. The more he learns—and for a man who truly wished to be out of the loop, Jack has learned an amazing amount—the more the poisons swim through his bloodstream, distorting his perceptions. He had come to Norway Valley in flight from a world that had abruptly turned unreliable and rubbery, as if liquefying under thermal pressure. During his last month in Los Angeles, the thermal pressure had become intolerable. Grotesque possibilities leered from darkened windows and the gaps between buildings, threatening to take form. On days off, the sensation of dishwater greasing his lungs made him gasp for breath and fight against nausea, so he worked without stopping, in the process solving more cases than ever before. (His diagnosis was that the work was getting to him, but we can hardly blame the captain for his astonishment at the ace boy's resignation.)

He had escaped to this obscure pocket of the countryside, this shelter, this haven at the edge of a yellow meadow, removed from the world of threat and madness, removed by nearly twenty miles from French Landing, removed a good distance even from Norway Valley Road. However, the layers of removal had failed to do their job. What he was trying to escape riots around him again, here in his redoubt. If he let himself succumb to self-centered fantasy, he would have to conclude that what he had fled had spent the last three years sniffing his trail and had finally succeeded in tracking him down.

In California, the rigors of his task had overwhelmed him; now the disorders of western Wisconsin must be kept at arm's length. Sometimes, late at night, he awakens to the echo of the little, poisoned voice wailing, *No more coppiceman, I won't, too close, too close.* What was too close, Jack Sawyer refuses to consider; the echo proves that he must avoid any further contamination.

Bad news for Dale, he knows, and he regrets both his inability to join the investigation and to explain his refusal to his friend. Dale's ass is on the line, no two ways about it. He is a good chief of police, more than good enough for French Landing, but he misjudged the politics and let the staties set him up. With every appearance of respect for local authority, state detectives Brown and Black had bowed low, stepped aside, and permitted Dale Gilbertson, who thought they were doing him a favor, to slip a noose around his neck. Too bad, but Dale has just figured out that he is standing on a trapdoor with a black bag over his face. If the Fisherman murders one more kid. . . . Well, Jack Sawyer sends his most profound regrets. He can't perform a miracle right now, sorry. Jack has more pressing matters on his mind.

Red feathers, for example. Small ones. Little red feathers are much on Jack's mind, and have been, despite his efforts to magic them away, since a month before the murders started. One morning as he emerged from his bedroom and began to go down to fix breakfast, a single red feather, a plume smaller than a baby's finger, *seemed to* float out of the slanted ceiling at the top of the stairs. In its wake, two or three others came drifting toward him. An oval section of plaster two inches across *seemed to* blink and open like an eye, and the eye released a tight, fat column of feathers that zoomed out of the ceiling as if propelled through a straw. A feather explosion, a feather hurricane, battered his chest, his raised arms, his head.

But this . . .

This never happened.

Something else happened, and it took him a minute or two to figure it out. A wayward brain neuron misfired. A mental receptor lapped up the wrong chemical, or lapped up too much of the right chemical. The switches that nightly triggered the image conduits responded to a false signal and produced a *waking dream.* The waking dream resembled a hallucination, but hallucinations were experienced by wet-brain alcoholics, drug takers, and crazy people, specifically paranoid schizophrenics, with whom Jack had dealt on many an occasion during his life as a coppiceman. Jack fit into none of those categories, including the last. He knew he was not a paranoid schizophrenic or any other variety of madman. If you thought Jack Sawyer was crazy, *you* were. He has complete, at least 99 percent complete, faith in his sanity.

Since he is not delusional, the feathers must have flown toward him in a waking dream. The only other explanation involves reality, and the feathers had no connection to reality. What kind of world would this be, if such things could happen to us?

Abruptly George Rathbun bellows, "It *pains* me to say this, truly it does, for *I love* our dear old Brew Crew, you know I do, but there come times when *love* must grit its teeth and face a *painful* reality—for example, take the sorrowful state of our pitching staff. Bud Selig, oh *BU-UD*, this is *Houston* calling. Could you *Please* return to earth immediately? A *blind man* could throw more strikes than that aggregation of WIMPS, LOSERS, AND AIRHEADS!"

Good old Henry. Henry has George Rathbun down so perfectly you can see the sweat stains under his armpits. But the best of Henry's inventions—in Jack's opinion—has to be that embodiment of hipster cool, the laid-back, authoritative Henry Shake ("the Sheik, the Shake, the Shook of Araby"), who can, if in the mood, tell you the color of the socks worn by Lester Young on the day he recorded "Shoe Shine Boy" and "Lady Be Good" and describe the interiors of two dozen famous but mostly long-departed jazz clubs.

*. . . and before we get into the very cool, very beautiful, very simpático music whispered one Sunday at the Village Vanguard by the Bill Evans Trio, we might pay our respects to the third, inner eye. Let us honor the inner eye, the eye of imagination. It is late on a hot July afternoon in Greenwich Village, New York City. On sun-dazzled Seventh Avenue South, we stroll into the shade of the Vanguard's marquee, open a white door, and proceed down a long, narrow flight of stairs to a roomy underground cave. The musicians climb onto the stand. Bill Evans slides onto the piano bench and nods at the audience. Scott La-Faro hugs his bass. Paul Motian picks up his brushes. Evans lowers his head way, way down and drops his hands on the keyboard. For those of us who are privileged to be there, nothing will ever be the same again.*

*"My Foolish Heart" by the Bill Evans Trio, live at the Vil-*

*lage Vanguard, the twenty-fifth of June, 1961. I am your host, Henry Shake—the Sheik, the Shake, the Shook of Araby.*

Smiling, Jack pours the beaten eggs into the frying pan, twice swirls them with a fork, and marginally reduces the gas flame. It occurs to him that he has neglected to make coffee. Nuts to coffee. Coffee is the last thing he needs; he can drink orange juice. A glance at the toaster suggests that he has also neglected to prepare the morning's toast. Does he require toast, is toast essential? Consider the butter, consider slabs of cholesterol waiting to corrupt his arteries. The omelette is risky enough; in fact, he has the feeling he cracked way too many eggs. Now Jack cannot remember why he wanted to make an omelette in the first place. He rarely eats omelettes. In fact, he tends to buy eggs out of a sense of duty aroused by the two rows of egg-sized depressions near the top of his refrigerator door. If people were not supposed to buy eggs, why would refrigerators come with egg holders?

He nudges a spatula under the edges of the hardening but still runny eggs, tilts the pan to slide them around, scrapes in the mushrooms and scallions, and folds the result in half. All right. Okay. Looks good. A luxurious forty minutes of freedom stretches out before him. In spite of everything, he seems to be functioning pretty well. Control is not an issue here.

Unfolded on the kitchen table, the *La Riviere Herald* catches Jack's eye. He has forgotten about the newspaper. The newspaper has not forgotten him, however, and demands its proper share of attention. FISHERMAN STILL AT LARGE IN, and so on. ARCTIC CIRCLE would be nice, but no, he moves nearer to the table and sees that the Fisherman remains a stubbornly local problem. From beneath the headline, Wendell Green's name leaps up and lodges in his eye like a pebble. Wendell Green is an all-around, comprehensive pest, an ongoing irritant. After reading the first two paragraphs of Green's article, Jack groans and clamps a hand over his eyes.

I'm a blind man, make me an umpire!

Wendell Green has the confidence of a small-town athletic hero who never left home. Tall, expansive, with a crinkly mat of red-blond hair and a senatorial waistline, Green swaggers through the bars, the courthouses, the public arenas of La Riviere and its surrounding communities, distributing wised-up charm. Wendell Green is a reporter who knows how to act like one, an old-fashioned print journalist, the *Herald*'s great ornament.

At their first encounter, the great ornament struck Jack as a third-rate phony, and he has seen no reason to change his mind since then. He distrusts Wendell Green. In Jack's opinion, the reporter's gregarious facade conceals a limitless capacity for treachery. Green is a blowhard posturing in front of a mirror, but a canny blowhard, and such creatures will do anything to gain their own ends.

After Thornberg Kinderling's arrest, Green requested an interview. Jack turned him down, as he declined the three invitations that followed his removal to Norway Valley Road. His refusals had not deterred the reporter from staging occasional "accidental" meetings.

The day after the discovery of Amy St. Pierre's body, Jack emerged from a Chase Street dry cleaner's shop with a box of freshly laundered shirts under his arm, began walking toward his car, and felt a hand close on his elbow. He looked back and beheld, contorted into a leer of spurious delight, the florid public mask of Wendell Green.

—Hey, hey, Holly—. A bad-boy smirk. I *mean,* Lieutenant Sawyer. Hey, I'm glad I ran into you. This is where you have your shirts done? They do a good job?

—If you leave out the part about the buttons.

—Good one. You're a funny guy, Lieutenant. Let me give you a tip. Reliable, on Third Street in La Riviere? They live up to their name. No smashee, no breakee. Want your shirts done right, go to a Chink every time. Sam Lee, try him out, Lieutenant.

—I'm not a lieutenant anymore, Wendell. Call me Jack or Mr. Sawyer. Call me Hollywood, I don't care. And now—

He walked toward his car, and Wendell Green walked beside him.

—Any chance of a few words, Lieutenant? Sorry, Jack? Chief Gilbertson is a close friend of yours, I know, and this tragic case, little girl, apparently mutilated, terrible things, can you can offer us your expertise, step in, give us the benefit of your thoughts?

—You want to know my thoughts?

—Anything you can tell me, buddy.

Pure, irresponsible malice inspired Jack to extend an arm over Green's shoulders and say:

—Wendell, old buddy, check out a guy named Albert Fish. It was back in the twenties.

—Fisch?

—F-i-s-h. From an old-line WASP New York family. An amazing case. Look it up.

Until that moment, Jack had been barely conscious of remembering the outrages committed by the bizarre Mr. Albert Fish. Butchers more up-to-date—Ted Bundy, John Wayne Gacy, and Jeffrey Dahmer—had eclipsed Albert Fish, not to mention exotics like Edmund Emil Kemper III, who, after committing eight murders, decapitated his mother, propped her head on his mantel, and used it as a dartboard. (By way of explanation, Edmund III said, "This seemed appropriate.") Yet the name of Albert Fish, an obscure back number, had surfaced in Jack's mind, and into Wendell Green's ready ear he had uttered it.

What had gotten *into* him? Well, that was the question, wasn't it?

Whoops, the omelette. Jack grabs a plate from a cabinet, silverware from a drawer, jumps to the stove, turns off the burner, and slides the mess in the pan onto his plate. He sits down and opens the *Herald* to page 5, where he reads about Milly Kuby's nearly winning third place at the big statewide spelling bee, but for the substitution of an *i* for an *a* in *opopanax,* the kind of thing that is supposed to be in a local paper. How can you expect a kid to spell *opopanax* correctly, anyhow?

Jack takes two or three bites of his omelette before the peculiar taste in his mouth distracts him from the monstrous unfairness done to Milly Kuby. The funny taste is like half-burned garbage. He spits the food out of his mouth and sees a wad of gray mush and raw, half-chewed vegetables. The uneaten part of his breakfast does not look any more appetizing. He did not cook this omelette; he ruined it.

He drops his head and groans. A shudder like a loose electrical wire travels here and there through his body, throwing off sparks that singe his throat, his lungs, his suddenly palpitating organs. *Opopanax,* he thinks. *I'm falling apart. Right here and now. Forget I said that. The savage opopanax has gripped me in its claws, shaken me with the fearful opopanax of its opopanax arms, and intends to throw me into the turbulent Opopanax River, where I shall meet my opopanax.*

"What is happening to me?" he says aloud. The shrill sound of his voice scares him.

Opopanax tears sting his opopanax eyes, and he gets groaning up off his opopanax, dumps the swill into the garbage disposal, rinses the plate, and decides that it is damn well time to start making sense around here. Opopanax me no opopanaxes. Everybody makes mistakes. Jack examines the door of the refrigerator, trying to remember if he still has an egg or two in there. Sure he does: a whole bunch of eggs, about nine or ten, had nearly filled the entire row of egg-shaped depressions at the top of the door. He could not have squandered all of them; he wasn't that out of it.

Jacks closes his fingers around the edge of the refrigerator door. Entirely unbidden, the vision of lights reflected on a black man's bald head.

*Not you.*

The person being addressed is not present; the person being addressed is scarcely a person at all.

*No, no, not you.*

The door swings open under the pressure of his fingers; the refrigerator light illuminates the laden shelves. Jack Sawyer regards the egg holders. They appear to be empty. A closer look reveals, nested within the rounded depression at the end of the first row, the presence of a small, egg-shaped object colored a pale and delicate shade of blue: a nostalgic, tender blue, quite possibly the half-remembered blue of a summer sky observed in early afternoon by a small boy lying face-up on the quarter acre of grass located behind a nice residential property on Roxbury Drive in Beverly Hills, California. Whoever owns this residential property, boy, you can put your money on one thing: they're in the entertainment business.

Jack knows the name of this precise shade of blue due to an extended consideration of color samples undertaken in the company of Claire Evinrude, M.D., an oncologist of lovely and brisk dispatch, during the period when they were planning to repaint their then-shared bungalow in the Hollywood Hills.

Claire, Dr. Evinrude, had marked this color for the master bedroom; he, recently returned from a big-deal, absurdly selective
VICAP course of instruction at Quantico, Virginia, and newly
promoted to the rank of lieutenant, had dismissed it as, um,
well, maybe a little cold.

Jack, have you ever seen an actual robin's egg? Dr. Evinrude
inquired. Do you have any idea how beautiful they are? Dr.
Evinrude's gray eyes enlarged as she grasped her mental
scalpel.

Jack inserts two fingers into the egg receptacle and lifts from
it the small, egg-shaped object the color of a robin's egg. What
do you know, this is a robin's egg. An "actual," in the words of
Dr. Claire Evinrude, robin's egg, hatched from the body of a
robin, sometimes called a robin redbreast. He deposits the egg
in the palm of his left hand. There it sits, this pale blue oblate
the size of a pecan. The capacity for thought seems to have left
him. What the hell did he do, *buy* a robin's egg? Sorry, no, this
relationship isn't working, the opopanax is out of whack, Roy's
Store doesn't sell robin's eggs, I'm gone.

Slowly, stiffly, awkward as a zombie, Jack progresses across
the kitchen floor and reaches the sink. He extends his left hand
over the maw at the sink's center and releases the robin's egg.
Down into the garbage disposal it drops, irretrievably. His right
hand switches the machine into action, with the usual noisy results. Growl, grind, snarl, a monster is enjoying a nice little
snack. Grrr. The live electrical wire shudders within him, shed-
ding sparks as it twitches, but he has become zombiefied and
barely registers the internal shocks. All in all, taking everything
into consideration, what Jack Sawyer feels most like doing at
this moment . . .

*When the red, red . . .*

For some reason, he has not called his mother in a long, long
while. He cannot think why he has not, and it is about time he
did. Robin me no red robins. The voice of Lily Cavanaugh
Sawyer, the Queen of the B's, once his only companion in a
rapture-flooded, transcendent, rigorously forgotten New Hampshire hotel room, is precisely the voice Jack needs to hear right
about now. Lily Cavanaugh is the one person in the world to
whom he can spill the ridiculous mess in which he finds himself. Despite the dim, unwelcome awareness of trespassing be-

yond the borders of strict rationality and therefore bringing further into question his own uncertain sanity, he moves down the kitchen counter, picks up his cell phone, and punches in the number of the nice residential property on Roxbury Drive, Beverly Hills, California.

The telephone in his old house rings five times, six times, seven. A man picks up and, in an angry, slightly drunken, sleep-distorted voice, says, "Kimberley . . . whatever the hell this is about . . . for your sake . . . I hope it's really, really important."

Jack hits END and snaps his phone shut. Oh God oh hell oh damn. It is just past five A.M. in Beverly Hills, or Westwood, or Hancock Park, or wherever that number now reaches. He forgot his mother was dead. Oh hell oh damn oh God, can you beat that?

Jack's grief, which has been sharpening itself underground, once again rises up to stab him, as if for the first time, bang, dead-center in the heart. At the same time the idea that even for a second he could have *forgotten that his mother was dead* strikes him, God knows why, as hugely and irresistibly funny. How ridiculous can you get? The goofy stick has whapped him on the back of the head, and without knowing if he is going to burst into sobs or shouts of laughter, Jack experiences a brief wave of dizziness and leans heavily against the kitchen counter.

*Jive-ass turkey,* he remembers his mother saying. Lily had been describing her late husband's recently deceased partner in the days after her suspicious accountants discovered that the partner, Morgan Sloat, had been diverting into his own pockets three-fourths of the income from Sawyer & Sloat's astonishingly vast real estate holdings. Every year since Phil Sawyer's death in a so-called hunting accident, Sloat had stolen millions of dollars, many millions, from his late partner's family. Lily diverted the flow back into the proper channels and sold half the company to its new partners, in the process guaranteeing her son a tremendous financial bonanza, not to mention the annual bonanza that produces the interest Jack's private foundation funnels off to noble causes. Lily had called Sloat things far more colorful than *jive-ass turkey,* but that is the term her voice utters in his inner ear.

Way back in May, Jack tells himself, he probably came across that robin's egg on an absentminded stroll through the meadow and put it in the refrigerator for safekeeping. To keep it safe. Because, after all, it was of a delicate shade of blue, a beautiful blue, to quote Dr. Evinrude. So long had he kept it safe that he'd forgotten all about it. Which, he gratefully recognizes, is why the waking dream presented him with an explosion of red feathers!

Everything happens for a reason, concealed though the reason may be; loosen up and relax long enough to stop being a jive-ass turkey, and the reason might come out of hiding.

Jack bends over the sink and, for the sake of refreshment internal and external, immerses his face in a double handful of cold water. For the moment, the cleansing shock washes away the ruined breakfast, the ridiculous telephone call, and the corrosive image flashes. It is time to strap on his skates and get going. In twenty-five minutes, Jack Sawyer's best friend and only confidant will, with his customary aura of rotary perception, emerge through the front door of KDCU-AM's cinder-block building and, applying his golden lighter's flame to the tip of a cigarette, glide down the walkway to Peninsula Drive. Should rotary perception inform him that Jack Sawyer's pickup awaits, Henry Leyden will unerringly locate the handle and climb in. This exhibition of blind-man cool is too dazzling to miss.

And miss it he does not, for in spite of the morning's difficulties, which from the balanced, mature perspective granted by his journey through the lovely countryside eventually seem trivial, Jack's pickup pulls in front of the Peninsula Drive end of KDCU-AM's walkway at 7:55, a good five minutes before his friend is to stroll out into the sunlight. Henry will be good for him: just the *sight* of Henry will be like a dose of soul tonic. Surely Jack cannot be the first man (or woman) in the history of the world who momentarily lost his (or her) grip under stress and kind of halfway forgot that his (or her) mother had shuffled off the old mortal coil and departed for a higher sphere. Stressed-out mortals turned naturally to their mothers for comfort and reassurance. The impulse is coded into our DNA. When he hears the story, Henry will chuckle and advise him to tighten his wig.

On second thought, why cloud Henry's sky with a story so

absurd? The same applies to the robin's egg, especially since Jack has not spoken to Henry about his waking dream of a feather eruption, and he does not feel like getting involved in a lot of pointless backtracking. Live in the present; let the past stretch out in its grave; keep your chin high and walk around the mud puddles. Don't look to your friends for therapy.

He switches on the radio and hits the button for KWLA-FM, the UW–La Riviere station, home to both the Wisconsin Rat and Henry the Sheik the Shake the Shook. What pours glittering from the cab's hidden speakers raises the hairs on his arms: Glenn Gould, inner eye luminously open, blazing through something by Bach, he could not say exactly what. But Glenn Gould, but Bach, for sure. One of the Partitas, maybe.

A CD jewel box in one hand, Henry Leyden strolls through the humble doorway at the side of the station, enters the sunlight, and without hesitation begins to glide down the flagged walkway, the rubber soles of his Hershey-brown suede loafers striking the center of each successive flagstone.

Henry . . . Henry is a vision.

Today, Jack observes, Henry comes attired in one of his Malaysian teak forest owner ensembles, a handsome collarless shirt, shimmering braces, and an heirloom straw fedora creased to a fare-thee-well. Had Jack not been so welcomed into Henry's life, he would not have known that his friend's capacity for flawless wardrobe assemblage depended upon the profound organization of his enormous walk-in closet long ago established by Rhoda Gilbertson Leyden, Henry's deceased wife: Rhoda had arranged every article of her husband's clothing by season, style, and color. Item by item, Henry memorized the entire system. Although blind since birth, therefore incapable of distinguishing between matching and mismatching shades, Henry never errs.

Henry extracts from his shirt pocket a gold lighter and a yellow pack of American Spirits, fires up, exhales a radiant cloud brightened by sunlight to the color of milk, and continues his unwavering progress down the flagstones.

The pink, back-slanting capitals of TROY LUVS MARYANN! YES! sprayed across the sign on the bare lawn suggest that 1) Troy spends a lot of time listening to KDCU-AM, and 2) Maryann loves him back. Good for Troy, good for Maryann. Jack applauds love's announcement, even in pink spray paint, and wishes the lovers happiness and good fortune. It occurs to him that if at this present stage of his existence he could be said to love anyone, that person would have to be Henry Leyden. Not in the sense that Troy luvs Maryann, or vice versa, but he luvs him all the same, a matter that has never been as clear as it is this moment.

Henry traverses the last of the flagstones and approaches the curb. A single stride brings him to the door of the pickup; his hand closes on the recessed metal bar; he opens the door, steps up, and slides in. His head tilts, cocking his right ear to the music. The dark lenses of his aviator glasses shine.

"How can you do that?" Jack asked. "This time, the music helped, but you don't need music."

"I can do that because I am totally, totally bitchrod," Henry says. "I learned that lovely word from our pothead intern, Morris Rosen, who kindly applied it to me. Morris thinks I am God, but he must have something on the ball, because he figured out that George Rathbun and the Wisconsin Rat are one and the same. I hope the kid keeps his mouth shut."

"I do, too," Jack says, "but I'm not going to let you change the subject. How can you always open the door right away? How do you find the handle without groping for it?"

Henry sighs. "The handle tells me where it is. Obviously. All I have to do is listen to it."

"The door handle makes a *sound*?"

"Not like your high-tech radio and *The Goldberg Variations,* no. More like a vibration. The sound of a sound. The sound *inside* a sound. Isn't Daniel Barenboim a great piano player? Man, listen to that—every note, a different coloration. Makes you want to kiss the lid of his Steinway, baby. Imagine the muscles in his hands."

"That's Barenboim?"

"Well, who else could it be?" Slowly, Henry turns his head to Jack. An irritating smile raises the corners of his mouth. "Ah. I see, yes. Knowing you as I do, you poor schmuck, I see you imagined you were listening to Glenn Gould."

"I did not," Jack says.

"Please."

"Maybe for a minute I wondered if it was Gould, but—"

"Don't, don't, don't. Don't even try. Your voice gives you away. There's a little, whiny topspin on every word; it's so pathetic. Are we going to drive back to Norway Valley, or would you like to sit here and keep lying to me? I want to tell you something on the way home."

He holds up the CD. "Let's put you out of your misery. The pothead gave this to me—Dirtysperm doing an old Supremes ditty. Me, I *loathe* that sort of thing, but it might be perfect for the Wisconsin Rat. Cue up track seven."

The pianist no longer sounds anything like Glenn Gould, and the music seems to have slowed to half its former velocity. Jack puts himself out of his misery and inserts the CD into the opening beneath the radio. He pushes a button, then another. At an insanely fast tempo, the screeches of madmen subjected to unspeakable tortures come blasting out of the speakers. Jack rocks backward into the seat, jolted. "My God, Henry," he says, and reaches for the volume control.

"Don't dare touch that dial," Henry says. "If this crap doesn't make your ears bleed, it isn't doing its job."

"Ears," Jack knows, is jazz-speak for the capacity to hear what is going on in music as it unfurls across the air. A musician with good ears soon memorizes the songs and arrangements he is asked to play, picks up or already knows the harmonic movement underlying the theme, and follows the transformations and substitutions to that pattern introduced by his fellow musicians. Whether or not he can accurately read notes written on a staff, a musician with *great* ears learns melodies and arrangements the first time he hears them, grasps harmonic intricacies through flawless intuition, and immediately identifies the notes and key signatures registered by taxi horns, elevator bells, and mewing cats. Such people inhabit a world defined by the particularities of individual sounds, and Henry Leyden is one of them. As far as Jack is concerned, Henry's ears are Olympian, in a class by themselves.

It was Henry's ears that gave him access to Jack's great secret, the role his mother, Lily Cavanaugh Sawyer, "Lily Cavanaugh," had occupied in life, and he is the only person ever to discover it. Shortly after Dale introduced them, Jack and Henry Leyden entered into an easy, companionable friendship surprising to both. Each the answer to the other's loneliness, they spent two or three nights of every week having dinner together, listening to music, and talking about whatever came into their well-stocked minds. Either Jack drove down the road to Henry's eccentric house, or he picked Henry up and drove him back to his place. After something like six or seven months, Jack wondered if his friend might enjoy spending an hour or so listening to him read aloud from books agreed upon by both parties. Henry replied, *Ivey-divey, my man, what a beautiful idea. How about starting with some whacked-out crime novels?* They began with Chester Himes and Charles Willeford, changed gear with a batch of contemporary novels, floated through S. J. Perelman and James Thurber, and ventured emboldened into fictional mansions erected by Ford Madox Ford and Vladimir Nabokov. (Marcel Proust lies somewhere ahead, they understand, but Proust can wait; at present they are to embark upon *Bleak House*.)

One night after Jack had finished the evening's installment of Ford's *The Good Soldier,* Henry cleared his throat and said, Dale said you told him your parents were in the entertainment industry. In show business.

—That's right.

—I don't want to pry, but would you mind if I asked you some questions? If you feel like answering, just say yes or no.

Already alarmed, Jack said, What's this about, Henry?

—I want to see if I'm right about something.

—Okay. Ask.

—Thank you. Were your parents in different aspects of the industry?

—Um.

—Was one of them in the business end of things, and the other a performer?

—Um.

—Was your mother an actress?

—Uh-huh.

—A famous actress, in a way. She never really got the respect she deserved, but she made a ton of movies all through the fifties and into the mid-sixties, and at the end of her career she won an Oscar for Best Supporting Actress.

—Henry, Jack said. Where did you—

—Clam up. I intend to relish this moment. Your mother was Lily Cavanaugh. That's wonderful. Lily Cavanaugh was always so much more talented than most people gave her credit for. Every time out, she brought those roles she played, those girls, those tough little waitresses and dames with guns in their handbags, up to a new level. Beautiful, smart, gutsy, no pretensions, just lock in and inhabit the part. She was about a hundred times better than anyone else around her.

—Henry . . .

—Some of those movies had nice sound tracks, too. *Lost Summer,* Johnny Mandel? Out of sight.

—Henry, how did—

—You told me; how else could I know? These little things your voice does, that's how. You slide over the tops of your *r*'s, and you hit the rest of your consonants in a kind of cadence, and that cadence runs through your sentences.

—A cadence?

—Bet your ass, junior. An underlying rhythm, like your own personal drummer. All through *The Good Soldier* I kept trying to remember where I'd heard it before. Faded in, faded back out. A couple of days ago, I nailed it. Lily Cavanaugh. You can't blame me for wanting to see if I was right, can you?

—Blame you? Jack said. I'm too stunned to blame anybody, but give me a couple of minutes.

—Your secret's safe. When people see you, you don't want their first thought to be, Hey, there's Lily Cavanaugh's son. Makes sense to me.

Henry Leyden has great ears, all right.

As the pickup rolls through French Landing the din filling the cab makes conversation impossible. Dirtysperm is burning a hole through the marzipan center of "Where Did Our Love Go" and in the process committing hideous atrocities upon those cute little Supremes. Henry, who claims to loathe this kind of thing, slouches in his seat, knees up on the dash, hands steepled below his chin, grinning with pleasure. The shops on Chase Street have opened for business, and half a dozen cars jut at an angle from parking spaces.

Four boys astride bicycles swerve off the sidewalk before Schmitt's Allsorts and into the road twenty feet in front of the moving pickup. Jack hits his brakes; the boys come to an abrupt halt and line up side by side, waiting for him to pass. Jack trolls forward. Henry straightens up, checks his mysterious sensors, and drops back into position. All is well with Henry. The boys, however, do not know what to make of the uproar growing ever louder as the pickup approaches. They stare at Jack's windshield in bafflement tinged with distaste, the way their great-grandfathers once stared at the Siamese twins and the Alligator Man in the freak show at the back of the fairground. Everybody knows that the drivers of pickup trucks listen to only two kinds of music, heavy metal or country, so what's with *this* creep?

As Jack drives past the boys, the first, a scowling heavy-weight with the inflamed face of a schoolyard bully, displays an upraised second finger. The next two continue the imitations of their great-grandfathers having a hot night out in 1921 and gape, idiotically, mouths slack and open. The fourth boy, whose dark blond hair beneath a Brewers cap, bright eyes, and general air of innocence make him the nicest-looking of the group, gazes directly into Jack's face and gives him a sweet, tentative smile. This is Tyler Marshall, out for a spin—though he is completely unaware of it—into no-man's-land.

The boys glide into the background, and Jack glances into the mirror to see them pedaling furiously up the street, Sluggo in front, the smallest, most appealing one in the rear, already falling behind.

"A sidewalk panel of experts has reported in on the Dirty-sperm," Jack says. "Four kids on bikes." Since he can scarcely make out his words, he does not think Henry will be able to hear them at all.

Henry, it seems, has heard him perfectly, and he responds with a question that disappears into the uproar. Having a reasonably good idea of what it must have been, Jack answers it anyhow. "One firm negative, two undecideds tending toward negative, and one cautious positive." Henry nods.

Violent marzipan-destruction crashes and thuds to a conclusion on Eleventh Street. As if a haze has blown from the cab, as if the windshield has been freshly washed, the air seems clearer, the colors more vibrant. "Interesting," Henry says. He reaches unerringly for the EJECT button, extracts the disc from the holder, and slips it into its case. "That was very revealing, don't you think? Raw, self-centered hatred should never be dismissed automatically. Morris Rosen was right. It's perfect for the Wisconsin Rat."

"Hey, I think they could be bigger than Glenn Miller."

"That reminds me," Henry says. "You'll never guess what I'm doing later. I have a gig! Chipper Maxton, actually his second in command, this Rebecca Vilas woman, who I am sure is as gorgeous as she sounds, hired me to put on a record hop as the slam-bang climax to Maxton's big Strawberry Fest. Well, not me—an old, long-neglected persona of mine, Symphonic Stan, the Big-Band Man."

"Do you need a ride?"

"I do not. The wondrous Miss Vilas has attended to my needs, in the form of a car with a comfy back seat for my turntable and a trunk spacious enough for the speakers and record cartons, which she will be sending. But thanks anyhow."

"Symphonic Stan?" Jack said.

"A knocked-out, all-frantic, all-zoot-suit embodiment of the big-band era, and a charming, mellifluous gentleman besides. For the residents of Maxton's, an evocation of their salad days and a joy to behold."

"Do you actually own a zoot suit?"

Magnificently inexpressive, Henry's face swings toward him.

"Sorry. I don't know what came over me. To change the subject, what you said, I mean what George Rathbun said, about the Fisherman this morning probably did a lot of good. I was glad to hear that."

Henry opens his mouth and summons George Rathbun in all his avuncular glory. " 'The original Fisherman, boys and girls, Albert Fish, has been dead and gone for sixty-seven years.' " It is uncanny, hearing the voice of that charged-up fat man leap from Henry Leyden's slender throat. In his own voice, Henry says, "I hope it did some good. After I read your buddy Wendell Green's nonsense in the paper this morning, I thought George had to say *something*."

Henry Leyden enjoys using terms like *I read, I was reading, I saw, I was looking at.* He knows these phrases disconcert his auditors. And he called Wendell Green "your buddy" because Henry is the only person to whom Jack has ever admitted that he alerted the reporter to the crimes of Albert Fish. Now Jack wishes he had confessed to no one. Glad-handing Wendell Green is not his buddy.

"Having been of some assistance to the press," Henry says, "you might reasonably be thought in a position to do the same for our boys in blue. Forgive me, Jack, but you opened the door, and I'll only say this once. Dale is my nephew, after all."

"I don't believe you're doing this to me," Jack says.

"Doing what, speaking my mind? Dale *is* my nephew, remember? He could use your expertise, and he is very much of the opinion that you owe him a favor. Hasn't it occurred to you that you could help him stay in his job? Or that if you love French Landing and Norway Valley as much as you say, you owe these folks a little of your time and talent?"

"Hasn't it occurred to you, Henry, that I'm retired?" Jack says through gritted teeth. "That investigating homicides is the last thing, I mean, the *last* thing in the world I want to do?"

"Of course it has," Henry says. "But—and again I hope you'll forgive me, Jack—here you are, the person I know you are, with the skills you have, which are certainly far beyond Dale's and probably well beyond all these other guys', and I can't help wondering what the hell your problem is."

"I don't have a *problem,*" Jack says. "I'm a civilian."

"You're the boss. We might as well listen to the rest of the Barenboim." Henry runs his fingers over the console and pushes the button for the tuner.

For the next fifteen minutes, the only voice to be heard in the pickup's cab is that of a Steinway concert grand meditating upon *The Goldberg Variations* in the Teatro Colón, Buenos Aires. A splendid voice it is, too, Jack thinks, and you'd have to be an ignoramus to mistake it for Glenn Gould. A person capable of making that mistake probably couldn't hear the vibration-like inner sound produced by a General Motors door handle.

When they turn right off Highway 93 onto Norway Valley Road, Henry says, "Stop sulking. I shouldn't have called you a schmuck. And I shouldn't have accused you of having a problem, because I'm the one with the problem."

"You?" Jack looks at him, startled. Long experience has immediately suggested that Henry is about to ask for some kind of unofficial investigative help. Henry is facing the windshield, giving nothing away. "What kind of problem can *you* have? Did your socks get out of order? Oh—are you having trouble with one of the stations?"

"That, I could deal with." Henry pauses, and the pause stretches into a lengthy silence. "What I was going to say is, I feel like I'm losing my mind. I think I'm going sort of crazy."

"Come on." Jack eases up on the gas pedal and cuts his speed in half. Has Henry witnessed a feather explosion? Of course he hasn't; Henry cannot see anything. And his own feather explosion was merely a waking dream.

Henry quivers like a tuning fork. He is still facing the windshield.

"Tell me what's going on," Jack says. "I'm starting to worry about you."

Henry opens his mouth to a crack that might accommodate a communion wafer, then closes it again. Another tremor runs through him.

"Hmm," he says. "This is harder than I thought." Astonishingly, his dry, measured voice, the true voice of Henry Leyden, wobbles with a wide, helpless vibrato.

Jack slows the pickup to a crawl, begins to say something, and decides to wait.

"I hear my wife," Henry says. "At night, when I'm lying in bed. Around three, four in the morning. Rhoda's footsteps are moving around in the kitchen, they're coming up the stairs. I must be losing my mind."

"How often does this happen?"

"How many times? I don't know, exactly. Three or four."

"Do you get up and look for her? Call out her name?"

Henry's voice again sails up and down on the vibrato trampoline. "I've done both those things. Because I was sure I heard her. Her *footsteps,* her way of walking, her *tread.* Rhoda's been gone for six years now. Pretty funny, huh? I'd think it was funny, if I didn't think I was going bats."

"You call out her name," Jack says. "And you get out of bed and go downstairs."

"Like a lunatic, like a madman. 'Rhoda? Is that you, Rhoda?' Last night, I went all around the house. 'Rhoda? Rhoda?' You'd think I was expecting her to answer." Henry pays no attention to the tears that leak from beneath his aviator glasses and slip down his cheeks. "And I was, that's the problem."

"No one else was in the house," Jack says. "No signs of disturbance. Nothing misplaced or missing, or anything like that."

"Not as far as I saw. Everything was still where it should have been. Right where I left it." He raises a hand and wipes his face.

The entrance to Jack's looping driveway slides past on the right side of the cab.

"I'll tell you what I think," Jack says, picturing Henry wandering through his darkened house. "Six years ago, you went through all the grief business that happens when someone you love dies and leaves you, the denial, the bargaining, the anger, the pain, whatever, acceptance, that whole range of emotions, but afterward you still missed Rhoda. No one ever says you keep on missing the dead people you loved, but you do."

"Now, that's profound," Henry says. "And comforting, too."

"Don't interrupt. Weirdness happens. Believe me, I know what I'm talking about. Your mind rebels. It distorts the evidence, it gives false testimony. Who knows why? It just does."

"In other words, you go batshit," Henry says. "I believe that is where we came in."

"What I mean," Jack says, "is that people can have waking dreams. That's what is happening to you. It's nothing to worry about. All right, here's your drive, you're home."

He turns into the grassy entrance and rolls up to the white farmhouse in which Henry and Rhoda Leyden had spent the fifteen lively years between their marriage and the discovery of Rhoda's liver cancer. For nearly two years after her death, Henry went wandering through his house every evening, turning on the lights.

"Waking dreams? Where'd you get that one?"

"Waking dreams aren't uncommon," Jack says. "Especially in people who never get enough sleep, like you." *Or like me,* he silently adds. "I'm not making this up, Henry. I've had one or two myself. One, anyhow."

"Waking dreams," Henry says in a different, considering tone of voice. "Ivey-divey."

"Think about it. We live in a rational world. People do not return from the dead. Everything happens for a reason, and the *reasons* are always rational. It's a matter of chemistry or coincidence. If they weren't rational, we'd never figure anything out, and we'd never know what was going on."

"Even a blind man can see that," Henry says. "Thanks. Words to live by." He gets out of the cab and closes the door. He moves away, steps back, and leans in through the window. "Do you want to start on *Bleak House* tonight? I should get home about eight-thirty, something like that."

"I'll turn up around nine."

By way of parting, Henry says, "Ding-dong." He turns away, walks to his doorstep, and disappears into his house, which is of course unlocked. Around here, only parents lock their doors, and even that's a new development.

Jack reverses the pickup, swings down the drive and onto Norway Valley Road. He feels as though he has done a doubly good deed, for by helping Henry he has also helped himself. It's nice, how things turn out sometimes.

When he turns into his own long driveway, a peculiar rattle comes from the ashtray beneath his dashboard. He hears it again at the last curve, just before his house comes into view. The sound is not so much a rattle as a small, dull clunk. A button, a coin—something like that. He rolls to a stop at the side of his house, turns off the engine, and opens his door. On an afterthought, he reaches over and pulls out the ashtray.

What Jack finds nestled in the grooves at the bottom of the sliding tray, a tiny robin's egg, a robin's egg the size of an almond M&M, expels all the air from his body.

The little egg is so blue a blind man could see it.

Jack's trembling fingers pluck the egg from the ashtray. Staring at it, he leaves the cab and closes the door. Still staring at the egg, he finally remembers to breathe. His hand revolves on his wrist and releases the egg, which falls in a straight line to the grass. Deliberately, he lifts his foot and smashes it down onto the obscene blue speck. Without looking back, he pockets his keys and moves toward the dubious safety of his house.

# PART TWO

# THE TAKING OF
# TYLER MARSHALL

# 5

We glimpsed a janitor on our whirlwind early-morning tour of Maxton Elder Care—do you happen to remember him? Baggy overalls? A wee bit thick in the gut? Dangling cigarette in spite of the NO SMOKING! LUNGS AT WORK! signs that have been posted every twenty feet or so along the patient corridors? A mop that looks like a clot of dead spiders? No? Don't apologize. It's easy enough to overlook Pete Wexler, a onetime nondescript youth (final grade average at French Landing High School: 79) who passed through a nondescript young manhood and has now reached the edge of what he expects to be a nondescript middle age. His only hobby is administering the occasional secret, savage pinch to the moldy oldies who fill his days with their grunts, nonsensical questions, and smells of gas and piss. The Alzheimer's assholes are the worst. He has been known to stub out the occasional cigarette on their scrawny backs or buttocks. He likes their strangled cries when the heat hits and the pain cores in. This small and ugly torture has a double-barreled effect: it wakes them up a little and satisfies something in him. Brightens his days, somehow. Refreshes the old outlook. Besides, who are they going to tell?

And oh God, there goes the worst of them now, shuffling slowly down the corridor of Daisy. Charles Burnside's mouth is agape, as is the back of his johnny. Pete has a better view of Burnside's scrawny, shit-smeared buttocks than he ever wanted. The chocolate stains go all the way down to the backs of his knees, by God. He's headed for the bathroom, but it's just a leetle bit late. A certain brown horse—call him Morning Thunder—has already bolted from its stall and no doubt galloped across Burny's sheets.

*Thank God cleaning 'em up isn't my job,* Pete thinks, and smirks around his cigarette. *Over to you, Butch.*

But the desk up there by the little boys' and girls' rooms is for the time being unattended. Butch Yerxa is going to miss the charming sight of Burny's dirty ass sailing by. Butch has apparently stepped out for a smoke, although Pete has told the idiot a hundred times that all those NO SMOKING signs mean nothing—Chipper Maxton could care less about who smoked where (or where the smokes were butted out, for that matter). The signs are just there to keep good old Drooler Manor in compliance with certain tiresome state laws.

Pete's smirk widens, and at that moment he looks a good deal like his son Ebbie, Tyler Marshall's sometime friend (it was Ebbie Wexler, in fact, who just gave Jack and Henry the finger). Pete is wondering whether he should go out and tell Butch he's got a little cleanup job in D18—plus D18's occupant, of course—or if he should just let Butch discover Burny's latest mess on his own. Perhaps Burny will go back to his room and do a little fingerpainting, kind of spread the joy around. That would be good, but it would also be good to see Butch's face fall when Pete tells him—

"Pete."

Oh no. Sandbagged by the bitch. She's a fine-looking bitch, but a bitch is still a bitch. Pete stands where he is for a moment, thinking that maybe if he ignores her, she'll go away.

Vain hope.

"Pete."

He turns. There is Rebecca Vilas, current squeeze of the big cheese. Today she is wearing a light red dress, perhaps in honor of Strawberry Fest!, and black high-heeled pumps, probably in honor of her own fine gams. Pete briefly imagines those fine gams wrapped around him, those high heels crossed at the small of his back and pointing like clock hands, then sees the cardboard box she's holding in her arms. Work for him, no doubt. Pete also notes the glinting ring on her finger, some sort of gemstone the size of a goddamn robin's egg, although considerably paler. He wonders, not for the first time, just what a woman does to earn a ring like that.

She stands there, tapping her foot, letting him have his look. Behind him, Charles Burnside continues his slow, tottery progress toward the men's. You'd think, looking at that old wreck with his scrawny legs and flyaway milkweed hair, that his running days were long behind him. But you'd be wrong. Terribly wrong.

"Miz Vilas?" Pete says at last.

"Common room, Pete. On the double. And how many times have you been told not to smoke in the patient wings?"

Before he can reply, she turns with a sexy little flirt of the skirt and starts off toward the Maxton common room, where that afternoon's Strawberry Fest! dance will be held.

Sighing, Pete props his mop against the wall and follows her.

Charles Burnside is now alone at the head of the Daisy corridor. The vacancy leaves his eyes and is replaced with a brilliant and feral gleam of intelligence. All at once he looks younger. All at once Burny the human shit machine is gone. In his place is Carl Bierstone, who reaped the young in Chicago with such savage efficiency.

Carl . . . and something else. Something not human.

He—*it*—grins.

On the unattended desk is a pile of paper weighed down with a round stone the size of a coffee cup. Written on the stone in small black letters is BUTCH'S PET ROCK.

Burny picks up Butch Yerxa's pet rock and walks briskly toward the men's room, still grinning.

In the common room, the tables have been arranged around the walls and covered with red paper cloths. Later, Pete will add small red lights (battery powered; no candles for the droolers, gosh, no). On the walls, great big cardboard strawberries have been taped up everywhere, some looking rather battered—they have been put up and taken down every July since Herbert Maxton opened this place at the end of the swingin' sixties. The linoleum floor is open and bare.

This afternoon and early evening, the moldy oldies who are still ambulatory and of a mind to do so will shuffle around out there to the big-band sounds of the thirties and forties, clinging to each other during the slow numbers and probably dampening their Depends with excitement at the end of the jitterbugs. (Three years ago a moldy oldie named Irving Christie had a minor heart attack after doing a particularly strenuous lindyhop to "Don't Sit Under the Apple Tree with Anyone Else but Me.") Oh yes, the Strawberry Fest Hop is always exciting.

Rebecca has all by herself pushed together three wooden flats and covered them with a white cloth, creating the basis for Symphonic Stan's podium. In the corner stands a brilliantly chromed microphone with a large round head, a genuine antique from the thirties that saw service at the Cotton Club. It is one of Henry Leyden's prize possessions. Beside it is the tall, narrow carton in which it arrived yesterday. On the podium, beneath a beam decorated with red and white crepe and more cardboard strawberries, is a stepladder. Seeing it, Pete feels a moment's possessive jealousy. Rebecca Vilas has been in his closet. Trespassing bitch! If she stole any of his weed, by God—

Rebecca sets her carton down on the podium with an audible grunt, then straightens up. She brushes a lock of silky chestnut hair off one flushed cheek. It's only midmorning, but the day is going to be a genuine Coulee Country scorcher. Air-condition your underwear and double up on the deodorant, folks, as George Rathbun has been known to bellow.

"Oi thought you'd never come, me foine bucko," Rebecca says.

"Well, I'm here," Pete says sullenly. "Looks like you're doing fine without me." He pauses, then adds: *"Foine."* For Pete, this is quite a witticism. He walks forward and peers into the carton, which, like the one by the mike, is stamped PROPERTY OF HENRY LEYDEN. Inside the box is a small spotlight with an electrical cord wrapped around it, and a circular pink gel that is meant to turn the light the color of candy canes and sugar strawberries.

"What's this shit?" Pete asks.

Rebecca gives him a brilliant, dangerous smile. Even to a relatively dull fellow like Pete, the message of that smile is clear: you're on the edge of the gator pool, buddy; how many more steps do you want to take?

"Light," she says. "L-I-G-H-T. Hangs up there, on that hook. H-O-O-K. It's something the deejay insists on. Says it gets him in the mood. M-O-O—"

"What happened to Weenie Erickson?" Pete grumbles.

"There was none of this shit with Weenie. He played the god-damn records for two hours, had a few out of his hip flask, then shut it down."

"He moved," Rebecca says indifferently. "Racine, I think."

"Well—" Pete is looking up, studying the beam with its in-tertwined fluffs of red and white crepe. "I don't see no hook, Miz Vilas."

"Christ on a bicycle," she says, and mounts the stepladder. "Here. Are you blind?"

Pete, most definitely not blind, has rarely been so grateful for his sighted state. From his position below her, he's got a clear view of her thighs, the red lace froth of her panties, and the twin curves of her buttocks, now nicely tensed as she stands on the fifth step of the ladder.

She looks down at him, sees the stunned look on his face, notes the direction of his sight line. Her expression softens a bit. As her dear mother so wisely observed, some men are just fools for a flash of panty.

"Pete. Earth to Pete."

"Uh?" He looks up at her, mouth agape, a dot of spittle on his lower lip.

"There is no hook of any kind on my underwear, I'm sure of that as of few things in life. But if you will direct your gaze up-ward . . . to my hand instead of my ass . . ."

He looks up, face still dazed, and sees one red-tipped nail (Rebecca is a through-and-through vision in strawberry red today, no doubt about it) tapping a hook that just gleams out of the crepe, like a fisherman's hook gleaming murderously out of a gaudy lure.

"Hook," she says. "Attach gel to light, attach light to hook. Light becomes warm pink spotlight, as per deejay's explicit in-structions. You get-um message, Kemo sabe?"

"Uh . . . yeah . . ."

"Then, if I may coin a phrase, will you please get it up?"

She comes down the ladder, deciding Pete Wexler has gotten the biggest free show he can reasonably expect for one lousy chore. And Pete, who has already achieved one erection, pulls Symphonic Stan's pink pinspot out of its box and prepares to achieve another. As he mounts the stepladder, his crotch rises past Rebecca's face. She notes the bulge there and gnaws the inside of one cheek to suppress a smile. Men are fools, all right. *Lovable* fools, some of them, but fools, all the same. It's just that some fools can afford rings and trips and midnight suppers at Milwaukee nightspots, and some fools cannot.

With some fools, the best you can get them to do is put up a lousy light.


"WAIT UP, YOU GUYS!" TY MARSHALL CALLS. "EBBIE! RONNIE! T.J.! WAIT UP!"

Over his shoulder, Ebbie Wexler (who really *does* look like Nancy's not-too-bright boyfriend, Sluggo) calls back: "Catch us, slowpoke!"

"Yeah!" Ronnie Metzger yells. "Catch us, po-sloke!" Ronnie, a kid with a lot of hours in the speech-therapy room ahead of him, looks back over his own shoulder, almost crashes his bike into a parking meter, and just manages to swerve around it. Then they are fleeing, the three of them filling the sidewalk with their bikes (God help the pedestrian headed the other way), their racing shadows fleeing beside them.

Tyler considers a final catch-up dash, then decides his legs are just too tired. His mother and father say that he *will* catch up in time, that he's just small for his age, but brother, Ty has his doubts. And he has had increasing doubts about Ebbie, Ronnie, and T.J., too. Are they really worth keeping up *with*? (If Judy Marshall knew of these doubts, she would stand and applaud—she has wondered for the last two years when her bright and thoughtful son will finally tire of hanging out with such a bunch of losers . . . what she calls "low-raters.")

"Suck an elf," Ty says disconsolately—he has picked up this harmless vulgarity from Sci-Fi Channel reruns of a miniseries called *The 10th Kingdom*—and dismounts his bike. There's no real reason to speed after them, anyway; he knows where he'll find them, in the parking lot of the 7-Eleven, drinking Slurpees and trading Magic cards. This is another problem Tyler is having with his friends. These days he'd much rather trade baseball cards. Ebbie, Ronnie, and T.J. could care less about the Cardinals, the Indians, the Red Sox, and the Brew Crew. Ebbie has gone so far as to say that baseball is gay, a comment Ty considers stupid (almost pitiable) rather than outrageous.

He walks his bike slowly up the sidewalk, catching his

breath. Here is the intersection of Chase and Queen streets. Ebbie calls Queen Street Queer Street. Of course. No surprise there. And isn't that a big part of the problem? Tyler is a boy who likes surprises; Ebbie Wexler is a boy who doesn't. Which makes their opposite reactions to the music pouring out of the pickup a little earlier that morning perfectly predictable.

Tyler pauses at the corner, looking down Queen Street. There are shaggy hedges on both sides. Above those on the right rise a number of interconnected red roofs. The old folks' home. Beside the main gate, some sort of sign has been placed. Curious, Tyler remounts his bike and rides slowly down the sidewalk for a look. The longest branches of the hedge beside him whisper against the handlebar of his bike.

The sign turns out to be a great big strawberry. TODAY IS STRAWBERRY FEST!!! is written below it. What, Ty Marshall wonders, is a Strawberry Fest? A party, something strictly for old folks? It's a question, but not a very interesting one. After mulling it over for a few seconds, he turns his bike and prepares to ride back down to Chase Street.

Charles Burnside enters the men's room at the head of the Daisy corridor, still grinning and clutching Butch's pet rock. To his right is a line of sinks with a mirror over each one—they are the sort of metal mirrors one finds in the toilets of lower-class bars and saloons. In one of these, Burny sees his own grinning reflection. In another, the one closest the window, he sees a small boy in a Milwaukee Brewers T-shirt. The boy is standing astride his bike, just outside the gate, reading the Strawberry Fest! sign.

Burny begins to drool. There is nothing discreet about it, either. Burny drools like a wolf in a fairy tale, white curds of foamy spit leaking from the corners of his mouth and flowing over the slack, liver-colored roll of his lower lip. The drool runs down his chin like a stream of soapsuds. He wipes at it absently with the back of one gnarled hand and shakes it to the floor in a splatter, never taking his eyes from the mirror. The boy in the mirror is not one of this creature's poor lost babies—Ty Marshall has lived in French Landing his whole life and knows exactly where he is—but he *could* be. He could very easily become lost, and wind up in a certain room. A certain cell. Or

trudging toward a strange horizon on burning, bleeding footsies.

Especially if Burny has his way. He will have to move fast,
but as we have already noted, Charles Burnside can, with the
proper motivation, move very fast indeed.

"Gorg," he says to the mirror. He speaks this nonsense word
in a perfectly clear, perfectly flat midwestern accent. "Come,
Gorg."

And without waiting to see what comes next—he *knows*
what comes next—Burny turns and walks toward the line of
four toilet stalls. He steps into the second from the left and
closes the door.

Tyler has just remounted his bike when the hedge rustles ten
feet from the Strawberry Fest! sign. A large black crow shrugs
its way out of the greenery and onto the Queen Street sidewalk.
It regards the boy with a lively, intelligent eye. It stands with its
black legs spread, opens its beak, and speaks. "Gorg!"

Tyler looks at it, beginning to smile, not sure he heard this
but ready to be delighted (at ten, he's always ready to be delighted, always primed to believe the unbelievable). "What?
Did you say something?"

The crow flutters its glossy wings and cocks its head in a
way that renders the ugly almost charming.

"Gorg! Ty!"

The boy laughs. It said his name! The crow said his name!

He dismounts his bike, puts it on the kickstand, and takes a
couple of steps toward the crow. Thoughts of Amy St. Pierre
and Johnny Irkenham are—unfortunately—the furthest things
from his mind.

He thinks the crow will surely fly away when he steps toward
it, but it only flutters its wings a little and takes a slide-step
toward the bushy darkness of the hedge.

"Did you say my name?"

"Gorg! Ty! Abbalah!"

For a moment Ty's smile falters. That last word is almost familiar to him, and the associations, although faint, are not exactly pleasant. It makes him think of his mother, for some
reason. Then the crow says his name again; surely it is saying
*Ty.*

Tyler takes another step away from Queen Street and toward the black bird. The crow takes a corresponding step, sidling closer still to the bulk of the hedge. There is no one on the street; this part of French Landing is dreaming in the morning sunshine. Ty takes another step toward his doom, and all the worlds tremble.

Ebbie, Ronnie, and T.J. come swaggering out of the 7-Eleven, where the raghead behind the counter has just served them blueberry Slurpees (*raghead* is just one of many pejorative terms Ebbie has picked up from his dad). They also have fresh packs of Magic cards, two packs each.

Ebbie, his lips already smeared blue, turns to T.J. "Go on downstreet and get the slowpoke."

T.J. looks injured. "Why me?"

"Because Ronnie bought the cards, dumbwit. Go on, hurry up."

"Why do we need him, Ebbie?" Ronnie asks. He leans against the bike rack, noshing on the cold, sweet chips of ice.

"Because I say so," Ebbie replies loftily. The fact is, Tyler Marshall usually has money on Fridays. In fact, Tyler has money almost every day. His parents are loaded. Ebbie, who is being raised (if you can call it that) by a single father who has a crappy janitor's job, has already conceived a vague hate for Tyler on this account; the first humiliations aren't far away, and the first beatings will follow soon after. But now all he wants is more Magic cards, a third pack for each of them. The fact that Tyler doesn't even *like* Magic that much will only make getting him to pony up that much sweeter.

But first they have to get the little slowpoke up here. Or the little po-sloke, as mush-mouthed Ronnie calls him. Ebbie likes that, and thinks he will start using it. Po-sloke. A good word. Makes fun of Ty and Ronnie at the same time. Two for the price of one.

"Go on, T.J. Unless you want an Indian burn."

T.J. doesn't. Ebbie Wexler's Indian burns hurt like a mad bastard. He gives a theatrical sigh, backs his bike out of the rack, mounts it, and rides back down the mild slope of the hill, holding a handlebar in one hand and his Slurpee in the other. He expects to see Ty right away, probably walking his bike because he's *just . . . so . . . tiyyy-urd,* but Ty doesn't seem to be on Chase Street at all—what's up with that?

T.J. pedals a little faster.

In the men's room, we are now looking at the line of toilet stalls. The door of the one second from the left is closed. The other three stand ajar on their chrome hinges. Beneath the closed door, we see a pair of gnarled, veiny ankles rising from a pair of filthy slippers.

A voice cries out with surprising strength. It is a young man's voice, hoarse, hungry, and angry. It echoes flatly back from the tile walls: "*Abbalah! Abbalah-doon! Munshun gorg!*"

Suddenly the toilets flush. Not just the one in the closed cubicle but all of them. Across the room the urinals also flush, their chromed handles dipping in perfect synchronicity. Water runs down their curved porcelain surfaces.

When we look back from the urinals to the toilets, we see that the dirty slippers—and the feet that were in them—are gone. And for the first time we have actually *heard* the sound of slippage, a kind of hot exhale, the sort of sound one hears escaping one's lungs when waking from a nightmare at two in the morning.

Ladies and gentlemen, Charles Burnside has left the building.

The crow has backed right up against the hedge now. Still it regards Tyler with its bright, eerie eyes. Tyler steps toward it, feeling hypnotized.

"Say my name again," he breathes. "Say my name again and you can go."

"*Ty!*" the crow croaks obligingly, then gives its wings a little shake and slips into the hedge. For a moment Tyler can still see it, a mixture of shiny black in the shiny green, and then it's gone.

"Holy crow!" Tyler says. He realizes what he's said and gives a small, shaky laugh. Did it happen? It did, didn't it?

He leans closer to where the crow reentered the hedge, thinking if it shed a feather he will take it for a souvenir, and when he does, a scrawny white arm shoots out through the green and seizes him unerringly by the neck. Tyler has time to give a single terrified squawk, and then he is dragged through the hedge. One of his sneakers is pulled off by the short, stiff branches. From the far side there is a single guttural, greedy cry—it might have been "*Boy!*"—and then a thud, the sound of a pet rock coming down on a small boy's head, perhaps. Then there's nothing but the distant drone of a lawn mower and the closer drone of a bee.

The bee is bumbling around the flowers on the far side of the hedge, the Maxton side. There is nothing else to be seen over there but green grass, and closer to the building, the tables where the elderly inhabitants will, at noon, sit down to the Strawberry Fest Picnic.

Tyler Marshall is gone.

T. J. Renniker coasts to a stop at the corner of Chase and Queen. His Slurpee is dripping dark blue juice over his wrist, but he barely notices. Halfway down Queen Street he sees Ty's bike, leaning neatly over on its kickstand, but no Ty.

Moving slowly—he has a bad feeling about this, somehow—T.J. rides over to the bike. At some point he becomes aware that what was a Slurpee has now dissolved into a soggy cup of melting goop. He tosses it into the gutter.

It's Ty's ride, all right. No mistaking that red twenty-inch Schwinn with the ape-hanger handlebars and the green Milwaukee Bucks decal on the side. The bike, and—

Lying on its side by the hedge that creates a border between the world of the old folks and the world of regular people, the *real* people, T.J. sees a single Reebok sneaker. Scattered around it are a number of shiny green leaves. One feather protrudes from the sneaker.

The boy stares at this sneaker with wide eyes. T.J. may not be as smart as Tyler, but he's a few watts brighter than Ebbie Wexler, and it's easy enough for him to imagine Tyler being dragged through the hedge, leaving his bike behind . . . and one sneaker . . . one lonely, overturned sneaker . . .

"Ty?" he calls. "Are you jokin' around? Because if you are, you better stop. I'll tell Ebbie to give you the biggest Indian burn you ever had."

No answer. Ty isn't joking around. T.J. somehow knows it.

Thoughts of Amy St. Pierre and Johnny Irkenham suddenly

explode in T.J.'s mind. He hears (or imagines he hears) stealthy footsteps behind the hedge: the Fisherman, having secured dinner, has come back for dessert!

T.J. tries to scream and cannot. His throat has shrunk down to a pinhole. Instead of screaming, he hunches himself over the handlebars of his bike and begins pedaling. He swerves off the sidewalk and into the street, wanting to get away from the dark bulk of that hedge just as fast as he can. When he leaves the curb, the front tire of his Huffy bike squashes through the remains of his Slurpee. As he pedals toward Chase Street, bent over his handlebars like a Grand Prix racer, he leaves a dark and shiny track on the pavement. It looks like blood. Somewhere nearby, a crow caws. It sounds like laughter.

16 Robin Hood Lane: we've been here before, as the chorus girl said to the archbishop. Peek through the kitchen window and we see Judy Marshall, asleep in the rocking chair in the corner. There's a book in her lap, the John Grisham novel we last saw on her bedside table. Sitting beside her on the floor is half a cup of cold coffee. Judy managed to read ten pages before dozing off. We shouldn't blame Mr. Grisham's narrative skills; Judy had a hard night last night, and it's not the first. It's been over two months since she last got more than two hours of sleep in one stretch. Fred knows something is wrong with his wife, but has no idea how deep it runs. If he did, he would be a lot more than frightened. Soon, God help him, he is going to have a better picture of her mental state.

Now she begins to moan thickly, and to turn her head from side to side. Those nonsense words begin to issue from her again. Most of them are too sleep-fuzzy to understand, but we catch *abbalah* and *gorg*.

Her eyes suddenly flash open. They are a brilliant, royal blue in the morning light, which fills the kitchen with summer's dusty gold.

"*Ty!*" she gasps, and her feet give a convulsive waking jerk. She looks at the clock over the stove. It is twelve minutes past nine, and everything seems twisted, as it so often does when we sleep deeply but not well or long. She has sucked some miserable, not-quite-a-nightmare dream after her like mucusy strings of afterbirth: men with fedora hats pulled down so as to shadow their faces, walking on long R. Crumb legs that ended in big round-toed R. Crumb shoes, sinister keep on truckin' sharpies who moved too fast against a city background—Milwaukee? Chicago?—and in front of a baleful orange sky. The dream's sound track was the Benny Goodman band playing "King Porter Stomp," the one her father had always played when he was getting a little shot, and the feeling of the dream had been a terrible darkwood mix of terror and grief: awful things had happened, but the worst was waiting.

There's none of the relief people usually feel upon waking from bad dreams—the relief she herself had felt when she had been younger and . . . and . . .

"And sane," she says in a croaky, just-woke-up voice. " 'King Porter Stomp.' Think of that." To her it had always sounded like the music you heard in the old cartoons, the ones where mice in white gloves ran in and out of ratholes with dizzying, feverish speed. Once, when her father was dancing her around to that one, she had felt something hard poking against her. Something in his pants. After that, when he put on his dance music, she tried to be somewhere else.

"Quit it," she says in the same croaky voice. It's a crow's voice, and it occurs to her that there was a crow in her dream. Sure, you bet. The Crow Gorg.

"Gorg means death," she says, and licks her dry upper lip without realizing it. Her tongue comes out even farther, and on the return swipe the tip licks across her nostrils, warm and wet and somehow comforting. "Over there, *gorg* means death. Over there in the—"

*Faraway* is the word she doesn't say. Before she can, she sees something on the kitchen table that wasn't there before. It's a wicker box. A sound is coming from it, some low sleepy sound.

Distress worms into her lower belly, making her bowels feel loose and watery. She knows what a box like that is called: a creel. It's a fisherman's creel.

There is a fisherman in French Landing these days. A bad fisherman.

"Ty?" she calls, but of course there is no answer. The house is empty except for her. Dale is at work, and Ty will be out playing—you bet. It's half-past July, the heart of summer vacation, and Ty will be rolling around the town, doing all the Ray Bradbury–August Derleth things boys do when they've got the whole endless summer day to do them in. But he won't be alone; Fred has talked with him about buddying up until the Fisherman is caught, at *least* until then, and so has she. Judy has no great liking for the Wexler kid (the Metzger or Renniker kids, either), but there's safety in numbers. Ty probably isn't having any great cultural awakenings this summer, but at least—

"At least he's safe," she says in her croaky Crow Gorg voice. Yet the box that has appeared on the kitchen table during her nap seems to deny that, to negate the whole concept of safety. Where did it come from? And what is the white thing on top of it?

"A note," she says, and gets up. She crosses the short length of floor between the rocker and the table like someone still in a dream. The note is a piece of paper, folded over. Written across the half she can see is Sweet Judy Blue Eyes. In college, just before meeting Dale, she had a boyfriend who used to call her that. She asked him to stop—it was annoying, sappy—and when he kept forgetting (on purpose, she suspected), she dropped him like a rock. Now here it is again, that stupid nickname, mocking her.

Judy turns on the sink tap without taking her eyes from the note, fills her cupped hand with cold water, and drinks. A few drops fall on Sweet Judy Blue Eyes. and the name smears at once. Written in fountain-pen ink? How antique! Who writes with a fountain pen these days?

She reaches for the note, then draws back. The sound from inside the box is louder now. It's a humming sound. It—

"It's flies," she says. Her throat has been refreshed by the water and her voice isn't so croaky, but to herself, Judy still sounds like the Crow Gorg. "You know the sound of flies."

*Get the note.*

*Don't want to.*

*Yes, but you NEED to! Now get it! What happened to your GUTS, you little chickenshit?*

Good question. *Fucking* good question. Judy's tongue comes out, slathers her upper lip and philtrum. Then she takes the note and unfolds it.

Sorry there is only one "kiddie-knee" (kidney). The other I fryed and ate. It was very good!

The Fisherman

The nerves in Judy Marshall's fingers, palms, wrists, and forearms suddenly shut down. The color drops so completely from her face that the blue veins in her cheeks become visible. It's surely a miracle that she doesn't pass out. The note drops from her fingers and goes seesawing to the floor. Shrieking her son's name over and over again, she throws back the lid of the fisherman's creel.

Inside are shiny red coils of intestine, crawling with flies. There are the wrinkled sacs of lungs and the fist-sized pump that was a child's heart. There is the thick purple pad of a liver . . . and one kidney. This mess of guts is crawling with flies and all the world is gorg, is gorg, is gorg.

In the sunny stillness of her kitchen Judy Marshall now begins to howl, and it is the sound of madness finally broken free of its flimsy cage, madness unbound.

Butch Yerxa intended to go in after a single smoke—there's always a lot to do on Strawberry Fest! days (although kindhearted Butch doesn't hate the little artificial holiday the way Pete Wexler does). Then Petra English, an orderly from Asphodel, wandered over and they started talking motorcycles, and before you know it twenty minutes have passed.

He tells Petra he has to go, she tells him to keep the shiny side up and the rubber side down, and Butch slips back in through the door to an unpleasant surprise. There is Charles Burnside, starkers, standing beside the desk with his hand on the rock Butch uses as a paperweight. (His son made it in camp last year—painted the words on it, anyway—and Butch thinks it's cute as hell.) Butch has nothing against the residents—certainly he would give Pete Wexler a pasting if he knew about the thing with the cigarettes, never mind just reporting him—but he doesn't like them touching his things. Especially this guy, who is fairly nasty when he has his few wits about him. Which he does now. Butch can see it in his eyes. The real Charles Burnside has come up for air, perhaps in honor of Strawberry Fest!

And speaking of strawberries, Burny has apparently been into them already. There are traces of red on his lips and tucked into the deep folds at the corners of his mouth.

Butch barely looks at this, though. There are other stains on Burny. Brown ones.

"Want to take your hand off that, Charles?" he asks.

"Off what?" Burny asks, then adds: "Asswipe."

Butch doesn't want to say *Off my pet rock,* that sounds stupid. "Off my paperweight."

Burny looks down at the rock, which he has just replaced (there was a little blood and hair on it when he emerged from the toilet stall, but cleanup is what bathroom sinks are for). He drops his hand from it and just stands there. "Clean me up, bozo. I shit myself."

"So I see. But first tell me if you've gone and spread your crap around the kitchen. And I know you've been down there, so don't lie."

"Warshed my hands first," Burny says, and shows them. They are gnarled, but pink and clean for all that. Even the nails are clean. He certainly has washed them. He then adds: "Jackoff."

"Come on down to the bathroom with me," Butch says. "The jackoff asswipe will get you cleaned up."

Burny snorts, but comes willingly enough.

"You ready for the dance this afternoon?" Butch asks him, just to be saying something. "Got your dancing shoes all polished, big boy?"

Burny, who can surprise you sometimes when he's actually home, smiles, showing a few yellow teeth. Like his lips, they are stained with red. "Yowza, I'm ready to rock," he says.

Although Ebbie's face doesn't show it, he listens with growing unease to T.J.'s story about Tyler Marshall's abandoned bike and sneaker. Ronnie's face, on the other hand, shows *plenty* of unease.

"So what're we gonna do, Ebbie?" T.J. asks when he's done. He's finally getting his breath back from his rapid pedal up the hill.

"What do you mean, what're we gonna do?" Ebbie says. "Same things we were gonna do anyway, go downstreet, see what we can find for returnable bottles. Go down the park and trade Magics."

"But . . . but what if—"

"Shut your yap," Ebbie says. He knows what two words T.J. is about to say, and he doesn't want to hear them. His dad says it's bad luck to toss a hat on the bed, and Ebbie never does it. If that's bad luck, mentioning some freako killer's name has got to be twice as bad.

But then that idiot Ronnie Metzger goes and says it anyway . . . sort of. "But Ebbie, what if it's the Misherfun? What if Ty got grabbed by the—"

"Shut the fuck up!" Ebbie says, and draws back his fist as if to hit the damn mushmouth.

At that moment the raghead clerk pops out of the 7-Eleven like a turbaned jack out of his box. "I want none of that talk here!" he cries. "You go now, do your filthy-talk another place! Or I call police!"

Ebbie starts to pedal slowly away, in a direction that will take him farther from Queer Street (under his breath he mutters *dune coon,* another charming term he has learned from his father), and the other two boys follow him. When they have put a block between them and the 7-Eleven, Ebbie stops and faces the other two, both his gut and his jaw jutting.

"He rode off on his own half an hour ago," he says.

*"Huh?"* says T.J.

"Who did what?" says Ronnie.

"Ty Marshall. If anyone asks, he rode off on his own half an hour ago. When we were . . . ummm . . ." Ebbie casts his mind back, something that's hard for him because he has had so little practice. In ordinary circumstances, the present is all Ebbie Wexler needs.

"When we were looking in the window of the Allsorts?" T.J. asks timidly, hoping he isn't buying himself one of Ebbie's ferocious Indian burns.

Ebbie looks at him blankly for a moment, then smiles. T.J. relaxes. Ronnie Metzger only goes on looking bewildered. With a baseball bat in his hands or a pair of hockey skates on his feet, Ronnie is prince of all he surveys. The rest of the time he's pretty much at sea.

"That's right," Ebbie says, "yeah. We was lookin' in the window of Schmitt's, then that truck came along, the one playin' the punk-ass music, and then Ty said he hadda split."

"Where'd he have to go?" T.J. asks.

Ebbie isn't bright, but he is possessed of what might be termed "low cunning." He knows instinctively that the best story is a *short* story—the less there is, the smaller the chance that someone will trip you up with an inconsistency. "He didn't tell us that. He just said he hadda go."

"He didn't go anywhere," Ronnie says. "He just got behind because he's a . . ." He pauses, arranging the word, and this time it comes out right. "Slowpoke."

"You never mind that," Ebbie says. "What if the . . . what if *that guy* got him, you dummocks? You want people sayin' it was because he couldn't keep up? That he got killed or somethin' because we left him behind? You want people sayin' it was our fault?"

"Gee," Ronnie says. "You don't really think the Misherfun—*Fisherman*—got Ty, do you?"

"I don't know and I don't care," Ebbie says, "but I don't mind it that he's gone. He was startin' to piss me off."

"Oh." Ronnie contrives to look both vacant and satisfied. *What a dummocks he is,* Ebbie marvels. *What a total and complete dummocks.* And if you didn't believe it, just think of how Ronnie, who's as strong as a horse, allows Ebbie to give him Indian burn after Indian burn. A day will probably come when Ronnie realizes he doesn't have to put up with that anymore, and on that day he may well pound Ebbie into the ground like a human tent peg, but Ebbie doesn't worry about such things; he's even worse at casting his mind forward than he is at casting it back.

"Ronnie," Ebbie says.

"What?"

"Where were we when Tyler took off?"

"Um . . . Schmitt's Allsorts?"

"Right. And where'd he go?"

"Didn't say."

Ebbie sees that for Ronnie this is already becoming the truth and is satisfied. He turns to T.J. "You got it?"

"I got it."

"Then let's go."

They pedal off. The dummocks pulls a little ahead of Ebbie and T.J. as they roll along the tree-lined street, and Ebbie allows this. He swings his bike a little closer to T.J.'s and says: "You see anything else back there? Anybody? Like a guy?"

T.J. shakes his head. "Just his bike and his sneaker." He pauses, remembering as hard as he can. "There were some leaves scattered around. From the hedge. And I think there might have been a feather. Like a crow feather?"

Ebbie dismisses this. He is grappling with the question of whether or not the Fisherman has actually come close to him this morning, close enough to snatch one of his buddies. There is a bloodthirsty part of him that likes the idea, that relishes the thought of some shadowy, no-face monster killing the increasingly annoying Ty Marshall and eating him for lunch. There is also a childish part of him that is terrified of the boogeyman (this part will be in charge tonight as he lies awake in his room, looking at shadows that seem to take form and slink ever closer around his bed). And there is the older-than-his-years part of him, which has taken instinctive and immediate measures to avoid the eye of authority, should Tyler's disappearance turn into what Ebbie's father calls "a fuckarow."

But mostly, as with Dale Gilbertson and Ty's father, Fred, there is a continent of fundamental disbelief inside of Ebbie Wexler. He simply cannot believe that anything *final* has happened to Tyler. Not even after Amy St. Pierre and Johnny Irkenham, who was carved into pieces and hung up in an old henhouse. These are kids of whom Ebbie has heard on the evening news, fictions from the Land of TV. He didn't know Amy or Johnny, so they could have died, just as make-believe people were always dying in the movies and on TV. Ty is different. Ty was just here. He talked to Ebbie, Ebbie talked to him. In Ebbie's mind, this equals immortality. Or *should*. If Ty could be snatched by the Fisherman, any kid could be snatched. Including him. Hence, like Dale and Fred, he just doesn't believe it. His most secret and fundamental heart, the part of him that assures the rest of him that everything is fine on Planet Ebbie, denies the Fisherman and all his works.

T.J. says: "Ebbie, do you think—"

"Nah," Ebbie says. "He'll turn up. Come on, let's go to the park. We can look for cans and bottles later."

• • •

Fred Marshall has left his sport coat and tie in his office, rolled up his sleeves, and is helping Rod Tisbury unpack a new Hiler rototiller. It's the first of the new Hiler line, and it's a beaut.

"I've been waiting for a gadget like this twenty years or more," Rod says. He expertly inserts the wide end of his crowbar at the top of the big crate, and one of the wooden sides falls to the concrete floor of the maintenance garage with a flat clap. Rod is Goltz's chief mechanic, and out here in maintenance he is king. "It's gonna work for the small farmer; it's gonna work for the town gardener, as well. If you can't sell a dozen of these by fall, you're not doing your job."

"I'll sell twenty by the end of August," Fred says with perfect confidence. All his worries have been temporarily swept away by this splendid little green machine, which can do a hell of a lot more than rototill; there are a number of sexy attachments that snap in and out as easily as the lining in a fall jacket. He wants to start it up, listen to it run. That two-cylinder engine looks pretty sweet.

"Fred?"

He looks around impatiently. It's Ina Gaitskill, Ted Goltz's secretary and the dealership receptionist. "What?"

"You've got a call on line one." She points across the floor—alive with clanging machinery and the noisy whir of pneumatic screwdrivers loosening bolts on an old Case tractor—to the phone on the wall, where several lights are blinking.

"Can you take a message, Ina? I was going to help Rod get a battery in this little beast and then—"

"I think you should take the call. It's a woman named Enid Purvis. A neighbor of yours?"

For a moment Fred blanks, and then his salesman's mind, which stores up names compulsively, comes to his rescue. Enid Purvis. Wife of Deke. Corner of Robin Hood and Maid Marian. He saw Deke just this morning. They waved to each other.

At the same time, he becomes aware that Ina's eyes are too big and her normally generous mouth is too small. She looks worried.

"What is it?" Dale asks. "Ina, what is it?"

"I don't know." Then, reluctantly: "Something about your wife."

"Better take it, hoss," Rod says, but Fred is already crossing the oil-stained concrete floor to the phone.

He arrives home ten minutes after leaving Goltz's, peeling out of the employees' parking lot and laying rubber like a teenager. The worst part had been Enid Purvis's calm and careful delivery, how hard she'd been trying not to sound frightened.

She had been walking Potsie past the Marshall house, she said, when she heard Judy scream. Not once, but twice. Of course Enid had done what any good neighbor would, God bless her: gone up to the door, rapped, then pushed open the letter slot and called through it. If there had been no answer, she told Fred, she probably would have phoned the police. She wouldn't even have gone back home to do it; she would have crossed the street to the Plotskys' house and called from there. But—

"I'm all right," Judy had called back, and then she had laughed. The laugh was shrill, ending in a tittery gasp. Enid had found this laugh somehow even more upsetting than the screams. "It was all a dream. Even Ty was a dream."

"Did you cut yourself, dear?" Enid had called through the letter slot. "Did you fall down?"

"There was no creel," Judy had called back. She might have said *keel,* but Enid was quite sure it was *creel.* "I dreamed that, too." Then, Enid reluctantly told Fred, Judy Marshall had begun crying. It had been very upsetting, listening to that sound come to her through the letter slot. It had even made the dog whine.

Enid had called through one more time, asking if she could come in and make sure Judy wasn't hurt.

"Go away!" Judy had called back. In the midst of her crying, she'd laughed again—an angry, distracted laugh. "You're a dream, too. This whole world is a dream." Then there had been the sound of shattering glass, as if she had struck a coffee mug or water tumbler and knocked it to the floor. Or thrown it at the wall.

"I didn't call the police, because she sounded all right," Enid told Fred (Fred standing with the phone jammed up against one ear and his hand plastered over the other to cut out all the yam-

mering mechanical sounds, which he ordinarily enjoys and
which at that moment seemed to go into his head like chrome
spikes). "*Physically* all right, anyway. But Fred . . . I think you
ought to go home and check on her."

All of Judy's recent oddities went through his mind in a
whirl. So did Pat Skarda's words. *Mental dysfunction. . . . We
hear people say "So-and-so snapped," but there are usually
signs . . .*

And he has *seen* the signs, hasn't he?

Seen them and done nothing.

Fred parks his car, a sensible Ford Explorer, in the driveway and
hurries up the steps, already calling his wife's name. There is no
answer. Even when he has stepped through the front door (he
pushes it open so hard the brass letter slot gives a nonsensical little clack), there is no answer. The air-conditioned interior of the
house feels too cold on his skin and he realizes he's sweating.

"Judy? Jude?"

Still no answer. He hurries down the hall to the kitchen,
where he is most apt to find her if he comes home for something in the middle of the day.

The kitchen is sun-washed and empty. The table and the
counter are clean; the appliances gleam; two coffee cups have
been placed in the dish drainer, winking sun from their freshly
washed surfaces. More sun winks from a heap of broken glass
in the corner. Fred sees a flower decal on one piece and realizes
it was the vase on the windowsill.

"Judy?" he calls again. He can feel the blood hammering in
his throat and at his temples.

She doesn't answer him, but he hears her upstairs, beginning
to sing.

*"Rock-a-bye baby . . . on the treetop . . . when the wind
blows . . ."*

Fred recognizes it, and instead of feeling relieved at the
sound of her voice, his flesh goes even colder. She used to sing
it to Tyler when their son was little. Ty's lullabye. Fred hasn't
heard that particular ditty come out of her mouth in years.

He goes back down the hall to the stairs, now seeing what he
missed on his first trip. The Andrew Wyeth print, *Christina's
World,* has been taken down and set against the baseboard

heater. The wallpaper below the picture hook has been scraped away in several places, revealing the plasterboard beneath. Fred, colder than ever, knows that Judy did this. It isn't intuition, exactly; not deduction, either. Call it the telepathy of the long married.

Floating down from above, beautiful and on-key yet at the same time perfectly empty: *". . . the cradle will rock. When the bough breaks, the cradle will fall . . ."*

Fred is up the stairs two at a time, calling her name.

The upper hall is a scary mess. This is where they have hung the gallery of their past: Fred and Judy outside Madison Shoes, a blues club they sometimes went to when there was nothing interesting going on at the Chocolate Watchband; Fred and Judy dancing the first dance at their wedding reception while their folks happily looked on; Judy in a hospital bed, exhausted but smiling, holding the wrapped bundle that was Ty; the photo of the Marshall family farm that she always sniffed at; more.

Most of these framed photographs have been taken down. Some, like the one of the farm, have been *thrown* down. Glass litters the hall in sparkling sprays. And she has been at the wallpaper behind half a dozen. In the spot where the picture of Judy and Ty in the hospital had hung, the paper has been torn almost completely away, and he can see where she scraped at the wallboard beneath. Some of the scratches are dappled with drying spots of blood.

"Judy! *Judy!*"

Tyler's door stands open. Fred sprints the length of the upstairs hall with glass crunching under his loafers.

*". . . and down will come Tyler, cradle and all."*

"Judy! Ju—"

He stands in the door, all words temporarily knocked out of him.

Ty's room looks like the aftermath of a rough search in a detective movie. The drawers have been yanked out of his bureau and lie everywhere, most overturned. The bureau itself has been pulled away from the wall. Summer clothes are spread hell to breakfast—jeans and T-shirts and underwear and white athletic socks. The closet door is open and more clothes have been struck from the hangers; that same spousal telepathy tells him she tore Ty's slacks and button-up shirts down so she could make sure nothing was behind them. The coat of Tyler's only suit hangs askew from the closet's doorknob. His posters have been pulled from the walls; Mark McGwire has been torn in half. In every case but one she has left the wallpaper behind the posters alone, but the one exception is a beaut. Behind the rectangle where the poster of the castle hung (COME BACK TO THE AULD SOD), the wallpaper has been almost entirely stripped away. There are more streaks of blood on the wallboard beneath.

Judy Marshall sits on the bare mattress of her son's bed. The sheets are heaped in the corner, along with the pillow. The bed itself has been yanked away from the wall. Judy's head is down. He can't see her face—her hair is screening it—but she's wearing shorts and he can see dapples and streaks of blood on her tanned thighs. Her hands are clasped below her knees, out of sight, and Fred is glad. He doesn't want to see how badly she has hurt herself until he has to. His heart is hammering in his chest, his nervous system is redlining with adrenaline overload, and his mouth tastes like a burnt fuse.

She begins to sing the chorus of Ty's lullabye again and he can't stand it. "Judy, no," he says, going to her through the strewn minefield that was, only last night when he came in to give Ty a good-night kiss, a reasonably neat little boy's room. "Stop, honey, it's okay."

For a wonder, she does stop. She raises her head, and when he sees the terrified look in her eyes, he loses what little breath he has left. It's more than terror. It's *emptiness,* as if something inside her has slipped aside and exposed a black hole.

"Ty's gone," she says simply. "I looked behind all the pictures I could . . . I was sure he'd be behind that one, if he was anywhere he'd be behind that one . . ."

She points toward the place where the Ireland travel poster hung, and he sees that four of the nails on her left hand have been ripped partly or completely away. His stomach does a flip-flop. Her fingers look as if they have been dipped in red ink. *If only it was ink,* Fred thinks. *If only.*

". . . but of course it's just a picture. They're all just pictures. I see that now." She pauses, then cries: "Abbalah! Munshun! Abbalah-gorg, Abbalah-doon!" Her tongue comes out—comes out to an impossible, cartoonish length—and swipes spittishly across her nose. Fred sees it but cannot believe it. This is like coming into a horror movie halfway through the show, discovering it's real, and not knowing what to do. What *is* he supposed to do? When you discover that the woman you love has gone mad—had a break with reality, at the very least— what are you supposed to *do*? How the hell do you deal with it?

But he loves her, has loved her from the first week he knew her, helplessly and completely and without the slightest regret ever after, and now love guides him. He sits down next to her on the bed, puts his arm around her, and simply holds her. He can feel her trembling from the inside out. Her body thrums like a wire.

"I love you," he says, surprised at his voice. It's amazing that seeming calmness can issue from such a crazy cauldron of confusion and fear. "I love you and everything is going to be all right."

She looks up at him and something comes back into her eyes. Fred cannot call it sanity (no matter how much he would like to), but it is at least some sort of marginal awareness. She knows where she is and who is with her. For a moment he sees gratitude in her eyes. Then her face cramps in a fresh agony of grief and she begins to weep. It is an exhausted, lost sound that wrenches at him. Nerves, heart, and mind, it wrenches at him.

"Ty's gone," Judy says. "Gorg fascinated him and the abbalah took him. Abbalah-doon!" The tears course down her cheeks. When she raises her hands to wipe them away, her fingers leave appalling streaks of blood.

Even though he's sure Tyler is fine (certainly *Fred* has had no premonitions today, unless we count his rosy sales prediction about the new Hiler roto), he feels a shudder course through him at the sight of those streaks, and it is not Judy's condition that causes it but what she's just said: *Ty's gone.* Ty is with his friends; he told Fred just last night that he, Ronnie, T.J., and the less-than-pleasant Wexler boy intended to spend the day "goofing off." If the other three boys go somewhere Ty doesn't want to be, he has promised to come directly home. All the bases seem to be covered, yet . . . is there not such a thing as mother's intuition? *Well,* he thinks, *maybe on the Fox Network.*

He picks Judy up in his arms and is appalled all over again, this time by how light she is. *She's lost maybe twenty pounds since the last time I picked her up like this,* he thinks. *At least ten. How could I not have noticed?* But he knows. Preoccupation with work was part of it; a stubborn refusal to let go of the idea that things were basically all right was the rest of it. *Well,* he thinks, carrying her out the door (her arms have crept tiredly up and locked themselves around his neck), *I'm over* that *little misconception.* And he actually believes this, in spite of his continued blind confidence in his son's safety.

Judy hasn't toured their bedroom during her rampage, and to Fred it looks like a cool oasis of sanity. Judy apparently feels the same way. She gives a tired sigh, and her arms drop away from her husband's neck. Her tongue comes out, but this time it gives only a feeble little lick at her upper lip. Fred bends and puts her down on the bed. She holds up her hands, looks at them.

"I cut myself . . . scraped myself . . ."

"Yes," he says. "I'm going to get something for them."

"How . . . ?"

He sits beside her for a moment. Her head has sunk into the soft double thickness of her pillows, and her eyelids are drooping. He thinks that, beyond the puzzlement in them, he can still see that terrifying blankness. He hopes he is wrong.

"Don't you remember?" he asks her gently.

"No . . . did I fall down?"

Fred chooses not to answer. He is starting to think again. Not much, he's not capable of much just yet, but a little. "Honey, what's a gorg? What's an abbalah? Is it a person?"

"Don't . . . know . . . Ty . . ."

"Ty's fine," he says.

"No . . ."

*"Yes,"* he insists. Perhaps he's insisting to both of the people in this pretty, tastefully decorated bedroom. "Honeybunch, you just lie there. I want to get a couple of things."

Her eyes drift closed. He thinks she will sleep, but her lids struggle slowly back up to half-mast.

"Lie right there," he says. "No getting up and wandering around. There's been enough of that. You scared poor Enid Purvis out of a year's life. You promise?"

"Promise . . ." Her eyelids drift back down.

Fred goes into the adjoining bathroom, ears alert for any

movement behind him. He has never seen anyone in his life who looks more bolt-shot than Judy does right now, but mad people are clever, and despite his prodigious capacity for denial in some areas, Fred can no longer fool himself about his wife's current mental state. Mad? Actually stark raving mad? Probably not. But off the rails, certainly. *Temporarily* off the rails, he amends as he opens the medicine cabinet.

He takes the bottle of Mercurochrome, then scans the prescription bottles on the shelf above. There aren't many. He grabs the one on the far left. Sonata, French Landing Pharmacy, one capsule at bedtime, do not use more than four nights in a row, prescribing physician Patrick J. Skarda, M.D.

Fred can't see the entire bed in the medicine-cabinet mirror, but he can see the foot of it . . . and one of Judy's feet, as well. Still on the bed. Good, good. He shakes out one of the Sonatas, then dumps their toothbrushes out of the glass—he has no intention of going all the way downstairs for a clean glass, does not want to leave her alone that long.

He fills the glass, then goes back into the bedroom with the water, the pill, and the bottle of Mercurochrome. Her eyes are shut. She is breathing so slowly that he has to put one hand on her chest to make sure she's breathing at all.

He looks at the sleeping pill, debates, then gives her a shake. "Judy! Jude! Wake up a little, hon. Just long enough to take a pill, okay?"

She doesn't even mutter, and Fred sets the Sonata aside. It won't be necessary after all. He feels some faint optimism at how fast she's fallen asleep and how deep she has gone. It's as if some vile sac has popped, discharged its poison, left her weak and tired but possibly okay again. Could that be? Fred doesn't know, but he's positive that she isn't just shamming sleep. All of Judy's current woes began with insomnia, and the insomnia has been the one constant throughout. Although she's only been exhibiting distressing symptoms for a couple of months—talking to herself and doing that odd and rather disgusting thing with her tongue, to mention only a couple of items—she hasn't been sleeping well since January. Hence the Sonata. Now it seems that she has finally tipped over. And is it too much to hope that when she wakes from a normal sleep she'll be her old normal self again? That her worries about her son's safety during the summer of the Fisherman have forced her to some sort of climax? Maybe, maybe not . . . but at least it has given Fred some time to think about what he should do next, and he had better use it well. One thing seems to him beyond argument: if Ty is here when his mother wakes up, Ty is going to have a much happier mother. The immediate question is how to locate Tyler as soon as possible.

His first thought is to call the homes of Ty's friends. It would be easy; those numbers are posted on the fridge, printed in Judy's neat back-slanting hand, along with the numbers of the fire department, the police department (including Dale Gilbertson's private number; he's an old friend), and French Landing Rescue. But it takes Fred only a moment to realize what a bad idea this is. Ebbie's mother is dead and his father is an unpleasant moron—Fred met him just once, and once is more than enough. Fred doesn't much like his wife labeling some people "low-raters" (*Who do you think you are,* he asked her once, *Queen of the doggone Realm?*), but in the case of Pete Wexler, the shoe fits. He won't have any idea of where the boys are today and won't care.

Mrs. Metzger and Ellen Renniker might, but having once been a boy on summer vacation himself—the whole world laid at your feet and at least two thousand places to go—Fred doubts it like hell. There's a chance the boys might be eating lunch (it's getting to be that time) at the Metzgers' or Rennikers', but is that slight chance worth scaring the hell out of two women? Because the killer will be the first thing they think of, just as sure as God made little fishes . . . and fishermen to catch 'em.

Once more sitting on the bed beside his wife, Fred feels his first real tingle of apprehension on his son's behalf and dismisses it brusquely. This is no time to give in to the heebie-jeebies. He has to remember that his wife's mental problems and his son's safety are not linked—except in her mind. His job is to present Ty, front and center and all squared away, thus proving her fears groundless.

Fred looks at the clock on his side of the bed and sees that it's quarter past eleven. *How the time flies when you're having fun,* he thinks. Beside him, Judy utters a single gaspy snore. It's a small sound, really quite ladylike, but Fred jumps anyway.

How she scared him when he first saw her in Ty's room! He's still scared.

Ty and his friends may come here for lunch. Judy says they often do because the Metzgers don't have much to eat and Mrs. Renniker usually serves what the boys call "goop," a mystery dish consisting of noodles and some gray meat. Judy makes them Campbell's soup and baloney sandwiches, stuff they like. But Ty has money enough to treat them all to McDonald's out by the little mall on the north side, or they could go into Sonny's Cruisin' Restaurant, a cheap diner with a cheesy fifties ambience. And Ty isn't averse to treating. He's a generous boy.

"I'll wait until lunch," he murmurs, completely unaware that he is talking as well as thinking. Certainly he doesn't disturb Judy; she has gone deep. "Then—"

Then what? He doesn't know, exactly.

He goes downstairs, kicks the Mr. Coffee back into gear, and calls work. He asks Ina to tell Ted Goltz he'll be out the rest of the day—Judy's sick. The flu, he tells her. Throwing up and everything. He runs down a list of people he was expecting to see that day and tells her to speak to Otto Eisman about handling them. Otto will be on that like white on rice.

An idea occurs to him while he's talking to her, and when he's done, he calls the Metzgers' and Rennikers' after all. At the Metzgers' he gets an answering machine and hangs up without leaving a message. Ellen Renniker, however, picks up on the second ring. Sounding casual and cheerful—it comes naturally, he's a hell of a salesman—he asks her to have Ty call home if the boys show up there for lunch. Fred says he has something to tell his son, making it sound like something good. Ellen says she will, but adds that T.J. had four or five dollars burning a hole in his jeans when he left the house that morning, and she doesn't expect to see him until suppertime.

Fred goes back upstairs and checks on Judy. She hasn't moved so much as a finger, and he supposes that's good.

No. There's nothing good about any of this.

Instead of receding now that the situation has stabilized— sort of—his fear seems to be intensifying. Telling himself that Ty is with his friends no longer seems to help. The sunny, silent house is creeping him out. He realizes he no longer wants Ty front and center simply for his wife's sake. Where would the boys go? Is there any one place—?

Of course there is. Where they can get Magic cards. That stupid, incomprehensible game they play.

Fred Marshall hurries back downstairs, grabs the phone book, hunts through the Yellow Pages, and calls the 7-Eleven. Like most of French Landing, Fred is in the 7-Eleven four or five times a week—a can of soda here, a carton of orange juice there—and he recognizes the lilt of the Indian day clerk's voice. He comes up with the man's name at once: Rajan Patel. It's that old salesman's trick of keeping as many names as possible in the active file. It sure helps here. When Fred calls the man Mr. Patel, the day clerk immediately becomes friendly, perfectly willing to help. Unfortunately, there isn't much help he can give. Lots of boys in. They are buying Magic cards, also Poké-mon and baseball cards. Some are trading these cards outside. He *does* recall three that came in that morning on bikes, he says. They bought Slurpees as well as cards, and then argued about something outside. (Rajan Patel doesn't mention the cursing, although this is chiefly why he remembers these boys.) After a little while, he says, they went on their way.

Fred is drinking coffee without even remembering when he poured it. Fresh threads of unease are spinning spider-silky webs in his head. Three boys. *Three.*

*It means nothing, you know that, don't you?* he tells himself. He *does* know it, and at the same time he *doesn't* know it. He can't even believe he's caught a little of Judy's freakiness, like a cold germ. This is just . . . well . . . freakiness for freakiness's sake.

He asks Patel to describe the kids and isn't too surprised when Patel can't. He thinks one of them was a bit of a fat boy, but he's not even sure of that. "Sorry, but I see so many," he says. Fred tells him he understands. He does, too, only all the understanding in the world won't ease his mind.

Three boys. Not four but three.

Lunchtime has come, but Fred is not the least bit hungry. The spooky, sunny silence maintains itself. The spiderwebs continue to spin.

Not four but three.

If it was Ty's bunch that Mr. Patel saw, the fattish boy was certainly Ebbie Wexler. The question is, who were the other two? And which one was missing? Which one had been stupid enough to go off on his own?

*Ty's gone. Gorg fascinated him and the abbalah took him.*

Crazy talk, no doubt about it . . . but Fred's arms nevertheless break out in a lush of goose bumps. He puts his coffee mug down with a bang. He'll clean up the broken glass, that's what he'll do. That's the next step, no doubt about it.

The *actual* next step, the *logical* next step, whispers through his mind as he climbs the stairs, and he immediately pushes it away. He's sure the cops are just lately overwhelmed with queries from hysterical parents who have lost track of their kids for an hour or so. The last time he saw Dale Gilbertson, the poor guy looked careworn and grim. Fred doesn't want to be marked down as part of the problem instead of part of the solution. Still . . .

Not four but three.

He gets the dustpan and broom out of the little utility closet next to the laundry room and begins sweeping up broken glass. When he's done he checks on Judy, sees she's still sleeping (more deeply than ever, from the look of her), and goes down to Ty's room. If Ty saw it like this, he'd be upset. He'd think his mom was a lot more than a Coke short of a Happy Meal.

*You don't have to worry about that,* his mind whispers. *He won't be seeing his room, not tonight, not ever. Gorg fascinated him and the abbalah took him.*

"Stop it," Fred tells himself. "Stop being an old woman."

But the house is too empty, too silent, and Fred Marshall is afraid.

Setting Tyler's room to rights takes longer than Fred ever would have expected; his wife went through it like a whirlwind. How can such a little woman have such strength in her? Is it the strength of the mad? Perhaps, but Judy doesn't *need* the strength of the mad. When she sets her mind to something, she is a formidable engine.

By the time he's finished cleaning up, almost two hours have passed and the only obvious scar is the scratched-out rectangle of wallpaper where the Irish travel poster hung. Sitting on Ty's remade bed, Fred finds that the longer he looks at that spot, the less he can stand the white wallboard, peering through as brazenly as a broken bone through outraged skin. He has washed away the streaks of blood, but can do nothing about the scratch marks she made with her nails.

*Yes I can,* he thinks. *Yes I can, too.*

Ty's dresser is mahogany, a piece of furniture that came to them from the estate of some distant relative on Judy's side. Moving it really isn't a one-man job, and under the circumstances, that suits Fred just fine. He slides a rug remnant under it to keep from marking up the floor, then pulls it across the room. Once it's been placed against the far wall, it covers most of the scratched area. With the bald spot out of sight, Fred feels better. Saner. Ty hasn't come home for lunch, but Fred didn't really expect he would. He'll be home by four, at the latest. Home for supper. Take it to the bank.

Fred strolls back to the master bedroom, massaging the small of his back as he walks. Judy *still* hasn't moved, and once again he puts an anxious hand on her chest. Her breathing is slow, but steady as she goes. *That's* all right. He lies down beside her on the bed, goes to loosen his tie, and laughs when he feels his open collar. Coat and tie, both back at Goltz's. Well, it's been a crazy day. For the time being it's just good to lie here in the air-conditioned cool, easing his aching back. Moving that dresser was a bitch, but he's glad he did it. Certainly there's no chance he'll drop off; he's far too upset. Besides, napping in the middle of the day has never been his thing.

So thinking, Fred falls asleep.

Beside him, in her own sleep, Judy begins to whisper. Gorg . . . abbalah . . . the Crimson King. And a woman's name. The name is Sophie.

# 6

In the ready room of the French Landing P.D., the phone on the desk rings. Bobby Dulac has been mining for nose-gold. Now he squashes his latest treasure on the sole of his shoe and picks up the phone.

"*Yell*-o, Police Department, Officer Dulac speaking, how can I help you?"

"Hey, Bobby. It's Danny Tcheda."

Bobby feels a prink of unease. Danny Tcheda—last name pronounced *Cheetah*—is one of French Landing's fourteen full-time RMP cops. He's currently on duty, and ordinary procedure dictates that duty cops radio in—that's what the *R* in RMP stands for, after all. The only exception to the rule has to do with the Fisherman. Dale has mandated that patrol officers call in on a landline if they think they have a situation involving the killer. Too many people have their ears on out there, doubtless including Wendell "Pisshead" Green.

"Danny, what's up?"

"Maybe nothing, maybe something not so good. I got a bike and a sneaker in the trunk of my car. I found 'em over on Queen Street. Near Maxton Elder Care?"

Bobby draws a pad toward him and begins to jot. The tickle of unease has become a sinking feeling.

"Nothing wrong with the bike," Danny continues, "just sitting there on its kickstand, but combined with the sneaker . . ."

"Yeah, yeah, I see your point, Danny, but you never should have fooled with what could be evidence of a crime." *Please God don't let it be evidence of a crime,* Bobby Dulac is thinking. *Please God don't let it be another one.*

Irma Freneau's mother has just been in to see Dale, and

while there was no screaming or shouting, she came out with tears on her cheeks and looking like death on the half shell. They can't still be sure the little girl has become the Fisherman's third victim, but—

"Bobby, I *had* to," Danny is saying. "I'm ridin' solo, I didn't want to put this out on the air, I hadda find a phone. If I'd left the bike there, someone *else* coulda monkeyed with it. Hell, stolen it. This is a good bike, Schwinn three-speed. Better'n the one my kid's got, tell you that."

"What's your twenty?"

"7-Eleven, up the hill on 35. What I did was mark the location of the bike and the sneaker with chalk X's on the sidewalk. I handled them with gloves and put the sneaker in an evidence bag." Danny is sounding more and more anxious. Bobby knows how he must feel, sympathizes with the choices Danny had to make. Riding solo is a bitch, but French Landing is already supporting as many cops—full-time and part-time—as the budget will bear. Unless, of course, this Fisherman business gets totally out of control; in that case, the town fathers will no doubt discover a bit more elastic in the budget.

*Maybe it's already out of control,* Bobby thinks.

"Okay, Danny. Okay. See your point." *Whether or not* Dale *sees it is a whole 'nother thing,* Bobby thinks.

Danny lowers his voice. "No one needs to know I broke the chain of evidence, do they? I mean, if the subject ever came up. In court, or something."

"I guess that's up to Dale." *Oh God,* Bobby thinks. A new problem has just occurred to him. All calls that come in on this phone are automatically taped. Bobby decides the taping machinery is about to have a malfunction, retroactive to about two o'clock in the afternoon.

"And you want to know the other thing?" Danny is asking. "The *big* thing? I didn't want people to see it. A bike standing all by itself that way, you don't have to be Sherlock Fucking Holmes to draw a certain conclusion. And folks're getting close to the panic line, especially after that goddamned irresponsible story in the paper this morning. I didn't want to call from Maxton's for the same reason."

"I'm gonna put you on hold. You better talk to Dale."

In a vastly unhappy voice, Danny says: "Oh boy."

• • •

In Dale Gilbertson's office there is a bulletin board dominated by enlarged photographs of Amy St. Pierre and Johnny Irkenham. A third photo will be added soon, he fears—that of Irma Freneau. Beneath the two current photos, Dale sits at his desk, smoking a Marlboro 100. He's got the fan on. It will, he hopes, blow the smoke away. Sarah would just about kill him if she knew he was smoking again, but dear Jesus Christ, he needs *something*.

His interview with Tansy Freneau had been short and nothing short of purgatorial. Tansy is a juicer, a regular patron of the Sand Bar, and during their interview the smell of coffee brandy was so strong it almost seemed to be coming out of her pores (another excuse for the fan). Half drunk, she had been, and Dale was glad. It kept her calm, at least. It didn't put any sparkle in her dead eyes, coffee brandy was no good for that, but she had been calm. Hideously, she had even said "Thank you for helping me, sir" before leaving.

Tansy's ex—Irma's father—lives across the state in Green Bay ("Green Bay is the devil's town," Dale's father used to say, God knows why), where he works in a garage and, according to Tansy, supports several bars with names like the End Zone and the Fifty-Yard Line. Until today, there has been some reason to believe—at least to hope—that Richard "Cubby" Freneau snatched his daughter. An e-mail from the Green Bay Police Department has put paid to that little idea. Cubby Freneau is living with a woman who has two kids of her own, and he was in jail—D & D—the day Irma disappeared. There is still no body, and Tansy hasn't received a letter from the Fisherman, but—

The door opens. Bobby Dulac sticks his head in. Dale mashes his cigarette out on the inside lip of the wastebasket, burning the back of his hand with sparks in the process.

"Gosh 'n' fishes, Bobby, do you know how to *knock*?"

"Sorry, Chief." Bobby looks at the smoke ribboning up from the wastebasket with neither surprise nor interest. "Danny Tcheda's on the phone. I think you better take it."

"What's it about?" But he knows. Why else would it be the phone?

Bobby only repeats, not without sympathy, "I think you better take it."

. . .

The car sent by Rebecca Vilas delivers Henry to Maxton Elder Care at three-thirty, ninety minutes before the Strawberry Fest! dance is scheduled to begin. The idea is for the old folks to work up an appetite on the floor, then troop down to the caff—suitably decorated for the occasion—for a glamorously late (seven-thirty is *quite* late for Maxton's) dinner. With wine, for those who drink it.

A resentful Pete Wexler has been drafted by Rebecca Vilas to bring in the deejay's shit (Pete thinks of Henry as "the blind record-hopper"). Said shit consists of two speakers (very large), one turntable (light, but awkward as a motherfucker to carry), one preamp (very heavy), assorted wires (all tangled up, but that's the blind record-hopper's problem), and four boxes of actual records, which went out of style about a hundred years ago. Pete guesses that the blind record-hopper never heard a CD in his whole life.

The last item is a suit bag on a hanger. Pete has peeked in and ascertained that the suit is white.

"Hang it in there, please," Henry says, pointing with unerring accuracy toward the supply closet that has been designated his dressing room.

"Okay," Pete says. "What exactly is it, if you don't mind me asking?"

Henry smiles. He knows perfectly well that Pete has already had a peep. He heard the plastic bag rattling and the zipper chinking in a duet that only occurs when someone pulls the bag away from the hanger at the neck. "Inside that bag, my friend, Symphonic Stan, the Big-Band Man, is just waiting for me to put him on and bring him to life."

"Oh, uh-huh," Pete says, not knowing if he has been answered or not. All he's really sure of is that those records were almost as heavy as the preamp. Someone should really give the blind record-hopper some information about CDs, the next great leap forward.

"You asked me one; may I ask you one?"

"Be my guest," Pete says.

"There appears to have been a police presence at Maxton

Elder Care this afternoon," the blind record-hopper says. "They're gone now, but they were here when I arrived. What's that about? There hasn't been a robbery or an assault among the geriatrics, I hope?"

Pete stops in his tracks beneath a large cardboard strawberry, holding the suit bag and looking at the blind record-hopper with an amazement Henry can almost touch. "How'd you know the cops were here?"

Henry puts a finger to the side of his nose and tips his head to one side. He replies in a hoarse, conspiratorial whisper. "Smelled something blue."

Pete looks puzzled, debates whether or not to inquire further, and decides not to. Resuming his march toward the supply closet–dressing room, he says: "They're playing it cagey, but I think they're looking for another lost kid."

The look of amused curiosity fades from Henry's face. "Good Christ," he says.

"They came and went in a hurry. No kids here, Mr . . . uh, Leyden?"

"Leyden," Henry confirms.

"A kid in this place would stand out like a rose in a patch of poison ivy, if you know what I mean."

Henry doesn't consider old folks in any way analogous to poison ivy, but he does indeed get Mr. Wexler's drift. "What made them think—?"

"Someone found sumpin' on the sidewalk," Pete says. He points out the window, then realizes the blind guy can't see him pointing. *Duh,* as Ebbie would say. He lowers his hand. "If a kid got snatched, someone probably came along in a car and snatched him. No kidnapers in here, I can tell you that much." Pete laughs at the very idea of a Maxton moldy oldie snatching any kid big enough to ride a bike. The kid would probably break the guy over his knee like a dry stick.

"No," Henry says soberly, "that hardly seems likely, does it?"

"But I guess the cops got to dot all the *t*'s and cross all the *i*'s." He pauses. "That's just a little joke of mine."

Henry smiles politely, thinking that with some people, Alzheimer's disease might be an actual improvement. "When you hang my suit up, Mr. Wexler, would you be so good as to give it a gentle shake? Just to banish any incipient wrinkles?"

"Okay. Want me to take it out of the bag forya?"

"Thanks, that won't be necessary."

Pete goes into the supply closet, hangs up the suit bag, and gives it a little shake. *Incipient,* just what the hell does *that* mean? There's a rudiment of a library here at Maxton's; maybe he'll look it up in the dictionary. It pays to increase your word power, as it says in the *Reader's Digest,* although Pete doubts it will pay him much in this job.

When he goes back out to the common room, the blind record-hopper—Mr. Leyden, Symphonic Stan, whoever the hell he is—has begun unraveling wires and plugging them in with a speed and accuracy Pete finds a trifle unnerving.

Poor old Fred Marshall is having a terrible dream. *Knowing* it's a dream should make it less horrible but somehow doesn't. He's in a rowboat with Judy, out on a lake. Judy is sitting in the bow. They are fishing. *He* is, at least; Judy is just holding her pole. Her face is an expressionless blank. Her skin is waxy. Her eyes have a stunned, hammered look. He labors with increasing desperation to make contact with her, trying one conversational gambit after another. None work. To make what is, under the circumstances, a fairly apt metaphor, she spits every lure. He sees that her empty eyes appear fixed on the creel sitting between them in the bottom of the boat. Blood is oozing through the wickerwork in fat red dribbles.

*It's nothing, just fishblood,* he tries to assure her, but she makes no reply. In fact, Fred isn't so sure himself. He's thinking he ought to take a look inside the creel, just to be sure, when his pole gives a tremendous jerk—if not for quick reflexes, he would have lost it over the side. He's hooked a big one!

Fred reels it in, the fish on the other end of the line fighting him for every foot. Then, when he finally gets it near the boat, he realizes he has no net. *Hell with it,* he thinks, *go for broke.* He whips the pole backward, just *daring* the line to snap, and the fish—biggest goddamned lake trout you'd ever hope to see—flies out of the water and through the air in a gleaming, fin-flipping arc. It lands in the bottom of the boat (beside the oozing creel, in fact) and begins thrashing. It also begins to make gruesome choking noises. Fred has never heard a fish make noises like that. He bends forward and is horrified to see that the trout has Tyler's face. His son has somehow become a weretrout, and now he's dying in the bottom of the boat. Strangling.

Fred grabs at it, wanting to remove the hook and throw it back while there's still time, but the terrible choking thing keeps slipping through his fingers, leaving only a shiny slime of scales behind. It would be tough to get the hook out, in any case. The Ty-fish has swallowed it whole, and the barbed tip is actually protruding from one of the gills, just below the point where the human face melts away. Ty's choking becomes louder, harsher, infinitely more horrible—

Fred sits up with a low cry, feeling as if he's choking himself. For a moment he's completely adrift as to place and time—lost in the slippage, we might say—and then he realizes he's in his own bedroom, sitting up on his side of the bed he shares with Judy.

He notices that the light in here is much dimmer, because the sun has moved to the other side of the house. *My God,* he thinks, *how long have I been asleep? How could I—*

Oh, but here is another thing: that hideous choking sound has followed him out of his dream. It's louder than ever. It will wake Judy, scare her—

Judy is no longer on the bed, though.

"Jude? *Judy?*"

She's sitting in the corner. Her eyes are wide and blank, just as they were in his dream. A corsage of crumpled paper is protruding from her mouth. Her throat is grotesquely swelled, looks to Fred like a sausage that has been grilled until the casing is ready to pop.

*More paper,* he thinks. *Christ, she's choking on it.*

Fred rolls himself across the bed, falls off, and lands on his knees like a gymnast doing a trick. He reaches for her. She makes no move to evade him. There's that, at least. And although she's choking, he still sees no expression in her eyes. They are dusty zeros.

Fred yanks the corsage of paper from her mouth. There's another behind it. Fred reaches between her teeth, tweezes this second ball of paper between the first two fingers of his right hand (thinking *Please don't bite me, Judy, please don't*), and pulls it out, too. There's a third ball of paper behind this one, way at the back of her mouth. He gets hold of this one as well, and extracts it. Although it's crumpled, he can see the printed words GREAT IDEA, and knows what she's swallowed: sheets of paper from the notepad Ty gave her for her birthday.

She's still choking. Her skin is turning slate.

Fred grabs her by her upper arms and pulls her up. She comes easily, but when he relaxes his hold her knees bend and she starts to go back down. She's turned into Raggedy Ann. The choking sound continues. Her sausage throat—

"Help me, Judy! Help me, you bitch!"

Unaware of what he is saying. He yanks her hard—as hard as he yanked the fishing pole in his dream—and spins her around like a ballerina when she comes up on her toes. Then he seizes her in a bear hug, his wrists brushing the undersides of her breasts, her bottom tight against his crotch, the kind of position he would find extremely sexy if his wife didn't happen to be choking to death.

He pops his thumb up between her breasts like a hitchhiker, then says the magic word as he pulls sharply upward and backward. The magic word is *Heimlich,* and it works. Two more wads of paper fly from Judy's mouth, propelled by a jet of vomit that is little more than bile—her intake of food over the last twelve hours amounts to three cups of coffee and a cranberry muffin.

She gives a gasp, coughs twice, then begins to breathe more or less normally.

He puts her on the bed . . . drops her on the bed. His lower back is spasming wildly, and it's really no wonder; first Ty's dresser, now this.

"Well, what did you think you were doing?" he asks her loudly. "What in the name of Christ did you think you were *doing*?"

He realizes that he has raised one hand over Judy's upturned face as if to strike her. Part of him *wants* to strike her. He loves her, but at this moment he also hates her. He has imagined plenty of bad things over the years they've been married—Judy getting cancer, Judy paralyzed in an accident, Judy first taking a lover and then demanding a divorce—but he has never imagined Judy going chickenshit on him, and isn't that what this amounts to?

"What did you think you were *doing*?"

She looks at him without fear . . . but without anything else, either. Her eyes are dead. Her husband lowers his hand, thinking: *I'd cut it off before I hit you. I might be pissed at you, I am pissed at you, but I'd cut it off before I did that.*

Judy rolls over, face-down on the coverlet, her hair spread around her head in a corona.

"Judy?"

Nothing. She just lies there.

Fred looks at her for a moment, then uncrumples one of the slimy balls of paper with which she has tried to strangle herself. It is covered with tangles of scribbled words. Gorg, abbalah, eeleelee, munshun, bas, lum, opopanax: these mean nothing to him. Others—drudge, asswipe, black, red, Chicago, and Ty— are actual words but have no context. Printed up one side of the sheet is IF YOU'VE GOT PRINCE ALBERT IN A CAN, HOW CAN YOU EVER GET HIM OUT? Up the other, like a teletype stuck in repeat mode, is this: BLACK HOUSE CRIMSON KING BLACK HOUSE CRIMSON KING BLACK

*If you waste time looking for sense in this, you're as crazy as she is,* Fred thinks. *You can't waste time—*

Time.

He looks at the clock on his side of the bed and cannot believe its news: 4:17 P.M. Is that possible? He looks at his watch and sees that it is.

Knowing it's foolish, knowing he would have heard his son come in even if in a deep sleep, Fred strides to the door on big nerveless legs. *"Ty!"* he yells. *"Hey, Ty! TYLER!"*

Waiting for an answer that will not come, Fred realizes that everything in his life has changed, quite possibly forever. People tell you this can happen—*in the blink of an eye,* they say, *before you know it,* they say—but you don't believe it. Then a wind comes.

Go down to Ty's room? Check? Be sure?

Ty isn't there—Fred knows this—but he does it just the same. The room is empty, as he knew it would be. And it looks oddly distorted, almost sinister, with the dresser now on the other side.

*Judy. You left her alone, you idiot. She'll be chewing paper again by now, they're clever, mad people are clever—*

Fred dashes back down to the master bedroom and exhales a sigh of relief when he sees Judy lying just as he left her, face-down, hair spread around her head. He discovers that his worries about his mad wife are now secondary to his worries about his missing son.

*He'll be home by four, at the latest . . . take it to the bank.* So he had thought. But four has come and gone. A strong wind has arisen and blown the bank away. Fred walks to his side of the bed and sits down beside his wife's splayed right leg. He picks up the phone and punches in a number. It's an easy number, only three digits.

"*Yell*-o, Police Department, Officer Dulac speaking, you've dialed 911, do you have an emergency?"

"Officer Dulac, this is Fred Marshall. I'd like to speak to Dale, if he's still there." Fred is pretty sure Dale is. He works late most nights, especially since—

He pushes the rest away, but inside his head the wind blows harder. Louder.

"Gee, Mr. Marshall, he's here, but he's in a meeting and I don't think I can—"

"Get him."

"Mr. Marshall, you're not hearing me. He's in with two guys from the WSP and one from the FBI. If you could just tell me—"

Fred closes his eyes. It's interesting, isn't it? Something interesting here. He called in on the 911 line, but the idiot on the other end seems to have forgotten that. Why? Because it's someone he knows. It's good old Fred Marshall, bought a Deere lawn tractor from him just the year before last. Must have dialed 911 because it was easier than looking up the regular number. Because *no one Bobby knows* can actually have an emergency.

Fred remembers having a similar idea himself that morning—a different Fred Marshall, one who believed that the Fisherman could never touch his son. Not *his* son.

*Ty's gone. Gorg fascinated him and the abbalah took him.*

"Hello? Mr. Marshall? Fred? Are you still—"

"Listen to me," Fred says, his eyes still closed. Down at Goltz's, he would be calling the man on the other end Bobby by now, but Goltz's has never seemed so far away; Goltz's is in the star-system Opopanax, on Planet Abbalah. "Listen to me carefully. Write it down if you have to. My wife has gone mad and my son is missing. Do you understand those things? Wife mad. Son missing. *Now put me through to the chief!*"

But Bobby Dulac doesn't, not right away. He has made a deduction. A more diplomatic police officer (Jack Sawyer as he was in his salad days, for instance) would have kept said deduction to himself, but Bobby can't do that. Bobby has hooked a big one.

"Mr. Marshall? Fred? Your son doesn't own a Schwinn, does he? Three-speed Schwinn, red? Got a novelty license plate that reads . . . uh . . . BIG MAC?"

Fred cannot answer. For several long and terrible moments he cannot even draw a breath. Between his ears, the wind blows both louder and harder. Now it's a hurricane.

*Gorg fascinated him . . . the abbalah took him.*

At last, just when it seems he will begin to strangle himself, his chest unlocks and he takes in a huge, tearing breath. *"PUT CHIEF GILBERTSON ON! DO IT NOW, YOU MOTHERFUCKER!"*

Although he shrieks this at the top of his lungs, the woman lying face-down on the coverlet beside him never moves. There is a click. He's on hold. Not for long, but it's long enough for him to see the scratched, bald place on his missing son's bedroom wall, the swelled column of his mad wife's throat, and blood dribbling through the creel in his dream. His back spasms cruelly, and Fred welcomes the pain. It's like getting a telegram from the real world.

Then Dale is on the phone, Dale is asking him what's wrong, and Fred Marshall begins to cry.

# 7

God may know where Henry Leyden found that astounding suit, but we certainly do not. A costume shop? No, it is too elegant to be a costume; this is the real thing, not an imitation. But what sort of real thing is it? The wide lapels sweep down to an inch below the waist, and the twin flaps of the swallowtail reach nearly to the ankles of the billowing, pleated trousers, which seem, beneath the snowfield expanse of the double-breasted waistcoat, to ride nearly at the level of the sternum. On Henry's feet, white, high-button spats adorn white patent-leather shoes; about his neck, a stiff, high collar turns its pointed peaks over a wide, flowing, white satin bow tie, perfectly knotted. The total effect is of old-fashioned diplomatic finery harmoniously wedded to a zoot suit: the raffishness of the ensemble outweighs its formality, but the dignity of the swallowtail and the waistcoat contribute to the whole a regal quality of a specific kind, the regality often seen in African-American entertainers and musicians.

Escorting Henry to the common room while surly Pete Wexler comes along behind, pushing a handcart loaded with boxes of records, Rebecca Vilas dimly remembers having seen Duke Ellington wearing a white cutaway like this in a clip from some old film . . . or was it Cab Calloway? She recalls an up-raised eyebrow, a glittering smile, a seductive face, an upright figure posed before a band, but little more. (If alive, either Mr. Ellington or Mr. Calloway could have informed Rebecca that Henry's outfit, including the "high-drape" pants with a "reet pleat," terms not in her vocabulary, had undoubtedly been handmade by one of four specific tailors located in the black neighborhoods of New York, Washington, D.C., Philadelphia, or Los Angeles, masters of their trade during the thirties and forties, underground tailors, men now alas as dead as their celebrated clients. Henry Leyden knows exactly who tailored his outfit, where it came from, and how it fell into his hands, but when it comes to persons such as Rebecca Vilas, Henry imparts no more information than is already likely to be known.) In the corridor leading to the common room, the white cutaway appears to shine from within, an impression only increased by Henry's oversized, daddy-cool dark glasses with bamboo frames, in which what may be tiny sapphires wink at the corners of the bows.

Is there maybe some shop that sells Spiffy Clothes of Great 1930s Bandleaders? Does some museum inherit this stuff and auction it off? Rebecca cannot contain her curiosity a moment longer. "Mr. Leyden, where did you get that beautiful outfit?"

From the rear and taking care to sound as though he is muttering to himself, Pete Wexler opines that obtaining an outfit like that probably requires chasing a person of an ethnicity beginning with the letter *n* for at least a couple of miles.

Henry ignores Pete and smiles. "It's all a matter of knowing where to look."

"Guess you never heard of CDs," Pete says. "They're like this big new breakthrough."

"Shut up and tote them bales, me bucko," says Ms. Vilas. "We're almost there."

"Rebecca, my dear, if I may," Henry says. "Mr. Wexler has every right to grouse. After all, there's no way he could know that I own about three thousand CDs, is there? And if the man who originally owned these clothes can be called a nigger, I'd be proud to call myself one, too. That would be an *incredible* honor. I wish I could claim it."

Henry has come to a halt. Each, in a different way, shocked by his use of the forbidden word, Pete and Rebecca have also stopped moving.

"And," Henry says, "we owe respect to those who assist us in the performance of our duties. I asked Mr. Wexler to shake out my suit when he hung it up, and he very kindly obliged me."

"Yeah," Pete says. "Plus I also hung up your light and put your turntable and speakers and shit right where you want 'em."

"Thank you very much, Mr. Wexler," Henry says. "I appreciate your efforts in my behalf."

"Well, shit," Pete says, "I was only doing my job, you know? But anything you want after you're done, I'll give you a hand."

Without benefit of a flash of panties or a glimpse of ass, Pete Wexler has been completely disarmed. Rebecca finds this amazing. All in all, sightless or not, Henry Leyden, it comes to her, is far and away the coolest human being she has ever been privileged to encounter in her entire twenty-six years on the face of the earth. Never mind his clothes—where did *guys* like this come from?

"Do you really think some little boy vanished from the sidewalk out in front of here this afternoon?" Henry asks.

"What?" Rebecca asks.

"Seems like it to me," Pete says.

"What?" Rebecca asks again, this time to Pete Wexler, not Henry. "What are you saying?"

"Well, he ast me, and I tol' him," Pete says. "That's all."

Simmering dangerously, Rebecca takes a stride toward him. "This happened on *our* sidewalk? Another kid, in front of *our building*? And you didn't say anything to me or Mr. Maxton?"

"There wasn't nothin' to say," Pete offers in self-defense.

"Maybe you could tell us what actually happened," Henry says.

"Sure. What happened was, I went outside for a smoke, see?" This is less than strictly truthful. Faced with the choice of walking ten yards to the Daisy corridor men's room to flush his cigarette down a toilet or walking ten feet to the entrance and pitching it into the parking lot, Pete had sensibly elected outdoor disposal. "So I get outside and that's when I saw it. This police car, parked right out there. So I walked up to the hedge, and there's this cop, a young guy, I think his name is Cheetah, or something like that, and he's loadin' this bike, like a kid's bike, into his trunk. And something else, too, only I couldn't see what it was except it was small. And after he did that, he got a piece a chalk outta his glove compartment and he came back and made like X marks on the sidewalk."

"Did you talk to him?" Rebecca asks. "Did you ask him what he was doing?"

"Miz Vilas, I don't talk to cops unless it's like you got no other choice, know what I mean? Cheetah, he never even saw me. The guy wouldn't of said nothing anyhow. He had this expression on his face—it was like, Jeez, I hope I get to the crapper before I drop a load in my pants, that kind of expression."

"Then he just drove away?"

"Just like that. Twenty minutes later, two other cops showed up."

Rebecca raises both hands, closes her eyes, and presses her fingertips to her forehead, giving Pete Wexler an excellent opportunity, of which he does not fail to take full advantage, to admire the shape of her breasts underneath her blouse. It may not be as great as the view from the bottom of the ladder, but it'll do, all right, yes it will. As far as Ebbie's dad is concerned, a sight like Rebecca Vilas's Hottentots pushing out against her dress is like a good fire on a cold night. They are bigger than you'd expect on a slender little thing like her, and you know what? When the arms go up, the Hottentots go up, too! Hey, if he had known she was going to put on a show like this, he would have told her about Cheetah and the bicycle as soon as it happened.

"All right, okay," she says, still flattening the tips of her fingers against her head. She lifts her chin, raising her arms another few inches, and frowns in concentration, for a moment looking like a figure on a plinth.

*Hoo-ray and hallelujah,* Pete thinks. *There's a bright side to everything. If another little snotnose gets grabbed off the sidewalk tomorrow morning, it won't be soon enough for me.*

Rebecca says, "Okay, okay, okay," opens her eyes, and lowers her arms. Pete Wexler is staring firmly at a point over her shoulder, his face blank with a false innocence she immediately comprehends. Good God, what a caveman. "It's not as bad as I thought. In the first place, all you saw was a policeman picking up a bike. Maybe it was stolen. Maybe some other kid borrowed the bike, dumped it, and ran away. The cop could have been looking for it. Or the kid who *owned* the bike could have been hit by a car or something. And even if the worst did happen, I don't see any way that it could hurt us. Maxton's isn't responsible for whatever goes on outside the grounds."

She turns to Henry, who looks as though he wishes he were a hundred miles away. "Sorry, I know that sounded awfully cold. I'm as distressed about this Fisherman business as everyone else, what with those two poor kids and the missing girl.

We're all so upset we can hardly think straight. But I'd hate to see *us* dragged into the mess, don't you see?"

"I see perfectly," Henry says. "Being one of those blind men George Rathbun is always yelling about."

"Hah!" Pete Wexler barks.

"And you agree with me, don't you?"

"I'm a gentleman, I agree with everybody," Henry says. "I agree with Pete that another child may well have been abducted by our local monster. Officer Cheetah, or whatever his name is, sounded too anxious to be just picking up a lost bicycle. And I agree with you that Maxton's cannot be blamed for anything that happened."

"Good," Rebecca says.

"Unless, of course, someone here is involved in the murders of these children."

"But that's impossible!" Rebecca says. "Most of our male clients can't even remember their own names."

"A ten-year-old girl could take most of these feebs," Pete says. "Even the ones who don't have old-timer's disease walk around covered in their own . . . you know."

"You're forgetting about the staff," Henry says.

"Oh, now," Rebecca says, momentarily rendered nearly wordless. "Come on. That's . . . that's a totally irresponsible thing to say."

"True. It is. But if this goes on, nobody will be above suspicion. That's my point."

Pete Wexler feels a sudden chill—if the town clowns start grilling Maxton's residents, his private amusements might come to light, and wouldn't Wendell Green have a field day with that stuff? A gleaming new idea comes to him, and he brings it forth, hoping to impress Miz Vilas. "You know what? The cops should talk to that California guy, the big-time detective who nailed that Kinderling asshole two–three years ago. He lives around here somewhere, don't he? Someone like that, he's the guy we need on this. The cops here, they're way outta their depth. That guy, he's like a whaddayacallit, a goddamn *resource*."

"Odd you should say that," Henry says. "I couldn't agree with you more. It is about time Jack Sawyer did his thing. I'll work on him again."

"You know him?" Rebecca asks.

"Oh, yes," Henry says. "That I do. But isn't it about time for me to do my own thing?"

"Soon. They're all still outside."

Rebecca leads him down the rest of the corridor and into the common room, where all three of them move across to the big platform. Henry's microphone stands beside a table mounted with his speakers and turntable. With unnerving accuracy, Henry says, "Lot of space in here."

"You can tell that?" she asks.

"Piece of cake," Henry says. "We must be getting close now."

"It's right in front of you. Do you need any help?"

Henry extends one foot and taps the side of the flat. He glides a hand down the edge of the table, locates the mike stand, says, "Not at the moment, darlin'," and steps neatly up onto the platform. Guided by touch, he moves to the back of the table and locates the turntable. "All is copacetic," he says. "Pete, would you please put the record boxes on the table? The one on top goes *here,* and the other one right next to it."

"What's he like, your friend Jack?" Rebecca asks.

"An orphan of the storm. A pussycat, but an extremely *difficult* pussycat. I have to say, he can be a real pain in the bunghole."

Crowd noises, a buzz of conversation interlaced with children's voices and songs thumped out on an old upright piano, have been audible through the windows since they entered the room, and when Pete has placed the record boxes on the table, he says, "I better get out there, 'cuz Chipper's probly lookin' for me. Gonna be a shitload of cleanup once they come inside."

Pete shambles out, rolling the handcart before him. Rebecca asks if there is anything more Henry would like her to do for him.

"The overhead lights are on, aren't they? Please turn them off, and wait for the first wave to come in. Then switch on the pink spot, and prepare to jitterbug your heart out."

"You want me to turn off the lights?"

"You'll see."

Rebecca moves back across to the door, turns off the overhead lights, and does see, just as Henry had promised. A soft, dim illumination from the rank of windows hovers in the air, replacing the former brightness and harshness with a vague mellow haze, as if the room lay behind a scrim. That pink spotlight is going to look pretty good in here, Rebecca thinks.

Outside on the lawn, the predance wingding is winding down. Lots of old men and women are busily polishing off their strawberry shortcakes and soda pop at the picnic tables, and the piano-playing gent in the straw boater and red sleeve garters comes to the end of "Heart and Soul," *ba bump ba bump ba ba bump bump bump,* no finesse but plenty of volume, closes the lid of the upright, and stands up to a scattering of applause. Grandchildren who had earlier complained about having to come to the great fest dodge through the tables and wheelchairs, evading their parents' glances and hoping to wheedle a last balloon from the balloon lady in the clown suit and frizzy red wig, oh joy unbounded.

Alice Weathers applauds the piano player, as well she might: forty years ago, he reluctantly absorbed the rudiments of pianism at her hands just well enough to pick up a few bucks at occasions like this, when not obliged to perform his usual function, that of selling sweatshirts and baseball caps on Chase Street. Charles Burnside, who, having been scrubbed clean by good-hearted Butch Yerxa, decked himself out in an old white shirt and a pair of loose, filthy trousers, stands slightly apart from the throng in the shade of a large oak, not applauding but sneering. The unbuttoned collar of the shirt droops around his ropy neck. Now and then he wipes his mouth or picks his teeth with a ragged thumbnail, but mainly he does not move at all. He looks as though someone plunked him down by the side of a road and drove off. Whenever the careering grandkids swerve near Burny, they instantly veer away, as if repelled by a force field.

Between Alice and Burny, three-fourths of the residents of Maxton's belly up to the tables, stump around on their walkers, sit beneath the trees, occupy their wheelchairs, hobble here and there—yakking, dozing, chuckling, farting, dabbing at fresh strawberry-colored stains on their clothing, staring at their relatives, staring at their trembling hands, staring at nothing. Half a dozen of the most vacant among them wear conical party hats of hard, flat red and hard, flat blue, the shades of enforced gaiety. The women from the kitchen have begun to circulate through the tables with big black garbage bags, for soon they must retire to their domain to prepare the evening's great feast of potato salad, mashed potatoes, creamed potatoes, baked beans, Jell-O salad, marshmallow salad, and whipped-cream salad, plus of course more mighty strawberry shortcake!

The undisputed and hereditary sovereign of this realm, Chipper Maxton, whose disposition generally resembles that of a skunk trapped in a muddy hole, has spent the previous ninety minutes ambling about smiling and shaking hands, and he has had enough. "Pete," he growls, "what the hell took you so long? Start racking up the folding chairs, okay? And help shift these people into the common room. Let's get a goddamn move on here. Wagons west."

Pete scurries off, and Chipper claps his hands twice, loudly, then raises his outstretched arms. "Hey, everybody," he bellows, "can you truly believe what a gol-durn gorgeous day the good Lord gave us for this beautiful event? Isn't this *something*?"

Half a dozen feeble voices rise in agreement.

"Come on, people, you can do better than that! I want to hear it for this wonderful day, this wonderful time we're all having, and for all the wonderful help and assistance given us by our volunteers and staff!"

A slightly more exuberant clamor rewards his efforts.

"All *right!* Hey, you know what? As George Rathbun would say, even a blind man could see what a great time we're all having. I know I am, and we're not done yet! We got the greatest deejay you ever heard, a fellow called Symphonic Stan, the Big-Band Man, waiting to put on a great, great show in the common room, music and dancing right up to the big Strawberry Fest dinner, and we got him cheap, too—but don't tell him I said that! So, friends and family, it's time to say your good-byes and let your loved ones cut a rug to the golden oldies, just like them, ha ha! Golden oldies one and all, that's all of us here at Maxton's. Even I'm not as young as I used to be, ha ha, so I might take a spin across the floor with some lucky lady.

"Seriously, folks, it's time for us to put on our dancing shoes.

Please kiss Dad or Mom, Granddad or Grandma good-bye, and on your way out, you may wish to leave a contribution toward our expenses in the basket on top of Ragtime Willie's piano right over here, ten dollars, five dollars, anything you can spare helps us cover the costs of giving your mom, your dad, a bright, bright day. *We* do it out of love, but half of that love is *your* love."

And in what may seem to us a surprisingly short amount of time, but does not to Chipper Maxton, who understands that very few people wish to linger in an elder-care facility any longer than they must, the relatives bestow their final hugs and kisses, round up the exhausted kiddies, and file down the paths and over the grass into the parking lot, along the way a good number depositing bills in the basket atop Ragtime Willie's upright piano.

No sooner does this exodus begin than Pete Wexler and Chipper Maxton set about persuading, with all the art available to them, the oldsters back into the building. Chipper says things like, "Now don't you know how much we all want to see you trip the light fantastic, Mrs. Syverson?" while Pete takes the more direct approach of, "Move along, bud, time to stir your stumps," but both men employ the techniques of subtle and not-so-subtle nudges, pushes, elbow grasping, and wheelchair rolling to get their doddering charges through the door.

At her post, Rebecca Vilas watches the residents enter the hazy common room, some of them traveling at a rate a touch too brisk for their own good. Henry Leyden stands motionless behind his boxes of LPs. His suit shimmers; his head is merely a dark silhouette before the windows. For once too busy to ogle Rebecca's chest, Pete Wexler moves past with one hand on the elbow of Elmer Jesperson, deposits him eight feet inside the room, and whirls around to locate Thorvald Thorvaldson, Elmer's dearest enemy and fellow inhabitant of D12. Alice Weathers wafts in under her own guidance and folds her hands beneath her chin, waiting for the music to begin. Tall, scrawny, hollow-cheeked, at the center of an empty space that is his alone, Charles Burnside slides through the door and quickly moves a good distance off to the side. When his dead eyes indifferently meet hers, Rebecca shivers. The next pair of eyes to meet hers belong to Chipper, who pushes Flora Flostad's wheelchair as if it held a crate of oranges and gives her an impatient glare completely at odds with the easy smile on his face. Time is money, you bet, but money is money, too, let's get this show on the road, pronto. The first wave, Henry had told her— is that what they have here, the first wave? She glances across the room, wondering how to ask, and sees that the question has already been answered, for as soon as she looks up, Henry flashes her the okay sign.

Rebecca flips the switch for the pink spot, and nearly everybody in the room, including a number of old parties who had appeared well beyond response of any kind, utters a soft *aaah*. His suit, his shirt, his spats blazing in the cone of light, a transformed Henry Leyden glides and dips toward the microphone as a twelve-inch LP, seemingly magicked out of the air, twirls like a top on the palm of his right hand. His teeth shine; his sleek hair gleams; the sapphires wink from the bows of his enchanted sunglasses. Henry seems almost to be dancing himself, with his sweet, clever sidestepping glide . . . only he is no longer Henry Leyden; no way, Renee, as George Rathbun likes to roar. The suit, the spats, the slicked-back hair, the shades, even the wondrously effective pink spot are mere stage dressing. The real magic here is Henry, that uniquely malleable creature. When he is George Rathbun, he is *all* George. Ditto the Wisconsin Rat; ditto Henry Shake. It has been eighteen months since he took Symphonic Stan from the closet and fit into him like a hand into a glove to dazzle the crowd at a Madison VFW record hop, but the clothes still fit, oh yes, they fit, and he fits within them, a hipster reborn whole into a past he never saw firsthand.

On his extended palm, the spinning LP resembles a solid, unmoving, black beachball.

Whenever Symphonic Stan puts on a hop, he always begins with "In the Mood." Although he does not detest Glenn Miller as some jazz aficionados do, over the years he has grown tired of this number. But it always does the job. Even if the customers have no choice but to dance with one foot in the grave and the other on the proverbial banana peel, they *do* dance. Besides, he knows that after Miller was drafted he told the arranger Billy May of his plan to "come out of this war as some kind of hero," and, hell, he was as good as his word, wasn't he?

Henry reaches the mike and slips the revolving record onto the platter with a negligent gesture of his right hand. The crowd applauds him with an exhaled *oooh.*

"Welcome, welcome, all you hepcats and hepkitties," Henry says. The words emerge from the speakers wrapped in the smooth, slightly above-it-all voice of a true broadcaster in 1938 or 1939, one of the men who did live remotes from dance halls and nightclubs located from Boston to Catalina. Honey poured through their throats, these muses of the night, and they never missed a beat. "Say, tell me this, you gates and gators, can you think of a better way to kick off a swingin' soiree than with Glenn Miller? Come on, brothers and sisters, give me *yeahhh.*"

From the residents of Maxton's—some of whom are already out on the floor, others wheelchair-bound on its edges in various postures of confusion or vacuity—comes a whispery response, less a party cry than the rustle of an autumn wind through bare branches. Symphonic Stan grins like a shark and holds up his hands as if to still a hopped-up multitude, then twirls and spins like a Savoy Ballroom dancer inspired by Chick Webb. His coattails spread like wings, his sparkling feet fly and land and fly again. The moment evaporates, and two black beachballs appear on the deejay's palms, one of them spinning back into its sleeve, the other down to meet the needle.

"All-reety all-righty all-rooty, you hoppin' hens and boppin' bunnies, here comes the Sentimental Gentleman, Mr. Tommy Dorsey, so get off your money and grab your honey while vocalist Dick Haymes, the pride of Buenos Aires, Argentina, asks the musical question 'How Am I to Know You?' Frank Sinatra hasn't entered the building yet, brethren and sistren, but life is still fine as mmm-mmm wine."

Rebecca Vilas cannot believe what she is seeing. This guy is getting just about everyone out onto the floor, even some of the wheelchair cases, who are dipping and swirling with the best of them. Dolled up in his exotic, astonishing outfit, Symphonic Stan—Henry Leyden, she reminds herself—is corny and breathtaking, absurd and convincing, all at once. He's like . . . some kind of *time capsule,* locked into both his role and what these old people want to hear. He has charmed them back into life, back into whatever youth they had left in them.

Unbelievable! No other word will do. People she had written off as shuffling basket cases are blooming right in front of her. As for Symphonic Stan, he's carrying on like an elegant dervish, making her think of words like *suave, polished, urbane, unhinged, sexy, graceful,* words that do not connect except in him. And that thing he does with the records! How is that possible?

She does not realize that she is tapping her foot and swaying in time to the music until Henry puts on Artie Shaw's "Begin the Beguine," when she literally begins her own beguine by starting to dance by herself. Henry's hepcat jive-dance, the sight of so many white-haired, blue-haired, and bald-headed people gliding around the floor, Alice Weathers beaming happily in the arms of none other than gloomy Thorvald Thorvaldson, Ada Meyerhoff and "Tom Tom" Boettcher twirling around each other in their wheelchairs, the sweeping pulse of the music driving everything beneath the molten radiance of Artie Shaw's clarinet, all of these things abruptly, magically coalesce into a vision of earthly beauty that brings tears stinging to her eyes. Smiling, she raises her arms, spins, and finds herself expertly grasped by Tom Tom's twin brother, eighty-six-year-old Hermie Boettcher, the retired geography teacher in A17 formerly considered something of a stick, who without a word fox-trots her right out to the middle of the floor.

"Shame to see a pretty girl dancing all on her lonesome," Hermie says.

"Hermie, I'd follow you anywhere," she tells him.

"Let's us get closer to the bandstand," he says. "I want a better look at that hotshot in the fancy suit. They say he's blind as a bat, but I don't believe it."

His hand planted firmly at the base of her spine, his hips swerving in time to Artie Shaw, Hermie guides her to within a foot of the platform, where the Symphonic One is already doing his trick with a new record as he waits for the last bar of the present one. Rebecca could swear that Stan/Henry not only senses her presence before him but actually *winks* at her! But that is truly impossible . . . isn't it?

The Symphonic One twirls the Shaw record into its sleeve, the new one onto the platter, and says, "Can you say 'Vout'? Can you say 'Solid'? Now that we're all limbered up, let's get

jumpin' and jivin' with Woody Herman and 'Wild Root.' This
tune is dedicated to all you beautiful ladies, especially the lady
wearing Calyx."

Rebecca laughs and says, "Oh, dear." He could smell her
perfume; he recognized it!

Undaunted by the steamy tempo of "Wild Root," Hermie
Boettcher slides into a back step, extends his arm, and spins
Rebecca around. On the first beat of the next bar, he catches her
in his arms and reverses direction, spinning them both toward
the far end of the platform, where Alice Weathers stands next to
Mr. Thorvaldson, gazing up at Symphonic Stan.

"The special lady must be you," Hermie says. "Because that
perfume of yours is worth a dedication."

Rebecca asks, "Where'd you learn to dance like this?"

"My brother and I, we were town boys. Learned how to
dance in front of the jukebox at Alouette's, over by Arden." Rebecca knows Alouette's, on Arden's Main Street, but what was
once a soda fountain is now a lunch counter, and the jukebox
disappeared around the time Johnny Mathis dropped off the
charts. "You want a good dancer, you find yourself a town boy.
Tom Tom, now he was always the slickest dancer around, and
you can plunk him in that chair, but you can't take away his
rhythm."

"Mr. Stan, yoo-hoo, Mr. Stan?" Alice Weathers has tilted her
head and cupped her hands around her mouth. "Do you take requests?"

A voice as flat and hard as the sound of two stones grinding
together says, "I was here first, old woman."

This implacable rudeness brings Rebecca to a halt. Hermie's
right foot comes gently down atop her left, then swiftly moves
off, doing her no more injury than a kiss. Towering over Alice,
Charles Burnside glares at Thorvald Thorvaldson. Thorvaldson
steps back and tugs at Alice's hand.

"Certainly, my dear," says Stan, bending down. "Tell me
your name and what you'd like to hear."

"I am Alice Weathers, and—"

"I was here first," Burny loudly repeats.

Rebecca glances at Hermie, who shakes his head and makes
a sour face. Town boy or not, he is as intimidated as Mr. Thorvaldson.

" 'Moonglow,' please. By Benny Goodman."

"It's my turn, you jackass. I want that Woody Herman number called 'Lady Magowan's Nightmare.' That one's *good*."

Hermie leans toward Rebecca's ear. "Nobody likes that fella, but he gets his own way."

"Not this time," Rebecca says. "Mr. Burnside, I want you to—"

Symphonic Stan silences her with a wave of his hand. He turns to face the owner of the remarkably unpleasant voice. "No can do, mister. The song is called 'Lady Magowan's Dream,' and I didn't bring that snappy little item with me this afternoon, sorry."

"Okay, bud, how about 'I Can't Get Started,' the one Bunny Berigan did?"

"Oh, I *love* that," Alice says. "Yes, play 'I Can't Get Started.' "

"Happy to oblige," Stan says in Henry Leyden's normal voice. Without bothering to jive around or spin the records on his hands, he simply exchanges the LP on the turntable for one from the first box. He seems oddly wilted as he steps to the mike and says, "I've flown around the world on a plane, I settled revolutions in Spain. Can't get started. Dedicated to the lovely Alice Blue Gown and the One Who Walks by Night."

"You're no better'n a monkey on a stick," says Burny.

The music begins. Rebecca taps Hermie on the arm and moves up alongside Charles Burnside, for whom she has never felt anything but mild revulsion. Now that she has him in focus, her outrage and disgust cause her to say, "Mr. Burnside, you are going to apologize to Alice and to our guest here. You're a crude, obnoxious bully, and after you apologize, I want you to get back into your room, where you belong."

Her words have no effect. Burnside's shoulders have slumped. He has a wide, sloppy grin on his face, and he is staring empty-eyed at nothing in particular. He looks too far gone to remember his own name, much less Bunny Berigan's. In any case, Alice Weathers has danced away, and Symphonic Stan, back at the far end of the platform and out of the pink spot, appears to be deep in thought. The elderly couples sway back and forth on the dance floor. Off to the side, Hermie Boettcher pantomimes dancing and quizzes her with a look.

"I'm sorry about that," she says to Stan/Henry.

"No need to apologize. 'I Can't Get Started' was my wife's favorite record. I've been thinking about her a lot, the past few days. Sort of took me by surprise." He runs a hand over his sleek hair and shakes out his arms, visibly getting back into his role.

Rebecca decides to leave him alone. In fact, she wants to leave everyone alone for a little while. Signaling regret and the press of duty to Hermie, she makes her way through the crowd and exits the common room. Somehow, old Burny has beaten her to the corridor. He shuffles absently toward Daisy wing, head drooping, feet scuffing the floor.

"Mr. Burnside," she says, "your act may fool everyone else, but I want you to know that it doesn't fool me."

Moving by increments, the old man turns around. First one foot shifts, then a knee, the spavined waist, the second foot, finally the cadaverous trunk. The ugly bloom of Burny's head droops on its thin stalk, offering Rebecca a view of his mottled scalp. His long nose protrudes like a warped rudder. With the same dreadful slowness, his head lifts to reveal muddy eyes and a slack mouth. A flash of sheer vindictiveness rises into the dull eyes, and the dead lips writhe.

Frightened, Rebecca takes an instinctive step backward. Burny's mouth has moved all the way into a horrible grin. Rebecca wants to escape, but anger at having been humiliated by this miserable jerk lets her hold her ground.

"Lady Magowan had a bad, bad nightmare," Burny informs her. He sounds drugged, or half asleep. "And Lady Sophie had a nightmare. Only hers was worse." He giggles. "The king was in his countinghouse, counting out his honeys. That's what Sophie saw when she fell asleep." His giggling rises in pitch, and he says something that might be "Mr. Munching." His lips flap, revealing yellow, irregular teeth, and his sunken face undergoes a subtle change. A new kind of intelligence seems to sharpen his features. "Does you know Mr. Munshun? Mr. Munshun and his li'l friend Gorg? Does you know what happened in Chicago?"

"Stop this right now, Mr. Burnside."

"Duz you know uff Fridz Haarman, him who wazz zo loffly? Dey called him, dey called him, dey called him 'da Vamp, Vamp, Vamp of Hanover,' yez dey dud, dud, dud. Evveybuddy,

evveybuddy, evveybuddy haz godz nide-marez all da dime, dime, dime, ha ha ho ho."

*"Stop talking like that!"* Rebecca shouts. *"You're not fooling me!"*

For a moment, the new intelligence flares within Burny's dim eyes. It almost instantly retreats. He licks his lips and says, "Way-gup, Burn-Burn."

"Whatever," Rebecca says. "Dinner is downstairs at seven, if you want it. Go take a nap or something, will you?"

Burny gives her a peeved, murky look and plops a foot down on the floor, beginning the tedious process that will turn him around again. "You could write it down. Fritz Haarman. In Hanover." His mouth twists into a smile of unsettling slyness. "When the king comes here, maybe we can dance together."

"No, thanks." Rebecca turns her back on the old horror and clacks down the hallway on her high heels, uncomfortably aware of his eyes following her.

Rebecca's nice little Coach handbag lies flat on her desk in the windowless vestibule to Chipper's office. Before going in, she pauses to rip off a sheet of notepaper, write down *Fritz Harmann(?)*, *Hanover(?)*, and slip the paper into the bag's central compartment. It might be nothing—it probably is—but who knows? She is furious that she let Burnside frighten her, and if she can find a way to use his nonsense against him, she will do her best to expel him from Maxton's.

"Kiddo, is that you?" Chipper calls out.

"No, it's Lady Magowan and her freakin' nightmare." She strides into Chipper's office and finds him behind his desk, happily counting out the bills contributed that afternoon by the sons and daughters of his clientele.

"My li'l Becky looks all ticked off," he says. "What happened, one of our zombies stomp on your foot?"

"Don't call me Becky."

"Hey, hey, cheer up. You won't believe how much your silver-tongued boyfriend conned out of the relatives today. A hundred and twenty-six smackers! Free money! Okay, what went wrong, anyhow?"

"Charles Burnside spooked me, that's what. He ought to be in a mental hospital."

"Are you kidding? That particular zombie is worth his weight in gold. As long as Charles Burnside can draw breath into his body, he will always have a place in my heart." Grinning, he brandishes a handful of bills. "And if you have a place in my heart, honey-baby, you'll always have a place at Maxton's."

The memory of Burnside saying, *The king was in his countinghouse, counting out his honeys* makes her feel unclean. If Chipper were not grinning in that exultant, loose-lipped way, Rebecca supposes, he would not remind her so unpleasantly of his favorite resident. *Evveybuddy haz godz nide-marez all da dime, dime, dime*—that wasn't a bad description of the Fisherman's French Landing. Funny, you wouldn't think Old Burny would take more notice of those murders than Chipper. Rebecca had never heard him mention the Fisherman's crimes, apart from the time he groused that he would not be able to tell anyone he was going fishing until Dale Gilbertson finally got off his big fat butt, and what kind of crappy deal was that?

# 8

Two telephone calls and another, private matter, one he is doing his best to deny, have conspired to pluck Jack Sawyer from his cocoon in Norway Valley and put him on the road to French Landing, Sumner Street, and the police station. The first call had been from Henry, and Henry, calling from the Maxton cafeteria during one of the Symphonic One's breaks, had insisted on speaking his mind. A child had apparently been abducted from the sidewalk in front of Maxton's earlier that day. Whatever Jack's reasons for staying out of the case, which by the way he had never explained, they didn't count anymore, sorry. This made four children who had been lost to the Fisherman, because Jack didn't really think Irma Freneau was going to walk in her front door anytime soon, did he? Four children!

—No, Henry had said, I didn't hear about it on the radio. It happened this morning.

—From a janitor at Maxton's, Henry had said. He saw a worried-looking cop pick up a bicycle and put it in his trunk.

—All right, Henry had said, maybe I don't *know* for certain, but I *am* certain. By tonight, Dale will identify the poor kid, and tomorrow his name will be all over the newspaper. And *then* this whole county is going to flip out. Don't you get it? Just knowing you are involved will do a lot to keep people calm. You no longer have the luxury of retirement, Jack. You have to do your part.

Jack had told him he was jumping to conclusions, and that they would talk about it later.

Forty-five minutes later, Dale Gilbertson had called with the news that a boy named Tyler Marshall had vanished from in front of Maxton's sometime that morning, and that Tyler's father, Fred Marshall, was down there right now, in the station, demanding to see Jack Sawyer. Fred was a great guy, a real straight arrow and family man, a solid citizen, a *friend* of Dale's, you could say, but at the moment he was at the end of his rope. Apparently Judy, his wife, had been having some kind of mental problems even before the trouble started, and Tyler's disappearance had driven her off the edge. She talked in gibberish, injured herself, tore the house apart.

—And I kind of know Judy Marshall, Dale had said. Beautiful, beautiful woman, a little thing but tough as all get-out on the inside, both feet on the ground, a great person, a tremendous person, someone you'd think would never lose her grip, no matter what. It seems she thought, knew, whatever, that Tyler had been snatched even before his bicycle turned up. Late this afternoon, she got so bad Fred had to call Dr. Skarda and get her over to French County Lutheran in Arden, where they took one look at her and put her in Ward D, the mental wing. So you can imagine what kind of shape Fred's in. He insists on talking to you. *I have no confidence in you,* he said to me.

—Well, Dale had said, if you don't come down here, Fred Marshall is going to show up at your house, that's what'll happen. I can't put the guy on a leash, and I'm not going to lock him up just to keep him away from you. On top of everything else, we need you here, Jack.

—All right, Dale had said. I know you're not making any promises. But you know what you should do.

Would these conversations have been enough to get him into his pickup and on the road to Sumner Street? Very likely, Jack imagines, which renders the third factor, the secret, barely acknowledged one, inconsequential. It means nothing. A silly attack of nerves, a buildup of anxiety, completely natural under the circumstances. The kind of thing that could happen to anybody. He felt like getting out of the house, so what? No one could accuse him of *escaping*. He was traveling toward, not running away from, that which he most wanted to *escape*—the dark undertow of the Fisherman's crimes. Neither was he committing himself to any deeper involvement. A friend of Dale's and the father of a child apparently missing, this Fred Marshall, insisted on talking to him; fine, let him talk. If half an hour with a retired detective could help Fred Marshall get a handle on his problems, the retired detective was willing to give him the time.

Everything else was merely personal. Waking dreams and robins' eggs messed with your mind, but that was merely personal. It could be outwaited, outwitted, figured out. No rational person took that stuff seriously: like a summer storm, it blew in, it blew out. Now, as he coasted through the green light at Centralia and noted, with a cop's reflexive awareness, the row of Harleys lined up in the Sand Bar's parking lot, he felt himself coming into alignment with the afternoon's difficulties. It made perfect sense that he should have found himself unable—well, let us say unwilling—to open the refrigerator door. Nasty surprises made you think twice. A light in his living room had expired, and when he had gone to the drawer that contained half a dozen new halogen bulbs, he had been unable to open it. In fact, he had not quite been able to open any drawer, cabinet, or closet in his house, which had denied him the capacity to make a cup of tea, change his clothes, prepare lunch, or do anything but leaf halfheartedly through books and watch television. When the flap of the mailbox had threatened to conceal a pyramid of small blue eggs, he had decided to put off collecting the mail until the next day. Anyhow, all he ever got were financial statements, magazines, and junk mail.

*Let's not make it sound worse than it was,* Jack says to himself. *I could have opened every door, drawer, and cabinet in the place, but I didn't want to. I wasn't afraid that robins' eggs were going to come spilling out of the refrigerator or the closet—it's just that I didn't want to take the chance of finding one of the blasted things. Show me a psychiatrist who says that's neurotic, and I'll show you a moron who doesn't understand psychology. All the old-timers used to tell me that working homicide messed with your head. Hell, that's why I retired in the first place!*

*What was I supposed to do, stay on the force until I ate my gun? You're a smart guy, Henry Leyden, and I love you, but there are some things you don't GET!*

All right, he was going to Sumner Street. Everybody was yelling at him to do something, and that's what he was doing. He'd say hello to Dale, greet the boys, sit down with this Fred Marshall, the solid citizen with a missing son, and give him the usual oatmeal about everything possible being done, blah blah, the FBI is working hand in glove with us on this one, and the bureau has the finest investigators in the world. *That* oatmeal. As far as Jack was concerned, his primary duty was to stroke Fred Marshall's fur, as if to soothe the feelings of an injured cat; when Marshall had calmed down, Jack's supposed obligation to the community—an obligation that existed entirely in the minds of others—would be fulfilled, freeing him to go back to the privacy he had earned. If Dale didn't like it, he could take a running jump into the Mississippi; if *Henry* didn't like it, Jack would refuse to read *Bleak House* and force him to listen instead to Lawrence Welk, Vaughn Monroe, or something equally excruciating. Bad Dixieland. Years ago, someone had given Jack a CD called *Fats Manassas & His Muskrat All Stars Stompin' the Ramble.* Thirty seconds of Fats Manassas, and Henry would be begging for mercy.

This image makes Jack feel comfortable enough to prove that his hesitation before cupboards and drawers had been merely a temporary unwillingness, not phobic inability. Even while his attention was elsewhere, as it chiefly was, the shoved-in ashtray below the dash has mocked and taunted him since he first climbed into the pickup. A kind of sinister suggestiveness, an aura of latent malice, surrounds the ashtray's flat little panel.

Does he fear that a small blue egg lurks behind the little panel?

Of course not. Nothing is in there but air and molded black plastic.

In that case, he can pull it out.

The buildings on the outskirts of French Landing glide past the pickup's windows. Jack has reached almost the exact point at which Henry pulled the plug on Dirtysperm. Obviously he can open the ashtray. Nothing could be simpler. You just get your fingers under there and tug. Easiest thing in the world. He extends a hand. Before his fingers touch the panel, he snatches the hand back. Drops of perspiration glide down his forehead and lodge in his eyebrows.

"It isn't a big deal," he says aloud. "You got some kind of problem here, Jacky-boy?"

Again, he extends his hand to the ashtray. Abruptly aware that he is paying more attention to the bottom of his dashboard than to the road, he glances up and cuts his speed by half. He refuses to hit his brakes. It's just an ashtray, for God's sake. His fingers meet the panel, then curl under its lip. Jack glances at the road once more. Then, with the decisivesness of a nurse ripping a strip of tape off a patient's hairy abdomen, he yanks out the sliding tray. The lighter attachment, which he had unknowingly dislodged in his driveway that morning, bounces three inches into the air, greatly resembling, to Jack's appalled eye, a flying black-and-silver egg.

He veers off the road, bumps over the weedy shoulder, and heads toward a looming telephone pole. The lighter drops back into the tray with a loud, metallic thwack no egg in the world could have produced. The telephone pole swims closer and nearly fills the windshield. Jack stamps on the brake and jerks to a halt, arousing a flurry of ticks and rattles from the ashtray. If he had not cut his speed before opening the ashtray, he would have driven straight into the pole, which stands about four feet from the hood of the pickup. Jack wipes the sweat off his face and picks up the lighter. "Shit on a shingle." He clicks the attachment into its receptacle and collapses backward against the seat. "No wonder they say smoking can kill you," he says. The joke is too feeble to amuse him, and for a couple of seconds he does nothing but slump against the seat and regard the sparse traffic on Lyall Road. When his heart rate drops back to something like normal, he reminds himself that he did, after all, open the ashtray.

Blond, rumpled Tom Lund has evidently been prepped for his arrival, for when Jack walks past three bicycles lined up next to the door and enters the station, the young officer takes off from behind his desk and rushes forward to whisper that Dale and Fred Marshall are waiting for him in Dale's office, and he will show him right in. They'll be glad to see him, that's for sure. "I am, too, Lieutenant Sawyer," Lund adds. "Boy, I gotta say it. What you got, I think, we need."

"Call me Jack. I'm not a lieutenant anymore. I'm not even a cop anymore." Jack had met Tom Lund during the Kinderling investigation, and he had liked the young man's eagerness and dedication. In love with his job, his uniform, and his badge, respectful of his chief and awed by Jack, Lund had uncomplain-

ingly logged hundreds of hours on the telephone, in records offices, and in his car, checking and rechecking the often contradictory details spun off by the collision between a Wisconsin
farm-insurance salesman and two Sunset Strip working girls.
All the while, Tom Lund had retained the energetic sparkle of a
high school quarterback running onto the field for his first
game.

He does not look that way anymore, Jack observes. Dark
smudges hang beneath his eyes, and the bones in his face are
more prominent. More than sleeplessness and exhaustion lie
behind Lund's affect: his eyes bear the helplessly startled expression of those who have suffered a great moral shock. The
Fisherman has stolen a good part of Tom Lund's youth.

"But I'll see what I can do," Jack says, offering the promise
of a commitment greater than he intends.

"We can sure use anything you can give us," Lund says. It is
too much, too servile, and as Lund turns away and leads him to
the office, Jack thinks, *I didn't come here to be your savior.*

The thought instantly makes him feel guilty.

Lund knocks, opens the door to announce Jack, shows him
in, and vanishes like a ghost, utterly unnoticed by the two men
who rise from their chairs and fasten their eyes upon their visitor's face, one with visible gratitude, the other with an enormous degree of the same emotion mixed with naked need,
which makes Jack even more uncomfortable.

Over Dale's garbled introduction, Fred Marshall says,
"Thank you for agreeing to come, thank you so much. That's all
I can . . ." His right arm sticks out like a pump handle. When
Jack takes his hand, an even greater quantity of feeling floods
into Fred Marshall's face. His hand fastens on Jack's and seems
almost to *claim* it, as an animal claims its prey. He squeezes,
hard, a considerable number of times. His eyes fill. "I can't . . ."
Marshall pulls his hand away and scrubs the tears off his face.
Now his eyes look raw and intensely vulnerable. "Boy oh boy,"
he says. "I'm really glad you're here, Mr. Sawyer. Or should I
say Lieutenant?"

"Jack is fine. Why don't the two of you fill me in on what
happened today?"

Dale points toward a waiting chair; the three men take their
places; the painful but essentially simple story of Fred, Judy,

and Tyler Marshall begins. Fred speaks first, at some length. In his version of the story, a valiant, lionhearted woman, a devoted wife and mother, succumbs to baffling, multifaceted transformations and disorders, and develops mysterious symptoms overlooked by her ignorant, stupid, self-centered husband. She blurts out nonsense words; she writes crazy stuff on sheets of notepaper, rams the papers into her mouth, and tries to swallow them. *She sees the tragedy coming in advance, and it unhinges her.* Sounds crazy, but the self-centered husband thinks it's the truth. That is, he *thinks* he thinks it's the truth, because he's been thinking about it since he first talked to Dale, and even though it sounds crazy, it kind of makes sense. Because what other explanation could there be? So that's what he thinks he thinks—that his wife started to lose her mind because she knew that the Fisherman was on the way. Things like that are possible, he guesses. For example, the brave afflicted wife knew that her beautiful wonderful son was missing even before the stupid selfish husband, who went to work exactly as if it were a normal day, told her about the bicycle. That pretty much proved what he was talking about. The beautiful little boy went out with his three friends, but only the three friends came back, and Officer Danny Tcheda found the little son's Schwinn bike and one of his poor sneakers on the sidewalk outside Maxton's.

"Danny Cheetah?" asks Jack, who, like Fred Marshall, is beginning to think he thinks a number of alarming things.

"Tcheda," says Dale, and spells it for him. Dale tells his own, far shorter version of the story. In Dale Gilbertson's story, a boy goes out for a ride on his bicycle and vanishes, perhaps as a result of abduction, from the sidewalk in front of Maxton's. That is all of the story Dale knows, and he trusts that Jack Sawyer will be able to fill in many of the surrounding blanks.

Jack Sawyer, at whom both of the other men in the room are staring, takes time to adjust to the three thoughts he now thinks he thinks. The first is not so much a thought as a response that embodies a hidden thought: from the moment Fred Marshall clutched his hand and said "Boy oh boy," Jack found himself liking the man, an unanticipated turn in the evening's plot. Fred Marshall strikes him as something like the poster boy for small-town life. If you put his picture on billboards advertising French County real estate, you could sell a lot of second homes to people in Milwaukee and Chicago. Marshall's friendly, good-looking face and slender runner's body are as good as testimonials to responsibility, decency, good manners and good neighborliness, modesty, and a generous heart. The more Fred Marshall accuses himself of selfishness and stupidity, the more Jack likes him. And the more he likes him, the more he sympathizes with his terrible plight, the more he wishes to help the man. Jack had come to the station expecting that he would respond to Dale's friend like a policeman, but his cop reflexes have rusted from disuse. He is responding like a fellow citizen. Cops, as Jack well knows, seldom view the civilians caught up in the backwash of a crime as fellow citizens, certainly never in the early stages of an investigation. (The thought hidden at the center of Jack's response to the man before him is that Fred Marshall, being what he is, cannot harbor suspicions about anyone with whom he is on good terms.)

Jack's second thought is that of both a cop and a fellow citizen, and while he continues his adjustment to the third, which is wholly the product of his rusty yet still accurate cop reflexes, he makes it public. "The bikes I saw outside belong to Tyler's friends? Is someone questioning them now?"

"Bobby Dulac," Dale says. "I talked to them when they came in, but I didn't get anywhere. According to them, they were all together on Chase Street, and Tyler rode off by himself. They claim they didn't see anything. Maybe they didn't."

"But you think there's more."

"Honest to God, I do. But I don't know what the dickens it could be, and we have to send them home before their parents get bent out of shape."

"Who are they, what are their names?"

Fred Marshall wraps his fingers together as if around the handle of an invisible baseball bat. "Ebbie Wexler, T. J. Renniker, and Ronnie Metzger. They're the kids Ty's been hanging around with this summer." An unspoken judgment hovers about this last sentence.

"It sounds like you don't consider them the best possible company for your son."

"Well, no," says Fred, caught between his desire to tell the truth and his innate wish to avoid the appearance of unfairness. "Not if you put it like that. Ebbie seems like kind of a bully, and the other two are maybe a little on the . . . slow side? I hope . . . or I was hoping . . . that Ty would realize he could do better and spend his free time with kids who are more on, you know . . ."

"More on his level."

"Right. The trouble is, my son is sort of small for his age, and Ebbie Wexler is . . . um . . ."

"Heavyset and tall for his age," Jack says. "The perfect situation for a bully."

"You're saying *you* know Ebbie *Wexler*?"

"No, but I saw him this morning. He was with the other two boys and your son."

Dale jolts upright in his chair, and Fred Marshall drops his invisible bat. "When was that?" Dale asks. At the same time, Fred Marshall asks, "Where?"

"Chase Street, about ten past eight. I came in to pick up Henry Leyden and drive him home. When we were on our way out of town, the boys drove their bikes into the road right in front of me. I got a good look at your son, Mr. Marshall. He seemed like a great kid."

Fred Marshall's widening eyes indicate that some kind of hope, some promise, is taking shape before him; Dale relaxes. "That pretty much matches their story. It would have been right before Ty took off on his own. If he did."

"Or they took off and left him," says Ty's father. "They were faster on their bikes than Ty, and sometimes they, you know . . . they teased him."

"By racing ahead and leaving him alone," Jack says. Fred Marshall's glum nod speaks of boyhood humiliations shared with this sympathetic father. Jack remembers the inflamed, hostile face and raised finger of Ebbie Wexler and wonders if and how the boy might be protecting himself. Dale had said that he smelled the presence of falsity in the boys' story, but why would they lie? Whatever their reasons, the lie almost certainly began with Ebbie Wexler. The other two followed orders.

For the moment setting aside the third of his thoughts, Jack says, "I want to talk to the boys before you send them home. Where are they?"

"The interrogation room, top of the stairs." Dale aims a finger at the ceiling. "Tom will take you up."

With its battleship-gray walls, gray metal table, and single window narrow as a slit in a castle wall, the room at the top of the stairs seems designed to elicit confessions through boredom and despair, and when Tom Lund leads Jack through the door, the four inhabitants of the interrogation room appear to have succumbed to its leaden atmosphere. Bobby Dulac looks sideways, stops drumming a pencil on the tabletop, and says, "Well, hooray for Hollywood. Dale said you were coming down." Even Bobby gleams a little less conspicuously in this gloom. "Did you want to interrogate these here hoodlums, Lieutenant?"

"In a minute, maybe." Two of the three hoodlums on the far side of the table watch Jack move alongside Bobby Dulac as if fearing he will clap them in a cell. The words "interrogate" and "Lieutenant" have had the bracing effect of a cold wind from Canada. Ebbie Wexler squints at Jack, trying to look tough, and the boy beside him, Ronnie Metzger, wriggles in his chair, his eyes like dinner plates. The third boy, T. J. Renniker, has dropped his head atop his crossed arms and appears to be asleep.

"Wake him up," Jack says. "I have something to say, and I want you all to hear it." In fact, he has nothing to say, but he needs these boys to pay attention to him. He already knows that Dale was right. If they are not lying, they are at least holding something back. That's why his abrupt appearance within their dozy scene frightened them. If Jack had been in charge, he would have separated the boys and questioned them individually, but now he must deal with Bobby Dulac's mistake. He has to treat them collectively, to begin with, and he has to work on their fear. He does not want to terrorize the boys, merely to get their hearts pumping a bit faster; after that, he can separate them. The weakest, guiltiest link has already declared himself. Jack feels no compunction about telling lies to get information.

Ronnie Metzger shoves T.J.'s shoulder and says, "Wake up, bumdell . . . *dumbbell*."

The sleeping boy moans, lifts his head from the table, begins to stretch out his arms. His eyes fasten on Jack, and blinking and swallowing he snaps into an upright position.

"Welcome back," Jack says. "I want to introduce myself and explain what I am doing here. My name is Jack Sawyer, and I am a lieutenant in the Homicide Division of the Los Angeles Police Department. I have an excellent record and a roomful of citations and medals. When I go after a bad guy, I usually wind up arresting him. Three years ago, I came here on a case from Los Angeles. Two weeks later, a man named Thornberg Kinderling was shipped back to L.A. in chains. Because I know this area and have worked with its law enforcement officers, the LAPD asked me to assist your local force in its investigation of the Fisherman murders." He glances down to see if Bobby Dulac is grinning at this nonsense, but Bobby is staring frozen-faced across the table. "Your friend Tyler Marshall was with you before he disappeared this morning. Did the Fisherman take him? I hate to say it, but I think he did. Maybe we can get Tyler back, and maybe we can't, but if I am going to stop the Fisherman, I need you to tell me exactly what happened, down to the last detail. You have to be completely honest with me, because if you lie or keep anything secret, you will be guilty of obstruction of justice. Obstruction of justice is a serious, serious crime. Officer Dulac, what is the minimum sentence for that crime in the state of Wisconsin?"

"Five years, I'm pretty sure," Bobby Dulac says.

Ebbie Wexler bites the inside of his cheek; Ronnie Metzger looks away and frowns at the table; T. J. Renniker dully contemplates the narrow window.

Jack sits down beside Bobby Dulac. "Incidentally, I was the guy in the pickup one of you gave the finger to this morning. I can't say I'm thrilled to see you again."

Two heads swivel toward Ebbie, who squints ferociously, trying to solve this brand-new problem. "I did not," he says, having settled on outright denial. "Maybe it looked like I did, but I didn't."

"You're lying, and we haven't even started to talk about Tyler Marshall yet. I'll give you one more chance. Tell me the truth."

Ebbie smirks. "I don't go around flipping the bird at people I don't know."

"Stand up," Jack says.

Ebbie glances from side to side, but his friends are unable to meet his gaze. He shoves back his chair and stands up, uncertainly.

"Officer Dulac," Jack says, "take this boy outside and hold him there."

Bobby Dulac performs his role perfectly. He uncoils from his chair and keeps his eyes on Ebbie as he glides toward him. He resembles a panther on the way to a sumptuous meal. Ebbie Wexler jumps back and tries to stay Bobby with a raised palm. "No, don't—I take it back—I did it, okay?"

"Too late," Jack says. He watches as Bobby grasps the boy's elbow and pulls him toward the door. Red-faced and sweating, Ebbie plants his feet on the floor, and the forward pressure applied to his arm folds him over the bulge of his stomach. He staggers forward, yelping and scattering tears. Bobbie Dulac opens the door and hauls him into the bleak second-floor corridor. The door slams shut and cuts off a wail of fear.

The two remaining boys have turned the color of skim milk and seem incapable of movement. "Don't worry about him," Jack says. "He'll be fine. In fifteen, twenty minutes, you'll be free to go home. I didn't think there was any point in talking to someone who lies from the git-go, that's all. Remember: even lousy cops know when they're being lied to, and I am a *great* cop. So this is what we are going to do now. We're going to talk about what happened this morning, about what Tyler was doing, the way you separated from him, where you were, what you did afterward, anyone you might have seen, that kind of thing." He leans back and flattens his hands on the table. "Go on, tell me what happened."

Ronnie and T.J. look at each other. T.J. inserts his right index finger into his mouth and begins to worry the nail with his front teeth. "Ebbie flipped you," Ronnie says.

"No kidding. After that."

"Uh, Ty said he hadda go someplace."

"He hadda go someplace," T.J. chimes in.

"Where were you right then?"

"Uh . . . outside the Allsorts Pomorium."

*"Emporium,"* T.J. says. "It's not a pomorium, mushhead, it's a *em-por-ee-um.*"

"And?"

"And Ty said—" Ronnie glances at T.J. "Ty said he hadda go somewhere."

"Which way did he go, east or west?"

The boys treat this question as though it were asked in a foreign language, by puzzling over it, mutely.

"Toward the river, or away from the river?"

They consult each other again. The question has been asked in English, but no proper answer exists. Finally, Ronnie says, "I don't know."

"How about you, T.J.? Do you know?"

T.J. shakes his head.

"Good. That's honest. You don't know because you didn't see him leave, did you? And he didn't really say he had to go somewhere, did he? I bet Ebbie made that up."

T.J. wriggles, and Ronnie gazes at Jack with wondering awe. He has just revealed himself to be Sherlock Holmes.

"Remember when I drove past in my truck?" They nod in unison. "Tyler was with you." They nod again. "You'd already left the sidewalk in front of the Allsorts Emporium, and you were riding east on Chase Street—away from the river. I saw you in my rearview mirror. Ebbie was pedaling very fast. The two of you could almost keep up with him. Tyler was smaller than the rest of you, and he fell behind. So I *know* he didn't go off on his own. He couldn't keep up."

Ronnie Metzger wails, "And he got way, way behind, and the Misherfun came out and grabbed him." He promptly bursts into tears.

Jack leans forward. "Did you see it happen? Either one of you?"

*"Nooooa,"* Ronnie sobs. T.J. slowly shakes his head.

"You didn't see anyone talking with Ty, or a car stopping, or him going into a shop, or anything like that?"

The boys utter an incoherent, overlapping babble to the effect that they saw nothing.

"When did you realize he was gone?"

T.J. opens his mouth, then closes it. Ronnie says, "When we were having the Slurpees." His face pursed with tension, T.J. nods in agreement.

Two more questions reveal that they had enjoyed the Slurpees at the 7-Eleven, where they also purchased Magic cards, and that it had probably taken them no more than a couple of minutes to notice Tyler Marshall's absence. "Ebbie said Ty would buy us some more cards," helpful Ronnie adds.

They have reached the moment for which Jack has been waiting. Whatever the secret may be, it took place soon after the boys came out of the 7-Eleven and saw that Tyler had still not joined them. And the secret is T.J.'s alone. The kid is practically sweating blood, while the memory of the Slurpees and Magic cards has calmed down his friend to a remarkable degree. There is only one more question he wishes to ask the two of them. "So Ebbie wanted to find Tyler. Did you all get on your bikes and search around, or did Ebbie send just one of you?"

"Huh?" Ronnie says. T.J. drops his chin and crosses his arms on the top of his head, as if to ward off a blow. "Tyler went somewheres," Ronnie says. "We didn't look for him, we went to the park. To trade the Magic cards."

"I see," Jack says. "Ronnie, thank you. You have been very helpful. I'd like you to go outside and stay with Ebbie and Officer Dulac while I have a short conversation with T.J. It shouldn't take more than five minutes, if that."

"I can go?" At Jack's nod, Ronnie moves hesitantly out of his chair. When he reaches the door, T.J. emits a whimper. Then Ronnie is gone, and T.J. jerks backward into his chair and tries to become as small as possible while staring at Jack with eyes that have become shiny, flat, and perfectly round.

"T.J.," Jack says, "you have nothing to worry about, I promise you." Now that he is alone with the boy who had declared his guilt by falling asleep in the interrogation room, Jack Sawyer wants above all to absolve him of that guilt. He knows T.J.'s secret, and the secret is nothing; it is useless. "No matter what you tell me, I'm not going to arrest you. That's a promise, too. You're not in any trouble, son. In fact, I'm glad you and your friends could come down here and help us straighten things out."

He goes on in this vein for another three or four minutes, in the course of which T. J. Renniker, formerly condemned to death by firing squad, gradually comprehends that his pardon has come through and his release from what his buddy Ronnie would call vurance dile is imminent. A little color returns to his face. He returns to his former size, and his eyes lose their horror-stricken glaze.

"Tell me what Ebbie did," Jack says. "Just between you and me. I won't tell him anything. Honest. I won't rat you out."

"He wanted Ty to buy more Magic cards," T.J. says, feeling his way through unknown territory. "If Ty was there, he woulda. Ebbie can get kind of mean. So . . . so he told me, go downstreet and get the slowpoke, or I'll give you an Indian burn."

"You got on your bike and rode back down Chase Street."

"Uh-huh. I looked, but I didn't see Ty anywheres. I thought I *would,* you know? Because where else could he be?"

"And . . . ?" Jack reels in the answer he knows is coming by winding his hand through the air.

"And I still didn't see him. And I got to Queen Street, where the old folks' home is, with the big hedge out front. And, um, I saw his bike there. On the sidewalk in front of the hedge. His sneaker was there, too. And some leaves off the hedge."

There it is, the worthless secret. Maybe not entirely worthless: it gives them a pretty accurate fix on the time of the boy's disappearance: 8:15, say, or 8:20. The bike lay on the sidewalk next to the sneaker for something like four hours before Danny Tcheda spotted them. Maxton's takes up just about all the land on that section of Queen Street, and no one was showing up for the Strawberry Fest until noon.

T.J. describes being afraid—if the Fisherman pulled Ty into that hedge, maybe he'd come back for more! In answer to Jack's final question, the boy says, "Ebbie told us to say Ty rode away from in front of the Allsorts, so people wouldn't, like, blame us. In case he was killed. Ty isn't really killed, is he? Kids like *Ty* don't get killed."

"I hope not," Jack says.

"Me, too." T.J. snuffles and wipes his nose on his arm.

"Let's get you on your way home," Jack says, leaving his chair.

T.J. stands up and begins to move along the side of the table. "Oh! I just remembered!"

"What?"

"I saw feathers on the sidewalk."

The floor beneath Jack's feet seems to roll left, then right, like the deck of a ship. He steadies himself by grasping the back of a chair. "Really." He takes care to compose himself before turning to the boy. "What do you mean, feathers?"

"Black ones. Big. They looked like they came off a crow. One was next to the bike, and the other was *in* the sneaker."

"That's funny," says Jack, buying time until he ceases to re-
verberate from the unexpected appearance of feathers in his
conversation with T. J. Renniker. That he should respond at all
is ridiculous; that he should have felt, even for a second, that he
was likely to faint is grotesque. T.J.'s feathers were real crow
feathers on a real sidewalk. His were dream feathers, feathers
from unreal robins, illusory as everything else in a dream. Jack
tells himself a number of helpful things like this, and soon he
does feel normal once again, but we should be aware that, for
the rest of the night and much of the next day, the word *feathers* floats, surrounded by an aura as charged as an electrical
storm, beneath and through his thoughts, now and then surfac-
ing with the sizzling crackle of a lightning bolt.

"It's weird," T.J. says. "Like, how did a feather get in his
*sneaker*?"

"Maybe the wind blew it there," Jack says, conveniently ignoring the nonexistence of wind this day. Reassured by the sta-
bility of the floor, he waves T.J. into the hallway, then follows
him out.

Ebbie Wexler pushes himself off the wall and stamps up
alongside Bobby Dulac. Still in character, Bobby might have
been carved from a block of marble. Ronnie Metzger sidles
away. "We can send these boys home," Jack says. "They've
done their duty."

"T.J., what did you say?" Ebbie asks, glowering.

"He made it clear that you know nothing about your friend's
disappearance," Jack says.

Ebbie relaxes, though not without distributing scowls all
around. The final and most malignant scowl is for Jack, who
raises his eyebrows. "I didn't cry," Ebbie says. "I was scared,
but I didn't cry."

"You were scared, all right," Jack says. "Next time, don't lie
to me. You had your chance to help the police, and you blew it."

Ebbie struggles with this notion and succeeds, at least partially, in absorbing it. "Okay, but I wasn't really flippin' at you.
It was the stupid music."

"I hated it, too. The guy who was with me insisted on playing it. You know who he was?"

In the face of Ebbie's suspicious glower, Jack says, "George
Rathbun."

It is like saying "Superman," or "Arnold Schwarzenegger"; Ebbie's suspicion evaporates, and his face transforms. Innocent wonder fills his small, close-set eyes. "You know George Rathbun?"

"He's one of my best friends," Jack says, not adding that most of his other best friends are, in a sense, also George Rathbun.

"Cool," Ebbie says.

In the background, T.J. and Ronnie echo, *"Cool."*

"George *is* pretty cool," Jack says. "I'll tell him you said that. Let's go downstairs and get you kids on your bikes."

Still wrapped in the glory of having gazed upon the great, the *tremendous* George Rathbun, the boys mount their bicycles, pedal away down Sumner Street, and swerve off onto Second. Bobby Dulac says, "That was a good trick, what you said about George Rathbun. Sent them away happy."

"It wasn't a trick."

So startled that he jostles back into the station house side by side with Jack, Bobby says, "George Rathbun is a friend of yours?"

"Yep," Jack says. "And sometimes, he can be a real pain in the ass."

Dale and Fred Marshall look up as Jack enters the office, Dale with a cautious expectancy, Fred Marshall with what Jack sees, heartbreakingly, as hope.

"Well?" Dale says.

*(feathers)*

"You were right, they were hiding something, but it isn't much."

Fred Marshall slumps against the back of his chair, letting some of his belief in a future hope leak out of him like air from a punctured tire.

"Not long after they got to the 7-Eleven, the Wexler boy sent T.J. down the street to look for your son," Jack says. "When T.J. got to Queen Street, he saw the bike and the sneaker lying on the sidewalk. Of course, they all thought of the Fisherman. Ebbie Wexler figured they might get blamed for leaving him behind, and he came up with the story you heard—that Tyler left them, instead of the other way around."

"If you saw all four boys around ten past eight, that means

Tyler disappeared only a few minutes later. What does this guy do, lurk in hedges?"

"Maybe he does exactly that," Jack says. "Did you have people check out that hedge?"

*( feathers)*

"The staties went over it, through it, and under it. Leaves and dirt, that's what they came up with."

As if driving a spike with his hand, Fred Marshall bangs his fist down onto the desk. "My son was gone for four hours before anyone noticed his bike. Now it's almost seven-thirty! He's been missing for most of the day! I shouldn't be sitting here, I should be driving around, looking for him."

"Everybody is looking for your son, Fred," Dale says. "My guys, the staties, even the FBI."

"I have no faith in them," Fred says. "They haven't found Irma Freneau, have they? Why should they find my son? As far as I can see, I've got one chance here." When he looks at Jack, emotion turns his eyes into lamps. "That chance is you, Lieutenant. Will you help me?"

Jack's third and most troubling thought, withheld until now and purely that of an experienced policeman, causes him to say, "I'd like to talk to your wife. If you're planning on visiting her tomorrow, would you mind if I came along?"

Dale blinks and says, "Maybe we should talk about this."

"Do you think it would do some good?"

"It might," Jack says.

"Seeing you might do *her* some good, anyhow," Fred says. "Don't you live in Norway Valley? That's on the way to Arden. I can pick you up about nine."

"Jack," Dale says.

"See you at nine," Jack says, ignoring the signals of mingled distress and anger emanating from his friend, also the little voice that whispers *( feather)*.

"Amazing," says Henry Leyden. "I don't know whether to thank you or congratulate you. Both, I suppose. It's too late in the game to make 'bitchrod,' like me, but I think you could have a shot at 'dope.' "

"Don't lose your head. The only reason I went down there was to keep the boy's father from coming to my house."

"That wasn't the only reason."

"You're right. I was feeling sort of edgy and hemmed in. I felt like getting out, changing the scenery."

"But there was also *another* reason."

"Henry, you are hip-deep in pigshit, do you know that? You want to think I acted out of civic duty, or honor, or compassion, or altruism, or something, but I didn't. I don't like having to say this, but I'm a lot less good-hearted and responsible than you think I am."

" 'Hip-deep in pigshit'? Man, you are absolutely on the money. I have been hip-deep in pigshit, not to mention chest-deep and even *chin*-deep in pigshit, most of my life."

"Nice of you to admit it."

"However, you misunderstand me. You're right, I do think you are a good, decent person. I don't just think it, I know it. You're modest, you're compassionate, you're honorable, you're responsible—no matter what you think of yourself right now. But that wasn't what I was talking about."

"What *did* you mean, then?"

"The other reason you decided to go to the police station is connected to this problem, this concern, whatever it is, that's been bugging you for the past couple of weeks. It's like you've been walking around under a shadow."

"Huh," Jack said.

"This problem, this *secret* of yours, takes up half your attention, so you're only half present; the rest of you is somewhere else. Sweetie, don't you think I can tell when you're worried and preoccupied? I might be blind, but I can see."

"Okay. Let's suppose that something has been on my mind lately. What could that have to do with going to the station house?"

"There are two possibilities. Either you were going off to confront it, or you were fleeing from it."

Jack does not speak.

"All of which suggests that this problem has to do with your life as a policeman. It could be some old case coming back to haunt you. Maybe a psychotic thug you put in jail was released and is threatening to kill you. Or, hell, I'm completely full of shit and you found out you have liver cancer and a life expectancy of three months."

"I don't have cancer, at least as far as I know, and no ex-con wants to kill me. All of my old cases, most of them, anyway, are safely asleep in the records warehouse of the LAPD. Of course, something has been bothering me lately, and I should have expected you to see that. But I didn't want to, I don't know, burden you with it until I managed to figure it out for myself."

"Tell me one thing, will you? Were you going toward it, or running away?"

"There's no answer to that question."

"We shall see. Isn't the food ready by now? I'm starving, literally *starving*. You cook too slow. I would have been done ten minutes ago."

"Hold your horses," Jack says. "Coming right up. The problem is this crazy kitchen of yours."

"Most rational kitchen in America. Maybe in the world."

After ducking out of the police station quickly enough to avoid a useless conversation with Dale, Jack had yielded to impulse and called Henry with the offer of making dinner for both of them. A couple of good steaks, a nice bottle of wine, grilled mushrooms, a big salad. He could pick up everything they needed in French Landing. Jack had cooked for Henry on three or four previous occasions, and Henry had prepared one stupendously bizarre dinner for Jack. (The housekeeper had taken all the herbs and spices off their rack to wash it, and she had put everything back in the wrong place.) What was he doing in French Landing? He'd explain that when he got there. At eight-thirty he had pulled up before Henry's roomy white farmhouse, greeted Henry, and carried the groceries and his copy of *Bleak House* into the kitchen. He had tossed the book to the far end of the table, opened the wine, poured a glass for his host and one for himself, and started cooking. He'd had to spend several minutes reacquainting himself with the eccentricities of Henry's kitchen, in which objects were not located by kind—pans with pans, knives with knives, pots with pots—but according to what sort of meal required their usage. If Henry wanted to whip up a grilled trout and some new potatoes, he had only to open the proper cabinet to find all the necessary utensils. These were arranged in four basic groups (meat, fish, poultry, and vegetables), with many subgroups and subsubgroups within each category. The filing system confounded Jack, who often had to peer into several widely separated realms before coming upon the frying pan or spatula he was looking for. As Jack chopped, wandered the shelves, and cooked, Henry had laid the table in the kitchen with plates and silverware and sat down to quiz his troubled friend.

Now the steaks, rare, are transported to the plates, the mushrooms arrayed around them, and the enormous wooden salad bowl installed on the center of the table. Henry pronounces the meal delicious, takes a sip of his wine, and says, "If you still won't talk about your trouble, whatever it is, you'd better at least tell me what happened at the station. I suppose there's very little doubt that another child was snatched."

"Next to none, I'm sorry to say. It's a boy named Tyler Marshall. His father's name is Fred Marshall, and he works out at Goltz's. Do you know him?"

"Been a long time since I bought a combine," Henry says.

"The first thing that struck me was that Fred Marshall was a very nice guy," Jack says, and goes on to recount, in great detail and leaving nothing out, the evening's events and revelations, except for one matter, that of his third, his unspoken, thought.

"You actually asked to visit Marshall's wife? In the mental wing at French County Lutheran?"

"Yes, I did," Jack says. "I'm going there tomorrow."

"I don't get it." Henry eats by hunting the food with his knife, spearing it with his fork, and measuring off a narrow strip of steak. "Why would you want to see the mother?"

"Because one way or another I think she's involved," Jack says.

"Oh, come off it. The boy's own mother?"

"I'm not saying she's the Fisherman, because of course she isn't. But according to her husband, Judy Marshall's behavior started to change before Amy St. Pierre disappeared. She got worse and worse as the murders went on, and on the day her son vanished, she flipped out completely. Her husband had to have her committed."

"Wouldn't you say she had an excellent reason to break down?"

"She flipped out *before* anyone told her about her son. Her husband thinks she has ESP! He said she saw the murders in advance, she knew the Fisherman was on the way. And she knew her son was gone before they found the bike—when Fred Marshall came home, he found her tearing at the walls and talking nonsense. Completely out of control."

"You hear about lots of cases where a mother is suddenly aware of some threat or injury to her child. A pyschic bond. Sounds like mumbo jumbo, but I guess it happens."

"I don't believe in ESP, and I don't believe in coincidence."

"So what are you saying?"

"Judy Marshall *knows* something, and whatever she knows is a real showstopper. Fred can't see it—he's much too close—and Dale can't see it, either. You should have heard him talk about her."

"So what is she supposed to know?"

"I think she may know the doer. I think it has to be someone close to her. Whoever he is, she knows his name, and it's driving her crazy."

Henry frowns and uses his inchworm technique to entrap another piece of steak. "So you're going to the hospital to open her up," he finally says.

"Yes. Basically."

A mysterious silence follows this statement. Henry quietly whittles away at the meat, chews what he whittles, and washes it down with Jordan cabernet.

"How did your deejay gig go? Was it okay?"

"It was a thing of beauty. All the adorable old swingers cut loose on the dance floor, even the ones in wheelchairs. One guy sort of rubbed me the wrong way. He was rude to a woman named Alice, and he asked me to play 'Lady Magowan's Nightmare,' which doesn't exist, as you probably know—"

"It's 'Lady Magowan's Dream.' Woody Herman."

"Good boy. The thing was, he had this *terrible* voice. It sounded like something out of hell! Anyhow, I didn't have the Woody Herman record, and he asked for the Bunny Berigan 'I Can't Get Started.' Which happened to be Rhoda's favorite record. What with my goofy ear hallucinations and all, it shook me up. I don't know why."

For a few minutes they concentrate on their plates.

Jack says, "What do you think, Henry?"

Henry tilts his head, auditing an inner voice. Scowling, he

sets down his fork. The inner voice continues to demand his attention. He adjusts his shades and faces Jack. "In spite of everything you say, you still think like a cop."

Jack bridles at the suspicion that Henry is not paying him a compliment. "What do you mean by that?"

"Cops see differently than people who aren't cops. When a cop looks at someone, he wonders what he's guilty of. The possibility of innocence never enters his mind. To a longtime cop, a guy who's put in ten years or more, everyone who isn't a cop is guilty. Only most of them haven't been caught yet."

Henry has described the mind-set of dozens of men Jack once worked with. "Henry, how do you know about that?"

"I can see it in their eyes," Henry says. "That's the way policemen approach the world. You are a policeman."

Jack blurts out, "I am a coppiceman." Appalled, he blushes. "Sorry, that stupid phrase has been running around and around in my head, and it just popped out."

"Why don't we clear the dishes and start on *Bleak House*?"

When their few dishes have been stacked beside the sink, Jack takes the book from the far side of the table and follows Henry toward the living room, pausing on the way to glance, as he always does, at his friend's studio. A door with a large glass insert opens into a small, soundproofed chamber bristling with electronic equipment: the microphone and turntable back from Maxton's and reinstalled before Henry's well-padded, swiveling chair; a disc changer and matching digital-analog converter mount, close at hand, beside a mixing board and a massive tape recorder adjacent to the other, larger window, which looks into the kitchen. When Henry had been planning the studio, Rhoda requested the windows, because, she'd said, she wanted to be able to see him at work. There isn't a wire in sight. The entire studio has the disciplined neatness of the captain's quarters on a ship.

"Looks like you're going to work tonight," Jack says.

"I want to get two more Henry Shakes ready to send, and I'm working on something for a birthday salute to Lester Young and Charlie Parker."

"Were they born on the same day?"

"Close enough. August twenty-seventh and twenty-ninth. You know, I can't quite tell if you'll want the lights on or not."

"Let's turn them on," Jack says.

And so Henry Leyden switches on the two lamps beside the window, and Jack Sawyer moves to the overstuffed chair near the fireplace and turns on the tall lamp at one of its rounded arms and watches as his friend walks unerringly to the light just inside the front door and the ornate fixture alongside his own, his favorite resting place, the Mission-style sofa, clicking first one, then the other into life, then settles down onto the sofa with one leg stretched out along its length. Even, low light pervades the long room and swells into greater brightness around Jack's chair.

"*Bleak House,* by Charles Dickens," he says. He clears his throat. "Okay, Henry, we're off to the races."

"London. Michaelmas Term lately over," he reads, and marches into a world made of soot and mud. Muddy dogs, muddy horses, muddy people, a day without light. Soon he has reached the second paragraph: "Fog everywhere. Fog up the river, where it flows among green aits and meadows; fog down the river, where it rolls defiled among the tiers of shipping, and the waterside pollutions of a great (and dirty) city. Fog on the Essex marshes, fog on the Kentish heights. Fog creeping into the cabooses of collier-brigs; fog lying out on the yards, and hovering in the rigging of great ships; fog drooping on the gunwales of barges and small boats."

His voice catches, and his mind temporarily drifts off-focus. What he is reading unhappily reminds him of French Landing, of Sumner Street and Chase Street, of the lights in the window of the Oak Tree Inn, the Thunder Five lurking in Nailhouse Row, and the gray ascent from the river, of Queen Street and Maxton's hedges, the little houses spreading out on grids, all of it choked by unseen fog;—which engulfs a battered NO TRESPASSING sign on the highway and swallows the Sand Bar and glides hungry and searching down the valleys.

"Sorry," he says. "I was just thinking—"

"I was, too," Henry says. "Go on, please."

But for that brief flicker of an old NO TRESPASSING sign completely unaware of the black house he one day will have to enter, Jack concentrates again on the page and continues reading *Bleak House.* The windows darken as the lamps grow warmer. The case of Jarndyce and Jarndyce grinds through the

courts, aided or impeded by attorneys Chizzle, Mizzle, and
Drizzle; Lady Dedlock leaves Sir Leicester Dedlock alone at
their great estate with its moldy chapel, stagnant river, and
"Ghost's Walk"; Esther Summerson begins to chirp away in the
first person. Our friends decide that the appearance of Esther
demands a small libation, if they are to get through much more
chirping. Henry unfolds from the sofa, sails into the kitchen,
and returns with two short, fat glasses one-third filled with Bal-
venie Doublewood single-malt whiskey, as well as a glass of
plain water for the reader. A couple of sips, a few murmurs of
appreciation, and Jack resumes. Esther, Esther, Esther, but beneath the water torture of her relentless sunniness the story
gathers steam and carries both reader and listener along in its
train.

Having come to a convenient stopping point, Jack closes the
book and yawns. Henry stands up and stretches. They move to
the door, and Henry follows Jack outside beneath a vast night
sky brilliantly scattered with stars. "Tell me one thing," Henry
says.

"Shoot."

"When you were in the station house, did you really feel like
a cop? Or did you feel like you were pretending to be one?"

"Actually, it was kind of surprising," Jack says. "In no time
at all, I felt like a cop again."

"Good."

"Why is that good?"

"Because it means you were running toward that mysterious
secret, not away from it."

Shaking his head and smiling, deliberately not giving Henry
the satisfaction of a reply, Jack steps up into his vehicle and
says good-bye from the slight but distinct elevation of the driver's seat. The engine coughs and churns, his headlights snap
into being, and Jack is on his way home.

# 9

Not many hours later, Jack finds himself walking down the midway of a deserted amusement park under a gray autumn sky. On either side of him are boarded-over concessions: the Fenway Franks hot dog stand, the Annie Oakley Shooting Gallery, the Pitch-Til-U-Win. Rain has fallen and more is coming; the air is sharp with moisture. Not far away, he can hear the lonely thunder of waves hurling themselves against a deserted shingle of beach. From closer by comes the snappy sound of guitar picking. It should be cheerful, but to Jack it is dread set to music. He shouldn't be here. This is an old place, a dangerous place. He passes a boarded-up ride. A sign out front reads: THE SPEEDY OPOPANAX WILL REOPEN MEMORIAL DAY 1982—SEE YA THEN!

*Opopanax,* Jack thinks, only he is no longer Jack; now he's Jacky. He's Jacky-boy, and he and his mother are on the run. From whom? From Sloat, of course. From hustlin', bustlin' Uncle Morgan.

*Speedy,* Jack thinks, and as if he has given a telepathic cue, a warm, slightly slurry voice begins to sing. *"When the red red robin comes bob bob bobbin' along, / There'll be no more sobbin' when he starts throbbin' his old sweet song . . ."*

*No,* Jack thinks. *I don't want to see you. I don't want to hear your old sweet song. You can't be here anyway, you're dead. Dead on the Santa Monica Pier. Old bald black man dead in the shadow of a frozen merry-go-round horse.*

Oh, but no. When the old cop logic comes back it takes hold like a tumor, even in dreams, and it doesn't take much of it to realize that this isn't Santa Monica—it's too cold and too old. This is the land of ago, when Jacky and the Queen of the B's fled out of California like the fugitives they had become. And didn't stop running until they got to the other coast, the place where Lily Cavanaugh Sawyer—

*No, I don't think of this, I never think of this*

—had come to die.

*"Wake up, wake up you sleepyhead!"*

The voice of his old friend.

*Friend, my ass. He's the one who put me on the road of trials, the one who came between me and Richard, my* real *friend. He's the one who almost got me killed, almost drove me crazy.*

*"Wake up, wake up, get out of bed!"*

*Way-gup, way-gup, way-gup. Time to face the fearsome opopanax. Time to get back to your not-so-sweet used-to-be.*

"No," Jacky whispers, and then the midway ends. Ahead is the carousel, sort of like the one on the Santa Monica Pier and sort of like the one he remembers from . . . well, from ago. It is a hybrid, in other words, a dream specialty, neither here nor there. But there's no mistaking the man who sits beneath one of the frozen rearing horses with his guitar on his knee. Jacky-boy would know that face anywhere, and all the old love rises in his heart. He fights it, but that is a fight few people win, especially not those who have been turned back to the age of twelve.

"Speedy!" he cries.

The old man looks at him and his brown face cracks open in a smile. "Travelin' Jack!" he says. "How I have missed you, son."

"I've missed you, too," he says. "But I don't travel anymore. I've settled down in Wisconsin. This . . ." He gestures at his magically restored boy's body, clad in jeans and a T-shirt. "This is just a dream."

"Maybe so, maybe not. In any case, you got a mite more traveling to do, Jack. I been telling you that for some time."

"What do you mean?"

Speedy's grin is sly in the middle, exasperated at the corners. "Don't play the fool with me, Jacky. Sent you the feathers, didn't I? Sent you a robin's egg, didn't I? Sent you more'n one."

"Why can't people leave me alone?" Jack asks. His voice is suspiciously close to a whine. Not a pretty sound. "You . . . Henry . . . Dale . . ."

"Quit on it now," Speedy says, growing stern. "Ain't got no

more time to ask you nice. The game has gotten rough. Ain't it?"

"Speedy—"

"You got your job and I got mine. Same job, too. Don't you whine at me, Jack, and don't make me chase you no mo'. You're a coppiceman, same as ever was."

"I'm retired—"

"*Shit* on your retired! The kids he killed, that's bad enough. The kids he *might* kill if he's let to go on, that's worse. But the one he's got . . ." Speedy leans forward, dark eyes blazing in his dark face. "That boy has got to be brought back, and *soon*. If you can't get him back, you got to kill him yourself, little as I like to think of it. Because he's a Breaker. A powerful one. One more might be all he needs to take it down."

"Who might need?" Jack asks.

"The Crimson King."

"And what is it this Crimson King wants to take down?"

Speedy looks at him a moment, then starts to play that perky tune again instead of answering. "There'll be no more sobbin' when he starts throbbin' his old sweet song . . ."

"Speedy, I *can't*!"

The tune ends in a discordant jangle of strings. Speedy looks at twelve-year-old Jack Sawyer with a coldness that chills the boy inward all the way to the hidden man's heart. And when he speaks again, Speedy Parker's faint southern accent has deepened. It has filled with a contempt that is almost liquid.

"You get busy now, hear me? Y'all quit whinin' and cryin' and slackin' off. Y'all pick up yo' guts from wherever you left 'em and *get busy*!"

Jack steps back. A heavy hand falls on his shoulder and he thinks, *It's Uncle Morgan. Him or maybe Sunlight Gardener. It's 1981 and I've got to do it all over again—*

But that is a boy's thought, and this is a man's dream. Jack Sawyer as he is now thrusts the child's acquiescing despair away. *No, not at all. I deny that. I have put those faces and those places aside. It was hard work, and I won't see it all undone by a few phantom feathers, a few phantom eggs, and one bad dream. Find yourself another boy, Speedy. This one grew up.*

He turns, ready to fight, but no one's there. Lying behind him on the boardwalk, on its side like a dead pony, is a boy's bicycle. There's a license plate on the back reading BIG MAC. Scattered around it are shiny crow's feathers. And now Jack hears another voice, cold and cracked, ugly and unmistakably evil. He knows it's the voice of the thing that touched him.

"That's right, asswipe. Stay out of it. You mess with me and I'll strew your guts from Racine to La Riviere."

A spinning hole opens in the boardwalk just in front of the bike. It widens like a startled eye. It continues to widen, and Jack dives for it. It's the way back. The way out. The contemptuous voice follows him.

"That's right, jackoff," it says. "Run! Run from the abbalah! Run from the King! Run for your miserable fucking life!" The voice dissolves into laughter, and it is the mad sound of that laughter which follows Jack Sawyer down into the darkness between worlds.

Hours later, Jack stands naked at his bedroom window, absently scratching his ass and watching the sky lighten in the east. He's been awake since four. He can't remember much of his dream (his defenses may be bending, but even now they have not quite broken), yet enough of it lingers for him to be sure of one thing: the corpse on the Santa Monica Pier upset him so badly that he quit his job because it reminded him of someone he once knew.

"All of that never happened," he tells the coming day in a falsely patient voice. "I had a kind of preadolescent breakdown, brought on by stress. My mother thought she had cancer, she grabbed me, and we ran all the way to the East Coast. All the way to New Hampshire. She thought she was going back to the Great Happy Place to die. Turned out to be mostly vapors, some goddamn actress midlife crisis, but what does a kid know? I was stressed. I had dreams."

Jack sighs.

"I dreamed I saved my mother's life."

The phone behind him rings, the sound shrill and broken in the shadowy room.

Jack Sawyer screams.

"I woke you up," Fred Marshall says, and Jack knows at once that this man has been up all night, sitting in his wifeless, son-less home. Looking at photo albums, perhaps, while the TV plays. Knowing he is rubbing salt into the wounds but unable to quit.

"No," Jack says, "actually I was—"

He stops. The phone's beside the bed and there's a pad beside the phone. There's a note written on the pad. Jack must have written it, since he's the only one here—ella-fucking-ment'ry, my dear Watson—but it isn't in his handwriting. At some point in his dream, he wrote this note in his dead mother's handwriting.

> *The Tower. The Beams. If the Beams are broken, Jacky-boy,*
> *if the Beams are broken and the Tower falls*

There's no more. There is only poor old Fred Marshall, who has discovered how quickly things can go bad in the sunniest midwestern life. Jack's mouth has attempted to say a couple of things while his mind is occupied with this forgery from his subconscious, probably not very sensible things, but that doesn't bother Fred; he simply goes droning along with none of the stops and drops that folks usually employ to indicate the ends of sentences or changes of thought. Fred is just getting it out, unloading, and even in his own distressed state Jack realizes that Fred Marshall of 16 Robin Hood Lane, that sweet little Cape Cod honey of a home, is nearing the edge of his endurance. If things don't turn around for him soon, he won't need to visit his wife in Ward D of French County Lutheran; they'll be roommates.

And it is their proposed visit to Judy of which Fred is speaking, Jack realizes. He quits trying to interrupt and simply listens, frowning down at the note he has written to himself as he does so. Tower and Beams. What kind of beams? Sunbeams? Hornbeams? Raise high the roof beam, carpenters?

"—know I said I'd pick you up at nine but Dr. Spiegleman that's her doctor up there Spiegleman his name is he said she had a very bad night with a lot of yelling and screaming and then trying to get up the wallpaper and eat it and maybe a seizure of some kind so they're trying her on a new medication he might have said Pamizene or Patizone I didn't write it down Spiegleman called me fifteen minutes ago I wonder if those guys ever sleep and said we should be able to see her around four he thinks she'll be more stabilized by four and we could see her then so could I pick you up at three or maybe you have—"

"Three would be fine," Jack says quietly.

"—other stuff to do other plans I'd understand that but I could come by if you don't it's mostly that I don't want to go alone—"

"I'll be waiting for you," Jack said. "We'll go in my pickup."

"—thought maybe I'd hear from Ty or from whoever snatched him like maybe a ransom demand but no one called only Spiegleman he's my wife's doctor up there at—"

"Fred, I'm going to find your boy."

Jack is appalled at this bald assurance, at the suicidal confidence he hears in his own voice, but it serves at least one purpose: bringing Fred's flood of dead words to an end. There is blessed silence from the other end of the line.

At last, Fred speaks in a trembling whisper. "Oh, sir. If only I could believe that."

"I want you to try," Jack says. "And maybe we can find your wife's mind while we're at it."

*Maybe both are in the same place,* he thinks, but this he does not say.

Liquid sounds come from the other end of the line. Fred has begun to cry.

"Fred."

"Yes?"

"You're coming to my place at three."

"Yes." A mighty sniff; a miserable cry that is mostly choked back. Jack has some comprehension of how empty Fred Marshall's house must feel at this moment, and even that dim understanding is bad enough.

"My place in Norway Valley. Come past Roy's Store, over Tamarack Creek—"

"I know where it is." A faint edge of impatience has crept into Fred's voice. Jack is very glad to hear it.

"Good. I'll see you."

"You bet." Jack hears a ghost of Fred's salesman cheer, and it twists his heart.

"What time?"

"Th-three?" Then, with marginal assurance: "Three."

"That's right. We'll take my truck. Maybe have a bite of supper at Gertie's Kitchen on our way back. Good-bye, Fred."

"Good-bye, sir. And thank you."

Jack hangs up the phone. Looks a moment longer at his memory's reproduction of his mother's handwriting and wonders what you'd call such a thing in cop-speak. Autoforgery? He snorts, then crumples the note up and starts getting dressed. He will drink a glass of juice, then go out walking for an hour or so. Blow all the bad dreams out of his head. And blow away the sound of Fred Marshall's awful droning voice while he's at it. Then, after a shower, he might or might not call Dale Gilbertson and ask if there have been any developments. If he's really going to get involved in this, there'll be a lot of paperwork to catch up on . . . he'll want to reinterview the parents . . . take a look at the old folks' home close to where the Marshall kid disappeared . . .

With his mind full of such thoughts (*pleasant* thoughts, actually, although if this had been suggested to him, he would have strenuously denied it), Jack almost stumbles over the box sitting on the welcome mat just outside his front door. It's where Buck Evitz, the postman, leaves packages when he has packages to leave, but it's not gone six-thirty yet, and Buck won't be along in his little blue truck for another three hours.

Jack bends down and cautiously picks the package up. It's the size of a shoe box, covered with brown paper that has been cut raggedly and secured not with tape but with big drools of red sealing wax. In addition to this, there are complicated loops of white string secured with a child's oversized bow. There's a cluster of stamps in the upper corner, ten or a dozen, featuring various birds. (No robins, however; Jack notes this with understandable relief.) There's something not right about those stamps, but at first Jack doesn't see what it is. He's too focused on the address, which is *spectacularly* not right. There's no box number, no RFD number, no zip code. No *name,* not really. The address consists of a single word, scrawled in large capital letters:

$$J A C K Y$$

Looking at those bedraggled letters, Jack imagines a fisted hand clutching a Sharpie marker; narrowed eyes; a tongue poked from the corner of some lunatic's mouth. His heartbeat has sped up to double-time. "I'm not liking this," he breathes. "I am *so* not liking this."

And of course there are perfectly good reasons, coppiceman reasons, not to. It *is* a shoe box; he can feel the edge of the top right through the brown paper, and nutters have been known to put bombs in shoe boxes. He'd be crazy to open it, but he has an idea he *will* open it, just the same. If it blows him sky-high, at least he'll be able to opt out of the Fisherman investigation.

Jack raises the package to listen for ticking, fully aware that ticking bombs are as out-of-date as Betty Boop cartoons. He hears nothing, but he *does* see what's wrong with the stamps, which aren't stamps at all. Someone has carefully cut the front panels from a dozen or so cafeteria sugar packets and taped them to this wrapped shoe box. A grunt of humorless laughter escapes Jack. Some nut sent him this, all right. Some nut in a locked facility, with easier access to sugar packets than to stamps. But how has it gotten *here*? Who left it (with the fake stamps uncanceled) while he was dreaming his confused dreams? And who, in this part of the world, could possibly know him as Jacky? His Jacky days are long gone.

*No they ain't, Travelin' Jack,* a voice whispers. *Not by half. Time to stop your sobbin' and get bob-bob-bobbin' along, boy. Start by seein' what's in that box.*

Resolutely ignoring his own mental voice, which tells him he's being dangerously stupid, Jack snaps the twine and uses his thumbnail to cut through the sloppy blobs of red wax. Who uses sealing wax in this day and age, anyway? He sets the wrapping paper aside. Something else for the forensics boys, maybe.

It isn't a shoe box but a sneaker box. A New Balance sneaker box, to be exact. Size 5. A child's size. And at that, Jack's heart speeds up to triple-time. He feels beads of cold sweat springing up on his forehead. His gorge and sphincter are both tightening up. This is also familiar. It is how coppicemen get cocked and locked, ready to look at something awful. And this *will* be awful. Jack has no doubt about it, and no doubt about who the package is from.

*This is my last chance to back out,* he thinks. *After this it's all aboard and heigh-ho for the . . . the wherever.*

But even that is a lie, he realizes. Dale will be looking for him at the police station on Sumner Street by noon. Fred Marshall is coming to Jack's place at three o'clock and they are going to see the Mad Housewife of Robin Hood Lane. The backout point has already come and gone. Jack still isn't sure how it happened, but it looks like he's back in harness. And if Henry Leyden has the temerity to congratulate him on this, Jack thinks, he'll probably kick Henry's blind ass for him.

A voice from his dream whispers up from beneath the floorboards of Jack's consciousness like a whiff of rotten air—*I'll strew your guts from Racine to La Riviere*—but this bothers him less than the madness inherent in the sugar-pack stamps and the laboriously printed letters of his old nickname. He has dealt with crazies before. Not to mention his share of threats.

He sits down on the steps with the sneaker box on his thighs. Beyond him, in the north field, all is still and gray. Bunny Boettcher, son of Tom Tom, came and did the second cutting only a week ago, and now a fine mist hangs above the ankle-high stubble. Above it, the sky has just begun to brighten. Not a single cloud as yet marks its calm no-color. Somewhere a bird calls out. Jack breathes deeply and thinks, *If this is where I go out, I could do worse. A lot worse.*

Then, very carefully, he takes the lid off the box and sets it aside. Nothing explodes. But it looks as if someone has filled the New Balance sneaker box with night. Then he realizes that it's been packed with shiny black crow feathers, and his arms roughen with goose bumps.

He reaches toward them, then hesitates. He wants to touch those feathers about as much as he'd want to touch the corpse of a half-decayed plague victim, but there's something beneath them. He can see it. Should he get some gloves? There are gloves in the front hall closet—

"Fuck the gloves," Jack says, and dumps the box onto the brown paper wrapping lying beside him on the porch. There's a flood of feathers, which swirl a bit even in the perfectly still morning air. Then a thump as the object around which the feathers were packed lands on Jack's porch. The smell hits Jack's nose a moment later, an odor like rotting baloney.

Someone has delivered a child's bloodstained sneaker chez Sawyer on Norway Valley Road. Something has gnawed at it pretty briskly, and even more briskly at what's inside it. He sees a lining of bloody white cotton—that would be a sock. And inside the sock, tatters of skin. This is a child's New Balance sneaker with a child's foot inside it, one that has been badly used by some animal.

*He sent it,* Jack thinks. *The Fisherman.*

Taunting him. Telling him *If you want in, come on in. The water's fine, Jacky-boy, the water is* fine.

Jack gets up. His heart is hammering, the beats now too close together to count. The beads of sweat on his forehead have swelled and broken and gone running down his face like tears, his lips and hands and feet are numb . . . yet he tells himself he is calm. That he has seen worse, much worse, piled up against bridge abutments and freeway underpasses in L.A. Nor is this his first severed body part. Once, in 1997, he and his partner Kirby Tessier found a single testicle sitting on top of a toilet tank in the Culver City public library like an ancient soft-boiled egg. So he tells himself he is calm.

He gets up and walks down the porch steps. He walks past the hood of his burgundy-colored Dodge Ram with the world-class sound system inside; he walks past the bird hotel he and Dale put up at the edge of the north field a month or two after Jack moved into this, the most perfect house in the universe. He tells himself he is calm. He tells himself that it's evidence, that's all. Just one more loop in the hangman's noose that the Fisherman will eventually put around his own neck. He tells himself not to think of it as part of a kid, part of a little girl named Irma, but as Exhibit A. He can feel dew wetting his sockless ankles and the cuffs of his pants, knows that any sort of extended stroll through the hay stubble is going to ruin a five-hundred-dollar pair of Gucci loafers. And so what if it does? He's rich well beyond the point of vulgarity; he can have as many shoes as Imelda Marcos, if he wants. The important thing is he's calm. Someone brought him a shoe box with a human foot inside it, laid it on his porch in the dark of night, but he's calm. It's evidence, that's all. And he? He is a coppice-man. Evidence is his meat and drink. He just needs to get a little air, needs to clear his nose of the rotted baloney smell that came puffing out of the box—

Jack makes a strangled gagging, urking sound and begins to hurry on a little faster. There is a sense of approaching climax growing in his mind (*my* calm *mind,* he tells himself). Something is getting ready to break . . . or change . . . or change *back.*

That last idea is particularly alarming and Jack begins to run across the field, knees lifting higher, arms pumping. His passage draws a dark line through the stubble, a diagonal that starts at the driveway and might end anywhere. Canada, maybe. Or the North Pole. White moths, startled out of their dew-heavy morning doze, flutter up in lacy swirls and then slump back into the cut stubble.

He runs faster, away from the chewed and bloody sneaker lying on the porch of the perfect house, away from his own horror. But that sense of coming climax stays with him. Faces begin to rise in his mind, each with its own accompanying snippet of sound track. Faces and voices he has ignored for twenty years or more. When these faces rise or those voices mutter, he has until now told himself the old lie, that once there was a frightened boy who caught his mother's neurotic terror like a cold and made up a story, a grand fantasy with good old Mom-saving Jack Sawyer at its center. None of it was real, and it was forgotten by the time he was sixteen. By then he was calm. Just as he's calm now, running across his north field like a lunatic, leaving that dark track and those clouds of startled moths behind him, but doing it *calmly.*

Narrow face, narrow eyes under a tilted white paper cap: *If you can run me out a keg when I need one, you can have the job.* Smokey Updike, from Oatley, New York, where they drank the beer and then ate the glass. Oatley, where there'd been something in the tunnel outside of town and where Smokey had kept him prisoner. Until—

Prying eyes, false smile, brilliant white suit: *I've met you before, Jack . . . where? Tell me. Confess.* Sunlight Gardener, an Indiana preacher whose name had also been Osmond. Osmond in some other world.

The broad, hairy face and frightened eyes of a boy who wasn't a boy at all: *This is a bad place, Jacky, Wolf knows.* And it was, it was a very bad place. They put him in a box, put good old Wolf in a box, and finally they killed him. Wolf died of a disease called America.

"Wolf!" the running man in the field gasps. "Wolf, ah, God, I'm sorry!"

Faces and voices, all those faces and voices, rising in front of his eyes, dinning into his ears, demanding to be seen and heard, filling him with that sense of climax, every defense on the verge of being washed away like a breakwater before a tidal wave.

Nausea roars through him and tilts the world. He makes that urking sound again, and this time it fills the back of his throat with a taste he remembers: the taste of cheap, rough wine. And suddenly it's New Hampshire again, Arcadia Funworld again. He and Speedy are standing beside the carousel again, all those frozen horses *("All carousel horses is named, don't you know that, Jack?"),* and Speedy is holding out a bottle of wine and telling him it's magic juice, one little sip and he'll go over, *flip over—*

"No!" Jack cries, knowing it's already too late. *"I don't want to go over!"*

The world tilts the other way and he falls into the grass on his hands and knees with his eyes squeezed shut. He doesn't need to open them; the richer, deeper smells that suddenly fill his nose tell him everything he needs to know. That, and the sense of coming home after so many dark years when almost every waking motion and decision has in some way been dedicated to canceling (or at least postponing) the arrival of this very moment.

This is Jack Sawyer, ladies and gentlemen, down on his knees in a vast field of sweet grass under a morning sky untainted by a single particle of pollution. He is weeping. He knows what has happened, and he is weeping. His heart bursts with fear and joy.

This is Jack Sawyer twenty years along, grown to be a man, and back in the Territories again at last.

It is the voice of his old friend Richard—sometimes known as Rational Richard—that saves him. Richard as he is now, head of his own law firm (Sloat & Associates, Ltd.), not Richard as he was when Jack perhaps knew him best, during long vacation days on Seabrook Island, in South Carolina. The Richard of

Seabrook Island had been imaginative, quick-spoken, fast on
his feet, mop-topped, skinny as a morning shadow. The current
Richard, Corporate Law Richard, is thinning on top, thick in
the middle, much in favor of sitting and Bushmills. Also, he
has crushed his imagination, so brilliantly playful in those
Seabrook Island days, like a troublesome fly. Richard Sloat's
life has been one of reduction, Jack has sometimes thought,
but one thing has been added (probably in law school): the
pompous, sheeplike sound of hesitation, particularly annoying
on the phone, which is now Richard's vocal signature. This
sound starts with the lips closed, then opens out as Richard's
lips spring wide, making him look like an absurd combination
of Vienna choirboy and Lord Haw-Haw.

Now, kneeling with his eyes shut in the vast green reach of
what used to be his very own north field, smelling the new,
deeper smells that he remembers so well and has longed for so
fiercely without even realizing it, Jack hears Richard Sloat
begin speaking in the middle of his head. What a relief those
words are! He knows it's only his own mind mimicking
Richard's voice, but it's still wonderful. If Richard were here,
Jack thinks he'd embrace his old friend and say, *May you pon-
tificate forever, Richie-boy. Sheep bray and all.*

Rational Richard says: *You realize you're dreaming, Jack,
don't you? . . .* ba-haaaa *. . . the stress of opening that package
no doubt . . .* ba-haaaa *. . . no doubt caused you to pass out, and
that in turn has caused . . .* ba-HAAAA! *. . . the dream you are
having now.*

Down on his knees, eyes still closed and hair hanging in his
face, Jack says, "In other words, it's what we used to call—"

*Correct! What we used to call . . . ba-haaaa . . .* "Seabrook
Island stuff." *But Seabrook Island was a long time ago, Jack, so
I suggest you open your eyes, get back on your feet, and remind yourself that should you see anything out of the ordinary . . . b'haa! . . . it's not really there.*

"Not really there," Jack murmurs. He stands up and opens
his eyes.

He knows from the very first look that it *is* really here, but
he holds Richard's pompous I-look-thirty-five-but-I'm-really-
sixty voice in his head, shielding himself with it. Thus he is able

to maintain a precarious balance instead of passing out for real, or—perhaps—cracking up entirely.

Above him, the sky is an infinitely clear dark blue. Around him, the hay and timothy is rib-high instead of ankle-high; there has been no Bunny Boettcher in this part of creation to cut it. In fact, there is no house back the way he came, only a picturesque old barn with a windmill standing off to one side.

*Where are the flying men?* Jack thinks, looking up into the sky, then shakes his head briskly. No flying men; no two-headed parrots; no werewolves. All that was Seabrook Island stuff, a neurosis he picked up from his mother and even passed on to Richard for a while. It was all nothing but . . . *ba-haaa* . . . bullshit.

He accepts this, knowing at the same time that the real bullshit would be not believing what's all around him. The smell of the grass, now so strong and sweet, mixed with the more flowery smell of clover and the deeper, basso profundo smell of black earth. The endless sound of the crickets in this grass, living their unthinking cricket lives. The fluttering white field moths. The unblemished cheek of the sky, not marked by a single telephone wire or electrical cable or jet contrail.

What strikes Jack most deeply, however, is the perfection of the field around him. There's a matted circle where he fell on his knees, the dew-heavy grass crushed to the ground. But there is no path *leading* to the circle, not a mark of passage through the wet and tender grass. He might have dropped out of the sky. That's impossible, of course, more Seabrook Island stuff, but—

"I *did* sort of fall out of the sky, though," Jack says in a remarkably steady voice. "I came here from Wisconsin. I *flipped* here."

Richard's voice protests this strenuously, exploding in a flurry of *hrrumph*s and *ba-haaa*s, but Jack hardly notices. It's just good old Rational Richard, doing his Rational Richard thing inside his head. Richard had lived through stuff like this once before and come out the other side with his mind more or less intact . . . but he'd been twelve. They'd both been twelve that fall, and when you're twelve, the mind and body are more elastic.

Jack has been turning in a slow circle, seeing nothing but

open fields (the mist over them now fading to a faint haze in the day's growing warmth) and blue-gray woods beyond them. Now there's something else. To the southwest, there's a dirt road about a mile away. Beyond it, at the horizon or perhaps just beyond, the perfect summer sky is a little stained with smoke.

*Not woodstoves,* Jack thinks, *not in July, but maybe small manufactories. And . . .*

He hears a whistle—three long blasts made faint with distance. His heart seems to grow large in his chest, and the corners of his mouth stretch up in a kind of helpless grin.

"The Mississippi's that way, by God," he says, and around him the field moths seem to dance their agreement, lace of the morning. "That's the Mississippi, or whatever they call it over here. And the whistle, friends and neighbors—"

Two more blasts roll across the making summer day. They are faint with distance, yes, but up close they would be mighty. Jack knows this.

"That's a riverboat. A damn big one. Maybe a paddle wheeler."

Jack begins to walk toward the road, telling himself that this is all a dream, not believing a bit of that but using it as an acrobat uses his balance pole. After he's gone a hundred yards or so, he turns and looks back. A dark line cuts through the timothy, beginning at the place where he landed and cutting straight to where he is. It is the mark of his passage. The *only* mark of it. Far to the left (in fact almost behind him now) are the barn and the windmill. *That's my house and garage,* Jack thinks. *At least that's what they are in the world of Chevrolets, Mideast warfare, and the* Oprah Winfrey *show.*

He walks on, and has almost reached the road when he realizes there is more than smoke in the southwest. There is a kind of vibration, as well. It beats into his head like the start of a migraine headache. And it's strangely variable. If he stands with his face pointed dead south, that unpleasant pulse is less. Turn east and it's gone. North and it's *almost* gone. Then, as he continues to turn, it comes all the way back to full. Worse than ever now that he's noticed it, the way the buzz of a fly or the knock of a radiator in a hotel room is worse after you really start to notice it.

Jack turns another slow, full circle. South, and the vibration sinks. East, it's gone. North, it's starting to come back. West, it's coming on strong. Southwest and he's locked in like the SEEK button on a car radio. Pow, pow, pow. A black and nasty vibration like a headache, a smell like ancient smoke . . .

"No, no, no, not smoke," Jack says. He's standing almost up to his chest in summer grass, pants soaked, white moths flittering around his head like a half-assed halo, eyes wide, cheeks once more pale. In this moment he looks twelve again. It is eerie how he has rejoined his younger (and perhaps better) self. "Not smoke, that smells like . . ."

He suddenly makes that urking sound again. Because the smell—not in his nose but in the center of his head—is rotted baloney. The smell of Irma Freneau's half-rotted, severed foot.

"I'm smelling him," Jack whispers, knowing it's not a smell he means. He can make that pulse whatever he wants . . . including, he realizes, gone. "I'm smelling the Fisherman. Either him or . . . I don't know."

He starts walking, and a hundred yards later he stops again. The pulse in his head is indeed gone. It has faded out the way radio stations do when the day warms and the temperature thickens. It's a relief.

Jack has almost reached the road, which no doubt leads one way to some version of Arden and the other way to versions of Centralia and French Landing, when he hears an irregular drumming sound. He feels it as well, running up his legs like a Gene Krupa backbeat.

He turns to the left, then shouts in mingled surprise and delight. Three enormous brown creatures with long, lolloping ears go leaping past Jack's position, rising above the grass, sinking back into it, then rising above it again. They look like rabbits crossed with kangaroos. Their protruding black eyes stare with comic terror. Across the road they go, their flat feet (white-furred instead of brown) slapping up dust.

"Christ!" Jack says, half-laughing and half-sobbing. He whacks himself in the center of his forehead with the heel of his palm. "What was that, Richie-boy? Got any comments on *that*?"

Richie, of course does. He tells Jack that Jack has just suffered an extremely vivid . . . *ba-haaa*! . . . hallucination.

"Of course," Jack says. "Giant bunny rabbits. Get me to the nearest A.A. meeting." Then, as he steps out onto the road, he looks toward the southwestern horizon again. At the haze of smoke there. A village. And do the residents fear as the shadows of the evening come on? Fear the coming of the night? Fear the creature that is taking their children? Do they need a coppiceman? Of course they do. Of course they—

Something is lying on the road. Jack bends down and picks up a Milwaukee Brewers baseball cap, jarringly out of place in this world of giant hopping range rabbits, but indubitably real. Judging from the plastic adjustment band in the back, it's a child's baseball cap. Jack looks inside, knowing what he'll find, and there it is, carefully inked on the bill: TY MARSHALL. The cap's not as wet as Jack's jeans, which are soaked with morning dew, but it's not dry, either. It has been lying here on the edge of the road, he thinks, since yesterday. The logical assumption would be that Ty's abductor brought Ty this way, but Jack doesn't believe that. Perhaps it is the lingering pulse of vibration that gives rise to a different thought, a different image: the Fisherman, with Ty carefully stashed away, walking out this dirt road. Under his arm is a wrapped shoe box decorated with bogus stamps. On his head is Ty's baseball hat, kind of balancing there because it's really too small for the Fisherman. Still, he doesn't want to change the adjustment band. Doesn't want Jack to mistake it for a man's cap, even for a single second. Because he is teasing Jack, inviting Jack into the game.

"Took the boy in our world," Jack mutters. "Escaped with him to *this* world. Stashed him someplace safe, like a spider stashing a fly. Alive? Dead? Alive, I think. Don't know why. Maybe it's just what I want to believe. Leave it. Then he went to wherever he stashed Irma. Took her foot and brought it to me. Brought it through *this* world, then flipped back to *my* world to leave it on the porch. Lost the hat on the way, maybe? Lost it off his head?"

Jack doesn't think so. Jack thinks this fuck, this skell, this world-hopping dirtbag, left the cap on purpose. Knew that if Jack walked this road he'd find it.

Holding the hat to his chest like a Miller Park fan showing respect to the flag during the national anthem, Jack closes his eyes and concentrates. It's easier than he would have expected, but he supposes some things you never forget—how to peel an orange, how to ride a bike, how to flip back and forth between worlds.

*Boy like you don't need no cheap wine, anyhow,* he hears his old friend Speedy Parker say, and there's the edge of a laugh in Speedy's voice. At the same time, that sense of vertigo twists through Jack again. A moment later he hears the alarming sound of an oncoming car.

He steps back, opening his eyes as he does so. Catches a glimpse of a tarred road—Norway Valley Road, but—

A horn blares and a dusty old Ford slams by him, the passenger side-view mirror less than nine inches from Jack Sawyer's nose. Warm air, once again filled with the faint but pungent odor of hydrocarbons, surfs over Jack's cheeks and brow, along with some farm kid's indignant voice:

"—hell out of the road, *assshollle—*"

"Resent being called an asshole by some cow-college graduate," Jack says in his best Rational Richard voice, and although he adds a pompous *Ba-haaa!* for good measure, his heart is pumping hard. Man, he'd almost flipped back right in front of that guy!

*Please, Jack, spare me,* Richard said. *You dreamed the whole thing.*

Jack knows better. Although he looks around himself in total amazement, the core of his heart isn't amazed at all, no, not even a little bit. He still has the cap, for one thing—Ty Marshall's Brewers cap. And for another, the bridge across Tamarack Creek is just over the next rise. In the other world, the one where giant rabbits went hopping past you, he has walked maybe a mile. In this one he's come at least *four.*

*That's the way it was before,* he thinks, *that's the way it was when Jacky was six. When everybody lived in California and nobody lived anywhere else.*

But that's wrong. Somehow wrong.

Jack stands at the side of the road that was dirt a few seconds ago and is tarred now, stands looking down into Ty Marshall's baseball cap and trying to figure out exactly what is wrong and *how* it's wrong, knowing he probably won't be able to turn the trick. All that was a long time ago, and besides, he's worked at burying his admittedly bizarre childhood memories since he was thirteen. More than half his life, in other words. A person can't dedicate that much time to forgetting, then suddenly just snap his fingers and expect—

Jack snaps his fingers. Says to the warming summer morning: "What happened when Jacky was six?" And answers his own question: "When Jacky was six, Daddy played the horn."

What does *that* mean?

"Not Daddy," Jack says suddenly. "Not *my* daddy. Dexter Gordon. The *tune* was called 'Daddy Played the Horn.' Or maybe the album. The LP." He stands there, shaking his head, then nods. "*Plays*. Daddy Plays. '*Daddy Plays the Horn.*' " And just like that it all comes back. Dexter Gordon playing on the hi-fi. Jacky Sawyer behind the couch, playing with his toy London taxi, so satisfying because of its weight, which somehow made it seem more real than a toy. His father and Richard's father talking. Phil Sawyer and Morgan Sloat.

*Imagine what this guy would be like over there,* Uncle Morgan had said, and that had been Jack Sawyer's first hint of the Territories. When Jacky was six, Jacky got the word. And—

"When Jacky was twelve, Jacky actually *went* there," he says.

*Ridiculous!* Morgan's son trumpets. *Utterly . . . ba-haaa! . . . ridiculous! Next you'll be telling me there really were men in the sky!*

But before Jack can tell his mental version of his old pal that or anything else, another car arrives. This one pulls up beside him. Looking suspiciously out of the driver's window (the expression is habitual, Jack has found, and means nothing in itself) is Elvena Morton, Henry Leyden's housekeeper.

"What in the tarnal are you doin' way down here, Jack Sawyer?" she asks.

He gives her a smile. "Didn't sleep very well, Mrs. Morton. Thought I'd take a little walk to clear my head."

"And do you always go walking through the dews and the damps when you want to clear your head?" she asks, casting her eyes down at his jeans, which are wet to the knee and even a bit beyond. "Does that help?"

"I guess I got lost in my own thoughts," he says.

"I guess you did," she says. "Get in and I'll give you a lift most of the way back to your place. Unless, that is, you've got a little more head clearing to do."

Jack has to grin. That's a good one. Reminds him of his late mother, actually. (When asked by her impatient son what was for dinner and when it would be served, Lily Cavanaugh was apt to say, "Fried farts with onions, wind pudding and air sauce for dessert, come and get it at ha' past a pickle.")

"I guess my head's as clear as I can expect today," he says, and goes around the front of Mrs. Morton's old brown Toyota. There's a brown bag on the passenger seat with leafy stuff poking out of it. Jack moves it to the middle, then sits down.

"I don't know if the early bird gets the worm," she says, driving on, "but the early shopper gets the best greens at Roy's, I can tell you that. Also, I like to get there before the layabouts."

"Layabouts, Mrs. Morton?"

She gives him her best suspicious look, eyes cutting to the side, right corner of her mouth quirked down as if at the taste of something sour.

"Take up space at the lunch counter and talk about the Fisherman this and the Fisherman that. Who he might be, *what* he might be—a Swede or a Pole or an Irish—and of course what they'll do to him when he's caught, which he would have been long ago if anyone but that nummie-squarehead Dale Gilbertson was in charge of things. So says they. Easy to take charge when you got your ass cozied down on one of Roy Soderholm's stools, cuppa coffee in one hand and a sinker in the other. So thinks I. Course, half of 'em's also got the unemployment check in their back pockets, but they won't talk about that. My father used to say, 'Show me a man who's too good to hay in July and I'll show you a man that won't turn a hand the rest of the year, neither.' "

Jack settles in the passenger bucket, knees against the dash, and watches the road unroll. They'll be back in no time. His pants are starting to dry and he feels oddly at peace. The nice thing about Elvena Morton is that you don't have to hold up your end of the conversation, because she is glad to take care of everything. Another Lily-ism occurs to him. Of a very talkative person (Uncle Morgan, for instance), she was apt to say that So-and-so's tongue was "hung in the middle and running on both ends."

He grins a little, and raises a casual hand to hide his mouth from Mrs. M. She'd ask him what was so funny, and what would he tell her? That he had just been thinking her tongue was hung in the middle? But it's also funny how the thoughts and memories are flooding back. Did he just yesterday try to call his mother, forgetting she was dead? That now seems like something he might have done in a different life. Maybe it *was* a different life. God knows he doesn't seem like the same man who swung his legs out of bed this morning, wearily, and with a feeling best described as doomish. He feels fully alive for the first time since . . . well, since Dale first brought him out this very same road, he supposes, and showed him the nice little place that had once belonged to Dale's father.

Elvena Morton, meanwhile, rolls on.

"Although I also admit that I take any excuse to get out of the house when he starts with the Mad Mongoloid," she says. The Mad Mongoloid is Mrs. Morton's term for Henry's Wisconsin Rat persona. Jack nods understanding, not knowing that before many hours are passed, he will be meeting a fellow nicknamed the Mad Hungarian. Life's little coincidences.

"It's always early in the morning that he takes it into his head to do the Mad Mongoloid, and I've told him, 'Henry, if you have to scream like that and say awful things and then play that awful music by kids who never should have been let near a *tuba,* let alone an *electrical guitar,* why do you do it in the morning when you know it spoils you for the whole day?' And it does, he gets a headache four times out of every five he pretends to be the Mad Mongoloid and by afternoon he's lying in his bedroom with an icebag on his poor forehead and not a bite of lunch will he take on those days, neither. Sometimes his supper will be gone when I check the next day—I always leave it in the same place in the refrigerator, unless he tells me he wants to cook himself—but half the time it's still there and even when it's gone I think that sometimes he just tips it down the garbage disposer."

Jack grunts. It's all he has to do. Her words wash over him and he thinks of how he will put the sneaker in a Baggie, handling it with the fire tongs, and when he turns it over at the police station, the chain of evidence will begin. He's thinking about how he needs to make sure there's nothing else in the sneaker box, and check the wrapping paper. He also wants to check those sugar packets. Maybe there's a restaurant name printed under the bird pictures. It's a long shot, but—

"And *he* says, 'Mrs. M., I can't help it. Some days I just wake up as the Rat. And although I pay for it later, there's such joy in it while the fit is on me. Such total *joy.*' And I asked him, I said, 'How can there be joy in music about children wanting to kill their parents and eat fetuses and have sex with animals'—as one of those songs really *was* about, Jack, I heard it clear as day—'and all of that?' I asked him, and he said— Uhhp, here we are."

They have indeed reached the driveway leading to Henry's house. A quarter of a mile further along is the roof of Jack's own place. His Ram pickup twinkles serenely in the driveway. He can't see his porch, most certainly can't see the horror that lies upon its boards, waiting for someone to clean it up. To clean it up in the name of decency.

"I *could* run you all the way up," she says. "Why don't I just do that?"

Jack, thinking of the sneaker and the rotten baloney smell hanging around it, smiles, shakes his head, and quickly opens the passenger door. "Guess I need to do a little more thinking after all," he says.

She looks at him with that expression of discontented suspicion which is, Jack suspects, love. She knows that Jack has brightened Henry Leyden's life, and for that alone he believes she loves him. He likes to hope so, anyway. It occurs to him that she never mentioned the baseball cap he's holding, but why would she? In this part of the world, every man's got at least four.

He starts up the road, hair flopping (his days of styled cuts at Chez-Chez on Rodeo Drive are long behind him now—this is the Coulee Country, and when he thinks of it at all, he gets his hair cut by old Herb Roeper down on Chase Street next to the Amvets), his gait as loose and lanky as a boy's. Mrs. Morton leans out her window and calls after him. "Change out of those jeans, Jack! The minute you get back! Don't let them dry on you! That's how arthritis starts!"

He raises a hand without turning and calls back, "Right!"

Five minutes later, he's walking up his own driveway again.

At least temporarily, the fear and depression have been burned out of him. The ecstasy as well, which is a relief. The last thing a coppiceman needs is to go charging through an investigation in a state of ecstasy.

As he sights the box on the porch—and the wrapping paper, and the feathers, and the ever-popular child's sneaker, can't forget that—Jack's mind turns back to Mrs. Morton quoting that great sage Henry Leyden.

*I can't help it. Some days I just wake up as the Rat. And although I pay for it later, there's such joy in it while the fit is on me. Such total* joy.

Total joy. Jack has felt this from time to time as a detective, sometimes while investigating a crime scene, more often while questioning a witness who knows more than he or she is telling . . . and this is something Jack Sawyer almost always knows, something he smells. He supposes carpenters feel that joy when they are carpentering particularly well, sculptors when they're having a good nose or chin day, architects when the lines are landing on their blueprints just right. The only problem is, someone in French Landing (maybe one of the surrounding towns, but Jack is guessing French Landing) gets that feeling of joy by killing children and eating parts of their little bodies.

Someone in French Landing is, more and more frequently, waking up as the Fisherman.

Jack goes into his house by the back door. He stops in the kitchen for the box of large-size Baggies, a couple of waste-basket liners, a dustpan, and the whisk broom. He opens the refrigerator's icemaker compartment and loads about half the cubes into one of the plastic liners—as far as Jack Sawyer is concerned, Irma Freneau's poor foot has reached its maximum state of decay.

He ducks into his study, where he grabs a yellow legal pad, a black marker, and a ballpoint pen. In the living room he gets the shorter set of fire tongs. And by the time he steps back onto the porch, he has pretty much put his secret identity as Jack Sawyer aside.

*I am COPPICEMAN,* he thinks, smiling. *Defender of the American Way, friend of the lame, the halt, and the dead.*

Then, as he looks down at the sneaker, surrounded by its pitiful little cloud of stink, the smile fades. He feels some of the tremendous mystery we felt when we first came upon Irma in the wreckage of the abandoned restaurant. He will do his absolute best to honor this remnant, just as we did our best to honor the child. He thinks of autopsies he has attended, of the true solemnity that lurks behind the jokes and butcher-shop crudities.

"Irma, is it you?" he asks quietly. "If it is, you help me, now. Talk to me. This is the time for the dead to help the living." Without thinking about it, Jack kisses his fingers and blows the kiss down toward the sneaker. He thinks, *I'd like to kill the man—or the thing—that did this. String him up alive and screaming while he filled his pants. Send him out in the stink of his own dirt.*

But such thoughts are not honorable, and he banishes them.

The first Baggie is for the sneaker with the remains of the foot inside it. Use the tongs. Zip it closed. Mark the date on the Baggie with the marker. Note the nature of the evidence on the pad with the ballpoint. Put it in the wastebasket liner with the ice in it.

The second is for the cap. No need for the tongs here; he's already handled the item. He puts it in the Baggie. Zips it closed. Marks the date, notes the nature of the evidence on the pad.

The third bag is for the brown wrapping paper. He holds it up for a moment in the tongs, examining the bogus bird stamps. MANUFACTURED BY DOMINO is printed below each picture, but that's all. No restaurant name, nothing of that sort. Into the Baggie. Zip it closed. Mark the date. Note the nature of the evidence.

He sweeps up the feathers and puts them in a fourth Baggie. There are more feathers in the box. He picks the box up with the tongs, dumps the feathers inside onto the dustpan, and then his heart takes a sudden hard leap in his chest, seeming to knock against the left side of his rib cage like a fist. Something is written on the box's bottom. The same Sharpie marker has been used to make the same straggling letters. And whoever wrote this knew who he was writing *to*. Not the outer Jack Sawyer, or else he—the Fisherman—would have no doubt called him Hollywood.

This message is addressed to the inner man, and to the child who was here before Jack "Hollywood" Sawyer was ever thought of.

> Try Ed's Eats and Dogs, coppiceman. Your fiend,
>
> THE FISHERMAN.

"Your fiend," Jack murmurs. "Yes." He picks up the box with the tongs and puts it into the second wastebasket liner; he doesn't have any Baggies quite big enough for it. Then he gathers all the evidence beside him in a neat little pile. This stuff always looks the same, at once grisly and prosaic, like the kind of photographs you used to see in those true-crime magazines.

He goes inside and dials Henry's number. He's afraid he'll get Mrs. Morton, but it turns out to be Henry instead, thank God. His current fit of Rat-ism has apparently passed, although there's a residue; even over the phone Jack can hear the faint thump and bray of "electrical guitars."

He knows Ed's Eats well, Henry says, but why in the world would *Jack* want to know about a place like that? "It's nothing but a wreck now; Ed Gilbertson died quite a time ago and there are people in French Landing who'd call that a blessing, Jack. The place was a ptomaine palace if ever there was one. A gutache waiting to happen. You'd have expected the board of health to shut him down, but Ed knew people. Dale Gilbertson, for one."

"The two of them related?" Jack asks, and when Henry replies "Fuck, yeah," something his friend would never say in the ordinary course of things, Jack understands that while Henry may have avoided a migraine this time, that Rat is still running in his head. Jack has heard similar bits of George Rathbun pop out from time to time, unexpected fat exultations from Henry's slim throat, and there is the way Henry often says good-bye, throwing a *Ding-dong* or *Ivey-divey* over his shoulder: that's just the Sheik, the Shake, the Shook coming up for air.

"Where exactly is it?" Jack asks.

"That's hard to say," Henry replies. He now sounds a bit testy. "Out by the farm equipment place . . . Goltz's? As I recall, the driveway's so long you might as well call it an access road. And if there was ever a sign, it's long gone. When Ed Gilbertson sold his last microbe-infested chili dog, Jack, you were probably in the first grade. What's all this about?"

Jack knows that what he's thinking of doing is ridiculous by normal investigatory standards—you don't invite a John Q. to a crime scene, especially not a murder scene—but this is no normal investigation. He has one piece of bagged evidence that he recovered in another world, how's that for abnormal? Of course he can find the long-defunct Ed's Eats; someone at Goltz's will no doubt point him right at it. But—

"The Fisherman just sent me one of Irma Freneau's sneakers," Jack says. "With Irma's foot still inside it."

Henry's initial response is a deep, sharp intake of breath.

"Henry? Are you all right?"

"Yes." Henry's voice is shocked but steady. "How terrible for the girl and her mother." He pauses. "And for you. For Dale." Another pause. "For this town."

"Yes."

"Jack, do you want me to take you to Ed's?"

Henry can do that, Jack knows. Easy as pie. Ivey-divey. And let's get real—why did he call Henry in the first place?

"Yes," he says.

"Have you called the police?"

"No."

*He'll ask me why not, and what will I say? That I don't want Bobby Dulac, Tom Lund, and the rest of them tromping around out there, mixing their scents with the doer's scent, until I get a chance to smell for myself? That I don't trust a mother's son of them not to fuck things up, and that includes Dale himself?*

But Henry doesn't ask. "I'll be standing at the end of my driveway," he said. "Just tell me when."

Jack calculates his remaining chores with the evidence, chores that will end with stowing everything in the lockbox in the bed of his truck. Reminds himself to take his cell phone, which usually does nothing but stand on its little charging device in his study. He'll want to call everything in as soon as he has seen Irma's remains in situ and finished that vital first walkthrough. Let Dale and his boys come then. Let them bring along the high school marching band, if they want to. He glances at his watch and sees that it's almost eight o'clock. How did it get so late so early? Distances are shorter in the other place, this he remembers, but does time go faster as well? Or has he simply lost track?

"I'll be there at eight-fifteen," Jack says. "And when we get to Ed's Eats, you're going to sit in my truck like a good little boy until I tell you you can get out."

"Understood, *mon capitaine.*"

"Ding-dong." Jack hangs up and heads back out to the porch.

Things aren't going to turn out the way Jack hopes. He's not going to get that clear first look and smell. In fact, by this afternoon the situation in French Landing, volatile already, will be on the verge of spinning out of control. Although there are many factors at work here, the chief cause of this latest escalation will be the Mad Hungarian.

There's a dose of good old small-town humor in this nickname, like calling the skinny bank clerk Big Joe or the trifocal-wearing bookstore proprietor Hawkeye. Arnold Hrabowski, at five foot six and one hundred and fifty pounds, is the smallest man on Dale Gilbertson's current roster. In fact, he's the smallest *person* on Dale's current roster, as both Debbi Anderson and Pam Stevens outweigh him and stand taller (at six-one, Debbi could eat scrambled eggs off Arnold Hrabowski's head). The Mad Hungarian is also a fairly inoffensive fellow, the sort of guy who continues to apologize for giving tickets no matter how many times Dale has told him that this is a very bad policy, and who has been known to start interrogations with such unfortunate phrases as *Excuse me, but I was wondering.* As a result, Dale keeps him on desk as much as possible, or downtown, where everyone knows him and most treat him with absent respect. He tours the county grammar schools as Officer Friendly. The little ones, unaware that they are getting their first lessons on the evils of pot from the Mad Hungarian, adore him. When he gives tougher lectures on dope, drink, and reckless driving at the high school, the kids doze or pass notes, although they do think the federally funded DARE car he drives—a low, sleek Pontiac with JUST SAY NO emblazoned on the doors—is way cool. Basically, Officer Hrabowski is about as exciting as a tuna on white, hold the mayo.

But in the seventies, you see, there was this relief pitcher for St. Louis and then the Kansas City Royals, a *very* fearsome fellow indeed, and his name was *Al* Hrabosky. He stalked rather than walked in from the bullpen, and before beginning to pitch (usually in the ninth inning with the bases juiced and the game on the line), Al Hrabosky would turn from the plate, lower his head, clench his fists, and pump them once, very hard, psyching himself up. Then he would turn and begin throwing nasty fastballs, many of them within kissing distance of the batters' chins. He was of course called the Mad Hungarian, and even a blind man could see he was the best damn reliever in the majors. And of course Arnold Hrabowski is now known, *must* be known, as the Mad Hungarian. He even tried to grow a Fu Manchu mustache a few years back, like the one the famed reliever wore. But whereas Al Hrabosky's Fu was as fearsome as Zulu warpaint, Arnold's only provoked chuckles—a Fu sprouting on that mild accountant's face, just imagine!—and so he shaved it off.

The Mad Hungarian of French Landing is not a bad fellow; he does his absolute level best, and under normal circumstances his level best is good enough. But these aren't ordinary days in French Landing, these are the slippery slippage days, the abbalah-opopanax days, and he is exactly the sort of officer of whom Jack is afraid. And this morning he is, quite without meaning to, going to make a bad situation very much worse.

The call from the Fisherman comes in to the 911 phone at 8:10 A.M., while Jack is finishing his notes on the yellow legal pad and Henry is strolling down his driveway, smelling the summer morning with great pleasure in spite of the shadow Jack's news has cast over his mind. Unlike some of the officers (Bobby Dulac, for instance), the Mad Hungarian reads the script taped next to the 911 phone word for word.

ARNOLD HRABOWSKI: Hello, this is the French Landing Police Department, Officer Hrabowski speaking. You've dialed 911. Do you have an emergency?

*[Unintelligible sound . . . throat-clearing?]*

AH: Hello? This is Officer Hrabowski answering on 911. Do you—

CALLER: Hello, asswipe.

AH: Who is this? Do you have an emergency?

C: You have an emergency. Not me. You.

AH: Who is this, please?

C: Your worst nightmare.

AH: Sir, could I ask you to identify yourself?

C: Abbalah. Abbalah-doon. [*Phonetic.*]

AH: Sir, I don't—

C: I'm the Fisherman.

[*Silence.*]

C: What's wrong? Scared? You ought to be scared.

AH: Sir. Ah, sir. There are penalties for false—

C: There are whips in hell and chains in shayol. [Caller may be saying "Sheol."]

AH: Sir, if I could have your name—

C: My name is legion. My number is many. I am a rat under the floor of the universe. Robert Frost said that. [*Caller laughs.*]

AH: Sir, if you hold, I can put on my chief—

C: Shut up and listen, asswipe. Your tape running? I hope so. I could shag [*Caller may be saying "scram" but word is indistinct*] it if I wanted to but I don't want to.

AH: Sir, I—

C: Kiss my scrote, you monkey. I left you one and I'm tired of waiting for you to find her. Try Ed's Eats and Dogs. Might be a little rotten now, but when she was new she was very [*Caller rolls r's, turning the word into "verrry"*] tasty.

AH: Where are you? Who is this? If this is a joke—

C: Tell the coppiceman I said hello.

When the call began, the Mad Hungarian's pulse was lub-dubbing along at a perfectly normal sixty-eight beats a minute. When it ends at 8:12, Arnold Hrabowski's ticker is in overdrive. His face is pale. Halfway through the call he looked at the Caller I.D. readout and wrote down the number displayed there with a hand shaking so badly that the numbers jigged up and down over three lines on his pad. When the Fisherman hangs up and he hears the sound of an open line, Hrabowski is so flustered that he tries to dial the callback on the red phone, forgetting that 911 is a one-way street. His fingers strike the smooth plastic front of the phone and he drops it back into the cradle with a frightened curse. He looks at it like something that has bitten him.

Hrabowski grabs the receiver from the black telephone beside 911, starts to punch in the callback, but his fingers betray him and hit two numbers at once. He curses again, and Tom Lund, passing by with a cup of coffee, says, "What's wrong there, Arnie?"

"Get Dale!" the Mad Hungarian shouts, startling Tom so badly he spills coffee on his fingers. "Get him out here *now!*"

"What the hell's wrong with y—"

*"NOW, goddamnit!"*

Tom stares at Hrabowski a moment longer, eyebrows raised, then goes to tell Dale that the Mad Hungarian seems to have really gone mad.

The second time Hrabowski tries, he succeeds in dialing the callback number. It rings. It rings. And it rings some more.

Dale Gilbertson appears with his own cup of coffee. There are dark circles under his eyes, and the lines at the corners of his mouth are a lot more prominent than they used to be.

"Arnie? What's—"

"Play back the last call," Arnold Hrabowski says. "I think it was . . . hello!" He barks this last, sitting forward behind the dispatch desk and shoving papers every which way. "Hello, who is this?"

Listens.

"It's the police, that's who it is. Officer Hrabowski, FLPD. Now you talk to me. Who is this?"

Dale, meanwhile, has got the earphones on his head and is listening to the most recent call to French Landing 911 with mounting horror. *Oh dear God,* he thinks. His first impulse—the very first—is to call Jack Sawyer and ask for help. To *bawl* for it, like a little kid with his hand caught in a door. Then he tells himself to take hold, that this is his job, like it or not, and he had better take hold and try to do it. Besides, Jack has gone up to Arden with Fred Marshall to see Fred's crazy wife. At least that was the plan.

Cops, meanwhile, are clustering around the dispatch desk: Lund, Tcheda, Stevens. What Dale sees when he looks at them is nothing but big eyes and pale, bewildered faces. And the ones on patrol? The ones currently off duty? No better. With the possible exception of Bobby Dulac, no better. He feels despair as well as horror. Oh, this is a nightmare. A truck with no brakes rolling downhill toward a crowded school playground.

He pulls the earphones off, tearing a small cut by his ear, not feeling it. "Where'd it come from?" he asks Hrabowski. The Mad Hungarian has hung up the telephone and is just sitting there, stunned. Dale grabs his shoulder and gives it a shake. *"Where'd it come from?"*

"The 7-Eleven," the Mad Hungarian replies, and Dale hears Danny Tcheda grunt. Not too far from where the Marshall boy's bike disappeared, in other words. "I just spoke with Mr. Rajan Patel, the day clerk. He says the callback number belongs to the pay phone, just outside."

"Did he see who made the call?"

"No. He was out back, taking a beer delivery."

"You positive Patel himself didn't—"

"Yeah. He's got an Indian accent. Heavy. The guy on 911 . . . Dale, you heard him. He sounded like *anybody.*"

"What's going on?" Pam Stevens asks. She has a good idea, though; they all do. It's just a question of details. "What's happened?"

Because it's the quickest way to get them up to speed, Dale replays the call, this time on speaker.

In the stunned silence that follows, Dale says: "I'm going out to Ed's Eats. Tom, you're coming with me."

"Yessir!" Tom Lund says. He looks almost ill with excitement.

"Four more cruisers to follow me." Most of Dale's mind is frozen; this procedural stuff skates giddily on top of the ice. *I'm okay at procedure and organization,* he thinks. *It's just catching the goddamn psycho murderer that's giving me a little trouble.* "All pairs. Danny, you and Pam in the first. Leave five minutes after Tom and I do. Five minutes by the clock, and no lights or siren. We're going to keep this quiet just as long as we can."

Danny Tcheda and Pam Stevens look at each other, nod, then look back at Dale. Dale is looking at Arnold "the Mad Hungarian" Hrabowski. He ticks off three more pairs, ending with Dit Jesperson and Bobby Dulac. Bobby is the only one he really wants out there; the others are just insurance and—God grant it not be necessary—crowd control. All of them are to come at five-minute intervals.

"Let me go out, too," Arnie Hrabowski pleads. "Come on, boss, what do you say?"

Dale opens his mouth to say he wants Arnie right where he is, but then he sees the hopeful look in those watery brown eyes. Even in his own deep distress, Dale can't help responding to that, at least a little. For Arnie, police life is too often standing on the sidewalk while the parade goes by.

*Some parade,* he thinks.

"I tell you what, Arn," he says. "When you finish all your other calls, buzz Debbi. If you can get her in here, you can come out to Ed's."

Arnold nods excitedly, and Dale almost smiles. The Mad Hungarian will have Debbi in here by nine-thirty, he guesses, even if he has to drag her by the hair like Alley Oop. "Who do I pair with, Dale?"

"Come by yourself," Dale says. "In the DARE car, why don't you? But, Arnie, if you leave this desk without relief waiting to drop into the chair the second you leave it, you'll be looking for a new job come tomorrow."

"Oh, don't worry," Hrabowski says, and, Hungarian or not, in his excitement he sounds positively Suh-vee-dish. Nor is that surprising, since Centralia, where he grew up, was once known as Swede Town.

"Come on, Tom," Dale says. "We'll grab the evidence kit on our—"

"Uh . . . boss?"

"*What,* Arnie?" Meaning, of course, *What now?*

"Should I call those State Police guys, Brown and Black?"

Danny Tcheda and Pam Stevens snicker. Tom smiles. Dale doesn't do either. His heart, already in the cellar, now goes even lower. *Subbasement, ladies and gentlemen—false hopes on your left, lost causes on your right. Last stop, everybody out.*

Perry Brown and Jeff Black. He had forgotten them, how funny. Brown and Black, who would now almost certainly take his case away from him.

"They're still out at the Paradise Motel," the Mad Hungarian goes on, "although I think the FBI guy went back to Milwaukee."

"I—"

"And County," the Hungarian plows relentlessly along. "Don't forget them. You want me to call the M.E. first, or the

evidence wagon?" The evidence wagon is a blue Ford Econoline van, packed with everything from quick-drying plaster for
taking tire impressions to a rolling video studio. Stuff the
French Landing P.D. will never have access to.

Dale stands where he is, head lowered, looking dismally at
the floor. They are going to take the case away from him. With
every word Hrabowski says, that is clearer. And suddenly he
wants it for his own. In spite of how he hates it and how it
scares him, he wants it with all his heart. The Fisherman is a
monster, but he's not a county monster, a state monster, or
a Federal Bureau of Investigation monster. The Fisherman is a
French Landing monster, *Dale Gilbertson's* monster, and he
wants to keep the case for reasons that have nothing to do with
personal prestige or even the practical matter of holding on to
his job. He wants him because the Fisherman is an offense
against everything Dale wants and needs and believes in. Those
are things you can't say out loud without sounding corny and
stupid, but they are true for all that. He feels a sudden, foolish
anger at Jack. If Jack had come on board sooner, maybe—

And if wishes were horses, beggars would ride. He has to
notify County, if only to get the medical examiner out at the
scene, and he has to notify the State Police, in the persons of
Detectives Brown and Black, as well. But not until he has a
look at what's out there, in the field beyond Goltz's. At what the
Fisherman has left. By God, not until then.

And, perhaps, has one final swing at the bastard.

"Get our guys rolling at five-minute intervals," he said, "just
as I told you. Then get Debbi in the dispatch chair. Have *her* call
State and County." Arnold Hrabowski's puzzled face makes
Dale feel like screaming, but somehow he retains his patience.
"I want some lead time."

"Oh," Arnie says, and then, when he actually *does* get it: *"Oh!"*

"And don't tell anyone other than our guys about the call or our
response. *Anyone.* You'd likely start a panic. Do you understand?"

"Absolutely, boss," says the Hungarian.

Dale glances at the clock: 8:26 A.M. "Come on, Tom," he
says. "Let's get moving. *Tempus fugit.*"

The Mad Hungarian has never been more efficient, and things
fall into place like a dream. Even Debbi Anderson is a good sport

about the desk. And yet through it all, the voice on the phone stays with him. Hoarse, raspy, with just a tinge of accent—the kind anyone living in this part of the world might pick up. Nothing unusual about that. Yet it haunts him. Not that the guy called him an asswipe—he's been called much worse by your ordinary Saturday night drunks—but some of the other stuff. *There are whips in hell and chains in shayol. My name is legion.* Stuff like that. And *abbalah.* What was an abbalah? Arnold Hrabowski doesn't know. He only knows that the very sound of it in his head makes him feel bad and scared. It's like a word in a secret book, the kind you might use to conjure up a demon.

When he gets the willies, there's only one person who can take them away, and that's his wife. He knows Dale told him not to tell anybody about what was going down, and he understands the reasons, but surely the chief didn't mean Paula. They have been married twenty years, and Paula isn't like another person at all. She's like the rest of him.

So (more in order to dispel his bad case of the willies than to gossip; let's at least give Arnold that much) the Mad Hungarian makes the terrible mistake of trusting his wife's discretion. He calls Paula and tells her that he spoke to the Fisherman not half an hour ago. Yes, really, the *Fisherman*! He tells her about the body that is supposedly waiting for Dale and Tom Lund out at Ed's Eats. She asks him if he's all right. Her voice is trembling with awe and excitement, and the Mad Hungarian finds this quite satisfying, since he's feeling awed and excited himself. They talk a little more, and when Arnold hangs up, he feels better. The terror of that rough, strangely knowing voice on the phone has receded a little.

Paula Hrabowski is discretion itself, the very soul of discretion. She tells only her two best friends about the call Arnie got from the Fisherman and the body at Ed's Eats, and swears them both to secrecy. Both say they will never tell a soul, and this is why, one hour later, even before the State Police and the county medical and forensics guys have been called, everyone knows that the police have found a slaughterhouse out at Ed's Eats. Half a dozen murdered kids.

Maybe more.

# 10

As the cruiser with Tom Lund behind the wheel noses down Third Street to Chase—roof-rack lights decorously dark, siren off—Dale takes out his wallet and begins digging through the mess in the back: business cards people have given him, a few dog-eared photographs, little licks of folded-over notebook paper. On one of the latter he finds what he wants.

"Whatcha doin', boss?" Tom asks.

"None of your beeswax. Just drive the car."

Dale grabs the phone from its spot on the console, grimaces and wipes off the residue of someone's powdered doughnut, then, without much hope, dials the number of Jack Sawyer's cell phone. He starts to smile when the phone is answered on the fourth ring, but the smile metamorphoses into a frown of puzzlement. He knows that voice and should recognize it, but—

"Hello?" says the person who has apparently answered Jack's cell phone. "Speak now, whoever you are, or forever hold your peace."

Then Dale knows. Would have known immediately if he had been at home or in his office, but in this context—

"Henry?" he says, knowing he sounds stupid but not able to help it. "Uncle Henry, is that you?"

Jack is piloting his truck across the Tamarack Bridge when the cell phone in his pants pocket starts its annoying little tweet. He takes it out and taps the back of Henry's hand with it. "Deal with this," he says. "Cell phones give you brain cancer."

"Which is okay for me but not for you."

"More or less, yeah."

"That's what I love about you, Jack," Henry says, and opens the phone with a nonchalant flick of the wrist. "Hello?" And, after a pause: "Speak now, whoever you are, or forever hold your peace." Jack glances at him, then back at the road. They're coming up on Roy's Store, where the early shopper gets the best greens. "Yes, Dale. It is indeed your esteemed—" Henry listens, frowning a little bit and smiling a little bit. "I'm in Jack's truck, with Jack," he says. "George Rathbun isn't working this morning because KDCU is covering the Summer Marathon over in La Riv—"

He listens some more, then says: "If it's a Nokia—which is what it feels like and sounds like—then it's digital rather than analog. Wait." He looks at Jack. "Your cell," he says. "It's a Nokia?"

"Yes, but why—"

"Because digital phones are supposedly harder to snoop," Henry says, and goes back to the phone. "It's a digital, and I'll put him on. I'm sure Jack can explain everything." Henry hands him the telephone, folds his hands primly in his lap, and looks out the window exactly as he would if surveying the scenery. *And maybe he is,* Jack thinks. *Maybe in some weird fruit-bat way, he really is.*

He pulls over to the shoulder on Highway 93. He doesn't like the cell phone to begin with—twenty-first-century slave bracelets, he thinks them—but he absolutely *loathes* driving while talking on one. Besides, Irma Freneau isn't going anywhere this morning.

"Dale?" he says.

"Where are you?" Dale asks, and Jack knows at once that the Fisherman has been busy elsewhere, too. *As long as it's not another dead kid,* he thinks. *Not that, not yet, please.* "How come you're with Henry? Is Fred Marshall there, too?"

Jack tells him about the change in plan, and is about to go on when Dale breaks in.

"Whatever you're doing, I want you to get your ass out to a place called Ed's Eats and Dawgs, near Goltz's. Henry can help you find it. The Fisherman called the station, Jack. He called 911. Told us Irma Freneau's body is out there. Well, not in so many words, but he did say *she*."

Dale is not quite babbling, but almost. Jack notes this as any good clinician would note the symptoms of a patient.

"I need you, Jack. I really—"

"That's where we were headed anyway," Jack says quietly, although they are going absolutely nowhere at this moment, just sitting on the shoulder while the occasional car blips past on 93.

*"What?"*

Hoping that Dale and Henry are right about the virtues of digital technology, Jack tells French Landing's police chief about his morning delivery, aware that Henry, although still looking out the window, is listening sharply. He tells Dale that Ty Marshall's cap was on top of the box with the feathers and Irma's foot inside it.

"Holy . . ." Dale says, sounding out of breath. "Holy shit."

"Tell me what you've done," Jack says, and Dale does. It sounds pretty good—so far, at least—but Jack doesn't like the part about Arnold Hrabowski. The Mad Hungarian has impressed him as the sort of fellow who will never be able to behave like a real cop, no matter how hard he tries. Back in L.A., they used to call the Arnie Hrabowskis of the world Mayberry RFDs.

"Dale, what about the phone at the 7-Eleven?"

"It's a *pay* phone," Dale says, as if speaking to a child.

"Yes, but there could be fingerprints," Jack says. "I mean, there are going to be *billions* of fingerprints, but forensics can isolate the freshest. *Easily*. He might have worn gloves, but maybe not. If he's leaving messages and calling cards as well as writing to the parents, he's gone Stage Two. Killing isn't enough for him anymore. He wants to play you now. Play *with* you. Maybe he even wants to be caught and stopped, like Son of Sam."

"The phone. Fresh fingerprints on the phone." Dale sounds badly humiliated, and Jack's heart goes out to him. "Jack, I can't do this. I'm lost."

This is something to which Jack chooses not to speak. Instead he says, "Who've you got who can see to the phone?"

"Dit Jesperson and Bobby Dulac, I guess."

Bobby, Jack thinks, is entirely too good to waste for long at the 7-Eleven outside town. "Just have them crisscross the phone with yellow tape and talk to the guy on duty. Then they can come on out to the site."

"Okay." Dale hesitates, then asks a question. The defeat in it, the sense of almost complete abrogation, makes Jack sad. "Anything else?"

"Have you called the State Police? County? Does that FBI guy know? The one who thinks he looks like Tommy Lee Jones?"

Dale snorts. "Uh . . . actually, I'd decided to sit on notification for a little while."

"Good," Jack says, and the savage satisfaction in his voice causes Henry to turn from his blind regard of the countryside and regard his friend instead, eyebrows raised.

Let us rise up again—on wings as eagles, as the Reverend Lance Hovdahl, French Landing's Lutheran pastor, might say—and fly down the black ribbon of Highway 93, back toward town. We reach Route 35 and turn right. Closer and to our right is the overgrown lane that leads not to a dragon's hidden gold or secret dwarf mines but to that peculiarly unpleasant black house. A little farther on, we can see the futuristic dome shape of Goltz's (well . . . it seemed futuristic in the seventies, at least). All our landmarks are in place, including the rubbly, weedy path that shoots off from the main road to the left. This is the track that leads to the remains of Ed Gilbertson's erstwhile palace of guilty pleasures.

Let us flutter onto the telephone line just across from this track. Hot gossip tickles our birdy feet: Paula Hrabowski's friend Myrtle Harrington passing on the news of the dead body (or bodies) at Ed's to Richie Bumstead, who will in turn pass it on to Beezer St. Pierre, grieving father and spiritual leader of the Thunder Five. This passage of voices through the wire probably shouldn't please us, but it does. Gossip is no doubt nasty stuff, but it *does* energize the human spirit.

Now, from the west comes the cruiser with Tom Lund at the wheel and Dale Gilbertson in the shotgun seat. And from the east comes Jack's burgundy-colored Ram pickup. They reach the turnoff to Ed's at the same time. Jack motions for Dale to go first, then follows him. We take wing, fly above and then ahead of them. We roost on the rusty Esso gas pump to watch developments.

Jack drives slowly down the lane to the half-collapsed building that stands in a scruff of high weeds and goldenrod. He's looking for any sign of passage, and sees only the fresh tracks made by Dale and Tom's police car.

"We've got the place to ourselves," he informs Henry.

"Yes, but for how long?"

*Not very* would have been Jack's answer, had he bothered to give one. Instead, he pulls up next to Dale's car and gets out. Henry rolls down his window but stays put, as ordered.

Ed's was once a simple wooden building about the length of a Burlington Northern boxcar and with a boxcar's flat roof. At the south end, you could buy sof'-serve ice cream from one of three windows. At the north end you could get your nasty hot dog or your even nastier order of fish and chips to go. In the middle was a small sit-down restaurant featuring a counter and red-top stools. Now the south end has entirely collapsed, probably from the weight of snow. All the windows have been broken in. There's some graffiti—So-and-so chugs cock, we fucked Patty Jarvis untill she howelled, TROY LUVS MARYANN— but not as much as Jack might have expected. All but one of the stools have been looted. Crickets are conversing in the grass. They're loud, but not as loud as the flies inside the ruined restaurant. There are *lots* of flies in there, a regular fly convention in progress. And—

"Do you smell it?" Dale asks him.

Jack nods. Of course he does. He's smelled it already today, but now it's worse. Because there's more of Irma out here to send up a stink. Much more than what would fit into a single shoe box.

Tom Lund has produced a handkerchief and is mopping his broad, distressed face. It's warm, but not warm enough to account for the sweat streaming off his face and brow. And his skin is pasty.

"Officer Lund," Jack says.

"Huh!" Tom jumps and looks rather wildly around at Jack.

"You may have to vomit. If you feel you must, do it over

there." Jack points to an overgrown track, even more ancient and ill-defined than the one leading in from the main road. This one seems to meander in the direction of Goltz's.

"I'll be okay," Tom says.

"I know you will. But if you need to unload, don't do it on what may turn out to be evidence."

"I want you to start stringing yellow tape around the entire building," Dale tells his officer. "Jack? A word?"

Dale puts a hand on Jack's forearm and starts walking back toward the truck. Although he's got a good many things on his mind, Jack notices how strong that hand is. And no tremble in it. Not yet, anyway.

"What is it?" Jack asks impatiently when they're standing near the passenger window of the truck. "We want a look before the whole world gets here, don't we? Wasn't that the idea, or am I—"

"You need to get the foot, Jack," Dale says. And then: "Hello, Uncle Henry, you look spiff."

"Thanks," Henry says.

"What are you talking about?" Jack asks. "That foot is *evidence.*"

Dale nods. "I think it ought to be evidence found here, though. Unless, of course, you relish the idea of spending twenty-four hours or so answering questions in Madison."

Jack opens his mouth to tell Dale not to waste what little time they have with arrant idiocies, then closes it again. It suddenly occurs to him how his possession of that foot might look to minor-league smarties like Detectives Brown and Black. Maybe even to a major-league smarty like John Redding of the FBI. Brilliant cop retires at an impossibly young age, and to the impossibly bucolic town of French Landing, Wisconsin. He has plenty of scratch, but the source of income is blurry, to say the least. And oh, look at this, all at once there's a serial killer operating in the neighborhood.

Maybe the brilliant cop has got a loose screw. Maybe he's like those firemen who enjoy the pretty flames so much they get into the arson game themselves. Certainly Dale's Color Posse would have to wonder why the Fisherman would send an early retiree like Jack a victim's body part. *And the hat,* Jack thinks. *Don't forget Ty's baseball cap.*

All at once he knows how Dale felt when Jack told him that the phone at the 7-Eleven had to be cordoned off. *Exactly.*

"Oh man," he says. "You're right." He looks at Tom Lund, industriously running yellow POLICE LINE tape while butterflies dance around his shoulders and the flies continue their drunken buzzing from the shadows of Ed's Eats. "What about him?"

"Tom will keep his mouth shut," Dale says, and on that Jack decides to trust him. He wouldn't, had it been the Hungarian.

"I owe you one," Jack says.

"Yep," Henry agrees from his place in the passenger seat. "Even a blind man could see he owes you one."

"Shut up, Uncle Henry," Dale says.

"Yes, *mon capitaine.*"

"What about the cap?" Jack asks.

"If we find anything else of Ty Marshall's . . ." Dale pauses, then swallows. "Or Ty himself, we'll leave it. If not, you keep it for the time being."

"I think maybe you just saved me a lot of major irritation," Jack says, leading Dale to the back of the truck. He opens the stainless steel box behind the cab, which he hasn't bothered to lock for the run out here, and takes out one of the trash-can liners. From inside it comes the slosh of water and the clink of a few remaining ice cubes. "The next time you get feeling dumb, you might remind yourself of that."

Dale ignores this completely. "Ohgod," he says, making it one word. He's looking at the Baggie that has just emerged from the trash-can liner. There are beads of water clinging to the transparent sides.

"The *smell* of it!" Henry says with undeniable distress. "Oh, the poor child!"

"You can smell it even through the plastic?" Jack asks.

"Yes indeed. And coming from there." Henry points at the ruined restaurant and then produces his cigarettes. "If I'd known, I would have brought a jar of Vicks and an El Producto."

In any case, there's no need to walk the Baggie with the gruesome artifact inside it past Tom Lund, who has now disappeared behind the ruins with his reel of yellow tape.

"Go on in," Dale instructs Jack quietly. "Get a look and take care of the thing in that Baggie if you find . . . you know . . . her. I want to speak to Tom."

Jack steps through the warped, doorless doorway into the thickening stench. Outside, he can hear Dale instructing Tom to send Pam Stevens and Danny Tcheda back down to the end of the access road as soon as they arrive, where they will serve as passport control.

The interior of Ed's Eats will probably be bright by afternoon, but now it is shadowy, lit mostly by crazed, crisscrossing rays of sun. Galaxies of dust spin lazily through them. Jack steps carefully, wishing he had a flashlight, not wanting to go back and get one from the cruiser until he's taken care of the foot. (He thinks of this as "redeployment.") There are human tracks through the dust, trash, and drifts of old gray feathers. The tracks are man-sized. Weaving in and out of them are a dog's pawprints. Off to his left, Jack spies a neat little pile of droppings. He steps around the rusty remains of an overturned gas grill and follows both sets of tracks around the filthy counter. Outside, the second French Landing cruiser is rolling up. In here, in this darker world, the sound of the flies has become a soft roar and the stench . . . the *stench* . . .

Jack fishes a handkerchief from his pocket and places it over his nose as he follows the tracks into the kitchen. Here the pawprints multiply and the human footprints disappear completely. Jack thinks grimly of the circle of beaten-down grass he made in the field of that other world, a circle with no path of beaten-down grass leading to it.

Lying against the far wall near a pool of dried blood is what remains of Irma Freneau. The mop of her filthy strawberry-blond hair mercifully obscures her face. Above her on a rusty piece of tin that probably once served as a heat shield for the deep-fat fryers, two words have been written with what Jack feels sure was a black Sharpie marker:

Hello boys

"Ah, *fuck,*" Dale Gilbertson says from almost directly behind him, and Jack nearly screams.

Outside, the snafu starts almost immediately.

Halfway back down the access road, Danny and Pam (not in the least disappointed to have been assigned guard duty once

they have actually seen the slumped ruin of Ed's and smelled
the aroma drifting from it) nearly have a head-on with an old
International Harvester pickup that is bucketing toward Ed's at
a good forty miles an hour. Luckily, Pam swings the cruiser to
the right and the driver of the pickup—Teddy Runkleman—
swings left. The vehicles miss each other by inches and swerve
into the grass on either side of this poor excuse for a road. The
pickup's rusty bumper thumps against a small birch.

Pam and Danny get out of their unit, hearts pumping, adrenaline spurting. Four men come spilling out of the pickup's cab
like clowns out of the little car in the circus. Mrs. Morton would
recognize them all as regulars at Roy's Store. Layabouts, she
would call them.

"What in the name of God are you *doing*?" Danny Tcheda
roars. His hand drops to the butt of his gun and then falls away
a bit reluctantly. He's getting a headache.

The men (Runkleman is the only one the officers know by
name, although between them they recognize the faces of the
other three) are goggle-eyed with excitement.

"How many ja find?" one of them spits. Pam can actually see
the spittle spraying out in the morning air, a sight she could
have done without. "How many'd the bastid kill?"

Pam and Danny exchange a single dismayed look. And before they can reply, holy God, here comes an old Chevrolet Bel
Air with another four or five men inside it. No, one of them is
a woman. They pull up and spill out, also like clowns from the
little car.

*But we're the real clowns,* Pam thinks. *Us.*

Pam and Danny are surrounded by eight semihysterical men
and one semihysterical woman, all of them throwing questions.

"Hell, I'm going up there and see for myself!" Teddy Runkleman shouts, almost jubilantly, and Danny realizes the situation is on the verge of spinning out of control. If these fools get
the rest of the way up the access road, Dale will first tear him a
new asshole and then salt it down.

*"HOLD IT RIGHT THERE, ALL OF YOU!"* he bawls, and
actually draws his gun. It's a first for him, and he hates the
weight of it in his hand—these are ordinary people, after all,
not bad guys—but it gets their attention.

"This is a crime scene," Pam says, finally able to speak in a normal tone of voice. They mutter and look at one another; worst fears confirmed. She steps to the driver of the Chevrolet. "Who are you, sir? A Saknessum? You look like a Saknessum."

"Freddy," he admits.

"Well, you get back in your vehicle, Freddy Saknessum, and the rest of you who came with him also get in, and you back the hell right out of here. Don't bother trying to turn around, you'll just get stuck."

"But—" the woman begins. Pam thinks she's a Sanger, a clan of fools if ever there was one.

"Stow it and go," Pam tells her.

"And you right behind him," Danny tells Teddy Runkleman. He just hopes to Christ no more will come along, or they'll end up trying to manage a parade in reverse. He doesn't know how the news got out, and at this moment can't afford to care. "Unless you want a summons for interfering with a police investigation. That can get you five years." He has no idea if there is such a charge, but it gets them moving even better than the sight of his pistol.

The Chevrolet backs out, rear end wagging from side to side like a dog's tail. Runkleman's pickup goes next, with two of the men standing up in back and peering over the cab, trying to catch sight of the old restaurant's roof, at least. Their curiosity lends them a look of unpleasant vacuity. The P.D. unit comes last, herding the old car and older truck like a corgi herding sheep, roof-rack lights now pulsing. Pam is forced to ride mostly on the brake, and as she drives she lets loose a low-pitched stream of words her mother never taught her.

"Do you kiss your kids good-night with that mouth?" Danny asks, not without admiration.

"Shut up," she says. Then: "You got any aspirin?"

"I was going to ask you the same thing," Danny says.

They get back out to the main road just in time. Three more vehicles are coming from the direction of French Landing, two from the direction of Centralia and Arden. A siren rises in the warming air. Another cruiser, the third in what was supposed to be an unobtrusive line, is coming along, passing the lookie-loos from town.

"Oh man." Danny sounds close to tears. "Oh man, oh man, oh man. It's gonna be a carnival, and I bet the staties *still* don't know. They'll have kittens. *Dale* is gonna have kittens."

"It'll be all right," Pam says. "Calm down. We'll just pull across the road and park. Also stick your gun back in the fucking holster."

"Yes, Mother." He stows his piece as Pam swings across the access road, pulling back to let the third cruiser through, then pulling forward again to block the way. "Yeah, maybe we caught it in time to put a lid on it."

"Course we did."

They relax a little. Both of them have forgotten the old stretch of road that runs between Ed's and Goltz's, but there are plenty of folks in town who know about it. Beezer St. Pierre and his boys, for instance. And while Wendell Green does not, guys like him always seem able to find the back way. They've got an instinct for it.

# 11

Beezer's journey began with Myrtle Harrington, the loving wife of Michael Harrington, whispering down the telephone line to Richie Bumstead, on whom she has an industrial-strength crush in spite of his having been married to her second-best friend, Glad, who dropped down dead in her kitchen at the amazing age of thirty-one. For his part, Richie Bumstead has had enough macaroni-tuna casseroles and whisper-voiced phone calls from Myrtle to last him through two more lifetimes, but this is one set of whispers he's glad, even oddly relieved, to listen to, because he drives a truck for the Kingsland Brewing Company and has come to know Beezer St. Pierre and the rest of the boys, at least a little bit.

At first, Richie thought the Thunder Five was a bunch of hoodlums, those big guys with scraggly shoulder-length hair and foaming beards roaring through town on their Harleys, but one Friday he happened to be standing alongside the one called Mouse in the pay-window line, and Mouse looked down at him and said something funny about how working for love never made the paycheck look bigger, and they got into a conversation that made Richie Bumstead's head spin. Two nights later he saw Beezer St. Pierre and the one called Doc shooting the breeze in the yard when he came off-shift, and after he got his rig locked down for the night he went over and got into another conversation that made him feel like he'd walked into a combination of a raunchy blues bar and a *Jeopardy!* championship. These guys—Beezer, Mouse, Doc, Sonny, and Kaiser Bill—looked like rockin', stompin', red-eyed violence, but they were *smart.* Beezer, it turned out, was head brewmaster in Kingsland Ale's special-projects division, and the other guys were just under him. They had all gone to *college.* They were interested in making great beer and having a good time, and Richie sort of wished he could get a bike and let it all hang out like them, but a long Saturday afternoon and evening at the Sand Bar proved that the line between a high old time and utter abandon was too fine for him. He didn't have the stamina to put away two pitchers of Kingsland, play a decent game of pool, drink two more pitchers while talking about the influences of Sherwood Anderson and Gertrude Stein on the young Hemingway, get into some serious head-butting, put down another couple of pitchers, emerge clearheaded enough to go barrel-assing through the countryside, pick up a couple of experimental Madison girls, smoke a lot of high-grade shit, and romp until dawn. You have to respect people who can do that and still hold down good jobs.

As far as Richie is concerned, he has a *duty* to tell Beezer that the police have finally learned the whereabouts of Irma Freneau's body. That busybody Myrtle said it was a secret Richie has to keep to himself, but he's pretty sure that right after Myrtle gave him the news, she called four or five other people. Those people will call their best friends, and in no time at all half of French Landing is going to be heading over on 35 to be in on the action. Beezer has a better right to be there than most, doesn't he?

Less than thirty seconds after getting rid of Myrtle Harrington, Richie Bumstead looks up Beezer St. Pierre in the directory and dials the number.

"Richie, I sure hope you aren't shitting me," Beezer says.

"He called in, yeah?" Beezer wants Richie to repeat it. "That worthless piece of shit in the DARE car, the Mad Hungarian? . . . And he said the girl was *where*?"

"Fuck, the whole town is gonna be out there," Beezer says. "But thanks, man, thanks a lot. I owe you." In the instant before the receiver slams down, Richie thinks he hears Beezer start to say something else that gets dissolved in a scalding rush of emotion.

And in the little house on Nailhouse Row, Beezer St. Pierre swipes tears into his beard, gently moves the telephone a few inches back on the table, and turns to face Bear Girl, his common-law spouse, his old lady, Amy's mother, whose real name is Susan Osgood, and who is staring up at him from beneath her thick blond bangs, one finger holding her place in a book.

"It's the Freneau girl," he says. "I gotta go."

"Go," Bear Girl tells him. "Take the cell phone and call me as soon as you can."

"Yeah," he says, and plucks the cell phone from its charger and rams it into a front pocket of his jeans. Instead of moving to the door, he thrusts a hand into the huge red-brown tangle of his beard and absentmindedly combs it with his fingers. His feet are rooted to the floor; his eyes have lost focus. "The Fisherman called 911," he says. "Can you believe this shit? They couldn't find the Freneau girl by themselves, they needed *him* to tell them where to find her body."

"Listen to me," Bear Girl says, and gets up and travels the space between them far more quickly than she seems to. She snuggles her compact little body into his massive bulk, and Beezer inhales a chestful of her clean, soothing scent, a combination of soap and fresh bread. "When you and the boys get out there, it's going to be up to you to keep them in line. So you have to keep *yourself* in line, Beezer. No matter how angry you are, you can't go nuts and start beating on people. Cops especially."

"I suppose you think I shouldn't go."

"You have to. I just don't want you to wind up in jail."

"Hey," he says, "I'm a brewer, not a brawler."

"Don't forget it," she says, and pats him on the back. "Are you going to call them?"

"Street telephone." Beezer walks to the door, bends down to pick up his helmet, and marches out. Sweat slides down his forehead and crawls through his beard. Two strides bring him to his motorcycle. He puts one hand on the saddle, wipes his forehead, and bellows, "THE FUCKING FISHERMAN TOLD THAT FUCKING HUNGARIAN COP WHERE TO FIND IRMA FRENEAU'S BODY. WHO'S COMING WITH ME?"

On both sides of Nailhouse Row, bearded heads pop out of windows and loud voices shout "Wait Up!" "Holy Shit!" and "Yo!" Four vast men in leather jackets, jeans, and boots come barreling out of four front doors. Beezer almost has to smile—he loves these guys, but sometimes they remind him of cartoon characters. Even before they reach him, he starts explaining about Richie Bumstead and the 911 call, and by the time he finishes, Mouse, Doc, Sonny, and Kaiser Bill are on their bikes and waiting for the signal.

"But this here's the deal," Beezer says. "Two things. We're going out there for Amy and Irma Freneau and Johnny Irkenham, not for ourselves. We want to make sure everything gets done the right way, and we're not gonna bust anybody's head open, not unless they ask for it. You got that?"

The others rumble, mumble, and grumble, apparently in assent. Four tangled beards wag up and down.

"And number two, when we *do* bust open somebody's head, it's gonna be the Fisherman's. Because we have put up with enough crap around here, and now I am pretty damn sure it's our turn to hunt down the fucking bastard who killed my little girl—" Beezer's voice catches in his throat, and he raises his fist before continuing. "And dumped this other little girl in that fucking shack out on 35. Because I am going to get my hands on that fucking fuckhead, and when I do, I am gonna get RIGHTEOUS on his ass!"

His boys, his crew, his posse shake their fists in the air and bellow. Five motorcycles surge noisily into life. "We'll take a look at the place from the highway and double back to the road behind Goltz's," Beezer shouts, and charges down the road and uphill on Chase Street with the others in his slipstream.

Through the middle of town they roll, Beezer in the lead, Mouse and Sonny practically on his tailpipe, Doc and the Kaiser right behind, their beards flowing in the wind. The thunder of their bikes rattles the windows in Schmitt's Allsorts and sends starlings flapping up from the marquee of the Agincourt Theater. Hanging over the bars of his Harley, Beezer looks a little bit like King Kong getting set to rip apart a jungle gym. Once they get past the 7-Eleven, Kaiser and Doc move up alongside Sonny and Mouse and take up the entire width of the highway. People driving west on 35 look at the figures charging toward them and swerve onto the shoulder; drivers who see them in their rearview mirrors drift to the side of the road, stick their arms out of their windows, and wave them on.

As they near Centralia, Beezer passes about twice as many cars as really ought to be traveling down a country highway on a weekend morning. The situation is even worse than he figured it would be: Dale Gilbertson is bound to have a couple of cops blocking traffic turning in from 35, but two cops couldn't handle more than ten or twelve ghouls dead set on seeing, really *seeing*, the Fisherman's handiwork. French Landing doesn't have enough cops to keep a lid on all the screwballs homing in on Ed's Eats. Beezer curses, picturing himself losing control, turning a bunch of twisted Fisherman geeks into tent pegs. Losing control is exactly what he cannot afford to do, not if he expects any cooperation from Dale Gilbertson and his flunkies.

Beezer leads his companions around a crapped-out old red Toyota and is visited by an idea so perfect that he forgets to strike unreasoning terror into the beater's driver by looking him in the eye and snarling, "I make Kingsland Ale, the best beer in the world, you dimwit cur." He has done this to two drivers this morning, and neither one let him down. The people who earn this treatment by either lousy driving or the possession of a truly ugly vehicle imagine that he is threatening them with some grotesque form of sexual assault, and they freeze like rabbits, they stiffen right up. Jolly good fun, as the citizens of Emerald City sang in *The Wizard of Oz*. The idea that has distracted Beezer from his harmless pleasures possesses the simplicity of most valid inspirations. *The best way to get cooperation is to give it.* He knows exactly how to soften up Dale Gilbertson: the answer is putting on a baseball cap, grabbing its car keys, and heading out the door—the answer lies all around him.

One small part of that answer sits behind the wheel of the red Toyota just being overtaken by Beezer and his jolly crew. Wendell Green earned the mock rebuke he failed to receive on both of the conventional grounds. His little car may not have been ugly to begin with, but by now it is so disfigured by multiple dents and scrapes that it resembles a rolling sneer; and Green drives with an unyielding arrogance he thinks of as "dash." He zooms through yellow lights, changes lanes recklessly, and tailgates as a means of intimidation. Of course, he blasts his horn at the slightest provocation. Wendell is a menace. The way he handles his car perfectly expresses his character, being inconsiderate, thoughtless, and riddled with grandiosity. At the moment, he is driving even worse than usual, because as he tries to overtake every other vehicle on the road, most of his concentration is focused on the pocket tape recorder he holds up to his mouth and the golden words his equally golden voice pours into the precious machine. (Wendell often regrets the shortsightedness of the local radio stations in devoting so much air time to fools like George Rathbun and Henry Shake, when they could move up to a new level simply by letting him give an ongoing commentary on the news for an hour or so every day.) Ah, the delicious combination of Wendell's words and Wendell's voice—Edward R. Murrow in his heyday never sounded so eloquent, so resonant.

Here is what he is saying: *This morning I joined a virtual caravan of the shocked, the grieving, and the merely curious in a mournful pilgrimage winding eastward along bucolic Highway 35. Not for the first time, this journalist was struck, and struck deeply, by the immense contrast between the loveliness and peace of the Coulee Country's landscape and the ugliness and savagery one deranged human being has wrought in its unsuspecting bosom. New paragraph.*

*The news had spread like wildfire. Neighbor called neighbor, friend called friend. According to a morning 911 call to the French Landing police station, the mutilated body of little Irma Freneau lies within the ruins of a former ice-cream parlor and café called Ed's Eats and Dawgs. And who had placed the call? Surely, some dutiful citizen. Not at all, ladies and gentlemen, not at all . . .*

Ladies and gentlemen, this is frontline reportage, this is the news being written *while it happens,* a concept that cannot but murmur "Pulitzer Prize" to an experienced journalist. The scoop had come to Wendell Green by way of his barber, Roy Royal, who heard it from his wife, Tillie Royal, who had been clued in by Myrtle Harrington herself, and Wendell Green has done his duty to his readers: he grabbed his tape recorder and his camera and ran out to his nasty little vehicle without pausing to telephone his editors at the *Herald.* He doesn't need a photographer; he can take all the photographs he needs with that dependable old Nikon F2A on the passenger seat. A seamless blend of words and pictures—a penetrating examination of

the new century's most hideous crime—a thoughtful explo-
ration into the nature of evil—a compassionate portrayal of one
community's suffering—an unsparing exposé of one police department's ineptitude—

With all this going on in his mind as his mellifluous words
drip one by one into the microphone of his upheld cassette
recorder, is it any wonder that Wendell Green fails to hear the
sound of motorcycles, or to take in the presence of the Thunder
Five in any way, until he happens to glance sideways in search
of the perfect phrase? Glance sideways he does, and with a spurt
of panic observes, no more than two feet to his left, Beezer St.
Pierre astride his roaring Harley, apparently singing, to judge
from his own moving lips

                    singing
                      huh?

Can't be, nope. In Wendell's experience, Beezer St. Pierre is
far more likely to be cursing like a navvy in a waterfront brawl.
When, after the death of Amy St. Pierre, Wendell, who was
merely obeying the ancient rules of his trade, dropped in at 1
Nailhouse Row, and inquired of the grieving father how it felt to
know that his daughter had been slaughtered like a pig and partially eaten by a monster in human form, Beezer had gripped the
innocent newshound by the throat, unleashed a torrent of obscenities, and concluded by bellowing that if he should ever see
Mr. Green again, he would tear off his head and use the stump
as a sexual orifice.

It is this threat that causes Wendell's moment of panic. He
glances into his rearview mirror and sees Beezer's cohorts
strung out across the road like an invading army of Goths. In
his imagination, they are waving skulls on ropes made of
human skin and yelling about what they are going to do to his
neck after they rip his head off. Whatever he was about to dic-
tate into the invaluable machine instantly evaporates, along
with his daydreams of winning the Pulitzer Prize. His stomach
clenches, and sweat bursts from every pore on his broad, ruddy
face. His left hand trembles on the wheel, his right shakes the
cassette recorder like a castanet. Wendell lifts his foot from the
accelerator and slides down on the car seat, turning his head as
far to the right as he dares. His basic desire is to curl up in the

well beneath the dashboard and pretend to be a fetus. The huge roar of sound behind him grows louder, and his heart leaps in his chest like a fish. Wendell whimpers. A rank of kettledrums batters the air beyond the fragile skin of the car door.

Then the motorcycles swoop past him and race off up the highway. Wendell Green wipes his face. Slowly, he persuades his body to sit up straight. His heart ceases its attempt to escape his chest. The world on the other side of his windshield, which had contracted to the size of a housefly, expands back to its normal size. It occurs to Wendell that he was no more afraid than any normal human being would be, under the circumstances. Self-regard fills him like helium fills a balloon. Most guys he knows would have driven right off the road, he thinks; most guys would have crapped in their pants. What did Wendell Green do? He slowed down a little, that's all. He acted like a gentleman and let the assholes of the Thunder Five drive past him. When it comes to Beezer and his apes, Wendell thinks, being a gentleman is the better part of valor. He picks up speed, watching the bikers race on ahead.

In his hand, the cassette recorder is still running. Wendell raises it to his mouth, licks his lips, and discovers that he has forgotten what he was going to say. Blank tape whirls from spool to spool. "Damn," he says, and pushes the OFF button. An inspired phrase, a melodious cadence, has vanished into the ether, perhaps for good. But the situation is far more frustrating than that. It seems to Wendell that a whole series of logical connections has vanished with the lost phrase: he can remember seeing the shape of a vast outline for at least half a dozen penetrating articles that would go beyond the Fisherman to . . . do what? Win him the Pulitzer, for sure, but how? The area in his mind that had given him the immense outline still holds its shape, but the shape is empty. Beezer St. Pierre and his goons murdered what now seems the greatest idea Wendell Green ever had, and Wendell has no certainty that he can bring it back to life.

What are these biker freaks doing out here, anyhow?

The question answers itself: some creepy do-gooder thought Beezer ought to know about the Fisherman's 911 call, and now the biker freaks are headed to the ruins of Ed's, just like him. Fortunately, so many other people are going to the same place that Wendell figures he can steer clear of his nemesis. Taking no chances, he drops a couple of cars behind the bikers.

The traffic thickens and slows down; up ahead, the bikers form a single line and zoom up alongside the line crawling toward the dusty old lane to Ed's place. From seventy or eighty yards back, Wendell can see two cops, a man and a woman, trying to wave the rubberneckers along. Every time a fresh car pulls up in front of them, they have to go through the same pantomine of turning its occupants away and pointing down the road. To reinforce the message, a police car is parked sideways across the lane, blocking anyone who should try to get fancy. This spectacle troubles Wendell not at all, for the press has automatic access to such scenes. Journalists are the medium, the aperture, through which otherwise prohibited places and events reach the general public. Wendell Green is the people's representative here, and the most distinguished journalist in western Wisconsin besides.

After he has inched along another thirty feet, he sees that the cops riding herd on the traffic are Danny Tcheda and Pam Stevens, and his complacency wavers. A couple of days ago, both Tcheda and Stevens had responded to his request for information by telling him to go to hell. Pam Stevens is a know-it-all bitch anyhow, a professional ballbreaker. Why else would a reasonably okay-looking dame want to be a cop? Stevens would turn him away from the scene for the sheer hell of it—she'd *enjoy* it! Probably, Wendell realizes, he will have to sneak in somehow. He pictures himself crawling through the fields on his belly and shivers with distaste.

At least he can have the pleasure of watching the cops giving the finger to Beezer and crew. The bikers roar past another half-dozen cars without slowing down, so Wendell supposes they plan on going into a flashy, skidding turn, dodging right by those two dumbbells in blue, and zooming around the patrol car as if it didn't exist. What will the cops do then, Wendell wonders—drag out their guns and try to look fierce? Fire warning shots and hit each other in the foot?

Astonishingly, Beezer and his train of fellow bikers pay no attention to the cars attempting to move into the lane, to Tcheda and Stevens, or to anything else up there. They do not even turn their heads to gape up at the ruined shack, the chief's car, the pickup truck—which Wendell instantly recognizes—and the men standing on the beaten grass, two of whom are Dale Gilbertson and the pickup's owner, Hollywood Jack Sawyer, that snooty L.A. prick. (The third guy, who is wearing an ice-cream hat, sunglasses, and a spiffy vest, makes no sense at all, at least not to Wendell. He looks like he dropped in from some old Humphrey Bogart movie.) No, they blast on by the whole messy scene with their helmets pointed straight ahead, as if all they have in mind is cruising into Centralia and busting up the fixtures in the Sand Bar. On they go, all five of the bastards, in-different as a pack of wild dogs. As soon as they hit open road again, the other four move into parallel formation behind Beezer and fan out across the highway. Then, as one, they veer off to the left, send up five great plumes of dust and gravel, and spin into five U-turns. Without breaking stride—without even appearing to slow down—they separate into their one-two-two pattern and come streaking back westward toward the crime scene and French Landing.

*I'll be damned,* Wendell thinks. *Beezer turned tail and gave up. What a wimp.* The knot of bikers grows larger and larger as it swoops toward him, and soon the amazed Wendell Green makes out Beezer St. Pierre's grim face, which beneath its hel-met also gets larger and larger as it approaches. "I never figured you for a quitter," Wendell says, watching Beezer loom ever nearer. The wind has parted his beard into two equal sections that flare out behind him on both sides of his head. Behind his goggles, Beezer's eyes look as if he is aiming down the barrel of a rifle. The thought that Beezer might turn those hunter's eyes on him makes Wendell's bowels feel dangerously loose. "Loser," he says, not very loudly. With an ear-pounding roar, Beezer flashes past the dented Toyota. The rest of the Thunder Five hammer the air, then streak down the road.

This evidence of Beezer's cowardice brightens Wendell's heart as he watches the bikers diminish in his rearview mirror, but a thought he cannot ignore begins to worm its way upward through the synapses of his brain. Wendell may not be the Ed-ward R. Murrow of the present day, but he has been a reporter for nearly thirty years, and he has developed a few instincts. The thought winding through his mental channels sets off a se-ries of wavelike alarms that at last push it into consciousness.

Wendell *gets* it—he sees the hidden design; he understands what's going down.

"Well, hot doggy," he says, and with a wide grin blasts his horn, cranks his wheel to the left, and jolts into a turn with only minimal damage to his fender and that of the car in front of him. "You sneaky bastard," he says, nearly chuckling with delight. The Toyota squeezes out of the line of vehicles pointed eastward and drifts over into the westbound lanes. Clanking and farting, it shoots away in pursuit of the crafty bikers.

There will be no crawling through cornfields for Wendell Green: that sneaky bastard Beezer St. Pierre knows a back way to Ed's Eats! All our star reporter has to do is hang back far enough to stay out of sight and he gets a free pass into the scene. Beautiful. Ah, the irony: Beezer gives the press a helpful hand—many thanks, you arrogant thug. Wendell hardly supposes that Dale Gilbertson will give him the run of the place, but it will be harder to throw him out than to turn him away. In the time he has, he can ask a few probing questions, snap a few telling photos, and—above all!—soak up enough atmosphere to produce one of his legendary "color" pieces.

With a cheerful heart, Wendell poodles down the highway at fifty miles per hour, letting the bikers race far ahead of him without ever letting them pass out of sight. The number of cars coming toward him thins out to widely spaced groups of two and three, then to a few single cars, then to nothing. As if they have been waiting to be unobserved, Beezer and his friends swerve across the highway and go blasting up the driveway to Goltz's space-age dome.

Wendell feels an unwelcome trickle of self-doubt, but he is not about to assume that Beezer and his louts have a sudden yearning for tractor hitches and riding lawn mowers. He speeds up, wondering if they have spotted him and are trying to throw him off their trail. As far as he knows, there is nothing up on that rise except the showroom, the maintenance garage, and the parking lot. Damn place looks like a wasteland. Beyond the parking lot . . . what? On one side, he remembers a scrubby field stretching away to the horizon, on the other a bunch of trees, like a forest, only not as thick. He can see the trees from where he is now, running downhill like a windbreak.

Without bothering to signal, he speeds across the oncoming

lanes and into Goltz's driveway. The sound of the motorcycles is still audible but growing softer, and Wendell experiences a jolt of fear that they have somehow tricked him and are getting away, jeering at him! At the top of the rise, he zooms around the front of the showroom and drives into the big lot. Two huge yellow tractors stand in front of the equipment garage, but his is the only car in sight. At the far end of the empty lot, a low concrete wall rises to bumper height between the asphalt and the meadow bordered by trees. On the other side of the tree line, the wall ends at the swoop of asphalt drive coming around from the back of the showroom.

Wendell cranks the wheel and speeds toward the far end of the wall. He can still hear the motorcycles, but they sound like a distant swarm of bees. They must be about a half mile away, Wendell thinks, and jumps out of the Toyota. He jams the cassette recorder in a jacket pocket, slings the Nikon on its strap around his neck, and runs around the low wall and into the meadow. Even before he reaches the tree line, he can see the remains of an old macadam road, broken and overgrown, cutting downhill between the trees.

Wendell imagines, overestimating, that Ed's old place is about a mile distant, and he wonders if his car could go the distance on this rough, uneven surface. In some places, the macadam has fissured into tectonic plates; in others, it has crumbled away to black gravel. Sinkholes and weedy rills radiate out from the thick, snaking roots of the trees. A biker could jounce over this mess reasonably well, but Wendell sees that his legs will manage the journey better than his Toyota, so he sets off down the old track through the trees. From what he took in while he was on the highway, he still has plenty of time before the medical examiner and the evidence wagon show up. Even with the help of the famous Hollywood Sawyer, the local cops are mooning around in a daze.

The sound of motorcycles grows louder as Wendell picks his way along, as if the boys stopped moving in order to talk things over when they came to the far end of the old back road. That's perfect. Wendell hopes they will keep jawing until he has nearly caught up with them; he hopes they are shouting at one another and waving their fists in the air. He wants to see them cranked to the gills on rage and adrenaline, plus God knows what else those savages might have in their saddlebags. Wendell would love to get a photograph of Beezer St. Pierre knocking out Dale Gilbertson's front teeth with a well-aimed right, or putting the choke hold on his buddy Sawyer. The photograph Wendell wants most, however, and for the sake of which he is prepared to bribe every cop, county functionary, state official, or innocent bystander capable of holding out his hand, is a good, clean, dramatic picture of Irma Freneau's naked corpse. Preferably one that leaves no doubt about the Fisherman's depredations, whatever they were. Two would be ideal—one of her face for poignancy, the other a full-body shot for the perverts—but he will settle for the body shot if he has to. An image like that would go around the world, generating millions as it went. The *National Enquirer* alone would fork over, what—two hundred thousand, three?—for a photo of poor little Irma sprawled out in death, mutilations clearly visible. Talk about your gold mines, talk about your Big Kahunas!

When Wendell has covered about a tenth of a mile of the miserable old road, his concentration divided between gloating over all the money little Irma is going to siphon into his pockets and his fears of falling down and twisting his ankle, the uproar caused by the Thunder Five's Harleys abruptly ceases. The resulting silence seems immense, then immediately fills with other, quieter sounds. Wendell can hear his breath struggling in and out, and also some other noise, a combined rattle and thud, from behind him. He whirls around and beholds, far up the ruined road, an ancient pickup lurching toward him.

It's almost funny, the way the truck rocks from side to side as one tire, then another, sinks into an invisible depression or rolls up a tilting section of road surface. That is, it would be funny if these people were not horning in on his private access route to Irma Freneau's body. Whenever the pickup climbs over a particularly muscular-looking length of tree root, the four dark heads in the cab bob like marionettes. Wendell takes a step forward, intending to send these yokels back where they came from. The truck's suspension scrapes against a flat rock, and sparks leap from the undercarriage. That thing must be thirty years old, at least, Wendell thinks—it's one of the few vehicles on the road that looks even worse than his car. When the truck jolts closer to him, he sees that it is an International Harvester.

Weeds and twigs decorate the rusty bumper. Does I.H. even make pickups anymore? Wendell holds up his hand like a juror taking the oath, and the truck jounces and dips over another few rutted feet before coming to a halt. Its left side sits noticeably higher than the right. In the darkness cast by the trees, Wendell cannot quite make out the faces peering at him through the windshield, but he has the feeling that at least two of them are familiar.

The man behind the wheel pokes his head out of the driver's window and says, "Hidey-ho, Mr. Bigshot Reporter. They slam the front door in your face, too?" It is Teddy Runkleman, who regularly comes to Wendell's attention while he is going over the day's police reports. The other three people in the cab bray like mules at Teddy's wit. Wendell knows two of them—Freddy Saknessum, part of a low-life clan that oozes in and out of various run-down shacks along the river, and Toots Billinger, a scrawny kid who somehow supports himself by scavenging scrap metal in La Riviere and French Landing. Like Runkleman, Toots has been arrested for a number of third-rate crimes but never convicted of anything. The hard-worn, scruffy woman between Freddy and Toots rings a bell too dim to identify.

"Hello, Teddy," Wendell says. "And you, Freddy and Toots. No, after I got a look at the mess out front, I decided to come in the back way."

"Hey, *Wen*-dell, doncha 'member me?" the woman says, a touch pathetically. "Doodles Sanger, in case your memory's all shot to hell. I started out with a whole buncha guys in Freddy's Bel Air, and Teddy was with a whole 'nother bunch, but after we got run off by Miss Bitch, the rest of 'em wanted to go back to their barstools."

Of course he does remember her, although the hardened face before him now only faintly resembles that of the bawdy party girl named Doodles Sanger who served up drinks at the Nelson Hotel a decade ago. Wendell thinks she got fired more for drinking too much on the job than for stealing, but God knows she did both. Back then, Wendell threw a lot of money across the bar at the Nelson Hotel. He tries to remember if he ever hopped in the sack with Doodles.

He plays it safe and says, "Cripes, Doodles, how the hell could I forget a pretty little thing like you?"

The boys get a big yuck out of this sally. Doodles jabs her elbow into Toots Billinger's vaporous ribs, gives Wendell a pouty little smile, and says, "Well thank-ee, kind sir." Yep, he boffed her, all right.

This would be the perfect time to order these morons back to their ratholes, but Wendell is visited by grade-A inspiration. "How would you charming people like to assist a gentleman of the press and earn fifty bucks in the process?"

"Fifty each, or all together?" asks Teddy Runkleman.

"Come on, all together," Wendell says.

Doodles leans forward and says, "Twenty each, all right, big-timer? If we agree to do what you want."

"Aw, you're breakin' my heart," Wendell says, and extracts his wallet from his back pocket and removes four twenties, leaving only a ten and three singles to see him through the day. They accept their payment and, in a flash, tuck it away. "Now this is what I want you to do," Wendell says, and leans toward the window and the four jack-o'-lantern faces in the cab.

# 12

A few minutes later, the pickup lurches to a halt between the last of the trees, where the macadam disappears into the weeds and tall grass. The Thunder Five's motorcycles stand tilted in a neat row a few yards ahead and off to his left. Wendell, who has replaced Freddy Saknessum on the seat, gets out and moves a few paces forward, hoping that none of the ripe aroma of dried sweat, unwashed flesh, and stale beer emerging from his fellow passengers has clung to his clothing. Behind him, he hears Freddy jumping down from the back of the truck as the others climb out and shut the doors without making any more than twice as much noise as necessary. All Wendell can see from his position is the colorless, rotting rear wall of Ed's Eats rising from a thick tangle of Queen Anne's lace and tiger lilies. Low voices, one of them Beezer St. Pierre's, come to him. Wendell gives the Nikon a quick once-over, removes the lens cap, and cranks a new roll of film into place before moving with slow, quiet steps past the bikes and along the side of the ruined structure.

Soon he is able to see the overgrown access road and the patrol car astride it like a barrier. Down close to the highway, Danny Tcheda and Pam Stevens wrangle with half a dozen men and women who have left their cars strewn like toys behind them. That's not going to work much longer: if Tcheda and Stevens are supposed to be a dam, the dam is about to spring some serious leaks. Good news for Wendell: a maximum amount of confusion would give him a lot more leeway and make for a more colorful story. He wishes he could murmur into his recorder right now.

*The inexperience of Chief Gilbertson's force was evident in the futile efforts of Officers Tcheda and Stevens to turn back the numbers of those citizens eager to witness for themselves the latest evidence of the Fisherman's insanity . . . Ah, something, something, then:* but this journalist was able to place himself at the heart of the scene, where he felt proud and humbled to serve as the eyes and ears of his readers . . .

Wendell hates to lose such splendid stuff, but he cannot be sure he will remember it, and he does not dare to take the risk of being overheard. He moves closer to the front of Ed's Eats.

The humble ears of the public take in the sound of Beezer St. Pierre and Dale Gilbertson having a surprisingly amiable conversation directly in front of the building; the humble eyes of the public observe Jack Sawyer walking into view, an empty plastic bag and a baseball cap swinging from the fingers of his right hand. The humble nose of the public reports a truly awful stench that guarantees the presence of a decomposing body in the shabby little structure to the right. Jack is moving a little more quickly than usual, and although it is clear that he is just going to his pickup, he keeps glancing from side to side.

What's going on here? Golden Boy looks more than a little furtive. He's acting like a shoplifter just stuffing the goodies under his coat, and golden boys shouldn't behave that way. Wendell raises his camera and focuses in on his target. There you are, Jack old boy, old fellow, old sport, crisp as a new bill and twice as sharp. Look pretty for the camera, now, and let us see what you've got in your hand, okay? Wendell snaps a picture and watches through his viewfinder as Jack approaches his truck. Golden Boy is going to stash those things in the glove compartment, Wendell thinks, and he doesn't want anyone to see him do it. Too bad, kid, you're on Candid Camera. And too bad for the proud yet humble eyes and ears of French County, because when Jack Sawyer reaches his truck he does not climb in but leans over the side and fiddles around with something, giving our noble journalist a fine view of his back and nothing else. The noble journalist takes a picture anyhow, to establish a sequence with the next photo, in which Jack Sawyer turns away from his truck empty-handed and no longer furtive. He stashed his grubby treasures back there and got them out of sight, but what made them treasures?

Then a lightning bolt strikes Wendell Green. His scalp shivers, and his crinkly hair threatens to straighten out. A great story just became *unbelievably* great. Fiendish Murderer, Mutilated Dead Child, and . . . the Downfall of a Hero! Jack Sawyer walks out of the ruin carrying a plastic bag and a Brewers cap, tries to make sure he is unobserved, and hides the stuff in his truck. He *found* those things in Ed's Eats, and he squirreled them away right under the nose of his friend and admirer Dale Gilbertson. Golden Boy removed *evidence* from *the scene of a crime!* And Wendell has the proof on film, Wendell has the goods on the high-and-mighty Jack Sawyer, Wendell is going to bring him down with one godalmighty huge crash. Man oh man, Wendell feels like dancing, he does, and is unable to restrain himself from executing a clumsy jig with the wonderful camera in his hands and a sloppy grin on his face.

He feels so good, so triumphant, that he almost decides to forget about the four idiots waiting for his signal and just pack it in. But hey, let's not get all warm and fuzzy here. The supermarket tabloids are panting for a nice, gruesome photograph of Irma Freneau's dead body, and Wendell Green is the man to give it to them.

Wendell takes another cautious step toward the front of the ruined building and sees something that stops him cold. Four of the bikers have gone down to the end of the overgrown lane, where they seem to be helping Tcheda and Stevens turn away the people who want to get a good look at all the bodies. Teddy Runkleman heard that the Fisherman stowed at least six, maybe eight half-eaten kids in that shack: the news grew more and more sensational as it filtered through the community. So the cops can use the extra help, but Wendell wishes that Beezer and crew were blowing the lid off things instead of helping to keep it on. He comes to the end of the building and peers around it to see everything that is going on. If he is to get what he wants, he will have to wait for the perfect moment.

A second FLPD car noses in through the vehicles hovering out on 35 and moves up past Tcheda's car to swing onto the weeds and rubble in front of the old store. Two youngish part-time cops named Holtz and Nestler get out and stroll toward Dale Gilbertson, trying hard not to react to the stench that gets more sickening with each step they take. Wendell can see that these lads have even more difficulty concealing their dismay and astonishment at seeing their chief engaged in apparently amiable conversation with Beezer St. Pierre, whom they probably suspect of myriad nameless crimes. They are farm boys, UW–River Falls dropouts, who split a single salary and are trying so hard to make the grade as police officers that they tend to see things in rigid black-and-white. Dale calms them down, and Beezer, who could pick each of them up with one hand and smash their skulls like soft-boiled eggs, smiles benignly. In response to what must have been Dale's orders, the new boys trot back down to the highway, on the way casting worshipful glances at Jack Sawyer, the poor saps.

Jack wanders up to Dale for a little confab. Too bad Dale doesn't know that his buddy is concealing evidence, hah! Or, Wendell considers, *does* he know—is he in on it, too? One thing's for sure: it will all come out in the wash, once the *Herald* runs the telltale pictures.

In the meantime, the dude in the straw hat and the sunglasses just stands there with his arms folded across his chest, looking serene and confident, like he has everything so under control that even the smell can't reach him. This guy is obviously a key player, Wendell thinks. He calls the shots. Golden Boy and Dale want to keep him happy; you can see it in their body language. A touch of respect, of deference. If they are covering something up, they're doing it for him. But why? And what the devil is he? The guy is middle-aged, somewhere in his fifties, a generation older than Jack and Dale; he is too stylish to live in the country, so he's from Madison, maybe, or Milwaukee. He is obviously not a cop, and he doesn't look like a businessman, either. This is one self-reliant mother; that comes through loud and clear.

Then another police car breaches the defenses down on 35 and rolls up beside the part-timers'. Golden Boy and Gilbertson walk up to it and greet Bobby Dulac and that other one, the fat boy, Dit Jesperson, but the dude in the hat doesn't even look their way. Now, *that's* cool. He stands there, all by himself, like a general surveying his troops. Wendell watches the mystery man produce a cigarette, light up, and exhale a plume of white smoke. Jack and Dale walk the new arrivals into the old store, and this bird keeps on smoking his cigarette, sublimely detached from everything around him. Through the rotting wall,

Wendell can hear Dulac and Jesperson complaining about the smell; then one of them grunts *Uh!* when he sees the body. "Hello boys?" Dulac says. "Is this shit for real? *Hello boys?*" The voices give Wendell a good fix on the location of the corpse, way back against the far wall.

Before the three cops and Sawyer begin to shuffle toward the front end of the store, Wendell leans out, aims his camera, and snaps a photograph of the mystery man. To his horror, the Cat in the Hat instantly looks in his direction and says, "Who took my picture?" Wendell jerks himself back into the protection of the wall, but he knows the guy must have seen him. Those sunglasses were pointed right at him! The guy has ears like a bat— he picked up the noise of the shutter. "Come on out," Wendell hears him say. "There's no point in hiding; I know you're there."

From his reduced vantage point, Wendell can just see a State Police car, followed by French Landing's DARE Pontiac, barreling up from the congestion at the end of the lane. Things seem to have reached the boiling point down there. Unless Wendell is wrong, he thinks he glimpses one of the bikers pulling a man out through the window of a nice-looking green Olds.

Time to call in the cavalry, for sure. Wendell steps back from the front of the building and waves to the troops. Teddy Runkleman yells, *"Hoo boy!"* Doodles screeches like a cat in heat, and Wendell's four assistants charge past him, making all the noise he could wish for.

# 13

Danny Tcheda and Pam Stevens already have their hands full with would-be gate-crashers when they hear the sound of motorcycles gunning toward them, and the arrival of the Thunder Five is all they need to make their day really complete. Getting rid of Teddy Runkleman and Freddy Saknessum had been easy enough, but not five minutes later the eastbound lanes of Highway 35 filled up with people who thought they had a perfect right to gawk at all the little corpses that were supposed to be stacked up in the wreckage of Ed's Eats. For every car they finally manage to send away, two more show up in its place. Everybody demands a long explanation of why they, as taxpayers and concerned citizens, should not be allowed to enter a crime scene, especially one so tragic, so poignant, so . . . well, so exciting. Most of them refuse to believe that the only body inside that tumbledown building is Irma Freneau's; three people in a row accuse Danny of abetting a cover-up, and one of them actually uses the word "Fishergate." Yikes. In a weird way, lots of these corpse hunters almost think that the local police are protecting the Fisherman!

Some of them finger rosaries while they chew him out. One lady waves a crucifix in his face and tells him he has a dirty soul and is bound for hell. At least half of the people he turns away are carrying cameras. What kind of person sets off on a Saturday morning to take pictures of dead children? What gets Danny is this: they all think they're perfectly normal. Who's the creep? *He* is.

The husband of an elderly couple from Maid Marian Way says, "Young man, apparently you are the only person in this county who does not understand that history is happening all around us. Madge and I feel we have the right to a keepsake."

*A keepsake?*

Sweaty, out of sorts, and completely fed up, Danny loses his cool. "Buddy, I agree with you right down the line," he says. "If it was up to me, you and your lovely wife would be able to drive away with a bloodstained T-shirt, maybe even a severed finger or two, in your trunk. But what can I say? The chief is a very unreasonable guy."

Off zooms Maid Marian Way, too shocked to speak. The next guy in line starts yelling the moment Danny leans down to his window. He looks exactly like Danny's image of George Rathbun, but his voice is raspier and slightly higher in pitch. *"Don't think I can't see what you're doing, buster!"* Danny says good, because he's trying to protect a crime scene, and the George Rathbun guy, who is driving an old blue Dodge Caravan minus the front bumper and the right side-view mirror, shouts, *"I been sitting here twenty minutes while you and that dame do doodly-squat! I hope you won't be surprised when you see some VIGILANTE ACTION around here!"*

It is at this tender moment that Danny hears the unmistakable rumble of the Thunder Five charging toward him down the highway. He has not felt right since he found Tyler Marshall's bicycle in front of the old folks' home, and the thought of wrangling with Beezer St. Pierre fills his brain with dark oily smoke and whirling red sparks. He lowers his head and stares directly into the eyes of the red-faced George Rathbun look-alike. His voice emerges in a low, dead monotone. "Sir, if you continue on your present course, I will handcuff you, park you in the back of my car until I am free to leave, and then take you to the station and charge you with everything that comes to mind. That is a promise. Now do yourself a favor and get the hell out of here."

The man's mouth opens and closes, goldfishlike. Splotches of brighter red appear on his jowly, already flushed face. Danny keeps staring into his eyes, almost hoping for an excuse to truss him in handcuffs and roast him in the back seat of his car. The guy considers his options, and caution wins. He drops his eyes, moves the shift lever to R, and nearly backs into the Miata behind him.

"I don't believe this is happening," Pam says. "What dumb so-and-so spilled the beans?"

Like Danny, she is watching Beezer and his friends roar toward them past the row of waiting cars.

"I don't know, but I'd like to ram my nightstick down his throat. And after him, I'm looking for Wendell Green."

"You won't have to look very far. He's about six cars back in the line." Pam points to Wendell's traveling sneer.

"Good God," Danny says. "Actually, I'm sort of glad to see that miserable blowhard. Now I can tell him exactly what I think of him." Smiling, he bends down to speak to the teenaged boy at the wheel of the Miata. The boy leaves, and Danny waves off the driver behind him while watching the Thunder Five get closer and closer. He says to Pam, "At this point, if Beezer climbs up in my face and even *looks* like he wants to get physical, I'm pulling out my roscoe, honest to God."

"Paperwork, paperwork," Pam says.

"I really don't give a damn."

"Well, here we go," she says, telling him that if he pulls his gun, she will back him up.

Even the drivers trying to argue their way into the lane are taking time out to watch Beezer and the boys. In motion, hair and beards blowing, faces set, they look ready to commit as much mayhem as possible. Danny Tcheda's heart begins to speed, and he feels his sphincter tighten.

But the Thunder Five bikers race past without so much as turning their heads, one after another. Beezer, Mouse, Doc, Sonny, and the Kaiser—there they go, leaving the scene.

"Well, *damn*," Danny says, unable to decide if he feels relieved or disappointed. The abrupt jolt of dismay he registers when the bikers wheel around in a comprehensive, gravel-spraying U-turn thirty yards up ahead tells him that what he had felt was relief.

"Oh, please, no," Pam says.

In the waiting automobiles, every head turns as the motorcycles flash by again, returning the way they came. For a couple of seconds, the only sound to be heard is the receding furor of five Harley-Davidson cycles. Danny Tcheda takes off his uniform hat and wipes his forehead. Pam Stevens arches her back and exhales. Then someone blasts his horn, and two other horns join in, and a guy with a graying walrus mustache and a denim shirt is holding up a three-quarter-sized badge in a leather case and explaining that he is the cousin of a county-circuit judge and an honorary member of the La Riviere police force, which basically means he never gets speeding or parking tickets and can go wherever he likes. The mustache spreads out in a big grin. "So just let me get by, and you can go back to your business, Officer."

Not letting him get by *is* his business, Danny says, and he is forced to repeat this message several times before he can get on to the next case. After sending away a few more disgruntled citizens, he checks to see how long he must wait before he can tell off Wendell Green. Surely the reporter cannot be more than two or three cars back. As soon as Danny raises his head, horns blast and people start shouting at him. *Let us in! Hey, bud, I pay your salary, remember? I wanna talk to Dale, I wanna talk to Dale!*

A few men have gotten out of their cars. Their fingers are pointing at Danny, their mouths are working, but he cannot make out what they are yelling. A band of pain runs like a red-hot iron bar from behind his left eye to the middle of his brain. Something is wrong; he cannot see Green's ugly red car. Where the hell is it? Damn damn and double damn, Green must have eased out of the line and driven into the field alongside Ed's. Danny snaps around and inspects the field. Angry voices and car horns boil up at his back. No beat-up red Toyota, no Wendell Green. What do you know, the windbag gave up!

A few minutes later the traffic thins out, and Danny and Pam think their job is pretty much over. All four lanes of Highway 35 are empty, their usual condition on a Saturday morning. The one truck that rolls along keeps on rolling, on its way to Centralia.

"Think we ought to go up there?" Pam asks, nodding toward the remains of the store.

"Maybe, in a couple minutes." Danny is not eager to get within range of that smell. He would be perfectly happy to stay down here until the M.E. and the evidence wagon come along. What gets into people, anyhow? He would happily surrender two days' pay to be spared the sight of Irma Freneau's poor body.

Then he and Pam hear two distinct sounds at once, and neither one makes them comfortable. The first is that of a fresh wave of vehicles racing down the highway to their position; the second, the rumble of motorcycles descending upon the scene from somewhere behind the old store.

"Is there a back road to this place?" he asks, incredulous.

Pam shrugs. "Sounds like it. But look—Dale'll have to deal with Beezer's goons, because we're gonna have our hands full down here."

"Aw, cripes," Danny says. Maybe thirty cars and pickups are converging on the end of the little lane, and both he and Pam can see that these people are angrier and more determined than the first bunch. At the far end of the crowd, some men and women are leaving their vehicles on the shoulder and walking toward the two officers. The drivers at the front of the pack are waving their fists and shouting even before they try to turn in. Incredibly, a woman and two teenage kids are holding up a long banner that reads WE WANT THE FISHERMAN! A man in a dusty old Caddy thrusts his arm through the window and displays a handmade placard: GILBERTSON MUST GO.

Danny looks over his shoulder and sees that the Thunder Five must have found a back road, because four of them are standing out in front of Ed's, looking oddly like Secret Service agents, while Beezer St. Pierre is deep in discussion with the chief. And what *they* look like, it occurs to Danny, is two heads of state working out a trade agreement. This makes no sense at all, and Danny turns back to the cars, the lunatics with signs, and the men and women working their way toward him and Pam.

A barrel-chested, seventy-one-year-old man with a white goatee, Hoover Dalrymple, plants himself in front of Pam and starts demanding his inalienable rights. Danny remembers his name because Dalrymple initiated a brawl in the bar of the Nelson Hotel about six months earlier, and now here he is all over again, getting his revenge. "I will *not* speak to your partner," he yells, "and I will *not* listen to anything he says, because your partner has no interest in the rights of the people of this community."

Danny sends away an orange Subaru driven by a sullen teenage boy in a Black Sabbath T-shirt, then a black Corvette with La Riviere dealer's plates and a strikingly pretty, strikingly foulmouthed young woman. Where do these people come from? He does not recognize anyone except Hoover Dalrymple. Most of the people in front of him now, Danny supposes, were hailed in from out of town.

He has set out to help Pam when a hand closes on his shoulder, and he looks behind him to see Dale Gilbertson side by side with Beezer St. Pierre. The four other bikers hover a few feet away. The one called Mouse, who is of course roughly the size of a haystack, catches Dale's eye and grins.

"What are you *doing*?" Danny asks.

"Calm down," Dale says. "Mr. St. Pierre's friends have volunteered to assist our crowd-control efforts, and I think we can use all the help they can give us."

Out of the side of his eye, Danny glimpses the Neary twins breaking out of the front of the crowd, and he holds up a hand to stop them. "What do they get out of this?"

"Simple information," the chief says. "Okay, boys, get to work."

Beezer's friends move apart and approach the crowd. The chief moves beside Pam, who first looks at him in amazement, then nods. Mouse snarls at Hoover Dalrymple and says, "By the power invested in me, I order you to get the fuck out of here, Hoover." The old man vanishes so quickly he seems to have dematerialized.

The rest of the bikers have the same effect on the angry sightseers. Danny hopes they can maintain their cool in the face of steady abuse: a three-hundred-pound man who looks like a Hells Angel on a knife edge between self-control and mounting fury works wonders on a rebellious crowd. The biker nearest Danny sends Floyd and Frank Neary away just by raising his fist at them. As they melt back to their car, the biker winks at Danny and introduces himself as Kaiser Bill. Beezer's friend enjoys the process of controlling a crowd, and an immense grin threatens to break through his scowl, yet molten anger bubbles underneath, just the same.

"Who are the other guys?" Danny asks.

Kaiser Bill identifies Doc and Sonny, who are dispersing the crowd to Danny's right.

"Why are you guys doing this?"

The Kaiser lowers his head so that his face hangs two inches from Danny's. It is like confronting a bull. Heat and rage pour from the broad features and hairy skin. Danny almost expects to see steam puffing from the man's wide nostrils. One of the pupils is smaller than the other; explosive red wires tangle through the whites. "Why? We're doing it for *Amy*. Isn't that clear to you, Officer Tcheda?"

"Sorry," Danny mutters. Of course. He hopes Dale will be able to keep a lid on these monsters. Watching Kaiser Bill rock an ancient Mustang belonging to a fool kid who failed to back up in time, he is extremely happy that the bikers don't have any blunt instruments.

Through the vacant space formerly occupied by the kid's Mustang, a police car rolls toward Danny and the Kaiser. As it makes its way through the crowd, a woman wearing a sleeveless T-shirt and Capri pants bangs her hand against the passenger windows. When the car reaches Danny the two part-timers, Bob Holtz and Paul Nestler, jump out, gape at the Kaiser, and ask if he and Pam need help. "Go up and talk to the chief," Danny says, though he should not have to. Holtz and Nestler are nice guys, but they have a lot to learn about chain of command, along with everything else.

About a minute and a half later, Bobby Dulac and Dit Jesperson show up. Danny and Pam wave them through as the bikers charge into the fray and drag chanting citizens off the sides and hoods of their vehicles. Sounds of struggle reach Danny over angry shouts coming from the mob before him. It seems that he has been out here for hours. Thrusting people out of the way with great backswings of his arms, Sonny emerges to stand beside Pam, who is doing her best. Mouse and Doc wade into the clear. A trail of blood leaking from his nose, a red smear darkening his beard at the corner of his mouth, the Kaiser strides up beside Danny.

Just as the crowd begins chanting, "HELL NO, WE WON'T GO! HELL NO, WE WON'T GO!" Holtz and Nestler return to bolster the line. *Hell no, we won't go?* Danny wonders. *Isn't that supposed to be about Vietnam?*

Only dimly aware of the sound of a police siren, Danny sees Mouse wade into the crowd and knock out the first three people he can reach. Doc settles his hands on the open window of an all-too-familiar Oldsmobile and asks the small, balding driver what the hell he thinks he is doing. "Doc, leave him alone," Danny says, but the siren whoops again and drowns out his words.

Although the little man at the wheel of the Olds looks like an ineffectual math teacher or a low-level civic functionary, he possesses the determination of a gladiator. He is the Reverend Lance Hovdahl, Danny's old Sunday school teacher.

"I thought I could help," the reverend says.

"What with all this racket, I can't really hear you too good. Let me help you get closer," Doc says. He reaches in through the window as the siren whoops again and a State Police car slides by on the other side.

"Hold it, Doc, STOP!" Danny shouts, seeing the two men in the state car, Brown and Black, craning their necks to stare at the spectacle of a bearded man built like a grizzly bear dragging a Lutheran minister out through the window of his car. Creeping along behind them, another surprise, is Arnold Hrabowski, the Mad Hungarian, goggling through the windshield of his DAREmobile as if terrified by the chaos around him.

The end of the lane is like a war zone now. Danny strides into the screaming mob and shoves a few people aside on his way to Doc and his old Sunday school teacher, who looks shaken but not at all injured. "Well, Danny, my *goodness,*" the minister says. "I'm certainly glad to see you here."

Doc glares at the two of them. "You know each other?"

"Reverend Hovdahl, this is Doc," Danny says. "Doc, this is Reverend Hovdahl, the pastor at Mount Hebron Lutheran."

"Holy moly," says Doc, and immediately begins to pat the little man's lapels and tug at the hem of his jacket, as if to pull him into shape. "Sorry, Reverend, I hope I didn't hurt you none."

The state cops and the Mad Hungarian manage at last to squeeze out of the crowd. The sound level decreases to a mild hubbub—one way or another, Doc's friends have silenced the loudest members of the opposition.

"Fortunately, the window is wider than I am," the reverend says.

"Say, maybe I could come over and talk to you someday,"

says Doc. "I've been doing a lot of reading about first-century Christianity lately. You know, Géza Vermès, John Dominic Crossan, Paula Fredriksen, stuff like that. I'd like to bounce some ideas off you."

Whatever Reverend Hovdahl intends to say is obliterated by the sudden explosion of noise from the other end of the lane. A woman's voice rises like a banshee's, in an inhuman screeching that shivers the hairs on the nape of Danny's neck. It sounds to him as though escaped lunatics a thousand times more dangerous than the Thunder Five are raving through the landscape. What the devil could have *happened* up there?

" 'Hello boys'?" Unable to contain his indignation, Bobby Dulac turns to stare first at Dale, then at Jack. His voice rises, hardens. "Is this shit for real? *'Hello boys'?*"

Dale coughs into his fist and shrugs. "He wanted us to find her."

"Well, of course," Jack says. "He told us to come here."

"Why would he do that, though?" Bobby asks.

"He's proud of his work." From some dim crossroads in Jack's memory, an ugly voice says, *Stay out of it. You mess with me and I'll strew your guts from Racine to La Riviere.* Whose voice had that been? With no more evidence than his conviction, Jack understands that if he could place that voice, he would put a name to the Fisherman. He cannot; all Jack Sawyer can do at this moment is remember a stink worse than the foul cloud that fills this crumbling building—a hideous smell that came from the southwest of another world. That was the Fisherman, too, or whatever the Fisherman was in that world.

A thought worthy of the former rising star of the LAPD's Homicide Division awakens in his mind, and he says, "Dale, I think you should let Henry hear that 911 tape."

"I don't get it. What for?"

"Henry's tuned in to stuff even bats can't hear. Even if he doesn't recognize the voice, he'll learn a hundred times more than what we know now."

"Well, Uncle Henry never forgets a voice, that's true. Okay, let's get out of here. The M.E. and the evidence wagon should show up in a couple of minutes."

Trailing behind the other two men, Jack thinks of Tyler Marshall's Brewers cap and where he found it—that world he has spent more than half his life denying, and his return to which this morning continues to send shocks through his system. The Fisherman left the cap for him in the Territories, the land he had first heard of when Jacky was six—when Jacky was six, and Daddy played the horn. It is all coming back to him, that immense adventure, not because he wishes it, but because it *has to* come back: forces outside himself are picking him up by the scruff of his neck and carrying him forward. Forward into his own past! The Fisherman is proud of his handiwork, yes, the Fisherman is deliberately taunting them—a truth so obvious none of the three men had to speak it aloud—but really the Fisherman is baiting only Jack Sawyer, who alone has seen the Territories. And if *that's* true, as it has to be, then—

—then the Territories and all they contain are involved somehow in these wretched crimes, and he has been thrust into a drama of enormous consequence he cannot possibly grasp right now. *The Tower. The Beam.* He had seen this in his mother's handwriting, something about the Tower falling and the Beams breaking: these things are parts of the puzzle, whatever they mean, as is Jack's gut conviction that Tyler Marshall is still alive, tucked away in some pocket of the other world. The recognition that he can never speak of all this to anyone else, not even Henry Leyden, makes him feel intensely alone.

Jack's thoughts blow away in the noisy chaos that erupts alongside and in front of the shack. It sounds like an Indian attack in a cowboy movie, whooping and yelling and the sound of running feet. A woman sends up a shrill scream eerily like the *blip-blip*s of the police siren he had half-noted a few moments ago. Dale mutters "Jeez," and breaks into a run, followed by Bobby and Jack.

Outside, what appears to be a half dozen crazy people are racing around in the weedy gravel in front of Ed's. Dit Jesperson and Beezer, still too stunned to react, watch them caper back and forth. The crazy people make an amazing amount of noise. One man yells, "KILL THE FISHERMAN! KILL THE DIRTY BASTARD!" Another is shouting "LAW 'N' ORDER 'N' FREE BEER!" A scrawny character in bib overalls picks up "FREE BEER! WE WANT FREE BEER!" A harpy too old for her tank top and blue jeans skitters around waving her arms and screeching at the top of her lungs. The grins on their faces indicate that these people are engaged in some dimwitted prank. They are having the time of their lives.

Up from the end of the lane comes a State Police car, with the Mad Hungarian's DARE Pontiac right behind it. In the middle of the chaos, Henry Leyden tilts his head and smiles to himself.

When he sees his chief take off after one of the men, fat Dit Jesperson lurches into action and spots Doodles Sanger, against whom he has borne a grudge ever since she turned him down late one night in the Nelson Hotel. Dit recognizes Teddy Runkleman, the tall galoot with the broken nose Dale is chasing; and he knows Freddy Saknessum, but Freddy is undoubtedly too fast for him and, besides, Dit has the feeling that if he put his hands on Freddy Saknessum, about eight hours later he would probably come down with something really nasty. Bobby Dulac is on the skinny guy's case, so Doodles is Dit's target, and he looks forward to pulling her down into the weeds and making her pay for calling him what she did, six years ago in the Nelson's filthy bar. (In front of maybe a dozen of French Landing's most raffish characters, Doodles had compared him to the then chief's smelly, waddling old mongrel, Tubby.)

Dit looks her in the eye, and for a second she stops jumping around to stand flat-footed on the ground and give him a little come-hither gesture with the fingers of both hands. He launches himself at her, but when he gets to where she was, she is six feet off to the right, shifting on her feet like a basketball player. "Tubby-Tubby," she says. "Come and get it, Tub-Tub." Furious, Dit reaches, misses, and nearly loses his balance. Doodles prances away laughing and mouths the hateful expression. Dit doesn't get it—why doesn't Doodles just break away and take off? It's like she almost wants to get caught, but first she has to run out the clock.

After another serious lunge that misses the target by only an inch or two, Dit Jesperson wipes the sweat off his face and checks out the scene. Bobby Dulac is snapping cuffs on the skinny guy, but Dale and Hollywood Sawyer are faring only a little better than he is. Teddy Runkleman and Freddy Saknessum dodge and bob away from their pursuers, both of them cackling like idiots and shouting their halfwit slogans. Why is low-life scum always so agile? Dit supposes that rodents like Runkleman and Saknessum get more practice in being light on their feet than regular people.

He charges Doodles, who slips past him and goes into a chuckling, high-stepping diddley-bop. Over her shoulder, Dit sees Hollywood finally fake out Saknessum, wrap an arm around his waist, and throw him to the ground.

"You didn't have to get all physical on my ass," Saknessum says. His eyes shift, and he gives a brief nod. "Hey, Runks."

Teddy Runkleman glances at him, and his eyes shift, too. He stops moving. The chief says, "What, you run out of gas?"

"Party's over," Runkleman says. "Hey, we were just funnin', you know?"

"Aw, Runksie, I wanna play some more," Doodles says, throwing a few hip wiggles into the diddley-bop. In a flash, Beezer St. Pierre thrusts his mountainous self between her and Dit. He steps forward, rumbling like a semi going up a steep grade. Doodles tries to dance backward, but Beezer envelops her and carries her toward the chief.

"Beezie, don'cha love me no more?" Doodles asks.

Beezer grunts in disgust and deposits her in front of the chief. The two state cops, Perry Brown and Jeff Black, are hanging back, looking even more disgusted than the biker. If Dit's mental processes were to be transcribed from their short-hand into standard English, the result would be, *He's gotta have something on the ball if he brews that Kingsland Ale, because that is some fine, fine beer. And look at the chief! He's so ready to bust a gut, he can't even see that we're about to lose this case.*

"You were FUNNIN'?" the chief roars. "What's the MAT-TER with you idiots? Don't you have any respect for that poor girl in there?"

As the state cops step forward to take charge, Dit sees Beezer go rigid with shock for a moment, then move as incon-spicuously as possible away from the group. No one but Dit Jesperson pays any attention to him—the enormous biker has done his bit, and now his part is over. Arnold Hrabowski, who had been more or less concealed behind Brown and Black, shoves his hands in his pockets, hunches his shoulders, and gives Dit a glance of shamefaced apology. Dit doesn't get it: What does the Mad Hungarian have to feel so guilty about? Hell, he just *got* here. Dit looks back at Beezer, who is advancing ponderously toward the side of the shack and—surprise, surprise!—everybody's best pal and favorite reporter, Mr. Wendell Green, now appearing a little alarmed. *Guess more than one kind of scum just rose to the surface,* Dit thinks.

Beezer likes women who are smart and levelheaded, like Bear Girl; brainless skanks like Doodles drive him crazy. He reaches out, grabs two handfuls of pasty, rayon-covered flesh, and scoops wriggling Doodles under his arm.

Doodles says, "Beezie, don'cha love me no more?"

He lowers the dumb mutt to the ground in front of Dale Gilbertson. When Dale finally explodes at these four grown-up juvenile delinquents, Beezer remembers the signal Freddy had given Runksie, and looks over the chief's shoulder at the front of the old store. To the left of the rotting gray entrance, Wendell Green is aiming his camera at the group before him, getting fancy, bending and leaning, stepping to one side and another as he snaps pictures. When he sees Beezer looking at him through his lens, Wendell straightens up and lowers his camera. He has an awkward little smile on his face.

Green must have slithered in through the back way, Beezer imagines, because there's no way the cops down front would give him a pass. Come to think of it, Doodles and the Dodos must have come the same way. He hopes all of them did not learn of the back road by following him, but that's a possibility.

The reporter lets his camera hang from its strap and, keeping his eyes on Beezer, sidles away from the old shanty. The guilty, frightened way he moves reminds Beezer of a hyena's slink toward its carrion. Wendell Green does fear Beezer, and Beezer cannot blame him. Green is lucky that Beezer did not actually rip off his head, instead of merely talking about it. Yet . . . Green's hyenalike crawl strikes Beezer as pretty strange, under the circumstances. He can't be afraid of getting beaten up in front of all these cops, can he?

Green's uneasiness forms a link in Beezer's mind to the communication he had seen pass between Runkleman and Freddy. When their eyes shifted, when they looked away, they were looking at the reporter! *He had set the whole thing up in advance.* Green was using the Dodos as a distraction from whatever he was doing with his camera, of course. Such total sleaziness, such moral ugliness, infuriates Beezer. Galvanized by loathing, he moves quietly away from Dale and the other policemen and walks toward Wendell Green, keeping his eyes locked on the reporter's.

He sees Wendell consider making a break for it, then reject the idea, most likely because he knows he doesn't have a chance of getting away.

When Beezer comes to within ten feet of him, Green says, "We don't need any trouble here, Mr. St. Pierre. I'm just doing my job. Surely you can understand that."

"I understand a lot of things," Beezer says. "How much did you pay those clowns?"

"Who? What clowns?" Wendell pretends to notice Doodles and the others for the first time. "Oh, them? Are they the ones who were making all that ruckus?"

"And why would they go do a thing like that?"

"Because they're animals, I guess." The expression on Wendell's face communicates a great desire to align himself with Beezer on the side of human beings, as opposed to animals like Runkleman and Saknessum.

Taking care to fix Green's eyes, instead of his camera, with his own, Beezer moves in closer and says, "Wendy, you're a real piece of work, you know that?"

Wendell holds up his hands to ward off Beezer. "Hey, we may have had our differences in the past, but—"

Still looking him in the eye, Beezer folds his right hand around the camera and plants his left on Wendell Green's chest. He jerks the right hand back and gives Green a massive shove with the left. One of two things is going to break, Green's neck or the camera strap, and he does not much care which it is to be.

To a sound like the crack of a whip, the reporter flails backward, barely managing to remain upright. Beezer is pulling the camera out of the case, from which dangle two strips of severed leather. He drops the case and rotates the camera in his big hands.

"Hey, don't do that!" Wendell says, his voice louder than speech but softer than a shout.

"What is it, an old F2A?"

"If you know that, you know it's a classic. Give it back to me."

"I'm not going to hurt it, I'm going to clean it out." Beezer snaps open the back of the camera, gets one thick finger under the exposed length of film, and rips out the entire roll. He smiles at the reporter and tosses the film into the weeds. "See how much better it feels without all that crap in there? This is a nice little machine—you shouldn't fill it with garbage."

Wendell does not dare show how furious he is. Rubbing the sore spot on the back of his neck, he growls, "That so-called garbage is my livelihood, you oaf, you moron. Now give me back my camera."

Beezer casually holds it out before him. "I didn't quite catch all of that. What did you say?"

His only response a bleak glance, Wendell snatches the camera from Beezer's hand.

When the two state cops finally step forward, Jack feels a mixture of disappointment and relief. What they are going to do is obvious, so let them do it. Perry Brown and Jeff Black will take the Fisherman case away from Dale and run their own investigation. From now on, Dale will be lucky to get random scraps from the state's table. Jack's greatest regret is that Brown and Black should have walked into this madhouse, this circus. They have been waiting for their moment all along—in a sense, waiting for the local guy to prove his incompetence—but what is going on now is a public humiliation for Dale, and Jack wishes it weren't happening. He could not have imagined feeling grateful for the arrival of a biker gang at a crime scene, but that's how bad it is. Beezer St. Pierre and his companions kept the crowd away more efficiently than Dale's officers. The question is, how did all those people find out?

Apart from the damage to Dale's reputation and self-esteem, however, Jack has few regrets about the case passing to another jurisdiction. Let Brown and Black scour every basement in French County: Jack has the feeling they won't get any further than the Fisherman permits. To go further, he thinks, you'd have to travel in directions Brown and Black could never understand, visit places they are certain do not exist. Going further means making friends with *opopanax,* and men like Brown and Black distrust anything that even smells like *opopanax.* Which means that, in spite of everything Jack has said to himself since the murder of Amy St. Pierre, he will have to catch the Fisherman by himself. Or maybe not entirely by himself. Dale is going to have a lot more time on his hands, after all, and no matter what the State Police do to him, Dale is too wrapped up in this case to walk away from it.

"Chief Gilbertson," says Perry Brown, "I believe we have seen enough here. Is this what you call securing an area?"

Dale gives up on Teddy Runkleman and turns in frustration to the state cops, who stand side by side, like storm troopers. In his expression, Jack can see that he knows exactly what is going to happen, and that he hopes it will not be humiliatingly brutal. "I did everything in my power to make this area secure," Dale says. "After the 911 call came in, I talked to my men face to face and ordered them to come out in pairs at reasonable intervals, to keep from arousing any curiosity."

"Chief, you must have used your radio," says Jeff Black. "Because for sure *somebody* was tuned in."

"I did not use the radio," Dale says. "And my people knew better than to spread the news. But you know what, Officer Black? If the Fisherman called us on 911, maybe he also made a couple of anonymous calls to the citizens."

Teddy Runkleman has been attending to this discussion like a spectator at a tennis final. Perry Brown says, "Let's handle first things first. What do you intend to do with this man and his friends? Are you going to charge them? The sight of his face is getting on my nerves."

Dale thinks for a moment, then says, "I'm not going to charge them. Get out of here, Runkleman." Teddy moves backward, and Dale says, "Hold it for a second. How did you get here?"

"The back road," Teddy says. "Comes straight down from behind Goltz's. Thunder Five came the same way. So did that big-shot reporter, Mr. Green."

"Wendell Green is here?"

Teddy points to the side of the ruin. Dale glances over his shoulder, and Jack looks in the same direction and witnesses Beezer St. Pierre ripping film from the back of a camera while Wendell Green watches in dismay.

"One more question," Dale says. "How did you learn that the Freneau girl's body was out here?"

"They was five or six bodies up at Ed's, is what I heard. My brother Erland called up and told me. He heard it from his girl-friend."

"Go on, get out of here," Dale says, and Teddy Runkleman ambles away as if he has been awarded a medal for good citizenship.

"All right," Perry Brown says. "Chief Gilbertson, you have reached the end of your leash. As of now, this investigation is to be conducted by Lieutenant Black and myself. I'll want a copy of the 911 tape and copies of all notes and statements taken by you and your officers. Your role *is* to be entirely subordinate to the state's investigation, and to cooperate fully when called upon. You *will* be given updates at the discretion of Lieutenant Black and myself.

"If you ask me, Chief Gilbertson, you are getting far more than you deserve. I have never seen a more disorganized crime scene. You violated the security of this site to an *unbelievable* degree. How many of you walked into the . . . the structure?"

"Three," Dale says. "Myself, Officer Dulac, and Lieutenant Sawyer."

"Lieutenant *Sawyer*," Brown says. "Excuse me, has Lieutenant *Sawyer* rejoined the LAPD? Has he become an official member of your department? And if not, why did you give him access to that structure? In fact, what is *Mr.* Sawyer doing here in the first place?"

"He's cleared more homicide cases than you and me ever will, no matter how long we live."

Brown gives Jack an evil glance, and Jeff Black stares straight ahead. Beyond the two state cops, Arnold Hrabowski also glances at Jack Sawyer, though not at all the way Perry Brown did. Arnold's expression is that of a man who deeply wishes to be invisible, and when he finds Jack's eye on him, he quickly glances sideways and shifts on his feet.

*Oh,* Jack thinks. *Of course, the Mad Mad Mad Mad Mad Hungarian, there you go.*

Perry Brown asks Dale what *Mr.* St. Pierre and his friends are doing on the scene, and Dale replies that they are assisting with crowd control. Did Dale advise Mr. St. Pierre that in exchange for this service he would be kept up-to-date on the investigation? It was something like that, yes.

Jack steps back and begins to move sideways along a gentle arc that will bring him to Arnold Hrabowski.

"Incredible," says Brown. "Tell me, Chief Gilbertson, did you decide to delay a little bit before passing the news on to Lieutenant Black and myself?"

"I did everything according to procedure," Dale says. In answer to the next question he says that yes, he has called for the medical examiner and the evidence wagon, which, by the way, he can see coming up the lane right now.

The Mad Hungarian's efforts at self-control succeed only in making him look as though he urgently needs to urinate. When Jack places a hand on his shoulder, he stiffens like a cigar-store Indian.

"Calm down, Arnold," Jack says, then raises his voice. "Lieutenant Black, if you're taking over this case, there's some information you should have."

Brown and Black turn their attention to him.

"The man who made the 911 call used the pay phone at the 7-Eleven store on Highway 35 in French Landing. Dale had the phone taped off, and the owner knows to keep people from handling it. You might get some useful prints from that phone."

Black scribbles something in his notebook, and Brown says, "Gentlemen, I think your role is finished here. Chief, use your people to disperse those individuals at the bottom of the lane. By the time the M.E. and I come out of that structure, I don't want to see a single person down there, including you and your officers. You'll get a call later in the week, if I have any new information."

Wordlessly, Dale turns away and points Bobby Dulac down the path, where the crowd has dwindled to a few stubborn souls leaning against their cars. Brown and Black shake hands with the medical examiner and confer with the specialists in charge of the evidence wagon.

"Now, Arnold," Jack says, "you like being a cop, don't you?"

"Me? I love being a cop." Arnold cannot quite force himself to meet Jack's eyes. "And I could be a good one, I know I could, but the chief doesn't have enough faith in me." He thrusts his trembling hands into his pants pockets.

Jack is torn between feeling pity for this pathetic wanna-be and the impulse to kick him all the way down to the end of the lane. A good cop? Arnold couldn't even be a good scoutmaster. Thanks to him, Dale Gilbertson got a public dressing-down that probably made him feel as though he'd been put in the stocks. "But you didn't follow orders, did you, Arnold?"

Arnold quivers like a tree struck by lightning. "What? I didn't do anything."

"You told someone. Maybe you told a couple of people."

"No!" Arnold shakes his head violently. "I just called my wife, that's all." He looks imploringly at Jack. "The Fisherman talked to *me,* he told *me* where he put the girl's body, and I wanted Paula to know. Honest, Holl— Lieutenant Sawyer, I didn't think she'd call anybody, I just wanted to *tell* her."

"Bad move, Arnold," Jack says. "You are going to tell the chief what you did, and you're going to do it right now. Because Dale deserves to know what went wrong, and he shouldn't have to blame himself. You like Dale, don't you?"

"The chief?" Arnold's voice wobbles with respect for his chief. "Sure I do. He's, he's . . . he's great. But isn't he going to fire me?"

"That's up to him, Arnold," Jack says. "If you ask me, you deserve it, but maybe you'll get lucky."

The Mad Hungarian shuffles off toward Dale. Jack watches their conversation for a second, then walks past them to the side of the old store, where Beezer St. Pierre and Wendell Green face each other in unhappy silence.

"Hello, Mr. St. Pierre," he says. "And hello to you, Wendell."

"I'm lodging a complaint," Green says. "I'm covering the biggest story of my life, and this lout spoils a whole roll of film. You can't treat the press that way; we have a *right* to photograph whatever the hell we like."

"I guess you woulda said you had a right to photograph my daughter's dead body, too." Beezer glares at Jack. "This piece of shit paid Teddy and the other lunkheads to go nuts so nobody would notice him sneaking inside there. He took pictures of the girl."

Wendell jabs a finger at Jack's chest. "He has no proof of that. But I'll tell you something, Sawyer. I did get pictures of you. You were concealing evidence in the back of your truck, and I got you dead to rights. So think twice before you try to mess with me, because I'll hang you out to dry."

A dangerous red mist seems to fill Jack's head. "Were you going to sell photographs of that girl's body?"

"What's it to you?" An ugly smirk widens Wendell Green's mouth. "You're not exactly lily-white either, are you? Maybe we can do each other some good, huh?"

The red mist darkens and fills Jack's eyes. "We can do each other some good?"

Standing beside Jack, Beezer St. Pierre clenches and un-clenches his enormous fists. Beezer, Jack knows, catches his tone perfectly, but the vision of dollar signs has so gripped Wendell Green that he hears Jack's threat as a straightforward question.

"You let me reload my camera and get the pictures I need, and I keep quiet about you."

Beezer lowers his head and balls his hands again.

"Tell you what. I'm a generous guy—maybe I could even cut you in, say ten percent of my total."

Jack would prefer to break his nose, but he contents himself with a hard punch to the reporter's stomach. Green clutches his gut and folds in half, then falls to the ground. His face has turned a hectic pink, and he struggles for breath. His eyes register shock and disbelief.

"See, I'm a generous guy, too, Wendell. I probably saved you thousands of dollars in dental work, plus a broken jaw."

"Don't forget the plastic surgery," says Beezer, grinding a fist into the palm of the other hand. He looks as if someone just stole his favorite dessert off the dinner table.

Wendell's face has become a reddish shade of purple.

"For your information, Wendell, no matter what you think you saw, I am not concealing evidence. If anything I am *revealing* it, though I hardly expect you to understand."

Green manages to wheeze in something like a cubic inch of air.

"When your wind starts to come back, get out of here. Crawl, if you have to. Go back to your car and drive away. And for God's sake, make it snappy, or our friend here is likely to put you in a wheelchair for the rest of your life."

Slowly, Wendell Green gets to his knees, takes another noisy sip of oxygen, and levers himself semi-upright. He waggles one open hand at them, but his meaning is unclear. He could be telling Beezer and Jack to stay away from him, or that he will trouble them no further, or both. His trunk tilted over his belt, his hands pressed to his stomach, Green stumbles around the side of the building.

"I guess I oughta thank you," Beezer says. "You let me keep my promise to my old lady. But I have to say, Wendell Green is one guy I'd really like to deconstruct."

"Man," Jack says, "I wasn't sure if I could get in before you did."

"It's true, my restraint was crumbling."

Both men smile. "Beezer St. Pierre," Beezer says, and sticks out a hand.

"Jack Sawyer." Jack takes his hand and experiences no more than a second of pain.

"Are you gonna let the state guys do all the work, or will you keep going on your own?"

"What do you think?" Jack says.

"If you ever need any help, or you want reinforcements, all you have to do is ask. Because I do want to get this son of a bitch, and I figure you have a better chance of finding him than anyone else."

On the drive back to Norway Valley, Henry says, "Oh, Wendell took a picture of the body, all right. When you came out of the building and went to your truck, I heard someone take a couple of pictures, but I thought it might have been Dale. Then I heard it again when you and Dale were inside with Bobby Dulac, and I realized someone was taking a picture of *me*! Well, now, I say to myself, *this must be Mr. Wendell Green,* and I told him to come out from behind the wall. That's when those people charged out, yelling and screaming. As soon as that happened, I heard Mr. Green trot around from the side, go into the building, and shoot a few pictures. Then he sneaked out and stood by the side of the building, which is where your friend Beezer caught up with him and took care of things. Beezer is a remarkable fellow, isn't he?"

"Henry, were you going to *tell* me about this?"

"Of course, but you were running around all over the place,

and I knew Wendell Green wasn't going to leave until he was thrown out. I'll never read another word he writes. Never."

"Same here," Jack says.

"But you're not giving up on the Fisherman, are you? In spite of what that pompous state cop said."

"I can't give up now. To tell you the truth, I think those waking dreams I mentioned yesterday were connected to this case."

"*I*vey-*di*vey. Now, let's get back to Beezer. Didn't I hear him say he wanted to 'deconstruct' Wendell?"

"Yeah, I think so."

"He must be a fascinating man. I gather from my nephew that the Thunder Five spends Saturday afternoons and evenings in the Sand Bar. Next week, maybe I'll start up Rhoda's old car and drive to Centralia, have a few beers and a nice gab with Mr. St. Pierre. I'm sure he has interesting taste in music."

"You want to drive to Centralia?" Jack stares at Henry, whose only concession to the absurdity of this suggestion is a little smile.

"Blind people can drive perfectly well," Henry says. "Probably, they can drive better than most sighted people. Ray Charles can, anyhow."

"Come on, Henry. Why would you think Ray Charles can drive a car?"

"Why, you ask? Because one night in Seattle, this was, oh, forty years ago, back when I had a gig at KIRO, Ray took me out for a spin. Smooth as Lady Godiva's backside. No trouble at all. We stuck to the side roads, of course, but Ray got up to fifty-five, I'm pretty sure."

"Assuming this really happened, weren't you scared?"

"Scared? Of course not. I was his navigator. I certainly don't think I'd have a problem navigating to Centralia along this sleepy stretch of backcountry highway. The only reason blind people don't drive is that other people won't let them. It's a power issue. They want us to stay marginalized. Beezer St. Pierre would understand perfectly."

"And here I was, thinking I was going to visit the madhouse this afternoon," Jack says.

# 14

At the top of the steep hill between Norway Valley and Arden, the zigzag, hairpin turns of Highway 93, now narrowed to two lanes, straighten out for the long, ski-slope descent into the town, and on the eastern side of the highway, the hilltop widens into a grassy plateau. Two weatherbeaten red picnic tables wait for those who choose to stop for a few minutes and appreciate the spectacular view. A patchwork of quilted farms stretches out over fifteen miles of gentle landscape, not quite flat, threaded with streams and country roads. A solid row of bumpy, blue-green hills form the horizon. In the immense sky, sun-washed white clouds hang like fresh laundry.

Fred Marshall steers his Ford Explorer onto the gravel shoulder, comes to a halt, and says, "Let me show you something."

When he climbed into the Explorer at his farmhouse, Jack was carrying a slightly worn black leather briefcase, and the case is now lying flat across his knees. Jack's father's initials, P.S.S., for Philip Stevenson Sawyer, are stamped in gold beside the handle at the top of the case. Fred has glanced curiously at the briefcase a couple of times, but has not asked about it, and Jack has volunteered nothing. There will be time for show-and-tell, Jack thinks, after he talks to Judy Marshall. Fred gets out of the car, and Jack slides his father's old briefcase behind his legs and props it against the seat before he follows the other man across the pliant grass. When they reach the first of the picnic tables, Fred gestures toward the landscape. "We don't have a lot of what you could call tourist attractions around here, but this is pretty good, isn't it?"

"It's very beautiful," Jack says. "But I think everything here is beautiful."

"Judy really likes this view. Whenever we go over to Arden on a decent day, she has to stop here and get out of the car, relax and look around for a while. You know, sort of store up on the important things before getting back into the grind. Me, sometimes I get impatient and think, Come on, you've seen that view a thousand times, I have to get back to work, but I'm a guy, right? So every time we turn in here and sit down for a few minutes, I realize my wife knows more than I do and I should just listen to what she says."

Jack smiles and sits down at the bench, waiting for the rest of it. Since picking him up, Fred Marshall has spoken only two or three sentences of gratitude, but it is clear that he has chosen this place to get something off his chest.

"I went over to the hospital this morning, and she—well, she's *different*. To look at her, to talk to her, you'd have to say she's in much better shape than yesterday. Even though she's still worried sick about Tyler, it's *different*. Do you think that could be due to the medication? I don't even know what they're giving her."

"Can you have a normal conversation with her?"

"From time to time, yeah. For instance, this morning she was telling me about a story in yesterday's paper on a little girl from La Riviere who nearly took third place in the statewide spelling bee, except she couldn't spell this crazy word nobody ever heard of. *Popoplax,* or something like that."

"Opopanax," Jack says. He sounds like he has a fishbone caught in his throat.

"You saw that story, too? That's interesting, you both picking up on that word. Kind of gave her a kick. She asked the nurses to find out what it meant, and one of them looked it up in a couple of dictionaries. Couldn't find it."

Jack had found the word in his *Concise Oxford Dictionary;* its literal meaning was unimportant. "That's probably the definition of *opopanax*," Jack says. " '1. A word not to be found in the dictionary. 2. A fearful mystery.' "

"Hah!" Fred Marshall has been moving nervously around the lookout area, and now he stations himself beside Jack, whose upward glance finds the other man surveying the long panorama. "Maybe that is what it means." Fred's eyes remain fixed on the landscape. He is still not quite ready, but he is making progress. "It was great to see her interested in something like that, a tiny little item in the *Herald* . . ."

He wipes tears from his eyes and takes a step toward the horizon. When he turns around, he looks directly at Jack. "Uh, before you meet Judy, I want to tell you a few things about her. Trouble is, I don't know how this is going to sound to you. Even to me, it sounds . . . I don't know."

"Give it a try," Jack says.

Fred says, "Okay," knits his fingers together, and bows his head. Then he looks up again, and his eyes are as vulnerable as a baby's. "Ahhh . . . I don't know how to put this. Okay, I'll just say it. With part of my brain, I think Judy *knows* something. Anyhow, I want to think that. On the other hand, I don't want to fool myself into believing that just because she seems to be better, she can't be crazy anymore. But I do want to believe that. Boy oh boy, do I ever."

"Believe that she knows something." The eerie feeling aroused by *opopanax* diminishes before this validation of his theory.

"Something that isn't even real clear to her," Fred says. "But do you remember? She knew Ty was gone even before I told her."

He gives Jack an anguished look and steps away. He knocks his fists together and stares at the ground. Another internal barrier topples before his need to explain his dilemma.

"Okay, look. This is what you have to understand about Judy. She's a special person. All right, a lot of guys would say their wives are special, but Judy's special in a special way. First of all, she's sort of amazingly beautiful, but that's not even what I'm talking about. And she's tremendously brave, but that's not it, either. It's like she's connected to something the rest of us can't even begin to understand. But can that be real? How crazy is that? Maybe when you're going crazy, at first you put up a big fight and get hysterical, and then you're too crazy to fight anymore and you get all calm and accepting. I have to talk to her doctor, because this is tearing me apart."

"What kinds of things does she say? Does she explain why she's so much calmer?"

Fred Marshall's eyes burn into Jack's. "Well, for one thing, Judy seems to think that Ty is still alive, and that you're the only person who can find him."

"All right," Jack says, unwilling to say more until after he can speak to Judy. "Tell me, does Judy ever mention someone she used to know—or a cousin of hers, or an old boyfriend—she thinks might have taken him?" His theory seems less convincing than it had in Henry Leyden's ultrarational, thoroughly bizarre kitchen; Fred Marshall's response weakens it further.

"Not unless he's named the Crimson King, or Gorg, or Abbalah. All I can tell you is, Judy thinks she *sees* something, and even though it makes no sense, I sure as hell hope it's there."

A sudden vision of the world where he found a boy's Brewers cap pierces Jack Sawyer like a steel-tipped lance. "And that's where Tyler is."

"If part of me didn't think that might just *possibly* be true, I'd go out of my mind right here and now," Fred says. "Unless I'm already out of my gourd."

"Let's go talk to your wife," Jack says.

From the outside, French County Lutheran Hospital resembles a nineteenth-century madhouse in the north of England: dirty red-brick walls with blackened buttresses and lancet arches, a peaked roof with finial-capped pinnacles, swollen turrets, miserly windows, and all of the long facade stippled black with ancient filth. Set within a walled parkland dense with oaks on Arden's western boundary, the enormous building, Gothic without the grandeur, looks punitive, devoid of mercy. Jack half-expects to hear the shrieking organ music from a Vincent Price movie.

They pass through a narrow, peaked wooden door and enter a reassuringly familiar lobby. A bored, uniformed man at a central desk directs visitors to the elevators; stuffed animals and sprays of flowers fill the gift shop's window; bathrobed patients tethered to I.V. poles occupy randomly placed tables with their families, and other patients perch on the chairs lined against the side walls; two white-coated doctors confer in a corner. Far overhead, two dusty, ornate chandeliers distribute a soft ocher light that momentarily seems to gild the luxurious heads of the lilies arrayed in tall vases beside the entrance of the gift shop.

"Wow, it sure looks better on the inside," Jack says.

"Most of it does," Fred says.

They approach the man behind the desk, and Fred says, "Ward D." With a mild flicker of interest, the man gives them two rectangular cards stamped VISITOR and waves them through. The elevator clanks down and admits them to a wood-paneled enclosure the size of a broom closet. Fred Marshall pushes the button marked 5, and the elevator shudders upward. The same soft, golden light pervades the comically tiny interior. Ten years ago, an elevator remarkably similar to this, though situated in a grand Paris hotel, had held Jack and a UCLA art-history graduate student named Iliana Tedesco captive for two and a half hours, in the course of which Ms. Tedesco announced that their relationship had reached its final destination, thank you, despite her gratitude for what had been at least until that moment a rewarding journey together. After thinking it over, Jack decides not to trouble Fred Marshall with this information.

Better behaved than its French cousin, the elevator trembles to a stop and with only a slight display of resistance slides open its door and releases Jack Sawyer and Fred Marshall to the fifth floor, where the beautiful light seems a touch darker than in both the elevator and the lobby. "Unfortunately, it's way over on the other side," Fred tells Jack. An apparently endless corridor yawns like an exercise in perspective off to their left, and Fred points the way with his finger.

They go through two big sets of double doors, past the corridor to Ward B, past two vast rooms lined with curtained cubicles, turn left again at the closed entrance to Gerontology, down a long, long hallway lined with bulletin boards, past the opening to Ward C, then take an abrupt right at the men's and women's bathrooms, pass Ambulatory Ophthalmology and Records Annex, and at last come to a corridor marked WARD D. As they proceed, the light seems progressively to darken, the walls to contract, the windows to shrink. Shadows lurk in the corridor to Ward D, and a small pool of water glimmers on the floor.

"We're in the oldest part of the building now," Fred says.

"You must want to get Judy out of here as soon as possible."

"Well, sure, soon as Pat Skarda thinks she's ready. But you'll be surprised; Judy kind of likes it in here. I think it's helping.

What she told me was, she feels completely safe, and the ones that can talk, some of them are extremely interesting. It's like being on a cruise, she says."

Jack laughs in surprise and disbelief, and Fred Marshall touches his shoulder and says, "Does that mean she's a lot better or a lot worse?"

At the end of the corridor, they emerge directly into a good-sized room that seems to have been preserved unaltered for a hundred years. Dark brown wainscoting rises four feet from the dark brown wooden floor. Far up in the gray wall to their right, two tall, narrow windows framed like paintings admit filtered gray light. A man seated behind a polished wooden counter pushes a button that unlocks a double-sized metal door with a WARD D sign and a small window of reinforced glass. "You can go in, Mr. Marshall, but who is he?"

"His name is Jack Sawyer. He's here with me."

"Is he either a relative or a medical professional?"

"No, but my wife wants to see him."

"Wait here a moment." The attendant disappears through the metal door and locks it behind him with a prisonlike clang. A minute later, the attendant reappears with a nurse whose heavy, lined face, big arms and hands, and thick legs make her look like a man in drag. She introduces herself as Jane Bond, the head nurse of Ward D, a combination of words and circumstances that irresistibly suggest at least a couple of nicknames. The nurse subjects Fred and Jack, then only Jack, to a barrage of questions before she vanishes back behind the great door.

"Ward Bond," Jack says, unable not to.

"We call her Warden Bond," says the attendant. "She's tough, but on the other hand, she's unfair." He coughs and stares up at the high windows. "We got this orderly, calls her Double-oh Zero."

A few minutes later, Head Nurse Warden Bond, Agent OO Zero, swings open the metal door and says, "You may enter now, but pay attention to what I say."

At first, the ward resembles a huge airport hangar divided into a section with a row of padded benches, a section with round tables and plastic chairs, and a third section where two long tables are stacked with drawing paper, boxes of crayons, and watercolor sets. In the vast space, these furnishings look like dollhouse furniture. Here and there on the cement floor, painted a smooth, anonymous shade of gray, lie padded rectangular mats; twenty feet above the floor, small, barred windows punctuate the far wall, of red brick long ago given a couple of coats of white paint. In a glass enclosure to the left of the door, a nurse behind a desk looks up from a book. Far down to the right, well past the tables with art supplies, three locked metal doors open into worlds of their own. The sense of being in a hangar gradually yields to a sense of a benign but inflexible imprisonment.

A low hum of voices comes from the twenty to thirty men and women scattered throughout the enormous room. Only a very few of these men and women are talking to visible companions. They pace in circles, stand frozen in place, lie curled like infants on the mats; they count on their fingers and scribble in notebooks; they twitch, yawn, weep, stare into space and into themselves. Some of them wear green hospital robes, others civilian clothes of all kinds: T-shirts and shorts, sweat suits, running outfits, ordinary shirts and slacks, jerseys and pants. No one wears a belt, and none of the shoes have laces. Two muscular men with close-cropped hair and in brilliant white T-shirts sit at one of the round tables with the air of patient watchdogs. Jack tries to locate Judy Marshall, but he cannot pick her out.

"I asked for your attention, Mr. Sawyer."

"Sorry," Jack says. "I wasn't expecting it to be so big."

"We'd better be big, Mr. Sawyer. We serve an expanding population." She waits for an acknowledgment of her significance, and Jack nods. "Very well. I'm going to give you some basic ground rules. If you listen to what I say, your visit here will be as pleasant as possible for all of us. Don't stare at the patients, and don't be alarmed by what they say. Don't act as though you find anything they do or say unusual or distressing. Just be polite, and eventually they will leave you alone. If they ask you for things, do as you choose, within reason. But please refrain from giving them money, any sharp objects, or edibles not previously cleared by one of the physicians—some medications interact adversely with certain kinds of food. At some point, an elderly woman named Estelle Packard will probably come up to you and ask if you are her father. Answer however you like, but if you say no, she will go away disappointed, and if you say yes, you'll make her day. Do you have any questions, Mr. Sawyer?"

"Where is Judy Marshall?"

"She's on this side, with her back to us on the farthest bench. Can you see her, Mr. Marshall?"

"I saw her right away," Fred says. "Have there been any changes since this morning?"

"Not as far as I know. Her admitting physician, Dr. Spiegleman, will be here in about half an hour, and he might have more information for you. Would you like me to take you and Mr. Sawyer to your wife, or would you prefer going by yourself?"

"We'll be fine," Fred Marshall says. "How long can we stay?"

"I'm giving you fifteen minutes, twenty max. Judy is still in the eval stage, and I want to keep her stress level at a minimum. She looks pretty peaceful now, but she's also deeply disconnected and, quite frankly, delusional. I wouldn't be surprised by another hysterical episode, and we don't want to prolong her evaluation period by introducing new medication at this point, do we? So please, Mr. Marshall, keep the conversation stress-free, light, and positive."

"You think she's delusional?"

Nurse Bond smiles pityingly. "In all likelihood, Mr. Marshall, your wife has been delusional for years. Oh, she's managed to keep it hidden, but ideations like hers don't spring up overnight, no no. These things take years to construct, and all the time the person can appear to be a normally functioning human being. Then something triggers the psychosis into full-blown expression. In this case, of course, it was your son's disappearance. By the way, I want to extend my sympathies to you at this time. What a terrible thing to have happened."

"Yes, it was," says Fred Marshall. "But Judy started acting strange even before . . ."

"Same thing, I'm afraid. She needed to be comforted, and her delusions—her delusional world—came into plain view, because that world provided exactly the comfort she needed. You must have heard some of it this morning, Mr. Marshall. Did your wife mention anything about going to other worlds?"

"Going to other worlds?" Jack asks, startled.

"A fairly typical schizophrenic ideation," Nurse Bond says. "More than half the people on this ward have similar fantasies."

"You think my wife is schizophrenic?"

Nurse Bond looks past Fred to take a comprehensive inventory of the patients in her domain. "I'm not a psychiatrist, Mr. Marshall, but I have had twenty long years of experience in dealing with the mentally ill. On the basis of that experience, I have to tell you, in my opinion your wife manifests the classic symptoms of paranoid schizophrenia. I wish I had better news for you." She glances back at Fred Marshall. "Of course, Dr. Spiegleman will make the final diagnosis, and he will be able to answer all your questions, explain your treatment options, and so forth."

The smile she gives Jack seems to congeal the moment it appears. "I always tell my new visitors it's tougher on the family than it is on the patient. Some of these people, they don't have a care in the world. Really, you almost have to envy them."

"Sure," Jack says. "Who wouldn't?"

"Go on, then," she says, with a trace of peevishness. "Enjoy your visit."

A number of heads turn as they walk slowly across the dusty wooden floor to the nearest row of benches; many pairs of eyes track their progress. Curiosity, indifference, confusion, suspicion, pleasure, and an impersonal anger show in the pallid faces. To Jack, it seems as though every patient on the ward is inching toward them.

A flabby middle-aged man in a bathrobe has begun to cut through the tables, looking as though he fears missing his bus to work. At the end of the nearest bench, a thin old woman with streaming white hair stands up and beseeches Jack with her eyes. Her clasped, upraised hands tremble violently. Jack forces himself not to meet her eyes. When he passes her, she half-croons, half-whispers, "My ducky-wucky was behind the door, but I didn't know it, and there he was, *in all that water.*"

"Um," Fred says. "Judy told me her baby son drowned in the bath."

Through the side of his eye, Jack has been watching the fuzzy-haired man in the bathrobe rush toward them, open-mouthed. When he and Fred reach the back of Judy Marshall's bench, the man raises one finger, as if signaling the bus to wait for him, and trots forward. Jack watches him approach; nuts to Warden Bond's advice. He's not going to let this lunatic climb all over him, no way. The upraised finger comes to within a foot of Jack's nose, and the man's murky eyes search his face. The eyes retreat; the mouth snaps shut. Instantly, the man whirls around and darts off, his robe flying, his finger still searching out its target.

*What was that,* Jack wonders. *Wrong bus?*

Judy Marshall has not moved. She must have heard the man rushing past her, his rapid breath when he stopped, then his flapping departure, but her back is still straight in the loose green robe, her head still faces forward at the same upright angle. She seems detached from everything around her. If her hair were washed, brushed, and combed, if she were conventionally dressed and had a suitcase beside her, she would look exactly like a woman on a bench at the train station, waiting for the hour of departure.

So even before Jack sees Judy Marshall's face, before she speaks a single word, there is about her this sense of leavetaking, of journeys begun and begun again—this suggestion of travel, this hint of a possible elsewhere.

"I'll tell her we're here," Fred whispers, and ducks around the end of the bench to kneel in front of his wife. The back of her head tilts forward over the erect spine as if to answer the tangled combination of heartbreak, love, and anxiety burning in her husband's handsome face. Dark blond hair mingled with gold lies flat against the girlish curve of Judy Marshall's skull. Behind her ear, dozens of varicolored strands clump together in a cobwebby knot.

"How you feeling, sweetie?" Fred softly asks his wife.

"I'm managing to enjoy myself," she says. "You know, honey, I should stay here for at least a little while. The head nurse is positive I'm absolutely crazy. Isn't that convenient?"

"Jack Sawyer's here. Would you like to see him?"

Judy reaches out and pats his upraised knee. "Tell Mr. Sawyer to come around in front, and you sit right here beside me, Fred."

Jack is already coming forward, his eyes on Judy Marshall's

once again upright head, which does not turn. Kneeling, Fred has taken her extended hand in both of his, as if he intends to kiss it. He looks like a lovelorn knight before a queen. When he presses her hand to his cheek, Jack sees the white gauze wrapped around the tips of her fingers. Judy's cheekbone comes into view, then the side of her gravely unsmiling mouth; then her entire profile is visible, as sharp as the crack of ice on the first day of spring. It is the regal, idealized profile on a cameo, or on a coin: the slight upward curve of the lips, the crisp, chis-eled downstroke of the nose, the sweep of the jawline, every angle in perfect, tender, oddly familiar alignment with the whole.

It staggers him, this unexpected beauty; for a fraction of a second it slows him with the deep, grainy nostalgia of its frag-mentary, not-quite evocation of another's face. Grace Kelly? Catherine Deneuve? No, neither of these; it comes to him that Judy's profile reminds him of someone he has still to meet.

Then the odd second passes: Fred Marshall gets to his feet, Judy's face in three-quarter profile loses its regal quality as she watches her husband sit beside her on the bench, and Jack re-jects what has just occurred to him as an absurdity.

She does not raise her eyes until he stands before her. Her hair is dull and messy; beneath the hospital gown she is wear-ing an old blue lace-trimmed nightdress that looked dowdy when it was new. Despite these disadvantages, Judy Marshall claims him for her own at the moment her eyes meet his.

An electrical current beginning at his optic nerves seems to pulse downward through his body, and he helplessly concludes that she has to be the most stunningly beautiful woman he has ever seen. He fears that the force of his reaction to her will knock him off his feet, then—even worse!—that she will see what is going on and think him a fool. He desperately does not want to come off as a fool in her eyes. Brooke Greer, Claire Evinrude, Iliana Tedesco, gorgeous as each of them was in her own way, look like little girls in Halloween costumes next to her. Judy Marshall puts his former beloveds on the shelf; she exposes them as whims and fancies, riddled with false ego and a hundred crippling insecurities. Judy's beauty is not put on in front of a mirror but grows, with breathtaking simplicity, straight from her innermost being: what you see is only the small, visible portion of a far greater, more comprehensive, radiant, and formal quality within.

Jack can scarcely believe that agreeable, good-hearted Fred Marshall actually had the fantastic luck to marry this woman. Does he know how great, how literally *marvelous,* she is? Jack would marry her in an instant, if she were single. It seems to him that he fell in love with her as soon as he saw the back of her head.

But he cannot be in love with her. She is Fred Marshall's wife and the mother of their son, and he will simply have to live without her.

She utters a short sentence that passes through him in a vibrating wave of sound. Jack bends forward muttering an apology, and Judy smilingly offers him a sweep of her hand that invites him to sit before her. He folds to the floor and crosses his ankles in front of him, still reverberating from the shock of having first seen her.

Her face fills beautifully with feeling. She has seen exactly what just happened to him, and it is all right. She does not think less of him for it. Jack opens his mouth to ask a question. Although he does not know what the question is to be, he must ask it. The nature of the question is unimportant. The most idiotic query will serve; he cannot sit here staring at that wondrous face.

Before he speaks, one version of reality snaps soundlessly into another, and without transition Judy Marshall becomes a tired-looking woman in her mid-thirties with tangled hair and smudges under her eyes who regards him steadily from a bench in a locked mental ward. It should seem like a restoration of his sanity, but it feels instead like a kind of trick, as though Judy Marshall has done this herself, to make their encounter easier on him.

The words that escape him are as banal as he feared they might be. Jack listens to himself say that it is nice to meet her.

"It's nice to meet you, too, Mr. Sawyer. I've heard so many wonderful things about you."

He looks for a sign that she acknowledges the enormity of the moment that has just passed, but he sees only her smiling warmth. Under the circumstances, that seems like acknowledgment enough. "How are you getting on in here?" he asks, and the balance shifts even more in his direction.

"The company takes some getting used to, but the people here got lost and couldn't find their way back, that's all. Some of them are very intelligent. I've had conversations in here that were a lot more interesting than the ones in my church group or the PTA. Maybe I should have come to Ward D sooner! Being here has helped me learn some things."

"Like what?"

"Like there are many different ways to get lost, for one, and getting lost is easier to do than anyone ever admits. The people in here can't hide how they feel, and most of them never found out how to deal with their fear."

"How are you supposed to deal with that?"

"Why, you deal with it by taking it on, that's how! You don't just say, I'm lost and I don't know how to get back—you keep on going in the same direction. You put one foot in front of the other until you get *more* lost. Everybody should know that. Especially you, Jack Sawyer."

"Especial—" Before he can finish the question, an elderly woman with a lined, sweet face appears beside him and touches his shoulder.

"Excuse me." She tucks her chin toward her throat with the shyness of a child. "I want to ask you a question. Are you my father?"

Jack smiles at her. "Let me ask you a question first. Is your name Estelle Packard?"

Eyes shining, the old woman nods.

"Then yes, I am your father."

Estelle Packard clasps her hands in front of her mouth, dips her head in a bow, and shuffles backward, glowing with pleasure. When she is nine or ten feet away, she gives Jack a little bye-bye wave of one hand and twirls away.

When Jack looks again at Judy Marshall, it is as if she has parted her veil of ordinariness just wide enough to reveal a small portion of her enormous soul. "You're a very nice man, aren't you, Jack Sawyer? I wouldn't have known that right away. You're a good man, too. Of course, you're also charming, but charm and decency don't always go together. Should I tell you a few other things about yourself?"

Jack looks up at Fred, who is holding his wife's hand and beaming. "I want you to say whatever you feel like saying."

"There are things I can't say, no matter how I feel, but you might hear them anyhow. I can say this, however: your good looks haven't made you vain. You're not shallow, and that might have something to do with it. Mainly, though, you had the gift of a good upbringing. I'd say you had a wonderful mother. I'm right, aren't I?"

Jack laughs, touched by this unexpected insight. "I didn't know it showed."

"You know one way it shows? In the way you treat other people. I'm pretty sure you come from a background people around here only know from the movies, but it hasn't gone to your head. You see us as people, not hicks, and that's why I know I can trust you. It's obvious that your mother did a great job. I was a good mother, too, or at least I tried to be, and I know what I'm talking about. I can *see*."

"You say you *were* a good mother? Why use—"

"The past tense? Because I was talking about before."

Fred's smile fades into an expression of ill-concealed concern. "What do you mean, 'before'?"

"Mr. Sawyer might know," she says, giving Jack what he thinks is a look of encouragement.

"Sorry, I don't think I do," he says.

"I mean, before I wound up here and finally started to think a little bit. Before the things that were happening to me stopped scaring me out of my mind—before I realized I could look inside myself and examine these feelings I've had over and over all my life. Before I had time to travel. I think I'm still a good mother, but I'm not exactly the *same* mother."

"Honey, please," says Fred. "You are the same, you just had a kind of breakdown. We ought to talk about Tyler."

"We are talking about Tyler. Mr. Sawyer, do you know that lookout point on Highway 93, right where it reaches the top of the big hill about a mile south of Arden?"

"I saw it today," Jack says. "Fred showed it to me."

"You saw all those farms that keep going and going? And the hills off in the distance?"

"Yes. Fred told me you loved the view from up there."

"I always want to stop and get out of the car. I love everything about that view. You can see for miles and miles, and then—whoops!—it stops, and you can't see any farther. But the sky keeps going, doesn't it? The sky proves that there's a world on the other side of those hills. If you travel, you can get there."

"Yes, you can." Suddenly, there are goose bumps on Jack's forearms, and the back of his neck is tingling.

"Me? I can only travel in my mind, Mr. Sawyer, and I only remembered how to do that because I landed in the loony bin. But it came to me that *you* can get there—to the other side of the hills."

His mouth is dry. He registers Fred Marshall's growing distress without being able to reduce it. Wanting to ask her a thousand questions, he begins with the simplest one:

"How did it come to you? What do you mean by that?"

Judy Marshall takes her hand from her husband and holds it out to Jack, and he holds it in both of his. If she ever looked like an ordinary woman, now is not the time. She is blazing away like a lighthouse, like a bonfire on a distant cliff.

"Let's say . . . late at night, or if I was alone for a long time, someone used to whisper to me. It wasn't that concrete, but let's say it was as if a person were whispering on the other side of a thick wall. A girl like me, a girl my age. And if I fell asleep then, I would almost always dream about the place where that girl lived. I called it Faraway, and it was like this world, the Coulee Country, only brighter and cleaner and more magical. In Faraway, people rode in carriages and lived in great white tents. In Faraway, there were men who could fly."

"You're right," he says. Fred looks from his wife to Jack in painful uncertainty, and Jack says, "It sounds crazy, but she's right."

"By the time these bad things started to happen in French Landing, I had pretty much forgotten about Faraway. I hadn't thought about it since I was about twelve or thirteen. But the closer the bad things came, to Fred and Ty and me, I mean, the worse my dreams got, and the less and less real my life seemed to be. I wrote words without knowing I was doing it, I said crazy things, I was falling apart. I didn't understand that Faraway was trying to tell me something. The girl was whispering to me from the other side of the wall again, only now she was grown up and scared half to death."

"What made you think I could help?"

"It was just a feeling I had, back when you arrested that

Kinderling man and your picture was in the paper. The first thing I thought when I looked at your picture was, *He knows about Faraway.* I didn't wonder how, or how I could tell from looking at a picture; I simply understood that you knew. And then, when Ty disappeared and I lost my mind and woke up in this place, I thought if you could see into some of these people's heads, Ward D wouldn't be all that different from Faraway, and I remembered seeing your picture. And that's when I started to understand about traveling. All this morning, I have been walking through Faraway in my head. Seeing it, touching it. Smelling that unbelievable air. Did you know, Mr. Sawyer, that over there they have jackrabbits the size of kangaroos? It makes you laugh just to look at them."

Jack breaks into a wide grin, and he bends to kiss her hand, in a gesture much like her husband's.

Gently, she takes her hand from his grasp. "When Fred told me he had met you, and that you were helping the police, I knew that you were here for a reason."

What this woman has done astonishes Jack. At the worst moment of her life, with her son lost and her sanity crumbling, she used a monumental feat of memory to summon all of her strength and, in effect, accomplish a miracle. She found within herself the capacity to *travel.* From a locked ward, she moved halfway out of this world and into another known only from childhood dreams. Nothing but the immense courage her husband had described could have enabled her to have taken this mysterious step.

"You *did* something once, didn't you?" Judy asks him. "You were there, in Faraway, and you *did* something—something tremendous. You don't have to say yes, because I can see it in you; it's as plain as day. But you have to say yes, so I can hear it, so say it, say yes."

"Yes."

"Did what?" Fred asks. "In this dream country? How can you say yes?"

"Wait," Jack tells him, "I have something to show you later," and returns to the extraordinary woman seated before him. Judy Marshall is aflame with insight, courage, and faith and, although she is forbidden to him, now seems to be the only woman in this world or any other whom he could love for the rest of his life.

"You were like me," she says. "You forgot all about that world. And you went out and became a policeman, a detective. In fact, you became one of the best detectives that ever lived. Do you know why you did that?"

"I guess the work appealed to me."

"What about it appealed to you in particular?"

"Helping the community. Protecting innocent people. Putting away the bad guys. It was interesting work."

"And you thought it would never stop being interesting. Because there would always be a new problem to solve, a new question in need of an answer."

She has struck a bull's-eye that, until this moment, he did not know existed. "That's right."

"You were a great detective because, even though you didn't know it, there was something—something vital—you needed to detect."

*I am a coppiceman,* Jack remembers. His own little voice in the night, speaking to him from the other side of a thick, thick wall.

"Something you had to find, for the sake of your own soul."

"Yes," Jack says. Her words have penetrated straight into the center of his being, and tears spring to his eyes. "I always wanted to find what was missing. My whole life was about the search for a secret explanation."

In memory as vivid as a strip of film, he sees a great tented pavilion, a white room where a beautiful and wasted queen lay dying, and a little girl two or three years younger than his twelve-year-old self amid her attendants.

"Did you call it Faraway?" Judy asks.

"I called it the Territories." Speaking the words aloud feels like the opening of a chest filled with a treasure he can share at last.

"That's a good name. Fred won't understand this, but when I was on my long walk this morning, I felt that my son was somewhere in Faraway—in your Territories. Somewhere out of sight, and hidden away. In grave danger, but still alive and unharmed. In a cell. Sleeping on the floor. But alive. Unharmed. Do you think that could be true, Mr. Sawyer?"

"Wait a second," Fred says. "I know you feel that way, and I want to believe it, too, but this is the real world we're talking about here."

"I think there are lots of real worlds," Jack says. "And yes, I believe Tyler is somewhere in Faraway."

"Can you rescue him, Mr. Sawyer? Can you bring him back?"

"It's like you said before, Mrs. Marshall," Jack says. "I must be here for a reason."

"Sawyer, I hope whatever you're going to show me makes more sense than the two of you do," says Fred. "We're through for now, anyhow. Here comes the warden."

Driving out of the hospital parking lot, Fred Marshall glances at the briefcase lying flat on Jack's lap but says nothing. He holds his silence until he turns back onto 93, when he says, "I'm glad you came with me."

"Thank you," Jack says. "I am, too."

"I feel sort of out of my depth here, you know, but I'd like to get your impressions of what went on in there. Do you think it went pretty well?"

"I think it went better than that. Your wife is . . . I hardly know how to describe her. I don't have the vocabulary to tell you how great I think she is."

Fred nods and sneaks a glance at Jack. "So you don't think she's out of her head, I guess."

"If that's crazy, I'd like to be crazy right along with her."

The two-lane blacktop highway that stretches before them lifts up along the steep angle of the hillside and, at its top, seems to extend into the dimensionless blue of the enormous sky.

Another wary glance from Fred. "And you say you've seen this, this *place* she calls Faraway."

"I have, yes. As hard as that is to believe."

"No crap. No b.s. On your mother's grave."

"On my mother's grave."

"You've been there. And not just in a dream, really *been* there."

"The summer I was twelve."

"Could I go there, too?"

"Probably not," Jack says. This is not the truth, since Fred could go to the Territories if Jack took him there, but Jack wants to shut this door as firmly as possible. He can imagine bringing Judy Marshall into that other world; Fred is another matter. Judy has more than earned a journey into the Territories, while Fred is still incapable of believing in its existence. Judy would feel at home over there, but her husband would be like an anchor Jack had to drag along with him, like Richard Sloat.

"I didn't think so," says Fred. "If you don't mind, I'd like to pull over again when we get to the top."

"I'd like that," Jack says.

Fred drives to the crest of the hill and crosses the narrow highway to park in the gravel turnout. Instead of getting out of the car, he points at the briefcase lying flat on Jack's knees. "Is what you're going to show me in there?"

"Yes," Jack says. "I was going to show it to you earlier, but after we stopped here the first time, I wanted to wait until I heard what Judy had to say. And I'm glad I did. It might make more sense to you, now that you've heard at least part of the explanation of how I found it."

Jack snaps open the briefcase, raises the top, and from its pale, leather-lined interior removes the Brewers cap he had found that morning. "Take a look," he says, and hands over the cap.

"Ohmygod," Fred Marshall says in a startled rush of words. "Is this . . . is it . . . ?" He looks inside the cap and exhales hugely at the sight of his son's name. His eyes leap to Jack's. "It's Tyler's. Good Lord, it's Tyler's. Oh, Lordy." He crushes the cap to his chest and takes two deep breaths, still holding Jack's gaze. "Where did you find this? How long ago was it?"

"I found it on the road this morning," Jack says. "In the place your wife calls Faraway."

With a long moan, Fred Marshall opens his door and jumps out of the car. By the time Jack catches up with him, he is at the far edge of the lookout, holding the cap to his chest and staring at the blue-green hills beyond the long quilt of farmland. He whirls to stare at Jack. "Do you think he's still alive?"

"I think he's alive," Jack says.

"In that world." Fred points to the hills. Tears leap from his eyes, and his mouth softens. "The world that's over there some-where, Judy says."

"In that world."

"Then you go there and find him!" Fred shouts. His face shining with tears, he gestures wildly toward the horizon with the baseball cap. "Go there and bring him back, damn you! *I* can't do it, so *you* have to." He steps forward as if to throw a punch, then wraps his arms around Jack Sawyer and sobs.

When Fred's shoulders stop trembling and his breath comes in gasps, Jack says, "I'll do everything I can."

"I know you will." He steps away and wipes his face. "I'm sorry I yelled at you like that. I know you're going to help us."

The two men turn around to walk back to the car. Far off to the west, a loose, woolly smudge of pale gray blankets the land beside the river.

"What's that?" Jack asks. "Rain?"

"No, fog," Fred says. "Coming in off the Mississippi."

# PART THREE

# NIGHT'S
# PLUTONIAN SHORE

# 15

By evening, the temperature has dropped fifteen degrees as a minor cold front pushes through our little patch of the Coulee Country. There are no thunderstorms, but as the sky tinges toward violet, the fog arrives. It's born out of the river and rises up the inclined ramp of Chase Street, first obscuring the gutters, then the sidewalks, then blurring the buildings themselves. It cannot completely hide them, as the fogs of spring and winter sometimes do, but the blurring is somehow worse: it steals colors and softens shapes. The fog makes the ordinary look alien. And there's the smell, the ancient, seagully odor that works deep into your nose and awakens the back part of your brain, the part that is perfectly capable of believing in monsters when the sight lines shorten and the heart is uneasy.

On Sumner Street, Debbi Anderson is still working dispatch. Arnold "the Mad Hungarian" Hrabowski has been sent home without his badge—in fact, suspended—and feels he must ask his wife a few pointed questions (his belief that he already knows the answers makes him even more heartsick). Debbi is now standing at the window, a cup of coffee in her hand and a puckery little frown on her face.

"Don't like this," she says to Bobby Dulac, who is glumly and silently writing reports. "It reminds me of the Hammer pictures I used to watch on TV back when I was in junior high."

"Hammer pictures?" Bobby asks, looking up.

"Horror pictures," she says, looking out into the deepening fog. "A lot of them were about Dracula. Also Jack the Ripper."

"I don't want to hear nothing about Jack the Ripper," Bobby says. "You mind me, Debster." And resumes writing.

In the parking lot of the 7-Eleven, Mr. Rajan Patel stands beside his telephone (still crisscrossed by yellow police tape, and when it will be all right again for using, this Mr. Patel could not be telling us). He looks toward downtown, which now seems to rise from a vast bowl of cream. The buildings on Chase Street descend into this bowl. Those at Chase's lowest point are visible only from the second story up.

"If he is down there," Mr. Patel says softly, and to no one but himself, "tonight he will be doing whatever he wants."

He crosses his arms over his chest and shivers.

Dale Gilbertson is at home, for a wonder. He plans to have a sit-down dinner with his wife and child even if the world ends because of it. He comes out of his den (where he has spent twenty minutes talking with WSP officer Jeff Black, a conversation in which he has had to exercise all his discipline to keep from shouting), and sees his wife standing at the window and looking out. Her posture is almost exactly the same as Debbi Anderson's, only she's got a glass of wine in her hand instead of a cup of coffee. The puckery little frown is identical.

"River fog," Sarah says dismally. "Isn't that ducky. If he's out there—"

Dale points at her. "Don't say it. Don't even think it."

But he knows that neither of them can help thinking about it. The streets of French Landing—the *foggy* streets of French Landing—will be deserted right now: no one shopping in the stores, no one idling along the sidewalks, no one in the parks. Especially no children. The parents will be keeping them in. Even on Nailhouse Row, where good parenting is the exception rather than the rule, the parents will be keeping their kids inside.

"I won't say it," she allows. "That much I can do."

"What's for dinner?"

"How does chicken pot pie sound?"

Ordinarily such a hot dish on a July evening would strike him as an awful choice, but tonight, with the fog coming in, it sounds like just the thing. He steps up behind her, gives her a brief squeeze, and says, "Great. And earlier would be better."

She turns, disappointed. "Going back in?"

"I shouldn't have to, not with Brown and Black rolling the ball—"

"Those pricks," she says. "I *never* liked them."

Dale smiles. He knows that the former Sarah Asbury has never cared much for the way he earns his living, and this makes her furious loyalty all the more touching. And tonight it feels vital, as well. It's been the most painful day of his career in law enforcement, ending with the suspension of Arnold Hrabowski. Arnie, Dale knows, believes he will be back on duty before long. And the shitty truth is that Arnie may be right. Based on the way things are going, Dale may need even such an exquisite example of ineptitude as the Mad Hungarian.

"Anyway, I shouldn't *have* to go back in, but . . ."

"You have a feeling."

"I do."

"Good or bad?" She has come to respect her husband's intuitions, not in the least because of Dale's intense desire to see Jack Sawyer settled close enough to reach with seven keystrokes instead of eleven. Tonight that looks to her like—pardon the pun—a pretty good call.

"Both," Dale says, and then, without explaining or giving Sarah a chance to question further: "Where's Dave?"

"At the kitchen table with his crayons."

At six, young David Gilbertson is enjoying a violent love affair with Crayolas, has gone through two boxes since school let out. Dale and Sarah's strong hope, expressed even to each other only at night, lying side by side before sleep, is that they may be raising a real artist. The next Norman Rockwell, Sarah said once. Dale—who helped Jack Sawyer hang his strange and wonderful pictures—has higher hopes for the boy. Too high to express, really, even in the marriage bed after the lights are out.

With his own glass of wine in hand, Dale ambles out to the kitchen. "What you drawing, Dave? What—"

He stops. The crayons have been abandoned. The picture—a half-finished drawing of what might be either a flying saucer or perhaps just a round coffee table—has also been abandoned.

The back door is open.

Looking out at the whiteness that hides David's swing and jungle gym, Dale feels a terrible fear leap up his throat, choking him. All at once he can smell Irma Freneau again, that terrible smell of raw spoiled meat. Any sense that his family lives in a protected, magic circle—*it may happen to others, but it can never, never happen to us*—is gone now. What has replaced it is stark certainty: David is gone. The Fisherman has enticed him out of the house and spirited him away into the fog. Dale can see the grin on the Fisherman's face. He can see the gloved hand—it's yellow—covering his son's mouth but not the bulging, terri-fied child's eyes.

Into the fog and out of the known world.

David.

He moves forward across the kitchen on legs that feel bone-less as well as nerveless. He puts his wineglass down on the table, the stem landing a-tilt on a crayon, not noticing when it spills and covers David's half-finished drawing with something that looks horribly like venous blood. He's out the door, and al-though he means to yell, his voice comes out in a weak and al-most strengthless sigh: "David? . . . Dave?"

For a moment that seems to last a thousand years, there is nothing. Then he hears the soft thud of running feet on damp grass. Blue jeans and a red-striped rugby shirt materialize out of the thickening soup. A moment later he sees his son's dear, grinning face and mop of yellow hair.

"Dad! Daddy! I was swinging in the fog! It was like being in a cloud!"

Dale snatches him up. There is a bad, blinding impulse to slap the kid across the face, to hurt him for scaring his father so. It passes as quickly as it came. He kisses David instead.

"I know," he says. "That must have been fun, but it's time to come in now."

"Why, Daddy?"

"Because sometimes little boys get lost in the fog," he says, looking out into the white yard. He can see the patio table, but it is only a ghost; he wouldn't know what he was looking at if he hadn't seen it a thousand times. He kisses his son again. "Sometimes little boys get lost," he repeats.

Oh, we could check in with any number of friends, both old and new. Jack and Fred Marshall have returned from Arden (neither suggested stopping at Gertie's Kitchen in Centralia when they passed it), and both are now in their otherwise deserted houses. For the balance of the ride back to French Landing, Fred never once let go of his son's baseball cap, and he has a hand on it even now, as he eats a microwaved TV dinner in his too empty living room and watches Action News Five.

Tonight's news is mostly about Irma Freneau, of course. Fred picks up the remote when they switch from shaky-cam footage of Ed's Eats to a taped report from the Holiday Trailer Park. The cameraman has focused on one shabby trailer in particular. A few flowers, brave but doomed, straggle in the dust by the stoop, which consists of three boards laid across two cement blocks. "Here, on the outskirts of French Landing, Irma Freneau's grieving mother is in seclusion," says the on-scene correspondent. "One can only imagine this single mother's feelings tonight." The reporter is prettier than Wendell Green but exudes much the same aura of glittering, unhealthy excitement.

Fred hits the OFF button on the remote and growls, "Why can't you leave the poor woman alone?" He looks down at his chipped beef on toast, but he has lost his appetite.

Slowly, he raises Tyler's hat and puts it on his own head. It doesn't fit, and Fred for a moment thinks of letting out the plastic band at the back. The idea shocks him. Suppose that was all it took to kill his son? That one simple, deadly modification? The idea strikes him as both ridiculous and utterly inarguable. He supposes that if this keeps up, he'll soon be as mad as his wife . . . or Sawyer. Trusting Sawyer is as crazy as thinking he might kill his son by changing the size of the boy's hat . . . and yet he believes in both things. He picks up his fork and begins to eat again, Ty's Brewers cap sitting on his head like Spanky's beanie in an old *Our Gang* one-reeler.

Beezer St. Pierre is sitting on his sofa in his underwear, a book open on his lap (it is, in fact, a book of William Blake's poems) but unread. Bear Girl's asleep in the other room, and he's fighting the urge to bop on down to the Sand Bar and score some crank, his old vice, untouched for going on five years now. Since Amy died, he fights this urge every single day, and lately he wins only by reminding himself that he won't be able to find the Fisherman—and punish him as he deserves to be punished—if he's fucked up on devil dust.

Henry Leyden is in his studio with a huge pair of Akai headphones on his head, listening to Warren Vaché, John Bunch, and Phil Flanigan dreamboat their way through "I Remember April." He can smell the fog even through the walls, and to him it smells like the air at Ed's Eats. Like bad death, in other words. He's wondering how Jack made out in good old Ward D at French County Lutheran. And he's thinking about his wife, who lately (especially since the record hop at Maxton's, although he doesn't consciously realize this) seems closer than ever. And unquiet.

Yes indeed, all sorts of friends are available for our inspection, but at least one seems to have dropped out of sight. Charles Burnside isn't in the common room at Maxton's (where an old episode of *Family Ties* is currently running on the ancient color TV bolted to the wall), nor in the dining hall, where snacks are available in the early evening, nor in his own room, where the sheets are currently clean (but where the air still smells vaguely of old shit). What about the bathroom? Nope. Thorvald Thorvaldson has stopped in to have a pee and a handwash, but otherwise the place is empty. One oddity: there's a fuzzy slipper lying on its side in one of the stalls. With its bright black and yellow stripes, it looks like the corpse of a huge dead bumblebee. And yes, it's the stall second from the left. Burny's favorite.

Should we look for him? Maybe we should. Maybe not knowing exactly where that rascal is makes us uneasy. Let us slip through the fog, then, silent as a dream, down to lower Chase Street. Here is the Nelson Hotel, its ground floor now submerged in river fog, the ocher stripe marking high water of that ancient flood no more than a whisper of color in the fading light. On one side of it is Wisconsin Shoe, now closed for the day. On the other is Lucky's Tavern, where an old woman with bowlegs (her name is Bertha Van Dusen, if you care) is currently bent over with her hands planted on her large knees, yarking a bellyful of Kingsland Old-Time Lager into the gutter. She makes sounds like a bad driver grinding a manual transmission. In the doorway of the Nelson Hotel itself sits a patient old mongrel, who will wait until Bertha has gone back into the tavern, then slink over to eat the half-digested cocktail franks floating in the beer. From Lucky's comes the tired, twanging voice of the late Dick Curless, Ole Country One-Eye, singing about those Hainesville Woods, where there's a tombstone every mile.

The dog gives a single disinterested growl as we pass him and slip into the Nelson's lobby, where moth-eaten heads—a wolf, a bear, an elk, and an ancient half-bald bison with a single glass eye—look at empty sofas, empty chairs, the elevator that hasn't worked since 1994 or so, and the empty registration desk. (Morty Fine, the clerk, is in the office with his feet propped up on an empty file-cabinet drawer, reading *People* and picking his nose.) The lobby of the Nelson Hotel always smells of the river—it's in the pores of the place—but this evening the smell is heavier than usual. It's a smell that makes us think of bad ideas, blown investments, forged checks, deteriorating health, stolen office supplies, unpaid alimony, empty promises, skin tumors, lost ambition, abandoned sample cases filled with cheap novelties, dead hope, dead skin, and fallen arches. This is the kind of place you don't come to unless you've been here before and all your other options are pretty much foreclosed. It's a place where men who left their families two decades before now lie on narrow beds with pee-stained mattresses, coughing and smoking cigarettes. The scuzzy old lounge (where scuzzy old Hoover Dalrymple once held court and knocked heads most every Friday and Saturday night) has been closed by unanimous vote of the town council since early June, when Dale Gilbertson scandalized the local political elite by showing them a video of three traveling strippers who billed themselves as the Anal University Trio, performing a synchronized cucumber routine on the tiny stage (FLPD cameraman: Officer Tom Lund, let's give him a hand), but the Nelson's residents still have only to go next door to get a beer; it's convenient. You pay by the week at the Nelson. You can keep a hot plate in your room, but only by permission and after the cord has been inspected. You can die on a fixed income at the Nelson, and the last sound you hear could well be the creaking of bedsprings over your head as some other helpless old loser jacks off.

Let us rise up the first flight, past the old canvas firehose in its glass box. Turn right at the second-floor landing (past the pay phone with its yellowing OUT OF ORDER sign) and continue to rise. When we reach the third floor, the smell of river fog is joined by the smell of chicken soup warming on someone's hot plate (the cord duly approved either by Morty Fine or George Smith, the day manager).

The smell is coming from 307. If we slip through the keyhole (there have never been keycards at the Nelson and never will be), we'll be in the presence of Andrew Railsback, seventy, balding, scrawny, good-humored. He once sold vacuum cleaners for Electrolux and appliances for Sylvania, but those days are behind him now. These are his golden years.

A candidate for Maxton's, we might think, but Andy Railsback knows that place, and places like it. Not for him, thanks. He's sociable enough, but he doesn't want people telling him when to go to bed, when to get up, and when he can have a little nip of Early Times. He has friends in Maxton's, visits them often, and has from time to time met the sparkling, shallow, predatory eye of our pal Chipper. He has thought on more than one such occasion that Mr. Maxton looks like the sort of fellow who would happily turn the corpses of his graduates into soap if he thought he could turn a buck on it.

No, for Andy Railsback, the third floor of the Nelson Hotel is good enough. He has his hot plate; he has his bottle of hooch; he's got four packs of Bicycles and plays big-picture solitaire on nights when the sandman loses his way.

This evening he has made three Lipton Cup-A-Soups, thinking he'll invite Irving Throneberry in for a bowl and a chat. Maybe afterward they'll go next door to Lucky's and grab a beer. He checks the soup, sees it has attained a nice simmer, sniffs the fragrant steam, and nods. He also has saltines, which go well with soup. He leaves the room to make his way upstairs and knock on Irv's door, but what he sees in the hallway stops him cold.

It's an old man in a shapeless blue robe, walking away from him with suspicious quickness. Beneath the hem of the robe, the stranger's legs are as white as a carp's belly and marked with blue snarls of varicose veins. On his left foot is a fuzzy black-and-yellow slipper. His right foot is bare. Although our new friend can't tell for sure—not with the guy's back to him—he doesn't look like anyone Andy knows.

Also, he's trying doorknobs as he wends his way along the

main third-floor hall. He gives each one a single hard, quick
shake. Like a turnkey. Or a thief. A fucking thief.

Yeah. Although the man is obviously old—older than Andy,
it looks like—and dressed as if for bed, the idea of thievery resonates in Andy's mind with queer certainty. Even the one bare
foot, arguing that the fellow probably didn't come in off the
street, has no power over this strong intuition.

Andy opens his mouth to call out—something like *Can I
help you?* or *Looking for someone?*—and then changes his
mind. He just has this feeling about the guy. It has to do with
the fleet way the stranger scurries along as he tries the knobs,
but that's not all of it. Not all of it by any means. It's a feeling
of darkness and danger. There are pockets in the geezer's robe,
Andy can see them, and there might be a weapon in one of
them. Thieves don't *always* have weapons, but . . .

The old guy turns the corner and is gone. Andy stands where
he is, considering. If he had a phone in his room, he might call
downstairs and alert Morty Fine, but he doesn't. So, what
to do?

After a brief interior debate, he tiptoes down the hall to the
corner and peeps around. Here is a cul-de-sac with three doors:
312, 313, and, at the very end, 314, the only room in that little
appendix which is currently occupied. The man in 314 has been
there since the spring, but almost all Andy knows about him is
his name: George Potter. Andy has asked both Irv and Hoover
Dalrymple about Potter, but Hoover doesn't know jack-shit and
Irv has learned only a little more.

"You must," Andy objected—this conversation took place in
late May or early June, around the time the Buckhead Lounge
downstairs went dark. "I seen you in Lucky's with him, havin'
a beer."

Irv had lifted one bushy eyebrow in that cynical way of his.
"Seen me havin' a beer with him. What are you?" he'd rasped.
"My fuckin' wife?"

"I'm just saying. You drink a beer with a man, you have a little conversation—"

"Usually, maybe. Not with him. I sat down, bought a pitcher,
and mostly got the dubious pleasure of listenin' to myself think.
I say, 'What do you think about the Brewers this year?' and he

says, 'They'll suck, same as last year. I can get the Cubs at night on my rah-dio—' "

"That the way he said it? *Rah*-dio?"

"Well, it ain't the way *I* say it, is it? You ever heard me say rah-dio? I say radio, same as any normal person. You want to hear this or not?"

"Don't sound like there's much to hear."

"You got that right, buddy. He says, 'I can get the Cubs at night on my rah-dio, and that's enough for me. I always went to Wrigley with my dad when I was a kid.' So I found out he was from Chi, but otherwise, *bupkes.*"

The first thought to pop into Andy's mind upon glimpsing the fucking thief in the third-floor corridor had been Potter, but Mr. George I-Keep-to-Myself Potter is a tall drink of water, maybe six-four, still with a pretty good head of salt-and-pepper hair. Mr. One-Slipper was shorter than that, hunched over like a toad. (*A* poison *toad, at that* is the thought that immediately rises in Andy's mind.)

*He's in there,* Andy thinks. *Fucking thief's in Potter's room, maybe going through Potter's drawers, looking for a little stash. Fifty or sixty rolled up in the toe of a sock, like I used to do. Or stealing Potter's radio. His fucking* rah-*dio.*

Well, and what was that to him? You passed Potter in the hallway, gave him a civil good morning or good afternoon, and what you got back was an uncivil grunt. *Bupkes,* in other words. You saw him in Lucky's, he was drinking alone, far side of the jukebox. Andy guessed you could sit down with him and he'd split a pitcher with you—Irv's little tête-à-tête with the man proved that much—but what good was that without a little chin-jaw to go along with it? Why should he, Andrew Railsback, risk the wrath of some poison toad in a bathrobe for the sake of an old grump who wouldn't give you a yes, no, or maybe?

Well . . .

Because this is his home, cheesy as it might be, that's why. Because when you saw some crazy old one-slipper fuck in search of loose cash or the easily lifted rah-dio, you didn't just turn your back and shuffle away. Because the bad feeling he got from the scurrying old elf (*the bad vibe,* his grandchildren would have said) was probably nothing but a case of the chick-enshits. Because—

Suddenly Andy Railsback has an intuition that, while not a direct hit, is at least adjacent to the truth. Suppose it *is* a guy from off the street? Suppose it's one of the old guys from Maxton Elder Care? It's not that far away, and he knows for a fact that from time to time an old feller (or old gal) will get mixed up in his (or her) head and wander off the reservation. Under ordinary circumstances that person would be spotted and hauled back long before getting this far downtown—kind of hard to miss on the street in an institutional robe and single slipper—but this evening the fog has come in and the streets are all but deserted.

*Look at you,* Andy berates himself. *Scared half to death of a feller that's probably got ten years on you and peanut butter for brains. Wandered in here past the empty desk—not a chance in the goddamn world Fine's out front; he'll be in back reading a magazine or a stroke book—and now he's looking for his room back at Maxton's, trying every knob on the goddamn corridor, no more idea of where he is than a squirrel on a freeway ramp. Potter's probably having a beer next door* (this, at least, turns out to be true) *and left his door unlocked* (this, we may be assured, is not).

And although he's still frightened, Andy comes all the way around the corner and walks slowly toward the open door. His heart is beating fast, because half his mind is still convinced the old man is maybe dangerous. There was, after all, that bad feeling he got just from looking at the stranger's *back*—

But he goes. God help him, he does.

"Mister?" he calls when he reaches the open door. "Hey, mister, I think you got the wrong room. That's Mr. Potter's room. Don't you—"

He stops. No sense talking, because the room is empty. How is that possible?

Andy steps back and tries the knobs of 312 and 313. Both locked up tight, as he knew they would be. With that ascertained, he steps into George Potter's room and has a good look around—curiosity killed the cat, satisfaction brought him back. Potter's digs are a little larger than his, but otherwise not much different: it's a box with a high ceiling (they made places a man could stand up in back in the old days, you had to say that much for them). The single bed is sagging in the middle but neatly made. On the night table is a bottle of pills (these turn out to be an antidepressant called Zoloft) and a single framed picture of a woman. Andy thinks she took a pretty good whopping with the ugly stick, but Potter must see her differently. He has, after all, put the picture in a place where it's the first thing he looks at in the morning and the last thing he sees at night.

"Potter?" Andy asks. "Anyone? Hello?"

He is suddenly overcome with a sense of someone standing behind him and whirls around, lips drawn back from his dentures in a grinning snarl that is half a cringe. One hand comes up to shield his face from the blow he is suddenly certain will fall . . . only there's no one there. Is he lurking behind the corner at the end of this short addendum to the main corridor? No. Andy *saw* the stranger go scurrying around that corner. No way he could have gotten behind him again . . . unless he crawled along the ceiling like some kind of fly . . .

Andy looks up there, knowing he's being absurd, giving in to the whim-whams big time, but there's no one here to see him, so what the hey? And nothing for him to see overhead, either. Just an ordinary tin ceiling, now yellowed by age and decades of cigar and cigarette smoke.

The radio—oh, excuse me all to hell, *rah*-dio—is sitting on the windowsill, unmolested. Damn fine one, too, a Bose, the kind Paul Harvey always talks about on his noon show.

Beyond it, on the other side of the dirty glass, is the fire escape.

*Ah-hah!* Andy thinks, and hurries across to the window. One look at the turned thumb lock and his triumphant expression fades. He peers out just the same, and sees a short stretch of wet black iron descending into the fog. No blue robe, no scaly bald pate. Of course not. The knob shaker didn't go out that way unless he had some magic trick to move the window's inside thumb lock back into place once he was on the fire escape landing.

Andy turns, stands where he is a moment, thinking, then drops to his knees and looks under the bed. What he sees is an old tin ashtray with an unopened pack of Pall Malls and a Kingsland Old-Time Lager disposable lighter in it. Nothing else except dust kittens. He puts his hand on the coverlet preparatory to standing up, and his eyes fix on the closet door. It's standing ajar.

"There," Andy breathes, almost too low for his own ears to hear.

He gets up and crosses to the closet door. The fog may or may not come in on little cat feet, as Carl Sandburg said, but that is certainly how Andy Railsback moves across George Potter's room. His heart is beating hard again, hard enough to start the prominent vein in the center of his forehead pulsing. The man he saw is in the closet. Logic demands it. Intuition screams it. And if the doorknob shaker's just a confused old soul who wandered into the Nelson Hotel out of the fog, why hasn't he spoken to Andy? Why has he concealed himself? Because he may be old but he's not confused, that's why. No more confused than Andy is himself. The doorknob shaker's a fucking thief, and he's in the closet. He's maybe holding a knife that he has taken from the pocket of his tatty old robe. Maybe a coat hanger that he's unwound and turned into a weapon. Maybe he's just standing there in the dark, eyes wide, fingers hooked into claws. Andy no longer cares. You can scare him, you bet—he's a retired salesman, not Superman—but if you load enough tension on top of fright you turn it into anger, same as enough pressure turns coal into a diamond. And right now Andy is more pissed off than scared. He closes his fingers around the cool glass knob of the closet door. He squeezes down on it. He takes one breath . . . a second . . . steeling himself, getting ready . . . psyching himself up, the grandkids would say . . . one more breath, just for good luck, and . . .

With a low, stressful sound—half growl and half howl— Andy yanks the closet door wide, setting off a chatter of hangers. He crouches, hands up in fists, looking like some ancient sparring partner from the Gym Time Forgot.

"Come outta there, you fucking—"

No one there. Four shirts, one jacket, two ties, and three pairs of pants hanging like dead skin. A battered old suitcase that looks as if it has been kicked through every Greyhound Bus terminal in North America. Nothing else. Not a goddamn th—

But there is. There's something on the floor beneath the

shirts. Several somethings. Almost half a dozen somethings. At first Andy Railsback either doesn't understand what he's seeing or doesn't *want* to understand. Then it gets through to him, imprints itself on his mind and memory like a hoofprint, and he tries to scream. He can't. He tries again and nothing comes out but a rusty wheeze from lungs that feel no larger than old prune skins. He tries to turn around and can't do that, either. He is sure George Potter is coming, and if Potter finds him here, Andy's life will end. He has seen something George Potter can never allow him to talk about. But he can't turn. Can't scream. Can't take his eyes from the secret in George Potter's closet.

Can't move.

Because of the fog, nearly full dark has arrived in French Landing unnaturally early; it's barely six-thirty. The blurry yellow lights of Maxton Elder Care look like the lights of a cruise ship lying becalmed at sea. In Daisy wing, home of the wonderful Alice Weathers and the far less wonderful Charles Burnside, Pete Wexler and Butch Yerxa have both gone home for the day. A broad-shouldered, peroxide blonde named Vera Hutchinson is now on the desk. In front of her is a book entitled *E-Z Minute Crosswords*. She is currently puzzling over 6 Across: *Garfield, for example.* Six letters, first is F, third is L, sixth is E. She hates these tricky ones.

There's the swoosh of a bathroom door opening. She looks up and sees Charles Burnside come shuffling out of the men's in his blue robe and a pair of yellow-and-black striped slippers that look like great fuzzy bumblebees. She recognizes them at once.

"Charlie?" she asks, putting her pencil in her crossword book and closing it.

Charlie just goes shuffling along, jaw hanging down, a long runner of drool also hanging down. But he has an unpleasant half grin on his face that Vera doesn't care for. This one may have lost most of his marbles, but the few left in his head are *mean* marbles. Sometimes she knows that Charlie Burnside genuinely doesn't hear her when she speaks (or doesn't understand her), but she's positive that sometimes he just *pretends* not to understand. She has an idea this is one of the latter times.

"Charlie, what are you doing wearing Elmer's bee slippers? You know his great-granddaughter gave those to him."

The old man—Burny to us, Charlie to Vera—just goes shuffling along, in a direction that will eventually take him back to D18. Assuming he stays on course, that is.

"Charlie, stop."

Charlie stops. He stands at the head of Daisy's corridor like a machine that has been turned off. His jaw hangs. The string of drool snaps, and all at once there's a little wet spot on the linoleum beside one of those absurd but amusing slippers.

Vera gets up, goes to him, kneels down before him. If she knew what we know, she'd probably be a lot less willing to put her defenseless white neck within reach of those hanging hands, which are twisted by arthritis but still powerful. But of course she does not.

She grasps the left bee slipper. "Lift," she says.

Charles Burnside lifts his right foot.

"Oh, quit being such a turkey," she says. "Other one."

Burny lifts his left foot a little, just enough for her to get the slipper off.

"*Now* the right one."

Unseen by Vera, who is looking at his feet, Burny pulls his penis from the fly of his loose pajama pants and pretends to piss on Vera's bowed head. His grin widens. At the same time, he lifts his right foot and she removes the other slipper. When she looks back up, Burny's wrinkled old tool is back where it belongs. He considered baptizing her, he really did, but he has created almost enough mischief for one evening. One more little chore and he'll be off to the land of dreamy dreams. He's an old monster now. He needs his rest.

"All right," Vera says. "Want to tell me why one of these is dirtier than the other?" No answer. She hasn't really expected one. "Okay, beautiful. Back to your room or down to the common room, if you want. There's microwave popcorn and Jell-O pops tonight, I think. They're showing *The Sound of Music.* I'll see that these slippers get back to where they belong, and you taking them will be our little secret. Take them again and I'll have to report you, though. *Capisce?*"

Burny just stands there, vacant . . . but with that nasty little grin lifting his wrinkled old chops. And that light in his eyes. He *capisces*, all right.

"Go on," Vera says. "And you better not have dropped a load on the floor in there, you old buzzard."

Again she expects no reply, but this time she gets one. Burny's voice is low but perfectly clear. "Keep a civil tongue, you fat bitch, or I'll eat it right out of your head."

She recoils as if slapped. Burny stands there with his hands dangling and that little grin on his face.

"Get out of here," she says. "Or I really *will* report you." And a great lot of good that would do. Charlie is one of Maxton's cash cows, and Vera knows it.

Charlie recommences his slow walk (Pete Wexler has dubbed this particular gait the Old Fucks' Shuffle), now in his bare feet. Then he turns back. The bleary lamps of his eyes regard her. "The word you're looking for is *feline.* Garfield's a *feline.* Got it? Stupid cow."

With that he continues his trip down the corridor. Vera stands where she is, looking at him with her own jaw hanging. She has forgotten all about her crossword puzzle.

In his room, Burny lies down on his bed and slips his hands into the small of his back. From there down he aches like a bugger. Later he will buzz for the fat old bitch, get her to bring him an ibuprofen. For now, though, he has to stay sharp. One more little trick still to do.

"Found you, Potter," he murmurs. "Good . . . old . . . Potsie."

Burny hadn't been shaking doorknobs at all (not that Andy Railsback will ever know this). He had been feeling for the fellow who diddled him out of a sweet little Chicago housing deal back in the late seventies. South Side, home of the White Sox. Blacktown, in other words. Lots of federal money in that one, and several bushels of Illinois dough as well. Enough skim available to last for years, more angles than on a baseball field, but George "Go Fuck Your Mother" Potter had gotten there first, cash had changed hands beneath the proverbial table, and Charles Burnside (or perhaps then he'd still been Carl Bierstone; it's hard to remember) had been out in the cold.

But Burny has kept track of the thief for lo these many years. (Well, not Burny himself, actually, but as we must by now have realized, this is a man with powerful friends.) Old Potsie—what his friends called him in the days when he still had a few—declared bankruptcy in La Riviere back in the nineties, and lost most of what he still had hidden away during the Great Dot-Com Wreck of Double Aught. But that's not good enough for Burny. Potsie requires further punishment, and the coincidence of that particular fuckhead washing up in this particular fuckhole of a town is just too good to pass up. Burny's principal motive—a brainless desire to keep stirring the pot, to make sure bad goes to worse—hasn't changed, but this will serve that purpose, too.

So he traveled to the Nelson, doing so in a way Jack understands and Judy Marshall has intuited, homing in on Potsie's room like some ancient bat. And when he sensed Andy Railsback behind him, he was of course delighted. Railsback will save him having to make another anonymous call, and Burny is, in truth, getting tired of doing *all* their work for them.

Now, back in his room, all comfy-cozy (except for the arthritis, that is), he turns his mind away from George Potter, and begins to Summon.

Looking up into the dark, Charles Burnside's eyes begin to glow in a distinctly unsettling way. *"Gorg,"* he says. *"Gorg t'eelee. Dinnit a abbalah. Samman Tansy. Samman a montah a Irma. Dinnit a abbalah, Gorg. Dinnit a Ram Abbalah."*

Gorg. Gorg, come. Serve the abbalah. Find Tansy. Find the mother of Irma. Serve the abbalah, Gorg.

Serve the Crimson King.

Burny's eyes slip closed. He goes to sleep with a smile on his face. And beneath their wrinkled lids, his eyes continue to glow like hooded lamps.


Morty Fine, the night manager of the Nelson Hotel, is half-asleep over his magazine when Andy Railsback comes bursting in, startling him so badly that Morty almost tumbles out of his chair. His magazine falls to the floor with a flat slap.

"Jesus Christ, Andy, you almost gave me a heart attack!" Morty cries. "You ever hear of knocking, or at least clearing your goddam *throat*?"

Andy takes no notice, and Morty realizes the old fella is as white as a sheet. Maybe *he's* the one having the heart attack. It wouldn't be the first time one occurred in the Nelson.

"You gotta call the police," Andy says. "They're *horrible*. Dear Jesus, Morty, they're the most horrible pictures I ever saw . . . Polaroids . . . and oh man, I thought he was going to come back in . . . come back in any second . . . but at first I was just *froze,* and I . . . I . . ."

"Slow down," Morty says, concerned. "What are you talking about?"

Andy takes a deep breath and makes a visible effort to get himself under control. "Have you seen Potter?" he asks. "The guy in 314?"

"Nope," Morty says, "but most nights he's in Lucky's around this time, having a few beers and maybe a hamburger. Although why anybody would eat anything in that place, I don't know." Then, perhaps associating one ptomaine palace with another: "Hey, have you heard what the cops found out at Ed's Eats? Trevor Gordon was by and he said—"

"Never mind." Andy sits in the chair on the other side of the desk and stares at Morty with wet, terrified eyes. "Call the police. Do it right now. Tell them that the Fisherman is a man named George Potter, and he lives on the third floor of the Nelson Hotel." Andy's face tightens in a hard grimace, then relaxes again. "Right down the hall from yours truly."

"*Potter?* You're dreaming, Andy. That guy's nothing but a retired builder. Wouldn't hurt a fly."

"I don't know about flies, but he hurt the *hell* out of some little kids. I seen the Polaroids he took of them. They're in his closet. They're the worst things you ever saw."

Then Andy does something that amazes Morty and convinces him that this isn't a joke, and probably not just a mistake, either: Andy Railsback begins to cry.

Tansy Freneau, a.k.a. Irma Freneau's grieving mother, is not actually grieving yet. She knows she should be, but grief has been deferred. Right now she feels as if she is floating in a cloud of warm bright wool. The doctor (Pat Skarda's associate, Norma Whitestone) gave her five milligrams of lorazepam four or five hours ago, but that's only the start. The Holiday Trailer Park, where Tansy and Irma have lived since Cubby Freneau took off for Green Bay in ninety-eight, is handy to the Sand Bar, and she has a part-time "thing" going with Lester Moon, one of the bartenders. The Thunder Five has dubbed Lester Moon "Stinky Cheese" for some reason, but Tansy unfailingly calls him Lester, which he appreciates almost as much as the occasional boozy grapple in Tansy's bedroom or out back of the Bar, where there's a mattress (and a black light) in the storeroom. Around five this evening, Lester ran over with a quart of coffee brandy and four hundred milligrams of OxyContin, all considerably crushed and ready for snorting. Tansy has done half a dozen lines already, and she is cruising. Looking over old pictures of Irma and just . . . you know . . . cruising.

*What a pretty baby she was,* Tansy thinks, unaware that not far away, a horrified hotel clerk is looking at a very different picture of her pretty baby, a nightmare Polaroid he will never be able to forget. It is a picture Tansy herself will never have to look at, suggesting that perhaps there *is* a God in heaven.

She turns a page (GOLDEN MEMORIES has been stamped on the front of her scrapbook), and here are Tansy and Irma at the Mississippi Electrix company picnic, back when Irma was four and Mississippi Electrix was still a year away from bankruptcy and everything was more or less all right. In the photo, Irma is wading with a bunch of other tykes, her laughing face smeared with chocolate ice cream.

Looking fixedly at this snapshot, Tansy reaches for her glass of coffee brandy and takes a small sip. And suddenly, from nowhere (or the place from which all our more ominous and unconnected thoughts float out into the light of our regard), she finds herself remembering that stupid Edgar Allan Poe poem they had to memorize in the ninth grade. She hasn't thought of it in years and has no reason to now, but the words of the opening stanza rise effortlessly and perfectly in her mind. Looking at Irma, she recites them aloud in a toneless, pauseless voice that no doubt would have caused Mrs. Normandie to clutch her stringy white hair and groan. Tansy's recitation doesn't affect us that way; instead it gives us a deep and abiding chill. It is like listening to a poetry reading given by a corpse.

"Once upon a mih'nigh' dreary while I ponnered weak 'n' weary over many a quaint 'n' curris volume of forgotten lore while I nodded nearly nappin' sun'ly there came a tappin' as of someone gen'ly rappin' rappin' at my chamber door—"

At this precise moment there comes a soft rapping at the

cheap fiberboard door of Tansy Freneau's Airstream. She looks up, eyes floating, lips pursed and glossed with coffee brandy.

"Les'ser? Is that you?"

It might be, she supposes. Not the TV people, at least she hopes not. She wouldn't talk to the TV people, sent them packing. She knows, in some deep and sadly cunning part of her mind, that they would lull her and comfort her only to make her look stupid in the glare of their lights, the way that the people on the *Jerry Springer Show* always end up looking stupid.

No answer . . . and then it comes again. Tap. Tap-tap.

"'Tis some visitor," she says, getting up. It's like getting up in a dream. "'Tis some visitor, I murmured, tappin' at my chamber door, only this 'n' nothin' more."

Tap. Tap-tap.

Not like curled knuckles. It's a thinner sound than that. A sound like a single fingernail.

Or a beak.

She crosses the room in her haze of drugs and brandy, bare feet whispering on carpet that was once nubbly and is now balding: the ex-mother. She opens the door onto this foggy summer evening and sees nothing, because she's looking too high. Then something on the welcome mat rustles.

Something, some black *thing*, is looking up at her with bright, inquiring eyes. It's a raven, omigod it's Poe's *raven*, come to pay her a visit.

"Jesus, I'm trippin'," Tansy says, and runs her hands through her thin hair.

"Jesus!" repeats the crow on the welcome mat. And then, chipper as a chickadee: "Gorg!"

If asked, Tansy would have said she was too stoned to be frightened, but this is apparently not so, because she gives out a disconcerted little cry and takes a step backward.

The crow hops briskly across the doorsill and strides onto the faded purple carpet, still looking up at her with its bright eyes. Its feathers glisten with condensed drops of mist. It bops on past her, then pauses to preen and fluff. It looks around as if to ask, *How'm I doin', sweetheart?*

"Go away," Tansy says. "I don't know what the fuck you are, or if you're here at all, but—"

"Gorg!" the crow insists, then spreads its wings and fleets

across the trailer's living room, a charred fleck burnt off the back of the night. Tansy screams and cringes, instinctively shielding her face, but Gorg doesn't come near her. It alights on the table beside her bottle, there not being any bust of Pallas handy.

Tansy thinks: *It got disoriented in the fog, that's all. It could even be rabid, or have that Key Lime disease, whatever you call it. I ought to go in the kitchen and get the broom. Shoo it out before it shits around . . .*

But the kitchen is too far. In her current state, the kitchen seems hundreds of miles away, somewhere in the vicinity of Colorado Springs. And there's probably no crow here at all. Thinking of that goddamn poem has caused her to hallucinate, that's all . . . that, and losing her daughter.

For the first time the pain gets through the haze, and Tansy winces from its cruel and wiry heat. She remembers the little hands that sometimes pressed so tidily against the sides of her neck. The cries in the night, summoning her from sleep. The smell of her, fresh from the bath.

"Her name was Irma!" she suddenly shouts at the figment standing so boldly beside the brandy bottle. "*Irma*, not fucking Lenore, what kind of stupid name is Lenore? Let's hear you say *Irma!*"

"Irma!" the visitor croaks obediently, stunning her to silence. And its eyes. Ah! Its glittering eyes draw her, like the eyes of the Ancient Mariner in that other poem she was supposed to learn but never did. "Irma-Irma-Irma-Irma—"

"*Stop it!*" She doesn't want to hear it after all. She was wrong. Her daughter's name out of that alien throat is foul, insupportable. She wants to put her hands over her ears and can't. They're too heavy. Her hands have joined the stove and the refrigerator (miserable half-busted thing) in Colorado Springs. All she can do is look into those glittering black eyes.

It preens for her, ruffling its ebony sateen feathers. They make a loathsome little scuttering noise all up and down its back and she thinks, *"Prophet!" said I, "thing of evil! prophet still, if bird or devil!"*

Certainty fills her heart like cold water. "What do you know?" she asks. "Why did you come?"

"Know!" croaks the Crow Gorg, nodding its beak briskly up and down. "Come!"

And does it wink? Good God, *does it wink at her?*

"Who killed her?" Tansy Freneau whispers. "Who killed my pretty baby?"

The crow's eyes fix her, turn her into a bug on a pin. Slowly, feeling more in a dream than ever (but this *is* happening, on some level she understands that perfectly), she crosses to the table. Still the crow watches her, still the crow draws her on. *Night's Plutonian shore,* she thinks. *Night's Plutonian fuckin' shore.*

"Who? Tell me what you know!"

The crow looks up at her with its bright black eyes. Its beak opens and closes, revealing a wet red interior in tiny peeks.

"Tansy!" it croaks. "Come!"

The strength runs out of her legs, and she drops to her knees, biting her tongue and making it bleed. Crimson drops splatter her U of W sweatshirt. Now her face is on a level with the bird's face. She can see one of its wings brushing up and down, sensuously, on the glass side of the coffee-brandy bottle. The smell of Gorg is dust and heaped dead flies and ancient urns of buried spice. Its eyes are shining black portholes looking into some other world. Hell, perhaps. Or Sheol.

*"Who?"* she whispers.

Gorg stretches its black and rustling neck until its black beak is actually in the cup of her ear. It begins to whisper, and eventually Tansy Freneau begins to nod. The light of sanity has left her eyes. And when will it return? Oh, I think we all know the answer to that one.

Can you say "Nevermore"?

# 16

6:45 P.M. French Landing is fogged out, fagged out, and uneasy in its heart, but quiet. The quiet won't last. Once it has started, *slippage* never stops for long.

At Maxton's, Chipper has stayed late, and considering the leisurely (and really quite sensational) blow job being administered to him by Rebecca Vilas as he sits sprawled in his office chair, his decision to put in a little overtime isn't that surprising.

In the common room, the old folks sit transfixed by Julie Andrews and *The Sound of Music*. Alice Weathers is actually crying with happiness—*Music* is her all-time favorite movie. *Singin' in the Rain* comes close, but close never won the cigar. Among those MEC inmates who are ambulatory, only Burny is missing . . . except no one here misses him at all. Burny is deep in sleep. The spirit that now controls him—the demon, we might as well say—has its own agenda in French Landing, and it has used Burny roughly over these last few weeks (not that Burny's complaining; he is a very willing accomplice).

On Norway Valley Road, Jack Sawyer is just pulling his Dodge Ram into Henry Leyden's driveway. The fog out here is thinner, but it still turns the truck's headlamps into soft coronas. Tonight he will recommence *Bleak House* at chapter 7 ("The Ghost's Walk") and hopefully reach the end of chapter 8 ("Covering a Multitude of Sins"). But before Dickens, he has promised to listen to the Wisconsin Rat's latest candidate for hot rotation, a number called "Gimme Back My Dog" by Slobberbone.

"Every five years or so, another great rock-'n'-roll song comes break-dancing out of the woodwork," Henry has told him over the phone, and Jack's damned if he can't hear the Rat screaming around the edges of his friend's voice, popping wheelies out there on the edge of darkness. "This is a *great* rock-'n'-roll song."

"If you say so," Jack replies dubiously. His idea of a great rock-'n'-roll song is "Runaround Sue," by Dion.

At 16 Robin Hood Lane (that sweet little Cape Cod honey of a home), Fred Marshall is down on his hands and knees, wearing a pair of green rubber gloves and washing the floor. He's still got Tyler's baseball cap balanced on his head, and he's weeping.

Out at the Holiday Trailer Park, the Crow Gorg is dripping poison into the porches of Tansy Freneau's ears.

In the sturdy brick house on Herman Street where he lives with the beautiful Sarah and the equally beautiful David, Dale Gilbertson is just getting ready to head back to the office, his movements slightly slowed by two helpings of chicken pot pie and a dish of bread pudding. When the telephone rings, he is not terribly surprised. He's had that feeling, after all. His caller is Debbi Anderson, and from her first word he knows that something has popped.

He listens, nodding, asking an occasional question. His wife stands in the kitchen doorway, watching him with worried eyes. Dale bends and jots on the pad beside the phone. Sarah walks over and reads two names: Andy Railsback and M. Fine.

"You've still got Railsback on the line?" he asks.

"Yes, on hold—"

"Patch me in."

"Dale, I don't know if I know how to do that." Debbi sounds uncharacteristically flustered. Dale closes his eyes a moment, reminds himself that this isn't her usual job.

"Ernie's not there yet?"

"No."

"Who is?"

"Bobby Dulac . . . I think Dit might be in the shower . . ."

"Put Bobby on," Dale says, and is relieved when Bobby is able to patch him quickly and painlessly through to Andy Railsback in Morty Fine's office. The two men have been upstairs to room 314, and one look at the Polaroids scattered on the floor of George Potter's closet has been enough for Morty. He's now as pale as Andy himself. Maybe paler.

Outside the police station, Ernie Therriault and Reginald "Doc" Amberson meet in the parking lot. Doc has just arrived on his old (but perfectly maintained) Harley Fat Boy. They exchange amiable greetings in the fog. Ernie Therriault is another cop—sort of—but relax: he's the last one we'll have to meet (well, there *is* an FBI agent running around here someplace, but never mind him right now; he's in Madison, and he's a fool).

Ernie is a trim sixty-five, retired from full-time police duty for almost twelve years, and still four times the cop Arnold Hrabowski will ever be. He supplements his pension by doing night dispatch at the FLPD (he doesn't sleep so well these days, thanks to a cranky prostate) and pulling private security time at First Bank of Wisconsin on Fridays, when the Wells Fargo people come at two and the Brinks people at four.

Doc looks every inch the Hells Angel, with his long black-and-gray beard (which he sometimes braids with ribbons in the style of the pirate Edward Teach), and he brews beer for a living, but the two men get along very well. For one thing, they recognize each other's intelligence. Ernie doesn't know if Doc really *is* a doctor, but he could be. Maybe at one point he was.

"Anything changed?" Doc asks.

"Not that I know of, my friend," Ernie says. One of the Five comes by every night, in turn, to check. Tonight Doc's got the duty.

"Mind if I walk in with you?"

"Nope," Ernie said. "Just as long as you respect the rule."

Doc nods. Some of the other Fives can be pissy about the rule (especially Sonny, who's pissy about lots of stuff), but Doc abides by it: one cup of coffee or five minutes, whichever comes first, then down the road you go. Ernie, who saw plenty of *real* Hells Angels when he was a cop in Phoenix back in the seventies, appreciates how deeply patient Beezer St. Pierre and his crew have been. But of course, they are *not* Hells Angels, or Pagans, or Beasts on Bikes, or any of that nonsense. Ernie doesn't know exactly *what* they are, but he knows that they listen to Beezer, and he suspects that Beezer's patience is growing thin. Ernie knows his would be by now.

"Well, then, come on in," Ernie says, clapping the big man on the shoulder. "Let's see what's shaking."

Quite a lot, as it turns out.

Dale finds he is able to think quickly and clearly. His earlier fear has left him, partly because the fuckup has already happened and the case—the *official* case, anyway—has been taken away from him. Mostly because he knows he can now call on Jack if he needs to, and Jack will answer. Jack's his safety net.

He listens to Railsback's description of the Polaroids—mostly letting the old fella vent and settle a bit—and then asks a single question about the two photos of the boy.

"Yellow," Railsback replies with no hesitation. "The shirt was yellow. I could read the word *Kiwanis* on it. Nothing else. The . . . the blood . . ."

Dale says he understands, and tells Railsback an officer will join them shortly.

There is the sound of the phone shifting hands, and then Fine is in his ear—a fellow Dale knows and doesn't much care for. "What if he comes back, Chief? What if Potter comes back here to the hotel?"

"Can you see the lobby from where you are?"

"No." Petulant. "We're in the office. I told you that."

"Then go out front. Look busy. If he comes in—"

"I don't want to do that. If you'd seen those pitchers, you wouldn't want to do it, either."

"You don't have to say boo to him," Dale says. "Just call if he goes by."

"But—"

"Hang up the telephone, sir. I've got a lot to do."

Sarah has put her hand on her husband's shoulder. Dale puts his free one over hers. There is a click in his ear, loud enough to sound disgruntled.

"Bobby, are you on?"

"Right here, Chief. Debbi, too, and Dit. Oh, and Ernie just walked in." He lowers his voice. "He's got one of those motor-cycle boys with him. The one who calls himself Doc."

Dale thinks furiously. Ernie, Debbi, Dit, and Bobby: all in uniform. Not good for what he wants. He comes to a sudden decision and says, "Put the hogger on."

*"What?"*

"You heard me."

A moment later he's talking to Doc Amberson. "You want to help bust the fucker who killed Armand St. Pierre's little girl?"

"Hell, yes." No hesitation.

"All right: don't ask questions and don't make me repeat myself."

"I'm listening," Doc says crisply.

"Tell Officer Dulac to give you the blue cell phone in evidence storage, the one we took off the doper who skipped. He'll know the one I mean." If anyone tries to star-69 a call originating from that phone, Dale knows, they won't be able to trace it back to his shop, and that's just as well. He is, after all, supposed to be off the case.

"Blue cell phone."

"Then walk down to Lucky's Tavern, next to the Nelson Hotel."

"I got my bike—"

"No. *Walk*. Go inside. Buy a lottery ticket. You'll be looking for a tall man, skinny, salt-and-pepper hair, about seventy, khaki pants, maybe a khaki shirt, too. Most likely alone. His favorite roost is between the jukebox and the little hall that goes to the johns. If he's there, call the station. Just hit 911. Got all that?"

"Yeah."

"Go. Really shuck your buns, Doctor."

Doc doesn't even bother to say good-bye. A moment later, Bobby's back on the phone. "What are we gonna do, Dale?"

"If he's there, we're gonna take the son of a bitch," Dale says. He's still under control, but he can feel his heartbeat accelerating, really starting to crank. The world stands out before him with a brilliance that hasn't been there since the first murder. He can feel every finger of his wife's hand on his shoulder. He can smell her makeup and her hairspray. "Get Tom Lund. And lay out three of the Kevlar vests." He thinks it over, then says: "Make it four."

"You're going to call Hollywood?"

"Yeah," he says, "but we're not gonna wait for him." On that he hangs up. Because he wants to bolt, he makes himself stand still for a moment. Takes a deep breath. Lets it out, then takes another.

Sarah grasps his hands. "Be careful."

"Oh yeah," Dale says. "You can take that to the bank." He starts for the door.

"What about Jack?" she calls.

"I'll get him from the car," he says without slowing. "If God's on our side, we'll have the guy in lockup before he makes it halfway to the station."

Five minutes later, Doc is standing at the bar in Lucky's, listening to Trace Adkins sing "I Left Something Turned On at Home" and scratching a Wisconsin instant-winner ticket. It actually *is* a winner—ten bucks—but most of Doc's attention is focused in the direction of the juke. He bops his shaggy head a little bit, as if he's really getting off on this particular example of Shitkicker Deluxe.

Sitting at the table in the corner with a plate of spaghetti in front of him (the sauce as red as a nosebleed) and a pitcher of beer close at hand is the man he's looking for: tall even sitting down, skinny, lines grooving his tanned hound dog's face, salt-and-pepper hair neatly combed back. Doc can't really see the shirt, because the guy's got a napkin tucked into the collar, but the long leg sticking out from under the table is dressed in khaki.

If Doc was entirely sure this was the baby-killing puke who did Amy, he'd make a citizen's arrest right now—an extremely rough one. Fuck the cops and their Miranda shit. But maybe the guy's only a witness, or an accomplice, or something.

He takes his ten-spot from the bartender, turns down the suggestion that he stay for a beer, and strolls back out into the fog. Ten steps up the hill, he takes the blue cell phone from his pocket and dials 911. This time it's Debbi who answers.

"He's there," Doc says. "What next?"

"Bring the phone back," she says, and hangs up.

"Well, fuck you very much," Doc says mildly. But he'll be a good boy. He'll play by their rules. Only first—

He dials another number on the blue phone (which has one more chore to do before it passes out of our tale forever) and Bear Girl answers. "Put him on, sweetness," he says, hoping she won't tell him that Beezer's gone down to the Sand Bar. If the

Beez ever goes down there alone, it'll be because he's after one thing. A bad thing.

But a moment later Beezer's voice is in his ear—rough, as if he's been crying. "Yeah? What?"

"Round 'em up and get your heavyset ass down to the police station parking lot," Doc tells him. "I'm not a hunnert percent certain, but I think they might be getting ready to nail the motherfucker done it. I might even have seen—"

Beezer is gone before Doc can get the phone off his ear and push the OFF button. He stands in the fog, looking up at the bleary lights of the French Landing cop shop, wondering why he didn't tell Beezer and the boys to meet him outside of Lucky's. He supposes he knows the answer. If Beezer got to that old guy before the cops, spaghetti might turn out to be the old guy's last meal.

Better to wait, maybe.

Wait and see.

There's nothing but a fine mist on Herman Street, but the soup thickens almost as soon as Dale turns toward downtown. He turns on his parking lights, but they're not enough. He goes to low beams, then calls Jack's. He hears the recorded announcement start, kills the call, and dials Uncle Henry's. And Uncle Henry answers. In the background, Dale can hear a howling fuzz-tone guitar and someone growling "Gimme back my *dog!*" over and over.

"Yes, he's just arrived," Henry allows. "We're currently in the Musical Appreciation phase of our evening. Literature to follow. We've reached a critical juncture in *Bleak House*—Chesney Wold, the Ghost's Walk, Mrs. Rouncewell, all of that—and so unless your need is actually *urgent*—"

"It is. Put him on *now,* Unc."

Henry sighs. *"Oui, mon capitaine."*

A moment later he's talking to Jack, who of course agrees to come at once. This is good, but French Landing's police chief finds some of his friend's reactions a trifle puzzling. No, Jack doesn't want Dale to hold the arrest until he arrives. Very considerate of him to ask, also very considerate of Dale to have saved him a Kevlar vest (part of the law enforcement booty showered on the FLPD and thousands of other small police departments during the Reagan years), but Jack believes Dale and his men can nab George Potter without much trouble.

The truth is, Jack Sawyer seems only slightly interested in George Potter. Ditto the horrific photos, although they must certainly be authentic; Railsback has I.D.'d Johnny Irkenham's yellow Kiwanis Little League shirt, a detail never given to the press. Even the loathsome Wendell Green never ferreted out that particular fact.

What Jack asks about—not once but several times—is the guy Andy Railsback saw in the hallway.

"... one slipper, and that's all I know!" Dale is finally ... to admit. "Jesus, Jack, what does it matter? Listen, I have to get off the telephone."

"Ding-dong," Jack replies, equally enough, and rings off.

Dale turns into the foggy parking lot. He sees Ernie Therriault and the biker-brewer called Doc standing outside the back door, talking. They are little more than shadows in the drifting fog.

Dale's conversation with Jack has left him feeling very uneasy, as if there are huge clues and signposts that he (dullard that he is) has entirely missed. But what clues? For Christ's sake, *what* signposts? And now a dash of resentment flavors his unease. Perhaps a high-powered Lucas Davenport type like Jack Sawyer just can't believe in the obvious. Perhaps guys like him are always more interested in the dog that *doesn't* bark.

Sound travels well in the fog, and halfway to the station's back door, Dale hears motorcycle engines explode into life down by the river. Down on Nailhouse Row.

"Dale," Ernie says. He nods a greeting as if this were any ordinary evening.

"Hey, Chief," Doc chips in. He's smoking an unfiltered cigarette, looks to Dale like a Pall Mall or a Chesterfield. *Some doctor,* Dale thinks. "If I may egregiously misquote Misterogers," Doc goes on, "it's a beautiful night in the neighborhood. Wouldn't you say?"

"You called them," Dale says, jerking his head in the direction of the revving motorcycles. Two pairs of headlights swing into the parking lot. Dale sees Tom Lund behind the wheel of the first car. The second vehicle is almost certainly

Danny Tcheda's personal. The troops are gathering once more. Hopefully this time they can avoid any cataclysmic fuckups. They better. This time they could be playing for all the marbles.

"Well, I couldn't comment on that directly," Doc says, "but I could ask, If they were your friends, what would you do?"

"Same damn thing," Dale says, and goes inside.

Henry Leyden once more sits primly in the passenger seat of the Ram pickup. Tonight he's dressed in an open-collared white shirt and a pair of trim blue khakis. Slim as a male model, silvering hair combed back. Did Sydney Carton look any cooler going to the guillotine? Even in Charles Dickens's mind? Jack doubts it.

"Henry—"

"I know," Henry says. "Sit here in the truck like a good little boy until I'm called."

"With the doors locked. And don't say *Oui, mon capitaine.* That one's wore out."

"Will *affirmative* do?"

"Nicely."

The fog thickens as they near town, and Jack dips his headlights—high beams are no good in this shit. He looks at the dashboard clock. 7:03 P.M. Things are speeding up. He's glad. Do more, think less, Jack Sawyer's recipe for E-Z care sanity.

"I'll whisk you inside as soon as they've got Potter jugged."

"You don't expect them to have a problem with that, do you?"

"No," Jack says, then changes the subject. "You know, you surprised me with that Slobberbone record." He can't really call it a song, not when the lead vocalist simply shrieked most of the lyrics at the top of his lungs. "That was good."

"It's the lead guitar that makes the record," Henry says, picking up on Jack's careful use of the word. "Surprisingly sophisticated. Usually the best you can hope for is in tune." He unrolls his window, sticks his head out like a dog, then pulls it back in. Speaking in that same conversational voice, he says: "The whole town reeks."

"It's the fog. It pulls up the river's stinkiest essence."

"No," Henry replies matter-of-factly, "it's death. I smell it, and I think you do, too. Only maybe not with your nose."

"I smell it," Jack admits.

"Potter's the wrong man."

"I think so."

"The man Railsback saw was a Judas goat."

"The man Railsback saw was almost certainly the Fisherman."

They drive in silence for a while.

"Henry?"

"Affirmative."

"What's the best record? The best record and the best song?"

Henry thinks about it. "Do you realize what a dreadfully personal question that is?"

"Yes."

Henry thinks some more, then says: " 'Stardust,' maybe. Hoagy Carmichael. For you?"

The man behind the wheel thinks back, all the way back to when Jacky was six. His father and Uncle Morgan had been the jazz fiends; his mother had had simpler tastes. He remembers her playing the same song over and over one endless L.A. summer, sitting and looking out the window and smoking. *Who is that lady, Mom?* Jacky asks, and his mother says, *Patsy Cline. She died in an airplane crash.*

" 'Crazy Arms,' " Jack says. "The Patsy Cline version. Written by Ralph Mooney and Chuck Seals. That's the best record. That's the best song."

Henry says no more for the rest of the drive. Jack is crying. Henry can smell his tears.

Let us now take the wider view, as some politician or other no doubt said. We almost have to, because things have begun to overlap. While Beezer and the rest of the Thunder Five are arriving in the FLPD parking lot just off Sumner Street, Dale and Tom Lund and Bobby Dulac—bulky in their Kevlar vests—are double-parking in front of Lucky's. They park in the street because Dale wants plenty of room to swing the back door of the cruiser wide, so that Potter can be bundled in as fast as possible. Next door, Dit Jesperson and Danny Tcheda are at the Nelson Hotel, where they will cordon off room 314 with yellow POLICE LINE tape. Once that's done, their orders are to bring Andy Railsback and Morty Fine to the police station. Inside the police station, Ernie Therriault is calling WSP officers Brown and Black, who will arrive after the fact . . . and if they're pissed about that, good deal. At the Sand Bar, a dead-eyed Tansy Freneau has just pulled the plug on the jukebox, killing the Wallflowers. *"Listen to me, everybody!"* she cries in a voice that's not her own. *"They've got him! They've got the baby-murdering son of a bitch! His name's Potter! They'll have him up in Madison by midnight, and unless we do something, some smart lawyer will have him back out on the street by next Monday! WHO WANTS TO HELP ME DO SOMETHING ABOUT IT?"* There is a moment of silence . . . and then a roar. The half-stoned, half-drunk habitués of the Sand Bar know *exactly* what they want to do about it. Jack and Henry, meanwhile, with no fog to slow them down until they hit town, swing into the police station parking lot just behind the Thunder Five, who park in a line around Doc's Fat Boy. The lot is filling up rapidly, mostly with cops' personal vehicles. Word of the impending arrest has spread like fire in dry grass. Inside, one of Dale's crew—we need not bother with exactly which one—spots the blue cell phone Doc used outside Lucky's. This cop grabs it and ducks into the closet-sized room marked EVIDENCE STORAGE.

At the Oak Tree Inn, where he has checked in for the duration of the Fisherman case, Wendell Green is getting sullenly drunk. In spite of three double whiskeys, his neck still aches from having his camera pulled off by the biker asshole, and his gut still aches from being sucker punched by the Hollywood asshole. The parts of him that hurt most of all, however, are his pride and his pocketbook. Sawyer concealed evidence just as sure as shit sticks to a blanket. Wendell is halfway to believing that Sawyer *himself* is the Fisherman . . . but how can he prove either thing with his film gone? When the bartender says he has a call, Wendell almost tells him to stick the call up his ass. But he's a professional, goddamnit, a *professional news hawk,* and so he goes over to the bar and takes the phone.

"Green," he growls.

"Hello, asshole," says the cop with the blue cell phone. Wendell doesn't yet know his caller is a cop, only that it's some cheery ghoul poaching on his valuable drinking time. "You want to print some good news for a change?"

"Good news doesn't sell papers, my pal."

"This will. We caught the guy."

*"What?"* In spite of the three doubles, Wendell Green is suddenly the most undrunk man on the planet.

"Did I stutter?" The caller is positively gloating, but Wendell Green no longer cares. "We caught the Fisherman. Not the staties, not the Feebs, *us.* Name's George Potter. Early seventies. Retired builder. Had Polaroids of all three dead kids. If you hustle, you can maybe be here to snap the picture when Dale takes him inside."

This thought—this *shining possibility*—explodes in Wendell Green's head like a firework. Such a photo could be worth five times as much as one of little Irma's corpse, because the reputable mags would want it. And TV! Also, think of this: What if someone shot the bastard as Marshall Dillon was taking him in? Given the town's mood, it's far from impossible. Wendell has a brief and brilliant memory of Lee Harvey Oswald clutching his stomach, mouth open in his dying yawp.

"Who is this?" he blurts.

"Officer Fucking Friendly," the voice on the other end says, and clicks off.

In Lucky's Tavern, Patty Loveless is now informing those assembled (older than the Sand Bar crowd, and a good deal less interested in nonalcoholic substances) that she can't get no satisfaction and her tractor can't get no traction. George Potter has finished his spaghetti, neatly folded his napkin (which in the end had to catch only a single drop of red-sauce), and turned seriously to his beer. Sitting close to the juke as he is, he doesn't notice that the room has quieted with the entrance of three men, only one in uniform but all three armed and wearing what look too much like bulletproof vests to be anything else.

"George Potter?" someone says, and George looks up. With his glass in one hand and his pitcher of suds in the other, he is a sitting duck.

"Yeah, what about it?" he asks, and then he is snatched by the arms and shoulders and yanked from his spot. His knees connect with the bottom of the table, overturning it. The spaghetti plate and the pitcher hit the floor. The plate shatters. The pitcher, made of sterner stuff, does not. A woman screams. A man says, "Yow!" in a low and respectful voice.

Potter holds on to his partly filled glass for a moment, and then Tom Lund plucks this potential weapon from his hand. A second later, Dale Gilbertson is snapping on the cuffs, and Dale has time to think that it's the most satisfying sound he's ever heard in his life. *His* tractor has finally gotten some traction, by God.

This deal is light-years from the snafu at Ed's; this is slick and tidy. Less than ten seconds after Dale asked the only question—"George Potter?"—the suspect is out the door and into the fog. Tom has one elbow, Bobby the other. Dale is still rattling off the Miranda warning, sounding like an auctioneer on amphetamines, and George Potter's feet never touch the sidewalk.

Jack Sawyer is fully alive for the first time since he was twelve years old, riding back from California in a Cadillac Eldorado driven by a werewolf. He has an idea that later on he will pay a high price for this regained vividness, but he hopes he will just button his lip and fork over when the time comes. Because the rest of his adult life now seems so *gray*.

He stands outside his truck, looking in the window at Henry. The air is dank and already charged with excitement. He can hear the blue-white parking lot lights sizzling, like something frying in hot juices.

"Henry."

"Affirmative."

"Do you know the hymn 'Amazing Grace'?"

"Of course I do. Everyone knows 'Amazing Grace.' "

Jack says, " 'Was blind but now I see.' I understand that now."

Henry turns his blind, fearfully intelligent face toward Jack. He is smiling. It is the second-sweetest smile Jack has ever seen. The blue ribbon still goes to Wolf, that dear friend of his wandering twelfth autumn. Good old Wolf, who liked everything right here and now.

"You're back, aren't you?"

Standing in the parking lot, our old friend grins. "Jack's back, that's affirmative."

"Then go do what you came back to do," Henry says.

"I want you to roll up the windows."

"And not be able to hear? I think not," Henry tells him, pleasantly enough.

More cops are coming, and this time the blue lights of the lead car are flashing and the siren is blurping. Jack detects a celebratory note to those little blurps and decides he doesn't have time to stand here arguing with Henry about the Ram's windows.

He heads for the back door of the police station, and two of the blue-white arcs cast his shadow double on the fog, one dark head north and one south.

Part-time officers Holtz and Nestler pull in behind the car bearing Gilbertson, Lund, Dulac, and Potter. We don't care much about Holtz and Nestler. Next in line is Jesperson and Tcheda, with Railsback and Morton Fine in the back seat (Morty is complaining about the lack of knee room). We care about Railsback, but he can wait. Next into the lot—oh, this is interesting, if not entirely unexpected: Wendell Green's beat-up red Toyota, with the man himself behind the wheel. Around his neck is his backup camera, a Minolta that'll keep taking pictures as long as Wendell keeps pressing the button. No one from the Sand Bar—not yet—but there *is* one more car waiting to turn into the already crowded lot. It's a discreet green Saab with a POLICE POWER sticker on the left side of the bumper and one reading HUGS NOT DRUGS on the right. Behind the wheel of the Saab, looking stunned but determined to do the right thing (whatever the right thing might be), is Arnold "the Mad Hungarian" Hrabowski.

Standing in a line against the brick wall of the police station are the Thunder Five. They wear identical denim vests with gold 5's on the left breast. Five sets of meaty arms are crossed on five broad chests. Doc, Kaiser Bill, and Sonny wear their hair in thick ponytails. Mouse's is cornrowed tonight. And Beezer's floods down over his shoulders, making him look to Jack a little like Bob Seger in his prime. Earrings twinkle. Tats flex on huge biceps.

"Armand St. Pierre," Jack says to the one closest the door. "Jack Sawyer. From Ed's?" He holds out his hand and isn't ex-

actly surprised when Beezer only looks at it. Jack smiles pleasantly. "You helped big-time out there. Thanks."

Nothing from the Beez.

"Is there going to be trouble with the intake of the prisoner,
do you think?" Jack asks. He might be asking if Beezer thinks
it will shower after midnight.

Beezer watches over Jack's shoulder as Dale, Bobby, and
Tom help George Potter from the back of the cruiser and begin
walking him briskly toward the back door. Wendell Green
raises his camera, then is nearly knocked off his feet by Danny
Tcheda, who doesn't even have the pleasure of seeing which
asshole he's bumped. "Watch it, dickweed," Wendell squawks.

Beezer, meanwhile, favors Jack—if that is the word—with a
brief, cold glance. "Wellnow," he says. "We'll have to see how
it shakes out, won't we?"

"Indeed we will," Jack agrees. He sounds almost happy. He
pushes in between Mouse and Kaiser Bill, making himself a
place: the Thunder Five Plus One. And perhaps because they
sense he doesn't fear them, the two wide-boys make room. Jack
crosses his own arms over his chest. If he had a vest, an earring,
and a tattoo, he really would fit right in.

The prisoner and his custodians kill the distance between the
car and the building quickly. Just before they reach it, Beezer
St. Pierre, spiritual leader of the Thunder Five and father of
Amy, whose liver and tongue were eaten, steps in front of the
door. His arms are still folded. In the heartless glare of the parking lot lights, his massive biceps are blue.

Bobby and Tom suddenly look like guys with a moderate
case of the flu. Dale looks stony. And Jack continues to smile
gently, arms placidly crossed, seeming to gaze everywhere and
nowhere at once.

"Get out of the way, Beezer," Dale says. "I want to book this
man."

And what of George Potter? Is he stunned? Resigned? Both?
It's hard to tell. But when Beezer's bloodshot blue eyes meet
Potter's brown ones, Potter does not drop his gaze. Behind him,
the lookie-loos in the parking lot fall silent. Standing between
Danny Tcheda and Dit Jesperson, Andy Railsback and Morty
Fine are gawking. Wendell Green raises his camera and then

holds his breath like a sniper who's lucked into a shot—just one, mind you—at the commanding general.

"Did you kill my daughter?" Beezer asks. The gentle inquiry is somehow more terrible than any raw yell could have been, and the world seems to hold its breath. Dale makes no move. In that moment he seems as frozen as the rest of them. The world waits, and the only sound is a low, mournful hoot from some fogbound boat on the river.

"Sir, I never killed no one," Potter says. He speaks softly and without emphasis. Although he has expected nothing else, the words still box Jack's heart. There is an unexpected painful dignity in them. It's as if George Potter is speaking for all the lost good men of the world.

"Stand aside, Beezer," Jack says gently. "You don't want to hurt this guy."

And Beezer, looking suddenly not at all sure of himself, does stand aside.

Before Dale can get his prisoner moving again, a raucously cheerful voice—it can only be Wendell's—yells out: "Hey! Hey, Fisherman! Smile for the camera!"

They all look around, not just Potter. They have to; that cry is as insistent as fingernails dragged slowly down a slate blackboard. White light strobes the foggy parking lot—one! two! three! four!—and Dale snarls. "Aw, fuck me till I cry! Come on, you guys! Jack! Jack, I want you!"

From behind them, one of the other cops calls, "Dale! You want me to grab this creep?"

"Leave him alone!" Dale shouts, and bulls his way inside. It's not until the door is closed behind him and he's in the lower hall with Jack, Tom, and Bobby that Dale realizes how certain he was that Beezer would simply snatch the old man away from him. And then crack his neck like a chicken bone.

"Dale?" Debbi Anderson calls uncertainly from halfway down the stairs. "Is everything all right?"

Dale looks at Jack, who still has his arms crossed over his chest and is still smiling his little smile. "I think it is," Dale says. "For now."

Twenty minutes later, Jack and Henry (the latter gentleman retrieved from the truck and still reet-petite) sit in Dale's office.

Beyond the closed door, the ready room roars with conversation and laughter: almost every cop on the FLPD force is out there, and it sounds like a goddamn New Year's Eve party. There are occasional shouts and smacking sounds that can only be relieved boys (and girls) in blue high-fiving each other. In a little while Dale will put a stop to that shit, but for now he's content to let them go ahead. He understands how they feel, even though he no longer feels that way himself.

George Potter has been printed and stuck in a cell upstairs to think things over. Brown and Black of the State Police are on their way. For now, that is enough. As for triumph . . . well, something about his friend's smile and his faraway eyes have put triumph on hold.

"I didn't think you were going to give Beezer his moment," Jack says. "It's a good thing you did. There might have been trouble right here in River City if you'd tried to face him down."

"I suppose I have a better idea tonight of how he feels," Dale replies. "I lost track of my own kid tonight, and it scared the living shit out of me."

"David?" Henry cries, leaning forward. "Is David okay?"

"Yeah, Uncle Henry, Dave's fine."

Dale returns his gaze to the man who now lives in his father's house. He's remembering the first time Jack ever laid eyes on Thornberg Kinderling. Dale had at that point known Jack only nine days—long enough to form some favorable opinions, but not long enough to realize how really extraordinary Jack Sawyer was. That was the day Janna Massengale at the Taproom told Jack about the trick Kinderling did when he was getting squiffy, that little trick of pinching his nostrils shut with his palm turned out to the world.

They had just arrived back at the police station from interviewing Janna, Dale in his personal unit that day, and he'd touched Jack on the shoulder just as Jack was about to get out of the car. "Speak a name, see the face it belongs to before suppertime, that's what my mother used to say." He pointed down to Second Street, where a broad-shouldered bald fellow had just come out of News 'n Notions, a newspaper under his arm and a fresh deck of smokes in his hand. "That's Thornberg Kinderling, his very own self."

Jack had bent forward without speaking, looking with the

sharpest (and perhaps the most merciless) eyes Dale had ever seen in his life.

"Do you want to approach him?" Dale had asked.

"No. Hush."

And Jack simply sat with one leg in Dale's car and one out of it, not moving, eyes narrowed. So far as Dale could tell, he didn't even breathe. Jack watched Kinderling open his cigarettes, tap one out, put it in his mouth, and light it. He watched Kinderling glance at the headline of the *Herald* and then saunter to his own car, an all-wheel-drive Subaru. Watched him get in. Watched him drive away. And by that time, Dale realized he was holding his own breath.

"Well?" he'd asked when the Kinderling-mobile was gone. "What do you think?"

And Jack had said, "I think he's the guy."

Only Dale had known better. Even then he had known better. Jack was saying *I think* only because he and Chief Dale Gilbertson of French Landing, Wisconsin, were still on short terms, getting-to-know-you, getting-to-work-with-you terms. What he had meant was *I know*. And although that was impossible, Dale had quite believed him.

Now, sitting in his office with Jack directly across the desk from him—his reluctant but scarily gifted deputy—Dale asks, "What do you think? Did he do it?"

"Come on, Dale, how can I—"

"Don't waste my time, Jack, because those assholes from WSP are going to be here any minute and they'll take Potter heigh-ho over the hills. You knew it was Kinderling the second you looked at him, and you were halfway down the block. You were close enough to Potter when I brought him in to count the hairs in his nose. So what do you think?"

Jack is quick, at least; spares him the suspense and just administers the chop. "No," he says. "Not Potter. Potter's not the Fisherman."

Dale has known that Jack believes this—knew it from his face outside—but hearing it is still an unhappy thump. He sits back, disappointed.

"Deduction or intuition?" Henry asks.

"Both," Jack says. "And stop looking like I plugged your mother, Dale. You may still have the key to this thing."

"Railsback?"

Jack makes a seesawing gesture with one hand—maybe, maybe not, it says. "Railsback probably saw what the Fisherman wanted him to see . . . although the single slipper is intriguing, and I want to ask Railsback about it. But if Mr. One-Slipper *was* the Fisherman, why would he lead Railsback—and us—to Potter?"

"To get us off his trail," Dale says.

"Oh, have we been on it?" Jack asks politely, and when neither of them answers: "But say he *thinks* we're on his trail. I can almost buy that, especially if he just remembered some goof he might have made."

"Nothing back yet on the 7-Eleven phone one way or the other, if that's what you're thinking of," Dale tells him.

Jack appears to ignore this. His eyes gaze off into the middle distance. That little smile is back on his face. Dale looks at Henry and sees Henry looking at Jack. Unc's smile is easier to read: relief and delight. *Look at that,* Dale thinks. *He's doing what he was built to do. By God, even a blind man can see it.*

"Why Potter?" Jack finally repeats. "Why not one of the Thunder Five, or the Hindu at the 7-Eleven, or Ardis Walker down at the bait shop? Why not Reverend Hovdahl? What motive usually surfaces when you uncover a frame job?"

Dale thinks it over. "Payback," he says at last. "Revenge."

In the ready room, a phone rings. "Shut up, shut up!" Ernie bellows to the others. "Let's try to act professional here for thirty seconds or so!"

Jack, meanwhile, is nodding at Dale. "I think I need to question Potter, and rather closely."

Dale looks alarmed. "Then you better get on it right away, before Brown and Black—" He comes to a halt, frowning, with his head cocked. A rumbling sound has impinged on his attention. It's low, but rising. "Uncle Henry, what's that?"

"Motors," Henry says promptly. "A lot of them. They're east of here, but coming this way. Edge of town. And I don't know if you've noticed this, but it sounds like the party next door is like, over, dude."

As if this were a cue, Ernie Therriault's distressed cry comes through the door. "Ohhhh, *shit*."

Dit Jesperson: "What's—"

Ernie: "Get the chief. Aw, never mind, I'll—" There is a single perfunctory knock and then Ernie's looking in at the brain trust. He's as collected and soldierly as ever, but his cheeks have paled considerably beneath his summer tan, and a vein is pulsing in the middle of his forehead.

"Chief, I just took a call on the 911, twenty was the Sand Bar?"

"*That* hole," Dale mutters.

"Caller was the bartender. Says about fifty to seventy people are on their way." By now the sound of approaching engines is very loud. It sounds to Henry like the Indy 500 just before the pace car runs for dear life and the checkered flag drops.

"Don't tell me," Dale says. "What do I need to make my day complete? Let me think. They're coming to take my prisoner."

"Umm, yes, sir, that's what the caller said," Ernie agrees. Behind him, the other cops are silent. In that moment they don't look like cops at all to Dale. They look like nothing but dismayed faces crudely drawn on a dozen or so white balloons (also two black ones—can't forget Pam Stevens and Bob Holtz). The sound of the engines continues to grow. "Also might want to know one other thing the caller said?"

"Christ, *what?*"

"Said the, um . . ." Ernie searches for a word that isn't *mob*. "The protest group was being led by the Freneau girl's mom?"

"Oh . . . my . . . Christ," Dale says. He gives Jack a look of sick panic and utter frustration—the look of a man who knows he is dreaming but can't seem to wake up no matter how hard he tries. "If I lose Potter, Jack, French Landing is going to be the lead story on CNN tomorrow morning."

Jack opens his mouth to reply, and the cell phone in his pocket picks that moment to start up its annoying tweet.

Henry Leyden immediately crosses his arms and tucks his hands into his armpits. "Don't hand it to me," he says. "Cell phones give you cancer. We agreed on that."

Dale, meanwhile, has left the room. As Jack digs for the cell phone (thinking someone has picked a cataclysmically shitty time to ask him about his network television preferences), Henry follows his nephew, walking briskly with his hands now held slightly out, fingers gently fluttering the air, seeming to read the currents for obstacles. Jack hears Dale saying that if he sees *a single drawn weapon,* the person who drew it will join Arnie Hrabowski on the suspension list. Jack is thinking exactly one thing: no one is taking Potter anywhere until Jack Sawyer has had time to put a few pointed questions. No way.

He flicks the cell phone open and says, "Not now, whoever you are. We've got—"

"Hidey-ho, Travelin' Jack," says the voice from the phone, and for Jack Sawyer the years once more roll away.

*"Speedy?"*

"The very one," Speedy says. Then the drawl is gone. The voice becomes brisk and businesslike. "And as one coppiceman to another, son, I think you ought to visit Chief Gilbertson's private bathroom. Right now."

Outside, there are enough vehicles arriving to shake the building. Jack has a bad feeling about this; has since he heard Ernie say who was leading the fools' parade.

"Speedy, I don't exactly have the time to visit the facilities right n—"

"You haven't got time to visit anyplace else," Speedy replies coldly. Only now he's the other one. The hard boy named Parkus. "What you're gonna find there you can use twice. But if you don't use it almighty quick the first time, you won't need it the second time. Because that man is gonna be up a lamppost."

And just like that, Speedy is gone.

When Tansy leads the willing patrons into the Sand Bar's parking lot, there is none of the carnival raucousness that was the keynote of the cluster fuck at Ed's Eats & Dawgs. Although most of the folks we met at Ed's have been spending the evening in the Bar, getting moderately to seriously tanked, they are quiet, even funereal, as they follow Tansy out and fire up their cars and pickups. But it's a savage funereality. She has taken something in from Gorg—some stone powerful poison—and passed it along to them.

In the belt of her slacks is a single crow feather.

Doodles Sanger takes her arm and guides her sweetly to Teddy Runkleman's International Harvester pickup. When Tansy heads for the truck bed (which already holds two men and one hefty female in a white rayon waitress's uniform), Doodles steers her toward the cab. "No, honey," Doodles says, "you sit up there. Be comfy."

Doodles wants that last place in the truck bed. She's spotted something, and knows just what to do with it. Doodles is quick with her hands, always has been.

The fog isn't thick this far from the river, but after two dozen cars and trucks have spun out of the Bar's dirt parking lot, following Teddy Runkleman's dented, one-taillight I.H., you can barely see the tavern. Inside, only half a dozen people are left— these were somehow immune to Tansy's eerily powerful voice. One of them is Stinky Cheese, the bartender. Stinky has a lot of liquid assets to protect out here and isn't going anywhere. When he calls 911 and speaks to Ernie Therriault, it will be mostly in the spirit of petulance. If he can't go along and enjoy the fun, by God, at least he can spoil it for the rest of those monkeys.

Twenty vehicles leave the Sand Bar. By the time the caravan passes Ed's Eats (the lane leading to it cordoned off by yellow tape) and the NO TRESPASSING sign alongside the overgrown lane to that queer forgotten house (not cordoned off; not even noticed, for that matter), the caravan has grown to thirty. There are fifty cars and trucks rolling down both lanes of Highway 35 by the time the mob reaches Goltz's, and by the time it passes the 7-Eleven, there must be eighty vehicles or more, and maybe two hundred and fifty people. Credit this unnaturally rapid swelling to the ubiquitous cell phone.

Teddy Runkleman, oddly silent (he is, in fact, afraid of the pallid woman sitting beside him—her snarling mouth and her wide, unblinking eyes), brings his old truck to a halt in front of the FLPD parking lot entrance. Sumner Street is steep here, and he sets the parking brake. The other vehicles halt behind him, filling the street from side to side, rumbling through rusty mufflers and blatting through broken exhaust pipes. Misaligned headlights stab the fog like searchlight beams at a movie premiere. The night's dank wet-fish smell has been overlaid with odors of burning gas, boiling oil, and cooking clutch lining. After a moment, doors begin to open and then clap shut. But there is no conversation. No yelling. No indecorous *yee-haw* whooping. Not tonight. The newcomers stand in clusters around the vehicles that brought them, watching as the people in the back of Teddy's truck either jump over the sides or slip off the end of the tailgate, watching as Teddy crosses to the passenger door, at this moment as attentive as a young man arriving with his date at the junior prom, watching as he helps down the slim young woman who has lost her daughter. The mist seems to outline her somehow, and give her a bizarre electric aura, the same blue of the sodium lights on Beezer's upper arms. The crowd gives out a collective (and weirdly amorous) sigh when it sees her. She is what connects them. All her life, Tansy Freneau has been the forgotten one—even Cubby Freneau forgot her eventually, running off to Green Bay and leaving her here to work odd jobs and collect the ADC. Only Irma remembered her, only Irma cared, and now Irma is dead. Not here to see (unless she's looking down from heaven, Tansy thinks in some distant and ever-receding part of her mind) her mother suddenly idolized. Tansy Freneau has tonight become the dearest subject of French Landing's eye and heart. Not its mind, because its mind is temporarily gone (perhaps in search of its conscience), but certainly of its eye and heart, yes. And now, as delicately as the girl she once was, Doodles Sanger approaches this woman of the hour. What Doodles spotted lying on the floor of Teddy's truck bed was an old length of rope, dirty and oily but thick enough to do the trick. Below Doodles's petite fist hangs the noose that her clever hands have fashioned on the ride into town. She hands it to Tansy, who holds it up in the misty light.

The crowd lets out another sigh.

Noose raised, looking like a female Diogenes in search of an honest man rather than of a cannibal in need of lynching, Tansy walks—delicate herself in her jeans and bloodstained sweatshirt—into the parking lot. Teddy, Doodles, and Freddy Saknessum walk behind her, and behind them come the rest. They move toward the police station like the tide.

The Thunder Five are still standing with their backs to the brick wall and their arms folded. "What the fuck do we do?" Mouse asks.

"I don't know about you," Beezer says, "but I'm gonna stand here until they grab me, which they probably will." He's looking at the woman with the upraised noose. He's a big boy and he's been in a lot of hard corners, but this chick frightens him with her blank, wide eyes, like the eyes of a statue. And there's something stuck in her belt. Something black. Is it a knife? Some kind of dagger? "And I'm not gonna fight, because it won't work."

"They'll lock the door, right?" Doc asks nervously. "I mean, the cops'll lock the door."

"I imagine," Beezer says, never taking his eyes from Tansy Freneau. "But if these folks want Potter, they'll have him on the half shell. *Look* at 'em, for Christ's sake. There's a couple of hundred."

Tansy stops, the noose still held up. "Bring him out," she says. Her voice is louder than it should be, as if some doctor has cunningly hidden an amplifying gadget in her throat. "Bring him out. Give us the killer!"

Doodles joins in. "Bring him out!"

And Teddy. *"Give us the killer!"*

And Freddy. *"Bring him out! Give us the killer!"*

And then the rest. It could almost be the sound track of George Rathbun's *Badger Barrage,* only instead of *"Block that kick!"* or *"On Wisconsin!"* they are screaming, *"BRING HIM OUT! GIVE US THE KILLER!"*

"They're gonna take him," Beezer murmurs. He turns to his troops, his eyes both fierce and frightened. Sweat stands out on his broad forehead in large perfect drops. "When she's got 'em pumped up to high, she'll come and they'll be right on her ass. Don't run, don't even unfold your arms. And when they grab you, let it happen. If you want to see daylight tomorrow, *let it happen.*"

The crowd stands knee-deep in fog like spoiled skim milk, chanting, *"BRING HIM OUT! GIVE US THE KILLER!"*

Wendell Green is chanting right along with them, but that doesn't keep him from continuing to take pictures.

Because shit, this is the story of a lifetime.

From the door behind Beezer, there's a click. *Yeah, they locked it,* he thinks. *Thanks, you whores.*

But it's the latch, not the lock. The door opens. Jack Sawyer steps out. He walks past Beezer without looking or reacting as Beez mutters, "Hey, man, I wouldn't go near her."

Jack advances slowly but not hesitantly into the no-man's-land between the building and the mob with the woman standing at its head, Lady Liberty with the upraised hangman's noose instead of a torch in her hand. In his simple gray collarless shirt and dark pants, Jack looks like a cavalier from some old romantic tale advancing to propose marriage. The flowers he holds in his own hand add to this impression. These tiny white blooms are what Speedy left for him beside the sink in Dale's bathroom, a cluster of impossibly fragrant white blossoms.

They are lilies of the vale, and they are from the Territories. Speedy left him no explanation about how to use them, but Jack needs none.

The crowd falls silent. Only Tansy, lost in the world Gorg has made for her, continues to chant: *"Bring him out! Give us the killer!"* She doesn't stop until Jack is directly in front of her, and he doesn't kid himself that it's his handsome face or dashing figure that ends the too loud repetition. It is the smell of the flowers, their sweet and vibrant smell the exact opposite of the meaty stench that hung over Ed's Eats.

Her eyes clear . . . a little, at least.

"Bring him out," she says to Jack. Almost a question.

"No," he says, and the word is filled with heartbreaking tenderness. "No, dear."

Behind them, Doodles Sanger suddenly thinks of her father for the first time in maybe twenty years and begins to weep.

"Bring him out," Tansy pleads. Now her own eyes are filling. "Bring out the monster who killed my pretty baby."

"If I had him, maybe I would," Jack says. "Maybe I would at that." Although he knows better. "But the guy we've got's not the guy you want. He's not the one."

"But Gorg said—"

Here is a word he knows. One of the words Judy Marshall tried to eat. Jack, not in the Territories but not entirely in this world right now either, reaches forward and plucks the feather from her belt. "Did Gorg give you this?"

"Yes—"

Jack lets it drop, then steps on it. For a moment he thinks—*knows*—that he feels it buzzing angrily beneath the sole of his shoe, like a half-crushed wasp. Then it stills. "Gorg lies, Tansy. Whatever Gorg is, he lies. The man in there is not the one."

Tansy lets out a great wail and drops the rope. Behind her, the crowd sighs.

Jack puts his arm around her and again he thinks of George Potter's painful dignity; he thinks of all the lost, struggling along without a single clean Territories dawn to light their way. He hugs her to him, smelling sweat and grief and madness and coffee brandy.

In her ear, Jack whispers: "I'll catch him for you, Tansy."
She stiffens. "You . . ."
"Yes."
"You . . . promise?"
"Yes."
"He's not the one?"
"No, dear."
"You swear?"
Jack hands her the lilies and says, "On my mother's name."

She lowers her nose to the flowers and inhales deeply. When her head comes up again, Jack sees that the danger has left her, but not the insanity. She's one of the lost ones now. Something has gotten to her. Maybe if the Fisherman is caught, it will leave her. Jack would like to believe that.

"Someone needs to take this lady home," Jack says. He speaks in a mild, conversational voice, but it still carries to the crowd. "She's very tired and full of sadness."

"I'll do it," Doodles says. Her cheeks gleam with tears. "I'll take her in Teddy's truck, and if he don't give me the keys, I'll knock him down. I—"

And that's when the chant starts again, this time from back in the crowd: *"Bring him out! Give us the killer! Give us the Fisherman! Bring out the Fisherman!"* For a moment it's a solo job, and then a few other hesitant voices begin to join in and lend harmony.

Still standing with his back against the bricks, Beezer St. Pierre says: "Ah, shit. Here we go again."

Jack forbade Dale to come out into the parking lot with him, saying that the sight of Dale's uniform might set off the crowd. He didn't mention the little bouquet of flowers he was holding, and Dale barely noticed them; he was too terrified of losing Potter to Wisconsin's first lynching of the new millennium. He followed Jack downstairs, however, and has now commandeered the peephole in the door by right of seniority.

The rest of the FLPD is still upstairs, looking out of the ready-room windows. Henry has ordered Bobby Dulac to give him a running play-by-play. Even in his current state of worry about Jack (Henry thinks there's at least a 40 percent chance the mob will either trample him or tear him apart), Henry is amused and flattered to realize that Bobby is doing George Rathbun without even realizing it.

"Okay, Hollywood's out there . . . he approaches the woman . . . no sign of fear . . . the rest of them are quiet . . . Jack and the woman appear to be talking . . . and holy jeezum, he's givin' her a bouquet of flowers! What a ploy!"

"Ploy" is one of George Rathbun's favorite sports terms, as in *The Brew Crew's hit-and-run ploy failed yet again last night at Miller Park.*

"She's *turnin' away!*" Bobby yells jubilantly. He grabs Henry's shoulder and shakes it. "Hot damn, I think it's over! *I think Jack turned her off!*"

"Even a blind man could see he turned her off," Henry says.

"Just in time, too," Bobby says. "Here's Channel Five and there's another truck with one of those big orange poles on it . . . Fox-Milwaukee, I think . . . and—"

*"Bring him out!"* a voice outside begins yelling. It sounds cheated and indignant. *"Give us the killer! Give us the Fisherman!"*

"Oh nooo!" Bobby says, even now sounding like George Rathbun, telling his morning-after audience how another Badger rally had started to fizzle. "Not nowwww, not with the TV here! That's—"

*"Bring out the Fisherman!"*

Henry already knows who that is. Even through two layers of chicken-wire-reinforced glass, that high, yapping cry is impossible to mistake.

Wendell Green understands his job—don't ever make the mistake of thinking he doesn't. His job is to *report* the news, to *analyze* the news, to sometimes *photojournalize* the news. His job

is not to *make* the news. But tonight he can't help it. This is the
second time in the last twelve hours that a career maker of a
story has been extended to his grasping, pleading hands, only
to be snatched away at the last second.

*"Bring him out!"* Wendell bawls. The raw strength in his
voice surprises, then thrills him. *"Give us the killer! Give us the
Fisherman!"*

The sound of other voices joining in with his provides an incredible rush. It is, as his old college roommate used to say, a
real zipper buster. Wendell takes a step forward, his chest
swelling, his cheeks reddening, his confidence building. He's
vaguely aware that the Action News Five truck is rolling slowly
toward him through the crowd. Soon there will be 10-k's and
5-k's shining through the fog; soon there will be TV cameras
rolling tape by their harsh light. So what? If the woman in the
blood-spattered sweatshirt was in the end too chicken to stand
up for her own kid, Wendell will do it for her! Wendell Green,
shining exemplar of civic responsibility! Wendell Green, *leader
of the people!*

He begins to pump his camera up and down. It's exhilarating. Like being back in college! At a Skynyrd concert! Stoned!
It's like—

There is a huge flash in front of Wendell Green's eyes. Then
the lights go out. All of them.

*"ARNIE HIT HIM WITH HIS FLASHLIGHT!"* Bobby is
screaming.

He grabs Dale's blind uncle by the shoulders and whirls him
in a delirious circle. A thick aroma of Aqua Velva descends
toward Henry, who knows Bobby's going to kiss him on both
cheeks, French style, a second before Bobby actually does this.
And when Bobby's narration resumes, he sounds as transported
as George Rathbun on those rare occasions when the local
sports teams actually buck the odds and grab the gold.

*"Can you believe it, the Mad Hungarian hit him with
his ever-lovin' flashlight and . . . GREEN'S DOWN! THE
FUCKIN' HUNGARIAN HAS PUT EVERYONE'S FAVORITE
ASSHOLE REPORTER ON THE MAT! WAY TO GO,
HRABOWSKI!"*

All around them, cops are cheering at the tops of their lungs.

Debbi Anderson starts chanting "We Are the Champions," and other voices quickly lend support.

*These are strange days in French Landing,* Henry thinks. He stands with his hands in his pockets, smiling, listening to the bedlam. There's no lie in the smile; he's happy. But he's also uneasy in his heart. Afraid for Jack.

Afraid for all of them, really.

"That was good work, man," Beezer tells Jack. "I mean, balls to the wall."

Jack nods. "Thanks."

"I'm not going to ask you again if that was the guy. You say he's not, he's not. But anything we can do to help you find the right one, you just call us."

The other members of the Thunder Five rumble assent; Kaiser Bill gives Jack a friendly bop on the shoulder. It will probably leave a bruise.

"Thanks," Jack says again.

Before he can knock on the door, it's opened. Dale grabs him and gives him a crushing embrace. When their chests touch, Jack can feel Dale's heart beating hard and fast.

"You saved my ass," Dale says into his ear. "Anything I can do—"

"You can do something, all right," Jack says, pulling him inside. "I saw another cop car behind the news trucks. Couldn't tell for sure, but I think this one was blue."

"Oh-oh," Dale says.

"Oh-oh is right. I need at least twenty minutes with Potter. It might not get us anything, but it might get us a lot. Can you hold off Brown and Black for twenty minutes?"

Dale gives his friend a grim little smile. "I'll see you get half an hour. Minimum."

"That's great. And the 911 tape of the Fisherman's call, do you still have that?"

"It went with the rest of the evidence we were holding after Brown and Black took the case. A trooper picked it up this afternoon."

"Dale, *no!*"

"Easy, big boy. I've got a cassette copy, safe in my desk." Jack pats his chest. "Don't scare me that way."

"Sorry," Dale says, thinking, *Seeing you out there, I wouldn't have guessed you were afraid of anything.*

Halfway up the stairs, Jack remembers Speedy telling him he could use what had been left in the bathroom twice . . . but he has given the flowers to Tansy Freneau. Shit. Then he cups his hands over his nose, inhales, and smiles.

Maybe he still has them after all.

# 17

George Potter is sitting on the bunk in the third holding cell down a short corridor that smells of piss and disinfectant. He's looking out the window at the parking lot, which has lately been the scene of so much excitement and which is still full of milling people. He doesn't turn at the sound of Jack's approaching footfalls.

As he walks, Jack passes two signs. ONE CALL MEANS ONE CALL, reads the first. A.A. MEETINGS MON. AT 7 P.M., N.A. MEETINGS THURS. AT 8 P.M., reads the second. There's a dusty drinking fountain and an ancient fire extinguisher, which some wit has labeled LAUGHING GAS.

Jack reaches the bars of the cell and raps on one with his house key. Potter at last turns away from the window. Jack, still in that state of hyperawareness that he now recognizes as a kind of Territorial residue, knows the essential truth of the man at a single look. It's in the sunken eyes and the dark hollows beneath them; it's in the sallow cheeks and the slightly hollowed temples with their delicate nestles of veins; it's in the too sharp prominence of the nose.

"Hello, Mr. Potter," he says. "I want to talk to you, and we have to make it fast."

"They wanted me," Potter remarks.

"Yes."

"Maybe you should have let 'em take me. Another three–four months, I'm out of the race anyway."

In his breast pocket is the Mag-card Dale has given him, and Jack uses it to unlock the cell door. There's a harsh buzzing as it trundles back on its short track. When Jack removes the key, the buzzing stops. Downstairs in the ready room, an amber light marked H.C. 3 will now be glowing.

Jack comes in and sits down on the end of the bunk. He has put his key ring away, not wanting the metallic smell to corrupt the scent of lilies. "Where have you got it?"

Without asking how Jack knows, Potter raises one large gnarled hand—a carpenter's hand—and touches his midsection. Then he lets it drop. "Started in the gut. That was five years ago. I took the pills and the shots like a good boy. La Riviere, that was. That stuff . . . man, I was throwing up ever'where. Corners and just about ever'where. Once I threw up in my own bed and didn't even know it. Woke up the next morning with puke drying on my chest. You know anything about that, son?"

"My mother had cancer," Jack says quietly. "When I was twelve. Then it went away."

"She get five years?"

"More."

"Lucky," Potter says. "Got her in the end, though, didn't it?" Jack nods.

Potter nods back. They're not quite friends yet, but it's edging that way. It's how Jack works, always has been.

"That shit gets in and waits," Potter tells him. "My theory is that it *never* goes away, not really. Anyway, shots is done. Pills is done, too. Except for the ones that kill the pain. I come here for the finish."

"Why?" This is not a thing Jack needs to know, and time is short, but it's his technique, and he won't abandon what works just because there are a couple of State Police jarheads downstairs waiting to take his boy. Dale will have to hold them off, that's all.

"Seems like a nice enough little town. And I like the river. I go down ever' day. Like to watch the sun on the water. Sometimes I think of all the jobs I did—Wisconsin, Minnesota, Illinois—and then sometimes I don't think about much of anything. Sometimes I just sit there on the bank and feel at peace."

"What was your line of work, Mr. Potter?"

"Started out as a carpenter, just like Jesus. Progressed to builder, then got too big for my britches. When that happens to a builder, he usually goes around calling himself a contractor. I made three–four million dollars, had a Cadillac, had a young woman who hauled my ashes Friday nights. Nice young woman. No trouble. Then I lost it all. Only thing I missed was the Cadillac. It had a smoother ride than the woman. Then I got my bad news and come here."

He looks at Jack.

"You know what I think sometimes? That French Landing's close to a better world, one where things look and smell better. Maybe where people *act* better. I don't go around with folks—I'm not a friendly type person—but that doesn't mean I don't feel things. I got this idea in my head that it's not too late to be decent. You think I'm crazy?"

"No," Jack tells him. "That's pretty much why I came here myself. I'll tell you how it is for me. You know how if you put a thin blanket over a window, the sun will still shine through?"

George Potter looks at him with eyes that are suddenly alight. Jack doesn't even have to finish the thought, which is good. He has found the wavelength—he almost always does, it's his gift—and now it's time to get down to business.

"You *do* know," Potter says simply.

Jack nods. "You know why you're here?"

"They think I killed that lady's kid." Potter nods toward the window. "The one out there that was holdin' up the noose. I didn't. That's what I know."

"Okay, that's a start. Listen to me, now."

Very quickly, Jack lays out the chain of events that has brought Potter to this cell. Potter's brow furrows as Jack speaks, and his big hands knot together.

"Railsback!" he says at last. "I shoulda known! Nosy goddamn old man, always askin' questions, always askin' do you want to play cards or maybe shoot some pool or, I dunno, play *Parcheesi,* for Christ's sake! All so he can ask questions. Goddamn nosey parker . . ."

There's more in this vein, and Jack lets him go on with it for a while. Cancer or no cancer, this old fellow has been ripped out of his ordinary routine without much mercy, and needs to vent a little. If Jack cuts him off to save time, he'll lose it instead. It's hard to be patient (how is Dale holding those two assholes off? Jack doesn't even want to know), but patience is necessary. When Potter begins to widen the scope of his attack, however (Morty Fine comes in for some abuse, as does Andy Railsback's pal Irv Throneberry), Jack steps in.

"The point is, Mr. Potter, that Railsback followed someone to your room. No, that's the wrong way to put it. Railsback was *led* to your room."

Potter doesn't reply, just sits looking at his hands. But he nods. He's old, he's sick and getting sicker, but he's four counties over from stupid.

"The person who led Railsback was almost certainly the same person who left the Polaroids of the dead children in your closet."

"Yar, makes sense. And if he had pictures of the dead kiddies, he was prob'ly the one who made 'em dead."

"Right. So I have to wonder—"

Potter waves an impatient hand. "I guess I know what you got to wonder. Who there is around these parts who'd like to see Chicago Potsie strung up by the neck. Or the balls."

"Exactly."

"Don't want to put a stick in your spokes, sonny, but I can't think of nobody."

"No?" Jack raises his eyebrows. "Never did business around here, built a house or laid out a golf course?"

Potter raises his head and gives Jack a grin. "Course I did. How else d'you think I knew how nice it is? Specially in the summer? You know the part of town they call Libertyville? Got all those 'ye olde' streets like Camelot and Avalon?"

Jack nods.

"I built half of those. Back in the seventies. There was a fella around then . . . some moke I knew from Chicago . . . or thought I knew. . . . Was he in the business?" This last seems to be Potter addressing Potter. In any case, he gives his head a brief shake. "Can't remember. Doesn't matter, anyway. How could it? Fella was gettin' on then, must be dead now. It was a long time ago."

But Jack, who interrogates as Jerry Lee Lewis once played the piano, thinks it *does* matter. In the usually dim section of his mind where intuition keeps its headquarters, lights are coming on. Not a lot yet, but maybe more than just a few.

"A moke," he says, as if he has never heard the word before. "What's that?"

Potter gives him a brief, irritated look. "A citizen who . . . well, not exactly a *citizen*. Someone who knows people who are connected. Or maybe sometimes connected people call him. Maybe they do each other favors. A moke. It's not the world's best thing to be."

*No,* Jack thinks, *but moking can get you a Cadillac with that nice smooth ride.*

"Were you ever a moke, George?" Got to get a little more intimate now. This is not a question Jack can address to a Mr. Potter.

"Maybe," Potter says after a grudging, considering pause. "Maybe I was. Back in Chi. In Chi, you had to scratch backs and wet beaks if you wanted to land the big contracts. I don't know how it is there now, but in those days, a clean contractor was a poor contractor. You know?"

Jack nods.

"The biggest deal I ever made was a housing development on the South Side of Chicago. Just like in that song about bad, bad Leroy Brown." Potter chuckles rustily. For a moment he's not thinking about cancer, or false accusations, or almost being lynched. He's living in the past, and it may be a little sleazy, but it's better than the present—the bunk chained to the wall, the steel toilet, the cancer spreading through his guts.

"Man, that one was *big,* I kid you not. Lots of federal money, but the local hotshots decided where the dough went home at night. And me and this other guy, this moke, we were in a horse race—"

He breaks off, looking at Jack with wide eyes.

"Holy shit, what are you, magic?"

"I don't know what you mean. I'm just sitting here."

"*That* guy was the guy who showed up here. That was the moke!"

"I'm not following you, George." But Jack thinks he is. And although he's starting to get excited, he shows it no more than he did when the bartender told him about Kinderling's little nose-pinching trick.

"It's probably nothing," Potter says. "Guy had plenty of reasons not to like yours truly, but he's got to be dead. He'd be in his eighties, for Christ's sake."

"Tell me about him," Jack says.

"He was a moke," Potter repeats, as if this explains everything. "And he must have got in trouble in Chicago or somewhere around Chicago, because when he showed up here, I'm pretty sure he was using a different name."

"When did you swink him on the housing-development deal, George?"

Potter smiles, and something about the size of his teeth and the way they seem to jut from the gums allows Jack to see how fast death is rushing toward this man. He feels a little shiver of gooseflesh, but he returns the smile easily enough. This is also how he works.

"If we're gonna talk about mokin' and swinkin', you better call me Potsie."

"All right, Potsie. When did you swink this guy in Chicago?"

"That much is easy," Potter says. "It was summer when the bids went out, but the hotshots were still bellerin' about how the hippies came to town the year before and gave the cops and the mayor a black eye. So I'd say 1969. What happened was I'd done the building commissioner a big favor, and I'd done another for this old woman who swung weight on this special Equal Opportunity Housing Commission that Mayor Daley had set up. So when the bids went out, mine got special consideration. This other guy—the moke—I have no doubt that his bid was lower. He knew his way around, and he musta had his own contacts, but that time I had the inside track."

He smiles. The gruesome teeth appear, then disappear again.

"Moke's bid? Somehow gets lost. Comes in too late. Bad luck. Chicago Potsie nails the job. Then, four years later, the moke shows up here, bidding on the Libertyville job. Only that time when I beat him, everything was square-john. I pulled no strings. I met him in the bar at the Nelson Hotel the night after the contract was awarded, just by accident. And he says, 'You were that guy in Chicago.' And I say, 'There are lots of guys in Chicago.' Now this guy was a moke, but he was a *scary* moke. He had a kind of smell about him. I can't put it any better than that. Anyway, I was big and strong in those days, I could be mean, but I was pretty meek that time. Even after a drink or two, I was pretty meek.

" 'Yeah,' he says, 'there are a lot of guys in Chicago, but only one who diddled me. I still got a sore ass from that, Potsie, and I got a long memory.'

"Any other time, any other *guy*, I might have asked how good his memory stayed after he got his head knocked on the floor, but with him I just took it. No more words passed between us. He walked out. I don't think I ever saw him again, but I heard about him from time to time while I was working the Libertyville job. Mostly from my subs. Seems like the moke was building a house of his own in French Landing. For his retirement. Not that he was old enough to retire back then, but he was gettin' up a little. Fifties, I'd say . . . and that was in '72."

"He was building a house here in town," Jack muses.

"Yeah. It had a name, too, like one of those English houses. The Birches, Lake House, Beardsley Manor, you know."

"What name?"

"Shit, I can't even remember the *moke's* name, how do you expect me to remember the name of the house he built? But one thing I *do* remember: none of the subs liked it. It got a reputation."

"Bad?"

"The worst. There were accidents. One guy cut his hand clean off on a band saw, almost bled to death before they got him to the hospital. Another guy fell off a scaffolding and ended up paralyzed . . . what they call a quad. You know what that is?"

Jack nods.

"Only house I ever heard of people were calling haunted even before it was all the way built. I got the idea that he had to finish most of it himself."

"What else did they say about this place?" Jack puts the question idly, as if he doesn't care much one way or the other, but he cares a lot. He has never heard of a so-called haunted house in French Landing. He knows he hasn't been here anywhere near long enough to hear all the tales and legends, but something like this . . . you'd think something like this would pop out of the deck early.

"Ah, man, I can't remember. Just that . . ." He pauses, eyes distant. Outside the building, the crowd is finally beginning to disperse. Jack wonders how Dale is doing with Brown and Black. The time seems to be racing, and he hasn't gotten what he needs from Potter. What he's gotten so far is just enough to tantalize.

"One guy told me the sun never shone there even when it shone," Potter says abruptly. "He said the house was a little way off the road, in a clearing, and it should have gotten sun at least five hours a day in the summer, but it somehow . . . didn't. He said the guys lost their shadows, just like in a fairy tale, and they didn't like it. And sometimes they heard a dog growling in the woods. Sounded like a big one. A mean one. But they never saw it. You know how it is, I imagine. Stories get started, and then they just kinda feed on themselves . . ."

Potter's shoulders suddenly slump. His head lowers.

"Man, that's all I can remember."

"What was the moke's name when he was in Chicago?"

"Can't remember."

Jack suddenly thrusts his open hands under Potter's nose. With his head lowered, Potter doesn't see them until they're right there, and he recoils, gasping. He gets a noseful of the dying smell on Jack's skin.

"What . . . ? Jesus, what's that?" Potter seizes one of Jack's hands and sniffs again, greedily. "Boy, that's nice. What is it?"

"Lilies," Jack says, but it's not what he thinks. What he thinks is *The memory of my mother.* "What was the moke's name when he was in Chicago?"

"It . . . something like beer stein. That's not it, but it's close. Best I can do."

"Beer stein," Jack says. "And what was his name when he got to French Landing three years later?"

Suddenly there are loud, arguing voices on the stairs. "I don't care!" someone shouts. Jack thinks it's Black, the more officious one. "It's our case, he's our prisoner, and we're taking him out! *Now!*"

Dale: "I'm not arguing. I'm just saying that the paperwork—"

Brown: "Aw, fuck the paperwork. We'll take it with us."

"What was his name in French Landing, Potsie?"

"I can't—" Potsie takes Jack's hands again. Potsie's own

hands are dry and cold. He smells Jack's palms, eyes closed. On the long exhale of his breath he says: "Burnside. Chummy Burnside. Not that he was chummy. The nickname was a joke. I think his real handle might have been Charlie."

Jack takes his hands back. Charles "Chummy" Burnside. Once known as Beer Stein. Or something like Beer Stein.

"And the house? What was the name of the house?"

Brown and Black are coming down the corridor now, with Dale scurrying after them. *There's no time,* Jack thinks. *Damnit all, if I had even five minutes more—*

And then Potsie says, "Black House. I don't know if that's what he called it or what the subs workin' the job got to calling it, but that was the name, all right."

Jack's eyes widen. The image of Henry Leyden's cozy living room crosses his mind: sitting with a drink at his elbow and reading about Jarndyce and Jarndyce. "Did you say *Bleak* House?"

*"Black,"* Potsie reiterates impatiently. "Because it really *was*. It was—"

"Oh dear to Christ," one of the state troopers says in a snotty look-what-the-cat-dragged-in voice that makes Jack feel like rearranging his face. It's Brown, but when Jack glances up, it's Brown's partner he looks at. The coincidence of the other trooper's name makes Jack smile.

"Hello, boys," Jack says, getting up from the bunk.

"What are you doing here, Hollywood?" Black asks.

"Just batting the breeze and waiting for you," Jack says, and smiles brilliantly. "I suppose you want this guy."

"You're goddamn right," Brown growls. "And if you fucked up our case—"

"Gosh, I don't think so," Jack says. It's a struggle, but he manages to achieve a tone of amiability. Then, to Potsie: "You'll be safer with them than here in French Landing, sir."

George Potter looks vacant again. Resigned. "Don't matter much either way," he says, then smiles as a thought occurs to him. "If old Chummy's still alive, and you run across him, you might ask him if his ass still hurts from that diddling I gave him back in '69. And tell him old Chicago Potsie says hello."

"What the hell are you talking about?" Brown asks, glowering. He has his cuffs out, and is clearly itching to snap them on George Potter's wrists.

"Old times," Jack says. He stuffs his fragrant hands in his pockets and leaves the cell. He smiles at Brown and Black. "Nothing to concern you boys."

Trooper Black turns to Dale. "You're out of this case," he says. "Those are words of one syllable. I can't make it any simpler. So tell me once and mean it forever, Chief: Do you understand?"

"Of course I do," Dale said. "Take the case and welcome. But get off the tall white horse, willya? If you expected me to simply stand by and let a crowd of drunks from the Sand Bar take this man out of Lucky's and lynch him—"

"Don't make yourself look any stupider than you already are," Brown snaps. "They picked his name up off your police calls."

"I doubt that," Dale says quietly, thinking of the doper's cell phone borrowed out of evidence storage.

Black grabs Potter's narrow shoulder, gives it a vicious twist, then thrusts him so hard toward the door at the end of the corridor that the man almost falls down. Potter recovers, his haggard face full of pain and dignity.

"Troopers," Jack says.

He doesn't speak loudly or angrily, but they both turn.

"Abuse that prisoner one more time in my sight, and I'll be on the phone to the Madison shoofly-pies the minute you leave, and believe me, Troopers, they will listen to me. Your attitude is arrogant, coercive, and counterproductive to the resolution of this case. Your interdepartmental cooperation skills are nonexistent. Your demeanor is unprofessional and reflects badly upon the state of Wisconsin. You will either behave yourselves or I guarantee you that by next Friday you will be looking for security jobs."

Although his voice remains even throughout, Black and Brown seem to shrink as he speaks. By the time he finishes, they look like a pair of chastened children. Dale is gazing at Jack with awe. Only Potter seems unaffected; he's gazing down at his cuffed hands with eyes that could be a thousand miles away.

"Go on, now," Jack says. "Take your prisoner, take your case records, and get lost."

Black opens his mouth to speak, then shuts it again. They

leave. When the door closes behind them, Dale looks at Jack
and says, very softly: "Wow."

"What?"

"If you don't know," Dale says, "I'm not going to tell you."

Jack shrugs. "Potter will keep them occupied, which frees us
up to do a little actual work. If there's a bright side to tonight,
that's it."

"What did you get from him? Anything?"

"A name. Might mean nothing. Charles Burnside. Nicknamed Chummy. Ever heard of him?"

Dale sticks out his lower lip and pulls it thoughtfully. Then
he lets go and shakes his head. "The name itself seems to ring
a faint bell, but that might only be because it's so common. The
nickname, no."

"He was a builder, a contractor, a wheeler-dealer in Chicago
over thirty years ago. According to Potsie, at least."

"Potsie," Dale says. The tape is peeling off a corner of the
ONE CALL MEANS ONE CALL sign, and Dale smoothes it back
down with the air of a man who doesn't really know what he's
doing. "You and he got pretty chummy, didn't you?"

"No," Jack says. "*Burnside's* Chummy. And Trooper Black
doesn't own the Black House."

"You've gone dotty. What black house?"

"First, it's a proper name. Black, capital *B*, house, capital *H*.
Black House. You ever heard of a house named that around
here?"

Dale laughs. "God, no."

Jack smiles back, but all at once it's his interrogation smile,
not his I'm-discussing-things-with-my-friend smile. Because
he's a coppiceman now. And he has seen a funny little flicker in
Dale Gilbertson's eyes.

"Are you sure? Take a minute. Think about it."

"Told you, no. People don't name their houses in these parts.
Oh, I guess old Miss Graham and Miss Pentle call their place
on the other side of the town library Honeysuckle, because of
the honeysuckle bushes all over the fence in front, but that's the
only one in these parts I ever heard named."

Again, Jack sees that flicker. Potter is the one who will be
charged for murder by the Wisconsin State Police, but Jack

didn't see that deep flicker in Potter's eyes a single time during their interview. Because Potter was straight with him.

Dale isn't being straight.

*But I have to be gentle with him,* Jack tells himself. *Because he doesn't know he's not being straight. How is that possible?*

As if in answer, he hears Chicago Potsie's voice: *One guy told me the sun never shone there even when it shone . . . he said the guys lost their shadows, just like in a fairy tale.*

*Memory* is a shadow; any cop trying to reconstruct a crime or an accident from the conflicting accounts of eyewitnesses knows it well. Is Potsie's Black House like this? Something that casts no shadow? Dale's response (he has now turned full-face to the peeling poster, working on it as seriously as he might work on a heart attack victim in the street, administering CPR right out of the manual until the ambulance arrives) suggests to Jack that it might be something like *just* that. Three days ago he wouldn't have allowed himself to consider such an idea, but three days ago he hadn't returned to the Territories.

"According to Potsie, this place got a reputation as a haunted house even before it was completely built," Jack says, pressing a little.

"Nope." Dale moves on to the sign about the A.A. and N.A. meetings. He examines the tape studiously, not looking at Jack. "Doesn't ring the old chimeroo."

"Sure? One man almost bled to death. Another took a fall that paralyzed him. People complained—listen to this, Dale, it's good—according to Potsie, people complained about losing their shadows. Couldn't see them even at midday, with the sun shining full force. Isn't that something?"

"Sure is, but I don't remember any stories like that." As Jack walks toward Dale, Dale moves away. Almost scutters away, although Chief Gilbertson is not ordinarily a scuttering man. It's a little funny, a little sad, a little horrible. He doesn't know he's doing it, Jack's sure of that. There *is* a shadow. Jack sees it, and on some level Dale *knows* he sees it. If Jack should force him too hard, Dale would have to see it, too . . . and Dale doesn't want that. Because it's a *bad* shadow. Is it worse than a monster who kills children and then eats selected portions of their bodies? Apparently part of Dale thinks so.

*I could make him see that shadow,* Jack thinks coldly. *Put my hands under his nose—my lily-scented hands—and make him see it. Part of him even* wants *to see it. The coppiceman part.*

Then another part of Jack's mind speaks up in the Speedy Parker drawl he now remembers from his childhood. *You could push him over the edge of a nervous breakdown, too, Jack. God knows he's close to one, after all the goin's-ons since the Irkenham boy got took. You want to chance that? And for what? He didn't know the name, about that he was* bein' straight.

"Dale?"

Dale gives Jack a quick, bright glance, then looks away. The furtive quality in that quick peek sort of breaks Jack's heart. "What?"

"Let's go get a cup of coffee."

At this change of subject, Dale's face fills with glad relief. He claps Jack on the shoulder. "Good idea!"

*God-pounding good idea, right here and now,* Jack thinks, then smiles. There's more than one way to skin a cat, and more than one way to find a Black House. It's been a long day. Best, maybe, to let this go. At least for tonight.

"What about Railsback?" Dale asks as they clatter down the stairs. "You still want to talk to him?"

"You bet," Jack replies, heartily enough, but he holds out little hope for Andy Railsback, a picked witness who saw exactly what the Fisherman wanted him to see. With one little exception . . . perhaps. The single slipper. Jack doesn't know if it will ever come to anything, but it might. In court, for instance . . . as an identifying link . . .

*This is never going to court and you know it. It may not even finish in this w—*

His thoughts are broken by a wave of cheerful sound as they step into the combination ready room and dispatch center. The members of the French Landing Police Department are standing and applauding. Henry Leyden is also standing and applauding. Dale joins in.

"Jesus, guys, quit it," Jack says, laughing and blushing at the same time. But he won't lie to himself, try to tell himself he takes no pleasure in that round of applause. He feels the warmth of them; can see the light of their regard. Those things aren't important. But it feels like coming home, and that is.

When Jack and Henry step out of the police station an hour or so later, Beezer, Mouse, and Kaiser Bill are still there. The other two have gone back to the Row to fill in the various old ladies on tonight's events.

"Sawyer," Beezer says.

"Yes," Jack says.

"Anything we can do, man. Can you dig that? *Anything.*"

Jack looks at the biker thoughtfully, wondering what his story is . . . other than grief, that is. A father's grief. Beezer's eyes remain steady on his. A little off to one side, Henry Leyden stands with his head raised to smell the river fog, humming deep down in his throat.

"I'm going to look in on Irma's mom tomorrow around eleven," Jack says. "Do you suppose you and your friends could meet me in the Sand Bar around noon? She lives close to there, I understand. I'll buy youse a round of lemonade."

Beezer doesn't smile, but his eyes warm up slightly. "We'll be there."

"That's good," Jack says.

"Mind telling me why?"

"There's a place that needs finding."

"Does it have to do with whoever killed Amy and the other kids?"

"Maybe."

Beezer nods. "Maybe's good enough."

Jack drives back toward Norway Valley slowly, and not just because of the fog. Although it's still early in the evening, he is tired to the bone and has an idea that Henry feels the same way. Not because he's quiet; Jack has become used to Henry's occasional dormant stretches. No, it's the quiet in the truck itself. Under ordinary circumstances, Henry is a restless, compulsive radio tuner, running through the La Riviere stations, checking KDCU here in town, then ranging outward, hunting for Milwaukee, Chicago, maybe even Omaha, Denver, and St. Louis, if conditions are right. An appetizer of bop here, a salad of spiritual music there, perhaps a dash of Perry Como way down at the foot of the dial: hot-diggity, dog-diggity, *boom* what-ya-do-to-me. Not tonight, though. Tonight Henry just sits quiet on his side of the truck with his hands folded in his lap. At last, when they're no more than two miles from his driveway, Henry says: "No Dickens tonight, Jack. I'm going straight to bed."

The weariness in Henry's voice startles Jack, makes him uneasy. Henry doesn't sound like himself or any of his radio personae; at this moment he just sounds old and tired, on the way to being used up.

"I am, too," Jack agrees, trying not to let his concern show in his voice. Henry picks up on every vocal nuance. He's eerie that way.

"What do you have in mind for the Thunder Five, may I ask?"

"I'm not entirely sure," Jack says, and perhaps because he's tired, he gets this untruth past Henry. He intends to start Beezer and his buddies looking for the place Potsie told him about, the place where shadows had a way of disappearing. At least way back in the seventies they did. He had also intended to ask Henry if he's ever heard of a French Landing domicile called Black House. Not now, though. Not after hearing how beat Henry sounds. Tomorrow, maybe. Almost certainly, in fact, because Henry is too good a resource not to use. Best to let him recycle a little first, though.

"You have the tape, right?"

Henry pulls the cassette with the Fisherman's 911 call on it partway out of his breast pocket, then puts it back. "Yes, Mother. But I don't think I can listen to a killer of small children tonight, Jack. Not even if you come in and listen with me."

"Tomorrow will be fine," Jack says, hoping he isn't condemning another of French Landing's children to death by saying this.

"You're not entirely sure of that."

"No," Jack agrees, "but you listening to that tape with dull ears could do more harm than good. I *am* sure of that."

"First thing in the morning. I promise."

Henry's house is up ahead now. It looks lonely with only the one light on over the garage, but of course Henry doesn't need lights inside to find his way.

"Henry, are you going to be all right?"

"Yes," Henry says, but to Jack he doesn't seem entirely sure.

"No Rat tonight," Jack tells him firmly.

"No."

"Ditto the Shake, the Shook, the Sheik."

Henry's lips lift in a small smile. "Not even a George Rathbun promo for French Landing Chevrolet, where price is king and you never pay a dime of interest for the first six months with approved credit. Straight to bed."

"Me too," Jack says.

But an hour after lying down and putting out the lamp on his bedside table, Jack is still unable to sleep. Faces and voices revolve in his mind like crazy clock hands. Or a carousel on a deserted midway.

Tansy Freneau: *Bring out the monster who killed my pretty baby.*

Beezer St. Pierre: *We'll have to see how it shakes out, won't we?*

George Potter: *That shit gets in and waits. My theory is that it* never *goes away, not really.*

Speedy, a voice from the distant past on the sort of telephone that was science fiction when Jack first met him: *Hidey-ho, Travelin' Jack . . . as one coppiceman to another, son, I think you ought to visit Chief Gilbertson's private bathroom. Right now.*

As one coppiceman to another, right.

And most of all, over and over again, Judy Marshall: *You don't just say, I'm lost and I don't know how to get back—you keep on going . . .*

Yes, but keep on going where? *Where?*

At last he gets up and goes out onto the porch with his pillow under his arm. The night is warm; in Norway Valley, where the fog was thin to begin with, the last remnants have now disappeared, blown away by a soft east wind. Jack hesitates, then goes on down the steps, naked except for his underwear. The porch is no good to him, though. It's where he found that hellish box with the sugar-packet stamps.

He walks past his truck, past the bird hotel, and into the north field. Above him are a billion stars. Crickets hum softly in the grass. His fleeing path through the hay and timothy has disappeared, or maybe now he's entering the field in a different place.

A little way in, he lies down on his back, puts the pillow under his head, and looks up at the stars. *Just for a little while,* he thinks. *Just until all those ghost voices empty out of my head. Just for a little while.*

Thinking this, he begins to drowse.

Thinking this, he goes over.

Above his head, the pattern of the stars changes. He *sees* the new constellations form. What is that one, where the Big Dipper was a moment before? Is it the Sacred Opopanax? Perhaps it is. He hears a low, pleasant creaking sound and knows it's the windmill he saw when he flipped just this morning, a thousand years ago. He doesn't need to look at it to be sure, any more than he needs to look at where his house was and see that it has once more become a barn.

*Creak . . . creak . . . creak:* vast wooden vanes turning in that same east wind. Only now the wind is infinitely sweeter, infinitely purer. Jack touches the waistband of his underpants and feels some rough weave. No Jockey shorts in this world. His pillow has changed, too. Foam has become goosedown, but it's still comfortable. More comfortable than ever, in truth. Sweet under his head.

"I'll catch him, Speedy," Jack Sawyer whispers up at the new shapes in the new stars. "At least I'll try."

He sleeps.

When he awakens, it's early morning. The breeze is gone. In the direction from which it came, there's a bright orange line on the horizon—the sun is on its way. He's stiff and his ass hurts and he's damp with dew, but he's rested. The steady, rhythmic creaking is gone, but that doesn't surprise him. He knew from the moment he opened his eyes that he's in Wisconsin again. And he knows something else: he can go back. Any time he wants. The real Coulee Country, the *deep* Coulee Country, is just a wish and a motion away. This fills him with joy and dread in equal parts.

Jack gets up and barefoots back to the house with his pillow under his arm. He guesses it's about five in the morning. Another three hours' sleep will make him ready for anything. On the porch steps, he touches the cotton of his Jockey shorts. Although his skin is damp, the shorts are almost dry. Of course they are. For most of the hours he spent sleeping rough (as he spent so many nights that autumn when he was twelve), they weren't on him at all. They were somewhere else.

"In the Land of Opopanax," Jack says, and goes inside. Three minutes later he's asleep again, in his own bed. When he wakes at eight, with the sensible sun streaming in through his window, he could almost believe that his latest journey was a dream.

But in his heart, he knows better.

# 18

Remember those news vans that drove into the parking lot behind the police station? And Wendell Green's contribution to the excitement, before Officer Hrabowski's giant flashlight knocked him into the Land of Nod? Once the crews inside the vans took in the seeming inevitability of a riot, we can be sure they rose to the occasion, for the next morning their footage of the wild night dominates television screens across the state. By nine o'clock, people in Racine and Milwaukee, people in Madison and Delafield, and people who live so far north in the state that they need satellite dishes to get any television at all are looking up from their pancakes, their bowls of Special K, their fried eggs, and their buttered English muffins to watch a small, nervous-looking policeman finishing off a large, florid reporter's budding career as a demagogue by clocking him with a blunt instrument. And we may also be sure of one other matter: that nowhere is this footage watched as widely and compulsively as in French Landing and the neighboring communities of Centralia and Arden.

Thinking about several matters at once, Jack Sawyer watches it all on a little portable TV placed on his kitchen counter. He hopes that Dale Gilbertson will not revoke Arnold Hrabowski's suspension, although he strongly suspects that the Mad Hungarian will soon be back in uniform. Dale only *thinks* he wants him off the force for good: he is too softhearted to listen to Arnie's pleas—and after last night, even a blind man can see that Arnie is going to plead—without relenting. Jack also hopes that the awful Wendell Green will get fired or move away in disgrace. Reporters are not supposed to thrust themselves into their stories, and here is good old loudmouth Wendell, bay-ing for blood like a werewolf. However, Jack has the depressing feeling that Wendell Green will talk his way out of his present difficulties (that is, *lie* his way out of them) and go on being a powerful nuisance. And Jack is pondering Andy Railsback's description of the creepy old man trying the doorknobs on the third floor of the Nelson Hotel.

There he was, *the Fisherman,* given form at last. An old man in a blue robe and one slipper striped black and yellow, like a bumblebee. Andy Railsback had wondered if this unpleasant-looking old party had wandered away from the Maxton Elder Care Facility. That was an interesting notion, Jack thought. If "Chummy" Burnside is the man who planted the photographs in George Potter's room, Maxton's would be a perfect hidey-hole for him.

Wendell Green is watching the news on the Sony in his hotel room. He cannot take his eyes off the screen, although what he sees there afflicts him with a mixture of feelings—anger, shame, and humiliation—that makes his stomach boil. The knot on his head throbs, and every time he witnesses that poor excuse for a cop sneaking up behind him with his flashlight raised, he pushes his fingers into the thick, curly hair at the back of his head and gently palpates it. The damn thing feels about the size of a ripe tomato and just as ready to burst. He's lucky not to have a concussion. That pipsqueak could have killed him!

Okay, maybe he went a little bit over the edge, maybe he took a tiny step across a professional boundary; he never claimed to be perfect. The local news guys, they piss him off, all that guff about Jack Sawyer. Who is the top guy covering the Fisherman story? Who has been all over it from day one, telling the citizens what they need to know? Who's been putting himself on the line, day after crummy goddamn day? Who *gave the guy his name?* Not those blow-dried airheads Bucky and Stacey, those wanna-be news reporters and local anchors who smile into the camera to show off their capped teeth, that's for sure. Wendell Green is a legend around here, a star, the closest thing to a giant of journalism ever to come out of western Wisconsin. Even over in Madison, the name Wendell Green stands for . . . well, unquestioned excellence. And if the name Wendell Green is like the gold standard now, just wait until he rides the

Fisherman's blood-spattered shoulders all the way to a Pulitzer Prize.

So Monday morning he has to go into the office and pacify his editor. Big deal. It isn't the first time, and it won't be the last. Good reporters make waves; nobody admits it, but that's the deal, that's the fine print nobody reads until it's too late. When he walks into his editor's office, he knows what he's going to say: *Biggest story of the day, and did you see any other reporters there?* And when he has the editor eating out of his hand again, which will take about ten minutes flat, he intends to drop in on a Goltz's salesman named Fred Marshall. One of Wendell's most valuable sources has suggested that Mr. Marshall has some interesting information about his special, special baby, the Fisherman case.

Arnold Hrabowski, now a hero to his darling wife, Paula, is watching the news in a postcoital glow and thinking that she is right: he really should call Chief Gilbertson and ask to be taken off suspension.

Wondering with half his mind where he might look for George Potter's old adversary, Dale Gilbertson watches Bucky and Stacey cut away yet again to the spectacle of the Mad Hungarian taking care of Wendell Green and thinks that he really should reinstate the little guy. Would you look at the beautiful swing Arnie took? Dale can't help it—that swing really brightens up his day. It's like watching Mark McGwire, like watching Tiger Woods.

Alone in her dark little house off the highway, Wanda Kinderling, to whom we have made passing mention from time to time, is listening to the radio. Why is she listening to the radio? Some months ago, she had to decide between paying her cable bill and buying another half gallon of Aristocrat vodka, and sorry, Bucky and Stacey, but Wanda followed her bliss, she went with her heart. Without cable service, her television set brings in little more than snow and a heavy dark line that scrolls up over her screen in an endless loop. Wanda always hated Bucky and Stacey anyhow, along with almost everyone else on television, especially if they looked content and well groomed. (She has a special loathing for the hosts of morning news programs and network anchors.) Wanda has not been content or well groomed since her husband, Thorny, was accused of terrible crimes he could never ever have committed by that high and mighty show-off Jack Sawyer. Jack Sawyer ruined her life, and Wanda is not about to forgive or forget.

That man trapped her husband. He *set him up.* He smeared Thorny's innocent name and packed him off to jail just to make himself look good. Wanda hopes they never catch the Fisherman, because the Fisherman is exactly what they deserve, those dirty bastards. *Play* dirty, you *are* dirty, and people like that can go straight to the deepest bowels of hell—that's what Wanda Kinderling thinks. The Fisherman is *retribution*—that's what Wanda thinks. Let him kill a hundred brats, let him kill a thousand, and after that he can start in on their parents. Thorny could not have killed those sluts down there in Los Angeles. Those were sex murders, and Thorny had no interest in sex, thank the Lord. The rest of him grew up, but his man-part never did; his thingie was about the size of his little finger. It was impossible for him to care about nasty women and sex things. But Jack Sawyer lived in Los Angeles, didn't he? So why couldn't *he* have killed those sluts, those whores, and blamed it all on Thorny?

The newscaster describes former Lieutenant Sawyer's actions of the previous night, and Wanda Kinderling spits up bile, grabs the glass from her bedside table, and douses the fire in her guts with three inches of vodka.

Gorg, who would seem a natural visitor to the likes of Wanda, pays no attention to the news, for he is far away in Faraway.

In his bed at Maxton's, Charles Burnside is enjoying dreams not precisely his, for they emanate from another being, from elsewhere, and depict a world he has never seen on his own. Ragged, enslaved children plod on their bleeding foodzies past leaping flames, turning giant wheels that turn yet larger wheels oho aha that power the beyoodiful engynes of destruction mounting mounting to the black-and-red sky. The Big Combination! An acrid stink of molten metal and something truly vile, something like dragon urine, perfumes the air, as does the leaden stench of despair. Lizard demons with thick, flickering tails whip the children along. A din of clattering and banging, of crashing and enormous thuds punishes the ears. These are the dreams of Burny's dearest friend and loving master, Mr. Munshun, a being of endless and perverse delight.

Down past the end of Daisy wing, across the handsome lobby, and through Rebecca Vilas's little cubicle, Chipper Maxton is concerned with matters considerably more mundane. The little TV on a shelf over the safe broadcasts the wondrous image of Mad Hungarian Hrabowski clobbering Wendell Green with a nice, clean sweep of his heavy-duty flashlight, but Chipper barely notices the splendid moment. He has to come up with the thirteen thousand dollars he owes his bookie, and he has only about half of that sum. Yesterday, lovely Rebecca drove to Miller to withdraw most of what he had stashed there, and he can use about two thousand dollars from his own account, as long as he replaces it before the end of the month. That leaves about six grand, an amount that will call for some seriously creative bookkeeping. Fortunately, creative bookkeeping is a speciality of Chipper's, and when he begins to think of his options, he sees his current difficulty as an opportunity.

After all, he went into business in the first place to steal as much money as possible, didn't he? Apart from being serviced by Ms. Vilas, stealing is about the only activity that makes him truly happy. The amount is almost irrelevant: as we have seen, Chipper derives as much pleasure from conning chump change out of the visiting relatives after the Strawberry Fest as from screwing the government out of ten or fifteen thousand dollars. The thrill lies in *getting away with it*. So he needs six thousand; why not take ten thousand? That way, he can leave his own account untouched and still have an extra two grand to play with. He has two sets of books on his computer, and he can easily draw the money from the company's bank account without setting off bells during his next state audit, which is coming up in about a month. Unless the auditors demand the bank records, and even then there are a couple of tricks he can use. It's too bad about the audit, though—Chipper would like to have a little more time to paper over the cracks. Losing the thirteen thousand wasn't the problem, he thinks. The problem was that he lost it at *the wrong time*.

In order to keep everything clear in his head, Chipper pulls his keyboard toward him and tells the computer to print out complete statements of both sets of books for the past month. By the time the auditors show up, baby, those pages will have been fed into the shredder and come out as macaroni.

Let us move from one form of insanity to another. After the owner of the Holiday Trailer Park has extended a trembling index finger to point out the Freneau residence, Jack drives toward it on the dusty path with gathering doubts. Tansy's Airstream is the last and least maintained of a row of four. Two of the others have flowers in a bright border around them, and the third has been dressed up with striped green awnings that make it look more like a house. The fourth trailer displays no signs of decoration or improvement. Dying flowers and skimpy weeds straggle in the beaten earth surrounding it. The shades are pulled down. An air of misery and waste hangs about it, along with a quality Jack might define, if he stopped to consider it, as *slippage.* In no obvious way, the trailer looks wrong. Unhappiness has distorted it, as it can distort a person, and when Jack gets out of his truck and walks toward the cinder blocks placed before the entrance, his doubts increase. He can no longer be sure why he has come to this place. It occurs to Jack that he can give Tansy Freneau nothing but his pity, and this thought makes him uneasy.

Then it occurs to him that these doubts mask his real feelings, which have to do with the discomfort the trailer arouses in him. He does not want to enter that thing. Everything else is a rationalization; he has no choice but to keep moving forward. His eyes find the welcome mat, a reassuring touch of the ordinary world he can feel already disappearing around him, and he steps up onto the topmost board and knocks on the door. Nothing happens. Maybe she really is still asleep and would prefer to stay that way. If he were Tansy, he would stay in bed as long as possible. If he were Tansy, he'd stay in bed for *weeks.* Once more pushing away his reluctance, Jack raps on the door again and says, "Tansy? Are you up?"

A little voice from within says, "Up where?"

*Uh-oh,* Jack thinks, and says, "Out of bed. I'm Jack Sawyer, Tansy. We met last night. I'm helping the police, and I told you I'd come over today."

He hears footsteps moving toward the door. "Are you the man who gave me the flowers? He was a nice man."

"That was me."

A lock clicks, and the knob revolves. The door cracks open. A sliver of a faintly olive-skinned face and a single eye shine out of the inner darkness. "It is you. Come in, fast. *Fast.*" She steps back, opening the door just wide enough for him to pass through. As soon as he is inside, she slams it shut and locks it again.

The molten light burning at the edges of the curtains and the window shades deepens the darkness of the long trailer's interior. One soft lamp burns above the sink, and another, just as low, illuminates a little table otherwise occupied by a bottle of coffee brandy, a smeary glass decorated with a picture of a cartoon character, and a scrapbook. The circle of light cast by the lamp extends to take in half of a low, fabric-covered chair next to the table. Tansy Freneau pushes herself off the door and takes two light, delicate steps toward him. She tilts her head and folds her hands together beneath her chin. The eager, slightly glazed expression in her eyes dismays Jack. By even the widest, most comprehensive definition of sanity, this woman is not sane. He has no idea what to say to her.

"Would you care to . . . sit down?" With a hostessy wave of her hand, she indicates a high-backed wooden chair.

"If it's all right with you."

"Why wouldn't it be all right? I'm going to sit down in *my* chair, why shouldn't you sit down in that one?"

"Thank you," Jack says, and sits down, watching her glide back to the door to check the lock. Satisfied, Tansy gives him a brilliant smile and pads back to her chair, moving almost with the duck-waddle grace of a ballerina. When she lowers herself to the chair, he says, "Are you afraid of someone who might come here, Tansy? Is there someone you want to keep locked out?"

"Oh, yes," she says, and leans forward, pulling her eyebrows together in an exaggerated display of little-girl seriousness. "But it isn't a *someone,* it's a *thing.* And I'm never, never going to let him in my house again, not ever. But I'll let you in, because you're a very nice man and you gave me those beautiful flowers. And you're very handsome, too."

"Is Gorg the thing you want to keep out, Tansy? Are you afraid of Gorg?"

"Yes," she says, primly. "Would you care for a cup of tea?"

"No, thank you."

"Well, *I'm* going to have some. It's very, very good tea. It tastes sort of like coffee." She raises her eyebrows and gives him a bright, questioning look. He shakes his head. Without moving from her chair, Tansy pours two fingers of the brandy into her glass and sets the bottle back down on the table. The figure on her glass, Jack sees, is Scooby-Doo. Tansy sips from the glass. "Yummy. Do you have a girlfriend? I could be your girlfriend, you know, especially if you gave me more of those lovely flowers. I put them in a vase." She pronounces the word like a parody of a Boston matron: *vahhhz.* "See?"

On the kitchen counter, the lilies of the vale droop in a mason jar half-filled with water. Removed from the Territories, they do not have long to live. This world, Jack supposes, is poisoning them faster than they are able to deal with. Every ounce of goodness they yield to their surroundings subtracts from their essence. Tansy, he realizes, has been kept afloat on the residue of the Territories remaining in the lilies—when they die, her protective little-girl persona will crumble into dust, and her madness may engulf her. That madness came from Gorg; he'd bet his life on it.

"I *do* have a boyfriend, but he doesn't count. His name is Lester Moon. Beezer and his friends call him Stinky Cheese, but I don't know why. Lester isn't all that stinky, at least not when he's sober."

"Tell me about Gorg," Jack says.

Extending her little finger away from the Scooby-Doo glass, Tansy takes another sip of coffee brandy. She frowns. "Oh, that's a real icky thing to talk about."

"I want to know about him, Tansy. If you help me, I can make sure he never bothers you again."

"Really?"

"And you'd be helping me find the man who killed your daughter."

"I can't talk about that now. It's too upsetting." Tansy flutters her free hand over her lap as if sweeping off a crumb. Her face contracts, and a new expression moves into her eyes. For a second, the desperate, unprotected Tansy rises to the surface, threatening to explode in a madness of grief and rage.

"Does Gorg look like a person, or like something else?"

Tansy shakes her head from side to side with great slowness. She is composing herself again, reinstating a personality that can ignore her real emotions. "Gorg does *not* look like a person. Not at all."

"You said he gave you the feather you were wearing. Does he look like a bird?"

"Gorg doesn't look like a bird, he *is* a bird. And do you know what kind?" She leans forward again, and her face takes on the expression of a six-year-old girl about to tell the worst thing she knows. "A *raven*. That's what he is, a big, old *raven*. All black. But not shiny black." Her eyes widen with the seriousness of what she has to say. "He came from Night's Plutonian shore. That's from a poem Mrs. Normandie taught us in the sixth grade. 'The Raven,' by Edgar Allan Poe."

Tansy straightens up, having passed on this nugget of literary history. Jack guesses that Mrs. Normandie probably wore the same satisfied, pedagogic expression that is now on Tansy's face, but without the bright, unhealthy glaze in Tansy's eyes.

"Night's Plutonian shore is not part of this world," Tansy continues. "Did you know that? It's *alongside* this world, and *outside* it. You need to find a door, if you want to go there."

This is like talking to Judy Marshall, Jack abruptly realizes, but a Judy without the depth of soul and the unbelievable courage that rescued her from madness. The instant that Judy Marshall comes into his mind, he wants to see her again, so strongly that Judy feels like the one essential key to the puzzle all around him. And if she is the key, she is also the door the key opens. Jack wants to be out of the dark, warped atmosphere of Tansy's Airstream; he wants to put off the Thunder Five and speed up the highway and over the hill to Arden and the gloomy hospital where radiant Judy Marshall has found freedom in a locked mental ward.

"But I don't ever want to find that door, because I don't want to go there," Tansy says in a singsong voice. "Night's Plutonian shore is a *bad* world. Everything's on *fire* there."

"How do you know that?"

"Gorg told me," she whispers. Tansy's gaze skitters away

from him and fastens on the Scooby-Doo glass. "Gorg likes fire. But not because it makes him warm. Because it burns things up, and that makes him happy. Gorg said . . ." She shakes her head and lifts the glass to her mouth. Instead of drinking from it, she tilts the liquid toward the lip of the glass and laps at it with her tongue. Her eyes slide up to meet his again. "I think my tea is magic."

*I bet you do,* Jack thinks, and his heart nearly bursts for delicate lost Tansy.

"You can't cry in here," she tells him. "You looked like you wanted to cry, but you can't. Mrs. Normandie doesn't allow it. You can kiss me, though. Do you want to kiss me?"

"Of course I do," he says. "But Mrs. Normandie doesn't allow kissing, either."

"Oh, well." Tansy laps again at her drink. "We can do it later, when she leaves the room. And you can put your arms around me, like Lester Moon. And everything Lester does, you can do. With me."

"Thank you," Jack says. "Tansy, can you tell me some of the other things Gorg said?"

She cants her head and pushes her lips in and out. "He said he came here through a burning hole. With folded-back edges. And he said I was a mother, and I had to help my daughter. In the poem, her name is Lenore, but her real name is Irma. And he said . . . he said a mean old man ate her leg, but there were worse things that could have happened to my Irma."

For a couple of seconds, Tansy seems to recede into herself, to vanish behind her stationary surface. Her mouth remains half open; she does not even blink. When she returns from where she has gone, it is like watching a statue slowly come to life. Her voice is almost too soft to be heard. "I was supposed to *fix* that old man, fix him but good. Only you gave me my beautiful lilies, and he wasn't the right man, was he?"

Jack feels like screaming.

"He said there were worse things," Tansy says in a whisper of disbelief. "But he didn't say what they were. He showed me, instead. And when I saw, I thought my eyes burned up. Even though I could still see."

"What did you see?"

"A big, big place all made of fire," Tansy says. "Going way

high up." She falls silent, and an internal temblor runs through her, beginning in her face and moving down and out through her fingers. "*Irma* isn't there. No, she isn't. She got dead, and a mean old man ate her leg. He sent me a letter, but I never got it. So Gorg read it to me. I don't want to think about that letter." She sounds like a little girl describing something she has heard about thirdhand, or has invented. A thick curtain lies between Tansy and what she has seen and heard, and that curtain allows her to function. Jack again wonders what will happen to her when the lilies die.

"And now," she says, "if you're not going to kiss me, it's time you left. I want to be alone for a while."

Surprised by her decisiveness, Jack stands up and begins to say something polite and meaningless. Tansy waves him toward the door.

Outside, the air seems heavy with bad odors and unseen chemicals. The lilies from the Territories retained more power than Jack had imagined, enough to sweeten and purify Tansy's air. The ground beneath Jack's feet has been baked dry, and a parched sourness hangs in the atmosphere. Jack has nearly to force himself to breathe as he walks toward his truck, but the more he breathes, the more quickly he will readjust to the ordinary world. *His* world, though now it feels poisoned. He wants to do one thing only: drive up Highway 93 to Judy Marshall's lookout point and keep on going, through Arden and into the parking lot, past the hospital doors, past the barriers of Dr. Spiegleman and Warden Jane Bond, until he can find himself once again in the life-giving presence of Judy Marshall herself.

He almost thinks he loves Judy Marshall. Maybe he does love her. He knows he needs her: Judy is his door and his key. His *door,* his *key.* Whatever that means, it is the truth. All right, the woman he needs is married to the extremely nice Fred Marshall, but he doesn't want to marry her; in fact, he doesn't even want to sleep with her, not exactly—he just wants to stand before her and see what happens. *Something* will happen, that's for sure, but when he tries to picture it, all he sees is an explosion of tiny red feathers, hardly the image he was hoping for.

Feeling unsteady, Jack props himself on the cab of his truck with one hand while he grabs the door handle with the other.

Both surfaces sear his hands, and he waves them in the air for a little while. When he gets into the cab, the seat is hot, too. He rolls down his window and, with a twinge of loss, notices that the world smells normal to him again. It smells fine. It smells like summer. Where is he going to go? That is an interesting question, he thinks, but after he gets back on the road and travels no more than a hundred feet, the low, gray wooden shape of the Sand Bar appears on his left, and without hesitating he turns into the absurdly extensive parking lot, as if he knew where he was going all along. Looking for a shady spot, Jack cruises around to the back of the building and sees the Bar's single hint of landscaping, a broad maple tree that rises out of the asphalt at the far end of the lot. He guides the Ram into the maple's shadow and gets out, leaving the windows cranked down. Waves of heat ripple upward from the only other two cars in the lot.

It is 11:20 A.M. He is getting hungry, too, since his breakfast consisted of a cup of coffee and a slice of toast smeared with marmalade, and that was three hours ago. Jack has the feeling that the afternoon is going to be a long one. He might as well have something to eat while he waits for the bikers.

The back door of the Sand Bar opens onto a narrow restroom alcove that leads into a long, rectangular space with a gleaming bar at one side and a row of substantial wooden booths on the other. Two big pool tables occupy the middle of the room, and a jukebox stands set back against the wall between them. At the front of the room, a big television screen hangs where it can be seen by everyone, suspended eight or nine feet above the clean wooden floor. The sound has been muted on a commercial that never quite identifies the purpose of its product. After the glare of the parking lot, the Bar seems pleasantly dark, and while Jack's eyes adjust, the few low lamps appear to send out hazy beams of light.

The bartender, whom Jack takes to be the famous Lester "Stinky Cheese" Moon, looks up once as Jack enters, then returns to the copy of the *Herald* folded open on the bar. When Jack takes a stool a few feet to his right, he looks up again. Stinky Cheese is not as awful as Jack had expected. He is wearing a clean shirt only a few shades whiter than his round, small-featured face and his shaven head. Moon has the unmistakable air, half professional and half resentful, of someone who has taken over the family business and suspects he could have done better elsewhere. Jack's intuition tells him that this sense of weary frustration is the source of his nickname among the bikers, because it gives him the look of one who expects to encounter a nasty smell any minute now.

"Can I get something to eat here?" Jack asks him.

"It's all listed on the board." The bartender turns sideways and indicates a white board with movable letters that spell out the menu. Hamburger, cheeseburger, hot dog, bratwurst, kielbasa, sandwiches, french fries, onion rings. The man's gesture is intended to make Jack feel unobservant, and it works.

"Sorry, I didn't see the sign."

The bartender shrugs.

"Cheeseburger, medium, with fries, please."

"Lunch don't start until eleven-thirty, which it says on the board. See?" Another half-mocking gesture toward the sign. "But Mom is setting up in back. I could give her the order now, and she'll start in on it when she's ready."

Jack thanks him, and the bartender glances up at the television screen and walks down to the end of the bar and disappears around a corner. A few seconds later, he returns, looks up at the screen, and asks Jack what he would like to drink.

"Ginger ale," Jack says.

Watching the screen, Lester Moon squirts ginger ale from a nozzle into a beer glass and pushes the glass toward Jack. Then he slides his hand down the bar to pick up the remote control and says, "Hope you don't mind, but I was watching this old movie. Pretty funny." He punches a button on the remote, and from over his left shoulder Jack hears his mother's voice say, *Looks like Smoky's coming in late today. I wish that little rascal would learn how to handle his liquor.*

Before he can turn sideways to face the screen, Lester Moon is asking him if he remembers Lily Cavanaugh.

"Oh, yes."

"I always liked her when I was a kid."

"Same here," Jack says.

As Jack had known instantly, the movie is *The Terror of Deadwood Gulch,* a 1950 comic Western in which the then-famous and still fondly remembered Bill Towns, a sort of poor man's Bob Hope, played a cowardly gambler and cardsharp who arrives in the little Potemkin community of Deadwood Gulch, Arizona, and is soon mistaken for a notorious gunfighter. As the beautiful, quick-witted owner of a saloon called the Lazy 8, the lively center of village social life, Lily Cavanaugh is much appreciated by the crowd of cowpokes, loungers, ranchers, merchants, lawmen, and riffraff who fill her place every night. She makes her patrons check their revolvers at the door and mind their manners, which tend toward the opopanax. In the scene playing now, which is about half an hour into the movie, Lily is alone in her saloon, trying to get rid of a persistent bee.

*A bee for the Queen of the B's,* Jack thinks, and smiles.

At the buzzing nuisance, Lily flaps a cleaning rag, a flyswatter, a mop, a broom, a gun belt. The bee eludes her every effort, zooming here and there, from the bar to a card table, to the top of a whiskey bottle, the tops of three other bottles all in a row, the lid of the upright piano, often waiting while its adversary comes sneaking up by subtle indirection, then taking off a second before the latest weapon slams down. It is a lovely little sequence that verges on slapstick, and when Jacky was six, six, six, or maybe seven, half hysterical with laughter at the sight of his competent mother failing repeatedly to vanquish this flying annoyance and suddenly curious as to how the movie guys had made the insect *do* all these things, his mother had explained that it was not a real bee but an enchanted one produced by the special-effects department.

Lester Moon says, "I could never figure out how they got the bee to go where they wanted. Like, what did they do, *train* it?"

"First they filmed her alone on the set," Jack says, having concluded that, after all, Stinky Cheese is a pretty decent fellow with great taste in actresses. "Special effects put the bee in later. It isn't a real bee, it's a drawing—an animation. You really can't tell, can you?"

"No way. Are you sure? How do you know that, anyhow?"

"I read it in a book somewhere," Jack says, using his all-purpose response to such questions.

Resplendent in fancy cardsharp getup, Bill Towns saunters through the Lazy 8's swinging doors and leers at its proprietress without noticing that she is edging toward the bee now once again installed upon the shiny bar. He has romance in mind, and he swaggers when he walks.

*I see you came back for more, hotshot,* Lily says. *You must like the place.*

*Baby, this is the sweetest joint west of the wide Missouri. Reminds me of the place where I beat Black Jack McGurk to the draw. Poor Black Jack. He never did know when to fold 'em.*

With a noise like the revving of a B-52, the enchanted bee, a creature of fiction inside the fiction, launches itself at Bill Towns's slickly behatted head. The comedian's face turns rubbery with comic terror. He waves his arms, he jigs, he screeches. The enchanted bee performs aeronautic stunts around the panicky pseudogunfighter. Towns's splendid hat falls off; his hair disarranges itself. He edges toward a table and, with a final flurry of hand waving, dives under it and begs for help.

Eye fixed on the ambling bee, Lily walks to the bar and picks up a glass and a folded newspaper. She approaches the table, watching the bee walking around in circles. She jumps forward and lowers the glass, trapping the bee. It flies up and bumps the bottom of the glass. Lily tilts the glass, slides the folded paper underneath it, and raises her hands, holding the newspaper against the top of the glass.

The camera pulls back, and we see the cowardly gambler peeking out from under the table as Lily pushes the doors open and releases the bee.

Behind him, Lester Moon says, "Cheeseburger's ready, mister."

For the next half hour, Jack eats his burger and tries to lose himself in the movie. The burger is great, world-class, with that juicy taste you can get only from a greased-up griddle, and the fries are perfect, golden and crunchy on the outside, but his concentration keeps wandering from *The Terror of Deadwood Gulch*. The problem is not that he has seen the movie perhaps a dozen times; the problem is Tansy Freneau. Certain things she said trouble him. The more he thinks about them, the less he understands what is going on.

According to Tansy, the crow—the *raven*—named Gorg came from a world alongside and outside the world we know. She had to be talking about the Territories. Using a phrase from

Poe's "The Raven," she called this other world "Night's Plutonian shore," which was pretty good for someone like Tansy, but
did not seem in any way applicable to the magical Territories.
Gorg had told Tansy that everything in his world was *on fire*,
and not even the Blasted Lands met that description. Jack could
remember the Blasted Lands and the odd train that had taken
him and Rational Richard, then a sick, wasted Rational
Richard, across that vast red desert. Strange creatures had lived
there, alligator-men and birds with the faces of bearded monkeys, but it had certainly not been on fire. The Blasted Lands
were the product of some past disaster, not the site of a present
conflagration. What had Tansy said? *A big, big place made all
of fire . . . going way high up.* What had she seen, to what landscape had Gorg opened her eyes? It sounded like a great burning tower, or a tall building consumed by fire. A burning tower,
a burning building in a burning world—how could that world
be the Territories?

Jack has been in the Territories twice in the past forty-eight
hours, and what he has seen has been beautiful. More than
beautiful—cleansing. The deepest truth Jack knows about the
Territories is that they contain a kind of sacred magic: the
magic he saw in Judy Marshall. Because of that magic, the Territories can confer a wondrous blessing on human beings. The
life of that extraordinarily tough beloved woman making fun of
Bill Towns on the big screen before him was saved by an object
from the Territories. Because Jack had been in the Territories—
and maybe because he had held the Talisman—almost every
horse he bets on comes in first, every stock he buys triples in
value, every poker hand he holds takes the pot.

So what world is Tansy talking about? And what's all this
stuff about Gorg coming here through a burning hole?

When Jack flipped over yesterday, he had sensed something
unhappy, something unhealthy, far off to the southwest, and he
suspected that was where he would find the Fisherman's Twinner. Kill the Fisherman, kill the Twinner; it didn't matter which
he did first, the other one would weaken. But . . .

It still didn't make sense. When you travel between worlds,
you just *flip*—you don't set a fire at the world's edge and run
through it into another one.

A few minutes before twelve, the rumble of motorcycles

drowns the voices on the screen. "Um, mister, you might want to take off," says Moon. "That's the—"

"The Thunder Five," Jack says. "I know."

"Okay. It's just, they scare the shit out of some of my customers. But as long as you treat 'em right, they act okay."

"I know. There's nothing to worry about."

"I mean, if you buy 'em a beer or something, they'll think you're all right."

Jack gets off his stool and faces the bartender. "Lester, there is no reason to be nervous. They're coming here to meet me."

Lester blinks. For the first time, Jack notices that his eyebrows are thin, curved wisps, like those of a 1920s vamp. "I'd better start pourin' a pitcher of Kingsland." He grabs a pitcher from beneath the bar, sets it under the Kingsland Ale tap, and opens the valve. A thick stream of amber liquid rushes into the pitcher and turns to foam.

The sound of the motorcycles builds to an uproar at the front of the building, then cuts off. Beezer St. Pierre bangs through the door, closely followed by Doc, Mouse, Sonny, and Kaiser Bill. They look like Vikings, and Jack is overjoyed to see them.

"Stinky, turn that TV the fuck off," Beezer roars. "And we didn't come here to drink, so empty that pitcher into the drain. The way you pour, it's all head anyhow. And when you're done, get back in the kitchen with your momma. Our business with this man's got nothin' to do with you."

"Okay, Beezer," Moon says in a shaky voice. "All I need is a second."

"Then that's what you got," Beezer says.

Beezer and the others line up in front of the bar, some of them staring at Stinky Cheese, some, more kindly, at Jack. Mouse is still wearing his cornrows, and he has daubed some black antiglare substance beneath his eyes, like a football player. Kaiser Bill and Sonny have pulled their manes back into ponytails again. Ale and foam slide out of the pitcher and seep into the drain. "Okay, guys," Moon says. His footsteps retreat along the back of the bar. A door closes.

The members of the Thunder Five separate and spread out in front of Jack. Most of them have crossed their arms on their chests, and muscles bulge.

Jack pushes his plate to the back of the bar, stands up, and says, "Before last night, had any of you guys ever heard of George Potter?"

From his perch on the edge of the pool table nearest to the front door, Jack faces Beezer and Doc, who lean forward on their bar stools. Kaiser Bill, one finger against his lips and his head bowed, stands beside Beezer. Mouse lies stretched out on the second pool table, propping his head up with one hand. Banging his fists together and scowling, Sonny is pacing back and forth between the bar and the jukebox.

"You sure he didn't say 'Bleak House,' like the Dickens novel?" Mouse says.

"I'm sure," says Jack, reminding himself that he should not be surprised every time one of these guys demonstrates that he went to college. "It was 'Black House.' "

"Jeez, I almost think I . . ." Mouse shakes his head.

"What was the builder's name again?" asks Beezer.

"Burnside. First name probably Charles, sometimes known as 'Chummy.' A long time ago, he changed it from something like 'Beer Stein.' "

"Beerstein? Bernstein?"

"You got me," Jack says.

"And you think he's the Fisherman."

Jack nods. Beezer is staring at him as if trying to see the back of his head.

"How sure are you?"

"Ninety-nine percent. He planted the Polaroids in Potter's room."

"Damn." Beezer pushes himself off his stool and walks around to the back of the bar. "I want to make sure nobody forgets the obvious." He bends down and straightens up with a telephone book in one hand. "Know what I mean?" Beezer opens the directory on the bar, flips a few pages, flips back, and runs his thick finger down a column of names. "No Burnside. Too bad."

"Good idea, though," Jack says. "This morning, I tried the same thing myself."

Sonny pauses on his return journey from the jukebox and jabs a finger at Jack. "How long ago was this damn house built?"

"Nearly thirty years ago. During the seventies."

"Hell, we were all kids then, back in Illinois. How are we supposed to know about that house?"

"You guys get around. I thought there was a pretty good chance you might have seen it. And the place is spooky. People tend to talk about houses like that." They did in normal cases, at least, Jack thought. In normal cases, spooky houses got that way because they had been empty for a couple of years, or because something terrible had happened in them. In this case, he thought, the house itself was terrible, and the people who otherwise would have talked about it could barely remember seeing it. Judging by Dale's response, Black House had vanished into its own nonexistent shadow.

He says, "Think about this. Try to remember. In the years you've been living in French Landing, have you ever heard of a house that seemed to have a curse on it? Black House caused injuries to the people who built it. The workmen hated the place; they were afraid of it. They said you couldn't see your shadow when you got near it. They were claiming it was haunted while they worked on it! Eventually, they all quit, and Burnside had to finish the job himself."

"It's off by itself somewhere," Doc says. "Obviously, this thing isn't sitting around in plain view. It's not in some development like Libertyville. You're not going to find it on Robin Hood Lane."

"Right," Jack says. "I should have mentioned that before. Potter told me it was built a little way off what he called 'the road,' in a kind of clearing. So it's in the woods, Doc, you're right. It's isolated."

"Hey, hey, hey," Mouse says, swinging his legs over the side of the pool table and grunting himself upright.

His eyes are screwed shut, and he claps one meaty hand on his forehead. "If I could only remember . . ." He lets out a howl of frustration.

*"What?"* Beezer's voice is at twice its normal volume, and the word sounds like a paving stone hitting a cement sidewalk.

"I *know* I saw that fucking place," he says. "As soon as you started talking about it, I had this feeling it sounded kinda familiar. It kept hanging at the back of my mind, but it wouldn't come out. When I tried to think about it—you know, make myself remember—I kept seeing these sparkly lights. When Jack said it was back in the woods, I knew what he was talking about. I had a clear picture of the place. Surrounded by all these sparkling lights."

"That doesn't sound much like Black House," Jack says.

"Sure it does. The lights weren't really there, I just *saw* them." Mouse offers this observation as though it is completely rational.

Sonny utters a bark of laughter, and Beezer shakes his head and says, "Shit."

"I don't get it," Jack says.

Beezer looks at Jack, holds up one finger, and asks Mouse, "Are we talking about July, August, two years ago?"

"Naturally," Mouse says. "The summer of the Ultimate Acid." He looks at Jack and smiles. "Two years ago, we got this amazing, amazing acid. Drop a tab, you're in for five or six hours of the most *unbelievable* head games. Nobody ever had a bad experience with the stuff. It was all *groove,* know what I mean?"

"I suppose I can guess," Jack says.

"You could even do your job behind it. For sure, you could *drive,* man. Get on your hog, go anywhere you could think of. Doing anything normal was a piece of cake. You weren't fucked up, you were operating way beyond your max."

"Timothy Leary wasn't *all* wrong," Doc says.

"God, that was great stuff," Mouse says. "We did it until there was no more to do, and then the whole thing was over. The *whole* acid thing. If you couldn't get that stuff, there was no point in taking anything else. I never knew where it came from."

"You don't want to know where it came from," says Beezer. "Trust me."

"So you were doing this acid when you saw Black House," Jack says.

"Sure. That's why I saw the lights."

Very slowly, Beezer asks, "Where is it, Mouse?"

"I don't exactly know. But hold on, Beezer, let me talk. That was the summer I was tight with Little Nancy Hale, remember?"

"Sure," Beezer says. "That was a damn shame." He glances at Jack. "Little Nancy died right after that summer."

"Tore me apart," Mouse says. "It was like she turned allergic to air and sunlight, all of a sudden. Sick all the time. Rashes all over her body. She couldn't stand being outside, because the light hurt her eyes. Doc couldn't figure out what was wrong with her, so we took her to the big hospital in La Riviere, but they couldn't find what was wrong, either. We talked to a couple of guys at Mayo, but they weren't any help. She died *hard,* man. Broke your heart to see it happen. Broke mine, for sure."

He falls silent for a long moment, during which he stares down at his gut and his knees and no one else says a word. "All right," Mouse finally says, raising his head. "Here's what I remember. On this Saturday, Little Nancy and I were tripping on the Ultimate, just riding around to some places we liked. We went to the riverfront park in La Riviere, drove over to Dog Island and Lookout Point. We came back this direction and went up on the bluff—beautiful, man. After that, we didn't feel like going home, so we just wheeled around. Little Nancy noticed this NO TRESPASSING sign I must have passed about a thousand times before without seeing it."

He looks at Jack Sawyer. "I can't say for certain, but I think it was on 35."

Jack nods.

"If we hadn't been on the Ultimate, I don't think she ever would have seen that sign, either. Oh man, it's all coming back to me. 'What's that?' she says, and I swear, I had to look two or three times before I saw that sign—it was all beat-up and bent, with a couple rusty bullet holes in it. Sort of leaning back into the trees. 'Somebody wants to keep us off that road,' Little Nancy says. 'What are they hiding up there, anyhow?' Something like that. 'What road?' I ask, and then I see it. It's hardly even what you could call a road. About wide enough for a car to fit in, if you have a compact. Thick trees on both sides. Hell, I didn't think anything interesting was hidden up there, unless it was an old shack. Besides that, I didn't like the way it looked." He glances at Beezer.

"What do you mean, you didn't like the way it looked?" Beezer asks. "I've seen you go into places you damn well knew were no good. Or are you getting *mystical* on me, Mouse?"

"Call it what you fucking want, I'm telling you how it was. It was like that sign was saying KEEP OUT IF YOU KNOW WHAT'S GOOD FOR YOU. Gave me a bad feeling."

"On account of it was a bad place," Sonny interrupts. "I've seen some bad places. They don't want you there, and they let you know."

Beezer shoots him a measured look and says, "I don't care how evil this *bad* place is, if it's where the Fisherman lives, I'm going there."

"And I'm going with you," says Mouse, "but just listen. I wanted to bag it and get some fried chicken or something, which combined with the Ultimate would have been like eating the food of Paradise, or whatever Coleridge said, but Little Nancy wanted to go in *because* she had the same feeling I did. She was a game broad, man. Ornery, too. So I turned in, and Little Nancy's hanging on in back of me, and she's saying, 'Don't be a pussy, Mouse, let's haul ass,' so I gun it a little bit, and everything feels all weird and shit, but all I can see's this track curving away into the trees and the shit I *know* isn't there."

"Like what?" asks Sonny, in what sounds like the spirit of scientific inquiry.

"These dark shapes coming up to the edge of the road and looking out through the trees. A couple of them ran toward me, but I rolled right through them like smoke. I don't know, maybe they *were* smoke."

"Fuck that, it was the acid," Beezer says.

"Maybe, but it didn't feel that way. Besides, the Ultimate never turned on you, remember? It wasn't about *darkness.* Anyhow, right before the shit hit the fan, all of a sudden I was thinking about Kiz Martin. I can remember that, all right. It was like I could practically see her, right in front of me—the way she looked when they loaded her in the ambulance."

"Kiz Martin," Beezer says.

Mouse turns to Jack. "Kiz was a girl I went out with when we were all at the university. She used to beg us to let her ride with us, and one day the Kaiser said, okay, she could borrow his bike. Kiz was having a *ball,* man, she's diggin' it. And then she rolls over some damn little twig, I think it was—"

"Bigger than a twig," Doc says. "Little branch. Maybe two inches in diameter."

"Which is just enough to test your balance, especially if you're not used to hogs," Mouse says. "She rolls over this little branch, and the bike flops over, and Kiz flies off and hits the road. My heart damn near stopped, man."

"I knew she was gone the second I came up close enough to see the angle of her head," says Doc. "There wasn't even any point in trying CPR. We covered her with our jackets, and I rode off to call an ambulance. Ten minutes later, they were loading her in. One of the guys recognized me from my stint in the ER, or they might have given us some trouble."

"I wondered if you were really a doctor," Jack says.

"Completed my residency in surgery at U.I., walked away from the whole deal right there." Doc smiles at him. "Hanging around with these guys, getting into beer brewing, sounded like more fun than spending all day cutting people up."

"Mouse," Beezer says.

"Yeah. I was just getting to the curve in the little road, and it was like Kiz was standing right in front of me, it was so vivid. Her eyes closed, and her head hanging like a leaf about to fall. *Oh man,* I said to myself, *this is not what I want to see at this particular moment.* I could feel it all over again—the way I felt when Kiz hit the road. Sick dread. That's the word for it, sick dread.

"And we come around the curve, and I hear this dog growling somewhere off in the woods. Not just growling, *growling.* Like twenty big dogs are out there, and they're all mad as hell. My head starts feeling like it wants to explode. And I look up ahead of me to see if a pack of wolves or something is running toward us, and it takes me a while to realize that the weird shadowy stuff I see up ahead is a house. A black house.

"Little Nancy is hitting me on the back and rapping my head, screaming at me to stop. Believe me, I can get with the program, because the last thing I want to do is get any closer to that place. I stop the bike, and Little Nancy jumps off and pukes on the side of the road. She holds her head and she pukes some more. I'm feeling like my legs turned to rubber, like something heavy is pressing on my chest. That *thing,* whatever it is, is still going nuts in the woods, and it's getting closer. I take another look up at the end of the road, and that ugly damn house is stretching back into the woods, like it's crawling into them, only it's standing still. It gets bigger the more you look at it! Then I see the sparkly lights floating around it, and they look dangerous—*Stay away,* they're telling me, *get out of here, Mouse.* There's another NO TRESPASSING sign leaning against the porch, and that sign, man . . . that sign kind of flashed, like it was saying THIS TIME I MEAN IT, BUDDY.

"My head is splitting in half, but I get Little Nancy on the bike, and she sags against me, like pure dead weight except she's hanging on, and I kick the hog on and spin around and take off. When we get back to my place, she goes to bed and stays there for three days. To me, it seemed like I could hardly remember what happened. The whole thing went kind of *dark.* In my mind. I hardly had time to think about it anyhow, because Little Nancy got sick and I had to take care of her whenever I wasn't at work. Doc gave her some stuff to get her temperature down, and she got better, so we could drink beer and smoke shit and ride around, like before, but she was never really the same. End of August, she started getting bad again, and I had to put her in the hospital. Second week of September, hard as she was fighting, Little Nancy passed away."

"How big was Little Nancy?" Jack asks, picturing a woman roughly the size of Mouse.

"Little Nancy Hale was about the size and shape of Tansy Freneau," Mouse says, looking surprised by the question. "If she stood on my hand, I could lift her up with one arm."

"And you never talked about this with anyone," Jack says.

"How could I talk about it?" Mouse asks. "First, I was crazy with worry about Little Nancy, and then it went clean out of my head. Weird shit will do that to you, man. Instead of sticking in your head, it erases itself."

"I know exactly what you mean," Jack says.

"I guess I do, too," says Beezer, "but I'd say that the Ultimate kicked the shit out of your reality there for a while. You did see the place, though—Black House."

"Damn straight," says Mouse.

Beezer focuses on Jack. "And you say the Fisherman, this creep Burnside, built it."

Jack nods.

"So maybe he's living there, and he rigged up a bunch of gadgets to scare people away."

"Could be."

"Then I think we're gonna let Mouse take us over on Highway 35 and see if he can find that little road he was talking about. Are you coming with us?"

"I can't," Jack says. "I have to see someone in Arden first, someone who I think can also help us. She has another piece of the puzzle, but I can't explain it to you until I see her."

"This woman knows something?"

"Oh, yes," Jack says. "She knows something."

"All right," Beezer says, and stands up from his stool. "Your choice. We'll have to talk to you afterward."

"Beezer, I want to be with you when you go inside Black House. Whatever we have to do in there, whatever we see . . ." Jack pauses, trying to find the right words. Beezer is rocking on his heels, practically jumping out of his skin in his eagerness to hunt down the Fisherman's lair. "You're going to want me there. There's more to this business than you can imagine, Beezer. You're going to know what I'm talking about in a little while, and you'll be able to stand up to it—I think all of you will—but if I tried to describe it now, you wouldn't believe me. When the time comes, you'll need me to see you through, if we get through. You'll be glad I was there. We're at a dangerous point here, and none of us wants to mess it up."

"What makes you think I'll mess it up?" Beezer asks, with deceptive mildness.

"Anyone would mess it up, if they didn't have the last piece of the puzzle. Go out there. See if Mouse can find the house he saw two years ago. Check it out. Don't go in—to do that, you need me. After you check it out, come back here, and I'll see you as soon as I can. I should be back before two-thirty, three at the latest."

"Where are you going in Arden? Maybe I'll want to call you."

"French County Lutheran Hospital. Ward D. If you can't get me, leave a message with a Dr. Spiegleman."

"Ward D, huh?" Beezer says. "Okay, I guess everybody's crazy today. And I guess I can be satisfied with only a look at this house, as long as I know that sometime this afternoon, I can count on you to explain all these pieces I'm too stupid to understand."

"It'll be soon, Beezer. We're closing in. And the last thing I'd call you is stupid."

"I guess you must have been one hell of a cop," Beezer says. "Even though I think half the stuff you say is crap, I can't help but believe it." He turns around and brings his fists down on the bar. "Stinky Cheese! It's safe now. Drag your pale ass out of the kitchen."

# 19

Jack follows the Thunder Five out of the parking lot, and for the moment we will let him go alone on his northward way on Highway 93 toward Judy Marshall's lookout and Judy Marshall's locked ward. Like Jack, the bikers are headed toward the unknown, but their unknown lies westward on Highway 35, into the land of the steadily accumulating past, and we want to know what they will find there. These men do not appear to be nervous; they still project the massive confidence with which they burst into the Sand Bar. In truth, they never really display nervousness, for situations that would make other people worried or anxious generally make them get physical. Fear affects them differently than it does other people, too: in the rare moments when they have experienced fear, they've tended on the whole to enjoy it. In their eyes, fear represents a God-given opportunity for focusing their collective concentration. Due to their remarkable solidarity, that concentration is formidable. For those of us who are not members of a biker gang or the Marine Corps, solidarity means little more than the compassionate impulse that leads us to comfort a bereft friend; for Beezer and his merry band, solidarity is the assurance that someone's always got your back. They are on each other's hands, and they know it. For the Thunder Five, safety really is in numbers.

Yet the encounter toward which they are flying has no precedents or analogues in their experience. Black House is something new, and its newness—the sheer *strangeness* of Mouse's story—sinks tendrils down into their guts, one and all.

Eight miles west of Centralia, where the flatland around Potsie's thirty-year-old development yields to the long stretch of woods that runs all the way to Maxton's, Mouse and Beezer ride side by side in front of the others. Beezer occasionally looks to his friend, asking a wordless question. The third time that Mouse shakes his head, he follows the gesture with a backward wave of his hand that says *Stop bugging me, I'll tell you when we're there.* Beezer drops back; Sonny, Kaiser Bill, and Doc automatically assume Beezer is giving them a signal, and they string out in a single line.

At the head of the column, Mouse keeps taking his eyes off the highway to inspect the right-hand side of the road. The little road is hard to see, Mouse knows, and by now it will be more overgrown than it was two years ago. He is trying to spot the white of the battered NO TRESPASSING sign. It, too, may be partially hidden by new growth. He slows down to thirty-five. The four men behind him match his change in pace with the smoothness of long practice.

Alone of the Thunder Five, Mouse has already seen their destination, and in the deepest places of his soul he can scarcely believe that he is going there again. At first, the ease and rapidity with which his memories had flown out of their dark vault had pleased him; now, instead of feeling that he has effortlessly reclaimed a lost part of his life, he has the sense of being at the mercy of that lost afternoon. A grave danger then—and he does not doubt that some great and dangerous *force* had brushed him with a warning hand—is an increased danger now. Memory has returned a miserable conclusion he thrust away long ago: that the hideous structure Jack Sawyer called Black House had killed Little Nancy Hale as surely as if its rafters had fallen in on her. Moral more than physical, Black House's ugliness exhaled toxic fumes. Little Nancy had been killed by the invisible poisons carried on the warning hand; now Mouse had to look at that knowledge without blinking. He can feel her hands on his shoulders, and their thin bones are covered with rotting flesh.

*If I'd been five foot three and weighed one hundred and five pounds instead of being six-two and two hundred and ninety, by now I'd be rotting, too,* he thinks.

Mouse may look for the narrow road and the sign beside it with the eyes of a fighter pilot, but someone else has to see them, because he never will. His unconscious has taken a vote, and the decision was unanimous.

Each of the other men, Sonny, Doc, the Kaiser, and even Beezer, have also connected Little Nancy's death with Black House, and the same speculations about comparative size and weight have passed through their minds. However, Sonny Cantinaro, Doc Amberson, Kaiser Bill Strassner, and especially Beezer St. Pierre assume that whatever poison surrounded Black House had been concocted in a laboratory by human beings who knew what they were doing. These four men derive the old, primitive reassurance from one another's company that they have enjoyed since college; if anything makes them feel a touch uneasy, it is that Mouse Baumann, not Beezer, leads their column. Even though Beezer let Mouse wave him back, Mouse's position contains a hint of insurrection, of mutiny: the universe has been subtly disordered.

Twenty yards from the back end of the Maxton property, Sonny decides to put an end to this farce, guns his Softail, roars past his friends, and moves up parallel to Mouse. Mouse glances at him with a trace of worry, and Sonny motions to the side of the road.

When they have all pulled over, Mouse says, "What's your problem, Sonny?"

"You are," Sonny says. "Either you missed the turnoff, or your whole story's all fucked up."

"I *said* I wasn't sure where it is." He notices with nearly immeasurable relief that Little Nancy's dead hands no longer grip his shoulders.

"Of course not. You were ripped on acid!"

"*Good* acid."

"Well, there's no road up ahead, I know that much. It's just trees all the way to the old fucks' home."

Mouse ponders the stretch of road ahead as if the road just might be up there, after all, although he knows it is not.

"Shit, Mouse, we're practically in town. I can see *Queen Street* from here."

"Yeah," Mouse says. "Okay." If he can get to Queen Street, he thinks, those hands will never fasten on him again.

Beezer walks his Electra Glide up to them and says, "Okay what, Mouse? You agree it's farther back, or is the road somewhere else?"

Frowning, Mouse turns his head to look back down the highway. "Goddamn. I *think* it's along here somewhere, unless I got totally turned around that day."

"Gee, how could that have happened?" says Sonny. "I looked at every inch of ground we passed, and I sure as hell didn't see a road. Did you, Beezer? How about a NO TRESPASSING sign, you happen to see one of those?"

"You don't get it," Mouse says. "This shit doesn't want to be seen."

"Maybe you shoulda gone to Ward D with Sawyer," Sonny says. "People in there appreciate visionaries."

"Can it, Sonny," Beezer says.

"I was there before, and you weren't," Mouse says. "Which one of us knows what he's talking about?"

"I've heard enough out of both of you guys," Beezer says. "Do you still think it's along here somewhere, Mouse?"

"As far as I can recollect, yeah."

"Then we missed it. We'll go back and check again, and if we don't find it, we'll look somewhere else. If it's not here, it's between two of the valleys along 93, or in the woods on the hill leading up to the lookout. We have plenty of time."

"What makes you so sure?" Sonny asks. Mild anxiety about what they might come across is making him belligerent. He would just as soon go back to the Sand Bar and down a pitcher of Kingsland while messing with Stinky's head as waste his time goofing along the highways.

Beezer looks at him, and his eyes crackle. "You know anywhere else there's enough trees to call it a woods?"

Sonny backs down immediately. Beezer is never going to give up and go back to the Sand Bar. Beezer is in this for keeps. Most of that has to do with Amy, but some of it relates to Jack Sawyer. Sawyer impressed the shit out of Beezer the other night, that's what happened, and now Beezer thinks everything the guy says is golden. To Sonny, this makes no sense at all, but Beezer's the one who calls the shots, so for now, Sonny guesses, they will all run around like junior G-men for a while. If this adopt-a-cop program goes on for more than a couple of days, Sonny plans to have a little chat with Mouse and the Kaiser. Doc will always side with Beezer no matter what, but the other two are capable of listening to reason.

"All right, then," Beezer says. "Scratch from here to Queen

Street. We *know* there's no fuckin' road along that stretch. We'll go back the way we came, give it one more shot. Single file the whole way. Mouse, you're point man again."

Mouse nods and prepares himself to feel those hands on his shoulders again. Gunning his Fat Boy, he rolls forward and takes his place at the head of the line. Beezer moves in behind him, and Sonny follows Beezer, with Doc and the Kaiser in the last two slots.

*Five pairs of eyes,* Sonny thinks. *If we don't see it this time, we never will. And we won't, because that damned road is halfway across the state. When Mouse and his old lady got buzzed on the Ultimate, they could go for hundreds of miles and think they'd taken a spin around the block.*

Everybody scans the opposite side of the road and the edge of the woods. Five pairs of eyes, as Sonny puts it, register an unbroken line of oaks and pine trees. Mouse has set a pace somewhere between a fast walk and a medium jog, and the trees crawl by. At this speed, they can notice the moss blistering the trunks of the oaks and the bright smears of sunlight on the forest's floor, which is brownish gray and resembles a layer of rumpled felt. A hidden world of upright trees, shafts of light, and deadfalls extends backward from the first, sentinel row. Within that world, paths that are not paths wind mazelike between the thick trunks and lead to mysterious clearings. Sonny becomes suddenly aware of a tribe of squirrels doing squirrel gymnastics in the map of branches that lace into an intermittent canopy. And with the squirrels, an aviary of birds pops into view.

All of this reminds him of the deep Pennsylvania woods he had explored as a boy, before his parents sold their house and moved to Illinois. Those woods had contained a rapture he had found nowhere else. Sonny's conviction that Mouse got things wrong and they are looking in the wrong place takes on greater inner density. Earlier, Sonny had spoken about bad places, of which he has seen at least one he was absolutely certain about. In Sonny's experience, *bad* places, the ones that let you know you were not welcome, tended to be on or near borders.

During the summer after his high school graduation, he and his two best buddies, all of them motorcycle freaks, had taken their bikes to Rice Lake, Wisconsin, where he had two cousins cute enough to show off to his friends. Sal and Harry were thrilled with the girls, and the girls thought the bikers were sexy and exotic. After a couple of days spent as a literal fifth wheel (or fifth *and* sixth wheel, depending on what you are counting), Sonny proposed extending their trip by a week and, in the interest of expanding their educations, ballin' the jack down to Chicago and spending the rest of their money on beer and hookers until they had to go home. Sal and Harry loved the whole idea, and on their third evening in Rice Lake, they packed their rolls on their bikes and roared south, making as much noise as possible. By 10:00 they had managed to get completely lost.

It might have been the beer, it might have been inattention, but for one reason or another they had wandered off the highway and, in the deep black of a rural night, found themselves on the edge of an almost nonexistent town named Harko. Harko could not be found on their gas-station road map, but it had to be close to the Illinois border, on either one side or the other. Harko seemed to consist of an abandoned motel, a collapsing general store, and an empty grain mill. When the boys reached the mill, Sal and Harry groused about being exhausted and hungry and wanted to turn back to spend the night in the motel.

Sonny, who was no less worn out, rode back with them; the second they rolled into the dark forecourt of the motel, he had a bad feeling about the place. The air seemed heavier, the darkness darker than they should have been. To Sonny, it seemed that malign, invisible presences haunted the place. He could all but make them out as they flitted between the cabins. Sal and Harry jeered at his reservations: he was a coward, a fairy, a *girl*. They broke down a door and unrolled their sleeping bags in a bare, dusty rectangular room. He carried his across the street and slept in a field.

Dawn awakened him, and his face was wet with dew. He jumped up, pissed into the high grass, and checked for the motorcycles on the other side of the road. There they were, all three of them, listing over their stands outside a broken door. The dead neon sign at the entrance of the forecourt read HONEYMOONER'S BOWER. He walked across the narrow road and swept a hand over the moisture shining black on the seats of the motorcycles. A funny sound came from the room where his friends were sleeping. Already tasting dread, Sonny pushed open the broken door. If he had not initially refused to make sense of what was before him, what he saw in the room would have made him pass out.

His face streaked with blood and tears, Sal Turso was sitting on the floor. Harry Reilly's severed head rested in his lap, and an ocean of blood soaked the floor and daubed the walls. Harry's body lay loose and disjointed on top of his blood-soaked sleeping bag. The body was naked; Sal wore only a blood-red T-shirt. Sal raised both his hands—the one holding his prize long-bladed knife and the one holding only a palmful of blood—and lifted his contorted face to Sonny's frozen gaze. *I don't know what happened.* His voice was high and screechy, not his. *I don't remember doing this, how could I have done this? Help me, Sonny. I don't know what happened.*

Unable to speak, Sonny had backed out and flown away on his cycle. He'd had no clear idea of where he was going except that it was out of Harko. Two miles down the road, he came to a little town, a real one, with people in it, and someone finally took him to the sheriff's office.

Harko: *there* was a bad place. In a way, both of his high school friends had died there, because Sal Turso hanged himself six months after being committed to a state penitentiary for life on a second-degree murder charge. In Harko, you saw no red-winged blackbirds or woodpeckers. Even sparrows steered clear of Harko.

This little stretch of 35? Nothing but a nice, comfortable woodland. Let me tell you, Senator, Sonny Cantinaro has seen Harko, and this ain't no Harko. This don't even come close. It might as well be in another world. What meets Sonny's appraising eye and increasingly impatient spirit is about a mile and a quarter of beautiful wooded landscape. You could call it a mini-forest. He thinks it would be cool to come out here by himself one day, tuck the Harley out of sight, and just walk around through the great oaks and pines, that big pad of felt beneath his feet, digging the birds and the crazy squirrels.

Sonny gazes at and through the sentinel trees on the far side of the road, enjoying his anticipation of the pleasure to come, and a flash of white jumps out at him from the darkness beside a huge oak tree. Caught up in the vision of walking alone under that green canopy, he almost dismisses it as a trick of the light, a brief illusion. Then he remembers what he is supposed to be looking for, and he slows down and leans sideways and sees, emerging from the tangle of underbrush at the base of the oak, a rusty bullet hole and a large, black letter N. Sonny swerves across the road, and the N expands into NO. He doesn't believe it, but there it is, Mouse's goddamn sign. He rolls ahead another foot, and the entire phrase comes into view.

Sonny puts the bike in neutral and plants one foot on the ground. The darkness next to the oak stretches like a web to the next tree at the side of the road, which is also an oak, though not as huge. Behind him, Doc and the Kaiser cross the road and come to a halt. He ignores them and looks at Beezer and Mouse, who are already some thirty feet up the road, intently scanning the trees.

"Hey," he shouts. Beezer and Mouse do not hear him. *"Hey! Stop!"*

"You got it?" Doc calls out.

"Go up to those assholes and bring them back," Sonny says.

"It's here?" Doc asks, peering into the trees.

"What, you think I found a body? Of course it's here."

Doc speeds up, stops just behind Sonny, and stares at the woods.

"Doc, you see it?" Kaiser Bill shouts, and he speeds up, too.

"Nope," Doc says.

"You can't see it from there," Sonny tells him. "Will you please get your ass in gear and tell Beezer to come back here?"

"Why don't you do it, instead?" Doc says.

"Because if I leave this spot, I might not ever be able to fucking find it again," Sonny says.

Mouse and Beezer, now about sixty feet up the road, continue blithely on their way.

"Well, I still don't see it," Doc says.

Sonny sighs. "Come up alongside me." Doc walks his Fat Boy to a point parallel with Sonny's bike, then moves a couple of inches ahead. "There," Sonny says, pointing at the sign.

Doc squints and leans over, putting his head above Sonny's handlebars. "Where? Oh, I see it now. It's all beat to hell."

The top half of the sign curls over and shades the bottom half. Some antisocial lad has happened along and creased the sign with his baseball bat. His older brothers, more advanced in the ways of crime, had tried to kill it with their .22 rifles, and he was just delivering the coup de grâce.

"Where's the road supposed to be?" Doc asks.

Sonny, who is a little troubled about this point, indicates the flat sheet of darkness to the right of the sign and extending to the next, smaller oak tree. As he looks at it, the darkness loses its two-dimensionality and deepens backward like a cave, or a black hole softly punched through the air. The cave, the black hole, melts and widens into the earthen road, about five and a half feet wide, that it must have been all along.

"That sure as hell is it," says Kaiser Bill. "I don't know how all of us could have missed it the first time."

Sonny and Doc glance at each other, realizing that the Kaiser came along too late to watch the road seem to materialize out of a black wall with the thickness of a sheet of paper.

"It's kind of tricky," Sonny says.

"Your eyes have to adjust," Doc says.

"Okay," says Kaiser Bill, "but if you two want to argue about who tells Mouse and the Beeze, let me put you out of your misery." He jams his bike into gear and tears off like a World War I messenger with a hot dispatch from the front. By now a long way up the road, Mouse and Beezer come to a halt and look back, having apparently heard the sound of his bike.

"I guess that's it," Sonny says, with an uneasy glance at Doc. "Our eyes had to adjust."

"Couldn't be anything else."

Less convinced than they would like to be, both men let it drop in favor of watching Kaiser Bill conversing with Beezer and Mouse. The Kaiser points at Sonny and Doc, Beezer points. Then Mouse points at them, and the Kaiser points again. It looks like a discussion in an extremely unevolved version of sign language. When everybody has gotten the point, Kaiser Bill spins his bike around and comes roaring back down the road with Beezer and Mouse on his tail.

There is always that feeling of disorder, of misrule, when Beezer is not in the lead.

The Kaiser stops on the side of the narrow road. Beezer and Mouse halt beside him, and Mouse winds up stationed directly in front of the opening in the woods.

"Shouldn't have been *that* hard to see," Beezer says. "But there she is, anyhow. I was beginning to have my doubts, Mousie."

"Uh-huh," says Mouse. His customary manner, that of an intellectual roughneck with a playful take on the world, has lost all of its buoyancy. Beneath his biker's fair-weather sunburn, his skin looks pale and curdlike.

"I want to tell you guys the truth," Beezer says. "If Sawyer is right about this place, the creepy fuck who built it could have set up booby traps and all sorts of surprises. It was a long time ago, but if he really is the Fisherman, he has more reason than ever to keep people away from his crib. So we gotta watch our backs. The best way to do that is to go in strong, and go in ready. Put your weapons where you can reach them in a hurry, all right?"

Beezer opens one of his saddlebags and draws out a Colt 9mm pistol with ivory grips and a blue-steel barrel. He chambers a round and unlocks the safety. Under his gaze, Sonny pulls his massive .357 Magnum from his bag, Doc a Colt identical to Beezer's, and Kaiser Bill an old S&W .38 Special he has owned since the late seventies. They shove the weapons, which until this moment have seen use only on firing ranges, into the pockets of their leather jackets. Mouse, who does not own a gun, pats the various knives he has secreted in the small of his back, in the hip and front pockets of his jeans, and sheathed within both of his boots.

"Okay," Beezer says. "Anybody in there is going to hear us coming no matter what we do, and maybe already *has* heard us, so there's no point in being sneaky about this. I want a fast, aggressive entrance—just what you guys are good at. We can use speed to our advantage. Depending on what happens, we get as close to the house as possible."

"What if nothing happens?" asks the Kaiser. "Like, if we roll on in there and just keep going until we get to the house? I mean, I don't see any particular reason to be spooked here. Okay, something bad happened to Mouse, but . . . you know. Doesn't mean it's going to happen all over again."

"Then we enjoy the ride," Beezer says.

"Don't you want to take a look inside?" the Kaiser asks. "He might have kids in there."

"*He* might be in there," Beezer tells him. "If he is, no matter what I said to Sawyer, we're bringing him out. Alive would be better than dead, but I wouldn't mind putting him in a serious state of bad health."

He gets a rumble of approval. Mouse does not contribute to this wordless, but otherwise universal agreement; he lowers his head and tightens his hands on the grips of his bike.

"Because Mouse has been here before, he goes in on point. Doc and I'll be right behind him, with Sonny and the Kaiser covering our asses." Beezer glances at them and says, "Stay about six, eight feet back, all right?"

*Don't put Mouse on point; you have to go in first,* speaks in Sonny's mind, but he says, "All right, Beeze."

"Line up," Beezer says.

They move their bikes into the positions Beezer has specified. Anyone driving fast along Highway 35 would have to hit his brakes to avoid running into at least two beefy men on motorcycles, but the road stays empty. Everyone, including Mouse, guns his engine and prepares to move. Sonny slaps his fist against the Kaiser's and looks back at that dark tunnel into the woods.

A big crow flaps onto a low-hanging branch, cocks its head, and seems to fix Sonny's eyes with its own. The crow must be looking at all of them, Sonny knows, but he cannot shake the illusion that the crow is staring directly at him, and that its black insatiable eyes are dancing with malice. The uncomfortable feeling that the crow is amused by the sight of him bent over his bike makes Sonny think of his Magnum.

*Turn you into a mess of bloody feathers, baby.*

Without unfolding its wings, the crow hops backward and disappears into the oak leaves.

"GO!" Beezer shouts.

The moment Mouse charges in, Little Nancy's rotting hands clamp down on his shoulders. Her thin bones press down on the leather hard enough to leave bruises on his skin. Although he knows this is impossible—you cannot get rid of what does not exist—the sudden flare of pain causes him to try to shake her off. He twitches his shoulders and wiggles the handlebars, and the bike wobbles. As the bike dips, Little Nancy

digs in harder. When Mouse rights himself, she pulls herself
forward, wraps her bony arms around his chest, and flattens
her body against his back. Her skull grinds against the nape
of his neck; her teeth bite down on his skin.

It is *too much.* Mouse had known she would reappear, but
not that she would put him in a vise. And despite his speed, he
has the feeling that he is traveling through a substance heavier
and more viscous than air, a kind of syrup that slows him down,
holds him back. Both he and the bike seem unnaturally dense,
as if gravity exerts a stronger pull on the little road than anywhere else. His head pounds, and already he can hear that dog
growling in the woods off to his right. He could take all of that,
he supposes, if it were not for what stopped him the last time he
drove up this path: a dead woman. Then she was Kiz Martin;
now the dead woman is Little Nancy, and she is riding him like
a dervish, slapping his head, punching him in the side, battering his ears. He feels her teeth leave his neck and sink into the
left shoulder of his jacket. One of her arms whips in front of
him, and he enters a deeper level of shock and horror when he
realizes that this arm is visible. Rags of skin flutter over long
bones; he glimpses white maggots wriggling into the few remaining knots of flesh.

A hand that feels both spongelike and bony flaps onto his
cheek and crawls up his face. Mouse cannot keep it together
anymore: his mind fills with white panic, and he loses control
of the bike. When he heads into the curve that leads to Black
House, the wheels are already tilting dangerously, and Mouse's
sideways jerk of revulsion pushes them over beyond the possibility of correction.

As the bike topples, he hears the dog snarling from only a
few yards away. The Harley smashes down on his left leg, then
skids ahead, and he and his ghastly passenger slide after it.
When Mouse sees Black House looming from its dark bower
amid the trees, a rotting hand flattens over his eyes. His scream
is a bright, thin thread of sound against the fury of the dog.

A few seconds after going in, Beezer feels the air thicken and
congeal around him. It's some *trick,* he tells himself, an illusion
produced by the Fisherman's mind-fuck toxins. Trusting that
the others will not be suckered by this illusion, he raises his

head and looks over Mouse's broad back and cornrowed head to see the road curve to the left about fifty feet ahead. The thick air seems to weigh down on his arms and shoulders, and he feels the onset of the mother and father of all headaches, a dull, insistent pain that begins as a sharp twinge behind his eyes and moves thudding deeper into his brain. Beezer gives Doc a half second of attention, and from what he sees, Doc is taking care of business. A glance at the speedometer tells him that he is traveling at thirty-five miles per hour and gathering steam, so they should be doing sixty by the time they come into the curve.

Off to his left, a dog growls. Beezer hauls his pistol out of his pocket and listens to the growling keep pace with them as they speed toward the curve. The band of pain in his head widens and intensifies; it seems to push at his eyes from the inside, making them bulge in their sockets. The big dog—it has to be a dog, what else could it be?—is getting closer, and the fury of its noises makes Beezer see a giant, tossing head with blazing red eyes and ropes of slather whipping from a gaping mouth filled with shark's teeth.

Two separate things destroy his concentration: the first is that he sees Mouse slamming himself back and forth on his bike as he goes into the curve, as if he is trying to scratch his back on the thickening air; the second is that the pressure behind his eyes triples in force, and immediately after he sees Mouse going into what is surely a fall, the blood vessels in his eyes explode. From deep red, his vision shifts rapidly to absolute black. An ugly voice starts up in his head, saying, *Amy zadt in my lap an huggedt mee. I made opp my mindt to eed hurr. How she dud, dud, dud kick an scrutch. I chokked hurr do deff—*

"No!" Beezer shouts, and the voice that is pushing at his eyes drops into a rasping chuckle. For less than a second, he gets a vision of a tall, shadowy creature and a single eye, a flash of teeth beneath a hat or a hood—

—and the world abruptly revolves around him, and he ends up flat on his back with the bike weighing on his chest. Everything he sees is stained a dark, seething red. Mouse is screaming, and when Beezer turns his head in the direction of the screams, he sees a red Mouse lying on a red road with a huge red dog barreling toward him. Beezer cannot find his pistol; it went sailing into the woods. Shouts, screams, and the roar of motorcycles fill his ears. He scrambles out from under the bike yelling he knows not what. A red Doc flashes by on his red bike and almost knocks him down again. He hears a gunshot, then another.

Doc sees Beezer glance at him and tries not to show how sick he feels. Dishwater boils in his stomach, and his guts are writhing. It feels like he is going about five miles an hour, the air is so thick and rancid. For some reason, his head weighs thirty or forty pounds, damnedest thing; it would almost be interesting if he could stop the disaster happening inside him. The air seems to *concentrate* itself, to *solidify,* and then *boom,* his head turns into a superheavyweight bowling ball that wants to drop onto his chest. A giant growling sound comes from out of the woods beside him, and Doc almost yields to the impulse to puke. He is dimly aware that Beezer is pulling out his gun, and he supposes he should do the same, but part of his problem is that the memory of a child named Daisy Temperly has moved into his mind, and the memory of Daisy Temperly paralyzes his will.

As a resident in surgery at the university hospital in Urbana, Doc had performed, under supervision, nearly a hundred operations of every sort and assisted at as many. Until Daisy Temperly was wheeled into the O.R., all of them had gone well. Complicated but not especially difficult or life-threatening, her case involved bone grafts and other repair work. Daisy was being put back together again after a serious auto accident, and she had already endured two previous surgeries. Two hours after the start of the procedure, the head of the department, Doc's supervisor, was called away for an emergency operation, and Doc was left in charge. Partly because he had been sleep-deprived for forty-eight hours, partly because in his exhaustion he had pictured himself cruising along the highway with Beezer, Mouse, and his other new friends, he made a mistake— not during the operation, but after it. While writing a prescription for medication, he miscalculated the dosage, and two hours later, Daisy Temperly was dead. There were things he could have done to rescue his career, but he did none of them. He was allowed to finish his residency, and then he left medicine for

good. Talking to Jack Sawyer, he had vastly simplified his motives.

The uproar in the middle of his body can no longer be contained. Doc turns his head and vomits as he races forward. It is
not the first time he has puked while riding, but it is the messi-
est and the most painful. The weight of his bowling-ball head
means that he cannot extend his neck, so vomit spatters against
his right shoulder and right arm; and what comes leaping out of
him feels alive and equipped with teeth and claws. He is not
surprised to see blood mixed with the vomit erupting from his
mouth. His stomach doubles in on itself with pain.

Without meaning to, Doc has slowed down, and when he ac-
celerates and faces forward again, he sees Mouse topple over
sideways and skid behind his bike into the curve up ahead. His
ears report a rushing sound, like that of a distant waterfall.
Dimly, Mouse screams; equally dimly, Beezer shouts "No!"
Right after that, the Beeze runs headlong into a big rock or
some other obstruction, because his Electra Glide leaves the
ground, flips completely over in the compacted air, and comes
down on top of him. It occurs to Doc that this mission is totally
FUBAR. The whole world has hung a left, and now they are in
deep shit. He does the only sensible thing: he yanks his trusty
9mm out of his pocket and tries to figure out what to shoot first.

His ears pop, and the sounds around him surge into life.
Mouse is still screeching. Doc cannot figure out how he missed
hearing the noise of the dog before, because even with the roaring of the cycles and Mouse's screams, that moving growl is the
loudest sound in the woods. The fucking Hound of the
Baskervilles is racing toward them, and both Mouse and Beezer
are out of commission. From the noise it makes, the thing must
be the size of a bear. Doc aims the pistol straight ahead and
steers with one hand as he blasts by Beezer, who is wriggling
out from beneath his bike. That enormous sound—Doc imagines a bear-sized dog widening its chops around Mouse's head,
and instantly erases the image. Things are happening too fast,
and if he doesn't pay attention, those jaws could close on *him*.

He has just time enough to think, *That's no ordinary dog, not
even a huge one*—

—when something enormous and black comes charging out

of the woods to his right and cuts on a diagonal toward Mouse. Doc pulls the trigger, and at the sound of the pistol the animal whirls halfway around and snarls at him. All Doc can see clearly are two red eyes and an open red mouth with a long tongue and a lot of sharp canine teeth. Everything else is smudgy and indistinct, with no more definition than if it were covered in a swirling cape. A lightning bolt of pure terror that tastes as clean and sharp as cheap vodka pierces Doc from gullet to testicles, and his bike slews its rear end around and comes to a halt—he has stopped it out of sheer reflex. Suddenly it feels like deep night. Of course he can't see it—how could you see a black dog in the middle of the night?

The creature whirls around again and streaks toward Mouse.

*It doesn't want to charge me because of the gun and because the other two guys are right behind me,* Doc thinks. His head and arms seem to have gained another forty pounds apiece, but he fights against the weight of his muscles and straightens his arms and fires again. This time he *knows* he hits that thing, but its only reaction is to shudder off-course for a moment. The big smudge of its head swings toward Doc. The growling gets even louder, and long, silvery streamers of dog drool fly from its open mouth. Something that suggests a tail switches back and forth.

When Doc looks into the open red gash, his resolve weakens, his arms get heavier, and he is scarcely capable of holding his head upright. He feels as though he is falling down into that red maw; his pistol dangles from his limp hand. In a moment suspended throughout eternity, the same hand scribbles a post-op prescription for Daisy Temperly. The creature trots toward Mouse. Doc can hear Sonny's voice, cursing furiously. A loud explosion on his right side seals both of his ears, and the world falls perfectly silent. *Here we are,* Doc says to himself. *Darkness at noon.*

For Sonny, the darkness strikes at the same time as the searing pain in his head and his stomach. A single band of agony rips right down through his body, a phenomenon so unparalleled and extreme that he assumes it has also erased the daylight. He and Kaiser Bill are eight feet behind Beezer and Doc, and about fifteen feet up the narrow dirt road. The Kaiser lets go of his handlebars and grips the sides of his head. Sonny understands exactly how he feels: a four-foot section of red-hot iron pipe has been thrust through the top of his head and pushed down into his guts, burning everything it touches. "Hey, man," he says, in his misery noticing that the air has turned sludgy, as though individual atoms of oxygen and carbon dioxide are gummy enough to stick to his skin. Then Sonny notices that the Kaiser's eyes are swimming up toward the back of his head, and he realizes that the man is passing out right next to him. Sick as he is, he has to do something to protect the Kaiser. Sonny reaches out for the other man's bike, watching as well as he can the disappearance of the Kaiser's irises beneath his upper eye-lids. Blood explodes out of his nostrils, and his body slumps backward on the seat and rolls over the side. For a couple of seconds, he is dragged along by a boot caught in the handle-bars, but the boot slips off, and the cycle drifts to a halt.

The red-hot iron bar seems to rupture his stomach, and Sonny has no choice; he lets the other bike fall and utters a groan and bends sideways and vomits out what feels like every meal he has ever eaten. When nothing is left inside him, his stomach feels better, but John Henry has decided to drive giant rail spikes through his skull. His arms and legs are made of rub-ber. Sonny focuses on his bike. It seems to be standing still. He does not understand how he can go forward, but he watches a blood-spattered hand gun his bike and manages to stay upright when it takes off. *Is that my blood?* he wonders, and remembers two long red flags unfurling from the Kaiser's nose.

A noise that had been gathering strength in the background turns into the sound of a 747 coming in for a landing. Sonny thinks that the last thing he wants to do today is get a look at the animal capable of making that sound. Mouse was right on the money: this is a bad, bad place, right up there with the charming town of Harko, Illinois. Sonny wishes to encounter no more Harkos, okay? One was enough. So why is he moving forward instead of turning around and running for the sunny peace of Highway 35? Why is he pulling that massive gun out of his pocket? It's simple. He is not about to let that jet-airplane-dog mess up his homeys, no matter how much his head hurts.

John Henry keeps pounding in those five-dollar spikes while

Sonny picks up speed and squints at the road ahead, trying to figure out what is going on. Someone screams, he cannot identify who. Through the growling, he hears the unmistakable sound of a motorcycle hitting the ground after a flip, and his heart shivers. *Beezer should always be point man,* he thinks, *otherwise we're asking for punishment.* A gun goes off with a loud explosion. Sonny forces himself to press through the gluey atoms in the air, and after another five or six seconds he spots Beezer, who is painfully pushing himself upward beside his toppled bike. A few feet beyond Beezer, Doc's bulky figure comes into view, sitting astride his bike and aiming his 9 at something in the road ahead of him. Doc fires, and red flame bursts from the barrel of his pistol.

Feeling more beat-up and useless than ever before in his life, Sonny jumps from his moving bike and runs toward Doc, trying to look past him. The first thing he sees is a flash of light off Mouse's bike, which comes into view flat on its side about twenty feet down the road, at the top of the curve. Then he finds Mouse, on his ass and scrambling backward from some animal Sonny can barely make out, except for its eyes and teeth. Unconscious of the stream of obscenities that pour from his mouth, Sonny levels his pistol at the creature and fires just as he runs past Doc.

Doc just stands there; Doc is out for the count. The weird animal up on the road closes its jaws on Mouse's leg. It is going to rip away a hamburger-sized chunk of muscle, but Sonny hits it with a fucking hollow-point *missile* from his Magnum, a bit show-offy for target practice but under the circumstances no more than prudent, thank you very much. Contrary to all expectations and the laws of physics, Sonny's amazing wonderbullet does not knock a hole the size of a football in the creature's hide. The wonderbullet pushes the animal sideways and distracts it from Mouse's leg; it does not even knock it down. Mouse sends up a howl of pain.

The dog whips around and glares at Sonny with red eyes the size of baseballs. Its mouth opens on jagged white teeth, and it snaps the air. Ropes of slime shoot out of its jaws. The creature lowers its shoulders and steps forward. Amazingly, its snarling grows in volume and ferocity. Sonny is being warned: if he does not turn and run, he is next on the menu.

"Fuck that," Sonny says, and fires straight at the animal's mouth. Its whole head should fly apart in bloody rags, but for a second after the Magnum goes off, nothing changes.

*Oh, shit,* Sonny thinks.

The dog-thing's eyes blaze, and its feral, wedge-shaped head seems to assemble itself out of the darkness in the air and emerge into view. As though an inky robe had been partially twitched aside, Sonny can see a thick neck descending to meaty shoulders and strong front legs. Maybe the tide is turning here, maybe this monster will turn out to be vulnerable after all. Sonny braces his right wrist with his left hand, aims at the dog-thing's chest, and squeezes off another round. The explosion seems to stuff his ears with cotton. All the railroad spikes in his head heat up like electric coils, and bright pain sings between his temples.

Dark blood gouts from the creature's brisket. At the center of Sonny Cantinaro's being, a pure, primitive triumph bursts into life. More of the monster melts into visibility, the wide back and a suggestion of its rear legs. Of no recognizable breed and four and a half feet high, the dog-thing is approximately the size of a gigantic wolf. When it moves toward him, Sonny fires again. Like an echo, the sound of his gun repeats from somewhere close behind; a bullet like a supercharged wasp zings past his chest.

The creature staggers back, limping on an injured leg. Its enraged eyes bore into Sonny's. He risks glancing over his shoulder and sees Beezer braced in the middle of the narrow road.

"Don't look at me, shoot!" Beezer yells.

His voice seems to awaken Doc, who raises his arm and takes aim. Then all three of them are pulling their triggers, and the little road sounds like the firing range on a busy day. The dog-thing (*hell hound,* Sonny thinks) limps back a step and opens wide its terrible mouth to howl in rage and frustration. Before the howl ends, the creature gathers its rear legs beneath its body, springs across the road, and vanishes into the woods.

Sonny fights off the impulse to collapse under a wave of relief and fatigue. Doc swivels his body and keeps firing into the darkness behind the trees until Beezer puts a hand on his arm and orders him to stop. The air stinks of cordite and some animal odor that is musky and disgustingly sweet. Pale gray smoke shimmers almost white as it filters upward through the darker air.

Beezer's haggard face turns to Sonny, and the whites of his eyes are crimson. "You hit that fucking animal, didn't you?" Through the wads of cotton in his ears, Beezer's voice sounds small and tinny.

"Shit, yes. At least twice, probably three times."

"And Doc and I hit it once apiece. What the hell is that thing?"

" 'What the hell' is right," Sonny says.

Weeping with pain, Mouse a third time repeats his cry of "Help me!" and the others hear him at last. Moving slowly and pressing their hands over whatever parts of their bodies hurt the most, they hobble up the road and kneel in front of Mouse. The right leg of his jeans is ripped and soaked with blood, and his face is contorted.

"Are you assholes deaf?"

"Pretty near," Doc says. "Tell me you didn't take a bullet in your leg."

"No, but it must be some kind of miracle." He winces and inhales sharply. Air hisses between his teeth. "Way you guys were shooting. Too bad you couldn't draw a bead before it bit my leg."

"I did," Sonny says. "Reason you still *got* a leg."

Mouse peers at him, then shakes his head. "What happened to the Kaiser?"

"He lost about a liter of blood through his nose and passed out," Sonny tells him.

Mouse sighs as if at the frailty of the human species. "I believe we might try to get out of this crazy shithole."

"Is your leg all right?" Beezer asks.

"It's not broken, if that's what you mean. But it's not all right, either."

"What?" Doc asks.

"I can't say," Mouse tells him. "I don't answer medical questions from guys all covered in puke."

"Can you ride?"

"Fuck yes, Beezer—you ever know me when I couldn't *ride*?"

Beezer and Sonny each take a side and, with excruciating effort, lift Mouse to his feet. When they release his arms, Mouse lumbers sideways a few steps. "This is not right," he says.

"That's brilliant," says Beezer.

"Beeze, old buddy, you know your eyes are, like, bright red? You look like fuckin' Dracula."

To the extent that hurry is possible, they are hurrying. Doc wants to get a look at Mouse's leg; Beezer wants to make sure that Kaiser Bill is still alive; and all of them want to get out of this place and back into normal air and sunlight. Their heads pound, and their muscles ache from strain. None of them can be sure that the dog-thing is not preparing for another charge.

As they speak, Sonny has been picking up Mouse's Fat Boy and rolling it toward its owner. Mouse takes the handles and pushes his machine forward, wincing as he goes. Beezer and Doc rescue their bikes, and six feet along Sonny pulls his upright out of a snarl of weeds.

Beezer realizes that when he was at the curve in the road, he failed to look for Black House. He remembers Mouse saying, *This shit doesn't want to be seen,* and he thinks Mouse got it just about right: the Fisherman did not want them there, and the Fisherman did not want his house to be seen. Everything else was spinning around in his head the way his Electra Glide had spun over after that ugly voice spoke up in his mind. Beezer is certain of one thing, however: Jack Sawyer is not going to hold out on him any longer.

Then a terrible thought strikes him, and he asks, "Did anything funny—anything really *strange*—happen to you guys before the dog from hell jumped out of the woods? Besides the physical stuff, I mean."

He looks at Doc, and Doc blushes. *Hello?* Beezer thinks.

Mouse says, "Go fuck yourself. I'm not gonna talk about that."

"I'm with Mouse," Sonny says.

"I guess the answer is yes," Beezer says.

Kaiser Bill is lying by the side of the road with his eyes closed and the front of his body wet with blood from mouth to waist. The air is still gray and sticky; their bodies seem to weigh a thousand pounds, the bikes to roll on leaden wheels. Sonny walks his bike up beside the Kaiser's supine body and kicks him, not all that gently, in the ribs.

The Kaiser opens his eyes and groans. "Fuck, Sonny," he says. "You kicked me." His eyelids flutter, and he lifts his head off the ground and notices the blood soaking into his clothing. "What happened? Am I shot?"

"You conducted yourself like a hero," Sonny says. "How do you feel?"

"Lousy. Where was I hit?"

"How am I supposed to know?" Sonny says. "Come on, we're getting out of here."

The others file past. Kaiser Bill manages to get to his feet and, after another epic struggle, hauls his bike upright beside him. He pushes it down the track after the others, marveling at the pain in his head and the quantity of blood on his body. When he comes out through the last of the trees and joins his friends on Highway 35, the sudden brightness stabs his eyes, his body feels light enough to float away, and he nearly passes out all over again. "I don't think I did get shot," he says.

No one pays any attention to the Kaiser. Doc is asking Mouse if he wants to go to the hospital.

"No hospital, man. Hospitals kill people."

"At least let me take a look at your leg."

"Fine, look."

Doc kneels at the side of the road and tugs the cuff of Mouse's jeans up to the bottom of his knee. He probes with surprisingly delicate fingers, and Mouse winces.

"Mouse," he says, "I've never seen a dog bite like this before."

"Never saw a dog like that before, either."

The Kaiser says, "What dog?"

"There's something funny about this wound," Doc says. "You need antibiotics, and you need them right away."

"Don't you have antibiotics?"

"Sure, I do."

"Then let's go back to Beezer's place, and you can stick me full of needles."

"Whatever you say," says Doc.

# 20

Around the time Mouse and Beezer first fail to see the little road and the NO TRESPASSING sign beside it, Jack Sawyer answers the annoying signal of his cell phone, hoping that his caller will turn out to be Henry Leyden with information about the voice on the 911 tape. Although an identification would be wonderful, he does not expect Henry to I.D. the voice; the Fisherman–Burnside is Potsie's age, and Jack does not suppose the old villain has much of a social life, here or in the Territories. What Henry *can* do, however, is to apply his finely tuned ears to the nuances of Burnside's voice and describe what he hears in it. If we did not know that Jack's faith in his friend's capacity to hear distinctions and patterns inaudible to other people was justified, that faith would seem as irrational as the belief in magic: Jack trusts that a refreshed, invigorated Henry Leyden will pick up at least one or two crucial details of history or character that will narrow the search. Anything that Henry picks up will interest Jack.

If someone else is calling him, he intends to get rid of whoever it is, fast.

The voice that answers his greeting revises his plans. Fred Marshall wants to talk to him, and Fred is so wound up and incoherent that Jack must ask him to slow down and start over.

"Judy's flipping out again," Fred says. "Just . . . babbling and raving, and getting crazy like before, trying to rip through the walls—oh God, they put her in restraints and she hates that, she wants to help Ty, it's all because of that tape. Christ, it's getting to be too much to handle, Jack, Mr. Sawyer, I mean it, and I know I'm running off at the mouth, but I'm really worried."

"Don't tell me someone sent her the 911 tape," Jack says.

"No, not . . . what 911 tape? I'm talking about the one that was delivered to the hospital today. Addressed to Judy. Can you believe they let her *listen* to that thing? I want to strangle Dr. Spiegleman and that nurse, Jane Bond. What's the matter with these people? The tape comes in, they say, oh goody, here's a nice tape for you to listen to, Mrs. Marshall, hold on, I'll be right back with a cassette player. On a *mental ward*? They don't even bother to listen to it first? Look, whatever you're doing, I'd be eternally grateful if you'd let me pick you up, so I could drive you over there. You could talk to her. You're the only person who can calm her down."

"You don't have to pick me up, because I'm already on the way. What was on the tape?"

"I don't get it." Fred Marshall has become considerably more lucid. "Why are you going there without me?"

After a second of thought, Jack tells him an outright lie. "I thought you would probably be there already. It's a pity you weren't."

"I would have had the sense to screen that tape before letting *her* hear it. Do you know what was on that thing?"

"The Fisherman," Jack says.

"How did you know?"

"He's a great communicator," Jack says. "How bad was it?"

"You tell me, and then we'll both know. I'm piecing it together from what I gathered from Judy and what Dr. Spiegleman told me later." Fred Marshall's voice begins to waver. "The Fisherman was taunting her. Can you believe that? He said, *Your little boy is very lonely.* Then he said something like, *He's been begging and begging to call home and say hello to his mommy.* Except Judy says he had a weird foreign accent, or a speech impediment, or something, so he wasn't easy to understand right away. Then he says, *Say hello to your mommy, Tyler,* and Tyler . . ." Fred's voice breaks, and Jack can hear him stifling his agony before he begins again. "Tyler, ah, Tyler was apparently too distressed to do much but scream for help." A long, uncertain inhalation comes over the phone. "And he *cried,* Jack, he *cried.*" Unable to contain his feelings any longer, Fred weeps openly, unguardedly. His breath rattles in his throat; Jack listens to all the wet, undignified, helpless noises people make when grief and sorrow cancel every other feeling, and his heart moves for Fred Marshall.

The sobbing relents. "Sorry. Sometimes I think they'll have to put *me* in restraints."

"Was that the end of the tape?"

"*He* got on again." Fred breathes noisily for a moment, clearing his head. "Boasting about what he was going to do. *Dere vill be morrr mur-derts, and morrr afder dat, Choo-dee, we are all goink zu haff sotch fun*—Spiegleman quoted this junk to me! The children of French Landing will be harvested like wheat. *Havv-uz-ted like wheed.* Who talks like that? What kind of person is this?"

"I wish I knew," Jack says. "Maybe he was putting on an accent to sound even scarier. Or to disguise his voice." *He'd never disguise his voice,* Jack thinks, *he's too delighted with himself to hide behind an accent.* "I'll have to get the tape from the hospital and listen to it myself. And I'll call you as soon as I have some information."

"There's one more thing," Marshall says. "I probably made a mistake. Wendell Green came over about an hour ago."

"Anything involving Wendell Green is automatically a mistake. So what happened?"

"It was like he knew all about Tyler and just needed me to confirm it. I thought he must have heard from Dale, or the state troopers. But Dale hasn't made us public yet, has he?"

"Wendell has a network of little weasels that feed him information. If he knows anything, that's how he heard about it. What did you tell him?"

"More or less everything," Marshall says. "Including the tape. Oh, God, I'm such a dope. But I thought it'd be all right— I thought it would all get out anyhow."

"Fred, did you tell him anything about me?"

"Only that Judy trusts you and that we're both grateful for your help. And I think I said that you would probably be going in to see her this afternoon."

"Did you mention Ty's baseball cap?"

"Do you think I'm *nuts*? As far as I'm concerned, that stuff is between you and Judy. If I don't get it, I'm not going to talk about it to Wendell Green. At least I got him to promise to stay away from Judy. He has a great reputation, but I got the feeling he isn't everything he's cracked up to be."

"You said a mouthful," Jack says. "I'll be in touch."

When Fred Marshall hangs up, Jack punches in Henry's number.

"I may be a little late, Henry. I'm on my way to French County Lutheran. Judy Marshall got a tape from the Fisherman, and if they'll let me have it, I'll bring it over. There's something strange going on here—on Judy's tape, I guess he has some kind of foreign accent."

Henry tells Jack there is no rush. He has not listened to the first tape yet, and now will wait until Jack comes over with the second one. He might hear something useful if he plays them in sequence. At least, he could tell Jack if they were made by the same man. "And don't worry about me, Jack. In a little while, Mrs. Morton is coming by to take me over to KDCU. George Rathbun butters my bread today, baby—six or seven radio ads. 'Even a *blind man* knows you want to treat your honey, your sweetheart, your lovey-dovey, your wife, your best friend through thick and thin, to a mm-mmm fine dinner tonight, and there's no better place to show your appreciation to the old ball and chain than to take her to Cousin Buddy's Rib Crib on South Wabash Street in beautiful downtown La Riviere!' "

" 'The old ball and chain'?"

"You pay for George Rathbun, you get George Rathbun, warts and all."

Laughing, Jack tells Henry he will see him later that day, and pushes the Ram up to seventy. What is Dale going to do, give him a speeding ticket?

He parks in front of the hospital instead of driving around to the parking lot, and trots across the concrete with his mind filled with the Territories and Judy Marshall. Things are hurtling forward, picking up pace, and Jack has the sense that everything converges on Judy—no, on Judy and *him.* The Fisherman has chosen them more purposefully than he did his first three victims: Amy St. Pierre, Johnny Irkenham, and Irma Freneau were simply the right age—any three children would have done—but Tyler was Judy Marshall's son, and that set him apart. Judy has glimpsed the Territories, Jack has traveled through them, and the Fisherman lives there the way a cancer cell lives in a healthy organism. The Fisherman sent Judy a tape, Jack a grisly present. At Tansy Freneau's, he had seen Judy as his key and the door it opened, and where did that door lead but into Judy's Faraway?

*Faraway.* God, that's pretty. Beautiful, in fact.

Aaah . . . the word evokes Judy Marshall's face, and when he sees that face, a door in his mind, a door that is his and his alone, flies open, and for a moment Jack Sawyer stops moving altogether, and in shock, dread, and joyous expectation, freezes on the concrete six feet from the hospital's entrance.

Through the door in his mind pours a stream of disconnected images: a stalled Ferris wheel, Santa Monica cops milling behind a strip of yellow crime-scene tape, light reflected off a black man's bald head. Yes, a bald man's black head, that which he really and truly, in fact most desperately, had not wished to see, so take a good look, kiddo, here it is again. There had been a guitar, but the guitar was elsewhere; the guitar belonged to the magnificent demanding comforting comfortless Speedy Parker, God bless him God damn his eyes God love him Speedy, who touched its strings and sang

> *Travelin' Jack, ole Travelin' Jack,*
> *Got a far long way to go,*
> *Longer way to come back.*

Worlds spin around him, worlds within worlds and other worlds alongside them, separated by a thin membrane composed of a thousand thousand doors, if only you know how to find them. A thousand thousand red feathers, tiny ones, feathers from a robin redbreast, hundreds of robin redbreasts, flew through one of those doors, Speedy's. Robin, as in robin's-egg blue, thank you, Speedy, and a song that said Wake up, wake up, you sleepyhead.

Or: *Wake up, wake up, you DUNDERHEAD!*

Crazily, Jack hears George Rathbun's now-not-so genial roar: *Eeeven a BLIIIND MAAAN coulda seen THIS one coming, you KNOTHEAD!*

"Oh, yeah?" Jack says out loud. It is a good thing Head Nurse Jane Bond, Warden Bond, Agent OO Zero, cannot hear him. She's tough, but on the other hand, she's unfair, and if she were to appear beside him now, she would probably clap him in irons, sedate him, and drag him back to her domain. "Well, I know something you don't know, old buddy: Judy Marshall has a Twinner, and the Twinner has been whispering through the wall for a considerable old time now. It's no surprise she finally started to shout."

A red-haired teenager in an ARDEN H.S. BASEBALL T-shirt shoves open the literal door six feet from Jack and gives him a wary, disconcerted look. *Man, grown-ups are weird,* the look says; *aren't I glad I'm a kid?* Since he is a high school student and not a mental-health professional, he does not clap our hero in irons and drag him sedated away to the padded room. He simply takes care to steer a wide course around the madman and keeps walking, albeit with a touch of self-conscious stiffness in his gait.

It is all about Twinners, of course. Rebuking his stupidity, Jack raps his knuckles against the side of his head. He should have seen it before; he should have understood *immediately.* If he has any excuse, it is that at first he refused to think about the case despite Speedy's efforts to wake him up, then became so caught up in concentrating on the Fisherman that until this morning, while watching his mother on the Sand Bar's big TV, he had neglected to consider the monster's Twinner. In Judy Marshall's childhood, her Twinner had spoken to her through that membrane between the two worlds; growing more and more alarmed over the past month, the Twinner had all but thrust her arms through the membrane and shaken Judy senseless. Because Jack is single-natured and has no Twinner, the corresponding task fell to Speedy. Now that everything seems to make sense, Jack cannot believe it has taken him so long to see the pattern.

And *this* is why he has resented everything that kept him from standing before Judy Marshall: Judy is the doorway to her Twinner, to Tyler, and to the destruction of both the Fisherman and his opposite number in the Territories, the builder of the satanic, fiery structure a crow named Gorg showed Tansy Freneau. Whatever happens on Ward D today, it is going to be world-altering.

Heart thrumming in anticipation, Jack passes from intense

sunlight into the vast ocher space of the lobby. The same bathrobed patients seem to occupy the many chairs; in a distant corner, the same doctors discuss a troublesome case or, who knows, that tricky tenth hole at Arden Country Club; the same golden lilies raise their luxuriant, attentive heads outside the gift shop. This repetition reassures Jack, it hastens his step, for it surrounds and cushions the unforeseeable events awaiting him on the fifth floor.

The same bored clerk responds to the proffer of the same password with an identical, if not the same, green card stamped VISITOR. The elevator surprisingly similar to one in the Ritz Hôtel on the Place Vendôme obediently trembles upward past floors two, three, and four, in its dowager-like progress pausing to admit a gaunt young doctor who summons the memory of Roderick Usher, then releases Jack on five, where the beautiful ocher light seems a shade or two darker than down there in the huge lobby. From the elevator Jack retraces the steps he took with his guide Fred Marshall down the corridor, through the two sets of double doors and past the way stations of Gerontology and Ambulatory Ophthalmology and Records Annex, getting closer and closer to the unforeseen unforeseeable as the corridors grow narrower and darker, and emerges as before into the century-old room with high, skinny windows and a lot of walnut-colored wood.

And there the spell breaks, for the attendant seated behind the polished counter, the person currently the guardian of this realm, is taller, younger, and considerably more sullen than his counterpart of the day before. When Jack asks to see Mrs. Marshall, the young person glances in disdain at his VISITOR card and inquires if he should happen to be a relative or—another glance at the card—a medical professional. Neither, Jack admits, but if the young person could trouble himself to inform Nurse Bond that Mr. Sawyer wishes to speak to Mrs. Marshall, Nurse Bond is practically guaranteed to swing open the forbidding metal doors and wave him inward, since that is more or less what she did yesterday.

That is all well and good, if it happens to be true, the young person allows, but Nurse Bond is not going to be doing any door opening and waving in today, for today Nurse Bond is off duty. Could it be that when Mr. Sawyer showed up to see Mrs.

Marshall yesterday he was accompanied by a family member, say Mr. Marshall?

Yes. And if Mr. Marshall were to be consulted, say via the telephone, he would urge the young fellow presently discussing the matter in a commendably responsible fashion with Mr. Sawyer to admit the gentleman promptly.

That may be the case, the young person grants, but hospital regulations require that nonmedical personnel in positions such as the young person's obtain authorization for any outside telephone calls.

And from whom, Jack wishes to know, would this authorization be obtained?

From the acting head nurse, Nurse Rack.

Jack, who is growing a little hot, as they say, under the collar, suggests in that case that the young person seek out the excellent Nurse Rack and obtain the required authorization, so that things might progress in the manner Mr. Marshall, the patient's husband, would wish.

No, the young person sees no reason to pursue such a course, the reason being that doing so would represent a pitiful waste of time and effort. Mr. Sawyer is not a member of Mrs. Marshall's family; therefore the excellent Nurse Rack would under no circumstances grant the authorization.

"Okay," Jack says, wishing he could strangle this irritating pip-squeak, "let's move a step up the administrative ladder, shall we? Is Dr. Spiegleman somewhere on the premises?"

"Could be," the young person says. "How'm I supposed to know? Dr. Spiegleman doesn't tell me everything he does."

Jack points to the telephone at the end of the counter. "I don't expect you to know, I expect you to find out. Get on that phone *now*."

The young man slouches down the counter to the telephone, rolls his eyes, punches two numbered keys, and leans against the counter with his back to the room. Jack hears him muttering about Spiegleman, sigh, then say, "All right, transfer me, whatever." Transferred, he mutters something that includes Jack's name. Whatever he hears in response causes him to jerk himself upright and sneak a wide-eyed look over his shoulder at Jack. "Yes, sir. He's here now, yes. I'll tell him."

He replaces the receiver. "Dr. Spiegleman'll be here right

away." The boy—he is no more than twenty—steps back and shoves his hands in his pockets. "You're that cop, huh?"

"What cop?" Jack says, still irritated.

"The one from California that came here and arrested Mr. Kinderling."

"Yes, that's me."

"I'm from French Landing, and boy, that was some shock. To the whole town. Nobody would have guessed. Mr. *Kinderling?* Are you kidding? You'd never believe that someone like that would . . . you know, kill people."

"Did you know him?"

"Well, in a town like French Landing, everybody sort of knows everybody, but I didn't really know Mr. Kinderling, except to say hi. The one I knew was his wife. She used to be my Sunday school teacher at Mount Hebron Lutheran."

Jack cannot help it; he laughs at the incongruity of the murderer's wife teaching Sunday school classes. The memory of Wanda Kinderling radiating hatred at him during her husband's sentencing stops his laughter, but it is too late. He sees that he has offended the young man. "What was she like?" he asks. "As a teacher."

"Just a teacher," the boy says. His voice is uninflected, resentful. "She made us memorize all the books of the Bible." He turns away and mutters, "Some people think he didn't do it."

"What did you say?"

The boy half-turns toward Jack but looks at the brown wall in front of him. "I said, Some people think he didn't do it. Mr. Kinderling. They think he got put in jail because he was a small-town guy who didn't know anybody out there."

"That's too bad," Jack says. "Do you want to know the real reason Mr. Kinderling went to prison?"

The boy turns the rest of the way and looks at Jack.

"Because he was guilty of murder, and he confessed. That's it, that's all. Two witnesses put him at the scene, and two other people saw him on a plane to L.A. when he told everyone he was flying to Denver. After that, he said, Okay, I did it. I always wanted to know what it was like to kill a girl, and one day I couldn't stand it anymore, so I went out and killed two whores. His lawyer tried to get him off on an insanity plea, but the jury at his hearing found him sane, and he went to prison."

The boy lowers his head and mumbles something.

"I couldn't hear that," Jack says.

"Lots of ways to make a guy confess." The boy repeats the sentence just loud enough to be heard.

Then footsteps ring in the hallway, and a plump, white-coated man with steel-rimmed glasses and a goatee comes striding toward Jack with his hand out. The boy has turned away. The opportunity to convince the attendant that he did not beat a confession out of Thornberg Kinderling has slipped away. The smiling man with the white jacket and the goatee seizes Jack's hand, introduces himself as Dr. Spiegleman, and declares it a pleasure to meet such a famous personage. (*Personage, persiflage,* Jack thinks.) From one step behind the doctor, a man unnoticed until this moment steps fully into view and says, "Hey, Doctor, do you know what would be perfect? If Mr. Famous and I interview the lady together. Twice the information in half the time—perfect."

Jack's stomach turns sour. Wendell Green has joined the party.

After greeting the doctor, Jack turns to the other man. "What are you doing here, Wendell? You promised Fred Marshall you'd stay away from his wife."

Wendell Green holds up his hands and dances back on the balls of his feet. "Are we calmer today, Lieutenant Sawyer? Not inclined to use a sucker punch on the hardworking press, are we? I have to say, I'm getting a little tired of being assaulted by the police."

Dr. Spiegleman frowns at him. "What are you saying, Mr. Green?"

"Yesterday, before that cop knocked me out with his flashlight, Lieutenant Sawyer here punched me in the stomach for no real reason at all. It's a good thing I'm a reasonable man, or I'd have filed lawsuits already. But, Doctor, you know what? I don't do things that way. I believe everything works out better if we cooperate with each other."

Halfway through this self-serving speech, Jack thinks, *Oh hell,* and glances at the young attendant. The boy's eyes burn with loathing. A lost cause: now Jack will never persuade the boy that he did not mistreat Kinderling. By the time Wendell Green finishes congratulating himself, Jack has had a bellyful of his specious, smarmy affability.

"Mr. Green offered to give me a percentage of his take, if I let him sell photographs of Irma Freneau's corpse," he tells the doctor. "What he is asking now is equally unthinkable. Mr. Marshall urged me to come here and see his wife, and he made Mr. Green promise *not* to come."

"Technically, that may be true," Green says. "As an experienced journalist, I know that people often say things they don't mean and will eventually regret. Fred Marshall understands that his wife's story is going to come out sooner or later."

"Does he?"

"Especially in the light of the Fisherman's latest communication," Green says. "This tape proves that Tyler Marshall is his fourth victim, and that, miraculously, he is still alive. How long do you think that can be kept from the public? And wouldn't you agree that the boy's mother should be able to explain the situation in her own words?"

"I refuse to be badgered like this." The doctor scowls at Green and gives Jack a look of warning. "Mr. Green, I am very close to ordering you out of this hospital. I wish to discuss several matters with Lieutenant Sawyer, in private. If you and the lieutenant can work out some agreement between the two of you, that is your affair. I am certainly not going to permit a joint interview with my patient. I am in no way certain that she should talk to Lieutenant Sawyer, either. She is calmer than she was this morning, but she is still fragile."

"The best way to deal with her problem is to let her express herself," Green says.

"You will be quiet *now,* Mr. Green," Dr. Spiegleman says. The double chins that fold under his goatee turn a warm pink. He glares at Jack. "What specifically is it that you request, Lieutenant?"

"Do you have an office in this hospital, Doctor?"

"I do."

"Ideally, I'd like to spend about half an hour, maybe less, talking to Mrs. Marshall in a safe, quiet environment where our conversation would be completely confidential. Your office would probably be perfect. There are too many people on the ward, and you can't talk without being interrupted or having other patients listen in."

"My office," Spiegleman says.

"If you're willing."

"Come with me," the doctor says. "Mr. Green, you will please stand back next to the counter while Lieutenant Sawyer and I step into the hallway."

"Anything you say." Green executes a mocking bow and moves lightly, with a suggestion of dance steps, to the counter. "In your absence, I'm sure this handsome young man and I will find something to talk about."

Smiling, Wendell Green props his elbows on the counter and watches Jack and Dr. Spiegleman leave the room. Their footsteps click against the floor tiles until it sounds as though they have gone more than halfway down the corridor. Then there is silence. Still smiling, Wendell about-faces and finds the attendant openly staring at him.

"I read you all the time," the boy says. "You write real good."

Wendell's smile becomes beatific. "Handsome *and* intelligent. What a stunning combination. Tell me your name."

"Ethan Evans."

"Ethan, we do not have much time here, so let's make this snappy. Do you think responsible members of the press should have access to information the public needs?"

"You bet."

"And wouldn't you agree that an informed press is one of our best weapons against monsters like the Fisherman?"

A single, vertical wrinkle appears between Ethan Evans's eyebrows. "Weapons?"

"Let me put it this way. Isn't it true that the more we know about the Fisherman, the better chance we have of stopping him?"

The boy nods, and the wrinkle disappears.

"Tell me, do you think the doctor is going to let Sawyer use his office?"

"Prob'ly, yeah," Evans says. "But I don't like the way that Sawyer guy works. He's a police brutality. Like when they hit people to make them confess. That's brutality."

"I have another question for you. Two questions, really. Is

there a closet in Dr. Spiegleman's office? And is there some way you could take me there without going through that corridor?"

"Oh." Evans's dim eyes momentarily shine with understanding. "You want to *listen*."

"Listen and record." Wendell Green taps the pocket that contains his cassette recorder. "For the good of the public at large, God bless 'em one and all."

"Well, maybe, yeah," the boy says. "But Dr. Spiegleman, he . . ."

A twenty-dollar bill has magically appeared folded around the second finger of Wendell Green's right hand. "Act fast, and Dr. Spiegleman will never know a thing. Right, Ethan?"

Ethan Evans snatches the bill from Wendell's hand and motions him back behind the counter, where he opens a door and says, "Come on, hurry."

Low lights burn at both ends of the dark corridor. Dr. Spiegleman says, "I gather that my patient's husband told you about the tape she received this morning."

"He did. How did it get here, do you know?"

"Believe me, Lieutenant, after I saw the effect that tape had on Mrs. Marshall and listened to it myself, I tried to learn how it reached my patient. All of our mail goes through the hospital's mailroom before being delivered, *all* of it, whether to patients, medical staff, or administrative offices. From there, a couple of volunteers deliver it to the addressees. I gather that the package containing the tape was in the hospital mailroom when a volunteer looked in there this morning. Because the package was addressed only with my patient's name, the volunteer went to our general information office. One of the girls brought it up."

"Shouldn't someone have consulted you before giving the tape and a cassette player to Judy?"

"Of course. Nurse Bond would have done so immediately, but she is not on duty today. Nurse Rack, who is on duty, assumed that the address referred to a childhood nickname and thought that one of Mrs. Marshall's old friends had sent her some music to cheer her up. And there is a cassette player in the nurses' station, so she put the tape in the player and gave it to Mrs. Marshall."

In the gloom of the corridor, the doctor's eyes take on a sardonic glint. "Then, as you might imagine, all hell broke loose. Mrs. Marshall reverted to the condition in which she was first hospitalized, which takes in a range of alarming behaviors. Fortunately, I happened to be in the hospital, and when I heard what had happened, I ordered her sedated and placed in a secure room. A secure room, Lieutenant, has padded walls—Mrs. Marshall had reopened the wounds to her fingers, and I did not want her to do any more damage to herself. Once the sedative had taken effect, I went in and talked to her. I listened to the tape. Perhaps I should have called the police immediately, but my first responsibility is to my patient, and I called Mr. Marshall instead."

"From where?"

"From the secure room, with my cell phone. Mr. Marshall of course insisted on speaking to his wife, and she wanted to speak to him. She became very distraught during their conversation, and I had to give her another mild sedative. When she calmed down, I went out of the room and called Mr. Marshall again, to tell him more specifically about the contents of the tape. Do you want to hear it?"

"Not now, Doctor, thanks. But I do want to ask you about one aspect of it."

"Then ask."

"Fred Marshall tried to imitate the way you had reproduced the accent of the man who made the tape. Did it sound like any recognizable accent to you? German, maybe?"

"I've been thinking about that. It was sort of like a Germanic pronunciation of English, but not really. If it sounded like anything recognizable, it was English spoken by a Frenchman trying to put on a German accent, if that makes sense to you. But really, I've never heard anything like it."

From the start of this conversation, Dr. Spiegleman has been measuring Jack, assessing him according to standards Jack cannot even begin to guess. His expression remains as neutral and impersonal as that of a traffic cop. "Mr. Marshall informed me that he intended to call you. It seems that you and Mrs. Marshall have formed a rather extraordinary bond. She respects your skill at what you do, which is to be expected, but she also seems to trust you. Mr. Marshall asks that you be allowed to interview his wife, and his wife tells me that she must talk to you."

"Then you should have no problems with letting me see her in private for half an hour."

Dr. Spiegleman's smile is gone as soon as it appears. "My patient and her husband have demonstrated their trust in you, Lieutenant Sawyer, but that is not the issue. The issue is whether or not I can trust you."

"Trust me to do what?"

"A number of things. Primarily, to act in the best interest of my patient. To refrain from unduly distressing her, also from giving her false hopes. My patient has developed a number of delusions centered on the existence of another world somehow contiguous to ours. She thinks her son is being held captive in this other world. I must tell you, Lieutenant, that both my patient and her husband believe you are familiar with this fantasy-world—that is, my patient accepts this belief wholly, and her husband accepts it only provisionally, on the grounds that it comforts his wife."

"I understand that." There is only one thing Jack can tell the doctor now, and he says it. "And what you should understand is that in all of my conversations with the Marshalls, I have been acting in my unofficial capacity as a consultant to the French Landing Police Department and its chief, Dale Gilbertson."

"Your unofficial capacity."

"Chief Gilbertson has been asking me to advise him on his conduct of the Fisherman investigation, and two days ago, after the disappearance of Tyler Marshall, I finally agreed to do what I could. I have no official status whatsoever. I'm just giving the chief and his officers the benefit of my experience."

"Let me get this straight, Lieutenant. You have been misleading the Marshalls as to your familiarity with Mrs. Marshall's delusional fantasy world?"

"I'll answer you this way, Doctor. We know from the tape that the Fisherman really is holding Tyler Marshall captive. We could say that he is no longer in this world, but in the Fisherman's."

Dr. Spiegleman raises his eyebrows.

"Do you think this monster inhabits the same universe that we do?" asks Jack. "I don't, and neither do you. The Fisherman lives in a world all his own, one that operates according to fantastically detailed rules he has made up or invented over the years. With all due respect, my experience has made me far more familiar with structures like this than the Marshalls, the police, and, unless you have done a great deal of work with psychopathic criminals, even you. I'm sorry if that sounds arrogant, because I don't mean it that way."

"You're talking about profiling? Something like that?"

"Years ago, I was invited into a special VICAP profiling unit run by the FBI, and I learned a lot there, but what I'm talking about now goes beyond profiling." *And that's the understatement of the year,* Jack says to himself. *Now it's in your court, Doctor.*

Spiegleman nods, slowly. The distant glow flashes in the lenses of his glasses. "I think I see, yes." He ponders. He sighs, crosses his arms over his chest, and ponders some more. Then he raises his eyes to Jack's. "All right. I'll let you see her. Alone. In my office. For thirty minutes. I wouldn't want to stand in the way of advanced investigative procedure."

"Thank you," Jack says. "This will be extremely helpful, I promise you."

"I have been a psychiatrist too long to believe in promises like that, Lieutenant Sawyer, but I hope you succeed in rescuing Tyler Marshall. Let me take you to my office. You can wait there while I get my patient and bring her there by another hallway. It's a little quicker."

Dr. Spiegleman marches to the end of the dark corridor and turns left, then left again, pulls a fat ball of keys from his pocket, and opens an unmarked door. Jack follows him into a room that looks as though it had been created by combining two small offices into one. Half of the room is taken up by a long wooden desk, a chair, a glass-topped coffee table stacked with journals, and filing cabinets; the other half is dominated by a couch and the leather recliner placed at its head. Georgia O'Keeffe posters decorate the walls. Behind the desk stands a door Jack assumes opens into a small closet; the door directly opposite, behind the recliner and at the midpoint between the two halves of the office, looks as though it leads into an adjoining room.

"As you see," Dr. Spiegleman says, "I use this space as both an office and a supplementary consulting room. Most of my patients come in through the waiting room, and I'll bring Mrs. Marshall in that way. Give me two or three minutes."

Jack thanks him, and the doctor hurries out through the door to the waiting room.

In the little closet, Wendell Green slides his cassette recorder from the pocket of his jacket and presses both it and his ear to the door. His thumb rests on the RECORD button, and his heart is racing. Once again, western Wisconsin's most distinguished journalist is doing his duty for the man in the street. Too bad it's so blasted dark in that closet, but being stuffed into a black hole is not the first sacrifice Wendell has made for his sacred calling; besides, all he really needs to see is the little red light on his tape recorder.

Then, a surprise: although Doctor Spiegleman has left the room, here is his voice, asking for Lieutenant Sawyer. How did that Freudian quack get back in without opening or closing a door, and what happened to Judy Marshall?

*Lieutenant Sawyer, I must speak to you. Pick up the receiver. You have a call, and it sounds urgent.*

Of course—he is on the intercom. Who can be calling Jack Sawyer, and why the urgency? Wendell hopes that Golden Boy will push the telephone's SPEAKER button, but alas Golden Boy does not, and Wendell must be content with hearing only one side of the conversation.

"A call?" Jack says. "Who's it from?"

"He refused to identify himself," the doctor says. "Someone you told you'd be visiting Ward D."

Beezer, with news of Black House. "How do I take the call?"

"Just punch the flashing button," the doctor says. "Line one. I'll bring in Mrs. Marshall when I see you're off the line."

Jack hits the button and says, "Jack Sawyer."

"Thank God," says Beezer St. Pierre's honey-and-tobacco voice. "Hey man, you gotta get over to my place, the sooner the better. Everything got messed up."

"Did you find it?"

"Oh yeah, we found Black House, all right. It didn't exactly welcome us. That place wants to stay *hidden,* and it lets you know. Some of the guys are hurting. Most of us will be okay, but Mouse, I don't know. He got something terrible from a dog bite, if it was a dog, which I doubt. Doc did what he could, but. . . . Hell, the guy is out of his mind, and he won't let us take him to the hospital."

"Beezer, why don't you take him anyway, if that's what he needs?"

"We don't do things that way. Mouse hasn't stepped inside a hospital since his old man croaked in one. He's twice as scared of hospitals as of what's happening to his leg. If we took him to La Riviere General, he'd probably drop dead in the E.R."

"And if he didn't, he'd never forgive you."

"You got it. How soon can you be here?"

"I still have to see the woman I told you about. Maybe an hour—not much longer than that, anyhow."

"Didn't you hear me? Mouse is dying on us. We got a whole lot of things to say to each other."

"I agree," Jack says. "Work with me on this, Beez." He hangs up, turns to the door near the consulting-room chair, and waits for his world to change.

*What the hell was that all about?* Wendell wonders. He has squandered two minutes' worth of tape on a conversation between Jack Sawyer and the dumb SOB who spoiled the film that should have paid for a nice car and a fancy house on a bluff above the river, and all he got was worthless crap. Wendell deserves the nice car and the fancy house, has earned them thrice over, and his sense of deprivation makes him seethe with resentment. Golden Boys get everything handed to them on diamond-studded salvers, people fall all over themselves to give them stuff they don't even need, but a legendary, selfless working stiff and gentleman of the press like Wendell Green? It costs Wendell Green *twenty bucks* to hide in a dark, crowded little closet just to do his job!

His ears tingle when he hears the door open. The red light burns, the faithful recorder passes the ready tape from spool to spool, and whatever happens now is going to change everything: Wendell's gut, that infallible organ, his best friend, warms with the assurance that justice will soon be his.

Dr. Spiegleman's voice filters through the closet door and registers on the spooling tape: "I'll leave you two alone now."

Golden Boy: "Thank you, Doctor. I'm very grateful."

Dr. Spiegleman: "Thirty minutes, right? That means I'll be back at, umm, ten past two."

Golden Boy: "Fine."

The soft closing of the door, the click of the latch. Then long seconds of silence. *Why aren't they talking to each other?* But of course . . . the question answers itself. *They're waiting for fat-ass Spiegleman to move out of hearing range.*

Oh, this is just delicious, that's what this is! The whisper of Golden Boy's footsteps moving toward that door all but confirms the sterling reporter's intuition. O gut of Wendell Green, O Instrument Marvelous and Trustworthy, once more you come through with the journalistic goods! Wendell hears, the machine records, the inevitable next sound: the click of the lock.

Judy Marshall: "Don't forget the door behind you."

Golden Boy: "How are you?"

Judy Marshall: "Much, much better, now that you're here. The door, Jack."

Another set of footsteps, another unmistakable sliding into place of a metal bolt.

Soon-To-Be-Ruined Boy: "I've been thinking about you all day. I've been thinking about *this.*"

The Harlot, the Whore, the Slut: "Is half an hour long enough?"

Him With Foot In Bear Trap: "If it isn't, he'll just have to bang on the doors."

Wendell barely restrains himself from crowing with delight. These two people are actually going to have sex together, they are going to rip off their clothes and have at it like animals. Man, talk about your paybacks! When Wendell Green is done with him, Jack Sawyer's reputation will be lower than the Fisherman's.

Judy's eyes look tired, her hair is limp, and her fingertips wear the startling white of fresh gauze, but besides registering the depth of her feeling, her face glows with the clear, hard-won beauty of the imaginative strength she called upon to earn what she has seen. To Jack, Judy Marshall looks like a queen falsely imprisoned. Instead of disguising her innate nobility of spirit, the hospital gown and the faded nightdress make it all the more apparent. Jack takes his eyes from her long enough to lock the second door, then takes a step toward her.

He sees that he cannot tell her anything she does not already know. Judy completes the movement he has begun; she moves before him and holds out her hands to be grasped.

"I've been thinking about you all day," he says, taking her hands. "I've been thinking about *this*."

Her response takes in everything she has come to see, everything they must do. "Is half an hour long enough?"

"If it isn't, he'll just have to bang on the doors."

They smile; she increases the pressure on his hands. "Then let him bang." With the smallest, slightest tug, she pulls him forward, and Jack's heart pounds with the expectation of an embrace.

What she does is far more extraordinary than a mere embrace: she lowers her head and, with two light, dry brushes of her lips, kisses his hands. Then she presses the back of his right hand against her cheek, and steps back. Her eyes kindle. "You know about the tape."

He nods.

"I went mad when I heard it, but sending it to me was a mistake. He pushed me too hard. Because I fell right back into being that child who listened to another child whispering through a wall. I went crazy and I tried to rip the wall apart. I heard my son screaming for my help. And he was there—on the other side of the wall. Where you have to go."

"Where *we* have to go."

"Where we have to go. Yes. But I can't get through the wall, and you can. So you have work to do, the most important work there could be. You have to find Ty, and you have to stop the abbalah. I don't know what that is, exactly, but stopping it is your *job*. Am I saying this right: you are a coppiceman?"

"You're saying it right," Jack says. "I am a coppiceman. That's why it's my job."

"Then this is right, too. You have to get *rid* of Gorg and his master, Mr. Munshun. That's not what his name really *is,* but it's what it sounds like: Mr. Munshun. When I went mad, and I tried to rip through the world, she told me, and she could whisper straight into my ear. I was so close!"

What does Wendell Green, ear and whirling tape recorder pressed to the door, make of this conversation? It is hardly what he expected to hear: the animal grunts and moans of desire busily being satisfied. Wendell Green grinds his teeth, he stretches his face into a grimace of frustration.

"I love that you've let yourself see," says Jack. "You're an amazing human being. There isn't a person in a thousand who could even understand what that means, much less do it."

"You talk too much," Judy says.

"I mean, I love you."

"In your way, you love me. But you know what? Just by coming here, you made me more than I was. There's this sort of *beam* that comes out of you, and I just locked on to that beam. Jack, you *lived* there, and all I could do was peek at it for a little while. That's enough, though. I'm satisfied. You and Ward D, you let me travel."

"What you have inside you lets you travel."

"Okay, three cheers for a well-examined spell of craziness. Now it's time. You have to be a coppiceman. I can only come halfway, but you'll need all your strength."

"I think your strength is going to surprise you."

"Take my hands and do it, Jack. Go over. She's waiting, and I have to give you to her. You know her name, don't you?"

He opens his mouth, but cannot speak. A force that seems to come from the center of the earth surges into his body, rolling electricity through his bloodstream, tightening his scalp, sealing his trembling fingers to Judy Marshall's, which also tremble. A feeling of tremendous lightness and mobility gathers within all the hollow spaces of his body; at the same time he has never been so aware of his body's obduracy, its resistance to flight. When they leave, he thinks, it'll be like a rocket launch. The floor seems to vibrate beneath his feet.

He manages to look down the length of his arms to Judy Marshall, who leans back with her head parallel to the shaking floor, eyes closed, smiling in a trance of accomplishment. A band of shivery white light surrounds her. Her beautiful knees, her legs shining beneath the hem of the old blue garment, her bare feet planted. That light shivers around him, too. *All of this comes from her,* Jack thinks, *and from—*

A rushing sound fills the air, and the Georgia O'Keeffe prints fly off the walls. The low couch dances away from the wall; papers swirl up from the jittering desk. A skinny halogen lamp crashes to the ground. All through the hospital, on every floor, in every room and ward, beds vibrate, television sets go black, instruments rattle in their rattling trays, lights flicker. Toys drop from the gift-shop shelves, and the tall lilies skid across the marble in their vases. On the fifth floor, light bulbs detonate into showers of golden sparks.

The hurricane noise builds, builds, and with a great whooshing sound becomes a wide, white sheet of light, which immediately vanishes into a pinpoint and is gone. Gone, too, is Jack Sawyer; and gone from the closet is Wendell Green.

Sucked *into the Territories, blown out of one world and* sucked *into another, blasted and dragged, man, we're a hundred levels up from the simple, well-known flip.* Jack is lying down, looking up at a ripped white sheet that flaps like a torn sail. A quarter of a second ago, he saw another white sheet, one made of pure light and not literal, like this one. The soft, fragrant air blesses him. At first, he is conscious only that his right hand is being held, then that an astonishing woman lies beside him. Judy Marshall. No, not Judy Marshall, whom he does love, in his way, but another astonishing woman, who once whispered to Judy through a wall of night and has lately drawn a great deal closer. He had been about to speak her name when—

Into his field of vision moves a lovely face both like and unlike Judy's. It was turned on the same lathe, baked in the same kiln, chiseled by the same besotted sculptor, but more delicately, with a lighter, more caressing touch. Jack cannot move for wonder. He is barely capable of breathing. This woman whose face is above him now, smiling down with a tender impatience, has never borne a child, never traveled beyond her native Territories, never flown in an airplane, driven a car, switched on a television, scooped ice ready-made from the freezer, or used a microwave: and she is radiant with spirit and inner grace. She is, he sees, lit from within.

Humor, tenderness, compassion, intelligence, strength, glow in her eyes and speak from the curves of her mouth, from the very molding of her face. He knows her name, and her name is perfect for her. It seems to Jack that he has fallen in love with this woman in an instant, that he enlisted in her cause on the spot, and at last he finds he can speak her perfect name:

*Sophie.*

# 21

"Sophie."

Still holding her hand, he gets to his feet, pulling her up with him. His legs are trembling. His eyes feel hot and too large for their sockets. He is terrified and exalted in equal, perfectly equal, measure. His heart is hammering, but oh the beats are sweet. The second time he tries, he manages to say her name a little louder, but there's still not much to his voice, and his lips are so numb they might have been rubbed with ice. He sounds like a man just coming back from a hard punch in the gut.

"Yes."

"Sophie."

"Yes."

"Sophie."

"Yes."

There's something weirdly familiar about this, him saying the name over and over and her giving back that simple affirmation. Familiar and funny. And it comes to him: there's a scene almost identical to this in *The Terror of Deadwood Gulch,* after one of the Lazy 8 Saloon's patrons has knocked Bill Towns unconscious with a whiskey bottle. Lily, in her role as sweet Nancy O'Neal, tosses a bucket of water in his face, and when he sits up, they—

"This is funny," Jack says. "It's a good bit. We should be laughing."

With the slightest of smiles, Sophie says, "Yes."

"Laughing our fool heads off."

"Yes."

"Our *tarnal* heads off."

"Yes."

"I'm not speaking English anymore, am I?"

"No."

He sees two things in her blue eyes. The first is that she doesn't know the word *English*. The second is that she knows exactly what he means.

"Sophie."

"Yes."

"Sophie-Sophie-Sophie."

Trying to get the reality of it. Trying to pound it home like a nail.

A smile lights her face and enriches her mouth. Jack thinks of how it would be to kiss that mouth, and his knees feel weak. All at once he is fourteen again, and wondering if he dares give his date a peck good-night after he walks her home.

"Yes-yes-yes," she says, the smile strengthening. And then: "Have you got it yet? Do you understand that you're here and how you got here?"

Above and around him, billows of gauzy white cloth flap and sigh like living breath. Half a dozen conflicting drafts gently touch his face and make him aware that he carried a coat of sweat from the other world, and that it stinks. He arms it off his brow and cheeks in quick gestures, not wanting to lose sight of her for longer than a moment at a time.

They are in a tent of some kind. It's huge—many-chambered—and Jack thinks briefly of the pavilion in which the Queen of the Territories, his mother's Twinner, lay dying. That place had been rich with many colors, filled with many rooms, redolent of incense and sorrow (for the Queen's death had seemed inevitable, sure—only a matter of time). This one is ramshackle and ragged. The walls and the ceiling are full of holes, and where the white material remains whole, it's so thin that Jack can actually see the slope of land outside, and the trees that dress it. Rags flutter from the edges of some of the holes when the wind blows. Directly over his head he can see a shadowy maroon shape. Some sort of cross.

"Jack, do you understand how you—"

"Yes. I flipped." Although that isn't the word that comes out of his mouth. The literal meaning of the word that comes out seems to be *horizon road*. "And it seems that I sucked a fair number of Spiegleman's accessories with me." He bends and picks up a flat stone with a flower carved on it. "I believe that in my world, this was a Georgia O'Keeffe print. And that—" He points to a blackened, fireless torch leaning against one of the pavilion's fragile walls. "I think that was a—" But there are no words for it in this world, and what comes out of his mouth sounds as ugly as a curse in German: "—halogen lamp."

She frowns. "Hal-do-jen . . . limp? Lemp?"

He feels his numb lips rise in a little grin. "Never mind."

"But you are all right."

He understands that she needs him to be all right, and so he'll say that he is, but he's not. He is sick and glad to be sick. He is one lovestruck daddy, and wouldn't have it any other way. If you discount how he felt about his mother—a very different kind of love, despite what the Freudians might think—it's the first time for him. Oh, he certainly *thought* he had been in and out of love, but that was before today. Before the cool blue of her eyes, her smile, and even the way the shadows thrown by the decaying tent fleet across her face like schools of fish. At this moment he would try to fly off a mountain for her if she asked, or walk through a forest fire, or bring her polar ice to cool her tea, and those things do *not* constitute being all right.

But she needs him to be.

*Tyler* needs him to be.

*I am a coppiceman,* he thinks. At first the concept seems insubstantial compared to her beauty—to her simple *reality*—but then it begins to take hold. As it always has. What else brought him here, after all? Brought him against his will and all his best intentions?

"Jack?"

"Yes, I'm all right. I've flipped before." *But never into the presence of such beauty,* he thinks. *That's the problem.* You're *the problem, my lady.*

"Yes. To come and go is your talent. *One* of your talents. So I have been told."

"By whom?"

"Shortly," she says. "Shortly. There's a great deal to do, and yet I think I need a moment. You . . . rather take my breath away."

Jack is fiercely glad to know it. He sees he is still holding her hand, and he kisses it, as Judy kissed his hands in the world on the other side of the wall from this one, and when he does, he sees the fine mesh of bandage on the tips of three of her fingers. He wishes he dared to take her in his arms, but she daunts him: her beauty and her presence. She is slightly taller than Judy—a matter of two inches, surely no more—and her hair is lighter, the golden shade of unrefined honey spilling from a broken comb. She is wearing a simple cotton robe, white trimmed with a blue that matches her eyes. The narrow V-neck frames her throat. The hem falls to just below her knees. Her legs are bare but she's wearing a silver anklet on one of them, so slim it's almost invisible. She is fuller-breasted than Judy, her hips a bit wider. *Sisters,* you might think, except that they have the same spray of freckles across the nose and the same white line of scar across the back of the left hand. Different mishaps caused that scar, Jack has no doubt, but he also has no doubt that those mishaps occurred at the same hour of the same day.

"You're her Twinner. Judy Marshall's Twinner." Only the word that comes out of his mouth isn't *Twinner;* incredibly, dopily, it seems to be *harp.* Later he will think of how the strings of a harp lie close together, only a finger's touch apart, and he will decide that word isn't so foolish after all.

She looks down, her mouth drooping, then raises her head again and tries to smile. "*Judy.* On the other side of the wall. When we were children, Jack, we spoke together often. Even when we grew up, although then we spoke in each other's dreams." He is alarmed to see tears forming in her eyes and then slipping down her cheeks. "Have I driven her mad? Run her to lunacy? Please say I haven't."

"Nah," Jack says. "She's on a tightrope, but she hasn't fallen off yet. She's tough, that one."

"You have to bring her Tyler back to her," Sophie tells him. "For both of us. I've never had a child. I *cannot* have a child. I was . . . mistreated, you see. When I was young. Mistreated by one you knew well."

A terrible certainty forms in Jack's mind. Around them, the ruined pavilion flaps and sighs in the wonderfully fragrant breeze.

"Was it Morgan? Morgan of Orris?"

She bows her head, and perhaps this is just as well. Jack's face is, at that moment, pulled into an ugly snarl. In that moment he wishes he could kill Morgan Sloat's Twinner all over again. He thinks to ask her how she was mistreated, and then realizes he doesn't have to.

"How old were you?"

"Twelve," she says . . . as Jack has known she would say. It happened that same year, the year when Jacky was twelve and came here to save his mother. Or *did* he come here? Is this really the Territories? Somehow it doesn't feel the same. Almost . . . but not quite.

It doesn't surprise him that Morgan would rape a child of twelve, and do it in a way that would keep her from ever having children. Not at all. Morgan Sloat, sometimes known as Morgan of Orris, wanted to rule not just one world or two, but the entire universe. What are a few raped children to a man with such ambitions?

She gently slips her thumbs across the skin beneath his eyes. It's like being brushed with feathers. She's looking at him with something like wonder. "Why do you weep, Jack?"

"The past," he says. "Isn't that always what does it?" And thinks of his mother, sitting by the window, smoking a cigarette, and listening while the radio plays "Crazy Arms." Yes, it's always the past. That's where the hurt is, all you can't get over.

"Perhaps so," she allows. "But there's no time to think about the past today. It's the future we must think about today."

"Yes, but if I could ask just a few questions . . . ?"

"All right, but only a few."

Jack opens his mouth, tries to speak, and makes a comical little gaping expression when nothing comes out. Then he laughs. "You take my breath away, too," he tells her. "I have to be honest about that."

A faint tinge of color rises in Sophie's cheeks, and she looks down. She opens her lips to say something . . . then presses them together again. Jack wishes she had spoken and is glad she hasn't, both at the same time. He squeezes her hands gently, and she looks up at him, blue eyes wide.

"Did I know you? When you were twelve?"

She shakes her head.

"But I saw you."

"Perhaps. In the great pavilion. My mother was one of the

Good Queen's handmaidens. I was another . . . the youngest. You could have seen me then. I think you *did* see me."

Jack takes a moment to digest the wonder of this, then goes on. Time is short. They both know this. He can almost feel it fleeting.

"You and Judy are Twinners, but neither of you travel—she's never been in your head over here and you've never been in *her* head, over there. You . . . talk through a wall."

"Yes."

"When she wrote things, that was you, whispering through the wall."

"Yes. I knew how hard I was pushing her, but I had to. *Had* to! It's not just a question of restoring her child to her, important as that may be. There are larger considerations."

"Such as?"

She shakes her head. "I am not the one to tell you. The one who will is much greater than I."

He studies the tiny dressings that cover the tips of her fingers, and muses on how hard Sophie and Judy have tried to get through that wall to each other. Morgan Sloat could apparently become Morgan of Orris at will. As a boy of twelve, Jack had met others with that same talent. Not him; he was single-natured and had always been Jack in both worlds. Judy and Sophie, however, have proved incapable of flipping back and forth in any fashion. Something's been left out of them, and they could only whisper through the wall between the worlds. There must be sadder things, but at this moment he can't think of a single one.

Jack looks around at the ruined tent, which seems to breathe with sunshine and shadow. Rags flap. In the next room, through a hole in the gauzy cloth wall, he sees a few overturned cots. "What *is* this place?" he asks.

She smiles. "To some, a hospital."

"Oh?" He looks up and once more takes note of the cross. Maroon now, but undoubtedly once red. *A red cross, stupid,* he thinks. "Oh! But isn't it a little . . . well . . . old?"

Sophie's smile widens, and Jack realizes it's ironic. Whatever sort of hospital this is, or was, he's guessing it bears little or no resemblance to the ones on *General Hospital* or *ER*. "Yes,

Jack. *Very* old. Once there were a dozen or more of these tents in the Territories, On-World, and Mid-World; now there are only a few. Mayhap just this one. Today it's here. Tomorrow . . ." Sophie raises her hands, then lowers them. "Anywhere! Perhaps even on Judy's side of the wall."

"Sort of like a traveling medicine show."

This is supposed to be a joke, and he's startled when she first nods, then laughs and claps her hands. "Yes! Yes, indeed! Although you wouldn't want to be treated here."

What exactly is she trying to say? "I suppose not," he agrees, looking at the rotting walls, tattered ceiling panels, and ancient support posts. "Doesn't exactly look sterile."

Seriously (but her eyes are sparkling), Sophie says: "Yet if you were a patient, you would think it beautiful out of all measure. And you would think your nurses, the Little Sisters, the most beautiful any poor patient ever had."

Jack looks around. "Where are they?"

"The Little Sisters don't come out when the sun shines. And if we wish to continue our lives with the blessing, Jack, we'll be gone our separate ways from here long before dark."

It pains him to hear her talk of separate ways, even though he knows it's inevitable. The pain doesn't dampen his curiosity, however; once a coppiceman, it seems, always a coppiceman.

"Why?"

"Because the Little Sisters are vampires, and their patients never get well."

Startled, uneasy, Jack looks around for signs of them. Certainly disbelief doesn't cross his mind—a world that can spawn werewolves can spawn anything, he supposes.

She touches his wrist. A little tremble of desire goes through him.

"Don't fear, Jack—they also serve the Beam. *All* things serve the Beam."

"What beam?"

"Never mind." The hand on his wrist tightens. "The one who can answer your questions will be here soon, if he's not already." She gives him a sideways look that contains a glimmer of a smile. "And after you hear him, you'll be more apt to ask questions that matter."

Jack realizes that he has been neatly rebuked, but coming

from her, it doesn't sting. He allows himself to be led through room after room of the great and ancient hospital. As they go, he gets a sense of how really huge this place is. He also realizes that, in spite of the fresh breezes, he can detect a faint, unpleasant undersmell, something that might be a mixture of fermented wine and spoiled meat. As to what sort of meat, Jack is afraid he can guess pretty well. After visiting over a hundred homicide crime scenes, he *should* be able to.

It would have been impolite to break away while Jack was meeting the love of his life (not to mention bad narrative business), so we didn't. Now, however, let us slip through the thin walls of the hospital tent. Outside is a dry but not unpleasant landscape of red rocks, broom sage, desert flowers that look a bit like sego lilies, stunted pines, and a few barrel cacti. Somewhere not too far distant is the steady cool sigh of a river. The hospital pavilion rustles and flaps as dreamily as the sails of a ship riding down the sweet chute of the trade winds. As we float along the great ruined tent's east side in our effortless and peculiarly pleasant way, we notice a strew of litter. There are more rocks with drawings etched on them, there is a beautifully made copper rose that has been twisted out of shape as if by some great heat, there is a small rag rug that looks as if it has been chopped in two by a meat cleaver. There's other stuff as well, stuff that has resisted any change in its cyclonic passage from one world to the other. We see the blackened husk of a television picture tube lying in a scatter of broken glass, several Duracell AA batteries, a comb, and—perhaps oddest—a pair of white nylon panties with the word *Sunday* written on one side in demure pink script. There has been a collision of worlds; here, along the east side of the hospital pavilion, is an intermingled detritus that attests to how hard that collision was.

At the end of that littery plume of exhaust—the head of the comet, we might say—sits a man we recognize. We're not used to seeing him in such an ugly brown robe (and he clearly doesn't know how to wear such a garment, because if we look at him from the wrong angle, we can see *much* more than we want to), or wearing sandals instead of wing tips, or with his hair pulled back into a rough horsetail and secured with a hank of rawhide, but this is undoubtedly Wendell Green. He is muttering to himself. Drool drizzles from the corners of his mouth. He is looking fixedly at an untidy crumple of foolscap in his right hand. He ignores all the more cataclysmic changes that have occurred around him and focuses on just this one. If he can figure out how his Panasonic minicorder turned into a little pile of ancient paper, perhaps he'll move on to the other stuff. Not until then.

Wendell (we'll continue to call him Wendell, shall we, and not worry about any name he might or might not have in this little corner of existence, since *he* doesn't know it or want to) spies the Duracell AA batteries. He crawls to them, picks them up, and begins trying to stick them into the little pile of foolscap. It doesn't work, of course, but that doesn't keep Wendell from trying. As George Rathbun might say, "Give that boy a flyswatter and he'd try to catch dinner with it."

"Geh," says the Coulee Country's favorite investigative reporter, repeatedly poking the batteries at the foolscap. "Geh . . . in. Geh . . . in! Gah-damnit, geh in th—"

A sound—the approaching jingle of what can only be, God help us, spurs—breaks into Wendell's concentration, and he looks up with wide, bulging eyes. His sanity may not be gone forever, but it's certainly taken the wife and kids and gone to Disney World. Nor is the current vision before his eyes apt to coax it back anytime soon.

Once in our world there was a fine black actor named Woody Strode. (Lily knew him; acted with him, as a matter of fact, in a late-sixties American International stinkeroo called *Execution Express*.) The man now approaching the place where Wendell Green crouches with his batteries and his handful of foolscap looks remarkably like that actor. He is wearing faded jeans, a blue chambray shirt, a neck scarf, and a heavy revolver on a wide leather gun belt in which four dozen or so shells twinkle. His head is bald, his eyes deep-set. Slung over one shoulder by a strap of intricate design is a guitar. Sitting on the other is what appears to be a parrot. The parrot has two heads.

"No, no," says Wendell in a mildly scolding voice. "Don't. Don't see. Don't see. That." He lowers his head and once more begins trying to cram the batteries into the handful of paper.

The shadow of the newcomer falls over Wendell, who resolutely refuses to look up.

"Howdy, stranger," says the newcomer.

Wendell carries on not looking up.

"My name's Parkus. I'm the law 'round these parts. What's your handle?"

Wendell refuses to respond, unless we can call the low grunts issuing from his drool-slicked mouth a response.

"I asked your name."

"Wen," says our old acquaintance (we can't really call him a friend) without looking up. "Wen. Dell. Gree . . . Green. I . . . I . . . I . . ."

"Take your time," Parkus says (not without sympathy). "I can wait till your branding iron gets hot."

"I . . . news hawk!"

"Oh? That what you are?" Parkus hunkers; Wendell cringes back against the fragile wall of the pavilion. "Well, don't that just beat the bass drum at the front of the parade? Tell you what, I've seen *fish* hawks, and I've seen *red* hawks, and I've seen *gos*hawks, but you're my first *news* hawk."

Wendell looks up, blinking rapidly.

On Parkus's left shoulder, one head of the parrot says: "God is love."

"Go fuck your mother," replies the other head.

"All must seek the river of life," says the first head.

"Suck my tool," says the second.

"We grow toward God," responds the first.

"Piss up a rope," invites the second.

Although both heads speak equally—even in tones of reasonable discourse—Wendell cringes backward even farther, then looks down and furiously resumes his futile work with the batteries and the handful of paper, which is now disappearing into the sweat-grimy tube of his fist.

"Don't mind 'em," Parkus says. "*I* sure don't. Hardly hear 'em anymore, and that's the truth. Shut up, boys."

The parrot falls silent.

"One head's Sacred, the other's Profane," Parkus says. "I keep 'em around just to remind me that—"

He is interrupted by the sound of approaching footsteps, and stands up again in a single lithe and easy movement. Jack and Sophie are approaching, holding hands with the perfect unconsciousness of children on their way to school.

"Speedy!" Jack cries, his face breaking into a grin.

"Why, Travelin' Jack!" Parkus says, with a grin of his own. "Well-met! Look at you, sir—you're all grown up."

Jack rushes forward and throws his arms around Parkus, who hugs him back, and heartily. After a moment, Jack holds Parkus at arm's length and studies him. "You were older—you looked older to *me,* at least. In both worlds."

Still smiling, Parkus nods. And when he speaks again, it is in Speedy Parker's drawl. "Reckon I did look older, Jack. You were just a child, remember."

"But—"

Parkus waves one hand. "Sometimes I look older, sometimes not so old. It all depends on—"

"Age is wisdom," one head of the parrot says piously, to which the other responds, "You senile old fuck."

"—depends on the place and the circumstances," Parkus concludes, then says: "And I told you boys to shut up. You keep on, I'm apt to wring your scrawny neck." He turns his attention to Sophie, who is looking at him with wide, wondering eyes, as shy as a doe. "Sophie," he says. "It's wonderful to see you, darling. Didn't I say he'd come? And here he is. Took a little longer than I expected, is all."

She drops him a deep curtsey, all the way down to one knee, her head bowed. *"Thankee-sai,"* she says. "Come in peace, gunslinger, and go your course along the Beam with my love."

At this, Jack feels an odd, deep chill, as if many worlds had spoken in a harmonic tone, low but resonant.

Speedy—so Jack still thinks of him—takes her hand and urges her to her feet. "Stand up, girl, and look me in the eye. I'm no gunslinger here, not in the borderlands, even if I do still carry the old iron from time to time. In any case, we have a lot to talk about. This's no time for ceremony. Come over the rise with me, you two. We got to make palaver, as the gunslingers say. Or used to say, before the world moved on. I shot a good brace of grouse, and think they'll cook up just fine."

"What about—" Jack gestures toward the muttering, crouched heap that is Wendell Green.

"Why, he looks right busy," Parkus says. "Told me he's a news hawk."

"I'm afraid he's a little above himself," Jack replies. "Old Wendell here's a news *vulture*."

Wendell turns his head a bit. He refuses to lift his eyes, but his lip curls in a sneer that may be more reflexive than real. "Heard. That." He struggles. The lip curls again, and this time the sneer seems less reflexive. It is, in fact, a snarl. "Gol. *Gol. Gol*-den boy. Holly. Wood."

"He's managed to retain at least some of his charm and his joi de vivre," Jack says. "Will he be okay here?"

"Not much with ary brain in its head comes near the Little Sisters' tent," Parkus says. "He'll be okay. And if he smells somethin' tasty on the breeze and comes for a look-see, why, I guess we can feed him." He turns toward Wendell. "We're going just over yonder. If you want to come and visit, why, you just up and do her. Understand me, Mr. News Hawk?"

"Wen. Dell. *Green*."

"Wendell Green, yessir." Parkus looks at the others. "Come on. Let's mosey."

"We mustn't forget him," Sophie murmurs, with a look back. "It will be dark in a few hours."

"No," Parkus agrees as they top the nearest rise. "Wouldn't do to leave him beside that tent after dark. That wouldn't do at all."


There's more foliage in the declivity on the far side of the rise—even a little ribbon of creek, presumably on its way to the river Jack can hear in the distance—but it still looks more like northern Nevada than western Wisconsin. Yet in a way, Jack thinks, that makes sense. The last one had been no ordinary flip. He feels like a stone that has been skipped all the way across a lake, and as for poor Wendell—

To the right of where they descend the far side of the draw, a horse has been tethered in the shade of what Jack thinks is a Joshua tree. About twenty yards down the draw to the left is a circle of eroded stones. Inside it a fire, not yet lit, has been carefully laid. Jack doesn't like the look of the place much—the stones remind him of ancient teeth. Nor is he alone in his dislike. Sophie stops, her grip on his fingers tightening.

"Parkus, do we have to go in there? Please say we don't."

Parkus turns to her with a kindly smile Jack knows well: a Speedy Parker smile for sure.

"The Speaking Demon's been gone from this circle many the long age, darling," he says. "And you know that such as yon are best for stories."

"Yet—"

"Now's no time to give in to the willies," Parkus tells her. He speaks with a trace of impatience, and "willies" isn't precisely the word he uses, but only how Jack's mind translates it. "You waited for him to come in the Little Sisters' hospital tent—"

"Only because *she* was there on the other side—"

"—and now I want you to come along." All at once he seems taller to Jack. His eyes flash. Jack thinks: *A gunslinger. Yes, I suppose he* could *be a gunslinger. Like in one of Mom's old movies, only for real.*

"All right," she says, low. "If we must." Then she looks at Jack. "I wonder if you'd put your arm around me?"

Jack, we may be sure, is happy to oblige.

As they step between two of the stones, Jack seems to hear an ugly twist of whispered words. Among them, one voice is momentarily clear, seeming to leave a trail of slime behind it as it enters his ear: *Drudge drudge drudge, oho the bledding foodzies, soon he cummz, my good friend Munshun, and such a prize I have for him, oho, oho—*

Jack looks at his old friend as Parkus hunkers by a tow sack and loosens the drawstring at the top. "He's close, isn't he? The Fisherman. And Black House, that's close, too."

"Yep," Parkus says, and from the sack he spills the gutted corpses of a dozen plump dead birds.

Thoughts of Irma Freneau reenter Jack's head at the sight of the grouse, and he thinks he won't be able to eat. Watching as Parkus and Sophie skewer the birds on greensticks reinforces this idea. But after the fire is lit and the birds begin to brown, his stomach weighs in, insisting that the grouse smell wonderful and will probably taste even better. Over here, he remembers, everything always does.

"And here we are, in the speaking circle," Parkus says. His smiles have been put away for the nonce. He looks at Jack and Sophie, who sit side by side and still holding hands, with somber gravity. His guitar has been propped against a nearby rock. Beside it, Sacred and Profane sleeps with its two heads tucked into its feathers, dreaming its no doubt bifurcated dreams. "The Demon may be long gone, but the legends say such things leave a residue that may lighten the tongue."

"Like kissing the Blarney Stone, maybe," Jack suggests.

Parkus shakes his head. "No blarney today."

Jack says, "If only we were dealing with an ordinary scumbag. That I could handle."

Sophie looks at him, puzzled.

"He means a dust-off artist," Parkus tells her. "A hardcase." He looks at Jack. "And in one way, that *is* what you're dealing with. Carl Bierstone isn't much—an ordinary monster, let's say. Which is *not* to say he couldn't do with a spot of killing. But as for what's going on in French Landing, he has been used. Possessed, you'd say in your world, Jack. Taken by the spirits, we'd say in the Territories—"

"Or brought low by pigs," Sophie adds.

"Yes." Parkus is nodding. "In the world just beyond this borderland—Mid-World—they would say he has been infested by a demon. But a demon far greater than the poor, tattered spirit that once lived in this circle of stones."

Jack hardly hears that. His eyes are glowing. *It sounded something like beer stein,* George Potter told him last night, a thousand years ago. *That's not it, but it's close.*

"Carl Bierstone," he says. He raises a clenched fist, then shakes it in triumph. "That was his name in Chicago. Burnside here in French Landing. Case closed, game over, zip up your fly. Where is he, Speedy? Save me some time h—"

*"Shut . . . up,"* Parkus says.

The tone is low and almost deadly. Jack can feel Sophie shrink against him. He does a little shrinking himself. This sounds nothing like his old friend, nothing at all. *You have to stop thinking of him as Speedy,* Jack tells himself. *That's not who he is or ever was. That was just a character he played, someone who could both soothe and charm a scared kid on the run with his mother.*

Parkus turns the birds, which are now browned nicely on one side and spitting juice into the fire.

"I'm sorry to speak harsh to you, Jack, but you have to realize that your Fisherman is pretty small fry compared to what's really going on."

*Why don't you tell Tansy Freneau he's small fry? Why don't you tell Beezer St. Pierre?*

Jack thinks these things, but doesn't say them out loud. He's more than a little afraid of the light he saw in Parkus's eyes.

"Nor is it about Twinners," Parkus says. "You got to get that idea out of your mind. That's just something that has to do with your world and the world of the Territories—a link. You can't kill some hardcase over here and end the career of your cannibal over there. And if you kill him over there, in Wisconsin, the thing inside will just jump to another host."

"The thing—?"

"When it was in Albert Fish, Fish called it the Monday Man. Fellow you're after calls it Mr. Munshun. Both are only ways of trying to say something that can't be pronounced by any earthly tongue on any earthly world."

"How many worlds are there, Speedy?"

"Many," Parkus says, looking into the fire. "And this business concerns every one of them. Why else do you think I've been after you like I have? Sending you feathers, sending you robins' eggs, doing every damned thing I could to make you wake up."

Jack thinks of Judy, scratching on walls until the tips of her fingers were bloody, and feels ashamed. Speedy has been doing much the same thing, it seems. "Wake up, wake up, you dunderhead," he says.

Parkus seems caught between reproof and a smile. "For sure you must have seen me in the case that sent you running out of L.A."

"Ah, man—why do you think I went?"

"You ran like Jonah, when God told him to go preach against the wickedness in Nineveh. Thought I was gonna have to send a whale to come and swallow you up."

"I *feel* swallowed," Jack tells him.

In a small voice, Sophie says: "I do, too."

"We've all been swallowed," says the man with the gun on his hip. "We're in the belly of the beast, like it or not. It's *ka,* which is destiny and fate. Your Fisherman, Jack, is now your *ka. Our ka.* This is more than murder. Much more."

And Jack sees something that frankly scares the shit out of him. Lester Parker, a.k.a. Speedy, a.k.a. Parkus, is himself scared almost to death.

"This business concerns the Dark Tower," he says.

Beside Jack, Sophie gives a low, desperate cry of terror and lowers her head. At the same time she raises one hand and forks the sign of the Evil Eye at Parkus, over and over.

That gentleman doesn't seem to take it amiss. He simply sets to work turning the birds again on their sticks. "Listen to me, now," he says. "Listen, and ask as few questions as you can. We still have a chance to get Judy Marshall's son back, but time is blowing in our teeth."

"Talk," Jack says.

Parkus talks. At some point in his tale he judges the birds done and serves them out on flat stones. The meat is tender, almost falling off the small bones. Jack eats hungrily, drinking deep of the sweet water from Parkus's waterskin each time it comes around to him. He wastes no more time comparing dead children to dead grouse. The furnace needs to be stoked, and he stokes it with a will. So does Sophie, eating with her fingers and licking them clean without the slightest reserve or embarrassment. So, in the end, does Wendell Green, although he refuses to enter the circle of old stones. When Parkus tosses him a golden-brown grouse, however, Wendell catches it with remarkable adroitness and buries his face in the moist meat.

"You asked how many worlds," Parkus begins. "The answer, in the High Speech, is *da fan:* worlds beyond telling." With one of the blackened sticks he draws a figure eight on its side, which Jack recognizes as the Greek symbol for infinity.

"There is a Tower that binds them in place. Think of it as an axle upon which many wheels spin, if you like. And there is an entity that would bring this Tower down. Ram Abbalah."

At these words, the flames of the fire seem to momentarily darken and turn red. Jack wishes he could believe that this is only a trick of his overstrained mind, but cannot. "The Crimson King," he says.

"Yes. His physical being is pent in a cell at the top of the Tower, but he has another manifestation, every bit as real, and this lives in Can-tah Abbalah—the Court of the Crimson King."

"Two places at once." Given his journeying between the world of America and the world of the Territories, Jack has little trouble swallowing this concept.

"Yes."

"If he—or it—destroys the Tower, won't that defeat his purpose? Won't he destroy his physical being in the process?"

"Just the opposite: he'll set it free to wander what will then be chaos . . . din-tah . . . the furnace. Some parts of Mid-World have fallen into that furnace already."

"How much of this do I actually need to know?" Jack asks. He is aware that time is fleeting by on his side of the wall, as well.

"Hard telling what you need to know and what you don't," Parkus says. "If I leave out the wrong piece of information, maybe all the stars go dark. Not just here, but in a thousand thousand universes. That's the pure hell of it. Listen, Jack—the King has been trying to destroy the Tower and set himself free for time out of mind. Forever, mayhap. It's slow work, because the Tower is bound in place by crisscrossing force beams that act on it like guy wires. The Beams have held for millennia, and would hold for millennia to come, but in the last two hundred years—that's speaking of time as you count it, Jack; to you, Sophie, it would be Full-Earth almost five hundred times over—"

"So long," she says. It's almost a sigh. "So very long."

"In the great sweep of things, it's as short as the gleam of a single match in a dark room. But while good things usually take a long time to develop, evil has a way of popping up full-blown and ready-made, like Jack out of his box. Ka is a friend to evil as well as to good. It embraces both. And, speaking of Jack . . ." Parkus turns to him. "You've heard of the Iron Age and the Bronze Age, of course?"

Jack nods.

"On the upper levels of the Tower, there are those who call the last two hundred or so years in your world the Age of Poisoned Thought. That means—"

"You don't have to explain it to me," Jack says. "I knew Morgan Sloat, remember? I knew what he planned for *Sophie's* world." Yes, indeed. The basic plan had been to turn one of the universe's sweetest honeycombs into first a vacation spot for the rich, then a source of unskilled labor, and finally a waste pit, probably radioactive. If that wasn't an example of poisoned thought, Jack doesn't know what is.

Parkus says, "Rational beings have always harbored telepaths among their number; that's true in all the worlds. But they're ordinarily rare creatures. Prodigies, you might say. But since the Age of Poisoned Thought came on your world, Jack— infested it like a demon—such beings have become much more common. Not as common as slow mutants in the Blasted Lands, but common, yes."

"You speak of mind readers," Sophie says, as if wanting to be sure.

"Yes," Parkus agrees, "but not *just* mind readers. Precognates. Teleports—world jumpers like old Travelin' Jack here, in other words—and telekinetics. Mind readers are the most common, telekinetics the rarest . . . and the most valuable."

"To *him,* you mean," Jack says. "To the Crimson King."

"Yes. Over the last two hundred years or so, the abbalah has spent a good part of his time gathering a crew of telepathic slaves. Most of them come from Earth and the Territories. *All* of the telekinetics come from Earth. This collection of slaves— this gulag—is his crowning achievement. We call them Breakers. They . . ." He trails off, thinking. Then: "Do you know how a galley travels?"

Sophie nods, but Jack at first has no idea what Parkus is talking about. He has a brief, lunatic vision of a fully equipped kitchen traveling down Route 66.

"Many oarsmen," Sophie says, then makes a rowing motion that throws her breasts into charming relief.

Parkus is nodding. "Usually slaves chained together. They—"

From outside the circle, Wendell suddenly sticks his own oar in. "Spart. Cus." He pauses, frowning, then tries it again. "*Spart*-a-cus."

"What's he on about?" Parkus asks, frowning. "Any idea, Jack?"

"A movie called *Spartacus,*" Jack says, "and you're wrong as usual, Wendell. I believe you're thinking about *Ben-Hur.*"

Looking sulky, Wendell holds out his greasy hands. "More. Meat."

Parkus pulls the last grouse from its sizzling stick and tosses it between two of the stones, where Wendell sits with his pallid, greasy face peering from between his knees. "Fresh prey for the news hawk," he says. "Now do us a favor and shut up."

"Or. What." The old defiant gleam is rising in Wendell's eyes.

Parkus draws his shooting iron partway from its holster. The grip, made of sandalwood, is worn, but the barrel gleams murder-bright. He has to say no more; holding his second bird in one hand, Wendell Green hitches up his robe and hies himself back over the rise. Jack is extremely relieved to see him go. Spartacus *indeed,* he thinks, and snorts.

"So the Crimson King wants to use these Breakers to destroy the Beams," Jack says. "That's it, isn't it? That's his plan."

"You speak as though of the future," Parkus says mildly. "This is happening *now,* Jack. Only look at your own world if you want to see the ongoing disintegration. Of the six Beams, only one still holds true. Two others still generate some holding power. The other three are dead. One of these went out thousands of years ago, in the ordinary course of things. The others . . . killed by the Breakers. All in two centuries or less."

"Christ," Jack says. He is beginning to understand how Speedy could call the Fisherman small-fry.

"The job of protecting the Tower and the Beams has always belonged to the ancient war guild of Gilead, called gunslingers in this world and many others. They also generated a powerful psychic force, Jack, one fully capable of countering the Crimson King's Breakers, but—"

"The gunslingers are all gone save for one," Sophie says, looking at the big pistol on Parkus's hip. And, with timid hope: "Unless you really *are* one, too, Parkus."

"Not I, darling," he says, "but there's more than one."

"I thought Roland was the last. So the stories say."

"He has made at least three others," Parkus tells her. "I've no idea how that can be possible, but I believe it to be true. If Roland were still alone, the Breakers would have toppled the Tower long since. But with the force of these others added to his—"

"I have no clue what you're talking about," Jack says. "I *did,* sort of, but you lost me about two turns back."

"There's no need for you to understand it all in order to do your job," Parkus says.

"Thank God for that."

"As for what you *do* need to understand, leave galleys and oarsmen and think in terms of the Western movies your mother used to make. To begin with, imagine a fort in the desert."

"This Dark Tower you keep talking about. That's the fort."

"Yes. And surrounding the fort, instead of wild Indians—"

"The Breakers. Led by Big Chief Abbalah."

Sophie murmurs: "The King is in his Tower, eating bread and honey. The Breakers in the basement, making all the money."

Jack feels a light but singularly unpleasant chill shake up his spine: he thinks of rat paws scuttering over broken glass. "What? Why do you say that?"

Sophie looks at him, flushes, shakes her head, looks down. "It's what *she* says, sometimes. Judy. It's how I hear her, sometimes."

Parkus seizes one of the charred greensticks and draws in the rocky dust beside the figure-eight shape. "Fort here. Marauding Indians here, led by their merciless, evil—and most likely insane—chief. But over here—" Off to the left, he draws a harsh arrow in the dirt. It points at the rudimentary shapes indicating the fort and the besieging Indians. "What always arrives at the last moment in all the best Lily Cavanaugh Westerns?"

"The cavalry," Jack says. "That's us, I suppose."

"No," Parkus says. His tone is patient, but Jack suspects it is costing him a great effort to maintain that tone. "The cavalry is Roland of Gilead and his new gunslingers. Or so those of us who want the Tower to stand—or to fall in its own time—dare hope. The Crimson King hopes to hold Roland back, and to finish the job of destroying the Tower while he and his band are still at a distance. That means gathering all the Breakers he can, especially the telekinetics."

"Is Tyler Marshall—"

"Stop interrupting. This is difficult enough without that."

"You used to be a hell of a lot cheerier, Speedy," Jack says reproachfully. For a moment he thinks his old friend is going to give him another tongue-lashing—or perhaps even lose his temper completely and turn him into a frog—but Parkus relaxes a little, and utters a laugh.

Sophie looks up, relieved, and gives Jack's hand a squeeze.

"Oh, well, maybe you're right to yank on my cord a little," Parkus says. "Gettin' all wound up won't help anything, will it?" He touches the big iron on his hip. "I wouldn't be surprised if wearin' this thing has given me a few delusions of grandeur."

"It's a step or two up from amusement-park janitor," Jack allows.

"In both the Bible—your world, Jack—and the Book of Good Farming—*yours,* Sophie dear—there's a scripture that goes something like 'For in my kingdom there are many mansions.' Well, in the Court of the Crimson King there are many *monsters.*"

Jack hears a short, hard laugh bolt out of his mouth. His old friend has made a typically tasteless policeman's joke, it seems.

"They are the King's courtiers . . . his knights-errant. They have all sorts of tasks, I imagine, but in these last years their chief job has been to find talented Breakers. The more talented the Breaker, the greater the reward."

"They're headhunters," Jack murmurs, and doesn't realize the resonance of the term until it's out of his mouth. He has used it in the business sense, but of course there is another more literal meaning. Headhunters are cannibals.

"Yes," Parkus agrees. "And they have mortal subcontractors who work for . . . one doesn't like to say for the joy of it, but what else could we call it?"

Jack has a nightmarish vision then: a cartoon Albert Fish standing on a New York sidewalk with a sign reading WILL WORK FOR FOOD. He tightens his arm around Sophie. Her blue eyes turn to him, and he looks into them gladly. They soothe him.

"How many Breakers did Albert Fish send his pal Mr. Monday?" Jack wants to know. "Two? Four? A dozen? And do they die off, at least, so the abbalah has to replace them?"

"They don't," Parkus replies gravely. "They are kept in a place—a basement, yes, or a cavern—where there is essentially no time."

"*Purgatory.* Christ."

"And it doesn't matter. Albert Fish is long gone. Mr. Monday is now Mr. Munshun. The deal Mr. Munshun has with your killer is a simple one: this Burnside can kill and eat all the children he wants, as long as they are *untalented* children. If he should find any who *are* talented—any Breakers—they are to be turned over to Mr. Munshun at once."

"Who will take them to the abbalah," Sophie murmurs.

"That's right," Parkus says.

Jack feels that he's back on relatively solid ground, and is extremely glad to be there. "Since Tyler hasn't been killed, he must be talented."

" 'Talented' is hardly the word. Tyler Marshall is, potentially, one of the two most powerful Breakers in all the history of all the worlds. If I can briefly return to the analogy of the fort surrounded by Indians, then we could say that the Breakers are like fire arrows shot over the walls . . . a new kind of warfare. But Tyler Marshall is no simple fire arrow. He's more like a guided missile."

"Or a nuclear weapon."

Sophie says, "I don't know what that is."

"You don't want to," Jack replies. "Believe me."

He looks down at the scribble of drawings in the dirt. Is he surprised that Tyler should be so powerful? No, not really. Not after experiencing the aura of strength surrounding the boy's mother. Not after meeting Judy's Twinner, whose plain dress and manner can't conceal a character that strikes him as almost regal. She's beautiful, but he senses that beauty is one of the least important things about her.

"Jack?" Parkus asks him. "You all right?" *There's no time to be anythin' else,* his tone suggests.

"Give me a minute," Jack says.

"We don't have much t—"

"That has been made perfectly clear to me," Jack says, biting off the words, and he feels Sophie shift in surprise at his tone of voice. "Now give me a minute. Let me do my job."

From beneath a ruffle of green feathers, one of the parrot's heads mutters: "God loves the poor laborer." The other replies: "Is that why he made so fucking many of them?"

"All right, Jack," Parkus says, and cocks his head up at the sky.

*Okay, what have we got here?* Jack thinks. *We've got a valu-*

*able little boy, and the Fisherman knows* he's *valuable. But this Mr. Munshun doesn't have him yet, or Speedy wouldn't be here. Deduction?*

Sophie, looking at him anxiously. Parkus, still looking up into the blameless blue sky above this borderland between the Territories—what Judy Marshall calls Faraway—and the Whatever Comes Next. Jack's mind is ticking faster now, picking up speed like an express train leaving the station. He is aware that the black man with the bald head is watching the sky for a certain malevolent crow. He is aware that the fair-skinned woman beside him is looking at him with the sort of fascination that could become love, given world enough and time. Mostly, though, he's lost in his own thoughts. They are the thoughts of a coppiceman.

*Now Bierstone's Burnside, and he's old. Old and not doing so well in the cognition department these days. I think maybe he's gotten caught between what he wants, which is to keep Tyler for himself, and what he's promised this Munshun guy. Somewhere there's a fuddled, creaky, dangerous mind trying to make itself up. If he decides to kill Tyler and stick him in the stewpot like the witch in* "Hansel and Gretel," *that's bad for Judy and Fred. Not to mention Tyler, who may already have seen things that would drive a Marine combat vet insane. If the Fisherman turns the boy over to Mr. Munshun, it's bad for everyone in creation. No wonder Speedy said time was blowing in our teeth.*

"You knew this was coming, didn't you?" he says. "Both of you. You must have. Because *Judy* knew. She's been weird for months, long before the murders started."

Parkus shifts and looks away, uncomfortable. "I knew something was coming, yes—there have been great disruptions on this side—but I was on other business. And Sophie can't cross. She came here with the flying men and will go back the same way when our palaver's done."

Jack turns to her. "You are who my mother once was. I'm sure of it." He supposes he isn't being entirely clear about this, but he can't help it; his mind is trying to go in too many directions at once. "You're Laura DeLoessian's successor. The Queen of this world."

Now Sophie is the one who looks uncomfortable. "I was nobody in the great scheme of things, really I wasn't, and that was the way I liked it. What I did mostly was write letters of commendation and thank people for coming to see me . . . only in my official capacity, I always said 'us.' I enjoyed walking, and sketching flowers, and cataloging them. I enjoyed hunting. Then, due to bad luck, bad times, and bad behavior, I found myself the last of the royal line. Queen of this world, as you say. Married once, to a good and simple man, but my Fred Marshall died and left me alone. Sophie the Barren."

"Don't," Jack says. He is surprised at how deeply it hurts him to hear her refer to herself in this bitter, joking way.

"Were you not single-natured, Jack, your Twinner would be my cousin."

She turns her slim fingers so that now she is gripping him instead of the other way around. When she speaks again, her voice is low and passionate. "Put all the great matters aside. All *I* know is that Tyler Marshall is Judy's child, that I love her, that I'd not see her hurt for all the worlds that are. He's the closest thing to a child of my own that I'll ever have. These things I know, and one other: that you're the only one who can save him."

"Why?" He has sensed this, of course—why else in God's name is he here?—but that doesn't lessen his bewilderment. "Why me?"

"Because you touched the Talisman. And although some of its power has left you over the years, much still remains."

Jack thinks of the lilies Speedy left for him in Dale's bathroom. How the smell lingered on his hands even after he had given the bouquet itself to Tansy. And he remembers how the Talisman looked in the murmuring darkness of the Queen's Pavilion, rising brightly, changing everything before it finally vanished.

He thinks: *It's still changing everything.*

"Parkus." Is it the first time he's called the other man—the other coppiceman—by that name? He doesn't know for sure, but he thinks it may be.

"Yes, Jack."

"What's left of the Talisman—is it enough? Enough for me to take on this Crimson King?"

Parkus looks shocked in spite of himself. "Never in your life,

Jack. Never in *any* life. The abbalah would blow you out like a candle. But it *may* be enough for you to take on Mr. Munshun—to go into the furnace-lands and bring Tyler out."

"There are machines," Sophie says. She looks caught in some dark and unhappy dream. "Red machines and black machines, all lost in smoke. There are great belts and children without number upon them. They trudge and trudge, turning the belts that turn the machines. Down in the foxholes. Down in the ratholes where the sun never shines. Down in the great caverns where the furnace-lands lie."

Jack is shaken to the bottom of his mind and spirit. He finds himself thinking of Dickens—not *Bleak House* but *Oliver Twist.* And, of course he thinks of his conversation with Transy Freneau. *At least Irma's not there,* he thinks. *Not in the furnace-lands, not she. She got dead, and a mean old man ate her leg. Tyler, though . . . Tyler . . .*

"They trudge until their feet bleed," he mutters. "And the way there . . . ?"

"I think you know it," Parkus says. "When you find Black House, you'll find your way to the furnace-lands . . . the machines . . . Mr. Munshun . . . and Tyler."

"The boy is alive. You're sure of that."

"Yes." Parkus and Sophie speak together.

"And where is Burnside now? That information might speed things up a bit."

"I don't know," Parkus says.

"Christ, if you know who he *was*—"

"That was the fingerprints," Parkus says. "The fingerprints on the telephone. Your first real idea about the case. The Wisconsin State Police got the Bierstone name back from the FBI's VICAP database. You have the Burnside name. That should be enough."

*Wisconsin State Police, FBI, VICAP, database:* these terms come out in good old American English, and in this place they sound unpleasant and foreign to Jack's ear.

"How do you know all that?"

"I have my sources in your world; I keep my ear to the ground. As you know from personal experience. And surely you're cop enough to do the rest on your own."

"Judy thinks you have a friend who can help," Sophie says unexpectedly.

"Dale? Dale Gilbertson?" Jack finds this a little hard to believe, but he supposes Dale may have uncovered something.

"I don't know the name. Judy thinks he's like many here in Faraway. A man who sees much because he sees nothing."

Not Dale, after all. It's Henry she's talking about.

Parkus rises to his feet. The heads of the parrot come up, revealing four bright eyes. Sacred and Profane flutters up to his shoulder and settles there. "I think our palaver is done," Parkus says. "It *must* be done. Are you ready to go back, my friend?"

"Yes. And I suppose I better take Green, little as I want to. I don't think he'd last long here."

"As you say."

Jack and Sophie, still holding hands, are halfway up the rise when Jack realizes Parkus is still standing in the speaking circle with his parrot on his shoulder. "Aren't you coming?"

Parkus shakes his head. "We go different ways now, Jack. I may see you again."

*If I survive,* Jack thinks. *If any of us survive.*

"Meantime, go your course. And be true."

Sophie drops another deep curtsey. *"Sai."*

Parkus nods to her and gives Jack Sawyer a little salute. Jack turns and leads Sophie back to the ruined hospital tent, wondering if he will ever see Speedy Parker again.

Wendell Green—ace reporter, fearless investigator, explicator of good and evil to the great unwashed—sits in his former place, holding the crumpled foolscap in one hand and the batteries in the other. He has resumed muttering, and barely looks up when Sophie and Jack approach.

"You'll do your best, won't you?" Sophie asks. "For her."

"And for you," Jack says. "Listen to me, now. If this were to end with all of us still standing . . . and if I were to come back here . . ." He finds he can say no more. He's appalled at his temerity. This is a queen, after all. A *queen.* And he's . . . what? Trying to ask her for a date?

"Perhaps," she says, looking at him with her steady blue eyes. "Perhaps."

"Is it a perhaps you want?" he asks softly.

"Yes."

He bends and brushes his lips over hers. It's brief, barely a kiss at all. It is also the best kiss of his life.

"I feel like fainting," she tells him when he straightens up again.

"Don't joke with me, Sophie."

She takes his hand and presses it against the underswell of her left breast. He can feel her heart pounding. "Is this a joke? If she were to run faster, she'd catch her feet and fall." She lets him go, but he holds his hand where it is a moment longer, palm curved against that springing warmth.

"I'd come with you if I could," she says.

"I know that."

He looks at her, knowing if he doesn't get moving now, right away, he never will. It's wanting not to leave her, but that's not all. The truth is that he's never been more frightened in his life. He searches for something mundane to bring him back to earth—to slow the pounding of his own heart—and finds the perfect object in the muttering creature that is Wendell Green. He drops to one knee. "Are you ready, big boy? Want to take a trip on the mighty Mississip'?"

"Don't. Touch. Me." And then, in a nearly poetic rush: "Fucking Hollywood asshole!"

"Believe me, if I didn't have to, I wouldn't. And I plan to wash my hands just as soon as I get the chance."

He looks up at Sophie and sees all the Judy in her. All the *beauty* in her. "I love you," he says.

Before she can reply, he seizes Wendell's hand, closes his eyes, and flips.

# 22

This time there's something that isn't quite silence: a lovely white rushing he has heard once before. In the summer of 1997, Jack went up way north to Vacaville with an LAPD skydiving club called the P.F. Flyers. It was a dare, one of those stupid things you got yourself into as a result of too many beers too late at night and then couldn't get yourself out of again. Not with any grace. Which was to say, not without looking like a chickenshit. He expected to be frightened; instead, he was exalted. Yet he had never done it again, and now he knows why: he had come too close to remembering, and some frightened part of him must have known it. It was the sound before you pulled the ripcord—that lonely white rushing of the wind past your ears. Nothing else to hear but the soft, rapid beat of your heart and—maybe—the click in your ears as you swallowed saliva that was in free fall, just like the rest of you.

*Pull the ripcord, Jack,* he thinks. *Time to pull the ripcord, or the landing's going to be awfully damn hard.*

Now there's a new sound, low at first but quickly swelling to a tooth-rattling bray. *Fire alarm,* he thinks, and then: *No, it's a symphony of fire alarms.* At the same moment, Wendell Green's hand is snatched out of his grip. He hears a faint, squawking cry as his fellow sky diver is swept away, and then there's a smell—

*Honeysuckle—*

*No, it's her hair—*

—and Jack gasps against a weight on his chest and his diaphragm, a feeling that the wind has been knocked out of him. There are hands on him, one on his shoulder, the other at the small of his back. Hair tickling his cheek. The sound of alarms.

The sound of people yelling in confusion. Running footfalls that clack and echo.

"jack jack jack are you all right"

"Ask a queen for a date, get knocked into the middle of next week," he mutters. Why is it so dark? Has he been blinded? Is he ready for that intellectually rewarding and financially remunerative job as an ump at Miller Park?

*"Jack!"* A palm smacks his cheek. Hard.

No, not blind. His eyes are just shut. He pops them open and Judy is bending over him, her face inches from his. Without thinking, he closes his left hand in the hair at the nape of her neck, brings her face down to his, and kisses her. She exhales into his mouth—a surprised reverse gasp that inflates his lungs with her electricity—and then kisses him back. He has never been kissed with such intensity in his entire life. His hand goes to the breast beneath her nightdress, and he feels the frenzied gallop of her heart—*If she were to run faster, she'd catch her feet and fall,* Jack thinks—beneath its firm rise. At the same moment her hand slips inside his shirt, which has somehow come unbuttoned, and tweaks his nipple. It's as hard and hot as the slap. As she does it, her tongue darts into his mouth in one quick plunge, there and gone, like a bee into a flower. He tightens his grip on the nape of her neck and God knows what would have happened next, but at that moment something falls over in the corridor with a huge crash of glass and someone screams. The voice is high and almost sexless with panic, but Jack believes it's Ethan Evans, the sullen young person from the hall. *"Get back here! Stop running, goldarnit!"* Of course it's Ethan; only a graduate of Mount Hebron Lutheran Sunday school would use *goldarnit,* even in extremis.

Jack pulls away from Judy. She pulls away from him. They are on the floor. Judy's nightdress is all the way up to her waist, exposing plain white nylon underwear. Jack's shirt is open, and so are his pants. His shoes are still on, but on the wrong feet, from the feel of them. Nearby, the glass-topped coffee table is overturned and the journals that were on it are scattered. Some seem to have been literally blown out of their bindings.

More screams from the corridor, plus a few cackles and mad ululations. Ethan Evans continues to yell at stampeding mental patients, and now a woman is yelling as well—Head Nurse Rack, perhaps. The alarms bray on and on.

All at once a door bursts open and Wendell Green gallops into the room. Behind him is a closet with clothes scattered everywhere, the spare items of Dr. Spiegleman's wardrobe all ahoo. In one hand Wendell's holding his Panasonic minicorder. In the other he has several gleaming tubular objects. Jack is willing to bet they're double-A Duracells.

Jack's clothes have been unbuttoned (or perhaps blown open), but Wendell has fared much worse. His shirt is in tatters. His belly hangs over a pair of white boxer shorts, severely pee-stained in front. He is dragging his brown gabardine slacks by one foot. They slide across the carpet like a shed snakeskin. And although his socks are on, the left one appears to have been turned inside out.

*"What did you do?"* Wendell blares. *"Oh you Hollywood son of a bitch, WHAT DID YOU DO TO M—"*

He stops. His mouth drops open. His eyes widen. Jack notes that the reporter's hair appears to be standing out like the quills on a porcupine.

Wendell, meanwhile, is noting Jack Sawyer and Judy Marshall, embracing on the glass- and paper-littered floor, with their clothes disarranged. They aren't quite in flagrant delicious, but if Wendell ever saw two people on the verge, dese are dem. His mind is whirling and filled with impossible memories, his balance is shot, his stomach is chugging like a washing machine that has been overloaded with clothes and suds; he desperately needs something to hold on to. He needs news. Even better, he needs *scandal*. And here, lying in front of him on the floor, are both.

*"RAPE!"* Wendell bellows at the top of his lungs. A mad, relieved grin twists up the corners of his mouth. *"SAWYER BEAT ME UP AND NOW HE'S RAPING A MENTAL PATIENT!"* It doesn't look much like rape to Wendell, in all truth, but who ever yelled *CONSENSUAL SEX!* at the top of his lungs and attracted any attention?

"Shut that idiot up," Judy says. She yanks down the hem of her nightgown and prepares to stand.

"Watch out," Jack says. "Broken glass everywhere."

"I'm okay," she snaps. Then, turning to Wendell with that perfect fearlessness Fred knew so well: "Shut up! I don't know who you are, but quit that bellowing! Nobody's being—"

Wendell backs away from Hollywood Sawyer, dragging his pants along with him. *Why doesn't someone come?* he thinks. *Why doesn't someone come before he shoots me, or something?* In his frenzy and near hysteria, Wendell has either not registered the alarms and general outcry or believes them to be going on inside his head, just a little more false information to go with his absurd "memories" of a black gunslinger, a beautiful woman in a robe, and Wendell Green himself crouching in the dust and eating a half-cooked bird like a caveman.

"Keep away from me, Sawyer," he says, backing up with his hands held out in front of him. "I have an extremely hungry lawyer. Caveet-emporer, you asshole, lay one finger on me and he and I will strip you of everything you—OW! *OW!*"

Wendell has stepped on a piece of broken glass, Jack sees— probably from one of the prints that formerly decorated the walls and are now decorating the floor. He takes one more off-balance lurch backward, this time steps on his own trailing slacks, and goes sprawling into the leather recliner where Dr. Spiegleman presumably sits while quizzing his patients on their troubled childhoods.

La Riviere's premier muckraker stares at the approaching Neanderthal with wide, horrified eyes, then throws the minicorder at him. Jack sees that it's covered with scratches. He bats it away.

*"RAPE!"* Wendell squeals. *"HE'S RAPING ONE OF THE LOONIES! HE'S—"*

Jack pops him on the point of the chin, pulling the punch just a little at the last moment, delivering it with almost scientific force. Wendell flops back in Dr. Spiegleman's recliner, eyes rolling up, feet twitching as if to some tasty beat that only the semiconscious can truly appreciate.

"The Mad Hungarian couldn't have done better," Jack murmurs. It occurs to him that Wendell ought to treat himself to a complete neurological workup in the not too distant future. His head has put in a hard couple of days.

The door to the hall bursts open. Jack steps in front of the recliner to hide Wendell, stuffing his shirt into his pants (at some point he's zipped his fly, thank God). A candy striper pokes her fluffy head into Dr. Spiegleman's office. Although she's probably eighteen, her panic makes her look about twelve.

"Who's yelling in here?" she asks. "Who's hurt?"

Jack has no idea what to say, but Judy manages like a pro. "It was a patient," she says. "Mr. Lackley, I think. He came in, yelled that we were all going to be raped, and then ran out again."

"You have to leave at once," the candy striper tells them. "Don't listen to that idiot Ethan. And don't use the elevator. We think it was an earthquake."

"Right away," Jack says crisply, and although he doesn't move, it's good enough for the candy striper; she heads out. Judy crosses quickly to the door. It closes but won't latch. The frame has been subtly twisted out of true.

There was a clock on the wall. Jack looks toward it, but it's fallen face-down to the floor. He goes to Judy and takes her by the arms. "How long was I over there?"

"Not long," she says, "but what an exit you made! Ka-*pow!* Did you get anything?" Her eyes plead with him.

"Enough to know I have to go back to French Landing right away," he tells her. *Enough to know that I love you—that I'll always love you, in this world or any other.*

"Tyler . . . is he alive?" She reverses his grip so she is holding him. Sophie did exactly the same thing in Faraway, Jack remembers. *"Is my son alive?"*

"Yes. And I'm going to get him for you."

His eye happens on Spiegleman's desk, which has danced its way into the room and stands with all its drawers open. He sees something interesting in one of those drawers and hurries across the carpet, crunching on broken glass and kicking aside one of the prints.

In the top drawer to the left of the desk's kneehole is a tape recorder, considerably bigger than Wendell Green's trusty Panasonic, and a torn piece of brown wrapping paper. Jack snatches up the paper first. Scrawled across the front in draggling letters he's seen at both Ed's Eats and on his own front porch is this:

*Deliver to JUDY MARSHALL*
*also known as SOPHIE*

There are what appear to be stamps in the upper corner of the torn sheet. Jack doesn't need to examine them closely to know that they are really cut from sugar packets, and that they were affixed by a dangerous old dodderer named Charles Burnside. But the Fisherman's identity no longer matters much, and Speedy knew it. Neither does his location, because Jack has an idea Chummy Burnside can flip to a new one pretty much at will.

*But he can't take the real doorway with him. The doorway to the furnace-lands, to Mr. Munshun, to Ty. If Beezer and his pals found that—*

Jack drops the wrapping paper back into the drawer, hits the EJECT button on the tape recorder, and pops out the cassette tape inside. He sticks it in his pocket and heads for the door.

"Jack."

He looks back at her. Beyond them, fire alarms honk and blat, lunatics scream and laugh, staff runs to and fro. Their eyes meet. In the clear blue light of Judy's regard, Jack can almost touch that other world with its sweet smells and strange constellations.

"Is it wonderful over there? As wonderful as in my dreams?"

"It's wonderful," he tells her. "And you are, too. Hang in there, okay?"

Halfway down the hallway, Jack comes upon a nasty sight: Ethan Evans, the young man who once had Wanda Kinderling as his Sunday school teacher, has laid hold of a disoriented old woman by her fat upper arms and is shaking her back and forth. The old woman's frizzy hair flies around her head.

*"Shut up!"* young Mr. Evans is shouting at her. *"Shut up, you crazy old cow! You're not going anywhere except back to your dadblame room!"*

Something about his sneer makes it obvious that even now, with the world turned upside down, young Mr. Evans is enjoying both his power to command and his Christian duty to brutalize. This is only enough to make Jack angry. What infuriates him is the look of terrified incomprehension on the old woman's face. It makes him think of boys he once lived with long ago, in a place called the Sunlight Home.

It makes him think of Wolf.

Without pausing or so much as breaking stride (they have entered the endgame phase of the festivities now, and somehow he knows it), Jack drives his fist into young Mr. Evans's temple. That worthy lets go of his plump and squawking victim, strikes the wall, then slides down it, his eyes wide and dazed.

"Either you didn't listen in Sunday school or Kinderling's wife taught you the wrong lessons," Jack says.

"You . . . hit . . . me . . ." young Mr. Evans whispers. He finishes his slow dive splay-legged on the hallway floor halfway between the Records Annex and Ambulatory Ophthalmology.

"Abuse another patient—this one, the one I was just talking to, *any* of them—and I'll do a lot more than that," Jack promises young Mr. Evans. Then he's down the stairs, taking them two at a time, not noticing a handful of johnny-clad patients who stare at him with expressions of puzzled, half-fearful wonder. They look at him as if at a vision who passes them in an envelope of light, some wonder as brilliant as it is mysterious.

Ten minutes later (long after Judy Marshall has walked composedly back to her room without professional help of any kind), the alarms cut off. An amplified voice—perhaps even Dr. Spiegleman's own mother wouldn't have recognized it as her boy's—begins to blare from the overhead speakers. At this unexpected roar, patients who had pretty much calmed down begin to shriek and cry all over again. The old woman whose mistreatment so angered Jack Sawyer is crouched below the admissions counter with her hands over her head, muttering something about the Russians and Civil Defense.

"THE EMERGENCY IS OVER!" Spiegleman assures his cast and crew. "THERE IS NO FIRE! PLEASE REPORT TO THE COMMON ROOMS ON EACH FLOOR! THIS IS DR. SPIEGLEMAN, AND I REPEAT THAT THE EMERGENCY IS *OVER*!"

Here comes Wendell Green, weaving his way slowly toward the stairwell, rubbing his chin gently with one hand. He sees young Mr. Evans and offers him a helping hand. For a moment it looks as though Wendell may be pulled over himself, but then young Mr. Evans gets his buttocks against the wall and manages to gain his feet.

"THE EMERGENCY IS OVER! I REPEAT, THE EMERGENCY IS *OVER*! NURSES, ORDERLIES, AND DOCTORS, PLEASE ESCORT ALL PATIENTS TO THE COMMON ROOMS ON EACH FLOOR!"

Young Mr. Evans eyes the purple bruise rising on Wendell's chin.

Wendell eyes the purple bruise rising on the temple of young Mr. Evans.

"Sawyer?" young Mr. Evans asks.

"Sawyer," Wendell confirms.

"Bastard sucker punched me," young Mr. Evans confides.

"Son of a bitch came up behind *me*," Wendell says. "The Marshall woman. He had her down." He lowers his voice. "He was getting ready to *rape* her."

Young Mr. Evans's whole manner says he is sorrowful but not surprised.

"Something ought to be done," Wendell says.

"You got that right."

"People ought to be told." Gradually, the old fire returns to Wendell's eyes. People *will* be told. By him! Because that is what he does, by God! He *tells* people!

"Yeah," young Mr. Evans says. He doesn't care as much as Wendell does—he lacks Wendell's burning commitment—but there's one person he *will* tell. One person who deserves to be comforted in her lonely hours, who has been left on her own Mount of Olives. One person who will drink up the knowledge of Jack Sawyer's evil like the very waters of life.

"This kind of behavior cannot just be swept under the rug," Wendell says.

"No way," young Mr. Evans agrees. "No way, José."

Jack has barely cleared the gates of French County Lutheran when his cell phone tweets. He thinks of pulling over to take the call, hears the sound of approaching fire engines, and decides for once to risk driving and talking at the same time. He wants to be out of the area before the local fire brigade shows up and slows him down.

He flips the little Nokia open. "Sawyer."

"Where the fuck *are* you?" Beezer St. Pierre bellows. "Man, I been hittin' redial so hard I damn near punched it off the phone!"

"I've been . . ." But there's no way he can finish that, not and stay within shouting distance of the truth, that is. Or maybe there is. "I guess I got into one of those dead zones where the cell phone just doesn't pick up—"

"Never mind the science lesson, chum. Get your ass over here right *now.* The actual address is 1 Nailhouse Row—it's County Road Double-O just south of Chase. It's the babyshit brown two-story on the corner."

"I can find it," Jack says, and steps down a little harder on the Ram's gas pedal. "I'm on my way now."

"What's your twenty, man?"

"Still Arden, but I'm rolling. I can be there in maybe half an hour."

*"Fuck!"* There is an alarming crash-rattle in Jack's ear as somewhere on Nailhouse Row Beezer slams his fist against something. Probably the nearest wall. "The fuck's *wrong* with you, man? Mouse is goin' down, I mean *fast.* We're doin' our best—those of us who're still here—but he is goin' *down.*" Beezer is panting, and Jack thinks he's trying not to cry. The thought of Armand St. Pierre in that particular state is alarming. Jack looks at the Ram's speedometer, sees it's touching seventy, and eases off a tad. He won't help anybody by getting himself greased in a road wreck between Arden and Centralia.

"What do you mean 'those of us who are still here'?"

"Never mind, just get your butt down here, if you want to talk to Mouse. And he sure wants to talk to you, because he keeps sayin' your name." Beezer lowers his voice. "When he ain't just ravin' his ass off, that is. Doc's doing his best—me and Bear Girl, too—but we're shovelin' shit against the tide here."

"Tell him to hold on," Jack says.

"Fuck that, man—tell him yourself."

There's a rattling sound in Jack's ear, the faint murmuring of voices. Then another voice, one which hardly sounds human, speaks in his ear. "Got to hurry . . . got to get over here, man. Thing . . . bit me. I can feel it in there. Like acid."

"Hold on, Mouse," Jack says. His fingers are dead white on the telephone. He wonders that the case doesn't simply crack in his grip. "I'll be there fast as I can."

"Better be. Others . . . already forgot. Not me." Mouse chuckles. The sound is ghastly beyond belief, a whiff straight out of an open grave. "I got . . . the memory serum, you know? It's eatin' me up . . . eatin' me alive . . . but I got it."

There's the rustling sound of the phone changing hands again, then a new voice. A woman's. Jack assumes it's Bear Girl.

"You got them moving," she says. "You brought it to this. Don't let it be for nothing."

There is a click in his ear. Jack tosses the cell phone onto the seat and decides that maybe seventy isn't too fast, after all.

A few minutes later (they seem like very long minutes to Jack), he's squinting against the glare of the sun on Tamarack Creek. From here he can almost see his house, and Henry's.

Henry.

Jack thumps the side of his thumb lightly against his breast pocket and hears the rattle of the cassette tape he took from the machine in Spiegleman's office. There's not much reason to turn it over to Henry now; given what Potter told him last night and what Mouse is holding on to tell him today, this tape and the 911 tape have been rendered more or less redundant. Besides, he's got to hurry to Nailhouse Row. There's a train getting ready to leave the station, and Mouse Baumann is very likely going to be on it.

And yet . . .

"I'm worried about him," Jack says softly. "Even a blind man could see I'm worried about Henry."

The brilliant summer sun, now sliding down the afternoon side of the sky, reflects off the creek and sends shimmers of light dancing across his face. Each time this light crosses his eyes, they seem to burn.

Henry isn't the only one Jack's worried about, either. He's got a bad feeling about all of his new French Landing friends and acquaintances, from Dale Gilbertson and Fred Marshall right down to such bit players as old Steamy McKay, an elderly gent who makes his living shining shoes outside the public library, and Ardis Walker, who runs the ramshackle bait shop down by the river. In his imagination, all these people now seem made of glass. If the Fisherman decides to sing high C, they'll vibrate and then shatter to powder. Only it's not really the Fisherman he's worried about anymore.

*This is a case,* he reminds himself. *Even with all the Territories weirdness thrown in, it's still a case, and it's not the first one you've ever been on where everything suddenly started to seem too big. Where all the shadows seemed to be too long.*

True enough, but usually that funhouse sense of false perspective fades away once he starts to get a handle on things. This time it's worse, and worse by far. He knows why, too. The Fisherman's long shadow is a thing called Mr. Munshun, an immortal talent scout from some other plane of existence. Nor is even that the end, because Mr. Munshun also casts a shadow. A *red* one.

"Abbalah," Jack mutters. "Abbalah-doon and Mr. Munshun and the Crow Gorg, just three old pals walking together on night's Plutonian shore." For some reason this makes him think of the Walrus and the Carpenter from *Alice.* What was it they took for a walk in the moonlight? Clams? Mussels? Jack's damned if he can remember, although one line surfaces and resonates in his mind, spoken in his mother's voice: *"The time has come," the Walrus said, "to talk of many things."*

The abbalah is presumably hanging out in his court (the part of him that isn't imprisoned in Speedy's Dark Tower, that is), but the Fisherman and Mr. Munshun could be anywhere. Do they know Jack Sawyer has been meddling? Of course they do. By today, that is common knowledge. Might they try to slow him down by doing something nasty to one of his friends? A certain blind sportscaster-headbanger-bebopper, for instance?

Yes indeed. And now, perhaps because he's been sensitized to it, he can once more feel that nasty pulse coming out of the southwestern landscape, the one he sensed when he flipped over for the first time in his adult life. When the road curves southeast, he almost loses it. Then, when the Ram points its nose southwest again, the poisonous throb regains strength, beating into his head like the onset of a migraine headache.

*That's Black House you feel, only it's not a house, not really. It's a wormhole in the apple of existence, leading all the way down into the furnace-lands. It's a door. Maybe it was only standing ajar before today, before Beezer and his pals turned up there, but now it's wide open and letting in one hell of a draft. Ty needs to be brought back, yes . . . but that door needs to be shut, as well. Before God knows what awful things come snarling through.*

Jack abruptly swings the Ram onto Tamarack Road. The tires scream. His seat belt locks, and for a moment he thinks the truck may overturn. It stays up, though, and he goes flying toward Norway Valley Road. Mouse will just have to hang on a little bit longer; he's not going to leave Henry way out here on his own. His pal doesn't know it, but he's going on a little field trip to Nailhouse Row. Until this situation stabilizes, it seems to Jack that the buddy system is very much in order.

Which would have been all well and good if Henry had been at home, but he's not. Elvena Morton, dust mop in hand, comes in response to Jack's repeated jabbing at the doorbell.

"He's been over at KDCU, doing commercials," Elvena says. "Dropped him off myself. I don't know why he doesn't just do them in his studio here, something about the sound effects, I think he might have said. I'm surprised he didn't tell you that."

The bitch of it is, Henry did. Cousin Buddy's Rib Crib. The old ball and chain. Beautiful downtown La Riviere. All that. He even told Jack that Elvena Morton was going to drive him. A few things have happened to Jack since that conversation—he's reencountered his old childhood friend, he's fallen in love with Judy Marshall's Twinner, and just by the way he's been filled in on your basic Secret of All Existence—but none of that keeps him from turning his left hand into a fist and then slamming himself directly between the eyes with it. Given how fast things are now moving, making this needless detour strikes him as an almost unforgivable lapse.

Mrs. Morton is regarding him with wide-eyed alarm.

"Are you going to be picking him up, Mrs. Morton?"

"No, he's going for a drink with someone from ESPN. Henry said the fellow would bring him back afterward." She lowers her voice to the timbre of confidentiality at which secrets are somehow best communicated. "Henry didn't come right out and say so, but I think there may be big things ahead for George Rathbun. Ver-ry big things."

*Badger Barrage* going national? Jack wouldn't be entirely surprised, but he has no time to be delighted for Henry now. He hands Mrs. Morton the cassette tape, mostly so he won't feel this was an *entirely* wasted trip. "Leave this for him where . . ."

He stops. Mrs. Morton is looking at him with knowing amusement. *Where he'll be sure to see it* is what Jack almost said. Another mental miscue. Big-city detective, indeed.

"I'll leave it by the soundboard in his studio," she says. "He'll find it there. Jack, maybe it's none of my business, but you don't look all right. You're very pale, and I'd swear you've lost ten pounds since last week. Also . . ." She looks a bit embarrassed. "Your shoes are on the wrong feet."

So they are. He makes the necessary change, standing first on one foot and then the other. "It's been a tough forty-eight hours, but I'm hanging in there, Mrs. M."

"It's the Fisherman business, isn't it?"

He nods. "And I have to go. The fat, as they say, is in the fire." He turns, reconsiders, turns back. "Leave him a message on the kitchen tape recorder, would you? Tell him to call me on my cell. Just as soon as he gets in." Then, one thought leading to another, he points to the unmarked cassette tape in her hand. "Don't play that, all right?"

Mrs. Morton looks shocked. "I'd never do such a thing! It would be like opening someone else's mail!"

Jack nods and gives her a scrap of a smile. "Good."

"Is it . . . him on the tape? Is it the Fisherman?"

"Yes," Jack says. "It's him." *And there are worse things waiting,* he thinks but doesn't say. *Worse things by far.*

He hurries back to his truck, not quite running.

Twenty minutes later Jack parks in front of the babyshit brown two-story at 1 Nailhouse Row. Nailhouse Row and the dirty snarl of streets around it strike him as unnaturally silent under the sun of this hot summer afternoon. A mongrel dog (it is, in fact, the old fellow we saw in the doorway of the Nelson Hotel just last night) goes limping across the intersection of Ames and County Road Oo, but that's about the extent of the traffic. Jack has an unpleasant vision of the Walrus and the Carpenter toddling along the east bank of the Mississippi with the hypnotized residents of Nailhouse Row following along behind them. Toddling along toward the fire. And the cooking pot.

He takes two or three deep breaths, trying to steady himself. Not far out of town—close to the road leading to Ed's Eats, in fact—that nasty buzzing in his head peaked, turning into something like a dark scream. For a few moments there it was so strong Jack wondered if he was perhaps going to drive right off the road, and he slowed the Ram to forty. Then, blessedly, it began to move around toward the back of his head and fade. He didn't see the NO TRESPASSING sign that marks the overgrown road leading to Black House, didn't even look for it, but he knew it was there. The question is whether or not he'll be able to approach it when the time comes without simply exploding.

"Come on," he tells himself. "No time for this shit."

He gets out of the truck and starts up the cracked cement walk. There's a fading hopscotch diagram there, and Jack swerves to avoid it without even thinking, knowing it's one of the few remaining artifacts which testify that a little person named Amy St. Pierre once briefly trod the boards of existence. The porch steps are dry and splintery. He's vilely thirsty and thinks, *Man, I'd kill for a glass of water, or a nice cold—*

The door flies open, cracking against the side of the house like a pistol shot in the sunny silence, and Beezer comes running out.

"Christ almighty, I didn't think you were *ever* gonna get here!"

Looking into Beezer's alarmed, agonized eyes, Jack realizes that he will never tell this guy that he might be able to find Black House without Mouse's help, that thanks to his time in the Territories he has a kind of range finder in his head. No, not even if they live the rest of their lives as close friends, the kind who usually tell each other everything. The Beez has suffered like Job, and he doesn't need to find out that his friend's agony may have been in vain.

"Is he still alive, Beezer?"

"By an inch. Maybe an inch and a quarter. It's just me and

Doc and Bear Girl now. Sonny and Kaiser Bill got scared, ran off like a couple of whipped dogs. March your boots in here, sunshine." Not that Beezer gives Jack any choice; he grabs him by the shoulder and hauls him into the little two-story on Nail-house Row like luggage.

# 23

"One more!" says the guy from ESPN.

It sounds more like an order than a request, and although Henry can't see the fellow, he knows this particular homeboy never played a sport in his life, pro or otherwise. He has the lardy, slightly oily aroma of someone who has been overweight almost from the jump. Sports is perhaps his compensation, with the power to still memories of clothes bought in the Husky section at Sears and all those childhood rhymes like "Fatty-fatty, two-by-four, had to do it on the floor, couldn't get through the bathroom door."

His name is Penniman. "Just like Little Richard!" he told Henry when they shook hands at the radio station. "Famous rock 'n' roller from back in the fifties? Maybe you remember him."

"Vaguely," Henry said, as if he hadn't at one time owned every single Little Richard had ever put out. "I believe he was one of the Founding Fathers." Penniman laughed uproariously, and in that laugh Henry glimpsed a possible future for himself. But was it a future he wanted? People laughed at Howard Stern, too, and Howard Stern was a dork.

"One more drink!" Penniman repeats now. They are in the bar of the Oak Tree Inn, where Penniman has tipped the bartender five bucks to switch the TV from bowling on ABC to ESPN, even though there's nothing on at this hour of the day except golf tips and bass fishing. "One more drink, just to seal the deal!"

But they *don't* have a deal, and Henry isn't sure he wants to make one. Going national with George Rathbun as part of the ESPN radio package should be attractive, and he doesn't have any serious problem with changing the name of the show from *Badger Barrage* to *ESPN Sports Barrage*—it would still focus primarily on the central and northern areas of the country—but . . .

But what?

Before he can even get to work on the question, he smells it again: My Sin, the perfume his wife used to wear on certain evenings, when she wanted to send a certain signal. Lark was what he used to call her on those certain evenings, when the room was dark and they were both blind to everything but scents and textures and each other.

Lark.

"You know, I think I'm going to pass on that drink," Henry says. "Got some work to do at home. But I'm going to think over your offer. And I mean seriously."

"Ah-ah-ah," Penniman says, and Henry can tell from certain minute disturbances in the air that the man is shaking a finger beneath his nose. Henry wonders how Penniman would react if Henry suddenly darted his head forward and bit off the offending digit at the second knuckle. If Henry showed him a little Coulee Country hospitality Fisherman-style. How loud would Penniman yell? As loud as Little Richard before the instrumental break of "Tutti Frutti," perhaps? Or not quite as loud as that?

"Can't go till I'm ready to take you," Mr. I'm Fat But It No Longer Matters tells him. "I'm your ride, y'know." He's on his fourth gimlet, and his words are slightly slurred. *My friend,* Henry thinks, *I'd poke a ferret up my ass before I'd get into a car with you at the wheel.*

"Actually, I can," Henry says pleasantly. Nick Avery, the bartender, is having a kick-ass afternoon: the fat guy slipped him five to change the TV channel, and the blind guy slipped him five to call Skeeter's Taxi while the fat guy was in the bathroom, making a little room.

"Huh?"

"I said, 'Actually, I can.' Bartender?"

"He's outside, sir," Avery tells him. "Pulled up two minutes ago."

There is a hefty creak as Penniman turns on his bar stool. Henry can't see the man's frown as he takes in the taxi now idling in the hotel turnaround, but he can sense it.

"Listen, Henry," Penniman says. "I think you may lack a certain understanding of your current situation. There are stars in the firmament of sports radio, damned right there are—people like the Fabulous Sports Babe and Tony Kornheiser make six figures a year just in speaking fees, six figures *easy*—but you ain't there yet. That door is currently closed to you. But I, my friend, am one helluva doorman. The upshot is that if I say we ought to have one more drink, then—"

"Bartender," Henry says quietly, then shakes his head. "I can't just call you bartender; it might work for Humphrey Bogart but it doesn't work for me. What's your name?"

"Nick Avery, sir." The last word comes out automatically, but Avery never would have used it when speaking to the other one, never in a million years. Both guys tipped him five, but the one in the dark glasses is the gent. It's got nothing to do with him being blind, it's just something he *is*.

"Nick, who else is at the bar?"

Avery looks around. In one of the back booths, two men are drinking beer. In the hall, a bellman is on the phone. At the bar itself, no one at all except for these two guys—one slim, cool, and blind, the other fat, sweaty, and starting to be pissed off.

"No one, sir."

"There's not a . . . lady?" *Lark,* he's almost said. *There's not a lark?*

"No."

"Listen here," Penniman says, and Henry thinks he's never heard anyone so unlike "Little Richard" Penniman in his entire life. This guy is whiter than Moby Dick . . . and probably about the same size. "We've got a lot more to discuss here." *Loh more t'dishcush* is how it comes out. "Unless, that is"—*Unlesh*—"you're trying to let me know you're not interested." *Never in a million years,* Penniman's voice says to Henry Leyden's educated ears. *We're talking about putting a money machine in your living room, sweetheart, your very own private ATM, and there ain't no way in hell you're going to turn that down.*

"Nick, you don't smell perfume? Something very light and old-fashioned? My Sin, perhaps?"

A flabby hand falls on Henry's shoulder like a hot-water bottle. "The sin, old buddy, would be for you to *refuse* to have another drink with me. Even a blindman could see th—"

"Suggest you get your hand off him," Avery says, and perhaps Penniman's ears aren't *entirely* deaf to nuance, because the hand leaves Henry's shoulder at once.

Then another hand comes in its place, higher up. It touches the back of Henry's neck in a cold caress that's there and then gone. Henry draws in breath. The smell of perfume comes with it. Usually scents fade after a period of exposure, as the receptors that caught them temporarily deaden. Not this time, though. Not this smell.

"No perfume?" Henry almost pleads. The touch of her hand on his neck he can dismiss as a tactile hallucination. But his nose never betrays him.

Never until now, anyway.

"I'm sorry," Avery says. "I can smell beer . . . peanuts . . . this man's gin and his aftershave . . ."

Henry nods. The lights above the backbar slide across the dark lenses of his shades as he slips gracefully off his stool.

"I think you want another drink, my friend," Penniman says in what he no doubt believes to be a tone of polite menace. "One more drink, just to celebrate, and then I'll take you home in my Lexus."

Henry smells his wife's perfume. He's sure of it. And he seemed to feel the touch of his wife's hand on the back of his neck. Yet suddenly it's skinny little Morris Rosen he finds himself thinking about—Morris, who wanted him to listen to "Where Did Our Love Go" as done by Dirtysperm. And of course for Henry to play it in his Wisconsin Rat persona. Morris Rosen, who has more integrity in one of his nail-chewed little fingers than this bozo has got in his entire body.

He puts a hand on Penniman's forearm. He smiles into Penniman's unseen face, and feels the muscles beneath his palm relax. Penniman has decided he's going to get his way. Again.

"You take my drink," Henry says pleasantly, "add it to *your* drink, and then stick them both up your fat and bepimpled ass. If you need something to hold them in place, why, you can stick your job up there right after them."

Henry turns and walks briskly toward the door, orienting himself with his usual neat precision and holding one hand out in front of him as an insurance policy. Nick Avery has broken into spontaneous applause, but Henry barely hears this and

Penniman he has already dismissed from his mind. What occupies him is the smell of My Sin perfume. It fades a little as he steps out into the afternoon heat . . . but is that not an amorous sigh he hears beside his left ear? The sort of sigh his wife sometimes made just before falling asleep after love? His Rhoda? His Lark?

"Hello, the taxi!" he calls from the curb beneath the awning.

"Right here, buddy—what're you, blind?"

"As a bat," Henry agrees, and walks toward the sound of the voice. He'll go home, he'll put his feet up, he'll have a glass of tea, and then he'll listen to the damned 911 tape. That as yet unperformed chore may be what's causing his current case of the heebie-jeebies and shaky-shivers, knowing that he must sit in darkness and listen to the voice of a child-killing cannibal. Surely that must be it, because there's no reason to be afraid of his Lark, is there? If she were to return—to return and haunt him—she would surely haunt with love.

Wouldn't she?

*Yes,* he thinks, and lowers himself into the taxi's stifling back seat.

"Where to, buddy?"

"Norway Valley Road," Henry says. "It's a white house with blue trim, standing back from the road. You'll see it not long after you cross the creek."

Henry settles back in the seat and turns his troubled face toward the open window. French Landing feels strange to him today . . . fraught. Like something that has slipped and slipped until it is now on the verge of simply falling off the table and smashing to pieces on the floor.

*Say that she* has *come back. Say that she* has. *If it's love she's come with, why does the smell of her perfume make me so uneasy? So almost revolted? And why was her touch (her* imagined *touch, he assures himself) so unpleasant?*

*Why was her touch so cold?*

After the dazzle of the day, the living room of Beezer's crib is so dark that at first Jack can't make out anything. Then, when his eyes adjust a little, he sees why: blankets—a double thickness, from the look—have been hung over both of the living-room windows, and the door to the other downstairs room, almost certainly the kitchen, has been closed.

"He can't stand the light," Beezer says. He keeps his voice low so it won't carry across to the far side of the room, where the shape of a man lies on a couch. Another man is kneeling beside him.

"Maybe the dog that bit him was rabid," Jack says. He doesn't believe it.

Beezer shakes his head decisively. "It isn't a phobic reaction. Doc says it's physiological. Where light falls on him, his skin starts to melt. You ever hear of anything like that?"

"No." And Jack has never smelled anything like the stench in this room, either. There's the buzz of not one but two table fans, and he can feel the cross-draft, but that stink is too gluey to move. There's the reek of spoiled meat—of gangrene in torn flesh—but Jack has smelled that before. It's the other smell that's getting to him, something like blood and funeral flowers and feces all mixed up together. He makes a gagging noise, can't help it, and Beezer looks at him with a certain impatient sympathy.

"Bad, yeah, I know. But it's like the monkey house at the zoo, man—you get used to it after a while."

The swing door to the other room opens, and a trim little woman with shoulder-length blond hair comes through. She's carrying a bowl. When the light strikes the figure lying on the couch, Mouse screams. It's a horribly thick sound, as if the man's lungs have begun to liquefy. Something—maybe smoke, maybe steam—starts to rise up from the skin of his forehead.

"Hold on, Mouse," the kneeling man says. It's Doc. Before the kitchen door swings all the way shut again, Jack is able to read what's pasted to his battered black bag. Somewhere in America there may be another medical man sporting a STEP-PENWOLF RULES bumper sticker on the side of his physician's bag, but probably not in Wisconsin.

The woman kneels beside Doc, who takes a cloth from the basin, wrings it out, and places it on Mouse's forehead. Mouse gives a shaky groan and begins to shiver all over. Water runs down his cheeks and into his beard. The beard seems to be coming out in mangy patches.

Jack steps forward, telling himself he will get used to the smell, sure he will. Maybe it's even true. In the meantime he wishes for a little of the Vicks VapoRub most LAPD homicide detectives carry in their glove compartments as a matter of course. A dab under each nostril would be very welcome right now.

There's a sound system (scruffy) and a pair of speakers in the corners of the room (huge), but no television. Stacked wooden crates filled with books line every wall without a door or a window in it, making the space seem even smaller than it is, almost cryptlike. Jack has a touch of claustrophobia in his makeup, and now this circuit warms up, increasing his discomfort. Most of the books seem to deal with religion and philosophy—he sees Descartes, C. S. Lewis, the Bhagavad-Gita, Steven Avery's *Tenets of Existence*—but there's also a lot of fiction, books on beer making, and (on top of one giant speaker) Albert Goldman's trash tome about Elvis Presley. On the other speaker is a photograph of a young girl with a splendid smile, freckles, and oceans of reddish-blond hair. Seeing the child who drew the hopscotch grid out front makes Jack Sawyer feel sick with anger and sorrow. Otherworldly beings and causes there may be, but there's also a sick old fuck prowling around who needs to be stopped. He'd do well to remember that.

Bear Girl makes a space for Jack in front of the couch, moving gracefully even though she's on her knees and still holding the bowl. Jack sees that in it are two more wet cloths and a heap of melting ice cubes. The sight of them makes him thirstier than ever. He takes one and pops it into his mouth. Then he turns his attention to Mouse.

A plaid blanket has been pulled up to his neck. His forehead and upper cheeks—the places not covered by his decaying beard—are pasty. His eyes are closed. His lips are drawn back to show teeth of startling whiteness.

"Is he—" Jack begins, and then Mouse's eyes open. Whatever Jack meant to ask leaves his head entirely. Around the hazel irises, Mouse's eyes have gone an uneasy, shifting scarlet. It's as if the man is looking into a terrible radioactive sunset. From the inner corners of his eyes, some sort of black scum is oozing.

"*The Book of Philosophical Transformation* addresses most

current dialectics," Mouse says, speaking mellowly and lucidly, "and Machiavelli also speaks to these questions." Jack can almost picture him in a lecture hall. Until his teeth begin to chatter, that is.

"Mouse, it's Jack Sawyer." No recognition in those weird red-and-hazel eyes. The black gunk at the corners of them seems to twitch, however, as if it is somehow sentient. Listening to him.

"It's Hollywood," Beezer murmurs. "The cop. Remember?"

One of Mouse's hands lies on the plaid blanket. Jack takes it, and stifles a cry of surprise when it closes over his with amazing strength. It's hot, too. As hot as a biscuit just out of the oven. Mouse lets out a long, gasping sigh, and the stench is fetid— bad meat, decayed flowers. *He's rotting,* Jack thinks. *Rotting from the inside out. Oh Christ, help me through this.*

Christ may not, but the memory of Sophie might. Jack tries to fix her eyes in his memory, that lovely, level, clear blue gaze.

"Listen," Mouse says.

"I'm listening."

Mouse seems to gather himself. Beneath the blanket, his body shivers in a loose, uncoordinated way that Jack guesses is next door to a seizure. Somewhere a clock is ticking. Somewhere a dog is barking. A boat hoots on the Mississippi. Other than these sounds, all is silence. Jack can remember only one other such suspension of the world's business in his entire life, and that was when he was in a Beverly Hills hospital, waiting for his mother to finish the long business of dying. Somewhere Ty Marshall is waiting to be rescued. Hoping to be rescued, at least. Somewhere there are Breakers hard at work, trying to destroy the axle upon which all existence spins. Here is only this eternal room with its feeble fans and noxious vapors.

Mouse's eyes close, then open again. They fix upon the newcomer, and Jack is suddenly sure some great truth is going to be confided. The ice cube is gone from his mouth; Jack supposes he crunched it up and swallowed it without even realizing, but he doesn't dare take another.

"Go on, buddy," Doc says. "You get it out and then I'll load you up with another hypo of dope. The good stuff. Maybe you'll sleep."

Mouse pays no heed. His mutating eyes hold Jack's. His

hand holds Jack's, tightening still more. Jack can almost feel the bones of his fingers grinding together.

"Don't . . . go out and buy top-of-the-line equipment," Mouse says, and sighs out another excruciatingly foul breath from his rotting lungs.

"Don't . . . ?"

"Most people give up brewing after . . . a year or two. Even dedicated . . . dedicated hobbyists. Making beer is not . . . is not for pussies."

Jack looks around at Beezer, who looks back impassively. "He's in and out. Be patient. Wait on him."

Mouse's grip tightens yet more, then loosens just as Jack is deciding he can take it no longer.

"Get a big pot," Mouse advises him. His eyes bulge. The reddish shadows come and go, come and go, fleeting across the curved landscape of his corneas, and Jack thinks, *That's its shadow. The shadow of the Crimson King. Mouse has already got one foot in its court.* "Five gallons . . . at least. You find the best ones are in . . . seafood supply stores. And for a fermentation vessel . . . plastic water-cooler jugs are good . . . they're lighter than glass, and . . . I'm burning up. Christ, Beez, I'm burning up!"

"Fuck this, I'm going to shoot it to him," Doc says, and snaps open his bag.

Beezer grabs his arm. "Not yet."

Bloody tears begin to slip out of Mouse's eyes. The black goo seems to be forming into tiny tendrils. These reach greedily downward, as if trying to catch the moisture and drink it.

"Fermentation lock and stopper," Mouse whispers. "Thomas Merton is shit, never let anyone tell you different. No real thought there. You have to let the gases escape while keeping dust out. Jerry Garcia wasn't God. Kurt Cobain wasn't God. The perfume he smells is not that of his dead wife. He's caught the eye of the King. *Gorg-ten-abbalah, ee-lee-lee.* The opopanax is dead, long live the opopanax."

Jack leans more deeply into Mouse's smell. "Who's smelling perfume? Who's caught the eye of the King?"

"The mad King, the bad King, the sad King. Ring-a-ding-ding, all hail the King."

"Mouse, *who's* caught the eye of the King?"

Doc says, "I thought you wanted to know about—"

*"Who?"* Jack has no idea why this seems important to him, but it does. Is it something someone has said to him recently? Was it Dale? Tansy? Was it, God save us, Wendell Green?

"Racking cane and hose," Mouse says confidentially. "That's what you need when the fermentation's done! And you can't put beer in screw-top bottles! You—"

Mouse turns his head away from Jack, nestles it cozily in the hollow of his shoulder, opens his mouth, and vomits. Bear Girl screams. The vomit is pus-yellow and speckled with moving black bits like the crud in the corners of Mouse's eyes. It is alive.

Beezer leaves the room in a hurry, not quite running, and Jack shades Mouse from the brief glare of kitchen sunlight as best he can. The hand clamped on Jack's loosens a little more.

Jack turns to Doc. "Do you think he's going?"

Doc shakes his head. "Passed out again. Poor old Mousie ain't getting off that easy." He gives Jack a grim, haunted look. "This better be worth it, Mr. Policeman. 'Cause if it ain't, I'm gonna replumb your sink."

Beezer comes back with a huge bundle of rags, and he's put on a pair of green kitchen gloves. Not speaking, he mops up the pool of vomit between Mouse's shoulder and the backrest of the couch. The black specks have ceased moving, and that's good. To have not seen them moving in the first place would have been even better. The vomit, Jack notices with dismay, has eaten into the couch's worn fabric like acid.

"I'm going to pull the blanket down for a second or two," Doc says, and Bear Girl gets up at once, still holding the bowl with the melting ice. She goes to one of the bookshelves and stands there with her back turned, trembling.

"Doc, is this something I really need to see?"

"I think maybe it is. I don't think you know what you're dealing with, even now." Doc takes hold of the blanket and eases it out from beneath Mouse's limp hand. Jack sees that more of the black stuff has begun to ooze from beneath the dying man's fingernails. "Remember that this happened only a couple of hours ago, Mr. Policeman."

He pulls the blanket down. Standing with her back to them, Susan "Bear Girl" Osgood faces the great works of Western

philosophy and begins to cry silently. Jack tries to hold back h
scream and cannot.

Henry pays off the taxi, goes into his house, takes a deep ar
soothing breath of the air-conditioned cool. There is a fai
aroma—sweet—and he tells himself it's just fresh-cut flower
one of Mrs. Morton's specialties. He knows better, but wants r
more to do with ghosts just now. He is actually feeling bette
and he supposes he knows why: it was telling the ESPN guy 
take his job and shove it. Nothing more apt to make a fellow
day, especially when the fellow in question is gainfully en
ployed, possessed of two credit cards that are nowhere near tl
max-out point, and has a pitcher of cold iced tea in the fridge

Henry heads kitchenward now, making his way down tl
hall with one hand held out before him, testing the air for ol
stacles and displacements. There's no sound but the whisper 
the air conditioner, the hum of the fridge, the clack of his hee
on the hardwood . . .

. . . and a sigh.

An amorous sigh.

Henry stands where he is for a moment, then turns ca
tiously. Is the sweet aroma a little stronger now, especially fa
ing back in this direction, toward the living room and the fro
door? He thinks yes. And it's not flowers; no sense fooling hin
self about that. As always, the nose knows. That's the aroma 
My Sin.

"Rhoda?" he says, and then, lower: "Lark?"

No answer. Of course not. He's just having the heebi
jeebies, that's all; those world-famous shaky-shivers, and wh
not?

"Because I'm the sheik, baby," Henry says. "The Sheik, tl
Shake, the Shook."

No smells. No sexy sighs. And yet he's haunted by the ide
of his wife back in the living room, standing there in perfume
cerements of the grave, watching him silently as he came in an
passed blindly before her. His Lark, come back from Nogg
Mound Cemetery for a little visit. Maybe to listen to the late
Slobberbone CD.

"Quit it," he says softly. "Quit it, you dope."

He goes into his big, well-organized kitchen. On his wa

through the door he slaps a button on the panel there without even thinking about it. Mrs. Morton's voice comes from the overhead speaker, which is so high-tech she might almost be in the room.

"Jack Sawyer was by, and he dropped off another tape he wants you to listen to. He said it was . . . you know, that man. That bad man."

"Bad man, right," Henry murmurs, opening the refrigerator and enjoying the blast of cold air. His hand goes unerringly to one of three cans of Kingsland Lager stored inside the door. Never mind the iced tea.

"Both of the tapes are in your studio, by the soundboard. Also, Jack wanted you to call him on his cell phone." Mrs. Morton's voice takes on a faintly lecturing tone. "If you do speak to him, I hope you tell him to be careful. And be careful yourself." A pause. "*Also,* don't forget to eat supper. It's all ready to go. Second shelf of the fridge, on your left."

"Nag, nag, nag," Henry says, but he's smiling as he opens his beer. He goes to the telephone and dials Jack's number.

On the seat of the Dodge Ram parked in front of 1 Nailhouse Row, Jack's cell phone comes to life. This time there's no one in the cab to be annoyed by its tiny but penetrating tweet.

"The cellular customer you are trying to reach is currently not answering. Please try your call again later."

Henry hangs up, goes back to the doorway, and pushes another button on the panel there. The voices that deliver the time and temperature are all versions of his own, but he's programmed a random shuffle pattern into the gadget, so he never knows which one he's going to get. This time it's the Wisconsin Rat, screaming crazily into the sunny air-conditioned silence of his house, which has never felt so far from town as it does today:

"Time's four twenty-two P.M.! Outside temperature's eighty-two! Inside temperature's seventy! What the hell do you care? What the hell does *anyone* care? Chew it up, eat it up, wash it down, *it aaall*—"

—comes out the same place. Right. Henry thumbs the button again, silencing the Rat's trademark cry. How did it get late so fast? God, wasn't it just noon? For that matter, wasn't he just young, twenty years old and so full of spunk it was practically coming out of his ears? What—

That sigh comes again, derailing his mostly self-mocking train of thought. A sigh? Really? More likely just the air conditioner's compressor, cutting off. He can tell himself that, anyway.

He can tell himself that if he wants to.

"Is anyone here?" Henry asks. There is a tremble in his voice that he hates, an old man's palsied quaver. "Is anyone in the house with me?"

For a terrible second he is almost afraid something will answer. Nothing does—of *course* nothing does—and he swallows half the can of beer in three long gulps. He decides he'll go back into the living room and read for a little while. Maybe Jack will call. Maybe he'll get himself a little more under control once he has a little fresh alcohol in his system.

*And maybe the world will end in the next five minutes,* he thinks. *That way you'll never have to deal with the voice on those damned tapes waiting in the studio. Those damned tapes lying there on the soundboard like unexploded bombs.*

Henry walks slowly back down the hall to the living room with one hand held out before him, telling himself he's not afraid, not a bit afraid of touching his wife's dead face.

Jack Sawyer has seen a lot, he's traveled to places where you can't rent from Avis and the water tastes like wine, but he's never encountered anything like Mouse Baumann's leg. Or rather, the pestilential, apocalyptic horror show that *was* Mouse Baumann's leg. Jack's first impulse once he's got himself back under something like control is to upbraid Doc for taking off Mouse's pants. Jack keeps thinking of sausages, and how the casing forces them to keep their shape even after the fry pan's sizzling on a red-hot burner. This is an undoubtedly stupid comparison, *primo stupido,* but the human mind under pressure puts on some pretty odd jinks and jumps.

There's still the *shape* of a leg there—sort of—but the flesh has spread away from the bone. The skin is almost completely gone, melted to a runny substance that looks like a mixture of milk and bacon fat. The interwoven mat of muscle beneath what remains of the skin is sagging and undergoing the same cataclysmic metamorphosis. The infected leg is in a kind of undisciplined motion as the solid becomes liquid and the liquid sizzles relentlessly into the couch upon which Mouse is lying. Along with the almost insupportable stench of decay, Jack can smell scorching cloth and melting fabric.

Poking out of this spreading, vaguely leglike mess is a foot that looks remarkably undamaged. *If I wanted to, I could pull it right off . . . just like a squash off a vine.* The thought gets to him in a way the sight of the grievously wounded leg hasn't quite been able to, and for a moment Jack can only bow his head, gagging and trying not to vomit down the front of his shirt.

What perhaps saves him is a hand on his back. It's Beezer, offering what comfort he can. The rowdy color has completely left the Beez's face. He looks like a motorcyclist come back from the grave in an urban myth.

"You see?" Doc is asking, and his voice seems to come from a great distance. "This ain't the chicken pox, my friend, although it looked a little like that while it was still getting cranked up. He's already exhibiting red spots on his left leg . . . his belly . . . his balls. That's pretty much what the skin around the bite looked like when we first got him back here, just some redness and swelling. I thought, 'Shit, ain't nothin' to this, I got enough Zithromax to put this on the run before sundown.' Well, you see what good the Zithro did. You see what good *anything* did. It's eating through the couch, and I'm guessing that when it finishes with the couch, it'll go right to work on the floor. This shit is *hungry.* So was it worth it, Hollywood? I guess only you and Mouse know the answer to that."

"He still knows where the house is," Beezer says. "Me, I don't have a clue, even though we just *came* from there. You, either. Do you?"

Doc shakes his head.

"But Mouse, he knows."

"Susie, honey," Doc says to Bear Girl. "Bring another blanket, would you? This one's damn near eaten through."

Bear Girl goes willingly enough. Jack gets to his feet. His

legs are rubbery, but they hold him. "Shield him," he tells Doc. "I'm going out to the kitchen. If I don't get a drink, I'm going to die."

Jack takes on water directly from the sink, swallowing until a spike plants itself in the center of his forehead and he belches like a horse. Then he just stands there, looking out into Beezer and Bear Girl's backyard. A neat little swing set has been planted there in the weedy desolation. It hurts Jack to look at it, but he looks anyway. After the lunacy of Mouse's leg, it seems important to remind himself that he's here for a reason. If the reminder hurts, so much the better.

The sun, now turning gold as it eases itself down toward the Mississippi, glares in his eyes. Time hasn't been standing still after all, it seems. Not outside this little house, anyway. Outside 1 Nailhouse Row, time actually seems to have sped up. He's haunted by the idea that coming here was as pointless as detouring to Henry's house; tormented by the thought that Mr. Munshun and his boss, the abbalah, are running him around like a windup toy with a key in its back while they do their work. He can follow that buzz in his head to Black House, so why the hell doesn't he just get back in his truck and *do* it?

*The perfume he smells is not that of his dead wife.*

What does that mean? Why does the idea of someone smelling perfume make him so crazy and afraid?

Beezer knocks on the kitchen door, making him jump. Jack's eye fixes on a sampler hung over the kitchen table. Instead of GOD BLESS OUR HOME, it reads HEAVY METAL THUNDER. With a carefully stitched HARLEY-DAVIDSON beneath.

"Get back in here, man," the Beez says. "He's awake again."

Henry's on a path in the woods—or maybe it's a lane—and something is behind him. Each time he turns to see—in this dream he can see, but seeing is no blessing—there's a little more of that something back there. It appears to be a man in evening dress, but the man is frightfully elongated, with spike teeth that jut over a smiling red lower lip. And he seems—is it possible?—to have only one eye.

The first time Henry looks back, the shape is only a milky blur amid the trees. The next time he can make out the uneasy dark swim of its coat and a floating red blotch that might be a tie or an ascot. Up ahead of him is this thing's den, a stinking hole that only coincidentally looks like a house. Its presence buzzes in Henry's head. Instead of pine, the woods pressing in on either side smell of heavy, cloying perfume: My Sin.

*It's driving me,* he thinks with dismay. *Whatever that thing back there is, it's driving me like a steer toward the slaughterhouse.*

He thinks of cutting off the lane to his left or right, of using the miracle of his new sight to escape through the woods. Only there are things there, too. Dark, floating shapes like sooty scarves. He can almost see the closest. It's some sort of gigantic dog with a long tongue as red as the apparition's tie and bulging eyes.

*Can't let it drive me to the house,* he thinks. *I have to get out of this before it can get me there . . . but how? How?*

It comes to him with startling simplicity. All he has to do is wake up. Because this is a dream. This is just a—

*"It's a dream!"* Henry cries out, and jerks forward. He's not walking, he's *sitting,* sitting in his very own easy chair, and pretty soon he's going to have a very wet crotch because he fell asleep with a can of Kingsland Lager balanced there, and—

But there's no spill, because there's no can of beer. He feels cautiously to his right and yep, there it is, on the table with his book, a braille edition of *Reflections in a Golden Eye.* He must have put it there before first falling asleep and then falling into that horrible nightmare.

Except Henry's pretty sure he didn't do any such thing. He was holding the book and the beer was between his legs, freeing his hands to touch the little upraised dots that tell the story. Something very considerately took both the book and the can after he dropped off, and put them on the table. Something that smells of My Sin perfume.

The air *reeks* of it.

Henry takes a long, slow breath with his nostrils flared and mouth tightly sealed shut.

"No," he says, speaking very clearly. "I can smell flowers . . . and rug shampoo . . . and fried onions from last night. Very faint but still there. The nose knows."

All true enough. But the smell *had* been there. It's gone now because *she's* gone, but she will be back. And suddenly he wants her to come. If he's frightened, surely it's the unknown he's frightened of, right? Only that and nothing more. He doesn't want to be alone here, with nothing for company but the memory of that rancid dream.

And the tapes.

He has to listen to the tapes. He promised Jack.

Henry gets shakily to his feet and makes his way to the living-room control panel. This time he's greeted by the voice of Henry Shake, a mellow fellow if ever there was one.

"Hey there, all you hoppin' cats and boppin' kitties, at the tone it's seven-fourteen P.M., Bulova Watch Time. Outside the temp is a very cool seventy-five degrees, and here in the Make-Believe Ballroom it's a very nifty seventy degrees. So why not get off your money, grab your honey, and make a little magic?"

Seven-fourteen! When was the last time he fell asleep for almost three hours in the daytime? For that matter, when was the last time he had a dream in which he could see? The answer to that second question, so far as he can remember, is never.

Where was that lane?

What was the thing behind him?

What was the place ahead of him, for that matter?

"Doesn't matter," Henry tells the empty room—if it *is* empty. "It was a dream, that's all. The tapes, on the other hand . . ."

He doesn't want to listen to them, has never wanted to listen to anything any less in his life (with the possible exception of Chicago singing "Does Anybody Really Know What Time It Is?"), but he has to. If it might save Ty Marshall's life, or the life of even one other child, he must.

Slowly, dreading every step, Henry Leyden makes his blind way to his studio, where two cassettes wait for him on the soundboard.

"In heaven there is no beer," Mouse sings in a toneless, droning voice.

His cheeks are now covered with ugly red patches, and his nose seems to be sinking sideways into his face, like an atoll after an undersea earthquake.

"That's why we drink it here. And when . . . we're

gone . . . from here . . . our friends will be drinking all the beer."

It's been like this for hours now: philosophical nuggets, instructions for the beginning beer-making enthusiast, snatches of song. The light coming through the blankets over the windows has dimmed appreciably.

Mouse pauses, his eyes closed. Then he starts another ditty.

"Hundred bottles of beer on the wall, one *hun*dred *bot*tles of *beer* . . . if one of those bottles should happen to fall . . ."

"I have to go," Jack says. He's hung in there as well as he can, convinced that Mouse is going to give him something, but he can wait no longer. Somewhere, Ty Marshall is waiting for *him.*

"Hold on," Doc says. He rummages in his bag and comes out with a hypodermic needle. He raises it in the dimness and taps the glass barrel with a fingernail.

"What's that?"

Doc gives Jack and Beezer a brief, grim smile. "Speed," he says, and injects it into Mouse's arm.

For a moment there's nothing. Then, as Jack is opening his mouth again to tell them he has to go, Mouse's eyes snap wide. They are now entirely red—a bright and bleeding red. Yet when they turn in his direction, Jack knows that Mouse is seeing him. Maybe really seeing him for the first time since he got here.

Bear Girl flees the room, trailing a single diminishing phrase behind her: "No more no more no more no more—"

"Fuck," Mouse says in a rusty voice. "Fuck, I'm fucked. Ain't I?"

Beezer touches the top of his friend's head briefly but tenderly. "Yeah, man. I think you are. Can you help us out?"

"Bit me once. Just once, and now . . . now . . ." His hideous red gaze turns to Doc. "Can barely see you. Fuckin' eyes are all weird."

"You're going down," Doc says. "Ain't gonna lie to you, man."

"Not yet I ain't," Mouse says. "Gimme something to write on. To draw a map on. Quick. Dunno what you shot me with, Doc, but the stuff from the dog's stronger. I ain't gonna be *compos* long. Quick!"

Beezer feels around at the foot of the couch and comes up

with a trade-sized paperback. Given the heavy shit on the book-cases, Jack could almost laugh—the book is *The 7 Habits of Highly Effective People.* Beezer tears off the back cover and hands it to Mouse with the blank side up.

"Pencil," Mouse croaks. "Hurry up. I got it all, man. I got it . . . up here." He touches his forehead. A patch of skin the size of a quarter sloughs off at his touch. Mouse wipes it on the blanket as if it were a booger.

Beezer pulls a gnawed stub of pencil from an inside pocket of his vest. Mouse takes it and makes a pathetic effort to smile. The black stuff oozing from the corners of his eyes has contin-ued to build up, and now it lies on his cheeks like smears of de-cayed jelly. More of it is springing out of the pores on his forehead in minute black dots that remind Jack of Henry's braille books. When Mouse bites his lower lip in concentration, the tender flesh splits open at once. Blood begins dribbling into his beard. Jack supposes the rotted-meat smell is still there, but Beezer had been right: he's gotten used to it.

Mouse turns the book cover sideways, then draws a series of quick squiggles. "Lookit," he says to Jack. "This the Missis-sippi, right?"

"Right," Jack says. When he leans in, he starts getting the smell again. Up close it's not even a stench; it's a miasma try-ing to crawl down his throat. But Jack doesn't move away. He knows what an effort Mouse is making. The least he can do is play his part.

"Here's downtown—the Nelson, Lucky's, the Agincourt Theater, the Taproom . . . here's where Chase Street turns into Lyall Road, then Route 35 . . . here's Libertyville . . . the VFW . . . Goltz's . . . ah, Christ—"

Mouse begins to thrash on the couch. Sores on his face and upper body burst open and begin leaking. He screams with pain. The hand not holding the pencil goes to his face and paws at it ineffectually.

Something inside Jack speaks up, then—speaks in a shining, imperative voice he remembers from his time on the road all those years ago. He supposes it's the voice of the Talisman, or whatever remains of it in his mind and soul.

*It doesn't want him to talk, it's trying to kill him before he can talk, it's in the black stuff, maybe it is the black stuff, you've got to get rid of it—*

Some things can only be done without the mind's prudish interference; when the work is nasty, instinct is often best. So it is without thinking that Jack reaches out, grasps the black slime oozing from Mouse's eyes between his fingers, and pulls. At first the stuff only stretches, as if made of rubber. At the same time Jack can feel it squirming and writhing in his grip, perhaps trying to pinch or bite him. Then it lets go with a *twang* sound. Jack throws the convulsing black tissue onto the floor with a cry.

The stuff tries to slither beneath the couch—Jack sees this even as he wipes his hands on his shirt, frantic with revulsion. Doc slams his bag down on one piece. Beezer squashes the other with the heel of a motorcycle boot. It makes a squittering sound.

"What the fuck is that shit?" Doc asks. His voice, ordinarily husky, has gone up into a near-falsetto range. "What the *fuck*—"

"Nothing from here," Jack says, "and never mind. Look at him! Look at Mouse!"

The red glare in Mouse's eyes has retreated; for the moment he looks almost normal. Certainly he's seeing *them,* and the pain seems gone. "Thanks," he breathes. "I only wish you could get it all that way, but man, it's already coming back. Pay attention."

"I'm listening," Jack says.

"You better," Mouse replies. "You think you know. You think you can find the place again even if these two can't, and maybe you can, but maybe you don't know quite so much as you . . . ah, *fuck.*" From somewhere beneath the blanket there is a ghastly bursting sound as something gives way. Sweat runs down Mouse's face, mixing with the black poison venting from his pores and turning his beard a damp and dirty gray. His eyes roll up to Jack's, and Jack can see that red glare starting to haze over them again.

"This sucks," Mouse pants. "Never thought I'd go out this way. Lookit, Hollywood . . ." The dying man draws a small rectangle on his makeshift scribble of map. "This—"

"Ed's Eats, where we found Irma," Jack says. "I know."

"All right," Mouse whispers. "Good. Now look . . . over on the other side . . . the Schubert and Gale side . . . and to the west . . ."

Mouse draws a line going north from Highway 35. He puts little circles on either side of it. Jack takes these to be representations of trees. And, across the front of the line like a gate: NO TRESPASSING.

"Yeah," Doc breathes. "That's where it was, all right. Black House."

Mouse takes no notice. His dimming gaze is fixed solely on Jack. "Listen to me, cop. Are you listening?"

"Yes."

"Christ, you better be," Mouse tells him.

As it always has, the work captures Henry, absorbs him, takes him away. Boredom and sorrow have never been able to stand against this old captivation with sound from the sighted world. Apparently fear can't stand against it, either. The hardest moment isn't listening to the tapes but mustering the courage to stick the first one in the big TEAC audio deck. In that moment of hesitation he's sure he can smell his wife's perfume even in the soundproofed and air-filtered environment of the studio. In that moment of hesitation he is positive he isn't alone, that someone (or some*thing*) is standing just outside the studio door, looking in at him through the glass upper half. And that is, in fact, the absolute truth. Blessed with sight as we are, we can see what Henry cannot. We want to tell him what's out there, to lock the studio door, for the love of God lock it *now,* but we can only watch.

Henry reaches for the PLAY button on the tape deck. Then his finger changes course and hits the intercom toggle instead.

"Hello? Is anyone out there?"

The figure standing in Henry's living room, looking in at him the way someone might look into an aquarium at a single exotic fish, makes no sound. The last of the sun's on the other side of the house and the living room is becoming quite dark, Henry being understandably forgetful when it comes to turning on the lights. Elmer Jesperson's amusing bee slippers (not that they amuse us much under these circumstances) are just about the brightest things out there.

"Hello? Anyone?"

The figure looking in through the glass half of the studio door is grinning. In one hand it is holding the hedge clippers from Henry's garage.

"Last chance," Henry says, and when there's still no response, he becomes the Wisconsin Rat, shrieking into the intercom, trying to startle whatever's out there into revealing itself: *"Come on now, honey, come on now, you muthafukkah, talk to Ratty!"*

The figure peering in at Henry recoils—as a snake might recoil when its prey makes a feint—but it utters no sound. From between the grinning teeth comes a leathery old tongue, wagging and poking in derision. This creature has been into the perfume that Mrs. Morton has never had the heart to remove from the vanity in the little powder room adjacent to the master bedroom, and now Henry's visitor reeks of My Sin.

Henry decides it's all just his imagination playing him up again—oy, such a mistake, Morris Rosen would have told him, had Morris been there—and hits PLAY with the tip of his finger.

He hears a throat-clearing sound, and then Arnold Hrabowski identifies himself. The Fisherman interrupts him before he can even finish: *Hello, asswipe.*

Henry rewinds, listens again: *Hello, asswipe.* Rewinds and listens yet again: *Hello, asswipe.* Yes, he has heard this voice before. He's sure of it. But where? The answer will come, answers of this sort always do—eventually—and getting there is half the fun. Henry listens, enrapt. His fingers dance back and forth over the tape deck's buttons like the fingers of a concert pianist over the keys of a Steinway. The feeling of being watched slips from him, although the figure outside the studio door—the thing wearing the bee slippers and holding the hedge clippers—never moves. Its smile has faded somewhat. A sulky expression is growing on its aged face. There is confusion in that look, and perhaps the first faint trace of fear. The old monster doesn't like it that the blind fish in the aquarium should have captured its voice. Of course it doesn't matter; maybe it's even part of the fun, but if it is, it's Mr. Munshun's fun, not *its* fun. And their fun should be the same . . . shouldn't it?

*You have an emergency. Not me. You.*

"Not me, *you*," Henry says. The mimicry is so good it's weird. "A little bit of sauerkraut in your salad, *mein* friend, *ja?*"

*Your worst nightmare . . . worst nightmare.*

*Abbalah.*

*I'm the Fisherman.*

Henry listening, intent. He lets the tape run awhile, then listens to the same phrase four times over: *Kiss my scrote, you monkey . . . kiss my scrote, you monkey . . . you monkey . . . monkey . . .*

No, not *monkey*. The voice is actually saying *munggey. MUNG-ghee.*

"I don't know where you are now, but you grew up in Chicago," Henry murmurs. "South Side. And . . ."

Warmth on his face. Suddenly he remembers warmth on his face. Why is that, friends and neighbors? Why is that, O great wise ones?

*You're no better'n a monkey on a stick.*

*Monkey on a stick.*

*Monkey—*

"Monkey," Henry says. He's rubbing his temples with the tips of his fingers now. "Monkey on a stick. MUNG-ghee on a stigg. Who said that?"

He plays the 911: *Kiss my scrote, you monkey.*

He plays his memory: *You're no better'n a monkey on a stick.*

Warmth on his face.

Heat? Light?

Both?

Henry pops out the 911 tape and sticks in the one Jack brought today.

*Hello, Judy. Are you Judy today, or are you Sophie? The abbalah sends his best, and Gorg says "Caw-caw-caw!"* [Husky, phlegmy laughter.] *Ty says hello, too. Your little boy is very lonely . . .*

When Tyler Marshall's weeping, terrified voice booms through the speakers, Henry winces and fast-forwards.

*Derr vill be morrr mur-derts.*

The accent much thicker now, a burlesque, a joke, *Katzenjammer Kids Meet the Wolfman,* but somehow even more revealing because of that.

*Der liddul chull-drun . . . havv-uz-ted like wheed. Like wheed. Havv-uz-ted like . . .*

"Harvested like a monkey on a stick," Henry says. "MUNG-ghee. HAVV-us-ted. Who are you, you son of a bitch?"

Back to the 911 tape.

*There are whips in hell and chains in Sheol.* But it's almost *vips in hell,* almost *chenz in Shayol.*

Vips. Chenz. MUNG-ghee on a stick. A *stigg.*

"You're no better'n—" Henry begins, and then, all at once, another line comes to him.

*"Lady Magowan's Nightmare." That one's good.*

A bad nightmare of what? Vips in hell? Chenz in Shayol? Mung-ghees on sticks?

"My God," Henry says softly. "Oh . . . my . . . God. The dance. *He was at the dance.*"

Now it all begins to fall into place. How stupid they have been! How criminally stupid! The boy's bike . . . it had been right there. *Right there,* for Christ's sake! They were all blind men, make them all umps.

"But he was so *old,*" Henry whispers. "And senile! How were we supposed to guess such a man could be the Fisherman?"

Other questions follow this one. If the Fisherman is a resident at Maxton Elder Care, for instance, where in God's name could he have stashed Ty Marshall? And how is the bastard getting around French Landing? Does he have a car somewhere?

"Doesn't matter," Henry murmurs. "Not now, anyway. Who is he and *where* is he? Those are the things that matter."

The warmth on his face—his mind's first effort to locate the Fisherman's voice in time and place—had been the spotlight, of course, Symphonic Stan's spotlight, the pink of ripening berries. And some woman, some nice old woman—

*Mr. Stan, yoo-hoo, Mr. Stan?*

—had asked him if he took requests. Only, before Stan could reply, a voice as flat and hard as two stones grinding together—

*I was here first, old woman.*

—had interrupted. Flat . . . and hard . . . and with that faint Germanic harshness that said South Side Chicago, probably second or even third generation. Not *vass* here first, not old *vumman,* but those telltale *v*'s had been lurking, hadn't they? Ah yes.

"Mung-ghee," Henry says, looking straight ahead. Looking straight at Charles Burnside, had he only known it. "Stigg. *Havv*-us-ted. *Hasta la vista . . .* baby."

Was that what it came down to, in the end? A dotty old maniac who sounded a bit like Arnold Schwarzenegger?

Who was the woman? If he can remember her name, he can call Jack . . . or Dale, if Jack's still not answering his phone . . . and put an end to French Landing's bad dream.

*Lady Magowan's Nightmare. That one's good.*

"Nightmare," Henry says, then adjusting his voice: "*Nahht*-mare." Once again the mimicry is good. Certainly too good for the old codger standing outside the studio door. He is now scowling bitterly and gnashing the hedge clippers in front of the glass. How can the blindman in there sound so much like him? It's not right; it's *completely* improper. The old monster longs to cut the vocal cords right out of Henry Leyden's throat. Soon, he promises himself, he will do that.

And eat them.

Sitting in the swivel chair, drumming his fingers nervously on the gleaming oak in front of him, Henry recalls the brief encounter at the bandstand. Not long into the Strawberry Fest dance, this had been.

*Tell me your name and what you'd like to hear.*

*I am Alice Weathers, and—*. *"Moonglow," please. By Benny Goodman.*

"Alice Weathers," Henry says. "That was her name, and if she doesn't know *your* name, my homicidal friend, then *I'm* a monkey on a stick."

He starts to get up, and that is when someone—some*thing*—begins to knock, very softly, on the glass upper half of the door.

Bear Girl has drawn close, almost against her will, and now she, Jack, Doc, and the Beez are gathered around the sofa. Mouse has sunk halfway into it. He looks like a person dying badly in quicksand.

*Well,* Jack thinks, *there's no quicksand, but he's dying badly, all right. Guess there's no question about that.*

"Listen up," Mouse tells them. The black goo is forming at the corners of his eyes again. Worse, it's trickling from the corners of his mouth. The stench of decay is stronger than ever as Mouse's inner workings give up the struggle. Jack is frankly amazed that they've lasted as long as they have.

"You talk," Beezer says. "We'll listen."

Mouse looks at Doc. "When I finish, give me the fireworks. The Cadillac dope. Understand?"

"You want to get out ahead of whatever it is you've got."

Mouse nods.

"I'm down with that," Doc agrees. "You'll go out with a smile on your face."

"Doubt that, bro, but I'll give it a try."

Mouse shifts his reddening gaze to Beezer. "When it's done, wrap me up in one of the nylon tents that're in the garage. Stick me in the tub. I'm betting that by midnight, you'll be able to wash me down the drain like . . . like so much beer foam. I'd be careful, though. Don't . . . touch what's left."

Bear Girl bursts into tears.

"Don't cry, darlin'," Mouse says. "I'm gonna get out ahead. Doc promised. Beez?"

"Right here, buddy."

"You have a little service for me. Okay? Read a poem . . . the one by Auden . . . the one that always used to frost your balls . . ."

" 'Thou shalt not read the Bible for its prose,' " Beezer says. He's crying. "You got it, Mousie."

"Play some Dead . . . 'Ripple,' maybe . . . and make sure you're full enough of Kingsland to christen me good and proper into the next life. Guess there won't . . . be any grave for you to piss on, but . . . do the best you can."

Jack laughs at that. He can't help it. And this time it's his turn to catch the full force of Mouse's crimson eyes.

"Promise me you'll wait until tomorrow to go out there, cop."

"Mouse, I'm not sure I can do that."

"You *gotta*. Go out there tonight, you won't have to worry about the devil dog . . . the other things in the woods around that house . . . the other things . . ." The red eyes roll horribly.

Black stuff trickles into Mouse's beard like tar. Then he some-how forces himself to go on. "The other things in those woods will eat you like candy."

"I think that's a chance I'll have to take," Jack says, frown-ing. "There's a little boy somewhere—"

"Safe," Mouse whispers.

Jack raises his eyebrows, unsure if he's heard Mouse right. And even if he has, can he trust what he's heard? Mouse has some powerful, evil poison working in him. So far he's been able to withstand it, to communicate in spite of it, but—

"Safe for a little while," Mouse says. "Not from every-thing . . . there's things that might still get him, I suppose . . . but for the time being he's safe from Mr. Munching. Is that his name? Munching?"

"Munshun, I think. How do you know it?"

Mouse favors Jack with a smile of surpassing eeriness. It is the smile of a dying sibyl. Once more he manages to touch his forehead, and Jack notes with horror that the man's fingers are now melting into one another and turning black from the nails down. "Got it up here, man. Got it *alll* up here. Told you that. And listen: it's better the kid should get eaten by some giant bug or rock crab over there . . . where he is . . . than that you should die trying to rescue him. If you do that, the abbalah will wind up with the kid for sure. That's what your . . . your friend says."

"What friend?" Doc asks suspiciously.

"Never mind," Mouse says. "*Hollywood* knows. Don'tcha, Hollywood?"

Jack nods reluctantly. It's Speedy, of course. Or Parkus, if you prefer.

"Wait until tomorrow," Mouse says. "High noon, when the sun's strongest in both worlds. *Promise.*"

At first Jack can say nothing. He's torn, in something close to agony.

"It'd be almost full dark before you could get back out High-way 35 anyway," Bear Girl says quietly.

"And there's bad shit in those woods, all right," Doc says. "Makes the stuff in that *Blair Witch Project* look fuckin' tame. I don't think you want to try it in the dark. Not unless you got a death wish, that is."

"When you're done . . ." Mouse whispers. "When you're done . . . if any of you are left . . . burn the place to the ground. That hole. That tomb. Burn it to the ground, do you hear me? *Close the door.*"

"Yeah," Beezer says. "Heard and understood, buddy."

"Last thing," Mouse says. He's speaking directly to Jack now. "You may be able to find it . . . but I think I got something else you need. It's a word. It's powerful to you because of something you . . . you touched. Once a long time ago. I don't understand that part, but . . ."

"It's all right," Jack tells him. "I do. What's the word, Mouse?"

For a moment he doesn't think Mouse will, in the end, be able to tell him. Something is clearly struggling to keep him from saying the word, but in this struggle, Mouse comes out on top. It is, Jack thinks, very likely his life's last W.

*"D'yamba,"* Mouse says. "Now you, Hollywood. You say it."

*"D'yamba,"* Jack says, and a row of weighty paperbacks slides from one of the makeshift shelves at the foot of the couch. They hang there in the dimming air . . . hang . . . hang . . . and then drop to the floor with a crash.

Bear Girl voices a little scream.

"Don't forget it," Mouse says. "You're gonna need it."

"How? *How* am I going to need it?"

Mouse shakes his head wearily. "Don't . . . know."

Beezer reaches over Jack's shoulder and takes the pitiful little scribble of map. "You're going to meet us tomorrow morning at the Sand Bar," he tells Jack. "Get there by eleven-thirty, and we should be turning into that goddamned lane right around noon. In the meantime, maybe I'll just hold on to this. A little insurance policy to make sure you do things Mouse's way."

"Okay," Jack says. He doesn't need the map to find Chummy Burnside's Black House, but Mouse is almost certainly right: it's probably not the sort of place you want to tackle after dark. He hates to leave Ty Marshall in the furnace-lands—it feels wrong in a way that's almost sinful—but he has to remember that there's more at stake here than one little boy lost.

"Beezer, are you sure you want to go back there?"

"Hell no, I don't want to go back," Beezer says, almost indignantly. "But something killed my daughter—my *daughter!*—and it got *here* from *there!* You want to tell me you don't know that's true?"

Jack makes no reply. Of course it's true. And of course he wants Doc and the Beez with him when he turns up the lane to Black House. If they can bear to come, that is.

*D'yamba,* he thinks. *D'yamba. Don't forget.*

He turns back to the couch. "Mouse, do you—"

"No," Doc says. "Guess he won't need the Cadillac dope, after all."

"Huh?" Jack peers at the big brewer-biker stupidly. He *feels* stupid. Stupid and exhausted.

"Nothin' tickin' but his watch," Doc says, and then he begins to sing. After a moment Beezer joins in, then Bear Girl. Jack steps away from the couch with a thought queerly similar to Henry's: How did it get late so early? Just how in hell did that happen?

"In heaven, there is no beer . . . that's why we drink it here . . . and when . . . we're gone . . . from here . . ."

Jack tiptoes across the room. On the far side, there's a lighted Kingsland Premium Golden Pale Ale bar clock. Our old friend—who is finally looking every year of his age and not quite so lucky—peers at the time with disbelief, not accepting it until he has compared it to his own watch. Almost eight. He has been here for *hours.*

Almost dark, and the Fisherman still out there someplace. Not to mention his otherworldly playmates.

*D'yamba,* he thinks again as he opens the door. And, as he steps out onto the splintery porch and closes the door behind him, he speaks aloud with great sincerity into the darkening day: "Speedy, I'd like to wring your neck."

# 24

D'YAMBA is a bright and powerful spell; powerful connections form a web that extends, ramifying, throughout infinity. When Jack Sawyer peels the living poison from Mouse's eyes, *d'yamba* first shines within the dying man's mind, and that mind momentarily expands into knowledge; down the filaments of the web flows some measure of its shining strength, and soon a touch of *d'yamba* reaches Henry Leyden. Along the way, the *d'yamba* brushes Tansy Freneau, who, seated in a windowed alcove of the Sand Bar, observes a wry, beautiful young woman take smiling shape in the pool of light at the far end of the parking lot and realizes, a moment before the young woman vanishes, that she has been given a glimpse of the person her Irma would have become; and it touches Dale Gilbertson, who while driving home from the station experiences a profound, sudden yearning for the presence of Jack Sawyer, a yearning like an ache in his heart, and vows to pursue the Fisherman case to the end with him, no matter what the obstacles; the *d'yamba* quivers flashing down a filament to Judy Marshall and opens a window into Faraway, where Ty sleeps in an iron-colored cell, awaiting rescue *and still alive;* within Charles Burnside, it touches the true Fisherman, Mr. Munshun, once known as the Monday Man, just as Burny's knuckles rap the glass. Mr. Munshun feels a subtle drift of cold air infiltrate his chest like a warning, and freezes with rage and hatred at this violation; Charles Burnside, who knows nothing of *d'yamba* and cannot hate it, picks up his master's emotion and remembers the time when a boy supposed dead in Chicago crept out of a canvas sack and soaked the back seat of his car in incriminating blood. *Damnably* incriminating blood, a substance that continued to mock him long after he had washed away its visible traces. But Henry Leyden, with whom we began this chain, is visited not by grace or rage; what touches Henry is a kind of informed clarity.

Rhoda's visits, he realizes, were one and all produced by his loneliness. The only thing he heard climbing the steps was his unending need for his wife. And the being on the other side of his studio door is the horrible old man from Maxton's, who intends to do to Henry the same thing he has done to three children. Who else would appear at this hour and knock on the studio window? Not Dale, not Jack, and certainly not Elvena Morton. Everyone else would stay outside and ring the doorbell.

It takes Henry no more than a couple of seconds to consider his options and work out a rudimentary plan. He supposes himself both quicker and stronger than the Fisherman, who sounded like a man in his mid- to late eighties; and the Fisherman does not know that his would-be victim is aware of his identity. To take advantage of this situation, Henry has to appear puzzled but amiable, as if he is merely curious about his visitor. And once he opens the studio door, which unfortunately he has left unlocked, he will have to act with speed and decisiveness.

*Are we up to this?* Henry asks himself, and thinks, *We'd better be.*

Are the lights on? No; because he expected to be alone, he never bothered with the charade of switching them on. The question then becomes: How dark is it outside? Maybe not quite dark enough, Henry imagines—an hour later, he would be able to move through the house entirely unseen and escape through the back door. Now his odds are probably no better than fifty-fifty, but the sun is sinking at the back of his house, and every second he can delay buys him another fraction of darkness in the living room and kitchen.

Perhaps two seconds have passed since the lurking figure rapped on the window, and Henry, who has maintained the perfect composure of one who failed to hear the sound made by his visitor, can stall no longer. Pretending to be lost in thought, with one hand he grips the base of a heavy Excellence in Broadcasting award accepted in absentia by George Rathbun some years before and with the other scoops from a shallow tray before him a switchblade an admirer once left at the university radio station as a tribute to the Wisconsin Rat. Henry uses the knife to unwrap CD jewel boxes, and not long ago, in search of something to do with his hands, he taught himself how to sharpen it. With its blade retracted, the knife resembles an odd, flat fountain pen. Two weapons are twice as good as one, he thinks, especially if your adversary imagines the second weapon to be harmless.

Now it has been four seconds since the rapping came from the window by his side, and in their individual ways both Burny and Mr. Munshun have grown considerably more restive. Mr. Munshun recoils in loathing from the suggestion of *d'yamba* that has somehow contaminated this otherwise delightful scene. Its appearance can mean one thing only, that some person connected to the blind man managed to get close enough to Black House to have tasted the poisons of its ferocious guardian. And that in turn means that now the hateful Jack Sawyer undoubtedly knows of the existence of Black House and intends to breach its defenses. It is time to destroy the blind man and return home.

Burny registers only an inchoate mixture of hatred and an emotion surprisingly like fear from within his master. Burny feels rage at Henry Leyden's appropriation of his voice, for he knows it represents a threat; even more than this self-protective impulse, he feels a yearning for the simple but profound pleasure of bloodletting. When Henry has been butchered, Charles Burnside wishes to claim one more victim before flying to Black House and entering a realm he thinks of as Sheol.

His big, misshapen knuckles rap once more against the glass.

Henry turns his head to the window in a flawless imitation of mild surprise. "I *thought* someone was out there. Who is it? . . . Come on, speak up." He toggles a switch and speaks into the mike: "If you're saying anything, I can't hear you. Give me a second or two to get organized in here, and I'll be right out." He faces forward again and hunches over his desk. His left hand seems idly to touch his handsome award; his right hand is hidden from sight. Henry appears to be deep in concentration. In reality, he is listening as hard as he ever has in his life.

He hears the handle on the studio door revolve clockwise with a marvelous slowness. The door whispers open an inch, two inches, three. The floral, musky scent of My Sin invades the studio, seeming to coat a thin chemical film over the mike, the tape canisters, all the dials, and the back of Henry's deliberately exposed neck. The sole of what sounds like a carpet slipper hushes over the floor. Henry tightens his hands on his weapons and waits for the particular sound that will be his signal. He hears another nearly soundless step, then another, and knows the Fisherman has moved behind him. He carries some weapon of his own, something that cuts through the mist of perfume with the grassy smell of front yards and the smoothness of machine oil. Henry cannot imagine what this is, but the movement of the air tells him it is heavier than a knife. Even a blind man can see that. An awkwardness in the way the Fisherman takes his next oh-so-quiet step suggests to Henry that the old fellow holds this weapon with both of his hands.

An image has formed in Henry's mind, that of his adversary standing behind him poised to strike, and to this image he now adds extended, upraised arms. The hands hold an instrument like garden shears. Henry has his own weapons, the best of these being surprise, but the surprise must be well timed to be effective. In fact, if Henry is to avoid a quick and messy death, his timing has to be perfect. He lowers his neck farther over the desk and awaits the signal. His calm surprises him.

A man standing unobserved with an object like garden shears or a heavy pair of scissors in his hands behind a seated victim will, before delivering the blow, take a long second to arch his back and reach up, to get a maximum of strength into the downward stroke. As he extends his arms and arches his back, his clothing will shift on his body. Fabric will slide over flesh; one fabric may pull against another; a belt may creak. There will be an intake of breath. An ordinary person would hear few or none of these telltale disturbances, but Henry Leyden can be depended upon to hear them all.

Then at last he does. Cloth rubs against skin and rustles against itself; air hisses into Burny's nasal passages. Instantly, Henry shoves his chair backward and in the same movement spins around and swings the award toward his assailant as he stands upright. It works! He feels the force of the blow run down his arm and hears a grunt of shock and pain. The odor of My Sin fills his nostrils. The chair bumps the top of his knees. Henry pushes the button on the switchblade, feels the long blade leap out, and thrusts it forward. The knife punches into flesh. From eight inches before his face comes a scream of outrage. Again, Henry batters the award against his attacker, then yanks the knife free and shoves it home again. Skinny arms tangle around his neck and shoulders, filling him with revulsion, and foul breath washes into his face.

He becomes aware that he has been injured, for a pain that is sharp on the surface and dull beneath announces itself on the left side of his back. *The goddamn hedge clippers,* he thinks and jabs again with the knife. This time, he stabs only empty air. A rough hand closes on his elbow, and another grips his shoulder. The hands pull him forward, and to keep upright he rests his knee on the seat of the chair. A long nose bangs against the bridge of his own nose and jars his sunglasses. What follows fills him with disgust: two rows of teeth like broken clamshells fasten on his left cheek and saw through the skin. Blood sluices down his face. The rows of teeth come together and rip away an oval wedge of Henry's skin, and over the white jolt of pain, which is incredible, worse by far than the pain in his back, he can hear his blood spatter against the old monster's face. Fear and revulsion, along with an amazing amount of adrenaline, give him the strength to lash out with the knife as he spins away from the man's grip. The blade connects with some moving part of the Fisherman's body—an arm, he thinks.

Before he can feel anything like satisfaction, he hears the sound of the hedge clippers slicing the air before they bite into his knife hand. It happens almost before he can take it in: the hedge clippers' blades tear through his skin, snap the bones, and sever the last two fingers on his right hand.

And then, as if the hedge clippers were the Fisherman's last contact with him, he is free. Henry's foot finds the edge of the door, kicks it aside, and he propels his body through the open space. He lands on a floor so sticky his feet slide when he tries to get up. Can all of that blood be his?

The voice he had been studying in another age, another era, comes from the studio door. "You stabbed me, you asswipe moke."

Henry is not waiting around to listen; Henry is on the move, wishing he did not feel that he was leaving a clear, wide trail of blood behind him. Somehow, he seems to be drenched in the stuff, his shirt is sodden with it, and the back of his legs are wet. Blood continues to gush down his face, and in spite of the adrenaline, Henry can feel his energy dissipating. How much time does he have before he bleeds to death—twenty minutes?

He slides down the hallway and runs into the living room.

*I'm not going to get out of this,* Henry thinks. *I've lost too much blood. But at least I can make it through the door and die outside, where the air is fresh.*

From the hallway, the Fisherman's voice reaches him. "I ate part of your cheek, and now I'm going to eat your fingers. Are you listening to me, you moke of an asshole?"

Henry makes it to the door. His hand slips and slips on the knob; the knob resists him. He feels for the lock button, which has been depressed.

"I said, are you *listening*?" The Fisherman is coming closer, and his voice is full of rage.

All Henry has to do is push the button that unlocks the door and turn the knob. He could be out of the house in a second, but his remaining fingers will not obey orders. *All right, I'm going to die,* he says to himself. *I'll follow Rhoda, I'll follow my Lark, my beautiful Lark.*

A sound of chewing, complete with smacking lips and crunching noises. "You taste like shit. I'm eating your fingers, and they taste like shit. You know what I like? Know my all-time favorite meal? The buttocks of a tender young child. Albert Fish liked that, too, oh yes he did. *Mmm-mmm!* BABY BUTT! That's GOOD EATIN'!"

Henry realizes that he has somehow slipped all the way down the unopenable door and is now resting, breathing far too heavily, on his hands and knees. He shoves himself forward and crawls behind the Mission-style sofa, from the comfort of which he had listened to Jack Sawyer reading a great many eloquent words written by Charles Dickens. Among the things he would now never be able to do, he realizes, is find out what finally happens in *Bleak House.* Another is seeing his friend Jack again.

The Fisherman's footsteps enter the living room and stop

moving. "All right, where the fuck are you, asshole? You can't hide from me." The hedge clippers' blades go *snick-snick*.

Either the Fisherman has grown as blind as Henry, or the room is too dark for vision. A little bit of hope, a match flame, flares in Henry's soul. Maybe his adversary will not be able to see the light switches.

"Asshole!" *Ahzz-hill.* "Damn it, where are you hiding?" *Dahmmut, vhey ah you high-dung?*

This is fascinating, Henry thinks. The more angry and frustrated the Fisherman gets, the more his accent melts into that weird non-German. It isn't the South Side of Chicago anymore, but neither is it anything else. It certainly isn't German, not really. If Henry had heard Dr. Spiegleman's description of this accent as that of a Frenchman trying to speak English like a German, he would have nodded in smiling agreement. It's like some kind of *outer space* German accent, like something that mutated toward German without ever having heard it.

"You hurt me, you stinking pig!" *You huhht me, you steenk-ung peek!*

The Fisherman lurches toward the easy chair and shoves it over on its side. In his Chicago voice, he says, "I'm gonna find you, buddy, and when I do, I'll cut your fucking head off."

A lamp hits the floor. The slippered footsteps move heavily toward the right side of the room. "A blind guy hides in the dark, huh? Oh, that's cute, that's really cute. Lemme tell you something. I haven't tasted a tongue in a while, but I think I'll try yours." A small table and the lamp atop it clunk and crash to the floor. "I got some information for you. Tongues are funny. An old guy's doesn't taste much different from a young fella's—though of course the tongue on a kid is twice as good as both. *Venn I vas Fridz Hahhmun I ade munny dungs, ha ha.*"

Strange—that extraterrestrial version of a German accent bursts out of the Fisherman like a second voice. A fist strikes the wall, and the footsteps plod nearer. Using his elbows, Henry crawls around the far end of the sofa and squirms toward the shelter of a long, low table. The footsteps squish in blood, and when Henry rests his head on his hands, warm blood pumps out against his face. The fiery agony in his fingers almost swallows the pain in his cheek and his back.

"You can't hide forever," the Fisherman says. Immediately,

he switches to the weird accent and replies, *"Eenuff ov dis, Burn-Burn. Vee huv murr impurdund vurk zu do."*

"Hey, you're the one who called him an *ahzz-hill*. He *hurt* me!"

*"Fogzes down fogzhulls, oho, radz in radhulls, dey too ahh huhht. My boor loss babbies ahh huhht, aha, vurze vurze vurze dan uz."*

"But what about him?"

*"Hee iz bledding zu deff, bledding zu deff, aha. Led hum dy."*

In the darkness, we can just make out what is happening. Charles Burnside appears to be performing an eerie imitation of the two heads of Parkus's parrot, Sacred and Profane. When he speaks in his own voice, he turns his head to the left; when speaking with the accent of an extraterrestrial, he looks to his right. Watching his head swivel back and forth, we might be watching a comic actor like Jim Carrey or Steve Martin pretending to be the two halves of a split personality—except that this man is not funny. Both of his personalities are awful, and their voices hurt our ears. The greatest difference between them is that left-head, the guttural extraterrestrial, runs the show: his hands hold the wheel of the other's vehicle, and right-head—our Burny—is essentially a slave. Since the difference between them has become so clear, we begin to get the impression that it will not be long before Mr. Munshun peels off Charles Burnside and discards him like a worn-out sock.

"But I WANT to kill him!" Burny screeches.

*"Hee iz alreddy dud, dud, dud. Chack Zawyuh's hardt iz go-ung do break. Chack Zawyuh vill nod know whud he iz do-ung. Vee go now du Muxtun'z and oho vee kull Chibbuh, yuzz? You vahhnd kull Chibbuh I ding, yuzz?"*

Burny snickers. "Yeah. I *vahhnd* to kill Chipper. I *vahhnd* to slice that asshole into little pieces and chew on his bones. And if his snippy bitch is there, I want to cut off her head and suck her juicy little tongue down my throat."

To Henry Leyden, this conversation sounds like insanity, demonic possession, or both. Blood continues to stream out of his back and from the ends of his mutilated fingers, and he is powerless to stop the flow. The smell of all the blood beneath and around him makes him feel nauseated, but nausea is the least of his problems. A light-headed sense of drift, of pleasing numbness—that is his real problem, and his best weapon against it is his own pain. He must remain conscious. Somehow, he must leave a message for Jack.

*"Zo vee go now, Burn-Burn, and vee hahhv ah blesh-ah vid Chibbuh, yuzz? End denn . . . oho end denn, denn, denn vee go do de beeyoodiful beeyoodiful Blagg Huzz, my Burn-Burn, end in Blagg Huzz vee mayyg reddy for de Grimsunn Ging!"*

"I *want* to meet the Crimson King," Burny says. A rope of drool sags from his mouth, and for an instant his eyes gleam in the darkness. "I'm gonna give the Marshall brat *to* the Crimson King, and the Crimson King is gonna love me, because all I'm gonna eat is like one little ass cheek, one little hand, something like that."

*"Hee vill lahhv you fuhr my zake, Burn-Burn, fuhr de Ging lahhvs mee bezzd, mee, mee, mee, Mizz-durr Munn-shunn! End venn de Ging roolz sooprumm, fogzes down fogzhulls veep and veep, dey gryy, gryy, gryy dere liddul hardz utt, on-cuzz you end mee, mee, mee, vee vull eed end eed end eed, eed, eed undill de vurrldz on all zydes are nudding bahd embdy bee-nudd shillz!"*

"Empty peanut shells." Burny chuckles, and noisily retracts another rope of slobber. "That's a hell of a lot of eatin'."

Any second now, Henry thinks, horrible old Burn-Burn is going to fork over a substantial down payment on the Brooklyn Bridge.

*"Gumm."*

"I'm coming," says Burnside. "First I want to leave a message."

There is a silence.

The next thing Henry hears is a curious whooshing sound and the joined *smack-smacks* of sodden footwear parting from a sticky floor. The door to the closet beneath the stairs bangs open; the studio door bangs shut. A smell of ozone comes and goes. They have gone; Henry does not know how it happened, but he feels certain that he is alone. Who cares how it happened? Henry has more important matters to think about. *"Murr impurdund vurk,"* he says aloud. "That guy's a German like I'm a speckled hen."

He crawls out from beneath the long table and uses its surface to lever himself up on his feet. When he straightens his back, his mind wobbles and goes gray, and he grasps a lampstand to stay upright. "Don't pass out," he says. "Passing out is not allowed, nope."

Henry can walk, he is sure of it. He's been walking most of his life, after all. Come to that, he can drive a car, too; driving is even easier than walking, only no one ever had the *cojones* to let him demonstrate his talents behind the wheel. Hell, if Ray Charles could drive—and he *could,* he *can,* Ray Charles is probably spinning into a left turn off the highway *at this moment*—why not Henry Leyden? Well, Henry does not happen to have an automobile available to him right now, so Henry is going to have to settle for taking a brisk walk. Well, as brisk as possible anyhow.

And where is Henry going on this delightful stroll through the blood-soaked living room? "Why," he answers himself, "the answer is obvious. I am going to my studio. I feel like taking a stroll into my lovely little studio."

His mind slides into gray once more, and gray is to be avoided. We have an antidote for the gray feeling, don't we? Yes, we do: the antidote is a good sharp taste of pain. Henry slaps his good hand against the stumps of his severed fingers—whoo boy, yes indeed, whole arm sort of went up in flames there. Flaming arm, that will work. Sparks shooting white hot from burning fingers *will* get us to the studio.

Let those tears flow. Dead folks don't cry.

"The smell of blood is like laughter," Henry says. "Who said that? Somebody. It's in a book. 'The smell of blood was like laughter.' Great line. Now put one foot in front of the other."

When he reaches the short hallway to the studio, he leans against the wall for a moment. A wave of luxurious weariness begins at the center of his chest and laps through his body. He snaps his head up, blood from his torn cheek spattering the wall. "Keep talking, you dope. Talking to yourself isn't crazy. It's a wonderful thing to do. And guess what? It's how you make your living—you talk to yourself all day long!"

Henry pushes himself off the wall, steps forward, and George Rathbun speaks through his vocal cords. "Friends, and you ARE my friends, let me be clear about that, we here at KDCU-AM seem to be experiencing some technical difficulties. The power levels are sinking, and brownouts have been recorded, yes they have. Fear not, my dear ones. Fear *not!* Even as I speak, we are but four paltry feet from the studio door, and in no time at all, we shall be up and running, yessir. No ancient cannibal and his space-alien sidekick can put this station out of business, uh-UHH, not before we make our last and final broadcast."

It is as if George Rathbun gives life to Henry Leyden, instead of the other way around. His back is straighter, and he holds his head upright. Two steps bring him to the closed studio door. "It's a tough catch, my friends, and if Pokey Reese is going to snag that ball, his mitt had better be clean as a whistle. What is he doing out there, folks? Can we believe our eyes? Can he be shoving one hand into his pants pocket? Is he pulling something out? Man oh man, it causes the mind to reel. . . . Pokey is using THE OLD HANDKERCHIEF PLOY! That's right! He is WIPING his mitt, WIPING his throwing hand, DROPPING the snotrag, GRABBING the handle. . . . And the door is OPEN! Pokey Reese has done it again, he is IN THE STUDIO!"

Henry winds the handkerchief around the ends of his fingers and fumbles for the chair. "And Rafael Furcal seems lost out there, the man is GROPING for the ball. . . . Wait, wait, does he have it? Has he caught an edge? YES! He has the ARM of the ball, he has the BACK of the ball, and he pulls it UP, ladies and gents, the ball is UP on its WHEELS! Furcal sits down, he pushes himself toward the console. We're facing a lot of blood here, but baseball is a bloody game when they come at you with their CLEATS up."

With the fingers of his left hand, from which most of the blood has been cleaned, Henry punches the ON switch for the big tape recorder and pulls the microphone close. He is sitting in the dark listening to the sound of tape hissing from reel to reel, and he feels oddly satisfied to be here, doing what he has done night after night for thousands of nights. Velvety exhaustion swims through his body and his mind, darkening whatever it touches. It is too early to yield. He will surrender soon, but first he must do his job. He must talk to Jack Sawyer by talking to himself, and to do that he calls upon the familiar spirits that give him voice.

George Rathbun: "Bottom of the ninth, and the home team is headed for the showers, pal. But the game ain't OVER till the last BLIND man is DEAD!"

Henry Shake: "I'm talking to *you*, Jack Sawyer, and I don't want you to flip out on me or nothin'. Keep cool and listen to your old friend Henry the Sheik the Shake the Shook, all right? The Fisherman paid me a visit, and when he left here he was on his way to Maxton's. He wants to kill Chipper, the guy who owns the place. Call the police, save him if you can. The Fisherman lives at Maxton's, did you know that? He's an old man with a demon inside him. He wanted to stop me from telling you that I recognized his voice. And he wanted to mess with your feelings—he thinks he can screw you up by killing me. Don't give him that satisfaction, all right?"

The Wisconsin Rat: *"BECAUSE THAT WOULD REALLY SUCK! FISH-BRAINS WILL BE WAITING FOR YOU IN A PLACE CALLED BLACK HOUSE, AND YOU HAVE TO BE READY FOR THE BASTARD! RIP HIS NUTS OFF!"*

The Rat's buzz-saw voice ends in a fit of coughing.

Henry Shake, breathing hard: "Our friend the Rat was suddenly called away. The boy has a tendency to get overexcited."

George Rathbun: "SON, are you trying to tell ME that—"

Henry Shake: "Calm down. Yes, he has a right to be excited. But Jack doesn't want us to scream at him. Jack wants information."

George Rathbun: "I reckon you better hurry up and give it to him, then."

Henry Shake: "This is the deal, Jack. The Fisherman's not very bright, and neither is his whatever, his demon, who's called something like Mr. Munching. He's incredibly vain, too."

Henry Leyden folds back into the chair and stares at nothing for a second or two. He can feel nothing from the waist down, and blood from his right hand has pooled around the microphone. From the stumps of his fingers comes a steady, diminishing pulse.

George Rathbun: "Not *now,* Chuckles!"

Henry Leyden shakes his head and says, "Vain and stupid you can beat, my friend. I have to sign off now. Jack, you don't have to feel too bad about me. I had a goddamn wonderful life, and I'm going to be with my darling Rhoda now." He smiles in the darkness; his smile widens. "Ah, Lark. Hello."

At times, it is possible for the smell of blood to be like laughter.

What is this, at the end of Nailhouse Row? A horde, a swarm of fat, buzzing things that circle and dart about Jack Sawyer, in the dying light seeming almost *illuminated,* like the radiant pages of a sacred text. Too small to be hummingbirds, they seem to carry their own individual, internal glow as they mesh through the air. If they are wasps, Jack Sawyer is going to be in serious trouble. Yet they do not sting; their round bodies brush his face and hands, blundering softly against his body as a cat will nudge its owner's leg, both giving and receiving comfort.

At present, they give much more comfort than they receive, and even Jack cannot explain why this should be so. The creatures surrounding him are not wasps, hummingbirds, or cats, but they *are* bees, honeybees, and ordinarily he would be frightened to be caught in a swarm of bees. Especially if they appeared to be members of a sort of master bee race, superbees, larger than any he has seen before, their golds more golden, their blacks vibrantly black. Yet Jack is not frightened. If they were going to sting him, they would already have done it. And from the first, he understood that they meant him no harm. The touch of their many bodies is surpassingly smooth and soft; their massed buzzing is low and harmonious, as peaceable as a Protestant hymn. After the first few seconds, Jack simply lets it happen.

The bees sift even closer, and their low noise pulses in his ears. It sounds like speech, or like song. For a moment, all he can see is a tightly woven network of bees moving this way and that; then the bees settle everywhere on his body but the oval of his face. They cover his head like a helmet. They blanket his arms, his chest, his back, his legs. Bees land on his shoes and obscure them from view. Despite their number, they are almost weightless. The exposed parts of Jack's body, his hands and neck, feel as though wrapped in cashmere. A dense, feather-light bee suit shimmers black and gold all over Jack Sawyer. He raises his arms, and the bees move with him.

Jack has seen photographs of beekeepers aswarm with bees, but this is no photograph and he is no beekeeper. His amazement—really, his sheer pleasure in the unexpectedness of this visitation—stuns him. For as long as the bees cling to him, he forgets Mouse's terrible death and the next day's fearsome task. What he does not forget is Sophie; he wishes Beezer and Doc would walk outside, so they could see what is happening, but more than that, he wishes Sophie could see it. Perhaps, by grace of *d'yamba,* she does. Someone is comforting Jack Sawyer, someone is wishing him well. A loving, invisible presence offers him support. It feels like a blessing, that support. Clothed in his glowing black-and-yellow bee suit, Jack has the idea that if he stepped toward the sky, he would be airborne. The bees would carry him over the valleys. They would carry him over the wrinkled hills. Like the winged men in the Territories who carried Sophie, he would fly. Instead of their two, he would have two thousand wings to bear him up.

In our world, Jack remembers, bees return to the hive before nightfall. As if reminded of their daily routine, the bees lift from Jack's head, his trunk, his arms and legs, not en masse, like a living carpet, but individually and in parties of five and six, wander a short distance above him, then swirl around, shoot like bullets eastward over the houses on the inland side of Nailhouse Row, and disappear one and all into the same dark infinity. Jack becomes aware of their sound only when it disappears with them.

In the seconds before he can once again begin moving toward his truck, he has the feeling that someone is watching over him. He has been . . . what? It comes to him as he turns his key in the Ram's ignition and flutters the gas pedal: he has been embraced.

Jack has no idea how much he will need the warmth of that embrace, nor of the manner in which it shall be returned to him, during the coming night.

First of all, he is exhausted. He has had the kind of day that *should* end in a surreal event like an embrace by a swarm of bees: Sophie, Wendell Green, Judy Marshall, Parkus—that cataclysm, that deluge!—and the strange death of Mouse Baumann, these things have stretched him taut, left him gasping.

His body aches for rest. When he leaves French Landing and drives into the wide, dark countryside, he is tempted to pull over to the side of the road and catch a half-hour nap. The deepening night promises the refreshment of sleep, and that is the problem: he could wind up sleeping in the truck all night, which would leave him feeling bleary and arthritic on a day when he must be at his best.

Right now, he is not at his best—not by a longshot, as his father, Phil Sawyer, used to say. Right now he is running on fumes, another of Phil Sawyer's pet expressions, but he figures that he can stay awake long enough to visit Henry Leyden. Maybe Henry cut a deal with the guy from ESPN—maybe Henry will move into a wider market and make a lot more money. Henry in no way needs any more money than he has, for Henry's life seems flawless, but Jack likes the idea of his dear friend Henry suddenly flush with cash. A Henry with extra money to throw around is a Henry Jack would love to see. Imagine the wondrous clothes he could afford! Jack pictures going to New York with him, staying in a nice hotel like the Carlyle or the St. Regis, walking him through half a dozen great men's stores, helping him pick out whatever he wants.

Just about everything looks good on Henry. He seems to improve all the clothes he wears, no matter what they are, but he has definite, particular tastes. Henry likes a certain classic, even old-fashioned, stylishness. He often dresses himself in pinstripes, windowpane plaids, herringbone tweeds. He likes cotton, linen, and wool. He sometimes wears bow ties, ascots, and little handkerchiefs that puff out of his breast pocket. On his feet, he puts penny loafers, wing tips, cap toes, and low boots of soft, fine leather. He never wears sneakers or jeans, and Jack has never seen him in a T-shirt that has writing on it. The question was, how did a man blind from birth evolve such a specific taste in clothing?

*Oh,* Jack realizes, *it was his mother. Of course. He got his taste from his mother.*

For some reason, this recognition threatens to bring tears to Jack's eyes. *I get too emotional when I get this tired,* he says to himself. *Watch out, or you'll go overboard.* But diagnosing a problem is not the same as fixing it, and he cannot follow his own advice. That Henry Leyden all of his life should have held to his mother's ideas about men's clothing strikes Jack as beautiful and moving. It implies a kind of loyalty he admires—unspoken loyalty. Henry probably got a lot from his mother: his quick-wittedness, his love of music, his levelheadedness, his utter lack of self-pity. Levelheadedness and lack of self-pity are a great combination, Jack thinks; they go a long way toward defining courage.

For Henry *is* courageous, Jack reminds himself. Henry is damn near fearless. It's funny, how he talks about being able to drive a car, but Jack feels certain that, if allowed, his friend would unhesitatingly jump behind the wheel of the nearest Chrysler, start the engine, and take off for the highway. He would not exult or show off, such behavior being foreign to his nature; Henry would nod toward the windshield and say things like, "Looks like the corn is nice and tall for this time of year," and "I'm glad Duane finally got around to painting his house." And the corn would be tall, and Duane Updahl would have recently painted his house, information delivered to Henry by his mysterious sensory systems.

Jack decides that if he makes it out of Black House alive, he will give Henry the opportunity to take the Ram out for a spin. They might wind up nose-down in a ditch, but it will be worth it for the expression on Henry's face. Some Saturday afternoon, he'll get Henry out on Highway 93 and let him drive to the Sand Bar. If Beezer and Doc do not get savaged by weredogs and survive their journey to Black House, they ought to have the chance to enjoy Henry's conversation, which, odd as it seems, is perfectly suited to theirs. Beezer and Doc *should* know Henry Leyden, they'd love the guy. After a couple of weeks, they'd have him up on a Harley, swooping toward Norway Valley from Centralia.

If only *Henry* could come with them to Black House. The thought pierces Jack with the sadness of an inspired idea that can never be put into practice. Henry would be brave and unfaltering, Jack knows, but what he most likes about the idea is that he and Henry would ever after be able to talk about what they had done. Those talks—the two of them, in one living room or another, snow piling on the roof—would be wonderful, but Jack cannot endanger Henry that way.

"That's a stupid thing to think about," Jack says aloud, and realizes that he regrets not having been completely open and unguarded with Henry—that's where the stupid worry comes from, his stubborn silence. It isn't what he will be unable to say in the future; it's what he failed to say in the past. He should have been honest with Henry from the start. He should have told him about the red feathers and the robins' eggs and his gathering uneasiness. Henry would have helped him open his eyes; he would have helped Jack resolve his own blindness, which was more damaging than Henry's.

All of that is over, Jack decides. No more secrets. Since he is lucky enough to have Henry's friendship, he will demonstrate that he values it. From now on, he will tell Henry everything, including the background: the Territories, Speedy Parker, the dead man on the Santa Monica Pier, Tyler Marshall's baseball cap. Judy Marshall. Sophie. Yes, he has to tell Henry about Sophie—how can he not have done so already? Henry will rejoice with him, and Jack cannot wait to see how he does it. Henry's rejoicing will be unlike anyone else's; Henry will impart some delicate, cool, good-hearted topspin to the expression of his delight, thereby increasing Jack's own delight. What an incredible, *literally* incredible friend! If you were to describe Henry to someone who had never met him, he would sound unbelievable. Someone like *that,* living alone in an outback of the boonies? But there he was, all alone in the entirely obscure area of Norway Valley, French County, Wisconsin, waiting for the latest installment of *Bleak House.* By now, in anticipation of Jack's arrival, he would have turned on the lights in his kitchen and living room, as he had done for years in honor of his dead, much-loved wife.

Jack thinks: *I must not be so bad, if I have a friend like that.*

And he thinks: *I really adore Henry.*

Now, even in the darkness, everything seems beautiful to him. The Sand Bar, ablaze with neon lights in its vast expanse of parking lot; the spindly, intermittent trees picked out by his headlights after the turn onto 93; the long, invisible fields; the glowing light bulbs hung like Christmas decorations from the porch of Roy's Store. The rattle over the first bridge and the sharp turn into the depths of the valley. Set back from the left side of the road, the first of the farmhouses gleam in the darkness, the lights in their windows burning like sacramental candles. Everything seems touched by a higher meaning, everything seems to *speak.* He is traveling, within a hush of sacred silence, through a sacred grove. Jack remembers when Dale first drove him into this valley, and that memory is sacred, too.

Jack does not know it, but tears are coursing down his cheeks. His blood sings in his veins. The pale farmhouses shine half-hidden by the darkness, and out of that darkness leans the stand of tiger lilies that greeted him on his first down-valley journey. The tiger lilies blaze in his headlights, then slip murmuring behind him. Their lost speech joins the speech of the tires rolling eagerly, gently toward Henry Leyden's warm house. Tomorrow he may die, Jack knows, and this may be the last night he will ever see. That he *must* win does not mean that he *will* win; proud empires and noble epochs have gone down in defeat, and the Crimson King may burst out of the Tower and rage through world after world, spreading chaos.

They could all die in Black House: he, Beezer, and Doc. If that happens, Tyler Marshall will be not only a Breaker, a slave chained to an oar in a timeless Purgatory, but a super-Breaker, a nuclear-powered Breaker the abbalah will use to turn all the worlds into furnaces filled with burning corpses. *Over my dead body,* Jack thinks, and laughs a little crazily—it's so literal!

What an extraordinary moment; he is laughing while he rubs tears off his face. The paradox suddenly makes him feel as though he is being torn in half. Beauty and terror, beauty and pain—there is no way out of the conundrum. Exhausted, strung out, Jack cannot hold off his awareness of the world's essential fragility, its constant, unstoppable movement toward death, or the deeper awareness that in that movement lies the source of all its meaning. Do you see all this heart-stopping beauty? Look closely, because in a moment your heart *will* stop.

In the next second, he remembers the swarm of golden bees that descended upon him: it was against this that they comforted him, exactly this, he tells himself. The blessing of blessings that vanish. What you love, you must love all the harder because someday it will be gone. It felt true, but it did not feel like all of the truth.

Against the vastness of the night, he sees the giant shape of the Crimson King holding aloft a small boy to use as a burning glass that will ignite the worlds into flaming waste. What

Parkus said was right: he cannot destroy the giant, but he may find it possible to rescue the boy.

The bees said: *Save Ty Marshall.*

The bees said: *Love Henry Leyden.*

The bees said: *Love Sophie.*

That is close enough, right enough, for Jack. To the bees, these were all the same sentence. He supposes that the bees might well also have said, *Do your job, coppiceman,* and that sentence was only slightly different. Well, he would do his job, all right. After having been given such a miracle, he could do nothing else.

His heart warms as he turns up Henry's drive. What was Henry but another kind of miracle?

Tonight, Jack gleefully resolves, he is going to give the amazing Henry Leyden a thrill he will never forget. Tonight, he will tell Henry the whole story, the entire long tale of the journey he took in his twelfth year: the Blasted Lands, Rational Richard, the Agincourt, and the Talisman. He will not leave out the Oatley Tap and the Sunlight Home, for these travails will get Henry wonderfully worked up. And Wolf! Henry is going to be crazy about Wolf; Wolf will tickle him right down to the soles of his chocolate-brown suede loafers. As Jack speaks, every word he says will be an apology for having been silent for so long.

And when he has finished telling the whole story, telling it at least as well as he can, the world, this world, will have been transformed, for one person in it besides himself will know everything that happened. Jack can barely imagine what it will feel like to have the dam of his loneliness so *obliterated,* so *destroyed,* but the very thought of it floods him with the anticipation of relief.

Now, this is strange . . . Henry has not turned on his lights, and his house looks dark and empty. He must have fallen asleep.

Smiling, Jack turns off the engine and gets out of the pickup's cab. Experience tells him that he won't get more than three paces into the living room before Henry rouses himself and pretends that he has been awake all along. Once, when Jack found him in the dark like this, he said, "I was just resting my eyes." So what is it going to be tonight? He was planning his

Lester Young–Charlie Parker birthday tribute, and he found it easier to concentrate this way? He was thinking about frying up some fish, and he wanted to see if food tasted different if you cooked it in the dark? Whatever it is, it'll be entertaining. And maybe they will celebrate Henry's new deal with ESPN!

"Henry?" Jack raps on the door, then opens it and leans in. "Henry, you faker, are you asleep?"

Henry does not respond, and Jack's question falls into a soundless void. He can see nothing. The room is a two-dimensional pane of blackness. "Hey, Henry, I'm here. And boy, do I have a story for you!"

More dead silence. "Huh," Jack says, and steps inside. Immediately, his instincts scream that he should *get out, take off, scram.* But why should he feel that? This is just Henry's house, that's all; he has been inside it hundreds of times before, and he knows Henry has either fallen asleep on his sofa or walked over to Jack's house, which come to think of it is probably exactly what happened. Henry got a terrific offer from the ESPN representative, and in his excitement—for even Henry Leyden can get excited, you just have to look a little closer than you do with most people—decided to surprise Jack at his house. When Jack failed to arrive by five or six, he decided to wait for him. And right now, he is probably sound asleep on Jack's sofa, instead of his own.

All of this is plausible, but it does not alter the message blasting from Jack's nerve endings. *Go! Leave! You don't want to be here!*

He calls Henry's name again, and his response is the silence he expects.

The transcendent mood that had carried him down the valley has already disappeared, but he never noted its passing, merely that it is a thing of the past. If he were still a homicide detective, this is the moment when he would unholster his weapon. Jack steps quietly into the living room. Two strong odors come to him. One is the scent of perfume, and the other . . .

He knows what the other one is. Its presence here means that Henry is dead. The part of Jack that is not a cop argues that the smell of blood means no such thing. Henry may have been wounded in a fight, and the Fisherman could have taken him across worlds, as he did with Tyler Marshall. Henry may be trussed up in some pocket of the Territories, salted away to be used as a bargaining chip, or as bait. He and Ty might be side by side, waiting for rescue.

Jack knows that none of this is true. Henry is dead, and the Fisherman killed him. It is his job now to find the body. He's a coppiceman; he has to act like one. That the last thing in the world he wants to do is look at Henry's corpse does not change the nature of his task. Sorrow comes in many forms, but the kind of sorrow that has been building within Jack Sawyer feels as if it is made of granite. It slows his step and clenches his jaw. When he moves to his left and reaches for the light switch, this stony sorrow directs his hand to the right spot on the wall as surely as if he were Henry.

Because he is looking at the wall when the lights go on, only his peripheral vision takes in the interior of the room, and the damage does not seem as extensive as he had feared. A lamp has been toppled, a chair knocked over. But when Jack turns his head, two aspects of Henry's living room sear themselves onto his retinas. The first is a red slogan on the cream-colored opposite wall; the second, the sheer amount of blood on the floor. The bloodstains are like a map of Henry's progress into and back out of the room. Gouts of blood like those left by a wounded animal begin at the hallway and trail, accompanied by many loops and spatters, to the back of the Mission sofa, where blood lies pooled. Another large pool covers the hardwood floor beneath the long, low table where Henry sometimes used to park his portable CD player and stack the evening's CDs. From the table, another series of splashes and gouts lead back into the hallway. To Jack, it looks as though Henry must have been very low on blood when he felt safe enough to crawl out from under the table. *If* that is the way it went.

While Henry lay dead or dying, the Fisherman had taken something made of cloth—his shirt? a handkerchief?—and used it like a fat, unwieldy paintbrush. He had dipped it in the blood behind the sofa, raised it dripping to the wall, and daubed a few letters. Then he'd repeated and repeated the action until he had wiped the last letter of his message onto the wall.

HELLO HOLLYWOOD CUM GET MEE
CK CK CK CK

But the Crimson King had not written the taunting initials, and neither had Charles Burnside. They had been daubed on the wall by the Fisherman's master, whose name, in our ears, sounds like *Mr. Munshun.*

*Don't worry, I'll come for you soon enough,* Jack thinks.

At this point, he could not be criticized for walking outside, where the air does not reek of blood and perfume, and using his cell phone to call Sumner Street. Maybe Bobby Dulac is on duty. He might even find Dale still at the station. To fulfill all of his civic obligations, he need speak only eight or nine words. After that, he could pocket the cell phone and sit on Henry's front steps until the guardians of law and order come barreling up the long drive. There would be a lot of them, at least four cars, maybe five. Dale would have to call the troopers, and Brown and Black might feel obliged to call the FBI. In about forty-five minutes, Henry's living room would be crowded with men taking measurements, writing in their notebooks, setting down evidence tags, and photographing bloodstains. There would be the M.E. and the evidence wagon. And when the first stage of everybody's various jobs came to an end, two men in white jackets would carry a stretcher through the front door and load the stretcher into whatever the hell they were driving.

Jack does not consider this option for much longer than a couple of seconds. He wants to see what the Fisherman and Mr. Munshun did to Henry—he has to see it, he has no choice. His grim sorrow demands it, and if he does not obey his sorrow's commands, he will never feel quite whole again.

His sorrow, which is closed like a steel vault around his love for Henry Leyden, drives him deeper into the room. Jack moves slowly, picking his way forward the way a man crossing a stream moves from rock to rock. He is looking for the bare places where he can set his feet. From across the room, dripping red letters eight inches high mock his progress.

HELLO HOLLYWOOD

It seems to wink on and off, like a neon sign. HELLO HOL-
LYWOOD HELLO HOLLYWOOD.

CUM GET MEE
CUM GET MEE

He wants to curse, but the weight of his sorrow will not permit him to utter the words that float into his mind. At the end of
the hallway to the studio and the kitchen, Jack steps over a long
smear of blood and turns his back on the living room and the
distracting flashes of neon. The light penetrates only three or
four feet into the hallway. The kitchen is solid, featureless darkness. The studio door hangs half open, and reflected light shines
softly in its window.

Blood lies spattered and smeared everywhere on the floor of
the hallway. He can no longer avoid stepping in it but moves
down the hallway with his eyes on the gaping studio door. Henry
Leyden never left this door yawning into the little corridor; he
kept it closed. Henry was *neat*. He had to be: if he left the studio
door hanging open, he would walk right into it the next time he
went to the kitchen. The mess, the disorder left in his wake by
Henry's murderer disturbs Jack more than he wishes to admit,
maybe even more than he recognizes. This messiness represents
a true violation, and, on his friend's behalf, Jack hugely resents
it.

He reaches the door, touches it, opens it wider. A concentrated stench of perfume and blood hangs in the air. Nearly as
dark as the kitchen, the studio offers Jack only the dim shape of
the console and the murky rectangles of the speakers fixed to the
wall. The window into the kitchen hovers like a black sheet, invisible. His hand still on the door, Jack moves nearer and sees,
or thinks he sees, the back of a tall chair and a shape stretched
over the desk in front of the console. Only then does he hear the
*whup-whup-whup* of tape hitting the end of a reel.

"Ohmygod," Jack says, all in one word, as if he had all along
not been expecting something precisely like what is before him.
With a terrible, insistent certainty, the sound of the tape drives
home the fact that Henry is dead. Jack's sorrow overrides his
chickenhearted desire to go outside and call every cop in the

state of Wisconsin by compelling him to grope for the light switch. He cannot leave; he must witness, as he did with Irma Freneau.

His fingers brush against the down-ticked plastic switch and settle on it. Into the back of his throat rises a sour, brassy taste. He flicks the switch up, and light floods the studio.

Henry's body leans out of the tall leather chair and over the desk, his hands on either side of his prize microphone, his face flattened on its left side. He is still wearing his dark glasses, but one of the thin metal bows is bent. At first, everything seems to have been painted red, for the nearly uniform coat of blood covering the desk has been dripping onto Henry's lap and the tops of his thighs for some time, and all the equipment has been sprayed with red. Part of Henry's cheek has been bitten off. He is missing two fingers from his right hand. To Jack's eyes, which have been taking an inventory as they register all the details of the room, most of Henry's blood loss came from a wound in his back. Blood-soaked clothing conceals the injury, but as much blood lies pooled, dripping, at the back of the chair as covers the desk. Most of the blood on the floor came from the chair. The Fisherman must have sliced an internal organ, or severed an artery.

Very little blood, apart from a fine mist over the controls, has hit the tape recorder. Jack can hardly remember how these machines work, but he has seen Henry change reels often enough to have a sense of what to do. He turns the recorder off and threads the end of the tape into the empty reel. Then he turns the machine on and pushes REWIND. The tape glides smoothly over the heads, spooling from one reel to the other.

"Did you make a tape for me, Henry?" Jack asks. "I bet you did, but I hope you didn't die telling me what I already know."

The tape clicks to a stop. Jack pushes PLAY and holds his breath.

In all his bull-necked, red-faced glory, George Rathbun booms from the speakers. "Bottom of the ninth, and the home team is headed for the showers, pal. But the game ain't OVER till the last BLIND man is DEAD!"

Jack sags against the wall.

Henry Shake enters the room and tells him to call Maxton's. The Wisconsin Rat sticks his head in and screams about Black

House. The Sheik the Shake the Shook and George Rathbun have a short debate, which the Shake wins. It is too much for Jack; he cannot stop his tears, and he does not bother to try. He lets them come. Henry's last performance moves him enormously. It is so *bountiful,* so *pure*—so purely Henry. Henry Leyden kept himself alive by calling on his alternate selves, and they did the job. They were a faithful crew, George and the Shake and the Rat, and they went down with the ship, not that they had much choice. Henry Leyden reappears, and in a voice that grows fainter with each phrase, says that Jack can beat *vain and stupid.* Henry's dying voice says he had a wonderful life. His voice drops to a whisper and utters three words filled to the brim with gratified surprise: *Ah, Lark. Hello.* Jack can hear the smile in those words.

Weeping, Jack staggers out of the studio. He wants to collapse into a chair and cry until he has no more tears, but he cannot fail either himself or Henry so greatly. He moves down the hallway, wipes his eyes, and waits for the stony sorrow to help him deal with his grief. It will help him deal with Black House, too. The sorrow is not to be deterred or deflected; it works like steel in his spine.

The ghost of Henry Shake whispers: *Jack, this sorrow is never going to leave you. Are you down with that?*

—*Wouldn't have it any other way.*

*Just as long as you know. Wherever you go, whatever you do. Through every door. With every woman. If you have children, with your children. You'll hear it in all the music you listen to, you'll see it in every book you read. It will be part of the food you eat. With you forever. In all the worlds. In Black House.*

—*I am it, and it is me.*

George Rathbun's whisper is twice as loud as the Sheik the Shake the Shook's: *Well, damnit, son, can I hear you say D'YAMBA?*

—*D'yamba.*

*I reckon now you know why the bees embraced you. Don't you have a telephone call to make?*

Yes, he does. But he cannot bear to be in this blood-soaked house any longer; he needs to be out in the warm summer night. Letting his feet land where they may, Jack walks across the ruined living room and passes through the doorway. His sorrow

walks with him, for he is it and it is he. The enormous sky
hangs far above him, pierced with stars. Out comes the trusty
cell phone.

And who answers the telephone at the French Landing Police Station? Arnold "Flashlight" Hrabowski, of course, with a
new nickname and just reinstated as a member of the force.
Jack's news puts Flashlight Hrabowski in a state of high agitation. What? Gosh! Oh, no. Oh, who woulda believed it? Gee.
Yeah, yessir. I'll take care of that right away, you bet.

So while the former Mad Hungarian tries to keep both his
hands and voice from trembling as he dials the chief's home
number and passes on Jack's two-sided message, Jack himself
wanders away from the house, away from the drive and his
pickup truck, away from anything that reminds him of human
beings, and into a meadow filled with high, yellow-green
grasses. His sorrow leads him, for his sorrow knows better than
he what he needs.

Above all, he needs rest. Sleep, if sleep is possible. A soft
spot on level ground far from the coming uproar of red lights
and sirens and furious, hyperactive policemen. Far from all that
desperation. A place where a man can lay his head and get a
representative view of the local heavens. Half a mile down the
fields, Jack comes to such a place between a cornfield and the
rocky beginnings of the wooded hills. His sorrowing mind tells
his sorrowing, exhausted body to lie down and make itself comfortable, and his body obeys. Overhead, the stars seem to vibrate and blur, though of course real stars in the familiar, real
heavens do not act that way, so it must be an optical illusion.
Jack's body stretches out, and the pad of grass and topsoil beneath his body seems to adjust itself around him, although this,
too, must be an illusion, for everyone knows that in real life, the
actual ground tends to be obdurate, inflexible, and stony. Jack
Sawyer's sorrowing mind tells his sorrowing ache of a body to
fall asleep, and impossible as it may seem, fall asleep it does.

Within minutes, Jack Sawyer's sleeping body undergoes a
subtle transformation. Its edges seem to soften, its colors—his
wheaten hair, his light tan jacket, his soft brown shoes—grow
paler. An odd translucency, a mistiness or cloudiness, enters the
process. It is as if we can peer through the cloudy, indistinct

mass of his slow-breathing body to see the soft, crushed blades of grass that form its mattress. The longer we peer, the more clearly we can take in the grass beneath him, for his body is getting vaguer and vaguer. At last it is only a shimmer over the grass, and by the time the Jack-shaped pad of green has again straightened itself, the body that shaped it is long gone.

# 25

Oh, forget about that. We know where Jack Sawyer went when he disappeared from the edge of the cornfield, and we know who he is likely to meet when he gets there. Enough of that stuff. We want fun, we want excitement! Luckily for us, that charming old party Charles Burnside, who can always be depended upon to slip a whoopee cushion under the governor's seat during a banquet, to pour a little hot sauce into the stew, to fart at the prayer meeting, is at this moment emerging from a toilet bowl and into a stall in the men's room on Daisy wing. We note that Ol' Burny, our Burn-Burn, hugs Henry Leyden's hedge clippers to his sunken chest with both arms, actually cradling them, as if he were holding a baby. On his bony right arm, blood slides out of a nasty gash and rolls down toward his elbow. When he gets one foot, clad in another resident's bee slipper, on the rim of the bowl, he pushes himself up and steps out, wobbling a bit. His mouth is twisted into a scowl, and his eyes look like bullet holes, but we do not suppose that he, too, carries a weight of heavy-duty sorrow. Blood soaks the bottoms of his trousers and the front of his shirt, which has darkened with the flow of blood from a knife wound to his abdomen.

Wincing, Burny opens the door of the stall and walks out into the empty men's room. Fluorescent lights on the ceiling reflect from the long mirror above the row of sinks; thanks to Butch Yerxa, who is working a double shift because the regular night man called in drunk, the white tiles of the floor gleam. In all this sparkling whiteness, the blood on Charles Burnside's clothes and body looks radiantly red. He peels off his shirt and tosses it into a sink before plodding down to the far end of the bathroom and a cabinet marked with a piece of tape on which someone has printed BANDAGES. Old men have a tendency to fall down in their bathrooms, and Chipper's father thoughtfully installed the cabinet where he thought it might be needed. Drops of blood lay spattered across the white tiles.

Burny rips a handful of paper towels from a dispenser, dampens them with cold water, and lays them on the side of the nearest sink. Then he opens the bandage cabinet, removes a wide roll of tape and a wad of gauze bandages, and tears off a six-inch strip of the tape. He wipes blood off the skin around the wound in his belly and presses the wet paper towels over the opening. He lifts away the towels and presses a pad of gauze to the cut. Awkwardly, he flattens the strip of tape over the gauze. He dresses the stab wound on his arm in the same fashion.

Now swirls and scoops of blood cover the white tiles.

He moves up the row of sinks and runs cold water over his shirt. The water turns red in the bowl. Burny keeps scrubbing the old shirt under cold running water until it has turned a pale rose only a few shades brighter than his skin. Satisfied, he wrings the shirt in his hands, flaps it once or twice, and puts it back on. That it clings to him bothers Burny not at all. His goal is a very basic version of acceptability, not elegance: insofar as it is possible, he wants to pass unnoticed. His cuffs are soaked with blood, and Elmer Jesperson's slippers are dark red and wet, but he thinks most people will not bother to look at his feet.

Within him, a coarse voice keeps saying, *Fazzdur, Burn-Burn, fazzdur!*

Burny's only mistake is that, while buttoning up his damp shirt, he looks at himself in the mirror. What he sees stops him cold with shock. Despite his ugliness, Charles Burnside has always approved of the image returned to him by mirrors. In his opinion, he looks like a guy who knows where to find the corners—sly, unpredictable, and foxy. The man staring at him from the other side of the mirror is nothing like the canny old operator Burny remembered. The man facing him looks dim-witted, worn-out, and seriously ill. Sunken, red-rimmed eyes, cheeks like craters, veins crawling across his bald, skull-like crown . . . even his nose looks bonier and more twisted than it once had. He is the sort of old man who frightens children.

*You shud fry-den cheerun, Burn-Burn. Dime do ged moo-vuhn.*

He couldn't really look that bad, could he? If he did, he would have noticed long before this. Nah, that wasn't how Charles Burnside faced the world. The bathroom's too damn white, that's all. A white like that makes you look bleached. Makes you look skinned, like a rabbit. The dying old horror in the mirror takes a step nearer, and the spotty discolorations on his skin seem to darken. The spectacle of his teeth makes him close his mouth.

Then his master is like a fishhook in his mind, pulling him toward the door and muttering, *Dime, dime.*

Burny knows why it's *dime:* Mr. Munshun wants to get back to Black House. Mr. Munshun comes from some place incredibly distant from French Landing, and certain parts of Black House, which they built together, feel like the world of his home—the deepest parts, which Charles Burnside seldom visits, and which make him feel hypnotized, weak with longing, and sick to his stomach when he does. When he tries to picture the world that gave birth to Mr. Munshun, he envisions a dark, craggy landscape littered with skulls. On the bare slopes and peaks stand houses like castles that change size, or vanish, when you blink. From the flickering defiles comes an industrial cacophony mingled with the cries of tortured children.

Burnside is eager to return to Black House, too, but for the simpler pleasures of the first set of rooms, where he can rest, eat canned food, and read his scrapbooks. He relishes the particular smell that inhabits those rooms, an order of rot, sweat, dried blood, must, sewage. If he could distill that fragrance, he would wear it like cologne. Also, a sweet little morsel named Tyler Marshall sits locked in a chamber located in another layer of Black House—and another world—and Burny cannot wait to torment little Tyler, to run his wrinkled hands over the boy's beautiful skin. Tyler Marshall *thrills* Burny.

But there are pleasures yet to be reaped in this world, and it is *dime* to attend to them. Burny peeks out through a crack in the bathroom door and sees that Butch Yerxa has succumbed to weariness and the cafeteria's meat loaf. He occupies his chair like an oversized doll, his arms on the desk and his fat chin resting on what would be a neck on a normal person. That useful little painted rock stands a few inches away from Butch's right hand, but Burny has no need of the rock, for he has acquired an instrument far more versatile. He wishes he had discovered the potential of hedge clippers long ago. Instead of one blade, you get two. One up, one down, *snick-snick!* And sharp! He had not intended to amputate the blind man's fingers. Back then he thought of the clippers as a big, primitive variety of knife, but when he got stabbed in the arm, he jerked the clippers toward the blind man and they more or less bit off his fingers by themselves, as neatly and swiftly as the old-time butchers in Chicago used to slice bacon.

Chipper Maxton is going to be fun. He deserves what he is going to get, too. Burny figures that Chipper is responsible for the way he has deteriorated. The mirror told him that he is about twenty pounds less than he should be, maybe even thirty, and no wonder—look at the slop they serve in the cafeteria. Chipper has been chiseling on the food, Burny thinks, the same way he chisels on everything else. The state, the government, Medicaid, Medicare, Chipper steals from all of them. A couple of times when he thought Charles Burnside was too out of it to know what was happening, Maxton had told him to sign forms that indicated he'd had an operation, prostate surgery, lung surgery. The way Burny sees it, half of the Medicaid money that paid for the nonexistent operation should have been his. It was his name on the form, wasn't it?

Burnside eases into the hallway and pads toward the lobby, leaving bloody footprints from the squishing slippers. Because he will have to pass the nurse's station, he shoves the clippers under his waistband and covers them with his shirt. The flabby cheeks, gold-rimmed glasses, and lavender hair of a useless old bag named Georgette Porter are visible to Burnside above the counter of the nurses' station. Things could be worse, he thinks. Ever since she waltzed into D18 and caught him trying to masturbate stark naked in the middle of the room, Georgette Porter has been terrified of him.

She glances his way, seems to suppress a shudder, and looks back down at whatever she is doing with her hands. Knitting, probably, or reading the kind of murder mystery in which a cat solves the crime. Burny slops nearer the station and considers using the clippers on Georgette's face, but decides it is not worth the waste of energy. When he reaches the counter, he looks over it and sees that she is holding a paperback book in her hands, just as he had imagined.

She looks up at him with profound suspicion in her eyes.

"We sure look yummy tonight, Georgie."

She glances up the hallway, then at the lobby, and realizes that she must deal with him by herself. "You should be in your room, Mr. Burnside. It's late."

"Mind your own business, Georgie. I got a right to take a walk."

"Mr. Maxton doesn't like the residents to go into the other wings, so please stay in Daisy."

"Is the big boss here tonight?"

"I believe so, yes."

"Good."

He turns away and continues on toward the lobby, and she calls after him. "Wait!"

He looks back. She is standing up, a sure sign of great concern.

"You aren't going to bother Mr. Maxton, are you?"

"Say any more, and I'll bother *you*."

She places a hand on her throat and finally notices the floor. Her chin drops, and her eyebrows shoot up. "Mr. Burnside, what do you have on your slippers? And your pants cuffs? You're tracking it everywhere!"

"Can't keep your mouth shut, can you?"

Grimly, he plods back to the nurses' station. Georgette Porter backs against the wall, and by the time she realizes that she could have tried to escape, Burny is already in front of her. She removes her hand from her throat and holds it out like a stop sign.

"Dumb bitch."

Burnside yanks the clippers out of his belt, grips the handles, and clips off her fingers as easily as if they were twigs. "Stupid."

Georgette has entered a stage of shocked disbelief that holds her in paralysis. She stares at the blood spilling from the four stumps on her hand.

"Goddamn moron."

He opens the clippers and rams one of the blades into her throat. Georgette makes a choked, gargling sound. She tries to get her hands on the clippers, but he pulls them from her neck and raises them to her head. Her hands flutter, scattering blood. The expression on Burny's face is that of a man who finally admits that he has to clean his cat's litter box. He levels the wet blade in front of her right eye and shoves it in, and Georgette is dead before her body slides down the wall and folds up on the floor.

Thirty feet up the hallway, Butch Yerxa mumbles in his sleep.

"They never listen," Burny mutters to himself. "You try and try, but they always ask for it in the end. Proves they want it—like those dumb little shits in Chicago." He tugs the clippers' blade out of Georgette's head and wipes it clean on the shoulder of her blouse. The memory of one or two of those little shits in Chicago sends a tingle down the length of his member, which begins to stiffen in his baggy old pants. *Hel*-lo! Ah . . . the magic of tender memories. Though, as we have seen, Charles Burnside now and again enjoys erections in his sleep, in his waking hours they are so rare as to be nearly nonexistent, and he is tempted to pull down his pants and see what he could make it do. But what if Yerxa wakes up? He would assume that *Georgette Porter,* or at least her corpse, aroused Burny's long-smoldering lusts. That wouldn't do—not at all. Even a monster has his pride. Best to carry on to Chipper Maxton's office, and hope that his hammer doesn't go limp before it is time to pound the nail.

Burny tucks the clippers into the back of his waistband and yanks at his wet shirt, pulling it away from his body. Down the corridor of Daisy wing he shuffles, across the empty lobby, and up to the burnished door further distinguished by the brass nameplate reading WILLIAM MAXTON, DIRECTOR. This he reverentially opens, summoning to mind the image of a long-dead ten-year-old boy named Herman Flagler, otherwise known as "Poochie," one of his first conquests. Poochie! Tender Poochie! Those tears, those sobs of mingled pain and joy, that yielding to utter helplessness: the faint crust of dirt over Poochie's scabby knees and slender forearms. Hot tears; a jet of urine from his terrified little rosebud.

There will be no such bliss from Chipper, but we may be sure there will be *something.* Anyhow, Tyler Marshall lies bound and waiting in Black House, helpless as helpless could be.

Charles Burnside plods through Rebecca Vilas's windowless cubicle, Poochie Flagler's pallid, deeply dimpled backside blazing in his mind. He places a hand on the next doorknob, takes a moment to calm himself, and noiselessly revolves the knob. The door opens just wide enough to reveal Chipper Maxton, only monarch of this realm, leaning over his desk, his head propped on one fist, and using a yellow pencil to make notations on two sets of papers. The trace of a smile softens the tight purse of his mouth; his damp eyes betray the suggestion of a gleam; the busy pencil glides back and forth between the two stacks of papers, making tiny marks. So happily absorbed in his task is Chipper that he fails to notice he is no longer alone until his visitor steps inside and gives the door a backward kick with his foot.

When the door slams shut, Chipper glances up in irritated surprise and peers at the figure before him. His attitude almost immediately changes to a sly, unpleasant heartiness he takes to be disarming. "Don't they knock on doors where you come from, Mr. Burnside? Just barge right on in, do they?"

"Barge right on in," says his visitor.

"Never mind. The truth is, I've been meaning to talk to you."

"Talk to me?"

"Yes. Come on in, will you? Take a seat. I'm afraid we might have a little problem, and I want to explore some possibilities."

"Oh," Burny says. "A problem." He plucks his shirt away from his chest and trudges forward, leaving behind him progressively fainter footprints Maxton fails to see.

"Take a pew," Chipper says, waving at the chair in front of his desk. "Pull up a bollard and rest your bones." This expression comes from Franky Shellbarger, the First Farmer's loan officer, who uses it all the time at the local Rotary meetings, and although Chipper Maxton has no idea what a bollard may be, he thinks it sounds cute as hell. "Old-timer, you and me have to have a heart-to-heart discussion."

"Ah," Burny says, and sits down, his back rigidly straight, due to the clippers. *"Hardz zu hardz."*

"Yeah, that's the idea. Hey, is that shirt wet? It is! We can't have that, old buddy—you might catch cold and die, and neither one of us would like that, would we? You need a dry shirt. Let me see what I can do for you."

"Don't bother, you fucking monkey."

Chipper Maxton is already on his feet and straightening his

shirt, and the old man's words throw him momentarily off his stride. He recovers nicely, grins, and says, "Stay right there, Chicago."

Although the mention of his native city sends a prickling sensation down his spine, Burnside gives nothing away as Maxton moves around the side of his desk and walks across his office. He watches the director leave the room. *Chicago.* Where Poochie Flagler and Sammy Hooten and Ferd Brogan and all the others had lived and died, God bless 'em. Stalks of grain, blades of grass, so foul so beautiful so enticing. With their smiles and their screams. Like all Caucasian slum children, pure pale ivory white under the crust of dirt, the fishy white of the city's poor, the soon-to-be-lost. The slender bones of their shoulder blades, sticking out as if to break through the thin layer of flesh. Burny's old organ stirs and stiffens as if *it* remembers the frolics of yesteryear. *Tyler Marshall,* he croons to himself, *pretty little Ty, we will have ourselves some fun before we turn you over to the boss, yes we will yes indeedy yes yes.*

The door slams behind him, yanking him out of his erotic reverie. But his old mule, his old hoss, it stays awake and on its mettle, bold and brash as ever it was in the glory days.

"No one in the lobby," Maxton complains. "That old bag, what'shername, Porter, Georgette Porter, down in the kitchen stuffing her face, I bet, and Butch Yerxa sound asleep in his chair. What am I supposed to do, ransack the *rooms* to find a dry shirt?"

He strides past Burnside, throws up his hands, and drops into his chair. It's all an act, but Burny has seen much better than this. Chipper cannot intimidate Burny, not even if he knows a few things about *Chicago.*

"I don't need a new shirt," he says. "Asswipe."

Chipper leans back in his chair and clasps his hands behind his head. He grins—this patient amuses him, he's a real card. "Now, now. There's no need for name-calling here. You don't fool me anymore, old man. I don't buy your Alzheimer's act. In fact, I don't buy any of it."

He is nice and relaxed and he oozes the confidence of a gambler holding four aces. Burny figures he is being set up for some kind of con job or blackmail, which makes the moment all the more delicious.

"I gotta hand it to you, though," Chipper goes on. "You fooled everybody in sight, including me. It must take an *incredible* amount of discipline to fake late-stage Alzheimer's. All that slumping in your chair, being fed baby food, crapping in your pants. Pretending you don't understand what people are saying."

"I wasn't faking, you jackass."

"So it's no wonder you staged a comeback—when was that, about a year ago? I would have done the same. I mean, it's one thing to go undercover, but it's another to do it as a vegetable. So we have ourselves a little miracle, don't we? Our Alzheimer's gradually reverses itself, it comes and it goes, like the common cold. It's a good deal all around. You get to walk around and make a nuisance of yourself, and there's less work for the staff. You're still one of my favorite patients, Charlie. Or should I call you Carl?"

"I don't give a shit what you call me."

"But Carl's your real name, isn't it?"

Burny does not even shrug. He hopes Chipper gets to the point before Butch Yerxa wakes up, notices the bloody prints, and discovers Georgette Porter's body, because while he is interested in Maxton's tale, he wants to get to Black House without *too* much interference. And Butch Yerxa would probably put up a decent fight.

Under the illusion that he is playing a cat-and-mouse game in which he is the cat, Chipper smiles at the old man in the wet pink shirt and rolls on. "A state detective called me today. Said I.D. on a local fingerprint had come back from the FBI. It belonged to a bad, bad man named Carl Bierstone who's been wanted for almost forty years. In 1964 he was sentenced to death for killing a couple of kids he molested, only he escaped from the car taking him to prison—killed two guards with his bare hands. No sign of him since then. He'd be eighty-five by now, and the detective thought Bierstone just might be one of our residents. What do you have to say, Charles?"

Nothing, evidently.

"Charles Burnside is pretty close to Carl Bierstone, isn't it? And we have no background information on you at all. That makes you a unique resident here. For everybody else, we damn near have a family tree, but you sort of come out of nowhere. The only information we have about you is your age. When you turned up at La Riviere General in 1996, you claimed to be seventy-eight. That would make you the same age as that fugitive."

Burnside gives him a truly unsettling smile. "I guess I must be the Fisherman, too, then."

"You're eighty-five years old. I don't think you're capable of dragging a bunch of kids halfway across the county. But I do think you're this Carl Bierstone, and the cops are still eager to get their hands on you. Which brings me to this letter that came a few days ago. I've been meaning to discuss it with you, but you know how busy things get around here." He opens his desk drawer and pulls out a single sheet torn from a yellow notepad. It bears a brief, neatly typed message. " 'De Pere, Wisconsin,' it says. No date. 'To Whom It May Concern' is how it starts. 'I regret to inform you that I am no longer able to continue monthly payments on behalf of my nephew, Charles Burnside.' That's it. Instead of writing her signature, she typed her name. 'Althea Burnside.' "

Chipper places the yellow notepaper before him and folds his hands together on top of it. "What's the deal here, Charles? There's no Althea Burnside living in De Pere, I know that much. And she can't be your aunt. How old would she be? At least a hundred. More like a hundred and ten. I don't believe it. But these checks have been coming in, regular as clockwork, since your first month here at Maxton's. Some buddy, some old partner of yours, has been looking out for you, my friend. And we want him to continue what he's been doing, don't we?"

"All the same to me, asswipe." This is not precisely truthful. All Burny knows of the monthly payments is that Mr. Munshun organized them long ago, and if these payments are to stop, well . . . what comes to an end with them? He and Mr. Munshun are in this together, aren't they?

"Come on, kiddo," Chipper says. "You can do better than that. I'm looking for a little cooperation here. I'm sure you don't want to go through all the mess and trouble of being taken into custody, getting fingerprinted, plus whatever might happen after that. And me, speaking personally, I wouldn't want to put you through all of that. Because the real rat here is your friend. It sure looks to me like this guy, whoever he is, is forgetting that you probably have something on him from the old days, right?

And he's thinking that he doesn't have to make sure that you have all your little comforts anymore. Only that's a mistake. I bet you could straighten the guy out, make him understand the situation."

Burny's mule, his old hoss, has softened up and dwindled like a punctured balloon, which increases his gloom. Since entering this oily crook's office, he has lost something vital: a feeling of purpose, a sense of immunity, an edge. He wants to get back to Black House. Black House will restore him, for Black House is magic, *dark* magic. The bitterness of his soul went into its making; the darkness of his heart soaked through every beam and joist.

Mr. Munshun helped Burny see the possibilities of Black House, and he contributed many and many a touch of his own devise. There are regions of Black House Charles Burnside has never truly understood, and that frighten him, badly: an underground wing seems to contain his secret career in Chicago, and when he drew near that part of the house, he could hear the pleading whimpers and pungent screams of a hundred doomed boys as well as his own rasps of command, his grunts of ecstasy. For some reason, the proximity of his earlier triumphs made him feel small and hunted, an outcast instead of a lord. Mr. Munshun had helped him remember the scale of his achievement, but Mr. Munshun had been of no use with another region of Black House, a small one, at best a room, more accurately a vault, which houses the whole of his childhood, and which he has never, ever visited. The merest hint of that room causes Burny to feel like an infant left outside to freeze to death.

The news of the fictitious Althea Burnside's defection has a lesser version of the same effect. This is intolerable, and he need not, in fact cannot, endure it.

"Yeah," he says. "Let's have some straightening out here. Let's have some understanding."

He rises from the chair, and a sound from what seems to be the center of French Landing speeds him along. It is the wail of police sirens, at least two, maybe three. Burny doesn't know for sure, but he supposes that Jack Sawyer has discovered the body of his friend Henry, only Henry was less than perfectly dead and managed to say that he had recognized his killer's voice. So Jack called the cop shop and here we are.

His next step brings him to the front of the desk. He glances at the papers on the desk and instantly grasps their meaning.

"Cooking the books, hey? You aren't just an asswipe, you're a sneaky little numbers juggler."

In an amazingly small number of seconds, Chipper Maxton's face registers a tremendous range of feeling states. Ire, surprise, confusion, wounded pride, anger, and disbelief chase across the landscape of his features as Burnside reaches back and produces the hedge clippers. In the office, they seem larger and more aggressive than they did in Henry Leyden's living room.

To Chipper, the blades look as long as scythes. And when Chipper tears his eyes away from them and raises them to the old man standing before him, he sees a face more demonic than human. Burnside's eyes gleam red, and his lips curl away from appalling, glistening teeth like shards of broken mirrors.

"Back off, buddy," Chipper squeaks. "The police are practically in the lobby."

"I ain't deaf." Burny rams one blade into Chipper's mouth and closes the clippers on his sweaty cheek. Blood shoots across the desk, and Chipper's eyes expand. Burny yanks on the clippers, and several teeth and a portion of Chipper's tongue fly from the yawning wound. He pushes himself upright and leans forward to grab the blades. Burnside steps back and lops off half of Chipper's right hand.

"*Damn,* that's sharp," he says.

Then Maxton comes reeling around the side of the desk, spraying blood in all directions and bellowing like a moose. Burny dodges away, dodges back, and punches the blades into the bulge of the blue button-down shirt over Chipper's belly. When he tugs them out, Chipper sags, groans, drops to his knees. Blood pours out of him as if from an overturned jug. He falls forward on his elbows. There is no fun left in Chipper Maxton; he shakes his head and mutters something that is a plea to be left alone. A bloodshot, oxlike eye revolves toward Charles Burnside and silently expresses an oddly impersonal desire for mercy.

"Mother of Mercy," Burny says, "is this the end of Rico?" What a laugh—he hasn't thought of that movie in years. Chuckling at his own wit, he leans over, positions the blades on either side of Chipper's neck, and nearly succeeds in cutting off his head.

The sirens turn blaring onto Queen Street. Soon policemen
will be running up the walk; soon they will burst into the lobby.
Burnside drops the clippers onto Chipper's broad back and regrets that he does not have the time to piss on his body or take
a dump on his head, but Mr. Munshun is grumbling about *dime,
dime, dime.*

"I ain't stupid, you don't have to tell me," Burny says.

He pads out of the office and through Miss Vilas's cubicle.
When he moves out into the lobby, he can see the flashing light
bars on the tops of two police cars rolling down the far side of
the hedge. They come to a halt not far from where he first put
his hand around Tyler Marshall's slender boy-neck. Burny
scoots along a little faster. When he reaches the beginning of
the Daisy corridor, two baby-faced policemen burst through the
opening in the hedge.

Down the hallway, Butch Yerxa is standing up and rubbing
his face. He stares at Burnside and says, "What happened?"

"Get out there," Burny says. "Take 'em to the office. Maxton's hurt."

"Hurt?" Incapable of movement, Butch is gaping at Burnside's bloody clothes and dripping hands.

"Go!"

Butch stumbles forward, and the two young policemen
charge in through the big glass door, from which Rebecca
Vilas's poster has been removed. "The office!" Butch yells,
pointing to his right. "The boss is hurt!"

While Yerxa indicates the office door by jabbing his hand at
the wall, Charles Burnside scuttles past him. A moment later,
he has entered the Daisy wing men's room and is hotfooting it
toward one of the stalls.


And what of Jack Sawyer? We already know. That is, we know
he fell asleep in a receptive place between the edge of a cornfield and a hill on the western side of Norway Valley. We know
that his body grew lighter, less substantial, cloudy. That it grew
vague and translucent. We can suppose that before his body attained transparency, Jack entered a certain nourishing dream.
And in that dream, we may suppose, a sky of robin's-egg blue
suggests an infinity of space to the inhabitants of a handsome
residential property on Roxbury Drive, Beverly Hills, wherein

Jacky is six, six, six, or twelve, twelve, twelve, or both at the same time, and Daddy played cool changes on his horn, horn, horn. ("Darn That Dream," Henry Shake could tell you, is the last song on *Daddy Plays the Horn,* by Dexter Gordon—a daddy-o if there ever was.) In that dream, everyone went on a journey and no one went anywhere else, and a traveling boy captured a most marvelous prize, and Lily Cavanaugh Sawyer captured a bumblebee in a glass. Smiling, she carried it to the swinging doors and launched it into the upper air. So the bumblebee traveled far and away to Faraway, and as it journeyed worlds upon worlds on their mysterious courses trembled and swayed, and Jack, too, journeyed on his own mysterious course into the infinite robin's-egg blue and, in the bee's accurate wake, returned to the Territories, where he lay sleeping in a silent field. So in that same darned dream, Jack Sawyer, a person younger than twelve and older than thirty, stunned by both grief and love, is visited in his sleep by a certain woman of tender regard. And she lies down beside him on his bed of sweet grass and takes him in her arms and his grateful body knows the bliss of her touch, her kiss, her deep blessing. What they do, alone in the faraway Territories, is none of our business, but we compound Sophie's blessing with our own and leave them to what is after all, with the gentlest possible urgency, *their* business, which blesses this boy and this girl, this man and this woman, this dear couple, as nothing else can, certainly not us.

Return comes as it should, with the clean, rich smells of topsoil and corn, and a rooster's alarm-clock crowing from the Gilbertson cousins' farm. A spiderweb shining with dew stitches the loafer on Jack's left foot to a mossy rock. An ant trundling across Jack's right wrist carries a blade of grass bearing in the V of its central fold a bright and trembling drop of newly made water. Feeling as wondrously refreshed as if he, too, were newly created, Jack eases the hardworking ant off his wrist, separates his shoe from the spiderweb, and gets to his feet. Dew sparkles in his hair and his eyebrows. Half a mile back across the field, Henry's meadow curves around Henry's house. Tiger lilies shiver in the cool morning breeze.

*Tiger lilies shiver . . .*

When he sees the hood of his pickup nosing out from behind

the house, everything comes back to him. Mouse, and the word given him by Mouse. Henry's house, Henry's studio, his dying message. By this time, all the police and investigators will have gone, and the house will be empty, echoing with bloodstains. Dale Gilbertson—and probably Troopers Brown and Black—will be looking for him. Jack has no interest in the troopers, but he does want to talk to Dale. It is time to let Dale in on some startling facts. What Jack has to say to Dale is going to peel his eyelids back, but we should remember what the Duke told Dean Martin about the whisking of eggs and the making of omelettes. In the words of Lily Cavanaugh, when the Duke spoke up, ever'-dang-body *lissened* up, and so must Dale Gilbertson, for Jack wants his faithful and resolute company on the journey through Black House.

Walking past the side of Henry's house, Jack puts the tips of his fingers to his lips and brushes them against the wood, transferring the kiss. *Henry. For all the worlds, for Tyler Marshall, for Judy, for Sophie, and for you, Henry Leyden.*

The cell phone in the cab of the Ram claims to have three saved messages, all from Dale, which he deletes unheard. At home, the answering machine's red light blinks 4-4-4, repeating itself with the ruthless insistence of a hungry infant. Jack pushes PLAYBACK. Four times, an increasingly unhappy Dale Gilbertson begs to know the whereabouts of his friend Jack Sawyer and communicates his great desire to converse with the same gentleman, largely in reference to the murder of his uncle and their friend, Henry, but it wouldn't hurt to talk about the goddamn *slaughter* at Maxton's, would it? And does the name Charles Burnside ring any bells?

Jack looks at his watch and, thinking that it cannot be correct, glances up at the clock in his kitchen. His watch was right after all. It is 5:42 A.M., and the rooster is still crowing behind Randy and Kent Gilbertson's barn. Tiredness suddenly washes through him, heavier than gravity. Someone is undoubtedly manning the telephone on Sumner Street, but Dale is just as certainly asleep in his bed, and Jack wishes to speak only to Dale. He yawns hugely, like a cat. The newspaper hasn't even been delivered yet!

He removes his jacket and tosses it onto a chair, then yawns again, even more widely than before. Maybe that cornfield was not so comfortable after all: Jack's neck feels pinched, and his back aches. He pulls himself up the staircase, shucks his clothes onto a love seat in his bedroom, and flops into bed. On the wall above the love seat hangs his sunny little Fairfield Porter painting, and Jack remembers how Dale responded to it, the night they uncrated and put up all the paintings. He had loved that picture the moment he saw it—it had probably been news to Dale that he could find such satisfaction in a painting. *All right,* Jack thinks, *if we manage to get out of Black House alive, I'll give it to him. And I'll make him take it: I'll threaten to chop it up and burn it in the woodstove if he doesn't. I'll tell him I'll give it to Wendell Green!*

His eyes are already closing; he sinks into the bedclothes and disappears, although this time not literally, from our world. He dreams.

He walks down a tricky, descending forest path toward a burning building. Beasts and monsters writhe and bellow on both sides, mostly unseen but now and then flicking out a gnarled hand, a spiky tail, a black, skeletal wing. These he severs with a heavy sword. His arm aches, and his entire body feels weary and sore. Somewhere he is bleeding, but he cannot see or feel the wound, merely the slow movement of blood running down the backs of his legs. The people who were with him at the start of his journey are all dead, and he is—he may be—dying. He wishes he were not so alone, for he is terrified.

The burning building grows taller and taller as he approaches. Screams and cries come from it, and around it lies a grotesque perimeter of dead, blackened trees and smoking ashes. This perimeter widens with every second, as if the building is devouring all of nature, one foot at a time. Everything is lost, and the burning building and the soulless creature who is both its master and its prisoner will triumph, blasted world without end, amen. Din-tah, the great furnace, eating all in its path.

The trees on his right side bend and contort their complaining branches, and a great stirring takes place in the dark, sharply pointed leaves. Groaning, the huge trunks bow, and the branches twine like snakes about one another, bringing into being a solid wall of gray, pointed leaves. From that wall emerges, with terrible slowness, the impression of a gaunt, bony face. Five feet tall from crown to chin, the face bulges out against the layer of leaves, weaving from side to side in search of Jack.

It is everything that has ever terrified him, injured him, wished him ill, either in this world or the Territories. The huge face vaguely resembles a human monster named Elroy who once tried to rape Jack in a wretched bar called the Oatley Tap, then it suggests Morgan of Orris, then Sunlight Gardener, then Charles Burnside, but as it continues its blind seeking from side to side, it suggests all of these malign faces layered on top of one another and melting into one. Utter fear turns Jack to stone.

The face bulging out of the massed leaves searches the downward path, then swings back and ceases its constant, flickering movement from side to side. It is pointed directly at him. The blind eyes see him, the nose without nostrils smells him. A quiver of pleasure runs through the leaves, and the face looms forward, getting larger and larger. Unable to move, Jack looks back over his shoulder to see a putrefying man prop himself up in a narrow bed. The man opens his mouth and shouts, *"D'YAMBA!"*

Heart thrashing in his chest, a shout dying before it leaves his throat, Jack vaults from his bed and lands on his feet before he quite realizes that he has awakened from a dream. His entire body seems to be trembling. Sweat runs down his forehead and dampens his chest. Gradually, the trembling ceases as he takes in what is really around him: not a giant face looming from an ugly wall of leaves but the familiar confines of his bedroom. Hanging on the wall opposite is a painting he intends to give to Dale Gilbertson. He wipes his face, he calms down. He needs a shower. His watch tells him that it is now 9:47 A.M. He has slept four hours, and it is time to get organized.

Forty-five minutes later, cleaned up, dressed, and fed, Jack calls the police station and asks to speak to Chief Gilbertson. At 11:25, he and a dubious, newly educated Dale—a Dale who badly wants to see some evidence of his friend's crazy tale—leave the chief's car parked beneath the single tree in the Sand Bar's lot and walk across the hot asphalt past two leaning Harleys and toward the rear entrance.

# PART FOUR

# BLACK HOUSE
# AND BEYOND

# 26

We have had our little conversation about *slippage,* and it's too late in the game to belabor the point more than a little, but wouldn't you say that most houses are an attempt to hold slippage back? To impose at least the illusion of normality and sanity on the world? Think of Libertyville, with its corny but endearing street names—Camelot and Avalon and Maid Marian Way. And think of that sweet little honey of a home in Libertyville where Fred, Judy, and Tyler Marshall once lived together. What else would you call 16 Robin Hood Lane but an ode to the everyday, a paean to the prosaic? We could say the same thing about Dale Gilbertson's home, or Jack's, or Henry's, couldn't we? Most of the homes in the vicinity of French Landing, really. The destructive hurricane that has blown through the town doesn't change the fact that the homes stand as brave bulwarks against slippage, as noble as they are humble. They are places of sanity.

Black House—like Shirley Jackson's Hill House, like the turn-of-the-century monstrosity in Seattle known as Rose Red—is *not* sane. It is not entirely of this world. It's hard to look at from the outside—the eyes play continual tricks—but if one *can* hold it steady for a few seconds, one sees a three-story dwelling of perfectly ordinary size. The color is unusual, yes—that dead black exterior, even the windows swabbed black—and it has a crouching, leaning aspect that would raise uneasy thoughts about its structural integrity, but if one could appraise it with the *glammer* of those other worlds stripped away, it would look almost as ordinary as Fred and Judy's place . . . if not so well maintained.

Inside, however, it is different.

Inside, Black House is *large*.

Black House is, in fact, almost infinite.

Certainly it is no place to get lost, although from time to time people have—hoboes and the occasional unfortunate runaway child, as well as Charles Burnside/Carl Bierstone's victims—and relics here and there mark their passing: bits of clothing, pitiful scratchings on the walls of gigantic rooms with strange dimensions, the occasional heap of bones. Here and there the visitor may see a skull, such as the ones that washed up on the banks of the Hanover River during Fritz Haarman's reign of terror in the early 1920s.

This is not a place where you want to get lost.

Let us pass through rooms and nooks and corridors and crannies, safe in the knowledge that we can return to the outside world, the sane antislippage world, anytime we want (and yet we are still uneasy as we pass down flights of stairs that seem all but endless and along corridors that dwindle to a point in the distance). We hear an eternal low humming and the faint clash of weird machinery. We hear the idiot whistle of a constant wind either outside or on the floors above and below us. Sometimes we hear a faint, houndly barking that is undoubtedly the abbalah's devil dog, the one that did for poor old Mouse. Sometimes we hear the sardonic caw of a crow and understand that Gorg is here, too—somewhere.

We pass through rooms of ruin and rooms that are still furnished with a pale and rotten grandeur. Many of these are surely bigger than the whole house in which they hide. And eventually we come to a humble sitting room furnished with an elderly horsehair sofa and chairs of fading red velvet. There is a smell of noisome cooking in the air. (Somewhere close by is a kitchen we must never visit . . . not, that is, if we ever wish to sleep without nightmares again.) The electrical fixtures in here are at least seventy years old. How can that be, we ask, if Black House was built in the 1970s? The answer is simple: much of Black House—*most* of Black House—has been here much longer. The draperies in this room are heavy and faded. Except for the yellowed news clippings that have been taped to the ugly green wallpaper, it is a room that would not be out of place on the ground floor of the Nelson Hotel. It's a place that is simultaneously sinister and oddly banal, a fitting mirror for the imagination of the old monster who has gone to earth here, who lies sleeping on the horsehair sofa with the front of his shirt turning a sinister red. Black House is not his, although in his pathological grandiosity he believes differently (and Mr. Munshun has not disabused him of this belief). This one room, however, is.

The clippings around him tell us all we need to know of Charles "Chummy" Burnside's lethal fascinations.

YES, I ATE HER, FISH DECLARES: *New York Herald Tribune*

BILLY GAFFNEY PLAYMATE AVERS "IT WAS THE GRAY MAN TOOK BILLY, IT WAS THE BOGEYMAN": New York *World Telegram*

GRACE BUDD HORROR CONTINUES: fish confesses!: *Long Island Star*

FISH ADMITS "ROASTING, EATING" WM GAFFNEY: *New York American*

FRITZ HAARMAN, SO-CALLED "BUTCHER OF HANOVER," EXECUTED FOR MURDER OF 24: New York *World*

WEREWOLF DECLARES: "I WAS DRIVEN BY LOVE, NOT LUST." HAARMAN DIES UNREPENTANT: *The Guardian*

CANNIBAL OF HANOVER'S LAST LETTER: "YOU CANNOT KILL ME, I SHALL BE AMONG YOU FOR ETERNITY": New York *World*

Wendell Green would *love* this stuff, would he not?

And there are more. God help us, there are so many more. Even Jeffrey Dahmer is here, declaring I WANTED ZOMBIES.

The figure on the couch begins to groan and stir.

*"Way-gup, Burny!"* This seems to come from thin air, not his mouth . . . although his lips move, like those of a second-rate ventriloquist.

Burny groans. His head turns to the left. "No . . . need to sleep. Everything . . . hurts."

The head turns to the right in a gesture of negation and Mr. Munshun speaks again. *"Way-gup, dey vill be gummink. You must move der buuuoy."*

The head switches back the other way. Sleeping, Burny thinks Mr. Munshun is still safe inside his head. He has forgotten things are different here in Black House. Foolish Burny, now nearing the end of his usefulness! But not quite there yet.

"Can't . . . lea' me 'lone . . . stomach hurts . . . the blind man . . . fucking blind man hurt my stomach . . ."

But the head turns back the other way and the voice speaks again from the air beside Burny's right ear. Burny fights it, not wanting to wake and face the full ferocious impact of the pain. The blind man has hurt him *much* worse than he thought at the time, in the heat of the moment. Burny insists to the nagging voice that the boy is safe where he is, that they'll never find him even if they can gain access to Black House, that they will become lost in its unknown depth of rooms and hallways and wander until they first go mad and then die. Mr. Munshun, however, knows that one of them is different from any of the others who have happened on this place. Jack Sawyer is acquainted with the infinite, and that makes him a problem. The boy must be taken out the back way and into End-World, into the very shadow of Din-tah, the great furnace. Mr. Munshun tells Burny that he may still be able to have some of the boy before turning him over to the abbalah, but not here. Too dangerous. Sorry.

Burny continues to protest, but this is a battle he will not win, and we know it. Already the stale, cooked-meat air of the room has begun to shift and swirl as the owner of the voice arrives. We see first a whirlpool of black, then a splotch of red—an ascot—and then the beginnings of an impossibly long white face, which is dominated by a single black shark's eye. This is the *real* Mr. Munshun, the creature who can only live in Burny's head outside of Black House and its enchanted environs. Soon he will be entirely here, he will pull Burny into wakefulness (torture him into wakefulness, if necessary), and he will put Burny to use while there is still use to be gotten from him. For Mr. Munshun cannot move Ty from his cell in the Black House.

Once he is in End-World—Burny's Sheol—things will be different.

At last Burny's eyes open. His gnarled hands, which have spilled so much blood, now reach down to feel the dampness of his own blood seeping through his shirt. He looks, sees what has bloomed there, and lets out a scream of horror and cowardice. It does not strike him as just that, after murdering so many children, he should have been mortally wounded by a blind man; it strikes him as hideous, unfair.

For the first time he is visited by an *extremely* unpleasant idea: What if there's more to pay for the things he has done over the course of his long career? He has seen End-World; he has seen Conger Road, which winds through it to Din-tah. The blasted, burning landscape surrounding Conger Road is like hell, and surely An-tak, the Big Combination, is hell itself. What if such a place waits for him? What if—

There's a horrible, paralyzing pain in his guts. Mr. Munshun, now almost fully materialized, has reached out and twisted one smoky, not-quite-transparent hand in the wound Henry inflicted with his switchblade knife.

Burny squeals. Tears run down the old child-murderer's cheeks. *"Don't hurt me!"*

"Zen do ass I zay."

"I *can't*," Burny snivels. "I'm dying. Look at all the blood! Do you think I can get past something like this? *I'm eighty-five fucking years old!*"

"Duff brayyg, Burn-Burn . . . but dere are zose on z'osser zide who could hill you off your wunds." Mr. Munshun, like Black House itself, is hard to look at. He shivers in and out of focus. Sometimes that hideously long face (it obscures most of his body, like the bloated head of a caricature on some newspaper's op-ed page) has two eyes, sometimes just one. Sometimes there seem to be tufted snarls of orange hair leaping up from his distended skull, and sometimes Mr. Munshun appears to be as bald as Yul Brynner. Only the red lips and the fangy pointed teeth that lurk inside them remain fairly constant.

Burny eyes his accomplice with a degree of hope. His hands, meanwhile, continue to explore his stomach, which is now hard and bloated with lumps. He suspects the lumps are clots. Oh, that someone should have hurt him so badly! That wasn't supposed to happen! That was *never* supposed to happen! He was supposed to be protected! He was supposed to—

"It iss not even peeyond ze realm of bossibility," Mr. Munshun says, "zat ze yearz could be rawled avey vrum you jusst as ze stunn vas rawled avey from ze mouse of Cheezus Chrizze's doom."

"To be young again," Burny says, and exhales a low, harsh

sigh. His breath stinks of blood and spoilage. "Yes, I'd like that."

"Of gorse! And soch zings are bossible," Mr. Munshun says, nodding his grotesquely unstable face. "Soch gifts are ze abbalah's to giff. But zey are not bromised, Charles, my liddle munching munchkin. But I *can* make you one bromise."

The creature in the black evening suit and red ascot leaps forward with dreadful agility. His long-fingered hand darts again into Chummy Burnside's shirt, this time clenches into a fist, and produces a pain beyond any the old monster has ever dreamed of in his own life . . . although he has inflicted this and more on the innocent.

Mr. Munshun's reeking countenance pushes up to Burny's. The single eye glares. "Do you feel dat, Burny? Do you, you mizz-er-a-ble old bag of dirt and zorrow? Ho-ho, ha-ha, of *gorse* you do! It iss your in-*des*-tines I haff in my hand! Und if you do not mooff now, *schweinhund,* I vill rip dem from your bledding body, ho-ho, ha-ha, und *vrap* dem arund your neg! You vill die knowing you are choking on your own *gudz*! A trick I learned from Fritz himzelf, Fritz Haarman, who vas so yunk und loff-ly! Now! *Vat* do you say? Vill you brink him, or vill you *choke*?"

*"I'll bring him!"* Burny screams. *"I'll bring him, only stop, stop, you're tearing me apart!"*

"Brink him to ze station. Ze *station,* Burn-Burn. Dis one iz nodd for ze radhulls, de fogzhulls—not for ze Com-bin-*ay*-shun. No bledding foodzies for Dyler; he works for his abbalah vid *dis.*" A long finger tipped with a brutal black nail goes to the huge forehead and taps it above the eyes (for the moment Burny sees two of them, and then the second is once more gone). "Understand?"

*"Yes! Yes!"* His guts are on fire. And still the hand in his shirt twists and twists.

The terrible highway of Mr. Munshun's face hangs before him. "Ze *station*—where you brought the other sbecial ones."

*"YES!"*

Mr. Munshun lets go. He steps back. Mercifully for Burny, he is beginning to grow insubstantial again, to discorporate. Yellowed clippings swim into view not behind him but *through* him. Yet the single eye hangs in the air above the paling blotch of the ascot.

"Mayg zure he vears za cab. Ziss one ezbeshully must wear za cab."

Burnside nods eagerly. He still smells faintly of My Sin perfume. "The cap, yes, I have the cap."

"Be gare-ful, Burny. You are old und hurt. Ze bouy is young und desberate. Flitt of foot. If you let him get avey—"

In spite of the pain, Burny smiles. One of the children getting away from *him*! Even one of the special ones! What an idea! "Don't worry," he says. "Just . . . if you speak to *him . . . to Abbalah-doon . . . tell him I'm not past it yet. If he makes me better, he won't regret it. And if he makes me young again, I'll bring him a thousand young. A thousand* Breakers."

Fading and fading. Now Mr. Munshun is again just a glow, a milky disturbance on the air of Burny's sitting room deep in the house he abandoned only when he realized he really did need someone to take care of him in his sunset years.

"Bring him just dis *vun,* Burn-Burn. Bring him just dis vun, und you vill be revarded."

Mr. Munshun is gone. Burny stands and bends over the horsehair sofa. Doing it squeezes his belly, and the resulting pain makes him scream, but he doesn't stop. He reaches into the darkness and pulls out a battered black leather sack. He grasps its top and leaves the room, limping and clutching at his bleeding, distended belly.


And what of Tyler Marshall, who has existed through most of these many pages as little more than a rumor? How badly has he been hurt? How frightened is he? Has he managed to retain his sanity?

As to his physical condition, he's got a concussion, but that's already healing. The Fisherman has otherwise done no more than stroke his arm and his buttocks (a creepy touch that made Tyler think of the witch in "Hansel and Gretel"). Mentally . . . would you be shocked to hear that, while Mr. Munshun is goading Burny onward, Fred and Judy's boy is *happy*?

He is. He is happy. And why not? He's at Miller Park.

The Milwaukee Brewers have confounded all the pundits this year, all the doomsayers who proclaimed they'd be in the cellar by July Fourth. Well, it's still relatively early, but the Fourth has come and gone and the Brew Crew has returned to Miller tied for first place with Cincinnati. They are in the hunt, in large part due to the bat of Richie Sexson, who came over to Milwaukee from the Cleveland Indians and who has been "really pickin' taters," in the pungent terminology of George Rathbun.

They are in the hunt, and *Ty is at the game! EXCELLENT!* Not only is he there, he's got a front-row seat. Next to him—big, sweating, red-faced, a Kingsland beer in one hand and another tucked away beneath his seat for emergencies—is the Gorgeous George himself, bellowing at the top of his leather lungs. Jeromy Burnitz of the Crew has just been called out at first on a bang-bang play, and while there can be no doubt that the Cincinnati shortstop handled the ball well and got rid of it fast, there can also be no doubt (at least not in George Rathbun's mind) that Burnitz was safe! He rises in the twilight, his sweaty bald pate glowing beneath a sweetly lavender sky, a foamy rill of beer rolling up one cocked forearm, his blue eyes twinkling (you can tell he sees a lot with those eyes, just about everything), and Ty waits for it, they all wait for it, and here it is, that avatar of summer in the Coulee Country, that wonderful bray that means everything is okay, terror has been denied, and slippage has been canceled.

*"COME ON, UMP, GIVE US A BREAK! GIVE US A FREEEEAKIN' BRAYYYYK! EVEN A BLIND MAN COULD SEE HE WAS SAFE!"*

The crowd on the first-base side goes wild at the sound of that cry, none wilder than the fourteen or so people sitting behind the banner reading MILLER PARK WELCOMES GEORGE RATHBUN AND THE WINNERS OF THIS YEAR'S KDCU BREWER BASH. Ty is jumping up and down, laughing, waving his Brew Crew hat. What makes this doubly boss is that he thought he forgot to enter the contest this year. He guesses his father (or perhaps his mother) entered it for him . . . and he won! Not the grand prize, which was getting to be the Brew Crew's batboy for the entire Cincinnati series, but what he got (besides this excellent seat with the other winners, that is) is, in his opinion, even better. Of course Richie Sexson isn't Mark McGwire—*nobody* can hit the tar out of the ball like

Big Mac—but Sexson has been awesome for the Brewers this year, just *awesome,* and Tyler Marshall has won—

Someone is shaking his foot.

Ty attempts to pull away, not wanting to lose this dream (this most excellent refuge from the horror that has befallen him), but the hand is relentless. It shakes. It shakes and shakes.

"Way-gup," a voice snarls, and the dream begins to darken.

George Rathbun turns to Ty, and the boy sees an amazing thing: the eyes that were such a shrewd, sharp blue only a few seconds ago have gone dull and milky. *Cripe, he's* blind, Ty thinks. *George Rathbun really* is *a*—

"Way-gup," the growling voice says. It's closer now. In a moment the dream will wink out entirely.

Before it does, George speaks to him. The voice is quiet, totally unlike the sportscaster's usual brash bellow. "Help's on the way," he says. "So be cool, you little cat. Be—"

"Way-*GUP,* you shit!"

The grip on his ankle is crushing, paralyzing. With a cry of protest, Ty opens his eyes. This is how he rejoins the world, and our tale.

He remembers where he is immediately. It's a cell with reddish-gray iron bars halfway along a stone corridor lit with cobwebby electric bulbs. There's a dish of some sort of stew in one corner. In the other is a bucket in which he is supposed to pee (or take a dump if he has to—so far he hasn't, thank goodness). The only other thing in the room is a raggedy old futon from which Burny has just dragged him.

"All right," Burny says. "Awake at last. That's good. Now get up. On your feet, asswipe. I don't have time to fuck with you."

Tyler gets up. A wave of dizziness rolls through him and he puts his hand to the top of his head. There is a spongy, crusted place there. Touching it sends a bolt of pain all the way down to his jaws, which clench. But it also drives the dizziness away. He looks at his hand. There are flakes of scab and dried blood on his palm. *That's where he hit me with his damned rock. Any harder, and I would have been playing a harp.*

But the old man has been hurt somehow, too. His shirt is covered with blood; his wrinkled ogre's face is waxy and pallid. Behind him, the cell door is open. Ty measures the distance to the hallway, hoping he's not being too obvious about it. But Burny has been in this game a long time. He has had more than one liddle one dry to esscabe on hiz bledding foodzies, oh ho.

He reaches into his bag and brings out a black gadget with a pistol grip and a stainless steel nozzle at the tip.

"Know what this is, Tyler?" Burny asks.

"Taser," Ty says. "Isn't it?"

Burny grins, revealing the stumps of his teeth. "Smart boy! A TV-watching boy, I'll be bound. It's a Taser, yes. But a special type—it'll drop a cow at thirty yards. Understand? You try to run, boy, I'll bring you down like a ton of bricks. Come out here."

Ty steps out of the cell. He has no idea where this horrible old man means to take him, but there's a certain relief just in being free of the cell. The futon was the worst. He knows, somehow, that he hasn't been the only kid to cry himself to sleep on it with an aching heart and an aching, lumpy head, nor the tenth.

Nor, probably, the fiftieth.

"Turn to your left."

Ty does. Now the old man is behind him. A moment later, he feels the bony fingers grip the right cheek of his bottom. It's not the first time the old man has done this (each time it happens he's reminded again of the witch in "Hansel and Gretel," asking the lost children to stick their arms out of their cage), but this time his touch is different. Weaker.

*Die soon,* Ty thinks, and the thought—its cold collectedness—is very, very Judy. *Die soon, old man, so I don't have to.*

"This one is mine," the old man says . . . but he sounds out of breath, no longer quite sure of himself. "I'll bake half, fry the rest. With bacon."

"I don't think you'll be able to eat much," Ty says, surprised at the calmness of his own voice. "Looks like somebody ventilated your stomach pretty g—"

There is a crackling, accompanied by a hideous, jittery burning sensation in his left shoulder. Ty screams and staggers against the wall across the corridor from his cell, trying to clutch the wounded place, trying not to cry, trying to hold on to just a little of his beautiful dream about being at the game with

George Rathbun and the other KDCU Brewer Bash winners. He knows he actually did forget to enter this year, but in dreams such things don't matter. That's what's so beautiful about them.

Oh, but it hurts so *bad*. And despite all his efforts—all the Judy Marshall in him—the tears begin to flow.

"You want another un?" the old man gasps. He sounds both sick and hysterical, and even a kid Ty's age knows that's a dangerous combination. "You want another un, just for good luck?"

"No," Ty gasps. "Don't zap me again, please don't."

"Then start walkin'! And no more smart goddamn remarks!"

Ty starts to walk. Somewhere he can hear water dripping. Somewhere, very faint, he can hear the laughing caw of a crow—probably the same one that tricked him, and how he'd like to have Ebbie's .22 and blow its evil shiny black feathers off. The outside world seems light-years away. But George Rathbun told him help was on the way, and sometimes the things you heard in dreams came true. His very own mother told him that once, and long before she started to go all wonky in the head, too.

They come to a stairway that seems to circle down forever. Up from the depths comes a smell of sulfur and a roast of heat. Faintly he can hear what might be screams and moans. The clank of machinery is louder. There are ominous creaking sounds that might be belts and chains.

Ty pauses, thinking the old guy won't zap him again unless he absolutely has to. Because Ty might fall down this long circular staircase. Might hit the place on his head the old guy already clipped with the rock, or break his neck, or tumble right off the side. And the old guy wants him alive, at least for now. Ty doesn't know why, but he knows this intuition is true.

"Where are we going, mister?"

"You'll find out," Burny says in his tight, out-of-breath voice. "And if you think I don't dare zap you while we're on the stairs, my little friend, you're very mistaken. Now get walking."

Tyler Marshall starts down the stairs, descending past vast galleries and balconies, around and down, around and down. Sometimes the air smells of putrid cabbage. Sometimes it smells of burned candles. Sometimes of wet rot. He counts a hundred and fifty steps, then stops counting. His thighs are burning. Behind him, the old man is gasping, and twice he stumbles, cursing and holding the ancient banister.

*Fall, old man,* Ty chants inside his head. *Fall and die, fall and die.*

But at last they are at the bottom. They arrive in a circular room with a dirty glass ceiling. Above them, gray sky hangs down like a filthy bag. There are plants oozing out of broken pots, sending greedy feelers across a floor of broken orange bricks. Ahead of them, two doors—French doors, Ty thinks they are called—stand open. Beyond them is a crumbling patio surrounded by ancient trees. Some are palms. Some—the ones with the hanging, ropy vines—might be banyans. Others he doesn't know. One thing he's sure of: they are no longer in Wisconsin.

Standing on the patio is an object he knows very well. Something from his own world. Tyler Marshall's eyes well up again at the sight of it, which is almost like the sight of a face from home in a hopelessly foreign place.

"Stop, monkey-boy." The old man sounds out of breath. "Turn around."

When Tyler does, he's pleased to see that the blotch on the old man's shirt has spread even farther. Fingers of blood now stretch all the way to his shoulders, and the waistband of his baggy old blue jeans has gone a muddy black. But the hand holding the Taser is rock-steady.

*God damn you,* Tyler thinks. *God damn you to hell.*

The old man has put his bag on a little table. He simply stands where he is for a moment, getting his breath. Then he rummages in the bag (something in there utters a faint metallic clink) and brings out a soft brown cap. It's the kind guys like Sean Connery sometimes wear in the movies. The old man holds it out.

"Put it on. And if you try to grab my hand, I'll zap you."

Tyler takes the cap. His fingers, expecting the texture of suede, are surprised by something metallic, almost like tinfoil. He feels an unpleasant buzzing in his hand, like a mild version of the Taser's jolt. He looks at the old man pleadingly. "Do I have to?"

Burny raises the Taser and bares his teeth in a silent grin.

Reluctantly, Ty puts the cap on.

This time the buzzing fills his head. For a moment he can't think . . . and then the feeling passes, leaving him with an odd sense of weakness in his muscles and a throbbing at his temples.

"Special boys need special toys," Burny says, and it comes out *sbecial boyz, sbecial toyz.* As always, Mr. Munshun's ridiculous accent has rubbed off a little, thickening that touch of South Chicago Henry detected on the 911 tape. *"Now* we can go out."

*Because with the cap on, I'm safe,* Ty thinks, but the idea breaks up and drifts away almost as soon as it comes. He tries to think of his middle name and realizes he can't. He tries to think of the bad crow's name and can't get that, either—was it something like Corgi? No, that's a kind of dog. The cap is messing him up, he realizes, and that's what it's *supposed* to do.

Now they pass through the open doors and onto the patio. The air is redolent with the smell of the trees and bushes that surround the back side of Black House, a smell that is heavy and cloying. *Fleshy,* somehow. The gray sky seems almost low enough to touch. Ty can smell sulfur and something bitter and electric and juicy. The sound of machinery is much louder out here.

The thing Ty recognized sitting on the broken bricks is an E-Z-Go golf cart. The Tiger Woods model.

"My dad sells these," Ty says. "At Goltz's, where he works."

"Where do you think it came from, asswipe? Get in. Behind the wheel."

Ty looks at him, amazed. His blue eyes, perhaps thanks to the effects of the cap, have grown bloodshot and rather confused. "I'm not old enough to drive."

"Oh, you'll be fine. A *baby* could drive this baby. Behind the wheel."

Ty does as he is told. In truth, he has driven one of these in the lot at Goltz's, with his father sitting watchfully beside him in the passenger seat. Now the hideous old man is easing himself into that same place, groaning and holding his perforated midsection. The Taser is in the other hand, however, and the steel tip remains pointed at Ty.

The key is in the ignition. Ty turns it. There's a click from the battery beneath them. The dashboard light reading CHARGE glows bright green. Now all he has to do is push the accelerator pedal. And steer, of course.

"Good so far," the old man says. He takes his right hand off his middle and points with a bloodstained finger. Ty sees a path of discolored gravel—once, before the trees and underbrush encroached, it was probably a driveway—leading away from the house. "Now go. And go slow. Speed and I'll zap you. Try to crash us and I'll break your wrist for you. Then you can drive one-handed."

Ty pushes down on the accelerator. The golf cart jerks forward. The old man lurches, curses, and waves the Taser threateningly.

"It would be easier if I could take off the cap," Ty says. "Please, I'm pretty sure that if you'd just let me—"

"No! Cap stays! *Drive!*"

Ty pushes down gently on the accelerator. The E-Z-Go rolls across the patio, its brand-new rubber tires crunching on broken shards of brick. There's a bump as they leave the pavement and go rolling up the driveway. Heavy fronds—they feel damp, sweaty—brush Tyler's arms. He cringes. The golf cart swerves. Burny jabs the Taser at the boy, snarling.

"Next time you get the juice! It's a promise!"

A snake goes writhing across the overgrown gravel up ahead, and Ty utters a little scream through his clenched teeth. He doesn't like snakes, didn't even want to touch the harmless little corn snake Mrs. Locher brought to school, and this thing is the size of a python, with ruby eyes and fangs that prop its mouth open in a perpetual snarl.

"Go! Drive!" The Taser, waving in his face. The cap, buzzing faintly in his ears. *Behind* his ears.

The drive curves to the left. Some sort of tree burdened with what look like tentacles leans over them. The tips of the tentacles tickle across Ty's shoulders and the goose-prickled, hair-on-end nape of his neck.

*Ourr boyy . . .*

He hears this in his head in spite of the cap. It's faint, it's distant, but it's there.

*Ourrrrr boyyyyy . . . yesssss . . . ourrrrs . . .*

Burny is grinning. "Hear 'em, don'tcha? They like you. So

do I. We're all friends here, don't you see?" The grin becomes
a grimace. He clutches his bloody middle again. "Goddamned
blind old fool!" he gasps.

Then, suddenly, the trees are gone. The golf cart rolls out
onto a sullen, crumbling plain. The bushes dwindle and Ty sees
that farther along they give way entirely to a crumbled, rocky
scree: hills rise and fall beneath that sullen gray sky. A few
birds of enormous size wheel lazily. A shaggy, slump-
shouldered creature staggers down a narrow defile and is gone
from sight before Ty can see exactly what it is . . . not that he
wanted to. The thud and pound of machinery is stronger, shaking the earth. The crump of pile drivers; the clash of ancient
gears; the squall of cogs. Tyler can feel the golf cart's steering
wheel thrumming in his hands. Ahead of them the driveway
ends in a wide road of beaten earth. Along the far side of it is a
wall of round white stones.

"That thing you hear, that's the Crimson King's power plant,"
Burny says. He speaks with pride, but there is more than a tinge
of fear beneath it. "The Big Combination. A million children
have died on its belts, and a zillion more to come, for all I know.
But that's not for you, Tyler. You might have a future after all.
First, though, I'll have my piece of you. Yes indeed."

His blood-streaked hand reaches out and caresses the top of
Ty's buttock.

"A good agent's entitled to ten percent. Even an old buzzard
like me knows that."

The hand draws back. Good thing. Ty has been on the verge of
screaming, holding the sound back only by thinking of sitting at
Miller Park with good old George Rathbun. *If I'd really entered
the Brewer Bash,* he thinks, *none of this would have happened.*

But he thinks that may not actually be true. Some things are
meant to be, that's all. *Meant.*

He just hopes that what this horrible old creature wants is
not one of them.

"Turn left," Burny grunts, settling back. "Three miles. Give
or take." And, as Tyler makes the turn, he realizes the ribbons
of mist rising from the ground aren't mist at all. They're ribbons
of smoke.

"Sheol," Burny says, as if reading his mind. "And this is the
only way through it—Conger Road. Get off it and there are

things out there that'd pull you to pieces just to hear you scream. My friend told me where to take you, but there might be just a *leedle* change of plan." His pain-wracked face takes on a sulky cast. Ty thinks it makes him look extraordinarily stupid. "He hurt me. Pulled my guts. I don't trust him." And, in a horrible child's singsong: "Carl Bierstone don't trust Mr. Munshun! Not no more! Not no more!"

Ty says nothing. He concentrates on keeping the golf cart in the middle of Conger Road. He risks one look back, but the house, in its ephemeral wallow of tropical greenery, is gone, blocked from view by the first of the eroded hills.

"He'll have what's his, but I'll have what's mine. Do you hear me, boy?" When Ty says nothing, Burny brandishes the Taser. *"Do you hear me, you asswipe monkey?"*

"Yeah," Ty says. "Yeah, sure." *Why don't you die? God, if You're there, why don't You just reach down and put Your finger on his rotten heart and stop it from beating?*

When Burny speaks again, his voice is sly. "You looked at the wall on t'other side, but I don't think you looked close enough. Better take another gander."

Tyler looks past the slumped old man. For a moment he doesn't understand . . . and then he does. The big white stones stretching endlessly away along the far side of Conger Road aren't stones at all. They're skulls.

What is this place? Oh God, how he wants his mother! How he wants to go *home*!

Beginning to cry again, his brain numbed and buzzing beneath the cap that looks like cloth but isn't, Ty pilots the golf cart deeper and deeper into the furnace-lands. Into Sheol.

Rescue—help of any kind—has never seemed so far away.

# 27

When Jack and Dale step into the air-conditioned cool, the Sand Bar is empty except for three people. Beezer and Doc are at the bar, with soft drinks in front of them—an End Times sign if there ever was one, Jack thinks. Far back in the shadows (any farther and he'd be in the dive's primitive kitchen), Stinky Cheese is lurking. There is a vibe coming off the two bikers, a bad one, and Stinky wants no part of it. For one thing, he's never seen Beezer and Doc without Mouse, Sonny, and Kaiser Bill. For another . . . oh God, it's the California detective and the freakin' chief of police.

The jukebox is dark and dead, but the TV is on and Jack's not exactly surprised to see that today's Matinee Movie on AMC features his mother and Woody Strode. He fumbles for the name of the film, and after a moment it comes to him: *Execution Express*.

"You don't want to be in on this, Bea," Woody says—in this film Lily plays a Boston heiress named Beatrice Lodge, who comes west and turns outlaw, mostly to spite her straitlaced father. "This is looking like the gang's last ride."

"Good," Lily says. Her voice is stony, her eyes stonier. The picture is crap, but as always, she is dead on character. Jack has to smile a little.

"What?" Dale asks him. "The whole world's gone crazy, so what's to smile about?"

On TV, Woody Strode says: "What do you mean, *good*? The whole damn world's gone crazy."

Jack Sawyer says, very softly: "We're going to gun down as many as we can. Let them know we were here."

On the screen, Lily says the same thing to Woody. The two

of them are about to step aboard the Execution Express, and heads will roll—the good, the bad, and the ugly.

Dale looks at his friend, dazed.

"I know most of her lines," Jack says, almost apologetically. "She was my mother, you see."

Before Dale can answer (supposing any answer came to mind), Jack joins Beezer and Doc at the bar. He looks up at the Kingsland Ale clock next to the television: 11:40. It should be high noon—in situations like this, it's always supposed to be high noon, isn't it?

"Jack," Beezer says, and gives him a nod. "How ya doin', buddy?"

"Not too bad. You boys carrying?"

Doc lifts his vest, disclosing the butt of a pistol. "It's a Colt 9. Beez has got one of the same. Good iron, all registered and proper." He glances at Dale. "You along for the ride, are you?"

"It's my town," Dale says, "and the Fisherman just murdered my uncle. I don't understand very much of what Jack's been telling me, but I know that much. And if he says there's a chance we can get Judy Marshall's boy back, I think we'd better try it." He glances at Jack. "I brought you a service revolver. One of the Ruger automatics. It's out in the car."

Jack nods absently. He doesn't care much about the guns, because once they're on the other side they'll almost certainly change into something else. Spears, possibly javelins. Maybe even slingshots. It's going to be the Execution Express, all right—the Sawyer Gang's last ride—but he doubts if it'll be much like the one in this old movie from the sixties. Although he'll take the Ruger. There might be work for it on this side. One never knows, does one?

"Ready to saddle up?" Beezer asks Jack. His eyes are deep-socketed, haunted. Jack guesses the Beez didn't get much sleep last night. He glances up at the clock again and decides—for no other reason than pure superstition—that he doesn't want to start for the Black House just yet, after all. They'll leave the Sand Bar when the hands on the Kingsland clock stand at straight-up noon, no sooner. The Gary Cooper witching hour.

"Almost," he says. "Have you got the map, Beez?"

"I got it, but I also got an idea you don't really need it, do you?"

"Maybe not," Jack allows, "but I'll take all the insurance I can get."

Beezer nods. "I'm down with that. I sent my old lady back to her ma's in Idaho. After what happened with poor old Mousie, I didn't have to argue too hard. Never sent her back before, man. Not even the time we had our bad rumble with the Pagans. But I got a terrible feeling about this." He hesitates, then comes right out with it. "Feel like none of us are coming back."

Jack puts a hand on Beezer's meaty forearm. "Not too late to back out. I won't think any less of you."

Beezer mulls it over, then shakes his head. "Amy comes to me in my dreams, sometimes. We talk. How am I gonna talk to her if I don't stand up for her? No, man, I'm in."

Jack looks at Doc.

"I'm with Beez," Doc says. "Sometimes you just gotta stand up. Besides, after what happened to Mouse . . ." He shrugs. "God knows what we might have caught from him. Or fucking around out there at that house. Future might be short after that, no matter what."

"How'd it turn out with Mouse?" Jack inquires.

Doc gives a short laugh. "Just like he said. Around three o'clock this morning, we just washed old Mousie down the tub drain. Nothing left but foam and hair." He grimaces as if his stomach is trying to revolt, then quickly downs his glass of Coke.

"If we're going to do something," Dale blurts, "let's just do it."

Jack glances up at the clock. It's 11:50 now. "Soon."

"I'm not afraid of dying," Beezer says abruptly. "I'm not even afraid of that devil dog. It can be hurt if you pour enough bullets into it, we found that out. It's how that fucking place makes you *feel*. The air gets thick. Your head aches and your muscles get weak." And then, with a surprisingly good British accent: "Hangovers ain't in it, old boy."

"My gut was the worst," Doc says. "That and . . ." But he falls silent. He doesn't ever talk about Daisy Temperly, the girl he killed with an errant scratch of ink on a prescription pad, but he can see her now as clearly as the make-believe cowboys on the Sand Bar's TV. Blond, she was. With brown eyes. Sometimes he'd made her smile (even in her pain) by singing that song to her, the Van Morrison song about the brown-eyed girl.

"I'm going for Mouse," Doc says. "I *have* to. But that place . . . it's a sick place. You don't know, man. You may think you understand, but you don't."

"I understand more than you think," Jack says. Now it's his turn to stop, to consider. Do Beezer and Doc remember the word Mouse spoke before he died? Do they remember *d'yamba*? They should, they were right there, they saw the books slide off their shelf and hang in the air when Jack spoke that word . . . but Jack is almost sure that if he asked them right now, they'd give him looks that are puzzled, or maybe just blank. Partly because *d'yamba* is hard to remember, like the precise location of the lane that leads from sane antislippage Highway 35 to Black House. Mostly, however, because the word was for him, for Jack Sawyer, the son of Phil and Lily. He is the leader of the Sawyer Gang because he is different. He has traveled, and travel is broadening.

How much of this should he tell them? None of it, probably. But they must believe, and for that to happen he must use Mouse's word. He knows in his heart that he must be careful about using it—*d'yamba* is like a gun; you can only fire it so many times before it clicks empty—and he hates to use it here, so far from Black House, but he will. Because they must believe. If they don't, their brave quest to rescue Ty is apt to end with them all kneeling in Black House's front yard, noses bleeding, eyes bleeding, vomiting and spitting teeth into the poison air. Jack can tell them that most of the poison comes from their own minds, but talk is cheap. They must believe.

Besides, it's still only 11:53.

"Lester," he says.

The bartender has been lurking, forgotten, by the swing door into the kitchen. Not eavesdropping—he's too far away for that—but not wanting to move and attract attention. Now it seems that he's attracted some anyway.

"Have you got honey?" Jack asks.

"H-honey?"

"Bees make it, Lester. Mokes make money and bees make honey."

Something like comprehension dawns in Lester's eyes. "Yeah, sure. I keep it to make Kentucky Getaways. Also—"

"Set it on the bar," Jack tells him.

Dale stirs restively. "If time's as short as you think, Jack—"

"This is important." He watches Lester Moon put a small plastic squeeze bottle of honey on the bar and finds himself thinking of Henry. How Henry would have enjoyed the pocket miracle Jack is about to perform! But of course, he wouldn't have needed to perform such a trick for Henry. Wouldn't have needed to waste part of the precious word's power. Because Henry would have believed at once, just as he had believed he could drive from Trempealeau to French Landing—hell, to the fucking *moon*—if someone just dared to give him the chance and the car keys.

"I'll bring it to you," Lester says bravely. "I ain't afraid."

"Just set it down on the far end of the bar," Jack tells him. "That'll be fine."

He does as asked. The squeeze bottle is shaped like a bear. It sits there in a beam of six-minutes-to-noon sun. On the television, the gunplay has started. Jack ignores it. He ignores everything, focusing his mind as brightly as a point of light through a magnifying glass. For a moment he allows that tight focus to remain empty, and then he fills it with a single word:

*(D'YAMBA)*

At once he hears a low buzzing. It swells to a drone. Beezer, Doc, and Dale look around. For a moment nothing happens, and then the sunshiny doorway darkens. It's almost as if a very small rain cloud has floated into the Sand Bar—

Stinky Cheese lets out a strangled squawk and goes flailing backward. "Wasps!" he shouts. "Them are wasps! *Get clear!*"

But they are not wasps. Doc and Lester Moon might not recognize that, but both Beezer and Dale Gilbertson are country boys. They know bees when they see one. Jack, meanwhile, only looks at the swarm. Sweat has popped out on his forehead. He's concentrating with all his might on what he wants the bees to do.

They cloud around the squeeze bottle of honey so thickly it almost disappears. Then their humming deepens, and the bottle begins to rise, wobbling from side to side like a tiny missile with a really shitty guidance system. Then, slowly, it wavers its way toward the Sawyer Gang. The squeeze bottle is riding a cushion of bees six inches above the bar.

Jack holds his hand out and open. The squeeze bottle glides into it. Jack closes his fingers. Docking complete.

For a moment the bees rise around his head, their drone competing with Lily, who is shouting: "Save the tall bastard for me! He's the one who raped Stella!"

Then they stream out the door and are gone.

The Kingsland Ale clock stands at 11:57.

"Holy Mary, mothera God," Beezer whispers. His eyes are huge, almost popping out of their sockets.

"You've been hiding your light under a bushel, looks like to me," Dale says. His voice is unsteady.

From the end of the bar there comes a soft thud. Lester "Stinky Cheese" Moon has, for the first time in his life, fainted.

"We're going to go now," Jack says. "Beez, you and Doc lead. We'll be right behind you in Dale's car. When you get to the lane and the NO TRESPASSING sign, *don't go in.* Just park your scoots. We'll go the rest of the way in the car, but first we're going to put a little of this under our noses." Jack holds up the squeeze bottle. It's a plastic version of Winnie-the-Pooh, grimy around the middle where Lester seizes it and squeezes it. "We might even dab some *in* our nostrils. A little sticky, but better than projectile vomiting."

Confirmation and approval are dawning in Dale's eyes. "Like putting Vicks under your nose at a murder scene," he says.

It's nothing like that at all, but Jack nods. Because this is about *believing.*

"Will it work?" Doc asks doubtfully.

"Yes," Jack replies. "You'll still feel some discomfort, I don't doubt that a bit, but it'll be mild. Then we're going to cross over to . . . well, to someplace else. After that, all bets are off."

"I thought the kid was in the house," Beez says.

"I think he's probably been moved. And the house . . . it's a kind of wormhole. It opens on another . . ." *World* is the first word to come into Jack's mind, but somehow he doesn't think it *is* a world, not in the Territories sense. "On another place."

On the TV, Lily has just taken the first of about six bullets. She dies in this one, and as a kid Jack always hated that, but at least she goes down shooting. She takes quite a few of the bastards with her, including the tall one who raped her friend, and that is good. Jack hopes he can do the same. More than any-thing, however, he hopes he can bring Tyler Marshall back to his mother and father.

Beside the television, the clock flicks from 11:59 to 12:00.

"Come on, boys," Jack Sawyer says. "Let's saddle up and ride."

Beezer and Doc mount their iron horses. Jack and Dale stroll toward the chief of police's car, then stop as a Ford Explorer bolts into the Sand Bar's lot, skidding on the gravel and hurry-ing toward them, pulling a rooster tail of dust into the summer air.

"Oh Christ," Dale murmurs. Jack can tell from the too small baseball cap sitting ludicrously on the driver's head that it's Fred Marshall. But if Ty's father thinks he's going to join the rescue mission, he'd better think again.

"Thank God I caught you!" Fred shouts as he all but tumbles from his truck. "Thank God!"

"Who next?" Dale asks softly. "Wendell Green? Tom Cruise? George W. Bush, arm in arm with Miss Fucking Uni-verse?"

Jack barely hears him. Fred is wrestling a long package from the bed of his truck, and all at once Jack is interested. The thing in that package could be a rifle, but somehow he doesn't think that's what it is. Jack suddenly feels like a squeeze bottle being levitated by bees, not so much acting as acted upon. He starts forward.

"Hey bro, let's roll!" Beezer yells. Beneath him, his Harley explodes into life. "Let's—"

Then Beezer *cries out.* So does Doc, who jerks so hard he al-most dumps the bike idling between his thighs. Jack feels something like a bolt of lightning go through his head and he reels forward into Fred, who is also shouting incoherently. For a moment the two of them appear to be either dancing with the long wrapped object Fred has brought them or wrestling over it.

Only Dale Gilbertson—who hasn't been to the Territories, hasn't been close to Black House, and who is not Ty Marshall's father—is unaffected. Yet even he feels something rise in his head, something like an interior shout. The world trembles. All at once there seems to be more color in it, more dimension.

"What was that?" he shouts. "Good or bad? Good or bad? *What the hell is going on here?*"

For a moment none of them answer. They are too dazed to answer.

While a swarm of bees is floating a squeeze bottle of honey along the top of a bar in another world, Burny is telling Ty Marshall to face the wall, goddamnit, just face the wall.

They are in a foul little shack. The sounds of clashing machinery are much closer. Ty can also hear screams and sobs and harsh yells and what can only be the whistling crack of whips. They are very near the Big Combination now. Ty has seen it, a great crisscrossing confusion of metal rising into the clouds from a smoking pit about half a mile east. It looks like a madman's conception of a skyscraper, a Rube Goldberg collection of chutes and cables and belts and platforms, everything run by the marching, staggering children who roll the belts and pull the great levers. Red-tinged smoke rises from it in stinking fumes.

Twice as the golf cart rolled slowly along, Ty at the wheel and Burny leaning askew in the passenger seat with the Taser pointed, squads of freakish green men passed them. Their features were scrambled, their skin plated and reptilian. They wore half-cured leather tunics from which tufts of fur still started in places. Most carried spears; several had whips.

*Overseers,* Burny said. *They keep the wheels of progress turning.* He began to laugh, but the laugh turned into a groan and the groan into a harsh and breathless shriek of pain.

*Good,* Ty thought coldly. And then, for the first time employing a favorite word of Ebbie Wexler's: *Die soon, you motherfucker.*

About two miles from the back of Black House, they came to a huge wooden platform on their left. A gantrylike thing jutted up from it. A long post projected out from the top, almost to the road. A number of frayed rope ends dangled from it, twitching in the hot and sulfurous breeze. Under the platform, on dead ground that never felt the sun, were litters of bones and ancient piles of white dust. To one side was a great mound of shoes. Why they'd take the clothes and leave the shoes was a question Ty probably couldn't have answered even had he not been wearing the cap

(*sbecial toyz for sbecial boyz*), but a disjointed phrase popped
into his head: custom of the country. He had an idea that was
something his father sometimes said, but he couldn't be sure. He
couldn't even remember his father's face, not clearly.

The gibbet was surrounded by crows. They jostled one another and turned to follow the humming progress of the E-Z-
Go. None was the special crow, the one with the name Ty could
no longer remember, but he knew why they were here. They
were waiting for fresh flesh to pluck, that's what they were
doing. Waiting for newly dead eyes to gobble. Not to mention
the bare toesies of the shoe-deprived dead.

Beyond the pile of discarded, rotting footwear, a broken
track led off to the north, over a fuming hill.

"Station House Road," Burny said. He seemed to be talking
more to himself than to Ty at that point, was perhaps edging
into delirium. Yet still the Taser pointed at Ty's neck, never wavering. "That's where I'm supposed to be taking the special
boy." *Taging the sbecial bouy.* "That's where the special ones
go. Mr. Munshun's gone to get the mono. The End-World
mono. Once there were two others. Patricia . . . and Blaine.
They're gone. Went crazy. Committed suicide."

Ty drove the cart and remained silent, but he had to believe
old Burn-Burn was the one who had gone crazy (crazi*er,* he reminded himself). He knew about monorails, had even ridden
one at Disney World in Orlando, but monorails named Blaine
and Patricia? That was stupid.

Station House Road fell behind them. Ahead, the rusty red
and iron gray of the Big Combination drew closer. Ty could see
moving ants on cruelly inclined belts. Children. Some from other
worlds, perhaps—worlds adjacent to this one—but many from
his own. Kids whose faces appeared for a while on milk cartons
and then disappeared forever. Kept a little longer in the hearts of
their parents, of course, but eventually growing dusty even there,
turning from vivid memories into old photographs. Kids presumed dead, buried somewhere in shallow graves by perverts
who had used them and then discarded them. Instead, they were
here. Some of them, anyway. *Many* of them. Struggling to yank
the levers and turn the wheels and move the belts while the
yellow-eyed, green-skinned overseers cracked their whips.

As Ty watched, one of the ant specks fell down the side of

the convoluted, steam-wreathed building. He thought he could hear a faint scream. Or perhaps it was a cry of relief?

"Beautiful day," Burny said faintly. "I'll enjoy it more when I get something to eat. Having something to eat always . . . always perks me up." His ancient eyes studied Ty, tightening a little at the corners with sudden warmth. "Baby butt's the best eatin', but yours won't be bad. Nope, won't be bad at all. He said to take you to the station, but I ain't sure he'd give me my share. My . . . commission. Maybe he's honest . . . maybe he's still my friend . . . but I think I'll just take my share first, and make sure. Most agents take their ten percent off the top." He reached out and poked Ty just below the belt-line. Even through his jeans, the boy could feel the tough, blunt edge of the old man's nail. "I think I'll take mine off the *bottom*." A wheezy, painful laugh, and Ty was not exactly displeased to see a bright bubble of blood appear between the old man's cracked lips. "Off the *bottom,* get it?" The nail poked the side of Ty's buttock again.

"I get it," Ty said.

"You'll be able to break just as well," Burny said. "It's just that when you fart, you'll have to do the old one-cheek sneak *every* time!" More wheezing laughter. Yes, he sounded delirious, all right—delirious or on the verge of it—yet still the tip of the Taser remained rock-steady. "Keep on going, boy. 'Nother half a mile up the Conger Road. You'll see a little shack with a tin roof, down in a draw. It's on the right. It's a special place. Special to me. Turn in there."

Ty, with no other choice, obeyed. And now—

"Do what I tell you! Face the fucking wall! Put your hands up and through those loops!"

Ty couldn't define the word *euphemism* on a bet, but he knows calling those metal circlets "loops" is bullshit. What's hanging from the rear wall are shackles.

Panic flutters in his brain like a flock of small birds, threatening to obscure his thoughts. Ty fights to hold on—fights with grim intensity. If he gives in to panic, starts to holler and scream, he's going to be finished. Either the old man will kill him in the act of carving him up, or the old man's friend will take him away to some awful place Burny calls Din-tah. In either case, Ty will never see his mother and father again. Or

French Landing. But if he can keep his head . . . wait for his chance . . .

Ah, but it's hard. The cap he's wearing actually helps a little in this respect—it has a dulling effect that helps hold the panic at bay—but it's still hard. Because he's not the first kid the old man has brought here, no more than he was the first to spend long, slow hours in that cell back at the old man's house. There's a blackened, grease-caked barbecue set up in the left corner of the shed, underneath a tin-plated smoke hole. The grill is hooked up to a couple of gas bottles with LA RIVIERE PROPANE stenciled on the sides. Hung on the wall are oven mitts, spatulas, tongs, basting brushes, and meat forks. There are scissors and tenderizing hammers and at least four keen-bladed carving knives. One of the knives looks almost as long as a ceremonial sword.

Hanging beside that one is a filthy apron with YOU MAY KISS THE COOK printed on it.

The smell in the air reminds Ty of the VFW picnic his mom and dad took him to the previous Labor Day. Maui Wowie, it had been called, because the people who went were supposed to feel like they were spending the day in Hawaii. There had been a great big barbecue pit in the center of La Follette Park down by the river, tended by women in grass skirts and men wearing loud shirts covered with birds and tropical foliage. Whole pigs had been roasting over a glaring hole in the ground, and the odor had been like the one in this shed. Except the smell in here is stale . . . and old . . . and . . .

*And not quite pork,* Ty thinks. *It's—*

"I should stand here and jaw at you all day, you louse?"

The Taser gives off a crackling sizzle. Tingling, debilitating pain sinks into the side of Ty's neck. His bladder lets go and he wets his pants. He can't help it. Is hardly aware of it, in truth. Somewhere (in a galaxy far, far away) a hand that is trembling but still terribly strong thrusts Ty toward the back wall and the shackles that have been welded to steel plates about five and a half feet off the ground.

"There!" Burny cries, and gives a tired, hysterical laugh. "Knew you'd get one for good luck eventually! Smart boy, ain'tcha? Little wisenheimer! Now put your hands through them loops and let's have no more foolishness about it!"

Ty has put out his hands in order to keep himself from crash-ing face-first into the shed's rear wall. His eyes are less than a foot from the wood, and he is getting a very good look at the old layers of blood that coat it. That *plate* it. The blood has an ancient metallic reek. Beneath his feet, the ground feels spongy. Jellylike. Nasty. This may be an illusion in the physical sense, but Ty knows that what he's feeling is nonetheless quite real. This is corpse ground. The old man may not prepare his terri-ble meals here every time—may not have that luxury—but this is the place he likes. As he said, it's special to him.

*If I let him lock both of my hands into those shackles,* Ty thinks, *I've had it. He'll cut me up. And once he starts cutting, he may not be able to stop himself—not for this Mr. Munching, not for anyone. So get ready.*

That last is not like one of his own thoughts at all. It's like hearing his mother's voice in his head. His mother, or someone like her. Ty steadies. The flock of panic birds is suddenly gone, and he is as clearheaded as the cap will allow. He knows what he must do. Or try to do.

He feels the nozzle of the Taser slip between his legs and thinks of the snake wriggling across the overgrown driveway, carrying its mouthful of fangs. "Put your hands through those loops right now, or I'm going to fry your balls like oysters." *Er-sters,* it sounds like.

"Okay," Ty says. He speaks in a high, whiny voice. He hopes he sounds scared out of his mind. God knows it shouldn't be hard to sound that way. "Okay, okay, just don't hurt me, I'm doing it now, see? See?"

He puts his hands through the loops. They are big and loose.

"Higher!" The growling voice is still in his ear, but the Taser is gone from between his legs, at least. "Shove 'em in as far as you can!"

Ty does as he is told. The shackles slide to a point just above his wrists. His hands are like starfish in the gloom. Behind him, he hears that soft clinking noise again as Burny rummages in his bag. Ty understands. The cap may be scrambling his thoughts a little, but this is too obvious to miss. The old bas-tard's got handcuffs in there. Handcuffs that have been used many, many times. He'll cuff Ty's wrists above the shackles, and here Ty will stand—or dangle, if he passes out—while the old monster carves him up.

"Now listen," Burny says. He sounds out of breath, but he also sounds *lively* again. The prospect of a meal has refreshed him, brought back a certain amount of his vitality. "I'm pointin' this shocker at you with one hand. I'm gonna slip a cuff around your left wrist with the other hand. If you move . . . if you so much as *twitch,* boy . . . you get the juice. Understand?"

Ty nods at the bloodstained wall. "I won't move," he gibbers. "Honest I won't."

"First one hand, then the other. That's how I do it." There is a revolting complacency in his voice. The Taser presses between Ty's shoulder blades hard enough to hurt. Grunting with effort, the old man leans over Ty's left shoulder. Ty can smell sweat and blood and age. It *is* like "Hansel and Gretel," he thinks, only he has no oven to push his tormentor into.

*You know what to do,* Judy tells him coldly. *He may not give you a chance, and if he doesn't, he doesn't. But if he does . . .*

A handcuff slips around his left wrist. Burny is grunting softly, repulsively, in Ty's ear. The old man reaches . . . the Taser shifts . . . but not quite far enough. Ty holds still as Burny snaps the handcuff shut and tightens it down. Now Ty's left hand is secured to the shed wall. Dangling down from his left wrist by its steel chain is the cuff Burny intends to put on his right wrist.

The old man, still panting effortfully, moves to the right. He reaches around Ty's front, groping for the dangling cuff. The Taser is once more digging into Ty's back. If the old man gets hold of the cuff, Ty's goose is probably cooked (in more ways than one). And he almost does. But the cuff slips out of his grip, and instead of waiting for it to pendulum back to where he can grab it, Burny leans farther forward. The bony side of his face is planted against Ty's right shoulder.

And when he leans to get the dangling handcuff, Ty feels the touch of the Taser first lighten, then disappear.

*Now!* Judy screams inside Ty's head. Or perhaps it is Sophie. Or maybe it's both of them together. *Now, Ty! It's your chance, there won't be another!*

Ty pistons his right arm downward, pulling free of the shackle. It would do him no good to try to shove Burny away from him—the old monster outweighs him by sixty pounds or more—and Ty doesn't try. He pulls away to his left instead, putting excruciating pressure on his shoulder and on his left wrist, which has been locked into the shackle holding it.

"What—" Burny begins, and then Ty's groping right hand has what it wants: the loose, dangling sac of the old man's balls. He squeezes with all the force in his body. He feels the monster's testicles squash toward each other; feels one of them rupture and deflate. Ty shouts, a sound of dismay and horror and savage triumph all mingled together.

Burny, caught entirely by surprise, howls. He tries to pull backward, but Ty has him in a harpy's grip. His hand—so small, so incapable (or so you would think) of any serious defense—has turned into a claw. If ever there was a time to use the Taser, this is it . . . but in his surprise, Burny's hand has sprung open. The Taser lies on the ancient, blood-impacted earth of the shed floor.

*"Let go of me! That HURTS! That hurr —"*

Before he can finish, Ty yanks forward on the spongy and deflating bag inside the old cotton pants; he yanks with all the force of panic, and something in there *rips.* Burny's words dissolve in a liquid howl of agony. This is more pain than he has ever imagined . . . certainly never in connection with *himself.*

But it is not enough. Judy's voice says it's not, and Ty might know it, anyway. He has hurt the old man—has given him what Ebbie Wexler would undoubtedly call "a fuckin' rupture"—but it's not enough.

He lets go and turns to his left, pivoting on his shackled hand. He sees the old man swaying before him in the shadows. Beyond him, the golf cart stands in the open door, outlined against a sky filled with clouds and burning smoke. The old monster's eyes are huge and disbelieving, bulging with tears. He gapes at the little boy who has done this.

Soon comprehension will return. When it does, Burny is apt to seize one of the knives from the wall—or perhaps one of the meat forks—and stab his chained prisoner to death, screaming curses and oaths at him as he does so, calling him a monkey, a bastard, a fucking asswipe. Any thought of Ty's great talent will be gone. Any fear of what may happen to Burny himself if Mr. Munshun—and the abbalah—is robbed of his prize will also be gone. In truth, Burny is nothing but a psychotic animal, and in another moment his essential nature will break loose and vent itself on this tethered child.

Tyler Marshall, son of Fred and the formidable Judy, does not give Burny this chance. During the last part of the drive he has thought repeatedly of what the old man said about Mr. Munshun—*he hurt me, he pulled my guts*—and hoped he might get his own opportunity to do some pulling. Now it's come. Hanging from the shackle with his left arm pulled cruelly up, he shoots his right hand forward. Through the hole in Burny's shirt. Through the hole Henry has made with his switchblade knife. Suddenly Ty has hold of something ropy and wet. He seizes it and pulls a roll of Charles Burnside's intestines out through the rip in his shirt.

Burny's head turns up toward the shed's ceiling. His jaw snaps convulsively, the cords on his wrinkled old neck stand out, and he voices a great, agonized bray. He tries to pull away, which may be the worst thing a man can do when someone has him by the liver and lights. A blue-gray fold of gut, as plump as a sausage and perhaps still trying to digest Burny's last Maxton cafeteria meal, comes out with the audible pop of a champagne cork leaving the neck of its bottle.

Charles "Chummy" Burnside's last words: *"LET GO, YOU LITTLE PIIIIG!"*

Tyler does not let go. Instead he shakes the loop of intestine furiously from side to side like a terrier with a rat in its jaws. Blood and yellowish fluid spray out of the hole in Burny's midsection. *"Die!"* Tyler hears himself screaming. *"Die, you old fuck, GO ON AND DIE!"*

Burny staggers back another step. His mouth drops open, and part of an upper plate tumbles out and onto the dirt. He is staring down at two loops of his own innards, stretching like gristle from the gaping red-black front of his shirt to the awful child's right hand. And he sees an even more terrible thing: a kind of white glow has surrounded the boy. It is feeding him more strength than he otherwise would have had. Feeding him the strength to pull Burny's living guts right out of his body and how it *hurt,* how it *hurt,* how it dud dud dud *hurrrrr*—

*"Die!"* the boy screams in a shrill and breaking voice. *"Oh please, WON'T YOU EVER DIE?"*

And at last—at long, long last—Burny collapses to his knees. His dimming gaze fixes on the Taser and he reaches one trembling hand toward it. Before it can get far, the light of consciousness leaves Burny's eyes. He hasn't endured enough pain to equal even the hundredth part of the suffering he has inflicted, but it's all his ancient body can take. He makes a harsh cawing sound deep in his throat, then tumbles over backward, more intestines pulling out of his lower abdomen as he does so. He is unaware of this or of anything else.

Carl Bierstone, also known as Charles Burnside, also known as "Chummy" Burnside, is dead.

For over thirty seconds, nothing moves. Tyler Marshall is alive but at first only hangs from the axis of his shackled left arm, still clutching a loop of Burny's intestine in his right hand. Clutching it in a death grip. At last some sense of awareness informs his features. He gets his feet under him and scrambles upright, easing the all but intolerable pressure on the socket of his left shoulder. He suddenly becomes aware that his right arm is splashed with gore all the way to the biceps, and that he's got a handful of dead man's insides. He lets go of them and bolts for the door, not remembering that he's still chained to the wall until he is yanked back, the socket of his shoulder once more bellowing with pain.

*You've done well,* the voice of Judy-Sophie whispers. *But you have to get out of here, and quick.*

Tears start to roll down his dirty, pallid face again, and Ty begins to scream at the top of his voice.

*"Help me! Somebody help me! I'm in the shed! I'M IN THE SHED!"*

Out in front of the Sand Bar, Doc stays where he is, with his scoot rumbling between his legs, but Beezer turns his off, levers the stand into place with one booted heel, and walks over to Jack, Dale, and Fred. Jack has taken charge of the wrapped object Ty's father has brought them. Fred, meanwhile, has gotten hold of Jack's shirt. Dale tries to restrain the man, but as far as Fred Marshall's concerned, there are now only two people in the world: him and Hollywood Jack Sawyer.

"It was him, wasn't it? It was Ty. *That was my boy, I heard him!*"

"Yes," Jack says. "It certainly was and you certainly did." He's gone rather pale, Beezer sees, but is otherwise calm. It's absolutely not bothering him that the missing boy's father has yanked his shirt out of his pants. No, all Jack's attention is on the wrapped package.

"What in God's name is going on here?" Dale asks plaintively. He looks at Beezer. "Do *you* know?"

"The kid's in a shed somewhere," Beezer says. "Am I right about that?"

"Yes," Jack says. Fred abruptly lets go of Jack's shirt and staggers backward, sobbing. Jack pays no attention to him and makes no effort to tuck in the tail of his crumpled shirt. He's still looking at the package. He half-expects sugar-packet stamps, but no, this is just a case of plain old metered mail. Whatever it is, it's been mailed Priority to Mr. Tyler Marshall, 16 Robin Hood Lane, French Landing. The return address has been stamped in red: Mr. George Rathbun, KDCU, 4 Peninsula Drive, French Landing. Below this, stamped in large black letters:

### EVEN A BLIND MAN CAN SEE THAT COULEE COUNTRY LOVES THE BREWER BASH!

"Henry, you never quit, do you?" Jack murmurs. Tears sting his eyes. The idea of life without his old friend hits him all over again, leaves him feeling helpless and lost and stupid and hurt.

"What about Uncle Henry?" Dale asks. "Jack, Uncle Henry's *dead*."

Jack's no longer so sure of that, somehow.

"Let's go," Beezer says. "We got to get that kid. He's alive, but he ain't safe. I got that clear as a bell. Let's go for it. We can figure the rest out later."

But Jack—who has not just heard Tyler's shout but has, for a moment, seen through Tyler's eyes—doesn't have much to figure out. In fact, figuring out now comes down to only one thing. Ignoring both Beezer and Dale, he steps toward Ty's weeping father.

"Fred."

Fred goes on sobbing.

"Fred, if you ever want to see your boy again, you get hold of yourself right now and listen to me."

Fred looks up, red eyes streaming. The ridiculously small baseball cap still perches on his head.

"What's in this, Fred?"

"It must be a prize in that contest George Rathbun runs every summer—the Brewer Bash. But I don't know how Ty could have won something in the first place. A couple of weeks ago he was pissing and moaning about how he forgot to enter. He even asked if maybe *I'd* entered the contest for him, and I kind of . . . well, I snapped at him." Fresh tears begin running down Fred's stubbly cheeks at the memory. "That was around the time Judy was getting . . . strange . . . I was worried about her and I just kind of . . . snapped at him. You know?" Fred's chest heaves. He makes a watery hitching sound and his Adam's apple bobs up and down. He wipes an arm across his eyes. "And Ty . . . all he said was, 'That's all right, Dad.' He didn't get mad at me, didn't sulk or anything. Because that's just the kind of boy he was. That he *is*."

"How did you know to bring it to me?"

"Your friend called," Fred says. "He told me the postman had brought something and I had to bring it to you here, right away. Before you left. He called you—"

"He called me Travelin' Jack."

Fred Marshall looks at him wonderingly. "That's right."

"All right." Jack speaks gently, almost absently. "We're going to get your boy now."

"I'll come. I've got my deer rifle in the truck—"

"And that's where it's going to stay. Go home. Make a place for him. Make a place for your wife. And let us do what we have to do." Jack looks first at Dale, then at Beezer. "Come on," he says. "Let's roll."

Five minutes later, the FLPD chief's car is speeding west on Highway 35. Directly ahead, like an honor guard, Beezer and Doc are riding side by side, the sun gleaming on the chrome of their bikes. Trees in full summer leaf crowd close to the road on either side.

Jack can feel the buzzing that is Black House's signature starting to ramp up in his head. He has discovered he can wall that noise off if he has to, keep it from spreading and blanketing his entire thought process with static, but it's still damned unpleasant. Dale has given him one of the Ruger .357s that are the police department's service weapons; it's now stuck in the waistband of his blue jeans. He was surprised at how good the weight of it felt in his hand, almost like a homecoming. Guns may not be of much use in the world behind Black House, but they have to get there first, don't they? And according to Beezer and Doc, the approach is not exactly undefended.

"Dale, do you have a pocketknife?"

"Glove compartment," Dale says. He glances at the long package on Jack's lap. "I presume you want to open that."

"You presume right."

"Can you explain a few things while you do it? Like whether or not, once we get inside Black House, we can expect Charles Burnside to jump out of a secret door with an axe and start—"

"Chummy Burnside's days of jumping out at folks are all over," Jack says. "He's dead. Ty Marshall killed him. That's what hit us outside the Sand Bar."

The chief's car swerves so extravagantly—all the way across to the left side of the road—that Beezer looks back for a moment, startled at what he's just seen in his rearview. Jack gives him a hard, quick wave—*Go on, don't worry about us*—and Beez faces forward again.

*"What?"* Dale gasps.

"The old bastard was hurt, but I have an idea that Ty still did one hell of a brave thing. Brave and crafty both." Jack is thinking that Henry softened Burnside up and Ty *finished* him up. What George Rathbun would undoubtedly have called a honey of a double play.

"How—"

"Disemboweled him. With his bare hands. *Hand.* I'm pretty sure the other one's chained up somehow."

Dale is silent for a moment, watching the motorcyclists ahead of him as they lean into a curve with their hair streaming out from beneath their token gestures at obeying Wisconsin's helmet law. Jack, meanwhile, is slitting open brown wrapping paper and revealing a long white carton beneath. Something rolls back and forth inside.

"You're telling me that a ten-year-old boy disemboweled a serial killer. A serial *cannibal.* You somehow know this."

"Yes."

"I find that extremely difficult to believe."

"Based on the father, I guess I can understand that.

Fred's . . ." *A wimp* is what comes to mind, but that is both unfair and untrue. "Fred's tenderhearted," Jack says. "Judy, though . . ."

"Backbone," Dale says. "She *does* have that, I'm told."

Jack gives his friend a humorless grin. He's got the buzzing confined to a small portion of his brain, but in that one small portion it's shrieking like a fire alarm. They're almost there. "She certainly does," he tells Dale. "And so does the boy. He's . . . brave." What Jack has almost said is *He's a prince.*

"*And* he's alive."

"Yes."

"Chained in a shed somewhere."

"Right."

"Behind Burnside's house."

"Uh-huh."

"If I've got the geography right, that places him somewhere in the woods near Schubert and Gale."

Jack smiles and says nothing.

"All right," Dale says heavily. "What have I got wrong?"

"It doesn't matter. Which is good, because it's impossible to explain." Jack just hopes Dale's mind is screwed down tightly, because it's apt to take one hell of a pounding in the next hour or so.

His fingernail slits the tape holding the box closed. He opens it. There's bubble wrap beneath. Jack pulls it out, tosses it into the footwell, and looks at Ty Marshall's Brewer Bash prize—a prize he won even though he apparently never entered the contest.

Jack lets out a little sigh of awe. There's enough kid left in him to react to the object that he sees, even though he never played the game once he was too old for Little League. Because there's something about a bat, isn't there? Something that speaks to our primitive beliefs about the purity of struggle and the strength of our team. The home team. Of the right and the *white.* Surely Bernard Malamud knew it; Jack has read *The Natural* a score of times, always hoping for a different ending (and when the movie offered him one, he hated it), always loving the fact that Roy Hobbs named his cudgel Wonderboy. And never mind the critics with all their stuffy talk about the Arthurian legend and phallic symbols; sometimes a cigar is just a smoke and sometimes a bat is just a bat. A big stick. Something to hit home runs with.

"Holy wow," Dale says, glancing over. And he looks *younger.* Boyish. Eyes wide. So Jack isn't the only one, it seems. "Whose bat?"

Jack lifts it carefully from the box. Written up the barrel in black Magic Marker is this message:

To Tyler Marshall    Keep Slugging! Your pal, Richie Sexson

"Richie Sexson," Jack says. "Who's Richie Sexson?"

"Big slugger for the Brewers," Dale says.

"Is he as good as Roy Hobbs?"

"Roy—" Then Dale grins. "Oh, in that movie! Robert Redford, right? No I don't think—. Hey, what are you doing?"

Still holding the bat (in fact he almost bashes Dale in the right cheekbone with the end of it), Jack reaches over and honks the horn. "Pull over," he says. "This is it. Those dopes were out here only yesterday and they're going right past it."

Dale pulls over on the shoulder, brings the cruiser to a jerky stop, and puts it in park. When he looks over at Jack, his face has gone remarkably pale. "Oh man, Jack—I don't feel so good. Maybe it was breakfast. Christ, I hope I'm not going to start puking."

"That buzzing you hear in your head, is that from breakfast?" Jack inquires.

Dale's eyes go wide. "How do you—"

"Because I hear it, too. And feel it in my stomach. It's not your breakfast. It's Black House." Jack holds out the squeeze bottle. "Go on. Dab some more around your nostrils. Get some right up in. You'll feel better." Projecting absolute confidence. Because it's not about secret weapons or secret formulas; it's certainly not about honey. It's about *belief.* They have left the realm of the rational and have entered the realm of slippage. Jack knows it for certain as soon as he opens the car door.

Ahead of him, the bikes swerve and come back. Beezer, an impatient look on his face, is shaking his head: *No, no, not here.*

Dale joins Jack at the front of the car. His face is still pale, but the skin around and below his nose is shiny with honey, and he looks steady enough on his feet. "Thanks, Jack. This is *so*

much better. I don't know how putting honey around my nose
could affect my *ears,* but the buzzing's better, too. It's nothing
but a low drone."

"Wrong place!" Beezer bawls as he pulls his Harley up to
the front of the cruiser.

"Nope," Jack says calmly, looking at the unbroken woods.
Sunlight on green leaves contrasting with crazy black zigzags
of shadow. Everything trembling and unsteady, making mock
of perspective. "This is it. The hideout of Mr. Munshun and the
Black House Gang, as the Duke never said."

Now Doc's bike adds to the din as he pulls up next to Beezer.
"Beez is right! We were just out here *yesterday,* y'damn fool!
Don't you think you know what we're talking about?"

"This is just scrap woods on both sides," Dale chimes in. He
points across the road where, fifty yards or so southeast of their
position, yellow police tape flutters from a pair of trees. "That's
the lane to Ed's Eats, there. The place we want is probably beyond it—"

*Even though you know it's here,* Jack thinks. Marvels, really.
*Why else have you gone and smeared yourself with honey like
Pooh-bear on a lucky day?*

He shifts his gaze to Beezer and Doc, who are also looking
remarkably unwell. Jack opens his mouth to speak to
them . . . and something flutters at the upper edge of his vision.
He restrains his natural impulse to look up and define the source
of that movement. Something—probably the old Travelin' Jack
part of him—thinks it would be a very bad idea to do that.
Something is watching them already. Better if it doesn't know
it's been spotted.

He puts the Richie Sexson bat down, leaning it against the
side of the idling cruiser. He takes the honey from Dale and
holds it out to the Beez. "Here you go," he says, "lather up."

"There's no *point* in it, you goddamn fool!" Beezer cries in
exasperation. *"This . . . ain't . . . the place!"*

"Your nose is bleeding," Jack says mildly. "Just a little. Yours
too, Doc."

Doc wipes a finger under his nose and looks at the red smear,
startled. He starts, "But I *know* this isn't—"

That flutter again, at the top of Jack's vision. He ignores it
and points straight ahead. Beezer, Doc, and Dale all look, and

Dale's the first one to see it. "I'll be damned," he says softly. "A NO TRESPASSING sign. Was it there before?"

"Yep," Jack says. "Been there for thirty years or more, I'd guess."

"Fuck," Beez says, and begins rubbing honey around his nose. He pokes generous wads of the stuff up his nostrils; resinous drops gleam in his red-brown Viking's beard. "We woulda gone right on, Doctor. All the way to town. Hell, maybe all the way to Rapid City, South Dakota." He hands the honey to Doc and grimaces at Jack. "I'm sorry, man. We should have known. No excuses."

"Where's the driveway?" Dale's asking, and then: "Oh. *There* it is. I could have *sworn*—"

"That there was nothing there, I know," Jack says. He's smiling. Looking at his friends. At the Sawyer Gang. He is certainly *not* looking at the black rags fluttering restively at the upper periphery of his vision, nor down at his waist, where his hand is slowly drawing the Ruger .357 from his waistband. He was always one of the best out there. He'd only won badges a couple of times when it was shooting from a stand, but when it came to the draw-and-fire competition, he did quite well. Top five, usually. Jack has no idea if this is a skill he's retained, but he thinks he's going to find out right now.

Smiling at them, watching Doc swab his schnozz with honey, Jack says in a conversational voice: "Something's watching us. Don't look up. I'm going to try and shoot it."

"What is it?" Dale asks, smiling back. He doesn't look up, only straight ahead. Now he can quite clearly see the shadowy lane that must lead to Burnside's house. It wasn't there, he could have sworn it wasn't, but now it is.

"It's a pain in the ass," Jack says, and suddenly swings the Ruger up, locking both hands around the stock. He's firing almost before he sees with his eyes, and he catches the great dark crow crouched on the overhanging branch of an oak tree entirely by surprise. It gives one loud, shocked cry— "AWWWWK!"—and then it is torn apart on its roost. Blood flies against the faded blue summer sky. Feathers flutter down in clumps as dark as midnight shadows. And a body. It hits the shoulder in front of the lane with a heavy thud. One dark, glazing eye peers at Jack Sawyer with an expression of surprise.

"Did you fire five or six?" Beezer asks in a tone of deep awe. "It was so fast I couldn't tell."

"All of them," Jack says. He guesses he's still not too bad at draw-and-fire after all.

"That's one big fucking crow," Doc says.

"It's not just any crow," Jack tells him. "It's Gorg." He advances to the blasted body lying on the dirt. "How you doin', fella? How do you feel?" He spits on Gorg, a luscious thick lunger. "That's for luring the kids," he says. Then, suddenly, he boots the crow's corpse into the underbrush. It flies in a limp arc, the wings wrapping around the body like a shroud. "And that's for fucking with Irma's mother."

They are looking at him, all three of them, with identical expressions of stunned awe. Almost of fear. It's a look that makes Jack tired, although he supposes he must accept it. He can remember his old friend Richard Sloat looking at him the same way, once Richard realized that what he called "Seabrook Island stuff " wasn't confined to Seabrook Island.

"Come on," Jack says. "Everybody in the car. Let's get it done." Yes, and they must move quickly because a certain one-eyed gent will shortly be looking for Ty, too. Mr. Munshun. *Eye of the King,* Jack thinks. *Eye of the abbalah. That's what Judy meant—Mr. Munshun. Whoever or whatever he really is.*

"Don't like leaving the bikes out here by the side of the road, man." Beezer says. "Anybody could come along and—"

"Nobody will see them," Jack tells him. "Three or four cars have gone by since we parked, and no one's so much as looked over at us. And you know why."

"We've already started to cross over, haven't we?" Doc asks. "This is the edge of it. The border."

"Opopanax," Jack says. The word simply pops out.

*"Huh?"*

Jack picks up Ty's Richie Sexson bat and gets in on the passenger side of the cruiser. "It means let's go," he says. "Let's get it done."

And so the Sawyer Gang takes its last ride—up the wooded, poisonous lane that leads to Black House. The strong afternoon light quickly fades to the sullen glow of an overcast November evening. In the close-pressing trees on either side, dark shapes twine and crawl and sometimes fly. They don't matter, much, Jack reckons; they are only phantoms.

"You gonna reload that Roogalator?" Beezer asks from the back seat.

"Nope," Jack says, looking at the Ruger without much interest. "Think it's done its job."

"What should we be ready for?" Dale asks in a thin voice.

"Anything," Jack replies. He favors Dale Gilbertson with a humorless grin. Ahead of them is a house that won't keep its shape but whirls and wavers in the most distressing way. Sometimes it seems no bigger than a humble ranch house; a blink, and it seems to be a ragged monolith that blots out the entire sky; another blink and it appears to be a low, uneven construction stretching back under the forest canopy for what could be miles. It gives off a low hum that sounds like voices.

"Be ready for anything at all."

# 28

But at first there is nothing.

The four of them get out and stand in front of Dale's cruiser, looking for all the world like men posing for the kind of group photo that will eventually show up on someone's den wall. Only the photographer would be on Black House's porch—that's the way they're facing—and the porch is empty except for the second NO TRESPASSING sign, which leans against a peeling newel post. Someone has drawn a skull on it with a Magic Marker or grease pencil. Burny? Some intrepid teenager who came all the way up to the house on a dare? Dale did some crazy things when he was seventeen, risked his life with a spray-paint can more than once, but he still finds that hard to believe.

The air is sullen and silent, as if before a thunderstorm. It stinks, too, but the honey seems to filter the worst of that out. In the woods, something makes a thick sound Dale has never heard before. *Groo-oooo.*

"What's that?" he asks Jack.

"I don't know," Jack replies.

Doc says, "I've heard bull gators. That's what they sound like when they're feeling horny."

"This isn't the Everglades," Dale says.

Doc gives him a thin smile. "It ain't Wisconsin anymore, either, Toto. Or maybe you didn't notice."

Dale has noticed plenty. There's the way the house won't hold its shape, for one thing—the way it sometimes seems *enormous,* as if it is many houses somehow all overlaid. A city perhaps the size of London folded under a single weird roof. And then there are the trees. There are old oaks and pines, there are birches like skinny ghosts, there are red maples—all of them indigenous to the area—but he also sees twisted, rooty growths that look like mutated banyan trees. And are these *moving*? Christ, Dale hopes not. But whether they are or not, they're *whispering*. He's almost sure of that. He can hear their words slithering through the buzzing in his head, and they're not encouraging words, not by a longshot.

*Killyew . . . eatchew . . . hatechew . . .*

"Where's the dog?" Beezer asks. He's holding his 9mm in one hand. "Here, doggy! Got something yummy for you! Hurry and get it!"

Instead, that guttural growl drifts out of the woods again, this time closer: *GROO-OOOOO!* And the trees whisper. Dale looks up at the house, watches it suddenly stack floors into a sky that has gone white and cold, and vertigo rolls through his head like a wave of warm grease. He has a faint sensation of Jack grabbing his elbow to steady him. A little help there, but not enough; French Landing's chief of police twists to the left and vomits.

"Good," Jack says. "Get it out. Get rid of it. What about you, Doc? Beez?"

The Thunder Two tell him they're okay. For now it's true, but Beezer doesn't know how long equilibrium is going to last. His stomach is churning, low and slow. *Well, so what if I blow my groceries in there?* he thinks. *According to Jack, Burnside's dead, he won't mind.*

Jack leads them up the porch steps, pausing to boot the rusted NO TRESPASSING sign with its death's-head graffiti over the side and into a clutch of weeds that close over it at once, like a greedy hand. Dale is reminded of how Jack spit on the crow. His friend seems different now, younger and stronger. "But we *are* going to trespass," Jack says. "We're going to trespass our *asses* off."

At first, however, it seems they will not. The front door of Black House isn't just locked. There's no crack at all between the door and the jamb. In fact, once they're close up, the door looks painted on, a trompe l'oeil.

Behind them, in the woods, something screams. Dale jumps. The scream rises to an excruciating high note, breaks into a peal of maniacal laughter, and is suddenly gone.

"Natives are fuckin' restless," Doc comments.

"Want to try a window?" Beezer asks Jack.

"Nope. We're going in the front way."

Jack has been raising the Richie Sexson bat as he speaks. Now he lowers it, looking puzzled. There is a droning sound from behind them, quickly growing louder. And the daylight, thin already in this strange forest dell, seems to be weakening even further.

"What now?" Beezer asks, turning back toward the drive and the parked cruiser. He's holding the 9mm up by his right ear. "What the—" And then he falls silent. The gun sags outward and downward. His mouth drops open.

"Holy shit," Doc says quietly.

Dale, even more quietly: "Is this your doing, Jack? If it is, you really *have* been hiding your light under a bushel."

The light has dimmed because the clearing in front of Black House has now acquired a canopy of bees. More are streaming in from the lane, a brownish-gold comet tail. They give off a sleepy, benevolent droning sound that drowns out the harsh fire-alarm buzz of the house entirely. The hoarse gator thing in the woods falls silent, and the flickering shapes in the trees disappear.

Jack's mind is suddenly filled with thoughts and images of his mother: Lily dancing, Lily pacing around behind one of the cameras before a big scene with a cigarette clamped between her teeth, Lily sitting at the living-room window and looking out as Patsy Cline sings "Crazy Arms."

In another world, of course, she'd been another kind of queen, and what is a queen without a loyal retinue?

Jack Sawyer looks at the vast cloud of bees—millions of them, perhaps billions; every hive in the Midwest must be empty this afternoon—and he smiles. This changes the shape of his eyes and the tears that have been growing there spill down his cheeks. *Hello,* he thinks. *Hello there, boys.*

The low pleasant hum of the bees seems to change slightly, as if in answer. Perhaps it's only his imagination.

"What are they *for,* Jack?" Beezer asks. His voice is resonant with awe.

"I don't exactly know," Jack says. He turns back to the door, raises the bat, and knocks it once, hard, against the wood.

*"Open!"* he cries. *"I demand it in the name of Queen Laura DeLoessian! And in the name of my mother!"*

There is a high-pitched crack, so loud and piercing that Dale and Beez both draw back, wincing. Beezer actually covers his ears. A gap appears at the top of the door and races along it left to right. At the door's upper right corner, the gap pivots and plunges straight down, creating a crack through which a musty draft blows. Jack catches a whiff of something both sour and familiar: the deathsmell they first encountered at Ed's Eats.

Jack reaches for the knob and tries it. It turns freely in his hand. He opens the way to Black House.

But before he can invite them in, Doc Amberson begins to scream.

Someone—maybe it's Ebbie, maybe T.J., maybe goofy old Ronnie Metzger—is yanking Ty's arm. It hurts like a son of a gun, but that's not the worst. The arm yanker is also making this weird humming noise that seems to vibrate deep inside his head. There's a clanking noise as well

(*the Big Combination, that's the Big Combination*)

but that humming . . . ! Man, that humming *hurts.*

"Quit it," Ty mumbles. "Quit it, Ebbie or I'll—"

Faint screams seep through that electric buzzing sound, and Ty Marshall opens his eyes. There's no merciful period of grace when he's unsure about where he is or what's happened to him. It all comes back with the force of some terrible picture—a car accident with dead people lying around, say—that is shoved into your face before you can look away.

He'd held on until the old man was dead; had obeyed the voice of his mother and kept his head. But once he started shouting for help, panic had come back and swallowed him. Or maybe it was shock. Or both. In any case, he'd passed out while still screaming for help. How long has he hung here by his shackled left arm, unconscious? It's impossible to tell from the light spilling through the shed door; that seems unchanged. So do the various clankings and groanings of the huge machine, and Ty understands that it goes on forever, along with the screams of the children and the crack of the whips as the unspeakable guards press the work ever onward. The Big Combination never shuts down. It runs on blood and terror and never takes a day off.

But that buzzing—that juicy electric buzzing, like the world's biggest Norelco razor—what the hell is that?

*Mr. Munshun's gone to get the mono.* Burny's voice in his head. A vile whisper. *The End-World mono.*

A terrible dismay steals into Ty's heart. He has no doubt at all that what he hears is that very monorail, even now pulling under the canopy at the end of Station House Road. Mr. Munshun will look for his boy, his sbecial bouy, and when he doesn't see him (nor Burn-Burn, either), will he come searching?

"Course he will," Ty croaks. "Oh boy. Suck an elf."

He looks up at his left hand. It would be so easy to yank it back through the oversized shackle if not for the handcuff. He yanks downward several times anyway, but the cuff only clashes against the shackle. The other cuff, the one Burny was reaching for when Ty grabbed his balls, dangles and twitches, making the boy think of the gibbet at this end of Station House Road.

That eye-watering, tooth-rattling buzz suddenly cuts out.

*He's shut it down. Now he's looking for me in the station, making sure I'm not there. And when he* is *sure, what then? Does he know about this place? Sure he does.*

Ty's dismay is turning into an icy chill of horror. Burny would deny it. Burny would say that the shack down here in this dry wash was his secret, a place special to him. In his lunatic arrogance, it would never have occurred to him how well that mistaken idea might serve his supposed friend's purpose.

His mother speaks in Ty's head again, and this time he's reasonably sure it really *is* his mother. *You can't depend on anyone else. They might come in time, but they might not. You have to assume they won't. You have to get out of this yourself.*

But *how?*

Ty looks at the twisted body of the old man, lying on the bloody dirt with his head almost out the door. The thought of Mr. Munshun tries to intrude, Burny's friend hurrying down Station House Road even now (or maybe driving in his own E-Z-Go golf cart), wanting to scoop him up and take him to the abbalah. Tyler pushes the image away. It will lead him back to panic, and he can't afford any more of that. He's all out of time.

"I can't reach him," Ty says. "If the key's in his pocket, I'm finished. Case closed, game over, zip up your f—"

His eye happens on something lying on the floor. It's the sack the old man was carrying. The one with the cap in it. And the handcuffs.

*If the handcuffs were in it, maybe the key's in there, too.*

Ty reaches forward with his left foot, stretching as far as he can. It's no good. He can't quite reach the bag. He's at least four inches short. Four inches short and Mr. Munshun is coming, coming.

Ty can almost smell him.

Doc shrieks and shrieks, distantly aware that the others are shouting at him to stop, it's all right, there's nothing to be afraid of, distantly aware that he is hurting his throat, probably making it bleed. Those things don't matter. What matters is that when Hollywood swung open the front door of Black House, he exposed the official greeter.

The official greeter is Daisy Temperly, Doc's brown-eyed girl. She's wearing a pretty pink dress. Her skin is pale as paper, except on the right side of her forehead, where a flap of skin falls down, exposing the red skull beneath.

"Come in, Doc," Daisy says. "We can talk about how you killed me. And you can sing. You can sing to me." She smiles. The smile becomes a grin. The grin exposes a mouthful of bulging vampire teeth. "You can sing to me *forever.*"

Doc takes a blunder-step backward, turns to flee, and that is when Jack grabs him and shakes him. Doc Amberson is a hefty fellow—two-sixty out of the shower, more like two-eighty when dressed in full Road Warrior regalia as he is now—but Jack shakes him easily, snapping the big man's head back and forth. Doc's long hair flops and flies.

"They're all illusions," Jack says. "Picture-shows designed to keep out unwanted guests like us. I don't know what you saw, Doc, but it's not there."

Doc looks cautiously past Jack's shoulder. For a moment he sees a pink, diminishing whirl—it's like the coming of the devil dog, only backward—and then it's gone. He looks up at Jack. Tears are rolling slowly down his sunburned face.

"I didn't mean to kill her," he says. "I *loved* her. But I was tired that night. Very tired. Do you know about being tired, Hollywood?"

"Yes," Jack says. "And if we get out of this, I intend to sleep for a week. But for now . . ." He looks from Doc to Beezer. From Beezer to Dale. "We're going to see more stuff. The house will use your worst memories against you: the things you did wrong, the people you hurt. But on the whole, I'm encouraged. I think a lot of the poison went out of this place when Burny died. All we have to do is find our way through to the other side."

"Jack," Dale says. He is standing in the doorway, in the very spot where Daisy greeted her old physician. His eyes are very large.

"What?"

"Finding our way through . . . that might be easier said than done."

They gather around him. Beyond the door is a gigantic circular foyer, a place so big it makes Jack think fleetingly of St. Peter's Basilica. On the floor is an acre of poison-green carpet entwined with scenes of torture and blasphemy. Doors open off this room everywhere. In addition, Jack counts four sets of crisscrossing stairways. He blinks and there are six. Blinks again and there are a dozen, as bewildering to the eye as an Escher drawing.

He can hear the deep idiot drone that is the voice of Black House. He can hear something else, as well: laughter.

*Come in,* Black House is telling them. *Come in and wander these rooms forever.*

Jack blinks and sees a *thousand* stairways, some moving, bulging in and out. Doors stand open on galleries of paintings, galleries of sculpture, on whirling vortexes, on emptiness.

"What do we do now?" Dale asks bleakly. "What the hell do we do now?"

Ty has never seen Burny's friend, but as he hangs from the shackle, he finds he can imagine him quite easily. In this world, Mr. Munshun is a real creature . . . but not a human being. Ty sees a shuffling, busy figure in a black suit and a flowing red tie bustling down Station House Road. This creature has a vast white face dominated by a red mouth and a single blurry eye. The abbalah's emissary and chief deputy looks, in the gaze of Ty's imagination, like Humpty-Dumpty gone bad. It wears a vest buttoned with bones.

*Got to get out of here. Got to get that bag . . . but how?*

He looks at Burny again. At the hideous tangle of Burny's spilled guts. And suddenly the answer comes. He stretches his foot out again, but this time not toward the bag. He hooks the toe of his sneaker under a dirt-smeared loop of Burny's intestines, instead. He lifts it, pivots, and then kicks softly. The loop of gut leaves the toe of his sneaker.

And loops over the leather bag.

So far, so good. Now if he can only drag it close enough to get his foot on it.

Trying not to think of the stocky, hurrying figure with the grotesquely long face, Ty gropes out with his foot again. He gets it under the dirty snarl of intestine and begins to pull, slowly and with infinite care.

"It's impossible," Beezer says flatly. "Nothing can be this big. You know that, don't you?"

Jack takes a deep breath, lets it out, takes another, and speaks a single word in a low, firm voice.

"Dee-*yamber*?" Beez asks suspiciously. "What the hell's dee-*yamber*?"

Jack doesn't bother answering. From the vast dark cloud of droning bees hanging over the clearing (Dale's cruiser is now nothing but a furry black-gold lump in front of the porch), a single bee emerges. It—*she,* for this is undoubtedly a queen bee—flies between Dale and Doc, pauses for a moment in front of Beezer, as if considering him (or considering the honey with which he has generously lathered himself), and then hovers in front of Jack. She is plump and aerodynamically unsound and ludicrous and somehow absolutely wonderful. Jack lifts a finger like a professor about to make a point or a bandleader about to deliver the downbeat. The bee lights on the end of it.

"Are you from her?" He asks this question in a low voice— too low for the others to hear, even Beezer, who is standing right next to him. Jack isn't quite sure who he means. His mother? Laura DeLoessian? Judy? Sophie? Or is there some other She, a counterbalancing force to the Crimson King? This somehow feels right, but he supposes he'll never know for sure.

In any case, the bee only looks at him with her wide black eyes, wings blurring. And Jack realizes that these are questions to which he needs no answer. He has been a sleepyhead, but now he's up, he's out of bed. This house is huge and deep, a place stacked with vileness and layered with secrets, but what of that? He has Ty's prize bat, he has friends, he has *d'yamba,* and here is the Queen of the Bees. Those things are enough. He's good to go. Better—perhaps best of all—he's *glad* to go.

Jack raises the tip of his finger to his mouth and blows the bee gently into Black House's foyer. She circles aimlessly for a moment, and then zips off to the left and through a door with an oddly bloated, obese shape.

"Come on," Jack says. "We're in business."

The other three exchange uneasy glances, then follow him into what has clearly been their destiny all along.

It is impossible to say how long the Sawyer Gang spends in Black House, that hole which spewed the slippery stuff into French Landing and the surrounding towns. It is likewise impossible to say with any clarity what they see there. In a very real sense, touring Black House is like touring the brain of a deranged madman, and in such a mental framework we can expect to find no plan for the future or memory of the past. In the brain of a madman only the fuming present exists, with its endless shouting urges, paranoid speculations, and grandiose assumptions. So it is not surprising that the things they see in Black House should fade from their minds almost as soon as they are gone from their eyes, leaving behind only vague whispers of unease that might be the distant cry of the opopanax. This amnesia is merciful.

The queen bee leads them, and the other bees follow in a swarm that discolors the air with its vastness and shivers through rooms that have been silent for centuries (for surely we understand—intuitively if not logically—that Black House existed long before Burny built its most recent node in French Landing). At one point the quartet descends a staircase of green glass. In the abyss below the steps, they see circling birds like vultures with the white, screaming faces of lost babies. In a long, narrow room like a Pullman car, living cartoons—two rabbits, a fox, and a stoned-looking frog wearing white gloves—sit around a table catching and eating what appear to be fleas. They are *cartoons,* 1940s-era black-and-white *cartoons,* and it hurts Jack's eyes to look at them because they are also real. The rabbit tips him a knowing wink as the Sawyer Gang goes by, and in the eye that doesn't close Jack sees flat murder. There is an empty salon filled with voices shouting in some foreign language that sounds like French but isn't. There is a room filled with vomitous green jungle and lit by a sizzling tropical sun. Hanging from one of the trees is a vast cocoon that appears to hold a baby dragon still wrapped in its own wings. "That can't be a dragon," Doc Amberson says in a weirdly reasonable voice. "They either come from eggs or the teeth of other dragons. Maybe both." They walk down a long corridor that slowly rounds itself off, becomes a tunnel, and then drops them down a long and greasy slide as crazy percussion beats from unseen speakers. To Jack it sounds like Cozy Cole, or maybe Gene Krupa. The sides fall away, and for a moment they are sliding over a chasm that literally seems to have no bottom. "Steer with your hands and feet!" Beezer shouts. "If you don't want to go over the side, STEER!" They are finally spilled off in what Dale calls the Dirt Room. They struggle over vast piles of filth-smelling earth under a rusty tin ceiling festooned with bare light bulbs. Platoons of tiny greenish-white spiders school back and forth like fish. By the time they reach the far side, they're all panting and out of breath, their shoes muddy, their clothes filthy. There are three doors here. Their leader is buzzing and doing Immelmann turns in front of the one in the middle. "No way," Dale says. "I want to trade for what's behind the curtain."

Jack tells him he's got a future in stand-up comedy, no doubt about it, and then opens the door the bee has chosen for them. Behind it is a huge automated laundry, which Beezer immediately dubs the Hall of Cleanliness. Bunched together, they follow the bee down a humid corridor lined with sudsing washers and humming, shuddering dryers. The air smells like baked bread. The washers—each with a single glaring portholed eye—are stacked up to a height of fifty feet or more. Above them, in an ocean of dusty air, pigeons flock in restless currents. Every now and then they pass piles of bones, or some other sign that human beings came (or were brought) this way. In a hallway they find a scooter overgrown with cobwebs. Farther on, a pair of girl's in-line skates, thick with dust. In a vast library room, the word LAUGH has been formed with human bones on a mahogany table. In a richly appointed (if obviously neglected) parlor through which the bee leads them in a nononsense straight line, Dale and Doc observe that the art on one wall appears to consist of human faces that have been cut off, cured, and then stretched on squares of wood. Huge bewildered eyes have been painted into the empty sockets. Dale thinks he recognizes at least one of the faces: Milton Wanderly, a schoolteacher who dropped out of sight three or four years back. Everyone had assumed that Don Wanderly's kid brother had simply left town. *Well,* Dale thinks, *he left, all right.* Halfway down a stone-throated corridor lined with cells, the bee darts into a squalid little chamber and circles above a ragged futon. At first none of them speak. They don't need to. Ty was here, and not that long ago. They can almost smell him—his fear. Then Beezer turns to Jack. The blue eyes above the lush red-brown beard are narrowed in fury.

"The old bastard burned him with something. Or zapped him."

Jack nods. He can smell that, too, although whether he does so with his nose or his mind he neither knows nor cares. "Burnside won't be zapping anyone else," he says.

The queen bee zips between them and whirls impatiently in the corridor. To the left, back the way they came, the corridor is black with bees. They turn to the right instead, and soon the bee is leading them down another seemingly endless stairway. At one point they walk through a brief, drippy drizzle—somewhere above this part of the stairs, a pipe in Black House's unimaginable guts has perhaps let go. Half a dozen of the risers are wet, and they all see tracks there. They're too blurry to do a forensics team much good (both Jack and Dale have the same thought), but the Sawyer Gang is encouraged: there's a big set and a little set, and both sets are relatively fresh. Now they are getting somewhere, by God! They begin to move faster, and behind them the bees descend in a vast humming cloud, like some plague out of the Old Testament.

Time may have ceased to exist for the Sawyer Gang, but for Ty Marshall it has become an agonizing presence. He can't be sure if his sense of Mr. Munshun's approach is imagination or precognition, but he's terribly afraid it's the latter. He has to get out of this shed, *has* to, but the damned bag keeps eluding him. He managed to pull it close to him with the loop of intestines; ironically, that was the easy part. The hard part is actually getting *hold* of the damned thing.

He can't reach it; no matter how he stretches or how cruelly he tests his left shoulder and shackled left wrist, he comes up at least two feet short. Tears of pain roll down his cheeks. Any moisture lost that way is quickly replaced by the sweat that runs stinging into his eyes from his greasy forehead.

"Foot it," he says. "Just like soccer." He looks at the disfigured sprawl in the doorway—his erstwhile tormentor. "Just like soccer, right, Burn-Burn?"

He gets the side of his foot against the bag, pushes it to the wall, and then begins to slide it up the bloodstained wood. At the same time he reaches down . . . now fourteen inches . . . now only a foot . . . reaching . . .

. . . and the leather bag tumbles off the toe of his sneaker and onto the dirt. Plop.

"You're watching out for him, aren't you, Burny?" Ty pants. "You have to, you know, my back's turned. You're the lookout, right? You're— *Fuck!*" This time the bag has tumbled off his foot before he can even begin to raise it. Ty slams his free hand against the wall.

*Why do you do that?* a voice inquires coolly. This is the one who sounds like his mother but *isn't* his mother, not quite. *Will that help you?*

"No," Ty says resentfully, "but it makes me feel better."

*Getting free will make you feel better. Now try again.*

Ty once more rolls the leather bag against the wall. He presses his foot against it, feeling for anything else that might be inside—a key, for instance—but he can't tell. Not through his sneaker. He begins to slide the bag up the wall again. Carefully . . . not too fast . . . like footing the ball toward the goal . . .

"Don't let him in, Burny," he pants to the dead man behind him. "You owe me that. I don't want to go on the mono. I don't want to go to End-World. And I don't want to be a Breaker. Whatever it is, I don't want to be it. I want to be an explorer . . . maybe underwater, like Jacques Cousteau . . . or a flier in the Air Force . . . or maybe . . . FUCK!" This time it's not irritation when the bag falls off his foot but rage and near panic.

Mr. Munshun, hustling and bustling. Getting closer. Meaning to take him away. *Din-tah. Abbalah-doon.* For ever and ever.

"Damn old key's probably not in there, anyway." His voice wavering, close to a sob. "Is it, Burny?"

"Chummy" Burnside offers no opinion.

"I bet there's nothing in there at all. Except maybe . . . I don't know . . . a roll of Tums, or something. Eating people's *got* to give you indigestion."

Nonetheless, Ty captures the bag with his foot again, and again begins the laborious job of sliding it up the wall far enough so that perhaps his stretching fingers can grasp it.

Dale Gilbertson has lived in the Coulee Country his entire life, and he's used to greenery. To him trees and lawns and fields that roll all the way to the horizon are the norm. Perhaps this is why he looks at the charred and smoking lands that surround Conger Road with such distaste and growing dismay.

"What *is* this place?" he asks Jack. The words come out in little puffs. The Sawyer Gang has no golf cart and must hoof it. In fact, Jack has set a pace quite a bit faster than Ty drove the E-Z-Go.

"I don't exactly know," Jack says. "I saw a place *like* it a long time ago. It was called the Blasted Lands. It—"

A greenish man with plated skin suddenly leaps at them from behind a tumble of huge boulders. In one hand he holds a stumpy whip—what Jack believes is actually called a quirt. *"Bahhrrr!"* this apparition cries, sounding weirdly like Richard Sloat when Richard laughs.

Jack raises Ty's bat and looks at the apparition questioningly—*Did you want some of this?* Apparently the apparition does not. It stands where it is for a moment, then turns and flees. As it disappears back into the maze of boulders, Jack sees that twisted thorns grow in a ragged line down both of its Achilles tendons.

"They don't like Wonderboy," Beezer says, looking appreciatively at the bat. It *is* still a bat, just as the 9mm's and .357 Rugers are still pistols and *they* are still *they:* Jack, Dale, Beezer, Doc. And Jack decides he isn't much surprised by that. Parkus *told* him that this wasn't about Twinners, told him that during their palaver near the hospital tent. This place may be adjacent to the Territories, but it's *not* the Territories. Jack had forgotten that.

*Well, yes—but I've had a few other things on my mind.*

"I don't know if you boys have taken a close look at the wall on the far side of this charming country lane," Doc says, "but those large white stones actually appear to be skulls."

Beezer gives the wall of skulls a cursory glance, then looks ahead again. "What worries me is *that* thing," he says. Over the broken teeth of the horizon rises a great complication of steel, glass, and machinery. It disappears into the clouds. They can see the tiny figures who surge and struggle there, can hear the crack of the whips. From this distance they sound like the pop of .22 rifles. "What's that, Jack?"

Jack's first thought is that he's looking at the Crimson King's Breakers, but no—there are too many of them. Yonder building is some sort of factory or power plant, powered by slaves. By children not talented enough to *qualify* as Breakers. A vast outrage rises in his heart. As if sensing it, the drone of the bees grows louder behind him.

Speedy's voice, whispering in his head: *Save your anger, Jack—your first job is that little boy. And time has grown very, very short.*

"Oh Christ," Dale says, and points. "Is that what I think it is?"

The gibbet hangs like a skeleton over the slanting road.

Doc says, "If you're thinking gallows, I believe you win the stainless steel flatware and get to go on to the next round."

"Look at all the shoes," Dale says. "Why would they pile the shoes up like that?"

"God knows," Beezer says. "Just the custom of the country, I guess. How close are we, Jack? Do you have any idea at all?"

Jack looks at the road ahead of them, then at the road leading away to the left, the one with the ancient gallows on its corner. "Close," he says. "I think we're—"

Then, from ahead of them, the shrieks begin. They are the cries of a child who has been pushed to the edge of madness. Or perhaps over it.

Ty Marshall can hear the approaching drone of the bees but believes it is only in his head, that it is no more than the sound of his own growing anxiety. He doesn't know how many times he's tried to slide Burny's leather bag up the side of the shed; he's lost count. It does not occur to him that removing the odd cap—the one that looks like cloth and feels like metal—might improve his coordination, for he's forgotten all about the cap. All he knows is that he's tired and sweating and trembling, probably in shock, and if he doesn't manage to snag the bag this time, he'll probably just give up.

*I'd probably go with Mr. Munshun if he just promised me a glass of water,* Ty thinks. But he *does* have Judy's toughness bred in his bones, and some of Sophie's regal insistence, as well. And, ignoring the ache in his thigh, he again begins sliding the bag up the wall, at the same time stretching down with his right hand.

Ten inches . . . eight . . . the closest he's gotten so far . . .

The bag slips to the left. It's going to fall off his foot. Again.

*"No,"* Ty says softly. "Not this time."

He presses his sneaker harder against the wood, then begins to raise it again.

Six inches . . . four inches . . . three and the bag starts to tilt farther and farther to the left, *it's going to fall off—*

*"No!"* Ty yells, and bends forward in a strenuous bow. His back creaks. So does his tortured left shoulder. But his fingers graze across the bag . . . and then snag it. He brings it toward him and then damned near drops it after all!

"No way, Burny," he pants, first juggling the leather sack and then clutching it against his chest. "You don't fool me with *that* old trick, no way in *hell* do you fool me with that one." He bites the corner of the bag with his teeth. The stink of it is awful, rotten—eau de Burnside. He ignores it and pulls the bag open. At first he thinks it's empty, and lets out a low, sobbing cry. Then he sees a single silver gleam. Crying through his clenched teeth, Ty reaches into the dangling bag with his right hand and brings the key out.

*Can't drop it,* he thinks. *If I drop it, I'll lose my mind. I really will.*

He doesn't drop it. He raises it above his head, sticks it in the little hole on the side of the cuff holding his left wrist, and turns it. The cuff springs open.

Slowly, slowly, Ty draws his hand through the shackle. The handcuffs fall to the shed's dirt floor. As he stands there, a queerly persuasive idea occurs to Ty: he's really still back in Black House, asleep on the ragged futon with the slop bucket in one corner of his cell and the dish of reheated Dinty Moore beef stew in the other. This is just his exhausted mind giving him a little hope. A last vacation before he goes into the stew-pot himself.

From outside comes the clank of the Big Combination and the screams of the children who march, march, march on their bleeding footsies, running it. Somewhere is Mr. Munshun, who wants to take him someplace even worse than this.

It's no dream. Ty doesn't know where he'll go from here or how he'll ever get back to his own world, but the first step is getting out of this shed and this general vicinity. Moving on trembling legs, like an accident victim getting out of bed for the first time after a long stay, Ty Marshall steps over Burny's sprawled corpse and out of the shed. The day is overcast, the landscape sterile, and even here that rickety skyscraper of pain and toil dominates the view, but still Ty feels an immense glad-ness just to be in the light again. To be *free*. It is not until he stands with the shed behind him that he truly realizes how com-pletely he expected to die there. For a moment Ty closes his eyes and turns his face up to the gray sky. Thus he never sees the figure that has been standing to one side of the shed, pru-dently waiting to make sure Ty is still wearing the cap when he comes out. Once he's sure he is, Lord Malshun—this is as close to his real name as we can come—steps forward. His grotesque face is like the bowl of a huge serving spoon upholstered in skin. The one eye bulges freakishly. The red lips grin. When he drops his arms around the boy, Ty begins to shriek—not just in fear and surprise, but in *outrage*. He has worked so hard to be free, so dreadfully hard.

"Hush," Lord Malshun whispers, and when Ty continues to loose his wild screams (on the upper levels of the Big Combination, some of the children turn toward those cries until the brutish ogres who serve as foremen whip them back to business), the abbalah's lord speaks again, a single word in the Dark Speech. *"Pnung."*

Ty goes limp. Had Lord Malshun not been hugging him from behind, he would have fallen. Guttural moans of protest continue to issue from the child's drooling, slack mouth, but the screams have ceased. Lord Malshun cocks his long, spoon-shaped face toward the Big Combination, and grins. Life is good! Then he peers into the shed—briefly, but with great interest.

"Did for him," Lord Malshun says. "And with the cap on, too. Amazing boy! The King wants to meet you in person before you go to Din-tah, you know. He may give you cake and coffee. Imagine, young Tyler! Cake and coffee with the abbalah! Cake and coffee with the King!"

". . . don't want go . . . want to go home . . . my maaaa . . ." These words spill out loose and low, like blood from a mortal wound.

Lord Malshun draws a finger across Ty's lips, and they press together behind his touch. "Hush," says the abbalah's talent scout again. "Few things in life are more annoying than a noisy traveling companion. And we have a long trip ahead of us. Far from your home and friends and family . . . ah, but don't cry." For Malshun has observed the tears that have begun to leak from the corners of the limp boy's eyes and roll down the planes of his cheeks. "Don't cry, little Ty. You'll make new friends. The Chief Breaker, for instance. All the boys like the Chief Breaker. His name is Mr. Brautigan. Perhaps he'll tell you tales of his many escapes. How funny they are! Perfectly *killing*! And now we must go! Cake and coffee with the King! Hold that thought!"

Lord Malshun is stout and rather bowlegged (his legs are, in fact, a good deal shorter than his grotesquely long face), but he is strong. He tucks Ty under his arm as if the boy weighed no more than two or three sheets bundled together. He looks back at Burny one last time, without much regret—there's a young fellow in upstate New York who shows great promise, and Burny was pretty well played out, anyway.

Lord Malshun cocks his head sideways and utters his almost soundless chuffing laugh. Then he sets out, not neglecting to give the boy's cap a good hard yank. The boy is not just a Breaker; he's perhaps the most powerful one to ever live. Luckily, he doesn't realize his own powers yet. Probably nothing would happen if the cap *did* fall off, yet it's best not to take chances.

Bustling—even humming a bit under his breath—Lord Malshun reaches the end of the draw, turns left onto Conger Road for the half-mile stroll back to Station House Road, and stops dead in his tracks. Standing in his way are four men from what Lord Malshun thinks of as Ter-tah. This is a slang term, and not a flattering one. In the Book of Good Farming, Ter is that period of Full-Earth in which breeding stock is serviced. Lord Malshun sees the world beyond the front door of Black House as a kind of vast *caldo largo,* a living soup into which he may dip his ladle—always on the abbalah's behalf, of course!—whenever he likes.

Four men from the Ter? Malshun's lip twists in contempt, causing upheavals all along the length of his face. What are they doing here? Whatever can they hope to *accomplish* here?

The smile begins to falter when he sees the stick one of them carries. It's glowing with a shifting light that is many colors but somehow always white at its core. A blinding light. Lord Malshun knows only one thing that has ever glowed with such light and that is the Globe of Forever, known by at least one small, wandering boy as the Talisman. That boy once touched it, and as Laura DeLoessian could have told him—as Jack himself now knows—the touch of the Talisman never completely fades.

The smile drops away entirely when Lord Malshun realizes that the man with the club *was that boy.* He has come again to annoy them, but if he thinks he will take back the prize of prizes, he's quite mistaken. It's only a stick, after all, not the Globe itself; perhaps a little of the Globe's residual power still lives within the man, but surely not much. Surely there can be no more than dust, after all the intervening years.

*And dust is what my life would be worth if I let them take this boy from me,* Lord Malshun thinks. *I must—*

His single eye is drawn to the black thunderhead hanging behind the men from the Ter. It gives off a vast, sleepy drone.

Bees? Bees with stingers? Bees with stingers between him and Station House Road?

Well, he will deal with them. In time. First is the business of these annoying men.

"Good day, gentlemen," Lord Malshun says in his most pleasant voice. The bogus German accent is gone; now he sounds like a bogus English aristocrat in a West End stage comedy from the 1950s. Or perhaps the World War II Nazi propagandist Lord Haw-Haw. "It's wonderful that you should come so far to visit, perfectly *wonderful,* and on such a rotten day, too. Yet I'm afraid most days *are* rotten here, the Dins of End-World were simply *made* for the pathetic fallacy, you know, and—dash it all—I can't stay. I'm afraid these are time-delivery goods, here."

Lord Malshun raises Ty and shakes him. Although Ty's eyes are open and he's obviously aware, his arms and legs flop as bonelessly as those of a rag doll.

"Put him down, Munshun," says the one with the club, and Lord Malshun realizes with growing dismay that he *could* have trouble with this one. He really could. Yet his smile widens, exposing the full, ghoulish range of his teeth. They are pointed and tip inward. Anything bitten by them would tear itself to shreds trying to pull free of that bony trap.

"Munshun? *Munshun?* No one here by that name. Or Mr. Monday either, for that matter. All gone, cheerio, ta-ta, toodle-oo. As for putting down the lad, couldn't do that, dear boy, simply *couldn't.* I've made commitments, you know. And really, you fellows should count yourselves fortunate. Your local reign of terror is over! Huzzah! The Fisherman is dead—dispatched by this boy right here, in fact, this perfectly admirable boy." He gives Ty another shake, always being careful to keep the head raised. Wouldn't want that cap falling off, oh no.

The bees trouble him.

Who has sent the bees?

"The boy's mother is in an insane asylum," says the man with the stick. That stick is glowing more fiercely than ever, Lord Malshun realizes with deepening fear. He now feels *very* afraid, and with fear comes anger. Is it possible they could take him? Really take the boy? "She's in an asylum, and she wants her son back."

If so, it's a corpse they'll have for their trouble.

Afraid or not, Lord Malshun's grin widens even further. (Dale Gilbertson has a sudden, nightmarish vision: William F. Buckley, Jr., with one eye and a face five feet long.) He lifts Ty's limp body close to his mouth and bites a series of needly little nips in the air less than an inch from the exposed neck.

"Have her husband stick his prick in her and make another 'un, old son—I'm sure he can do it. They live in Ter-tah, after all. Women get pregnant in Ter-tah just walking down the street."

One of the bearded men says, "She's partial to this one."

"But so am *I,* dear boy. So am *I.*" Lord Malshun actually nips Ty's skin this time and blood flows, as if from a shaving cut. Behind them, the Big Combination grinds on and on, but the screams have ceased. It's as if the children driving the machine realize that something has changed or might change; that the world has come to a balancing point.

The man with the glowing stick takes a step forward. Lord Malshun cringes back in spite of himself. It's a mistake to show weakness and fear, he knows this but can't help it. For this is no ordinary tah. This is someone like one of the old gunslingers, those warriors of the High.

"Take another step and I'll tear his throat open, dear boy. I'd hate doing that, would hate it awfully, but never doubt that I'll do it."

"You'd be dead yourself two seconds later," the man with the stick says. He seems completely unafraid, either for himself or for Ty. "Is that what you want?"

Actually, given the choice between dying and going back to the Crimson King empty-handed, death is what Lord Malshun would choose, yes. But it may not come to that. The quieting word worked on the boy, and it will work on at least three of these—the ordinary three. With them lying open-eyed and insensible on the road, Lord Malshun can deal with the fourth. It's Sawyer, of course. That's his name. As for the bees, surely he has enough protective words to get him up Station House Road to the mono. And if he's stung a few times, what of that?

"*Is* it what you want?" Sawyer asks.

Lord Malshun smiles. *"Pnung!"* he cries, and behind Jack Sawyer, Dale, Beezer, and Doc fall still.

Lord Malshun's smile widens into a grin. "Now what are you going to do, my meddling friend? What are you going to do with no friends to back you u—"

Armand "Beezer" St. Pierre steps forward. The first step is an effort, but after that it's easy. His own cold little smile exposes the teeth inside his beard. "You're responsible for the death of my daughter," he says. "Maybe you didn't do it yourself, but you egged Burnside on to it. Didn't you? I'm her *father,* asshole. You think you can stop me with a single word?"

Doc lurches to his friend's side.

"You fucked up my town," Dale Gilbertson growls. He also moves forward.

Lord Malshun stares at them in disbelief. The Dark Speech hasn't stopped them. Not *any* of them. They are blocking the road! They dare to block his proposed route of progress!

"I'll kill him!" he growls at Jack. "I'll kill him. So what do you say, sunshine? What's it going to be?"

And so here it is, at long last: the showdown. We cannot watch it from above, alas, as the crow with whom we have hitched so many rides (all unknown by Gorg, we assure you) is dead, but even standing off to one side, we recognize this archetypal scene from ten thousand movies—at least a dozen of them starring Lily Cavanaugh.

Jack levels the bat, the one even Beezer has recognized as Wonderboy. He holds it with the knob pressing into the underside of his forearm and the barrel pointing directly at Lord Malshun's head.

"Put him down," he says. "Last chance, my friend."

Lord Malshun lifts the boy higher. "Go on!" he shouts. "Shoot a bolt of energy out of that thing! I know you can do it! But you'll hit the boy, too! You'll hit the boy, t—"

A line of pure white fire jumps from the head of the Richie Sexson bat; it is as thin as the lead of a pencil. It strikes Lord Malshun's single eye and cooks it in its socket. The thing utters a shriek—it never thought Jack would call its bluff, not a creature from the *ter,* no matter how temporarily elevated—and it jerks forward, opening its jaws to bite, even in death.

Before it can, *another* bolt of white light, this one from the beaten silver commitment ring on Beezer St. Pierre's left hand, shoots out and strikes the abbalah's emissary square in the mouth. The red plush of Lord Malshun's red lips bursts into flame . . . and still he staggers upright in the road, the Big Combination a skeletal skyscraper behind him, trying to bite, trying to end the life of Judy Marshall's gifted son.

Dale leaps forward, grabs the boy around the waist and the shoulders, and yanks him away, reeling toward the side of the road. His honest face is pale and grim and set. *"Finish him, Jack!"* Dale bawls. *"Finish the sonofabitch!"*

Jack steps forward to where the blinded, howling, charred thing reels back and forth in the Conger Road, his bony vest smoking, his long white hands groping. Jack cocks the bat back on his right shoulder and sets his grip all the way down to the knob. No choking up this afternoon; this afternoon he's wielding a bat that blazes with glowing white fire, and he'd be a fool not to swing for the fences.

"Batter up, sweetheart," he says, and uncoils a swing that would have done credit to Richie Sexson himself. Or Big Mac. There is a punky, fleshy sound as the bat, still accelerating, connects with the side of Lord Malshun's huge head. It caves in like the rind of a rotted watermelon, and a spray of bright crimson flies out. A moment later the head simply explodes, spattering them all with its gore.

"Looks like the King's gonna have to find a new boy," Beezer says softly. He wipes his face, looks at a handful of blood and shriveling tissue, then wipes it casually on his faded jeans. "Home run, Jack. Even a blind man could see that."

Dale, cradling Tyler, says: "Game over, case closed, zip up your fly."

French Landing's police chief sets Ty carefully on his feet. The boy looks up at him, then at Jack. A bleary sort of light is dawning in his eyes. It might be relief; it might be actual comprehension.

"Bat," he says. His voice is husky and hoarse, almost impossible for them to understand. He clears his throat and tries again. "Bat. Dreamed about it."

"Did you?" Jack kneels in front of the boy and holds the bat out. Ty shows no inclination to actually take possession of the Richie Sexson wonder bat, but he touches it with one hand.

Strokes the bat's gore-spattered barrel. His eyes look only at Jack. It's as if he's trying to get the sense of him. The *truth* of him. To understand that he has, after all, been rescued.

"George," the boy says. "George. Rathbun. Really is blind."

"Yes," Jack says. "But sometimes blind isn't blind. Do you know that, Tyler?"

The boy nods. Jack has never in his life seen anyone who looks so fundamentally exhausted, so shocked and lost, so completely worn out.

"Want," the boy says. He licks his lips and clears his throat again. "Want . . . drink. Water. Want mother. See my mother."

"Sounds like a plan to me," Doc says. He is looking uneasily at the splattered remains of the creature they still think of as Mr. Munshun. "Let's get this young fellow back to Wisconsin before some of Old One Eye's friends show up."

"Right," Beezer says. "Burning Black House to the ground is also on my personal agenda. I'll throw the first match. Or maybe I can shoot fire out of my ring again. I'd like that. First thing, though, is to make tracks."

"I couldn't agree more," Dale says. "I don't think Ty's going to be able to walk either very far or very fast, but we can take turns giving him piggyb—"

"No," Jack says.

They look at him with varying degrees of surprise and consternation.

"Jack," Beezer says. He speaks with an odd gentleness. "There's such a thing as overstaying your welcome, man."

"We aren't finished," Jack tells him. Then he shakes his head and corrects himself. "*Ty's* not finished."

Jack Sawyer kneels in Conger Road, thinking: *I wasn't much older than this kid when I took off across America—and the Territories—to save my mother's life.* He knows this is true and at the same time absolutely can't believe it. Can't remember what it was to be twelve and never anything else, to be small and terrified, mostly below the world's notice and running just ahead of all the world's shadows. It *should* be over; Ty has been through nine kinds of hell, and he deserves to go home.

Unfortunately, it's *not* over. There's one more thing to do.

"Ty."

"Want. Home."

If there was light in the boy's eyes, it has gone out now. He wears the dull shockface of refugees at border checkpoints and the gates of deathcamps. His is the emptied visage of someone who has spent too long in the slippery opopanax landscape of slippage. And he is a child, damnit, only a *child*. He deserves better than what Jack Sawyer is about to serve out. But then, Jack Sawyer once deserved better than what he got and lived to tell the tale. That justifies nothing, of course, but it *does* give him the courage to be a bastard.

"Ty." He grasps the boy's shoulder.

"Water. Mother. Home."

"No," Jack says. "Not yet." He pivots the boy. The spatters of Lord Malshun's blood on his face are very bright. Jack can sense the men he came with—men who have risked their lives and sanity for him—beginning to frown. Never mind. He has a job to do. He is a coppiceman, and there's still a crime in progress here.

"Ty."

Nothing. The boy stands slumped. He's trying to turn himself into meat that does nothing but breathe.

Jack points at the ugly complication of struts and belts and girders and smoking chimneys. He points at the straining ants. The Big Combination disappears up into the clouds and down into the dead ground. How far in each direction? A mile? Two? Are there children above the clouds, shivering in oxygen masks as they trudge the treadmills and yank the levers and turn the cranks? Children below who bake in the heat of underground fires? Down there in the foxholes and the ratholes where the sun never shines?

"What is it?" Jack asks him. "What do you call it? What did *Burny* call it?"

Nothing from Ty.

Jack gives the boy a shake. Not a gentle one, either. "What do you *call* it?"

"Hey, man," Doc says. His voice is heavy with disapproval. "There's no need of that."

"Shut up," Jack says without looking at him. He's looking at Ty. Trying to see anything in those blue eyes but shocked vacancy. He needs for Ty to see the gigantic, groaning machine that stands yonder. To really see it. For until he does, how can he abominate it? "What is it?"

After a long pause, Ty says: "Big. The Big. The Big Combination." The words come out slowly and dreamily, as if he's talking in his sleep.

"The Big Combination, yes," Jack says. "Now stop it."

Beezer gasps. Dale says, "Jack, have you gone—" and then falls silent.

"I. Can't." Ty gives him a wounded look, as if to say Jack should know that.

"You can," Jack says. "You can and you will. What do you think, Ty? That we're going to just turn our backs on them and take you back to your mother and she'll make you Ovaltine and put you to bed and everyone will live happily ever after?" His voice is rising, and he makes no attempt to stop it, even when he sees that Tyler is crying. He shakes the boy again. Tyler cringes, but makes no actual attempt to get away. "Do you think there's going to be any happily ever after for you while those children go on and on, until they drop and get replaced with new ones? You'll see their faces in your dreams, Tyler. You'll see their faces and their dirty little hands and their bleeding feet in your fucking *dreams*."

"Stop it!" Beezer says sharply. "Stop it right now or I'll kick your ass."

Jack turns, and Beezer steps back from the ferocious blaze in his eyes. Looking at Jack Sawyer in this state is like looking into din-tah itself.

"Tyler."

Tyler's mouth trembles. Tears roll down his dirty, bloody cheeks. "Stop it. *I want to go home!*"

"Once you make the Big Combination quit. Then you go home. Not before."

*"I can't!"*

"Yes, Tyler. You can."

Tyler looks at the Big Combination, and Jack can feel the boy making some puny, faltering effort. Nothing happens. The belts continue to run; the whips continue to pop; the occasional screaming dot tumbles (or jumps) from the rust-ragged south side of the building.

Tyler looks back at him, and Jack hates the vacant stupidity in the kid's eyes, *loathes* it. "I *caann't*," Tyler whines, and Jack wonders how such a puler ever managed to survive over here in the first place. Did he use up all his ability in one mad, willful effort to escape? Is that it? He won't accept it. Anger blazes up in him and he slaps Tyler. Hard. Dale gasps. Ty's head rocks to the side, his eyes widening in surprise.

And the cap flies off his head.

Jack has been kneeling in front of the boy. Now he is knocked back, sprawling on his ass in the middle of Conger Road. The kid has . . . what?

*Pushed me. Pushed me with his mind.*

Yes. And Jack is suddenly aware of a new bright force in this dull place, a blazing bundle of light to rival the one that illuminated the Richie Sexson bat.

"Whoa, shit, what happened?" Doc cries.

The bees feel it, too, perhaps more than the men. Their sleepy drone rises to a strident cry, and the cloud darkens as they pull together. Now it looks like a gigantic dark fist below the pendulous, swag-bellied clouds.

*"Why did you hit me?"* Ty shouts at Jack, and Jack is suddenly aware that the boy could kill him at a stroke, if he wanted to. In Wisconsin, this power has been hidden (except from eyes trained to see it). Here, though . . . here . . .

*"To wake you up!"* Jack shouts back. He pushes himself up. "Was it that?" he points at the cap.

Ty looks at it, then nods. *Yes. The cap. But you didn't know, couldn't know, how much the cap was stealing from you until you took it off. Or someone knocked it off your forgetful head.* He returns his gaze to Jack. His eyes are wide and level. There is no shock in them now, no dullness. He doesn't glow, exactly, but he blazes with an inner light they all feel—with a power that dwarfs Lord Malshun's.

"What do you want me to do?" he asks. Tyler Marshall: the lioness's cub.

Once more Jack points at the Big Combination. "You're what all this has been about, Ty. You're a Breaker." He takes a deep breath and then whispers into the pink cup of the boy's ear.

*"Break it."*

Tyler Marshall turns his head and gazes deep into Jack's eyes. He says, "Break it?"

Jack nods his head, and Ty looks back at the Big Combination.

"Okay," he says, speaking not to Jack but to himself. He blinks, settles his feet, clasps his hands in front of his waist. A tiny wrinkle appears between his eyebrows, and the corners of his mouth lift in the suggestion of a smile. "Okay," Ty whispers.

For a second, nothing happens.

Then a rumble emerges from the bowels of the Big Combination. Its upper portion wavers like a heat mirage. The guards hesitate, and the screams of tortured metal rip through the air. Visibly confused, the toiling children look up, look in all directions. The mechanical screaming intensifies, then divides into a hundred different versions of torture. Gears reverse. Cogs jam smoking to a halt; cogs accelerate and strip their teeth. The whole of the Big Combination shivers and quakes. Deep in the earth, boilers detonate, and columns of fire and steam shoot upward, halting, sometimes shredding belts that have run for thousands of years, powered by billions of bleeding footsies.

It is as if an enormous metal jug has sprung a hundred leaks at once. Jack watches children leap from the lower levels and climb down the exterior of the structure in long, continuous lines. Children pour from the trembling building in dozens of unbroken streams.

Before the green-skinned whipslingers can make an organized attempt to stop their slaves from escaping, the bees assemble massively around the great foundry. When the guards begin to turn on the children, the bees descend in a furious tide of buzzing wings and needling stings. Some of Ty's power has passed into them, and their stings are fatal. Guards topple and fall from the unmoving belts and trembling girders. Others turn maddened on their own, whipping and being whipped until they tumble through the dark air.

The Sawyer Gang does not linger to see the end of the slaughter. The queen bee sails toward them out of the swarming chaos, floats above their upturned heads, and leads them back toward Black House.

In world upon world—in worlds strung side by side in multiple dimensions throughout infinity—evils shrivel and disperse: despots choke to death on chicken bones; tyrants fall before assassins' bullets, before the poisoned sweetmeats arrayed by their treacherous mistresses; hooded torturers collapse dying on bloody stone floors. Ty's deed reverberates through the great, numberless string of universes, revenging evil as it spreads. Three worlds over from ours and in the great city there known as Londinorium, Turner Topham, for two decades a respected member of Parliament and for three a sadistic pedophile, bursts abruptly into flame as he strides along the crowded avenue known as Pick-a-Derry. Two worlds down, a nice-looking young welder named Freddy Garver from the Isle of Irse, another, less seasoned member of Topham's clan, turns his torch upon his own left hand and incinerates every particle of flesh off his bones.

Up, up in his high, faraway confinement, the Crimson King feels a deep pain in his gut and drops into a chair, grimacing. Something, he knows, something fundamental, has changed in his dreary fiefdom.

In the wake of the queen bee, Tyler Marshall, his eyes alight and his face without fear, sits astride Jack's shoulders like a boy king. Behind Jack and his friends, hundreds upon hundreds of children who are fleeing from the disintegrating structure of the Big Combination come streaming on to Conger Road and the desolate fields beside it. Some of these children are from our world; many are not. Children move across the dark, empty plains in ragged armies, advancing toward the entrances to their own universes. Limping battalions of children stagger off like columns of drunken ants.

The children following the Sawyer Gang are no less ragged than the rest. Half of them are naked, or as good as naked. These children have faces we have seen on milk cartons and flyers headed MISSING and on child-find Web sites, faces from the dreams of heartbroken mothers and desolate fathers. Some of them are laughing, some are weeping, some are doing both. The stronger ones help the weaker ones along. They do not know where they are going, and they do not care. That they are going is enough for them. All they know is that they are free. The great machine that had stolen their strength and their joy and their hope is behind them, and a silken, protective canopy of bees is above them, and they are free.

At exactly 4:16 P.M., the Sawyer Gang steps out through the front door of Black House. Tyler is now riding on Beezer's

burly shoulders. They descend the steps and stand in front of
Dale Gilbertson's cruiser (there's a litter of dead bees on the
hood and in the well where the windshield wipers hide).

"Look at the house, Hollywood," Doc murmurs.

Jack does. It's *only* a house, now—a three-story job that
might once have been a respectable ranch but has fallen into
disrepair over the years. To make matters worse, someone has
slopped it with black paint from top to bottom and stem to
stern—even the windows have been blurred with swipes of that
paint. The overall effect is sad and eccentric, but by no means
sinister. The house's slippery shifting shape has solidified, and
with the abbalah's glammer departed, what remains is only the
abandoned home of an old fellow who was pretty crazy and *extremely* dangerous. An old fellow to put beside such human
monsters as Dahmer, Haarman, and Albert Fish. The leering,
rampant evil that once inhabited this building has been dissipated, blown away, and what remains is as mundane as an old
man mumbling in a cell on Death Row. There is something Jack
must do to this wretched place—something the dying Mouse
made him promise to do.

"Doc," Beezer says. "Look yonder."

A large dog—large but not monstrous—staggers slowly
down the lane that leads back to Highway 35. It looks like a
cross between a boxer and a Great Dane. The side of its head
and one of its rear paws have been blown away.

"It's your devil dog," the Beez says.

Doc gapes. "What, *that*?"

"That," Beezer confirms. He draws his 9mm, meaning to put
the thing out of its misery, but before he can, it collapses on its
side, takes a single deep, shuddering breath, and then lies still.
Beezer turns to Jack and Dale. "It's all a lot smaller with the
machine turned off, isn't it?"

"I want to see my mother," Ty says quietly. "Please, may I?"

"Yes," Jack says. "Do you mind swinging by your house and
picking up your father? I think he might like to go, too."

Tyler breaks into a tired grin. "Yes," he says. "Let's do that."

"You got it," Jack tells him.

Dale swings the car carefully around the yard and has
reached the beginning of the lane when Ty calls out, "Look!
Look, you guys! Here they come!"

Dale stops, peers in the rearview mirror, and whispers: "Oh, Jack. Holy Mother of God." He puts the cruiser in park and gets out. They all get out, looking back at Black House. Its shape remains ordinary, but it has not quite given up all of its magic after all, it seems. Somewhere a door—perhaps in the cellar or a bedroom or a dirty and neglected but otherwise perfectly ordinary kitchen—remains open. On this side is the Coulee Country; on the other is Conger Road, the smoking, newly stopped hulk of the Big Combination, and the Din-tah.

Bees are coming out onto the porch of Black House. Bees, and the children the bees are leading. They come in droves, laughing and crying and holding hands. Jack Sawyer has a brief, brilliant image of animals leaving Noah's Ark after the flood.

"Holy Mary, Mother of God," Dale whispers again. The yard is filling with laughing, crying, murmuring children.

Jack walks up to Beezer, who turns to him with a brilliant smile.

"After all the children come through, we have to close the door," Jack says. "For good."

"I know we do," says Beezer.

"You happen to have any brilliant ideas?"

"Well," Beezer says, "let me put it this way. If you promise me, and I mean promise me, not to ask any awkward questions or say anything about it later, before midnight tonight I might find it possible to lay my hands on a substantial quantity of something pretty damn effective."

"What? Dynamite?"

"Please," Beezer says. "Didn't I say effective?"

"You mean . . . ?"

Beezer smiles, and his eyes become slits.

"I'm glad you're on my side," Jack says. "See you back on the road before midnight. We'll have to sneak in, but I don't think we'll have any trouble."

"Sure won't have any on the way out," Beezer says.

Doc claps Dale on the shoulder. "I hope you've got some on-the-ball child-welfare organizations in this part of the world, Chiefy. I think you're going to need them."

"Holy . . ." Dale turns stricken eyes to Jack. "What am I going to *do*?"

Jack grins. "I think you better make a call to . . . what does Sarah call them? The Color Posse?"

A gleam of hope dawns in Dale Gilbertson's eyes. Or maybe it's incipient triumph. John P. Redding of the FBI, officers Perry Brown and Jeffrey Black of the Wisconsin State Police. He imagines this trio of bungholes faced with the appearance of a medieval children's crusade in western Wisconsin. Imagines the Dickensian piles of paperwork such an unheard-of event must certainly generate. It will keep them occupied for months or years. It may generate nervous breakdowns. Certainly it will give them something to think about other than Chief Dale Gilbertson of French Landing.

"Jack," he says. "What exactly do you suggest?"

"In broad strokes," Jack says, "I suggest that they should get stuck with all the work and you should hog all the credit. How does that sound to you?"

Dale thinks about it. "Very fair," he says. "What do you say we get this kiddo to his dad, then both of them up to Arden to see his mom?"

"Good," Jack says. "I only wish Henry was here, too."

"That makes us a pair," Dale says, and slides back behind the wheel. A moment later, they are rolling up the lane.

"What about all those kids?" Ty asks, looking out through the back window. "Are you just going to *leave* them?"

"I'll call WSP as soon as we're back on the highway," Dale says. "I think they should get on this right away, don't you guys? And the Feebs, of course."

"Right," Beezer says.

"Fuckin' A," Doc says.

"An excellent administrative call," Jack says, and sits Tyler down on his lap. "In the meantime they'll be fine," he says in the boy's ear. "They've seen a lot worse than Wisconsin."

Let us slip now from the driver's window like the breeze we are and watch them go—four brave men and one brave child who will never be so young (or so innocent) again. Behind them, the now harmless and unmagicked yard of Black House is alive with children, their faces dirty, their eyes wide with wonder. English is a minority tongue here, and some of the languages being spoken will puzzle the world's best linguists in the years ahead. This is the beginning of a worldwide sensation (*Time*'s cover story the following week will be "The Miracle Children from Nowhere") and, as Dale has already surmised, a bureaucratic nightmare.

Still, they are safe. And our guys are safe, too. All of them came back in one piece from the other side, and surely we did not expect that; most quests of this type usually demand at least one sacrifice (a relatively minor character like Doc, for instance). All's well that ends well. And this *can* be the end, if you want it to be; neither of the scribbling fellows who have brought you this far would deny you that. If you *do* choose to go on, never say you weren't warned: you're not going to like what happens next.

XXXXX DRUDGE REPORT XXXXX

FRENCH LANDING PD CHIEF REFUSES TO CANCEL PRESS CONFERENCE, CITES SUPPORT OF TOWN OFFICIALS; SOURCES CONFIRM CELEB L.A. COP WILL ATTEND; FBI, WISC S.P. EXPRESS STRONG DISAPPROVAL

\*\*Exclusive\*\*

One of them, Tyler Marshall, is from French Landing itself. Another, Josella Rakine, is from Bating, a small village in the south of England. A third is from Baghdad. All told, 17 of the so-called Miracle Children have been identified in the week since they were discovered walking along a rural highway (Rte 35) in western Wisconsin.

Yet these 17 are only the tip of the iceberg.

Sources close to the joint FBI/WSP (and now CIA?) investigation tell the Drudge Report that there are at least 750 children, far more than have been reported in the mainstream press. Who are they? Who took them, and to where? How did they get to the town of French Landing, which has been plagued by a serial killer (now reported deceased) in recent weeks? What part was played by Jack Sawyer, the Los Angeles detective who rose to stardom only to retire at age 31? And who was responsible for the massive explosion that destroyed a mysterious dwelling in the woods, reputedly central to the Fisherman case?

Some of these questions may be answered tomorrow in French Landing's La Follette Park, when P.D. Chief Dale Gilbertson holds a press conference. His longtime friend Jack Sawyer—reputed to have broken the Fisherman case singlehandedly—will be standing next to him when he takes the podium. Also expected to be present are two deputies, Armand St. Pierre and Reginald Amberson, who participated in last week's rescue mission.

The press conference will take place over the strong—almost strident—objections of an FBI/WSP task force headed by FBI agent John P. Redding and Wisconsin State Police Detective Jeffrey Black. "They [task force leaders] believe this is nothing but a last-ditch effort on the part of Gilbertson to save his job," a source said. "He botched everything, but luckily has a friend who knows a lot about public relations."

French Landing town officials sing a different tune. "This summer has been a nightmare for the people of French Landing," says town treasurer Beth Warren. "Chief Gilbertson wants to assure the people that the nightmare is over. If he can give us some answers about the children in the process of doing that, so much the better."

Interest focuses on Jack "Hollywood" Sawyer, who got to know Chief Gilbertson and the town of French Landing during the case of Thornberg Kinderling, the so-called Prostitute Killer. Sawyer was urged by Gilbertson to take an active role in the Fisherman case, and apparently played a large part in the events that followed.

What events, exactly, were they? That is what the world is waiting to find out. The first answers may come tomorrow, in La Follette Park, on the banks of the mighty Mississippi.

Developing . . .

# 29

"You guys ready?" Dale asks.

"Aw, man, I don't know," Doc says. This isn't the fifth time he's said it, maybe not even the fifteenth. He's pale, almost hyperventilating. The four of them are in a Winnebago—kind of a rolling green room—that has been set up on the edge of La Follette Park. Nearby is the podium on which they'll stand (always assuming Doc can keep his legs under him) and deliver their carefully crafted answers. On the slope running down to the broad river are gathered nearly four hundred newspeople, plus camera crews from six American networks and God knows how many foreign stations. The gentlemen of the press aren't in the world's best mood, because the prime space in front of the podium has been reserved for a representative sampling (drawn by lottery) of French Landing's residents. This was Dale's one ironclad demand for the press conference.

The idea for the press conference itself came from Jack Sawyer.

"Mellow out, Doc," Beezer says. He looks bigger than ever in his gray linen slacks and open-collared white shirt—almost like a bear in a tuxedo. He has even made an effort to comb his acres of hair. "And if you really think you're going to do one of the Three P's—piss, puke, or pass out—stay here."

"Nah," Doc says miserably. "In for a penny, in for a fuckin' pound. If we're gonna give it a try, let's give it a try."

Dale, resplendent in his dress uniform, looks at Jack. The latter is if anything more resplendent in his gray summerweight suit and dark blue silk tie. A matching blue handkerchief pokes from the breast pocket of his coat. "You sure this is the right thing?"

Jack is completely sure. It's not a matter of refusing to allow Sarah Gilbertson's Color Posse to steal the limelight; it's a matter of making certain that his old friend is in an unassailable position. He can do this by telling a very simple story, which the three other men will back up. Ty will do the same, Jack is confident. The story is this: Jack's *other* old friend, the late Henry Leyden, figured out the Fisherman's identity from the 911 tape. This tape was supplied by Dale, his nephew. The Fisherman killed Henry, but not before the heroic Mr. Leyden had mortally wounded him and passed his name to the police. ( Jack's other interest in this press conference, understood perfectly and supported completely by Dale, is to make sure Henry gets the credit he deserves.) An examination of French Landing property records and plats uncovered the fact that Charles Burnside owned a house on Highway 35, not far out of town. Dale deputized Jack and two widebodies who just happened to be in the vicinity (that would be Messrs. Amberson and St. Pierre), and they went on out there.

"From that point on," Jack told his friends repeatedly in the days leading up to the press conference, "it's vital that you remember the three little words that lead to most acquittals in criminal trials. And what are those words?"

" 'I can't remember,' " Dale said.

Jack nodded. "Right. If you don't have a story to remember, the bastards can never trip you up. There was something in the air inside that place—"

"No lie," Beezer rumbled, and grimaced.

"—and it messed us up. What we *do* remember is this: Ty Marshall was in the backyard, handcuffed to the clothesline whirligig." Before Beezer St. Pierre and Jack Sawyer slipped through the police barricades and vaporized Black House with plastic explosive, one reporter got out there and took numerous pictures. We know which reporter it was, of course; Wendell Green has finally realized his dreams of fame and fortune.

"And Burnside was dead at his feet," Beezer said.

"Right. With the key to the handcuffs in his pocket. Dale, you found that and released the boy. There were a few other kids in the backyard, but as to how many—"

"We don't remember," Doc said.

"As to their sexes—"

"A few boys, a few girls," Dale said. "We don't remember exactly how many of each."

"And as for Ty, how he was taken, what happened to him—"

"He said he didn't remember," Dale said, smiling.

"We left. We think we called to the other kids—"

"But don't exactly remember—" the Beez chips in.

"Right, and in any case they seemed safe enough where they were for the time being. It was when we were putting Ty into the cruiser that we saw them all streaming out."

"And called the Wisconsin State Police for backup," Dale said. "I *do* remember *that.*"

"Of course you do," Jack said benevolently.

"But we have no idea how that darn place got blasted all to hell, and we don't know who did it."

"Some people," Jack said, "are all too eager to take justice into their own hands."

"Lucky they didn't blow their heads clean off," said Dale.

"All right," Jack tells them now. They're standing at the door. Doc has produced half a joint, and four quick, deep tokes have calmed him visibly. "Just remember why we're doing this. The message is that we were there first, we found Ty, we saw *only a few other children,* we deemed their situation secure due to the death of Charles Burnside, also known as Carl Bierstone, the South Side Monster, and the Fisherman. The message is that Dale behaved properly—that we all did—and he then handed the investigation off to the FBI and WSP, who are now holding the baby. *Babies,* I guess in this case. The message is that French Landing is okay again. Last but far from least, the message is that Henry Leyden's the real star. The heroic blind man who I.D.'d Charles Burnside and broke the Fisherman case, mortally wounding the monster and losing his own life in the process."

"Amen," Dale says. "Sweet old Uncle Henry."

Beyond the door of the Winnebago, he can hear the surflike rumble of hundreds of people. Maybe even a thousand. He thinks, *This is what rock acts hear before they hit the stage.* A lump suddenly rises in his throat and he does his best to gulp it back down. He reckons that if he keeps thinking of Uncle Henry he will be okay.

"Anything else," Jack says, "questions that get too specific—"

"We can't remember," Beezer says.

"Because the air was bad," Doc agrees. "Smelled like ether or chloro or something like that."

Jack surveys them, nods, smiles. This will be a happy occasion, on the whole, he thinks. A love feast. Certainly the idea that he might be dying in a few minutes has not occurred to him.

"Okay," he says, "let's go out there and do it. We're politicians this afternoon, politicians at a press conference, and it's the politicians who stay on message who get elected."

He opens the RV's door. The rumble of the crowd deepens in anticipation.

They cross to the jury-rigged platform this way: Beezer, Dale, Jack, and the good Doctor. They move in a warm white nova glare of exploding flashbulbs and 10-k TV lights. Jack has no idea why they need such things—the day is bright and warm, a Coulee Country charmer—but it seems they do. That they always do. Voices cry, "Over here!" repeatedly. There are also thrown questions, which they ignore. When it comes time to answer questions they will—as best they can—but for now they are simply stunned by the crowd.

The noise begins with the two hundred or so French Landing residents sitting on folding chairs in a roped-off area directly in front of the podium. They rise to their feet, some clapping, others waving clenched fists in the air like winning boxers. The press picks it up from them, and as our four friends mount the steps to the podium, the roar becomes a thunder. We are with them, up on the platform with them, and God, we see so many faces we know looking up at us. There's Morris Rosen, who slipped Henry the Dirtysperm CD on our first day in town. Behind him is a contingent from the now defunct Maxton Elder Care: the lovely Alice Weathers is surrounded by Elmer Jesperson, Ada Meyerhoff (in a wheelchair), Flora Flostad, and the Boettcher brothers, Hermie and Tom Tom. Tansy Freneau, looking a bit spaced out but no longer outright insane, is standing next to Lester Moon, who has his arm around her. Arnold "Flashlight" Hrabowski, Tom Lund, Bobby Dulac, and the other members of Dale's department are up on their feet, dancing around and cheering crazily. Look, over there—that's Enid

Purvis, the neighbor who called Fred at work on the day Judy finally high-sided it. There's Rebecca Vilas, looking almost nunnish in a high-collared dress (but cry no tears for her, Argentina; Becky has stashed away quite a nice bundle, thank you very much). Butch Yerxa is with her. At the back of the crowd, lurking shamefully but unable to stay away from the triumph of their friends, are William Strassner and Hubert Cantinaro, better known to us as Kaiser Bill and Sonny. Look there! Herb Roeper, who cuts Jack's hair, standing beside Buck Evitz, who delivers his mail. So many others we know, and to whom we must say good-bye under less than happy circumstances. In the front row, Wendell Green is hopping around like a hen on a hot griddle (God knows how he got into the roped-off area, being from La Riviere instead of French Landing, but he's there), taking pictures. Twice he bumps into Elvena Morton, Henry's housekeeper. The third time he does it, she bats him a damned good one on top of the head. Wendell hardly seems to notice. His head has taken worse shots during the course of the Fisherman investigation. And off to one side, we see someone else we may or may not recognize. An elderly, dark-skinned gentleman wearing shades. He looks a little bit like an old blues singer. He also looks a little bit like a movie actor named Woody Strode.

The applause thunders and thunders. Folks cheer. Hats are thrown in the air and sail on the summer breeze. Their welcome becomes a kind of miracle in itself, an affirmation, perhaps even an acceptance of the children, who are widely supposed to have been held in some bizarre sexual bondage linked to the Internet. (Isn't all that weird stuff somehow linked to the Internet?) And of course they applaud because the nightmare is over. The boogeyman died in his own backyard, died at the foot of a prosaic, now vaporized aluminum clothes whirligig, and they are safe again.

Oh how the cheers ring in these few last moments of Jack Sawyer's life on planet Earth! Birds are startled up from the bank of the river and go squawking and veering into the sky, seeking quieter environs. On the river itself, a freighter responds to the cheers—or perhaps joins in—by blasting its air horn over and over. Other boats get the idea and add to the cacophony.

Without thinking about what he's doing, Jack takes Doc's right hand in his left, Dale's left hand in his right. Dale takes Beezer's hand, and the Sawyer Gang raises their arms together, facing the crowd.

Which, of course, goes nuts. If not for what is going to happen next, it would be the picture of the decade, perhaps of the century. They stand there in triumph, living symbols of victory with their linked hands in the sky, the crowd cheering, the videocams rolling, the Nikons flashing, and that is when the woman in the third row begins to make her move. This is someone else we know, but it takes us a second or two to recognize her, because she has had nothing at all to do with the case we have been following. She's just been . . . sort of lurking around. The two hundred seats up front have been awarded by random drawing from the French Landing voter rolls, the lucky lottery winners notified by Debbi Anderson, Pam Stevens, and Dit Jesperson. This woman was No. 199. Several people shrink from her as she passes them, although in their happy frenzy they are hardly aware of doing it; this pale woman with clumps of straw-colored hair sticking to her cheeks smells of sweat and sleeplessness and vodka. She's got a little purse. The little purse is open. She's reaching into it. And we who have lived through the second half of the twentieth century and have through the miracle of TV witnessed a dozen assassinations and near assassinations know exactly what she is reaching *for.* We want to scream a warning to the four men standing with their linked hands raised to the sky, but all we can do is watch.

Only the black man with the sunglasses sees what's happening. He turns and starts to move, aware that she has probably beaten him, that he is probably going to be too late.

*No,* Speedy Parker thinks. *It can't end like this, it can't.*

*"Jack, get down!"* he shouts, but no one hears him over the clapping, the cheering, the wild hurrahs. The crowd seems to block him on purpose, surging back and forth in front of him no matter which way he moves. For a moment Wendell Green, still bobbing around like a man in the throes of an epileptic seizure, is in the assassin's path. Then she heaves him aside with the strength of a madwoman. Why not? She *is* a madwoman.

"Folks—" Dale's got his mouth practically *on* the microphone, and the P.A. horns mounted to the nearby trees whine with feedback. He's still holding up Jack's hand on his left and Beezer's on his right. There's a small, dazed smile on his face. "Thank you, folks, we sure do appreciate the support, but if you could just quiet down . . ."

That's when Jack sees her.

It's been a long time, years, but he recognizes her at once. He should; she spat in his face one day as he left the Los Angeles courthouse. Spat at him and called him a railroading bastard. *She's lost fifty pounds since then,* Jack thinks. *Maybe more.* Then he sees the hand in the purse, and even before it comes back out, he knows what's happening here.

The worst is that he can do nothing about it. Doc and Dale have his hands in a death grip. He drags in a deep breath and shouts as he has been taught to do in just such a situation as this—*"Gun!"*—and Dale Gilbertson nods as if to say, *Yes it is, it is fun.* Behind her, pushing through the clapping, cheering crowd, he sees Speedy Parker, but unless Speedy's got a particularly good magic trick up his sleeve—

He doesn't. Speedy Parker, known in the Territories as Parkus, is just fighting his way into the aisle when the woman standing below the platform brings out her gun. It's an ugly little thing, a bulldog .32 with its handle wrapped in black kitchen tape, and Jack has just half a second to think that maybe it will blow up in her hand.

*"Gun!"* Jack shouts again, and it's Doc Amberson who hears him and sees the snarling woman crouched just below them.

"Ohfuck," Doc says.

*"Wanda, no!"* Jack cries. Doc has let go of his left hand (Dale has still got his right one hoisted high in the summer air) and Jack holds it out to her like a traffic cop. Wanda Kinderling's first bullet goes right through the palm, mushrooms slightly, begins to tumble, and punches into the hollow of Jack's left shoulder.

Wanda speaks to him. There's too much noise for Jack to hear her, but he knows what she's saying, just the same: *Here you go, you railroading son of a bitch—Thorny says hello.*

She empties the remaining five bullets into Jack Sawyer's chest and throat.

• • •

No one hears the insignificant popping sounds made by Wanda's bulldog .32, not over all that clapping and cheering, but Wendell Green has got his camera tilted up, and when the detective jerks backward, our favorite reporter's finger punches the Nikon's shutter-release button in simple reflex. It snaps off eight shots. The third is the picture, the one that will eventually become as well known as the photo of the Marines raising the flag on Iwo Jima and that of Lee Harvey Oswald clutching his belly in the parking garage of the Dallas police station. In Wendell's photo, Jack Sawyer looks calmly down toward the shooter (who is just a blur at the very bottom of the frame). The expression on his face might be one of forgiveness. Daylight is clearly visible through the hole in the palm of his outstretched hand. Droplets of blood, as red as rubies, hang frozen in the air beside his throat, which has been torn open.

The cheering and the applause stop as if amputated. There is a moment of awful, uncomprehending silence. Jack Sawyer, shot twice in the lungs and once in the heart, as well as in the hand and the throat, stands where he is, gazing at the hole below his spread fingers and above his wrist. Wanda Kinderling peers up at him with her dingy teeth bared. Speedy Parker is looking at Jack with an expression of naked horror that his wraparound sunglasses cannot conceal. To his left, up on one of four media towers surrounding the platform, a young cameraman faints and falls to the ground.

Then, suddenly, the freeze-frame that Wendell has captured without even knowing it bursts open and everything is in motion.

Wanda Kinderling screams *"See you in hell, Hollywood"*— several people will later verify this—and then puts the muzzle of her .32 to her temple. Her look of vicious satisfaction gives way to a more typical one of dazed incomprehension when the twitch of her finger produces nothing but a dry click. The bulldog .32 is empty.

A moment later she is pretty much obliterated—broken neck, broken left shoulder, four broken ribs—as Doc stage-dives onto her and drives her to the ground. His left shoe strikes the side of Wendell Green's head, but this time Wendell sustains no more than a bloody ear. Well, he was due to catch a break, wasn't he?

On the platform, Jack Sawyer looks unbelievingly at Dale, tries to speak, and cannot. He staggers, remains upright a moment longer, then collapses.

Dale's face has gone from bemused delight to utter shock and dismay in a heartbeat. He seizes the microphone and screams, "HE'S SHOT! WE NEED A DOCTOR!" The P.A. horns shriek with more feedback. No doctor comes forward. Many in the crowd panic and begin to run. The panic spreads.

Beezer is down on one knee, turning Jack over. Jack looks up at him, still trying to speak. Blood pours from the corners of his mouth.

"Ah fuck, it's bad, Dale, it's *really bad*," Beezer cries, and then he is knocked sprawling. One wouldn't expect that the scrawny old black man who's vaulted up onto the stage could knock around a bruiser like Beezer, but this is no ordinary old man. As we well know. There is a thin but perfectly visible envelope of white light surrounding him. Beezer sees it. His eyes widen.

The crowd, meanwhile, flees to the four points of the compass. Panic infects some of the ladies and gentlemen of the press, as well. Not Wendell Green; he holds his ground like a hero, snapping pictures until his Nikon is as empty as Wanda Kinderling's gun. He snaps the black man as he stands with Jack Sawyer in his arms; snaps Dale Gilbertson putting a hand on the black man's shoulder; snaps the black man turning and speaking to Dale. When Wendell later asks French Landing's chief of police what the old fellow said, Dale tells him he doesn't remember—besides, in all that pandemonium, he could hardly make it out, anyway. All bullshit, of course, but we may be sure that if Jack Sawyer had heard Dale's response, he would have been proud. When in doubt, tell 'em you can't remember.

Wendell's last picture shows Dale and Beezer watching with identical dazed expressions as the old fellow mounts the steps to the Winnebago with Jack Sawyer still in his arms. Wendell has no idea how such an old party can carry such a big man— Sawyer is six-two and must go a hundred and ninety at least— but he supposes it's the same sort of deal that allows a distraught mother to lift up the car or truck beneath which her kid is pinned. And it doesn't matter. It's small beans compared to what happens next. Because when a group of men led by Dale, Beez, and Doc burst into the Winnebago (Wendell is at the rear of this group), they find nothing but a single overturned chair and several splashes of Jack Sawyer's blood in the kitchenette where Jack gave his little gang their final instructions. The trail of blood leads toward the rear, where there's a foldout bed and a toilet cubicle. And there the drops and splashes simply stop.

Jack and the old man who carried him in here have vanished.

Doc and Beezer are babbling, almost in hysterics. They bounce between questions of where Jack might have gone to distraught recollections of the final few moments on the platform before the shooting started. They can't seem to let that go, and Dale has an idea it will be quite a while before he can let go of it himself. He realizes now that Jack saw the woman coming, that he was trying to get his hand free of Dale's so he could respond.

Dale thinks it may be time to quit the chief's job after all, find some other line of work. Not right now, though. Right now he wants to get Beezer and Doc away from the Color Posse, get them calmed down. He has something to tell them that may help with that.

Tom Lund and Bobby Dulac join him, and the three of them escort Beez and Doc away from the Winnebago, where Special Agent Redding and WSP Detective Black are already establishing a CIP (crime investigation perimeter). Once they're behind the platform, Dale looks into the stunned faces of the two burly bikers.

"Listen to me," Dale says.

"I should have stepped in front of him," Doc says. "I saw her coming, why didn't I step in front—"

"Shut up and *listen*!"

Doc shuts up. Tom and Bobby are also listening, their eyes wide.

"That black man said something to me."

"What?" Beezer asks.

"He said, 'Let me take him—there may still be a chance.' "

Doc, who has treated his share of gunshot wounds, gives a forlorn little chuckle. "And you *believed* him?"

"Not then, not exactly," Dale says. "But when we went in there and the place was empty—"

"No back door, either," Beezer adds.

Doc's skepticism has faded a little. "You really think . . . ?"

"I do," Dale Gilbertson says, and wipes his eyes. "I have to hope. And you guys have to help me."

"All right," Beezer says. "Then we will."

And we think that here we must leave them for good, standing under a blue summer sky close to the Father of Waters, standing beside a platform with blood on the boards. Soon life will catch them up again and pull them back into its furious current, but for a few moments they are together, joined in hope for our mutual friend.

Let us leave them so, shall we?

Let us leave them hoping.

# ONCE UPON A
# TIME IN THE
# TERRITORIES . . .

Once upon a time (as all the best old stories used to begin when we all lived in the forest and nobody lived anywhere else), a scarred Captain of the Outer Guards named Farren led a frightened little boy named Jack Sawyer through the Queen's Pavilion. That small boy did not see the Queen's court, however; no, he was taken through a maze of corridors behind the scenes, secret and seldom-visited places where spiders spun in the high corners and the warm drafts were heavy with the smells of cooking from the kitchen.

Finally, Farren placed his hands in the boy's armpits and lifted him up. *There's a panel in front of you now,* he whispered—do you remember? I think you were there. I think we both were, although we were younger then, weren't we? *Slide it to the left.*

Jack did as he was bidden, and found himself peeking into the Queen's chamber; the room in which almost everyone expected her to die . . . just as Jack expected his mother to die in her room at the Alhambra Inn and Gardens in New Hampshire. It was a bright, airy room filled with bustling nurses who had assumed a busy and purposeful manner because they had no real idea of how to help their patient. The boy looked through the peephole into this room, at a woman he at first thought was his own mother somehow magically transported to this place, and we looked with him, none of us guessing that years later, grown to a man, Jack Sawyer would be lying in the same bed where he first saw his mother's Twinner.

Parkus, who has brought him from French Landing to the Inner Baronies, now stands at the panel through which Jack, hoisted by Captain Farren, once looked. Beside him is Sophie of

Canna, now known in the Territories as both the Young Queen and Sophie the Good. There are no nurses in the sleeping chamber today; Jack lies silent beneath a slowly turning fan. Where he is not wrapped in bandages, his skin is pale. His closed eyelids are hazed with a delicate purple bruise-blush. The rise and fall of the fine linen sheet drawn up to his chin can hardly be seen . . . but it's there. He breathes.

For now, at least, he lives.

Speaking quietly, Sophie says, "If he'd never touched the Talisman—"

"If he'd never touched the Talisman, actually held it in his arms, he would have been dead there on that platform before I could even get close to him," Parkus says. "But of course, if not for the Talisman, he never would have been there in the first place."

"What chance has he?" She looks at him. Somewhere, in another world, Judy Marshall has already begun to subside back into her ordinary suburban life. There will be no such life for her Twinner, however—hard times have come again in this part of the universe—and her eyes gleam with an imperious, regal light. "Tell me the truth, sir; I would not have a lie."

"Nor would I give you one, my lady," he tells her. "I believe that, thanks to the residual protection of the Talisman, he will recover. You'll be sitting next to him one morning or evening and his eyes will open. Not today, and probably not this week, but soon."

"And as for returning to his world? The world of his friends?"

Parkus has brought her to this place because the spirit of the boy Jack was still lingers, ghostly and child-sweet. He was here before the road of trials opened ahead of him, and in some ways hardened him. He was here with his innocence still intact. What has surprised him about Jack as a grown man—and touched him in a way Parkus never expected to be touched again—is how much of that innocence still remained in the man the boy has become.

That, too, is the Talisman's doing, of course.

"Parkus? Your mind wanders."

"Not far, my lady; not far. You ask if he may return to his world after being mortally wounded three, perhaps even four times—after being heart-pierced, in fact. I brought him here because all the magic that has touched and changed his life is stronger here; for good or ill, the Territories have been Jack Sawyer's wellspring since he was a child. And it worked. He lives. But he will wake different. He'll be like . . ."

Parkus pauses, thinking hard. Sophie waits quietly beside him. Distantly, from the kitchen, comes the bellow of a cook lacing into one of the 'prentices.

"There are animals that live in the sea, breathing with gills," Parkus says at last. "And over time's long course, some of them develop lungs. Such creatures can live both under the water and on the land. Yes?"

"So I was taught as a girl," Sophie agrees patiently.

"But some of these latter creatures lose their gills and can live only on the land. Jack Sawyer is that sort of creature now, I think. You or I could dive into the water and swim beneath the surface for a little while, and he may be able to go back and visit his own world for short periods . . . in time, of course. But if either you or I were to try *living* beneath the water—"

"We'd drown."

"Indeed we would. And if Jack were to try living in his own world again, returning to his little house in Norway Valley, for instance, his wounds would return in a space of days or weeks. Perhaps in different forms—his death certificate might specify heart failure, for instance—but it would be Wanda Kinderling's bullet that killed him, all the same. Wanda Kinderling's heart shot." Parkus bares his teeth. "Hateful woman! I believe the abbalah was aware of her no more than I was, but look at the damage she's caused!"

Sophie ignores this. She is looking at the silent, sleeping man in the other room.

"Condemned to live in such a pleasant land as this . . ." She turns to him. "It *is* a pleasant land, isn't it, sirrah? Still a pleasant land, in spite of all?"

Parkus smiles and bows. Around his neck, a shark's tooth swings at the end of a fine gold necklace. "Indeed it is."

She nods briskly. "So living here might not be so terrible."

He says nothing. After a moment or two, her assumed briskness departs, and her shoulders sag.

"I'd hate it," she says in a small voice. "To be barred from my own world except for occasional brief visits . . . paroles . . . to have to leave at the first cough or twinge in my chest . . . I'd hate it."

Parkus shrugs. "He'll have to accept what is. Like it or not, his gills are gone. He's a creature of the Territories now. And God the Carpenter knows there's work for him over here. The business of the Tower is moving toward its climax. I believe Jack Sawyer may have a part to play in that, although I can't say for sure. In any case, when he heals, he won't want for work. He's a coppiceman, and there's always work for such."

She looks through the slit in the wall, her lovely face troubled.

"You must help him, dear," Parkus says.

"I love him," she says, speaking very low.

"And he loves you. But what's coming will be difficult."

"Why must that be, Parkus? Why must life always demand so much and give so little?"

He draws her into his arms and she goes willingly, her face pressed against his chest.

In the dark behind the chamber in which Jack Sawyer sleeps, Parkus answers her question with a single word:

*Ka.*

# Epilogue

She sits by his bed on the first night of Full-Earth Moon, ten days after her conversation with Parkus in the secret passageway. Outside the pavilion, she can hear children singing "The Green Corn A-Dayo." On her lap is a scrap of embroidery. It is summer, still summer, and the air is sweet with summer's mystery.

And in this billowing room where his mother's Twinner once lay, Jack Sawyer opens his eyes.

Sophie lays aside her embroidery, leans forward, and puts her lips soft against the shell of his ear.

"Welcome back," she says. "My heart, my life, and my love: welcome back."

*April 14, 2001*

Don't miss the bestselling prequel to *Black House*
**by STEPHEN KING and
PETER STRAUB**

# THE TALISMAN

One of the most influential and heralded works of
fantasy ever written, *The Talisman* is an extraordinary novel of loyalty, awakening, terror, and
mystery. Jack Sawyer, on a desperate quest to save
his mother's life, must search for a prize across an
epic landscape of innocents and monsters, of
incredible dangers and even more incredible truths.
The prize is essential, but the journey means
even more. Let the quest begin. . . .

**"EXTRAORDINARY. . .
MAKES YOUR HAIR STAND ON END."**
**—*The Washington Post***

**"A CLASSIC. . .RARE AND DAZZLING."**
**—*New York Daily News***